Marcel Proust's continuous novel *A la recherche du temps perdu* (REMEMBRANCE OF THINGS PAST) was originally published in eight parts, the titles and dates of which were: I. *Du côté de chez Swann* (1913); II. *A l'ombre des jeunes filles en fleurs* (1919), awarded the Prix Goncourt in the year of publication; III. *Le côté de Guermantes* I (1920); IV. *Le côté de Guermantes* II, *Sodome et Gomorrhe* I (1921); V. *Sodome et Gomorrhe* II (1922); VI. *La prisonnière* (1923); VII. *Albertine disparue* (1925); VIII. *Le temps retrouvé* (1927).

Du côté de chez Swann was published in English as SWANN'S WAY; *A l'ombre des jeunes filles en fleurs* as WITHIN A BUDDING GROVE; *Le côté de Guermantes* as THE GUERMANTES WAY; *Sodome et Gomorrhe* as CITIES OF THE PLAIN; *La prisonnière* as THE CAPTIVE; *Albertine disparue* as THE SWEET CHEAT GONE; and *Le temps retrouvé* as TIME REGAINED. The first seven parts were translated by C. K. Scott Moncrieff, and the eighth was first translated by Stephen Hudson and then by Andreas Mayor.

In 1954 a text of *A la recherche du temps perdu* derived by Pierre Clarac and André Ferré from holograph and other sources was published in the Bibliothèque de la Pléiade (Gallimard, Paris). The Pléiade edition contains material not available to C. K. Scott Moncrieff and this, together with extensive revision by Terence Kilmartin of the original English translation, is incorporated in the present three-volume edition.

REMEMBRANCE OF THINGS PAST

"When to the sessions of sweet silent thought
I summon up remembrance of things past . . ."

VOLUME TWO

*

THE GUERMANTES WAY

CITIES OF THE PLAIN

MARCEL PROUST

VOLUME TWO

THE GUERMANTES WAY

CITIES OF THE PLAIN

Translated by
C. K. Scott Moncrieff
and Terence Kilmartin

RANDOM HOUSE

NEW YORK

Library of Congress Cataloging in Publication Data
Proust, Marcel, 1871-1922.
Remembrance of things past.
Vol. 3's Time regained, translated by Andreas Mayor.
Translation of A la recherche du temps perdu.
Includes notes.
CONTENTS: v. 1. Swann's way. Within a budding
grove.—v. 2. The Guermantes way. Cities of the
plain.—v. 3. The captive. The fugitive. Time
regained.
I. Title.
PQ2631.R63A72 1981   843'.912   79-5542
ISBN 0-394-50644-8 (v. 1)
ISBN 0-394-50645-6 (v. 2)
ISBN 0-394-50646-4 (v. 3)
ISBN 0-394-50643-x (3 vol. set)

A

LÉON DAUDET

l'auteur
du VOYAGE DE SHAKESPEARE
du PARTAGE DE L'ENFANT
de L'ASTRE NOIR
de FANTÔMES ET VIVANTS
du MONDE DES IMAGES
de tant de chefs-d'œuvre

A l'incomparable ami
en témoignage
de reconnaissance et d'admiration

M. P.

CONTENTS

*

CONTENTS

Numerals in the text refer the reader to explanatory notes
while asterisks indicate the position of textual addenda. The
notes and the addenda follow the text in each volume.

NOTE ON THE TRANSLATION

C. K. Scott Moncrieff's version of *A la recherche du temps perdu* has in the past fifty years earned a reputation as one of the great English translations, almost as a masterpiece in its own right. Why then should it need revision? Why tamper with a work that has been enjoyed and admired, not to say revered, by several generations of readers throughout the English-speaking world?

The answer is that the original French edition from which Scott Moncrieff worked (the "abominable" edition of the *Nouvelle Revue Française*, as Samuel Beckett described it in a marvellous short study of Proust which he published in 1931) was notoriously imperfect. This was not so much the fault of the publishers and printers as of Proust's methods of composition. Only the first volume (*Du côté de chez Swann*) of the novel as originally conceived—and indeed written—was published before the 1914-1918 war. The second volume was set up in type, but publication was delayed, and moreover by that time Proust had already begun to reconsider the scale of the novel; the remaining eight years of his life (1914-1922) were spent in expanding it from its original 500,000 words to more than a million and a quarter. The margins of proofs and typescripts were covered with scribbled corrections and insertions, often overflowing on to additional sheets which were glued to the galleys or to one another to form interminable strips—what Françoise in the novel calls the narrator's "*paperoles*." The unravelling and deciphering of these copious additions cannot have been an enviable task for editors and printers.

Furthermore, the last three sections of the novel (*La prisonnière*, *La fugitive* and *Le temps retrouvé*) had not yet been published at the time of Proust's death in November 1922 (he was still correcting a typed copy of *La prisonnière* on his deathbed). Here the original editors had to take it upon themselves to prepare a coherent text from a manuscript littered with sometimes hasty corrections, revisions and afterthoughts and leaving a number of unresolved contradictions, obscurities and chronological inconsistencies. As a result of all this the original editions—even of the volumes published in Proust's lifetime—pullulate with errors, misreadings and omissions.

In 1954 a revised three-volume edition of *A la recherche* was published in Gallimard's Bibliothèque de la Pléiade. The editors, M. Pierre Clarac and M. André Ferré, had been charged by Proust's heirs with the task of "establishing a text of his novel as faithful as possible to his intentions." With infinite care and patience they examined all the relevant material—manuscripts, notebooks, typescripts, proofs, as well as the original edition—and produced what is generally agreed to be a virtually impeccable transcription of Proust's text. They scrupulously avoided the arbitrary emendations, the touchings-up, the wholesale reshufflings of paragraphs in which the original editors indulged, confining themselves to clarifying the text wherever necessary, correcting errors due to haste or inadvertence, eliminating careless repetitions and rationalising the punctuation (an area where Proust was notoriously casual). They justify and explain their editorial decisions in detailed critical notes, occupying some 200 pages over the three volumes, and print all the significant variants as well as a number of passages that Proust did not have time to work into his book.

The Pléiade text differs from that of the original edition, mostly in minor though none the less significant ways, throughout the novel. In the last three sections (the third Pléiade volume and the third volume of this present translation) the differences are sometimes considerable. In particular, MM. Clarac and Ferré have included a number of passages, sometimes of a paragraph or two, sometimes of several pages, which the original editors omitted for no good reason.

The present translation is a reworking, on the basis of the Pléiade edition, of Scott Moncrieff's version of the first six sections of *A la recherche*—or the first eleven volumes of the twelve-volume English edition. A post-Pléiade version of the final volume, *Le temps retrouvé* (originally translated by Stephen

Hudson after Scott Moncrieff's death in 1930), was produced
by the late Andreas Mayor and published in 1970; with some
minor emendations, it is incorporated in this edition. There
being no indication in Proust's manuscript as to where *La
fugitive* should end and *Le temps retrouvé* begin, I have followed
the Pléiade editors in introducing the break some pages earlier
than in the previous editions, both French and English—at the
beginning of the account of the Tansonville episode.

The need to revise the existing translation in the light of the
Pléiade edition has also provided an opportunity of correcting
mistakes and misinterpretations in Scott Moncrieff's version.
Translation, almost by definition, is imperfect; there is always
"room for improvement," and it is only too easy for the late-
comer to assume the *beau rôle*. I have refrained from officious
tinkering for its own sake, but a translator's loyalty is to the
original author, and in trying to be faithful to Proust's meaning
and tone of voice I have been obliged, here and there, to make
extensive alterations.

A general criticism that might be levelled against Scott
Moncrieff is that his prose tends to the purple and the precious
—or that this is how he interpreted the tone of the original:
whereas the truth is that, complicated, dense, overloaded
though it often is, Proust's style is essentially natural and
unaffected, quite free of preciosity, archaism or self-conscious
elegance. Another pervasive weakness of Scott Moncrieff's is
perhaps the defect of a virtue. Contrary to a widely-held view,
he stuck very closely to the original (he is seldom guilty of
short-cuts, omissions or loose paraphrases), and in his efforts
to reproduce the structure of those elaborate sentences with
their spiralling subordinate clauses, not only does he sometimes
lose the thread but he wrenches his syntax into oddly un-
English shapes: a whiff of Gallicism clings to some of the
longer periods, obscuring the sense and falsifying the tone. A
corollary to this is a tendency to translate French idioms and
turns of phrase literally, thus making them sound weirder,
more outlandish, than they would to a French reader. In
endeavouring to rectify these weaknesses, I hope I have
preserved the undoubted felicity of much of Scott Moncrieff
while doing the fullest possible justice to Proust.

Pace those Proust scholars who feel that "Remembrance of Things Past" distorts the meaning of Proust's title and who would prefer a more literal rendering, Scott Moncrieff's title has been retained for this edition. Of the titles of the seven separate sections, only one has been altered: "The Sweet Cheat Gone" (never Scott Moncrieff's happiest invention) becomes *The Fugitive*, in conformity with the Pléiade edition, which reverts from *Albertine disparue* to Proust's original title *La fugitive*, discarded in 1922 when a book of that title by Rabindranath Tagore was published in France.

There could of course be no question of reproducing the elaborate Pléiade "Notes and Variants" in an English edition, but I have included as addenda a selection of passages which, for one reason or another, did not find a place in Proust's final text. The most substantial of these—the tragi-comedy of the Princesse de Guermantes's unrequited passion for Charlus—will be found at the end of Volume Two and should on no account be overlooked.

I should like to thank Professor J. G. Weightman for his generous help and advice and Mr D. J. Enright for his patient and percipient editing.

TERENCE KILMARTIN

Numerals in the text refer the reader to explanatory notes while asterisks indicate the position of textual addenda. The notes and the addenda follow the text in each volume.

THE
GUERMANTES
WAY

CHAPTER ONE

THE twittering of the birds at daybreak sounded insipid to Françoise. Every word uttered by the maids upstairs made her jump; disturbed by all their running about, she kept asking herself what they could be doing. In other words, we had moved. True, the servants had made no less commotion in the attics of our old home; but she knew them, she had made of their comings and goings something friendly and familiar. Now she listened to the very silence with painful attentiveness. And as our new neighbourhood appeared to be as quiet as the boulevard on to which we had hitherto looked had been noisy, the song (distinct even at a distance, when it was still quite faint, like an orchestral *motif*) of a passer-by brought tears to the eyes of the exiled Françoise. Hence, if I had been tempted to scoff at her when, in her misery at having to leave a house in which one was "so well respected by all and sundry," she had packed her trunks weeping, in accordance with the rites of Combray, and declaring superior to all possible houses that which had been ours, on the other hand, finding it as hard to assimilate the new as I found it easy to abandon the old, I felt myself drawn towards our old servant when I saw that moving into a building where she had not received from the hall-porter, who did not yet know us, the marks of respect necessary to her spiritual wellbeing, had brought her positively to the verge of prostration. She alone could understand what I was feeling; certainly her young footman was not the person to do so; for him, who was as unlike the Combray type as it was possible to conceive, moving house, going to live in another neighbourhood, was like taking a holiday in which the novelty of one's surroundings gave one the same sense of refreshment as if one had actually travelled; he felt he was in the country; and a cold in the head afforded him, as though he had been sitting in a draughty railway carriage, the delicious sensation of having seen something of the world; at each fresh sneeze he rejoiced that he had found so "posh" a situation, having always longed to work for people who travelled a lot. And so, without giving him a thought, I went straight to Françoise, who, in return for my having laughed at her tears over a departure which had left me cold, now showed an icy indifference to my sorrow, because she shared it. The alleged "sensitivity" of neurotic people is matched by their egotism; they cannot abide the flaunting by others of the sufferings to which they pay an ever-increasing attention in themselves. Françoise, who would not allow the least of her own ailments to pass unnoticed, if I were in pain would turn her head away so that I should not have the satisfaction of seeing my sufferings pitied, or so much as observed. It was the same as soon as I tried to speak to her about our new house. Moreover, having been obliged, a day or two later, to return to the house we had just left, to retrieve some clothes which had been overlooked in our removal, while I, as a result of it, still had a "temperature," and like a boa constrictor that has just swallowed an ox felt myself painfully distended by the sight of a long sideboard which my eyes had still to digest, Françoise, with true feminine inconstancy, came back saying that she had really thought she would stifle on our old boulevard, that she had found it quite a day's journey to get there, that never had she seen such stairs, that she would not go back to live there for a king's ransom, not if you were to offer her millions—gratuitous hypotheses—and that *everything* (everything, that is to say, to do with the kitchen and "usual offices") was much better fitted up in our new home. Which, it is high time now that the reader should be told—and told also that we had moved into it because my grandmother, not having been at all well (though we took care to keep this reason from her), was in need of better air—was a flat forming part of the Hôtel de Guermantes.

At the age when Names, offering us an image of the unknowable which we have poured into their mould, while at the same moment connoting for us also a real place, force us accordingly to identify one with the other to such a point that we set out to seek in a city for a soul which it cannot enshrine but which we have no longer the power to expel from its name,

it is not only to towns and rivers that they give an individuality, as do allegorical paintings, it is not only the physical
universe which they speckle with differences, people with
marvels, it is the social universe also; and so every historic
house, in town or country, has its lady or its fairy, as every
forest has its genie, every stream its deity. Sometimes, hidden
in the heart of its name, the fairy is transformed to suit the life
of our imagination, by which she lives; thus it was that the
atmosphere in which Mme de Guermantes existed in me, after
having been for years no more than the reflection of a magic
lantern slide and of a stained glass window, began to lose its
colours when quite other dreams impregnated it with the
bubbling coolness of swift-flowing streams.

However, the fairy languishes if we come in contact with
the real person to whom her name corresponds, for the name
then begins to reflect that person, who contains nothing of the
fairy; the fairy may revive if we absent ourselves from the
person, but if we remain in the person's presence the fairy
ultimately dies and with her the name, as happened to the
family of Lusignan which was fated to become extinct on
the day when the fairy Mélusine should disappear. Then the
Name, beneath the successive "retouchings" of which we may
end by finding the original handsome portrait of a strange
woman whom we have never met, becomes no more than the
mere identity card photograph to which we refer in order to
decide whether we know, whether or not we ought to bow
to a person who passes us in the street. But should a sensation
from a bygone year—like those recording instruments which
preserve the sound and the manner of the various artists who
have sung or played into them—enable our memory to make
us hear that name with the particular ring with which it then
sounded in our ears, we feel at once, though the name itself
has apparently not changed, the distance that separates the
dreams which at different times its same syllables have meant
to us. For a moment, from the clear echo of its warbling in
some distant spring-time, we can extract, as from the little
tubes used in painting, the exact, forgotten, mysterious,
fresh tint of the days which we had believed ourselves to be
recalling, when, like a bad painter, we were giving to the whole

of our past, spread out on the same canvas, the conventional
and undifferentiated tones of voluntary memory. Whereas, on
the contrary, each of the moments that composed it employed,
for an original creation, in a unique harmony, the colours of
that time which are now lost to us and which, for example,
still suddenly enrapture me if by some chance the name
"Guermantes," resuming for a moment after all these years the
sound, so different from its sound to-day, which it had for me
on the day of Mlle Percepied's marriage, brings back to me
that mauve—so soft and smooth but almost too bright, too
new—with which the billowy scarf of the young Duchess
glowed, and, like two inaccessible, ever-flowering periwinkles,
her eyes, sunlit with an azure smile. And the name Guermantes of those days is also like one of those little balloons
which have been filled with oxygen or some other gas; when
I come to prick it, to extract its contents from it, I breathe the
air of the Combray of that year, of that day, mingled with a
fragrance of hawthorn blossom blown by the wind from the
corner of the square, harbinger of rain, which now sent the
sun packing, now let it spread itself over the red woollen carpet
of the sacristy, clothing it in a bright geranium pink and in
that, so to speak, Wagnerian sweetness and solemnity in joy
that give such nobility to a festive occasion. But even apart
from rare moments such as these, in which suddenly we feel
the original entity quiver and resume its form, carve itself out
of syllables now dead, if in the dizzy whirl of daily life, in
which they serve only the most practical purpose, names have
lost all their colour, like a prismatic top that spins too quickly
and seems only grey, when, on the other hand, we reflect
upon the past in our day-dreams and seek, in order to recapture
it, to slacken, to suspend the perpetual motion by which we
are borne along, gradually we see once more appear, side by
side but entirely distinct from one another, the tints which in
the course of our existence have been successively presented to
us by a single name.

What shape was projected in my mind's eye by this name
Guermantes when my wet-nurse—knowing no more, probably, than I know to-day in whose honour it had been composed—sang me to sleep with that old ditty, *Gloire à la*

Marquise de Guermantes, or when, some years later, the veteran
Maréchal de Guermantes, making my nurserymaid's bosom
swell with pride, stopped in the Champs-Elysées to remark:
"A fine child, that!" and gave me a chocolate drop from his
comfit-box, I cannot, of course, now say. Those years of my
earliest childhood are no longer a part of myself; they are
external to me; I can learn nothing of them save—as we learn
things that happened before we were born—from the accounts
given me by other people. But more recently I find in the period
of that name's occupation of me seven or eight different
figures. The earliest were the most beautiful: gradually my
daydream, forced by reality to abandon a position that was no
longer tenable, established itself anew in one slightly less advanced until it was obliged to retire still further. And, together
with Mme de Guermantes, her dwelling was simultaneously
transformed; itself also the offspring of that name, fertilised
from year to year by some word or other that came to my ears
and modified my reveries, that dwelling of hers mirrored them
in its very stones, which had become reflectors, like the surface
of a cloud or of a lake. A two-dimensional castle, no more
indeed than a strip of orange light, from the summit of which
the lord and his lady disposed of the lives and deaths of their
vassals, had given place—right at the end of that "Guermantes
way" along which, on so many summer afternoons, I followed
with my parents the course of the Vivonne—to that land of
bubbling streams where the Duchess taught me to fish for
trout and to know the names of the flowers whose red and
purple clusters adorned the walls of the neighbouring
gardens; then it had been the ancient heritage, the poetic
domain from which the proud race of Guermantes, like a
mellow, crenellated tower that traverses the ages, had risen
already over France, at a time when the sky was still empty at
those points where later were to rise Notre-Dame of Paris and
Notre-Dame of Chartres; a time when on the summit of the
hill of Laon the nave of its cathedral had not yet been poised
like the Ark of the Deluge on the summit of Mount Ararat,
crowded with Patriarchs and Judges anxiously leaning from
its windows to see whether the wrath of God has yet subsided,
carrying with it specimens of the plants that will multiply on

the earth, brimming over with animals which have even
climbed out through the towers, between which oxen grazing
calmly on the roof look down over the plains of Champagne;
when the traveller who left Beauvais at the close of day did not
yet see, following him and turning with his road, the black,
ribbed wings of the cathedral spread out against the golden
screen of the western sky. It was, this "Guermantes," like the
setting of a novel, an imaginary landscape which I could with
difficulty picture to myself and longed all the more to discover,
set in the midst of real lands and roads which all of a sudden
would become alive with heraldic details, within a few miles
of a railway station; I recalled the names of the places round it
as if they had been situated at the foot of Parnassus or of
Helicon, and they seemed precious to me as the physical
conditions—in the realm of topographical science—required
for the production of an unaccountable phenomenon. I saw
again the escutcheons blazoned beneath the windows of
Combray church; their quarters filled, century after century,
with all the fiefs which, by marriage or conquest, this illustrious house had appropriated to itself from all the corners of
Germany, Italy and France; vast territories in the North,
powerful cities in the South, assembled there to group themselves in Guermantes, and, losing their material quality, to
inscribe allegorically their sinople keep or castle triple-towered
argent upon its azure field. I had heard of the famous tapestries
of Guermantes, and could see them, mediaeval and blue, a
trifle coarse, stand out like floating clouds against the legendary,
amaranthine name at the edge of the ancient forest in which
Childebert so often went hunting; and it seemed to me that,
as effectively as by travelling to see them, I might penetrate
the secrets of the mysterious reaches of these lands, these vistas
of the centuries, simply by coming in contact for a moment in
Paris with Mme de Guermantes, the princess paramount of
the place and lady of the lake, as if her face and her speech
must possess the local charm of forest groves and streams, and
the same time-honoured characteristics as the old customs
recorded in her archives. But then I had met Saint-Loup; he
had told me that the castle had borne the name of Guermantes
only since the seventeenth century, when his family had

acquired it. They had lived, until then, in the neighbourhood, but their title did not come from those parts. The village of Guermantes had received its name from the manor round which it had been built, and so that it should not destroy the manorial view, a servitude that was still in force had traced the line of its streets and limited the height of its houses. As for the tapestries, they were by Boucher, bought in the nineteenth century by a Guermantes with a taste for the arts, and hung, interspersed with a number of mediocre sporting pictures which he himself had painted, in a hideous drawing-room upholstered in "adrianople" and plush. By these revelations, Saint-Loup had introduced into the castle elements foreign to the name of Guermantes which made it impossible for me to continue to extract solely from the resonance of the syllables the stone and mortar of its walls. Then in the depths of this name the castle mirrored in its lake had faded, and what now became apparent to me, surrounding Mme de Guermantes as her dwelling, had been her house in Paris, the Hôtel de Guermantes, limpid like its name, for no material and opaque element intervened to interrupt and blind its transparency. As the word church signifies not only the temple but also the assembly of the faithful, this Hôtel de Guermantes comprised all those who shared the life of the Duchess, but these intimates on whom I had never set eyes were for me only famous and poetic names, and, knowing exclusively persons who themselves too were only names, served to enhance and protect the mystery of the Duchess by extending all round her a vast halo which at the most declined in brilliance as its circumference increased.

In the entertainments which she gave, since I could not imagine the guests as possessing bodies, moustaches, boots, as making any utterance that was commonplace, or even original in a human and rational way, this vortex of names, introducing less material substance than would a phantom banquet or a spectral ball, round that statuette in Dresden china which was Mme de Guermantes, gave her mansion of glass the transparency of a showcase. Then, after Saint-Loup had told me various anecdotes about his cousin's chaplain, her gardeners and the rest, the Hôtel de Guermantes had

become—as the Louvre might have been in days gone by—
a kind of palace surrounded, in the very heart of Paris, by its
own domains, acquired by inheritance, by virtue of an ancient
right that had quaintly survived, over which she still enjoyed
feudal privileges. But this last dwelling had itself vanished
when we came to live near Mme de Villeparisis in one of the
apartments adjoining that occupied by Mme de Guermantes
in a wing of the Hôtel. It was one of those old town houses, a
few of which for all I know may still be found, in which the
main courtyard was flanked—alluvial deposits washed there by
the rising tide of democracy, perhaps, or a legacy from a more
primitive time when the different trades were clustered round
the overlord—by little shops and workrooms, a shoemaker's,
for instance, or a tailor's, such as we see nestling between the
buttresses of those cathedrals which the aesthetic zeal of the
restorer has not swept clear of such accretions, and a porter
who also did cobbling, kept hens, grew flowers—and, at the
far end, in the main house, a "Countess" who, when she
drove out in her old carriage and pair, flaunting on her hat a
few nasturtiums which seemed to have escaped from the plot
by the lodge (with, by the coachman's side on the box, a
footman who got down to leave cards at every aristocratic
mansion in the neighbourhood), dispensed smiles and little
waves of the hand impartially to the porter's children and
to any bourgeois tenants who might happen to be passing
and whom, in her disdainful affability and her egalitarian
arrogance, she found indistinguishable from one another.

In the house in which we had now come to live, the great
lady at the end of the courtyard was a Duchess, elegant and
still young. She was, in fact, Mme de Guermantes and, thanks
to Françoise, I soon came to know all about her household.
For the Guermantes (to whom Françoise regularly alluded as
the people "below," or "downstairs") were her constant
preoccupation from the first thing in the morning when, as
she did Mamma's hair, casting a forbidden, irresistible, furtive
glance down into the courtyard, she would say: "Look at that,
now, a pair of holy Sisters: they'll be for downstairs, surely";
or, "Oh! just look at the fine pheasants in the kitchen window.
No need to ask where they've become from: the Duke's

been out with his gun!"—until the last thing at night when, if her ear, while she was putting out my night-things, caught the sound of a piano or a few notes of a song, she would conclude: "They're having company down below; gay doings, I'll be bound"; whereupon, in her symmetrical face, beneath her snow-white hair, a smile from her young days, sprightly but proper, would for a moment set each of her features in its place, arranging them in an arch and formal pattern, as though for a quadrille.

But the moment in the life of the Guermantes which excited the keenest interest in Françoise, gave her the most complete satisfaction and at the same time the sharpest annoyance, was that at which, the carriage gates having been flung open, the Duchess stepped into her barouche. It was generally a little while after our servants had finished celebrating that sort of solemn passover which none might disturb, called their mid-day dinner, during which they were so far "taboo" that my father himself would not have taken the liberty of ringing for them, knowing moreover that none of them would have paid any more attention to the fifth peal than to the first, and that he would thus have committed this impropriety to no purpose, though not without detriment to himself. For Françoise (who, in her old age, lost no opportunity of standing upon her dignity) would not have failed to present him, for the rest of the day, with a face covered with the tiny red cuneiform hiero-glyphs by which she made visible—though by no means legible—to the outer world the long tale of her grievances and the underlying causes of her displeasure. She would enlarge upon them, too, in a running "aside," but not so that we could catch her words. She called this practice—which, she imagined, must be shattering for us, "mortifying," "vexing," as she put it—saying "low masses" to us the whole "blessed" day.

The last rites accomplished, Françoise, who was at one and the same time, as in the primitive church, the celebrant and one of the faithful, helped herself to a final glass, undid the napkin from her throat, folded it after wiping from her lips the vestiges of watered wine and coffee, slipped it into its ring, turned a doleful eye to thank "her" young footman who, to show his zeal in her service, was saying: "Come, ma'am, a

few more grapes—they're d'licious to-day," and went straight
across to the window, which she flung open, protesting that it
was too hot to breathe in "this wretched kitchen." Dexter-
ously casting, as she turned the latch and let in the fresh air, a
glance of studied indifference into the courtyard below, she
furtively ascertained that the Duchess was not yet ready to
start, gazed for a moment with scornful and impassioned eyes
at the waiting carriage, and, this meed of attention once paid
to the things of the earth, raised them towards the heavens,
whose purity she had already divined from the sweetness of the
air and the warmth of the sun; and let them rest on a corner of
the roof, at the place where, every spring, there came to nest,
immediately over the chimney of my bedroom, a pair of
pigeons like those she used to hear cooing from her kitchen at
Combray.

"Ah! Combray, Combray!" she cried. And the almost singing tone in which she declaimed this invocation might, taken
with the Arlesian purity of her features, have prompted a
stranger to surmise that she was of Southern origin and that
the lost homeland she was lamenting was no more than a land
of adoption. If so, he would have been wrong, for it seems that
there is no province that has not its own South-country; do
we not indeed constantly meet Savoyards and Bretons in
whose speech we find all those pleasing transpositions of
longs and shorts that are characteristic of the Southerner?
"Ah, Combray, when will I see you again, poor old place?
When will I spend the whole blessed day among your hawthorns, under our own poor lilac trees, hearing the finches
sing and the Vivonne making a little noise like someone
whispering, instead of that wretched bell from our young
master, who can never stay still for half an hour on end without
having me run the length of that blessed corridor. And even
then he makes out I don't come quick enough; you'd need to
hear the bell before he rung it, and if you're a minute late, he
flies into the most horrible rage. Ah, poor Combray! maybe
I'll only see you when I'm dead, when they drop me like a
stone into a hole in the ground. And so, nevermore will I
smell your lovely hawthorns, so white and all. But in the sleep
of death I dare say I shall still hear those three peals of the bell

which will already have driven me to damnation in this world."

Her soliloquy was interrupted by the voice of the waistcoat-maker in the courtyard below, the same who had so pleased my grandmother once, long ago, when she had gone to pay a call on Mme de Villeparisis, and now occupied no less high a place in Françoise's affections. Having raised his head when he heard our window open, he had already been trying for some time to attract his neighbour's attention, in order to bid her good day. The coquetry of the young girl that Françoise had once been softened and refined for M. Jupien the querulous face of our old cook, dulled by age, ill-temper and the heat of the kitchen stove, and it was with a charming blend of reserve, familiarity and modesty that she bestowed a gracious salutation on the waistcoat-maker, but without making any audible response, for if she infringed Mamma's injunctions by looking into the courtyard, she would never have dared to go the length of talking from the window, which would have been quite enough (according to her) to bring down on her "a whole chapter" from the Mistress. She pointed to the waiting carriage, as who should say: "A fine pair, eh!" though what she actually muttered was: "What an old rattle-trap!"—but principally because she knew that he would be bound to answer, putting his hand to his lips so as to be audible without having to shout: "*You* could have one too if you liked, as good as they have and better, I dare say, only you don't care for that sort of thing."

And Françoise, after a modest, evasive and delighted signal, the meaning of which was, more or less: "Tastes differ, you know; simplicity's the rule in this house," shut the window again in case Mamma should come in. The "you" who might have had more horses than the Guermantes were ourselves, but Jupien was right in saying "you" since, except for a few purely personal self-gratifications (such as, when she coughed all day long without ceasing and everyone in the house was afraid of catching her cold, that of insisting, with an irritating little titter, that she had not got a cold), Françoise, like those plants that an animal to which they are wholly attached keeps alive with food which it catches, eats and digests for them and of which it offers them the ultimate and easily assimilable residue, lived with us in a symbiotic relationship; it was we who, with our virtues, our wealth, our style of living, must take on ourselves the task of concocting those little sops to her vanity out of which was formed—with the addition of the recognised right to practise freely the cult of the midday dinner according to the traditional custom, which included a gulp of air at the window when the meal was finished, a certain amount of loitering in the street when she went out to do her marketing, and a holiday on Sundays when she paid a visit to her niece— the portion of contentment indispensable to her existence.

And so it can be understood why Françoise pined in those first days of our migration, a prey—in a house where my father's claims to distinction were not yet known—to a malady which she herself called "ennui," ennui in the strong sense in which the word is employed by Corneille, or in the last letters of soldiers who end by taking their own lives because they are pining after[1] their sweethearts or their native villages. Françoise's ennui had soon been cured by none other than Jupien, for he at once procured her a pleasure no less keen and more refined than she would have felt if we had decided to keep a carriage. "Very good class, those Juliens" (for Françoise readily assimilated new names to those with which she was already familiar), "very decent people; you can see it written on their faces." Jupien was indeed able to understand, and to inform the world, that if we did not keep a carriage it was because we had no wish to do so.

This new friend of Françoise's was seldom at home, having obtained a post in a Government office. A waistcoat-maker first of all, with the "chit of a girl" whom my grandmother had taken for his daughter, had lost all interest in the exercise of that calling after the girl (who, when still little more than a child, had shown great skill in darning a torn skirt, that day when my grandmother had gone to call on Mme de Villeparisis) had turned to ladies' fashions and become a skirt-maker. A prentice hand, to begin with, in a dressmaker's workroom, employed to stitch a seam, to sew up a flounce, to fasten a button or a press-stud, to fix a waistband with hooks and eyes, she had quickly risen to be second and then chief

assistant, and having formed a clientele of her own among
ladies of fashion, now worked at home, that is to say in our
courtyard, generally with one or two of her young friends from
the workroom, whom she had taken on as apprentices. After
this, Jupien's presence had become less essential. No doubt
the little girl (a big girl by this time) had often to cut out
waistcoats still. But with her friends to assist her she needed
no one besides. And so Jupien, her uncle, had sought employment outside. He was free at first to return home at midday;
then, when he had definitely succeeded the man whose assistant
only he had begun by being, not before dinner-time. His
appointment to the "regular establishment" was, fortunately,
not announced until some weeks after our arrival, so that
his amiability could be brought to bear on Françoise long
enough to help her through the first, most difficult phase
without undue pain. At the same time, and without under-
rating his value to Françoise as, so to speak, an interim sedative, I am bound to say that my first impression of Jupien had
been far from favourable. From a few feet away, entirely
destroying the effect that his plump cheeks and florid complexion would otherwise have produced, his eyes, brimming
with a compassionate, mournful, dreamy gaze, led one to
suppose that he was seriously ill or had just suffered a great
bereavement. Not only was this not so, but as soon as he
spoke (quite perfectly as it happened) he was inclined rather
to be cold and mocking. There resulted from this discord
between his look and his speech a certain falsity which was
not attractive, and by which he himself had the air of being
made as uncomfortable as a guest who arrives in day clothes
at a party where everyone else is in evening dress, or as someone who, having to speak to a royal personage, does not know
exactly how he ought to address him and gets round the
difficulty by cutting down his remarks to almost nothing.
Jupien's (here the comparison ends) were, on the contrary,
charming. Indeed, corresponding perhaps to that inundation
of the face by the eyes (which one ceased to notice when one
came to know him), I soon discerned in him a rare intelligence,
one of the most spontaneously literary that it has been my
privilege to come across, in the sense that, probably without

education, he possessed or had assimilated, with the help only of a few books hastily perused, the most ingenious turns of speech. The most gifted people that I had known had died young. And so I was convinced that Jupien's life would soon be cut short. He was kind and sympathetic, and had the most delicate and the most generous feelings.

His role in Françoise's life had soon ceased to be indispensable. She had learned to stand in for him. Even when a tradesman or servant came to our door with a parcel or message, while seeming to pay no attention to him and merely pointing vaguely to an empty chair, Françoise so skilfully put to the best advantage the few moments that he spent in the kitchen while he waited for Mamma's answer, that it was very seldom that he went away without having ineradicably engraved in his mind the conviction that, if we "did not have" any particular thing, it was because we had "no wish" for it. If she made such a point of other people's knowing that we "had money"[2] (for she knew nothing of what Saint-Loup used to call partitive articles, and said simply "have money," "fetch water"), of their knowing us to be rich, it was not because wealth with nothing else besides, wealth without virtue, was in her eyes the supreme good; but virtue without wealth was not her ideal either. Wealth was for her, so to speak, a necessary condition failing which virtue would lack both merit and charm. She distinguished so little between them that she had come in time to invest each with the other's attributes, to expect some material comfort from virtue, to discover something edifying in wealth.

As soon as she had shut the window again, fairly quickly—otherwise Mamma would, it appeared, have heaped on her "every imaginable insult"—Françoise began with many groans and sighs to put the kitchen table straight.

"There's some Guermantes who stay in the Rue de la Chaise," began my father's valet. "I had a friend used to work there; he was their second coachman. And I know a fellow, not my old pal but his brother-in-law, who did his time in the Army with one of the Baron de Guermantes's grooms. 'And after all, he ain't my father,' "[3] added the valet, who was in the habit, just as he used to hum the popular airs of the season, of peppering his conversation with all the latest witticisms.

Françoise, with the tired eyes of an ageing woman, eyes which moreover saw everything from Combray, in a hazy distance, perceived, not the witticism that underlay these words, but the fact that there must be something witty in them since they bore no relation to the rest of the observation and had been uttered with considerable emphasis by one whom she knew to be a joker. She therefore smiled with an air of dazzled benevolence, as who should say: "Always the same, that Victor!" And she was genuinely pleased, knowing that listening to smart sayings of this sort was akin—if remotely— to those reputable social pleasures for which, in every class of society, people make haste to dress themselves in their best and run the risk of catching cold. Furthermore, she believed the valet to be a friend after her own heart, for he never ceased to denounce with fierce indignation the appalling measures which the Republic was about to enforce against the clergy. Françoise had not yet learned that our cruellest adversaries are not those who contradict and try to convince us, but those who magnify or invent reports which are liable to distress us, taking care not to give them any appearance of justification which might lessen our pain and perhaps give us some slight regard for an attitude which they make a point of displaying to us, to complete our torment, as being at once terrible and triumphant.

"The Duchess must be allianced with all that lot," said Françoise, taking up the conversation again at the Guermantes of the Rue de la Chaise, as one resumes a piece of music at the andante. "I can't recall who it was told me one of them married a cousin of the Duke. It's the same kindred, anyway. Ay, they're a great family, the Guermantes!" she added, in a tone of respect, founding the greatness of the family at once on the number of its branches and the brilliance of its connexions, as Pascal founds the truth of Religion on Reason and on the authority of the Scriptures. For since she had only the single word "great" to express both meanings, it seemed to her that they formed a single idea, her vocabulary, like certain cut stones, showing thus on certain of its facets a flaw which projected a ray of darkness into the recesses of her mind.

"I wonder now if it wouldn't be them that have their castle at Guermantes, not a score of miles from Combray; then they must be kin to their cousin in Algiers, too." (My mother and I had wondered for a long time who this cousin in Algiers could be until finally we discovered that Françoise meant by the name "Algiers" the town of Angers. What is far off may be more familiar to us than what is quite near. Françoise, who knew the name "Algiers" from some particularly unpleasant dates that used to be given us at the New Year, had never heard of Angers. Her language, like the French language itself, and especially its toponymy, was thickly strewn with errors.) "I meant to talk to their butler about it. . . . What is it now they call him?" She broke off as though putting to herself a question of protocol, which she went on to answer with: "Oh, of course, it's Antoine they call him!" as though Antoine had been a title. "He's the one could tell me, but he's quite the gentleman, he is, a great pedant, you'd think they'd cut his tongue out, or that he'd forgotten to learn to speak. He makes no reply when you talk to him," went on Françoise, who said "make reply" like Mme de Sévigné. "But," she added, quite untruthfully, "so long as I know what's boiling in my pot I don't bother my head about what's in other people's. In any case it's not Catholic. And what's more, he's not a courageous man." (This criticism might have led one to suppose that Françoise had changed her mind about physical bravery which according to her, in Combray days, lowered men to the level of wild beasts. But it was not so. "Courageous" meant simply hard-working.) "They do say, too, that he's thievish as a magpie, but it doesn't do to believe all you hear. The staff never stay long there because of the lodge; the porters are jealous and set the Duchess against them. But it's safe to say that he's a real idler, that Antoine, and his Antoinesse is no better," concluded Françoise, who, in furnishing the name "Antoine" with a feminine suffix that would designate the butler's wife, was inspired, no doubt, in her act of word-formation by an unconscious memory of the words *chanoine* and *chanoinesse*. If so, she was not far wrong. There is still a street near Notre-Dame called Rue Chanoinesse, a name which must have been given to it (since it was inhabited only by

canons) by those Frenchmen of olden days of whom Françoise
was in reality the contemporary. She proceeded, moreover, at
once to furnish another example of this way of forming
feminines, for she added: "But one thing sure and certain is
that it's the Duchess that has Guermantes Castle. And it's she
that is the Lady Mayoress down in those parts. That's something."

"I should think it *is* something," said the footman with
conviction, having failed to detect the irony.

"You think so, do you, my boy, you think it's something?
Why, for folk like them to be Mayor and Mayoress, it's just
thank you for nothing. Ah, if it was mine, that Guermantes
Castle, you wouldn't see me setting foot in Paris, I can tell you.
I'm sure a family who've got something to go on with, like
Monsieur and Madame here, must have queer ideas to stay on
in this wretched town sooner than get away down to Combray
the moment they're free to start, and no one hindering them.
Why do they put off retiring when they've got everything they
want? Why wait till they're dead? Ah, if only I had a crust of
dry bread to eat and a faggot to keep me warm in winter,
I'd have been back home long since in my brother's poor old
house at Combray. Down there at least you feel you're alive;
you don't have all these houses stuck up in front of you, and
there's so little noise at night-time you can hear the frogs
singing five miles off and more."

"That must be really nice, Madame," exclaimed the young
footman with enthusiasm, as though this last attraction had
been as peculiar to Combray as the gondola is to Venice.
A more recent arrival in the household than my father's
valet, he used to talk to Françoise about things which might
interest not himself so much as her. And Françoise, whose face
wrinkled up in disgust when she was treated as a mere cook,
had for the young footman, who referred to her always as the
"housekeeper," that peculiar tenderness which certain princes
of the second rank feel towards the well-intentioned young
men who dignify them with a "Highness."

"At any rate you know what you're about there, and what
time of year it is. It isn't like here where you won't find one
wretched buttercup flowering at holy Easter any more than

you would at Christmas, and I can't hear so much as the tiniest angelus ring when I lift my old bones out of bed in the morning. Down there, you can hear every hour. It's only a poor old bell, but you say to yourself: 'My brother will be coming in from the fields now,' and you watch the daylight fade, and the bell rings to bless the fruits of the earth, and you have time to take a turn before you light the lamp. But here it's day-time and it's night-time, and you go to bed, and you can't say any more than the dumb beasts what you've been about."

"They say Méséglise is a fine place, too, Madame," broke in the young footman, who found that the conversation was becoming a little too abstract for his liking, and happened to remember having heard us, at table, mention Méséglise.

"Oh! Méséglise, is it?" said Françoise with the broad smile which one could always bring to her lips by uttering any of those names—Méséglise, Combray, Tansonville. They were so intimate a part of her life that she felt, on meeting them outside it, on hearing them used in conversation, a hilarity more or less akin to that which a teacher excites in his class by making an allusion to some contemporary personage whose name the pupils had never supposed could possibly greet their ears from the height of the academic rostrum. Her pleasure arose also from the feeling that these places meant something to her which they did not to the rest of the world, old companions with whom one has shared many an outing; and she smiled at them as if she found in them something witty, because there was in them a great part of herself.

"Yes, you may well say so, son, it's a pretty enough place is Méséglise," she went on with a tinkling laugh, "but how did you ever come to hear tell of Méséglise?"

"How did I hear of Méséglise? But it's a well-known place. People have told me about it oftentimes," he assured her with that criminal inexactitude of the informant who, whenever we attempt to form an impartial estimate of the importance that a thing which matters to us may have for other people, makes it impossible for us to do so.

"Ah! I can tell you it's better down there under the cherry trees than standing in front of the kitchen stove all day."

She spoke to them even of Eulalie as a good person. For

since Eulalie's death Françoise had completely forgotten that she had loved her as little in her lifetime as she loved anyone whose cupboard was bare, who was "perishing poor" and then came, like a good for nothing, thanks to the bounty of the rich, to "put on airs." It no longer pained her that Eulalie had so skilfully managed, Sunday after Sunday, to secure her "tip" from my aunt. As for the latter, Françoise never ceased to sing her praises.

"So it was at Combray itself that you used to be, with a cousin of Madame?" asked the young footman.

"Yes, with Mme Octave—ah, a real saintly woman, I can tell you, and a house where there was always more than enough, and all of the very best—a good woman, and no mistake, who didn't spare the partridges, or the pheasants, or anything. You might turn up five to dinner or six, it was never the meat that was lacking, and of the first quality too, and white wine, and red wine, and everything you could wish." (Françoise used the word "spare" in the same sense as La Bruyère.)⁴ "It was she that always paid the damages, even if the family stayed for months and years." (This reflexion was not really meant as a slur upon us, for Françoise belonged to an epoch when the word "damages" was not restricted to a legal use and meant simply expense.) "Ah, I can tell you people didn't go away empty from that house. As his reverence the Curé impressed on us many's the time, if there ever was a woman who could count on going straight before the Throne of God, it was her. Poor Madame, I can still hear her saying in that faint little voice of hers: 'You know, Françoise, I can eat nothing myself, but I want it all to be just as nice for the others as if I could.' They weren't for her, the victuals, you may be quite sure. If you'd only seen her, she weighed no more than a bag of cherries; there wasn't that much of her. She would never listen to a word I said, she'd never send for the doctor. Ah, it wasn't in that house that you'd have to gobble down your dinner. She liked her servants to be fed properly. Here, it's been just the same again to-day; we've hardly had time to sit down. Everything has to be done holus-bolus."

What exasperated her more than anything were the slices of

thin toast that my father used to eat. She was convinced that he indulged in them simply to give himself airs and to keep her "dancing." "I can tell you frankly," the young footman assured her, "that I never saw the like." He said this as if he had seen everything, and as if for him the range of an inexhaustible experience extended over all countries and their customs, among which was nowhere to be found the custom of eating slices of toast. "Yes, yes," the butler muttered, "but that may all be changed; the workers are going on strike in Canada, and the Minister told Monsieur the other evening that he's clearing two hundred thousand francs out of it." There was no note of censure in his tone, not that he was not himself entirely honest, but since he regarded all politicians as shady, the crime of peculation seemed to him less serious than the pettiest larceny. He did not even stop to ask himself whether he had heard this historic utterance aright, and seemed not to have been struck by the improbability that such a thing should have been said by the guilty party himself to my father without my father's immediately turning him out of the house. But the philosophy of Combray made it impossible for Françoise to expect that the strikes in Canada could have any repercussion on the consumption of toast. "Ah, well, as long as the world goes round, there'll be masters to keep us on the trot, and servants to do their bidding." In disproof of this theory of perpetual trotting, for the last quarter of an hour my mother (who probably did not employ the same measures of time as Françoise in reckoning the duration of the latter's dinner) had been saying: "What on earth can they be doing? They've been at table for at least two hours." And she rang timidly three or four times. Françoise, "her" footman and the butler heard the bell ring, not as a summons to themselves, and with no thought of answering it, but rather as the first sounds of the instruments being tuned when the next part of a concert will soon begin, and one knows that there will be only a few minutes more of interval. And so, when the peals were repeated and became more urgent, our servants began to pay attention, and, judging that they had not much time left and that the resumption of work was at hand, at a peal somewhat louder than the rest gave a collective sigh and went their several ways, the footman slipping downstairs to smoke a cigarette outside the door, Françoise, after a string of reflexions on ourselves, such as: "They've got the jumps to-day all right," going up to tidy her attic, while the butler, having supplied himself first with note-paper from my bedroom, polished off the arrears of his private correspondence.

Despite the arrogant air of their butler, Françoise had been in a position, from the first, to inform me that the Guermantes occupied their mansion by virtue not of an immemorial right but of a quite recent tenancy, and that the garden over which it looked on the side that I did not know was quite small and just like all the neighbouring gardens, and I realised at last that there were not to be seen there pit and gallows or fortified mill, secret chamber, pillared dovecote, manorial bakehouse, tithe-barn or fortress, drawbridge or fixed bridge or even flying or toll bridge, charters, muniments, ramparts or commemorative mounds. But just as Elstir, when the bay of Balbec, losing its mystery, had become for me simply a portion, interchangeable with any other, of the total quantity of salt water distributed over the earth's surface, had suddenly restored to it a personality of its own by telling me that it was the gulf of opal painted by Whistler in his "Harmonies in Blue and Silver," so the name Guermantes had seen the last of the dwellings that had issued from its syllables perish under Françoise's blows, when one day an old friend of my father said to us, speaking of the Duchess: "She has the highest position in the Faubourg Saint-Germain; hers is the leading house in the Faubourg Saint-Germain." No doubt the most exclusive drawing-room, the leading house in the Faubourg Saint-Germain was little or nothing after all those other mansions of which in turn I had dreamed. And yet this one too (and it was to be the last of the series), however humble it was, possessed something, quite apart from its material components, that amounted to an obscure differentiation.

And it became all the more essential that I should be able to explore in the "salon" of Mme de Guermantes, among her friends, the mystery of her name, since I did not find it in her person when I saw her leave the house in the morning on foot, or in the afternoon in her carriage. Once before, indeed, in the

church at Combray, she had appeared to me in the blinding
flash of a transfiguration, with cheeks that were irreducible to,
impervious to the colour of the name Guermantes and of
afternoons on the banks of the Vivonne, taking the place of
my shattered dream, like a swan or a willow into which a god
or nymph has been changed, and which henceforward, subjected to natural laws, will glide over the water or be shaken
by the wind. And yet scarcely had I left her presence than those
glittering fragments had reassembled like the green and
roseate reflexions of the sunset behind the oar that has broken
them, and in the solitude of my thoughts the name had quickly
appropriated to itself my impression of the face. But now,
frequently, I saw her at her window, in the courtyard, in the
street, and for myself at least, if I did not succeed in inte-
grating into the living woman the name Guermantes, in
thinking of her as Mme de Guermantes, I could cast the blame
on the impotence of my mind to carry through the act that
I demanded of it; but she herself, our neighbour, seemed to
commit the same error, commit it without discomfiture
moreover, without any of my scruples, without even suspecting that it was an error. Thus Mme de Guermantes showed
in her dresses the same anxiety to follow the fashion as if,
believing herself to have become a woman like any other,
she had aspired to that elegance in her attire in which ordinary
women might equal and perhaps surpass her; I had seen her
in the street gaze admiringly at a well-dressed actress; and in
the morning, before she sallied forth on foot, as if the opinion
of the passers-by, whose vulgarity she accentuated by parading
familiarly through their midst her inaccessible life, could be a
tribunal competent to judge her, I would see her in front of
the glass playing, with a conviction free from all pretence or
irony, with passion, with ill-humour, with conceit, like a queen
who has consented to appear as a servant-girl in theatricals at
court, the role, so unworthy of her, of a fashionable woman;
and in this mythological oblivion of her native grandeur, she
looked to see whether her veil was hanging properly, smoothed
her cuffs, adjusted her cloak, as the divine swan performs all
the movements natural to his animal species, keeps his eyes
painted on either side of his beak without putting into them

any glint of life, and darts suddenly after a bud or an umbrella, as a swan would, without remembering that he is a god. But as the traveller, disappointed by his first impression of a strange town, tells himself that he will doubtless succeed in penetrating its charm if he visits its museums and galleries, strikes up an acquaintance with its people, works in its libraries, so I assured myself that, had I been given the right of entry into Mme de Guermantes's house, were I one of her friends, were I to penetrate into her life, I should then know what, within its glowing amber envelope, her name enclosed in reality, objectively, for other people, since, after all, my father's friend had said that the Guermantes set was in a class of its own in the Faubourg Saint-Germain.

The life which I supposed them to lead there flowed from a source so different from anything in my experience, and must, I felt, be so out of the ordinary, that I could not have imagined the presence at the Duchess's parties of people in whose company I myself had already been, of people who really existed. For, not being able suddenly to change their nature, they would have carried on conversations there of the sort that I knew; their partners would perhaps have stooped to reply to them in the same human speech; and, in the course of an evening spent in the leading house in the Faubourg Saint-German, there would have been moments identical with moments that I had already lived. Which was impossible. It is true that my mind was perplexed by certain difficulties, and the presence of the body of Jesus Christ in the host seemed to me no more obscure a mystery than this leading house in the Faubourg being situated on the right bank of the river and so near that from my bedroom in the morning I could hear its carpets being beaten. But the line of demarcation that separated me from the Faubourg Saint-Germain seemed to me all the more real because it was purely ideal; I sensed that it was already part of the Faubourg when I saw, spread out on the other side of that Equator, the Guermantes doormat of which my mother had ventured to say, having like myself caught a glimpse of it one day when their door stood open, that it was in a shocking state. Besides, how could their dining-room, their dim gallery upholstered in red plush, into which I could

see sometimes from our kitchen window, have failed to possess
in my eyes the mysterious charm of the Faubourg Saint-
Germain, to form an essential part of it, to be geographically
situated within it, since to have been entertained to dinner in
that dining-room was to have gone into the Faubourg Saint-
Germain, to have breathed its atmosphere, since the people
who, before going to table, sat down beside Mme de Guermantes on the leather-covered sofa in that gallery were all of
the Faubourg Saint-Germain? No doubt elsewhere than in the
Faubourg, at certain parties, one might see now and then,
majestically enthroned amid the vulgar herd of fashion, one of
those men who are no more than names and who alternately
assume, when one tries to picture them to oneself, the aspect
of a tourney or of a royal forest. But here, in the leading salon
in the Faubourg Saint-Germain, in the dim gallery, there was
no one but them. They were the columns, wrought of precious
materials, that upheld the temple. Even for small and intimate
gatherings it was from among them only that Mme de Guermantes could choose her guests, and in the dinners for twelve,
assembled around the dazzling napery and plate, they were
like the golden statues of the apostles in the Sainte-Chapelle,
symbolic, dedicative pillars before the Lord's Table. As for
the tiny strip of garden that stretched between high walls at
the back of the house, where in summer Mme de Guermantes
had liqueurs and orangeade brought out after dinner, how
could I not have felt that to sit there of an evening, between
nine and eleven, on its iron chairs—endowed with a magic as
potent as the leather sofa—without inhaling at the same time
the breezes peculiar to the Faubourg Saint-Germain, was as
impossible as to take a siesta in the oasis of Figuig without
thereby being necessarily in Africa? Only imagination and
belief can differentiate from the rest certain objects, certain
people, and create an atmosphere. Alas, those picturesque sites,
those natural features, those local curiosities, those works of
art of the Faubourg Saint-Germain, doubtless I should never
be permitted to set my feet among them. And I must content
myself with a shiver of excitement as I sighted from the open
sea (and without the least hope of ever landing there), like
a prominent minaret, like the first palm, like the first signs of

some exotic industry or vegetation, the well-trodden doormat
of its shore.

But if the Hôtel de Guermantes began for me at its hall-
door, its dependencies must be regarded as extending a long
way further, in the estimation of the Duke, who, looking on all
the tenants as peasants, yokels, appropriators of national assets,
whose opinion was of no account, shaved himself every
morning in his nightshirt at the window, came down into the
courtyard, according to the warmth or coldness of the day, in
his shirt-sleeves, in pyjamas, in a plaid jacket of startling
colours with a shaggy nap, in little light-coloured covert coats
shorter than his jacket, and made one of his grooms lead past
him at a trot some horse that he had just bought. More than
once, indeed, the horse damaged Jupien's shop-front, whereupon Jupien, to the Duke's indignation, demanded compensation. "If it were only in consideration of all the good that
Madame la Duchesse does in the house here and in the parish,"
said M. de Guermantes, "it's an outrage on this fellow's part
to claim a sou from us." But Jupien had stuck to his guns,
apparently not having the faintest idea what "good" the
Duchess had ever done. And yet she did do good, but—since
one cannot do good to everybody at once—the memory of the
benefits that we have heaped on one person is a valid reason for
our abstaining from helping another, whose discontent we
thereby arouse the more. From other points of view than that of
philanthropy, the quarter appeared to the Duke—and this over
a considerable area—to be merely an extension of his courtyard, a longer track for his horses. After seeing how a new
acquisition trotted by itself he would have it harnessed and
taken through all the neighbouring streets, the groom running
beside the carriage holding the reins, making it pass to and
fro before the Duke who stood on the pavement, erect,
gigantic, enormous in his vivid clothes, a cigar between his
teeth, his head in the air, his eyeglass quizzical, until the moment when he sprang on to the box, drove the horse up and
down for a little to try it, then set off with his new turn-out
to pick up his mistress in the Champs-Elysées. M. de Guermantes would bid good day in the courtyard to two couples
who belonged more or less to his world: the first, some cousins

of his who, like working-class parents, were never at home to look after their children, since every morning the wife went off to the Schola to study counterpoint and fugue, and the husband to his studio to carve wood and tool leather; and then the Baron and Baronne de Norpois, always dressed in black, she like a pew-opener and he like an undertaker, who emerged several times daily on their way to church. They were the nephew and niece of the old Ambassador whom we knew, and whom my father had in fact met at the foot of the staircase without realising where he was coming from; for my father supposed that so considerable a personage, one who had come in contact with the most eminent men in Europe and was probably quite indifferent to the empty distinctions of social rank, was hardly likely to frequent the society of these obscure, clerical and narrow-minded nobles. They had not been long in the place; Jupien, who had come out into the courtyard to say a word to the husband just as he was greeting M. de Guermantes, called him "M. Norpois," not being certain of his name.

"Monsieur Norpois, indeed! Oh, that really is good! Just wait a little! This individual will be calling you Citizen Norpois next!" exclaimed M. de Guermantes, turning to the Baron. He was at last able to vent his spleen against Jupien who addressed him as "Monsieur" instead of "Monsieur le Duc."

One day when M. de Guermantes required some information upon a matter of which my father had professional knowledge, he had introduced himself to him with great courtesy. After that, he had often some neighbourly service to ask of my father and, as soon as he saw him coming downstairs, his mind occupied with his work and anxious to avoid any interruption, the Duke, leaving his stable-boys, would come up to him in the courtyard, straighten the collar of his greatcoat with the obliging deftness inherited from a line of royal body-servants, take him by the hand, and, holding it in his own, stroking it even, to prove to him, with the shamelessless of a courtesan, that he did not begrudge him the privilege of contact with the ducal flesh, would steer him, extremely irked and thinking only how he might escape, through the carriage entrance out into the street. He had given us a sweeping bow one day when he had passed us as he was setting out in the carriage with his wife; he was bound to have told her my name, but what likelihood was there of her remembering it, or my face either? And besides, what a feeble recommendation to be pointed out simply as being one of her tenants! Another, more valuable, would have been to meet the Duchess at the house of Mme de Villeparisis, who, as it happened, had sent word by my grandmother that I was to go and see her, and, remembering that I had been intending to go in for literature, had added that I should meet several authors there. But my father felt that I was still a little young to go into society, and as the state of my health continued to cause him disquiet he was reluctant to allow me unnecessary occasions for renewed outings.

As one of Mme de Guermantes's footmen was in the habit of gossiping with Françoise, I picked up the names of several of the houses which she frequented, but formed no impression of any of them: the moment they were a part of her life, of that life which I saw only through the veil of her name, were they not inconceivable?

"To-night there's a big party with a shadow theatre show at the Princesse de Parme's," said the footman, "but we shan't be going, because at five o'clock Madame is taking the train to Chantilly, to spend a few days with the Duc d'Aumale; but it'll be the lady's maid and valet that go with her. I'm to stay here. She won't be at all pleased, the Princesse de Parme won't, that's four times already she's written to Madame la Duchesse."

"Then you won't be going down to Guermantes Castle this year?"

"It's the first time we shan't be going there: it's because of Monsieur le Duc's rheumatics, the doctor says he's not to go there till the hot pipes are in, but we've been there every year till now, right on to January. If the hot pipes aren't ready, perhaps Madame will go for a few days to Cannes to the Duchesse de Guise, but nothing's settled yet."

"And do you ever go to the theatre?"

"We go now and then to the Opéra, usually on the evenings when the Princesse de Parme has her box, that's once a week.

It seems it's a fine show they give there, plays, operas, everything. Madame refused to rent a box herself, but we go all the
same to the boxes Madame's friends take, now one, now
another, often the Princesse de Guermantes, the Duke's
cousin's lady. She's sister to the Duke of Bavaria. . . . And so
you've got to run upstairs again now, have you?" went on
the footman, who, though identified with the Guermantes,
looked upon "masters" in general as a political estate, a view
which allowed him to treat Françoise with as much respect as
if she too were in service with a duchess. "You enjoy good
health, ma'am."

"Oh, if it wasn't for these cursed legs of mine! On the plain
I can still get along" ("on the plain" meant in the courtyard
or in the streets, where Françoise was not averse from walking,
in other words on flat ground), "but it's these stairs that do
me in, devil take them. Good day to you. Perhaps we'll meet
again this evening."

She was all the more anxious to continue her conversations
with the footman after learning from him that the sons of dukes
often bore a princely title which they retained until their
fathers were dead. Evidently the cult of the nobility, blended
with and accommodating itself to a certain spirit of revolt
against it, must, springing hereditarily from the soil of France,
be very strongly implanted still in her people. For Françoise,
to whom you might speak of the genius of Napoleon or of
wireless telegraphy without succeeding in attracting her
attention, and without her pausing for a moment in the job
she was doing, whether clearing the grate or laying the table,
if she learnt of these idiosyncrasies of nomenclature, and that
the younger son of the Duc de Guermantes was generally
called the Prince d'Oléron, would at once exclaim: "Now isn't
that nice!" and stand there bemused, as though in contemplation of a stained-glass window.

Françoise learned also from the Prince d'Agrigente's valet,
who had become friends with her by often calling round with
notes for the Duchess, that he had been hearing a great deal
of talk in society about the marriage of the Marquis de Saint-
Loup to Mlle d'Ambresac, and that it was practically settled.

That villa, that opera-box, into which Mme de Guermantes

transfused the current of her life, must, it seemed to me, be places no less magical than her home. The names of Guise, of Parme, of Guermantes-Bavière, differentiated from all possible others the holiday places to which the Duchess resorted, the daily festivities which the track of her carriage wheels linked to her mansion. If they told me that the life of Mme de Guermantes consisted of a succession of such holidays and such festivities, they brought no further light to bear on it. Each of them gave to the life of the Duchess a different determination, but merely brought it a change of mystery without allowing any of its own mystery to evaporate, so that it simply floated, protected by a watertight covering, enclosed in a bell, amid the waves of others' lives. The Duchess might have lunch on the shore of the Mediterranean at Carnival time, but in the villa of Mme de Guise, where the queen of Parisian society was no more, in her white piqué dress, among numberless princesses, than a guest like any other, and on that account more moving still to me, more herself by being thus made new, like a star of the ballet who in the intricacies of a dance figure takes the place of each of her humbler sisters in succession; she might look at shadow theatre shows, but at a party given by the Princesse de Parme; listen to tragedy or opera, but from the Princesse de Guermantes's box.

Since we localise in the body of a person all the potentialities of that person's life, our recollections of the people he knows and has just left or is on his way to meet, if, having learned from Françoise that Mme de Guermantes was going on foot to luncheon with the Princesse de Parme, I saw her emerge from the house about midday in a gown of flesh-coloured satin above which her face was of the same shade, like a cloud at sunset, it was all the pleasures of the Faubourg Saint-Germain that I saw before me, contained in that small compass, as though between the glossy pearl-pink valves of a shell.

My father had a friend at the Ministry, one A. J. Moreau, who, to distinguish himself from the other Moreaus, took care always to prefix his name with these two initials, with the result that people called him "A. J." for short. For some reason or other, this A. J. found himself in possession of a stall for a gala night at the Opéra. He sent the ticket to my father, and since Berma, whom I had not seen again since my first disappointment, was to give an act of *Phèdre*, my grandmother persuaded my father to pass it on to me.

Truth to tell, I set little store by this opportunity of seeing and hearing Berma which, a few years earlier, had plunged me in such a state of agitation. And it was not without a sense of melancholy that I registered to myself my indifference to what at one time I had put before health, comfort, everything. It was not that there had been any diminution in my desire to be able to contemplate at first hand the precious particles of reality which my imagination envisioned. But it no longer located them in the diction of a great actress; since my visits to Elstir, it was on to certain tapestries, certain modern paintings that I had transferred the inner faith I had once had in the acting, the tragic art of Berma; my faith and my desire no longer coming forward to pay incessant worship to the diction and the presence of Berma, the "double" that I possessed of them in my heart had gradually shrivelled, like those other "doubles" of the dead in ancient Egypt which had to be fed continually in order to maintain their originals in eternal life. That art had become a poor and pitiable thing. It was no longer inhabited by a deep-rooted soul.

That evening, as, armed with the ticket my father had received from his friend, I was climbing the grand staircase of the Opéra, I saw in front of me a man whom I took at first for M. de Charlus, whose bearing he had; when he turned his head to ask some question of an attendant I saw that I had been mistaken, but I nevertheless had no hesitation in placing the stranger in the same class of society, from the way not only in which he was dressed but in which he spoke to the man who took the tickets and to the box-openers who were keeping him waiting. For, apart from individual characteristics, there was still at this period a very marked difference between any rich and well-dressed man of that section of the aristocracy and any rich and well-dressed man of the world of finance or "big business." Where one of the latter would have thought he was giving proof of his exclusiveness by adopting a sharp and haughty tone in speaking to an inferior, the nobleman, affable and mild, gave the impression of considering, of

practising an affectation of humility and patience, a pretence
of being just an ordinary member of the audience, as a
prerogative of his good breeding. It is probable that on seeing
him thus dissemble behind a smile overflowing with good
nature the inaccessible threshold of the little world apart
which he carried in his person, more than one wealthy banker's
son entering the theatre at that moment, would have taken this
nobleman for a person of humble condition if he had not
remarked in him an astonishing resemblance to the portrait
that had recently appeared in the illustrated papers of a nephew
of the Austrian Emperor, the Prince of Saxony, who happened to be in Paris at the time. I knew him to be a great
friend of the Guermantes. As I myself reached the ticket
attendant I heard the Prince of Saxony (or his double) say
with a smile: "I don't know the number. My cousin told me
I had only to ask for her box."

He may well have been the Prince of Saxony; it was perhaps
the Duchesse de Guermantes (whom, in that event, I should
be able to watch in the process of living one of the moments
of her unimaginable life in her cousin's box) that he saw in his
mind's eye when he referred to "my cousin who told me I
had only to ask for her box," so much so that that distinctive
smiling gaze and those so simple words caressed my heart
(far more than any abstract reverie would have done) with
the alternative antennae of a possible happiness and a vague
glamour. At least, in uttering this sentence to the attendant,
he grafted on to a commonplace evening in my everyday
life a potential entry into a new world; the passage to
which he was directed after having spoken the word "box"
and along which he now proceeded was moist and mildewed
and seemed to lead to subaqueous grottoes, to the mythological kingdom of the water-nymphs. I had before me a
gentleman in evening dress who was walking away from me,
but I kept playing upon and around him, as with a badly
fitting projector, without ever succeeding in focusing it on him
exactly, the idea that he was the Prince of Saxony and was
on his way to join the Duchesse de Guermantes. And for all
that he was alone, that idea, external to himself, impalpable,
immense, unsteady as a searchlight beam, seemed to precede

and guide him like that deity, invisible to the rest of mankind, who stands beside the Greek warrior in the hour of battle.

I took my seat, trying to recapture a line from *Phèdre* which I could not quite remember. In the form in which I repeated it to myself it did not have the right number of feet, but as I made no attempt to count them, between its unwieldiness and a classical line of poetry it seemed as though no common measure could exist. It would not have surprised me to learn that I must subtract at least half a dozen syllables from that portentous phrase to reduce it to alexandrine dimensions. But suddenly I remembered it, the irremediable asperities of an inhuman world vanished as if by magic; the syllables of the line at once filled up the requisite measure, and what there was in excess floated off with the ease, the dexterity of a bubble of air that rises to burst on the surface of the water. And, after all, this excrescence with which I had been struggling consisted of only a single foot.

A certain number of orchestra stalls had been offered for sale at the box office and bought, out of snobbishness or curiosity, by such as wished to study the appearance of people whom they might not have another opportunity of seeing at close quarters. And it was indeed a fragment of their true social life, ordinarily concealed, that one could examine here in public, for, the Princesse de Parme having herself distributed among her friends the seats in stalls, balconies and boxes, the house was like a drawing-room in which everyone changed places, went to sit here or there, next to friends.

Next to me were some vulgar people who, not knowing the regular seat-holders, were anxious to show that they were capable of identifying them and named them aloud. They went on to remark that these "regulars" behaved there as though they were in their own drawing-rooms, meaning that they paid no attention to what was being played. In fact it was the opposite that took place. A budding genius who has taken a stall in order to see Berma thinks only of not soiling his gloves, of not disturbing, of conciliating the neighbour whom chance has put beside him, of pursuing with an intermittent smile the fleeting glance, and avoiding with apparent want of politeness the intercepted glance, of a person of his acquaintance whom he has discovered in the audience and to whom, after endless indecisions, he makes up his mind to go and talk just as the three knocks from the stage, resounding before he has had time to reach his friend, force him to take flight, like the Hebrews in the Red Sea, through a heaving tide of spectators and spectatresses whom he has forced to rise to their feet and whose dresses he tears and boots he crushes as he passes. On the other hand, it was because the society people sat in their boxes (behind the tiered circle) as in so many little suspended drawing-rooms, the fourth walls of which had been removed, or in so many little cafés to which one might go for refreshment without letting oneself be intimidated by the mirrors in gilt frames or the red plush seats, in the Neapolitan style, of the establishment,—it was because they rested an indifferent hand on the gilded shafts of the columns which upheld this temple of the lyric art,—it was because they remained unmoved by the extravagant honours which seemed to be being paid them by a pair of carved figures which held out towards the boxes branches of palm and laurel, that they alone would have had the equanimity of mind to listen to the play, if only they had had minds.

At first there were only vague shadows, in which one suddenly caught—like the gleam of a precious stone which one cannot see—the phosphorescence of a pair of famous eyes, or, like a medallion of Henri IV on a dark background, the bent profile of the Duc d'Aumale, to whom an invisible lady was exclaiming "Your Royal Highness must allow me to take his coat," to which the prince replied, "Oh, come, come! Really, Madame d'Ambresac." She took it, in spite of this vague demurral, and was envied by one and all for being thus honoured.

But in the other boxes, almost everywhere, the white deities who inhabited those sombre abodes had taken refuge against their shadowy walls and remained invisible. Gradually, however, as the performance went on, their vaguely human forms detached themselves languidly one after the other from the depths of the night which they spangled, and, raising themselves towards the light, allowed their half-naked bodies to emerge into the chiaroscuro of the surface where their

gleaming faces appeared behind the playful, frothy undulations
of their ostrich-feather fans, beneath their hyacinthine, pearl-
studded headdresses which seemed to bend with the motion
of the waves. Beyond began the orchestra stalls, abode of
mortals for ever separated from the sombre and transparent
realm to which here and there, in their smooth liquid surface,
the limpid, reflecting eyes of the water-goddesses served as
frontier. For the folding seats on its shore and the forms of
the monsters in the stalls were mirrored in those eyes in simple
obedience to the laws of optics and according to their angle of
incidence, as happens with those two sections of external
reality to which, knowing that they do not possess any soul,
however rudimentary, that can be considered analogous to
our own, we should think ourselves insane to address a smile
or a glance: namely, minerals and people to whom we have not
been introduced. Within the boundaries of their domain,
however, the radiant daughters of the sea were constantly
turning round to smile up at the bearded tritons who clung
to the anfractuosities of the cliff, or towards some aquatic
demi-god whose skull was a polished stone on to which the
tide had washed a smooth covering of seaweed, and his gaze
a disc of rock crystal. They leaned towards these creatures,
offering them sweetmeats; from time to time the flood parted
to admit a new nereid who, belated, smiling, apologetic, had
just floated into blossom out of the shadowy depths; then,
the act ended, having no further hope of hearing the melodious sounds of earth which had drawn them to the surface,
plunging back all at once, the several sisters vanished into
the night. But of all these retreats to the thresholds of which
their frivolous desire to behold the works of man brought the
curious goddesses who let none approach them, the most
famous was the cube of semi-darkness known to the world as
the stage box of the Princesse de Guermantes.

Like a tall goddess presiding from afar over the frolics of
the lesser deities, the Princess had deliberately remained somewhat in the background on a sofa placed sideways in the box,
red as a coral reef, beside a large vitreous expanse which was
probably a mirror and suggested a section, perpendicular,
opaque and liquid, cut by a ray of sunlight in the dazzling

crystal of the sea. At once plume and corolla, like certain
subaqueous growths, a great white flower, downy as the wing
of a bird, hung down from the Princess's forehead along one
of her cheeks, the curve of which it followed with coquettish,
amorous, vibrant suppleness, as if half enclosing it like a pink
egg in the softness of a halcyon's nest. Over her hair, reaching
in front to her eyebrows and caught back lower down at the
level of her throat, was spread a net composed of those little
white shells which are fished up in certain southern seas and
which were intermingled with pearls, a marine mosaic barely
emerging from the waves and at moments plunged back again
into a darkness in the depths of which even then a human
presence was revealed by the glittering motility of the Princess's eyes. The beauty which set her far above all the other
fabulous daughters of the twilight was not altogether materially
and comprehensively inscribed in the nape of her neck, in
her shoulders, her arms, her waist. But the exquisite, unfinished line of the last was the exact starting-point, the
inevitable focus of invisible lines into which the eye could not
help prolonging them—lines marvellously engendered round
the woman like the spectre of an ideal figure projected against
the darkness.

"That's the Princesse de Guermantes," said my neighbour
to the gentleman beside her, taking care to begin the word
"Princesse" with a string of 'P's, to show that the designation
was absurd. "She hasn't been sparing with her pearls. I'm
sure if I had as many as that I wouldn't make such a display
of them; it doesn't look at all genteel to my mind."

And yet, when they caught sight of the Princess, all those
who were looking round to see who was in the audience felt
the rightful throne of beauty rise up in their hearts. The fact
was that, with the Duchesse de Luxembourg, with Mme de
Morienval, with Mme de Saint-Euverte, with any number of
others, what enabled one to identify their faces would be the
juxtaposition of a big red nose and a hare-lip, or of a pair of
wrinkled cheeks and a faint moustache. These features were
moreover sufficient in themselves to charm the eye, since,
having merely the conventional value of a specimen of handwriting, they gave one to read a famous and impressive name;

but also, in the long run, they gave one the idea that ugliness had something aristocratic about it, and that it was immaterial whether the face of a great lady, provided it possessed distinction, was beautiful as well. But like certain artists who, instead of the letters of their names, set at the foot of their canvases a figure that is beautiful in itself, a butterfly, a lizard, a flower, so it was the figure of a delicious face and body that the Princess affixed at the corner of her box, thereby showing that beauty can be the noblest of signatures; for the presence there of Mme de Guermantes-Bavière, who brought to the theatre only such persons as at other times formed part of her intimate circle, was in the eyes of connoisseurs of the aristocracy the best possible certificate of the authenticity of the picture which her box presented, a sort of evocation of a scene from the intimate and exclusive life of the Princess in her palaces in Munich and in Paris.

Our imagination being like a barrel-organ out of order, which always plays some other tune than that shown on its card, every time I had heard any mention of the Princesse de Guermantes-Bavière, a recollection of certain sixteenth-century masterpieces had begun singing in my brain. I was obliged to rid myself of this association now that I saw her engaged in offering crystallised fruit to a stout gentleman in tails. Certainly I was very far from concluding that she and her guests were mere human beings like the rest of the audience. I understood that what they were doing there was only a game, and that as a prelude to the acts of their real life (of which, presumably, this was not where they lived the important part) they had arranged, in obedience to a ritual unknown to me, to pretend to offer and decline sweets, a gesture robbed of its ordinary significance and regulated beforehand like the steps of a dancer who alternately raises herself on her toes and circles around a scarf. For all I knew, perhaps at the moment of offering him her sweets, the goddess was saying, with that note of irony in her voice (for I saw her smile): "Will you have a sweet?" What did it matter to me? I should have found a delicious refinement in the deliberate dryness, in the style of Mérimée or Meilhac, of these words addressed by a goddess to a demi-god who knew what sublime thoughts they both had

in their minds, in reserve, doubtless, for the moment when
they would begin again to live their real life, and, joining in the
game, answered with the same mysterious playfulness: "Thanks,
I should like a cherry." And I should have listened to this
dialogue with the same avidity as to a scene from *Le Mari de la
Débutante*, where the absence of poetry, of lofty thoughts,
things which were so familiar to me and which, I suppose,
Meilhac would have been eminently capable of putting into it,
seemed to me in itself a refinement, a conventional refinement
and therefore all the more mysterious and instructive.

"That fat fellow is the Marquis de Ganançay," came in a
knowing tone from the man next to me, who had not quite
caught the name whispered in the row behind.

The Marquis de Palancy, his face bent downwards at the
end of his long neck, his round bulging eye glued to the glass
of his monocle, moved slowly around in the transparent shade
and appeared no more to see the public in the stalls than a fish
that drifts past, unconscious of the press of curious gazers,
behind the glass wall of an aquarium. Now and again he
paused, venerable, wheezing, moss-grown, and the audience
could not have told whether he was in pain, asleep, swimming,
about to spawn, or merely taking breath. No one aroused in
me so much envy as he, on account of his apparent familiarity
with this box and the indifference with which he allowed the
Princess to hold out to him her box of sweets, throwing him
as she did so a glance from her fine eyes, cut from a diamond
which at such moments intelligence and friendliness seemed
to liquefy, whereas, when they were in repose, reduced to
their purely material beauty, to their mineral brilliance alone,
if the least reflected light displaced them ever so slightly, they
set the depths of the pit ablaze with their inhuman, horizontal
and resplendent fires. But now, because the act of *Phèdre* in
which Berma was playing was due to start, the Princess came
to the front of the box; whereupon, as if she herself were a
theatrical apparition, in the different zone of light which she
traversed, I saw not only the colour but the material of her
adornments change. And in the box, now drained dry, emer-
gent, no longer a part of the watery realm, the Princess,
ceasing to be a nereid, appeared turbanned in white and blue

like some marvellous tragic actress dressed for the part of Zaïre, or perhaps of Orosmane; then, when she had taken her place in the front row, I saw that the halcyon's nest which tenderly shielded the pearly pink of her cheeks was an immense bird of paradise, soft, glittering and velvety.

But now my gaze was diverted from the Princesse de Guermantes's box by an ill-dressed, plain little woman who came in, her eyes ablaze with indignation, followed by two young men, and sat down a few seats away from me. Then the curtain rose. I could not help being saddened by the reflexion that there remained now no trace of my former predispositions in regard to Berma and the dramatic art, at the time when, in order to miss nothing of the extraordinary phenomenon which I would have gone to the ends of the earth to see, I kept my mind prepared like the sensitive plates which astronomers take out to Africa or the West Indies with a view to the scrupulous observation of a comet or an eclipse; when I trembled for fear lest some cloud (a fit of ill-humour on the artist's part or an incident in the audience) should prevent the spectacle from taking place with the maximum of intensity; when I should not have believed that I was watching it in the best conditions had I not gone to the very theatre which was consecrated to her like an altar, in which I then felt to be an inseparable if accessory part of her appearance from behind the little red curtain, the officials with their white carnations appointed by her, the vaulted balcony over a pit filled with a shabbily dressed crowd, the women selling programmes bearing her photograph, the chestnut trees in the square outside, all those companions, those confidants of my impressions of those days which seemed to me to be inseparable from them. *Phèdre*, the "Declaration Scene," Berma, had had then for me a sort of absolute existence. Standing aloof from the world of current experience, they existed by themselves, I must go out to meet them, I would penetrate what I could of them, and if I opened my eyes and my soul to their fullest extent I would still absorb only too little of them. But how pleasant life seemed to me! The insignificance of the form of it that I myself was leading mattered nothing, no more than the time we spend on dressing, on getting ready to go out, since

beyond it there existed in an absolute form, difficult to approach, impossible to possess in their entirety, those more
solid realities, *Phèdre* and the way in which Berma spoke her
lines. Steeped in these dreams of perfection in the dramatic
art (a strong dose of which dreams anyone who had at that
time subjected my mind to analysis at any moment of the day
or even the night would have been able to extract from it), I
was like a battery that accumulates and stores up electricity.
And a time had come when, ill as I was, even if I had believed
that I should die of it, I should still have been compelled to
go and hear Berma. But now, like a hill which from a distance
seems azure-clad but as we draw nearer returns to its place in
our commonplace vision of things, all this had left the world of
the absolute and was no more than a thing like other things,
of which I took cognisance because I was there; the actors were
people of the same substance as the people I knew, trying to
declaim as well as possible these lines of *Phèdre* which themselves no longer formed a sublime and individual essence,
distinct from everything else, but were simply more or less
effective lines ready to slip back into the vast corpus of French
poetry, of which they were merely a part. I felt a despondency
that was all the more profound in that, if the object of my
headstrong and active desire no longer existed, on the other
hand the same tendency to indulge in an obsessional day-
dream, which varied from year to year but led me always to
sudden impulses, regardless of danger, still persisted. The
evening on which I rose from my bed of sickness and set out to
see a picture by Elstir or a mediaeval tapestry in some country
house or other was so like the day on which I ought to have
set out for Venice, or that on which I had gone to see Berma
or left for Balbec, that I felt in advance that the immediate
object of my sacrifice would leave me cold after a very short
while, that then I might pass close by the place without stopping even to look at that picture or those tapestries for which I
would at this moment risk so many sleepless nights, so many
hours of pain. I discerned in the instability of its object the
vanity of my effort, and at the same time its immensity, which
I had not noticed before, like one of those neurasthenics whose
exhaustion is doubled when it is pointed out to them that they

are exhausted. In the meantime my musings gave a certain glamour to anything that might be related to them. And even in my most carnal desires, orientated always in a particular direction, concentrated round a single dream, I might have recognised as their primary motive an idea, an idea for which I would have laid down my life, at the innermost core of which, as in my daydreams while I sat reading all afternoon in the garden at Combray, lay the notion of perfection.

I no longer felt the same indulgence as on the former occasion for the scrupulous efforts to express tenderness or anger which I had then remarked in the delivery and gestures of Aricie, Ismène and Hippolyte. It was not that the players—they were the same—did not still seek, with the same intelligent application, to impart now a caressing inflexion or a calculated ambiguity to their voices, now a tragic amplitude or a suppliant gentleness to their movements. Their tones bade the voice: "Be gentle, sing like a nightingale, caress and woo," or else, "Now wax furious," and then hurled themselves upon it, trying to carry it along with them in their frenzy. But it, mutinous, independent of their diction, remained unalterably their natural voice with its material defects or charms, its everyday vulgarity or affectation, and thus presented a complex of acoustic or social phenomena which the sentiment contained in the lines they were declaiming was powerless to alter.

Similarly the gestures of the players said to their arms, to their garments: "Be majestic." But the unsubmissive limbs allowed a biceps which knew nothing of the part to flaunt itself between shoulder and elbow; they continued to express the triviality of everyday life and to bring into prominence, instead of fine shades of Racinian meaning, mere muscular relationships; and the draperies which they held up fell back again along vertical lines in which the natural law that governs falling bodies was challenged only by an insipid textile pliancy. At this point the little woman who was sitting near me exclaimed:

"Not a clap! And did you ever see such a get-up? She's too old; she can't do it any more; she ought to have retired ages ago."

Amid a sibilant protest from their neighbours the two young men with her quietened her down and her fury raged now only in her eyes. This fury could be prompted only by the notion of success and fame, for Berma, who had earned so much money, was overwhelmed with debts. Since she was always making business or social appointments which she was prevented from keeping, she had messengers flying with apologies along every street in Paris, hotel suites booked in advance which she would never occupy, oceans of scent to bathe her dogs, heavy penalties for breaches of contract with all her managers. Failing any more serious expenses, and being less voluptuous than Cleopatra, she would have found the means of squandering provinces and kingdoms on telegrams and hired carriages. But the little woman was an actress who had never tasted success, and had vowed a deadly hatred against Berma. The latter had just come on to the stage. And then, miraculously, like those lessons which we have laboured in vain to learn overnight and find intact, got by heart, on waking up next morning, and like those faces of dead friends which the impassioned efforts of our memory pursue without recapturing and which, when we are no longer thinking of them, are there before our eyes just as they were in life, the talent of Berma, which had evaded me when I sought so greedily to grasp its essence, now, after these years of oblivion, in this hour of indifference, imposed itself on my admiration with the force of self-evidence. Formerly, in my attempts to isolate this talent, I deducted, so to speak, from what I heard, the part itself, a part, the common property of all the actresses who appeared as Phèdre, which I myself had studied beforehand so that I might be capable of subtracting it, of gleaning as a residuum Mme Berma's talent alone. But this talent which I sought to discover outside the part itself was indissolubly one with it. So with a great musician (it appears that this was the case with Vinteuil when he played the piano), his playing is that of so fine a pianist that one is no longer aware that the performer is a pianist at all, because (by not interposing all that apparatus of digital effort, crowned here and there with brilliant effects, all that spattering shower of notes in which at least the listener who does not quite know where he is thinks that he can discern talent in its material, tangible reality) his playing has become so transparent, so imbued with what he is interpreting, that one no longer sees the performer himself— he is simply a window opening upon a great work of art. I had been able to distinguish the intentions underlying the voices and the mime of Aricie, Ismène and Hippolyte, but Phèdre had interiorised hers, and my mind had not succeeded in wresting from her diction and attitudes, in apprehending in the miserly simplicity of their unbroken surfaces, those inventions, those effects of which no sign emerged, so completely had they been absorbed into it. Berma's voice, in which there subsisted not one scrap of inert matter refractory to the mind, betrayed no visible sign of that surplus of tears which, because they had been unable to soak into it, one could feel trickling down the voice of Aricie or of Ismène, but had been delicately refined down to its smallest cells like the instrument of a master violinist in whom, when one says that he produces a beautiful sound, one means to praise not a physical peculiarity but a superiority of soul; and, as in the classical landscape where in the place of a vanished nymph there is an inanimate spring, a discernible and concrete intention had been transformed into a certain limpidity of tone, strange, appropriate and cold. Berma's arms, which the lines of verse themselves, by the same emissive force that made the voice issue from her lips, seemed to raise on to her bosom like leaves displaced by a gush of water; her stage presence, her poses, which she had gradually built up, which she was to modify yet further, and which were based upon reasonings altogether more profound than those of which traces could be seen in the gestures of her fellow-actors, but reasonings that had lost their original deliberation, had melted into a sort of radiance whereby they sent throbbing, round the person of the heroine, rich and complex elements which the fascinated spectator nevertheless took not for a triumph of dramatic artistry but for a manifestation of life; those white veils themselves, which, tenuous and clinging, seemed to be of a living substance and to have been woven by the suffering, half-pagan, half-Jansenist, around which they drew themselves like a frail and shrinking cocoon— all these, voice, posture, gestures, veils, round this embodiment of an idea which a line of poetry is (an embodiment that, unlike our human bodies, is not an opaque screen, but a purified, spiritualised garment), were merely additional envelopes which, instead of concealing, showed up in greater splendour the soul that had assimilated them to itself and had spread itself through them, lava-flows of different substances, grown translucent, the superimposition of which causes only a richer refraction of the imprisoned, central ray that pierces through them, and makes more extensive, more precious and more beautiful the flame-drenched matter in which it is enshrined. So Berma's interpretation was, around Racine's work, a second work, quickened also by the breath of genius.

My impression, to tell the truth, though more agreeable than on the earlier occasion, was not really different. Only, I no longer confronted it with a pre-existent, abstract and false idea of dramatic genius, and I understood now that dramatic genius was precisely this. It had just occurred to me that if I had not derived any pleasure from my first encounter with Berma, it was because, as earlier still when I used to meet Gilberte in the Champs-Elysées, I had come to her with too strong a desire. Between my two disappointments there was perhaps not only this resemblance, but another, deeper one. The impression given us by a person or a work (or an inter-pretation of a work) of marked individuality is peculiar to that person or work. We have brought with us the ideas of "beauty," "breadth of style," "pathos" and so forth which we might at a pinch have the illusion of recognising in the banality of a conventional face or talent, but our critical spirit has before it the insistent challenge of a form of which it possesses no intellectual equivalent, in which it must detect and isolate the unknown element. It hears a shrill sound, an oddly inter-rogative inflexion. It asks itself: "Is that good? Is what I am feeling now admiration? Is that what is meant by richness of colouring, nobility, strength?" And what answers it again is a shrill voice, a curiously questioning tone, the despotic impres-sion, wholly material, caused by a person whom one does not know, in which no scope is left for "breadth of interpretation." And for this reason it is the really beautiful works that, if we listen to them with sincerity, must disappoint us most keenly, because in the storehouse of our ideas there is none that responds to an individual impression.

This was precisely what Berma's acting showed me. This was indeed what was meant by nobility, by intelligence of diction. Now I could appreciate the merits of a broad, poetical, powerful interpretation, or rather it was to this that those epithets were conventionally applied, but only as we give the names of Mars, Venus, Saturn to planets which have nothing mythological about them. We feel in one world, we think, we give names to things in another; between the two we can establish a certain correspondence, but not bridge the gap. It was to some extent this gap, this fault, that I had to cross when, that afternoon on which I first went to see Berma, having strained my ears to catch every word, I had found some difficulty in correlating my ideas of "nobility of interpretation," of "originality," and had broken out in applause only after a moment of blankness and as if my applause sprang not from my actual impression but was connected in some way with my preconceived ideas, with the pleasure that I found in saying to myself: "At last I am listening to Berma." And the difference which exists between a person or a work of art that are markedly individual and the idea of beauty exists just as much between what they make us feel and the idea of love or of admiration. Wherefore we fail to recognise them. I had found no pleasure in listening to Berma (any more than, when I loved her, in seeing Gilberte). I had said to myself: "Well, I don't admire her." But meanwhile I was thinking only of mastering the secret of Berma's acting, I was preoccupied with that alone, I was trying to open my mind as wide as possible to receive all that her acting contained. I realised now that that was precisely what admiration meant.

Was this genius, of which Berma's interpretation was only the revelation, solely the genius of Racine?

I thought so at first. I was soon to be undeceived, when the act from *Phèdre* came to an end, after enthusiastic curtain-calls during which my furious old neighbour, drawing her little body up to its full height, turning sideways in her seat, stiffened the muscles of her face and folded her arms over her bosom to show that she was not joining the others in their applause, and to make more noticeable a protest which to her appeared sensational though it passed unperceived. The piece that followed was one of those novelties which at one time I had expected, since they were not famous, to be inevitably trivial and of no general application, devoid as they were of any existence outside the performance that was being given of them at the moment. But also I did not have the disappointment of seeing the eternity of a masterpiece occupy no more space or time than the width of the footlights and the length of a performance which would accomplish it as effectively as an occasional piece. Then at each set speech which I felt that the audience liked and which would one day be famous, in the absence of the celebrity it could not have won in the past I added the fame it would enjoy in the future, by a mental process the converse of that which consists in imagining masterpieces on the day of their first frail appearance, when it seemed inconceivable that a title which no one had ever heard before could one day be set, bathed in the same mellow light, beside those of the author's other works. And this role would eventually figure in the list of her finest impersonations, next to that of Phèdre. Not that in itself it was not destitute of all literary merit; but Berma was as sublime in it as in *Phèdre*. I realised then that the work of the playwright was for the actress no more than the raw material, more or less irrelevant in itself, for the creation of her masterpiece of interpretation, just as the great painter whom I had met at Balbec, Elstir, had found the inspiration for two pictures of equal merit in a school building devoid of character and a cathedral which was itself a work of art. And as the painter dissolves houses, carts, people, in some broad effect of light which makes them homogeneous, so Berma spread out great sheets of terror or tenderness over the words which were equally blended, all planed down or heightened, and which a lesser artist would have carefully detached from one another. Of course each of them had an inflexion of its own, and Berma's diction did not prevent one from distinguishing the lines. Is it not already a first element of ordered complexity, of beauty, when, on hearing a rhyme, that is to say something that is at once similar to and different from the preceding rhyme, which is prompted by it, but introduces the variety of a new idea, one is conscious of two systems overlapping each other, one intellectual, the other prosodic? But Berma at the same time made the words, the lines, whole speeches even, flow into lakes of sound vaster than themselves, at the margins of which it was a joy to see them obliged to stop, to break off; thus it is that a poet takes pleasure in making the word which is about to spring forth pause for a moment at the rhyming point, and a composer in merging the various words of the libretto in a single rhythm which runs counter to them and yet sweeps them along. Thus into the prose sentences of the modern playwright as into the verse of Racine Berma contrived to introduce those vast images of grief, nobility, passion, which were the masterpieces of her own personal art, and in which she could be recognised as, in the portraits which he has made of different sitters, we recognise a painter.

I had no longer any desire, as on the former occasion, to be able to arrest Berma's poses, or the beautiful effect of colour which she gave for a moment only in a beam of limelight which at once faded never to reappear, or to make her repeat a single line a hundred times over. I realised that my original desire had been more exacting than the intentions of the poet, the actress, the great decorative artist who directed the production, and that the charm which floated over a line as it was spoken, the shifting poses perpetually transformed into others, the successive tableaux, were the fleeting result, the momentary object, the mobile masterpiece which the art of the theatre intended and which the attentiveness of a too-enraptured audience would destroy by trying to arrest. I did not even wish to come back another day and hear Berma again; I was satisfied with her; it was when I admired too keenly not to be disappointed by the object of my admiration, whether that object was Gilberte or Berma, that I demanded in advance, of the impression to be received on the morrow, the pleasure that yesterday's impression had denied me. Without seeking to analyse the joy which I had just felt, and might perhaps have turned to some more profitable use, I said to myself, as in the old days some of my schoolfellows used to say: "Certainly, I put Berma first," not without a confused feeling that Berma's genius was not perhaps very accurately represented by this affirmation of my preference and this award to her of a "first" place, whatever the peace of mind that they might incidentally restore to me.

Just as the curtain was rising on this second play I looked up at Mme de Guermantes's box. The Princess, with a movement that called into being an exquisite line which my mind pursued into the void, had just turned her head towards the back of her box; the guests were all on their feet, and also turned towards the door, and between the double hedge which they thus formed, with all the triumphant assurance, the grandeur of the goddess that she was, but with an unwonted meekness due to her feigned and smiling embarrassment at arriving so late and making everyone get up in the middle of the performance, the Duchesse de Guermantes entered, enveloped in white chiffon. She went straight up to her cousin, made a deep curtsey to a young man with fair hair who was seated in the front row, and turning towards the amphibian monsters floating in the recesses of the cavern, gave to these demi-gods of the Jockey Club—who at that moment, and among them all M. de Palancy in particular, were the men I should most have liked to be—the familiar "good evening" of an old friend, an allusion to her day-to-day relations with them during the last fifteen years. I sensed but could not decipher the mystery of that smiling gaze which she addressed to her friends, in the azure brilliance with which it glowed while she surrendered her hand to them one after another, a gaze which, could I have broken up its prism, analysed its crystallisations, might perhaps have revealed to me the essence of the unknown life which was apparent in it at that moment. The Duc de Guermantes followed his wife, the gay flash of his monocle, the gleam of his teeth, the whiteness of his carnation or of his pleated shirt-front relegating, to make room for their light, the darkness of his eyebrows, lips and coat; with a wave of his outstretched hand which he let fall on to their shoulders, vertically, without moving his head, he commanded the inferior tritons who were making way for him to resume their seats, and made a deep bow to the fair young man. It was as though the Duchess had guessed that her cousin, of whom, it was rumoured, she was inclined to make fun for what she called her "exaggerations" (a noun which, from her point of view, so wittily French and restrained, was instantly applicable to the poetry and enthusiasm of the Teuton), would be wearing this evening one of those costumes in which the Duchess considered her "dressed up," and that she had decided to give her a lesson in good taste. Instead of the wonderful downy plumage which descended from the crown of the Princess's head to her throat, instead of her net of shells and pearls, the Duchess wore in her hair only a simple aigrette which, surmounting her arched nose and prominent eyes, reminded one of the crest on the head of a bird. Her neck and shoulders emerged from a drift of snow-white chiffon, against which fluttered a swansdown fan, but below this her gown, the bodice of which had for its sole ornament innumerable spangles (either little sticks and beads of metal, or brilliants), moulded her figure with a precision that was positively British. But different as their two costumes were, after the Princess had given her cousin the chair in which she herself had previously been sitting, they could be seen turning to gaze at one another in mutual appreciation.

Perhaps Mme de Guermantes would smile next day when she referred to the headdress, a little too complicated, which the Princess had worn, but certainly she would declare that the latter had been none the less quite lovely and marvellously got up; and the Princess, whose own tastes found something a little cold, a little austere, a little "tailor-made" in her cousin's way of dressing, would discover in this strict sobriety an exquisite refinement. Moreover, the harmony that existed between them, the universal and pre-established gravitational pull of their upbringing, neutralised the contrasts not only in their apparel but in their attitude. At those invisible magnetic longitudes which the refinement of their manners traced between them, the natural expansiveness of the Princess died away, while towards them the formal correctness of the Duchess allowed itself to be attracted and loosened, turned to sweetness and charm. As, in the play which was now being performed, to realise how much personal poetry Berma extracted from it one had only to entrust the part which she was playing, which she alone could play, to any other actress, so the spectator who raised his eyes to the balcony would have seen in two smaller boxes there how an "arrangement" intended to suggest that of the Princesse de Guermantes simply made the Baronne de Morienval appear eccentric, pretentious and ill-bred, while an effort as painstaking as it must have been costly to imitate the clothes and style of the Duchesse de Guermantes only made Mme de Cambremer look like some provincial schoolgirl, mounted on wires, rigid, erect, desiccated, angular, with a plume of raven's feathers stuck vertically in her hair. Perhaps this lady was out of place in a theatre in which it was only with the brightest stars of the season that the boxes (even those in the highest tier, which from below seemed like great hampers studded with human flowers and attached to the ceiling of the auditorium by the red cords of their plush-covered partitions) composed an ephemeral panorama which deaths, scandals, illnesses, quarrels would soon alter, but which this evening was held motionless by attentiveness, heat, dizziness, dust, elegance and boredom, in the sort of eternal tragic instant of unconscious expectancy and calm torpor which, in retrospect, seems always to have preceded the explosion of a bomb or the first flicker of a fire.

The explanation for Mme de Cambremer's presence on this occasion was that the Princesse de Parme, devoid of snobbishness as are most truly royal personages, and by contrast eaten up with a pride in and passion for charity which rivalled her taste for what she believed to be the Arts, had bestowed a few boxes here and there upon women like Mme de Cambremer who were not numbered among the highest aristocratic society but with whom she was in communication with regard to charitable undertakings. Mme de Cambremer never took her eyes off the Duchesse and Princesse de Guermantes, which was all the easier for her since, not being actually acquainted with either, she could not be suspected of angling for a sign of recognition. Inclusion in the visiting lists of these two great ladies was nevertheless the goal towards which she had been striving for the last ten years with untiring patience. She had calculated that she might possibly reach it in five years more.

But having been smitten by a fatal disease, the inexorable character of which—for she prided herself upon her medical knowledge—she thought she knew, she was afraid that she might not live so long. This evening she was happy at least in the thought that all these women whom she scarcely knew would see in her company a man who was one of their own set, the young Marquis de Beausergent, Mme d'Argencourt's brother, who moved impartially in both worlds and whom the women of the second were very keen to parade before the eyes of those of the first. He was seated behind Mme de Cambremer on a chair placed at an angle, so that he might be able to scan the other boxes. He knew everyone in them, and to bow to his friends, with the exquisite elegance of his delicately arched figure, his fine features and fair hair, he half-raised his upright torso, a smile brightening his blue eyes, with a blend of deference and detachment, a picture etched with precision in the rectangle of the oblique plane in which he was placed, like one of those old prints which portray a great nobleman in his courtly pride. He often accepted these invitations to go to the theatre with Mme de Cambremer. In the auditorium, and, on the way out, in the lobby, he stood gallantly by her side amid the throng of more brilliant friends whom he saw about him, and to whom he refrained from speaking, to avoid any awkwardness, just as though he had been in doubtful company. If at such moments the Princesse de Guermantes swept by, lightfoot and fair as Diana, trailing behind her the folds of an incomparable cloak, making every head turn round and followed by all eyes (and, most of all, by Mme de Cambremer's), M. de Beausergent would become engrossed in conversation with his companion, acknowledging the friendly and dazzling smile of the Princess only with constraint, and with the well-bred reserve, the considerate coldness of a person whose friendliness might have become momentarily embarrassing.

Had not Mme de Cambremer known already that the box belonged to the Princess, she could still have told that the Duchesse de Guermantes was the guest from the air of greater interest with which she was surveying the spectacle of stage and auditorium, out of politeness to her hostess. But simultaneously with this centrifugal force, an equal and opposite force generated by the same desire to be sociable drew her attention back to her own attire, her plume, her necklace, her bodice and also to that of the Princess herself, whose subject, whose slave her cousin seemed to proclaim herself, come there solely to see her, ready to follow her elsewhere should the titular holder of the box have taken it into her head to get up and go, and regarding the rest of the house as composed merely of strangers, worth looking at simply as curiosities, though she numbered among them many friends to whose boxes she regularly repaired on other evenings and with regard to whom she never failed on those occasions to demonstrate a similar loyalty, exclusive, relativistic and weekly. Mme de Cambremer was surprised to see her there that evening. She knew that the Duchess stayed on very late at Guermantes, and had supposed her to be there still. But she had been told that sometimes, when there was some special function in Paris which she considered it worth her while to attend, Mme de Guermantes would order one of her carriages to be brought round as soon as she had taken tea with the guns, and, as the sun was setting, drive off at a spanking pace through the gathering darkness of the forest, then along the high road, to join the train at Combray and so be in Paris the same evening. "Perhaps she has come up from Guermantes especially to see Berma," thought Mme de Cambremer, and marvelled at the thought. And she remembered having heard Swann say in that ambiguous jargon which he shared with M. de Charlus: "The Duchess is one of the noblest souls in Paris, the cream of the most refined, the choicest society." For myself, who derived from the names Guermantes, Bavaria and Condé what I imagined to be the lives and the thoughts of the two cousins (I could no longer do so from their faces, having seen them), I would rather have had their opinion of *Phèdre* than that of the greatest critic in the world. For in his I should have found merely intelligence, an intelligence superior to my own but similar in kind. But what the Duchesse and Princesse de Guermantes might think, an opinion which would have furnished me with an invaluable clue to the nature of these two poetic creatures, I imagined with the aid of their names, I endowed with an irrational charm, and, with the thirst and the longing of a fever-stricken patient, what I demanded that their opinion of *Phèdre* should yield to me was the charm of the summer afternoons that I had spent wandering along the Guermantes way.

Mme de Cambremer was trying to make out how exactly the cousins were dressed. For my own part, I never doubted that their garments were peculiar to themselves, not merely in the sense in which the livery with red collar or blue facings had once belonged exclusively to the houses of Guermantes and Condé, but rather as for a bird its plumage which, as well as being a heightening of its beauty, is an extension of its body. The costumes of these two ladies seemed to me like the materialisation, snow-white or patterned with colour, of their inner activity, and, like the gestures which I had seen the Princesse de Guermantes make and which, I had no doubt, corresponded to some latent idea, the plumes which swept down from her forehead and her cousin's glittering spangled bodice seemed to have a special meaning, to be to each of these women an attribute which was hers, and hers alone, the significance of which I should have liked to know: the bird of paradise seemed inseparable from its wearer as her peacock is from Juno, and I did not believe that any other woman could usurp that spangled bodice, any more than the fringed and flashing shield of Minerva. And when I turned my eyes to their box, far more than on the ceiling of the theatre, painted with cold and lifeless allegories, it was as though I had seen, thanks to a miraculous rending of the customary clouds, the assembly of the Gods in the act of contemplating the spectacle of mankind, beneath a crimson canopy, in a clear lighted space, between two pillars of Heaven. I gazed on this momentary apotheosis with a perturbation which was partly soothed by the feeling that I myself was unknown to the Immortals; the Duchess had indeed seen me once with her husband, but could surely have kept no memory of that, and I was not distressed that she should find herself, owing to the position that she occupied in the box, gazing down upon the nameless, collective madrepores of the audience in the stalls, for I was happily aware that my being was dissolved in their midst, when, at the moment in which, by virtue of the laws of refraction, the blurred shape of the protozoon devoid of any individual existence which was myself must have come to be reflected in the impassive current of those two blue eyes, I saw a ray illumine them: the Duchess, goddess turned woman, and appearing in that moment a thousand times more lovely, raised towards me the white-gloved hand which had been resting on the balustrade of the box and waved it in token of friendship, my gaze was caught in the spontaneous incandescence of the flashing eyes of the Princess, who had unwittingly set them ablaze merely by turning her head to see who it might be that her cousin was thus greeting, and the latter, who had recognised me, showered upon me the sparkling and celestial torrent of her smile.

Now, every morning, long before the hour at which she left her house, I went by a devious route to post myself at the corner of the street along which she generally came, and, when the moment of her arrival seemed imminent, I strolled back with an air of being absorbed in something else, looking the other way, and raised my eyes to her face as I drew level with her, but as though I had not in the least expected to see her. Indeed, for the first few mornings, so as to be sure of not missing her, I waited in front of the house. And every time the carriage gate opened (letting out one after another so many people who were not the one for whom I was waiting) its grinding rattle prolonged itself in my heart in a series of oscillations which took a long time to subside. For never was devotee of a famous actress whom he does not know, kicking his heels outside the stage door, never was angry or idolatrous crowd, gathered to insult or to carry in triumph through the streets the condemned assassin or the national hero whom it believes to be on the point of coming whenever a sound is heard from the inside of the prison or the palace, never were these so stirred by emotion as I was, awaiting the emergence of this great lady who in her simple attire was able, by the grace of her movements (quite different from the gait she affected on entering a drawing-room or a box), to make of her morning walk—and for me there was no one in the world but she out walking—a whole poem of elegant refinement and the loveliest ornament, the rarest flower of the season. But after the third day, so that the porter should not discover my stratagem, I betook myself much further afield, to some point upon the Duchess's usual route. Often before that evening at the theatre I had made similar little excursions before lunch, when the weather was fine; if it had been raining, at the first gleam of sunshine I would hasten downstairs to take a stroll, and if, suddenly, coming towards me along the still wet pavement, changed by the sun into a golden lacquer, in the transformation scene of a crossroads powdered with mist which the sun tanned and bleached, I caught sight of a schoolgirl followed by her governess or of a dairy-maid with her white sleeves, I stood motionless, my hand pressed to my heart which was already leaping towards an unexplored life; I tried to bear in mind the street, the time, the number of the door through which the girl (whom I followed sometimes) had vanished and failed to reappear. Fortunately the fleeting nature of these cherished images, which I promised myself that I would make an effort to see again, prevented them from fixing themselves with any vividness in my memory. No matter, I was less depressed now at the thought of my own ill health, of my never having summoned up the energy to set to work, to begin a book, for the world appeared to me a pleasanter place to live in, life a more interesting experience to go through, now that I had learned that the streets of Paris, like the roads round Balbec, were aflower with those unknown beauties whom I had so often sought to conjure from the woods of Méséglise, each of whom aroused a voluptuous longing which she alone seemed capable of assuaging.

On coming home from the Opéra I had added for the following morning to the list of those whom for some days past I had been hoping to meet again the image of Mme de Guer-mantes, tall, with her high-piled crown of silky, golden hair, with the tenderness promised by the smile which she had directed at me from her cousin's box. I would follow the route which Françoise had told me that the Duchess generally took, and I would try at the same time, in the hope of meeting two girls whom I had seen a few days earlier, not to miss the

break-up of a school lesson or a catechism class. But meanwhile, from time to time, the scintillating smile of Mme de
Guermantes, and the warm feeling it had engendered, came
back to me. And without exactly knowing what I was doing,
I tried to find a place for them (as a woman studies the effect
a certain kind of jewelled buttons that have just been given
her might have on a dress) beside the romantic ideas which I
had long held and which Albertine's coldness, Gisèle's premature departure, and before them my deliberate and too long
sustained separation from Gilberte had set free (the idea for
instance of being loved by a woman, of having a life in common with her); then it was the image of one or other of the two
girls seen in the street that I coupled with those ideas, to which
immediately afterwards I tried to adapt my memory of the
Duchess. Compared with those ideas, the memory of Mme de
Guermantes at the Opéra was a very insignificant thing, a tiny
star twinkling beside the long tail of a blazing comet; moreover
I had been quite familiar with the ideas long before I came to
know Mme de Guermantes; whereas the memory of her
I possessed but imperfectly; at moments it escaped me; it was
during the hours when, from floating vaguely in my mind in
the same way as the images of various other pretty women,
it gradually developed into a unique and definitive association
—exclusive of every other feminine image—with those romantic ideas of mine which were of so much longer standing
than itself, it was during those few hours in which I remembered it most clearly, that I ought to have taken steps to find
out exactly what it was; but I did not then know the importance
it was to assume for me; I cherished it simply as a first private
meeting with Mme de Guermantes inside myself; it was the
first, the only accurate sketch, the only one made from life, the
only one that was really Mme de Guermantes; during the few
hours in which I was fortunate enough to retain it without
giving it any conscious thought, it must have been charming,
though, that memory, since it was always to it, freely still at
that moment, without haste, without strain, without the
slightest compulsion or anxiety, that my ideas of love returned;
then, as gradually those ideas fixed it more permanently, it
acquired from them a greater strength but itself became more

vague; presently I could no longer recapture it; and in my
dreams I no doubt distorted it completely, for whenever I
saw Mme de Guermantes I realised the disparity—always, as
it happened, different—between what I had imagined and
what I saw. True, every morning now, at the moment when
Mme de Guermantes emerged from her doorway at the top of
the street, I saw again her tall figure, her face with its bright
eyes and crown of silken hair—all the things for which I was
waiting there; but, on the other hand, a minute or two later,
when, having first turned my eyes away so as to appear not to
be expecting this encounter which I had come to seek, I
raised them to look at the Duchess at the moment in which we
converged, what I saw then were red patches (as to which I
did not know whether they were due to the fresh air or to a
blotchy skin) on a sullen face which with the curtest of nods,
a long way removed from the affability of the *Phèdre* evening,
acknowledged the greeting which I addressed to her daily
with an air of surprise and which did not seem to please her.
And yet, after a few days during which the memory of the two
girls fought against heavy odds for the mastery of my amorous
feelings against that of Mme de Guermantes, it was in the end
the latter which, as though of its own accord, generally prevailed while its competitors withdrew; it was to it that I finally
found myself, on the whole voluntarily still and as though from
choice and with pleasure, to have transferred all my thoughts of
love. I had ceased to dream of the little girls coming from their
catechism, or of a certain dairy-maid; and yet I had also lost all
hope of encountering in the street what I had come to seek,
either the affection promised to me at the theatre in a smile, or
the profile, the bright face beneath its pile of golden hair which
were so only when seen from afar. Now I should not even have
been able to say what Mme de Guermantes was like, what I
recognised her by, for every day, in the picture which she
presented as a whole, the face was as different as were the dress
and the hat.

Why, on such and such a morning, when I saw advancing
towards me beneath a violet hood a sweet, smooth face whose
charms were symmetrically arranged about a pair of blue
eyes and into which the curve of the nose seemed to have

been absorbed, did I gauge from a joyous commotion in my breast that I was not going to return home without having caught a glimpse of Mme de Guermantes? Why did I feel the same perturbation, affect the same indifference, turn away my eyes with the same abstracted air as on the day before, at the appearance in profile in a side street, beneath a navy-blue toque, of a beak-like nose alongside a red cheek with a piercing eye, like some Egyptian deity? Once it was not merely a woman with a bird's beak that I saw but almost the bird itself; Mme de Guermantes's outer garments, even her toque, were of fur, and since she thus left no cloth visible, she seemed naturally furred, like certain vultures whose thick, smooth, tawny, soft plumage looks like a sort of animal's coat. In the midst of this natural plumage, the tiny head arched out its beak and the bulging eyes were piercing and blue.

One day I would be pacing up and down the street for hours on end without seeing Mme de Guermantes when suddenly, inside a dairy shop tucked in between two of the mansions of this aristocratic and plebeian quarter, there would emerge the vague and unfamiliar face of a fashionably dressed woman who was asking to see some *petits suisses*, and, before I had had time to distinguish her I would be struck, as by a flash of light reaching me sooner than the rest of the image, by the glance of the Duchess; another time, having failed to meet her and hearing midday strike, realising that it was not worth my while to wait for her any longer, I would be sorrowfully making my way homewards absorbed in my disappointment and gazing absent-mindedly at a receding carriage, when suddenly I realised that the nod which a lady had given through the carriage window was meant for me, and that this lady, whose features, relaxed and pale, or alternatively tense and vivid, composed, beneath a round hat or a towering plume, the face of a stranger whom I had supposed that I did not know, was Mme de Guermantes, by whom I had let myself be greeted without so much as an acknowledgement. And sometimes I would come upon her as I entered the carriage gate, standing outside the lodge where the detestable porter whose inquisitive eyes I loathed was in the act of making her a a profound obeisance and also, no doubt, his daily report. For the entire staff of the Guermantes household, hidden behind the window curtains, would tremble with fear as they watched a conversation which they were unable to overhear, but which meant as they very well knew that one or other of them would certainly have his "day out" stopped by the Duchess to whom this Cerberus had betrayed him.

In view of the succession of different faces which Mme Guermantes displayed thus one after another, faces that occupied a relative and varying expanse, sometimes narrow, sometimes large, in her person and attire as a whole, my love was not attached to any particular one of those changeable elements of flesh and fabric which replaced one another as day followed day, and which she could modify and renew almost entirely without tempering my agitation because beneath them, beneath the new collar and the strange cheek, I felt that it was still Mme de Guermantes. What I loved was the invisible person who set all this outward show in motion, the woman whose hostility so distressed me, whose approach threw me into a turmoil, whose life I should have liked to make my own, expropriating her friends. She might flaunt a blue feather or reveal an inflamed complexion, and her actions would still lose none of their importance for me.

I should not myself have felt that Mme de Guermantes was irritated at meeting me day after day, had I not learned it indirectly by reading it on the face, stiff with coldness, disapproval and pity, which Françoise wore when she was helping me to get ready for these morning walks. The moment I asked her for my outdoor things I felt a contrary wind arise in her worn and shrunken features. I made no attempt to win her confidence, for I knew that I should not succeed. She had a power the nature of which I have never been able to fathom for at once becoming aware of anything unpleasant that might happen to my parents and myself. Perhaps it was not a supernatural power, but was to be explained by sources of information that were peculiar to herself: as it may happen that the news which often reaches a savage tribe several days before the post has brought it to the European colony has really been transmitted to them not by telepathy but from hill-top to hill-top by a chain of beacon fires. Thus, in the particular instance of my morning walks, possibly Mme de Guermantes's servants had heard their mistress say how tired she was of running into me every day without fail wherever she went, and had repeated her remarks to Françoise. My parents might, it is true, have attached some servant other than Françoise to my person, but I should have been no better off. Françoise was in a sense less of a servant than the others. In her way of feeling things, of being kind and compassionate, harsh and disdainful, shrewd and narrow-minded, of combining a white skin with red hands, she was still the village girl whose parents had had "a place of their own" but having come to grief had been obliged to put her into service. Her presence in our houschold was the country air, the social life of a farm of fifty years ago transported into our midst by a sort of reversal of the normal order of travel whereby it is the countryside that comes to visit the traveller. As the glass cases in a local museum are filled with specimens of the curious handiwork which the peasants still carve or embroider in certain parts of the country, so our flat in Paris was decorated with the words of Françoise, inspired by a traditional and local sentiment and governed by extremely ancient laws. And she could trace her way back as though by clues of coloured thread to the songbirds and cherry trees of her childhood, to the bed in which her mother had died, and which she still vividly saw. But in spite of all this wealth of background, once she had come to Paris and had entered our service she had acquired—as, *a fortiori*, anyone else would have done in her place—the ideas, the system of interpretation used by the servants on the other floors, compensating for the respect which she was obliged to show to us by repeating the rude words that the cook on the fourth floor had used to her mistress, with a servile gratification so intense that, for the first time in our lives, feeling a sort of solidarity with the detestable occupant of the fourth floor flat, we said to ourselves that possibly we too were "employers" after all. This alteration in Françoise's character was perhaps inevitable. Certain ways of life are so abnormal that they are bound to produce certain characteristic faults; such was the life led by the King at Versailles among his courtiers, a life as strange as that of a Pharaoh or a Doge—and, far more even than his, the life of his courtiers. The life led by servants is probably of an even more monstrous abnormality, which only its familiarity can prevent us from seeing. But it was actually in details more intimate still that I should have been obliged, even if I had dismissed Françoise, to keep the same servant. For various others were to enter my service in the years to come; already endowed with the defects common to all servants, they underwent nevertheless a rapid transformation with me. As the laws of attack govern those of riposte, in order not to be worsted by the asperities of my character, all of them effected in their own an identical withdrawal, always at the same point, and to make up for this took advantage of the gaps in my line to thrust out advanced posts. Of these gaps I knew nothing, any more than of the salients to which they gave rise, precisely because they were gaps. But my servants, by gradually becoming spoiled, taught me of their existence. It was from the defects which they invariably acquired that I learned what were my own natural and invariable shortcomings; their character offered me a sort of negative of my own. We had always laughed, my mother and I, at Mme Sazerat, who used, in speaking of servants, to say "that race" or "that class." But I am bound to admit that what made it useless to think of replacing Françoise by anyone else was that her successor would inevitably have belonged just as much to the race of servants in general and to the class of my servants in particular.

To return to Françoise, I never in my life experienced a humiliation without having seen beforehand on her face the signs of ready-made condolences, and when in my anger at the thought of being pitied by her I tried to pretend that on the contrary I had scored a distinct success, my lies broke feebly against the wall of her respectful but obvious unbelief and the consciousness that she enjoyed of her own infallibility. For she knew the truth. She refrained from uttering it, and made only a slight movement with her lips as if she still had her mouth full and was finishing a tasty morsel. She refrained from uttering it? So at least I long believed, for at that time I still supposed that it was by means of words that one communicated the truth to others. Indeed the words that people said to me recorded their meaning so unalterably on the sensitive

plate of my mind that I could no more believe it possible that
someone who had professed to love me did not love me than
Françoise herself could have doubted when she had read it
"in the paper" that some priest or gentleman or other was
prepared, on receipt of a stamped envelope, to furnish us free
of charge with an infallible remedy for every known complaint
or with the means of multiplying our income a hundredfold.
(If, on the other hand, our doctor were to prescribe for her the
simplest cure for a cold in the head, she, so stubborn to
endure the keenest suffering, would complain bitterly of what
she had been made to sniff, insisting that it tickled her nose and
that life was not worth living.) But she was the first person
to prove to me by her example (which I was not to understand
until long afterwards, when it was given me afresh and more
painfully, as will be seen in the later volumes of this work, by
a person who was dearer to me than Françoise) that the truth
has no need to be uttered to be made apparent, and that one
may perhaps gather it with more certainty, without waiting
for words and without even taking any account of them, from
countless outward signs, even from certain invisible phenomena, analogous in the sphere of human character to what
atmospheric changes are in the physical world. I might perhaps
have suspected this, since it frequently occurred to me at that
time to say things myself in which there was no vestige of
truth, while I made the real truth plain by all manner of involuntary confidences expressed by my body and in my actions
(which were only too accurately interpreted by Françoise); I
ought perhaps to have suspected it, but to do so I should first
have had to be conscious that I myself was occasionally
mendacious and deceitful. Now mendacity and deceitfulness
were with me, as with most people, called into being in so
immediate, so contingent a fashion, in the defence of some
particular interest, that my mind, fixed on some lofty ideal,
allowed my character to set about those urgent, sordid tasks
in the darkness below and did not look down to observe
them.

When Françoise, in the evening, was nice to me, and asked
my permission to sit in my room, it seemed to me that her
face became transparent and that I could see the kindness and

honesty that lay beneath. But Jupien, who had lapses into indiscretion of which I learned only later, revealed afterwards that she had told him that I was not worth the price of a rope to hang me, and that I had tried to do her every conceivable harm. These words of Jupien's set up at once before my eyes, in new and strange colours, a print of my relations with Françoise so different from the one which I often took pleasure in contemplating and in which, without the least shadow of doubt, Françoise adored me and lost no opportunity of singing my praises, that I realised that it is not only the physical world that differs from the aspect in which we see it; that all reality is perhaps equally dissimilar from what we believe ourselves to be directly perceiving and which we compose with the aid of ideas that do not reveal themselves but are none the less efficacious, just as the trees, the sun and the sky would not be the same as what we see if they were apprehended by creatures having eyes differently constituted from ours, or else en-dowed for that purpose with organs other than eyes which would furnish equivalents of trees and sky and sun, though not visual ones. However that might be, this sudden glimpse that Jupien afforded me of the real world appalled me. And yet it concerned only Françoise, about whom I cared little. Was it the same with all one's social relations? And into what depths of despair might this not some day plunge me, if it were the same with love? That was the future's secret. For the present only Françoise was concerned. Did she sincerely believe what she had said to Jupien? Had she said it to embroil Jupien with me, possibly so that we should not appoint Jupien's girl as her successor? At any rate I realised the im-possibility of obtaining any direct and certain knowledge of whether Françoise loved or hated me. And thus it was she who first gave me the idea that a person does not, as I had imagined, stand motionless and clear before our eyes with his merits, his defects, his plans, his intentions with regard to ourselves (like a garden at which we gaze through a railing with all its borders spread out before us), but is a shadow which we can never penetrate, of which there can be no such thing as direct knowledge, with respect to which we form countless beliefs, based upon words and sometimes actions, neither of which

can give us anything but inadequate and as it proves contradictory information—a shadow behind which we can alternately
imagine, with equal justification, that there burns the flame of
hatred and of love.

I was genuinely in love with Mme de Guermantes. The
greatest happiness that I could have asked of God would have
been that he should send down on her every imaginable
calamity, and that ruined, despised, stripped of all the privileges
that separated her from me, having no longer any home of her
own or people who would condescend to speak to her, she
should come to me for asylum. I imagined her doing so. And
indeed on those evenings when some change in the atmosphere
or in my own state of health brought to the surface of my consciousness some forgotten scroll on which were recorded
impressions of other days, instead of profiting by the forces of
renewal that had been generated in me, instead of using them
to unravel in my own mind thoughts which as a rule escaped
me, instead of setting myself at last to work, I preferred to
relate aloud, to excogitate in a lively, external manner, with a
flow of invention as useless as was my declamation of it, a
whole novel crammed with adventure, in which the Duchess,
fallen upon misfortune, came to implore assistance from me—
who had become, by a converse change of circumstances,
rich and powerful. And when I had thus spent hours on
end imagining the circumstances, rehearsing the sentences with
which I should welcome the Duchess beneath my roof, the
situation remained unaltered; I had, alas, in reality, chosen to
love the woman who in her own person combined perhaps
the greatest possible number of different advantages; in whose
eyes, accordingly, I could not hope to cut any sort of figure;
for she was as rich as the richest commoner—and noble also;
not to mention that personal charm which set her at the pinnacle
of fashion, made her among the rest a sort of queen.

I felt that I displeased her by crossing her path every morning; but even if I had had the heart to refrain from doing so
for two or three days consecutively, Mme de Guermantes
might not have noticed that abstention, which would have
represented so great a sacrifice on my part, or might have
attributed it to some obstacle beyond my control. And indeed

I could not have brought myself to cease to dog her footsteps except by arranging that it should be impossible for me to do so, for the perpetually recurring need to meet her, to be for a moment the object of her attention, the person to whom her greeting was addressed, was stronger than my fear of arousing her displeasure. I should have had to go away for some time; and for that I had not the heart. I did think of it more than once. I would then tell Françoise to pack my boxes, and immediately afterwards to unpack them. (And as the spirit of imitation, the desire not to appear behind the times, alters the most natural and most positive form of oneself, Françoise, borrowing the expression from her daughter's vocabulary, used to remark that I was "dippy.") She did not approve of my tergiversations; she said that I was always "balancing," for when she was not aspiring to rival the moderns, she employed the very language of Saint-Simon. It is true that she liked it still less when I spoke to her authoritatively. She knew that this was not natural to me, and did not suit me, a condition which she expressed in the phrase "where there isn't a will." I should never have had the heart to leave Paris except in a direction that would bring me closer to Mme de Guermantes. This was by no means an impossibility. Would I not indeed find myself nearer to her than I was in the morning, in the street, solitary, humiliated, feeling that not a single one of the thoughts which I should have liked to convey to her ever reached her, in that weary marking time of my daily walks, which might go on indefinitely without getting me any further, if I were to go miles away from Mme de Guermantes, but to someone of her acquaintance, someone whom she knew to be particular in the choice of his friends and who appreciated me, who might speak to her about me, and if not obtain from her at least make her aware of what I wanted, someone thanks to whom at all events, simply because I should discuss with him whether or not it would be possible for him to convey this or that message to her, I should give to my solitary and silent meditations a new form, spoken, active, which would seem to me an advance, almost a realisation? What she did during the mysterious daily life of the "Guermantes" that she was—this was the constant object of my thoughts; and to break into

that life, even by indirect means, as with a lever, by employing the services of a person who was not excluded from
the Duchess's house, from her parties, from prolonged
conversation with her, would not that be a contact more distant but at the same time more effective than my contemplation
of her every morning in the street?

The friendship and admiration that Saint-Loup had shown
me seemed to me undeserved and had hitherto left me unmoved. All at once I set great store by them; I would have
liked him to disclose them to Mme de Guermantes, was quite
prepared even to ask him to do so. For when we are in love,
we long to be able to divulge to the woman we love all the
little privileges we enjoy, as the deprived and the boring do
in everyday life. We are distressed by her ignorance of them
and we seek to console ourselves with the thought that
precisely because they are never visible she has perhaps added
to the opinion which she already has of us this possibility of
further undisclosed virtues.

Saint-Loup had not for a long time been able to come to
Paris, either, as he himself claimed, because of his military
duties, or, as was more likely, because of the trouble he was
having with his mistress, with whom he had twice now been
on the point of breaking off relations. He had often told me
what a pleasure it would be to him if I came to visit him in that
garrison town the name of which, a couple of days after his
leaving Balbec, had caused me so much joy when I had read it
on the envelope of the first letter I had received from my friend.
Not so far from Balbec as its wholly inland surroundings might
have led one to think, it was one of those little fortified towns,
aristocratic and military, set in a broad expanse of country
over which on fine days there floats so often in the distance a
sort of intermittent haze of sound which—as a screen of
poplars by its sinuosities outlines the course of a river which
one cannot see—indicates the movements of a regiment on
manoeuvre that the very atmosphere of its streets, avenues
and squares has been gradually tuned to a sort of perpetual
vibrancy, musical and martial, and the most commonplace
sound of cartwheel or tramway is prolonged in vague trumpet
calls, indefinitely repeated, to the hallucinated ear, by the

silence. It was not too far away from Paris for me to be able, if I took the express, to return to my mother and grandmother and sleep in my own bed. As soon as I realised this, troubled by a painful longing, I had too little will-power to decide not to return to Paris but rather to stay in the little town; but also too little to prevent a porter from carrying my luggage to a cab and not to adopt, as I walked behind him, the destitute soul of a traveller looking after his belongings with no grandmother in attendance, not to get into the carriage with the complete detachment of a person who, having ceased to think of what it is that he wants, has the air of knowing what he wants, and not to give the driver the address of the cavalry barracks. I thought that Saint-Loup might come and sleep that night in the hotel at which I should be staying, in order to make the first shock of contact with this strange town less painful for me. One of the guard went to find him, and I waited at the barracks gate, in front of that huge ship of stone, booming with the November wind, out of which, every moment, for it was now six o'clock, men were emerging in pairs into the street, staggering as if they were coming ashore in some exotic port where they found themselves temporarily anchored.

Saint-Loup appeared, moving like a whirlwind, his monocle spinning in the air before him. I had not given my name, and was eager to enjoy his surprise and delight.

"Oh, what a bore!" he exclaimed, suddenly catching sight of me, and blushing to the tips of his ears. "I've just had a week's leave, and I shan't be off duty again for another week."

And, preoccupied by the thought of my having to spend this first night alone, for he knew better than anyone my bed-time agonies, which he had often noticed and soothed at Balbec, he broke off his lamentation to turn and look at me, coax me with little smiles, with tender though unsymmetrical glances, half of them coming directly from his eye, the other half through his monocle, but both sorts alike testifying to the emotion that he felt on seeing me again, testifying also to that important matter which I still did not understand but which now vitally concerned me, our friendship.

"I say, where are you going to sleep? Really, I can't recommend the hotel where we mess; it's next to the Exhibition ground, where there's a show just starting; you'll find it beastly crowded. No, you'd better go to the Hôtel de Flandre; it's a little eighteenth-century palace with old tapestries. It's quite the (*ça fait assez*) 'old historical dwelling.' ".

Saint-Loup employed in every connexion the verb *faire* for "have the air of," because the spoken language, like the written, feels from time to time the need of these alterations in the meanings of words, these refinements of expression. And just as journalists often have not the least idea what school of literature the "turns of phrase" they use originate from, so the vocabulary, the very diction of Saint-Loup were formed in imitation of three different aesthetes none of whom he knew but whose modes of speech had been indirectly inculcated into him. "Besides," he concluded, "the hotel I mean is more or less adapted to your auditory hyperaesthesia. You will have no neighbours. I quite see that it's a slender advantage, and as, after all, another guest may arrive to-morrow, it would not be worth your while to choose that particular hotel on such precarious grounds. No, it's for its appearance that I recommend it. The rooms are rather attractive, all the furniture is old and comfortable; there's something reassuring about it." But to me, less of an artist than Saint-Loup, the pleasure that an attractive house might give one was superficial, almost nonexistent, and could not calm my incipient anguish, as painful as that which I used to feel long ago at Combray when my mother did not come upstairs to say good night, or that which I felt on the evening of my arrival at Balbec in the room with the unnaturally high ceiling, which smelt of vetiver. Saint-Loup read all this in my fixed stare.

"A lot you care, though, about this charming palace, my poor fellow; you're quite pale; and here am I like a great brute talking to you about tapestries which you won't even have the heart to look at. I know the room they'll put you in; personally I find it most cheerful, but I can quite understand that it won't have the same effect on you with your sensitive nature. You mustn't think I don't understand you. I don't feel the same myself, but I can put myself in your place."

At that moment a sergeant who was exercising a horse on

the square, entirely absorbed in making the animal jump, disregarding the salutes of passing troopers, but hurling volleys of oaths at such as got in his way, turned with a smile to Saint-Loup and, seeing that he had a friend with him, saluted us. But his horse, frothing, at once reared. Saint-Loup flung himself at its head, caught it by the bridle, succeeded in quieting it and returned to my side.

"Yes," he resumed, "I assure you that I fully understand and sympathise with what you are going through. I feel wretched," he went on, laying his hand affectionately on my shoulder, "when I think that if I could have stayed with you to-night, I might have been able, by chatting to you till morning, to relieve you of a little of your unhappiness. I could lend you some books, but you won't want to read if you're feeling like that. And I shan't be able to get anyone else to stand in for me here: I've done it twice running because my girl came down to see me."

And he knitted his brows with vexation and also in the effort to decide, like a doctor, what remedy he might best apply to my disease.

"Run along and light the fire in my quarters," he called to a trooper who passed by. "Hurry up; get a move on!"

Then, once more, he turned towards me, and once more his monocle and his peering, myopic gaze testified to our great friendship.

"No, really, you here, in these barracks where I've thought so much about you, I can scarcely believe my eyes, I feel I must be dreaming! But how is your health on the whole? A little better, I hope. You must tell me all about yourself presently. We'll go up to my room; we mustn't hang about too long on the square, there's the devil of a wind. I don't feel it now myself, but you aren't accustomed to it, I'm afraid of your catching cold. And what about your work? Have you settled down to it yet? No? You are an odd fellow! If I had your talent I'm sure I should be writing morning, noon and night. It amuses you more to do nothing. What a pity it is that it's the useless fellows like me who are always ready to work, and the ones who could if they wanted to, won't. There, and I've clean forgotten to ask you how your grandmother is. Her Proudhon is in safe keeping. I never part from it."

A tall, handsome, majestic officer emerged with slow and solemn steps from the foot of a staircase. Saint-Loup saluted him and arrested the perpetual mobility of his body for the time it took him to hold his hand against the peak of his cap. But he had flung himself into the action with such force, straightening himself with so sharp a movement, and, the salute ended, brought his hand down with so abrupt a release, altering all the positions of shoulder, leg and monocle, that this moment was one not so much of immobility as of a throbbing tension in which the excessive movements which he had just made and those on which he was about to embark were neutralised. Meanwhile the officer, without coming any nearer, calm, benevolent, dignified, imperial, representing, in short, the direct opposite of Saint-Loup, also raised his hand, but unhurriedly, to the peak of his cap.

"I must just say a word to the Captain," whispered Saint-Loup. "Be a good fellow, and go and wait for me in my room. It's the second on the right, on the third floor. I'll be with you in a minute."

And setting off at the double, preceded by his monocle which fluttered in every direction, he made straight for the slow and stately captain whose horse had just been brought round and who, before preparing to mount, was giving orders with a studied nobility of gesture as in some historical painting, and as though he were setting forth to take part in some battle of the First Empire, whereas he was simply going to ride home, to the house which he had taken for the period of his service at Doncières, and which stood in a square that was named, as though in an ironical anticipation of the arrival of this Napoleonid, Place de la République. I started to climb the staircase, nearly slipping on each of its nail-studded steps, catching glimpses of barrack-rooms, their bare walls bordered with a double line of beds and kits. I was shown Saint-Loup's room. I stood for a moment outside its closed door, for I could hear movement—something stirring, something being dropped. I felt the room was not empty, that there was some-body there. But it was only the freshly lighted fire beginning

to burn. It could not keep quiet; it kept shifting its logs about,
and very clumsily. As I entered the room, it let one roll into
the fender and set another smoking. And even when it was
not moving, like an ill-bred person it made noises all the time,
which, from the moment I saw the flames rising, revealed
themselves to me as noises made by a fire, although if I had
been on the other side of a wall I should have thought that
they came from someone who was blowing his nose and walking about. I sat down in the room and waited. Liberty hangings
and old German stuffs of the eighteenth century preserved it
from the smell exuded by the rest of the building, a coarse,
stale, mouldy smell like that of wholemeal bread. It was here,
in this charming room, that I could have dined and slept with
a calm and happy mind. Saint-Loup seemed almost to be
present in it by reason of the text-books which littered his
table, between his photographs, among which I recognised
my own and that of the Duchesse de Guermantes, by reason
of the fire which had at length grown accustomed to the grate,
and, like an animal crouching in an ardent, noiseless, faithful
watchfulness, merely let fall now and then a smouldering log
which crumbled into sparks, or licked with a tongue of flame
the sides of the chimney. I heard the tick of Saint-Loup's
watch, which could not be far away. This tick changed place
every moment, for I could not see the watch; it seemed to
come from behind, from in front of me, from my right, from
my left, sometimes to die away as though it were a long way off.
Suddenly I caught sight of the watch on the table. Then I
heard the tick in a fixed place from which it did not move again.
That is to say, I thought I heard it at this place; I did not hear
it there, I saw it there, for sounds have no position in space.
At least we associate them with movements, and in that way
they serve the purpose of warning us of those movements, of
appearing to make them necessary and natural. True, it
sometimes happens that a sick man whose ears have been
stopped with cotton-wool ceases to hear the noise of a fire
such as was crackling at that moment in Saint-Loup's fireplace,
labouring at the formation of brands and cinders, which it then
dropped into the fender, nor would he hear the passage of the
tram-cars whose music rose at regular intervals over the

main square of Doncières. Then, if the sick man reads, the pages will turn silently as though they were flicked by the fingers of a god. The dull thunder of a bath being filled becomes thin, faint and distant as the twittering of birds high up in the sky. The withdrawal of sound, its dilution, rob it of all its aggressive power; alarmed a moment ago by hammer-blows which seemed to be shattering the ceiling above our head, it is with a quiet delight that we now absorb their sound, light, caressing, distant, like the murmur of leaves playing by the roadside with the passing breeze. We play games of patience with cards which we do not hear, so much so that we imagine that we have not touched them, that they are moving of their own accord, and, anticipating our desire to play with them, have begun to play with us. And in this connexion we may wonder whether, in the case of love (to which we may even add the love of life and the love of fame, since there are, it appears, persons who are acquainted with these latter sentiments), we ought not to act like those who, when a noise disturbs them, instead of praying that it may cease, stop their ears; and, in emulation of them, bring our attention, our defensive strength to bear on ourselves, give ourselves as an objective to subdue not the "other person" with whom we are in love but our capacity for suffering at that person's hands.

To return to the problem of sound, we have only to thicken the wads which close the aural passages, and they confine to a pianissimo the girl who has been playing a boisterous tune overhead; if we go further, and steep one of these wads in grease, at once the whole household must obey its despotic rule; its laws extend even beyond our portals. Pianissimo is no longer enough; the wad instantly closes the piano and the music lesson is abruptly ended; the gentleman who was walking up and down in the room above breaks off in the middle of his beat; the movement of carriages and trams is interrupted as though a sovereign were expected to pass. And indeed this attenuation of sounds sometimes disturbs our sleep instead of protecting it. Only yesterday the incessant noise in our ears, by describing to us in a continuous narrative all that was happening in the street and in the house, succeeded at length in sending us to sleep like a boring book;

to-day, on the surface of silence spread over our sleep, a shock
louder than the rest manages to make itself heard, gentle as a
sigh, unrelated to any other sound, mysterious; and the demand
for an explanation which it exhales is sufficient to awaken us.
On the other hand, take away for a moment from the sick man
the cotton-wool that has been stopping his ears and in a flash
the broad daylight, the dazzling sun of sound dawns afresh,
blinding him, is born again in the universe; the multitude of
exiled sounds comes hastening back; we are present, as though
it were the chanting of choirs of angels, at the resurrection of
the voice. The empty streets are filled for a moment with the
whirr of the swift and recurrent wings of the singing tram-
cars. In the bedroom itself the sick man has created, not, like
Prometheus, fire, but the sound of fire. And when we increase
or reduce the wads of cotton-wool, it is as though we were
pressing alternately one and then the other of the two pedals
with which we have extended the sonority of the outer world.

Only there are also suppressions of sound which are not
temporary. The man who has become completely deaf cannot
even heat a pan of milk by his bedside without having to keep
an eye open to watch, on the tilted lid, for the white hyper-
borean reflexion, like that of a coming snowstorm, which is
the premonitory sign it is wise to obey by cutting off (as the
Lord bade the waves be still) the electric current; for already
the fitfully swelling egg of the boiling milk is reaching its
climax in a series of sidelong undulations, puffs out and fills a
few drooping sails that had been puckered by the cream,
sending a nacreous spinnaker bellying out in the hurricane,
until the cutting off of the current, if the electric storm is
exorcised in time, will make them all twirl round on themselves
and scatter like magnolia petals. But should the sick man not
have been quick enough in taking the necessary precautions,
presently, his drowned books and watch scarcely emerging
from the milky tidal wave, he will be obliged to call the old
nurse, who, though he be himself an eminent statesman or a
famous writer, will tell him that he has no more sense than a
child of five. At other times in the magic chamber, standing
inside the closed door, a person who was not there a moment
ago will have made his appearance; it is a visitor who has

entered unheard, and who merely gesticulates, like a figure in
one of those little puppet theatres, so restful for those who
have taken a dislike to the spoken tongue. And for this stone-
deaf man, since the loss of a sense adds as much beauty to the
world as its acquisition, it is with ecstasy that he walks now
upon an earth become almost an Eden, in which sound has not
yet been created. The highest waterfalls unfold for his eyes
alone their sheets of crystal, stiller than the glassy sea, pure as
the cascades of Paradise. Since sound was for him, before his
deafness, the perceptible form which the cause of a movement
assumed, objects moved soundlessly now seem to be moved
without cause; deprived of the quality of sound, they show a
spontaneous activity, seem to be alive. They move, halt, become alight of their own accord. Of their own accord they
vanish in the air like the winged monsters of prehistory. In the
solitary and neighbourless house of the deaf man, the service
which, before his infirmity was complete, was already showing
more reserve, was being executed silently, is now carried out,
with a sort of surreptitious deftness, by mutes, as at the court
of a fairy-tale king. And again as on the stage, the building
which the deaf man looks out on from his window—be it
barracks, church, or town hall—is only so much scenery. If
one day it should fall to the ground, it may emit a cloud of dust
and leave visible ruins; but, less substantial even than a palace
on the stage, though it has not the same exiguity, it will subside
in the magic universe without letting the fall of its heavy
blocks of stone tarnish the chastity of the prevailing silence
with the vulgarity of noise.

The silence, altogether more relative, which reigned in the
little barrack-room where I sat waiting was now broken. The
door opened and Saint-Loup rushed in, dropping his monocle.

"Ah, my dear Robert, how very comfortable it is here,"
I said to him. "How nice it would be if one were allowed to
dine and sleep here."

And indeed, had it not been against the regulations, what
repose untinged by sadness I could have enjoyed there, guarded
by that atmosphere of tranquillity, vigilance and gaiety which
was maintained by a thousand ordered and untroubled wills,
a thousand carefree minds, in that great community called a

barracks where, time having taken the form of action, the sad bell that tolled the hours outside was replaced by the same joyous clarion of those martial calls, the ringing memory of which was kept perpetually alive in the paved streets of the town, like the dust that floats in a sunbeam—a voice sure of being heard, and musical because it was the command not only of authority to obedience but of wisdom to happiness.

"So you'd rather stay with me and sleep here, would you, than go to the hotel by yourself?" Saint-Loup asked me, smiling.

"Oh, Robert, it's cruel of you to be sarcastic about it," I answered. "You know it's not possible, and you know how wretched I shall be over there."

"Well, you flatter me!" he replied. "Because it actually occurred to me that you'd rather stay here to-night. And that is precisely what I went to ask the Captain."

"And he has given you leave?" I cried.

"He hadn't the slighest objection."

"Oh! I adore him!"

"No, that would be going too far. But now, let me just get hold of my batman and tell him to see about our dinner," he went on, while I turned away to hide my tears.

We were several times interrupted by the entry of one or other of Saint-Loup's fellow-N.C.O.'s. He drove them all out again.

"Get out of here. Buzz off!"

I begged him to let them stay.

"No, really, they would bore you stiff. They're absolutely uncouth people who can talk of nothing but racing or stable shop. Besides, I don't want them here either; they would spoil these precious moments I've been looking forward to. Mind you, when I tell you that these fellows are brainless, it isn't that everything military is devoid of intellectuality. Far from it. We have a major here who's an admirable man. He's given us a course in which military history is treated like a demonstration, like a problem in algebra. Even from the aesthetic point of view there's a curious beauty, alternately inductive and deductive, about it which you couldn't fail to appreciate."

"That's not the officer who's given me leave to stay here to-night?"

"No, thank God! The man you 'adore' for so very trifling a service is the biggest fool that ever walked the face of the earth. He's perfect at looking after messing, and at kit inspections; he spends hours with the senior sergeant and the master tailor. There you have his mentality. Besides, he has a vast contempt, like everyone here, for the excellent major in question, whom no one speaks to because he's a freemason and doesn't go to confession. The Prince de Borodino would never have an outsider like that in his house. Which is pretty fair cheek, when all's said and done, from a man whose great-grandfather was a small farmer, and who would probably be a small farmer himself if it hadn't been for the Napoleonic wars. Not that he isn't a little aware of his own rather ambiguous position in society, neither flesh nor fowl. He hardly ever shows his face at the Jockey, it makes him feel so deuced awkward, this so-called Prince," added Robert, who, having been led by the same spirit of imitation to adopt the social theories of his teachers and the worldly prejudices of his relatives, unconsciously combined a democratic love of humanity with a contempt for the nobility of the Empire.

I looked at the photograph of his aunt, and the thought that, since Saint-Loup had this photograph in his possession, he might perhaps give it to me, made me cherish him all the more and long to do him a thousand services, which seemed to me a very small exchange for it. For this photograph was like a supplementary encounter added to all those that I had already had with Mme de Guermantes; better still, a prolonged encounter, as if, by a sudden stride forward in our relations, she had stopped beside me, in a garden hat, and had allowed me for the first time to gaze at my leisure at that rounded cheek, that arched neck, that tapering eyebrow (veiled from me hitherto by the swiftness of her passage, the bewilderment of my impressions, the imperfection of memory); and the contemplation of them, as well as of the bare throat and arms of a woman whom I had never seen save in a high-necked and long-sleeved dress, was to me a voluptuous discovery, a priceless favour. Those forms, which had seemed to me almost a forbidden spectacle, I could study there as in a text-book of the only geometry that had any value for me. Later on, looking at Robert, it struck me that he too was a little like the photograph of his aunt, by a mysterious process which I found almost as moving, since, if his face had not been directly produced by hers, the two had nevertheless a common origin. The features of the Duchesse de Guermantes, which were pinned to my vision of Combray, the nose like a falcon's beak, the piercing eyes, seemed to have served also as a pattern for the cutting out—in another copy analogous and slender, with too delicate a skin—of Robert's face, which might almost be superimposed upon his aunt's. I looked longingly at those features of his so characteristic of the Guermantes, of that race which had remained so individual in the midst of a world in which it remained isolated in its divinely ornithological glory, for it seemed to have sprung, in the age of mythology, from the union of a goddess with a bird.

Robert, without being aware of its cause, was touched by my evident affection. This was moreover increased by the sense of well-being inspired in me by the heat of the fire and by the champagne which simultaneously bedewed my forehead with beads of sweat and my eyes with tears; it washed down some young partridges which I ate with the wonderment of a layman, of whatever sort he may be, who finds in a way of life with which he is not familiar what he has supposed it to exclude—the wonderment, for instance, of an atheist who sits down to an exquisitely cooked dinner in a presbytery. And next morning, when I awoke, I went over to Saint-Loup's window, which being at a great height overlooked the whole countryside, curious to make the acquaintance of my new neighbour, the landscape which I had not been able to see the day before, having arrived too late, at an hour when it was already sleeping beneath the outspread cloak of night. And yet, early as it had awoken, I could see it, when I opened the window and looked out, only as though from the window of a country house overlooking the lake, shrouded still in its soft white morning gown of mist which scarcely allowed me to make out anything at all. But I knew that, before the troopers who were busy with their horses in the square had finished grooming them, it would have cast its gown aside. In the meantime, I could see only a bare hill, raising its lean and rugged flanks, already swept clear of darkness, over the back of the barracks. Through the translucent screen of hoar-frost I could not take my eyes from this stranger who was looking at me too for the first time. But when I had formed the habit of coming to the barracks, my consciousness that the hill was there, more real, consequently, even when I did not see it, than the hotel at Balbec, than our house in Paris, of which I thought as of absent—or dead—friends, that is to say scarcely believing any longer in their existence, caused its reflected form, even without my realising it, to be silhouetted against the slightest impressions that I formed at Doncières, and among them, to begin with this first morning, the pleasing impression of warmth given me by the cup of chocolate, prepared by Saint-Loup's batman in this comfortable room, which seemed like a sort of optical centre from which to look out at the hill—the idea of doing anything else but just gaze at it, the idea of actually climbing it, being rendered impossible by this same mist. Imbued with the shape of the hill, associated with the taste of hot chocolate and with the whole web of my fancies at that particular time, this mist, without my having given it the least thought, came to infuse all my thoughts of that time, just as a massive and unmelting lump of gold had remained allied to my impressions of Balbec, or as the proximity of the outside steps of sandstone gave a greyish background to my impressions of Combray. It did not, however, persist late into the day; the sun began by hurling at it in vain a few darts which sprinkled it with brilliants, then finally overcame it. The hill might expose its grizzled rump to the sun's rays, which, an hour later, when I went into the town, gave to the russet tints of the autumn leaves, to the reds and blues of the election posters pasted on the walls, an exaltation which raised my spirits also and made me stamp, singing as I went, on the paving-stones from which I could hardly keep myself from jumping in the air for joy.

But after that first night I had to sleep at the hotel. And I knew beforehand that I was doomed to find sadness there. It was like an unbreathable aroma which all my life long had been exhaled for me by every new bedroom, that is to say by every bedroom—for in the one which I usually occupied

I was not present, my mind remained elsewhere and sent mere
Habit to take its place. But I could not employ this servant, less
sensitive than myself, to look after things for me in a new place,
where I preceded him, where I arrived alone, where I must
bring into contact with its environment that "Self" which I
rediscovered only at year-long intervals, but always the same,
not having grown at all since Combray, since my first arrival at
Balbec, weeping inconsolably on the edge of an unpacked trunk.

As it happened, I was mistaken. I had no time to be sad, for
I was not alone for an instant. The fact of the matter was that
there remained of the old palace a surplus refinement of structure and decoration, out of place in a modern hotel, which,
released from any practical assignment, had in its long spell of
leisure acquired a sort of life: passages winding about in all
directions, which one was continually crossing in their aimless
wanderings, lobbies as long as corridors and as ornate as
drawing-rooms, which had the air rather of dwelling there
themselves than of forming part of the dwelling, which could
not be induced to enter and settle down in any of the rooms
but roamed about outside mine and came up at once to offer
me their company—neighbours of a sort, idle but never noisy,
menial ghosts of the past who had been granted the privilege
of staying quietly by the doors of the rooms which were let to
visitors, and who whenever I came across them greeted me
with a silent deference. In short, the idea of a lodging, a
mere container for our present existence, simply shielding us
from the cold and from the sight of other people, was absolutely inapplicable to this dwelling, an assembly of rooms, as
real as a colony of people, living, it was true, in silence, but
which one was obliged to encounter, to avoid, to greet when
one came in. One tried not to disturb, and one could not look
at without respect, the great drawing-room which had formed,
far back in the eighteenth century, the habit of stretching itself
at its ease among its hangings of old gold beneath the clouds
of its painted ceiling. And one was seized with a more personal
curiosity as regards the smaller rooms which, without the least
concern for symmetry, ran all round it, innumerable, startled,
fleeing in disorder as far as the garden, to which they had so
easy an access down three broken steps.

If I wished to go out or come in without taking the lift or
being seen on the main staircase, a smaller private staircase,
no longer in use, offered me its steps so skilfully arranged, one
close above another, that there seemed to exist in their grada-
tion a perfect proportion of the same kind as those which, in
colours, scents, savours, often arouse in us a peculiar sensuous
pleasure. But the pleasure to be found in going up and downstairs I had had to come here to learn, as once in a mountain
resort I had found that the act—as a rule not noticed—
of breathing can be a perpetual delight. I received that dispensation from effort which is granted to us only by the things
to which long use has accustomed us, when I set my feet for
the first time on those steps, familiar before ever I knew them,
as if they possessed, stored up, incorporated in them perhaps
by the masters of old whom they used to welcome every day,
the prospective charm of habits which I had not yet contracted and which indeed could only dwindle once they had
become my own. I went into a room; the double doors closed
behind me, the hangings let in a silence in which I felt myself
invested with a sort of exhilarating royalty; a marble fireplace
with ornaments of wrought brass—of which one would have
been wrong to think that its sole idea was to represent the
art of the Directory—offered me a fire, and a little easy chair on
short legs helped me to warm myself as comfortably as if I
had been sitting on the hearthrug. The walls held the room in
a close embrace, separating it from the rest of the world and,
to let into it, to enclose in it what made it complete, parted to
make way for the bookcase, reserved a place for the bed, on
either side of which columns airily upheld the lofty ceiling of
the alcove. And the room was prolonged in depth by two
closets as wide as itself, one of which had hanging from its wall,
to scent the occasion on which one had recourse to it, a
voluptuous rosary of orris-roots; the doors, if I left them open
when I withdrew into this innermost retreat, were not content
with tripling its dimensions without spoiling its harmonious
proportions, and not only allowed my eyes to enjoy the delights of extension after those of concentration, but added
further to the pleasure of my solitude—which, while still
inviolable, was no longer shut in—the sense of liberty. This

closet gave on to a courtyard, a solitary fair stranger whom I
was glad to have for a neighbour when next morning my eyes
fell on her, a captive between her high walls in which no other
window opened, with nothing but two yellowing trees which
contrived to give a pinkish softness to the pure sky above.

Before going to bed I left the room to explore the whole of
my enchanted domain. I walked down a long gallery which
displayed to me successively all that it had to offer me if I
could not sleep, an armchair placed in a corner, a spinet, a
blue porcelain vase filled with cinerarias on a console table, and,
in an old frame, the phantom of a lady of long ago with
powdered hair mingled with blue flowers, holding in her hand
a bunch of carnations. When I came to the end, the bare wall
in which no door opened said to me simply: "Now you must
turn and go back, but, you see, you are at home here, the
house is yours," while the soft carpet, not to be left out, added
that if I could not sleep that night I could perfectly well come
in my bare feet, and the unshuttered windows looking out over
the countryside assured me that they would keep a sleepless
vigil and that, at whatever hour I chose to come, I need not
be afraid of disturbing anyone. And behind a hanging curtain
I came upon a little closet which, stopped by the outer wall
and unable to escape, had hidden itself there shamefacedly
and gave me a frightened stare from its little round window,
glowing blue in the moonlight. I went to bed, but the presence
of the eiderdown, of the slim columns, of the little fireplace, by
screwing up my attention to a pitch beyond that of Paris,
prevented me from surrendering to the habitual routine of
my musings. And as it is this particular state of attention that
enfolds our slumbers, acts upon them, modifies them, brings
them into line with this or that series of past impressions, the
images that filled my dreams that first night were borrowed
from a memory entirely distinct from that on which I was in
the habit of drawing. If I had been tempted while asleep to
let myself be swept back into my usual current of remembrance, the bed to which I was not accustomed, the careful
attention which I was obliged to pay to the position of my
limbs when I turned over, were sufficient to adjust or maintain
the new thread of my dreams. It is the same with sleep as with

our perception of the external world. It needs only a modification in our habits to make it poetic, it is enough that while undressing we should have dozed off on top of the bed for the dimensions of our dream-world to be altered and its beauty felt. We wake up, look at our watch and see "four o'clock"; it is only four o'clock in the morning, but we imagine that the whole day has gone by, so vividly does this unsolicited nap of a few minutes appear to have come down to us from heaven, by virtue of some divine right, huge and solid as an Emperor's orb of gold. In the morning, worried by the thought that my grandfather was ready and they were waiting for me to set out for our walk along the Méséglise way, I was awakened by the blare of a regimental band which passed every day beneath my windows. But two or three times—and I say this because one cannot properly describe human life unless one bathes it in the sleep into which it plunges night after night and which sweeps round it as a promontory is encircled by the sea—the intervening layer of sleep was resistant enough to withstand the impact of the music and I heard nothing. On other mornings it gave way for a moment; but my consciousness, still muffled from sleep (like those organs by which, after a local anaesthetic, a cauterisation, not perceived at first, is felt only at the very end and then as a faint smarting), was touched only gently by the shrill points of the fifes which caressed it with a vague, cool, matutinal warbling; and after this fragile interruption in which the silence had turned to music it relapsed into my slumber before even the dragoons had finished passing, depriving me of the last blossoming sheafs of the surging bouquet of sound. And the zone of my consciousness which its springing stems had brushed was so narrow, so circumscribed with sleep that later on, when Saint-Loup asked me whether I had heard the band, I was not certain that the sound of its brasses had not been as imaginary as that which I heard during the day echoing, after the slightest noise, from the paved streets of the town. Perhaps I had heard it only in my dreams, prompted by my fear of being awakened, or else of not being awakened and so not seeing the regiment march past. For often when I remained asleep at the moment when on the contrary I had supposed that the noise would awaken me, for the next hour I imagined that I was awake, while still dozing, and I enacted to myself with tenuous shadow-shapes on the screen of my slumber the various scenes of which it deprived me but at which I had the illusion of looking on.

Indeed, what one has meant to do during the day it turns out, sleep intervening, that one accomplishes only in one's dreams, that is to say after it has been diverted by drowsiness into following a different path from that which one would have chosen when awake. The same story branches off and has a different ending. When all is said, the world in which we live when we are asleep is so different that people who have difficulty in going to sleep seek first of all to escape from the waking world. After having desperately, for hours on end, with their eyes closed, revolved in their minds thoughts similar to those which they would have had with their eyes open, they take heart again on noticing that the preceding minute has been weighed down by a line of reasoning in strict contradiction to the laws of logic and the reality of the present, this brief "absence" signifying that the door is now open through which they may perhaps presently be able to escape from the perception of the real, to advance to a resting-place more or less remote from it, which will mean their having a more or less "good" night. But already a great stride has been made when we turn our backs on the real, when we reach the outer caves in which "auto-suggestions" prepare—like witches—the hell-broth of imaginary illnesses or of the recurrence of nervous disorders, and watch for the hour when the spasms which have been building up during the unconsciousness of sleep will be unleashed with sufficient force to make sleep cease.

Not far thence is the secret garden in which the kinds of sleep, so different one from another, induced by datura, by Indian hemp, by the multiple extracts of ether—the sleep of belladonna, of opium, of valerian—grow like unknown flowers whose petals remain closed until the day when the predestined stranger comes to open them with a touch and to liberate for long hours the aroma of their peculiar dreams for the delectation of an amazed and spellbound being. At the

end of the garden stands the convent with open windows
through which we hear voices repeating the lessons learned
before we went to sleep, which we shall know only at the
moment of awakening; while, presaging that moment, our
inner alarm-clock ticks away, so well regulated by our preoccupation that when our housekeeper comes in and tells us
it is seven o'clock she will find us awake and ready. The dim
walls of that chamber which opens upon our dreams and
within which the sorrows of love are wrapped in that oblivion
whose incessant toil is interrupted and annulled at times by a
nightmare heavy with reminiscences, but quickly resumed, are
hung, even after we are awake, with the memories of our
dreams, but they are so murky that often we catch sight of
them for the first time only in the broad light of the afternoon
when the ray of a similar idea happens by chance to strike
them; some of them, clear and harmonious while we slept,
already so distorted that, having failed to recognise them, we
can but hasten to lay them in the earth, like corpses too quickly
decomposed or relics so seriously damaged, so nearly crumbling into dust that the most skilful restorer could not give them
back a shape or make anything of them.

Near the gate is the quarry to which our heavier slumbers
repair in search of substances which coat the brain with so
unbreakable a glaze that, to awaken the sleeper, his own will
is obliged, even on a golden morning, to smite him with
mighty blows, like a young Siegfried. Beyond this, again, are
nightmares, of which the doctors foolishly assert that they tire
us more than does insomnia, whereas on the contrary they
enable the thinker to escape from the strain of thought—
nightmares with their fantastic picture-books in which our
relatives who are dead are shown meeting with serious accidents which at the same time do not preclude their speedy
recovery. Until then we keep them in a little rat-cage, in which
they are smaller than white mice and, covered with big red
spots out of each of which a feather sprouts, regale us with
Ciceronian speeches. Next to this picture-book is the revolving
disc of awakening, by virtue of which we submit for a moment
to the tedium of having to return presently to a house which
was pulled down fifty years ago, the image of which is gradually

effaced by a number of others as sleep recedes, until we arrive at the image which appears only when the disc has ceased to revolve and which coincides with the one we shall see with opened eyes.

Sometimes I had heard nothing, being in one of those slumbers into which we fall as into a pit from which we are heartily glad to be drawn up a little later, heavy, overfed, digesting all that has been brought to us (as by the nymphs who fed the infant Hercules) by those agile vegetative powers whose activity is doubled while we sleep.

That kind of sleep is called "sleeping like a log," and it seems as though, even for a few moments after such a sleep is ended, one is a sort of lay figure. One is no longer a person. How then, searching for one's thoughts, one's personality, as one searches for a lost object, does one recover one's own self rather than any other? Why, when one begins again to think, is it not a personality other than the previous one that becomes incarnate in one. One fails to see what dictates the choice, or why, among the millions of human beings one might be, it is on the being one was the day before that unerringly one lays one's hand. What is it that guides us, when there has been a real interruption—whether it be that our unconsciousness has been complete or our dreams entirely different from ourselves? There has indeed been death, as when the heart has ceased to beat and a rhythmical traction of the tongue revives us. No doubt the room, even if we have seen it only once before, awakens memories to which other, older memories cling, or perhaps some were dormant in us, of which we now become conscious. The resurrection at our awakening—after that beneficent attack of mental alienation which is sleep—must after all be similar to what occurs when we recall a name, a line, a refrain that we had forgotten. And perhaps the resurrection of the soul after death is to be conceived as a phenomenon of memory.

When I had finished sleeping, tempted by the sunlit sky but held back by the chill of those last autumn mornings, so luminous and so cold, which herald winter, in order to look at the trees on which the leaves were indicated now only by a few strokes of gold or pink which seemed to have been left in

the air, on an invisible web, I raised my head from the pillow
and stretched my neck, keeping my body still hidden beneath
the bedclothes; like a chrysalis in the process of metamorphosis,
I was a dual creature whose different parts were not adapted
to the same environment; for my eyes colour was sufficient,
without warmth; my chest on the other hand was anxious for
warmth and not for colour. I got up only after my fire had
been lighted, and studied the picture, so delicate and transparent, of the pink and golden morning, to which I had now
added by artificial means the element of warmth that it lacked,
poking my fire which burned and smoked like a good pipe and
gave me, as a pipe would have given me, a pleasure at once
coarse because it was based upon a material comfort and delicate because behind it were the soft outlines of a pure vision.
The walls of my dressing-room were papered in a violent red,
sprinkled with black and white flowers to which it seemed that
I should have some difficulty in growing accustomed. But
they succeeded only in striking me as novel, in forcing me to
enter not into conflict but into contact with them, in modulating the gaiety and the songs of my morning ablutions; they
succeeded only in imprisoning me in the heart of a sort of poppy,
out of which to look at a world which I saw quite otherwise
than in Paris, from the gay screen which was this new dwelling-
place, of a different aspect from the house of my parents, and
into which flowed a purer air.

On certain days, I was agitated by the desire to see my grandmother again or by the fear that she might be ill, or else by
the memory of some business left half-finished in Paris,
which seemed to have made no progress, or sometimes, again,
by some difficulty in which, even here, I had managed to become involved. One or other of these anxieties would have
prevented me from sleeping, and I would be powerless to face
up to my depression, which in an instant would fill the whole
of my existence. Then I would send a messenger from the
hotel to the barracks with a note for Saint-Loup, telling him
that if it was physically possible—I knew that it was extremely
difficult for him—I should be most grateful if he would look
in for a minute. An hour later he would arrive; and on hearing
his ring at the door I felt myself liberated from my obsessions.

I knew that, if they were stronger than I, he was stronger than they, and my attention was diverted from them and turned towards him, who would know how to settle them. On entering the room he would at once envelop me in the fresh air in which from early morning he had been active and busy, a vital atmosphere very different from that of my room, to which I at once adapted myself by appropriate reactions.

"I hope you weren't angry with me for bothering you. There is something that's worrying me, as you probably guessed."

"Not at all. I just supposed you wanted to see me, and I thought it very nice of you. I was delighted that you sent for me. But what's the trouble? Things not going well? What can I do to help?"

He would listen to my explanations, and give precise answers; but before he uttered a word he would have transformed me to his own likeness; compared with the important occupations which kept him so busy, so alert, so happy, the worries which a moment ago I had been unable to endure for another instant seemed to me as negligible as they did to him. I was like a man who, having been unable to open his eyes for some days, sends for a doctor, who neatly and gently raises his eyelids, removes from beneath it a grain of sand, and shows it to him; the sufferer is healed and comforted. All my cares resolved themselves in a telegram which Saint-Loup undertook to dispatch. Life seemed to me so different, so delightful, I was flooded with such a surfeit of strength, that I longed for action.

"What are you doing now?" I asked him.

"I must leave you, I'm afraid. We're going on a route march in three quarters of an hour, and I have to be on parade."

"Then it's been a great bother to you, coming here?"

"No, no bother at all, the Captain was very good about it. He told me that if it was for you I must go at once. But I don't like to seem to be abusing the privilege."

"But if I got up and dressed quickly and went by myself to the place where you'll be training, it would interest me immensely, and I could perhaps talk to you during the breaks."

"I shouldn't advise you to do that. You've been lying awake, fretting about something that I assure you is not of the slightest importance, but now that it has ceased to worry you, you should turn over and go to sleep—you'll find it an excellent antidote to the demineralisation of your nerve-cells. Only you mustn't go to sleep too soon, because our band-boys will be coming along under your windows. But as soon as they've passed I think you'll be left in peace, and we shall meet again this evening at dinner."

But soon I was constantly going to see the regiment doing field manoeuvres, when I began to take an interest in the military theories which Saint-Loup's friends used to expound over the dinner-table, and when it had become the chief desire of my life to see at close quarters their various leaders, just as a person who makes music his principal study and spends his life in the concert halls finds pleasure in frequenting the cafés in which one can share the life of the members of the orchestra. To reach the training ground I used to have to make long journeys on foot. In the evening after dinner the longing for sleep made my head droop every now and then as in a fit of vertigo. Next morning I realised that I had not heard the band any more than, at Balbec, after the evenings on which Saint-Loup had taken me to dinner at Rivebelle, I used to hear the concert on the beach. And when I wanted to get up I had a delicious sensation of being incapable of doing so; I felt myself fastened to a deep, invisible soil by the articulations (of which my tiredness made me conscious) of muscular and nutritious roots. I felt myself full of strength; life seemed to extend more amply before me; for I had reverted to the healthy tiredness of my childhood at Combray on mornings after the days when we had taken the Guermantes walk. Poets claim that we recapture for a moment the self that we were long ago when we enter some house or garden in which we used to live in our youth. But these are most hazardous pilgrimages, which end as often in disappointment as in success. It is in ourselves that we should rather seek to find those fixed places, contemporaneous with different years. And great fatigue followed by a good night's rest can to a certain extent help us to do so. For in order to make us descend into the most subterranean galleries of sleep, where no reflexion from overnight, no gleam of memory comes to light up the interior monologue—if the latter does not itself cease—fatigue followed by rest will so throughly turn over the soil and penetrate the bedrock of our bodies that we discover down there, where our muscles plunge and twist in their ramifications and breathe in new life, the garden where we played in our childhood. There is no need to travel in order to see it again; we must dig down inwardly to discover it. What once covered the earth is no longer above but beneath it; a mere excursion does not suffice for a visit to the dead city: excavation is necessary also. But we shall see how certain fugitive and fortuitous impressions carry us back even more effectively to the past, with a more delicate precision, with a more light-winged, more immaterial, more headlong, more unerring, more immortal flight, than these organic dislocations.

Sometimes my exhaustion was greater still. I had followed the manoeuvres for several days on end without being able to go to bed. How blissful then was my return to the hotel! As I got into bed I seemed to have escaped at last from the hands of enchanters and sorcerers like those who people the "romances" beloved of our forebears in the seventeenth century. My sleep that night and the lazy morning that followed it were no more than a charming fairy tale. Charming; beneficent perhaps also. I reminded myself that the worst sufferings have their place of sanctuary, that one can always, when all else fails, find rest. These thoughts carried me far.

On days when, although there was no parade, Saint-Loup had to stay in barracks, I used often to go and visit him there. It was a long way; I had to leave the town and cross the viaduct, from either side of which I had an immense view. A strong breeze blew almost always over this high ground, and swept round the buildings erected on three sides of the barrack-square, which howled incessantly like a cave of the winds. While I waited for Robert—he being engaged on some duty or other—outside the door of his room or in the mess, talking to some of his friends to whom he had introduced me (and whom later I came to see from time to time, even when he was not going to be there), looking down from the window at the countryside three hundred feet below me, bare now except where recently sown fields, often still soaked with rain and glittering in the sun, showed a few strips of green, of the brilliance and translucent limpidity of enamel, I often heard him discussed by the others, and I soon learned what a popular favourite he was. Among many of the volunteers, belonging to other squadrons, sons of rich business or professional men who looked at aristocratic high society only from outside and without penetrating its enclosure, the attraction which they naturally felt towards what they knew of Saint-Loup's character was reinforced by the glamour that attached in their eyes to the young man whom, on Saturday evenings, when they went on pass to Paris, they had seen supping in the Café de la Paix with the Duc d'Uzès and the Prince d'Orléans. And on that account they associated his handsome face, his casual way of walking and saluting, the perpetual dance of his monocle, the jaunty eccentricity of his service dress—the caps always too high, the breeches of too fine a cloth and too pink a shade— with a notion of elegance and "tone" which, they averred, was lacking in the best turned-out officers in the regiment, even the majestic Captain to whom I had been indebted for the privilege of sleeping in barracks, who seemed, in comparison, too pompous and almost common.

One of them mentioned that the Captain had bought a new horse. "He can buy as many horses as he likes. I passed Saint-Loup on Sunday morning in the Allée des Acacias. He's got altogether more style on a horse!" replied his companion with the knowledge of experience, for these young men belonged to a class which, if it does not frequent the same houses and know the same people, yet, thanks to money and leisure, does not differ from the nobility in its experience of all those refinements of life which money can procure. At most their elegance, in the matter of clothes, for instance, had something more studied, more impeccable about it than that relaxed and careless elegance which had so delighted my grandmother in Saint-Loup. It gave quite a thrill to these sons of big stockbrokers or bankers, as they sat eating oysters after the theatre, to see Sergeant Saint-Loup at an adjoining table. And what a tale there was to tell in barracks on Monday night, after a week-end leave, by one of them who was in

Robert's squadron, and to whom he had said how d'ye do "most civilly," while another, who was not in the same squadron, was quite positive that in spite of this Saint-Loup had recognised him, for two or three times he had put up his monocle and stared in the speaker's direction.

"Yes, my brother saw him at the Paix," said another, who had been spending the day with his mistress. "Apparently his dress coat was cut too loose and didn't fit him."

"What was the waistcoat like?"

"He wasn't wearing a white waistcoat; it was purple, with sort of palms on it; stunning!"

To the "old soldiers" (sons of the soil who had never heard of the Jockey Club and simply put Saint-Loup in the category of ultra-rich non-commissioned officers, in which they included all those who, whether bankrupt or not, lived in a certain style, whose income or debts ran into several figures, and who were generous towards their men), the gait, the monocle, the breeches, the caps of Saint-Loup, even if they saw in them nothing particularly aristocratic, furnished nevertheless just as much interest and meaning. They recognised in these peculiarities the character, the style which they had assigned once and for all to this most popular of the "stripes" in the regiment, manners like no one else's, scornful indifference to what his superior officers might think, which seemed to them the natural corollary of his kindness to his subordinates. The morning cup of coffee in the canteen, the afternoon "lay-down" in the barrack-room, seemed pleasanter, somehow, when some old soldier fed the greedy and idle squad with some savoury tit-bit about a cap in which Saint-Loup had appeared on parade.

"It was the height of my pack."

"Come off it, old chap, you're having us on, it couldn't have been the height of your pack," interrupted a young college graduate who hoped by using these slang terms not to appear a greenhorn, and by venturing on this contradiction to obtain confirmation of a fact the thought of which enchanted him.

"Oh, so it wasn't the height of my pack, wasn't it? You measured it, I suppose! I tell you this much, the C.O. glared at him as if he'd have liked to put him in clink. But you needn't think the great Saint-Loup was rattled, oh no, he came and he went, and down with his head and up with his head, and that blinking glass screwed in his eye all the time. We'll see what the 'Capstan' has to say when he hears. Oh, very likely he'll say nothing, but you may be sure he won't be pleased. But there's nothing so wonderful about that cap. I hear he's got thirty of 'em and more at home in town."

"How come you heard about it, old man? From our blasted corporal?" asked the young graduate, pedantically displaying the new grammatical forms which he had only recently acquired and with which he took a pride in garnishing his conversation.

"How come I heard it? From his batman of course!"

"Ah, there's a bloke who knows when he's well off!"

"I should think so! He's got more brass than I have, that's for sure! And besides he gives him all his own belongings and everything. He wasn't getting enough grub in the canteen, he says. So along comes de Saint-Loup and gives cooky hell: 'I want him to be properly fed, d'you hear,' he says, 'and I don't care what it costs.' "

The old soldier made up for the triviality of the words quoted by the emphasis of his tone, in a feeble imitation of the speaker which had an immense success.

On leaving the barracks I would take a stroll, and then, to fill up the time before I went, as I did every evening, to dine with Saint-Loup at the hotel in which he and his friends had established their mess, I walked back to my own, as soon as the sun went down, so as to have a couple of hours in which to rest and read. In the square, the evening sky bedecked the pepper-pot turrets of the castle with little pink clouds which matched the colour of the bricks, and completed the harmony by softening the tone of the latter with a sunset glow. So strong a current of vitality coursed through my veins that no movement on my part could exhaust it; each step I took, after touching a paving-stone of the square, rebounded off it. I seemed to have the wings of Mercury growing on my heels. One of the fountains was filled with a ruddy glow, while in the other the moonlight had already begun to turn the water opalescent. Between them were children at play, uttering shrill cries, wheeling in circles, obeying some necessity of the hour, like swifts or bats. Next door to the hotel, the old law-courts and the Louis XVI orangery, in which were now installed the savings-bank and the Army Corps headquarters, were lit from within by the palely gilded globes of their gas-jets which, already aglow though it was still daylight outside, suited those vast, tall, eighteenth-century windows from which the last gleams of the setting sun had not yet departed, as a headdress of yellow tortoise-shell might suit a complexion heightened with rouge, and persuaded me to seek out my fireside and the lamp which, alone in the shadowy façade of my hotel, was striving to resist the gathering darkness, and for the sake of which I went indoors before it was quite dark, for pleasure, as to an appetising meal. I retained, in my lodgings, the same fullness of sensation that I had felt outside. It gave such an apparent convexity of surface to things which as a rule seem flat and insipid—to the yellow flame of the fire, the coarse blue paper of the sky on which the setting sun had scribbled corkscrews and whirligigs like a schoolboy with a piece of red chalk, the curiously patterned cloth on the round table on which a ream of essay paper and an inkpot lay in readiness for me together with one of Bergotte's novels—that ever since then these things have continued to seem to me to abound in a richly particular form of existence which I feel that I should be able to extract from them if it were granted me to set eyes on them again. I thought with joy of the barracks I had just left and of its weather-cock turning with every wind that blew. Like a diver breathing through a pipe which rises above the surface of the water, I felt that I was in some sense linked to a healthy, open-air life through my connexion with those barracks, that towering observatory dominating a country-side furrowed with strips of green enamel, into whose various buildings I esteemed it a priceless privilege, which I hoped would last, to be free to go whenever I chose, always certain of a welcome.

At seven o'clock I dressed and went out again to dine with Saint-Loup at the hotel where he took his meals. I liked to go there on foot. It was by now pitch dark, and after the third day of my visit, as soon as night had fallen an icy wind began blowing which seemed a harbinger of snow. As I walked, I ought not, one might have supposed, to have ceased for a moment to think of Mme de Guermantes; it was only in an attempt to draw nearer to her that I had come to visit Robert's garrison. But memories and griefs are fleeting things. There are days when they recede so far that we are barely conscious of them, we think that they have gone for ever. Then we pay attention to other things. And the streets of this town had not yet become for me what streets are in the place where one is accustomed to live, simply means of getting from one place to another. The life led by the inhabitants of this unknown world must, it seemed to me, be a thing of wonder, and often the lighted windows of some dwelling kept me standing for a long while motionless in the dark by laying before my eyes the actual and mysterious scenes of an existence into which I might not penetrate. Here the fire-spirit displayed to me in a crimson tableau a chestnut-seller's booth in which a couple of non-commissioned officers, their belts slung over the backs of chairs, were playing cards, never dreaming that a magician's wand was conjuring them out of the night like an apparition on the stage and presenting them as they actually were at that very moment to the eyes of a spellbound passer-by whom they could not see. In a little curio shop a half-spent candle, projecting its warm glow over an engraving, reprinted it in sanguine, while, battling against the darkness, the light of a big lamp bronzed a scrap of leather, inlaid a dagger with glittering spangles, spread a film of precious gold like the patina of time or the varnish of an old master on pictures which were only bad copies, made in fact of the whole hovel, in which there was nothing but pinchbeck rubbish, a marvellous composition by Rembrandt. Sometimes I lifted my eyes to gaze at some huge old dwelling-house whose shutters had not been closed and in which amphibious men and women, adapting themselves anew each evening to living in a different element from their day-time one, floated slowly to and fro in the rich liquid that after nightfall rose incessantly from the wells of the lamps to fill the rooms to the very brink of their outer walls of stone and glass, the displacement of their bodies

sending oleaginous golden ripples through it. I proceeded on
my way, and often, in the dark alley that ran past the cathedral,
as long ago on the road to Méséglise, the force of my desire
caught and held me; it seemed that a woman must be on the
point of appearing, to satisfy it; if, in the darkness, I suddenly
felt a skirt brush past me, the violence of the pleasure which
I then felt made it impossible for me to believe that the contact
was accidental and I attempted to seize in my arms a terrified
stranger. This gothic alley meant for me something so real
that if I had been successful in picking up and enjoying a
woman there, it would have been impossible for me not to
believe that it was the ancient charm of the place that was
bringing us together, even if she were no more than a common street-walker, stationed there every evening, whom the
wintry night, the strange place, the darkness, the mediaeval
atmosphere had invested with their mysterious glamour. I
thought of what might be in store for me; to try to forget
Mme de Guermantes seemed to me to be painful, but sensible,
and for the first time possible, even perhaps easy. In the absolute quiet of this neighbourhood I could hear ahead of me
shouted words and laughter which must come from tipsy
revellers staggering home. I waited to see them; I stood peering in the direction from which I had heard the noise. But I was
obliged to wait for some time, for the surrounding silence
was so intense that it had allowed sounds that were still a long
way off to penetrate it with the utmost clarity and force.
Finally the revellers did appear; not, as I had supposed, in
front of me, but far behind. Whether because the intersection
of side streets and the interposition of buildings had, by
reverberation, brought about this acoustic error, or because
it is very difficult to locate a sound when its position is unknown to us, I had been as mistaken about direction as about
distance.

The wind grew stronger. It was grainy and bristling with
coming snow. I returned to the main street and jumped on
board the little tram, from the platform of which an officer was
acknowledging, without seeming to see them, the salutes of the
uncouth soldiers who trudged past along the pavement, their
faces daubed crimson by the cold, reminding me, in this little

town which the sudden leap from autumn into early winter seemed to have transported further north, of the rubicund faces which Breughel gives to his merry, junketing, frostbound peasants.

And indeed at the hotel where I was to meet Saint-Loup and his friends and to which the festive season now beginning attracted a number of people from near and far, I found, as I hurried across the courtyard with its glimpses of glowing kitchens in which chickens were turning on spits, pigs were roasting, lobsters were being flung alive into what the landlord called the "everlasting fire," an influx (worthy of some *Numbering of the People at Bethlehem* such as the Old Flemish masters used to paint) of new arrivals who assembled there in groups, asking the landlord or one of his staff (who, if they did not like the look of them, would recommend lodgings elsewhere in the town) for bed and board, while a scullion hurried past holding a struggling fowl by the neck. And similarly, in the big dining-room which I passed through on the first day before coming to the little room where my friend was waiting for me, it was of some Biblical repast portrayed with mediaeval naïvety and Flemish exaggeration that one was reminded by the quantity of fish, chickens, grouse, woodcock, pigeons, brought in dressed and garnished and piping hot by breathless waiters who slid along the polished floor for greater speed and set them down on the huge sideboard where they were carved at once, but where—for many diners were finishing when I arrived—they piled up untouched, as though their profusion and the haste of those who brought them were inspired far less by a desire to meet the requirements of the diners than by respect for the sacred text, scrupulously followed in the letter but naïvely illustrated with real details borrowed from local custom, and by an aesthetic and religious anxiety to make evident to the eye the splendour of the feast by the profusion of the victuals and the assiduity of the servers. One of these stood lost in thought by a sideboard at the far end of the room; and to find out from him, who alone appeared calm enough to be capable of answering me, in which room our table had been laid, I made my way forward among the chafing-dishes that had been lighted here and there to keep the late-comers' plates from growing cold (which did not, however, prevent the dessert, in the centre of the room, from being piled in the outstretched hands of a huge mannikin, sometimes supported on the wings of a duck, apparently of crystal but really of ice, carved afresh every day with a hot iron by a sculptor-cook, quite in the Flemish manner), and, at the risk of being knocked down by his colleagues, went straight towards this servitor in whom I felt I recognised a character traditionally present in these sacred subjects, for he reproduced with scrupulous accuracy the simple, snub-nosed, ill-drawn features and dreamy expression, already half aware of the miracle of a divine presence which the others have not yet begun to suspect. In addition—doubtless in view of the coming festivities the cast was reinforced by a celestial contingent recruited entirely from a reserve of cherubim and seraphim. A young angel musician, with fair hair framing a fourteen-year-old face, was not, it was true, playing an instrument, but stood musing before a gong or a pile of plates, while other less infantile angels flew swiftly across the boundless expanse of the room, beating the air with the ceaseless fluttering of the napkins which dangled from them like the wings in "primitive" paintings, with pointed ends. Fleeing those ill-defined regions, screened by a hedge of palms, from which the angelic servitors looked, at a distance, as though they had floated down out of the empyrean, I forced my way through to the smaller room in which Saint-Loup's table was laid. I found there several of his friends who dined with him regularly, nobles except for one or two commoners in whom the young nobles had, as early as their school-days, detected likely friends, and with whom they readily fraternised, proving thereby that they were not in principle hostile to the middle classes, even if they were Republican, provided they had clean hands and went to mass. On the first of these evenings, before we sat down to dinner, I drew Saint-Loup into a corner and, in front of all the rest but so that they should not hear me, said to him:

"Robert, this is hardly the time or the place for what I am going to say, but I shan't be a second. I keep forgetting to ask you when I'm in the barracks: isn't that Mme de Guermantes's photograph that you have on your table?"

"Why, yes, she's my dear aunt."

"Of course she is; what a fool I am. I used to know that, but I'd never thought about it. I say, your friends will be getting impatient, we must be quick, they're looking at us. Or another time will do; it isn't at all important."

"That's all right, carry on. They can wait."

"No, no, I do want to be polite to them; they're so nice. Besides, it doesn't really matter in the least, I assure you."

"Do you know the worthy Oriane, then?"

This "worthy Oriane," as he might have said "the good Oriane," did not imply that Saint-Loup regarded Mme de Guermantes as especially good. In this instance the words "good," "excellent," "worthy," are mere reinforcements of the definite article indicating a person who is known to both parties and of whom the speaker does not quite know what to say to someone outside the family circle. The word "good" does duty as a stop-gap and keeps the conversation going for a moment until the speaker has hit upon "Do you see much of her?" or "I haven't set eyes on her for months," or "I shall be seeing her on Tuesday," or "She must be getting on, now, you know."

"I can't tell you how funny it is that it should be her photograph, because we're living in her house now, and I've been hearing the most astounding things about her" (I should have been hard put to it to say what) "which have made me immensely interested in her, only from a literary point of view, you understand, from a—how shall I put it—from a Balzacian point of view. You're so clever you can see what I mean without my having to explain. But we must hurry up. What on earth will your friends think of my manners?"

"They'll think absolutely nothing. I've told them you're sublime, and they're a great deal more nervous than you are."

"You really are too kind. But listen, what I want to say is this: I suppose Mme de Guermantes hasn't any idea that I know you, has she?"

"I can't say. I haven't seen her since the summer, because I haven't had any leave since she's been in town."

"The fact of the matter is, I've been told that she regards me as an absolute idiot."

"That I do not believe. Oriane isn't exactly a genius, but all the same she's by no means stupid."

"You know that as a rule I'm not at all keen on your advertising the good opinion you're kind enough to hold of me; I'm not conceited. That's why I'm sorry you should have said flattering things about me to your friends here (whom we'll join in two seconds). But Mme de Guermantes is different. If you could let her know—even with a bit of exaggeration —what you think of me, you would give me great pleasure."

"Why, of course I will. If that's all you want me to do, it's not very difficult. But what difference can it possibly make to you what she thinks of you? I suppose you think her no end of a joke, really. Anyhow, if that's all you want we can discuss it in front of the others or when we're by ourselves; I'm afraid of your tiring yourself if you stand talking, especially in such awkward conditions, when we have heaps of opportunities of being alone together."

It was precisely these awkward conditions that had given me courage to approach Robert; the presence of the others was for me a pretext that justified my giving my remarks a brief and disjointed form, under cover of which I could more easily dissemble the falsehood of my saying to my friend that I had forgotten his connexion with the Duchess, and also for not giving him time to frame—with regard to my reasons for wishing Mme de Guermantes to know that I was his friend, was clever, and so forth—questions which would have been all the more disturbing in that I should not have been able to answer them.

"Robert, I'm surprised that a man of your intelligence should fail to understand that one doesn't discuss the things that will give one's friends pleasure; one does them. Now I, if you were to ask me no matter what—and indeed I only wish you would ask me to do something for you—I can assure you I shouldn't demand any explanations. I've gone further than I really meant; I have no desire to know Mme de Guermantes, but just to test you I ought to have said that I was anxious to dine with Mme de Guermantes and I'm sure you would never have done it."

"Not only would I have done it, but I will do it."

"When?"

"Next time I'm in Paris, three weeks from now, I expect."

"We shall see. I dare say she won't want to see me, though. I can't tell you how grateful I am."

"Not at all, it's nothing."

"Don't say that; it's everything in the world because now I can see what a friend you are. Whether what I ask you to do is important or not, disagreeable or not, whether I'm really keen about it or ask you only as a test, it makes no difference: you say you will do it, and there you show the fineness of your mind and heart. A stupid friend would have argued."

This was exactly what he had just been doing; but perhaps I wanted to flatter his self-esteem; perhaps also I was sincere, the sole touchstone of merit seeming to me to be the extent to which a friend could be useful in respect of the one thing that seemed to me to have any importance, namely my love. Then I added, perhaps out of duplicity, perhaps in a genuine access of affection inspired by gratitude, by self-interest, and by all the similarities with Mme de Guermantes's very features which nature had reproduced in her nephew Robert:

"But now we really can't keep them waiting any longer, and I've mentioned only one of the two things I wanted to ask you, the less important; the other is more important to me, but I'm afraid you'll never consent. Would it annoy you if we were to call each other *tu*?"

"Annoy me? My dear fellow! *Joy! Tears of joy! Undreamed-of happiness!*"[5]

"Thank you so much. I'll wait for you to start first. It's such a pleasure to me that you needn't do anything about Mme de Guermantes if you'd rather not."

"I can do both."

"I say, Robert! Listen to me a minute," I said to him later during dinner. "Oh, it's really too absurd, this conversation in fits and starts, I can't think why—you remember the lady I was speaking to you about just now."

"Yes."

"You're quite sure you know who I mean?"

"Why, what do you take me for, a village idiot?"

"You wouldn't care to give me her photograph, I suppose?"

I had meant to ask him only for the loan of it. But as I was about to speak I was overcome with shyness, feeling that the request was indiscreet, and in order to hide my confusion I formulated it more bluntly and amplified it, as if it had been quite natural.

"No, I should have to ask her permission first," was his answer.

He blushed as he spoke. I could see that he had a reservation in his mind, that he attributed one to me as well, that he would further my love only partially, subject to certain moral principles, and for this I hated him.

At the same time I was touched to see how differently Saint-Loup behaved towards me now that I was no longer alone with him, and that his friends formed an audience. His increased affability would have left me cold had I thought that it was deliberately assumed; but I could feel that it was spontaneous and simply consisted of all that he was wont to say about me in my absence and refrained as a rule from saying when I was alone with him. True, in our private conversations I could detect the pleasure that he found in talking to me, but that pleasure almost always remained unexpressed. Now, at the same remarks of mine which ordinarily he enjoyed without showing it, he watched from the corner of his eye to see whether they produced on his friends the effect on which he had counted and which evidently corresponded to what he had promised them beforehand. The mother of a debutante could be no more anxiously attentive to her daughter's repartee and to the attitude of the audience. If I had made some remark at which, alone in my company, he would merely have smiled, he was afraid that the others might not have seen the point, and kept saying "What? What?" to make me repeat what I had said, to attract their attention, and turning at once to his friends with a hearty laugh, making himself willy-nilly the fugleman of their laughter, presented me for the first time with the opinion that he had of me and must often have expressed to them. So that I caught sight of myself suddenly from the outside, like someone who reads his name in a newspaper or sees himself in a mirror.

It occurred to me on one of these evenings to tell a mildly amusing story about Mme Blandais, but I stopped at once, remembering that Saint-Loup knew it already, and that when I had started to tell it to him the day after my arrival he had interrupted me with: "You told me that before, at Balbec." I was surprised, therefore, to find him begging me to go on and assuring me that he did not know the story and that it would amuse him immensely. "You've forgotten it for the moment," I said to him, "but you'll soon remember." "No, really, I swear to you, you're mistaken. You've never told it to me. Do go on." And throughout the story he kept his feverish and enraptured gaze fixed alternately on myself and on his friends. I realised only after I had finished, amid general laughter, that it had struck him that this story would give his comrades a good idea of my wit, and that it was for this reason that he had pretended not to know it. Such is the stuff of friendship.

On the third evening, one of his friends, to whom I had not had an opportunity of speaking before, conversed with me at great length; and at one point I overheard him telling Saint-Loup how much he was enjoying himself. And indeed we sat talking together almost the entire evening, leaving our glasses of Sauterne untouched on the table before us, separated, sheltered from the others by the imposing veils of one of those instinctive likings between men which, when they are not based on physical attraction, are the only kind that is altogether mysterious. Of such an enigmatic nature had seemed to me to be, at Balbec, the feeling which Saint-Loup had for me, a feeling not to be confused with the interest of our conversations, free from any material association, invisible, intangible, and yet of whose presence in himself like a sort of combustible gas he had been sufficiently conscious to refer to with a smile. And perhaps there was something more surprising still in this fellow-feeling born here in a single evening, like a flower that had blossomed in a few minutes in the warmth of this little room.

I could not help asking Robert when he spoke to me about Balbec whether it was really settled that he was to marry Mlle d'Ambresac. He assured me that not only was it not settled, but that there had never been any question of such a match, that he had never seen her, that he did not know who she was. If at that moment I had happened to see any of the social gossips who had told me of this coming event, they would promptly have announced the engagement of Mlle d'Ambresac to someone who was not Saint-Loup and that of Saint-Loup to someone who was not Mlle d'Ambresac. I should have surprised them greatly had I reminded them of their incompatible and still so recent predictions. In order that this little game should continue, and should multiply false reports by attaching the greatest possible number to every name in turn, nature has furnished those who play it with a memory as short as their credulity is long.

Saint-Loup had spoken to me of another of his comrades who was present also, one with whom he was on particularly good terms since they were the only two advocates in their mess of the revision of the Dreyfus case.

Just as a brother of this friend of Saint-Loup, who had been trained at the Schola Cantorum, thought about every new musical work not at all what his father, his mother, his cousins, his club-mates thought, but exactly what the other students at the Schola thought, so this non-commissioned nobleman (of whom Bloch formed an extraordinary opinion when I told him about him, because, touched to hear that he was on the same side as himself, he nevertheless imagined him, on account of his aristocratic birth and religious and military upbringing, to be as different as possible, endowed with the romantic attraction of a native of a distant country) had a "mentality," as people were now beginning to say, analogous to that of the whole body of Dreyfusards in general and of Bloch in particular, on which the traditions of his family and the interests of his career could retain no hold whatever. (Similarly, one of Saint-Loup's cousins had married a young Eastern princess who was said to write poetry quite as fine as Victor Hugo's or Alfred de Vigny's, and in spite of this was presumed to have a different type of mind from what could normally be imagined, the mind of an Eastern princess immured in an Arabian Nights palace. It was left to the writers who had the privilege of meeting her to savour the disappoint-

ment, or rather the joy, of listening to conversation which gave
the impression not of Scheherazade but of a person of genius
of the type of Alfred de Vigny or Victor Hugo.)[6]

"That fellow? Oh, he's not like Saint-Loup, he's a crank,"
my new friend told me. "He's not even sincere. At first he
used to say: 'Just wait a little, there's a man I know well, a
very shrewd and kind-hearted fellow, General de Boisdeffre;
you need have no hesitation in accepting his opinion.' But
as soon as he heard that Boisdeffre had pronounced Dreyfus
guilty, Boisdeffre ceased to count: clericalism, the prejudices
of the General Staff, prevented him from forming a candid
opinion, although there is, or rather was, before this Dreyfus
business, no one as clerical as our friend. Next he told us that
in any event we were to get the truth, because the case had been
put in the hands of Saussier, and he, a Republican soldier (our
friend coming of an ultra-monarchist family, if you please), was
a man of steel, with a stern unyielding conscience. But when
Saussier pronounced Esterhazy innocent, he found fresh
reasons to account for the verdict, reasons damaging not to
Dreyfus but to General Saussier. Saussier was blinded by the
militarist spirit (and our friend, by the way, is as militarist as
he is clerical, or at least was; I don't know what to make of
him any more). His family are broken-hearted at seeing him
possessed by such ideas."

"Don't you think," I suggested, half turning towards Saint-
Loup so as not to appear to be cutting myself off from him, and
in order to bring him into the conversation, "that the influence we ascribe to environment is particularly true of an
intellectual environment. Each of us is conditioned by an idea.
There are far fewer ideas than men, therefore all men with
similar ideas are alike. As there is nothing material in an idea,
the people who are only materially connected to the man with
an idea in no way modify it."

At this point I was interrupted by Saint-Loup, because
another of the young soldiers had leaned across to him with
a smile and, pointing to me, exclaimed: "Duroc! Duroc all
over!" I had no idea what this might mean, but I felt the
expression on the shy young face to be more than friendly.
While I was speaking, even the approbation of the others

seemed supererogatory to Saint-Loup; he insisted on silence.
And just as a conductor stops his orchestra with a rap from
his baton because someone has made a noise, so he rebuked
the author of this disturbance: "Gibergue, you must be silent
when people are speaking. You can tell us about it afterwards."
And to me: "Please go on."

I gave a sigh of relief, for I had been afraid that he was going
to make me begin all over again.

"And as an idea," I went on, "is a thing that cannot partake
of human interests and would be incapable of deriving any
benefit from them, the men who are governed by an idea are
not swayed by self-interest."

When I had finished speaking, "Fairly takes your breath
away, doesn't it, my boys," exclaimed Saint-Loup, who had
been following me with his eyes with the same anxious
solicitude as if I had been walking a tight-rope. "What were
you going to say, Gibergue?"

"I was just saying that your friend reminded me of Major
Duroc. I could almost hear him speaking."

"Why, I've often thought so myself," replied Saint-Loup.
"They have several points in common, but you'll find that this
man has all kinds of qualities Duroc hasn't."

Saint-Loup was not satisfied with this comparison. In an
ecstasy of joy, no doubt intensified by the joy he felt in making
me shine before his friends, with extreme volubility, he
reiterated, stroking and patting me as though I were a horse
that had just come first past the post: "You're the cleverest
man I know, do you hear?" He corrected himself, and added:
"Together with Elstir.—You don't mind my bracketing him
with you, I hope? Scrupulous accuracy, don't you know. As
one might have said to Balzac, for example: 'You're the
greatest novelist of the century—together with Stendhal.'
Scrupulous to a fault, you see, but nevertheless, immense
admiration. No? You don't agree about Stendhal?" he went
on, with a naïve confidence in my judgment which found
expression in a charming, smiling, almost childish glance of
interrogation from his green eyes. "Oh, good! I see you're on
my side. Bloch can't stand Stendhal. I think it's idiotic of him.
The *Chartreuse* is after all a stunning work, don't you think?

I'm so glad you agree with me. What is it you like best in the *Chartreuse?* Answer me," he urged with boyish impetuosity. And the menace of his physical strength made the question almost terrifying. "Mosca? Fabrice?" I answered timidly that Mosca reminded me a little of M. de Norpois. Whereupon there were peals of laughter from the young Siegfried Saint-Loup. And no sooner had I added: "But Mosca is far more intelligent, not so pedantic," than I heard Robert exclaim "Bravo," actually clapping his hands, and, helpless with laughter, gasp: "Oh, perfect! Admirable! You really are astounding."

I took a particular pleasure in talking to my new friend, as for that matter to all Robert's comrades and to Robert himself, about the barracks, the officers of the garrison, and the Army in general. Thanks to the immensely exaggerated scale on which we see the things, however petty they may be, in the midst of which we eat, and talk, and lead our real life; thanks to that formidable enlargement which they undergo, and the effect of which is that the rest of the world, not being present, cannot compete with them, and assumes in comparison the unsubstantiality of a dream, I had begun to take an interest in the various personalities of the barracks, in the officers whom I saw in the square when I went to visit Saint-Loup, or, if I was awake then, when the regiment passed beneath my windows. I should have liked to know more about the major whom Saint-Loup so greatly admired, and about the course in military history which would have appealed to me "even from an aesthetic point of view." I knew that all too often Robert indulged in a rather hollow verbalism, but at other times gave evidence of the assimilation of profound ideas which he was fully capable of grasping. Unfortunately, in respect of Army matters Robert was chiefly preoccupied at this time with the Dreyfus case. He spoke little about it, since he alone of the party at table was a Dreyfusard; the others were violently opposed to the idea of a fresh trial, except my other neighbour, my new friend, whose opinions appeared to be somewhat wavering. A firm admirer of the colonel, who was regarded as an exceptionally able officer and had denounced the current agitation against the Army in several of his regimental orders

which had earned him the reputation of being an anti-Dreyfusard, my neighbour had heard that his commanding officer had
let fall certain remarks leading to suppose that he had his
doubts as to the guilt of Dreyfus and retained his admiration
for Picquart. On this last point at any rate, the rumour of
the colonel's relative Dreyfusism was ill-founded, as are all
the rumours, springing from no one knows where, which float
around any great scandal. For, shortly afterwards, this colonel
having been detailed to interrogate the former Chief of the
Intelligence Branch, had treated him with a brutality and
contempt the like of which had never been known before.
However this might be (and although he had not taken the
liberty of making a direct inquiry of the colonel), my neighbour had been kind enough to tell Saint-Loup—in the tone
in which a Catholic lady might tell a Jewish lady that her parish
priest denounced the pogroms in Russia and admired the
generosity of certain Jews—that their colonel was not, with
regard to Dreyfusism—to a certain kind of Dreyfusism, at
least—the fanatical, narrow opponent that he had been made
out to be.

"I'm not surprised," was Saint-Loup's comment, "as he's
a sensible man. But in spite of everything he's blinded by the
prejudices of his caste, and above all, by his clericalism. By
the way," he turned to me, "Major Duroc, the lecturer on
military history I was telling you about—there's a man who is
whole-heartedly in support of our views, or so I'm told. And
I should have been surprised to hear that he wasn't, for he's
not only a brilliantly clever man, but a Radical-Socialist and a
freemason."

Partly out of courtesy to his friends, to whom Saint-Loup's
professions of Dreyfusard faith were painful, and also because
the subject was of more interest to me, I asked my neighbour
if it were true that this major gave a demonstration of military
history which had a genuine aesthetic beauty.

"It's absolutely true."

"But what do you mean by that?"

"Well, all that you read, let us say, in the narrative of a
military historian, the smallest facts, the most trivial happenings, are only the outward signs of an idea which has to be

elucidated and which often conceals other ideas, like a palimpsest. So that you have a field of study as intellectual as any science you care to name, or any art, and one that is satisfying to the mind."

"Give me an example or two, if you don't mind."

"It's not very easy to explain," Saint-Loup broke in. "You read, let us say, that this or that corps has tried . . . but before we go any further, the serial number of the corps, its order of battle, are not without their significance. If it isn't the first time that the operation has been attempted, and if for the same operation we find a different corps being brought up, it's perhaps a sign that the previous corps has been wiped out or has suffered heavy casualties in the said operation, that it's no longer in a fit state to carry it through successfully. Next, we must ask ourselves what this corps which is now out of action consisted of; if it was made up of shock troops, held in reserve for big attacks, a fresh corps of inferior quality will have little chance of succeeding where the first has failed. Furthermore, if we are not at the start of a campaign, this fresh corps may itself be a composite formation of odds and ends drawn from other corps, and this provides an indication of the strength of the forces the belligerent still has at its disposal, and the proximity of the moment when its forces will definitely be inferior to the enemy's, which puts the operation on which this corps is about to engage in a different perspective, because, if it is no longer in a condition to make good its losses, its successes themselves will, with arithmetical certainty, only bring it nearer to its ultimate destruction. Moreover, the serial number of the corps that it has facing it is of no less significance. If, for instance, it is a much weaker unit, which has already accounted for several important units of the attacking force, the whole nature of the operation is changed, since, even if it should end in the loss of the position which the defending force has been holding, simply to have held it for any length of time may be a great success if a very small defending force has been sufficient to destroy considerable forces on the other side. You can understand that if, in the analysis of the various corps engaged on both sides, there are all these points of importance, the study of the position itself, of the roads and railways which it commands, of the supply lines which it protects, is of even greater consequence. One must study what I may call the whole geographical context," he added with a laugh. (And indeed he was so delighted with this expression that, every time he employed it, even months afterwards, it was always accompanied by the same laugh.) "While the operation is being prepared by one of the belligerents, if you read that one of its patrols has been wiped out in the neighbourhood of the position by the other belligerent, one of the conclusions which you are entitled to draw is that one side was attempting to reconnoitre the defensive works with which the other intended to resist the attack. An exceptional burst of activity at a given point may indicate the desire to capture that point, but equally well the desire to hold the enemy in check there, not to retaliate at the point at which he has attacked you; or it may indeed be only a feint, intended to cover by an intensification of activity withdrawals of troops in that sector. (This was a classic feint in Napoleon's wars.) On the other hand, to appreciate the significance of a manoeuvre, its probable object, and, as a corollary, other manoeuvres by which it will be accompanied or followed, it is not immaterial to consult, not so much the announcements issued by the High Command, which may be intended to deceive the enemy, to mask a possible setback, as the manual of field operations in use in the country in question. We are always entitled to assume that the manoeuvre which an army has attempted to carry out is that prescribed by the rules in force for analogous circumstances. If, for instance, the rules lay down that a frontal attack should be accompanied by a flank attack and if, this flank attack having failed, the High Command claims that it had no connexion with the main attack and was merely a diversion, there is a strong likelihood that the truth will be found by consulting the field regulations rather than the statements issued from Headquarters. And there are not only the regulations governing each army to be considered, but their traditions, their habits, their doctrines. The study of diplomatic activity, which is constantly acting or reacting upon military activity, must not be neglected either. Incidents apparently insignificant, misinterpreted at the time, will explain to you how the enemy, counting on support which these incidents prove to have been denied him, was able to carry out only a part of his strategic plan. So that, if you know how to read your military history, what is a confused jumble for the ordinary reader becomes a chain of reasoning as rational as a painting is for the picture-lover who knows how to look and can see what the person portrayed is wearing, what he has in his hands, whereas the average visitor to a gallery is bewildered by a blur of colour which gives him a headache. But just as with certain pictures it isn't enough to observe that the figure is holding a chalice, but one must know why the painter chose to place a chalice in his hands, what it's intended to symbolise, so these military operations, quite apart from their immediate objective, are habitually modelled, in the mind of the general who is directing the campaign, on earlier battles which represent, so to speak, the past, the literature, the learning, the etymology, the aristocracy of the battles of to-day. Mind you, I'm not speaking for the moment of the local, the (what shall I call it?) spatial identity of battles. That exists also. A battlefield has never been, and never will be throughout the centuries, simply the ground upon which a single battle has been fought. If it has been a battlefield, that was because it combined certain conditions of geographical position, of geological formation, even of certain defects calculated to hinder the enemy (a river, for instance, cutting it in two), which made it a good battlefield. And so what it has been it will continue to be. You don't make an artist's studio out of any old room; so you don't make a battlefield out of any old piece of ground. There are predestined sites. But, once again, that's not what I was talking about so much as the type of battle a general takes as his model, a sort of strategic carbon copy, a tactical pastiche, if you like. Battles like Ulm, Lodi, Leipzig, Cannae. I don't know whether there'll ever be another war, or what nations will fight in it, but, if a war does come, you may be sure that it will include (and deliberately, on the commander's part) a Cannae, an Austerlitz, a Rosbach, a Waterloo, to mention a few. Some people make no bones about it. Marshal von Schlieffen and General von Falkenhausen have planned in advance a Battle of Cannae against France, in the Hannibal style, pinning their enemy down along his whole front, and advancing on both flanks, especially on the right through Belgium, while Bernhardi prefers the oblique advance of Frederick the Great, Leuthen rather than Cannae. Others expound their views less crudely, but I can tell you one thing, my boy, and that is that Beauconseil, the squadron commander I introduced you to the other day and who's an officer with a very great future before him, has swotted up a little Pratzen attack of his own which he knows inside out and is keeping up his sleeve, and if he ever has an opportunity to put it into practice he won't miss the boat but will let us have it good and proper. The breakthrough in the centre at Rivoli, too—that will crop up again if there's ever another war. It's no more obsolete than the *Iliad*. I may add that we're more or less condemned to frontal attacks, because we can't afford to repeat the mistake we made in '70; we must assume the offensive, nothing but the offensive. The only thing that troubles me is that although I see only the slower, more antiquated minds among us opposing this splendid doctrine, nevertheless one of the youngest of my masters, who is a genius, I mean Mangin, feels that there ought to be a place, provisional of course, for the defensive. It isn't very easy to answer him when he cites the example of Austerlitz, where the defensive was simply a prelude to attack and victory."

The enunciation of these theories by Saint-Loup was cheering. They gave me to hope that perhaps I was not being led astray, in my life at Doncières, with regard to these officers whom I heard being discussed as I sat sipping a Sauterne which bathed them in its charming golden glint, by the same magnifying power that had blown up to such huge dimensions in my eyes, while I was at Balbec, the King and Queen of the South Seas, the little group of the four gastronomes, the young gambler, and Legrandin's brother-in-law, who were now so shrunken as to appear non-existent. What gave me pleasure to-day would not perhaps leave me indifferent to-morrow, as had always happened hitherto; the person that I still was at this moment was not perhaps doomed to imminent destruction, since to the ardent and fugitive passion which I felt on these few evenings for everything that concerned the military life, Saint-Loup, by what he had just been saying to me about the art of war, added an intellectual foundation, of a permanent character, capable of gripping me so strongly that I could believe, without any attempt at self-deception, that after I had left Doncières I should continue to take an interest in the work of my friends there, and should not be long in coming to pay them another visit. However, in order to be quite sure that this art of war was indeed an art in the true sense of the word I said to Saint-Loup:

"You interest me enormously. But tell me, there's one point that puzzles me. I feel that I could become passionately involved in the art of war, but first I should want to be sure that it is not so very different from the other arts, that knowing the rules is not everything. You tell me that battles are reproduced. I do find something aesthetic, just as you said, in seeing beneath a modern battle the plan of an older one; I can't tell you how attractive the idea sounds. But then, does the genius of the commander count for nothing? Does he really do no more than apply the rules? Or, granted equal knowledge, are there great generals as there are great surgeons, who, when the symptoms exhibited by two cases of illness are identical to the outward eye, nevertheless feel, for some infinitesimal reason, founded perhaps on their experience, but interpreted afresh, that in one case they ought to do this, in another case that; that in one case it is better to operate, in another to wait?"

"But of course! You'll find Napoleon not attacking when all the rules demanded that he should attack, but some obscure divination warned him not to. For instance, look at Austerlitz, or, in 1806, his instructions to Lannes. But you will find certain generals slavishly imitating one of Napoleon's manoeuvres and arriving at a diametrically opposite result. There are a dozen examples of that in 1870. But even as regards the interpretation of what the enemy *may* do, what he actually does is only a symptom which may mean any number of different things. Each of them has an equal chance of being the right one, if you confine yourself to logic and science, just as in certain difficult cases all the medical science in the world will

be powerless to decide whether the invisible tumour is malig-
nant or not, whether or not the operation ought to be performed. It is his flair, his divination, his crystal-gazing (if you
know what I mean) which decides, in the case of the great general as of the great doctor. Thus I explained to you, to take one
instance, what a reconnaissance on the eve of a battle might
signify. But it may mean a dozen other things, such as making
the enemy think you're going to attack him at one point
whereas you intend to attack him at another, putting up a
screen which will prevent him from seeing the preparations
for your real operation, forcing him to bring up fresh troops,
to fix them there, to immobilise them in a different place from
where they are needed, forming an estimate of the forces at
his disposal, sounding him out, forcing him to show his hand.
Sometimes, even, the fact that you deploy an immense number
of troops in an operation is by no means a proof that that is
your true objective; for you may carry it out in earnest, even if
it is only a feint, so that the feint may have a better chance of
deceiving the enemy. If I had time now to go through the
Napoleonic wars from this point of view, I assure you that
these simple classic movements which we study here, and which
you'll come and see us practising in the field, just for the pleasure of an outing, you young rotter (no, I know you're not
well, I'm sorry!), well, in a war, when you feel behind you the
vigilance, the judgment, the profound study of the High
Command, you're as moved by them as by the beam of a lighthouse, a purely physical light but none the less an emanation
of the mind, sweeping through space to warn ships of danger.
In fact I may perhaps be wrong in speaking to you only of the
literature of war. In reality, as the formation of the soil, the
direction of wind and light tell us which way a tree will grow,
so the conditions in which a campaign is fought, the features of
the country through which you manoeuvre, prescribe, to a
certain extent, and limit the number of the plans among which
the general has to choose. Which means that along a mountain
range, through a system of valleys, over certain plains, it's
almost with the inevitability and the grandiose beauty of an
avalanche that you can predict the line of an army on the
march."

"Now you deny me that freedom of choice in the commander, that power of divination in the enemy who is trying to
read his intentions, which you allowed me a moment ago."

"Not at all. You remember that book of philosphy we read
together at Balbec, the richness of the world of possibilities
compared with the real word. Well, it's exactly the same with
the art of war. In a given situation there will be four plans that
apply and among which the general may choose, as a disease
may take various courses for which the doctor has to be prepared. And there again human weakness and human greatness
are fresh causes of uncertainty. For of these four plans let us
assume that contingent reasons (such as the attainment of
minor objectives, or the time factor, or numerical inferiority
and inadequate supplies) lead the general to prefer the first,
which is less perfect but less costly and swifter to execute, and
has for its terrain a richer country for feeding his troops. He
may, after having begun with this plan, which the enemy,
uncertain at first, will soon detect, find that success lies beyond
his grasp, the difficulties being too great (that is what I call
the element of human weakness), abandon it and try the second
or third or fourth. But it may equally be that he has tried the
first plan (and this is what I call human greatness) merely as a
feint to pin down the enemy, so as to surprise him later at a
point where he has not been expecting an attack. Thus at Ulm,
Mack, who expected the enemy to attack from the west, was
encircled from the north where he thought he was perfectly
safe. My example is not a very good one, as a matter of fact.
Actually Ulm is a better example of the battle of encirclement,
which the future will see reproduced because it is not only a
classic example from which generals will draw inspiration, but
a form that is to some extent logically necessary (like several
others, thus leaving room for choice and variety) like a type
of crystallisation. But it doesn't much matter really, because
these conditions are after all artificial. To go back to our
philosophy book; it's like the rules of logic or scientific laws,
reality conforms to them more or less, but remember the
great mathematician Poincaré: he's by no means certain that
mathematics is a rigorously exact science. As to the rules
themselves, which I mentioned to you, they are of secondary

importance really, and besides they're altered from time to time. We cavalrymen, for instance, live by the *Field Service* of 1895, which may be said to be out of date since it is based on the old and obsolete doctrine which maintains that cavalry action has little more than a psychological effect by creating panic in the enemy ranks. Whereas the more intelligent of our teachers, all the best brains in the cavalry, and particularly the major I was telling you about, consider on the contrary that the issue will be decided in a real free-for-all with sabre and lance and the side that can hold out longer will be the winner, not merely psychologically, by creating panic, but physically."

"Saint-Loup is quite right, and it's likely that the next *Field Service* will reflect this new school of thought," my neighbour observed.

"I'm glad to have your support, since your opinions seem to make more impression upon my friend than mine," said Saint-Loup with a smile, whether because the growing liking between his comrade and myself annoyed him slightly or because he thought it graceful to solemnise it with this official acknowledgement. "Perhaps I may have underestimated the importance of the rules. They do change, that must be admitted. But in the meantime they control the military situation, the plans of campaign and troop concentration. If they reflect a false conception of strategy they may be the initial cause of defeat. All this is a little too technical for you," he remarked to me. "Always remember that, when all's said and done, what does most to accelerate the evolution of the art of war is wars themselves. In the course of a campaign, if it is at all long, you will see one belligerent profiting by the lessons provided by the enemy's successes and mistakes, perfecting the methods of the latter, who will improve on them in turn. But all that is a thing of the past. With the terrible advance of artillery, the wars of the future, if there are to be any more wars, will be so short that, before we have had time to think of putting our lessons into practice, peace will have been signed."

"Don't be so touchy," I told Saint-Loup, reverting to the first words of this speech. "I was listening to you quite avidly!"

"If you will kindly not take offence, and will allow me to

speak," his friend went on, "I shall add to what you've just been saying that if battles reproduce themselves indistinguishably it isn't merely due to the mind of the commander. It may happen that a mistake on his part (for instance, his failure to appreciate the strength of the enemy) will lead him to call upon his men for extravagant sacrifices, sacrifices which certain units will make with an abnegation so sublime that the part they play will be analogous to that of some other unit in some other battle, and they'll be quoted in history as interchangeable examples: to stick to 1870, we have the Prussian Guard at Saint-Privat, and the Turcos at Frœschviller and Wissembourg."

"Ah, interchangeable; precisely! Excellent! The lad has brains," was Saint-Loup's comment.

I was not insensible to these last examples, as always when, beneath the particular instance, I was afforded a glimpse of the general law. What really interested me, however, was the genius of the commander; I was anxious to discover in what it consisted, how, in given circumstances, when the commander who lacked genius could not withstand the enemy, the inspired commander would set about restoring his jeopardised position, which, according to Saint-Loup, was quite possible and had been done several times by Napoleon. And to understand what good generalship meant I asked for comparisons between the various commanders whom I knew by name, which of them had most markedly the character of a leader, the gifts of a tactician—at the risk of boring my new friends, who however showed no signs of boredom, but continued to answer me with an inexhaustible good-nature.

I felt cut off—not only from the great icy darkness which stretched out into the distance and in which we could hear from time to time the whistle of a train which only accentuated the pleasure of being there, or the chimes of an hour still happily distant from that at which these young men would have to buckle on their sabres and go—but also from all external preoccupations, almost from the memory of Mme de Guermantes, by the kindness of Saint-Loup, to which that of his friends, reinforcing it, gave, so to speak, a greater solidity; by the warmth, too, of that little dining-room, by the savour of the exquisite dishes that were set before us. These gave as much pleasure to my imagination as to my palate; sometimes the little piece of nature from which they had been extracted, the rugged holy-water stoup of the oyster in which lingered a few drops of brackish water, or the gnarled stem, the yellowed branches of a bunch of grapes, still enveloped them, inedible, poetic and distant as a landscape, evoking as we dined successive images of a siesta in the shade of a vine or of an excursion on the sea; on other evenings it was the cook alone who brought out these original properties of the viands, presenting them in their natural setting, like works of art, and a fish cooked in a court-bouillon was brought in on a long earthenware platter, on which, standing out in relief on a bed of bluish herbs, intact but still contorted from having been dropped alive into boiling water, surrounded by a ring of satellite shell-fish, of animalcules, crabs, shrimps and mussels, it had the appearance of a ceramic dish by Bernard Palissy.

"I'm furiously jealous," Saint-Loup said to me, half laughing, half in earnest, alluding to the interminable conversations apart which I had been having with his friend. "Is it because you find him more intelligent than me? Do you like him better than me? Ah, well, I suppose he's everything now, and no one else is to have a look in!" (Men who are enormously in love with a woman, who live in a society of woman-lovers, allow themselves pleasantries which others, seeing less innocence in them, would never dare to contemplate.)

When the conversation became general, the subject of Dreyfus was avoided for fear of offending Saint-Loup. A week later, however, two of his friends remarked how curious it was that, living in so military an environment, he was so keen a Dreyfusard, almost an anti-militarist. "The reason is," I suggested, not wishing to enter into details, "that the influence of environment is not so important as people think . . ." I intended of course to stop at this point, and not to reiterate the observations which I had made to Saint-Loup a week earlier. Since, however, I had made this particular remark almost word for word, I was about to excuse myself by adding: "Just as I was saying the other day . . ." But I had reckoned without the reverse side of Robert's cordial admiration for myself and

certain other people. That admiration was complemented by
so entire an assimilation of their ideas that after a day or two,
he would have completely forgotten that those ideas were not
his own. And so, in the matter of my modest thesis, Saint-
Loup, for all the world as though it had always dwelt in his
own brain, and as though I was merely poaching on his
preserves, felt it incumbent upon him to greet my discovery
with warm approval.

"Why, yes; environment is of no importance."

And with as much vehemence as if he were afraid I might
interrupt or fail to understand him:

"The real influence is that of the intellectual environment!
One is conditioned by an idea!"

He paused for a moment, with the satisfied smile of one who
has digested his dinner, dropped his monocle, and, fixing me
with a gimlet-like stare, said to me challengingly:

"All men with similar ideas are alike."

No doubt he had completely forgotten that I myself had
said to him only a few days earlier what on the other hand
he had remembered so well.

I did not arrive at Saint-Loup's restaurant every evening in
the same state of mind. If a memory, a sorrow that weigh on
us are capable of leaving us, to the extent that we are no longer
aware of them, they can also return and sometimes remain
with us for a long time. There were evenings when, as I
passed through the town on my way to the restaurant, I felt
so keen a longing for Mme de Guermantes that I could
scarcely breathe; it was as though part of my breast had been
cut out by a skilled anatomist and replaced by an equal part
of immaterial suffering, by its equivalent in nostalgia and love.
And however neatly the wound may have been stitched together, one lives rather uncomfortably when regret for the
loss of another person is substituted for one's entrails; it
seems to be occupying more room than they; one feels it
perpetually; and besides, what a contradiction in terms to be
obliged to *think* a part of one's body. Only it seems that we are
worth more, somehow. At the whisper of a breeze we sigh,
with oppression but also with languor. I would look up at the

sky. If it was clear, I would say to myself: "Perhaps she is in the country; she's looking at the same stars; and, for all I know, when I arrive at the restaurant Robert may say to me: 'Good news! I've just heard from my aunt. She wants to meet you, she's coming down here.'" It was not the firmament alone that I associated with the thought of Mme de Guermantes. A passing breath of air, more fragrant than the rest, seemed to bring me a message from her, as, long ago, from Gilberte in the wheatfields of Méséglise. We do not change; we introduce into the feeling which we associate with a person many slumbering elements which it awakens but which are foreign to it. Besides, with these feelings for particular people, there is always something in us that strives to give them a larger truth, that is to say, to absorb them in a more general feeling, common to the whole of humanity, with which individuals and the suffering that they cause us are merely a means to enable us to communicate. What mixed a certain pleasure with my pain was that I knew it to be a tiny fragment of universal love. True, from the fact that I seemed to recognise the same sorts of sadness that I had felt on Gilberte's account, or else when in the evenings at Combray Mamma did not stay in my room, and also the memory of certain pages of Bergotte, in the suffering which I now felt and to which Mme de Guermantes, her coldness, her absence, were not clearly linked as cause is to effect in the mind of a philosopher, I did not conclude that Mme de Guermantes was not that cause. Is there not such a thing as a diffused bodily pain, extending, radiating out into other parts, which, however, it leaves, to vanish altogether, if the practitioner lays his finger on the precise spot from which it springs? And yet, until that moment, its extension made it seem to us so vague and sinister that, powerless to explain or even to locate it, we imagined that there was no possibility of its being healed. As I made my way to the restaurant I said to myself: "A fortnight already since I last saw Mme de Guermantes" (a fortnight, which did not appear so enormous an interval except to me, who, where Mme de Guermantes was concerned, counted in minutes). For me it was no longer the stars and the breeze alone, but the arithmetical divisions of time that assumed a dolorous and poetic aspect.

Each day now was like the mobile crest of an indistinct hill, down one side of which I felt that I could descend towards forgetfulness, but down the other was carried along by the need to see the Duchess again. And I was continually inclining one way or the other, having no stable equilibrium. One day I said to myself: "Perhaps there'll be a letter to-night"; and on entering the dining-room I found courage to ask Saint-Loup:

"You don't happen to have had any news from Paris?"

"Yes," he replied gloomily, "bad news."

I breathed a sigh of relief when I realised that it was only he who had cause for unhappiness, and that the news was from his mistress. But I soon saw that one of its consequences would be to prevent Robert for a long time from taking me to see his aunt.

I learned that a quarrel had broken out between him and his mistress, through the post presumably, unless she had come down to pay him a flying visit between trains. And the quarrels, even when relatively slight, which they had previously had, had always seemed as though they must prove insoluble. For she had a violent temper, and would stamp her foot and burst into tears for reasons as incomprehensible as those that make children shut themselves into dark cupboards, not come out for dinner, refuse to give any explanation, and only redouble their sobs when, our patience exhausted, we give them a slap.

To say that Saint-Loup suffered terribly from this estrangement would be an oversimplification, would give a false impression of his grief. When he found himself alone, with nothing else to think about but his mistress parting from him with the respect for him which she had felt on seeing him so full of energy and vigour, the agony he had experienced during the first few hours at first gave way before the irreparable, and the cessation of pain is such a relief that the rupture, once it was certain, assumed for him something of the same kind of charm as a reconciliation. What he began to suffer from a little later was a secondary and accidental grief, the tide of which flowed incessantly from within himself, at the idea that perhaps she would have been glad to make it up, that it was not inconceivable that she was waiting for a word from him, that in the meantime, by way of revenge, she would perhaps on a certain evening, in a certain place, do a certain thing, and that he had only to telegraph to her that he was coming for it not to happen, that others perhaps were taking advantage of the time which he was letting slip, and that in a few days it would be too late to get her back, for she would be already bespoken. Among all these possibilities he was certain of nothing; his mistress preserved a silence which wrought him up to such a frenzy of grief that he began to ask himself whether she might not be in hiding at Doncières, or have set sail for the Indies.

It has been said that silence is strength; in a quite different sense it is a terrible strength in the hands of those who are loved. It increases the anxiety of the one who waits. Nothing so tempts us to approach another person as what is keeping us apart; and what barrier is so insurmountable as silence? It has been said also that silence is torture, capable of goading to madness the man who is condemned to it in a prison cell. But what an even greater torture than that of having to keep silence it is to have to endure the silence of the person one loves! Robert said to himself: "What can she be doing, to keep so silent as this? Obviously she's being unfaithful to me with others." He also said to himself: "What have I done that she should be so silent? Perhaps she hates me, and will go on hating me forever." And he reproached himself. Thus silence indeed drove him mad with jealousy and remorse. Besides, more cruel than the silence of prisons, that kind of silence is in itself a prison. It is an intangible enclosure, true, but an impenetrable one, this interposed slice of empty atmosphere through which nevertheless the visual rays of the abandoned lover cannot pass. Is there a more terrible form of lighting than that of silence, which shows us not one absent love but a thousand, and shows us each of them in the act of indulging in some new betrayal? Sometimes, in a sudden slackening of tension, Robert would imagine that this silence was about to cease, that the letter was on its way. He saw it, it had arrived, he started at every sound, his thirst was already quenched, he murmured: "The letter! The letter!" After this glimpse of a phantom oasis of tenderness, he found himself once more toiling across the real desert of a silence without end.

He suffered in anticipation, without missing a single one, all the griefs and pains of a rupture which at other moments he fancied he might somehow contrive to avoid, like people who put all their affairs in order with a view to an expatriation which will never take place, and whose minds, no longer certain where they will find themselves living next day, flutter momentarily, detached from them, like a heart that is taken out of a dying man and continues to beat, though separated from the rest of his body. At all events, this hope that his mistress would return gave him courage to persevere in the rupture, as the belief that one may return alive from the battle helps one to face death. And inasmuch as habit is, of all the plants of human growth, the one that has least need of nutritious soil in order to live, and is the first to appear on the most seemingly barren rock, perhaps had he begun by thinking of the rupture as a feint he would in the end have become genuinely accustomed to it. But his uncertainty kept him in a state which, linked with the memory of the woman herself, was akin to love. He forced himself, nevertheless, not to write to her, thinking perhaps that it was a less cruel torment to live without his mistress than with her in certain conditions, or else that, after the way in which they had parted, it was essential to wait for her apologies if she was to retain what he believed her to feel for him in the way, if not of love, at any rate of esteem and regard. He contented himself with going to the telephone, which had recently been installed at Doncières, and asking for news from, or giving instructions to, a lady's maid whom he had hired for his mistress. These communications were complicated and time-consuming, since, influenced by what her literary friends preached to her about the ugliness of the capital, but principally for the sake of her animals, her dogs, her monkey, her canaries and her parakeet, whose incessant din her Paris landlord had ceased to tolerate, Robert's mistress had taken a little house in the neighbourhood of Versailles. Meanwhile he, at Doncières, no longer slept a wink all night. Once, in my room, overcome by exhaustion, he dozed off for a while. But suddenly he began to speak, tried to get up and run to stop something from happening, said: "I hear her; you shan't . . . you shan't. . . ." He awoke. He had been dreaming, he told me, that he was in the country with the senior sergeant. His host had tried to keep him away from a certain part of the house. Saint-Loup had discovered that the senior sergeant had staying with him a subaltern, extremely rich and extremely vicious, whom he knew to have a violent passion for his mistress. And suddenly in his dream he had distinctly heard the intermittently regular cries which his mistress was in the habit of uttering at the moment of gratification. He had tried to force the senior sergeant to take him to the room in which she was. And the other had held on to him to keep him from going there, with an air of annoyance at such a want of discretion in a guest which, Robert said, he would never be able to forget.

"It was an idiotic dream," he concluded, still quite out of breath.

All the same I could see that, during the hour that followed, he was more than once on the point of telephoning to his mistress to beg for a reconciliation. My father now had the telephone, but I doubt whether that would have been of much use to Saint-Loup. Besides, it hardly seemed to me quite proper to make my parents, or even a mechanical instrument installed in their house, play pander between Saint-Loup and his mistress, however ladylike and high-minded the latter might be. His bad dream began to fade from his memory. With a fixed and absent stare, he came to see me on each of those cruel days which traced in my mind as they followed one after the other the splendid sweep of a staircase painfully forged, from the steps of which Robert stood asking himself what decision his beloved was going to take.

At length she wrote to ask whether he would consent to forgive her. As soon as he realised that a definite rupture had been avoided he saw all the disadvantages of a reconciliation. Besides, he had already begun to suffer less acutely, and had almost accepted a grief of which, in a few months perhaps, he would have to suffer the sharp bite again if their liaison were to be resumed. He did not hesitate for long. And perhaps he hesitated only because he was now certain of being able to recover his mistress, of being able to do so and therefore of doing so. However, she asked him, so that she might have time to recover her equanimity, not to come to Paris at the New Year. And he did not have the heart to go to Paris without seeing her. On the other hand, she had declared her willingness to go abroad with him, but for that he would need to make a formal application for leave, which Captain de Borodino was unwilling to grant.

"I'm sorry about it because of our visit to my aunt, which which will have to be put off. I dare say I shall be in Paris at Easter."

"We shan't be able to call on Mme de Guermantes then, because I shall have gone to Balbec. But, really, it doesn't matter in the least, I assure you."

"To Balbec? But you didn't go there till August."

"I know, but next year I'm being sent there earlier, for my health."

His main fear was that I might form a bad impression of his mistress after what he had told me. "She is violent simply because she's too frank, too headstrong in her feelings. But she's a sublime creature. You can't imagine the poetic delicacy there is in her. She goes every year to spend All Souls' Day at Bruges. Rather good, don't you think? If you ever meet her you'll see what I mean: she has a sort of greatness. . . ." And, as he was infected with certain of the linguistic mannerisms current in the literary circles in which the lady moved: "There's something astral about her, in fact something vatic. You know what I mean, the poet merging into the priest."

I searched all through dinner for a pretext which would enable Saint-Loup to ask his aunt to see me without my having to wait until he came to Paris. Such a pretext was finally furnished me by the desire I cherished to see some more pictures by Elstir, the famous painter whom Saint-Loup and I had met at Balbec—a pretext behind which there was, moreover, an element of truth, for if, on my visits to Elstir, I had asked of his painting that it should lead me to the understanding and love of things better than itself, a real thaw, an authentic square in a country town, live women on a beach (at most I would have commissioned from him portraits of realities I had not been able to fathom, such as a hedge of hawthorns, not so much that it might perpetuate their beauty for me as that it might reveal that beauty to me), now, on the contrary, it was the originality, the seductive attraction of those paintings that aroused my desire, and what I wanted above all else was to look at other pictures by Elstir.

It seemed to me, moreover, that the least of his pictures were something quite different from the masterpieces even of greater painters than himself. His work was like a realm apart, with impenetrable frontiers, peerless in substance. Eagerly collecting the infrequent periodicals in which articles on him and his work had appeared, I had learned that it was only recently that he had begun to paint landscape and still life, and that he had started with mythological subjects (I had seen photographs of two of these in his studio), and had then been for long under the influence of Japanese art.

Several of the works most characteristic of his various manners were scattered about the provinces. A certain house at Les Andelys, in which there was one of his finest landscapes, seemed to me as precious, gave me as keen a desire to go there, as might a village near Chartres among whose millstone walls was enshrined a glorious stained-glass window; and towards the possessor of this treasure, towards the man who, inside his rough-hewn house, on the main street, closeted like an astrologer, sat questioning one of those mirrors of the world which Elstir's pictures were, and who had perhaps bought it for many thousands of francs, I felt myself borne by that instinctive sympathy which joins the very hearts, the inmost natures of those who think alike upon a vital subject. Now three important works by my favourite painter were described in one of these articles as belonging to Mme de Guermantes. So that it was on the whole quite sincerely that, on the evening on which Saint-Loup told me of his lady's projected visit to Bruges, I was able, during dinner, in front of his friends, to say to him casually, as though on the spur of the moment:

"I say, if you don't mind, just one last word on the subject of the lady we were speaking about. You remember Elstir, the painter I met at Balbec?"

"Why, of course I do."

"You remember how much I admired his work?"

"I do, very well; and the letter we sent him."

"Well, one of the reasons—not one of the chief reasons, an incidental reason—why I should like to meet the said lady—you do know who I mean, don't you?"

"Of course I do. All these digressions!"

"Is that she has in her house at least one very fine picture by Elstir."

"Really, I never knew that."

"Elstir will probably be at Balbec at Easter; you know he now spends almost the entire year on that coast. I should very much like to have seen this picture before I leave Paris. I don't know whether you're on sufficiently intimate terms with your aunt: but couldn't you manage, somehow, giving her so good an impression of me that she won't refuse, to ask her to let me come and see the picture without you, since you won't be there?"

"Certainly. I'll answer for her; leave it to me."

"Oh, Robert, you're an angel; I do like you."

"It's very nice of you to like me, but it would be equally nice if you were to call me *tu*, as you promised, and as you began to do."

"I hope it's not your departure that you two are plotting together," one of Robert's friends said to me. "You know, if Saint-Loup does go on leave, it needn't make any difference, we shall still be here. It will be less amusing for you, perhaps, but we'll do all we can to make you forget his absence."

The fact was that, just when it had been generally assumed that Robert's mistress would be going to Bruges alone, the news came that Captain de Borodino, hitherto obdurate in his refusal, had given authority for Sergeant Saint-Loup to proceed on long leave to Bruges. What had happened was this. The Prince, extremely proud of his luxuriant head of hair, was an assiduous customer of the principal hairdresser in the town, who had started life as an apprentice to Napoleon III's barber. Captain de Borodino was on the best of terms with the hairdresser, being, in spite of his majestic airs, extremely simple in his dealings with his inferiors. But the hairdresser, through whose books the Prince's account had been running without payment for at least five years, swollen no less by bottles of "Portugal" and "Eau des Souverains," curling-tongs, razors, and strops, than by the ordinary charges for

shampooing, haircutting and the like, had a greater respect for
Saint-Loup, who always paid on the nail and kept several
carriages and saddle-horses. Having learned of Saint-Loup's
vexation at not being able to go with his mistress, he had
spoken warmly about it to the Prince at a moment when he
was trussed up in a white surplice with his head held firmly over
the back of the chair and his throat menaced by a razor. This
account of a young man's amatory adventures won from the
princely Captain a smile of Bonapartist indulgence. It is hardly
probable that he thought of his unpaid bill, but the barber's
recommendation inclined him to good humour as much as a
duke's would have inclined him to bad. While his chin was
still smothered in soap, the leave was promised and the warrant
was signed that evening. As for the hairdresser, who was in
the habit of boasting incessantly, and in order to be able to
do so laid claim, with an astonishing faculty for lying, to
exploits that were entirely fictitious, having for once rendered
a signal service to Saint-Loup, not only did he refrain from
publicly claiming credit for it, but, as if vanity were obliged to
lie, and when there is no call to do so gives way to modesty,
he never mentioned the matter to Robert again.

All Robert's friends assured me that, as long as I stayed at
Doncières, or if I should come there again at any time, even
though Robert was away, their horses, their quarters, their
free time would be at my disposal, and I felt that it was with the
greatest cordiality that these young men put their comfort and
youth and strength at the service of my weakness.

"Why at any rate," they went on after insisting that I should
stay, "don't you come down here every year? You see how our
humble life appeals to you! Besides, you're so keen about
everything that goes on in the regiment: quite the old soldier."

For I continued to ask them eagerly to classify the different
officers whose names I knew according to the degree of
admiration which they felt them to deserve, just as, in the old
days, I used to make my schoolfriends classify the actors of the
Théâtre-Français. If, in the place of one of the generals whom
I had always heard mentioned at the head of the list, such as
Galliffet or Négrier, one of Saint-Loup's friends remarked,
"But Négrier is one of the feeblest of our general officers,"

and put in the new, untarnished, appetising name of Pau or
Geslin de Bourgogne, I felt the same happy surprise as long
ago when the outworn names of Thiron or Febvre were ousted
by the sudden blossoming of the unfamiliar name of Amaury.
"Better even than Négrier? But in what respect? Give me an
example." I should have liked there to exist profound differences even among the junior officers of the regiment, and I
hoped, in the reason for these differences, to grasp the essence
of what constituted military superiority. One of those whom
I should have been most interested to hear discussed, because
he was the one whom I had most often seen, was the Prince de
Borodino. But neither Saint-Loup nor his friends, while giving
him credit for being a fine officer who kept his squadron up
to an incomparable pitch of efficiency, liked the man. Without
speaking of him, naturally, in the same tone as of certain other
officers, rankers and freemasons, who did not fraternise much
with the rest and had, in comparison, an uncouth, barrack-
room manner, they seemed not to include M. de Borodino
among the other officers of noble birth, from whom indeed
he differed considerably in his attitude even towards Saint-
Loup. These, taking advantage of the fact that Robert was only
an N.C.O., and that therefore his influential relatives might be
grateful were he invited to the houses of superior officers on
whom otherwise they would have looked down, lost no
opportunity of having him to dine when any bigwig was
expected who might be of use to a young cavalry sergeant.
Captain de Borodino alone confined himself to his official
relations (which for that matter were always excellent) with
Robert. The fact was that the Prince, whose grandfather had
been made a Marshal and a Prince-Duke by the Emperor, into
whose family he had subsequently married, and whose father
had then married a cousin of Napoleon III and had twice been
a minister after the coup d'état, felt that in spite of all this
he did not count for much with Saint-Loup and the Guermantes set, who in turn, since he did not look at things from
the same point of view as they, counted for very little with him.
He suspected that, for Saint-Loup, he—a kinsman of the
Hohenzollerns—was not a true noble but the grandson of a
farmer, but at the same time he regarded Saint-Loup as the

son of a man whose countship had been confirmed by the Emperor—one of what were known in the Faubourg Saint-Germain as "touched-up" counts—and who had besought him first for a Prefecture, then for some other post a long way down the list of subordinates to His Highness the Prince de Borodino, Minister of State, who was styled on his letters "Monseigneur" and was a nephew of the sovereign.

More than a nephew, possibly. The first Princesse de Borodino was reputed to have bestowed her favours on Napoleon I, whom she followed to the Isle of Elba, and the second hers on Napoleon III. And if, in the Captain's placid countenance, one caught a trace of Napoleon I—if not his actual features, at least the studied majesty of the expression—the officer had, particularly in his melancholy and kindly gaze, in his drooping moustache, something that reminded one also of Napoleon III; and this in so striking a fashion that, when he asked leave, after Sedan, to join the Emperor in captivity, and was shown the door by Bismarck, before whom he had been brought, the latter, happening to look up at the young man who was preparing to leave the room, was instantly struck by the likeness and, reconsidering his decision, recalled him and gave him the authorisation which, in common with everyone else, he had just been refused.

If the Prince de Borodino was not prepared to make overtures either to Saint-Loup or to the other representatives of the Faubourg Saint-Germain in the regiment (whereas he frequently invited two subalterns of plebeian origin who were pleasant companions) it was because, looking down on them all from the height of his Imperial grandeur, he drew between these two classes of inferiors the distinction that one set consisted of inferiors who knew themselves to be such and with whom he was delighted to consort, being beneath his outward majesty of a simple, jovial nature, and the other of inferiors who thought themselves his superiors, a claim which he could not allow. And so, while all the other officers of the regiment made much of Saint-Loup, the Prince de Borodino, to whom the young man had been recommended by Marshal X———, confined himself to being kindly towards him in the matter of military duty, where Saint-Loup was in fact exemplary, but

never had him to his house, except on one special occasion
when he found himself practically compelled to invite him,
and, since this occurred during my stay at Doncières, asked
him to bring me too. I had no difficulty that evening, as I
watched Saint-Loup sitting at his Captain's table, in distinguishing, in their respective manners and refinements, the
difference that existed between the two aristocracies: the old
nobility and that of the Empire. The product of a caste whose
faults, even if he repudiated them with all the force of his
intellect, had been absorbed into his blood, a caste which,
having ceased to exert any real authority for at least a century,
no longer saw in the patronising affability which was part and
parcel of its education anything more than an exercise, like
horsemanship or fencing, cultivated without any serious
purpose, as a diversion, Saint-Loup, on meeting representatives of that middle class which the old nobility so far
despised as to believe that they were flattered by its intimacy
and would be honoured by its informality, would cordially
shake hands with any bourgeois to whom he was introduced,
and whose name he had probably failed to catch, and as he
talked to him (constantly crossing and uncrossing his legs,
flinging himself back in his chair in an attitude of abandon, one
foot in the palm of his hand) would call him "my dear fellow."
Belonging, on the other hand, to a nobility whose titles still
preserved their meaning, possessed as they still were of the
rich emoluments given in reward for glorious services and
bringing to mind the record of high offices in which one is in
command of numberless men and must know how to deal
with men, the Prince de Borodino—not perhaps very distinctly
or in the personal awareness of his conscious mind, but at any
rate in his body, which revealed it by its attitudes and manners
—regarded his rank as a prerogative that was still effective;
those same commoners whom Saint-Loup would have slapped
on the shoulder and taken by the arm he addressed with a
majestic affability, in which a reserve instinct with grandeur
tempered the smiling good-fellowship that came naturally
to him, in a tone marked at once by a genuine kindliness and a
stiffness deliberately assumed. This was due, no doubt, to his
being not so far removed from the chancelleries and the Court

itself, at which his father had held the highest posts, and where the manners of Saint-Loup, his elbow on the table and his foot in his hand, would not have been well received; but principally it was due to the fact that he was less contemptuous of the middle class since it was the great reservoir from which the first Emperor had chosen his marshals and his nobles and in which the second had found a Rouher or a Fould.

Son or grandson of an Emperor though he might be, with nothing more important to do than to command a squadron, the preoccupations of his putative father and grandfather could not, of course, for want of an object on which to fasten themselves, survive in any real sense in the mind of M. de Borodino. But as the spirit of an artist continues, for many years after he is dead, to model the statue which he carved, so those preoccupations had taken shape in him, were materialised, incarnate in him, it was them that his face reflected. It was with the sharpness of the first Emperor in his voice that he addressed a reprimand to a corporal, with the dreamy melancholy of the second that he exhaled a puff of cigarette-smoke. When he passed in plain clothes through the streets of Doncières, a certain glint in his eyes, issuing from under the brim of his bowler hat, surrounded the Captain with the aura of a regal incognito; people trembled when he strode into the senior sergeant's office, followed by the sergeant-major and the quartermaster, as though by Berthier and Masséna. When he chose the cloth for his squadron's breeches, he fastened on the master-tailor a look capable of baffling Talleyrand and deceiving Alexander; and at times, in the middle of a kit inspection, he would pause, a dreamy look in his handsome blue eyes, and twist his moustache with the air of one building up a new Prussia and a new Italy. But a moment later, reverting from Napoleon III to Napoleon I, he would point out that the equipment was not properly polished, and insist on tasting the men's rations. And at home, in his private life, it was for the wives of middle-class officers (provided they were not freemasons) that he would bring out not only a dinner service of royal blue Sèvres, fit for an ambassador (which had been given to his father by Napoleon, and appeared even more priceless in the commonplace house he inhabited on the avenue, like those rare porcelains which tourists admire with a special delight in the rustic china-cupboard of some old manor that has been converted into a comfortable and prosperous farmhouse), but other gifts of the Emperor also: those noble and charming manners, which too would have done wonders in a diplomatic post abroad (if for some it did not mean a lifelong condemnation to the most unjust form of ostracism merely to have a "name"), the easy gestures, the kindness, the grace, and, enclosing images of glory in an enamel that was also royal blue, the mysterious, illuminated, living reliquary of his gaze.

And in regard to the social relations with the middle classes which the Prince had at Doncières, it may be appropriate to add the following. The lieutenant-colonel played the piano beautifully; the senior medical officer's wife sang like a Conservatoire medallist. This latter couple, as well as the lieutenant-colonel and his wife, used to dine every week with M. de Borodino. They were certainly flattered, knowing that when the Prince went to Paris on leave he dined with Mme de Pourtalès, with the Murats and suchlike. "But," they said to themselves, "he's just a captain, after all; he's only too glad to get us to come. Still, he's a real friend to us." But when M. de Borodino, who had long been pulling every possible wire to secure an appointment nearer Paris, was posted to Beauvais, he packed up and went, and forgot the two musical couples as completely as he forgot the Doncières theatre and the little restaurant to which he used often to send out for his lunch, and, to their great indignation, neither the lieutenant-colonel nor the senior medical officer, who had so often sat at his table, ever had so much as a single word from him for the rest of their lives.

One morning, Saint-Loup confessed to me that he had written to my grandmother to give her news of me and to suggest to her that, since there was a telephone service functioning between Paris and Doncières, she might make use of it to speak to me. In short, that very day she was to give me a call, and he advised me to be at the post office at about a quarter to four. The telephone was not yet at that date as commonly in use as it is to-day. And yet habit requires so short a time to divest of their mystery the sacred forces with which

we are in contact, that, not having had my call at once, my
immediate thought was that it was all very long and very
inconvenient, and I almost decided to lodge a complaint. Like
all of us nowadays, I found too slow for my liking, in its
abrupt changes, the admirable sorcery whereby a few moments
are enough to bring before us, invisible but present, the
person to whom we wish to speak, and who, while still sitting
at his table, in the town in which he lives (in my grandmother's
case, Paris), under another sky than ours, in weather that is not
necessarily the same, in the midst of circumstances and preoccupations of which we know nothing and of which he is
about to inform us, finds himself suddenly transported hundreds of miles (he and all the surroundings in which he remains immured) within reach of our ear, at the precise moment
which our fancy has ordained. And we are like the person in
the fairy-tale for whom a sorceress, at his express wish, con-
jures up, in a supernatural light, his grandmother or his betrothed in the act of turning over a book, of shedding tears,
of gathering flowers, close by the spectator and yet very far
away, in the place where she actually is at the moment. We
need only, so that the miracle may be accomplished, apply our
lips to the magic orifice and invoke—occasionally for rather
longer than seems to us necessary, I admit—the Vigilant
Virgins to whose voices we listen every day without ever
coming to know their faces, and who are our guardian angels
in the dizzy realm of darkness whose portals they so jealously
guard; the All-Powerful by whose intervention the absent
rise up at our side, without our being permitted to set eyes on
them; the Danaids of the unseen who incessantly empty and
fill and transmit to one another the urns of sound; the ironic
Furies who, just as we were murmuring a confidence to a
loved one, in the hope that no one could hear us, cry brutally:
"I'm listening!"; the ever-irritable handmaidens of the Mystery,
the umbrageous priestesses of the Invisible, the Young Ladies
of the Telephone.

And as soon as our call has rung out, in the darkness filled
with apparitions to which our ears alone are unsealed, a tiny
sound, an abstract sound—the sound of distance overcome—
and the voice of the dear one speaks to us.

It is she, it is her voice that is speaking, that is there. But how far away it is! How often have I been unable to listen without anguish, as though, confronted by the impossibility of seeing, except after long hours of journeying, her whose voice was so close to my ear, I felt more clearly the illusoriness in the appearance of the most tender proximity, and at what a distance we may be from the persons we love at the moment when it seems that we have only to stretch out our hands to seize and hold them. A real presence, perhaps, that voice that seemed so near—in actual separation! But a premonition also of an eternal separation! Many were the times, as I listened thus without seeing her who spoke to me from so far away, when it seemed to me that the voice was crying to me from the depths out of which one does not rise again, and I felt the anxiety that was one day to wring my heart when a voice would thus return (alone and attached no longer to a body which I was never to see again), to murmur in my ear words I longed to kiss as they issued from lips for ever turned to dust.

That afternoon, alas, at Doncières, the miracle did not occur. When I reached the post office, my grandmother's call had already been received. I stepped into the booth; the line was engaged; someone was talking who probably did not realise that there was nobody to answer him, for when I raised the receiver to my ear, the lifeless piece of wood began to squeak like Punchinello; I silenced it, as one silences a puppet, by putting it back on its hook, but, like Punchinello, as soon as I picked it up again it resumed its gabblings. At length, giving up in despair and hanging up the receiver once and for all, I stifled the convulsions of this vociferous stump which kept up its chatter until the last moment, and went in search of the telephonist, who told me to wait a while; then I spoke, and after a few seconds of silence, suddenly I heard that voice which I mistakenly thought I knew so well; for always until then, every time that my grandmother had talked to me, I had been accustomed to follow what she said on the open score of her face, in which the eyes figured so largely; but her voice itself I was hearing this afternoon for the first time. And because that voice appeared to me to have altered in its proportions from the moment that it was a whole, and reached me thus alone and without the accompaniment of her face and features, I discovered for the first time how sweet that voice was; perhaps indeed it had never been so sweet as it was now, for my grandmother, thinking of me as being far away and unhappy, felt that she might abandon herself to an outpouring of tenderness which, in accordance with her principles of upbringing, she usually restrained and kept hidden. It was sweet, but also how sad it was, first of all on account of its very sweetness, a sweetness drained almost— more than any but a few human voices can ever have been— of every element of hardness, of resistance to others, of selfishness! Fragile by reason of its delicacy, it seemed constantly on the verge of breaking, of expiring in a pure flow of tears; then, too, having it alone beside me, seen without the mask of her face, I noticed in it for the first time the sorrows that had cracked it in the course of a lifetime.

Was it, however, solely the voice that, because it was alone, gave me this new impression which tore my heart? Not at all; it was rather that this isolation of the voice was like a symbol, an evocation, a direct consequence of another isolation, that of my grandmother, for the first time separated from me. The commands or prohibitions which she constantly addressed to me in the ordinary course of life, the tedium of obedience or the fire of rebellion which neutralised the affection that I felt for her, were at this moment eliminated and indeed might be eliminated for ever (since my grandmother, no longer insisting on having me with her under her control, was in the act of expressing her hope that I would stay at Doncières altogether, or would at any rate extend my visit for as long as possible, since both my health and my work might benefit by the change); and so, what I held compressed in this little bell at my ear was our mutual affection, freed from the conflicting pressures which had daily counteracted it, and henceforth irresistible, uplifting me entirely. My grandmother, by telling me to stay, filled me with an anxious, an insensate longing to return. This freedom she was granting me henceforward, and to which I had never dreamed that she would consent, appeared to me suddenly as sad as my freedom of action might be after her death (when I should still love her and she would for ever have abandoned me). "Granny!" I cried to her, "Granny!" and I longed to kiss her, but I had beside me only the voice, a phantom as impalpable as the one that would perhaps come back to visit me when my grandmother was dead. "Speak to me!" But then, suddenly, I ceased to hear the voice, and was left even more alone. My grandmother could no longer hear me; she was no longer in communication with me; we had ceased to be close to each other, to be audible to each other; I continued to call her, groping in the empty darkness, feeling that calls from her must also be going astray. I quivered with the same anguish which I had felt once before in the distant past, when, as a little child, I had lost her in a crowd, an anguish due less to my not finding her than to the thought that she must be searching for me, must be saying to herself that I was searching for her, an anguish not unlike that which I was later to feel, on the day when we speak to those who can no longer reply and when we long for them at least to hear all the things we never said to them, and our assurance that we are not unhappy. It seemed to me as though it was already a beloved ghost that I had allowed to lose herself in the ghostly world, and, standing alone before the instrument, I went on vainly repeating: "Granny! Granny!" as Orpheus, left alone, repeats the name of his dead wife. I decided to leave the post office, and go and find Robert at his restaurant in order to tell him that, as I was half expecting a telegram which would oblige me to return to Paris, I wanted, just in case, to know the times of the trains. And yet, before reaching this decision, I felt I must make one more attempt to invoke the Daughters of the Night, the Messengers of the Word, the faceless divinities; but the capricious Guardians had not deigned once again to open the miraculous portals, or, more probably, had been unable to do so; untiringly though they invoked, as was their custom, the venerable inventor of printing and the young prince, collector of Impressionist paintings and driver of motor-cars (who was Captain de Borodino's nephew), Gutenberg and Wagram left their supplications unanswered, and I came away, feeling that the Invisible would continue to turn a deaf ear.

When I joined Robert and his friends, I withheld the confession that my heart was no longer with them, that my departure was now irrevocably fixed. Saint-Loup appeared to believe me, but I learned afterwards that he had from the first moment realised that my uncertainty was feigned and that he would not see me again next day. While he and his friends, letting their plates grow cold, searched through the time-table for a train which would take me to Paris, and while the whistling of the locomotives in the cold, starry night could be heard on the line, I certainly no longer felt the same peace of mind as on so many evenings I had derived from the friendship of the former and the latter's distant passage. And yet they did not fail, this evening, to perform the same office in a different form. My departure oppressed me less when I was no longer obliged to think of it alone, when I felt that the more normal and healthy exertions of my energetic friends, Robert's brothers-in-arms, were being applied to what was to be done, and of those other strong creatures, the trains, whose comings and goings, morning and night, between Doncières and Paris, broke up in retrospect what had been too compact and unendurable in my long isolation from my grandmother into daily possibilities of return.

"I don't doubt the truth of what you say, and that you aren't thinking of leaving us just yet," said Saint-Loup, smiling, "but pretend you are going, and come and say good-bye to me to-morrow morning early, otherwise there's a risk of my not seeing you. I'm going out to lunch, I've got leave from the Captain, but I shall have to be back in barracks by two, as we are to be on the march all afternoon. I suppose the man to whose house I'm going, a couple of miles out, will manage to get me back in time."

Scarcely had he uttered these words than a messenger came for me from my hotel: the post office had asked for me on the telephone. I ran there, for it was nearly closing time. The word "trunks" recurred incessantly in the answers given me by the clerks. I was in a fever of anxiety, for it was my grandmother who had asked for me. The post office was closing for the night. Finally I got my connexion. "Is that you, Granny?" A woman's voice, with a strong English accent, answered:

"Yes, but I don't recognise your voice." Neither did I recognise the voice that was speaking to me; besides, my grandmother called me *tu*, and not *vous*. And then all was explained. The young man for whom his grandmother had called on the telephone had a name almost identical with mine, and was staying in an annex of my hotel. This call coming on the very day on which I had been telephoning to my grandmother, I had never for a moment doubted that it was she who was asking for me. Whereas it was by pure coincidence that the post office and the hotel had combined to make a twofold error.

The following morning I was late, and failed to catch Saint-Loup, who had already left for the country house where he was invited to lunch. About half past one, having decided to go to the barracks so as to be there as soon as he returned, I was crossing one of the avenues on the way there when I noticed, coming behind me in the same direction as myself, a tilbury which, as it overtook me, obliged me to jump out of its way. An N.C.O. was driving it, wearing a monocle; it was Saint-Loup. By his side was the friend whose guest he had been at lunch, and whom I had met once before at the hotel where we dined. I did not dare shout to Robert since he was not alone, but, in the hope that he would stop and pick me up, I attracted his attention with a sweep of my hat which was by way of being motivated by the presence of a stranger. I knew that Robert was short-sighted, but I should have supposed that if he saw me at all he could not fail to recognise me. He did indeed see my salute, and returned it, but without stopping; driving on at full speed, without a smile, without moving a muscle of his face, he confined himself to keeping his hand raised for a minute to the peak of his cap, as though he were acknowledging the salute of a trooper whom he did not know. I ran to the barracks, but it was a long way; when I arrived, the regiment was forming up on the square, where I was not allowed to remain, and I was heart-broken at not having been able to say good-bye to Saint-Loup. I went up to his room, but there was no sign of him. I inquired after him from a group of sick troopers—recruits who had been excused route-marches, the young graduate, one of the "old soldiers," who were watching the regiment form up.

"You haven't seen Sergeant Saint-Loup, by any chance?" I asked.

"He's already gone down, sir," said the old soldier.

"I never saw him," said the graduate.

"You never saw him," exclaimed the old soldier, losing all interest in me, "you never saw our famous Saint-Loup, the figure he's cutting with his new breeches! When the Capstan sees that, officer's cloth, my word!"

"Oh, that's a good one, officer's cloth," replied the young graduate, who, reported "sick in quarters," was excused marching and ventured, not without some trepidation, to be brashly familiar with the veterans. "It isn't officer's cloth, it's just ordinary cloth."

"Monsieur?" inquired the old soldier angrily.

He was indignant that the young graduate should question his assertion that the breeches were made of officer's cloth, but, being a Breton, born in a village that went by the name of Penguern-Stereden, and having learned French with as much difficulty as if it had been English or German, whenever he felt himself overcome by emotion he would go on saying "Monsieur?" to give himself time to find words, then, after this preparation, let loose his eloquence, confining himself to the repetition of certain words which he knew better than others, but without haste, taking every precaution to gloss over his unfamiliarity with the pronunciation.

"Ah! so it's just ordinary cloth?" he broke out eventually with a fury whose intensity increased in direct proportion to the sluggishness of his speech. "Ah! so it's just ordinary cloth! When I tell you that it is officer's cloth, when-I-tell-you, if-I-tell-you, it's because I know, I should think."

"Oh, well, if you say so," replied the young graduate, overcome by the force of this argument.

"There, look, there's the Capstan coming along. No, but just look at Saint-Loup, the way he throws his leg out, and his head. Would you call that a non-com? And his eyeglass— it's all over the shop."

I asked these troopers, who did not seem at all embarrassed by my presence, whether I too might look out of the window. They neither objected to my doing so nor moved to make room

for me. I saw Captain de Borodino go majestically by, putting
his horse into a trot, and seemingly under the illusion that he
was taking part in the Battle of Austerlitz. A few loiterers
had stopped by the gate to see the regiment file out. Erect on
his charger, his face rather plump, his cheeks of an Imperial
fullness, his eye clear-sighted, the Prince must have been the
victim of some hallucination, as I was myself whenever,
after the tram-car had passed, the silence that followed its
rumble seemed to me to throb and echo with a vaguely musical
palpitation.

I was wretched at having failed to say good-bye to Saint-
Loup, but I went nevertheless, for my only concern was to
return to my grandmother; always until then, in this little
country town, when I thought of what my grandmother must
be doing by herself, I had pictured her as she was when with
me, but eliminating myself without taking into account the
effects on her of such an elimination; now, I had to free myself
at the first possible moment, in her arms, from the phantom,
hitherto unsuspected and suddenly called into being by her
voice, of a grandmother really separated from me, resigned,
having (something I had never yet thought of her as having)
a definite age, who had just received a letter from me in the
empty house in which I had already imagined Mamma when
I had left her to go to Balbec.

Alas, it was this phantom that I saw when, entering the
drawing-room before my grandmother had been told of my
return, I found her there reading. I was in the room, or rather
I was not yet in the room since she was not aware of my
presence, and, like a woman whom one surprises at a piece of
needlework which she will hurriedly put aside if anyone comes
in, she was absorbed in thoughts which she had never allowed
to be seen by me. Of myself—thanks to that privilege which
does not last but which gives one, during the brief moment of
return, the faculty of being suddenly the spectator of one's
own absence—there was present only the witness, the observer,
in travelling coat and hat, the stranger who does not belong
to the house, the photographer who has called to take a
photograph of places which one will never see again. The
process that automatically occurred in my eyes when I caught

sight of my grandmother was indeed a photograph. We never
see the people who are dear to us save in the animated system,
the perpetual motion of our incessant love for them, which,
before allowing the images that their faces present to reach us,
seizes them in its vortex and flings them back upon the idea
that we have always had of them, makes them adhere to it,
coincide with it. How, since into the forehead and the cheeks
of my grandmother I had been accustomed to read all the
most delicate, the most permanent qualities of her mind, how,
since every habitual glance is an act of necromancy, each face
that we love a mirror of the past, how could I have failed to
overlook what had become dulled and changed in her, seeing
that in the most trivial spectacles of our daily life, our eyes,
charged with thought, neglect, as would a classical tragedy,
every image that does not contribute to the action of the play
and retain only those that may help to make its purpose
intelligible. But if, instead of our eyes, it should happen to be
a purely physical object, a photographic plate, that has
watched the action, then what we see, in the courtyard of
the Institute, for example, instead of the dignified emergence
of an Academician who is trying to hail a cab, will be his
tottering steps, his precautions to avoid falling on his back,
the parabola of his fall, as though he were drunk or the
ground covered in ice. So it is when some cruel trick of chance
prevents our intelligent and pious tenderness from coming
forward in time to hide from our eyes what they ought never
to behold, when it is forestalled by our eyes, and they, arriving
first in the field and having it to themselves, set to work
mechanically, like films, and show us, in place of the beloved
person who has long ago ceased to exist but whose death
our tenderness has always hitherto kept concealed from us, the
new person whom a hundred times daily it has clothed with a
loving and mendacious likeness. And—like a sick man who,
not having looked at his own reflexion for a long time, and
regularly composing the features which he never sees in
accordance with the ideal image of himself that he carries in
his mind, recoils on catching sight in the glass, in the middle
of an arid desert of a face, of the sloping pink protuberance
of a nose as huge as one of the pyramids of Egypt—I, for

whom my grandmother was still myself, I who had never seen her save in my own soul, always in the same place in the past, through the transparency of contiguous and overlapping memories, suddenly, in our drawing-room which formed part of a new world, that of time, that which is inhabited by the strangers of whom we say "He's begun to age a good deal," for the first time and for a moment only, since she vanished very quickly, I saw, sitting on the sofa beneath the lamp, red-faced, heavy and vulgar, sick, vacant, letting her slightly crazed eyes wander over a book, a dejected old woman whom I did not know.

My request to be allowed to inspect the Elstirs in Mme de Guermantes's collection had been met by Saint-Loup with: "I'll answer for her." And indeed, unfortunately, it was he and he alone who did answer. We answer readily enough for other people when, setting our mental stage with the little puppets that represent them, we manipulate these to suit our fancy. No doubt even then we take into account the difficulties due to another person's nature being different from our own, and we do not fail to appeal to motives with the power to influence that nature—self-interest, conviction, anxiety—which will neutralise any contrary tendencies. But it is still our own nature which imagines these divergences; it is we who eliminate these difficulties; it is we who determine these compelling motives. And when we wish to see the other person perform in real life the actions which in our mind's eye we have made him rehearse, the case is altered, we come up against unseen resistances which may prove insuperable. One of the strongest is doubtless that which may be developed in a woman who does not love by the rank and unconquerable repulsion she feels for the man who loves her: during the long weeks in which Saint-Loup still did not come to Paris, his aunt, to whom I had no doubt of his having written begging her to do so, never once asked me to call at her house to see the Elstirs.

I perceived signs of coldness on the part of another occupant of the building. This was Jupien. Did he consider that I ought to have gone in and said good-day to him, on my return from Doncières, before even going upstairs to our own flat? My

mother said that it was nothing to be surprised about.
Françoise had told her that he was like that, subject to sudden
fits of ill humour, without any cause. These invariably passed
off after a while.

Meanwhile the winter was drawing to an end. One morning,
after several weeks of showers and storms, I heard in my
chimney—instead of the formless, elastic, sombre wind which
stirred in me a longing to go to the sea—the cooing of the
pigeons, nesting in the wall outside; shimmering and unexpected like a first hyacinth gently tearing open its nutritious
heart to release its flower of sound, mauve and satin-soft,
letting into my still dark and shuttered bedroom as through an
opened window the warmth, the brightness, the fatigue of a
first fine day. That morning, I caught myself humming a
music-hall tune which had never entered my head since the
year when I had been due to go to Florence and Venice—
so profoundly, and so unpredictably, does the atmosphere act
on our organism and draw from dim reserves where we had
forgotten them the melodies written there which our memory
has failed to decipher. Presently a more conscious dreamer
accompanied this musician to whom I was listening inside
myself, without even having recognised at first what he was
playing.

I realised that it was not for any reason peculiar to Balbec
that on my arrival there I had failed to find in its church the
charm which it had had for me before I knew it; that in
Florence or Parma or Venice my imagination could no more
take the place of my eyes when I looked at the sights there. I
realised this; similarly, one New Year's evening at nightfall,
standing before a column of playbills, I had discovered the
illusion that lies in our thinking that certain feast-days differ
essentially from the other days in the calendar. And yet I
could not prevent my memory of the time during which I
had looked forward to spending Easter in Florence from
continuing to make that festival the atmosphere, so to speak,
of the City of Flowers, to give at once to Easter Day something
Florentine and to Florence something paschal. Easter was still
a long way off; but in the range of days that stretched out
before me the days of Holy Week stood out more clearly at the

end of those that came between. Touched by a ray, like certain
houses in a village which one sees from a distance when the
rest are in shadow, they had caught and kept all the sun.

The weather had now become milder. And my parents
themselves, by urging me to take more exercise, gave me an
excuse for continuing my morning walks. I had wanted to give
them up, since they meant my meeting Mme de Guermantes.
But it was for that very reason that I kept thinking all the time
of those walks, and this induced me to go on finding fresh
reasons for taking them, reasons which had no connexion with
Mme de Guermantes and which easily convinced me that, had
she never existed, I should still have gone for a walk at that
hour every morning.

Alas, if for me meeting any person other than herself would
have been a matter of indifference, I felt that, for her, meeting
anyone in the world except myself would have been only too
endurable. It happened that, in the course of her morning
walks, she received the salutations of plenty of fools whom she
regarded as such. But the appearance of these in her path
seemed to her, if not to hold out any promise of pleasure, to
be at any rate the result of mere accident. And she stopped
them at times, for there are moments in which one wants to
escape from oneself, to accept the hospitality offered by the
soul of another, provided always that this soul, however
modest and plain it may be, is a different soul, whereas in my
heart she felt with exasperation that what she would have
found was herself. And so, even when I had another reason
for taking the same route than my desire to see her, I trembled
like a guilty man as she came past; and sometimes, in order to
neutralise what might seem to be excessive in my overtures,
I would barely acknowledge her salute, or would stare at her
without raising my hat, and succeed only in irritating her even
more and making her begin to regard me as insolent and ill-
bred besides.

She was now wearing lighter, or at any rate brighter clothes,
and would come strolling down the street in which already,
as though it were spring, in front of the narrow shops that
were squeezed in between the spacious fronts of the old
aristocratic mansions, over the booths of the butter-woman

and the fruit-woman and the vegetable-woman, awnings were
spread to protect them from the sun. I told myself that the
woman whom I could see in the distance, walking, opening
her sunshade, crossing the street, was, in the opinion of those
best qualified to judge, the greatest living exponent of the art
of performing those movements and of making of them
something exquisite. Meanwhile she advanced towards me,
and, unconscious of this widespread reputation, her narrow,
refractory body, which had absorbed nothing of it, was arched
forward under a scarf of violet silk; her clear, sullen eyes
looked absently in front of her, and had perhaps caught sight
of me; she was biting the corner of her lip; I watched her
adjust her muff, give alms to a beggar, buy a bunch of violets
from a flower-seller, with the same curiosity that I should have
felt in watching the brush-strokes of a great painter. And when,
as she passed me, she gave me a bow that was accompanied
sometimes by a faint smile, it was as though she had sketched
for me, adding a personal dedication, a water-colour that was
a masterpiece of art. Each of her dresses seemed to me her
natural and necessary setting, like the projection of a particular aspect of her soul. On one of these Lenten mornings,
when she was on her way out to lunch, I met her wearing a
dress of bright red velvet, cut slightly low at the neck. Her
face appeared dreamy beneath its pile of fair hair. I was less
sad than usual because the melancholy of her expression, the
sort of claustration which the startling hue of her dress set
between her and the rest of the world, made her seem somehow
lonely and unhappy, and this comforted me. The dress struck
me as being the materialisation round about her of the scarlet
rays of a heart which I did not recognise in her and might
perhaps have been able to console; sheltered in the mystical
light of the garment with its soft folds, she reminded me of
some saint of the early ages of Christianity. After which I
felt ashamed of inflicting my presence on this holy martyr.
"But, after all, the streets belong to everybody."

The streets belong to everybody, I repeated to myself,
giving a different meaning to the words, and marvelling that
indeed in the crowded street, often soaked with rain, which
gave it a precious lustre like the streets, at times, in the old

towns of Italy, the Duchesse de Guermantes mingled with the public life of the world moments of her own secret life, showing herself thus in all her mystery to everyone, jostled by all and sundry, with the splendid gratuitousness of the greatest works of art. As I often went out in the morning after staying awake all night, in the afternoon my parents would tell me to lie down for a little and try to get some sleep. There is no need, when one is trying to find sleep, to give much thought to the quest, but habit is very useful, and even the absence of thought. But in these afternoon hours I lacked both. Before going to sleep, I devoted so much time to thinking that I should be unable to do so that even after I was asleep a little of my thought remained. It was no more than a glimmer in the almost total darkness, but it was enough to cast a reflexion in my sleep, first of the idea that I could not sleep, and then, a reflexion of this reflexion, that it was in my sleep that I had had the idea that I was not asleep, then, by a further refraction, my awakening . . . to a fresh doze in which I was trying to tell some friends who had come into my room that, a moment earlier, when I was asleep, I had imagined that I was not asleep. These shadows were barely distinguishable; it would have required a keen—and quite useless—delicacy of perception to seize them. Similarly, in later years, in Venice, long after the sun had set, when it seemed to be quite dark, I have seen, thanks to the echo, itself imperceptible, of a last note of light held indefinitely on the surface of the canals as though by the effect of some optical pedal, the reflexions of the palaces displayed as though for all time in a darker velvet on the crepuscular greyness of the water. One of my dreams was the synthesis of what my imagination had often sought to depict, in my waking hours, of a certain seagirt place and its mediaeval past. In my sleep I saw a gothic city rising from a sea whose waves were stilled as in a stained-glass window. An arm of the sea divided the town in two; the green water stretched to my feet; on the opposite shore it washed round the base of an oriental church, and beyond it houses which existed already in the fourteenth century, so that to go across to them would have been to ascend the stream of time. This dream in which nature had learned from art, in which the sea had turned

Gothic, this dream in which I longed to attain, in which I believed that I was attaining to the impossible, was one that I felt I had often dreamed before. But as it is the nature of what we imagine in sleep to multiply itself in the past, and to appear, even when new, to be familiar, I supposed that I was mistaken. I noticed, however, that I did indeed frequently have this dream.

The diminutions, too, that characterise sleep were reflected in mine, but in a symbolic manner; I could not in the darkness make out the faces of the friends who were in the room, for we sleep with our eyes shut; I, who could carry on endless verbal arguments with myself while I dreamed, as soon as I tried to speak to these friends felt the words stick in my throat, for we do not speak distinctly in our sleep; I wanted to go to them, and I could not move my limbs, for we do not walk when we are asleep either; and, suddenly, I was ashamed to be seen by them, for we sleep without our clothes. So, my eyes blinded, my lips sealed, my limbs fettered, my body naked, the image of sleep which my sleep itself projected had the appearance of those great allegorical figures (in one of which Giotto has portrayed Envy with a serpent in her mouth) of which Swann had given me photographs.

Saint-Loup came to Paris for a few hours only. While affirming that he had not yet had an opportunity of speaking to his cousin, "She's not at all nice, Oriane," he told me with innocent self-betrayal. "She's not my old Oriane any longer, they've gone and changed her, I assure you it's not worth while bothering your head about her. You pay her far too great a compliment. You wouldn't care to meet my cousin Poictiers?" he went on, without stopping to reflect that this could not possibly give me any pleasure. "There's an intelligent young woman whom you'd like. She's married to my cousin, the Duc de Poictiers, who is a good fellow, but a bit slow for her. I've told her about you. She said I was to bring you to see her. She's much prettier than Oriane, and younger, too. She's a really nice person, you know, a really excellent person." Then there were expressions newly—and all the more ardently—adopted by Robert, which meant that the person in question had a delicate nature. "I don't go so far as to say she's a Dreyfusard, you must remember her background; still, she did say to me: 'If he was innocent, how ghastly for him to have been shut up on Devil's Island.' You see what I mean, don't you? And then she's the sort of woman who does a tremendous lot for her old governesses; she's given orders that they're never to be sent in by the servants' staircase when they come to the house. She's a very good sort, I assure you. Oriane doesn't really like her because she feels she's more intelligent than herself."

Although completely absorbed in the pity which she felt for one of the Guermantes footmen—who could not go to see his girl, even when the Duchess was out, because it would immediately have been reported to her from the lodge—Françoise was heartbroken at not having been in the house at the moment of Saint-Loup's visit, but this was because now she herself paid visits too. She never failed to go out on the days when I most needed her. It was always to see her brother, her niece and, more particularly, her own daughter, who had recently come to live in Paris. The family nature of these visits itself increased the irritation that I felt at being deprived of her services, for I foresaw that she would speak of them as being among those duties which could not be avoided, according to the laws laid down at Saint-André-des-Champs. And so I never listened to her excuses without an ill humour which was highly unjust to her, and was brought to a climax by the way Françoise had of saying not: "I've been to see my brother," or "I've been to see my niece," but "I've been to see the brother," "I just looked in to say good-day to the niece" (or "to my niece the butcheress"). As for her daughter, Françoise would have been glad to see her return to Combray. But the latter, who went in for abbreviations like a woman of fashion, though hers were of a vulgar kind, protested that the week she was shortly going to spend at Combray would seem quite long enough without so much as a sight of "the *Intran*."[7] She was even less willing to go to Françoise's sister, who lived in a mountainous region, for "mountains aren't really interesting," said the daughter, giving to the adjective a new and terrible meaning. She could not make up her mind to go back to Méséglise, where "the people are so stupid," where in the market the gossips at their stalls would claim cousinhood with her and say "Why, it's never poor Bazireau's daughter?" She would sooner die than go back and bury herself down there, now that she had "tasted the life of Paris," and Françoise, traditionalist as she was, smiled complacently nevertheless at the spirit of innovation embodied in this new "Parisian" when she said: "Very well, mother, if you don't get your day off, you've only to send me a wire."

The weather had turned chilly again. "Go out? What for? To catch your death?" said Françoise, who preferred to remain in the house during the week which her daughter and brother and the butcher-niece had gone to spend at Combray. Being, moreover, the last adherent in whom survived obscurely the doctrine of my aunt Léonie in matters of natural philosophy, Françoise would add, speaking of this unseasonable weather: "It's the remains of the wrath of God!" But I responded to her complaints only with a languid smile; all the more indifferent to these predictions in that whatever happened it would be fine for me; already, I could see the morning sun shining on the slope of Fiesole, and I warmed myself smilingly in its rays; their strength obliged me to half-open and half-shut my eyelids, which, like alabaster lamps, were filled with a roseate glow. It was not only the bells that came from Italy, Italy had come with them. My faithful hands would not lack flowers to honour the anniversary of the pilgrimage which I ought to have made long ago, for since, here in Paris, the weather had turned cold again as in another year at the time of our preparations for departure at the end of Lent, in the liquid, freezing air which bathed the chestnuts and planes on the boulevards and the tree in the courtyard of our house, the narcissi, the jonquils, the anemones of the Ponte Vecchio were already opening their petals as in a bowl of pure water.

My father had informed us that he now knew, through his friend A. J., where M. de Norpois went when he met him about the place.

"It's to see Mme de Villeparisis. They're great friends; I never knew anything about it. It seems she's a delightful person, a most superior woman. You ought to go and call on her," he told me. "Another thing that surprised me very

much: he spoke to me of M. de Guermantes as a most distinguished man; I'd always taken him for a boor. It seems
he knows an enormous amount, and has perfect taste, only
he's very proud of his name and his connexions. But as a
matter of fact, according to Norpois, he has a tremendous
position, not only here but all over Europe. It appears the
Austrian Emperor and the Tsar treat him just like one of themselves. Old Norpois told me that Mme de Villeparisis had
taken quite a fancy to you, and that you meet all sorts of
interesting people in her house. He praised you very highly.
You'll see him if you go there, and he may have some good
advice for you even if you are going to be a writer. For I can
see you won't do anything else. It might turn out quite a good
career; it's not what I should have chosen for you myself,
but you'll be a man in no time now, we shan't always be here
to look after you, and we mustn't prevent you from following
your vocation."

If only I had been able to start writing! But, whatever the
conditions in which I approached the task (as, too, alas, the
undertakings not to touch alcohol, to go to bed early, to sleep,
to keep fit), whether it was with enthusiasm, with method,
with pleasure, in depriving myself of a walk, or postponing it
and keeping it in reserve as a reward for industry, taking
advantage of an hour of good health, utilising the inactivity
forced on me by a day's illness, what always emerged in the end
from all my efforts was a virgin page, undefiled by any writing,
ineluctable as that forced card which in certain tricks one
invariably is made to draw, however carefully one may first
have shuffled the pack. I was merely the instrument of habits
of not working, of not going to bed, of not sleeping, which
must somehow be realised at all costs; if I offered them no
resistance, if I contented myself with the pretext they seized
from the first opportunity that the day afforded them of
acting as they chose, I escaped without serious harm, I slept
for a few hours after all towards morning, I read a little, I did
not over-exert myself; but if I attempted to thwart them, if I
decided to go to bed early, to drink only water, to work, they
grew restive, they adopted strong measures, they made me
really ill, I was obliged to double my dose of alcohol, did not

lie down in bed for two days and nights on end, could not even read, and I vowed that another time I would be more reasonable, that is to say less wise, like the victim of an assault who allows himself to be robbed for fear, should he offer resistance, of being murdered.

My father, in the meantime, had met M. de Guermantes once or twice, and, now that M. de Norpois had told him that the Duke was a remarkable man, had begun to pay more attention to what he said. As it happened, they met in the courtyard and discussed Mme de Villeparisis. "He tells me she's his aunt; 'Viparisi,' he pronounces it. He tells me, too, she's an extraordinarily able woman. In fact he said she kept a School of Wit," my father added, impressed by the vagueness of this expression, which he had indeed come across now and then in volumes of memoirs, but without attaching to it any definite meaning. My mother had so much respect for him that when she saw that he did not dismiss as of no importance the fact that Mme de Villeparisis kept a School of Wit, she decided that this must be of some consequence. Although she had always known through my grandmother the Marquise's intellectual worth, it was immediately enhanced in her eyes. My grandmother, who was not very well just then, was not in favour at first of the suggested visit, and afterwards lost interest in the matter. Since we had moved into our new flat, Mme de Villeparisis had several times asked my grandmother to call upon her. And invariably my grandmother had replied that she was not going out just at present, in one of those letters which, by a new habit of hers which we did not understand, she no longer sealed herself but employed Françoise to stick down for her. As for myself, without any very clear picture in my mind of this School of Wit, I should not have been greatly surprised to find the old lady from Balbec installed behind a desk, as, for that matter, I eventually did.

My father would in addition have been glad to know whether the Ambassador's support would be worth many votes to him at the *Institut*, for which he had thoughts of standing as an independent candidate. To tell the truth, while he did not venture to doubt that he would have M. de Norpois's support, he was by no means certain of it. He had thought it merely malicious gossip when he was told at the Ministry that M. de Norpois, wishing to be himself the only representative there of the *Institut*, would put every possible obstacle in the way of my father's candidature, which would moreover embarrass him at the moment since he was supporting another candidate. And yet, when M. Leroy-Beaulieu had first advised him to stand, and had calculated his chances, my father had been struck by the fact that, among the colleagues upon whom he could count for support, the eminent economist had not mentioned M. de Norpois. He dared not ask the Ambassador point-blank, but hoped that I would return from my visit to Mme de Villeparisis with his election as good as secured. This visit was now imminent. M. de Norpois's endorsement, capable of ensuring my father the votes of at least two thirds of the Academy,[8] seemed to him all the more probable since the Ambassador's willingness to oblige was proverbial, those who liked him least admitting that no one else took such pleasure in being of service. And besides, at the Ministry, his patronage was extended to my father far more markedly than to any other official.

My father had another encounter about this time, which caused him extreme indignation as well as astonishment. One day he ran into Mme Sazerat, whose life in Paris was restricted by her comparative poverty to occasional visits to a friend. There was no one who bored my father quite so intensely as did Mme Sazerat, so much so that Mamma was obliged, once a year, to intercede with him in sweet and suppliant tones: "My dear, I really must invite Mme Sazerat to the house, just once; she won't stay long"; and even: "Listen, dear, I'm going to ask you to make a great sacrifice; do go and call on Mme Sazerat. You know I hate bothering you, but it would be so nice of you." He would laugh, raise various objections, and go to pay the call. And so, for all that Mme Sazerat did not appeal to him, on catching sight of her in the street my father went towards her, doffing his hat; but to his profound astonishment Mme Sazerat confined her greeting to the frigid bow enforced by politeness towards a person who is guilty of some disgraceful action or has been condemned to live henceforth in another hemisphere. My father had come home speechless with rage.

Next day my mother met Mme Sazerat in someone's house. She did not offer my mother her hand, but merely smiled at her with a vague and melancholy air as one smiles at a person with whom one used to play as a child, but with whom one has since severed all connexions because she has led an abandoned life, has married a jailbird or (what is worse still) a divorced man. Now, from time immemorial my parents had accorded to Mme Sazerat, and inspired in her, the most profound respect. But (and of this my mother was ignorant) Mme Sazerat, alone of her kind at Combray, was a Dreyfusard. My father, a friend of M. Méline,[9] was convinced that Dreyfus was guilty. He had flatly refused to listen to some of his colleagues who had asked him to sign a revisionist petition. He refused to speak to me for a week after learning that I had chosen to take a different line. His opinions were well known. He came near to being looked upon as a Nationalist. As for my grandmother, who alone of the family seemed likely to be stirred by a generous doubt, whenever anyone spoke to her of the possible innocence of Dreyfus, she gave a shake of her head the meaning of which we did not at the time understand, but which was like the gesture of a person who has been interrupted while thinking of more serious things. My mother, torn between her love for my father and her hope that I might turn out to have brains, preserved an impartiality which she expressed by silence. Finally my grandfather, who adored the Army (albeit his duties with the National Guard had been the bugbear of his riper years), could never see a regiment march past the garden railings at Combray without baring his head as the colonel and the colours passed. All this was quite enough to make Mme Sazerat, who was thoroughly aware of the disinterestedness and integrity of my father and grandfather, regard them as pillars of Injustice. We forgive the crimes of individuals, but not their participation in a collective crime. As soon as she knew my father to be an anti-Dreyfusard she put continents and centuries between herself and him. Which explains why, across such an interval of time and space, her greeting had been imperceptible to my father, and why it had not occurred to her to shake hands or to say a few words which would never have carried across the worlds that lay between.

Saint-Loup, who was due to come to Paris, had promised to take me to Mme de Villeparisis's, where I hoped, though I had not said so to him, that we might meet Mme de Guermantes. He invited me to lunch in a restaurant with his mistress, whom we were afterwards to accompany to a rehearsal. We were to go out in the morning and call for her at her home on the outskirts of Paris.

I had asked Saint-Loup if the restaurant to which we went for lunch (in the lives of young noblemen with money to spend the restaurant plays as important a part as do bales of merchandise in Arabian tales) could for preference be the one to which Aimé had told me that he would be going as head waiter until the Balbec season opened. It was a great attraction to me who dreamed of so many journeys and made so few to see again someone who formed part not merely of my memories of Balbec but of Balbec itself, who went there year after year and, when ill health or my studies compelled me to stay in Paris, would be watching just the same, during the long July afternoons while he waited for the guests to come in to dinner, the sun creep down the sky and set in the sea, through the glass panels of the great dining-room behind which, at the hour when the light died, the motionless wings of vessels, smoky blue in the distance, looked like exotic and nocturnal butterflies in a show-case. Himself magnetised by his contact with the powerful lodestone of Balbec, this head waiter became in turn a magnet for me. I hoped by talking to him to enter in advance into communication with Balbec, to have realised here in Paris something of the delights of travel.

I left the house early, with Françoise complaining bitterly because the footman who was engaged to be married had once again been prevented, the evening before, from going to see his betrothed. Françoise had found him in tears; he had been itching to go and strike the porter, but had restrained himself, for he valued his place.

Before reaching Saint-Loup's, where he was to be waiting for me at the door, I ran into Legrandin, of whom we had lost sight since our Combray days, and who, though now quite grey, had preserved his air of youthful candour. Seeing me, he stopped:

"Ah! so it's you," he exclaimed, "a man of fashion, and in a frock coat too! That is a livery in which my independent spirit would be ill at ease. It is true that you are a man of the world, I suppose, and go out paying calls! In order to go and meditate, as I do, beside some half-ruined tomb, my bow tie and jacket are not out of place. You know how I admire the charming quality of your soul; that is why I tell you how deeply I regret that you should go forth and betray it among the Gentiles. By being capable of remaining for a moment in the for me nauseating, unbreathable atmosphere of the salons, you pronounce on your own future the condemnation, the damnation of the Prophet. I can see it all: you frequent the frivolous-minded, the gracious livers—that is the vice of our contemporary bourgeoisie. Ah, those aristocrats! The Terror was greatly to blame for not cutting the heads off every one of them. They are all disreputable scum, when they are not simply dreary idiots. Still, my poor boy, if that sort of thing amuses you! While you are on your way to some tea-party your old friend will be more fortunate than you, for alone in an outlying suburb he will be watching the pink moon rise in a violet sky. The truth is that I scarcely belong to this earth upon which I feel myself such an exile; it takes all the force of the law of gravity to hold me here, to keep me from escaping into another sphere. I belong to a different planet. Good-bye; do not take amiss the old-time frankness of the peasant of the Vivonne, who has also remained a peasant of the Danube. To prove my sincere regard for you, I shall send you my latest novel. But you will not care for it; it is not deliquescent enough, not *fin de siècle* enough for you; it is too frank, too honest. What you want is Bergotte, you have confessed it, gamy stuff for the jaded palates of refined voluptuaries. I suppose I am looked upon, in your set, as an old campaigner; I make the mistake of putting my heart into what I write: that is no longer done; besides, the life of the people is not distinguished enough to interest your little snobbicules. Go, get you gone, try to recall at times the words of Christ: 'Do this and ye shall live.' Farewell, friend."

It was not with any particular ill-humour against Legrandin that I parted from him. Certain memories are like friends in common, they can bring about reconciliations; set down amid fields of buttercups strewn with the ruins of feudal battlements, the little wooden bridge still joined us, Legrandin and me, as it joined the two banks of the Vivonne.

After coming out of a Paris in which, although spring had begun, the trees on the boulevards had hardly put on their first leaves, it was a marvel to Saint-Loup and myself, when the circle train had set us down at the suburban village in which his mistress was living, to see each little garden decked with the huge festal altars of the fruit-trees in blossom. It was like one of those peculiar, poetic, ephemeral, local festivals which people travel long distances to attend on certain fixed occasions, but this one was given by Nature. The blossom of the cherry tree is stuck so close to its branches, like a white sheath, that from a distance, among the other trees that showed as yet scarcely a flower or leaf, one might on this day of sunshine that was still so cold have taken it for snow that had remained clinging there, having melted everywhere else. But the tall pear-trees enveloped each house, each modest courtyard, in a more spacious, more uniform, more dazzling whiteness, as if all the dwellings, all the enclosed spaces in the village, were on their way to make their first communion on the same solemn day.

It had been a country village, and still had its old *mairie*, sunburned and mellow, in front of which, in the place of may-poles and streamers, three tall pear-trees were elegantly beflagged with white satin as though for some local civic festival. These villages in the environs of Paris still have at their gates parks of the seventeenth and eighteenth centuries which were the "follies" of the stewards and mistresses of the great. A market gardener had utilised one of these, which was situated on low ground beside the road, for his fruit-trees (or had simply, perhaps, preserved the plan of an immense orchard of former days). Laid out in quincunxes, these pear-trees, more spaced-out and less advanced than those that I had seen, formed great quadrilaterals—separated by low walls —of white blossom, on each side of which the light fell differently, so that all these airy roofless chambers seemed to belong to a Palace of the Sun, such as one might find in Crete;

and they reminded one also of the different ponds of a reservoir, or of those parts of the sea which man has subdivided for some fishery, or to plant oyster-beds, when one saw, according to their orientation, the light play upon the espaliers as upon springtime waters, and coax into unfolding here and there, gleaming amid the open-work, azure-panelled trellis of the branches, the foaming whiteness of a creamy, sunlit flower.

Never had Robert spoken to me so tenderly of his mistress as he did during this journey. I sensed that she alone had taken root in his heart; to his future career in the Army, his position in society, his family, he was not, of course, indifferent, but they counted for nothing beside the smallest thing that concerned his mistress. That alone had any importance in his eyes, infinitely more importance than the Guermantes and all the kings of the earth put together. I do not know whether he formulated to himself the notion that she was of a superior essence to the rest of the world, but he was exclusively preoccupied and concerned with what affected her. Through her and for her he was capable of suffering, of being happy, perhaps of killing. There was really nothing that interested, that could excite him except what his mistress wanted, what she was going to do, what was going on, discernible at most in fleeting changes of expression, in the narrow expanse of her face and behind her privileged brow. So nice-minded in all else, he looked forward to the prospect of a brilliant marriage, solely in order to be able to continue to maintain and keep her. If one had asked oneself what was the value that he set on her, I doubt whether one could ever have imagined a figure high enough. If he did not marry her, it was because a practical instinct warned him that as soon as she had nothing more to expect from him she would leave him, or would at least live as she pleased, and that he must retain his hold on her by keeping her in expectation. For he admitted the possibility that she did not love him. No doubt the general malady called love must have forced him—as it forces all men—to believe at times that she did. But in his heart of hearts he felt that her love for him was not inconsistent with her remaining with him only on account of his money, and that as soon as she had nothing more to expect from him she would make haste (the dupe of her literary friends and their theories, and yet still loving him, he thought) to leave him.

"To-day, if she's nice," he confided to me, "I'm going to give her a present that will make her very happy. It's a necklace she saw at Boucheron's. It's rather too much for me just at present—thirty thousand francs. But, poor puss, she doesn't have much pleasure in her life. She will be jolly pleased with it, I know. She mentioned it to me and told me she knew somebody who would perhaps give it to her. I don't believe it's true, but just in case, I arranged with Boucheron, who is our family jeweller, to reserve it for me. I'm so happy to think that you're going to meet her. She's nothing so very wonderful to look at, you know" (I could see that he thought just the opposite and had said this only to make my admiration the greater). "What she has above all is marvellous judgment; she'll perhaps be afraid to talk much in front of you, but by Jove! the things she'll say to me about you afterwards. You know she says things one can go on thinking about for hours; there's really something about her that's quite Pythian."

On our way to her house we passed a row of little gardens, and I was obliged to stop, for they were all dazzlingly aflower with pear and cherry blossom; as empty, no doubt, and lifeless only yesterday as a house that is still to let, they were suddenly peopled and adorned by these newcomers, arrived overnight, whose beautiful white garments could be seen through the railings along the garden paths.

"I'll tell you what—I can see you'd rather stop and look at all that and feel poetical about it," said Robert, "so don't budge from here, will you—my friend's house is quite close, and I'll go and fetch her."

While I waited I strolled up and down the road, past these modest gardens. If I raised my head I could see now and then girls sitting at the windows, but outside, in the open air, at the height of a half-landing, dangling here and there among the foliage, light and pliant in their fresh mauve frocks, clusters of young lilacs swayed in the breeze without heeding the passer-by who raised his eyes towards their green arbour. I recognised in them the purple-clad platoons posted at the entrance to M. Swann's park in the warm spring afternoons, like an enchanting rustic tapestry. I took a path which led me into a meadow. A cold wind swept through it, as at Combray, but in the middle of this rich, moist, rural land, which might have been on the banks of the Vivonne, there had nevertheless arisen, punctual at the trysting place like all its band of brothers, a great white pear-tree which waved smilingly in the sun's face, like a curtain of light materialised and made palpable, its flowers shaken by the breeze but polished and glazed with silver by the sun's rays.

Suddenly Saint-Loup appeared, accompanied by his mistress, and then, in this woman who was for him the epitome of love, of all the sweet things of life, whose personality, mysteriously enshrined as in a tabernacle, was the object that occupied incessantly his toiling imagination, whom he felt that he would never really know, as to whom he asked himself what could be her secret self, behind the veil of eyes and flesh—in this woman I recognised instantaneously "Rachel when from the Lord," she who, but a few years since (women change their situation so rapidly in that world, when they do change) used to say to the procuress: "To-morrow evening, then, if you want me for someone, you'll send round for me, won't you?"

And when they had "come round" for her, and she found herself alone in the room with the "someone," she knew so well what was required of her that after locking the door, as a womanly precaution or a ritual gesture, she would quickly remove all her clothes, as one does before the doctor who is going to examine one, and did not pause in the process unless the "someone," not caring for nudity, told her that she might keep on her shift, as specialists do sometimes, who, having an extremely fine ear and being afraid of their patient's catching a chill, are satisfied with listening to his breathing and the beating of his heart through his shirt. On this woman whose whole life, whose every thought, whose entire past and all the men by whom at one time or another she had been had, were to me so utterly unimportant that if she had told me about them I should have listened only out of politeness and scarcely heard what she said, the anxiety, the torment, the love of Saint-Loup had been concentrated in such a way as to make, out of what was for me a mechanical toy, the cause of endless suffering, the very object and reward of existence. Seeing these two elements separately (because I had known "Rachel when from the Lord" in a house of ill fame), I realised that many women for the sake of whom men live, suffer, take their own lives, may be in themselves or for other people what Rachel was for me. The idea that anyone could be tormented by curiosity with regard to her life amazed me. I could have told Robert of any number of her unchastities, which seemed to me the most uninteresting things in the world. And how they would have pained him! And what had he not given to learn them, without avail!

I realised then how much a human imagination can put behind a little scrap of a face, such as this woman's was, if it is the imagination that has come to know it first; and conversely into what wretched elements, crudely material and utterly valueless, something that had been the inspiration of countless dreams might be decomposed if, on the contrary, it had been perceived in the opposite manner, by the most casual and trivial acquaintance. I saw that what had appeared to me to be not worth twenty francs when it had been offered to me for twenty francs in the brothel, where it was then for me simply a woman desirous of earning twenty francs, might be worth more than a million, more than family affection, more than all the most coveted positions in life, if one had begun by imagining her as a mysterious being, interesting to know, difficult to seize and to hold. No doubt it was the same thin and narrow face that we saw, Robert and I. But we had arrived at it by two opposite ways which would never converge, and we would never both see it from the same side. That face, with its looks, its smiles, the movements of its mouth, I had known from the outside as being that of a woman of the sort who for twenty francs would do anything that I asked. And so her looks, her smiles, the movements of her mouth had seemed to me expressive merely of generalised actions with no individual quality, and beneath them I should not have had the curiosity to look for a person. But what to me had in a sense been offered at the start, that consenting face, had been for Robert an ultimate goal towards which he had made his way through endless hopes and doubts, suspicions and dreams. Yes, he had given more than a million francs in order to have, in order that others should not have, what had been offered to me, as to all and sundry, for twenty. That he too should not have had her at that price may have been due to the chance of a moment, the instant in which she who seemed ready to give herself suddenly jibs, having perhaps an assignation elsewhere, some reason which makes her more difficult of access that day. If the man in question is a sentimentalist, then, even if she has not noticed it, but infinitely more if she has, the direst game begins. Unable to swallow his disappointment, to make himself forget about the woman, he pursues her afresh, she rebuffs him, until a mere smile for which he no longer dared to hope is bought at a thousand times what should have been the price of the last, the most intimate favours. It sometimes even happens in such a case, when a man has been led by a mixture of naïvety of judgment and cowardice in the face of suffering to commit the crowning folly of making an inaccessible idol of a whore, that he never obtains these ultimate favours, or even the first kiss, and no longer even ventures to ask for them in order not to belie his assurances of Platonic love. And it is then a bitter anguish to leave the world without ever having experienced the embraces of the woman one has most passionately loved. As for Rachel's favours, however, Saint-Loup had fortunately succeeded in winning them all. True, if he had now learned that they had been offered to all the world for a louis, he would have suffered terribly, but would still have given a million francs to keep them, for nothing that he might have learned could have diverted him (what is important in man can only happen in spite of him, through the action of some great natural law) from the path he had taken and from which that face could appear to him only through the web of the dreams that he had already spun. The immobility of that thin face, like that of a sheet of paper subjected to the colossal pressure of two atmospheres, seemed to me to be held in equilibrium by two infinites which converged on her without meeting, for she held them apart. Looking at her, Robert and I, we did not both see her from the same side of the mystery.

It was not "Rachel when from the Lord" who seemed to me of little significance, it was the power of the human imagination, the illusion on which were based the pains of love, that I found very great. Robert noticed that I seemed moved. I turned my eyes to the pear and cherry trees of the garden opposite, so that he might think that it was their beauty that had touched me. And it did touch me in somewhat the same way; it also brought close to me things of the kind which we not only see with our eyes but feel also in our hearts. In likening those trees that I had seen in the garden to strange deities, had I not been mistaken like Magdalene when, in another garden, on a day whose anniversary was soon to come, she saw a human form and "supposed it was the gardener." Treasurers of our memories of the golden age, keepers of the promise that reality is not what we suppose, that the splendour of poetry, the wonderful radiance of innocence may shine in it and may be the recompense which we strive to earn, were they not, these great white creatures miraculously bowed over that shade so propitious for rest, for angling or for reading, were they not rather angels? I exchanged a few words with Saint-Loup's mistress. We cut across the village. Its houses were sordid. But by each of the most wretched, of those that looked as though they had been scorched and branded by a rain of brimstone, a mysterious traveller halting for a day in the accursed city, a resplendent angel stood erect, stretching over it the dazzling protection of his widespread wings of innocence: it was a pear tree in blossom. Saint-Loup drew me a little way ahead to explain:

"I should have liked you and me to have been able to stay together, in fact I'd much rather have had lunch just with you, and stayed with you until it was time to go to my aunt's. But this poor girl of mine here, it gives her so much pleasure, and she's so nice to me, don't you know, I hadn't the heart to refuse her. In any case you'll like her, she's literary, you know, very sensitive and receptive, and besides it's such a pleasure to be with her in a restaurant, she's so charming, so simple, always delighted with everything."

I fancy nevertheless that, on that precise morning, and probably for the first and only time, Robert detached himself for a moment from the woman whom out of successive layers of tenderness he had gradually created, and suddenly saw at some distance from himself another Rachel, the double of his but entirely different, who was nothing more nor less than a little whore. We had left the blossoming orchard and were making for the train which was to take us back to Paris when, at the station, Rachel, who was walking by herself, was recognised and hailed by a pair of common little "tarts" like herself, who first of all, thinking that she was alone, called out: "Hello, Rachel, why don't you come with us? Lucienne and Germaine are in the train, and there's room for one more. Come on, we'll all go to the rink together." They were just going to introduce to her two counter-jumpers, their lovers, who were accompanying them, when, noticing that she seemed a little ill at ease, they looked up and beyond her, caught sight of us, and with apologies bade her a good-bye to which she responded in a somewhat embarrassed but none the less friendly tone. They were two poor little tarts with collars of sham otter-skin, looking more or less as Rachel must have looked when Saint-Loup first met her. He did not know them, or their names even, and seeing that they appeared to be on intimate terms with his mistress, he could not help wondering whether she too might not once have had, had not still, perhaps, her place in an unsuspected life, utterly different from the life she led with him, a life in which one had women for a louis apiece. He not only glimpsed this life, but saw also in the thick of it a Rachel quite different from the one he knew, a Rachel like those two little tarts, a twenty-franc Rachel. In short, Rachel had for the moment duplicated herself in his eyes; he had seen, at some distance from his own Rachel, the little tart Rachel, the real Rachel, if it can be said that Rachel the tart was more real than the other. It may then have occurred to Robert that from the hell in which he was living, with the prospect and the necessity of a rich marriage, of the sale of his name, to enable him to go on giving Rachel a hundred thousand francs a year, he might easily perhaps have escaped, and have enjoyed the favours of his mistress, as the two counter-jumpers enjoyed those of their girls, for next to nothing. But how was it to be done? She had done nothing blameworthy. Less generously rewarded, she would be less nice to him, would stop saying and writing the things that so deeply touched him, things which he would quote, with a touch of boastfulness, to his comrades, taking care to point out how nice it was of her to say them, but omitting to mention that he was maintaining her in the most lavish fashion, or even that he ever gave her anything at all, that these inscriptions on photographs, or tender greetings at the end of telegrams, were but the transmutation of gold in its most exiguous but most precious form. If he took care not to admit that these rare kindnesses on Rachel's part were handsomely paid for, it would be wrong to say—and yet this oversimplification is applied, absurdly, to every lover who has to pay cash, and to a great many husbands—that this was from self-esteem or vanity. Saint-Loup was intelligent enough to realise that all the pleasures of vanity were freely available to him in society, thanks to his historic name and handsome face, and that his liaison with Rachel had if anything tended to cut him off from society, had led to his being less sought after. No; this pride which seeks to appear to be getting for nothing the apparent marks of predilection of the woman one loves is simply a consequence of love, the need to figure in one's own eyes and in other people's as being loved by the person whom one loves so much. Rachel rejoined us, leaving the two tarts to get into their compartment; but, no less than their sham otter-skins and the self-conscious appearance of their young men, the names Lucienne and Germaine kept the new Rachel alive for a moment longer. For a moment Robert imagined a Place Pigalle existence with unknown associates, sordid couplings, afternoons spent in naïve pleasures, in that Paris in which the sunny brightness of the streets from the Boulevard de Clichy onwards did not seem the same as the solar radiance in which he himself strolled with his mistress, for love, and suffering that is inseparable from it, have, like intoxication, the power to differentiate things for us. It was almost another Paris in the heart of Paris itself that he suspected; his liaison appeared to him like the exploration of a strange life, for if when with him Rachel was somewhat similar to himself, it was nevertheless a part of her real life that she lived with him, indeed the most precious part in view of his reckless expenditure on her, the part that made her so greatly envied

by her friends and would enable her one day to retire to the
country or to establish herself in the leading theatres, when
she had made her pile. Robert longed to ask her who Lucienne
and Germaine were, what they would have said to her if she
had joined them in their compartment, how they would all
have spent a day which would perhaps have ended, as a
supreme diversion, after the pleasures of the skating-rink, at the
Olympia Tavern, if Robert and I had not been there. For a
moment the purlieus of the Olympia, which until then had
seemed to him deadly dull, stirred his curiosity and anguish,
and the sunshine of this spring day beating down on the Rue
Caumartin where, possibly, if she had not known Robert,
Rachel might have gone that afternoon and have earned a louis,
filled him with a vague longing. But what would be the use of
plying Rachel with questions when he already knew that her
answer would be merely silence, or a lie, or something extremely painful for him to hear, which would yet explain
nothing. The deutero-Rachel had lasted long enough. The
porters were shutting the doors; we hurriedly climbed into a
first-class carriage; Rachel's magnificent pearls reminded
Robert that she was a woman of great price; he caressed her,
restored her to her place in his heart where he could contemplate her, interiorised, as he had always done hitherto—save
during this brief instant in which he had seen her in the Place
Pigalle of an Impressionist painter—and the train moved
off.

It was true that she was "literary." She never stopped talking
to me about books, Art Nouveau and Tolstoyism, except to
rebuke Saint-Loup for drinking too much wine:

"Ah! if you could live with me for a year, we'd see a fine
change. I should keep you on water and you'd be ever so much
better."

"Right you are. Let's go a long way away."

"But you know quite well I have a great deal of work to do"
(for she took her dramatic art very seriously). "Besides, what
would your family say?"

And she began to abuse his family to me in terms which
seemed to me highly justified, and with which Saint-Loup,
while disobeying Rachel in the matter of champagne, entirely

concurred. I, who was so afraid of the effect of wine on him, and felt the good influence of his mistress, was quite prepared to advise him to let his family go hang. Tears sprang to the young woman's eyes when I was rash enough to mention Dreyfus.

"The poor martyr!" she almost sobbed; "it will be the death of him in that dreadful place."

"Don't upset yourself, Zézette, he'll come back, he'll be acquitted all right, they'll admit they made a mistake."

"But long before then he'll be dead! Ah well, at least his children will bear a stainless name. But just think of the agony he must be going through: that's what I can't stand! And would you believe that Robert's mother, a pious woman, says that he ought to be left on Devil's Island even if he's innocent. Isn't that appalling?"

"Yes, it's absolutely true, she does say that," Robert assured me. "She's my mother, I can't contradict her, but it's quite clear she hasn't got a sensitive nature like Zézette."

In reality these luncheons which were said to be "such a pleasure" always led to trouble. For as soon as Saint-Loup found himself in a public place with his mistress, he would imagine that she was looking at every other man in the room, and his brow would darken; she would notice his ill-humour, which she perhaps took pleasure in fanning, but which more probably, out of stupid pride, feeling wounded by his tone, she did not wish to appear to be seeking to disarm; she would pretend not to be able to take her eyes off some man or other, and indeed this was not always purely for fun. In fact the man who happened to be sitting next to them in a theatre or a café, or, to go no further, the driver of the cab they had engaged, need only have something attractive about him, and Robert, his perception quickened by jealousy, would have noticed it before his mistress; he would see in him immediately one of those foul creatures whom he had denounced to me at Balbec, who corrupted and dishonoured women for their own amusement, and would beg his mistress to avert her eyes from the man, thereby drawing her attention to him. And sometimes she found that Robert had shown such good taste in his suspicions that after a while she even left off teasing him in order that he might calm down and consent to go off by himself on some errand which would give her time to enter into conversations with the stranger, often to make an assignation, sometimes even to bring matters to a head there and then.

I could see as soon as we entered the restaurant that Robert was looking troubled. For he had at once observed—what had escaped our notice at Balbec—that among his coarser colleagues Aimé exuded not only a modest distinction but, quite unconsciously of course, that air of romance which emanates for a certain number of years from fine hair and a Grecian nose, features thanks to which he stood out among the crowd of other waiters. These, almost all of them well on in years, presented a series of types, extraordinarily ugly and pronounced, of hypocritical priests, sanctimonious confessors, more numerously of actors of the old school whose sugar-loaf foreheads are scarcely to be seen nowadays outside the collections of portraits that hang in the humbly historic green-rooms of antiquated little theatres, where they are represented in the roles of servants or pontiffs, though this restaurant seemed, thanks to selective recruiting and perhaps to some system of hereditary nomination, to have preserved their solemn type in a sort of College of Augurs. As ill luck would have it, Aimé having recognised us, it was he who came to take our order, while the procession of operatic high-priests swept past us to other tables. Aimé inquired after my grandmother's health; I asked for news of his wife and children. He gave it to me with feeling, for he was a family man. He had an intelligent and vigorous but respectful air. Robert's mistress began to gaze at him with a strange attentiveness. But Aimé's sunken eyes, to which a slight short-sightedness gave a sort of veiled depth, betrayed no sign of awareness in his still face. In the provincial hotel in which he had served for many years before coming to Balbec, the charming sketch, now a trifle discoloured and faded, which was his face, and which, for all those years, like some engraved portrait of Prince Eugene, had been visible always in the same place, at the far end of a dining-room that was almost always empty, had probably not attracted many curious looks. He had thus for long remained, doubtless for want of connoisseurs, in ignorance of the artistic value of his face, and moreover but little inclined to draw attention to it, for he was temperamentally cold. At most some passing Parisian lady, stopping for some reason in the town, had raised her eyes to his, had asked him perhaps to serve her in her room before she took the train again, and, in the pellucid, monotonous, profound void of the existence of this good husband and provincial hotel servant, had buried the secret of a short-lived whim which no one would ever bring to light. And yet Aimé must have been conscious of the insistence with which the eyes of the young actress were fastened upon him now. At all events it did not escape Robert, beneath whose skin I saw a flush begin to gather, not vivid like that which burned his cheeks when he felt sudden emotion, but faint and diffused.

"Anything specially interesting about that waiter, Zézette?" he inquired, after sharply dismissing Aimé. "One would think you were making a study of him."

"There we go again; I knew it would happen!"

"You knew what would happen, my dear girl? If I was mistaken, I'm quite prepared to take it all back. But I have after all the right to warn you against that flunkey whom I know all about from Balbec (otherwise I shouldn't give a damn), and who is the biggest scoundrel that ever walked the face of the earth."

She seemed anxious to pacify Robert and began to engage me in a literary conversation in which he joined. I did not find her boring to talk to, for she had a thorough knowledge of the works I admired, and her opinion of them agreed more or less with mine; but since I had heard Mme de Villeparisis declare that she had no talent, I attached little importance to this evidence of culture. She discoursed wittily on all manner of topics, and would have been genuinely entertaining had she not affected to an irritating degree the jargon of the coteries and studios. She extended it, moreover, to everything under the sun; for instance, having acquired the habit of saying of a picture, if it were Impressionist, or an opera, if Wagnerian, "Ah! that's *good*," one day when a young man had kissed her on the ear, and, touched by her pretence of being thrilled, had affected modesty, she said: "But really, as a sensation I call it distinctly *good*." But what most surprised me was that the

expressions peculiar to Robert (which in any case had probably
come to him from literary men whom she knew) were used by
her to him and by him to her as though they had been a
necessary form of speech, and without any conception of the
pointlessness of an originality that is universal.

She was so clumsy with her hands when eating that one felt
she must appear extremely awkward on the stage. She recovered her dexterity only when making love, with that
touching prescience of women who love the male so intensely
that they immediately guess what will give most pleasure to
that body which is yet so different from their own.

I ceased to take part in the conversation when it turned upon
the theatre, for on that topic Rachel was too malicious for my
liking. She did, it was true, take up in a tone of commiseration
—against Saint-Loup, which proved that he was accustomed
to hearing Rachel attack her—the defence of Berma, saying:
"Oh, no, she's a remarkable woman really. Of course, the
things she does no longer appeal to us, they don't correspond
quite to what we're after, but one must think of her at the
time when she made her first appearance; we owe her a great
deal. She has done good work, you know. And, besides she's
such a splendid woman, she has such a good heart. Naturally
she doesn't care about the things that interest us, but in her
time she had, as well as a rather moving face, quite a shrewd
intelligence." (Our fingers, by the way, do not play the same
accompaniment to all our aesthetic judgments. If it is a picture
that is under discussion, to show that it is a fine piece of work,
painted with a full brush, it is enough to stick out one's thumb.
But the "shrewd intelligence" is more exacting. It requires
two fingers, or rather two fingernails, as though one were trying to flick away a particle of dust.) But, with this single
exception, Saint-Loup's mistress spoke of the best-known actresses in a tone of ironical superiority which annoyed me
because I believed—quite mistakenly, as it happened—that it
was she who was inferior to them. She was clearly aware that
I must regard her as an indifferent actress and conversely have
a great regard for those she despised. But she showed no
resentment, because there is in all great talent while it is still,
as hers was then, unrecognised, however sure it may be of

itself, a vein of humility, and because we make the consideration that we expect from others proportionate not to our
latent powers but to the position to which we have attained.
(An hour or so later, at the theatre, I was to see Saint-Loup's
mistress show a great deal of deference towards those very
artists whom she now judged so harshly.) And so, however
little doubt my silence may have left her in, she insisted none
the less on our dining together that evening, assuring me that
never had anyone's conversation delighted her so much as
mine. If we were not yet in the theatre, to which we were to go
after lunch, we had the sense of being in a green-room hung
with portraits of old members of the company, so markedly
were the waiters' faces of a kind that seems to have perished
with a whole generation of outstanding actors. They had a
look, too, of Academicians: one of them, standing in front of
a sideboard, was examining a dish of pears with the expression
of detached curiosity that M. de Jussieu[10] might have worn.
Others, on either side of him, were casting about the room
the sort of gaze, instinct with curiosity and coldness, with
which Members of the Institute who have arrived early
scrutinise the audience, while they exchange a few murmured
words which one fails to catch. They were faces well known
to all the regular customers. One of them, however, was being
pointed out, a newcomer with a wrinkled nose and sanctimonious lips who, as Rachel remarked in her jargon, "had a
whiff of the sacristy," and everyone gazed with interest at this
newly elected candidate. But presently, perhaps to drive
Robert away so that she might be alone with Aimé, Rachel
began to make eyes at a young student who was lunching with a
friend at a neighbouring table.

"Zézette, would you mind not looking at that young man
like that," said Saint-Loup, on whose face the hesitant flush of
a moment ago had gathered now into a scarlet cloud which
dilated and darkened his swollen features. "If you must make
an exhibition of us I shall go and lunch elsewhere and join
you at the theatre afterwards."

At this point a messenger came up to tell Aimé that a
gentleman wished him to go and speak to him at the door of his
carriage. Saint-Loup, ever uneasy, and afraid now that it

might be some message of an amorous nature that was to be conveyed to his mistress, looked out of the window and saw there, sitting in the back of his brougham, his hands tightly buttoned in white gloves with black seams and a flower in his buttonhole, M. de Charlus.

"There, you see!" he said to me in a low voice, "my family hunt me down even here. Will you, please—I can't very well do it myself—but since you know the head waiter well, ask him not to go to the carriage. He's certain to give us away. Ask him to send some other waiter who doesn't know me. I know my uncle; if they tell him I'm not known here, he'll never come inside to look for me, he loathes this sort of place. Really, it's pretty disgusting that an old womaniser like him, who's still at it, too, should be perpetually lecturing me and coming to spy on me!"

Aimé, on receiving my instructions, sent one of his under-lings to explain that he was busy and could not come out at the moment, and (should the gentleman ask for the Marquis de Saint-Loup) that they did not know any such person. Presently the carriage departed. But Saint-Loup's mistress, who had failed to catch our whispered conversation and thought that it was about the young man whom Robert had been reproach-ing her for making eyes at, broke out in a torrent of abuse.

"Ah, so that's it! So it's the young man over there, now, is it? Thank you for telling me; it's a real pleasure to have this sort of thing with one's meals! Don't pay any attention to him," she added, turning to me, "he's a bit piqued to-day, and any-way he just says these things because he thinks it's smart and rather aristocratic to appear to be jealous."

And she began to drum her feet and her fingers in nervous irritation.

"But, Zézette, it's for me that it's unpleasant. You're making us ridiculous in the eyes of that fellow, who will begin to imagine you're making advances to him, and who looks an impossible bounder, too."

"Oh, no, I think he's charming. For one thing, he's got the most adorable eyes, and a way of looking at women—you can feel he must love them."

"If you've lost your senses, you can at least keep quiet until

I've left the room," cried Robert. "Waiter, my things."

I did not know whether I was expected to follow him.

"No, I need to be alone," he told me in the same tone in which he had just been addressing his mistress, and as if he were quite as furious with me. His anger was like a single musical phrase to which in an opera several lines of dialogue are sung which are entirely different from one another in meaning and character in the libretto, but which the music gathers into a common sentiment. When Robert had gone, his mistress called Aimé and asked him various questions. She then wanted to know what I thought of him.

"He has an amusing expression, hasn't he? You see, what would amuse me would be to know what he really thinks about things, to have him wait on me often, to take him travelling. But that would be all. If we were expected to love all the people we find attractive, life would be pretty ghastly, wouldn't it? It's silly of Robert to imagine things. It all begins and ends in my head: Robert has nothing to worry about." She was still gazing at Aimé. "Do look what dark eyes he has. I should love to know what goes on behind them."

Presently she received a message that Robert was waiting for her in a private room, to which he had gone by another door to finish his lunch without having to pass through the restaurant again. I thus found myself alone, until I too was summoned by Robert. I found his mistress stretched out on a sofa laughing under the kisses and caresses that he was showering on her. They were drinking champagne. "Hallo, you!" she said to him from time to time, having recently picked up this expression which seemed to her the last word in affection and wit. I had had little lunch, I was extremely uncomfortable, and, though Legrandin's words had no bearing on the matter, I was sorry to think that I was beginning this first afternoon of spring in a back room in a restaurant and would finish it in the wings of a theatre. Looking first at the time to see that she was not making herself late, Rachel offered me a glass of champagne, handed me one of her Turkish cigarettes and unpinned a rose for me from her bodice. Whereupon I said to myself: "I needn't regret my day too much, after all. These hours spent in this young woman's company are not wasted, since I have had from her—charming gifts which cannot be bought too dear—a rose, a scented cigarette and a glass of champagne." I told myself this because I felt that it would endow with an aesthetic character, and thereby justify and rescue, these hours of boredom. I ought perhaps to have reflected that the very need which I felt of a reason that would console me for my boredom was sufficient to prove that I was experiencing no aesthetic sensation. As for Robert and his mistress, they appeared to have no recollection of the quarrel which had been raging between them a few minutes earlier, or of my having been a witness to it. They made no allusion to it, offered no excuse for it, any more than for the contrast with it which their present conduct provided. By dint of drinking champagne with them, I began to feel a little of the intoxication that had come over me at Rivebelle, though probably not quite the same. Not only every kind of intoxication, from that which we get from the sun or from travelling to that which is induced by exhaustion or wine, but every degree of intoxication—and each should have a different "reading," like fathoms on a chart—lays bare in us, at the precise depth which it has reached, a different kind of man. The room which Saint-Loup had taken was small, but the single mirror which decorated it was of such a kind that it seemed to reflect a score of others in an endless vista; and the electric bulb placed at the top of the frame must at night, when it was lit, followed by the procession of twenty or more reflexions similar to its own, give to the drinker, even when alone, the idea that the surrounding space was multiplying itself simultaneously with his sensations, heightened by intoxication, and that, shut up by himself in this little cell, he was reigning nevertheless over something far more extensive in its indefinite luminous curve than a passage in the "Jardin de Paris." Being then myself at this moment the said drinker, suddenly, looking for him in the glass, I caught sight of him, a hideous stranger, staring at me. The joy of intoxication was stronger than my disgust; from gaiety or bravado, I gave him a smile which he returned. And I felt myself so much under the ephemeral and potent sway of the minute in which our sensations are so strong, that I am not sure whether my sole regret was not at the thought that the hideous self whom I had just caught sight of in the glass was perhaps on his last legs, and that I should never meet that stranger again for the rest of my life.

Robert was annoyed only because I did not seem to want to shine more in the eyes of his mistress.

"What about that fellow you met this morning who combines snobbery with astronomy? Do tell her about him, I've forgotten the story," and he watched her out of the corner of his eye.

"But, my dear boy, there's nothing more to say than what you've just said."

"What a bore you are. Then tell her about Françoise in the Champs-Elysées. She'll enjoy that."

"Oh, do! Bobby has told me so much about Françoise." And taking Saint-Loup by the chin, she said once more, for want of anything more original, drawing the said chin nearer to the light: "Hallo, you!"

Since actors had ceased to be for me exclusively the depositaries, in their diction and playing, of an artistic truth, they had begun to interest me in themselves; I was amused, imagining that I was contemplating the characters in some old comic novel, to see the heroine of the play, struck by the new face of the young man who had just come into the stalls, listen abstractedly to the declaration of love which the juvenile lead was addressing to her, while he, through the running fire of his impassioned speech, still kept a gleaming eye fixed on an old lady seated in a stage box, whose magnificent pearls had caught his fancy; and thus, thanks mainly to the information that Saint-Loup had given me as to the private lives of actors, I saw another drama, mute but expressive, enacted beneath the words of the spoken drama which in itself, although of little merit, interested me too; for I could feel germinating and blossoming within it for an hour in the glare of the footlights, created out of the agglutination on the face of an actor of another face of grease-paint and pasteboard, and on his individual soul of the words of a part, those robust if ephemeral, and rather captivating, personalities which are the characters in a play, whom one loves, admires, pities,

whom one would like to see again after one has left the theatre,
but who by that time have already disintegrated into an actor
who is no longer in the situation which was his in the play,
into a text which no longer shows the actor's face, into a
coloured powder which a handkerchief wipes off, who have
returned, in short, to elements that contain nothing of them,
because of their dissolution, effected as soon as the play is over
—a dissolution which, like that of a loved one, causes one
to doubt the reality of the self and to meditate on the mystery
of death.

One number in the programme I found extremely painful.
A young woman whom Rachel and some of her friends disliked was to make her debut with a recital of old songs—a
debut on which she had based all her hopes for the future of
herself and her family. This young woman was possessed of an
unduly, almost grotesquely prominent rump and a pretty but
too slight voice, reduced still further by her nervousness and
in marked contrast to her muscular development. Rachel had
posted among the audience a certain number of friends, male
and female, whose business it was by their sarcastic comments
to disconcert the novice, who was known to be timid, and
to make her lose her head so that her recital should prove a
complete fiasco, after which the manager would refuse to
give her a contract. At the first notes uttered by the wretched
woman, several of the male spectators, recruited for that purpose, began pointing to her hindquarters with jocular comments, several of the women who were also in the plot laughed
out loud, and each fluty note from the stage increased the
deliberate hilarity until it verged on the scandalous. The
unhappy woman, sweating with anguish under her grease-
paint, tried for a little longer to hold out, then stopped and
gazed round the audience with a look of misery and rage
which succeeded only in increasing the uproar. The instinct
to imitate others, the desire to show off their own wit and
daring, added to the party several pretty actresses who had
not been forewarned but now exchanged with the others
glances charged with malicious connivance, and gave vent to
such violent peals of laughter that at the end of the second
song, although there were still five more on the programme,

the stage manager rang down the curtain. I did my utmost to
pay no more heed to the incident than I had paid to my grandmother's sufferings when my great-uncle, to tease her, used to
give my grandfather brandy, the idea of deliberate unkindness being too painful for me to bear. And yet, just as our pity
for misfortune is perhaps not very precise since in our imagination we recreate a whole world of grief by which the unfortunate who has to struggle against it has no thought of being
moved to self-pity, so unkindness has probably not in the
minds of the unkind that pure and voluptuous cruelty which
we find it so painful to imagine. Hatred inspires them, anger
prompts them to an ardour and an activity in which there is
no great joy; sadism is needed to extract any pleasure from it;
whereas unkind people suppose themselves to be punishing
someone equally unkind. Rachel certainly imagined that the
actress whom she had tortured was far from being of interest
to anyone, and that in any case, by having her hissed off the
stage, she was herself avenging an outrage on good taste and
teaching an unworthy colleague a lesson. Nevertheless, I preferred not to speak of this incident since I had had neither the
courage nor the power to prevent it, and it would have been
too painful for me, by speaking well of their victim, to assimilate the sentiments which animated the tormentors of the
novice singer to the gratifications of cruelty.

But the beginning of the afternoon's entertainment interested
me in quite another way. It made me realise in part the nature
of the illusion of which Saint-Loup was a victim with regard to
Rachel, and which had set a gulf between the images that he
and I respectively had of his mistress, when we saw her that
morning among the blossoming pear trees. Rachel had scarcely
more than a walking-on part in the little play. But seen thus,
she was another woman. She had one of those faces to which
distance—and not necessarily that between stalls and stage,
the world being merely a larger theatre—gives form and outline and which, seen from close to, crumble to dust. Standing
beside her one saw only a nebula, a milky way of freckles, of
tiny spots, nothing more. At a respectable distance, all this
ceased to be visible and, from cheeks that withdrew, were
reabsorbed into her face, there rose like a crescent moon a

nose so fine and so pure that one would have liked to be the
object of Rachel's attention, to see her again and again, to
keep her near one, provided that one had never seen her
differently and at close range. This was not my case, but it had
been Saint-Loup's when he first saw her on the stage. Then
he had asked himself how he might approach her, how get to
know her, a whole miraculous world had opened up in his
imagination—the world in which she lived—from which
emanated an exquisite radiance but into which he could never
penetrate. He had left the theatre in the little provincial town
where this had happened several years before, telling himself
that it would be madness to write to her, that she would not
answer his letter, quite prepared to give his fortune and his
name for the creature who now lived within him in a world so
vastly superior to those too familiar realities, a world made
beautiful by desire and dreams of happiness, when he saw
emerging from the stage door the gay and charmingly hatted
band of actresses who had just been playing. Young men
who knew them were waiting for them outside. The number
of pawns on the human chessboard being less than the number
of combinations that they are capable of forming, in a theatre
from which all the people we know and might have expected
to find are absent, there turns up one whom we never imagined
that we should see again and who appears so opportunely that
the coincidence seems to us providential, although no doubt
some other coincidence would have occurred in its stead had
we been not in that place but in some other, where other desires
would have been born and another old acquaintance forthcom-
ing to help us to satisfy them. The golden portals of the world
of dreams had closed upon Rachel before Saint-Loup saw her
emerge from the theatre, so that the freckles and spots were of
little importance. They displeased him nevertheless, especially
as, being no longer alone, he had not now the same power to
dream as in the theatre. But she, for all that he could no longer
see her, continued to dictate his actions, like those stars which
govern us by their attraction even during the hours in which
they are not visible to our eyes. And so his desire for the
actress with the delicate features which were not now even
present in Robert's memory caused him to fling himself at the

old friend whom chance had brought to the spot and get himself introduced to the person with no features and with freckles, since she was the same person, telling himself that later on he would take care to find out which of the two the actress really was. She was in a hurry, she did not on this occasion address a single word to Saint-Loup, and it was only some days later that he finally induced her to leave her companions and allow him to escort her home. He loved her already. The need for dreams, the desire to be made happy by the woman one has dreamed of, ensure that not much time is required before one entrusts all one's chances of happiness to someone who a few days since was no more than a fortuitous, unknown, insignificant apparition on the boards of a theatre.

When, the curtain having fallen, we moved on to the stage, alarmed at finding myself there for the first time, I felt the need to begin a spirited conversation with Saint-Loup. In this way my demeanour, since I did not know which one to adopt in a setting that was new to me, would be entirely dominated by our talk, and people would think that I was so absorbed in it, so unobservant of my surroundings, that it was quite natural for me not to be wearing the facial expressions proper to a place in which, to judge by what I appeared to be saying, I was barely conscious of standing; and seizing, for the sake of speed, upon the first topic that came to my mind:

"You know," I said, "I did come to say good-bye to you the day I left Doncières. I've never had a chance to mention it. I waved to you in the street."

"Don't speak about it," he replied, "I was so sorry. I passed you just outside the barracks, but I couldn't stop because I was late already. I assure you I felt quite wretched about it."

So he had recognised me! I saw again in my mind the utterly impersonal salute which he had given me, raising his hand to his cap, without a glance to indicate that he knew me, without a gesture to show that he was sorry he could not stop. Evidently the fiction of not recognising me which he had adopted at that moment must have simplified matters for him greatly. But I was amazed that he had hit upon it so swiftly and before a reflex had betrayed his original impression. I had already observed at Balbec that, side by side with that childlike sincerity of his face, the skin of which by its transparency made visible the sudden surge of his emotions, his body had been admirably trained to perform a certain number of well-bred dissimulations, and that, like a consummate actor, he could, in his regimental and in his social life, play alternately quite different roles. In one of his roles he loved me tenderly, and behaved towards me almost as if he was my brother; my brother he had been, and was now again, but for a moment that day he had been another person who did not know me and who, holding the reins, his monocle screwed into his eye, without a look or a smile had lifted his disengaged hand to the peak of his cap to give me a correct military salute.

The stage sets, still in their place, among which I was passing, seen thus at close range and deprived of those effects of lighting and distance on which the eminent artist whose brush had painted them had calculated, were a depressing sight, and Rachel, when I came near her, was subjected to a no less destructive influence. The curves of her charming nostrils had remained in the perspective between auditorium and stage, like the relief of the scenery. It was no longer she: I recognised her only by her eyes, in which her identity had taken refuge. The form, the radiance of this young star, so brilliant a moment ago, had vanished. On the other hand—as though we were to look more closely at the moon so that it ceased to present the appearance of a disk of pink and gold—on this face that had seemed so smooth a surface I could now distinguish only protuberances, discolourations, cavities.

I was delighted to observe, in the thick of a crowd of journalists or men of fashion, admirers of the actresses, who were greeting one another, talking, smoking, as though at a party in town, a young man in a black velvet cap and hortensia-coloured skirt, his cheeks chalked in red like a page from a Watteau album, who with smiling lips and eyes raised to the ceiling, describing graceful patterns with the palms of his hands and springing lightly into the air, seemed so entirely of another species from the sensible people in everyday clothes in the midst of whom he was pursuing like a madman the course of his ecstatic dream, so alien to the preoccupations of their life, so anterior to the habits of their civilisation, so enfranchised from the laws of nature, that it was as restful and refreshing a spectacle as watching a butterfly straying through a crowd to follow with one's eyes, between the flats, the natural arabesques traced by his winged, capricious, painted curvetings. But at that moment Saint-Loup conceived the notion that his mistress was paying undue attention to this dancer, who was now engaged in a final rehearsal of a dance-figure for the ballet performance in which he was about to appear, and his face darkened.

"You might look the other way," he said to her sombrely. "You know that those dancer-fellows are not worth the rope which one hopes they'll fall off and break their necks, and they're the sort of people who go about afterwards boasting that you've taken notice of them. Besides, you know very well you've been told to go to your dressing-room and change. You'll be missing your call again."

A group of men—journalists—noticing the look of fury on Saint-Loup's face, came nearer, amused, to listen to what was being said. And as the stage-hands had just set up some scenery on our other side we were forced into close contact with them.

"Oh, but I know him; he's a friend of mine," cried Saint-Loup's mistress, her eyes still fixed on the dancer. "Look how beautifully made he is; just watch those little hands of his dancing away by themselves like the rest of him!"

The dancer turned his head towards her, and his human person appeared beneath the sylph that he was endeavouring to be, the clear grey jelly of his eyes trembled and sparkled between eyelashes stiff with paint, and a smile extended the corners of his mouth in a face plastered with rouge; then, to amuse the young woman, like a singer who obligingly hums the tune of the song in which we have told her that we admired her singing, he began to repeat the movement of his hands, counterfeiting himself with the subtlety of a mime and the good humour of a child.

"Oh, it's too lovely, the way he mimics himself," cried Rachel, clapping her hands.

"I implore you, my dearest girl," Saint-Loup broke in, in a

tone of utter misery, "don't make an exhibition of yourself, I
can't stand it. I swear if you say another word I won't go with
you to your room, I shall walk straight out. Come on, don't
be nasty. . . . You oughtn't to stand about in the cigar smoke
like that, it'll make you ill," he added, turning to me, with the
solicitude he had shown for me in our Balbec days.

"Oh! what bliss it would be if you did go."

"I warn you, if I do, I shan't come back."

"That's more than I should dare to hope."

"Look here, I promised you the necklace if you behaved
nicely to me, but since you treat me like this. . . ."

"Ah! that doesn't surprise me in the least. You gave me a
promise, but I ought to have known you'd never keep it.
You want the whole world to know you're made of money,
but I'm not self-interested and money-grubbing like you. You
can keep your blasted necklace; I know someone else who'll
give it to me."

"No one else can possibly give it to you. I've told Boucheron
he's to keep it for me, and I have his promise not to sell it to
anyone else."

"So that's it! You wanted to blackmail me, so you took all
your precautions in advance. It's just what they say: Marsantes,
Mater Semita, it smells of the race," retorted Rachel, quoting
an etymology which was founded on a wild misinterpretation,
for *Semita* means "path" and not "Semite," but one which the
Nationalists applied to Saint-Loup on account of the Dreyfusard views for which, as it happened, he was indebted to the
actress. (She was less justified than anyone in applying the
appellation of Jewess to Mme de Marsantes, in whom the
ethnologists of society could succeed in finding no trace of
Jewishness apart from her kinship with the Lévy-Mirepoix
family.) "But this isn't the last of it, I can tell you. An agreement like that isn't binding. You've behaved treacherously towards me. Boucheron shall be told of it and he'll be paid twice
as much for his necklace. You'll hear from me before long,
don't you worry."

Robert was in the right a hundred times over. But circumstances are always so entangled that the man who is in the
right a hundred times may have been once in the wrong. (Lord

Derby himself acknowledges that England does not always seem right *vis-à-vis* Ireland.) And I could not help recalling that unpleasant and yet quite innocent remark he had made at Balbec: "In that way I keep a hold over her."

"You don't understand what I mean about the necklace. I made no formal promise. Once you start doing everything you possibly can to make me leave you, it's only natural, surely, that I shouldn't give it to you. I fail to understand what treachery you can see in that, or in what way I'm supposed to be self-interested. You can't seriously maintain that I brag about my money, I'm always telling you that I'm only a poor devil without a cent to my name. It's foolish of you to take it that way, my sweet. How am I self-interested? You know very well that my one interest in life is you."

"Yes, yes, please go on," she retorted ironically, with the sweeping gesture of a barber wielding his razor.[11] And turning towards the dancer:

"Isn't he too wonderful with his hands! I couldn't do the things he's doing there, even though I'm a woman." She went closer to him and, pointing to Robert's stricken face: "Look, he's hurt," she murmured, in a momentary impulse of sadistic cruelty totally out of keeping with her genuine feelings of affection for Saint-Loup.

"Listen; for the last time, I swear to you that you can try as hard as you like, that in a week's time you can have all the regrets in the world, but I shan't come back, I've had enough, do you hear, it's irrevocable; you'll be sorry one day, when it's too late."

Perhaps he was sincere in saying this, and the torture of leaving his mistress may have seemed to him less cruel than that of remaining with her in certain circumstances.

"But, my dear boy," he added, addressing me, "you oughtn't to stay here, I tell you, you'll start coughing."

I pointed to the scenery which barred my way. He touched his hat and said to one of the journalists:

"Would you mind, sir, throwing away your cigar? The smoke is bad for my friend."

His mistress, not waiting for him to accompany her, was on her way to the dressing-room when she turned round and addressed the dancer from the back of the stage, in an artificially melodious tone of girlish innocence:

"Do they do those tricks with women too, those nice little hands? You look just like a woman yourself. I'm sure I could have a wonderful time with you and a girl I know."

"There's no rule against smoking that I know of," said the journalist. "If people aren't well, they have only to stay at home."

The dancer smiled mysteriously at the actress.

"Oh! Do stop! You're driving me crazy," she cried to him. "The larks we'll have!"

"In any case, sir, you are not very civil," observed Saint-Loup to the journalist, still in a mild and courteous tone, with the air of appraisal of a man judging retrospectively the rights and wrongs of an incident that is already closed.

At that moment I saw Saint-Loup raise his arm vertically above his head as if he were making a sign to someone I could not see, or like the conductor of an orchestra, and indeed—without any greater transition than when, at a simple stroke of a violin bow, in a symphony or a ballet, violent rhythms succeed a graceful andante—after the courteous words that he had just uttered, he brought down his hand with a resounding smack upon the journalist's cheek.

Now that to the measured conversations of the diplomats, to the smiling arts of peace, had succeeded the furious onthrust of war, since blows lead to blows, I should not have been surprised to see the combatants wading in one another's blood. But what I could not understand (like people who feel that it is not according to the rules for war to break out between two countries when up till then it has been a question merely of the rectification of a frontier, or for a sick man to die when there was talk of nothing more serious than a swelling of the liver) was how Saint-Loup had contrived to follow up those words, which implied a hint of affability, with a gesture which in no way arose out of them, which they had not foreshadowed, the gesture of that arm raised in defiance not only of international law but of the principle of causality, in a spontaneous generation of anger, a gesture created *ex nihilo*. Fortunately the journalist who, staggering back from the violence of the blow, had turned pale and hesitated for a moment, did not retaliate. As for his friends, one of them had promptly turned away his head and was staring fixedly into the wings at someone who was evidently not there; the second pretended that a speck of dust had got into his eye, and began rubbing and squeezing his eyelid with every sign of being in pain; while the third had rushed off, exclaiming: "Good heavens, I believe the curtain's going up; we shan't get into our seats."

I wanted to speak to Saint-Loup, but he was so full of his indignation with the dancer that it clung to the very surface of his eyeballs; like a subcutaneous integument it distended his cheeks, so that, his inner agitation expressing itself externally in total immobility, he had not even the elasticity, the "play" necessary to take in a word from me and to answer it. The journalist's friends, seeing that the incident was at an end, gathered round him again, still trembling. But, ashamed of having deserted him, they were absolutely determined that he should be made to suppose that they had noticed nothing. And so they expatiated, one upon the speck of dust in his eye, one upon the false alarm which had made him think that the curtain was going up, the third upon the astonishing resemblance between a man who had just gone by and the speaker's brother. Indeed they seemed quite to resent their friend's not having shared their several emotions.

"What, didn't it strike you? You must be going blind."

"What I say is that you're a pack of cowards," growled the journalist who had been struck.

Forgetting the fictions they had adopted, to be consistent with which they ought—but they did not think of it—to have pretended not to understand what he meant, they fell back on certain expressions traditional in the circumstances: "What's all the excitement? Keep your hair on, old chap. You seem to be rather het up."

I had realised that morning beneath the pear blossom how illusory were the grounds upon which Robert's love for "Rachel when from the Lord" was based. On the other hand, I was no less aware how very real was the pain to which that love gave rise. Gradually the pain he had suffered without ceasing for the last hour receded, withdrew inside him, and a zone of accessibility appeared in his eyes. The two of us left the theatre and began to walk. I had stopped for a moment at a corner of the Avenue Gabriel from which I had often in the past seen Gilberte appear. I tried for a few seconds to recall those distant impressions, and was hurrying almost "at the double" to overtake Saint-Loup when I saw that a somewhat shabbily attired gentleman appeared to be talking to him confidentially. I concluded that this was a personal friend of Robert; meanwhile they seemed to be drawing even closer to one another; suddenly, as an astral phenomenon flashes through the sky, I saw a number of ovoid bodies assume with a giddy swiftness all the positions necessary for them to compose a flickering constellation in front of Saint-Loup. Flung out like stones from a catapult, they seemed to me to be at the very least seven in number. They were merely, however, Saint-Loup's two fists, multiplied by the speed with which they were changing place in this—to all appearance ideal and decorative —arrangement. But this elaborate display was nothing more than a pummelling which Saint-Loup was administering, the aggressive rather than aesthetic character of which was first revealed to me by the aspect of the shabbily dressed gentleman who appeared to be losing at once his self-possession, his lower jaw and a quantity of blood. He gave mendacious explanations to the people who came up to question him, turned his head and, seeing that Saint-Loup had made off and was hastening to rejoin me, stood gazing after him with an offended, crushed, but by no means furious expression on his face. Saint-Loup, on the other hand, was furious, although he himself had received no blow, and his eyes were still blazing with anger when he reached me. The incident was in no way connected (as I had supposed) with the assault in the theatre. It was an impassioned loiterer who, seeing the handsome young soldier that Saint-Loup was, had made a proposition to him. My friend could not get over the audacity of this "clique" who no longer even waited for the shades of night to venture forth, and spoke of the proposition that had been made to him with the same indignation as the newspapers use in reporting an armed assault and robbery in broad daylight in the centre of

Paris. And yet the recipient of his blows was excusable in one respect, for the trend of the downward slope brings desire so rapidly to the point of enjoyment that beauty in itself appears to imply consent. And that Saint-Loup was beautiful was beyond dispute. Castigation such as he had just administered has this value, for men of the type that had accosted him, that it makes them think seriously of their conduct, though never for long enough to enable them to mend their ways and thus escape correction at the hands of the law. And so, although Saint-Loup had administered the thrashing without much preliminary thought, all such punishments, even when they reinforce the law, are powerless to bring uniformity to morals.

These incidents, particularly the one that was weighing most on his mind, seemed to have prompted in Robert a desire to be left alone for a while. For after a time he asked me to leave him, and go by myself to call on Mme de Villeparisis. He would join me there, but preferred that we should not go in together, so that he might appear to have only just arrived in Paris instead of having spent half the day already with me.

As I had supposed before making the acquaintance of Mme de Villeparisis at Balbec, there was a vast difference between the world in which she lived and that of Mme de Guermantes. Mme de Villeparisis was one of those women who, born of an illustrious house, entering by marriage into another no less illustrious, do not for all that enjoy any great position in the social world, and, apart from a few duchesses who are their nieces or sisters-in-law, perhaps even a crowned head or two, old family connexions, have their drawing-rooms patronised only by third-rate people, drawn from the middle classes or from a nobility either provincial or tainted in some way, whose presence there has long since driven away all such smart and snobbish folk as are not obliged to come to the house by ties of blood or the claims of a friendship too old to be ignored. Certainly I had no difficulty after the first few minutes in understanding how Mme de Villeparisis, at Balbec, had come to be so well informed, better than ourselves even, as to the smallest details of the tour through Spain which my father was then making with M. de Norpois. It was impossible, for all that, to entertain the theory that the intimacy—of more than twenty years' standing—between Mme de Villeparisis and the Ambassador could have been responsible for the lady's loss of caste in a world where the smartest women boasted lovers far less respectable than him, quite apart from the fact that it was probably years since he had been anything more to the Marquise than an old friend. Had Mme de Villeparisis then had other adventures in the past? Being then of a more passionate temperament than now, in a calm and pious old age which nevertheless owed some of its mellow colouring to those ardent, vanished years, had she somehow failed, in the country neighbourhood where she had lived for so long, to avoid certain scandals unknown to a younger generation which merely noted their effect in the mixed and defective composition of a visiting list bound otherwise to have been among those least tarnished by any base alloy? Had that "sharp tongue" which her nephew ascribed to her made her enemies in those far-off days? Had it driven her into taking advantage of certain successes with men to avenge herself upon women? All this was possible; nor could the exquisitely sensitive way in which—modulating so delicately her choice of words as well as her tone of voice—Mme de Villeparisis spoke of modesty or kindness be held to invalidate this supposition; for the people who not only speak with approval of certain virtues but actually feel their charm and understand them admirably (who will be capable of painting a worthy picture of them in their memoirs) are often sprung from, but do not themselves belong to, the inarticulate, rough-hewn, artless generation which practised them. That generation is reflected but not continued in them. Instead of the character which it possessed, one finds a sensibility, an intelligence which are not conducive to action. And whether or not there had been in the life of Mme de Villeparisis any of those scandals which the lustre of her name had expunged, it was this intelligence, resembling rather that of a writer of the second rank than that of a woman of position, that was undoubtedly the cause of her social decline.

It is true that the qualities, such as level-headedness and moderation, which Mme de Villeparisis chiefly extolled were not especially exalting; but in order to describe moderation in an entirely convincing way, moderation will not suffice, and some of the qualities of authorship which presuppose a quite immoderate exaltation are required. I had remarked at Balbec that the genius of certain great artists was completely unintelligible to Mme de Villeparisis, and that all she could do was to make delicate fun of them and to express her incomprehension in a graceful and witty form. But this wit and grace, in the degree to which they were developed in her, became themselves—on another plane, and even though they were employed to belittle the noblest masterpieces—true artistic qualities. Now the effect of such qualities on any social position is a morbid activity of the kind which doctors call selective, and so disintegrating that the most firmly established pillars of society are hard put to it to hold out against it for any length of time. What artists call intelligence seems pure presumption to the fashionable world which, incapable of adopting the angle of vision from which they, the artists, judge things, incapable of understanding the particular attraction to which they yield when they choose an expression or draw a parallel, feel in their company an exhaustion, an irritation, from which antipathy rapidly springs. And yet in her conversation, and the same may be said of the *Memoirs* which she afterwards published, Mme de Villeparisis showed nothing but a sort of graciousness that was eminently social. Having passed by great works without considering them deeply, sometimes without even noticing them, she had retained from the period in which she had lived, and which indeed she described with great aptness and charm, little but the most trivial things it had had to offer. But a piece of writing, even if it treats exclusively of subjects that are not intellectual, is still a work of the intelligence, and to give a consummate impression of frivolity in a book, or in a talk which is not dissimilar, requires a touch of seriousness which a purely frivolous person would be incapable of. In a certain book of memoirs written by a woman and regarded as a masterpiece, such and such a sentence that people quote as a model of airy grace has always made me suspect that, in order to arrive at such a degree of lightness, the author must once have been imbued with a rather ponderous learning, a stodgy culture, and that as a girl she probably appeared to her friends an insufferable bluestocking. And between certain literary qualities and lack of social success the connexion is so inevitable that when we open Mme de Villeparisis's *Memoirs* to-day, on any page an apt epithet, a sequence of metaphors will suffice to enable the reader to reconstruct the deep but icy bow which must have been bestowed on the old Marquise on the staircase of an embassy by a snob such as Mme Leroi, who may perhaps have left a card on her when she went to call on the Guermantes, but never set foot in her house for fear of losing caste among all the doctors' or solicitors' wives whom she would find there. A bluestocking Mme de Ville-parisis had perhaps been in her earliest youth, and, intoxicated with her learning, had perhaps been unable to resist applying to people in society, less intelligent and less educated than herself, those cutting taunts which the injured party never forgets.

Moreover, talent is not a separate appendage which can be artificially attached to those qualities which make for social success, in order to create from the whole what people in society call a "complete woman." It is the living product of a certain moral conformation from which as a rule many quali-ties are lacking and in which there predominates a sensibility of which other manifestations not discernible in a book may make themselves fairly acutely felt in the course of a life, certain curiosities for instance, certain whims, the desire to go to this place or that for one's own amusement and not with a view to the extension, the maintenance or even the mere exercise of one's social relations. I had seen Mme de Villeparisis at Balbec hemmed in by a bodyguard of her own servants and not even glancing at the people sitting in the hall of the hotel. But I had had a presentiment that this abstention was not due to indifference, and it seemed that she had not always confined herself to it. She would get a sudden craze to know such and such an individual who had no claim to be received in her house, sometimes because she had thought him good-looking, or merely because she had been told that he was amusing, or because he had struck her as different from the people she knew, who at this period, when she had not yet begun to appreciate them because she imagined that they would never

abandon her, belonged, all of them, to the purest Faubourg
Saint-Germain. To this or that bohemian or petty bourgeois
whom she had marked out with her favour she was obliged to
address her invitations, the value of which he was unable to
appreciate, with an insistence that gradually depreciated her in
the eyes of the snobs who were in the habit of judging a salon
by the people whom its mistress excluded rather than by those
whom she entertained. True, if at some point in her youth Mme
de Villeparisis, surfeited with the satisfaction of belonging
to the flower of the aristocracy, had somehow amused herself
by scandalising the people among whom she lived, and deliberately impairing her own position in society, she had begun
to attach importance to that position once she had lost it.
She had wished to show the duchesses that she was better
than they, by saying and doing all the things that they dared
not say or do. But now that the latter, except for those who
were closely related to her, had ceased to call, she felt herself
diminished, and sought once more to reign, but with another
sceptre than that of wit. She would have liked to attract to her
house all those whom she had taken such pains to discard. How
many women's lives, lives of which little enough is known (for
we all live in different worlds according to our age, and the
discretion of their elders prevents the young from forming
any clear idea of the past and taking in the whole spectrum),
have been divided thus into contrasting periods, the last being
entirely devoted to the reconquest of what in the second has
been so light-heartedly flung to the winds! Flung to the winds
in what way? The young are all the less capable of imagining
it, since they see before them an elderly and respectable
Marquise de Villeparisis and have no idea that the grave
memorialist of to-day, so dignified beneath her pile of snowy
hair, can ever have been a gay midnight-reveller who was
perhaps in those days the delight, who perhaps devoured the
fortunes, of men now sleeping in their graves. That she should
also have set to work, with a persevering and natural industry,
to destroy the social position which she owed to her high
birth does not in the least imply that even at that remote period
Mme de Villeparisis did not attach great importance to her
position. In the same way the web of isolation, of inactivity

in which a neurasthenic lives may be woven by him from morning to night without thereby seeming endurable, and while he is hastening to add another mesh to the net which holds him captive, it is possible that he is dreaming only of dancing, sport and travel. We strive all the time to give our life its form, but we do so by copying willy-nilly, like a drawing, the features of the person that we are and not of the person we should like to be. Mme Leroi's disdainful bows might to some extent be expressive of the true nature of Mme de Villeparisis; they in no way corresponded to her ambition.

No doubt at the same moment in which Mme Leroi was—to use an expression dear to Mme Swann—"cutting" the Marquise, the latter could seek consolation in remembering how Queen Marie-Amélie had once said to her: "You are just like a daughter to me." But such royal civilities, secret and unknown to the world, existed for the Marquise alone, as dusty as the diploma of an old Conservatoire medallist. The only real social advantages are those that create life, that can disappear without the person who has benefited by them needing to try to cling on to them or to make them public, because on the same day a hundred others will take their place. Remember as she might the words of the Queen, Mme de Villeparisis would have bartered them gladly for the permanent capacity for being invited everywhere which Mme Leroi possessed, just as, in a restaurant, a great but unknown artist whose genius is written neither in the lines of his shy face nor in the antiquated cut of his threadbare coat, would willingly change places with the young stock-jobber from the lowest ranks of society, who is sitting with a couple of actresses at a neighbouring table to which in an obsequious and incessant chain come hurrying owner, manager, waiters, bell-hops and even the scullions who file out of the kitchen to salute him, as in the fairy-tales, while the wine waiter advances, as dust-covered as his bottles, limping and dazed, as if, on his way up from the cellar, he had twisted his foot before emerging into the light of day.

It must be remarked, however, that the absence of Mme Leroi from Mme de Villeparisis's salon, if it distressed the lady of the house, passed unperceived by the majority of her guests.

They were entirely ignorant of the peculiar position which Mme Leroi occupied, a position known only to the fashionable world, and never doubted that Mme de Villeparisis's receptions were, as the readers of her *Memoirs* to-day are convinced that they must have been, the most brilliant in Paris.

On the occasion of this first call which, after leaving Saint-Loup, I went to pay on Mme de Villeparisis following the advice given by M. de Norpois to my father, I found her in a drawing-room hung with yellow silk, against which the settees and the admirable armchairs upholstered in Beauvais tapestry stood out with the almost purple redness of ripe raspberries. Side by side with the Guermantes and Villeparisis portraits were to be seen—gifts from the sitters themselves—those of Queen Marie-Amélie, the Queen of the Belgians, the Prince de Joinville and the Empress of Austria. Mme de Villeparisis herself, wearing an old-fashioned bonnet of black lace (which she preserved with the same shrewd instinct for local or historical colour as a Breton innkeeper who, however Parisian his clientele may have become, thinks it more astute to keep his maids dressed in coifs and wide sleeves), was seated at a little desk on which, as well as her brushes, her palette and an unfinished flower-piece in water-colour, were arranged—in glasses, in saucers, in cups—moss-roses, zinnias, maidenhair ferns, which on account of the sudden influx of callers she had just left off painting, and which gave the impression of being arrayed on a florist's counter in some eighteenth-century mezzotint. In this drawing-room, which had been slightly heated on purpose because the Marquise had caught cold on the journey from her house in the country, there were already, among those present when I arrived, an archivist with whom Mme de Villeparisis had spent the morning selecting the autograph letters to herself from various historical personages which were to figure in facsimile as documentary evidence in the *Memoirs* which she was preparing for the press, and a solemn and tongue-tied historian, who, hearing that she had inherited and still possessed a portrait of the Duchesse de Montmorency, had come to ask her permission to reproduce it as a plate in his work on the Fronde—guests who were presently joined by my old schoolfriend Bloch, now a rising dramatist upon whom she counted to secure the gratuitous services of actors and actresses at her next series of afternoon parties. It was true that the social kaleidoscope was in the act of turning and that the Dreyfus case was shortly to relegate the Jews to the lowest rung of the social ladder. But, for one thing, however fiercely the anti-Dreyfus cyclone might be raging, it is not in the first hour of a storm that the waves are at their worst. In the second place, Mme de Villeparisis, leaving a whole section of her family to fulminate against the Jews, had remained entirely aloof from the Affair and never gave it a thought. Lastly, a young man like Bloch whom no one knew might pass unnoticed, whereas leading Jews who were representative of their side were already threatened. His chin was now decorated with a goatee beard, he wore a pince-nez and a long frock coat, and carried a glove like a roll of papyrus in his hand. The Rumanians, the Egyptians, the Turks may hate the Jews. But in a French drawing-room the differences between those peoples are not so apparent, and a Jew making his entry as though he were emerging from the desert, his body crouching like a hyaena's, his neck thrust forward, offering profound "salaams," completely satisfies a certain taste for the oriental. Only it is essential that the Jew in question should not be actually "in" society, otherwise he will readily assume the aspect of a lord and his manners become so Gallicised that on his face a refractory nose, growing like a nasturtium in unexpected directions, will be more reminiscent of Mascarille's than of Solomon's. But Bloch, not having been limbered up by the gymnastics of the Faubourg, nor ennobled by a crossing with England or Spain, remained for a lover of the exotic as strange and savoury a spectacle, in spite of his European costume, as a Jew in a painting by Decamps. How marvellous the power of the race which from the depths of the ages thrusts forward even into modern Paris, in the corridors of our theatres, behind the desks of our public offices, at a funeral, in the street, a solid phalanx, setting their mark upon our modern ways of hairdressing, absorbing, making us forget, disciplining the frock coat which on the whole has remained almost identical with the garment in which Assyrian scribes are depicted in ceremonial attire on the frieze of a monument at Susa before the gates of the Palace of Darius. (An hour later, Bloch was to feel that it was out of anti-semitic malice that M. de Charlus inquired whether his first name was Jewish, whereas it was simply from aesthetic interest and love of local colour.) But in any case to speak of racial persistence is to convey inaccurately the impression we receive from the Jews, the Greeks, the Persians, all those peoples whose variety is worth preserving. We know from classical paintings the faces of the ancient Greeks, we have seen Assyrians on the walls of a palace at Susa. And so we feel, on encountering in a Paris drawing-room Orientals belonging to such and such a group, that we are in the presence of supernatural creatures whom the forces of necromancy must have called into being. Hitherto we had only a superficial image; suddenly it has acquired depth, it extends into three dimensions, it moves. The young Greek lady, daughter of a rich banker and one of the latest society favourites, looks exactly like one of those dancers who in the chorus of a ballet at once historical and aesthetic symbolise Hellenic art in flesh and blood; but in the theatre the setting somehow vulgarises these images; whereas the spectacle to which the entry into a drawing-room of a Turkish lady or a Jewish gentleman admits us, by animating their features makes them appear stranger still, as if they really were creatures evoked by the efforts of a medium. It is the soul (or rather the pigmy thing which—up to the present, at any rate—the soul amounts to in this sort of materialisation), it is the soul, glimpsed by us hitherto in museums alone, the soul of the ancient Greeks, of the ancient Hebrews, torn from a life at once insignificant and transcendental, which seems to be enacting before our eyes this disconcerting pantomime. What we seek in vain to embrace in the shy young Greek is the figure admired long ago on the side of a vase. It struck me that if in the light of Mme de Villeparisis's drawing-room I had taken some photographs of Bloch, they would have given an image of Israel identical with those we find in spirit photographs— so disturbing because it does not appear to emanate from humanity, so deceptive because it none the less resembles humanity all too closely. There is nothing, to speak more generally, even down to the insignificance of the remarks

made by the people among whom we spend our lives, that
does not give us a sense of the supernatural, in our poor
everyday world where even a man of genius from whom,
gathered as though around a table at a séance, we expect to
learn the secret of the infinite, simply utters these words,
which had just issued from the lips of Bloch: "Take care of
my top hat."

"Oh, ministers, my dear sir," Mme de Villeparisis was
saying, addressing in particular my old schoolfriend and
picking up the thread of a conversation which had been
interrupted by my arrival, "ministers, nobody ever wanted to
see them. I was only a child at the time, but I can well remember the King begging my grandfather to invite M.
Decazes[12] to a rout at which my father was to dance with the
Duchesse de Berry. 'It will give me pleasure, Florimond,'
said the King. My grandfather, who was a little deaf, thought
he had said M. de Castries, and found the request perfectly
natural. When he understood that it was M. Decazes, he was
furious at first, but he gave in, and wrote the same evening
to M. Decazes, begging him to do him the honour of attending
the ball which he was giving the following week. For we
were polite in those days, and no hostess would have dreamed
of simply sending her card and writing on it 'Tea' or 'Dancing'
or 'Music.' But if we understood politeness, we were not
incapable of impertinence either. M. Decazes accepted, but the
day before the ball it was given out that my grandfather felt
indisposed and had cancelled the ball. He had obeyed the
King, but he had not had M. Decazes at his ball. . . . Yes,
indeed, I remember M. Molé very well, he was a man of wit—
he showed that in his reception of M. de Vigny at the Academy
—but he was very pompous, and I can see him now coming
downstairs to dinner in his own house with his top hat in his
hand."

"Ah! how evocative that is of what must have been a pretty
perniciously philistine epoch, for it was no doubt a universal
habit to carry one's hat in one's hand in one's own house,"
observed Bloch, anxious to make the most of so rare an
opportunity of learning from an eyewitness details of the
aristocratic life of another day, while the archivist, who was a

sort of intermittent secretary to the Marquise, gazed at her
tenderly as though he were saying to the rest of us: "There,
you see what she's like, she knows everything, she has met
everybody, you can ask her anything you like, she's quite
amazing."

"Oh dear, no," replied Mme de Villeparisis, drawing
towards her as she spoke the glass containing the maidenhair which presently she would continue painting. "It was
simply a habit of M. de Molé's. I never saw my father carry
his hat in the house, except of course when the King came,
because the King being at home wherever he is, the master of
the house is then only a visitor in his own drawing-room."

"Aristotle tells us in the second chapter of . . ." ventured
M. Pierre, the historian of the Fronde, but so timidly that no
one paid any attention. Having been suffering for some weeks
from a nervous insomnia which resisted every attempt at
treatment, he had given up going to bed, and, half-dead with
exhaustion, went out only whenever his work made it imperative. Incapable of repeating too often these expeditions which,
simple enough for other people, cost him as much effort as if
he was obliged to come down from the moon, he was surprised
to be brought up so frequently against the fact that other
people's lives were not organised on a constant and permanent
basis with a view to providing the maximum utility to the
sudden eruptions of his own. He sometimes found closed a
library which he had set out to visit only after planting himself
artificially on his feet and in a frock coat like some automaton
in a story by Wells. Fortunately he had found Mme de Villeparisis at home and was going to be shown the portrait.

Meanwhile he was cut short by Bloch. "Really," the latter
observed, referring to what Mme de Villeparisis had said as to
the etiquette for royal visits. "Do you know, I never knew
that" (as though it were strange that he should not have
known it).

"Talking of that sort of visit, do you know the stupid joke
my nephew Basin played on me yesterday morning?" Mme de
Villeparisis asked the librarian. "He told my people, instead of
announcing him, to say that it was the Queen of Sweden who
had called to see me."

"What! He made them tell you just like that! I say, he must have a nerve," exclaimed Bloch with a shout of laughter, while the historian smiled with a stately timidity.

"I was rather surprised, because I had only been back from the country a few days; I had given instructions, so as to be left in peace for a while, that no one was to be told that I was in Paris, and I wondered how the Queen of Sweden could have heard so soon, and in any case didn't leave me a couple of days to get my breath," went on Mme de Villeparisis, leaving her guests under the impression that a visit from the Queen of Sweden was in itself nothing unusual for their hostess.

And it was true that if earlier in the day Mme de Villeparisis had been checking the documentation of her *Memoirs* with the archivist, she was now quite unconsciously trying out their effect on an average audience representative of that from which she would eventually have to recruit her readers. Hers might differ in many ways from a really fashionable salon from which many of the bourgeois ladies whom she entertained would have been absent and where one would have seen instead such brilliant leaders of fashion as Mme Leroi had in course of time managed to secure, but this distinction is not perceptible in her *Memoirs*, in which certain mediocre connexions of the author's have disappeared because there is no occasion to refer to them; while the absence of ladies who did not visit her leaves no gap because, in the necessarily restricted space at the author's disposal, only a few persons can appear, and if these persons are royal personages, historic personalities, then the maximum impression of elegance which any volume of memoirs can convey to the public is achieved. In the opinion of Mme Leroi, Mme de Villeparisis's salon was third-rate; and Mme de Villeparisis felt the sting of Mme Leroi's opinion. But hardly anyone to-day remembers who Mme Leroi was, her opinions have vanished into thin air, and it is the salon of Mme de Villeparisis, frequented as it was by the Queen of Sweden, and as it had been by the Duc d'Aumale, the Duc de Broglie, Thiers, Montalembert, Mgr. Dupanloup, which will be regarded as one of the most brilliant of the nineteenth century by that posterity which has not changed since the days of Homer and Pindar, and for which the enviable

things are exalted birth, royal or quasi-royal, and the friendship of kings, of leaders of the people and other eminent
men.

Now of all these Mme de Villeparisis had her share in her
present salon and in the memories—sometimes slightly
"touched up"—by means of which she extended it into the
past. And then there was M. de Norpois who, while unable to
restore his friend to any substantial position in society, on the
other hand brought to her house such foreign or French
statesmen as might have need of his services and knew that the
only effective method of securing them was to pay court to
Mme de Villeparisis. Perhaps Mme Leroi also knew these
European celebrities. But, as an agreeable woman who shunned
anything that smacked of the bluestocking, she would as little
have thought of mentioning the Eastern Question to a Prime
Minister as of discussing the nature of love with a novelist or
a philosopher. "Love?" she had once replied to a lady who had
asked for her views on love, "I make it often but I never talk
about it." When she had any of these literary or political lions
in her house she contented herself, as did the Duchesse de
Guermantes, with setting them down to play poker. They often
preferred this to the serious conversations on general ideas
in which Mme de Villeparisis forced them to engage. But these
conversations, ridiculous as in the social sense they may have
been, have furnished the *Memoirs* of Mme de Villeparisis
with those admirable passages, those political dissertations
which read well in volumes of autobiography as they do in
Cornelian tragedies. Furthermore, the salons of the Mme de
Villeparisis of this world are alone destined to be handed down
to posterity, because the Mme Lerois of this world cannot
write, and, if they could, would not have the time. And if the
literary dispositions of the Mme de Villeparisis are the cause of
the disdain of the Mme Lerois, in its turn the disdain of the
Lerois does a singular service to the literary dispositions of
the Mme de Villeparisis by affording those bluestocking ladies
that leisure which the career of letters requires. God, whose
will it is that there should be a few well-written books in the
world, breathes with that purpose such disdain into the hearts
of the Mme Lerois, for he knows that if these should invite the

Mme Villeparisis to dinner, the latter would at once rise from their writing tables and order their carriages to be round at eight.

Presently there entered with slow and solemn tread an old lady of tall stature who, beneath the raised brim of her straw hat, revealed a monumental pile of snowy hair in the style of Marie-Antoinette. I did not then know that she was one of three women still to be seen in Parisian society who, like Mme de Villeparisis, while all of the noblest birth, had been reduced, for reasons which were now lost in the mists of time and could have been explained to us only by some old gallant of their period, to entertaining only certain of the dregs of society who were not sought after elsewhere. Each of these ladies had her own "Duchesse de Guermantes," the brilliant niece who came regularly to pay her respects, but none of them could have succeeded in attracting to her house the "Duchesse de Guermantes" of either of the others. Mme de Villeparisis was on the best of terms with these three ladies, but she did not like them. Perhaps the similarity between their social position and her own gave her a disagreeable impression of them. Besides, soured bluestockings as they were, seeking, by the number and frequency of the dramatic entertainments which they arranged in their houses, to give themselves the illusion of a regular salon, there had grown up among them a rivalry which the erosion of their wealth in the course of somewhat tempestuous lives, obliging them to watch their expenditure, to count on the services of professional actors or actresses free of charge, transformed into a sort of struggle for existence. Furthermore, the lady with the Marie-Antoinette hair-style, whenever she set eyes on Mme de Villeparisis, could not help being reminded of the fact that the Duchesse de Guermantes did not come to her Fridays. Her consolation was that at these same Fridays she could always count on having, blood being thicker than water, the Princesse de Poix, who was her own personal Guermantes, and who never went near Mme de Villeparisis, albeit Mme de Poix was an intimate friend of the Duchess.

Nevertheless from the mansion on the Quai Malaquais to the drawing-rooms of the Rue de Tournon, the Rue de la

Chaise and the Faubourg Saint-Honoré, a bond as compelling
as it was hateful united the three fallen goddesses, as to whom
I should have been interested to learn, from some dictionary
of social mythology, what amorous adventure, what sacrilegious presumption, had brought about their punishment.
The same illustrious origins, the same present decline, no
doubt had much to do with the necessity which compelled
them, while hating each other, to frequent one another's
society. Besides, each of them found in the others a convenient
way of impressing her guests. How should these fail to suppose
that they had scaled the most inaccessible peak of the Faubourg
when they were introduced to a lady with a string of titles
whose sister was married to a Duc de Sagan or a Prince de
Ligne? Especially as there was infinitely more in the newspapers about these sham salons than about the genuine ones.
Indeed these old ladies' "swell" nephews—and Saint-Loup the
foremost of them—when asked by a friend to introduce him
into society would say: "I'll take you to my aunt Villeparisis's, or to my aunt X's—you meet interesting people
there." They knew very well that this would mean less trouble
for themselves than trying to get the said friend invited by
the smart nieces or sisters-in-law of these ladies. Certain very
old men, and young women who had heard it from those men,
told me that if these ladies were no longer received in society
it was because of the extraordinary dissoluteness of their
conduct, which, when I objected that dissolute conduct was
not necessarily a barrier to social success, was represented to
me as having gone far beyond anything to be met with to-day.
The misconduct of these solemn dames who held themselves
so erect assumed on the lips of those who hinted at it something that I was incapable of imagining, something proportionate to the magnitude of prehistoric days, to the age of the
mammoth. In a word, these three Parcae with their white or
blue or pink hair had been the ruin of an incalculable number
of gentlemen. It struck me that the men of to-day exaggerated
the vices of those fabulous times, like the Greeks who created
Icarus, Theseus, Heracles out of men who had been but little
different from those who long afterwards deified them. But
one does not tabulate the sum of a person's vices until he has

almost ceased to be in a fit state to practise them, when from
the magnitude of his social punishment, which is then nearing
the completion of its term and which alone one can estimate,
one measures, one imagines, one exaggerates the magnitude
of the crime that has been committed. In that gallery of
symbolical figures which is "society," the really dissolute
women, the true Messalinas, invariably present the solemn
aspect of a lady of at least seventy, with an air of lofty distinction, who entertains everyone she can but not everyone she
would like to, to whose house women whose own conduct is
not above reproach refuse to go, to whom the Pope regularly
sends his Golden Rose, and who as often as not has written
a book about Lamartine's early years that has been crowned by
the French Academy.

"How d'ye do, Alix?" Mme de Villeparisis greeted the lady
with the Marie-Antoinette hair-style, which lady cast a searching glance round the assembly to see whether there was not in
this drawing-room any item that might be a valuable addition
to her own, in which case she would have to discover it for
herself, for Mme de Villeparisis, she was sure, would be
malevolent enough to hide it from her. Thus Mme de Villeparisis took good care not to introduce Bloch to the old lady
for fear of his being asked to produce the same play that he was
arranging for her in the drawing-room of the Quai Malaquais.
Besides, it was only tit for tat. For the evening before the old
lady had had Mme Ristori reciting verses, and had taken
care that Mme de Villeparisis, from whom she had filched the
Italian artist, should not hear of this function until it was over.
So that she should not read it first in the newspapers and feel
ruffled, the old lady had come in person to tell her about it,
showing no sense of guilt. Mme de Villeparisis, judging that
the introduction of myself was unlikely to have the same
drawbacks as that of Bloch, made me known to the Marie-
Antoinette of the Quai Malaquais. The latter, who sought, by
making the fewest possible movements, to preserve in her old
age those lines, as of a Coysevox goddess, which had years
ago charmed the young men of fashion and which spurious
poets still celebrated in rhyming couplets—and had acquired
the habit of a lofty and compensating stiffness common to all

those whom a personal uncomeliness obliges to be continually making advances—just perceptibly lowered her head with a frigid majesty, and, turning the other way, took no more notice of me than if I had not existed. Her dual-purpose attitude seemed to be saying to Mme de Villeparisis: "You see, I'm not as hard up for acquaintance as all that, and I'm not interested—in any sense of the word, you old cat—in young men." But when, twenty minutes later, she took her leave, taking advantage of the general hubbub she slipped into my ear an invitation to come to her box the following Friday with another of the three, whose high-sounding name—she had been born a Choiseul, moreover—made a prodigious impression on me.

"I understand, M'sieur, that you want to write somethin' about Mme la Duchesse de Montmorency," said Mme de Villeparisis to the historian of the Fronde in the gruff tone with which her genuine affability was furrowed by the shrivelled crotchiness, the physiological spleen of old age, as well as by the affectation of imitating the almost rustic speech of the old nobility. "I'll show you her portrait, the original of the copy they have in the Louvre."

She rose, laying down her brushes beside the flowers, and the little apron which then came into sight at her waist, and which she wore so as not to stain her dress with paint, added still further to the impression of an old peasant given by her bonnet and her big spectacles, and offered a sharp contrast to the luxury of her household, the butler who had brought in the tea and cakes, the liveried footman for whom she now rang to light up the portrait of the Duchesse de Montmorency, abbess of one of the most famous chapters in the east of France. Everyone had risen. "What is rather amusin'," said our hostess, "is that in these chapters where our great-aunts were so often made abbesses, the daughters of the King of France would not have been admitted. They were very exclusive chapters." "The King's daughters not admitted!" cried Bloch in amazement, "why ever not?" "Why, because the House of France had not enough quarterin's after that misalliance." Bloch's bewilderment increased. "A misalliance? The House of France? When was that?" "Why, when they married into the Medicis," replied Mme de Villeparisis in the most natural tone in the world. "It's a fine picture, is it not, and in a perfect state of preservation," she added.

"My dear," said the lady with the Marie-Antoinette hair-style, "surely you remember that when I brought Liszt to see you he said that it was this one that was the copy."

"I shall bow to any opinion of Liszt's on music, but not on painting. Besides, he was already gaga, and I don't remember his ever saying anything of the sort. But it wasn't you who brought him here. I had met him any number of times at dinner at Princess Sayn-Wittgenstein's."

Alix's shot had misfired; she stood silent, erect and motionless. Plastered with layers of powder, her face had the appearance of stone. And, since the profile was noble, she seemed, on a triangular, moss-grown pedestal hidden by her cape, like a crumbling goddess in a park.

"Ah, I see another fine portrait," said the historian.

The door opened and the Duchesse de Guermantes entered the room.

"Oh, good evening," Mme de Villeparisis greeted her without even a nod of the head, taking from her apron-pocket a hand which she held out to the newcomer; and ceasing at once to pay any further attention to her niece, turned back to the historian: "That is the portrait of the Duchesse de La Rochefoucauld. . . ."

A young servant with a bold manner and a charming face (but so finely chiselled to ensure its perfection that the nose was a little red and the rest of the skin slightly inflamed as though they were still smarting from the recent sculptural incision) came in bearing a card on a salver.

"It is that gentleman who has been several times to see Mme la Marquise."

"Did you tell him I was at home?"

"He heard the voices."

"Oh, very well then, show him in. It's a gentleman who was introduced to me," she explained. "He told me he was very anxious to come to my house. I certainly never said he might. But he's taken the trouble to call five times now, and it doesn't do to hurt people's feelings. Monsieur," she added to me, "and you, Monsieur," to the historian of the Fronde, "let me introduce my niece, the Duchesse de Guermantes."

The historian made a low bow, as I did too, and since he seemed to suppose that some friendly remark ought to follow this salute, his eyes brightened and he was preparing to open his mouth when he was chilled by the demeanour of Mme de Guermantes, who had taken advantage of the independence of her torso to throw it forward with an exaggerated politeness and bring it neatly back to a position of rest without letting face or eyes appear to have noticed that anyone was standing before them; after breathing a little sigh she contented herself with manifesting the nullity of the impression that had been made on her by the sight of the historian and myself by performing certain movements of her nostrils with a precision that testified to the absolute inertia of her unoccupied attention.

The importunate visitor entered the room, making straight for Mme de Villeparisis with an ingenuous, fervent air: it was Legrandin.

"Thank you so very much for letting me come and see you," he began, laying stress on the word "very." "It is a pleasure of a quality altogether rare and subtle that you confer on an old solitary. I assure you that its repercussion . . ."

He stopped short on catching sight of me.

"I was just showing this gentleman a fine portrait of the Duchesse de La Rochefoucauld, the wife of the author of the *Maxims*; it's a family heirloom."

Mme de Guermantes meanwhile had greeted Alix, with apologies for not having been able, that year as in every previous year, to go and see her. "I hear all about you from Madeleine," she added.

"She was at luncheon with me to-day," said the Marquise of the Quai Malaquais, with the satisfying reflexion that Mme de Villeparisis could never say the same.

Meanwhile I had been talking to Bloch, and fearing, from what I had been told of his father's change of attitude towards him, that he might be envying my life, I said to him that his must be happier. My remark was prompted simply by a desire to be friendly. But such friendliness readily convinces those who cherish a high opinion of themselves of their own good

fortune, or gives them a desire to convince other people of it.
"Yes, I do lead a delightful existence," Bloch assured me with
a beautific smile. "I have three great friends—I do not wish for
one more—and an adorable mistress; I am infinitely happy.
Rare is the mortal to whom Father Zeus accords so much
felicity." I fancy that he was anxious principally to congratulate
himself and to make me envious. Perhaps, too, his optimism
reflected a desire to be original. It was evident that he did not
wish to reply with the usual banalities—"Oh, it was nothing,
really," and so forth—when, to my question: "Was it nice?" à
propos of an afternoon dance at his house to which I had been
prevented from going, he replied in a level, careless tone, as if
the dance had been given by someone else: "Why, yes, it was
very nice, couldn't have been more successful. In fact it was
really delightful."

"What you have just told us interests me enormously," said
Legrandin to Mme de Villeparisis, "for I was saying to myself
only the other day that you showed a marked resemblance to
him in the agile sharpness of your turn of phrase, in a quality
which I will venture to describe by two contradictory terms,
monumental rapidity and immortal instantaneousness. I
should have liked this afternoon to take down all the things you
say; but I shall remember them. They are, in a phrase which
comes, I think, from Joubert, congenial to the memory. You
have never read Joubert? Oh! he would have admired you so!
I will take the liberty this very evening of sending you his
works: it will be a privilege to make you a present of his
mind. He had not your force. But he had a similar gracefulness."

I had wanted to go and greet Legrandin at once, but he kept
as far away from me as he could, no doubt in the hope that I
might not overhear the stream of flattery which, with a remarkable preciosity of expression, he kept pouring out to
Mme de Villeparisis whatever the subject.

She shrugged her shoulders, smiling, as though he had been
trying to make fun of her, and turned to the historian.

"And this is the famous Marie de Rohan, Duchesse de
Chevreuse, who was previously married to M. de Luynes."

"My dear, Mme de Luynes reminds me of Yolande; she
came to me yesterday evening, and if I had known that you

weren't engaged I'd have sent round to ask you to come. Mme Ristori turned up quite by chance, and recited some poems by Queen Carmen Sylva[13] in the author's presence. It was too beautiful!"

"What treachery!" thought Mme de Villeparisis. "Of course that was what she was whispering about the other day to Mme de Beaulaincourt and Mme de Chaponay ... I was free," she replied, "but I would not have come. I heard Ristori in her great days, she's a mere wreck now. Besides, I detest Carmen Sylva's poetry. Ristori came here once—the Duchess of Aosta brought her—to recite a canto of Dante's *Inferno*. In that sort of thing she's incomparable."

Alix bore the blow without flinching. She remained marble. Her gaze was piercing and blank, her nose proudly arched. But the surface of one cheek was flaking. A faint, strange vegetation, green and pink, was invading her chin. Perhaps another winter would finally lay her low.

"There, Monsieur, if you are fond of painting, look at the portrait of Mme de Montmorency," Mme de Villeparisis said to Legrandin to interrupt the flow of compliments which was beginning again.

Taking the opportunity of his back being turned, Mme de Guermantes pointed to him with an ironical, questioning look at her aunt.

"It's M. Legrandin," murmured Mme de Villeparisis. "He has a sister called Mme de Cambremer, not that that will mean any more to you than it does to me."

"What! Oh, but I know her very well!" exclaimed Mme de Guermantes, clapping her hand to her mouth. "Or rather I don't know her, but for some reason or other Basin, who meets the husband heaven knows where, took it into his head to tell the wretched woman she might call on me. And she did. I can't tell you what it was like. She told me she had been to London, and gave me a complete catalogue of all the things in the British Museum. And just as you see me now, the moment I leave your house, I'm going to drop a card on the monster. And don't think it's as easy as all that, because on the pretext that she's dying of some disease she's always at home, no matter whether you arrive at seven at night or nine in the morning, she's ready for you with a plate of strawberry tarts. No, but seriously, you know, she is a monstrosity," Mme de Guermantes went on in reply to a questioning glance from her aunt. "She's an impossible person, she talks about 'scriveners' and things like that." "What does 'scrivener' mean?" asked Mme de Villeparisis. "I haven't the slightest idea!" cried the Duchess in mock indignation. "I don't want to know. I don't speak that sort of language." And seeing that her aunt really did not know what a scrivener was, to give herself the satisfaction of showing that she was a scholar as well as a purist, and to make fun of her aunt after having made fun of Mme de Cambremer: "Why, of course," she said, with a half-laugh which the last traces of her feigned ill-humour kept in check, "everybody knows what it means; a scrivener is a writer, a person who scribbles. But it's a horror of a word. It's enough to make your wisdom teeth drop out. Nothing will ever make me use words like that ... And so that's the brother, is it? I can't get used to the idea. But after all it's not inconceivable. She has the same doormat humility and the same mass of information like a circulating library. She's just as much of a toady as he is, and just as boring. Yes, I'm beginning to see the family likeness now quite plainly."

"Sit down, we're just going to take a dish of tea," said Mme de Villeparisis to her niece. "Help yourself; you don't want to look at the pictures of your great-grandmothers, you know them as well as I do."

Presently Mme de Villeparisis sat down again at her desk and went on with her painting. The rest of the party gathered round her, and I took the opportunity to go up to Legrandin and, seeing no harm myself in his presence in Mme de Villeparisis's drawing-room and never dreaming how much my words would at once hurt him and make him believe that I had deliberately intended to hurt him, say: "Well, Monsieur, I am almost excused for being in a salon when I find you here too." M. Legrandin concluded from these words (at least this was the opinion which he expressed of me a few days later) that I was a thoroughly spiteful young wretch who delighted only in doing mischief.

"You might at least have the civility to begin by saying

how d'ye do to me," he replied, without offering me his hand
and in a coarse and angry voice which I had never suspected
him of possessing, a voice which, having no rational connexion with what he ordinarily said, had another more immediate
and striking connexion with something he was feeling. For
the fact of the matter is that, since we are determined always
to keep our feelings to ourselves, we have never given any
thought to the manner in which we should express them. And
suddenly there is within us a strange and obscene animal
making itself heard, whose tones may inspire as much alarm
in the person who receives the involuntary, elliptical and almost
irresistible communication of one's defect or vice as would
the sudden avowal indirectly and outlandishly proffered by a
criminal who can no longer refrain from confessing to a
murder of which one had never imagined him to be guilty. I
knew, of course, that idealism, even subjective idealism, did
not prevent great philosophers from still having hearty appetites or from presenting themselves with untiring perseverance for election to the Academy. But really Legrandin
had no need to remind people so often that he belonged to
another planet when all his uncontrollable impulses of anger
or affability were governed by the desire to occupy a good
position on this one.

"Naturally, when people pester me twenty times on end to
go somewhere," he went on in lower tones, "although I am
perfectly free to do what I choose, still I can't behave like an
absolute boor."

Mme de Guermantes had sat down. Her name, accompanied
as it was by her title, added to her physical person the duchy
which cast its aura round about her and brought the shadowy,
sun-splashed coolness of the woods of Guermantes into this
drawing-room, to surround the pouf on which she was sitting.
I was surprised only that the likeness of those woods was not
more discernible on the face of the Duchess, about which
there was nothing suggestive of vegetation, and on which the
ruddiness of her cheeks—which ought, one felt, to have been
emblazoned with the name Guermantes—was at most the
effect, and not the reflexion, of long gallops in the open air.
Later on, when I had become indifferent to her, I came to

know many of the Duchess's distinctive features, notably (to
stick for the moment only to those of which I already at this
time felt the charm though without yet being able to identify
it) her eyes, which captured as in a picture the blue sky of a
French country afternoon, broadly expansive, bathed in light
even when no sun shone; and a voice which one would have
thought, from its first hoarse sounds, to be almost plebeian,
in which there lingered, as over the steps of the church at
Combray or the pastry-cook's in the square, the rich and lazy
gold of a country sun. But on this first day I discerned nothing,
my ardent attention volatilised at once the little that I might
otherwise have been able to take in and from which I might
have been able to grasp something of the name Guermantes.
In any case, I told myself that it was indeed she who was
designated for all the world by the title Duchesse de Guermantes: the inconceivable life which that name signified was
indeed contained in this body; it had just introduced that life
into the midst of a group of disparate people, in this room
which enclosed it on every side and on which it produced so
vivid a reaction that I felt I could see, where the extent of that
mysterious life ceased, a fringe of effervescence outline its
frontiers—in the circumference of the circle traced on the
carpet by the balloon of her blue pekin skirt, and in the bright
eyes of the Duchess at the point of intersection of the preoccupations, the memories, the incomprehensible, scornful,
amused and curious thoughts which filled them from within
and the outside images that were reflected on their surface.
Perhaps I should have been not quite so deeply stirred had I
met her at Mme de Villeparisis's at an evening party, instead of
seeing her thus at one of the Marquise's "at homes," at one of
those tea-parties which are for women no more than a brief
halt in the course of their afternoon's outing, when, keeping
on the hats in which they have been doing their shopping, they
waft into a succession of salons the quality of the fresh air
outside, and offer a better view of Paris in the late afternoon
than do the tall open windows through which one can hear
the rumble of victorias: Mme de Guermantes wore a straw hat
trimmed with cornflowers, and what they recalled to me was
not the sunlight of bygone years among the tilled fields round

Combray where I had so often gathered them on the slope adjoining the Tansonville hedge, but the smell and the dust of twilight as they had been an hour ago when Mme de Guermantes had walked through them in the Rue de la Paix. With a smiling, disdainful, absent-minded air, and a pout on her pursed lips, she was tracing circles on the carpet with the point of her sunshade, as with the extreme tip of an antenna of her mysterious life; then, with that indifferent attention which begins by eliminating every point of contact between oneself and what one is considering, her gaze fastened upon each of us in turn, then inspected the settees and chairs, but softened now by that human sympathy which is aroused by the presence, however insignificant, of a thing one knows, a thing that is almost a person: these pieces of furniture were not like us, they belonged vaguely to her world, they were bound up with the life of her aunt; then from a Beauvais chair her gaze was carried back to the person sitting on it, and thereupon resumed the same air of perspicacity and that same disapproval which the respect that Mme de Guermantes felt for her aunt would have prevented her from expressing in words, but which she would have felt had she noticed on the chairs, instead of our presence, that of a spot of grease or a layer of dust.

The excellent writer G—— entered the room, having come to pay a call on Mme de Villeparisis which he regarded as a tiresome duty. The Duchess, although delighted to see him again, gave him no sign of welcome, but instinctively he made straight for her, the charm that she possessed, her tact, her simplicity making him look upon her as a woman of intelligence. He was bound, in any case, in common politeness to go and talk to her, for, since he was a pleasant and distinguished man, Mme de Guermantes frequently invited him to lunch even when her husband and herself were alone, or, in the autumn, took advantage of this intimacy to have him to dinner occasionally at Guermantes with royal personages who were curious to meet him. For the Duchess liked to entertain certain eminent men, on condition always that they were bachelors, a condition which, even when married, they invariably fulfilled for her, for since their wives, who were always more or less common, would have been a blot on a salon in which there were never any but the most fashionable beauties of Paris, it was always without them that their husbands were invited; and the Duke, to forestall any hurt feelings, would explain to these involuntary widowers that the Duchess never had women in the house, could not endure feminine company, almost as though this had been under doctor's orders, and as he might have said that she could not stay in a room in which there were smells, or eat over-salted food, or travel with her back to the engine, or wear stays. It was true that these eminent men used to see at the Guermantes' the Princesse de Parme, the Princesse de Sagan (whom Françoise, hearing her constantly mentioned, had taken to calling, in the belief that this feminine ending was required by the laws of accidence, "the Sagante"), and plenty more, but their presence was accounted for by the explanation that they were relations, or such very old friends that it was impossible to exclude them. Whether or not they were convinced by the explanations which the Duc de Guermantes had given of the singular malady that made it impossible for the Duchess to associate with other women, the great men duly transmitted them to their wives. Some of these thought that the malady was only an excuse to cloak her jealousy, because the Duchess wished to reign alone over a court of worshippers. Others more simple still thought that perhaps the Duchess had some peculiar habit, or even a scandalous past, so that women did not care to go to her house and that she gave the name of a whim to what was stern necessity. The better among them, hearing their husbands expatiate on the Duchess's wit, assumed that she must be so far superior to the rest of womankind that she found their society boring since they could not talk intelligently about anything. And it was true that the Duchess was bored by other women, if their princely rank did not give them an exceptional interest. But the excluded wives were mistaken when they imagined that she chose to entertain men only in order to be able to discuss with them literature, science, and philosophy. For she never spoke of these, at least with the great intellectuals. If, by virtue of a family tradition such as makes the daughters of great soldiers preserve a respect for military matters in the midst of their most frivolous distractions, she felt, as the granddaughter of women who had been on terms of friendship with Thiers, Mérimée and Augier, that a place must always be kept in her drawing-room for men of intellect, she had at the same time derived from the manner, at once condescending and familiar, in which those famous men had been received at Guermantes, the foible of looking on men of talent as family friends whose talent does not dazzle one, to whom one does not speak of their work, and who would not be at all interested if one did. Moreover the type of mind illustrated by Mérimée and Meilhac and Halévy, which was also hers, led her, by contrast with the verbal sentimentality of an earlier generation, to a style of conversation that rejects everything to do with fine language and the expression of lofty thoughts, so that she made it a sort of point of good breeding when she was with a poet or a musician to talk only of the food that they were eating or the game of cards to which they would afterwards sit down. This abstention had, on a third person not conversant with her ways, a disturbing effect which amounted to mystification. Mme de Guermantes having asked him if he would like to be invited to meet this or that famous poet, devoured by curiosity he would arrive at the appointed hour. The Duchess would talk to the poet about the weather. They would sit down to lunch. "Do you like this way of doing eggs?" she would ask the poet. On hearing his approval, which she shared, for everything in her own house appeared to her exquisite, down to a horrible cider which she imported from Guermantes: "Give Monsieur some more eggs," she would tell the butler, while the anxious fellow-guest sat waiting for what must surely have been the object of the occasion, since they had arranged to meet, in spite of every sort of difficulty, before the Duchess, the poet and he himself left Paris. But the meal went on, one after another the courses would be cleared away, not without having provided Mme de Guermantes with opportunities for clever witticisms or well-judged anecdotes. Meanwhile the poet would go on eating without either the Duke or Duchess showing any sign of remembering that he was a poet. And presently the luncheon would come to an end and the party would break up, without a word having been said about poetry which they nevertheless all admired but to which, by a reserve analogous to that of which Swann had given me a foretaste, no one referred. This reserve was simply a matter of good form. But for the fellow-guest, if he thought about the matter, there was something strangely melancholy about it all, and these meals in the Guermantes household were reminiscent of the hours which timid lovers often spend together in talking trivialities until it is time to part, without—whether from shyness, from modesty or from awkwardness—the great secret which they would have been happier to confess ever having succeeded in passing from their hearts to their lips. It must, however, be added that this silence with regard to deeper things which one was always waiting in vain to see broached, if it might pass as characteristic of the Duchess, was by no means absolute with her. Mme de Guermantes had spent her girlhood in a somewhat different environment, equally aristocratic but less brilliant and above all less futile than that in which she now lived, and one of wide culture. It had left beneath her present frivolity a sort of firmer bedrock, invisibly nutritious, to which indeed the Duchess would repair in search (very rarely, though, for she detested pedantry) of some quotation from Victor Hugo or Lamartine which, extremely appropriate, uttered with a look of true feeling from her fine eyes, never failed to surprise and charm her audience. Sometimes, even, unpretentiously, with pertinence and simplicity, she would give some dramatist and Academician a piece of sage advice, would make him modify a situation or alter an ending.

If, in the drawing-room of Mme de Villeparisis, as in the church at Combray on the day of Mlle Percepied's wedding, I had difficulty in discovering in the handsome but too human face of Mme de Guermantes the unknown element of her name, I thought at least that, when she spoke, her conversation, profound, mysterious, would have the strangeness of a mediaeval tapestry or a Gothic window. But in order that I should not be disappointed by the words that I should hear uttered by a person who called herself Mme de Guermantes, even if I had not been in love with her, it would not have sufficed that those words should be shrewd, beautiful and profound, they would have had to reflect that amaranthine colour of the closing syllable of her name, that colour which on first seeing her I had been disappointed not to find in her person and had fancied as having taken refuge in her mind. True, I had already heard Mme de Villeparisis and Saint-Loup, people whose intelligence was in no way extraordinary, pronounce quite casually this name Guermantes, simply as that of a person who was coming to see them or with whom they were going to dine, without seeming to feel that there were latent in her name the glow of yellowing woods and a whole mysterious tract of country. But this must have been an affectation on their part, as when the classic poets give us no warning of the profound intentions which they nevertheless had, an affectation which I myself also strove to imitate, saying in the most natural tone: "The Duchesse de Guermantes," as though it were a name that was just like other names. Besides, everyone declared that she was a highly intelligent woman, a witty conversationalist, living in a small circle of most interesting people: words which became accomplices of my dream. For when they spoke of an intelligent group, of witty talk, it was in no way intelligence as I knew it that I imagined, not even that of the greatest minds; it was not at all with men like Bergotte that I peopled this group. No, by intelligence I understood an ineffable faculty gilded by the sun, impregnated with a sylvan coolness. Indeed, had she made the most intelligent remarks (in the sense in which I understood the word when it was used of a philosopher or critic), Mme de Guermantes would perhaps have disappointed even more keenly my expectation of so special a faculty than if, in the course of a trivial conversation, she had confined herself to discussing cooking recipes or the furnishing of a country house, to mentioning the names of neighbours or relatives of hers, which would have given me a picture of her life.

"I thought I should find Basin here. He was meaning to come and see you to-day," said Mme de Guermantes to her aunt.

"I haven't set eyes on your husband for some days," replied Mme de Villeparisis in a somewhat nettled tone. "In fact, I haven't seen him—well, perhaps once—since that charming joke he played on me of having himself announced as the Queen of Sweden."

Mme de Guermantes formed a smile by contracting the corners of her mouth as though she were biting her veil.

"We met her at dinner last night at Blanche Leroi's. You wouldn't know her now, she's positively enormous. I'm sure she must be ill."

"I was just telling these gentlemen that you said she looked like a frog."

Mme de Guermantes emitted a sort of raucous noise which meant that she was laughing for form's sake.

"I don't remember making such a charming comparison, but if she was one before, now she's the frog that has succeeded in swelling to the size of the ox. Or rather, it isn't quite that, because all her swelling is concentrated in her stomach: she's more like a frog in an interesting condition."

"Ah, I do find that funny," said Mme de Villeparisis, secretly proud that her guests should be witnessing this display of her niece's wit.

"It is purely *arbitrary*, though," answered Mme de Guermantes, ironically detaching this selected epithet, as Swann would have done, "for I must admit I never saw a frog in the family way. Anyhow, the frog in question, who, by the way, does not require a king, for I never saw her so skittish as she's been since her husband died, is coming to dine with us one day next week. I promised I'd let you know just in case."

Mme de Villeparisis gave vent to an indistinct growl, from which emerged: "I know she was dining with the Mecklenburgs the night before last. Hannibal de Bréauté was there. He came and told me about it, quite amusingly, I must say."

"There was a man there who's a great deal wittier than Babal," said Mme de Guermantes who, intimate though she was with M. de Bréauté-Consalvi, felt the need to advertise the fact by the use of this diminutive. "I mean M. Bergotte."

I had never imagined that Bergotte could be regarded as witty; moreover, I thought of him always as part of the intellectual section of humanity, that is to say infinitely remote from that mysterious realm of which I had caught a glimpse through the purple hangings of a theatre box behind which, making the Duchess laugh, M. de Bréauté had been holding with her, in the language of the gods, that unimaginable thing, a conversation between people of the Faubourg Saint-Germain. I was distressed to see the balance upset and Bergotte rise above M. de Bréauté. But above all I was dismayed to think that I had avoided Bergotte on the evening of *Phèdre*, that I had not gone up and spoken to him, when I heard Mme de Guermantes, in whom one could always, as at the turn of a mental tide, see the flow of curiosity with regard to well-known intellectuals sweep over the ebb of her aristocratic snobbishness, say to Mme de Villeparisis: "He's the only person I have any wish to know. It would be such a pleasure."

The presence of Bergotte by my side, which it would have been so easy for me to secure but which I should have thought liable to give Mme de Guermantes a bad impression of me, would no doubt, on the contrary, have resulted in her signalling to me to join her in her box, and inviting me to bring the eminent writer to lunch one day.

"I gather that he didn't behave very well. He was presented to M. de Cobourg, and never uttered a word to him," Mme de Guermantes went on, dwelling on this odd fact as she might have recounted that a Chinese had blown his nose on a sheet of paper. "He never once said 'Your Royal Highness' to him," she added, with an air of amusement at this detail, as important to her mind as the refusal of a Protestant, during an audience with the Pope, to go on his knees before His Holiness.

Interested by these idiosyncrasies of Bergotte's, she did not, however, appear to consider them reprehensible, and seemed rather to give him credit for them, though she would have been hard put to it to say why. Despite this unusual mode of appreciating Bergotte's originality, it was a fact which I was later to regard as not wholly negligible that Mme de Guermantes, greatly to the surprise of many of her friends, considered Bergotte wittier than M. de Bréauté. Thus it is that such judgments, subversive, isolated, and yet after all right, are delivered in the world of society by those rare people who are superior to the rest. And they sketch then the first rough outlines of the hierarchy of values as the next generation will establish it, instead of abiding eternally by the old standards.

The Comte d'Argencourt, Chargé d'Affaires at the Belgian

Legation and a second cousin by marriage of Mme de Villeparisis, came in limping, followed presently by two young men,
the Baron de Guermantes and H. H. the Duc de Châtellerault,
whom Mme de Guermantes greeted with: "Good evening,
my dear Châtellerault," with a nonchalant air and without
moving from her pouf, for she was a great friend of the young
Duke's mother, which had given him a deep and lifelong respect for her. Tall, slim, with golden hair and skin, thoroughly
Guermantes in type, these two young men looked like a con-
densation of the light of the spring evening which was flooding
the spacious room. Following a custom which was the fashion
at that time, they laid their top hats on the floor beside them.
The historian of the Fronde assumed that they must be
embarrassed, like peasants coming into the mayor's office and
not knowing what to do with their hats. Feeling that he ought
in charity to come to the rescue of the awkwardness and
timidity which he ascribed to them:

"No, no," he said, "don't leave them on the floor, they'll
be trodden on."

A glance from the Baron de Guermantes, tilting the plane
of his pupils, shot suddenly from them a wave of pure and
piercing blue which froze the well-meaning historian.

"What is that person's name?" the Baron asked me, having
just been introduced to me by Mme de Villeparisis.

"M. Pierre," I whispered.

"Pierre what?"

"Pierre: it's his name, he's a very distinguished historian."

"Really? You don't say so."

"No, it's a new fashion with these young men to put their
hats on the floor," Mme de Villeparisis explained. "I'm like
you, I can never get used to it. Still, it's better than my nephew
Robert, who always leaves his in the hall. I tell him, when I see
him come in like that, that he looks just like a clockmaker, and
I ask him if he's come to wind the clocks."

"You were speaking just now, Madame la Marquise, of
M. Molé's hat; we shall soon be able, like Aristotle, to compile
a chapter on hats," said the historian of the Fronde, somewhat
reassured by Mme de Villeparisis's intervention, but in so faint
a voice that no one heard him except me.

"She really is astonishing, the little Duchess," said M. d'Argencourt, pointing to Mme de Guermantes who was talking to G——. "Whenever there's a prominent person in the room you're sure to find him sitting with her. Evidently that must be the lion of the party over there. It can't always be M. de Borelli, of course, or M. Schlumberger or M. d'Avenel. But then it's bound to be M. Pierre Loti or M. Edmond Rostand. Yesterday evening at the Doudeauvilles', where by the way she was looking splendid in her emerald tiara and a pink dress with a long train, she had M. Deschanel on one side and the German Ambassador on the other: she was holding forth to them about China. The general public, at a respectful distance where they couldn't hear what was being said, were wondering whether there wasn't going to be war. Really, you'd have said she was a queen holding her circle."

Everyone had gathered round Mme de Villeparisis to watch her painting.

"Those flowers are a truly celestial pink," said Legrandin, "I should say sky-pink. For there is such a thing as sky-pink just as there is sky-blue. But," he lowered his voice in the hope that he would not be heard by anyone but the Marquise, "I think I still plump for the silky, living flesh tint of your rendering of them. Ah, you leave Pisanello and Van Huysum a long way behind, with their laborious, dead herbals."

An artist, however modest, is always willing to hear himself preferred to his rivals, and tries only to see that justice is done them.

"What gives you that impression is that they painted flowers of their time which no longer exist, but they did it with great skill."

"Ah! Flowers of their time! That is a most ingenious theory," exclaimed Legrandin.

"I see you're painting some fine cherry blossoms—or are they mayflowers?" began the historian of the Fronde, in some doubt as to the flower, but with a note of confidence in his voice, for he was beginning to forget the incident of the hats.

"No, they're apple blossom," said the Duchesse de Guermantes, addressing her aunt.

"Ah! I see you're a good countrywoman like me; you can tell one flower from another."

"Why yes, so they are! But I thought the season for apple blossom was over now," hazarded the historian, to cover his mistake.

"Not at all; on the contrary it's not out yet; it won't be out for another fortnight, or three weeks perhaps," said the archivist who, since he helped with the management of Mme de Villeparisis's estates, was better informed upon country matters.

"Yes, even round Paris, where they're very far forward," put in the Duchess. "Down in Normandy, don't you know, at his father's place," she pointed to the young Duc de Châtellerault, "where they have some splendid apple trees close to the sea, like a Japanese screen, they're never really pink until after the twentieth of May."

"I never see them," said the young Duke, "because they give me hay fever. Such a bore."

"Hay fever? I never heard of that before," said the historian.

"It's the fashionable complaint just now," the archivist informed him.

"It all depends: you won't get it at all, probably, if it's a good year for apples. You know the Norman saying: 'When it's a good year for apples...'," put in M. d'Argencourt who, not being quite French, was always trying to give himself a Parisian air.

"You're quite right," Mme de Villeparisis said to her niece, "these are from the South. It was a florist who sent them round and asked me to accept them as a present. You're surprised, I dare say, Monsieur Vallenères," she turned to the archivist, "that a florist should make me a present of apple blossom. Well, I may be an old woman, but I'm not quite on the shelf yet, I still have a few friends," she went on with a smile that might have been taken as a sign of her simplicity but meant rather, I could not help feeling, that she thought it intriguing to pride herself on the friendship of a mere florist when she had such grand connexions.

Bloch rose and in his turn came over to look at the flowers which Mme de Villeparisis was painting.

"Never mind, Marquise," said the historian, sitting down

again, "even if we were to have another of those revolutions
which have stained so many pages of our history with blood—
and, upon my soul, in these days one can never tell," he added
with a circular and circumspect glance, as though to make sure
that there were no "dissidents" in the room, though he had
not the least suspicion that there actually were, "with a talent
like yours and your five languages you would be certain to
get on all right."

The historian of the Fronde was feeling quite refreshed, for
he had forgotten his insomnia. But he suddenly remembered
that he had not slept for six nights, whereupon a crushing
weariness, born of his mind, took hold of his legs and bowed
his shoulders, and his melancholy face began to droop like
an old man's.

Bloch wanted to express his admiration in an appropriate
gesture, but only succeeded in knocking over the glass containing the spray of apple blossom with his elbow, and all the
water was spilled on the carpet.

"You really have a fairy's touch," the historian said to the
Marquise; having his back turned to me at that moment, he
had not noticed Bloch's clumsiness.

But Bloch took the remark as a jibe at him, and to cover his
shame with a piece of insolence, retorted: "It's not of the
slightest importance; I'm not wet."

Mme de Villeparisis rang the bell and a footman came to
wipe the carpet and pick up the fragments of glass. She invited
the two young men to her theatricals, and also Mme de Guermantes, with the injunction:

"Remember to tell Gisèle and Berthe" (the Duchesses
d'Auberjon and de Portefin) "to be here a little before two to
help me," as she might have told hired waiters to come early
to arrange the tables.

She treated her princely relatives, as she treated M. de
Norpois, without any of the little courtesies which she showed
to the historian, Cottard, Bloch and myself, and they seemed
to have no interest for her beyond the possibility of serving
them up as food for our social curiosity. This was because she
knew that she need not put herself out to entertain people for
whom she was not a more or less brilliant woman but the

touchy old sister—who needed and received tactful handling—
of their father or uncle. There would have been no object in
her trying to shine in front of them; she could never have
deceived them as to the strength or weakness of her situation,
for they knew her whole story only too well and respected the
illustrious race from which she sprang. But, above all, they
had ceased to be anything more for her than a dead stock
that would never bear fruit again; they would never introduce
her to their new friends, or share their pleasures with her. She
could obtain from them only their occasional presence, or the
possibility of speaking of them, at her five o'clock receptions
as, later on, in her *Memoirs*, of which these receptions were
only a sort of rehearsal, a preliminary reading aloud of the
manuscript before a selected audience. And the society which
all these noble kinsmen and kinswomen served to interest, to
dazzle, to enthral, the society of the Cottards, of the Blochs,
of well-known dramatists, historians of the Fronde and such-
like, it was this society that, for Mme de Villeparisis—in the
absence of that section of the fashionable world which did not
go to her house—represented movement, novelty, entertainment and life; it was from people like these that she was able
to derive social advantages (which made it well worth her
while to let them meet, now and then, though without ever
getting to know her, the Duchesse de Guermantes): dinners
with remarkable men whose work had interested her, a light
opera or a pantomime staged complete by its author in her
drawing-room, boxes for interesting shows.

Bloch got up to go. He had said aloud that the incident of
the broken flower-glass was of no importance, but what he
said under his breath was different, more different still what he
thought: "If people can't train their servants to put vases
where they won't risk being knocked over and wetting and
even injuring their guests, they ought not to go in for such
luxuries," he muttered angrily. He was one of those susceptible, highly-strung persons who cannot bear to have made a
blunder which, though they do not admit it to themselves,
is enough to spoil their whole day. In a black rage, he was
just making up his mind never to go into society again. He
had reached the point at which some distraction was impera-

tive. Fortunately in a moment Mme de Villeparisis would press him to stay. Either because she was aware of the opinions of her friends and the rising tide of anti-semitism, or simply from absent-mindedness, she had not introduced him to any of the people in the room. He, however, being little used to society, felt that he ought to take leave of them all before going, out of good manners, but without warmth; he lowered his head several times, buried his bearded chin in his stiff collar, and scrutinised each of the party in turn through his glasses with a cold and peevish glare. But Mme de Villeparisis stopped him; she had still to discuss with him the little play which was to be performed in her house, and also she did not wish him to leave before he had had the satisfaction of meeting M. de Norpois (whose failure to appear surprised her), although as an inducement to Bloch this introduction was quite super-fluous, he having already decided to persuade the two actresses whose names he had mentioned to her to come and sing for nothing in the Marquise's drawing-room, in the interest of their careers, at one of those receptions to which the elite of Europe thronged. He had even offered in addition a tragic actress "with sea-green eyes, fair as Hera," who would recite lyrical prose with a sense of plastic beauty. But on hearing this lady's name Mme de Villeparisis had declined, for it was that of Saint-Loup's mistress.

"I have better news," she murmured in my ear. "I really believe it's on its last legs, and that before very long they'll have separated—in spite of an officer who has played an abominable part in the whole business," she added. (For Robert's family were beginning to look with a deadly hatred on M. de Borodino, who had given him leave, at the hair-dresser's instance, to go to Bruges, and accused him of giving countenance to an infamous liaison.) "He's a very bad man," said Mme de Villeparisis with that virtuous accent common to all the Guermantes, even the most depraved. "Very, very bad," she repeated, emphasising the word "very" and rolling the 'r's. One felt that she had no doubt of the Prince's being present at all their orgies. But, as kindness of heart was the old lady's dominant quality, her expression of frowning severity to-wards the horrible captain, whose name she articulated with an ironical emphasis: "The Prince de Borodino!"—as a woman for whom the Empire simply did not count—melted into a gentle smile at myself with a mechanical twitch of the eyelid indicating a vague connivance between us.

"I was quite fond of de Saint-Loup-en-Bray," said Bloch, "dirty dog though he is, because he's extremely well-bred. I have a great admiration for well-bred people, they're so rare," he went on, without realising, since he was himself so extremely ill-bred, how displeasing his words were. "I will give you an example which I consider most striking of his perfect breeding. I met him once with a young man just as he was about to spring into his wheelèd chariot, after he himself had buckled their splendid harness on a pair of steeds nourished with oats and barley, who had no need of the flashing whip to urge them on. He introduced us, but I did not catch the young man's name— one never does catch people's names when one's introduced to them," he added with a laugh, this being one of his father's witticisms. "De Saint-Loup-en-Bray remained perfectly natural, made no fuss about the young man, seemed absolutely at his ease. Well, I found out by pure chance a day or two later that the young man was the son of Sir Rufus Israels!"

The end of this story sounded less shocking than its preface, for it remained quite incomprehensible to everyone in the room. The fact was that Sir Rufus Israels, who seemed to Bloch and his father an almost royal personage before whom Saint-Loup ought to tremble, was in the eyes of the Guermantes world a foreign upstart, tolerated in society, on whose friendship nobody would ever have dreamed of priding himself—far from it.

"I learned this," said Bloch, "from Sir Rufus Israels' agent, who is a friend of my father and a quite remarkable man. Oh, an absolutely wonderful individual," he added with that affirmative energy, that note of enthusiasm which one puts only into convictions that do not originate from oneself.

"But tell me," Bloch asked me, lowering his voice, "how much money do you suppose Saint-Loup has? Not that it matters to me in the least, you quite understand. I'm interested from the Balzacian point of view. You don't happen to know what it's in, French stocks, foreign stocks, or land or what?"

I could give him no information whatsoever. Suddenly raising his voice, Bloch asked if he might open the windows, and without waiting for an answer, went across the room to do so. Mme de Villeparisis said that it was out of the question, as she had a cold. "Oh, well, if it's bad for you!" Bloch was downcast. "But you can't say it's not hot in here." And breaking into a laugh, he swept a glance round the room in an appeal for support against Mme de Villeparisis. He received none, from these well-bred people. His blazing eyes, having failed to seduce any of the other guests, resignedly reverted to their former gravity of expression. He acknowledged his defeat with: "What's the temperature? Twenty-two at least, I should say. Twenty-five? I'm not surprised. I'm simply dripping. And I have not, like the sage Antenor, son of the river Alpheus, the power to plunge myself in the paternal wave to staunch my sweat before laying my body in a bath of polished marble and anointing my limbs with fragrant oils." And with that need which people feel to outline for the benefit of others medical theories the application of which would be beneficial to their own health: "Well, if you believe it's good for you! I must say, I think the opposite. It's exactly what gives you your cold."

Bloch had expressed delight at the idea of meeting M. de Norpois. He would like, he said, to get him to talk about the Dreyfus case.

"There's a mentality at work there which I don't altogether understand, and it would be rather intriguing to have an interview with this eminent diplomat," he said in a sarcastic tone, so as not to appear to be rating himself below the Ambassador.

Mme de Villeparisis was sorry that he had said this so loud, but minded less when she saw that the archivist, whose strong Nationalist views kept her, so to speak, on a leash, was too far off to have overheard. She was more shocked to hear Bloch, led on by that demon of ill-breeding which made him permanently blind to the consequences of what he said, inquiring with a laugh at the paternal pleasantry:

"Haven't I read a learned treatise by him in which he sets forth a string of irrefutable arguments to prove that the Russo-Japanese war was bound to end in a Russian victory and a Japanese defeat? And isn't he a bit senile? I'm sure he's the old boy I've seen *taking aim* at his chair before sliding across the room to it, as if he was on casters."

"Good gracious, no!" the Marquise protested. "Just wait a minute. I don't know what he can be doing."

She rang the bell and, when the servant appeared, as she made no secret of, and indeed liked to advertise, the fact that her old friend spent the greater part of his time in her house: "Go and tell M. de Norpois to come," she ordered. "He's sorting some papers in my library; he said he would be twenty minutes, and I've been waiting now for an hour and three-quarters. He'll talk to you about the Dreyfus case, or anything else you like," she said grumpily to Bloch. "He doesn't much approve of what's happening."

For M. de Norpois was not on good terms with the Government of the day, and Mme de Villeparisis, although he had never taken the liberty of bringing any governmental personalities to her house (she still preserved all the unapproachable dignity of a great lady of the aristocracy and remained outside and above the political relations which he was obliged to cultivate), was kept well informed by him of everything that went on. Equally, these politicians of the present regime would never have dared to ask M. de Norpois to introduce them to Mme de Villeparisis. But several of them had gone down to see him at her house in the country when they needed his advice or help at critical junctures. They knew the address. They went to the house. They did not see its mistress. But at dinner that evening she would say: "I hear they've been down here bothering you. I trust things are going better."

"You're not in a hurry?" she now asked Bloch.

"No, not at all. I was thinking of going because I'm not very well; in fact there's a possibility of my taking a cure at Vichy for my gall bladder," he explained, articulating these words with a fiendish irony.

"Why, that's just where my nephew Châtellerault's got to go. You must fix it up together. Is he still here? He's a nice boy, you know," said Mme de Villeparisis, sincerely perhaps, thinking that two people whom she knew had no reason not to be friends with each other.

"Oh, I dare say he wouldn't care about that—I don't . . . I scarcely know him. He's over there," stammered Bloch, overwhelmed with delight.

The butler had evidently failed to deliver his mistress's message properly, for M. de Norpois, to give the impression that he had just come in from the street and had not yet seen his hostess, had picked up the first hat that he found in the vestibule, one which I thought I recognised, and came forward to kiss Mme de Villeparisis's hand with great ceremony, asking after her health with all the interest that people show after a long separation. He was not aware that the Marquise had removed in advance any semblance of verisimilitude from this charade, which indeed she eventually cut short by introducing him to Bloch. The latter, who had observed all the polite attentions that were being shown to a person whom he had not yet discovered to be M. de Norpois, and the formal, gracious, deep bows with which the Ambassador replied to them, evidently felt inferior to all this ceremonial and vexed to think that it would never be addressed to him, and said to me in order to appear at ease: "Who is that old idiot?" Perhaps, too, all this bowing and scraping by M. de Norpois had really shocked the better element in Bloch's nature, the freer and more straightforward manners of a younger generation, and he was partly sincere in condemning it as absurd. However that might be, it ceased to appear absurd and indeed delighted him the moment it was himself, Bloch, to whom the salutations were addressed.

"Monsieur l'Ambassadeur," said Mme de Villeparisis, "I should like you to meet this gentleman. Monsieur Bloch, Monsieur le Marquis de Norpois." She made a point, in spite of the way she bullied M. de Norpois, of addressing him always as "Monsieur l'Ambassadeur," as a point of etiquette as well as from an exaggerated respect for his ambassadorial rank, a respect which the Marquis had inculcated in her, and also with the intention of applying that less familiar, more ceremonious posture towards one particular man which, in the salon of a distinguished woman, in contrast to the freedom with which she treats her other regular guests, marks that man out instantly as her lover.

M. de Norpois sank his azure gaze in his white beard, bent
his tall body deep down as though he were bowing before all
the renowned and imposing connotations of the name Bloch,
and murmured: "I'm delighted . . ." whereat his young interlocutor, moved, but feeling that the illustrious diplomat was
going too far, hastened to correct him, saying: "Not at all!
On the contrary, it is I who am delighted." But this ceremony,
which M. de Norpois, out of friendship for Mme de Villeparisis, repeated for the benefit of every new person that his
old friend introduced to him, did not seem to her adequate to
the deserts of Bloch, to whom she said:

"Just ask him anything you want to know. Take him aside
if it's more convenient; he will be delighted to talk to you. I
think you wished to speak to him about the Dreyfus case,"
she went on, no more considering whether this would be
agreeable to M. de Norpois than she would have thought of
asking leave of the Duchesse de Montmorency's portrait
before having it lighted up for the historian, or of the tea
before offering a cup of it.

"You must speak loud," she warned Bloch, "he's a little
deaf, but he will tell you anything you want to know; he
knew Bismarck very well, and Cavour. That is so, isn't it?"
she raised her voice, "you knew Bismarck well."

"Have you got anything on the stocks?" M. de Norpois
asked me with a knowing air as he shook my hand warmly.
I took the opportunity to relieve him politely of the hat which
he had felt obliged to bring ceremonially into the room, for
I saw that it was my own which he had picked up at random.
"You showed me a somewhat laboured little thing in which
you went in for a good deal of hair-splitting. I gave you my
frank opinion; what you had written was not worth the trouble
of putting on paper. Are you preparing something for us?
You were greatly smitten with Bergotte, if I remember
rightly." "You're not to say anything against Bergotte," put
in the Duchess. "I don't dispute his pictorial talent; no one
would, Duchess. He understands all about etching and engraving, if not brush-work on a large canvas like M. Cher-
buliez. But it seems to me that in these days there is a tendency
to mix up the genres and forget that the novelist's business

is rather to weave a plot and edify his readers than to fiddle away at producing a frontispiece or tailpiece in drypoint. I shall be seeing your father on Sunday at our good friend A. J.'s," he went on, turning again to me.

I had hoped for a moment, when I saw him talking to Mme de Guermantes, that he would perhaps afford me, for getting myself asked to her house, the help he had refused me for getting to Mme Swann's. "Another of my great favourites," I told him, "is Elstir. It seems the Duchesse de Guermantes has some wonderful examples of his work, particularly that admirable *Bunch of Radishes* which I remember at the Exhibition and should so much like to see again; what a masterpiece it is!" And indeed, if I had been a prominent person and had been asked to state what picture I liked best, I should have named this *Bunch of Radishes*.

"A masterpiece?" cried M. de Norpois with a surprised and reproachful air. "It makes no pretence of being even a picture, it's merely a sketch." (He was right.) "If you label a clever little thing of that sort 'masterpiece,' what will you say about Hébert's *Virgin* or Dagnan-Bouveret?"

"I heard you refusing to have Robert's woman," said Mme de Guermantes to her aunt, after Bloch had taken the Ambassador aside. "I don't think you'll miss much: she's a perfect horror, you know, without a vestige of talent, and besides she's grotesquely ugly."

"Do you mean to say you know her, Duchess?" asked M. d'Argencourt.

"Yes, didn't you know that she performed in my house before anyone else's—not that that's anything to be proud of," replied Mme de Guermantes with a laugh, glad nevertheless, since the actress was under discussion, to let it be known that she herself had had the first taste of her absurdities. "Hallo, I suppose I ought to go now," she added, without moving.

She had just seen her husband enter the room, and these words were an allusion to the absurdity of their appearing to be paying a call together like a newly married couple, rather than to the often strained relations that existed between her and the strapping individual she had married, who, despite his advancing years, still led the life of a gay bachelor. Casting over the considerable party that was gathered round the tea-table the genial, cynical gaze—dazzled a little by the slanting rays of the setting sun—of the little round pupils lodged in the exact centre of his eyes, like the "bulls" which the excellent marksman that he was could always hit with such perfect aim and precision, the Duke advanced with a wondering, gingerly deliberation as though, alarmed by so brilliant a gathering, he was afraid of treading on ladies' skirts and interrupting conversations. A permanent smile suggesting a slightly tipsy "Good King Wenceslas," and a half-open hand floating like a shark's fin by his side, which he allowed to be clasped indiscriminately by his old friends and by the strangers who were introduced to him, enabled him, without having to make a single movement, or to interrupt his genial, lazy, royal progress, to reward the alacrity of them all by simply murmuring: "How do, my boy; how do, my dear fellow; charmed, Monsieur Bloch; how do, Argencourt"; and, on coming to myself, who was the most favoured of all when he had been told my name: "How do, young neighbour, how's your father? What an admirable man!" He made no great demonstration except to Mme de Villeparisis, who greeted him with a nod of her head, drawing one hand from a pocket of her little apron.

Being formidably rich in a world where people were becoming steadily less so, and having adapted himself long since to the idea of this enormous fortune, he had all the vanity of the great nobleman combined with that of the man of means, the refinement and breeding of the former only just managing to counterbalance the smugness of the latter. One could understand, moreover, that his success with women, which made his wife so unhappy, was not due merely to his name and his wealth, for he was still remarkably handsome, and his profile retained the purity, the firmness of outline of a Greek god's.

"Do you mean to tell me she performed in your house?" M. d'Argencourt asked the Duchess.

"Well, you know, she came to recite, with a bunch of lilies in her hand, and more lilies on her *dwess*." (Mme de Guermantes shared her aunt's affectation of pronouncing certain words in an exceedingly rustic fashion, though she never rolled her 'r's like Mme de Villeparisis.)

Before M. de Norpois, under constraint from his hostess, had taken Bloch into the little recess where they could talk more freely, I went up to the old diplomat for a moment and put in a word about my father's academic chair. He tried first of all to postpone the conversation to another day. I pointed out that I was going to Balbec. "What? Going to Balbec again? Why, you're a regular *globe-trotter*." Then he listened to what I had to say. At the name of Leroy-Beaulieu, he looked at me suspiciously. I conjectured that he had perhaps said something disparaging to M. Leroy-Beaulieu about my father and was afraid that the economist might have repeated it to him. All at once he seemed to be filled with a positive affection for my father. And after one of those decelerations in the flow of speech out of which suddenly a word explodes as though in spite of the speaker, whose irresistible conviction overcomes his stuttering efforts at silence: "No, no," he said to me with emotion, "your father *must not* stand. In his own interest he must not, for his own sake, out of respect for his merits, which are great, and which would be compromised by such an adventure. He is too big a man for that. If he were elected, he would have everything to lose and nothing to gain. He is not an orator, thank heaven. And that is the one thing that counts with my dear colleagues, even if you only talk platitudes. Your father has an important goal in life; he should march straight ahead towards it, and not beat about the bush, even the bushes (more thorny than flowery) of the groves of Academe. Besides, he would not get many votes. The Academy likes to keep a postulant waiting for some time before taking him to its bosom. For the present, there is nothing to be done. Later on, I can't say. But he must wait until the Society itself comes to seek him out. It observes with more fetishism than success the maxim *Fara da sè* of our friends across the Alps. Leroy-Beaulieu spoke to me about it all in a way I found highly displeasing. I should have said at a guess that he was hand in glove with your father? . . . I pointed out to him, a little sharply perhaps, that a man accustomed as he is to dealing with textiles and metals could not be expected to understand the part played by the imponderables, as Bismarck used to say. But, whatever happens, your father must on no account put himself forward as a candidate. *Principiis obsta.* His friends would find themselves placed in a delicate position if he presented them with a *fait accompli.* Indeed," he went on brusquely with an air of candour, fixing his blue eyes on my face, "I am going to tell you something that will surprise you coming from me, who am so fond of your father. Well, precisely because I am fond of him (we are known as the inseparables—*Arcades ambo*), precisely because I know the immense service that he can still render to his country, the reefs from which he can steer her if he remains at the helm; out of affection, out of high regard for him, out of patriotism, I would not vote for him. I fancy, moreover, that I have given him to understand that I wouldn't." (I seemed to discern in his eyes the stern Assyrian profile of Leroy-Beaulieu.) "So that to give him my vote now would be a sort of recantation on my part." M. de Norpois repeatedly dismissed his brother Academicians as old fossils. Other reasons apart, every member of a club or academy likes to ascribe to his fellow members the type of character that is the direct converse of his own, less for the advantage of being able to say: "Ah! if it only rested with me!" than for the satisfaction of making the honour which he himself has managed to secure seem less accessible, a greater distinction. "I may tell you," he concluded, "that in the best interests of you all, I should prefer to see your father triumphantly elected in ten or fifteen years' time." Words which I assumed to have been dictated, if not by jealousy, at any rate by an utter lack of willingness to oblige, and which were later, in the event, to acquire a different meaning.

"You haven't thought of giving the *Institut* an address on the price of bread during the Fronde, I suppose," the historian of that movement timidly inquired of M. de Norpois. "It might be an enormous success" (which was to say, "give me a colossal advertisement"), he added, smiling at the Ambassador with an obsequious tenderness which made him raise his eyelids and reveal eyes as wide as the sky. I seemed to have seen this look before, though I had met the historian for the first time this afternoon. Suddenly I remembered having seen the same expression in the eyes of a Brazilian doctor who claimed to be able to cure breathless spasms of the kind from which I suffered by absurd inhalations of plant essences. When, in the hope that he would pay more attention to my case, I had told him that I knew Professor Cottard, he had replied, as though speaking in Cottard's interest: "Now this treatment of mine, if you were to tell him about it, would give him the material for a most sensational paper for the Academy of Medicine!" He had not ventured to press the matter but had stood gazing at me with the same air of interrogation, timid, suppliant and self-seeking, which I had just wonderingly observed on the face of the historian of the Fronde. Obviously the two men were not acquainted and had little or nothing in common, but psychological laws, like physical laws, have a more or less general application. And if the requisite conditions are the same, an identical expression lights up the eyes of different human animals, as an identical sunrise lights up places that are a long way apart and that have no connexion with one another. I did not hear the Ambassador's reply, for the whole party, with a good deal of commotion, had again gathered round Mme de Villeparisis to watch her at work.

"You know who we're talking about, Basin?" the Duchess asked her husband.

"I can make a pretty good guess," said the Duke. "As an actress she's not, I'm afraid, in what one would call the great tradition."

"You can't imagine anything more ridiculous," went on Mme de Guermantes to M. d'Argencourt.

"In fact, it was drolatic," put in M. de Guermantes, whose odd vocabulary enabled society people to declare that he was no fool and literary people, at the same time, to regard him as a complete imbecile.

"What I fail to understand," resumed the Duchess, "is how in the world Robert ever came to fall in love with her. Oh, of course I know one must never discuss that sort of thing," she added, with the charming pout of a philosopher and senti-mentalist whose last illusion had long been shattered. "I know that anybody may fall in love with anybody else. And," she went on, for, though she might still make fun of modern literature, it had to some extent seeped into her, either through popularisation in the press or through certain conversations, "that is the really nice thing about love, because it's what makes it so 'mysterious.'"

"Mysterious! Oh, I must say, cousin, that's a bit beyond me," said the Comte d'Argencourt.

"Oh dear, yes, it's a very mysterious thing, love," declared the Duchess, with the sweet smile of a good-natured woman of the world, but also with the uncompromising conviction with which a Wagnerian assures a clubman that there is something more than just noise in the *Walküre*. "After all, one never does know what makes one person fall in love with another; it may not be at all what we think," she added with a smile, repudiating at once by this interpretation the idea she had just put forward. "After all, one never knows anything, does one?" she concluded with an air of weary scepticism. "So you see it's wiser never to discuss other people's choices in love."

But having laid down this principle she proceeded at once to violate it by criticising Saint-Loup's choice.

"All the same, don't you know, it's amazing to me that people can find any attraction in a ridiculous person."

Bloch, hearing Saint-Loup's name mentioned and gathering that he was in Paris, began to slander him so outrageously that everybody was shocked. He was beginning to nourish hatreds, and one felt that he would stop at nothing to gratify them. Having established the principle that he himself was of great moral integrity and that the sort of people who frequented La Boulie (a sporting club which he supposed to be highly fashionable) deserved penal servitude, he regarded every injury he could do to them as praiseworthy. He once went so far as to threaten to bring a lawsuit against one of his La Boulie friends. In the course of the trial he proposed to give certain evidence which would be entirely false, though the defendant would be unable to disprove it. In this way Bloch (who never in fact put his plan into action) counted on tormenting and alarming him still further. What harm could there be in that, since the man he sought to injure was a man who was interested only in fashion, a La Boulie man, and against people like that any weapon was justified, especially in the hands of a saint such as Bloch himself?

"I say, though, what about Swann?" objected M. d'Argencourt, who having at last succeeded in grasping the point of his cousin's remarks, was impressed by their shrewdness and was racking his brains for instances of men who had fallen in love with women in whom he himself would have seen no attraction.

"Oh, but Swann's case was quite different," the Duchess protested. "It was a great surprise, I admit, because she was a bit of an idiot, but she was never ridiculous, and she was at one time pretty."

"Oh, oh!" muttered Mme de Villeparisis.

"You never thought so? Surely, she had some charming points, very fine eyes, good hair, and she used to dress and still dresses wonderfully. Nowadays, I quite agree, she's unspeakable, but she has been a lovely woman in her time. Not that that made me any less sorry when Charles married her, because it was so unnecessary."

The Duchess had not intended to say anything out of the common, but as M. d'Argencourt began to laugh she repeated these last words—either because she thought them amusing or because she thought it nice of him to laugh—and looked up at him with a coy smile, to add the enchantment of her femininity to that of her wit. She went on:

"Yes, really, it wasn't worth the trouble, was it? Still, after all, she did have some charm and I can quite understand why people might fall for her, but if you saw Robert's young lady, I assure you you'd simply die laughing. Oh, I know somebody's going to quote Augier at me: 'What matters the bottle so long as one gets drunk?'[14] Well, Robert may have got drunk all right, but he certainly hasn't shown much taste in his choice of a bottle! First of all, would you believe it, she actually expected me to fit up a staircase right in the middle of my drawing-room. Oh, a mere nothing—what?—and she announced that she was going to lie flat on her stomach on the steps. And then, if you'd heard the things she recited! I only remember one scene, but I'm sure nobody could imagine anything like it: it was called *The Seven Princesses*."

"*Seven Princesses*! Dear, dear, what a snob she must be!" cried M. d'Argencourt. "But, wait a minute, why, I know the whole play. The author sent a copy to the King, who couldn't understand a word of it and called on me to explain it to him."

"It isn't, by any chance, by Sâr Péladan?" asked the historian of the Fronde, meaning to make a subtle and topical illusion, but in such a low voice that his question passed unnoticed.

"So you know *The Seven Princesses*, do you?" said the Duchess. "I congratulate you! I only know one, but she's quite enough; I have no wish to make the acquaintance of the other six. If they're all like the one I've seen!"

"What a goose!" I thought to myself, irritated by her icy greeting. I found a sort of bitter satisfaction in this proof of her total incomprehension of Maeterlinck. "To think that's the woman I walk miles every morning to see. Really, I'm too kind. Well, it's my turn now to ignore her." Those were the words I said to myself, but they were the opposite of what I thought; they were purely conversational words such as we say to ourselves at those moments when, too excited to remain quietly alone with ourselves, we feel the need, for want of another listener, to talk to ourselves, without meaning what we say, as we talk to a stranger.

"I can't tell you what it was like," the Duchess went on. "It was enough to make you howl with laughter. Most people did, rather too much, I'm sorry to say, for the young person was not at all pleased and Robert has never really forgiven me. Though I can't say I'm sorry, actually, because if it had been a success the lady would perhaps have come again, and I don't think Marie-Aynard would have been exactly thrilled."

Marie-Aynard was the name given in the family to Robert's mother, Mme de Marsantes, the widow of Aynard de Saint-Loup, to distinguish her from her cousin, the Princesse de Guermantes-Bavière, also a Marie, to whose Christian name her nephews and cousins and brothers-in-law added, to avoid confusion, either that of her husband or another of her own, making her Marie-Gilbert or Marie-Hedwige.

"To begin with, there was a sort of rehearsal the night before, which was a wonderful affair!" went on Mme de Guermantes in ironical pursuit of her theme. "Just imagine, she uttered a sentence, no, not so much, not a quarter of a sentence, and then she stopped; after which she didn't open her mouth—I'm not exaggerating—for a good five minutes."

"Oh, I say," cried M. d'Argencourt.

"With the utmost politeness I took the liberty of suggesting to her that this might seem a little unusual. And she said—I give you her actual words—'One ought always to recite a thing as though one were just composing it oneself.' It's really monumental, that reply, when you come to think of it!"

"But I understood she wasn't at all bad at reciting poetry," said one of the two young men.

"She hasn't the ghost of a notion what poetry is," replied Mme de Guermantes. "However, I didn't need to listen to her to tell that. It was quite enough to see her arriving with her lilies. I knew at once that she couldn't have any talent when I saw those lilies!"

Everybody laughed.

"I hope, my dear aunt, you weren't annoyed by my little joke the other day about the Queen of Sweden. I've come to ask your forgiveness."

"Oh, no, I'm not at all angry, I even give you leave to eat at my table, if you're hungry.—Come along, M. Vallenères, you're the daughter of the house," Mme de Villeparisis went on to the archivist, repeating a time-honoured pleasantry.

M. de Guermantes sat up in the armchair into which he had sunk, his hat on the carpet by his side, and examined with a satisfied smile the plate of cakes that was being held out to him.

"Why, certainly, now that I'm beginning to feel at home in this distinguished company, I will take a sponge-cake; they look excellent."

"This gentleman makes you an admirable daughter," commented M. d'Argencourt, whom the spirit of imitation prompted to keep Mme de Villeparisis's little joke in circulation.

The archivist handed the plate of cakes to the historian of the Fronde.

"You perform your functions admirably," said the latter, startled into speech, and hoping also to win the sympathy of the crowd. At the same time he cast a covert glance of connivance at those who had anticipated him.

"Tell me, my dear aunt," M. de Guermantes inquired of

Mme de Villeparisis, "who was that rather handsome-looking gentleman who was leaving just now as I came in? I must know him, because he gave me a sweeping bow, but I couldn't place him at all; you know I never can remember names, it's such a nuisance," he added with a self-satisfied air.

"M. Legrandin."

"Oh, but Oriane has a cousin whose mother, if I'm not mistaken, was a Grandin. Yes, I remember quite well, she was a Grandin de l'Eprevier."

"No," replied Mme de Villeparisis, "no relation at all. These are plain Grandins. Grandins of nothing at all. But they'd be only too glad to be Grandins of anything you choose to name. This one has a sister called Mme de Cambremer."

"Why, Basin, you know quite well who my aunt means," cried the Duchess indignantly. "He's the brother of that great graminivorous creature you had the weird idea of sending to call on me the other day. She stayed a solid hour; I thought I'd go mad. But I began by thinking it was she who was mad when I saw a person I didn't know come browsing into the room looking exactly like a cow."

"Look here, Oriane; she asked me what afternoon you were at home; I couldn't very well be rude to her; and besides, you do exaggerate so, she's not in the least like a cow," he added in a plaintive tone, though not without a furtive smiling glance round the audience.

He knew that his wife's conversational zest needed the stimulus of contradiction, the contradiction of common sense which protests that one cannot, for instance, mistake a woman for a cow. It was in this way that Mme de Guermantes, improving on a preliminary notion, had been inspired to produce many of her wittiest sallies. And the Duke would come forward with feigned naïvety to help her to bring off her effects, like the unacknowledged partner of a three-card trickster in a railway carriage.

"I admit she doesn't look like *a* cow, she looks like several," exclaimed Mme de Guermantes. "I assure you, I didn't know what to do when I saw a herd of cattle come marching into my drawing-room in a hat and asking me how I was. I had half a mind to say: 'Please, herd of cattle, you must be making a mistake, you can't possibly know me, because you're a herd of cattle,' but after racking my brains I came to the conclusion that your Cambremer woman must be the Infanta Dorothea, who had said she was coming to see me one day and who is rather bovine too, so that I was just on the point of saying 'Your Royal Highness' and using the third person to a herd of cattle. She's also got the same sort of dewlap as the Queen of Sweden. But actually this mass attack had been prepared for by long-range artillery fire, according to all the rules of war. For I don't know how long before, I was bombarded with her cards; I used to find them lying about all over the house, on all the tables and chairs, like prospectuses. I couldn't think what they were supposed to be advertising. You saw nothing in the house but 'Marquise et Marquis de Cambremer' with some address or other which I've forgotten and which you may be quite sure I shall never make use of."

"But it's very flattering to be taken for a queen," said the historian of the Fronde.

"Gad, sir, kings and queens don't amount to much these days," said M. de Guermantes, partly because he liked to be thought broad-minded and modern, and also so as not to seem to attach any importance to his own royal connections, which he valued highly.

Bloch and M. de Norpois had risen and were now in our vicinity.

"Well, Monsieur," asked Mme de Villeparisis, "have you been talking to him about the Dreyfus case?"

M. de Norpois raised his eyes to the ceiling, but with a smile, as though calling on heaven to witness the enormity of the whims to which his Dulcinea compelled him to submit. Nevertheless he spoke to Bloch with great affability of the terrible, perhaps fatal period through which France was passing. As this presumably meant that M. de Norpois (to whom Bloch had confessed his belief in the innocence of Dreyfus) was an ardent anti-Dreyfusard, the Ambassador's geniality, his air of tacit admission that his interlocutor was in the right, of never doubting that they were both of the same opinion, of joining forces with him to denounce the Government, flattered Bloch's vanity and aroused his curiosity. What were the important points which M. de Norpois never specified but on which he seemed implicitly to affirm that he was in agreement with Bloch? What opinion did he hold of the case that could bring them together? Bloch was all the more astonished at the mysterious unanimity which seemed to exist between him and M. de Norpois, in that it was not confined to politics, Mme de Villeparisis having spoken at some length to M. de Norpois of Bloch's literary work.

"You are not of your age," the former Ambassador told him, "and I congratulate you upon that. You are not of this age in which disinterested work no longer exists, in which writers offer the public nothing but obscenities or inanities. Efforts such as yours ought to be encouraged, and would be if we had a Government."

Bloch was flattered by this picture of himself swimming alone amid a universal shipwreck. But here again he would have been glad of details, would have liked to know what were the inanities to which M. de Norpois referred. Bloch had the feeling that he was working along the same lines as plenty of others; he had never supposed himself to be so exceptional. He returned to the Dreyfus case, but did not succeed in elucidating M. de Norpois's own views. He tried to induce him to speak of the officers whose names were appearing constantly in the newspapers at that time; they aroused more curiosity than the politicians who were involved in the affair, because they were not, like the politicians, well known already, but, wearing a special garb, emerging from the obscurity of a different kind of life and a religiously guarded silence, had only just appeared on the scene and spoken, like Lohengrin landing from a skiff drawn by a swan. Bloch had been able, thanks to a Nationalist lawyer of his acquaintance, to secure admission to several hearings of the Zola trial. He would arrive there in the morning and stay until the court rose, with a supply of sandwiches and a flask of coffee, as though for the final examination for a degree, and this change of routine stimulating a nervous excitement which the coffee and the emotional interest of the trial worked up to a climax, he would come away so enamoured of everything that had happened in court that when he returned home in the evening he longed to immerse himself again in the thrilling drama and would hurry out to a restaurant frequented by both parties in search of friends with whom he would go over the day's proceedings interminably and make up, by a supper ordered in an imperious tone which gave him the illusion of power, for the hunger and exhaustion of a day begun so early and unbroken by any interval for lunch. The human mind, hovering perpetually between the two planes of experience and imagination, seeks to fathom the ideal life of the people it knows and to know the people whose life it has had to imagine. To Bloch's questions M. de Norpois replied:

"There are two officers in the case now being tried of whom I remember hearing some time ago from a man whose judgment inspired me with the greatest confidence, and who had a high opinion of them both—I mean M. de Miribel. They are Lieutenant-Colonel Henry and Lieutenant-Colonel Picquart."

"But," exclaimed Bloch, "the divine Athena, daughter of Zeus, has put in the mind of one the opposite of what is in the mind of the other. And they are fighting against one another like two lions. Colonel Picquart had a splendid position in the Army, but his *Moira* has led him to the side that was not rightly his. The sword of the Nationalists will carve his tender flesh, and he will be cast out as food for the beasts of prey and the birds that wax fat upon the bodies of dead men."

M. de Norpois made no reply.

"What are those two palavering about over there?" M. de Guermantes asked Mme de Villeparisis, pointing to M. de Norpois and Bloch.

"The Dreyfus case."

"The devil they are. By the way, do you know who is a rabid supporter of Dreyfus? I give you a thousand guesses. My nephew Robert! I can tell you that when they heard of his goings on at the Jockey there was a fine gathering of the clans, a regular hue and cry. And as he's coming up for election next week . . ."

"Of course," broke in the Duchess, "if they're all like Gilbert, who's always maintained that all the Jews ought to be sent back to Jerusalem . . ."

"Ah! then the Prince de Guermantes is quite of my way of thinking," put in M. d'Argencourt.

The Duke showed off his wife, but did not love her. Extremely self-important, he hated to be interrupted, and was moreover in the habit of being rude to her at home. Quivering with the twofold rage of a bad husband when his wife speaks to him, and a glib talker when he is not listened to, he stopped short and transfixed the Duchess with a glare which made everyone feel uncomfortable.

"What makes you think we want to hear about Gilbert and Jerusalem?" he said at last. "That's got nothing to do with it. But," he went on in a gentler tone, "you must admit that if one of our family were to be pilled at the Jockey, especially Robert whose father was president for ten years, it would be a fine kettle of fish. What do you expect, my dear, it's got 'em on the raw, those fellows; can't get over it. I don't blame them, either; personally, you know that I have no racial prejudice, all that sort of thing seems to me out of date, and I do claim to move with the times; but damn it all, when one goes by the name of 'Marquis de Saint-Loup' one isn't a Dreyfusard. I'm sorry, but there it is."

M. de Guermantes uttered the words "when one goes by the name of Marquis de Saint-Loup" with some emphasis. And yet he knew very well that it was a far greater thing to go by that of Duc de Guermantes. But if his self-esteem had a tendency to exaggerate if anything the superiority of the title Duc de Guermantes over all others, it was perhaps not so much the rules of good taste as the laws of imagination that prompted him thus to diminish it. Each of us sees in brighter colours what he sees at a distance, what he sees in other people. For the general laws which govern perspective in imagination apply just as much to dukes as to ordinary mortals. And not only the laws of imagination, but those of speech. Now, one or other of two laws of speech might apply here. One of them demands that we should express ourselves like others of our mental category and not of our caste. Under this law M. de Guermantes might, in his choice of expressions, even when he wished to talk about the nobility, be indebted to the humblest little tradesman, who would have said: "When one goes by the name of Duc de Guermantes," whereas an educated man, a Swann, a Legrandin, would not have said it. A duke may write novels worthy of a grocer, even about life in high society, titles and pedigrees being of no help to him there, and the writings of a plebeian may deserve the epithet "aristocratic." Who in this instance had been the inferior from whom M. de Guermantes had picked up "when one goes by the name," he had probably not the least idea. But another law of speech is that, from time to time, as diseases appear and then vanish of which nothing more is ever heard, there come into being, no one knows how, spontaneously perhaps or by an accident like that which introduced into France a certain weed from America the seeds of which, caught in the wool of a travelling rug, fell on a railway embankment, modes of expression which one hears in the same decade on the lips of people who have not in any way combined together to that end. So, just as in a certain year I heard Bloch say, referring to himself, that "the most charming people, the most brilliant, the best known, the most exclusive had discovered that there was only one man in Paris whom they felt to be intelligent and agreeable, whom they could not do without—namely Bloch," and heard the same remark used by countless other young men who did not know him and varied it only by substituting their own names for his, so I was often to hear this "when one goes by the name."

"What do you expect," the Duke went on, "with the attitude he's adopted, it's fairly understandable."

"It's more comic than anything else," said the Duchess, "when you think of his mother's attitude, how she bores us to tears with her *Patrie française*, morning, noon and night."

"Yes, but there's not only his mother to be thought of, you can't humbug us like that. There's a wench, too, a fly-by-night of the worst type; she has far more influence over him than his mother, and she happens to be a compatriot of Master Dreyfus. She has infected Robert with her way of thinking."

"You may not have heard, Duke, that there is a new word to describe that sort of attitude," said the archivist, who was Secretary to the Antirevisionist Committee. "One says

'mentality.' It means exactly the same thing, but it has
the advantage that nobody knows what you're talking
about. It's the *ne plus ultra* just now, the 'latest thing,' as they
say."

Meanwhile, having heard Bloch's name, he watched him
question M. de Norpois with misgivings which aroused others
as strong though of a different order in the Marquise. Trembling before the archivist, and always acting the anti-Dreyfusard
in his presence, she dreaded what he would say were he to find
out that she had asked to her house a Jew more or less affiliated
to the "Syndicate."[15]

"Indeed," said the Duke, " 'mentality,' you say. I must
make a note of that and trot it out one of these days." (This
was no figure of speech, the Duke having a little pocket-
book filled with "quotations" which he used to consult before
dinner-parties). "I like 'mentality.' There are a lot of new words
like that which people suddenly start using, but they never
last. Some time ago I read that a writer was 'talentuous.'
Damned if I know what it means. And since then I've never
come across the word again."

"But 'mentality' is more widely used than 'talentuous,' "
the historian of the Fronde put in his oar. "I'm on a committee
at the Ministry of Education where I've heard it used several
times, as well as at my club, the Volney, and even at dinner at
M. Emile Ollivier's."

"I who have not the honour to belong to the Ministry of
Education," replied the Duke with a feigned humility but
with a vanity so intense that his lips could not refrain from
curving in a smile, nor his eyes from casting round his audience
a glance sparkling with joy, the ironical scorn in which made
the poor historian blush, "I who have not the honour to belong to the Ministry of Education," he repeated, relishing the
sound of his own voice, "nor to the Volney Club. My only
clubs are the Union and the Jockey—you aren't in the Jockey,
I think, sir?" he asked the historian, who, scenting an insult
and failing to understand it, began to tremble in every limb.
"I who am not even invited to dine with M. Emile Ollivier,
I must confess that I had never heard 'mentality.' I'm sure
you're in the same boat, Argencourt . . . You know," he went

on, "why they can't produce the proofs of Dreyfus's guilt. Apparently it's because the War Minister's wife was his mistress, that's what people are saying on the sly."

"Ah! I thought it was the Prime Minister's wife," said M. d'Argencourt.

"I think you're all equally tiresome about this wretched case," said the Duchesse de Guermantes, who, in the social sphere, was always anxious to show that she did not allow herself to be led by anyone. "It can't make any difference to me so far as the Jews are concerned, for the simple reason that I don't know any of them and I intend to remain in that state of blissful ignorance. But on the other hand I do think it perfectly intolerable that just because they're supposed to be right-thinking and don't deal with Jewish tradesmen, or have 'Down with the Jews' written on their sunshades, we should have a swarm of Durands and Dubois and so forth, women we should never have known but for this business, forced down our throats by Marie-Aynard or Victurnienne. I went to see Marie-Aynard a couple of days ago. It used to be so nice there. Nowadays one finds all the people one has spent one's life trying to avoid, on the pretext that they're against Dreyfus, and others of whom you have no idea who they can be."

"No, it was the War Minister's wife; at least, that's the tavern gossip," went on the Duke, who liked to flavour his conversation with certain expressions which he imagined to be of the old school. "Personally, of course, as everyone knows, I take just the opposite view to my cousin Gilbert. I'm not feudal like him, I'd go about with a negro if he was a friend of mine, and I shouldn't care two straws what anybody thought; still, after all you must agree with me that when one goes by the name of Saint-Loup one doesn't amuse oneself by flying in the face of public opinion, which has more sense than Voltaire or even my nephew. Nor does one go in for what I may be allowed to call these acrobatics of conscience a week before one comes up for a club. It really is a bit stiff! No, it's probably that little tart of his who worked him up to it. I expect she told him he would be classed among the 'intellectuals.' The intellectuals, that's what those gentry are always harping on. It's given rise, by the way, to a rather amusing pun, though a very naughty one."

And the Duke murmured, lowering his voice, for his wife's and M. d'Argencourt's benefit, "Mater Semita," which had already made its way into the Jockey Club, for, of all the flying seeds in the world, that to which are attached the most solid wings, enabling it to be disseminated at the greatest distance from its point of origin, is still a joke.

"We might ask this gentleman, who has a *nerudite* air, to explain it to us," he went on, pointing to the historian. "But it's better not to repeat it, especially as there's not a vestige of truth in the suggestion. I'm not so ambitious as my cousin Mirepoix, who claims that she can trace the descent of her family before Christ to the Tribe of Levi, and I'll guarantee to prove that there has never been a drop of Jewish blood in our family. Still it's no good shutting our eyes to the fact that my dear nephew's charming views are liable to make a considerable stir in Landerneau. Especially as Fezensac is ill just now, and Duras will be running the election; you know how he likes to draw the longbow," concluded the Duke, who had never succeeded in learning the exact meaning of certain phrases, and supposed drawing the longbow to mean making complications.

"In any case, if this man Dreyfus is innocent," the Duchess broke in, "he hasn't done much to prove it. What idiotic, turgid letters he writes from his island! I don't know whether M. Esterhazy is any better, but at least he has more of a knack of phrase-making, a different tone altogether. That can't be very welcome to the supporters of M. Dreyfus. What a pity for them that they can't exchange innocents."

Everyone burst out laughing. "Did you hear what Oriane said?" the Duc de Guermantes inquired eagerly of Mme de Villeparisis. "Yes, I thought it most amusing." This was not enough for the Duke: "Well, I don't know, I can't say that I thought it amusing; or rather it doesn't make the slightest difference to me whether a thing is amusing or not. I set no store by wit." M. d'Argencourt protested. "He doesn't believe a word he says," murmured the Duchess. "It's probably because I've been a Member of Parliament, where I've listened to brilliant speeches that meant absolutely nothing. I learned there to value logic more than anything else. That's probably why I wasn't re-elected. Amusing things leave me cold." "Basin, don't play the humbug like that, my sweet, you know quite well that no one admires wit more than you do." "Please let me finish. It's precisely because I'm unmoved by a certain type of humour that I appreciate my wife's wit. For you will find it based, as a rule, upon sound observation. She reasons like a man; she expresses herself like a writer."

Meanwhile Bloch was trying to pin M. de Norpois down on Colonel Picquart.

"There can be no question," replied M. de Norpois, "that the Colonel's evidence became necessary if only because the Government felt that there might well be something in the wind. I am well aware that, by maintaining this attitude, I have drawn shrieks of protest from more than one of my colleagues, but to my mind the Government were bound to let the Colonel speak. One can't get out of that sort of fix simply by performing a pirouette, or if one does there's always the risk of falling into a quagmire. As for the officer himself, his statement made a most excellent impression at the first hearing. When one saw him, looking so well in that smart Chasseur uniform, come into court and relate in a perfectly simple and frank tone what he had seen and what he had deduced, and say: 'On my honour as a soldier'" (here M. de Norpois's voice shook with a faint patriotic throb) "'such is my conviction,' it is impossible to deny that the impression he made was profound."

"There, he's a Dreyfusard, there's not the least doubt of it," thought Bloch.

"But where he entirely forfeited all the sympathy that he had managed to attract was when he was confronted with the registrar, Gribelin. When one heard that old public servant, a man of his word if ever there was one" (here M. de Norpois began to accentuate his words with the energy of sincere conviction), "when one saw him look his superior officer in the face, not afraid to hold his head up to him, and say to him in an unanswerable tone: 'Come, come, Colonel, you know very well that I have never told a lie, you know that at this moment, as always, I am speaking the truth,' the wind changed; M. Picquart might move heaven and earth at the subsequent hearings, but he came completely to grief."

"No, he's definitely an anti-Dreyfusard; it's quite obvious," said Bloch to himself. "But if he considers Picquart a traitor and a liar, how can he take his revelations seriously, and quote them as if he found them charming and believed them to be sincere? And if, on the other hand, he sees him as an honest man unburdening his conscience, how can he suppose him to have been lying when he was confronted with Gribelin?"

Perhaps the reason why M. de Norpois spoke thus to Bloch as though they were in agreement arose from the fact that he himself was so keen an anti-Dreyfusard that, finding the Government not anti-Dreyfusard enough, he was its enemy just as much as the Dreyfusards were. Perhaps it was because the object to which he devoted himself in politics was something more profound, situated on another plane, from which Dreyfusism appeared as an unimportant issue which did not deserve the attention of a patriot interested in large questions of foreign policy. Perhaps, rather, it was because, the maxims of his political wisdom being applicable only to questions of form, of procedure, of expediency, they were as powerless to solve questions of fact as, in philosophy, pure logic is powerless to tackle the problems of existence; or else because that very wisdom made him see danger in handling such subjects and so, in his caution, he preferred to speak only of minor circumstances. But where Bloch was mistaken was in assuming that M. de Norpois, even had he been less cautious by nature and of a less exclusively formal cast of mind, could, if he had wished, have told him the truth as to the part played by Henry, Picquart or du Paty de Clam, or as to any of the different aspects of the case. For Bloch had no doubt that M. de Norpois knew the truth as to all these matters. How could he fail to know it, seeing that he was a friend of all the ministers? Naturally, Bloch thought that the truth in politics could be approximately reconstructed by the most lucid minds, but he imagined, like the man in the street, that it resided permanently, beyond the reach of argument and in a material form, in the secret files of the President of the Republic and the Prime

Minister, who imparted it to the Cabinet. Whereas, even when a political truth is enshrined in written documents, it is seldom that these have any more value than a radiographic plate on which the layman imagines that the patient's disease is inscribed in so many words, whereas in fact the plate furnishes simply one piece of material for study, to be combined with a number of others on which the doctor's reasoning powers will be brought to bear and on which he will base his diagnosis. Thus the truth in politics, when one goes to well-informed men and imagines that one is about to grasp it, eludes one. Indeed, later on (to confine ourselves to the Dreyfus case), when so startling an event occurred as Henry's confession, followed by his suicide, this fact was at once interpreted in opposite ways by the Dreyfusard ministers and by Cavaignac and Cuignet who had themselves made the discovery of the forgery and conducted the interrogation; more remarkable still, among the Dreyfusard ministers themselves, men of the same shade of opinion, judging not only from the same documents but in the same spirit, the part played by Henry was explained in two entirely opposite ways, one set seeing in him an accomplice of Esterhazy, the others assigning that role to du Paty de Clam, thus adopting a thesis of their opponent Cuignet and in complete opposition to their supporter Reinach. All that Bloch could elicit from M. de Norpois was that if it were true that the Chief of the General Staff, General de Boisdeffre, had had a secret communication sent to M. Rochefort, it was evident that a singularly regrettable irregularity had occurred.

"You may be quite sure that the War Minister must (*in petto* at any rate) have called down every curse on his Chief of Staff. An official disclaimer would not have been (to my mind) a work of supererogation. But the War Minister expresses himself very bluntly on the matter *inter pocula*. There are certain subjects, moreover, about which it is highly imprudent to create an agitation over which one cannot afterwards retain control."

"But those documents are obviously fake," said Bloch.

M. de Norpois made no reply to this, but declared that he did not approve of the public demonstrations of Prince Henri d'Orléans:[16]

"Besides, they can only ruffle the calm of the praetorium, and encourage disturbances which, looked at from either point of view, would be deplorable. Certainly we must put a stop to the anti-militarist intrigues, but neither can we tolerate a brawl encouraged by those elements on the Right who instead of serving the patriotic ideal themselves are hoping to make it serve them. Heaven be praised, France is not a South American Republic, and the need has not yet been felt here for a military pronunciamento."

Bloch could not get him to pronounce on the question of Dreyfus's guilt, nor would he utter any forecast as to the judgment in the civil trial then proceeding. On the other hand, M. de Norpois seemed only too ready to expatiate on the consequences of the verdict.

"If it is a conviction," he said, "it will probably be quashed, for it is seldom that, in a case where there has been such a number of witnesses, there is not some flaw in the procedure which counsel can raise on appeal. To return to Prince Henri's outburst, I greatly doubt whether it met with his father's approval."

"You think Chartres is for Dreyfus?" asked the Duchess with a smile, her eyes rounded, her cheeks bright, her nose buried in her plate of *petits fours*, her whole manner deliciously scandalised.

"Not at all. I meant only that there runs through the whole family, on that side, a political sense of which we have seen the *ne plus ultra* in the admirable Princess Clémentine, and which her son, Prince Ferdinand, has kept as a priceless inheritance. You would never have found the Prince of Bulgaria clasping Major Esterhazy to his bosom."

"He would have preferred a private soldier," murmured Mme de Guermantes, who often met the Bulgarian at dinner at the Prince de Joinville's, and had said to him once, when he asked if she was not jealous: "Yes, Your Highness, of your bracelets."

"You aren't going to Mme de Sagan's ball this evening?" M. de Norpois asked Mme de Villeparisis, to cut short his conversation with Bloch.

The latter had made a not unpleasing impression on the

Ambassador, who told us afterwards, with some naïvety, thinking no doubt of the traces that survived in Bloch's speech of the neo-Homeric manner which he had on the whole outgrown: "He is quite amusing, with his old-fashioned, rather solemn way of speaking. You expect him to come out with 'the Learned Sisters,' like Lamartine or Jean-Baptiste Rousseau. It has become quite rare in the youth of the present day, as it was indeed in the generation before them. We ourselves were inclined to be a bit romantic." But however interesting his interlocutor may have seemed to him, M. de Norpois considered that the conversation had lasted long enough.

"No, I don't go to balls any more," Mme de Villeparisis replied with a charming grandmotherly smile. "You're going, all of you, I suppose? You're the right age for that sort of thing," she added, embracing in a comprehensive glance M. de Châtellerault, his friend and Bloch. "I was asked too," she went on, coyly pretending to be flattered by the distinction. "In fact, they came specially to invite me." ("They" being the Princesse de Sagan.)

"I haven't had a card," said Bloch, thinking that Mme de Villeparisis would at once offer to procure him one, and that Mme de Sagan would be happy to welcome the friend of a woman whom she had called in person to invite.

The Marquise made no reply, and Bloch did not press the point, for he had another, more serious matter to discuss with her, and, with that in view, had already asked her whether he might call again in a couple of days. Having heard the two young men say that they had both just resigned from the Rue Royale Club, which was letting in every Tom, Dick and Harry, he wished to ask Mme de Villeparisis to arrange for his election there.

"Aren't they rather bad form, rather stuck-up snobs, these Sagans?" he inquired in a sarcastic tone of voice.

"Not at all, they're the best we can do for you in that line," replied M. d'Argencourt, who adopted all the witticisms of Parisian society.

"Then," said Bloch, still half in irony, "I suppose it's one of the solemnities, the great social fixtures of the season."

Mme de Villeparisis turned merrily to Mme de Guermantes:

"Tell us, is it a great social solemnity, Mme de Sagan's ball?"

"It's no good asking me," answered the Duchess, "I have never yet succeeded in finding out what a social solemnity is. Besides, society isn't my forte."

"Oh, I thought it was just the opposite," said Bloch, who supposed Mme de Guermantes to have spoken seriously.

He continued, to the desperation of M. de Norpois, to ply him with questions about the Dreyfus case. The Ambassador declared that at first sight Colonel du Paty de Clam gave him the impression of a somewhat woolly mind, which had perhaps not been very happily chosen to conduct that delicate operation, which required so much coolness and discernment, a judicial inquiry.

"I know that the Socialist Party are clamouring for his head on a charger, as well as for the immediate release of the prisoner from Devil's Island. But I trust that we are not yet reduced to the necessity of going through the Caudine Forks of MM. Gérault-Richard and company. So far, the whole case has been in appalling muddle. I don't say that on both sides there isn't some pretty dirty work to be hushed up. That certain of your client's more or less disinterested patrons may have the best intentions I will not attempt to deny. But you know that hell is paved with such things," he added, with a look of great subtlety. "The great thing is that the Government should make it clear that it is no more in the hands of the factions of the Left than it is prepared to surrender, bound hand and foot, to the demands of some praetorian guard or other which, believe me, is not the same thing as the Army. It goes without saying that, should any fresh evidence come to light, a new trial would be ordered. It's as plain as a pike-staff; to demand that is to push at an open door. When that day comes the Government will speak out loud and clear—otherwise it would forfeit what is its essential prerogative. Cock and bull stories will no longer suffice. We must appoint judges to try Dreyfus. And that will be an easy matter because, although we have acquired the habit in our beloved France, where we love to speak ill of ourselves, of thinking or letting it be thought that in order to hear the words Truth and Justice it is necessary to cross the Channel, which is very often only a

roundabout way of reaching the Spree, there are judges to be
found outside Berlin. But once the machinery of Government
has been set in motion, will you have ears for the voice of
authority? When it bids you perform your duty as a citizen
will you take your stand in the ranks of law and order? When
its patriotic appeal sounds, will you have the wisdom not to
turn a deaf ear but to answer: 'Present!' ?"

M. de Norpois put these questions to Bloch with a vehemence which, while it alarmed my old schoolfriend,
flattered him also; for the Ambassador seemed to be addressing
a whole party in Bloch's person, to be interrogating him as
though he had been in the confidence of that party and might
be held responsible for the decisions which it would adopt.
"Should you fail to disarm," M. de Norpois went on without
waiting for Bloch's collective answer, "should you, before
even the ink has dried on the decree ordering the retrial,
obeying I know not what insidious word of command, fail,
I say, to disarm, and band yourselves in a sterile opposition
which seems to some minds the *ultima ratio* of policy, should
you retire to your tents and burn your boats, you would be
doing so to your own detriment. Are you the prisoner of those
who foment disorder? Have you given them pledges?" Bloch
was at a loss for an answer. M. de Norpois gave him no time.
"If the negative be true, as I sincerely hope and trust, and if
you have a little of what seems to me to be lamentably lacking
in certain of your leaders and your friends, namely political
sense, then, on the day when the Criminal Court assembles, if
you do not allow yourselves to be dragooned by the fishers in
troubled waters, you will have won the day. I do not guarantee
that the whole of the General Staff is going to get away unscathed, but it will be so much to the good if some of them at
least can save their faces without putting a match to the powder-
barrel. It goes without saying, of course, that it rests with the
Government to pronounce judgment and to close the list—
already too long—of unpunished crimes, not, certainly, at the
bidding of Socialist agitators, nor yet of any obscure military
rabble," he added, looking Bloch in the eyes, perhaps with
the instinct that leads all Conservatives to try to win support
for themselves in the enemy's camp. "Government action

is not to be dictated by the highest bid, wherever it may come from. The Government is not, thank heaven, under the orders of Colonel Driant, nor, at the other end of the scale, under M. Clemenceau's. We must curb the professional agitators and prevent them from raising their heads again. France, the vast majority here in France, desires only to be allowed to work in orderly conditions. As to that, there can be no question whatever. But we must not be afraid to enlighten public opinion; and if a few sheep, of the kind our friend Rabelais knew so well, should dash headlong into the water, it would be as well to point out to them that the water in question is troubled water, that it has been troubled deliberately by an agency not within our borders, in order to conceal the dangers lurking in its depths. And the Government must not give the impression that it is emerging from its passivity under duress when it exercises the right which is essentially its own and no one else's, I mean that of setting the wheels of justice in motion. The Government will accept all your suggestions. If there should prove to have been a judicial error, it can be assured of an overwhelming majority which would give it some elbow-room."

"You, sir," said Bloch, turning to M. d'Argencourt, to whom he had been introduced with the rest of the party on that gentleman's arrival, "you are a Dreyfusard, of course. Everyone is, abroad."

"It is a question that concerns only the French themselves, don't you think?" replied M. d'Argencourt with that peculiar form of insolence which consists in ascribing to the other person an opinion which one plainly knows that he does not share since he has just expressed one directly its opposite.

Bloch coloured; M. d'Argencourt smiled, looking round the room, and if this smile, so long as it was directed at the rest of the company, was charged with malice at Bloch's expense, he tempered it with cordiality when finally it came to rest on the face of my friend, so as to deprive him of any excuse for annoyance at the words he had just heard, though those words remained just as cruel. Mme de Guermantes muttered something in M. d'Argencourt's ear which I could not catch but which must have referred to Bloch's religion, for there flitted at that moment over the face of the Duchess that expression to which one's fear of being noticed by the person one is speaking of gives a certain hesitancy and falseness mixed with the inquisitive, malicious amusement inspired by a human group to which one feels oneself to be fundamentally alien. To retrieve himself, Bloch turned to the Duc de Châtellerault. "You, Monsieur, as a Frenchman, you must be aware that people abroad are all Dreyfusards, although everyone pretends that in France we never know what is going on abroad. Anyhow, I know I can talk freely to you; Saint-Loup told me so." But the young Duke, who felt that everyone was turning against Bloch, and was a coward as people often are in society, employing a mordant and precious form of wit which he seemed, by a sort of collateral atavism, to have inherited from M. de Charlus, replied: "Forgive me, Monsieur, if I don't discuss the Dreyfus case with you; it is a subject which, on principle, I never mention except among Japhetics." Everyone smiled, except Bloch, not that he was not himself in the habit of making sarcastic references to his Jewish origin, to that side of his ancestry which came from somewhere near Sinai. But instead of one of these remarks (doubtless because he did not have one ready) the trigger of his inner mechanism brought to Bloch's lips something quite different. And all one heard was: "But how on earth did you know? Who told you?" as though he had been the son of a convict. Whereas, given his name, which had not exactly a Christian sound, and his face, his surprise argued a certain naïvety.

What M. de Norpois had said to him not having completely satisfied him, he went up to the archivist and asked him whether M. du Paty de Clam or M. Joseph Reinach were not sometimes to be seen at Mme de Villeparisis's. The archivist made no reply; he was a Nationalist, and never ceased preaching to the Marquise that the social revolution might break out at any moment, and that she ought to show more caution in the choice of her acquaintances. He wondered whether Bloch might not be a secret emissary of the Syndicate, come to collect information, and went off at once to repeat to Mme de Villeparisis the questions that Bloch had put to him. She decided that he was ill-bred at best and that he might perhaps

be in a position to compromise M. de Norpois. She also wished
to give satisfaction to the archivist, who was the only person
she was a little afraid of, and by whom she was being indoctri-
nated, though without much success (every morning he read
her M. Judet's article in the *Petit Journal*). She decided,
therefore, to make it plain to Bloch that he need not come to
the house again, and had no difficulty in choosing from her
social repertory the scene by which a great lady shows someone her door, a scene which does not in the least involve the
the raised finger and blazing eyes that people imagine. As
Bloch came up to her to say good-bye, buried in her deep
armchair she seemed only half-awakened from a vague somnolence. Her filmy eyes held only the faint and charming gleam
of a pair of pearls. Bloch's farewells, barely unwrinkling
the Marquise's face in a languid smile, drew from her not a
word, and she did not offer him her hand. This scene left
Bloch in utter bewilderment, but as he was surrounded by a
circle of bystanders he felt that it could not be prolonged
without embarrassment to himself, and, to force the Marquise,
he himself thrust out the hand which she had just refused to
shake. Mme de Villeparisis was shocked. But doubtless, while
still bent on giving immediate satisfaction to the archivist
and the anti-Dreyfus clan, she wished at the same time to
insure against the future, and so contented herself with letting
her eyelids droop over her half-closed eyes.

"I think she's asleep," said Bloch to the archivist who,
feeling that he had the support of the Marquise, assumed an
air of indignation. "Good-bye, Madame," shouted Bloch.

The old lady made the slight movement with her lips of a
dying woman who wants to open her mouth but whose eyes
betray no hint of recognition. Then she turned, overflowing
with restored vitality, towards M. d'Argencourt, while Bloch
took himself off, convinced that she must be "soft" in the head.
Full of curiosity and anxious to clear up such a strange incident, he came to see her again a few days later. She received
him in the most friendly fashion, because she was a good-
natured woman, because the archivist was not there, because
she was keen on the little play which Bloch was to put on in
her house, and finally because she had staged the appropriate

grande dame act which was universally admired and commented upon that very evening in various drawing-rooms, but in a version that had already ceased to bear the slightest relation to the truth.

"You were speaking just now of *The Seven Princesses*, Duchess. You know (not that it's anything to be proud of) that the author of that—what shall I call it?—that object is a compatriot of mine," said M. d'Argencourt with an irony blended with the satisfaction of knowing more than anyone else in the room about the author of a work which had been under discussion. "Yes, he's a Belgian, by nationality," he went on.

"Indeed? No, we don't accuse you of any responsibility for *The Seven Princesses*. Fortunately for yourself and your compatriots you are not like the author of that absurdity. I know several charming Belgians, yourself, your King, who is a little shy but full of wit, my Ligne cousins, and heaps of others, but none of you, I'm happy to say, speak the same language as the author of *The Seven Princesses*. Besides, if you want to know, it's not worth talking about, because really there is absolutely nothing in it. You know the sort of people who are always trying to seem obscure, and don't even mind making themselves ridiculous to conceal the fact that they haven't an idea in their heads. If there was anything behind it all, I may tell you that I'm not in the least afraid of a little daring," she added in a serious tone, "provided there's a little thought. I don't know if you've seen Borelli's play. Some people seem to have been shocked by it, but I must say, even if they stone me through the streets for saying it," she went on, without stopping to think that she ran no very great risk of such a punishment, "I found it immensely interesting. But *The Seven Princesses*! One of them may have a fondness for my nephew, but I can't carry family feeling quite . . ."

The Duchess broke off abruptly, for a lady came in who was the Comtesse de Marsantes, Robert's mother. Mme de Marsantes was regarded in the Faubourg Saint-Germain as a superior being, of a goodness and resignation that were positively angelic. So I had been told, and had had no particular reason to feel surprised, not knowing at the time that she was the sister of the Duc de Guermantes. Later, I was always taken aback when I learned, in that society, that melancholy, pure, self-sacrificing women, venerated like ideal saints in stained-glass windows, had flowered from the same genealogical stem as brothers who were brutal, debauched and vile. Brothers and sisters, when they are identical in features as were the Duc de Guermantes and Mme de Marsantes, ought (I felt) to have a single intellect in common, a similar heart, like a person who may have good or bad moments but in whom nevertheless one cannot expect to find a vast breadth of outlook if his mental range is narrow or a sublime abnegation if he is hard-hearted.

Mme de Marsantes attended Brunetière's lectures. She inspired the Faubourg Saint-Germain with enthusiasm and, by her saintly life, edified it as well. But the morphological link of handsome nose and piercing gaze none the less led me to classify Mme de Marsantes in the same intellectual and moral family as her brother the Duke. I could not believe that the mere fact of her being a woman, and perhaps of her having had an unhappy life and won everyone's high opinion, could make a person so different from the rest of her family, as in the medieval romances where all the virtues and graces are combined in the sister of wild and lawless brothers. It seemed to me that nature, less unfettered than the old poets, must make use almost exclusively of the elements common to the family, and I was unable to credit her with enough power of invention to construct, out of materials analogous to those that composed a fool and a lout, a lofty mind without the least strain of foolishness, a saint without the least taint of brutality. Mme de Marsantes was wearing a gown of white surah embroidered with large palms, on which stood out flowers of a different material, these being black. This was because, three weeks earlier, she had lost her cousin M. de Montmorency, a bereavement which did not prevent her from paying calls or even from going to small dinners, but always in mourning. She was a great lady. Atavism had filled her with the frivolity of generations of life at court, with all the superficial and rigorous duties that that implies. Mme de Marsantes had not had the strength to mourn her father and mother for any length of time, but she would not for anything in the world have appeared in colours in the month following the death of a cousin. She was more than friendly to me, both because I was Robert's friend and because I did not move in the same world as he. This friendliness was accompanied by a pretence of shyness, by a sort of intermittent withdrawal of the voice, the eyes, the mind, as though she were drawing in a wayward skirt, so as not to take up too much room, to remain stiff and erect even in her suppleness, as good breeding demands—a good breeding that must not, however, be taken too literally, many of these ladies lapsing very swiftly into moral licentiousness without ever losing the almost childlike correctness of their manners. Mme de Marsantes was a trifle irritating in conversation since, whenever she had occasion to speak of a commoner, as for instance Bergotte or Elstir, she would say, isolating the word, giving it its full value, intoning it on two different notes with a modulation peculiar to the Guermantes: "I have had the *honour*, the great *hon*-our of meeting Monsieur Bergotte," or "of making the acquaintance of Monsieur Elstir," either in order that her hearers might marvel at her humility, or from the same tendency evinced by M. de Guermantes to revert to obsolete forms as a protest against the slovenly usages of the present day, in which people never professed themselves sufficiently "honoured." Whichever of these was the true reason, one felt that when Mme de Marsantes said: "I have had the *honour*, the great *hon*-our," she felt she was fulfilling an important role and showing that she could take in the names of distinguished men as she would have welcomed the men themselves at her country seat had they happened to be in the neighbourhood. On the other hand, as her family was large, as she was devoted to all her relations, as, slow of speech and fond of explaining things at length, she was always trying to make clear the exact degrees of kinship, she found herself (without any desire to create an effect and while genuinely preferring to talk only about touching peasants and sublime gamekeepers) referring incessantly to all the mediatised houses in Europe, a failing which people less brilliantly connected than herself could not forgive her and, if they were at all intellectual, derided as a sign of stupidity.

In the country, Mme de Marsantes was adored for the good that she did, but principally because the purity of a blood-line into which for many generations there had flowed only what was greatest in the history of France had rid her manner of everything that the lower orders call "airs" and had endowed her with perfect simplicity. She never shrank from embracing a poor woman who was in trouble, and would tell her to come up to the house for a cartload of wood. She was, people said, the perfect Christian. She was determined to find an immensely rich wife for Robert. Being a great lady means playing the great lady, that is to say, to a certain extent, playing at simplicity. It is a pastime which costs a great deal of money, all the more because simplicity charms people only on condition that they know that you are capable of not living simply, that is to say that you are very rich. Someone said to me afterwards, when I mentioned that I had seen her: "You saw of course that she must have been lovely as a young woman." But true beauty is so individual, so novel always, that one does not recognise it as beauty. I said to myself that afternoon only that she had a tiny nose, very blue eyes, a long neck and a sad expression.

"By the way," said Mme de Villeparisis to the Duchesse de Guermantes, "I'm expecting a woman at any moment whom you don't wish to know. I thought I'd better warn you, to avoid any unpleasantness. But you needn't be afraid, I shall never have her here again, only I was obliged to let her come to-day. It's Swann's wife."

Mme Swann, seeing the dimensions that the Dreyfus case had begun to assume, and fearing that her husband's racial origin might be used against herself, had besought him never again to allude to the prisoner's innocence. When he was not present she went farther and professed the most ardent nationalism; in doing which she was only following the example of Mme Verdurin, in whom a latent bourgeois anti-semitism had awakened and grown to a positive fury. Mme Swann had won by this attitude the privilege of membership in several of the anti-semitic leagues of society women that were beginning to be formed and had succeeded in establishing relations with various members of the aristocracy. It may seem

strange that, so far from following their example, the Duchesse
de Guermantes, so close a friend of Swann, had on the contrary always resisted the desire which he had not concealed
from her to introduce his wife to her. But we shall see in
due course that this was an effect of the peculiar character of
the Duchess, who held that she was not "bound to" do such
and such a thing, and laid down with despotic force what had
been decided by her social "free will," which was extremely
arbitrary.

"Thank you for warning me," said the Duchess. "It would
indeed be most disagreeable. But as I know her by sight I shall
be able to get away in time."

"I assure you, Oriane, she is really quite nice; an excellent
woman," said Mme de Marsantes.

"I have no doubt she is, but I feel no need to assure myself
of it in person."

"Have you been invited to Lady Israels's?" Mme de Villeparisis asked the Duchess, to change the subject.

"Why, thank heaven, I don't know the woman," replied
Mme de Guermantes. "You must ask Marie-Aynard. She
knows her. I never could make out why."

"I did indeed know her at one time," said Mme de Marsantes. "I confess my sins. But I have decided not to know
her any more. It seems she's one of the very worst of them,
and makes no attempt to conceal it. Besides, we have all been
too trusting, too hospitable. I shall never go near anyone of that
race again. While we closed our doors to old country cousins,
people of our own flesh and blood, we threw them open to
Jews. And now we see what thanks we get from them. But
alas, I've no right to speak; I have an adorable son who, young
fool that he is, goes round talking the most utter nonsense,"
she went on, having caught some allusion by M. d'Argencourt to Robert. "But, talking of Robert, haven't you seen
him?" she asked Mme de Villeparisis. "Since it's Saturday, I
thought he might have come to Paris for twenty-four hours,
and in that case would have been sure to pay you a visit."

As a matter of fact Mme de Marsantes thought that her
son would not obtain leave that week; but knowing that, even
if he did, he would never dream of coming to see Mme de

Villeparisis, she hoped, by making herself appear to have expected to find him there, to make his susceptible aunt forgive him for all the visits that he had failed to pay her.

"Robert here! But I haven't even had a word from him. I don't think I've seen him since Balbec."

"He is so busy; he has so much to do," said Mme de Marsantes.

A faint smile made Mme de Guermantes's eyelashes quiver as she studied the circle which she was tracing on the carpet with the point of her sunshade. Whenever the Duke had been too openly unfaithful to his wife, Mme de Marsantes had always taken up the cudgels against her own brother on her sister-in-law's behalf. The latter had a grateful and bitter memory of this support, and was not herself seriously shocked by Robert's pranks. At this point the door opened again and Robert himself came in.

"Well, talk of the Saint!"[17] said Mme de Guermantes.

Mme de Marsantes, who had her back to the door, had not seen her son come in. When she caught sight of him, her motherly bosom was convulsed with joy as by the beating of a wing, her body half rose from her seat, her face quivered and she fastened on Robert eyes that glowed with wonderment.

"What, you've come! How delightful! What a surprise!"

"Ah! *talk of the Saint!*—I see," cried the Belgian diplomat with a shout of laughter.

"Delicious, isn't it?" the Duchess retorted curtly, for she hated puns, and had ventured this one only with a pretence of self-mockery.

"Good evening, Robert," she said. "Well, so this is how we forget our aunt."

They talked for a moment, doubtless about me, for as Saint-Loup was leaving her to join his mother Mme de Guermantes turned to me:

"Good evening, how are you?" was her greeting.

She showered me with the light of her azure gaze, hesitated for a moment, unfolded and stretched towards me the stem of her arm, and leaned forward her body which sprang rapidly backwards like a bush that has been pulled down to the ground and, on being released, returns to its natural position. Thus she acted under the fire of Saint-Loup's eyes, which kept her under observation from a distance and made frantic efforts to obtain some further concession still from his aunt. Fearing that our conversation might dry up altogether, he came across to fuel it, and answered for me:

"He's not very well just now, he gets rather tired. I think he would be a great deal better, by the way, if he saw you more often, for I don't mind telling you that he admires you immensely."

"Oh, but that's very nice of him," said Mme de Guermantes in a deliberately casual tone, as if I had brought her her coat. "I'm most flattered."

"Look, I must go and talk to my mother for a minute; take my chair," said Saint-Loup, thus forcing me to sit down next to his aunt.

We were both silent.

"I see you sometimes in the morning," she said, as though she were giving me a piece of news and as though I for my part never saw her. "It's so good for one, a walk."

"Oriane," said Mme de Marsantes in a low voice, "you said you were going on to Mme de Saint-Ferréol's. Would you be so very kind as to tell her not to expect me to dinner. I shall stay at home now that I've got Robert. And one other thing, if you wouldn't mind my asking you to leave word as you pass to tell them to send out at once for a box of the cigars Robert likes. 'Corona,' they're called. I've none in the house."

Robert came up to us. He had caught only the name of Mme de Saint-Ferréol.

"Who in the world is Mme de Saint-Ferréol?" he inquired in a tone of studied surprise, for he affected ignorance of everything to do with society.

"But, my darling boy, you know perfectly well," said his mother, "She's Vermandois's sister. It was she who gave you that nice billiard table you liked so much."

"What, she's Vermandois's sister, I had no idea. Really, my family are amazing," he went on, half-turning towards me and unconsciously adopting Bloch's intonation just as he borrowed his ideas, "they know the most unheard-of people,

people called Saint-Ferréol" (emphasising the final consonant of each word) "and names like that; they go to balls, they drive in victorias, they lead a fabulous existence. It's prodigious."

Mme de Guermantes made a slight, short, sharp sound in her throat as of an involuntary laugh choked back, which was intended to show that she acknowledged her nephew's wit to the degree which kinship demanded. A servant came in to say that the Prince von Faffenheim-Munsterburg-Weinigen sent word to M. de Norpois that he had arrived.

"Go and fetch him, Monsieur," said Mme de Villeparisis to the ex-Ambassador, who set off in quest of the German Prime Minister.

"Wait, Monsieur. Do you think I ought to show him the miniature of the Empress Charlotte?"

"Why, I'm sure he'll be delighted," said the Ambassador in a tone of conviction, as though he envied the fortunate Minister the favour that was in store for him.

"Oh, I know he's very *sound*," said Mme de Marsantes, "and that is so rare among foreigners. But I've found out all about him. He's anti-semitism personified."

The Prince's name preserved, in the boldness with which its opening syllables were—to borrow an expression from music —attacked, and in the stammering repetition that scanned them, the energy, the mannered simplicity, the heavy refinements of the Teutonic race, projected like green boughs over the "heim" of dark blue enamel which glowed with the mystic light of a Rhenish window behind the pale and finely wrought gildings of the German eighteenth century. This name included, among the several names of which it was composed, that of a little German watering-place to which as a small child I had gone with my grandmother, at the foot of a mountain honoured by the feet of Goethe, from the vineyards of which we used to drink at the Kurhof the illustrious vintages with their compound and sonorous names like the epithets which Homer applies to his heroes. And so, scarcely had I heard it spoken than, before I had recalled the watering-place, the Prince's name seemed to shrink, to become imbued with humanity, to find large enough for itself a little place in my memory to which it clung, familiar, earthbound, picturesque, appetising, light, with something about it that was authorised, prescribed. Furthermore, M. de Guermantes, in explaining who the Prince was, quoted a number of his titles, and I recognised the name of a village traversed by a river on which, every evening, the cure finished for the day, I used to go boating amid the mosquitoes, and that of a forest far enough away for the doctor not to allow me to make the excursion to it. And indeed it was comprehensible that the suzerainty of the noble gentleman should extend to the surrounding places and associate afresh in the enumeration of his titles the names which one could read side by side on a map. Thus beneath the visor of the Prince of the Holy Roman Empire and Knight of Franconia it was the face of a beloved, smiling land, on which the rays of the evening sun had often lingered for me, that I saw, at any rate before the Prince, Rhinegrave and Elector Palatine, had entered the room. For I speedily learned that the revenues which he drew from the forest and the river peopled with gnomes and undines, and from the magic mountain on which rose the ancient Burg that still cherished memories of Luther and Louis the German, he employed in keeping five Charron motor-cars, a house in Paris and another in London, a box on Mondays at the Opéra and another for the "Tuesdays" at the "Français." He did not seem to me to be—nor did he himself seem to believe that he was—different from other men of similar wealth and age who had a less poetic origin. He had their culture, their ideals, he was proud of his rank but purely on account of the advantages it conferred on him, and had now only one ambition in life, to be elected a corresponding member of the Academy of Moral and Political Sciences, which was the reason of his coming to see Mme de Villeparisis.

If he, whose wife was a leader of the most exclusive set in Berlin, had solicited an introduction to the Marquise, it was not the result of any desire on his part for her acquaintance. Devoured for years past by this ambition to be elected to the *Institut*, he had unfortunately never been in a position to reckon above five the number of Academicians who seemed prepared to vote for him. He knew that M. de Norpois could by himself command at least a dozen votes, a number which he was capable, by skilful negotiations, of increasing still

further. And so the Prince, who had known him in Russia
when they were both there as ambassadors, had gone to see
him and had done everything in his power to win him over.
But in vain might he intensify his friendly overtures, procure
for the Marquis Russian decorations, quote him in articles on
foreign policy, he had been faced with a heartless ingrate, a
man in whose eyes all these attentions appeared to count as
nothing, who had not advanced the prospects of his candidature one inch, had not even promised him his own vote.
True, M. de Norpois received him with extreme politeness,
indeed begged him not to put himself out and "take the trouble
to come so far out of his way," went himself to the Prince's
residence, and when the Teutonic knight had launched his: "I
should very much like to be your colleague," replied in a tone
of deep emotion: "Ah! I should be most happy!" And no
doubt a simpleton, a Dr Cottard, would have said to himself:
"Well, here he is in my house; it was he who insisted on
coming because he regards me as a more important person than
himself; he tells me he'd be happy to see me in the Academy;
words do have some meaning after all, damn it, so if he
doesn't offer to vote for me it's probably because it hasn't
occurred to him. He lays so much stress on my power and
influence he presumably imagines that the plums fall into
my lap, that I have all the support I need and that's why
he doesn't offer me his; but I've only to corner him here and
now and just say to him quietly: 'Very well, vote for me, will
you?' and he'll be obliged to do it."

But Prince von Faffenheim was no simpleton. He was what
Dr Cottard would have called "a shrewd diplomat" and he
knew that M. de Norpois was a no less shrewd one and a
man who would have realised without needing to be told that
he could confer a favour on a candidate by voting for him.
The Prince, in his ambassadorial missions and as Foreign
Minister, had conducted, on his country's behalf instead of, as
in the present instance, his own, many of those conversations
in which one knows beforehand just how far one is prepared to
go and at what point one will decline to commit oneself. He
was not unaware that in diplomatic parlance to talk means to
offer. And it was for this reason that he had arranged for M.

de Norpois to receive the Cordon of Saint Andrew. But if he had had to report to his Government the conversation which he had subsequently had with M. de Norpois, he would have stated in his dispatch: "I realised that I had taken the wrong tack." For as soon as he had returned to the subject of the *Institut*, M. de Norpois had repeated:

"I should like nothing better; nothing could be better for my colleagues. They ought, I consider, to feel genuinely honoured that you should have thought of them. It's a really interesting candidature, a little outside our normal practice. As you know, the Academy is very hide-bound; it takes fright at anything that smacks of novelty. Personally, I deplore this. How often have I not had occasion to say as much to my colleagues! I cannot be sure, God forgive me, that I did not even once let the term 'stick-in-the-mud' escape my lips," he added with a scandalised smile in an undertone, almost an aside, as though on the stage, giving the Prince a rapid, sidelong glance from his blue eyes, like a veteran actor studying an effect on his audience. "You understand, Prince, that I should not care to allow a personality so eminent as yourself to embark on a venture which was hopeless from the start. So long as my colleagues' ideas linger so far behind the times, I consider that the wiser course will be to abstain. But you may rest assured that if I were ever to discern a slightly more modern, a slightly more lively spirit emerge in that college, which is tending to become a mausoleum, if I felt you had a genuine chance of success, I should be the first to inform you of it."

"The Cordon was a mistake," thought the Prince; "the negotiations have not advanced one step. That's not what he wanted. I have not yet laid my hand on the right key."

This was a kind of reasoning of which M. de Norpois, formed in the same school as the Prince, would also have been capable. One may mock at the pedantic silliness which makes diplomats of the Norpois type go into ecstasies over some piece of official wording which is to all intents and purposes meaningless. But their childishness has this compensation: diplomats know that, in the scales which ensure that balance of power, European or otherwise, which we call peace, good feeling, fine speeches, earnest entreaties weigh very little;

and that the heavy weight, the true determinant consists in something else, in the possibility which the adversary enjoys, if he is strong enough, or does not enjoy, of satisfying a desire in exchange for something in return. With this order of truths, which an entirely disinterested person, such as my grandmother for instance, would not have understood, M. de Norpois and Prince von Faffenheim had frequently to deal. As an envoy in countries with which we had been within an ace of going to war, M. de Norpois, in his anxiety as to the turn which events were about to take, knew very well that it was not by the word "Peace," nor by the word "War," that it would be revealed to him, but by some other, apparently commonplace word, a word of terror or blessing, which the diplomat, by the aid of his cipher, would immediately know how to interpret and to which, to safeguard the dignity of France, he would respond in another word, quite as commonplace, but one beneath which the minister of the enemy nation would at once decipher: "War." Moreover, in accordance with a time-honoured custom, analogous to that which used to give to the first meeting between two young people promised to one another in marriage the form of a chance encounter at a performance in the Théâtre du Gymnase, the dialogue in the course of which destiny was to dictate the word "War" or the word "Peace" took place, as a rule, not in the ministerial sanctum but on a bench in a Kurgarten where the minister and M. de Norpois went independently to a thermal spring to drink at its source their little tumblers of some curative water. By a sort of tacit convention they met at the hour appointed for their cure, and began by taking together a short stroll which, beneath its benign appearance, the two interlocutors knew to be as tragic as an order for mobilisation. And so, in a private matter like this nomination for election to the Institute, the Prince had employed the same system of induction which had served him in the diplomatic service, the same method of reading beneath superimposed symbols.

And certainly it would be wrong to pretend that my grandmother and the few who resembled her would have been alone in their failure to understand this kind of calculation. For one thing, the average run of humanity, practising professions the lines of which have been laid down in advance, approximate in their lack of intuition to the ignorance which my grandmother owed to her lofty disinterestedness. Often one has to come down to "kept" persons, male or female, before one finds the hidden spring of actions or words, apparently of the most innocent nature, in self-interest, in the necessity to keep alive. What man does not know that when a woman whom he is going to pay says to him: "Don't let's talk about money," the speech must be regarded as what is called in music "a silent bar" and that if, later on, she declares: "You make me too unhappy, you're always keeping things from me; I can't stand it any longer," he must interpret this as: "Someone else has been offering her more"? And yet this is only the language of the woman of easy virtue, not so far removed from society women. The ponce furnishes more striking examples. But M. de Norpois and the German prince, if ponces and their ways were unknown to them, had been accustomed to living on the same plane as nations, which are also, for all their grandeur, creatures of selfishness and cunning, which can be tamed only by force, by consideration of their material interests which may drive them to murder, a murder that is also often symbolic, since its mere hesitation or refusal to fight may spell for a nation the word "Perish." But since all this is not set forth in the various Yellow Books or elsewhere, the people as a whole are naturally pacific; if they are warlike, it is instinctively, from hatred, from a sense of injury, not for the reasons which have made up the mind of their ruler on the advice of his Norpois.

The following winter the Prince was seriously ill. He recovered, but his heart was permanently affected.

"The devil!" he said to himself, "I can't afford to lose any time over the *Institut*. If I wait too long, I may be dead before they elect me. That really would be disagreeable."

He wrote an essay for the *Revue des Deux Mondes* on European politics over the past twenty years, in which he referred more than once to M. de Norpois in the most flattering terms. The latter called upon him to thank him. He added that he did not know how to express his gratitude. The Prince said to himself, like a man who has just tried to fit another key into a stubborn lock: "Still not the right one!" and, feeling somewhat out of breath as he showed M. de Norpois to the door, thought: "Damn it, these fellows will see me in my grave before letting me in. We must hurry up."

That evening, he met M. de Norpois again at the Opéra.

"My dear Ambassador," he said to him, "you told me this morning that you did not know how to prove your gratitude to me. It's entirely superfluous, since you owe me none, but I am going to be so indelicate as to take you at your word."

M. de Norpois had a no less high esteem for the Prince's tact than the Prince had for his. He understood at once that it was not a request that Prince von Faffenheim was about to put to him, but an offer, and with a radiant affability he made ready to hear it.

"Well now, you will think me highly indiscreet. There are two people to whom I am greatly attached—in quite different ways, as you will understand in a moment—two people both of whom have recently settled in Paris, where they intend to live henceforth: my wife, and the Grand Duchess John. They are thinking of giving a few dinners, notably in honour of the King and Queen of England, and what they would have liked more than anything in the world would have been to be able to offer their guests the company of a person for whom, without knowing her, they both of them feel a great admiration. I confess that I did not know how I was going to gratify their wish when I learned just now, by the merest chance, that you were a friend of this person. I know that she lives a most retired life, and sees only a very few people—'happy few'— but if you were to give me your support, with the kindness you have always shown me, I am sure that she would allow you to present me to her so that I might convey to her the wish of the Grand Duchess and the Princess. Perhaps she would consent to come to dinner with the Queen of England, and then (who knows) if we don't bore her too much, to spend the Easter holidays with us at Beaulieu, at the Grand Duchess John's. The person I allude to is called the Marquise de Ville-parisis. I confess that the hope of becoming an habitué of such a school of wit would console me, would make me contemplate without regret the abandoning of my candidature for the *Institut*. For in her house, too, I understand, there is intellectual intercourse and brilliant talk."

With an inexpressible sense of pleasure the Prince felt that the lock no longer resisted and that at last the key was turning.

"Such an alternative is wholly unnecessary, my dear Prince," replied M. de Norpois. "Nothing could be more in harmony with the *Institut* than the house you speak of, which is a regular breeding-ground of academicians. I shall convey your request to Mme la Marquise de Villeparisis: she will undoubtedly be flattered. As for her dining with you, she goes out very little, and that will perhaps be more difficult to arrange. But I shall introduce you to her and you will plead your cause in person. You must on no account give up the Academy; to-morrow fortnight, as it happens, I shall be having luncheon, before going on with him to an important meeting, with Leroy-Beaulieu, without whom nobody can be elected; I had already allowed myself in conversation with him to let fall your name, with which, naturally, he was perfectly familiar. He raised certain objections. But it so happens that he requires the support of my group at the next election, and I fully intend to return to the charge; I shall tell him frankly of the extremely cordial ties that unite us, I shall not conceal from him that, if you were to stand, I should ask all my friends to vote for you" (here the Prince breathed a deep sigh of relief), "and he knows that I have friends. I consider that if I were to succeed in obtaining his co-operation, your chances would become very real. Come that evening, at six, to Mme de Villeparisis's. I will introduce you, and at the same time will be able to give you an account of my morning meeting."

Thus it was that Prince von Faffenheim had been led to call upon Mme de Villeparisis. My profound disillusionment occurred when he spoke. It had never struck me that, whereas a period has features both particular and general which are stronger than those of a nationality, so that in an illustrated dictionary which goes so far as to include an authentic portrait of Minerva, Leibniz with his periwig and his neckerchief differs little from Marivaux or Samuel Bernard, a nationality has particular features stronger than those of a caste. In the present instance these found expression not in a discourse in which I had expected to hear the rustling of the elves and the dance of the kobolds, but by a transposition which certified no less plainly that poetic origin: the fact that as he bowed, short, red-faced and portly, over the hand of Mme de Ville-parisis, the Rhinegrave said to her: "Aow to you too, Matame la Marquise," in the accent of an Alsatian porter.

"Won't you let me give you a cup of tea or a little of this tart, it's so good?" Mme de Guermantes asked me, anxious to have shown herself as friendly as possible. "I do the honours in this house just as if it was mine," she explained in an ironical tone which gave a slightly guttural sound to her voice, as though she were trying to stifle a hoarse laugh.

"Monsieur," said Mme de Villeparisis to M. de Norpois, "you won't forget that you have something to say to the Prince about the Academy?"

Mme de Guermantes lowered her eyes and gave a semi-circular turn to her wrist to look at the time.

"Gracious! I must fly at once if I'm to get to Mme de Saint-Ferréol's, and I'm dining with Mme Leroi."

And she rose without bidding me good-bye. She had just caught sight of Mme Swann, who appeared somewhat embarrassed at finding me in the room. Doubtless she remembered that she had been the first to assure me that she was convinced of Dreyfus's innocence.

"I don't want my mother to introduce me to Mme Swann," Saint-Loup said to me. "She's an ex-whore. Her husband's a Jew, and she comes here to pose as a Nationalist. Hallo, here's my uncle Palamède."

The arrival of Mme Swann had a special interest for me, owing to an incident which had occurred a few days earlier and which it is necessary to relate because of the consequences which it was to have at a much later date and which the reader will follow in detail in due course. A few days before this visit to Mme de Villeparisis, I had myself received a visitor whom I little expected, namely Charles Morel, the son, whom I did not know, of my great-uncle's old valet. This great-uncle (he in whose house I had met the lady in pink) had died the year before. His servant had more than once expressed his intention of coming to see me; I had no idea of the object of his visit,

but should have been glad to see him, for I had learned from
Françoise that he had a genuine veneration for my uncle's
memory and made a pilgrimage regularly to the cemetery in
which he was buried. But, being obliged for reasons of health
to retire to his home in the country, where he expected to
remain for some time, he had delegated the duty to his son. I
was surprised to see a handsome young man of eighteen come
into my room, dressed expensively rather than with taste, but
looking, all the same, like anything but the son of a valet. He
made a point, moreover, from the start, of emphasising his
aloofness from the domestic class from which he sprang, by
informing me with a complacent smile that he had won a first
prize at the Conservatoire. The object of his visit to me was
as follows: his father on going through the effects of my uncle
Adolphe, had set aside some which he felt it unseemly to send
to my parents but which he considered to be of a nature to
interest a young man of my age. These were photographs of the
famous actresses, the notorious courtesans whom my uncle
had known, the last fading pictures of that gay life of a man
about town which he kept separated by a watertight compartment from his family life. While the young Morel was showing
them to me, I noticed that he affected to speak to me as to an
equal. He derived from saying "you" to me as often and "sir"
as seldom as possible the pleasure of one whose father had
never ventured, when addressing my parents, upon anything
but the third person. Almost all the photographs bore an
inscription such as: "To my best friend." One actress, less
grateful and more circumspect than the rest, had written: "To
the best of friends," which enabled her (so I have been assured)
to say afterwards that my uncle was in no sense and had never
been her best friend but was merely the friend who had done
the most small services for her, the friend she made use of, a
good, kind man, in other words an old fool. In vain might
young Morel seek to divest himself of his lowly origin, one
felt that the shade of my uncle Adolphe, venerable and gigantic in the eyes of the old servant, had never ceased to hover,
almost a sacred vision, over the childhood and youth of the
son. While I was turning over the photographs Charles Morel
examined my room. And as I was looking for somewhere to

put them, "How is it," he asked me (in a tone in which the
reproach had no need to be emphasised, so implicit was it in
the words themselves), "that I don't see a single photograph
of your uncle in your room?" I felt the blood rise to my cheeks
and stammered: "Why, I don't believe I have one." "What, you
haven't a single photograph of your uncle Adolphe, who was
so fond of you! I'll send you one of the governor's—he's got
stacks of them—and I hope you'll put it in the place of honour
above that chest of drawers, which incidentally came to you
from your uncle." It is true that, as I had not even a photograph
of my father or mother in my room, there was nothing so
very shocking in there not being one of my uncle Adolphe.
But it was easy enough to see that for old Morel, who had
trained his son in the same way of thinking, my uncle was the
important person in the family, from whom my parents
derived only a dim reflected glory. I was in higher favour,
because my uncle used constantly to say to his valet that I was
going to turn out a sort of Racine, or Vaulabelle, and Morel
regarded me almost as an adopted son, as a favourite child
of my uncle. I soon discovered that Morel's son was extremely
"go-getting." Thus at this first meeting he asked me, being
something of a composer as well and capable of setting short
poems to music, whether I knew any poet who had a good
position in "aristo" society. I mentioned one. He did not know
the work of this poet and had never heard his name, of which
he made a note. And I was to discover that shortly afterwards
he wrote to the poet telling him that, being a fanatical admirer
of his work, he, Morel, had composed a musical setting for one
of his sonnets and would be grateful if the author would
arrange for its performance at the Comtesse so-and-so's. This
was going a little too fast and exposing his hand. The poet,
taking offence, made no reply.

For the rest, Charles Morel seemed to possess, besides
ambition, a strong leaning towards more concrete realities.
He had noticed, as he came through the courtyard, Jupien's
niece at work upon a waistcoat, and although he explained to
me only that he happened to want a fancy waistcoat at that
very moment, I felt that the girl had made a vivid impression
on him. He had no hesitation in asking me to come down-

stairs and introduce him to her, "but not as a connexion of
your family, you follow me, I rely on your discretion not to
drag in my father, say just a distinguished artist of your acquaintance, you know how important it is to make a good impression
on tradespeople." Although he had suggested to me that, not
knowing him well enough to call him, he quite realised, "dear
friend," I might address him, in front of the girl, in some such
terms as "not dear master, of course, ... although ... well, if
you like, dear distinguished artist," I avoided "qualifying" him,
as Saint-Simon would have said, in the shop and contented
myself with returning his "you's." He picked out from several
patterns of velvet one of the brightest red imaginable, so
loud that, for all his bad taste, he was never able to wear the
waistcoat when it was made. The girl settled down to work
again with her two "apprentices," but it struck me that the
impression had been mutual, and that Charles Morel, whom
she regarded as of my "station" (only smarter and richer), had
proved singularly attractive to her. As I had been greatly
surprised to find among the photographs which his father
had sent me one of the portrait of Miss Sacripant (otherwise
Odette) by Elstir, I said to Charles Morel as I accompanied
him to the carriage gateway: "I don't suppose you can tell
me, but did my uncle know this lady well? I can't think what
stage of his life she fits into exactly; and it interests me, because
of M. Swann ..." "Why, if I wasn't forgetting to tell you
that my father asked me specially to draw your attention to that
lady's picture. As a matter of fact, she was lunching with your
uncle the last time you saw him. My father was in two minds
whether to let you in. It seems you made a great impression
on the wench, and she hoped to see you again. But just at that
time there was a row in the family, from what my father tells
me, and you never set eyes on your uncle again." He broke
off to give Jupien's niece a smile of farewell across the courtyard. She gazed after him, doubtless admiring his thin but
regular features, his fair hair and sparkling eyes. For my part,
as I shook hands with him I was thinking of Mme Swann and
saying to myself with amazement, so far apart, so different
were they in my memory, that I should have henceforth to
identify her with the "Lady in pink."

M. de Charlus was soon seated by the side of Mme Swann. At every social gathering at which he appeared, contemptuous towards the men, courted by the women, he promptly attached himself to the most elegantly dressed of the latter, by whose garments he felt himself to be embellished. The Baron's frock coat or swallowtails were reminiscent of a portrait by some great colourist of a man dressed in black but having by his side, thrown over a chair, the brilliant cloak which he is about to wear at some fancy dress ball. These tête-à-têtes, generally with some royal lady, secured for M. de Charlus various privileges which he cherished. For instance, one consequence of them was that his hostesses, at theatricals or recitals, allowed the Baron alone to have a front seat in a row of ladies, while the rest of the men jostled one another at the back of the room. Furthermore, completely absorbed, it seemed, in telling amusing stories to the enraptured lady at the top of his voice, M. de Charlus was dispensed from the necessity of going to shake hands with any of the others, was set free, in other words, from all social duties. Behind the scented barrier which the chosen beauty provided for him, he was isolated in the middle of a crowded drawing-room, as, in a crowded theatre or concert-hall, behind the rampart of a box; and when anyone came up to greet him, through, as it were, the beauty of his companion, it was permissible for him to reply quite curtly and without interrupting his business of conversation with a lady. True, Mme Swann was scarcely of the rank of the persons with whom he liked thus to flaunt himself. But he professed admiration for her and friendship for Swann, knew that she would be flattered by his attentions, and was himself flattered at being compromised by the prettiest woman in the room.

Mme de Villeparisis meanwhile was not too well pleased to receive a visit from M. de Charlus. The latter, while admitting serious defects in his aunt's character, was genuinely fond of her. But every now and then in a fit of anger or imaginary grievance, he would sit down and write to her, without making the slightest attempt to resist his impulse, letters full of the most violent abuse, in whch he made the most of trifling incidents which until then he seemed not even to have noticed.

Among other examples I may instance the following, which my stay at Balbec brought to my knowledge: Mme de Ville-parisis, fearing that she had not brought enough money with her to Balbec to enable her to prolong her holiday there, and not caring, since she was of a thrifty disposition and shrank from superfluous expenditure, to have money sent to her from Paris, had borrowed three thousand francs from M. de Charlus. A month later, annoyed with his aunt for some trivial reason, he asked her to repay him this sum by telegraphic money order. He received two thousand nine hundred and ninety-odd francs. Meeting his aunt a few days later in Paris, in the course of a friendly conversation he drew her attention, very mildly, to the mistake that her bank had made when sending the money. "But there was no mistake," replied Mme de Villeparisis, "the money order cost six francs seventy-five." "Ah, well, if it was intentional, that's fine," said M. de Charlus. "I mentioned it only in case you didn't know, because in that case, if the bank had done the same thing with anyone who didn't know you as well as I do, it might have led to unpleasantness." "No, no, there was no mistake." "Actually you were quite right," M. de Charlus concluded gaily, stooping to kiss his aunt's hand. And in fact he bore her no ill will and was only amused at this little instance of her stinginess. But some time after-wards, imagining that, in a family matter, his aunt had been trying to cheat him and had "worked up a regular conspiracy" against him, as she rather foolishly took shelter behind the lawyers with whom he suspected her of having plotted to do him down, he had written her a letter boiling over with insolence and rage. "I shall not be satisfied with having my revenge," he added as a postscript, "I shall make you a laughing-stock. To-morrow I shall tell everyone the story of the money order and the six francs seventy-five you kept back from me out of the three thousand I lent you. I shall disgrace you publicly." Instead of so doing, he had gone to his aunt the next day to apologise, having already regretted a letter in which he had used some really appalling language. In any case, to whom could he have told the story of the money order? Since he no longer sought vengeance but a sincere reconciliation, now would have been the time for him to keep silence. But he had already told the story everywhere, while still on the best of terms with his aunt, had told it without malice, as a joke, and because he was the soul of indiscretion. He had told the story, but without Mme de Villeparisis's knowledge. With the result that, having learned from his letter that he intended to disgrace her by divulging a transaction in which he had assured her personally that she had acted rightly, she concluded that he had deceived her then and had lied when he pretended to be fond of her. All this had now died down, but neither of them knew precisely what the other thought of him or her. This sort of intermittent quarrel is of course somewhat exceptional. Of a different order were the quarrels of Bloch and his friends. Of a different order again were those of M. de Charlus, as we shall presently see, with people wholly unlike Mme de Villeparisis. In spite of this we must bear in mind that the opinions which we hold of one another, our relations with friends and family, far from being static, save in appearance, are as eternally fluid as the sea itself. Whence all the rumours of divorce between couples who have always seemed so perfectly united and will soon afterwards speak of one another with affection; all the terrible things said by one friend of another from whom we supposed him to be inseparable and with whom we shall find him once more reconciled before we have had time to recover from our surprise; all the reversals of alliances between nations after the briefest of spells.

"I say, my uncle and Mme Swann are getting on all right!" remarked Saint-Loup. "And look at Mamma in the innocence of her heart going across to disturb them. To the pure all things are pure!"

I studied M. de Charlus. The tuft of his grey hair, his twinkling eye, the brow of which was raised by his monocle, the red flowers in his buttonhole, formed as it were the three mobile apexes of a convulsive and striking triangle. I had not ventured to greet him, for he had given me no sign of recognition. And yet, though he was not facing in my direction, I was convinced that he had seen me; while he sat spinning some yarn to Mme Swann, whose sumptuous, pansy-coloured cloak floated over his knee, the Baron's roving eye, like that of

a street hawker who is watching all the time for the "law" to
appear, had certainly explored every corner of the room and
taken note of all the people who were in it. M. de Châtellerault
came up to say good evening to him without there being the
slightest hint on M. de Charlus's face that he had seen the
young Duke until he was actually standing in front of him. In
this way, in fairly numerous gatherings such as this, M. de
Charlus kept almost continuously on show a smile without
determinate direction or particular object, which, thereby pre-
existing the greetings of new arrivals, remained, when the
latter entered its zone, devoid of any amiable implication towards them. Nevertheless, I felt obliged to go across and
speak to Mme Swann. But as she was not certain whether I
knew Mme de Marsantes and M. de Charlus, she was distinctly
cold, fearing no doubt that I might ask her to introduce me
to them. I then turned to M. de Charlus, and at once regretted
it, for though he could not have helped seeing me he showed
no sign of having done so. As I stood before him and bowed I
found, at some distance from his body which it prevented
me from approaching by the full length of his outstretched arm,
a finger bereft, one would have said, of an episcopal ring,
of which he appeared to be offering the consecrated site for
the kiss of the faithful, and I was made to appear to have penetrated, without leave from the Baron and by an act of trespass
for which he left me the entire responsibility, the unalterable,
anonymous and vacant dispersion of his smile. This coldness
was hardly of a kind to encourage Mme Swann to depart from
hers.

"How tired and worried you look," said Mme de Marsantes
to her son who had come up to greet M. de Charlus.

And indeed the expression in Robert's eyes seemed now and
then to reach a depth from which it rose at once like a diver
who has touched bottom. This bottom which hurt Robert so
much when he touched it that he left it at once, to return to it
a moment later, was the thought that he had broken with his
mistress.

"Never mind," his mother went on, stroking his cheek,
"never mind; it's good to see my little boy again."

This show of affection seeming to irritate Robert, Mme de

Marsantes led her son away to the other end of the room where in an alcove hung with yellow silk a group of Beauvais armchairs massed their violet-hued tapestries like purple irises in a field of buttercups. Mme Swann, finding herself alone and having realised that I was a friend of Saint-Loup, beckoned me to come and sit beside her. Not having seen her for so long, I did not know what to talk to her about. I was keeping an eye on my hat among all those that littered the carpet, and I wondered with a vague curiosity to whom could belong one that was not the Duc de Guermantes's and yet in the lining of which a capital 'G' was surmounted by a ducal coronet. I knew who everyone in the room was, and could not think of anyone whose hat this could possibly be.

"What a pleasant man M. de Norpois is," I said to Mme Swann, pointing him out to her. "It's true that Robert de Saint-Loup says he's a pest, but . . ."

"He's quite right," she replied.

Seeing from her face that she was thinking of something which she was keeping from me, I plied her with questions. Pleased, perhaps, to appear to be very taken up with someone in this room where she hardly knew anyone, she took me into a corner.

"I'm sure this is what M. de Saint-Loup meant," she began, "but you must never tell him I said so, for he would think me indiscreet, and I value his esteem very highly—I'm an 'honest Injun,' you know. The other day, Charlus was dining at the Princesse de Guermantes's, and for some reason or other your name was mentioned. It appears that M. de Norpois told them—it's all too silly for words, don't go and worry yourself to death over it, nobody paid any attention, they all knew only too well the mischievous tongue that said it—that you were a hysterical little flatterer."

I have recorded a long way back my stupefaction at the discovery that a friend of my father such as M. de Norpois was could have expressed himself thus in speaking of me. I was even more astonished to learn that my emotion on that evening long ago when I had spoken about Mme Swann and Gilberte was known to the Princesse de Guermantes, whom I imagined never to have heard of my existence. Each of our actions, our words, our attitudes is cut off from the "world," from the people who have not directly perceived it, by a medium the permeability of which is infinitely variable and remains unknown to ourselves; having learned from experience that some important utterance which we eagerly hoped would be disseminated (such as those so enthusiastic speeches which I used at one time to make to everyone and at every opportunity on the subject of Mme Swann, thinking that among so many scattered seeds one at least would germinate) has at once, often because of our very anxiety, been hidden under a bushel, how immeasurably less do we suppose that some tiny word which we ourselves have forgotten, which may not even have been uttered by us but formed along its way by the imperfect refraction of a different word, could be transported, without ever being halted in its progress, infinite distances—in the present instance to the Princesse de Guermantes—and succeed in diverting at our expense the banquet of the gods! What we remember of our conduct remains unknown to our nearest neighbour; what we have forgotten that we ever said, or indeed what we never did say, flies to provoke hilarity in another planet, and the image that other people form of our actions and demeanour no more resembles our own than an inaccurate tracing, on which for the black line we find an empty space and for a blank area an inexplicable contour, resembles the original drawing. It may happen however that what has not been transcribed is a non-existent feature which only our purblind self-esteem reveals to us, and what seems to us to have been added does indeed belong to us, but so quintessentially that it escapes us. So that this strange print which seems to us to have so little resemblance to us bears sometimes the same stamp of truth, unflattering, certainly, but profound and useful, as an X-ray photograph. Not that that is any reason why we should recognise ourselves in it. A man who is in the habit of smiling in the glass at his handsome face and stalwart figure will, if he is shown an X-ray of them, have the same suspicion of error at the sight of this rosary of bones labelled as being a picture of himself as the visitor to an art gallery who, on coming to the portrait of a girl, reads in his catalogue: "Dromedary resting." Later on, this discrepancy in the picture of ourselves according to whether it is drawn by one's own hand or another's was something I was to register in the case of others than myself, living placidly in the midst of a collection of photographs which they had taken of themselves while round about them grinned frightful faces, invisible to them as a rule, but stunning them with amazement if some chance revealed them to them, saying: "It's you."

A few years earlier I should have been only too glad to tell Mme Swann in what connexion I had behaved so tenderly towards M. de Norpois, since the connexion had been my desire to get to know her. But I no longer felt this desire, since I was no longer in love with Gilberte. At the same time I found it difficult to identify Mme Swann with the lady in pink of my childhood. Accordingly I spoke of the woman who was on my mind at the moment.

"Did you see the Duchesse de Guermantes just now?" I asked Mme Swann.

But since the Duchess did not greet Mme Swann when they met, the latter chose to appear to regard her as a person of no interest, whose presence in a room one did not even notice.

"I don't know; I didn't *realise* she was here," she replied sourly, using an expression borrowed from English.

I was anxious nevertheless for information with regard not only to Mme de Guermantes but to all the people who came in contact with her, and (for all the world like Bloch), with the tactlessness of people who seek in their conversations not to give pleasure to others but to eludicate, from sheer egoism, points that are of interest to themselves, in my effort to form an exact idea of the life of Mme de Guermantes I questioned Mme de Villeparisis about Mme Leroi.

"Oh, yes, I know who you mean," she replied with an affectation of contempt, "the daughter of those rich timber merchants. I've heard that she's begun to go about quite a lot lately, but I must explain to you that I'm rather old now to make new acquaintances. I've known such interesting, such delightful people in my time that really I don't believe Mme Leroi would add much to what I already have."

Mme de Marsantes, who was playing lady in waiting to the Marquise, presented me to the Prince, and scarcely had she finished doing so than M. de Norpois also presented me in the most glowing terms. Perhaps he found it opportune to pay me a compliment which could in no way damage his credit since I had just been introduced; perhaps it was that he thought that a foreigner, even so distinguished a foreigner, was unfamiliar with French society and might think that he was being introduced to a young man of fashion; perhaps it was to exercise one of his prerogatives, that of adding the weight of his personal recommendation as an ambassador, or in his taste for the archaic to revive in the Prince's honour the old custom, flattering to his rank, whereby two sponsors were necessary if one wished to be presented to a royal personage.

Mme de Villeparisis appealed to M. de Norpois, feeling it imperative that I should have his assurance that she had nothing to regret in not knowing Mme Leroi.

"Isn't it true, M. l'Ambassadeur, that Mme Leroi is of no interest, very inferior to all the people who come here, and that I'm quite right not to have cultivated her?"

Whether from independence or because he was tired, M. de Norpois replied merely in a bow full of respect but devoid of meaning.

"Do you know," went on Mme de Villeparisis with a laugh, "there are some absurd people in the world. Would you believe that I had a visit this afternoon from a gentleman who tried to persuade me that he found more pleasure in kissing my hand than a young woman's?"

I guessed at once that this was Legrandin. M. de Norpois smiled with a slight quiver of the eyelid, as though he felt that such a remark had been prompted by a concupiscence so natural that one could not feel any resentment against the person who had felt it, almost as though it were the beginning of a romance which he was prepared to forgive, even to encourage, with the perverse tolerance of a Voisenon or a Crébillon *fils*.

"Many young women's hands would be incapable of doing what I see there," said the Prince, pointing to Mme de Villeparisis's unfinished water-colours. And he asked her whether she had seen the flower paintings by Fantin-Latour which had recently been exhibited.

"They are first class, the work, as they say nowadays, of a fine painter, one of the masters of the palette," declared M. de Norpois. "Nevertheless, in my opinion, they cannot stand comparison with those of Mme de Villeparisis, which give a better idea of the colouring of the flower."

Even supposing that the partiality of an old lover, the habit of flattery, the prevailing opinions in a social circle, had dictated these words to the ex-Ambassador, they nevertheless proved on what a negation of true taste the judgment of society people is based, so arbitrary that the smallest trifle can make it rush to the wildest absurdities, on the way to which it comes across no genuinely felt impression to arrest it.

"I claim no credit for knowing about flowers, since I've lived all my life in the fields," replied Mme de Villeparisis modestly. "But," she added graciously, turning to the Prince, "if, when I was very young, I had some rather more serious notions about them than other country children, I owe it to a distinguished fellow-countryman of yours, Herr von Schlegel. I met him at Broglie, where I was taken by my aunt Cordelia (Marshal de Castellane's wife, don't you know?). I remember so well M. Lebrun, M. de Salvandy, M. Doudan, getting him to talk about flowers. I was only a little girl, and I couldn't understand all he said. But he liked playing with me, and when he went back to your country he sent me a beautiful botany book to remind me of a drive we took together in a phaeton to the Val Richer, when I fell asleep on his knee. I've always kept the book, and it taught me to observe many things about flowers which I should not have noticed otherwise. When Mme de Barante published some of Mme de Broglie's letters, charming and affected like herself, I hoped to find among them some record of those conversations with Herr von Schlegel. But she was a woman who only looked to nature for arguments in support of religion."

Robert called me away to the far end of the room where he and his mother were.

"How very nice you've been," I said to him, "I don't know how to thank you. Can we dine together to-morrow?"

"To-morrow? Yes, if you like, but it will have to be with Bloch. I met him just now on the doorstep. He was rather stiff with me at first because I had quite forgotten to answer his last two letters (he didn't tell me that was what had offended him, but I guessed it), but after that he was so friendly to me that I simply can't disappoint him. Between ourselves, on his side at least, I feel it's a friendship for life."

I do not think that Robert was altogether mistaken. Furious detraction was often, with Bloch, the effect of a keen affection which he had supposed to be unrequited. And as he made little effort to imagine other people's lives, and never dreamed that one might have been ill, or away from home, or otherwise occupied, a week's silence was at once interpreted by him as arising from deliberate coldness. And so I never believed that his most violent outbursts as a friend, or in later years as a writer, went very deep. They were exacerbated if one replied to them with an icy dignity, or with a platitude which encouraged him to redouble his onslaught, but yielded often to a warmly sympathetic response. "As for my being nice to you," went on Saint-Loup, "I haven't really been nice at all. My aunt tells me that it's you who avoid her, that you never utter a word to her. She wonders whether you have anything against her."

Fortunately for myself, if I had been taken in by these words, our departure for Balbec, which I believed to be imminent, would have prevented my making any attempt to see Mme de Guermantes again, to assure her that I had nothing against her, and so put her under the necessity of proving that it was she who had something against me. But I had only to remind myself that she had not even offered to let me see her Elstirs. Moreover, this was not a disappointment; I had never expected her to talk to me about them; I knew that I did not appeal to her, that I had no hope of ever making her like me; the most that I had been able to look forward to was that, since I should not be seeing her again before I left Paris, her kindness would afford me an entirely soothing impression of her, which I could take with me to Balbec indefinitely prolonged, intact, instead of a memory mixed with anxiety and gloom.

Mme de Marsantes kept on interrupting her conversation with Robert to tell me how often he had spoken to her about me, how fond he was of me; she treated me with a deference

which I found almost painful because I felt it to be prompted
by her fear of falling out because of me with this son whom
she had not seen all day, with whom she was eager to be alone,
and over whom she must accordingly have supposed that the
influence which she wielded was not equal to and must conciliate mine. Having heard me earlier asking Bloch for news
of his uncle, M. Nissim Bernard, Mme de Marsantes inquired
whether it was he who had at one time lived at Nice.

"In that case, he knew M. de Marsantes there before our
marriage," she told me. "My husband used often to speak of
him as an excellent man, with such a delicate, generous nature."

"To think that for once in his life he wasn't lying! It's
incredible," Bloch would have thought.

All this time I should have liked to explain to Mme de
Marsantes that Robert felt infinitely more affection for her than
for myself, and that even if she had shown hostility towards me
it was not in my nature to attempt to set him against her, to
detach him from her. But now that Mme de Guermantes had
gone I had more leisure to observe Robert, and it was only
then that I noticed that a sort of fury seemed to have taken
possession of him once more, rising to the surface of his
stern and sombre features. I was afraid lest, remembering the
scene in the theatre that afternoon, he might be feeling humiliated in my presence at having allowed himself to be treated
so harshly by his mistress without making any rejoinder.

Suddenly he broke away from his mother, who had put her
arm round his neck, and, coming towards me, led me behind
the little flower-strewn counter at which Mme de Villeparisis
had resumed her seat and beckoned me to follow him into the
smaller drawing-room. I was hurrying after him when M. de
Charlus, who may have supposed that I was leaving the house,
turned abruptly from Prince von Faffenheim, to whom he had
been talking, and made a rapid circuit which brought him
face to face with me. I saw with alarm that he had taken the
hat in the lining of which were a capital 'G' and a ducal
coronet. In the doorway into the small drawing-room he
said without looking at me:

"As I see that you have taken to going into society, you
must give me the pleasure of coming to see me. But it's a little

complicated," he went on with a distracted but calculating air, as if the pleasure had been one that he was afraid of not securing again once he had let slip the opportunity of arranging with me the means by which it might be realised. "I am very seldom at home; you will have to write to me. But I should prefer to explain things to you more quietly. I shall be leaving soon. Will you walk a short way with me? I shall only keep you for a moment."

"You'd better take care, Monsieur," I warned him. "You have picked up the wrong hat by mistake."

"Do you want to prevent me from taking my own hat?"

I assumed, a similar mishap having recently occurred to myself, that, someone else having taken his hat, he had seized upon one at random so as not to go home bare-headed, and that I had placed him in a difficulty by exposing his stratagem. So I did not pursue the matter. I told him that I must say a few words to Saint-Loup. "He's talking to that idiotic Duc de Guermantes," I added. "That's a charming thing to say: I shall tell my brother." "Oh! you think that would interest M. de Charlus?" (I imagined that, if he had a brother, that brother must be called Charlus too. Saint-Loup had indeed explained his family tree to me at Balbec, but I had forgotten the details.) "Who's talking about M. de Charlus?" said the Baron in an insolent tone. "Go to Robert. I know that you took part this morning in one of those lunch-time orgies that he has with a woman who is disgracing him. You would do well to use your influence with him to make him realise the pain he is causing his poor mother and all of us by dragging our name in the dirt."

I should have liked to reply that at this degrading luncheon the conversation had been entirely about Emerson, Ibsen and Tolstoy, and that the young woman had lectured Robert to make him drink nothing but water. In the hope of bringing some balm to Robert, whose pride I thought had been wounded, I sought to excuse his mistress. I did not know that at that moment, in spite of his anger with her, it was on himself that he was heaping reproaches. But it always happens, in quarrels between a good man and a worthless woman and when the right is all on one side, that some trifle crops up which enables the woman to appear not to have been in the wrong on one point. And since she ignores all the other points, if the man feels the need of her, if he is upset by the separation, his weakness will make him exaggeratedly scrupulous, he will remember the absurd reproaches that have been flung at him and will ask himself whether they have not some foundation in fact.

"I've come to the conclusion that I was wrong about that necklace," Robert said to me. "Of course, I didn't do it with any ill intent, but I know very well that other people don't look at things in the same way as oneself. She had a very hard time when she was young. In her eyes I'm bound to appear the rich man who thinks he can get anything he wants with his money and against whom a poor person can't compete, whether in trying to influence Boucheron or in a lawsuit. Of course she has been horribly cruel to me, when I've never thought of anything but her good. But I do see clearly that she thinks I wanted to make her feel that one could keep a hold on her with money, and that's not true. And she's so fond of me—what must she be thinking? Poor darling, if you only knew how sweet and thoughtful she is, I simply can't tell you what adorable things she's often done for me. How wretched she must be feeling now! In any case, whatever happens I don't want to let her think me a cad; I shall dash off to Boucheron's and get the necklace. Who knows? Perhaps when she sees what I've done she'll admit that she's been partly in the wrong. You see, it's the idea that she's suffering at this moment that I can't bear. What one suffers oneself one knows—it's nothing. But to tell oneself that *she's* suffering and not to be able to form any idea of what she feels—I think I should go mad, I'd rather not see her ever again than let her suffer. All I ask is that she should be happy without me if need be. You know, for me everything that concerns her is enormously important, it becomes something cosmic; I shall run to the jeweller's and then go and ask her to forgive me. Until I get down there, what will she be thinking of me? If she could only know that I was on my way! Why don't you come to her house on the off chance; perhaps everything will be all right. Perhaps," he went on with a smile, as though hardly daring to believe in so idyllic a possibility, "we can all three dine together in the country. But one can't tell yet. I'm so bad at handling her; poor sweet, I may perhaps hurt her feelings again. Besides, her decision may be irrevocable."

Robert swept me back to his mother.

"Good-bye," he said to her. "I've got to go now. I don't know when I shall get leave again. Probably not for a month. I shall write to you as soon as I know."

Certainly Robert was not in the least the sort of son who, when he goes out with his mother, feels that an attitude of exasperation towards her ought to counterbalance the smiles and greetings which he bestows on strangers. Nothing is more prevalent than this odious form of vengeance on the part of those who appear to believe that rudeness to one's own family is the natural complement to ceremonial behaviour. Whatever the wretched mother may say, her son, as though he had been brought along against his will and wished to make her pay dearly for his presence, immediately refutes the timidly ventured assertion with a sarcastic, precise, cruel contradiction; the mother at once conforms, though without thereby disarming him, to the opinion of this superior being whose delightful nature she will continue to vaunt to all and sundry in his absence, but who, for all that, spares her none of his most wounding remarks. Saint-Loup was not at all like this; but the anguish which Rachel's absence provoked in him caused him for different reasons to be no less harsh with his mother than those other sons are with theirs. And as she listened to him I saw the same throb, like the beating of a wing, which Mme de Marsantes had been unable to repress when her son first entered the room, convulse her whole body once again; but this time it was an anxious face and woe-begone eyes that she fastened on him.

"What, Robert, you're going off? Seriously? My little son— the one day I had a chance to see something of you!"

And then quite softly, in the most natural tone, in a voice from which she strove to banish all sadness so as not to inspire her son with a pity which would perhaps have been painful to him, or else useless and simply calculated to irritate him, as a simple common-sense assertion she added: "You know it's not at all nice of you."

But to this simplicity she added so much timidity, to show him that she was not trespassing on his freedom, so much affection, so that he should not reproach her for interfering with his pleasures, that Saint-Loup could not help but observe in himself as it were the possibility of a similar wave of affection, in other words an obstacle to his spending the evening with his mistress. And so he reacted angrily: "It's unfortunate, but, nice or not, that's how it is."

And he heaped on his mother the reproaches which no doubt he felt that he himself perhaps deserved; thus it is that egoists have always the last word; having posited at the start that their resolution is unshakeable, the more susceptible the feeling to which one appeals in them to make them abandon their resolution, the more reprehensible they find, not themselves who resist that appeal, but those who put them under the necessity of resisting it, so that their own harshness may be carried to the utmost degree of cruelty without having any effect in their eyes but to aggravate the culpability of the person who is so indelicate as to be hurt, to be in the right, and to cause them thus treacherously the pain of acting against their natural instinct of pity. But of her own accord Mme de Marsantes ceased to pursue the matter, for she sensed that she would be unable to dissuade him.

"Well, I'm off," he said to me, "but you're not to keep him long, Mamma, because he's got to go and pay a call elsewhere quite soon."

I was fully aware that my company could not afford any pleasure to Mme de Marsantes, but I was glad not to give her the impression by leaving with Robert that I was involved in these pleasures which deprived her of him. I should have liked to find some excuse for her son's conduct, less from affection for him than from pity for her. But it was she who spoke first:

"Poor boy," she began, "I'm sure I must have hurt him dreadfully. You see, Monsieur, mothers are such selfish creatures. After all, he hasn't many pleasures, he comes so seldom to Paris. Oh, dear, if he hadn't gone already I should have liked to stop him, not to keep him of course, but just to tell him that I'm not vexed with him, that I think he was quite right. Will you excuse me if I go and look over the staircase?"

I accompanied her there.

"Robert! Robert!" she called. "No, he's gone. It's too late."

At that moment I would as gladly have undertaken a mission to make Robert break with his mistress as, a few hours earlier, to make him go and live with her altogether. In the one case Saint-Loup would have regarded me as a false friend, in the other his family would have called me his evil genius. Yet I was the same man at an interval of a few hours.

We returned to the drawing-room. Seeing that Saint-Loup was not with us, Mme de Villeparisis exchanged with M. de Norpois one of those sceptical, mocking and not too compassionate glances with which people point out to one another an over-jealous wife or an over-fond mother (traditional laughing-stocks), as much as to say: "Well, well, there's been trouble."

Robert went to his mistress, taking with him the splendid ornament which, after what had been said on both sides, he ought not to have given her. But it came to the same thing, for she would not look at it, and even after their reconciliation he could never persuade her to accept it. Certain of Robert's friends thought that these proofs of disinterestedness were deliberately calculated to bind him to her. And yet she was not greedy for money, except perhaps in order to be able to spend it freely. I often saw her lavish on people whom she believed to be in need the most extravagant largesse. "At this moment," Robert's friends would say to him, seeking to invalidate by their malicious words a disinterested action on Rachel's part, "at this moment she will be in the promenade at the Folies-Bergère. She's an enigma, that Rachel, a regular sphinx." In any case, how many mercenary women, women who are kept by men, does one not see setting countless little limits to the generosity of their lovers out of a delicacy that flowers in the midst of that sordid existence!

Robert was ignorant of almost all the infidelities of his mistress, and tormented himself over what were mere nothings compared with the real life of Rachel, a life which began every day only after he had left her. He was ignorant of almost all these infidelities. One could have told him of them without shaking his confidence in Rachel. For it is a charming law of nature, which manifests itself in the heart of the most complex social organisms, that we live in perfect ignorance of those we love. On the one hand the lover says to himself: "She is an angel, she will never give herself to me, I may as well die—and yet she loves me; she loves me so much that perhaps . . . but no, it can never possibly happen." And in the exaltation of his desire, in the anguish of his expectation, what jewels he flings at the feet of this woman, how he runs to borrow money to save her from financial worries! Meanwhile, on the other side of the glass screen, through which these conversations will no more carry than those which visitors exchange in front of an aquarium in a zoo, the public are saying: "You don't know her? You can count yourself lucky—she has robbed, in fact ruined, I don't know how many men. She's a common swindler. And crafty isn't the word!" And perhaps this last epithet is not absolutely wrong, for even the sceptical man who is not really in love with the woman but merely physically attracted says to his friends: "No, no, my dear fellow, she's not at all a whore. I don't say she hasn't had an adventure or two in her time, but she's not a woman one pays, she'd be a damned sight too expensive if she was. With her it's fifty thousand francs or nothing." The fact of the matter is that he himself has spent fifty thousand francs for the privilege of having her once, but she (finding a willing accomplice in the man himself) has managed to persuade him that he is one of those who have had her for nothing. Thus, in society, the most blatant, the most notorious creature will never be known to a certain other person save wrapped in a delicious cocoon of natural sweetness. There were in Paris two thoroughly decent men whom Saint-Loup no longer greeted when he saw them and to whom he could not refer without a tremor in his voice, calling them exploiters of women: this was because they had both been ruined by Rachel.

"There's only one thing I blame myself for," Mme de Marsantes murmured in my ear, "and that is for telling him that he wasn't nice. Such an adorable, unique son, like no one else in the world—to have told him, the only time I see him, that he wasn't nice to me! I'd sooner have been given a beating, because I'm sure that whatever pleasure he may be having this evening, and he hasn't many, will be spoiled for him by that unfair word. But I mustn't keep you, Monsieur, since you're in a hurry."

Everything that Mme de Marsantes had just said concerned Robert. It was sincere. But she ceased to be sincere, and became a patrician lady once more, when she said:

"I have been so *interested*, so *glad*, so *happy* to have this little talk with you. Thank you! Thank you!"

And with a humble air she fastened on me a look of ecstatic gratitude, as though my conversation had been one of the keenest pleasures she had experienced in her life. This charming expression went very well with the black flowers on her white patterned skirt; they were those of a great lady who knew her business.

"I can't leave at once. I must wait for M. de Charlus. I'm going with him."

Mme de Villeparisis overheard these last words. They appeared to vex her. Had the matter in question not been one which could not possibly involve such a sentiment, it might have struck me that what seemed to be at that moment aroused in Mme de Villeparisis was prudishness. But this hypothesis never even entered my mind. I was delighted with Mme de Guermantes, with Saint-Loup, with Mme de Marsantes, with M. de Charlus, with Mme de Villeparisis; I did not stop to reflect, and I spoke light-heartedly, and at random.

"You're leaving here with my nephew Palamède?" she asked me.

Thinking that it might produce a highly favourable impression on Mme de Villeparisis if she learned that I was on intimate terms with a nephew whom she esteemed so greatly, "He has asked me to walk home with him," I answered blithely. "I'm delighted. As a matter of fact, we're better friends than you think, and I've quite made up my mind that we're going to be better friends still."

From being vexed, Mme de Villeparisis seemed to have become anxious. "Don't wait for him," she said to me with a preoccupied air. "He is talking to M. de Faffenheim. He's certain to have forgotten what he said to you. You'd much better go now quickly while his back is turned."

I was not myself in any hurry to join Robert and his mistress. But Mme de Villeparisis seemed so anxious for me to go that, thinking perhaps that she had some important business to discuss with her nephew, I bade her good-bye. Next to her M. de Guermantes, superb and Olympian, was ponderously seated. One felt that the notion, omnipresent in all his limbs, of his vast riches, as though they had been smelted in a crucible into a single human ingot, gave an extraordinary density to this man who was worth so much. When I said good-bye to him he rose politely from his seat, and I sensed the inert and compact mass of thirty millions which his old-fashioned French education set in motion, raised, until it stood before me. I seemed to be looking at that statue of Olympian Zeus which Phidias is said to have cast in solid gold. Such was the power that a Jesuit education had over M. de Guermantes, over the body of M. de Guermantes at least, for it did not reign with equal mastery over the ducal mind. M. de Guermantes laughed at his own jokes, but did not even smile at other people's.

On my way downstairs I heard a voice calling out to me from behind: "So this is how you wait for me, is it?"

It was M. de Charlus.

"You don't mind if we go a little way on foot?" he asked dryly, when we were in the courtyard. "We'll walk until I find a cab that suits me."

"You wished to speak to me, Monsieur?"

"Ah, yes, as a matter of fact there were some things I wanted to say to you, but I'm not so sure now whether I shall. As far as you are concerned, I am sure that they could be the starting-point for inestimable benefits. But I can see also that they would bring into my existence, at an age when one begins to value tranquillity, a great deal of time-wasting, all sorts of inconvenience. I ask myself whether you are worth all the pains that I should have to take with you, and I have not the pleasure of knowing you well enough to be able to say. I found you very unsatisfactory at Balbec, even when allowances are made for the stupidity inseparable from the image of the "bather" and the wearing of the objects called *espadrilles*. Perhaps in any case you are not sufficiently desirous of what I could do for you to make it worth my while, for I must repeat to you quite frankly, Monsieur, that for me it can mean" (he hammered out the words with great force) "nothing but trouble."

I protested that, in that case, he must not dream of it. This summary end to negotiations did not seem to be to his liking.

"That sort of politeness means nothing," he rebuked me coldly. "There is nothing so agreeable as to put oneself out for a person who is worth one's while. For the best of us, the study of the arts, a taste for old things, collections, gardens, are all mere ersatz, surrogates, alibis. From the depths of our tub, like Diogenes, we cry out for a man. We cultivate begonias, we trim yews, as a last resort, because yews and begonias submit to treatment. But we should prefer to give our time to a plant of human growth, if we were sure that he was worth the trouble. That is the whole question. You must know yourself a little. Are you worth my trouble or not?"

"I would not for anything in the world, Monsieur, be a cause of anxiety to you," I said to him, "but so far as I am concerned you may be sure that everything that comes to me from you will give me very great pleasure. I am deeply touched that you should be so kind as to take an interest in me in this way and try to help me."

Greatly to my surprise, it was almost with effusion that he thanked me for these words. Slipping his arm through mine with that intermittent familiarity which had already struck me at Balbec, and was in such contrast to the harshness of his tone, he went on:

"With the want of consideration common at your age, you are liable to say things at times which would open an unbridgeable gulf between us. What you have said just now, on the other hand, is exactly the sort of thing that is capable of touching me, and of inducing me to do a great deal, perhaps too much for you."

As he walked arm in arm with me and uttered these words, which, though tinged with contempt, were so affectionate, M. de Charlus now fastened his gaze on me with that intense fixity, that piercing hardness which had struck me the first morning, when I saw him outside the casino at Balbec, and indeed many years before that, through the pink hawthorns,

standing beside Mme Swann, whom I supposed then to be his
mistress, in the park at Tansonville, now let it stray around him
and examine the cabs which at this time of day were passing
in considerable numbers, staring so insistently at them that
several stopped, the drivers supposing that he wished to engage
them. But M. de Charlus immediately dismissed them.

"None of them is suitable," he explained to me, "it's all a
question of the colour of their lamps, and the direction they're
going in. I hope, Monsieur," he went on, "that you will not
in any way misinterpret the purely disinterested and charitable
nature of the proposal which I am going to make to you."

I was struck by the number of ways, even more than at
Balbec, his diction resembled Swann's.

"You are intelligent enough, I dare say, not to imagine that
it is inspired by 'lack of connections,' by fear of solitude and
boredom. I need not speak to you of my family, for I assume
that a youth of your age belonging to the lower middle class"
(he accentuated the phrase in a tone of self-satisfaction) "must
know the history of France. It is the people of my world who
read nothing and are as ignorant as lackeys. In the old days the
King's valets were recruited among the nobility; now the
nobility are scarcely better than valets. But young bourgeois
like you do read, and you must certainly know Michelet's
fine passage about my family: 'I see them as being very great,
these powerful Guermantes. And what is the poor little King
of France beside them, shut up in his palace in Paris?' As for
what I am personally, that, Monsieur, is a subject which I do
not much care to talk about, but you may possibly have heard
—it was alluded to in a leading article in *The Times*, which made
a considerable impression—that the Emperor of Austria, who
has always honoured me with his friendship, and is good
enough to maintain cousinly relations with me, declared the
other day in an interview which was made public that if the
Comte de Chambord had had at his side a man as thoroughly
conversant with the undercurrents of European politics as
myself he would be King of France to-day. I have often
thought, Monsieur, that there was in me, thanks not to my
own humble gifts but to circumstances which you may one
day have occasion to learn, a wealth of experience, a sort of

secret dossier of inestimable value, of which I have not felt myself at liberty to make use for my own personal ends, which would be a priceless acquisition to a young man to whom I would hand over in a few months what it has taken me more than thirty years to acquire, and which I am perhaps alone in possessing. I do not speak of the intellectual enjoyment which you would find in learning certain secrets which a Guizot of to-day would give years of his life to know, and in the light of which certain events would assume an entirely different aspect. And I do not speak only of events that have already occurred, but of the chain of circumstances." (This was a favourite expression of M. de Charlus's, and often, when he used it, he joined his hands as if in prayer, but with his fingers stiffened, as though by this complexus to illustrate the said circumstances, which he did not specify, and the links between them.) "I could give you an explanation that no one has dreamed of, not only of the past but of the future."

M. de Charlus broke off to question me about Bloch, whom he had heard discussed, though without appearing to be listening, in his aunt's drawing-room. And in that tone which he was so skilful at detaching from what he was saying that he seemed to be thinking of something else altogether, and to be speaking mechanically, simply out of politeness, he asked if my friend was young, good-looking and so forth. Bloch, if he had heard him, would have been more puzzled even than with M. de Norpois, but for very different reasons, to know whether M. de Charlus was for or against Dreyfus. "It is not a bad idea, if you wish to learn about life," went on M. de Charlus when he had finished questioning me about Bloch, "to have a few foreigners among your friends." I replied that Bloch was French. "Indeed," said M. de Charlus, "I took him to be a Jew." His assertion of this incompatibility made me suppose that M. de Charlus was more anti-Dreyfusard than anyone I had met. He protested, however, against the charge of treason levelled against Dreyfus. But his protest took this form: "I believe the newspapers say that Dreyfus has committed a crime against his country—so I understand; I pay no attention to the newspapers; I read them as I wash my hands, without considering it worth my while to take an interest in what I

am doing. In any case, the crime is non-existent. This compatriot of your friend would have committed a crime if he
had betrayed Judaea, but what has he to do with France?"
I pointed out that if there should be a war the Jews would be
mobilised just as much as anyone else. "Perhaps so, and I am
not sure that it would not be an imprudence. If we bring over
Senegalese or Malagasies, I hardly suppose that their hearts will
be in the task of defending France, and that is only natural.
Your Dreyfus might rather be convicted of a breach of the
laws of hospitality. But enough of that. Perhaps you could
ask your friend to allow me to attend some great festival in
the Temple, a circumcision, or some Hebrew chants. He
might perhaps hire a hall and give me some biblical entertainment, as the young ladies of Saint-Cyr performed scenes taken
from the Psalms by Racine, to amuse Louis XIV. You might
perhaps arrange that, and even some comic exhibitions. For
instance a contest between your friend and his father, in
which he would smite him as David smote Goliath. That would
make quite an amusing farce. He might even, while he was
about it, give his hag (or, as my old nurse would say, his
"haggart") of a mother a good thrashing. That would be an
excellent show, and would not be unpleasing to us, eh, my
young friend, since we like exotic spectacles, and to thrash that
non-European creature would be giving a well-earned punishment to an old cow."

As he poured out these terrible, almost insane words, M. de
Charlus squeezed my arm until it hurt. I reminded myself of
all that his family had told me of his wonderful kindness to
this old nurse, whose Moliéresque vocabulary he had just
recalled, and thought to myself that the connexions, hitherto,
I felt, little studied, between goodness and wickedness in the
same heart, various as they might be, would be an interesting
subject for research.

I warned him that in any case Mme Bloch no longer existed,
while as for M. Bloch, I questioned to what extent he would
enjoy a sport which might easily result in his being blinded.
M. de Charlus seemed annoyed. "That," he said, "is a woman
who made a great mistake in dying. As for blinding him, surely
the Synagogue is blind, since it does not perceive the truth of

the Gospel. Besides, just think, at this moment when all those unhappy Jews are trembling before the stupid fury of the Christians, what an honour it would be for him to see a man like myself condescend to be amused by their sports."

At this point I caught sight of M. Bloch senior coming towards us, probably on his way to meet his son. He did not see us, but I offered to introduce him to M. de Charlus. I had no idea of the torrent of rage which my words were to let loose. "Introduce him to me! But you must have singularly little idea of social values! People do not get to know me as easily as that. In the present instance, the impropriety would be two-fold, on account of the youth of the introducer and the unworthiness of the person introduced. At the most, if I am ever permitted to enjoy the Asiatic spectacle which I outlined to you, I might address to the frightful fellow a few affable words. But on condition that he should have allowed himself to be thoroughly thrashed by his son. I might go so far as to express my satisfaction."

In any event M. Bloch paid no attention to us. He was in the process of greeting Mme Sazerat with a sweeping bow, which was very favourably received. I was surprised at this, for in the old days at Combray she was so anti-semitic that she had been highly indignant with my parents for having young Bloch in the house. But Dreyfusism, like a strong gust of wind, had, a few days before this, wafted M. Bloch to her feet. My friend's father had found Mme Sazerat charming and was particularly gratified by that lady's anti-semitism which he regarded as a proof of the sincerity of her faith and the soundness of her Dreyfusard opinions, and which also enhanced the value of the call which she had authorised him to pay her. He had not even been offended when she had said to him without thinking: "M. Drumont has the impudence to put the Revisionists in the same bag as the Protestants and the Jews. A charming juxtaposition!" "Bernard," he had said proudly to M. Nissim Bernard on returning home, "she has the prejudice, you know!" But M. Nissim Bernard had said nothing, raising his eyes to heaven in an angelic gaze. Saddened by the misfortunes of the Jews, remembering his old Christian friendships, grown mannered and precious with increasing years for reasons which the reader will learn in due course, he had now the air of a pre-Raphaelite grub on to which hair had been incongruously grafted, like threads in the heart of an opal.

"All this Dreyfus business," went on the Baron, still clasping me by the arm, "has only one drawback. It destroys society (I don't mean polite society; society has long ceased to deserve that laudatory epithet) by the influx of Mr and Mrs Beasts and Beastlies and Fitz Beastlies, whom I find even in the houses of my own cousins, because they belong to the Patriotic League, the Anti-Jewish League, or some such league, as if a political opinion entitled one to a social qualification."

This frivolity in M. de Charlus brought out his family likeness to the Duchesse de Guermantes. I remarked on the resemblance. As he appeared to think that I did not know her, I reminded him of the evening at the Opéra when he had seemed to be trying to avoid me. He assured me so forcefully that he had never seen me there that I should have ended by believing him if presently a trifling incident had not led me to think that M. de Charlus, in his excessive pride perhaps, did not care to be seen with me.

"Let us return to yourself," he said, "and my plans for you. There exists among certain men a freemasonry of which I cannot now say more than that it numbers in its ranks four of the reigning sovereigns of Europe. Now, the entourage of one of these, who is the Emperor of Germany, is trying to cure him of his fancy. That is a very serious matter, and may lead us to war. Yes, my dear sir, that is a fact. You remember the story of the man who believed that he had the Princess of China shut up in a bottle. It was a form of insanity. He was cured of it. But as soon as he ceased to be mad he became merely stupid. There are maladies which we must not seek to cure because they alone protect us from others that are more serious. A cousin of mine had a stomach ailment: he could digest nothing. The most learned stomach specialists treated him, to no avail. I took him to a certain doctor (another highly interesting man, by the way, of whom I could tell you a great deal). He guessed at once that the malady was nervous, persuaded his patient of this, advised him to eat whatever he

liked unhesitatingly, and assured him that his digestion would
stand it. But my cousin also had nephritis. What the stomach
digested perfectly well the kidneys ceased after a time to be
able to eliminate, and my cousin, instead of living to a fine
old age with an imaginary disease of the stomach which
obliged him to keep to a diet, died at forty with his stomach
cured but his kidneys ruined. Given a very considerable lead
over your contemporaries, who knows whether you may not
perhaps become what some eminent man of the past might
have been if a beneficent spirit had revealed to him, among a
generation that knew nothing of them, the secrets of steam and
electricity. Do not be foolish, do not refuse for reasons of tact
and discretion. Try to understand that, if I do you a great
service, I do not expect my reward from you to be any less
great. It is many years now since people in society ceased to
interest me. I have but one passion left, to seek to redeem the
mistakes of my life by conferring the benefit of my knowledge
on a soul that is still virgin and capable of being fired by virtue.
I have had great sorrows, of which I may tell you perhaps
some day; I have lost my wife, who was the loveliest, the
noblest, the most perfect creature that one could dream of. I
have young relatives who are not—I do not say worthy, but
capable of accepting the intellectual heritage of which I have
been speaking. Who knows but that you may be the person
into whose hands it is to pass, the person whose life I shall be
able to guide and to raise to so lofty a plane. My own would
gain in return. Perhaps in teaching you the great secrets of
diplomacy I might recover a taste for them myself, and begin
at last to do things of real interest in which you would have an
equal share. But before I can discover this I must see you often,
very often, every day."

I was thinking of taking advantage of these unexpectedly
ardent predispositions on M. de Charlus's part to ask him
whether he could not arrange for me to meet his sister-in-law
when suddenly I felt my arm violently jerked as though by an
electric shock. It was M. de Charlus who, for some reason
which had arisen to counter the "cosmic" laws of which until
a second before he had been the "inspired visionary," had
hurriedly withdrawn his arm from mine. Although as he talked

he had allowed his eyes to wander in all directions, he had only just caught sight of M. d'Argencourt emerging from a side street. On seeing us, the Belgian Minister appeared annoyed and gave me a look of distrust, almost that look intended for a creature of another race with which Mme de Guermantes had scrutinised Bloch, and tried to avoid us. But it was as though M. de Charlus was determined to show him that he was not at all anxious not to be seen by him, for he called after him to tell him something of extreme insignificance. And fearing perhaps that M. d'Argencourt had not recognised me, M. de Charlus informed him that I was a great friend of Mme de Villeparisis, of the Duchesse de Guermantes, of Robert de Saint-Loup, and that he himself, Charlus, was an old friend of my grandmother, glad to be able to show her grandson a little of the affection that he felt for her. Nevertheless I observed that M. d'Argencourt, although I had barely been introduced to him at Mme de Villeparisis's and M. de Charlus had now spoken to him at great length about my family, was distinctly colder to me than he had been an hour ago, and thereafter, for a long time, he showed the same aloofness whenever we met. He examined me now with a curiosity in which there was no sign of friendliness, and seemed even to have to overcome an instinctive repulsion when, on leaving us, after a moment's hesitation, he held out a hand to me which he at once withdrew.

"I'm sorry about that," said M. de Charlus. "That fellow Argencourt, well born but ill bred, a worse than second-rate diplomat, an execrable husband and a womaniser, as double-faced as a villain in a play, is one of those men who are incapable of understanding but perfectly capable of destroying the things in life that are really great. I hope that our friendship will be one of them, if it is ever to be formed, and that you will do me the honour of keeping it—as I shall—well clear of the heels of any of those donkeys who, from idleness or clumsiness or sheer malice, trample on what seemed destined to endure. Unfortunately, that is the mould in which most society people have been cast."

"The Duchesse de Guermantes seems to be very intelligent. We were talking this afternoon about the possibility of war. It appears that she is especially knowledgeable on that subject."

"She is nothing of the sort," replied M. de Charlus tartly. "Women, and most men for that matter, understand nothing about what I wished to speak to you of. My sister-in-law is an agreeable woman who imagines that we are still living in the days of Balzac's novels, when women had an influence on politics. Association with her could at present only have a most unfortunate effect on you, as for that matter all social intercourse. That was one of the very things I was about to tell you when that fool interrupted me. The first sacrifice that you must make for me—I shall claim them from you in proportion to the gifts I bestow on you—is to give up going into society. It distressed me this afternoon to see you at that idiotic gathering. You will tell me that I was there myself, but for me it was not a social gathering, it was simply a family visit. Later on, when you are a man of established position, if it amuses you to stoop for a moment to that sort of thing, it may perhaps do no harm. And then I need not point out how invaluable I can be to you. The 'Open Sesame' to the Guermantes house, and any others that it is worth while throwing open the doors of to you, rests with me. I shall be the judge, and intend to remain in control of the situation. At present you are a catechumen. There was something scandalous about your presence up there. You must at all costs avoid impropriety."

Since M. de Charlus had mentioned this visit to Mme de Villeparisis's, I wanted to ask him his exact relationship to the Marquise, the latter's birth, and so on, but the question took another form on my lips than I had intended, and I asked him instead what the Villeparisis family was.

"Dear me, it's not an easy question to answer," M. de Charlus replied in a voice that seemed to skate over the words. "It's as if you had asked me to tell you what nothing was. My aunt, who is capable of anything, took it into her whimsical head to plunge the greatest name in France into oblivion by marrying for the second time a little M. Thirion. This Thirion thought that he could assume an extinct aristocratic name with impunity, as people do in novels. History doesn't relate whether he was tempted by La Tour d'Auvergne, whether he hesitated between Toulouse and Montmorency. At all events

he made a different choice and became Monsieur de Villeparisis. Since there have been no Villeparisis since 1702, I
thought that he simply meant to indicate modestly that he was
a gentleman from Villeparisis, a little place near Paris, that he
had a solicitor's practice or a barber's shop at Villeparisis.
But my aunt didn't see things that way—as a matter of fact
she's reaching the age when she can scarcely see at all. She
tried to make out that such a marquisate existed in the family;
she wrote to us all and wanted to put things on a proper foot-
ing, I don't know why. When one takes a name to which one
has no right, it's best not to make too much fuss, like our
excellent friend the so-called Comtesse de M. who, against
the advice of Mme Alphonse Rothschild, refused to swell the
coffers of the State for a title which would not have been made
more authentic thereby. The joke is that ever since then my
aunt has claimed a monopoly of all the paintings connected
with the real Villeparisis family, to whom the late Thirion was
in no way related. My aunt's country house has become a sort
of repository for their portraits, genuine or not, under the
rising flood of which several Guermantes and several Condés
who are by no means small beer have had to disappear. The
picture dealers manufacture new ones for her every year. And
she even has in her dining-room in the country a portrait of
Saint-Simon because of his niece's first marriage to a M. de
Villeparisis, as if the author of the *Memoirs* hadn't perhaps
other claims to the interest of visitors than not to have been
the great-grandfather of M. Thirion."

Mme de Villeparisis being merely Mme Thirion completed
the decline and fall in my estimation of her which had begun
when I had seen the mixed composition of her salon. It seemed
to me to be unfair that a woman whose title and name were
of quite recent origin should be able thus to delude her contemporaries and might similarly delude posterity by virtue of her
friendships with royal personages. Now that she had become
once again what I had supposed her to be in my childhood, a
person who had nothing aristocratic about her, these distinguished kinsfolk by whom she was surrounded struck me
as somehow extraneous to her. She did not cease to be charming to us all. I went occasionally to see her and she sent me

little presents from time to time. But I had never any impression that she belonged to the Faubourg Saint-Germain, and if I had wanted any information about it she was one of the last people to whom I should have applied.

"At present," M. de Charlus went on, "by going into society you will only damage your position, warp your intellect and character. Moreover, you must be particularly careful in choosing your friends. Keep mistresses if your family have no objection—that doesn't concern me, and indeed I can only encourage it, you young rascal—a young rascal who will soon have to start shaving," he added, touching my chin. "But your choice of men friends is more important. Eight out of ten young men are little bounders, little wretches capable of doing you an injury which you will never be able to repair. My nephew Saint-Loup, now, he might be a suitable companion for you at a pinch. As far as your future is concerned, he can be of no possible use to you, but for that I will suffice. And really, when all's said and done, as a person to go about with, at times when you have had enough of me, he does not seem to present any serious drawback that I know of. At least he's a man, not one of those effeminate creatures one sees so many of nowadays, who look like little renters and at any moment may bring their innocent victims to the gallows." (I did not know the meaning of this slang word "renter"; anyone who had known it would have been as greatly surprised by his use of it as myself. Society people always like talking slang, and people who may be suspected of certain things like to show that they are not afraid to mention them. A proof of innocence in their eyes. But they have lost their sense of proportion, they are no longer capable of realising the point beyond which a certain pleasantry will become too technical, too flagrant, will be a proof rather of corruption than of ingenuousness.) "He's not like the rest of them: he's very nice, very serious."

I could not help smiling at this epithet "serious," to which the intonation that M. de Charlus gave it seemed to impart the sense of "virtuous," of "steady," as one says of a little shop-girl that she is "serious." At that moment a cab passed, zigzagging along the streeet. A young cabman, who had deserted his box, was driving it from inside, where he lay sprawling on the cushions, apparently half-tipsy. M. de Charlus instantly stopped him. The driver began to parley:

"Which way are you going?"

"Yours." (This surprised me, for M. de Charlus had already refused several cabs with similarly coloured lamps.)

"Well, I don't want to get up on the box. D'you mind if I stay inside?"

"No, but lower the hood. Well, think over my proposal," said M. de Charlus, preparing to leave me, "I give you a few days to consider it. Write to me. I repeat, I shall need to see you every day, and to receive from you guarantees of loyalty and discretion which, I must admit, you do seem to offer. But in the course of my life I have been so often deceived by appearances that I never wish to trust them again. Damn it, it's the least I can expect that before giving up a treasure I should know into what hands it is going to pass. Anyway, bear in mind what I'm offering you. You are like Hercules (though, unfortunately for yourself, you do not appear to me to have quite his muscular development) at the parting of the ways. Remember that you may regret for the rest of your life not having chosen the way that leads to virtue. Hallo," he turned to the cabman, "haven't you put the hood down? I'll do it myself. I think, too, I'd better drive, seeing the state you appear to be in."

He jumped in beside the cabman, and the cab set off at a brisk trot.

As for myself, no sooner had I turned in at our gate than I came across the pendant to the conversation which I had heard that afternoon between Bloch and M. de Norpois, but in another form, brief, inverted and cruel. This was a dispute between our butler, who was a Dreyfusard, and the Guermantes's, who was an anti-Dreyfusard. The truths and counter-truths which fought up above among the intellectuals of the rival Leagues, the Patrie Française and the Droits de l'Homme, were fast spreading downwards into the subsoil of popular opinion. M. Reinach manipulated through their feelings people whom he had never seen, whereas for him the Dreyfus case simply presented itself to his reason as an irrefutable theorem which he "demonstrated" in the sequel by the most astonishing victory for rational politics (a victory against France, according to some) that the world has ever seen. In two years he replaced a Billot ministry by a Clemenceau ministry, revolutionised public opinion from top to bottom, took Picquart from his prison to install him, ungrateful, in the Ministry of War. Perhaps this rationalist crowd-manipulator was himself manipulated by his ancestry. When we find that the systems of philosophy which contain the most truths were dictated to their authors, in the last analysis, by reasons of sentiment, how are we to suppose that in a simple affair of politics like the Dreyfus case reasons of that sort may not, unbeknownst to the reasoner, have ruled his reason? Bloch believed himself to have been led by a logical chain of reasoning to choose Dreyfusism, yet he knew that his nose, his skin and his hair had been imposed on him by his race. Doubtless the reason enjoys more freedom; yet it obeys certain laws which it has not prescribed for itself. The case of the Guermantes's butler and our own was peculiar. The waves of the two currents of Dreyfusism and anti-Dreyfusism which now divided France from top to bottom were, on the whole, silent, but the occasional echoes which they emitted were sincere. When you heard anyone in the middle of a talk which was being deliberately kept off the Affair announce furtively some piece of political news, generally false but always devoutly to be wished, you could induce from the nature of his predictions where his heart lay. Thus there came into conflict on certain points, on one side a timid apostolate, on the other a righteous indignation. The two butlers whom I heard arguing as I came in furnished an exception to the rule. Ours insinuated that Dreyfus was guilty, the Guermantes's that he was innocent. This was done not to conceal their personal convictions, but from cunning and competitive ruthlessness. Our butler, being uncertain whether the re-trial would be ordered, wanted in case of failure to deprive the Duke's butler in advance of the joy of seeing a just cause vanquished. The Duke's butler thought that, in the event of a refusal to grant a re-trial, ours would be more indignant at the detention of an innocent man on Devil's Island. The porter looked on. I had the impression that it was not he who was the cause of dissension in the Guermantes household.

I went upstairs, and found my grandmother not at all well. For some time past, without knowing exactly what was wrong, she had been complaining of her health. It is in sickness that we are compelled to recognise that we do not live alone but are chained to a being from a different realm, from whom we are worlds apart, who has no knowledge of us and by whom it is impossible to make ourselves understood: our body. Were we to meet a brigand on the road, we might perhaps succeed in making him sensible of his own personal interest if not of our plight. But to ask pity of our body is like discoursing in front of an octopus, for which our words can have no more meaning than the sound of the tides, and with which we should be appalled to find ourselves condemned to live. My grand-mother's ailments often passed unnoticed by her attention, which was always directed towards us. When they gave her too much pain, in the hope of curing them she tried in vain to understand them. If the morbid phenomena of which her body was the theatre remained obscure and beyond the reach of her mind, they were clear and intelligible to certain beings belonging to the same natural kingdom as themselves, beings to whom the human mind has learned gradually to have recourse in order to understand what its body is saying to it, as when a foreigner addresses us we try to find someone of his country who will act as interpreter. These can talk to our body, can tell us if its anger is serious or will soon be appeased. Cottard, who had been called in to examine my grandmother—and who had infuriated us by asking with a subtle smile, the moment we told him she was ill: "Ill? You're sure it's not what they call a diplomatic illness?"—tried to soothe his patient's restlessness by a milk diet. But incessant bowls of milk soup gave her no relief, because my grandmother sprinkled them liberally with salt, the injurious effects of which were then unknown (Widal not yet having made his dis-coveries). For, medicine being a compendium of the successive and contradictory mistakes of medical practitioners, when we summon the wisest of them to our aid the chances are that we may be relying on a scientific truth the error of which will be recognised in a few years' time. So that to believe in medicine would be the height of folly, if not to believe in it were not a

greater folly still, for from this mass of errors a few truths have
in the long run emerged. Cottard had told us to take her temperature. A thermometer was fetched. Almost throughout its
entire length the tube was empty of mercury. One could
scarcely make out, nestling at the bottom of its trough, the
silver salamander. It seemed dead. The little glass pipe was
slipped into my grandmother's mouth. We had no need to
leave it there for long; the little sorceress had not been slow
in casting her horoscope. We found her motionless, perched
half-way up her tower and declining to move, showing us with
precision the figure that we had asked of her, a figure with
which all the most careful thought that my grandmother's
mind might have devoted to herself would have been incapable of furnishing her: 101°. For the first time we felt
some anxiety. We shook the thermometer well, to erase the
ominous sign, as though we were able thus to reduce the
patient's fever simultaneously with the temperature indicated.
Alas, it was only too clear that the little sibyl, bereft of reason
though she was, had not pronounced judgment arbitrarily,
for the next day, scarcely had the thermometer been inserted
between my grandmother's lips when almost at once, as though
with a single bound, exulting in her certainty and in her
intuition of a fact that to us was imperceptible, the little
prophetess had come to a halt at the same point, in an implacable immobility, and pointed once again to that figure 101
with the tip of her gleaming wand. She said nothing else; in
vain had we longed, wished, prayed, she was deaf to our
entreaties; it seemed as though this were her final word, a
warning and a threat.

Then, in an attempt to constrain her to modify her response,
we had recourse to another creature of the same kingdom, but
more potent, a creature not content with questioning the body
but capable of commanding it, a febrifuge of the same order
as the modern aspirin, which had not then come into use. We
had not brought the thermometer down below 99.5, in the
hope that it would not have to rise from there. We made my
grandmother swallow this drug and then replaced the thermometer in her mouth. Like an implacable warder to whom
one presents a permit signed by a higher authority whose

patronage one enjoys, and who, finding it to be in order, replies: "All right, I've nothing to say; if that's how it is you may pass," this time the vigilant out-sister did not move. But sullenly she seemed to be saying: "What good will it do you? Since you know quinine, she may give me the order not to go up once, ten times, twenty times. And then she'll grow tired of telling me, I know her, believe me. This won't last for ever. And then where will it have got you?"

Thereupon my grandmother felt the presence within her of a being who knew the human body better than she; the presence of a contemporary of the races that have vanished from the earth, the presence of earth's first inhabitant—far earlier than the creation of thinking man; she felt that primeval ally probing in her head, her heart, her elbow; he was reconnoitring the ground, organising everything for the prehistoric combat which began at once to be fought. In a moment, a crushed Python, the fever was vanquished by the potent chemical element to which my grandmother, across all the kingdoms, reaching out beyond all animal and vegetable life, would have liked to be able to give thanks. And she remained moved by this glimpse which she had caught, through the mists of so many centuries, of an element anterior to the creation even of plants. Meanwhile the thermometer, like one of the Parcae momentarily vanquished by a more ancient god, held motionless her silver spindle. Alas! other inferior creatures which man has trained to hunt the mysterious quarry which he himself is incapable of pursuing in the depths of his being, reported cruelly to us every day a certain quantity of albumin, not large, but constant enough for it also to appear to be related to some persistent malady which we could not detect. Bergotte had shaken that scrupulous instinct in me which made me subordinate my intellect when he spoke to me of Dr du Boulbon as of a physician who would not bore me, who would discover methods of treatment which, however strange they might appear, would adapt themselves to the singularity of my intelligence. But ideas transform themselves in us, overcome the resistance we put up to them at first, and feed upon rich intellectual reserves which were ready-made for them without our realising it. So, of happens

whenever remarks we have heard made about someone we
do not know have had the faculty of awakening in us the idea
of great talent, of a sort of genius, in my inmost mind I now
gave Dr du Boulbon the benefit of that unlimited confidence
which is inspired in us by the man who, with an eye more penetrating than other men's, perceives the truth. I knew indeed
that he was more of a specialist in nervous diseases, the man
to whom Charcot before his death had predicted that he would
reign supreme in neurology and psychiatry. "Ah, I don't know
about that. It's quite possible," put in Françoise, who was in
the room and who was hearing Charcot's name, as indeed du
Boulbon's, for the first time. But this in no way prevented her
from saying "It's possible." Her "possibles," her "perhapses,"
her "I don't knows" were peculiarly irritating at such moments. One wanted to say to her: "Naturally you didn't know,
since you haven't the faintest idea what we are talking about.
How can you even say whether it's possible or not, since you
know nothing about it? Anyhow, you can't say now that you
don't know what Charcot said to du Boulbon. You do know
because we've just told you, and your 'perhapses' and 'possibles'
are out of place, because it's a fact."

In spite of this more special competence in cerebral and
nervous matters, as I knew that du Boulbon was a great
physician, a superior man with a profound and inventive
intellect, I begged my mother to send for him, and the hope
that, by a clear perception of the malady, he might perhaps
cure it, finally prevailed over the fear that we had that by
calling in a consultant we would alarm my grandmother.
What decided my mother was the fact that, unwittingly
encouraged by Cottard, my grandmother no longer went out
of doors, and scarcely rose from her bed. In vain might she
answer us in the words of Mme de Sévigné's letter on Mme de
la Fayette: "Everyone said she was mad not to wish to go out.
I said to these persons so precipitate in their judgment: 'Mme
de la Fayette is not mad!' and I stuck to that. It has taken her
death to prove that she was quite right not to go out." Du
Boulbon when he came decided against, if not Mme de
Sévigné, whom we did not quote to him, at any rate my grandmother. Instead of sounding her chest, he gazed at her with

his wonderful eyes, in which there was perhaps the illusion that he was making a profound scrutiny of his patient, or the desire to give her that illusion, which seemed spontaneous but must have become mechanical, or not to let her see that he was thinking of something quite different, or to establish his authority over her, and began to talk about Bergotte.

"Ah yes, indeed, Madame, he's splendid. How right you are to admire him! But which of his books do you prefer? Oh, really? Why, yes, perhaps that is the best after all. In any case it is the best composed of his novels. Claire is quite charming in it. Which of his male characters appeals to you most?"

I supposed at first that he was making her talk about literature because he himself found medicine boring, perhaps also to display his breadth of mind and even, with a more therapeutic aim, to restore confidence to his patient, to show her that he was not alarmed, to take her mind off the state of her health. But afterwards I realised that, being chiefly distinguished as an alienist and for his work on the brain, he had been seeking to ascertain by these questions whether my grandmother's memory was in good order. With seeming reluctance he began to inquire about her life, fixing her with a stern and sombre eye. Then suddenly, as though he had glimpsed the truth and was determined to reach it at all costs, with a preliminary rubbing of his hands to shake off any lingering hesitations which he himself might feel and any objections which we might have raised, looking down at my grandmother with a lucid eye, boldly and as though he were at last upon solid ground, punctuating his words in a quietly impressive tone, every inflexion of which was instinct with intelligence (his voice, indeed, thoughout his visit remained what it naturally was, caressing, and under his bushy brows his ironical eyes were full of kindness), he said:

"You will be cured, Madame, on the day, whenever it comes—and it rests entirely with you whether it comes to-day —on which you realise that there is nothing wrong with you and resume your ordinary life. You tell me that you have not been eating, not going out?"

"But, Doctor, I have a temperature."

"Not just now at any rate. Besides, what a splendid excuse! Don't you know that we feed up tuberculosis patients with temperatures of 102 and keep them out in the open air?"

"But I have a little albumin as well."

"You ought not to know anything about that. You have what I have had occasion to call 'mental albumin.' We have all of us had, when we have not been very well, little albuminous phases which our doctor has done his best to prolong by calling our attention to them. For one disorder that doctors cure with medicaments (as I am assured that they do occasionally succeed in doing) they produce a dozen others in healthy subjects by inoculating them with that pathogenic agent a thousand times more virulent than all the microbes in the world, the idea that one is ill. A belief of that sort, which has a potent effect on any temperature, acts with special force on neurotic people. Tell them that a shut window is open behind their backs, and they will begin to sneeze; persuade them that you have put magnesia in their soup, and they will be seized with colic; that their coffee is stronger than usual, and they will not sleep a wink all night. Do you imagine, Madame, that I needed to do more than look you in the eyes, listen to the way in which you express yourself, observe, if I may say so, your daughter and your grandson who are so like you, to realise what was the matter with you?"

"Your grandmother might perhaps go and sit, if the doctor allows it, in some quiet path in the Champs-Elysées, near that clump of laurels where you used to play when you were little," said my mother to me, thus indirectly consulting Dr du Boulbon and her voice for that reason assuming a tone of timid deference which it would not have had if she had been addressing me alone. The doctor turned to my grandmother and, being a man of letters no less than a man of science, adjured her as follows:

"Go to the Champs-Elysées, Madame, to the clump of laurels which your grandson loves. The laurel will be beneficial to your health. It purifies. After he had exterminated the serpent Python, it was with a branch of laurel in his hand that Apollo made his entry into Delphi. He sought thus to guard himself from the deadly germs of the venomous monster. So you see that the laurel is the most ancient, the most venerable and, I may add—something that has its therapeutic as well as its prophylactic value—the most beautiful of antiseptics."

Inasmuch as a great part of what doctors know is taught them by the sick, they are easily led to believe that this knowledge which patients exhibit is common to them all, and they fondly imagine that they can impress the patient of the moment with some remark picked up at a previous bedside. Thus it was with the superior smile of a Parisian who, in conversation with a peasant, might hope to surprise him by using a word of the local dialect, that Dr du Boulbon said to my grandmother: "Probably a windy night will help to put you to sleep when the strongest soporifics would have no effect." "On the contrary, the wind always keeps me wide awake." But doctors are touchy people. "Ach!" muttered du Boulbon with a frown, as if someone had trodden on his toe, or as if my grandmother's sleeplessness on stormy nights were a personal insult to himself. He had not, however, an undue opinion of himself, and since, in his character as a "superior" person, he felt himself bound not to put any faith in medicine, he quickly recovered his philosophic serenity.

My mother, in her passionate longing for reassurance from Bergotte's friend, added in support of his verdict that a first cousin of my grandmother's, who suffered from a nervous complaint, had remained for seven years shut up in her bedroom at Combray, without getting up more than once or twice a week.

"You see, Madame, I didn't know that, and yet I could have told you."

"But, Doctor, I'm not in the least like her; on the contrary, my doctor complains that he cannot get me to stay in bed," said my grandmother, either because she was a little irritated by the doctor's theories, or because she was anxious to submit to him all the objections that might be made to them, in the hope that he would refute these and that, once he had gone, she would no longer have any doubts as to the accuracy of his encouraging diagnosis.

"Why, naturally, Madame, one cannot have—if you'll forgive the expression—every form of mental derangement. You have others, but not that particular one. Yesterday I visited a home for neurasthenics. In the garden, I saw a man standing on a bench, motionless as a fakir, his neck bent in a position which must have been highly uncomfortable. On my asking him what he was doing there, he replied without turning his head or moving a muscle: 'You see, Doctor, I am extremely rheumatic and catch cold very easily. I have just been taking a lot of exercise, and while I was foolishly getting too hot, my neck was touching my flannels. If I move it away from my flannels now before letting myself cool down, I'm sure to get a stiff neck and possibly bronchitis.' Which he would, in fact, have done. 'You're a real neurotic, that's what you are,' I told him. And do you know what argument he advanced to prove that I was mistaken? It was this: that while all the other patients in the establishment had a mania for testing their weight, so much so that the weighing machine had to be padlocked so that they shouldn't spend the whole day on it, he had to be lifted on to it bodily, so little did he care to be weighed. He prided himself on not sharing the mania of the others, oblivious of the fact that he had one of his own, and that it was this that saved him from another. You must not be offended by the comparison, Madame, for that man who dared not turn his neck for fear of catching a chill is the greatest poet of our day. That poor lunatic is the most lofty intellect that I know. Submit to being called a neurotic. You belong to that splendid and pitiable family which is the salt of the earth. Everything we think of as great has come to us from neurotics. It is they and they alone who found religions and create great works of art. The world will never realise how much it owes to them, and what they have suffered in order to bestow their gifts on it. We enjoy fine music, beautiful pictures, a thousand exquisite things, but we do not know what they cost those who wrought them in insomnia, tears, spasmodic laughter, urticaria, asthma, epilepsy, a terror of death which is worse than any of these, and which you perhaps have experienced, Madame," he added with a smile at my grandmother, "for confess now, when I came, you were not feeling very confident.

You thought you were ill, dangerously ill, perhaps. Heaven only knows what disease you thought you had detected the symptoms of in yourself. And you were not mistaken; they were there. Neurosis has an absolute genius for malingering. There is no illness which it cannot counterfeit perfectly. It will produce lifelike imitations of the dilatations of dyspepsia, the nausea of pregnancy, the arythmia of the cardiac, the feverishness of the consumptive. If it is capable of deceiving the doctor, how should it fail to deceive the patient? Ah, do not think that I am mocking your sufferings. I should not undertake to cure them unless I understood them thoroughly. And, may I say, there is no good confession that is not reciprocal. I have told you that without nervous disorder there can be no great artist. What is more," he added, raising a solemn forefinger, "there can be no great scientist either. I will go further, and say that, unless he himself is subject to nervous trouble, he is not, I won't say a good doctor, but I do say the right doctor to treat nervous troubles. In the pathology of nervous diseases, a doctor who doesn't talk too much nonsense is a half-cured patient, just as a critic is a poet who has stopped writing verse and a policeman a burglar who has retired from practice. I, Madame, I do not, like you, fancy myself to be suffering from albuminuria, I have not your neurotic fear of food, or of fresh air, but I can never go to sleep without getting out of bed at least twenty times to see if my door is shut. And yesterday I went to that nursing-home, where I came across the poet who wouldn't move his neck, for the purpose of booking a room, for, between ourselves, I spend my holidays there looking after myself when I have aggravated my own troubles by wearing myself out in the attempt to cure those of others."

"But, Doctor, ought I to take a similar cure?" asked my grandmother, aghast.

"It is not necessary, Madame. The symptoms you betray here will vanish at my bidding. Besides, you have a very efficient person whom I appoint as your doctor from now onwards. That is your malady itself, your nervous hyperactivity. Even if I knew how to cure you of it, I should take good care not to. All I need do is to control it. I see on your table there one of Bergotte's books. Cured of your nervous diathesis, you would no longer care for it. Now, how could I take it upon myself to substitute for the joys that it procures you a nervous stability which would be quite incapable of giving you those joys? But those joys themselves are a powerful remedy, the most power-ful of all perhaps. No, I have nothing to say against your nervous energy. All I ask is that it should listen to me; I leave you in its charge. It must reverse its engines. The force which it has been using to prevent you from going out, from taking sufficient food, must be directed towards making you eat, making you read, making you go out, and distracting you in every possible way. Don't tell me that you feel tired. Tiredness is the organic realisation of a preconceived idea. Begin by not thinking it. And if ever you have a slight indisposition, which is a thing that may happen to anyone, it will be just as if you hadn't, for your nervous energy will have endowed you with what M. de Talleyrand astutely called 'imaginary good health.' See, it has begun to cure you already. You've been sitting up in bed listening to me without once leaning back on your pillows, your eyes bright, colour in your cheeks. I've been talking to you for a good half-hour and you haven't noticed the time. Well, Madame, I shall now bid you good-day."

When, after seeing Dr du Boulbon to the door, I returned to the room in which my mother was alone, the anguish that had been weighing me down for several weeks suddenly lifted, I sensed that my mother was going to give vent to her joy and would observe mine too, and I felt that inability to endure the suspense of the coming moment when a person is about to be overcome with emotion in our presence, which *mutatis mutandis* is not unlike the thrill of fear that runs through one when one knows that somebody is going to come in and startle one by a door that is still closed. I tried to speak to Mamma but my voice broke, and, bursting into tears, I remained for a long time with my head on her shoulder, weeping, savouring, accepting, cherishing my grief, now that I knew that it had departed from my life, as we like to work ourselves up into a state of exaltation with virtuous plans which circumstances do not permit us to put into execution.

Françoise annoyed me by refusing to share in our joy. She was in a state of great excitement because there had been a

terrible scene between the lovesick footman and the tale-
bearing porter. It had required the Duchess herself, in her
unfailing benevolence, to intervene, restore a semblance of
calm to the household, and forgive the footman. For she was a
kind mistress, and it would have been the ideal "place" if only
she didn't listen to "tittle-tattle."

During the last few days people had begun to hear of my
grandmother's illness and to ask after her. Saint-Loup had
written to me: "I do not wish to take advantage of a time
when your dear grandmother is unwell to convey to you what
is far more than mere reproach on a matter with which she
has no concern. But I should not be speaking the truth were I
to say to you, if only by preterition, that I shall ever forget the
perfidy of your conduct, or that there can ever be any forgiveness for so scoundrelly a betrayal." But some other friends,
supposing that my grandmother was not seriously ill, or not
knowing that she was ill at all, had asked me to meet them
next day in the Champs-Elysées, to go with them from there to
pay a call together, ending up with a dinner in the country,
the thought of which appealed to me. I had no longer any
reason to forgo these two pleasures. When my grandmother
had been told that it was now imperative, if she was to obey
Dr du Boulbon's orders, that she should go out as much as
possible, she had herself at once suggested the Champs-
Elysées. It would be easy for me to escort her there; and,
while she sat reading, to arrange with my friends where I
should meet them later; and I should still be in time, if I
made haste, to take the train with them to Ville d'Avray. When
the time came, my grandmother did not want to go out,
saying that she felt tired. But my mother, acting on du Boulbon's instructions, had the strength of mind to be firm and to
command obedience. She was almost in tears at the thought that
my grandmother was going to relapse again into her nervous
weakness and might not recover from it. Never had there been
such a fine, warm day for an outing. The sun as it moved
through the sky interposed here and there in the broken
solidity of the balcony its insubstantial muslins, and gave to the
freestone ledge a warm epidermis, an ill-defined halo of gold.
As Françoise had not had time to send a "wire" to her

daughter, she left us immediately after lunch. She considered it kind enough of her as it was to call first at Jupien's to get a stitch put in the cape which my grandmother was going to wear. Returning at that moment from my morning walk, I accompanied her into the shop. "Is it your young master who brings you here," Jupien asked Françoise, "is it you who have brought him to see me, or is it a fair wind and Dame Fortune that brings you both?" For all his want of education, Jupien respected the laws of syntax as instinctively as M. de Guermantes, in spite of every effort, broke them. With Françoise gone and the cape mended, it was time for my grandmother to get ready. Having obstinately refused to let Mamma stay in the room with her, left to herself she took an endlessly long time over her dressing, and now that I knew that she was not ill, with that strange indifference which we feel towards our relations so long as they are alive, and which makes us put everyone else before them, I thought it very selfish of her to take so long and to risk making me late when she knew that I had an appointment with my friends and was dining at Ville d'Avray. In my impatience I finally went downstairs without waiting for her, after I had twice been told that she was just ready. At last she joined me, without apologising to me as she generally did for having kept me waiting, flushed and bothered like a person who has come to a place in a hurry and has forgotten half her belongings, just as I was reaching the half-opened glass door which, without warming them with it in the least, let in the liquid, throbbing, tepid air from the street (as though the sluices of a reservoir had been opened) between the frigid walls of the passage.

"Oh, dear, if you're going to meet your friends I ought to to have put on another cape. I look rather wretched in this one."

I was startled to see her so flushed, and supposed that having begun by making herself late she had had to hurry over her dressing. When we left the cab at the corner of the Avenue Gabriel, in the Champs-Elysées, I saw my grandmother turn away without a word and make for the little old pavilion with its green trellis at the door of which I had once waited for Françoise. The same park-keeper who had been there then was still there beside Françoise's "Marquise" as, following my grandmother who, doubtless because she was feeling sick, had her hand in front of her mouth, I climbed the steps of the little rustic theatre erected there in the middle of the gardens. At the entrance, as in those circus booths where the clown, dressed for the ring and smothered in flour, stands at the door and takes the money himself for the seats, the "Marquise," at the receipt of custom, was still in her place with her huge, irregular face smeared with coarse paint and her little bonnet of red flowers and black lace surmounting her auburn wig. But I do not think she recognised me. The park-keeper, abandoning the supervision of the greenery, with the colour of which his uniform had been designed to harmonise, was sitting beside her chatting.

"So you're still here," he was saying. "You don't think of retiring?"

"And why should I retire, Monsieur? Will you tell me where I should be better off than here, where I'd be more comfy and snug? And then there's all the coming and going, plenty of distraction. My own little Paris, I call it; my customers keep me in touch with everything that's going on. Just to give you an example, there's one of them went out not five minutes ago; he's a judge, a proper high-up. Well!" she exclaimed heatedly, as though prepared to maintain the truth of this assertion by violence, should the agent of civic authority show any sign of challenging its accuracy, "for the last eight years, do you hear me, every blessed day, regular on the stroke of three he comes here, always polite, never saying one word louder than another, never making any mess; and he stays half an hour and more to read his papers and do his little jobs. There was one day he didn't come. I never noticed it at the time, but that evening, all of a sudden I says to myself: 'Why, that gentleman never came to-day; perhaps he's dead!' And that gave me a regular turn, you know, because of course, I get quite fond of people when they behave nicely. And so I was very glad when I saw him come in again next day, and I said to him: 'I hope nothing happened to you yesterday, sir?' And he told me nothing had happened to *him*, it was his wife that had died, and it had given him such a turn he hadn't been able to come. He looked sad, of course—well, you know, people who've been married five-and-twenty years—but he seemed pleased, all the same, to be back here. You could see that all his little habits had been quite upset. I did what I could to cheer him up. I said to him: 'You mustn't let go of things, sir. Just keep coming here the same as before, it will be a little distraction for you in your sorrow.'"

The "Marquise" resumed a gentler tone, for she had observed that the guardian of groves and lawns was listening to her good-naturedly and with no thought of contradiction, keeping harmlessly in its scabbard a sword which looked more like a gardening implement or some horticultural emblem.

"And besides," she went on, "I choose my customers, I don't let everyone into my little parlours, as I call them. Doesn't it just look like a parlour with all my flowers? Such friendly customers I have; there's always someone or other brings me a spray of nice lilac, or jasmine or roses; my favourite flowers, roses are."

The thought that we were perhaps viewed with disfavour by this lady because we never brought any sprays of lilac or fine roses to her bower made me blush, and in the hope of escaping physically (or of being condemned only by default) from an adverse judgement, I moved towards the exit. But it is not always in this world the people who bring us fine roses to whom we are most friendly, for the "Marquise," thinking that I was bored, turned to me:

"You wouldn't like me to open a little cabin for you?"

And, on my declining:

"No? You're sure you won't?" she persisted, smiling. "Well, just as you please. You're welcome to it, but of course, not having to pay for a thing won't make you want to do it if you've got nothing to do."

At this moment a shabbily dressed woman hurried into the place who seemed to be feeling precisely the want in question. But she did not belong to the "Marquise's" world, for the latter, with the ferocity of a snob, said to her curtly:

"I've nothing vacant, Madame."

"Will they be long?" asked the poor lady, flushed beneath the yellow flowers in her hat.

"Well, ma'am, if you want my advice you'd better try some-where else. You see, there's still these two gentlemen waiting, and I've only one closet; the others are out of order."

"Looked like a bad payer to me," she explained when the other had gone. "That's not the sort we want here, either; they're not clean, don't treat the place with respect. It'd be me who'd have to spend the next hour cleaning up after her lady-ship. I'm not sorry to lose her couple of sous."

At last, after a good half-hour, my grandmother emerged, and fearing that she might not seek to atone by a lavish gratuity for the indiscretion she had shown by remaining so long inside, I beat a retreat so as not to have to share in the scorn which the "Marquise" would no doubt heap on her, and strolled down a path, but slowly, so that my grandmother should not have to hurry to overtake me, as presently she did. I expected her to begin: "I'm afraid I've kept you waiting; I hope you'll still be in time for your friends," but she did not utter a single word, so much so that, feeling a little hurt, I was disinclined to speak first. Finally, looking up at her I noticed that as she walked beside me she kept her face turned the other way. I was afraid that she might be feeling sick again. I looked at her more closely and was struck by the disjointedness of her gait. Her hat was crooked, her cloak stained; she had the dishevelled and disgruntled appearance, the flushed, slightly dazed look of a person who had just been knocked down by a carriage or pulled out of a ditch.

"I was afraid you were feeling sick, Grandmamma; are you feeling better now?" I asked her.

Doubtless she thought that it would be impossible for her not to make some answer without alarming me.

"I heard the whole of the 'Marquise's' conversation with the keeper," she told me. "Could anything have been more typical of the Guermantes, or the Verdurins and their little clan? 'Ah! in what courtly terms those things were put!' "[18] And she added, with deliberate application, this from her own special Marquise, Mme de Sévigné: "As I listened to them I thought that they were preparing for me the delights of a farewell."

Such were the remarks that she addressed to me, remarks

into which she had put all her critical delicacy, her love of quotation, her memory of the classics, more thoroughly even than she would normally have done, and as though to prove that she retained possession of all these faculties. But I guessed rather than heard what she said, so inaudible was the voice in which she mumbled her sentences, clenching her teeth more than could be accounted for by the fear of vomiting.

"Come!" I said lightly enough not to seem to be taking her illness too seriously, "since you're feeling a little sick I suggest we go home. I don't want to trundle a grandmother with indigestion about the Champs-Elysées."

"I didn't like to suggest it because of your friends," she replied. "Poor pet! But if you don't mind, I think it would be wiser."

I was afraid of her noticing the strange way in which she uttered these words.

"Come," I said to her brusquely, "you mustn't tire yourself talking when you're feeling sick—it's silly; wait till we get home."

She smiled at me sorrowfully and gripped my hand. She had realised that there was no need to hide from me what I had at once guessed, that she had had a slight stroke.

We made our way back along the Avenue Gabriel through the strolling crowds. I left my grandmother to rest on a bench and went in search of a cab. She, in whose heart I always placed myself in order to form an opinion of the most insignificant person, she was now closed to me, had become part of the external world, and, more than from any casual passer-by, I was obliged to keep from her what I thought of her condition, to betray no sign of my anxiety. I could not have spoken of it to her with any more confidence than to a stranger. She had suddenly returned to me the thoughts, the griefs which, from my earliest childhood, I had entrusted to her for all time. She was not yet dead. But I was already alone. And even those allusions which she had made to the Guermantes, to Molière, to our conversations about the little clan, assumed a baseless, adventitious, fantastical air, because they sprang from this same being who to-morrow perhaps would have ceased to exist, for whom they would no longer have any meaning, from the

non-being—incapable of conceiving them—which my grandmother would shortly be.

"Monsieur, I don't like to say no, but you have not made an
appointment, you haven't a number. Besides, this is not my day
for seeing patients. You surely have a doctor of your own. I
cannot stand in for him, unless he calls me in for consultation.
It's a question of professional etiquette . . ."

Just as I was signalling to a cabman, I had caught sight of
the famous Professor E——, almost a friend of my father and
grandfather, acquainted at any rate with them both, who lived
in the Avenue Gabriel, and, on a sudden inspiration, had
stopped him just as he was entering his house, thinking that
he would perhaps be the very person to examine my grandmother. But, being evidently in a hurry, after collecting his
letters he seemed anxious to get rid of me, and I could only
speak to him by going up with him in the lift, of which he
begged me to allow him to press the buttons himself, this
being an idiosyncrasy of his.

"But Doctor, I'm not asking you to see my grandmother
here; you will realise when I've explained to you that she isn't
in a fit state; what I'm asking is that you should call at our
house in half an hour's time, when I've taken her home."

"Call at your house! Really, Monsieur, you can't mean such
a thing. I'm dining with the Minister of Commerce. I have a
call to pay first. I must change at once, and to make matters
worse my tail-coat is torn and the other one has no buttonhole
for my decorations. Would you please oblige me by not
touching the lift-buttons. You don't know how the lift works;
one can't be too careful. Getting that buttonhole made means
more delay. However, out of friendship for your family, if
your grandmother comes here at once I'll see her. But I warn
you I shan't be able to give her more than a quarter of an hour."

I had set off again at once, without even getting out of the
lift, which Professor E—— had himself set in motion to take
me down again, eyeing me distrustfully as he did so.

We may, indeed, say that the hour of death is uncertain,
but when we say this we think of that hour as situated in a
vague and remote expanse of time; it does not occur to us that
it can have any connexion with the day that has already

dawned and can mean that death—or its first assault and partial possession of us, after which it will never leave hold of us again —may occur this very afternoon, so far from uncertain, this afternoon whose time-table, hour by hour, has been settled in advance. One insists on one's daily outing so that in a month's time one will have had the necessary ration of fresh air; one has hesitated over which coat to take, which cabman to call; one is in the cab, the whole day lies before one, short because one must be bac'k home early, as a friend is coming to see one; one hopes that it will be as fine again to-morrow; and one has no suspicion that death, which has been advancing within one on another plane, shrouded in an impenetrable darkness, has chosen precisely this particular day to make its appearance, in a few minutes' time, more or less at the moment when the carriage reaches the Champs-Elysées. Perhaps those who are habitually haunted by the fear of the utter strangeness of death will find something reassuring in this kind of death—in this kind of first contact with death—because death thus assumes a known, familiar, everyday guise. A good lunch has preceded it, and the same outing that people take who are in perfect health. A drive home in an open carriage comes on top of its first onslaught; ill as my grandmother was, there were, after all, several people who could testify that at six o'clock, as we came home from the Champs-Elysées, they had bowed to her as she drove past in an open carriage, in perfect weather. Legrandin, making his way towards the Place de la Concorde, raised his hat to us, stopping to look after us with an air of surprise. I, who was not yet detached from life, asked my grandmother if she had acknowledged his greeting, reminding her of his touchiness. My grandmother, thinking me no doubt very frivolous, raised her hand in the air as though to say: "What does it matter? It's of no importance."

Yes, it might have been said that a few minutes earlier, while I was looking for a cab, my grandmother was resting on a bench in the Avenue Gabriel, and that a little later she had driven past in an open carriage. But would it have been really true? A bench, in order to maintain its position at the side of an avenue—although it may also be subject to certain conditions of equilibrium—has no need of energy. But in order for a living being to be stable, even when supported by a bench or in a carriage, there must be a tension of forces which we do not ordinarily perceive, any more than we perceive (because its action is multi-dimensional) atmospheric pressure. Perhaps if a vacuum were created within us and we were left to bear the pressure of the air, we should feel, in the moment that preceded our extinction, the terrible weight which there was now nothing else to neutralise. Similarly, when the abyss of sickness and death opens up within us, and we have nothing left to oppose to the tumult with which the world and our own body rush upon us, then to sustain even the thought of our muscles, even the shudder that pierces us to the marrow, then even to keep ourselves still, in what we ordinarily regard as no more than the simple negative position of a thing, demands, if one wants one's head to remain erect and one's demeanour calm, an expense of vital energy and becomes the object of an exhausting struggle.

And if Legrandin had looked back at us with that air of astonishment, it was because to him, as to the other people who passed us then, in the cab in which my grandmother was apparently sitting on the back seat, she had seemed to be foundering, slithering into the abyss, clinging desperately to the cushions which could scarcely hold back the headlong plunge of her body, her hair dishevelled, her eyes wild, no longer capable of facing the assault of the images which their pupils no longer had the strength to bear. She had appeared, although I was beside her, to be plunged in that unknown world in the heart of which she had already received the blows of which she bore the marks when I had looked up at her in the Champs-Elysées, her hat, her face, her coat deranged by the hand of the invisible angel with whom she had wrestled.

I have thought, since, that this moment of her stroke cannot have altogether surprised my grandmother, that indeed she had perhaps foreseen it a long time back, had lived in expectation of it. She had not known, naturally, when this fatal moment would come, had never been certain, any more than those lovers whom a similar doubt leads alternately to found unreasonable hopes and unjustified suspicions on the fidelity of their mistresses. But it is rare for these grave illnesses, such as that which now at last had struck her full in the face, not to take up residence in a sick person a long time before killing him, during which period they hasten, like a "sociable" neighbour or tenant, to make themselves known to him. A terrible acquaintance, not so much for the sufferings that it causes as for the strange novelty of the terminal restrictions which it imposes upon life. We see ourselves dying, in these cases, not at the actual moment of death but months, sometimes years before, when death has hideously come to dwell in us. We make the acquaintance of the Stranger whom we hear coming and going in our brain. True, we do not know him by sight, but from the sounds we hear him regularly make we can form an idea of his habits. Is he a malefactor? One morning, we can no longer hear him. He has gone. Ah! if only it were for ever! In the evening he has returned. What are his plans? The consultant, put to the question, like an adored mistress, replies with avowals that one day are believed, another day questioned. Or rather it is not the mistress's role but that of interrogated servants that the doctor plays. They are only third parties. The person whom we press for an answer, whom we suspect of being about to play us false, is Life itself, and although we feel her to be no longer the same, we believe in her still, or at least remain undecided until the day on which she finally abandons us.

I helped my grandmother into Professor E——'s lift and a moment later he came to us and took us into his consulting room. But there, pressed for time though he was, his offensive manner changed, such is the force of habit, and his habit was to be friendly, not to say playful, with his patients. Since he knew that my grandmother was a great reader, and was himself one, he devoted the first few minutes to quoting various favourite passages of poetry appropriate to the glorious summer weather. He had placed her in an armchair and himself with his back to the light so as to have a good view of her. His examination was minute and thorough, even obliging me to leave the room for a moment. He continued it after my return, then, having finished, went on, although the quarter of an hour was almost at an end, repeating various quotations to my grandmother. He even made a few jokes, which were witty enough, though I should have preferred to hear them on some other occasion, but which completely reassured me by the tone of amusement in which he uttered them. I then remembered that M. Fallières, the President of the Senate, had, many years earlier, had a false seizure, and that to the consternation of his political rivals he had taken up his duties again a few days later and had begun, it was said, to prepare an eventual candidature for the Presidency of the Republic. My confidence in my grandmother's prompt recovery was all the more complete in that, just as I was recalling the example of M. Fallières, I was distracted from pursuing the parallel by a shout of laughter which served as conclusion to one of the Professor's jokes. After which he took out his watch, frowned feverishly on seeing that he was five minutes late, and while he bade us good-bye rang for his dress clothes to be brought to him at once. I waited until my grandmother had left the room, closed the door and asked him to tell me the truth.

"Your grandmother is doomed," he said to me. "It is a stroke brought on by uraemia. In itself, uraemia is not necessarily fatal, but this case seems to me hopeless. I need not tell you that I hope I am mistaken. At all events, with Cottard you're in excellent hands. Excuse me," he broke off as a maid came into the room with his tail-coat over her arm. "As I told you, I'm dining with the Minister of Commerce, and I have a call to pay first. Ah! life is not all a bed of roses, as one is apt to think at your age."

And he graciously offered me his hand. I had shut the door behind me, and a footman was ushering us into the hall, when my grandmother and I heard a great shout of rage. The maid had forgotten to cut and hem the buttonhole for the decorations. This would take another ten minutes. The Professor continued to storm while I stood on the landing gazing at my grandmother who was doomed. Each of us is indeed alone. We set off homewards.

The sun was sinking; it burnished an interminable wall along which our cab had to pass before reaching the street in which we lived, a wall against which the shadow of horse and carriage cast by the setting sun stood out in black on a ruddy background, like a hearse on some Pompeian terra-cotta. At

length we arrived at the house. I sat the invalid down at the
foot of the staircase in the hall, and went up to warn my
mother. I told her that my grandmother had come home feeling
slightly unwell, after an attack of giddiness. As soon as I began
to speak, my mother's face was convulsed by a paroxysm of
despair, a despair which was yet already so resigned that I
realised that for many years she had been holding herself
quietly in readiness for an indeterminate but inexorable day.
She asked me no questions; it seemed that, just as malevolence
likes to exaggerate the sufferings of others, she in her loving
tenderness did not want to admit that her mother was seriously
ill, especially with a disease which might have affected the brain.
Mamma shuddered, her eyes wept without tears, she ran to give
orders for the doctor to be fetched at once; but when Françoise
asked who was ill she could not reply, her voice stuck in her
throat. She came running downstairs with me, struggling to
banish from her face the sob that crumpled it. My grandmother was waiting below on the sofa in the hall, but as soon
as she heard us coming she drew herself up, rose to her feet,
and waved her hand cheerfully at Mamma. I had partially
wrapped her head in a white lace shawl, telling her that this
was to prevent her from catching cold on the stairs. I had hoped
that my mother might not immediately notice the alteration
in the face, the distortion of the mouth. My precaution proved
unnecessary: my mother went up to my grandmother, kissed
her hand as though it were that of her God, raised her up and
supported her to the lift with an infinite care which reflected,
together with the fear of being clumsy and hurting her,
the humility of one who felt herself unworthy to touch what
was for her the most precious thing in the world, but not once
did she raise her eyes and look at the sufferer's face. Perhaps
this was in order that my grandmother should not be saddened
by the thought that the sight of her might have alarmed her
daughter. Perhaps from fear of a grief so piercing that she
dared not face it. Perhaps from respect, because she did not feel
it permissible for her without impiety to notice the trace of
any mental enfeeblement on those revered features. Perhaps
to be better able to preserve intact in her memory the image of
the true face of my grandmother, radiant with wisdom and

goodness. So they went up side by side, my grandmother half-hidden in her shawl, my mother averting her eyes.

Meanwhile there was one person who never took hers from what could be discerned of my grandmother's altered features at which her daughter dared not look, a person who fastened on them a dumbfounded, indiscreet and ominous look: this was Françoise. Not that she was not sincerely attached to my grandmother (indeed she had been disappointed and almost scandalised by the coldness shown by Mamma, whom she would have liked to see fling herself weeping into her mother's arms), but she had a certain tendency always to look at the worse side of things, and had retained from her childhood two characteristics which would seem to be mutually exclusive, but which, when combined, reinforce one another: the lack of restraint common among uneducated people who make no attempt to conceal the impression, indeed the painful alarm aroused in them by the sight of a physical change which it would be more tactful to appear not to notice, and the unfeeling roughness of the peasant who tears the wings off dragon-flies until she gets a chance to wring the necks of chickens, and lacks that sense of shame which would make her conceal the interest that she feels in the sight of suffering flesh.

When, thanks to the faultless ministrations of Françoise, my grandmother had been put to bed, she discovered that she could speak much more easily, the little rupture or obstruction of a blood-vessel which had produced the uraemia having apparently been quite slight. And at once she was anxious not to fail Mamma in her hour of need, to assist her in the most cruel moments through which she had yet had to pass.

"Well, my child," she began, taking my mother's hand in one of hers, and keeping the other in front of her lips, in order thus to account for the slight difficulty which she still found in pronouncing certain words. "So this is all the pity you show your mother! You look as if you thought that indi-gestion was quite a pleasant thing!"

Then for the first time my mother's eyes gazed passionately into those of my grandmother, not wishing to see the rest of her face, and she replied, beginning the list of those false promises which we swear but are unable to keep:

"Mamma, you'll soon be quite well again, your daughter will see to that."

And gathering up all her most ardent love, all her determination that her mother should recover, she entrusted them to a kiss which she accompanied with her whole mind, with her whole being until it flowered upon her lips, and bent down to lay it humbly, reverently, on the beloved forehead.

My grandmother complained of a sort of alluvial deposit of bedclothes which kept gathering all the time in the same place, over her left leg, and which she could never manage to lift off. But she did not realise that she was herself the cause of this (so that day after day she accused Françoise unjustly of not "doing" her bed properly). By a convulsive movement she kept flinging to that side the whole flood of those billowing blankets of fine wool, which gathered there like the sand in a bay which is very soon transformed into a beach (unless a breakwater is built) by the successive deposits of the tide.

My mother and I (whose mendacity was exposed before we spoke by the obnoxious perspicaciousness of Françoise) would not even admit that my grandmother was seriously ill, as though such an admission might give pleasure to her enemies (not that she had any) and it was more loving to feel that she was not so bad as all that, in short from the same instinctive sentiment which had led me to suppose that Andrée pitied Albertine too much to be really fond of her. The same individual phenomena are reproduced in the mass, in great crises. In a war, the man who does not love his country says nothing against it, but regards it as doomed, pities it, sees everything in the blackest colours.

Françoise was infinitely helpful to us owing to her faculty of doing without sleep, of performing the most arduous tasks. And if, when she had gone to bed after several nights spent in the sickroom, we were obliged to call her a quarter of an hour after she had fallen asleep, she was so happy to be able to perform painful duties as if they had been the simplest things in the world that, far from baulking, she would show signs of satisfaction tinged with modesty. Only when the time came for mass, or for breakfast, even if my grandmother had been in her death throes, Françoise would have slipped away in order not to be late. She neither could nor would let her place be taken by her young footman. It was true that she had brought from Combray an extremely exalted idea of everyone's duty towards ourselves; she would not have tolerated that any of our servants should "fail" us. This doctrine had made her so noble, so imperious, so efficient an instructor that we had never had in our house any servants, however corrupt, who had not speedily modified and purified their conception of life so far as to refuse to touch the usual commissions from tradesmen and to come rushing—however little they might previously have sought to oblige—to take from my hands and not let me tire myself by carrying the smallest parcel. But at Combray Françoise had contracted also—and had brought with her to Paris—the habit of not being able to put up with any assistance in her work. The sight of anyone coming to help her seemed to her like a deadly insult, and servants had remained for weeks without receiving from her any response to their morning greeting, had even gone off on their holidays without her bidding them good-bye or their guessing her reason, which was simply and solely that they had offered to do a share of her work on some day when she had not been well. And at this moment when my grandmother was so ill, Françoise's duties seemed to her peculiarly her own. She would not allow herself, as the official incumbent, to be done out of her role in the ritual of these gala days. And so her young footman, discarded by her, did not know what to do with himself, and not content with having copied the butler's example and supplied himself with note-paper from my desk, had begun as well to borrow volumes of poetry from my bookshelves. He sat reading them for a good half of the day, out of admiration for the poets who had written them, but also in order, during the rest of his time, to sprinkle with quotations the letters which he wrote to his friends in his native village. True, his intention was to dazzle them. But since he was somewhat lacking in logic he had formed the notion that these poems, picked out at random from my shelves, were things of common currency to which it was customary to refer. So much so that in writing to these peasants whom he expected to impress, he interspersed his own reflexions with lines from Lamartine,

just as he might have said "Who laughs last, laughs longest!"
or merely "How are you keeping?"

Because of her acute pain my grandmother was given
morphine. Unfortunately, if this relieved the pain it also
increased the quantity of albumin. The blows which we aimed
at the evil which had settled inside her were always wide of the
mark, and it was she, it was her poor interposed body that
had to bear them, without her ever uttering more than a faint
groan by way of complaint. And the pain that we caused her
found no compensation in any benefit that we were able to
give her. The ferocious beast we were anxious to exterminate
we barely succeeded in grazing; we merely enraged it even
more, hastening perhaps the moment when the captive would
be devoured. On certain days when the discharge of albumin
had been excessive Cottard, after some hesitation, stopped the
morphine. During these brief moments in which he deliberated,
in which the relative dangers of one and another course of
treatment fought it out between them in his mind until he
arrived at a decision, this man who was so insignificant and so
commonplace had something of the greatness of a general who,
vulgar in all things else, moves us by his decisiveness when
the fate of the country is at stake and, after a moment's
reflexion, he decides upon what is from the military point of
view the wisest course, and gives the order: "Advance east-
wards." Medically, however little hope there might be of
bringing this attack of uraemia to an end, it was important not
to put a strain on the kidneys. But, on the other hand, when
my grandmother was given no morphine, her pain became
unbearable; she would perpetually attempt a certain movement which it was difficult for her to perform without
groaning: to a great extent, pain is a sort of need on the part
of the organism to take cognisance of a new state which
is troubling it, to adapt its sensibility to that state. We can
discern this origin of pain in the case of certain discomforts
which are not such for everyone. Into a room filled with
pungent smoke two men of coarse fibre will come and attend
to their business; a third, more sensitively constituted,
will betray an incessant discomfort. His nostrils will continue
to sniff anxiously the odour which he ought, one would think,

to try not to notice but which he will keep on attempting to accommodate, by a more exact apprehension of it, to his troubled sense of smell. Hence the fact that an intense pre-occupation will prevent one from complaining of a toothache. When my grandmother was suffering thus the sweat trickled over the pink expanse of her forehead, glueing her white locks to it, and if she thought that none of us was in the room she would cry out: "Oh, it's dreadful!"—but if she caught sight of my mother, at once she devoted all her energy to banishing from her face every sign of pain, or alternatively repeated the same plaints accompanying them with explanations which gave a different sense retrospectively to those which my mother might have overheard:

"Ah! my dear, it's dreadful to have to stay in bed on a beauti-ful sunny day like this when one wants to be out in the fresh air—I've been weeping with rage against your instructions."

But she could not get rid of the anguish in her eyes, the sweat on her forehead, the convulsive start, checked at once, of her limbs.

"I'm not in pain, I'm complaining because I'm not lying very comfortably, I feel my hair is untidy, I feel sick, I knocked my head against the wall."

And my mother, at the foot of the bed, rivetted to that suffering as though, by dint of piercing with her gaze that pain-racked forehead, that body which contained the evil thing, she must ultimately succeed in reaching and removing it, my mother said:

"No, no, Mamma dear, we won't let you suffer like that, we'll find something to take it away, have patience just for a moment; let me give you a kiss, darling—no, you're not to move."

And stooping over the bed, with her knees bent, almost kneeling on the ground, as though by an exercise of humility she would have a better chance of making acceptable the impassioned gift of herself, she lowered towards my grand-mother her whole life contained in her face as in a ciborium which she was holding out to her, adorned with dimples and folds so passionate, so sorrowful, so sweet that one could not have said whether they had been engraved on it by a kiss, a sob or a smile. My grandmother too tried to lift up her face to

Mamma's. It was so altered that probably, had she been strong
enough to go out, she would have been recognised only by
the feather in her hat. Her features, as though during a modelling session, seemed to be straining, with an effort which
distracted her from everything else, to conform to some
particular model which we failed to identify. The work of the
sculptor was nearing its end, and if my grandmother's face had
shrunk in the process, it had at the same time hardened. The
veins that traversed it seemed those not of marble, but of some
more rugged stone. Permanently thrust forward by the difficulty
that she found in breathing, and as permanently withdrawn into
itself by exhaustion, her face, worn, diminished, terrifyingly
expressive, seemed like the rude, flushed, purplish, desperate
face of some wild guardian of a tomb in a primitive, almost
prehistoric sculpture. But the work was not yet complete.
Next, the mould must be broken, and then, into that tomb
which had been so painfully guarded, with that tense exertion,
the finished effigy lowered.

At one of those moments when, as the saying goes, we
did not know which way to turn, since my grandmother was
coughing and sneezing a good deal, we took the advice of a
relative who assured us that if we sent for the specialist X——
the trouble would be over in a couple of days. Society people
say that sort of thing about their own doctors, and their friends
believe them just as Françoise always believed the advertise-
ments in the newspapers. The specialist came with his bag
packed with all the colds and coughs of his other patients, like
Aeolus's goatskin. My grandmother refused point-blank to let
herself be examined. And we, out of consideration for this
doctor who had come out of his way for nothing, deferred to
the desire that he expressed to inspect each of our noses in
turn, although there was nothing the matter with any of them.
According to him, however, there was; everything, whether
headache or colic, heart-disease or diabetes, was a disease of the
nose that had been wrongly diagnosed. To each of us he said:
"I should like to have another look at that little nozzle. Don't
put it off too long. I'll soon clear it for you with a hot needle."
Of course we paid no attention whatsoever. And yet we asked
ourselves: "Clear it of what?" In a word, every one of our

noses was infected; his mistake lay only in his use of the present tense. For by the following day his examination and provisional treatment had taken effect. Each of us had his or her catarrh. And when in the street he ran into my father doubled up with a cough, he smiled to think that an ignorant layman might suppose the attack to be due to his intervention. He had examined us at a moment when we were already ill.

My grandmother's illness gave occasion to various people to manifest an excess or deficiency of sympathy which surprised us quite as much as the sort of chance which led one or another of them to reveal to us connecting links of circumstances, or even of friendships, which we had never suspected. And the signs of interest shown by the people who called incessantly at the house to inquire revealed to us the gravity of an illness which, until then, we had not sufficiently detached from the countless painful impressions that we received by my grandmother's sickbed. Informed by telegram, her sisters declined to leave Combray. They had discovered a musician there who gave them excellent chamber recitals, in listening to which they felt they could enjoy better than by the invalid's bedside a contemplative melancholy, a sorrowful exaltation, the form of which was, to say the least of it, unusual. Mme Sazerat wrote to Mamma, but in the tone of a person whom the sudden breaking off of an engagement (the cause of the rupture being Dreyfusism) has separated from one for ever. Bergotte, on the other hand, came every day and spent several hours with me.

He had always enjoyed going regularly for some time to the same house where he had no need to stand on ceremony. But formerly it had been in order that he might talk without being interrupted; now it was so that he might sit for as long as he chose in silence, without being expected to talk. For he was very ill, some people said with albuminuria, like my grandmother, while according to others he had a tumour. He grew steadily weaker; it was with difficulty that he climbed our staircase, with greater difficulty still that he went down it. Even though he held on to the banisters he often stumbled, and he would, I believe, have stayed at home had he not been afraid of losing altogether the habit and the capacity of

going out, he, the "man with the goatee beard" whom I remembered as being so alert not very long since. He was now
quite blind, and often he even had trouble with his speech.

But at the same time, by a directly opposite process, the
corpus of his work, known only to a few literary people at the
period when Mme Swann used to patronise their timid efforts
to disseminate it, now grown in stature and strength in the
eyes of all, had acquired an extraordinary power of expansion
among the general public. No doubt it often happens that only
after his death does a writer become famous. But it was while
he was still alive, and during his own slow progress towards
approaching death, that this writer was able to watch the
progress of his works towards Renown. A dead writer can at
least be illustrious without any strain on himself. The efful-
gence of his name stops short at his grave-stone. In the deafness
of eternal sleep he is not importuned by Glory. But for Bergotte the antithesis was still incomplete. He existed still
sufficiently to suffer from the tumult. He still moved about,
though with difficulty, while his books, skipping and cavort-
ing like daughters whom one loves but whose impetuous
youthfulness and noisy pleasures tire one, brought day after
day to his very bedside a crowd of fresh admirers.

The visits which he now began to pay us came for me
several years too late, for I no longer had the same admiration
for him as of old. This was in no sense incompatible with the
growth of his reputation. A man's work seldom becomes
completely understood and successful before that of another
writer, still obscure, has begun, among a few more exigent
spirits, to substitute a fresh cult for the one that has almost
ceased to command observance. In Bergotte's books, which
I constantly re-read, his sentences stood out as clearly before
my eyes as my own thoughts, the furniture in my room and the
carriages in the street. All the details were easily visible, not
perhaps precisely as one had always seen them, but at any rate
as one was accustomed to see them now. But a new writer had
recently begun to publish work in which the relations between
things were so different from those that connected them for me
that I could understand hardly anything of what he wrote. He
would say, for instance: "The hose-pipes admired the splendid

upkeep of the roads" (and so far it was simple, I followed him smoothly along those roads) "which set out every five minutes from Briand and Claudel." At that point I ceased to understand, because I had expected the name of a place and was given that of a person instead. Only I felt that it was not the sentence that was badly constructed but I myself that lacked the strength and agility necessary to reach the end. I would start afresh, striving tooth and nail to reach the point from which I would see the new relationships between things. And each time, after I had got about half-way through the sentence, I would fall back again, as later on, in the Army, in my attempts at the exercises on the horizontal bar. I felt nevertheless for the new writer the admiration which an awkward boy who gets nought for gymnastics feels when he watches another more nimble. And from then onwards I felt less admiration for Bergotte, whose limpidity struck me as a deficiency. There was a time when people recognised things quite easily when it was Fromentin who had painted them, and could not recognise them at all when it was Renoir.

People of taste tell us nowadays that Renoir is a great eighteenth-century painter. But in so saying they forget the element of Time, and that it took a great deal of time, even at the height of the nineteenth century, for Renoir to be hailed as a great artist. To succeed thus in gaining recognition, the original painter or the original writer proceeds on the lines of the oculist. The course of treatment they give us by their painting or by their prose is not always pleasant. When it is at an end the practitioner says to us: "Now look!" And, lo and behold, the world around us (which was not created once and for all, but is created afresh as often as an original artist is born) appears to us entirely different from the old world, but perfectly clear. Women pass in the street, different from those we formerly saw, because they are Renoirs, those Renoirs we persistently refused to see as women. The carriages, too, are Renoirs, and the water, and the sky; we feel tempted to go for a walk in the forest which is identical with the one which when we first saw it looked like anything in the world except a forest, like for instance a tapestry of innumerable hues but lacking precisely the hues peculiar to forests. Such is the new and perishable universe which has just been created. It will last until the next geological catastrophe is precipitated by a new painter or writer of original talent.

The writer who had taken Bergotte's place in my affections wearied me not by the incoherence but by the novelty—perfectly coherent—of associations which I was unaccustomed to following. The point, always the same, at which I felt myself falter indicated the identity of each renewed feat of acrobatics that I must undertake. Moreover, when once in a thousand times I did succeed in following the writer to the end of his sentence, what I saw there always had a humour, a truthfulness and a charm similar to those which I had found long ago in reading Bergotte, only more delightful. I reflected that it was not so many years since a renewal of the world similar to that which I now expected his successor to produce had been wrought for me by Bergotte himself. And I was led to wonder whether there was any truth in the distinction which we are always making between art, which is no more advanced now than in Homer's day, and science with its continuous progress. Perhaps, on the contrary, art was in this respect like science; each new original writer seemed to me to have advanced beyond the stage of his immediate predecessor; and who was to say whether in twenty years' time, when I should be able to accompany without strain or effort the new-comer of to-day, another might not emerge in the face of whom the present one would go the way of Bergotte?

I spoke to the latter of the new writer. He put me off him not so much by assuring me that his art was uncouth, facile and vacuous, as by telling me that he had seen him and had almost mistaken him (so strong was the likeness) for Bloch. The latter's image thenceforth loomed over the printed pages, and I no longer felt under compulsion to make the effort necessary to understand them. If Bergotte had decried him to me it was less, I fancy, from jealousy of a success that was yet to come than from ignorance of his work. He read scarcely anything. The bulk of his thought had long since passed from his brain into his books. He had grown thin, as though they had been extracted from him by a surgical operation. His reproductive instinct no longer impelled him to any activity, now that

he had given an independent existence to almost all his
thoughts. He led the vegetative life of a convalescent, of a
woman after childbirth; his fine eyes remained motionless,
vaguely dazed, like the eyes of a man lying on the sea-shore
and in a vague day-dream contemplating only each little
breaking wave. However, if it was less interesting to talk to
him now than I should once have found it, I felt no compunction about that. He was so far a creature of habit that the
simplest as well as the most luxurious habits, once he had
formed them, became indispensable to him for a certain
length of time. I do not know what made him come to our
house the first time, but thereafter he came every day simply
because he had been there the day before. He would turn up
at the house as he might have gone to a café, in order that no
one should talk to him, in order that he might—very rarely—
talk himself, so that it would have been difficult on the whole
to say whether he was moved by our grief or that he enjoyed
my company, had one sought to draw any conclusion from
such assiduity. But it did not fail to impress my mother,
sensitive to everything that might be regarded as an act of
homage to her invalid. And every day she reminded me: "See
that you don't forget to thank him nicely."

We had also—a discreet feminine attention like the refreshments that are brought to one, between sittings, by a painter's
mistress—as a supplement, free of charge, to those which her
husband paid us professionally, a visit from Mme Cottard.
She came to offer us her "lady's maid," or, if we preferred the
services of a man, she would "scour the country" for one, and
on our declining, said that she did hope this was not just a
"put-off" on our part, a word which in her world signified a
false pretext for not accepting an invitation. She assured us
that the Professor, who never referred to his patients when he
was at home, was as sad about it as if it had been she herself
who was ill. We shall see in due course that even if this had
been true it would have meant at once very little and a great
deal on the part of the most unfaithful and the most attentive
of husbands.

Offers as helpful, and infinitely more touching in the way in
which they were expressed (which was a blend of the highest

intelligence, the warmest sympathy, and a rare felicity of expression), were addressed to me by the heir to the Grand Duchy of Luxembourg. I had met him at Balbec where he had come on a visit to one of his aunts, the Princesse de Luxembourg, being himself at that time merely Comte de Nassau. He had married, some months later, the beautiful daughter of another Luxembourg princess, extremely rich because she was the only daughter of a prince who was the proprietor of an immense flour-milling business. Whereupon the Grand Duke of Luxembourg, who had no children of his own and was devoted to his nephew Nassau, had obtained parliamentary approval for declaring the young man his heir. As with all marriages of this nature, the origin of the bride's fortune was the obstacle, as it was also the efficient cause. I remembered this Comte de Nassau as one of the most striking young men I had ever met, already devoured, at that time, by a dark and blazing passion for his betrothed. I was deeply touched by the letters which he wrote to me regularly during my grandmother's illness, and Mamma herself, in her emotion, quoted sadly one of her mother's expressions: "Sévigné would not have put it better."

On the sixth day Mamma, yielding to my grandmother's entreaties, left her for a little and pretended to go and lie down. I should have liked (so that Grandmamma should go to sleep) Françoise to stay quietly at her bedside. In spite of my supplications, she got up and left the room. She was genuinely devoted to my grandmother, and with her perspicacity and her natural pessimism she regarded her as doomed. She would therefore have liked to give her every possible care and attention. But word had just come that an electrician had arrived, a veteran member of his firm, the head of which was his brother-in-law, highly esteemed throughout the building, where he had been coming for many years, and especially by Jupien. This man had been sent for before my grandmother's illness. It seemed to me that he could have been sent away again, or asked to wait. But Françoise's code of manners would not permit this; it would have been to show a lack of courtesy towards this excellent man; my grandmother's condition ceased at once to matter. When, after waiting a quarter of an hour, I lost patience and went to look for her in the kitchen, I found her chatting to him on the landing of the back staircase, the door of which stood open, a device which had the advantage, should any of us come on the scene, of letting it be thought that they were just saying good-bye, but had also the drawback of sending a terrible draught through the house. Françoise tore herself from the workman, not without turning to shout down after him various greetings, forgotten in her haste, to his wife and his brother-in-law. This concern, characteristic of Combray, not to be found wanting in politeness was one which Françoise extended even to foreign policy. People foolishly imagine that the broad generalities of social phenomena afford an excellent opportunity to penetrate further into the human soul; they ought, on the contrary, to realise that it is by plumbing the depths of a single personality that they might have a chance of understanding those phenomena. Françoise had told the gardener at Combray over and over again that war was the most senseless of crimes, that life was the only thing that mattered. Yet, when the Russo-Japanese war broke out, she was quite ashamed, vis-à-vis the Tsar, that we had not gone to war to help the "poor Russians," "since," she reminded us, "we're allianced to them." She felt this abstention to be discourteous to Nicholas II, who had always "said such nice things about us"; it was a corollary of the same code which would have prevented her from refusing a glass of brandy from Jupien, knowing that it would "upset" her digestion, and which caused her, with my grandmother lying at death's door, to feel that, by failing to go in person to make her apologies to this trusty electrician who had been put to so much trouble, she would have been committing the same discourtesy of which she considered France guilty in remaining neutral between Russia and Japan.

Luckily, we were soon rid of Françoise's daughter, who was obliged to be away for some weeks. To the regular stock of advice which people at Combray gave to the family of an invalid: "You haven't tried a little excursion . . . the change of air, you know . . . pick up an appetite . . . etc," she had added the almost unique idea, which she herself had thought up specially and which she repeated accordingly whenever we saw her, without fail, as though hoping by dint of reiteration to force it through the thickness of people's heads: "She ought to have looked after herself *radically* from the first." She did not recommend one particular kind of cure rather than another, provided it was "radical." As to Françoise herself, she noticed that my grandmother was not being given many medicaments. Since, according to her, they only upset the stomach, she was quite glad of this, but at the same time even more humiliated. She had, in the South of France, some relatively well-to-do cousins whose daughter, after falling ill in her adolescence, had died at twenty-three; for several years the father and mother had ruined themselves on drugs and cures, on different doctors, on pilgrimages from one thermal spa to another, until her decease. Now all this seemed to Françoise, for the parents in question, a kind of luxury, as though they had owned racehorses or a place in the country. They themselves, in the midst of their affliction, derived a certain pride from such lavish expenditure. They had now nothing left, least of all their most precious possession, their child, but they enjoyed telling people how they had done as much for her and more than the richest in the land. The ultra-violet rays to which the poor girl had been subjected several times a day for months on end particularly gratified them. The father, elated in his grief by the glory of it all, was so carried away as to speak of his daughter at times as though she had been an opera star for whose sake he had ruined himself. Françoise was not insensible to such a wealth of scenic effect; that which framed my grandmother's sickbed seemed to her a trifle meagre, suited rather to an illness on the stage of a small provincial theatre.

There was a moment when her uraemic trouble affected my grandmother's eyes. For some days she could not see at all. Her eyes were not at all like those of a blind person, but remained just the same as before. And I gathered that she could see nothing only from the strangeness of a certain smile of welcome which she assumed the moment one opened the door, until one had come up to her and taken her hand, a smile which began too soon and remained stereotyped on her lips, fixed, but always full-faced, and endeavouring to be visible from every quarter, because it could no longer rely on the eyes to regulate it, to indicate the right moment, the proper direction, to focus it, to make it vary according to the change of position or of facial expression of the person who had come in; because it was left isolated, without the accompanying smile in her eyes which would have diverted the attention of the visitor from it for a while, it assumed in its awkwardness an undue importance, giving an impression of exaggerated amiability. Then her sight was completely restored, and from her eyes the wandering affliction passed to her ears. For several days my grandmother was deaf. And as she was afraid of being taken by surprise by the sudden entry of someone whom she would not have heard come in, all day long (although she was lying with her face to the wall) she kept turning her head sharply towards the door. But the movement of her neck was awkward, for one cannot adapt oneself in a few days to this transposition of faculties, so as, if not actually to see sounds, at least to listen with one's eyes. Finally her pain grew less, but the impediment in her speech increased. We were obliged to ask her to repeat almost everything that she said.

And now my grandmother, realising that we could no longer understand her, gave up altogether the attempt to speak and lay perfectly still. When she caught sight of me she gave a sort of convulsive start like a person who suddenly finds himself unable to breathe, but could make no intelligible sound. Then, overcome by her sheer powerlessness, she let her head fall back on the pillows, stretched herself out flat on her bed, her face grave and stony, her hands motionless on the sheet or occupied in some purely mechanical action such as that of wiping her fingers with her handkerchief. She made no effort to think. Then came a state of perpetual agitation. She was incessantly trying to get up. But we restrained her so far as we could from doing so, for fear of her discovering how paralysed she was. One day when she had been left alone for a moment I found her out of bed, standing in her nightdress trying to open the window.

At Balbec, once, when a widow who had flung herself into the sea had been rescued against her will, my grandmother had told me (moved perhaps by one of those presentiments we discern at times in the mystery of our organic life which remains so obscure but in which nevertheless it seems that the future is foreshadowed) that she could think of nothing so cruel as to snatch a desperate woman away from the death that she had deliberately sought and restore her to her living martyrdom.

We were just in time to catch my grandmother; she put up an almost savage resistance to my mother, then, overpowered, seated forcibly in an armchair, she ceased to will, to regret, her face resumed its impassivity and she began laboriously to pick off the hairs that had been left on her nightdress by a fur coat which had been thrown over her shoulders.

The look in her eyes changed completely; often uneasy, plaintive, haggard, it was no longer the look we knew, it was the sullen expression of a senile old woman. . . .

By dint of repeatedly asking her whether she would like her hair done, Françoise ended up by persuading herself that the request had come from my grandmother. She armed herself with brushes, combs, eau de Cologne, a wrapper. "It can't hurt Madame Amédée," she said, "if I just comb her hair; nobody's ever too weak to be combed." In other words, one is never too weak for another person to be able, for her own satisfaction, to comb one's hair. But when I came into the room I saw between the cruel hands of Françoise, as blissfully happy as though she were in the act of restoring my grandmother to health, beneath aged straggling tresses which scarcely had the strength to withstand the contact of the comb, a head which, incapable of maintaining the position into which it had been forced, was rolling about in a ceaseless whirl in which sheer debility alternated with spasms of pain. I felt that the moment at which Françoise would have finished her task was approaching, and I dared not hasten it by suggesting to her: "That's enough," for fear of her disobeying me. But I did forcibly intervene when, in order that my grandmother might see whether her hair had been done to her liking, Françoise, with innocent savagery, brought her a mirror. I was glad for the moment that I had managed to snatch it from her in time, before my grandmother, whom we had carefully kept away from mirrors, caught even a stray glimpse of a face unlike anything she could have imagined. But alas, when, a moment later, I bent over her to kiss that beloved forehead which had been so harshly treated, she looked up at me with a puzzled, distrustful, shocked expression: she had not recognised me.

According to our doctor, this was a symptom that the congestion of her brain was increasing. It must be relieved in some way. Cottard was in two minds. Françoise hoped at first that they were going to apply "clarified cups." She looked up the effects of this treatment in my dictionary, but could find no reference to it. Even if she had said "scarified" instead of "clarified" she still would not have found any reference to this adjective, since she did not look for it under "C" any more than under "S"—she did indeed say "clarified" but she wrote (and consequently assumed that the printed word was) "esclarified." Cottard, to her disappointment, gave the preference, though without much hope, to leeches. When, a few hours later, I went into my grandmother's room, fastened to her neck, her temples, her ears, the tiny black reptiles were writhing among her bloodstained locks, as on the head of Medusa. But in her pale and peaceful, entirely motionless face I saw her beautiful eyes, wide open, luminous and calm as of old (perhaps even more charged with the light of intelligence than they had been before her illness, since, as she could not speak and must not move, it was to her eyes alone that she entrusted her thought, that thought which can be reborn, as though by spontaneous generation, thanks to the withdrawal of a few drops of blood), her eyes, soft and liquid as oil, in which the rekindled fire that was now burning lit up for the sick woman the recaptured universe. Her calm was no longer the wisdom of despair but of hope. She realised that she was better, wished, to be careful, not to move, and made me the present only of a beautiful smile so that I should know that she was feeling better, as she gently pressed my hand.

I knew the disgust that my grandmother felt at the sight of certain animals, let alone at being touched by them. I knew that it was in consideration of a higher utility that she was enduring the leeches. And so it infuriated me to hear Françoise repeating to her with the little chuckle one gives to a baby one is trying to amuse: "Oh, look at the little beasties running all over Madame." This was moreover to treat our patient with a lack of respect, as though she had lapsed into second child-hood. But my grandmother, whose face had assumed the calm fortitude of a stoic, did not even seem to hear her.

Alas! no sooner had the leeches been removed than the congestion returned and grew steadily worse. I was surprised to find that at this stage, when my grandmother was so ill, Françoise was constantly disappearing. The fact was that she had ordered herself a mourning dress, and did not wish to keep the dressmaker waiting. In the lives of most women, every-thing, even the greatest sorrow, resolves itself into a question of "trying-on."

A few days later, while I was asleep in bed, my mother came to call me in the early hours of the morning. With that tender concern which in the gravest circumstances people who are overwhelmed by grief show for the comfort and convenience of others, "Forgive me for disturbing your sleep," she said to me.

"I wasn't asleep," I answered as I awoke.

I said this in good faith. The great modification which the act of awakening effects in us is not so much that of ushering us into the clear life of consciousness, as that of making us lose all memory of the slightly more diffused light in which our mind had been resting, as in the opaline depths of the sea. The tide of thought, half veiled from our perception, on which we were still drifting a moment ago, kept us in a state of motion perfectly sufficient to enable us to refer to it by the name of wakefulness. But then our actual awakenings produce an interruption of memory. A little later we describe these states as sleep because we no longer remember them. And when that bright star shines which at the moment of waking lights up behind the sleeper the whole expanse of his sleep, it makes him imagine for a few moments that it was not a sleeping but a waking state; a shooting star indeed, which blots out with the fading of its light not only the illusory existence but every aspect of our dream, and merely enables him who has awoken to say to himself: "I was asleep."

In a voice so gentle that it seemed to be afraid of hurting me, my mother asked whether it would tire me too much to get up, and, stroking my hands, went on:

"My poor child, you have only your Papa and Mamma to rely on now."

We went into the sickroom. Bent in a semi-circle on the bed, a creature other than my grandmother, a sort of beast that had put on her hair and crouched among her bedclothes, lay panting, groaning, making the blankets heave with its convulsions. The eyelids were closed, and it was because they did not shut properly rather than because they opened that they disclosed a chink of eyeball, blurred, rheumy, reflecting the dimness of an organic vision and of a hidden, internal pain. All this agitation was not addressed to us, whom she neither saw nor knew. But if it was only a beast that was stirring there, where was my grandmother? Yes, I could recognise the shape of her nose, which bore no relation now to the rest of her face, but to the corner of which a beauty spot still adhered, and the hand that kept thrusting the blankets aside with a gesture which formerly would have meant that those blankets were oppressing her, but now meant nothing.

Mamma asked me to go for a little vinegar and water with which to sponge my grandmother's forehead. It was the only thing that refreshed her, thought Mamma, who saw that she was trying to push back her hair. But now one of the servants was signalling to me from the doorway. The news that my grandmother was *in extremis* had spread like wildfire through the house. One of those "extra helps" whom people engage at exceptional times to relieve the strain on their servants (a practice which gives deathbeds something of the air of social functions) had just opened the front door to the Duc de Guermantes, who was now waiting in the hall and had asked for me: I could not escape him.

"I have just, my dear sir, heard your tragic news. I should like, as a mark of sympathy, to shake your father by the hand."

I pleaded the difficulty of disturbing him for the moment. M. de Guermantes was like a caller who turns up just as one is about to set out on a journey. But he was so intensely aware of the importance of the courtesy he was showing us that it blinded him to all else, and he insisted upon being taken into the drawing-room. As a rule, he made a point of carrying out to the last letter the formalities with which he had decided to honour anyone, and took little heed that the trunks were packed or the coffin ready.

"Have you sent for Dieulafoy? No? That was a grave error. And if you had only asked me, I would have got him to come— he never refuses me anything, although he has refused the Duchesse de Chartres before now. You see, I set myself above a Princess of the Blood. However, in the presence of death we are all equal," he added, not in order to assure me that my grandmother was becoming his equal, but perhaps because he felt that a prolonged discussion of his power over Dieulafoy and his pre-eminence over the Duchesse de Chartres would not be in very good taste.

His advice did not in the least surprise me. I knew that, in the Guermantes family, the name of Dieulafoy was regularly quoted (only with slightly more respect) among those of other tradesmen who were "quite the best" in their respective lines. And the old Duchesse de Mortemart, *née* Guermantes (I never could understand, by the way, why the moment one speaks of a Duchess, one almost invariably says: "The old Duchess of So-and-so," or, alternatively, in a delicate Watteau tone, if she is still young, "The little Duchess of So-and-so") would prescribe almost automatically, with a droop of the eyelid, in serious cases: "Dieulafoy, Dieulafoy!" as, if one wanted a place for ices, she would advise "Poiré Blanche," or for cakes "Rebattet, Rebattet." But I was not aware that my father had, as a matter of fact, just sent for Dieulafoy.

At this point my mother, who was waiting impatiently for some cylinders of oxygen which would help my grandmother to breathe more easily, came out herself to the hall where she little expected to find M. de Guermantes. I should have liked to conceal him, no matter where. But convinced in his own mind that nothing was more essential, could be more gratifying to her or more indispensable to the maintenance of his reputation as a perfect gentleman, he seized me violently by the arm and, although I defended myself as though against an assault with repeated protestations of "Sir, Sir, Sir," dragged me across to Mamma, saying: "Will you do me the great honour of presenting me to your lady mother?" going slightly off pitch on the word "mother." And it was so plain to him that the honour was hers that he could not help smiling at her even while he was composing a grave face. I had no alternative but to effect the introduction, which triggered off a series of bowings and scrapings: he was about to begin the complete ritual of salutation, and even proposed to enter into conversation, but my mother, beside herself with grief, told me to come at once and did not reply to the speeches of M. de Guermantes who, expecting to be received as a visitor and finding himself instead left alone in the hall, would have been obliged to leave had he not at that moment caught sight of Saint-Loup who had arrived in Paris that morning and had come to us in haste to ask for news. "I say, this is a piece of luck!" cried the Duke joyfully, grabbing his nephew by a button which he nearly tore off, regardless of the presence of my mother who was again crossing the hall. Saint-Loup was not, I think, despite his genuine sympathy, altogether sorry to avoid seeing me, considering his attitude towards me. He left, dragged off by his uncle who, having had something very important to say to him and having very nearly gone down to Doncières on purpose to say it, was beside himself with joy at being able to save himself the trouble. "Upon my soul, if anybody had told me I had only to cross the courtyard to find you here, I should have thought they were pulling my leg. As your friend M. Bloch would say, it's rather droll." And as he disappeared down the stairs with his arm round Robert's shoulder: "All the same," he went on, "it's quite clear I must have touched the hangman's rope or something; I do have the devil's own luck." It was not that the Duc de Guermantes was bad-mannered; far from it. But he was one of those men who are incapable of putting themselves in the place of others, who resemble in that respect undertakers and the majority of doctors, and who, after having composed their faces and said "This is a very painful occasion," having embraced you at a pinch and advised you to rest, cease to regard a deathbed or a funeral as anything but a social gathering of a more or less restricted kind at which, with a joviality that has been checked for a moment only, they scan the room in search of the person whom they can talk to about their own little affairs, or ask to introduce them to someone else, or offer

a "lift" in their carriage when it is time to go home. The Duc
de Guermantes, while congratulating himself on the "good
wind" that had blown him into the arms of his nephew, was
still so surprised at the reception—natural as it was—that he
had had from my mother that he declared later on that she
was as disagreeable as my father was civil, that she had
"aberrations" during which she seemed literally not to hear
a word you said to her, and that in his opinion she was out of
sorts and perhaps even not quite "all there." At the same time
he was prepared (according to what I was told) to put it down
partly at least to the "circumstances" and to aver that my
mother had seemed to him greatly "affected" by the sad event.
But his limbs were still twitching with all the residue of bows
and heel-clickings and backings-out which he had been prevented from using up, and he had so little idea of the real nature
of Mamma's grief that he asked me, the day before the funeral,
if I was doing anything to distract her.

A brother-in-law of my grandmother's, who was a monk,
and whom I had never seen, had telegraphed to Austria,
where the head of his order was, and having as a special
dispensation received permission, arrived that day. Bowed
down with grief, he sat by the bedside reading prayers and
meditations without, however, taking his gimlet eyes from
the invalid's face. At one point when my grandmother was
unconscious, the sight of the priest's grief began to upset me,
and I looked at him tenderly. He appeared surprised by my pity,
and then an odd thing happened. He joined his hands in front
of his face like a man absorbed in sorrowful meditation, but,
on the assumption that I would then cease to watch him, left,
as I observed, a tiny chink between his fingers. And just I as
was looking away, I saw his sharp eye, which had been taking
advantage of the shelter of his hands to observe whether my
sympathy was sincere. He was crouched there as in the shadow
of a confessional. He saw that I had noticed him and at once
shut tight the lattice which he had left ajar. I met him again
later, but never was any reference made by either of us to that
minute. It was tacitly agreed that I had not noticed that he
was spying on me. With priests as with alienists, there is always
an element of the examining magistrate. Besides, what friend

is there, however dear to us, in whose past as in ours there has
not been some such episode which we find it more convenient
to believe that he must have forgotten?

The doctor gave my grandmother an injection of morphine,
and to make her breathing less painful ordered cylinders of
oxygen. My mother, the doctor, the nursing sister held these
in their hands; as soon as one was exhausted another was put
in its place. I had left the room for a few minutes. When I
returned I found myself in the presence of a sort of miracle.
Accompanied by an incessant low murmur, my grandmother
seemed to be singing us a long, joyous song which filled
the room, rapid and musical. I soon realised that it was scarcely
less unconscious, that it was as purely mechanical, as the
hoarse rattle that I had heard before leaving the room. Perhaps
to a slight extent it reflected some improvement brought about
by the morphine. Principally it was the result (the air not
passing quite in the same way through the bronchial tubes) of a
change in the register of her breathing. Released by the twofold
action of the oxygen and the morphine, my grandmother's
breath no longer laboured, no longer whined, but, swift and
light, glided like a skater towards the delicious fluid. Perhaps
the breath, imperceptible as that of the wind in the hollow
stem of a reed, was mingled in this song with some of those
more human sighs which, released at the approach of death,
suggest intimations of pain or happiness in those who have
already ceased to feel, and came now to add a more melodious
accent, but without changing its rhythm, to that long phrase
which rose, soared still higher, then subsided, to spring up
once more, from the alleviated chest, in pursuit of the oxygen.
Then, having risen to so high a pitch, having been sustained
with so much vigour, the chant, mingled with a murmur of
supplication in the midst of ecstasy, seemed at times to stop
altogether like a spring that has ceased to flow.

Françoise, in any great sorrow, felt the need, however futile
—but did not possess the art, however simple—to give it
expression. Realising that my grandmother was doomed, it
was her own personal impressions that she felt impelled to
communicate to us. And all that she could do was to repeat:
"I feel quite upset," in the same tone in which she would say,

when she had taken too large a plateful of cabbage broth: "I've got a sort of weight on my stomach," sensations both of which were more natural than she seemed to think. Though so feebly expressed, her grief was nevertheless very great, and was aggravated moreover by the fact that her daughter, detained at Combray (to which this young Parisian now disdainfully referred as "the back of beyond" and where she felt herself becoming a "country bumpkin"), would probably not be able to return in time for the funeral ceremony, which was certain, Françoise felt, to be a superb spectacle. Knowing that we were not inclined to be expansive, she had taken the precaution of bespeaking Jupien in advance for every evening that week. She knew that he would not be free at the time of the funeral. She was determined at least to "go over it all" with him on his return.

For several nights now my father, my grandfather and one of our cousins had been keeping vigil and no longer left the house. Their continuous devotion ended by assuming a mask of indifference, and their interminable enforced idleness around this deathbed made them indulge in the sort of small talk that is an inseparable accompaniment of prolonged confinement in a railway carriage. Besides, this cousin (a nephew of my great-aunt) aroused in me an antipathy as strong as the esteem which he deserved and generally enjoyed. He was always in the offing on such occasions, and was so assiduous in his attentions to the dying that their mourning families, on the pretext that he was delicate, despite his robust appearance, his bass voice and bristling beard, invariably besought him, with the customary euphemisms, not to come to the cemetery. I could tell already that Mamma, who thought of others in the midst of the most crushing grief, would soon be saying to him in different terms what he was in the habit of hearing said on all such occasions:

"Promise me that you won't come 'to-morrow.' Please, for 'her sake.' At any rate, you won't go 'all the way.' It's what she would have wished."

But it was no use; he was always the first to arrive "at the house," by reason of which he had been given, in another circle, the nickname (unknown to us) of "No flowers by request." And before attending "everything" he had always "attended to everything," which entitled him to the formula: "We don't know how to thank you."

"What's that?" came in a loud voice from my grandfather, who had grown rather deaf and had failed to catch something which our cousin had just said to my father.

"Nothing," answered the cousin. "I was just saying that I'd heard from Combray this morning. The weather is appalling down there, and here we've got almost too much sun."

"And yet the barometer is very low," put in my father.

"Where did you say the weather was bad?" asked my grandfather.

"At Combray."

"Ah! I'm not surprised; whenever the weather's bad here it's fine at Combray, and vice versa. Good gracious! Talking of Combray, has anyone remembered to tell Legrandin?"

"Yes, don't worry about that, it's been done," said my cousin, whose cheeks, bronzed by an irrepressible growth of beard, dimpled slightly with the satisfaction of having "thought of" it.

At this point my father hurried from the room. I supposed that a sudden change, for better or worse, had occurred. It was simply that Dr Dieulafoy had just arrived. My father went to receive him in the drawing-room, like the actor who is next to appear on the stage. He had been sent for not to cure but to certify, almost in a legal capacity. Dr Dieulafoy may indeed have been a great physician, a marvellous teacher; to the several roles in which he excelled, he added another, in which he remained for forty years without a rival, a role as original as that of the confidant, the clown or the noble father, which consisted in coming to certify that a patient was *in extremis*. His name alone presaged the dignity with which he would sustain the part, and when the servant announced: "M. Dieulafoy," one thought one was in a Molière play. To the dignity of his bearing was added, without being conspicuous, the litheness of a perfect figure. His exaggerated good looks were tempered by a decorum suited to distressing circumstances. In the sable majesty of his frock coat the Professor would enter the room, melancholy without affectation, uttering not one word of condolence that could have been construed as insincere, nor being guilty of the slightest infringement of the rules of tact. At the foot of a deathbed it was he and not the Duc de Guermantes who was the great nobleman. Having examined my grandmother without tiring her, and with an excess of reserve which was an act of courtesy to the doctor in charge of the case, he murmured a few words to my father, and bowed respectfully to my mother, to whom I felt that my father had positively to restrain himself from saying: "Professor Dieulafoy." But already the latter had turned away, not wishing to seem intrusive, and made a perfect exit, simply accepting the sealed envelope that was slipped into his hand. He did not appear to have seen it, and we ourselves were left wondering for a moment whether we had really given it to him, with such a conjurer's dexterity had he made it vanish without sacrificing one iota of the gravity— which was if anything accentuated—of the eminent consultant in his long frock coat with its silk lapels, his noble features engraved with the most dignified commiseration. His deliberation and his vivacity combined to show that, even if he had a hundred other calls to make, he did not wish to appear to be in a hurry. For he was the embodiment of tact, intelligence and kindness. The eminent man is no longer with us. Other physicians, other professors, may have rivalled, may indeed have surpassed him. But the "capacity" in which his knowledge, his physical endowments, his distinguished manners made him supreme exists no longer, for want of any successor capable of taking his place.

Mamma had not even noticed M. Dieulafoy: everything that was not my grandmother no longer existed. I remember (and here I anticipate) that at the cemetery, where we saw her, like a supernatural apparition, tremulously approach the grave, her eyes seeming to gaze after a being that had taken wing and was already far away, my father having remarked to her: "Old Norpois came to the house and to the church and on here; he gave up a most important committee meeting to come; you ought really to say a word to him, he'd be very touched," my mother, when the Ambassador bowed to her, could do no more than gently lower her face, which showed no sign of tears. A couple of days earlier—to anticipate still before returning to the bedside of the dying woman—while we were watching over her dead body, Françoise, who, not disbelieving entirely in ghosts, was terrified by the least sound, had said: "I believe that's her." But instead of fear, it was an ineffable sweetness that her words aroused in my mother, who would have dearly wished that the dead could return, so as to have her mother with her sometimes still.

To return now to those last hours, "You heard about the telegram her sisters sent us?" my grandfather asked the cousin.

"Yes, Beethoven, I've been told. It's worth framing. Still, I'm not surprised."

"And my poor wife was so fond of them, too," said my grandfather, wiping away a tear. "We mustn't blame them. They're stark mad, both of them, as I've always said. What's the matter now? Aren't you going on with the oxygen?"

My mother spoke: "Oh, but then Mamma will be having trouble with her breathing again."

The doctor reassured her: "Oh, no! The effect of the oxygen will last a good while yet. We can begin it again presently."

It seemed to me that he would not have said this of a dying woman, that if this good effect was going to last it meant that it was still possible to do something to keep her alive. The hiss of the oxygen ceased for a few moments. But the happy plaint of her breathing still poured forth, light, troubled, unfinished, ceaselessly recommencing. Now and then it seemed that all was over; her breath stopped, whether owing to one of those transpositions to another octave that occur in the respiration of a sleeper, or else from a natural intermittence, an effect of anaesthesia, the progress of asphyxia, some failure of the heart. The doctor stooped to feel my grandmother's pulse, but already, as if a tributary had come to irrigate the dried-up river-bed, a new chant had taken up the interrupted phrase, which resumed in another key with the same inexhaustible momentum. Who knows whether, without my grandmother's even being conscious of them, countless happy and tender memories compressed by suffering were not escaping from her now, like those lighter gases which had long been compressed in the cylinders? It was as though everything that she had to tell us was pouring out, that it was us that she was addressing with this prolixity, this eagerness, this effusion. At the foot of the bed, convulsed by every gasp of this agony, not weeping but at moments drenched with tears, my mother stood with the unheeding desolation of a tree lashed by the rain and shaken by the wind. I was made to dry my eyes before I went up to kiss my grandmother.

"But I thought she could no longer see," said my father.

"One can never be sure," replied the doctor.

When my lips touched her face, my grandmother's hands quivered, and a long shudder ran through her whole body—a reflex, perhaps, or perhaps it is that certain forms of tenderness have, so to speak, a hyperaesthesia which recognises through the veil of unconsciousness what they scarcely need senses to enable them to love. Suddenly my grandmother half rose, made a violent effort, like someone struggling to resist an attempt on his life. Françoise could not withstand this sight and burst out sobbing. Remembering what the doctor had just said I tried to make her leave the room. At that moment my grandmother opened her eyes. I thrust myself hurriedly in front of Françoise to hide her tears, while my parents were speaking to the patient. The hiss of the oxygen had ceased; the doctor moved away from the bedside. My grandmother was dead.

An hour or two later Françoise was able for the last time, and without causing it any pain, to comb that beautiful hair which was only tinged with grey and hitherto had seemed less old than my grandmother herself. But now, on the contrary, it alone set the crown of age on a face grown young again, from which had vanished the wrinkles, the contractions, the swellings, the strains, the hollows which pain had carved on it over the years. As in the far-off days when her parents had chosen for her a bridegroom, she had the features, delicately traced by purity and submission, the cheeks glowing with a chaste expectation, with a dream of happiness, with an innocent gaiety even, which the years had gradually destroyed. Life in withdrawing from her had taken with it the disillusionments of life. A smile seemed to be hovering on my grandmother's lips. On that funeral couch, death, like a sculptor of the Middle Ages, had laid her down in the form of a young girl.

CHAPTER TWO

ALTHOUGH it was simply a Sunday in autumn, I had been born again, life lay intact before me, for that morning, after a succession of mild days, there had been a cold fog which had not cleared until nearly midday: and a change in the weather is sufficient to create the world and ourselves anew. Formerly, when the wind howled in my chimney, I would listen to the blows which it struck on the iron trap with as keen an emotion as if, like the famous chords with which the Fifth Symphony opens, they had been the irresistible calls of a mysterious destiny. Every change in the aspect of nature offers us a similar transformation by adapting our desires so as to harmonise with the new form of things. The mist, from the moment of my awakening, had made of me, instead of the centrifugal being which one is on fine days, a man turned in on himself, longing for the chimney corner and the shared bed, a shivering Adam in quest of a sedentary Eve, in this different world.

Between the soft grey tint of a morning landscape and the taste of a cup of chocolate I incorporated all the originality of the physical, intellectual and moral life which I had taken with me to Doncières about a year earlier and which, blazoned with the oblong form of a bare hillside—always present even when it was invisible—formed in me a series of pleasures entirely distinct from all others, incommunicable to my friends in the sense that the impressions, richly interwoven with one another, which orchestrated them were a great deal more characteristic of them to my unconscious mind than any facts that I might have related. From this point of view the new world in which this morning's fog had immersed me was a world already known to me (which only made it more real) and forgotten for some time (which restored all its novelty). And I was able to

look at several of the pictures of misty landscapes which my
memory had acquired, notably a series of "Mornings at
Doncières," including my first morning there in barracks and
another in a neighbouring country house where I had gone
with Saint-Loup to spend the night, from the windows of
which, when I had drawn back the curtains at daybreak before
getting back into bed, in the first a trooper, in the second (on
the thin margin of a pond and a wood, all the rest of which was
engulfed in the uniform and liquid softness of the mist) a
coachman busy polishing harness, had appeared to me like
those rare figures, scarcely visible to the eye that is obliged to
adapt itself to the mysterious vagueness of their half-lights,
which emerge from a faded fresco.

It was from my bed that I was contemplating these memories
that afternoon, for I had returned to it to wait until the hour
came at which, taking advantage of the absence of my parents
who had gone for a few days to Combray, I proposed to get
up and go to a little play which was being given that evening
in Mme de Villeparisis's drawing-room. Had they been at
home I should perhaps not have ventured to do so; my mother,
in the delicacy of her respect for my grandmother's memory,
wished the tokens of regret that were paid to it to be freely
and sincerely given; she would not have forbidden me this
outing, but she would have disapproved of it. From Combray,
on the other hand, had I consulted her wishes, she would not
have replied with a melancholy: "Do just as you like; you're
old enough now to know what is right or wrong," but,
reproaching herself for having left me alone in Paris, and
measuring my grief by her own, would have wished for it
distractions of a sort which she herself would have eschewed
and which she persuaded herself that my grandmother,
solicitious above all things for my health and my nervous
equilibrium, would have recommended for me.

That morning the boiler of the new central heating installa-
tion had been turned on for the first time. Its disagreeable
sound—an intermittent hiccough—had no connexion with my
memories of Doncières. But its prolonged encounter with them
in my thoughts that afternoon was to give it so lasting an
affinity with them that whenever, after succeeding more or

less in forgetting it, I heard the central heating again it would bring them back to me.

There was no one else in the house but Françoise. The fog had lifted. The grey light, falling like a fine rain, wove without ceasing a transparent web through which the Sunday strollers appeared in a silvery sheen. I had flung to the foot of my bed the *Figaro*, for which I had been sending out religiously every morning ever since I had sent in an article which it had not yet printed; despite the absence of sun, the intensity of the daylight was an indication that we were still only half-way through the afternoon. The tulle window-curtains, vaporous and friable as they would not have been on a fine day, had that same blend of softness and brittleness that dragon-flies' wings have, and Venetian glass. It depressed me all the more that I should be spending this Sunday alone because I had sent a note that morning to Mlle de Stermaria. Robert de Saint-Loup, whom his mother had at length succeeded—after painful abortive attempts—in parting from his mistress, and who immediately afterwards had been sent to Morocco in the hope of forgetting the woman he had already for some time ceased to love, had sent me a line, which had reached me the day before, announcing his imminent arrival in France for a short spell of leave. As he would only be passing through Paris (where his family were doubtless afraid of seeing him renew relations with Rachel), he informed me, to show me that he had been thinking of me, that he had met at Tangier Mlle or rather Mme (for she had divorced her husband after three months of marriage) de Stermaria. And Robert, remembering what I had said to him at Balbec, had asked on my behalf for an assignation with the young woman. She would be delighted to dine with me, she had told him, on one of the evenings which she would be spending in Paris before her return to Brittany. He told me to lose no time in writing to Mme de Stermaria, for she must certainly have arrived.

Saint-Loup's letter had come as no surprise to me, even though I had had no news of him since, at the time of my grandmother's illness, he had accused me of perfidy and treachery. I had grasped at once what must have happened. Rachel, who liked to provoke his jealousy (she also had other causes for resentment against me), had persuaded her lover that I had made sly attempts to have relations with her in his absence. It is probable that he continued to believe in the truth of this allegation, but he had ceased to be in love with her, which meant that its truth or falsehood had become a matter of complete indifference to him, and our friendship alone remained. When, on meeting him again, I tried to talk to him about his accusations, he merely gave me a benign and affectionate smile which seemed to be a sort of apology, and then changed the subject. All this was not to say that he did not, a little later, see Rachel occasionally when he was in Paris. Those who have played a big part in one's life very rarely disappear from it suddenly for good. They return to it at odd moments (so much so that people suspect a renewal of old love) before leaving it for ever. Saint-Loup's breach with Rachel had very soon become less painful to him, thanks to the soothing pleasure that was given him by her incessant demands for money. Jealousy, which prolongs the course of love, is not capable of containing many more ingredients than the other products of the imagination. If one takes with one, when one starts on a journey, three or four images which incidentally one is sure to lose on the way (such as the lilies and anemones heaped on the Ponte Vecchio, or the Persian church shrouded in mist), one's trunk is already pretty full. When one leaves a mistress, one would be just as glad, until one has begun to forget her, that she should not become the property of three or four potential protectors whom one pictures in one's mind's eye, of whom, that is to say, one is jealous: all those whom one does not so picture count for nothing. Now frequent demands for money from a cast-off mistress no more give one a complete idea of her life than charts showing a high temperature would of her illness. But the latter would at any rate be an indication that she was ill, and the former furnish a presumption, vague enough it is true, that the forsaken one or forsaker (whichever she be) cannot have found anything very remarkable in the way of rich protectors. And so each demand is welcomed with the joy which a lull produces in the jealous one's sufferings, and answered with the immediate dispatch of money, for naturally one does not like to think of her being in want of anything except lovers (one of the three lovers one has in one's mind's eye), until time has enabled one to regain one's composure and to learn one's successor's name without wilting. Sometimes Rachel came in so late at night that she could ask her former lover's permission to lie down beside him until the morning. This was a great comfort to Robert, for it reminded him how intimately, after all, they had lived to-together, simply to see that even if he took the greater part of the bed for himself it did not in the least interfere with her sleep. He realised that she was more comfortable, lying close to his familiar body, than she would have been elsewhere, that she felt herself by his side—even in an hotel—to be in a bed-room known of old in which one has one's habits, in which one sleeps better. He felt that his shoulders, his limbs, all of him, were for her, even when he was unduly restless from insomnia or thinking of the things he had to do, so entirely usual that they could not disturb her and that the perception of them added still further to her sense of repose.

To revert to where we were, I had been all the more excited by Robert's letter in that I could read between the lines what he had not ventured to write more explicitly. "You can most certainly ask her to dine in a private room," he told me. "She is a charming young person, with a delightful nature—you will get on splendidly with her, and I am sure you will have a most enjoyable evening together." As my parents were re-turning at the end of the week, on Saturday or Sunday, and after that I should be obliged to dine every evening at home, I had written at once to Mme de Stermaria proposing any evening that might suit her up to Friday. A message was brought back that I should hear from her in writing that very evening at about eight o'clock. This time would have passed quickly enough if I had had, during the afternoon that separated me from her letter, the help of a visit from someone else. When the hours are wrapped in conversation one ceases to measure, or indeed to notice them; they vanish, and sud-denly it is a long way beyond the point at which it escaped you that the nimble truant time impinges once more on your atten-tion. But if we are alone, our preoccupation, by bringing before us the still distant and incessantly awaited moment with the frequency and uniformity of a ticking pendulum, divides, or rather multiplies, the hours by all the minutes which, had we been with friends, we should not have counted. And confronted, by the incessant return of my desire, with the ardent pleasure which I was to enjoy—not for some days, though, alas!—in Mme de Stermaria's company, this afternoon, which I was going to have to spend alone, seemed to me very empty and very melancholy.

Every now and then I heard the sound of the lift coming up, but it was followed by a second sound, not the one I was hoping for, namely its coming to a halt at our landing, but another very different sound which the lift made in continuing its progress to the floors above and which, because it so often meant the desertion of my floor when I was expecting a visitor, remained for me later, even when I had ceased to wish for visitors, a sound lugubrious in itself, in which there echoed, as it were, a sentence of solitary confinement. Weary, resigned, occupied for several hours still with its immemorial task, the grey day stitched its shimmering needlework of light and shade, and it saddened me to think that I was to be left alone with a thing that knew me no more than would a seamstress who, installed by the window so as to see better while she finishes her work, pays no attention to the person present with her in the room. Suddenly, although I had heard no bell, Françoise opened the door to introduce Albertine, who entered smiling, silent, plump, containing in the plenitude of her body, made ready so that I might continue living them, come in search of me, the days we had spent together in that Balbec to which I had never since returned. No doubt, whenever we see again a person with whom our relations—however trivial they may be—have now changed, it is like a juxtaposition of two different periods. For this, there is no need for a former mistress to call round to see us as a friend; all that is required is the visit to Paris of someone we have known day by day in a certain kind of life, and that this life should have ceased for us, if only a week ago. On each of Albertine's smiling, questioning, self-conscious features I could read the questions: "And what about Madame de Villeparisis? And the dancing-master? And the pastry-cook?"

When she sat down, her back seemed to be saying: "Well, well, there are no cliffs here, but you don't mind if I sit down beside you, all the same, as I used to do at Balbec?" She was like an enchantress offering me a mirror that reflected time. In this she resembled all the people whom we seldom see now but with whom at one time we lived on more intimate terms. With Albertine, however, there was something more than this. True, even in our daily encounters at Balbec, I had always been surprised when I caught sight of her, so changeable was her appearance. But now she was scarcely recognisable. Freed from the pink haze that shrouded them, her features had emerged in sharp relief like those of a statue. She had another face, or rather she had a face at last; her body too had grown. There remained scarcely anything now of the sheath in which she had been enclosed and on the surface of which, at Balbec, her future outline had been barely visible.

This time, Albertine had returned to Paris earlier than usual. As a rule she did not arrive until the spring, so that, already disturbed for some weeks past by the storms that were beating down the first flowers, I did not distinguish, in the pleasure that I felt, the return of Albertine from that of the fine weather. It was enough that I should be told that she was in Paris and that she had called at my house, for me to see her again like a rose flowering by the sea. I cannot say whether it was the desire for Balbec or for her that took possession of me then; perhaps my desire for her was itself a lazy, cowardly, and incomplete form of possessing Balbec, as if to possess a thing materially, to take up residence in a town, were tantamount to possessing it spiritually. Besides, even materially, when she was no longer swaying in my imagination before a horizon of sea, but motionless in a room beside me, she seemed to me often a very poor specimen of a rose, so much so that I wanted to shut my eyes in order not to observe this or that blemish of its petals, and to imagine instead that I was inhaling the salt air on the beach.

I may say all this here, although I was not then aware of what was to happen later on. Certainly, it is more reasonable to devote one's life to women than to postage stamps or old snuff-boxes, even to pictures or statues. But the example of other collections should be a warning to us to diversify, to have not one woman only but several. Those charming associations that a young girl affords with a sea-shore, with the braided tresses of a statue in a church, with an old print, with everything that causes one to love in her, whenever she appears, a delightful picture, those associations are not very stable. Live with a woman altogether and you will soon cease to see any of the things that made you love her; though it is true that the two sundered elements can be reunited by jealousy. If, after a long period of living together, I was to end by seeing no more in Albertine than an ordinary woman, an intrigue between her and someone she had loved at Balbec would still perhaps have sufficed to reincorporate in her, to amalgamate with her, the beach and the unrolling of the tide. But these secondary associations no longer captivate our eyes; it is to the heart that they are perceptible and fatal. We cannot, under so dangerous a form, regard the renewal of the miracle as a thing to be desired. But I am anticipating the course of years. And here I need only register my regret that I did not have the sense simply to keep my collection of women as people keep their collections of old quizzing glasses, never so complete, in their cabinet, that there is not room always for another and rarer still.

Contrary to the habitual order of her holiday movements, this year she had come straight from Balbec, where furthermore she had not stayed nearly so late as usual. It was a long time since I had seen her. And since I did not know even by name the people with whom she was in the habit of mixing in Paris, I knew nothing of her life during the periods in which she abstained from coming to see me. These lasted often for quite a time. Then, one fine day, in would burst Albertine whose rosy apparitions and silent visits left me little if any better informed as to what she might have been doing during an interval which remained plunged in that darkness of her hidden life which my eyes felt little anxiety to penetrate.

This time, however, certain signs seemed to indicate that some new experience must have entered into that life. And yet, perhaps, all that one was entitled to conclude from them was that girls change very rapidly at the age which Albertine had now reached. For instance, her intelligence was now more in evidence, and on my reminding her of the day when she had insisted with so much ardour on the superiority of her idea of making Sophocles write "My dear Racine," she was the first to laugh, quite whole-heartedly. "Andrée was quite right, it was stupid of me," she admitted. "Sophocles ought to have begun: 'Sir.' " I replied that Andrée's "Sir" and "Dear Sir" were no less comic than her own "My dear Racine," or Gisèle's "My dear friend," but that after all the really stupid people were the professors for making Sophocles write letters to Racine. Here, however, Albertine was unable to follow me. She could not see what was stupid about it; her intelligence was opening up, but was not fully developed. There were other more attractive novelties in her; I sensed, in this same pretty girl who had just sat down by my bed, something that was different; and in those lines which, in the look and the features of the face, express a person's habitual volition, a change of front, a partial conversion, as though something had happened to break down those resistances I had come up against in Balbec one long-ago evening when we had formed a couple symmetrical with but the converse of our present arrangement, for then it had been she who was lying down and I by her bedside. Wishing and not daring to ascertain whether she would now let herself be kissed, every time that she rose to go I asked her to stay a little longer. This was a concession not very easy to obtain, for although she had nothing to do (otherwise she would have rushed out of the house) she was a person methodical in her habits and moreover not very gracious towards me, seeming no longer to take pleasure in my company. Yet each time, after looking at her watch, she sat down again at my request until finally she had spent several hours with me without my having asked her for anything; the things I said to her were connected with those I had said during the preceding hours, and were totally unconnected with what I was thinking about, what I desired from her, remained obstinately parallel thereto. There is nothing like desire for preventing the things one says from bearing any resemblance to what one has in one's mind. Time presses, and yet it seems as though we were seeking to gain time by speaking of subjects absolutely alien to the one that preoccupies us. We go on chatting, whereas the sentence we should like to utter would have been accompanied by a gesture, if indeed we have not (to give ourselves the pleasure of immediate action and to gratify the curiosity we feel as to the reactions which will follow it, without saying a word, without a by-your-leave) already made this gesture. Certainly I was not in the least in love with Albertine; child of the mists outside, she could simply satisfy the fanciful desire which the change of weather had awakened in me and which was midway between the desires that are satisfied by the arts of the kitchen and of monumental sculpture respectively, for it made me dream simultaneously of mingling with my flesh a substance different and warm, and of attaching at some point to my recumbent body a divergent one, as the body of Eve barely holds by the feet to the side of Adam, to whose body hers is almost perpendicular, in those Romanesque bas-reliefs in the church at Balbec which represent in so noble and so reposeful a fashion, still almost like a classical frieze, the creation of woman; God in them is everywhere, followed, as by two ministers, by two little angels in whom one recognises—like those winged, swarming summer creatures which winter has caught by surprise and spared—cupids from Herculaneum still surviving well into the thirteenth century, and winging their last slow flight, weary but never failing in the grace that might be expected of them, over the whole front of the porch.

As for this pleasure which by accomplishing my desire would have released me from these musings and which I should have sought quite as readily from any other pretty woman, had I been asked upon what—in the course of this endless chatter throughout which I was at pains to keep from Albertine the one thing that was in my mind—my optimistic assumption with regard to her possible complaisances was based, I should perhaps have answered that this assumption was due (while the forgotten outlines of Albertine's voice retraced for me the contour of her personality) to the advent of certain words which had not formed part of her vocabulary, or at least not in the acceptation which she now gave them. Thus, when she said to me that Elstir was stupid and I protested: "You don't understand," she replied, smiling, "I mean that he was stupid in that instance, but of course I know he's a very distinguished person, really."

Similarly, wishing to say of the Fontainebleau golf club that it was smart, she declared: "It's really quite a selection."

Speaking of a duel I had fought, she said of my seconds: "What very choice seconds," and looking at my face confessed that she would like to see me "sport a moustache." She even went so far (and at this point my chances appeared to me very great) as to announce, in a phrase of which I would have sworn that she was ignorant a year earlier, that since she had last seen Gisèle there had passed a certain "lapse of time." This was not to say that Albertine had not already possessed, when I was at Balbec, a quite adequate assortment of those expressions which reveal at once that one comes of a well-to-do family and which, year by year, a mother passes on to her daughter just as she gradually bestows on her, as the girl grows up, her own jewels on important occasions. It was evident that Albertine had ceased to be a little girl when one day, to express her thanks for a present which a strange lady had given her, she had said: "I'm quite overcome." Mme Bontemps had been unable to refrain from looking across at her husband, whose comment was: "Well, well, and she's only fourteen."

Her more pronounced nubility had struck home when Albertine, speaking of another girl whom she considered ill-bred, said: "One can't even tell whether she's pretty, because she paints her face a *foot thick*." Finally, though still only a girl, she already displayed the manner of a grown woman of her upbringing and station when she said, of someone whose face twitched: "I can't look at him, because it makes me want to do the same," or, if someone else were being imitated: "The absurd thing about it is that when you imitate her voice you look exactly like her." All this is drawn from the social treasury. But the point was that it did not seem to me possible that Albertine's natural environment could have supplied her with "distinguished" in the sense in which my father would say of a colleague whom he had not actually met but whose intellectual attainments he had heard praised: "It appears he's a very distinguished person." "Selection," even when used of a golf club, struck me as being as incompatible with the Simonet family as it would be, if preceded by the adjective "natural," with a text published centuries before the researches of Darwin. "Lapse of time" seemed to me to augur better still. Finally there appeared the evidence of certain upheavals, the nature of which was unknown to me, but sufficient to justify me in all my hopes, when Albertine observed, with the self-satisfaction of a person whose opinion is by no means to be despised:

"*To my mind*, that is the best thing that could possibly happen. I regard it as the best solution, the stylish way out."

This was so novel, so manifestly an alluvial deposit leading one to suspect such capricious wanderings over ground hitherto unknown to her, that on hearing the words "to my mind" I drew Albertine towards me, and at "I regard" sat her down on my bed.

No doubt it happens that women of moderate culture, on marrying well-read men, receive such expressions as part of their dowry. And shortly after the metamorphosis which follows the wedding night, when they start paying calls and are stand-offish with their old friends, one notices with surprise that they have turned into matrons if, in decreeing that some person is intelligent, they sound both 'l's in the word; but that is precisely the sign of a change of state, and it seemed to me that there was a world of difference between the new expressions and the vocabulary of the Albertine I had known of old—a vocabulary in which the most daring flights were to say of any unusual person: "He's a type," or, if you suggested a game of cards to her: "I don't have money to burn," or again, if any of her friends were to reproach her in terms which she felt to be unjustified: "You really are the limit!"—expressions dictated in such cases by a sort of bourgeois tradition almost as old as the *Magnificat* itself, which a girl slightly out of temper and confident that she is in the right employs, as the saying is, "quite naturally," that is to say because she has learned them from her mother, just as she has learned to say her prayers or to curtsey. All these expressions Mme Bontemps had imparted to her at the same time as a hatred of the Jews and a respect for black because it is always suitable and becoming, even without any formal instruction, but as the piping of the parent goldfinches serves as a model for that of the newborn goldfinches so that they in turn grow into true goldfinches also. But when all was said, "selection" appeared to me of alien growth and "I regard" encouraging. Albertine was no longer the same; therefore she might not perhaps act, might not react in the same way.

Not only did I no longer feel any love for her, but I no longer had to consider, as I might have at Balbec, the risk of shattering in her an affection for myself, since it no longer existed. There could be no doubt that she had long since become quite indifferent to me. I was well aware that to her I was no longer in any sense a member of the "little band" into which I had at one time so anxiously sought and had then been so happy to have secured admission. Besides, since she no longer even had, as in the Balbec days, an air of frank good nature, I felt no serious scruples. However, I think what finally decided me was another philological discovery. As, continuing to add fresh links to the external chain of talk behind which I hid my inner desire, I spoke (having Albertine secure now on the corner of my bed) of one of the girls of the little band who was less striking than the rest but whom nevertheless I had thought quite pretty. "Yes," answered Albertine, "she reminds me of a little *mousmé*."[19] Clearly, when I first knew Albertine the word was unknown to her. It was probable that, had things followed their normal course, she would never have learned it, and for my part I should have seen no cause for regret in that, for there is no more repulsive word in the language. The mere sound of it sets one's teeth on edge as when one has put too large a spoonful of ice in one's mouth. But coming from Albertine, pretty as she was, not even "*mousmé*" could strike me as unpleasing. On the contrary, I felt it to be a revelation, if not of an external initiation, at any rate of an internal evolution. Unfortunately it was now time for me to bid her good-bye if I wished her to reach home in time for her dinner, and myself to be out of bed and dressed in time for my own. It was Françoise who was preparing it; she did not like it to be delayed, and must already have found it an infringement of one of the articles of her code that Albertine,

in the absence of my parents, should be paying me so prolonged a visit, and one which was going to make everything
late. But before *"mousmé"* all these arguments fell to the
ground and I hastened to say:

"You know, I'm not in the least ticklish. You could go on
tickling me for a whole hour and I wouldn't feel it."

"Really?"

"I assure you."

She understood, doubtless, that this was the awkward
expression of a desire on my part, for, like a person who offers
to give you an introduction for which you have not ventured
to ask, though what you have said has shown him that it would
be of great service to you:

"Would you like me to try?" she inquired with womanly
meekness.

"Just as you like, but you would be more comfortable if you
lay down properly on the bed."

"Like that?"

"No, further in."

"You're sure I'm not too heavy?"

As she uttered these words the door opened and Françoise
walked in carrying a lamp. Albertine just had time to scramble
back on to her chair. Perhaps Françoise had chosen this moment to confound us, having been listening at the door or
even peeping through the keyhole. But there was no need to
suppose anything of the sort; she might well have scorned to
assure herself by the use of her eyes of what her instinct must
plainly enough have detected, for by dint of living with me and
my parents she had succeeded in acquiring, through fear,
prudence, alertness and cunning, that instinctive and almost
divinatory knowledge of us all that the mariner has of the sea,
the quarry has of the hunter, and if not the physician, often at
any rate the invalid has of disease. The amount of knowledge
that she managed to acquire would have astounded a stranger
with as good reason as does the advanced state of certain arts
and sciences among the ancients, given the almost non-existent means of information at their disposal (hers were no less
exiguous; they consisted of a few casual remarks forming barely
a twentieth part of our conversation at dinner, caught on the

wing by the butler and inaccurately transmitted to the kitchen).
And even her mistakes were due, like theirs, like the fables in
which Plato believed, rather to a false conception of the world
and to preconceived ideas than to inadequacy of material
resources. Thus even in our own day it has been possible for the
most important discoveries as to the habits of insects to be
made by a scientist who had access to no laboratory and no
apparatus of any sort. But if the drawbacks arising from her
menial position had not prevented her from acquiring a stock
of learning indispensable to the art which was its ultimate goal
—and which consisted in putting us to confusion by communicating to us the results of her discoveries—the limitations
under which she worked had done more; in this case the
impediment, not content with merely not paralysing the flight
of her imagination, had powerfully reinforced it. Of course
Françoise neglected no artificial aids, those for example of
diction and attitude. Since (if she never believed what we said
to her in the hope that she would believe it) she accepted
without the slightest hesitation the truth of anything, however
absurd, that a person of her own condition in life might tell
her which might at the same time offend our notions, just as
her way of listening to our assertions bore witness to her
incredulity, so the accents in which (the use of indirect speech
enabling her to hurl the most deadly insults at us with impunity) she reported the narrative of a cook who had told her
how she had threatened her employers and, by calling them
"dung" in public, had wrung from them any number of
privileges and concessions, showed that she regarded the story
as gospel. Françoise went so far as to add: "I'm sure if I had
been the mistress I should have been quite vexed." In vain
might we, despite our original dislike of the lady on the fourth
floor, shrug our shoulders, as though at an unlikely fable, at
this unedifying report, the teller knew how to invest her tone
with the trenchant assertiveness of the most irrefutable and
most irritating affirmation.

But above all, just as writers, when they are bound hand and
foot by the tyranny of a monarch or of a school of poetry, by
the constraints of prosodic laws or of a state religion, often
attain a power of concentration from which they would have

been dispensed under a system of political liberty or literary anarchy, so Françoise, not being able to reply to us in an explicit fashion, spoke like Tiresias and would have written like Tacitus. She managed to embody everything that she could not express directly in a sentence for which we could not find fault with her without accusing ourselves, indeed in less than a sentence, in a silence, in the way in which she placed an object in a room.

Thus, whenever I inadvertently left on my table, among a pile of other letters, one which it was imperative that she should not see, because, for instance, it referred to her with a malevolence which afforded a presumption of the same feeling towards her in the recipient as in the writer, that evening, if I came home with a feeling of uneasiness and went straight to my room, there on top of my letters, neatly arranged in a symmetrical pile, the compromising document caught my eye as it could not possibly have failed to catch the eye of Françoise, placed by her right at the top, almost apart from the rest, in a prominence that was a form of speech, that had an eloquence all its own, and, as soon as I crossed the threshold, made me start as I would at a cry. She excelled in the preparation of these stage effects, intended to so enlighten the spectator, in her absence, that he already knew that she knew everything when in due course she made her entry. She possessed, for thus making an inanimate object speak, the art, at once inspired and painstaking, of an Irving or a Frédérick Lemaître. On this occasion, holding over Albertine and myself the lighted lamp whose searching beams missed none of the still visible depressions which the girl's body had made in the counterpane, Françoise conjured up a picture of "Justice shedding light upon Crime." Albertine's face did not suffer by this illumination. It revealed on her cheeks the same sunny burnish that had charmed me at Balbec. This face of hers, which sometimes, out of doors, made a general effect of livid pallor, now showed, in the light of the lamp, surfaces so glowingly, so uniformly coloured, so firm and so smooth, that one might have compared them to the sustained flesh tints of certain flowers. Taken aback meanwhile by Françoise's unexpected entry, I exclaimed:

"What, the lamp already? Heavens, how bright it is!"

My object, as may be imagined, was by the second of these ejaculations to dissimulate my confusion, by the first to excuse my lateness in rising. Françoise replied with cruel ambiguity:

"Do you want me to extinglish it?"

"Guish?" Albertine murmured in my ear, leaving me charmed by the familiar quick-wittedness with which, taking me at once for master and accomplice, she insinuated this psychological affirmation in the interrogative tone of a grammatical question.[20]

When Françoise had left the room and Albertine was seated once again on my bed:

"Do you know what I'm afraid of?" I asked her. "It is that if we go on like this I may not be able to resist the temptation to kiss you."

"That would be a happy misfortune."

I did not respond at once to this invitation. Another man might even have found it superfluous, for Albertine's way of pronouncing her words was so carnal, so seductive that merely in speaking to you she seemed to be caressing you. A word from her was a favour, and her conversation covered you with kisses. And yet it was highly gratifying to me, this invitation. It would have been so, indeed, coming from any pretty girl of Albertine's age; but that Albertine should be now so accessible to me gave me more than pleasure, brought before my eyes a series of images fraught with beauty. I remembered Albertine first of all on the beach, almost painted upon a background of sea, having for me no more real an existence than those theatrical tableaux in which one does not know whether one is looking at the actress herself who is supposed to appear, at an understudy who for the moment is taking her principal's part, or simply at a projection. Then the real woman had detached herself from the beam of light and had come towards me, but only for me to perceive that in the real world she had none of the amorous facility with which one had credited her in the magic tableau. I had learned that it was not possible to touch her, to kiss her, that one might only talk to her, that for me she was no more a woman than jade grapes, an inedible decoration at one time in fashion on dinner tables, are really fruit. And now she was appearing to me on a third plane, real as in the second experience that I had had of her but available as in the first; available, and all the more deliciously so in that I had long imagined that she was not. My surplus of knowledge of life (life as being less uniform, less simple than I had at first supposed it to be) inclined me provisionally towards agnosticism. What can one positively affirm, when the thing that one thought probable at first has then shown itself to be false and in the third instance turns out true? (And alas, I was not yet at the end of my discoveries with regard to Albertine.) In any case, even if there had not been the romantic attraction of this disclosure of a greater wealth of planes revealed one after another by life (an attraction the opposite of that which Saint-Loup had felt during our dinners at Rivebelle on recognising, beneath the masks which life had superimposed on a calm face, features to which his lips had once been pressed), the knowledge that to kiss Albertine's cheeks was a possible thing was a pleasure perhaps greater even than that of kissing them. What a difference there is between possessing a woman to whom one applies one's body alone, because she is no more than a piece of flesh, and possessing the girl whom one used to see on the beach with her friends on certain days without even knowing why one saw her on those days and not on others, so that one trembled at the thought that one might not see her again! Life had obligingly revealed to one in its whole extent the novel of this little girl's life, had lent one, for the study of her, first one optical instrument, then another, and had added to carnal desire the accompaniment, which multiplies and diversifies it, of those other desires, more spiritual and less easily assuaged, which do not emerge from their torpor but leave it to carry on alone when it aims only at the conquest of a piece of flesh, but which, to gain possession of a whole tract of memories from which they have felt nostalgically exiled, come surging round it, enlarge and extend it, are unable to follow it to the fulfilment, to the assimilation, impossible in the form in which it is looked for, of an immaterial reality, but wait for this desire half-way and at the moment of return, provide it once more with their escort; to kiss, instead of the

cheeks of the first comer, anonymous, without mystery or
glamour, however cool and fresh they may be, those of which
I had so long been dreaming, would be to know the taste,
the savour, of a colour on which I had endlessly gazed. One
has seen a woman, a mere image in the decorative setting of
life, like Albertine silhouetted against the sea, and then one
has been able to take that image, to detach it, to bring it close
to oneself, gradually to discern its volume, its colours, as
though one had placed it behind the lens of a stereoscope. It is
for this reason that women who are to some extent resistant,
whom one cannot possess at once, of whom one does not indeed know at first whether one will ever possess them, are
alone interesting. For to know them, to approach them, to
conquer them, is to make the human image vary in shape, in
dimension, in relief, is a lesson in relativity in the appreciation
of a woman's body, a woman's life, so delightful to see afresh
when it has resumed the slender proportions of a silhouette
against the back-drop of life. The women one meets first of all
in a brothel are of no interest because they remain invariable.

At the same time, Albertine preserved, inseparably attached
to her, all my impressions of a series of seascapes of which I
was particularly fond. I felt that in kissing her cheeks I should
be kissing the whole of Balbec beach.

"If you really don't mind my kissing you, I'd rather put it
off for a while and choose a good moment. Only you mustn't
forget that you've said I may. I want a voucher: 'Valid for
one kiss.' "

"Do I have to sign it?"

"But if I took it now, should I be entitled to another later
on?"

"You do make me laugh with your vouchers: I shall issue a
new one every now and then."

"Tell me, just one thing more. You know, at Balbec, before
I got to know you, you used often to have a hard, calculating
look. You couldn't tell me what you were thinking about when
you looked like that?"

"No, I don't remember at all."

"Wait, this may remind you: one day your friend Gisèle
jumped with her feet together over the chair an old gentleman

was sitting in. Try to remember what was in your mind at that moment."

"Gisèle was the one we saw least of. She did belong to the group, I suppose, but not properly. I expect I thought that she was very ill-bred and common."

"Oh, is that all?"

I should have liked, before kissing her, to be able to breathe into her anew the mystery which she had had for me on the beach before I knew her, to discover in her the place where she had lived earlier still; in its stead at least, if I knew nothing of it, I could insinuate all the memories of our life at Balbec, the sound of the waves breaking beneath my window, the shouts of the children. But when I let my eyes glide over the charming pink globe of her cheeks, the gently curving surfaces of which expired beneath the first foothills of her beautiful black hair which ran in undulating ridges, thrust out its escarpments, and moulded the hollows and ripples of its valleys, I could not help saying to myself: "Now at last, after failing at Balbec, I am going to discover the fragrance of the secret rose that blooms in Albertine's cheeks. And, since the cycles through which we are able to make things and people pass in the course of our existence are comparatively few, perhaps I shall be able to consider mine in a certain sense fulfilled when, having taken out of its distant frame the blossoming face that I had chosen from among all others, I shall have brought it onto this new plane, where I shall at last have knowledge of it through my lips." I told myself this because I believed that there was such a thing as knowledge acquired by the lips; I told myself that I was going to know the taste of this fleshly rose, because I had not stopped to think that man, a creature obviously less rudimentary than the sea-urchin or even the whale, nevertheless lacks a certain number of essential organs, and notably possesses none that will serve for kissing. For this absent organ he substitutes his lips, and thereby arrives perhaps at a slightly more satisfying result than if he were reduced to caressing the beloved with a horny tusk. But a pair of lips, designed to convey to the palate the taste of whatever whets their appetite, must be content, without understanding their mistake or admitting their disappointment, with roaming over the surface and with coming to a halt at the barrier of the impenetrable but irresistible cheek. Moreover at that moment of actual contact with the flesh, the lips, even on the assumption that they might become more expert and better endowed, would doubtless be unable to enjoy any more fully the savour which nature prevents their ever actually grasping, for in that desolate zone in which they are unable to find their proper nourishment they are alone, the sense of sight, then that of smell, having long since deserted them. At first, as my mouth began gradually to approach the cheeks which my eyes had recommended it to kiss, my eyes, in changing position, saw a different pair of cheeks; the neck, observed at closer range and as though through a magnifying-glass, showed in its coarser grain a robustness which modified the character of the face.

Apart from the most recent applications of photography— which huddle at the foot of a cathedral all the houses which so often, from close to, appeared to us to reach almost to the height of the towers, drill and deploy like a regiment, in file, in extended order, in serried masses, the same monuments, bring together the two columns on the Piazzetta which a moment ago were so far apart, thrust away the adjoining dome of the Salute, and in a pale and toneless background manage to include a whole immense horizon within the span of a bridge, in the embrasure of a window, among the leaves of a tree that stands in the foreground and is portrayed in a more vigorous tone, frame a single church successively in the arcades of all the others—I can think of nothing that can to so great a degree as a kiss evoke out of what we believed to be a thing with one definite aspect, the hundred other things which it may equally well be, since each is related to a no less legitimate perspective. In short, just as at Balbec Albertine had often appeared different to me, so now—as if, prodigiously accelerating the speed of the changes of perspective and changes of colouring which a person presents to us in the course of our various encounters, I had sought to contain them all in the space of a few seconds so as to reproduce experimentally the phenomenon which diversifies the individuality of a fellow-creature, and to draw out one from another, like a nest of boxes, all the possibilities that it contains—so now, during this brief journey of my lips towards her cheek, it was ten Albertines that I saw; this one girl being like a many-headed goddess, the head I had seen last, when I tried to approach it, gave way to another. At least so long as I had not touched that head, I could still see it, and a faint perfume came to me from it. But alas—for in this matter of kissing our nostrils and eyes are as ill-placed as our lips are ill-made—suddenly my eyes ceased to see, then my nose, crushed by the collision, no longer perceived any odour, and, without thereby gaining any clearer idea of the taste of the rose of my desire, I learned, from these ob-noxious signs, that at last I was in the act of kissing Albertine's cheek.

Was it because we were enacting (represented by the rotation of a solid body) the converse of our scene together at Balbec, because it was I who was lying in bed and she who was up, capable of evading a brutal attack and of controlling the course of events, that she allowed me to take so easily now what she had refused me on the former occasion with so forbidding a look? (No doubt from the same look the voluptuous expression which her face assumed now at the approach of my lips differed only by an infinitesimal deviation of its lines but one in which may be contained all the disparity that there is between the gesture of "finishing off" a wounded man and that of giving him succour, between a sublime and a hideous portrait.) Not knowing whether I had to give credit and thanks for this change of attitude to some unwitting benefactor who in these last months, in Paris or at Balbec, had been working on my behalf, I supposed that the respective positions in which we were now placed was the principal cause of it. It was quite another explanation, however, that Albertine offered me; precisely this: "Oh, well, you see, that time at Balbec I didn't know you properly. For all I knew, you might have meant mischief." This argument left me perplexed. Albertine was no doubt sincere in advancing it—so difficult is it for a woman to recognise in the movements of her limbs, in the sensations felt by her body in the course of an intimate encounter with a male friend, the unknown sin into which she trembled to think that a stranger might be planning her fall!

In any case, whatever the modifications that had occurred

recently in her life and that might perhaps have explained why it was that she now so readily accorded to my momentary and purely physical desire what at Balbec she had refused with horror to allow to my love, an even more surprising one manifested itself in Albertine that same evening as soon as her caresses had procured in me the satisfaction which she could not fail to notice and which, indeed, I had been afraid might provoke in her the instinctive movement of revulsion and offended modesty which Gilberte had made at a similar moment behind the laurel shrubbery in the Champs-Elysées.

The exact opposite happened. Already, when I had first made her lie on my bed and had begun to fondle her, Albertine had assumed an air which I did not remember in her, of docile good will, of an almost childish simplicity. Obliterating every trace of her customary preoccupations and pretensions, the moment preceding pleasure, similar in this respect to the moment that follows death, had restored to her rejuvenated features what seemed like the innocence of earliest childhood. And no doubt everyone whose special talent is suddenly brought into play becomes modest, diligent and charming; especially if by this talent such persons know that they are giving us a great pleasure, are themselves made happy by it, and want us to enjoy it to the full. But in this new expression on Albertine's face there was more than disinterestedness and professional conscientiousness and generosity, there was a sort of conventional and unexpected zeal; and it was further than to her own childhood, it was to the infancy of her race that she had reverted. Very different from myself, who had looked for nothing more than a physical alleviation, which I had finally secured, Albertine seemed to feel that it would indicate a certain coarseness on her part were she to think that this material pleasure could be unaccompanied by a moral sentiment or was to be regarded as terminating anything. She, who had earlier been in so great a hurry, now, doubtless because she felt that kisses implied love and that love took precedence over all other duties, said when I reminded her of her dinner:

"Oh, but that doesn't matter in the least. I've got plenty of time."

She seemed embarrassed at the idea of getting up and going immediately after what had happened, embarrassed from a sense of propriety, just as Françoise when, without feeling thirsty, she had felt herself bound to accept with a seemly gaiety the glass of wine which Jupien offered her, would never have dared to leave him as soon as the last drops were drained, however urgent the call of duty. Albertine—and this was perhaps, with another which the reader will learn in due course, one of the reasons which had made me unconsciously desire her—was one of the incarnations of the little French peasant whose type may be seen in stone at Saint-André-des-Champs. As in Françoise, who presently, however, was to become her deadly enemy, I recognised in her a courtesy towards the host and the stranger, a sense of propriety, a respect for the bedside.

Françoise, who after the death of my aunt felt obliged to speak only in a doleful tone, would, in the months that preceded her daughter's marriage, have been quite shocked if the girl had not taken her lover's arm when the young couple walked out together. Albertine lying motionless beside me said:

"What nice hair you have; what nice eyes—you're sweet."

When, after pointing out to her that it was getting late, I added: "You don't believe me?", she replied, what was perhaps true, but only since the minute before and for the next few hours:

"I always believe you."

She spoke to me of myself, my family, my social background. She said: "Oh, I know your parents know some very nice people. You're a friend of Robert Forestier and Suzanne Delage." For a moment these names conveyed absolutely nothing to me. But suddenly I remembered that I had indeed played as a child in the Champs-Elysées with Robert Forestier, whom I had never seen since. As for Suzanne Delage, she was the great-niece of Mme Blandais, and I had once been due to go to a dancing lesson, and even to take a small part in a play in her parents' house. But the fear of getting a fit of giggles and a nose-bleed had at the last moment prevented me, so that I had never set eyes on her. I had at the most a vague idea

that I had once heard that the Swanns' feather-hatted governess had at one time been with the Delages, but perhaps it was
only a sister of this governess, or a friend. I protested to
Albertine that Robert Forestier and Suzanne Delage occupied
a very small place in my life. "That may be; but your mothers
are friends, I can place you by that. I often pass Suzanne
Delage in the Avenue de Messine. I admire her style." Our
mothers were acquainted only in the imagination of Mme
Bontemps, who having heard that I had at one time played with
Robert Forestier, to whom, it appeared, I used to recite
poetry, had concluded from that that we were bound by family
ties. She could never, I gathered, hear my mother's name
mentioned without observing: "Oh yes, she belongs to the
Delage-Forestier set," giving my parents a good mark which
they had done nothing to deserve.

Quite apart from this, Albertine's social notions were fatuous
in the extreme. She regarded the Simonnets with a double "n"
as inferior not only to the Simonets with a single "n" but to
everyone in the world. That someone else should bear the same
name as yourself without belonging to your family is an excellent reason for despising him. Of course there are exceptions.
It may happen that two Simonnets (introduced to one another
at one of those gatherings where one feels the need to talk, no
matter what about, and where moreover one is instinctively
well disposed towards strangers, for instance in a funeral
procession on its way to the cemetery), finding that they have
the same name, will seek with mutual affability though without
success to discover a possible kinship. But that is only an exception. Plenty of people are disreputable, without our either
knowing or caring. If, however, a similarity of names brings
to our door letters addressed to them, or vice versa, we at once
feel a mistrust, often justified, as to their moral worth. We are
afraid of being confused with them, and forestall the mistake
by a grimace of disgust when anyone refers to them in our
hearing. When we read our own name, as borne by them, in
the newspaper, they seem to have usurped it. The trans-
gressions of other members of the social organism are a matter
of indifference to us. We lay the burden of them the more
heavily upon our namesakes. The hatred which we bear to-

wards the other Simonnets is all the stronger in that it is not a personal feeling but has been transmitted hereditarily. After the second generation we remember only the expression of disgust with which our grandparents used to refer to the other Simonnets; we know nothing of the reason; we should not be surprised to learn that it had begun with a murder. Until, as is not uncommon, the day comes when a male Simonnet and a female Simonnet who are not in any way related are joined together in matrimony and so repair the breach.

Not only did Albertine speak to me of Robert Forestier and Suzanne Delage, but spontaneously, with that impulse to confide which the juxtaposition of two human bodies creates, at the beginning at least, during a first phase before it has engendered a special duplicity and reticence in one person towards the other, she told me a story about her own family and one of Andrée's uncles, of which, at Balbec, she had refused to say a word; but she now felt that she ought not to appear to have any secrets from me. Now, had her dearest friend said anything to her against me, she would have made a point of repeating it to me.

I insisted on her going home, and finally she did go, but she was so ashamed on my account at my discourtesy that she laughed almost as though to apologise for me, as a hostess to whose party you have gone without dressing makes the best of you but is offended nevertheless.

"What are you laughing at?" I inquired.

"I'm not laughing, I'm smiling at you," she replied tenderly. "When am I going to see you again?" she went on, as though declining to admit that what had just happened between us, since it is generally the consummation of it, might not be at least the prelude to a great friendship, a pre-existent friendship which we owed it to ourselves to discover, to confess, and which alone could account for what we had indulged in.

"Since you give me leave, I shall send for you when I can."

I dared not let her know that I was subordinating everything else to the chance of seeing Mme de Stermaria.

"It will have to be at short notice, unfortunately," I went on, "I never know beforehand. Would it be possible for me to send round for you in the evenings when I'm free?"

"It will be quite possible soon, because I'm going to have an independent entrance. But just at present it's impracticable. Anyhow I shall come round to-morrow or the next day in the afternoon. You needn't see me if you're busy."

On reaching the door, surprised that I had not preceded her, she offered me her cheek, feeling that there was no need now for any coarse physical desire to prompt us to kiss one another. The brief relations in which we had just indulged being of the sort to which a profound intimacy and a heartfelt choice sometimes lead. Albertine had felt it incumbent upon her to improvise and add provisionally to the kisses which we had exchanged on my bed the sentiment of which those kisses would have been the symbol for a knight and his lady such as they might have been conceived by a Gothic minstrel.

When she had left me, this young Picarde who might have been carved on his porch by the sculptor of Saint-André-des-Champs, Françoise brought me a letter which filled me with joy, for it was from Mme de Stermaria, who accepted my invitation to dinner for Wednesday. From Mme de Stermaria—that was to say, for me, not so much from the real Mme de Stermaria as from the one of whom I had been thinking all day before Albertine's arrival. It is the terrible deception of love that it begins by engaging us in play not with a woman of the external world but with a doll fashioned in our brain—the only woman moreover that we have always at our disposal, the only one we shall ever possess—whom the arbitrary power of memory, almost as absolute as that of the imagination, may have made as different from the real woman as the Balbec of my dreams had been from the real Balbec; an artificial creation which by degrees, and to our own hurt, we shall force the real woman to resemble.

Albertine had made me so late that the play had just finished when I entered Mme de Villeparisis's drawing-room; and having little desire to be caught in the stream of guests who were pouring out, discussing the great piece of news, the separation, which was said to have been already effected, between the Duc de Guermantes and his wife, I had taken a seat on a *bergère* in the outer room while waiting for an opportunity to greet my hostess, when from the inner one, where she had no doubt been sitting in the front row, I saw emerging, majestic, ample and tall in a flowing gown of yellow satin upon which huge black poppies were picked out in relief, the Duchess herself. The sight of her no longer disturbed me in the least. One fine day my mother, laying her hands on my forehead (as was her habit when she was afraid of hurting my feelings) and saying: "You really must stop hanging about trying to meet Mme de Guermantes. You're becoming a laughing-stock. Besides, look how ill your grandmother is, you really have something more serious to think about than waylaying a woman who doesn't care a straw about you," instantaneously—like a hypnotist who brings you back from the distant country in which you imagined yourself to be, and opens your eyes for you, or like the doctor who, by recalling you to a sense of duty and reality, cures you of an imaginary disease in which you have been wallowing—had awakened me from an unduly protracted dream. The rest of the day had been consecrated to a last farewell to this malady which I was renouncing; I had sung, for hours on end and weeping as I sang, the sad words of Schubert's *Adieu*:

Farewell, strange voices call thee
Away from me, dear sister of the angels.

And then it was over. I had given up my morning walks, and with so little difficulty that I thought myself justified in the prophecy (which we shall see was to prove false later on) that I should easily grow accustomed, during the course of my life, to no longer seeing a woman. And when, shortly afterwards, Françoise had reported to me that Jupien, anxious to enlarge his business, was looking for a shop in the neighbourhood, anxious to find one for him (delighted, too, while strolling along a street which already from my bed I had heard luminously vociferous like a peopled beach, to see behind the raised iron shutters of the dairies the young milk-maids with their white sleeves), I had been able to begin those outings again. Nor did I feel the slightest constraint; for I was conscious that I was no longer going out with the object of seeing Mme de Guermantes—much as a married woman, who has taken endless precautions so long as she has a lover, from the day she breaks with him leaves his letters lying about, at the risk of disclosing to her husband an infidelity which ceased to alarm her the moment she ceased to be guilty of it.

What troubled me now was the discovery that almost every house sheltered some unhappy person. In one the wife was always in tears because her husband was unfaithful to her. In the next it was the other way about. In another a hardworking mother, beaten black and blue by a drunkard son, tried to conceal her sufferings from the eyes of the neighbours. Quite half of the human race was in tears. And when I came to know it I saw that it was so exasperating that I asked myself whether it might not be the adulterous husband and wife (who were unfaithful only because their lawful happiness had been denied them, and showed themselves charming and loyal to everyone but their respective spouses) who were in the right. Presently I ceased to have even the excuse of being useful to Jupien for continuing my morning peregrinations. For we learned that the cabinet-maker in our courtyard, whose workrooms were separated from Jupien's shop only by the flimsiest of partitions, was shortly to be "given notice" by the Duke's agent because his hammering made too much noise. Jupien could have hoped for nothing better. The workrooms had a basement for storing timber, which communicated with our cellars. He could keep his coal there, could knock down the partition, and would then have one huge shop. Indeed, since Jupien, finding the rent that M. de Guermantes was asking him exorbitant, allowed the premises to be inspected in the hope that, discouraged by his failure to find a tenant, the Duke would resign himself to accepting a lower offer, Françoise, noticing that, even at an hour when no prospective tenant was likely to call, the concierge left the door of the empty shop on the latch with the "To let" sign still up, scented a trap laid by him to entice the young woman who was engaged to the Guermantes footman (they would find a lovers' retreat there) and to catch them red-handed.

However that might be, and for all that I had no longer to find Jupien a new shop, I still went out before lunch. Often, on these excursions, I met M. de Norpois. It would happen that, conversing as he walked with a colleague, he cast at me a glance which, after making a thorough scrutiny of my person, turned back towards his companion without his having smiled at me or given me any more sign of recognition than if he had never set eyes on me before. For, with these eminent diplomats, looking at you in a certain way is intended to let you know not that they have seen you but that they have not seen you and that they have some serious matter to discuss with the colleague who is accompanying them. A tall woman whom I frequently encountered near the house was less discreet with me. For although I did not know her, she would turn round to look at me, would wait for me, unavailingly, in front of shop windows, smile at me as though she were going to kiss me, make gestures indicative of complete surrender. She resumed an icy coldness towards me if anyone appeared whom she knew. For a long time now in these morning walks, according to what I had to do, even if it was the most trivial purchase of a newspaper, I chose the shortest way, with no regret if it was off the Duchess's habitual route, and if on the other hand it did lie along that route, without either compunction or concealment, because it no longer appeared to me the forbidden road on which I extorted from an ungrateful woman the favour of setting eyes on her against her will. But it had never occurred to me that my recovery, in restoring me to a normal attitude towards Mme de Guermantes, would have a corresponding effect on her and make possible a friendliness, even a friendship, which no longer mattered to me. Until then, the efforts of the entire world banded together to bring me into touch with her would have been powerless to counteract the evil spell that is cast by an ill-starred love. Fairies more powerful than mankind have decreed that in such cases nothing can avail us until the day we utter sincerely in our hearts the formula: "I am no longer in love." I had been vexed with Saint-Loup for not having taken me to see his aunt. But he was no more capable than anyone else of breaking a spell. So long as I was in love with Mme de Guermantes, the marks of cordiality that I received from others, their compliments, actually distressed me, not only because they did not come from her but because she would never hear of them. And yet even if she had known of them it would not have been of the slightest use to me. But even in the details of an attachment, an absence, the declining of an invitation to dinner, an unintentional, unconscious harshness are of more service then all the cosmetics and fine clothes in the world. There would be plenty of social success if people were taught upon these lines the art of succeeding.

As she swept through the room in which I was sitting, her thoughts filled with the memory of friends whom I did not know and whom she would perhaps be meeting again presently at some other party, the Duchess caught sight of me on my *bergère*, genuinely indifferent and seeking only to be polite whereas while I was in love I had tried so desperately, without ever succeeding, to assume an air of indifference. She swerved aside, came towards me and, reproducing the smile she had worn that evening at the Opéra, which the painful feeling of being loved by someone she did not love no longer obliterated, "No, don't move," she said, gracefully gathering in her immense skirt which otherwise would have occupied the entire *bergère*. "You don't mind if I sit down beside you a moment?"

She was taller than me, and further enlarged by the volume of her dress, and I felt myself almost touching her handsome bare arm, round which a faint and ubiquitous down exhaled as it were a perpetual golden mist, and the blonde coils of her hair which wafted their fragrance over me. Having barely room to sit down, she could not turn easily to face me, and so, obliged to look straight in front of her rather than in my direction, assumed the sort of soft and dreamy expression one sees in a portrait.

"Have you any news of Robert?" she inquired.

At that moment Mme de Villeparisis entered the room.

"Well, what a fine time you arrive when we do see you here for once in a way!"

And noticing that I was talking to her niece, and concluding, perhaps, that we were more intimate than she had supposed: "But don't let me interrupt your conversation with Oriane," she went on (for the good offices of the procuress are part of the duties of the perfect hostess). "You wouldn't care to dine with her here on Wednesday?"

It was the day on which I was to dine with Mme de Stermaria, so I declined.

"Saturday, then?"

As my mother was returning on Saturday or Sunday, it would have been unkind not to stay at home every evening to dine with her. I therefore declined this invitation also.

"Ah, you're not an easy person to get hold of."

"Why do you never come to see me?" inquired Mme de Guermantes when Mme de Villeparisis had left us to go and congratulate the performers and present the leading lady with a bunch of roses upon which the hand that offered it conferred all its value, for it had cost no more than twenty francs. (This, incidentally, was as high as she ever went when an artist had performed only once. Those who gave their services at all her afternoons and evenings throughout the season received roses painted by the Marquise.) "It's such a bore never to see each other except in other people's houses. Since you won't dine with me at my aunt's, why not come and dine at my house?"

Various people who had stayed to the last possible moment on one pretext or another, but were at last preparing to leave, seeing that the Duchess had sat down to talk to a young man on a seat so narrow as just to contain them both, thought that they must have been misinformed, that it was not the Duchess but the Duke who was seeking a separation, on my account. Whereupon they hastened to spread abroad this intelligence. I had better grounds than anyone for being aware of its falsity. But I was myself surprised that at one of those difficult periods in which a separation is being effected but is not yet complete, the Duchess, instead of withdrawing from society, should go out of her way to invite a person whom she knew so slightly. The suspicion crossed my mind that it had been the Duke alone who had been opposed to her having me in the house, and that now that he was leaving her she saw no further obstacle to her surrounding herself with the people she liked.

A few minutes earlier I should have been amazed had anyone told me that Mme de Guermantes was going to ask me to come and see her, let alone to dine with her. However much I might be aware that the Guermantes salon could not present those distinctive features which I had extracted from the name, the fact that it had been forbidden territory to me, by obliging me to give it the same kind of existence that we give to the

salons of which we have read the description in a novel or seen
the image in a dream, made me, even when I was certain that it
was just like any other, imagine it as quite different; between
myself and it was the barrier at which reality ends. To dine with
the Guermantes was like travelling to a place I had long wished
to see, making a desire emerge from my head and take shape
before my eyes, making acquaintance with a dream. At least
I might have supposed that it would be one of those dinners
to which someone is invited whom his hosts are reluctant to
exhibit, saying: "Do come; there'll be *absolutely* nobody but
ourselves," pretending to attribute to the pariah the alarm
which they themselves feel at the thought of his mixing with
their friends, and seeking indeed to convert into an enviable
privilege, reserved for their intimates alone, the quarantine
of the involuntarily reclusive outsider they are befriending. I
felt on the contrary that Mme de Guermantes was anxious for
me to enjoy the most delightful society that she had to offer
me when she went on to say, projecting before my eyes as it
were the violet-hued loveliness of a visit to Fabrice's aunt and
the miracle of an introduction to Count Mosca:

"You wouldn't be free on Friday, now, for a small dinner-
party? It would be so nice. There'll be the Princesse de Parme,
who's charming, not that I'd ask you to meet anyone who
wasn't agreeable."

Discarded in the intermediate social grades which are
engaged in a perpetual climbing movement, the family still
plays an important part in certain stationary grades, such as
the middle class and the semi-royal aristocracy, which latter
cannot seek to raise itself since above it, from its own special
point of view, there exists nothing. The friendship shown me
by her "aunt Villeparisis" and Robert had perhaps made me,
for Mme de Guermantes and her friends, living always upon
themselves and in the same little circle, the object of an attentive curiosity of which I had no suspicion.

With these two kinsfolk she had a familiar, everyday,
homely relationship of a sort, very different from what we
imagine, in which, if we happen to be included, so far from
our actions being ejected therefrom like a speck of dust from
the eye or a drop of water from the windpipe, they are capable

of remaining engraved, and will still be related and discussed years after we ourselves have forgotten them, in the palace in which we are astonished to find them preserved like a letter in our own handwriting among a priceless collection of autographs.

People who are merely fashionable may close their doors against undue invasion. But the Guermantes door did not suffer from that. Hardly ever did a stranger have occasion to appear at it. If, for once in a way, the Duchess had one pointed out to her, she never dreamed of troubling herself about the social distinction that he might bring, since this was a thing that she conferred and could not receive. She thought only of his real merits. Both Mme de Villeparisis and Saint-Loup had testified to mine. And doubtless she would not have believed them if she had not at the same time observed that they could never manage to secure me when they wanted me, and that therefore I attached no importance to society, which seemed to the Duchess a sign that a stranger was to be numbered among what she called "agreeable people."

It was worth seeing, when one spoke to her of women for whom she did not care, how her face changed as soon as one named, in connexion with one of these, let us say her sister-in-law. "Oh, she's charming!" the Duchess would say in an assured and judicious tone. The only reason she gave was that this lady had declined to be introduced to the Marquise de Chaussegros and the Princesse de Silistrie. She did not add that the lady had also refused to be introduced to herself, the Duchesse de Guermantes. This had nevertheless been the case, and ever since, the mind of the Duchess had been at work trying to unravel the motives of a woman who was so hard to know. She was dying to be invited to her house. People in society are so accustomed to being sought after that the person who shuns them seems to them a phoenix and at once monopolises their attention.

Was the real motive in the mind of Mme de Guermantes for thus inviting me (now that I was no longer in love with her) that I did not seek the society of her relatives, although apparently sought after by them? I cannot say. In any case, having made up her mind to invite me, she was anxious to do me the honours of her house to the fullest extent and to keep away those of her friends whose presence might have dissuaded me from coming again, those whom she knew to be boring. I had not known to what to attribute her change of direction, when I had seen her diverge from her stellar path, come to sit down beside me, and invite me to dinner, the effect of unexplained causes: for want of a special sense to enlighten us in this respect, we imagine the people we know only slightly— as was my case with the Duchesse de Guermantes—as thinking of us only at the rare moments in which they set eyes on us. Whereas in fact this ideal oblivion in which we picture them as holding us is purely arbitrary. So much so that while in the silence of solitude, reminiscent of a clear and starlit night, we imagine the various queens of society pursuing their course in the heavens at an infinite distance, we cannot help an involuntary start of dismay or pleasure if there falls upon us from that starry height, like a meteorite engraved with our name which we supposed to be unknown on Venus or Cassiopeia, an invitation to dinner or a piece of gossip.

Perhaps from time to time when, following the example of the Persian princes who, according to the Book of Esther, made their scribes read out to them the registers in which were enrolled the names of those of their subjects who had shown zeal in their service, Mme de Guermantes consulted her list of the well-disposed, she had said to herself, on coming to my name: "A man we must ask to dine some day." But other thoughts had distracted her

> (Beset by surging cares, a Prince's mind
> Towards fresh matters ever is inclined)

until the moment she caught sight of me sitting alone like Mordecai at the palace gate; and, the sight of me having refreshed her memory, she wished, like Ahasuerus, to lavish her gifts upon me.

I must however add that a surprise of a totally different sort was to follow the one which I had had on hearing Mme de Guermantes ask me to dine with her. Since I had felt that it would show great modesty on my part, and gratitude also, not to conceal this initial surprise but rather to exaggerate my expression of the delight that it gave me, Mme de Guermantes, who was getting ready to go on to another, final party, had said to me, almost as a justification and for fear of my not being quite certain who she was since I appeared so astonished at being invited to dine with her: "You know I'm the aunt of Robert de Saint-Loup who is very fond of you, and besides, we've already met each other here." In replying that I was aware of this I added that I also knew M. de Charlus, "who had been very kind to me at Balbec and in Paris." Mme de Guermantes appeared surprised and her eyes seemed to turn, as though for a verification of this statement, to some much earlier page of her internal register. "What, so you know Palamède, do you?" This name took on a considerable charm on the lips of Mme de Guermantes because of the instinctive simplicity with which she spoke of a man who was socially so brilliant a figure but for her was no more than her brother-in-law and the cousin with whom she had grown up. And on the dim greyness which the life of the Duchesse de Guermantes represented for me this name Palamède shed as it were the radiance of long summer days when she had played with him as a girl in the garden at Guermantes. Moreover, in that long-forgotten period of their lives, Oriane de Guermantes and her cousin Palamède had been very different from what they had since become: M. de Charlus in particular, entirely absorbed in artistic pursuits which he had so effectively curbed in later life that I was amazed to learn that it was he who had painted the huge fan decorated with black and yellow irises which the Duchess was at this moment unfurling. She could also have shown me a little sonatina which he had once composed for her. I was completely unaware that the Baron possessed all these talents, of which he never spoke. Let me remark in passing that M. de Charlus did not at all relish being called "Palamède" by his family. That the form "Mémé" might not please him one could easily understand. These stupid abbreviations are a sign of the utter inability of the aristocracy to appreciate its own poetry (in Jewry, too, we may see the same defect, since a nephew of Lady Israels, whose name was Moses, was commonly known as "Momo") at the same time as its anxiety not to appear to attach any importance to what is aristocratic. Now on this point M. de Charlus had more poetic imagination

and a more blatant pride. But the reason for his distaste for
"Mémé" could not be this, since it extended also to the fine
name Palamède. The truth was that, considering himself,
knowing himself, to be of princely stock, he would have liked
his brother and sister-in-law to refer to him as "Charlus,"
just as Queen Marie-Amélie and the Duc d'Orléans might
speak of their sons and grandsons, brothers and nephews as
"Joinville, Nemours, Chartres, Paris."

"What a humbug Mémé is!" she exclaimed. "We talked to
him about you for hours, and he told us he would be delighted
to make your acquaintance, just as if he had never set eyes on
you. You must admit he's odd, and—though it's not very nice
of me to say such a thing about a brother-in-law I'm devoted
to and really do admire immensely—a trifle mad at times."

I was struck by the application of this last epithet to M.
de Charlus, and thought to myself that this half-madness might
perhaps account for certain things, such as his having appeared
so delighted with his proposal that I should ask Bloch to
beat his own mother. I decided that, by reason not only of the
things he said but of the way in which he said them, M. de
Charlus must be a little mad. The first time one listens to a
barrister or an actor, one is surprised by his tone, so different
from the conversational. But, observing that everyone else
seems to find this quite natural, one says nothing about it to
other people, one says nothing in fact to oneself, one is content
to appreciate the degree of talent shown. At the most one
may think, of an actor at the Théâtre-Français: "Why, instead
of letting his raised arm fall naturally, did he bring it down
in a series of little jerks broken by pauses for at least ten
minutes?" or of a Labori: "Why, whenever he opened his
mouth, did he utter those tragic, unexpected sounds to express
the simplest things?" But as everybody accepts these things *a
priori* one is not shocked by them. In the same way, on thinking
it over, one said to oneself that M. de Charlus spoke of himself
very grandiloquently, in a tone which was not in the least that
of ordinary speech. One felt that people should have been
saying to him every other minute: "But why are you shouting
so loud? Why are you so offensive?" But everyone seemed to
have tacitly agreed that it was quite all right. And one took

one's place in the circle which applauded his perorations. But certainly there were moments when a stranger might have thought that he was listening to the ravings of a maniac.

"But," went on the Duchess with the faint insolence that went with her natural simplicity, "are you absolutely sure you're not thinking of someone else? Do you really mean my brother-in-law Palamède? I know he loves mystery, but this seems a bit much."

I replied that I was absolutely sure, and that M. de Charlus must have misheard my name.

"Well, I must leave you," said Mme de Guermantes, as though with regret. "I have to look in for a moment at the Princesse de Ligne's. You aren't going on there? No? You don't care for parties? You're very wise, they're too boring for words. If only I didn't have to go! But she's my cousin; it wouldn't be polite. I'm sorry, selfishly, for my own sake, because I could have taken you there, and brought you back afterwards, too. Good-bye then; I look forward to seeing you on Friday."

That M. de Charlus should have blushed to be seen with me by M. d'Argencourt was all very well. But that to his own sister-in-law, who had so high an opinion of him besides, he should deny all knowledge of me, a knowledge that was perfectly natural since I was a friend of both his aunt and his nephew, was something I could not understand.

I must end my account of this incident with the remark that from one point of view there was an element of true grandeur in Mme de Guermantes which consisted in the fact that she entirely obliterated from her memory what other people would have only partially forgotten. Had she never seen me waylaying her, following her, tracking her down on her morning walks, had she never responded to my daily salute with an irritated impatience, had she never sent Saint-Loup about his business when he begged her to invite me to her house, she could not have been more graciously and naturally amiable to me. Not only did she waste no time in retrospective inquiries, in hints, allusions or ambiguous smiles, not only was there in her present affability, without any harking back to the past, without the slightest reticence, something as proudly rectilinear as her majestic stature, but any resentment which she might have felt against someone in the past was so entirely reduced to ashes, and those ashes were themselves cast so utterly from her memory, or at least from her manner, that on studying her face whenever she had occasion to treat with the most exquisite simplicity what in so many other people would have been a pretext for reviving stale antipathies and recriminations, one had the impression of a sort of purification.

But if I was surprised by the modification that had occurred in her opinion of me, how much more did it surprise me to find an even greater change in my feelings for her! Had there not been a time when I could regain life and strength only if—always building new castles in the air!—I had found someone who would obtain for me an invitation to her house and, after this initial boon, would procure many others for my increasingly exacting heart? It was the impossibility of making any headway that had made me leave Paris for Doncières to visit Robert de Saint-Loup. And now it was indeed by the consequence of a letter from him that I was agitated, but on account this time of Mme de Stermaria, not of Mme de Guermantes.

Let me add further, to conclude my account of this evening, that in the course of it there occurred an incident, contradicted a few days later, which surprised me not a little, which caused a breach between myself and Bloch, and which constitutes in itself one of those curious paradoxes the explanation of which will be found in the next part of this work. At this party at Mme de Villeparisis's, Bloch kept on boasting to me about the friendly attentions shown him by M. de Charlus, who, when he passed him in the street, looked him straight in the face as though he recognised him, was anxious to know him personally, knew quite well who he was. I smiled at first, Bloch having expressed himself so violently at Balbec on the subject of the said M. de Charlus. And I supposed merely that Bloch, like his father in the case of Bergotte, knew the Baron "without actually knowing him," and that what he took for a friendly glance was an absent-minded stare. But finally Bloch produced such circumstantial details, and appeared so confident that on two or three occasions M. de Charlus had wished to address him that, remembering that I had spoken of my friend to the Baron, who had asked me various questions about him as we walked together from this very house, I came to the conclusion that Bloch was not lying, that M. de Charlus had heard his name, realised that he was my friend, and so forth. And so, some time later, at the theatre one evening, I asked M. de Charlus if I might introduce Bloch to him, and, on his assenting, went in search of my friend. But as soon as M. de Charlus caught sight of him an expression of astonishment, instantly repressed, appeared on his face, where it gave way to a blazing fury. Not only did he not offer Bloch his hand but whenever Bloch spoke to him he replied in the rudest manner, in an irate and wounding tone. So that Bloch, who, according to his version, had received nothing until then from the Baron but smiles, assumed that I had disparaged rather than recommended him during the brief conversation which, knowing M. de Charlus's liking for etiquette, I had had with him about my friend before bringing him up to be introduced. Bloch left us, exhausted and broken, like a man who has been trying to mount a horse which is constantly on the verge of bolting, or to swim against waves which continually fling him back on the shingle, and did not speak to me again for six months.

The days that preceded my dinner with Mme de Stermaria, far from being delightful, were almost unbearable for me. For as a general rule, the shorter the interval that separates us from our planned objective the longer it seems to us, because we apply to it a more minute scale of measurement, or simply because it occurs to us to measure it. The Papacy, we are told, reckons by centuries, and indeed may perhaps not bother to reckon time at all, since its goal is in eternity. Mine being no more than three days off, I counted by seconds, I gave myself up to those imaginings which are the adumbrations of caresses, of caresses which one itches to be able to make the woman herself reciprocate and complete—precisely those caresses, to the exclusion of all others. And on the whole, if it is true that in general the difficulty of attaining the object of a desire enhances that desire (the difficulty, not the impossibility, for that suppresses it altogether), yet in the case of a desire that is

purely physical, the certainty that it will be realised at a speci-
fic and fairly imminent point in time is not much more stirring
than uncertainty; almost as much as anxious doubt, the absence
of doubt makes intolerable the period of waiting for the
pleasure that is bound to come, because it makes of that suspense an innumerably rehearsed accomplishment and, by the
frequency of our proleptic representations, divides time into
sections as minute as any that could be carved by anguished
uncertainty.

What I wanted was to possess Mme de Stermaria: for several
days my desires had been actively and incessantly preparing
my imagination for this pleasure, and this pleasure alone; any
other pleasure (pleasure with another woman) would not have
been ready, pleasure being but the realisation of a prior
craving which is not always the same but changes according
to the endless variations of one's fancies, the accidents of one's
memory, the state of one's sexual disposition, the order of
availability of one's desires, the most recently assuaged of
which lie dormant until the disappointment of their fulfilment has been to some extent forgotten; I had already turned
from the main road of general desires and had ventured along
the path of a more particular desire; I should have had—in
order to wish for a different assignation—to retrace my steps
too far before rejoining the main road and taking another path.
To take possession of Mme de Stermaria on the island in the
Bois de Boulogne where I had asked her to dine with me:
this was the pleasure that I pictured to myself all the time. It
would naturally have been destroyed if I had dined on that
island without Mme de Stermaria; but perhaps as greatly
dimished had I dined, even with her, somewhere else. Besides,
the attitudes according to which one envisages a pleasure are
prior to the woman, to the type of woman suitable thereto.
They dictate the pleasure, and the place as well, and for that
reason bring to the fore alternatively, in our capricious fancy,
this or that woman, this or that setting, this or that room, which
in other weeks we should have dismissed with contempt.
Daughters of the attitude that produced them, certain women
will not appeal to us without the double bed in which we find
peace by their side, while others, to be caressed with a more

secret intention, require leaves blown by the wind, water rippling in the night, are as frail and fleeting as they.

No doubt in the past, long before I received Saint-Loup's letter and when there was as yet no question of Mme de Stermaria, the island in the Bois had seemed to me to be specially designed for pleasure, because I had found myself going there to taste the bitterness of having no pleasure to enjoy there. It is to the shores of the lake from which one goes to that island, and along which, in the last weeks of summer, those ladies of Paris who have not yet left for the country take the air, that, not knowing where to look for her, or whether indeed she has not already left Paris, one wanders in the hope of seeing the girl go by with whom one fell in love at the last ball of the season, whom one will not have a chance of meeting again on any evening until the following spring. Sensing it to be at least the eve, if not the morrow, of the beloved's departure, one follows along the brink of the shimmering water those pleasant paths by which already a first red leaf is blooming like a last rose, one scans that horizon where, by a contrivance the opposite of that employed in those panoramas beneath whose rotundas the wax figures in the foreground impart to the painted canvas beyond them the illusory appearance of depth and mass, our eyes, travelling without transition from the cultivated park to the natural heights of Meudon and the Mont Valérien, do not know where to set the boundary, and make the natural country trespass upon the handiwork of the gardener, the artificial charm of which they project far beyond its own limits; like those rare birds reared in liberty in a botanical garden which every day, wherever their winged excursions may chance to take them, sound an exotic note here or there in the surrounding woods. Between the last festivity of summer and one's winter exile, one anxiously ranges that romantic world of chance encounters and lover's melancholy, and one would be no more surprised to learn that it was situated outside the mapped universe than if, at Versailles, looking down from the terrace, an observatory round which the clouds gather against the blue sky in the manner of Van der Meulen, after having thus risen above the bounds of nature, one were informed that, there where nature begins again at the end of the great canal, the villages which one cannot make out, on a horizon as dazzling as the sea, are called Fleurus or Nijmegen.

And then, the last carriage having rolled by, when one feels with a throb of pain that she will not now come, one goes to dine on the island; above the quivering poplars which endlessly recall the mysteries of evening more than they respond to them, a pink cloud puts a last touch of living colour into the tranquil sky. A few drops of rain fall soundlessly on the ancient water which, in its divine infancy, remains always the colour of the weather and continually forgets the reflexions of clouds and flowers. And after the geraniums have vainly striven, by intensifying the brilliance of their scarlet, to resist the gathering twilight, a mist rises to envelop the now slumbering island; one walks in the moist darkness along the water's edge, where at the most the silent passage of a swan startles one like the momentarily wide-open eyes and the swift smile of a child in bed at night whom one did not suppose to be awake. Then one longs all the more to have a lover by one's side because one feels alone and can believe oneself to be far away from the world.

But to this island, where even in summer there was often a mist, how much more gladly would I have brought Mme de Stermaria now that the cold season, the end of autumn had come! If the weather that had prevailed since Sunday had not in itself rendered grey and maritime the scenes in which my imagination was living—as other seasons made them balmy, luminous, Italian—the hope of making Mme de Stermaria mine in a few days' time would have been quite enough to raise, twenty times in an hour, a curtain of mist in my monotonously lovesick imagination. In any event the fog which since yesterday had risen even in Paris not only made me think incessantly of the native province of the young woman whom I had invited to dine with me, but since it was probable that it must after sunset invade the Bois, and especially the shores of the lake, far more thickly than the streets of the town, I felt that for me it would give the Isle of Swans a hint of that Breton island whose marine and misty atmosphere had always enveloped in my mind like a garment the pale silhouette

of Mme de Stermaria. Of course when we are young, at the
age I had reached at the time of my walks along the Méséglise
way, our desires, our beliefs confer on a woman's clothing an
individual personality, an irreducible essence. We pursue the
reality. But by dint of allowing it to escape we end by noticing
that, after all those vain endeavours which have led to nothing,
something solid subsists, which is what we have been seeking.
We begin to isolate, to identify what we love, we try to procure
it for ourselves, if only by a stratagem. Then, in the absence of
our vanished faith, costume fills the gap, by means of a
deliberate illusion. I knew quite well that within half an hour
of home I should not find myself in Brittany. But in walking
arm in arm with Mme de Stermaria in the dusk of the island,
by the water's edge, I should be acting like other men who,
unable to penetrate the walls of a convent, do at least, before
enjoying a woman, clothe her in the habit of a nun.

I could even look forward to hearing with her a lapping of
waves, for, on the day before our dinner, a storm broke over
Paris. I was beginning to shave before going to the island to
engage the room (although at this time of year the island was
empty and the restaurant deserted) and order the food for our
dinner next day when Françoise came in to announce the
arrival of Albertine. I had her shown in at once, indifferent to
her finding me disfigured by a bristling chin, although at
Balbec I had never felt smart enough for her and she had cost
me as much agitation and distress as Mme de Stermaria did now.
The latter, I was determined, must go away with the best
possible impression from our evening together. Accordingly
I asked Albertine to come with me there and then to the island
to choose the menu. She to whom one gives everything is so
quickly replaced by another that one is surprised to find oneself
giving all that one has afresh at every moment, without any
hope of future reward. At my suggestion the smiling rosy
face beneath Albertine's flat toque, which came down very low,
over her eyebrows, seemed to hesitate. She had probably other
plans; if so she sacrificed them willingly, to my great satisfaction, for I attached the utmost importance to having with me
a young housewife who would know a great deal more than
me about ordering dinner.

It is certain that she had represented something utterly different for me at Balbec. But our intimacy with a woman with whom we are in love, even when we do not consider it close enough at the time, creates between her and us, in spite of the shortcomings that pain us while our love lasts, social ties which outlast our love and even the memory of our love. Then, in the woman who is now no more to us than a means of approach, an avenue towards others, we are just as astonished and amused to learn from our memory what her name meant originally to that other person we formerly were as if, after giving a cabman an address in the Boulevard des Capucines or the Rue du Bac, thinking only of the person we are going to see there, we remind ourselves that these names were once those of the Capuchin nuns whose convent stood on the site and of the ferry across the Seine.

At the same time, my Balbec desires had so generously ripened Albertine's body, had gathered and stored in it savours so fresh and sweet that, during our expedition to the Bois, while the wind like a careful gardener shook the trees, brought down the fruit, swept up the fallen leaves, I told myself that had there been any risk of Saint-Loup's being mistaken, or of my having misunderstood his letter, so that my dinner with Mme de Stermaria might lead to no satisfactory result, I should have made an appointment for later the same evening with Albertine, in order to forget, during an hour of purely sensual pleasure, holding in my arms a body of which my curiosity had once computed, weighed up all the possible charms in which it now abounded, the emotions and perhaps the regrets of this burgeoning love for Mme de Stermaria. And certainly, if I could have supposed that Mme de Stermaria would grant me none of her favours at our first meeting, I should have formed a slightly depressing picture of my evening with her. I knew only too well from experience how bizarrely the two stages which succeed one another in the first phase of our love for a woman whom we have desired without knowing her, loving in her rather the particular kind of existence in which she is steeped than her still unfamiliar self—how bizarrely those two stages are reflected in the domain of reality, that is to say no longer in ourselves but in our meetings with her. Without ever having talked to her, we have hesitated, tempted as we were by the poetic charm which she represented for us. Shall it be this woman or another? And suddenly our dreams become focused on her, are indistinguishable from her. The first meeting with her which will shortly follow should reflect this dawning love. Nothing of the sort. As if it were necessary for material reality to have its first phase also, loving her already we talk to her in the most trivial fashion: "I asked you to come and dine on this island because I thought the surroundings would amuse you. Mind you, I've nothing particular to say to you. But it's rather damp, I'm afraid, and you may find it cold——" "Oh, no, not at all!" "You just say that out of politeness. Very well, Madame, I shall allow you to battle against the cold for another quarter of an hour, as I don't want to pester you, but in fifteen minutes I shall take you away by force. I don't want to have you catching a chill." And without having said anything to her we take her home, remembering nothing about her, at the most a certain look in her eyes, but thinking only of seeing her again. Then at the second meeting (when we do not even find that look, our sole memory of her, but nevertheless still only thinking— indeed even more so—of seeing her again), the first stage is transcended. Nothing has happened in the interval. And yet, instead of talking about the comfort or want of comfort of the restaurant, we say, without apparently surprising the new person, who seems to us positively plain but to whom we should like to think that people were talking about us at every moment in her life: "We're going to have our work cut out to overcome all the obstacles in our way. Do you think we shall be successful? Do you think we'll get the better of our enemies —live happily ever afterwards, and all that sort of thing?" But these contrasting conversations, trivial to begin with, then hinting at love, would not be required; Saint-Loup's letter was a guarantee of that. Mme de Stermaria would give herself on the very first evening, so that I should have no need to engage Albertine to come to me as a substitute later in the evening. It would be unnecessary; Robert never exaggerated, and his letter was quite clear.

Albertine spoke hardly at all, sensing that my thoughts were elsewhere. We went a little way on foot into the greenish, almost submarine grotto of a dense grove on the dome of which we heard the wind howl and the rain splash. I trod underfoot dead leaves which sank into the soil like sea-shells, and poked with my stick at fallen chestnuts prickly as sea-urchins.

On the boughs of the trees, the last clinging leaves, shaken by the wind, followed it only as far as their stems would allow, but sometimes these broke and they fell to the ground, along which they coursed to overtake it. I thought joyfully how much more remote still, if this weather lasted, the island would be the next day, and in any case quite deserted. We returned to our carriage and, as the squall had subsided, Albertine asked me to take her on to Saint-Cloud. As on the ground the drifting leaves, so up above the clouds were chasing the wind. And a stream of migrant evenings, of which a sort of conic section cut into the sky made visible the successive layers, pink, blue and green, were gathered in readiness for departure to warmer climes. To obtain a closer view of a marble goddess who had been carved in the act of springing from her pedestal and, alone in a great wood which seemed to be consecrated to her, filled it with the mythological terror, half animal, half divine, of her frenzied leaps, Albertine climbed a knoll while I waited for her in the road. She herself, seen thus from below, no longer coarse and plump as a few days earlier on my bed when the grain of her neck appeared under the magnifying-glass of my eyes, but delicately chiselled, seemed like a little statue on which our happy hours together at Balbec had left their patina. When I found myself alone again at home, remembering that I had been for an expedition that afternoon with Albertine, that I was to dine in two days' time with Mme de Guermantes and that I had to answer a letter from Gilberte, three women I had loved, I said to myself that our social existence, like an artist's studio, is filled with abandoned sketches in which we fancied for a moment that we could set down in permanent form our need of a great love, but it did not occur to me that sometimes, if the sketch is not too old, it may happen that we return to it and make of it a wholly different work, and one that is possibly more important than what we had originally planned.

The next day was cold and fine; winter was in the air—indeed the season was so far advanced that it was a miracle that we should have found in the already ravaged Bois a few domes of gilded green. When I awoke I saw, as from the window of the barracks at Doncières, a uniform, dead white mist which hung gaily in the sunlight, thick and soft as a web of spun sugar. Then the sun withdrew, and the mist thickened still further in the afternoon. Night fell early, and I washed and changed, but it was still too soon to start. I decided to send a carriage for Mme de Stermaria. I did not like to go for her in it myself, not wishing to force my company on her, but I gave the driver a note for her in which I asked whether she would mind my coming to call for her. Meanwhile I lay down on my bed, shut my eyes for a moment, then opened them again. Over the top of the curtains there was now only a thin strip of daylight which grew steadily dimmer. I recognised that vacant hour, the vast ante-room of pleasure, the dark, delicious emptiness of which I had learned at Balbec to know and to enjoy when, alone in my room as I was now, while everyone else was at dinner, I saw without regret the daylight fade from above my curtains, knowing that presently, after a night of polar brevity, it was to be resuscitated in a more dazzling brightness in the lighted rooms at Rivebelle. I sprang from my bed, tied my black tie, brushed my hair, final gestures of a belated tidying-up, carried out at Balbec with my mind not on myself but on the women whom I should see at Rivebelle, while I smiled at them in anticipation in the mirror that stood across a corner of my room, gestures which for that reason had remained the harbingers of an entertainment in which music and lights would be mingled. Like magic signs they conjured it up, indeed already brought it into being; thanks to them I had as positive a notion of its reality, as complete an enjoyment of its intoxicating frivolous charm, as I had had at Combray, in the month of July, when I heard the hammer-blows ring on the packing cases and enjoyed the warmth and the sunshine in the coolness of my darkened room.

Thus it was no longer entirely Mme de Stermaria that I should have wished to see. Forced now to spend my evening with her, I should have preferred, as it was almost the last before the

return of my parents, that it should remain free and that I should
be able to seek out some of the women I had seen at Rivebelle.
I gave my hands one more final wash and, my sense of pleasure
keeping me on the move, dried them as I walked through the
shuttered dining-room. It appeared to be open on to the
lighted hall, but what I had taken for the bright crevice of the
door, which in fact was closed, was only the gleaming reflexion
of my towel in a mirror that had been laid against the wall in
readiness to be fixed in its place before Mamma's return. I
thought again of all the other illusions of the sort which I had
discovered in different parts of the house, and which were not
optical only, for when we first came there I had thought that
our next door neighbour kept a dog on account of the prolonged, almost human, yapping which came from a kitchen
pipe whenever the tap was turned on. And the door on to the
outer landing never closed by itself, very gently, against the
draughts of the staircase, without rendering those broken,
voluptuous, plaintive phrases that overlap the chant of the
pilgrims towards the end of the Overture to *Tannhäuser*. I
had in fact, just as I had put my towel back on its rail, an
opportunity of hearing a fresh rendering of this dazzling symphonic fragment, for at a peal of the bell I hurried out to open
the door to the driver who had come with Mme de Stermaria's
answer. I thought that his message would be: "The lady is
downstairs," or "The lady is waiting." But he had a letter in
his hand. I hesitated for a moment before looking to see what
Mme de Stermaria had written, which as long as she held the
pen in her hand might have been different, but was now,
detached from her, an engine of fate pursuing its course alone,
which she was utterly powerless to alter. I asked the driver to
wait downstairs for a moment, although he grumbled about
the fog. As soon as he had gone I opened the envelope. On
her card, inscribed *Vicomtesse Alix de Stermaria*, my guest had
written: "Am so sorry—am unfortunately prevented from
dining with you this evening on the island in the Bois. Had been
so looking forward to it. Will write you a proper letter from
Stermaria. Very sorry. Kindest regards." I stood motionless,
stunned by the shock that I had received. At my feet lay the
card and envelope, fallen like the spent cartridge from a gun

when the shot has been fired. I picked them up, and tried to analyse her message. "She says that she cannot dine with me on the island in the Bois. One might conclude from that that she might be able to dine with me somewhere else. I shall not be so indiscreet as to go and fetch her, but, after all, that is quite a reasonable interpretation." And from the island in the Bois, since for the last few days my thoughts had been installed there in advance with Mme de Stermaria, I could not succeed in bringing them back to where I was. My desire continued to respond automatically to the gravitational force which had been impelling it now for so many hours, and in spite of this message, too recent to counteract that force, I went on instinctively getting ready to set out, just as a student, although ploughed by the examiners, tries to answer one question more. At last I decided to tell Françoise to go down and pay the driver. I went along the passage, and failing to find her, passed through the dining-room, where suddenly my feet ceased to ring out on the bare boards as they had been doing until then and were hushed to a silence which, even before I had realised the explanation of it, gave me a feeling of suffocation and confinement. It was the carpets which, with a view to my parents' return, the servants had begun to put down again, those carpets which look so well on bright mornings when amid their disorder the sun awaits you like a friend come to take you out to lunch in the country, and casts over them the dappled light and shade of the forest, but which now on the contrary were the first installations of the wintry prison from which, obliged as I should be to live and take my meals at home, I should no longer be free to escape when I chose.

"Take care you don't slip, sir; they're not tacked yet," Françoise called to me. "I ought to have lighted up. Oh, dear, it's the end of 'September' already, the fine days are over."

In no time, winter; at the corner of a window, as in a Gallé glass, a vein of crusted snow; and even in the Champs-Elysées, instead of the girls one waits to see, nothing but solitary sparrows.

What added to my despair at not seeing Mme de Stermaria was that her answer led me to suppose that whereas, hour by hour, since Sunday, I had been living for this dinner alone, she had presumably never given it a second thought. Later on I learned of an absurd love match that she made with a young man whom she must already have been seeing at this time, and who had presumably made her forget my invitation. For if she had remembered it she would surely never have waited for the carriage, which I had not in fact arranged to send for her, to inform me that she was otherwise engaged. My dreams of a young feudal maiden on a misty island had opened up a path to a still non-existent love. Now my disappointment, my rage, my desperate desire to recapture her who had just refused me, were able, by bringing my sensibility into play, to make definite the possible love which until then my imagination alone had —though more feebly—offered me.

How many they are in our memories, how many more we have forgotten—those faces of girls and young women, all different, on which we have superimposed a certain charm and a frenzied desire to see them again only because at the last moment they eluded us! In the case of Mme de Stermaria there was a good deal more than this, and it was enough now, in order to love her, for me to see her again so that I might refresh those impressions, so vivid but all too brief, which my memory would not otherwise have the strength to keep alive in her absence. Circumstances decided against me; I did not see her again. It was not she that I loved, but it might well have been. And one of the things that made most painful, perhaps, the great love which was presently to come to me was telling myself, when I thought of this evening, that given a slight modification of very simple circumstances, my love might have been transferred elsewhere, on to Mme de Stermaria; that, applied to her who inspired it in me so soon afterwards, it was not therefore—as I so longed, so needed to believe—absolutely necessary and predestined.

Françoise had left me by myself in the dining-room with the remark that it was foolish of me to stay there before she had lighted the fire. She went to get me some dinner, for from this very evening, even before the return of my parents, my seclusion was beginning. I caught sight of a huge bundle of carpets, still rolled up, and propped against one end of the sideboard; and burying my head in it, swallowing its dust together with my own tears, as the Jews used to cover their heads with ashes in times of mourning, I began to sob. I shivered, not only because the room was cold, but because a distinct lowering of temperature (against the danger and, it must be said, the by no means disagreeable sensation of which we make no attempt to react) is brought about by a certain kind of tears which fall from our eyes, drop by drop, like a fine, penetrating, icy rain, and seem as though they will never cease to flow. Suddenly I heard a voice:

"May I come in? Françoise told me you might be in the dining-room. I looked in to see whether you would care to come out and dine somewhere, if it isn't bad for your throat—there's a fog outside you could cut with a knife."

It was Robert de Saint-Loup, who had arrived in Paris that morning, when I imagined him to be still in Morocco or on the sea.

I have already said (and it was precisely Robert himself who at Balbec had helped me, quite unwittingly, to arrive at this conclusion) what I think about friendship: to wit, that it is so trivial a thing that I find it hard to understand how men with some claim to genius—Nietzsche, for instance—can have been so ingenuous as to ascribe to it a certain intellectual merit, and consequently to deny themselves friendships in which intellectual esteem would have no part. Yes, it has always been a surprise to me to think that a man who carried honesty with himself to the point of cutting himself off from Wagner's music from scruples of conscience could have imagined that the truth can ever be attained by the mode of expression, by its very nature vague and inadequate, which actions in general and acts of friendship in particular constitute, or that there can be any kind of significance in the fact of one's leaving one's work to go and see a friend and shed tears with him on hearing the false report that the Louvre has been burned down. I had reached the point, at Balbec, of regarding the pleasure of playing with a troop of girls as less destructive of the spiritual life, to which at least it remains alien, than friendship, the whole effort of which is directed towards making us sacrifice the only part of ourselves that is real and incommunicable (other-

wise than by means of art) to a superficial self which, unlike
the other, finds no joy in its own being, but rather a vague,
sentimental glow at feeling itself supported by external props,
hospitalised in an extraneous individuality, where, happy in the
protection that is afforded it there, it expresses its well-being in
warm approval and marvels at qualities which it would denounce as failings and seek to correct in itself. Besides, the
scorners of friendship can, without illusion and not without
remorse, be the finest friends in the world, in the same way as
an artist who is carrying a masterpiece within him and feels it
his duty to live and carry on his work, nevertheless, in order
not to be thought or to run the risk of being selfish, gives his
life for a futile cause, and gives it all the more gallantly in that
the reasons for which he would have preferred not to give it
were disinterested. But whatever might be my opinion of
friendship, to mention only the pleasure that it procured me,
of a quality so mediocre as to be like something half-way
between physical exhaustion and mental boredom, there is no
brew so deadly that it cannot at certain moments become
precious and invigorating by giving us just the stimulus that
was necessary, the warmth that we cannot generate ourselves.

It never entered my mind of course to ask Saint-Loup to take
me to see some of the Rivebelle women, as I had wanted to
do an hour ago; the scar left by my regret about Mme de
Stermaria was too recent to be so quickly healed, but at the
moment when I had ceased to feel in my heart any reason for
happiness Saint-Loup's arrival was like a sudden apparition of
kindness, gaiety, life, which were external to me, no doubt, but
offered themselves to me, asked only to be made mine. He did
not himself understand my cry of gratitude, my tears of affection. And is there anything indeed more paradoxically affectionate than one of those friends, be he diplomat, explorer,
airman, or soldier like Saint-Loup, who, having to leave next
day for the country whence they will go on heaven knows
where, seem to derive from the evening they devote to us an
impression which we are astonished to find so heart-warming
for them, so rare and fleeting is it, and equally astonished,
since it delights them so much, not to see them prolong further
or repeat more often? A meal with us, an event so natural in

itself, gives these travellers the same strange and exquisite
pleasure as our boulevards give to an Asiatic.

We set off together to dine, and on the way downstairs I
thought of Doncières, where every evening I used to meet
Robert at his restaurant, and the little dining-rooms there that
I had forgotten. I remembered one of these to which I had
never given a thought, and which was not in the hotel where
Saint-Loup dined but in another, far humbler, a cross between
an inn and a boarding-house, where the waiting was done by
the landlady and one of her servants. I had been forced to take
shelter there once from a snowstorm. Besides, Robert was not
to be dining at the hotel that evening and I had not cared to
go any further. My food was brought to me in a little panelled
room upstairs. The lamp went out during dinner and the
serving-girl lighted a couple of candles. Pretending that I could
not see very well as I held out my plate while she helped me to
potatoes, I took her bare fore-arm in my hand, as though to
guide her. Seeing that she did not withdraw it, I began to
fondle it, then, without saying a word, pulled her towards me,
blew out the candles and told her to feel in my pocket for some
money. For the next few days physical pleasure seemed to me
to require, to be properly enjoyed, not only this serving-girl
but the timbered dining-room, so remote and isolated. And yet
it was to the other, in which Saint-Loup and his friends dined,
that I returned every evening, from force of habit and from
friendship, until I left Doncières. But even of this hotel, where
he boarded with his friends, I had long ceased to think. We
make little use of our experience, we leave unfulfilled on long
summer evenings or premature winter nights the hours in
which it had seemed to us that there might nevertheless be
contained some element of peace or pleasure. But those hours
are not altogether wasted. When new moments of pleasure
call to us in their turn, moments which would pass by in the
same way, equally bare and one-dimensional, the others recur,
bringing them the groundwork, the solid consistency of a rich
orchestration. They thus prolong themselves into one of those
classic examples of happiness which we recapture only now and
again but which continue to exist; in the present instance it
was the abandonment of everything else to dine in comfortable

surroundings, which by the help of memory embody in a scene from nature suggestions of the rewards of travel, with a friend who is going to stir our dormant life with all his energy, all his affection, to communicate to us a tender pleasure, very different from anything that we could derive from our own efforts or from social distractions; we are going to exist solely for him, to make vows of friendship which, born within the confines of the hour, remaining imprisoned in it, will perhaps not be kept on the morrow but which I need have no scruple in making to Saint-Loup since, with a courage that enshrined a great deal of common sense and the presentiment that friendship cannot be very deeply probed, on the morrow he would be gone.

If as I came downstairs I relived those evenings at Doncières, suddenly, when we reached the street, the almost total darkness, in which the fog seemed to have extinguished the lamps, which one could make out, glimmering very faintly, only when close at hand, took me back to a dimly remembered arrival by night at Combray, when the streets there were still lighted only at distant intervals and one groped one's way through a moist, warm, hallowed crib-like darkness in which there flickered here and there a dim light that shone no brighter than a candle. Between that year—to which in any case I could ascribe no precise date—of my Combray life and the evenings at Rivebelle which had, an hour earlier, been reflected above my drawn curtains, what a world of differences! I felt on perceiving them an enthusiasm which might have borne fruit had I remained alone and would thus have saved me the detour of many wasted years through which I was yet to pass before the invisible vocation of which this book is the history declared itself. Had the revelation come to me that evening, the carriage in which I sat would have deserved to rank as more memorable for me than Dr Percepied's, on the box seat of which I had composed that little sketch—which, as it happened, I had recently unearthed, altered and sent in vain to the *Figaro*—of the spires of Martinville. Is it because we relive our past years not in their continuous sequence, day by day, but in a memory focused upon the coolness or sunshine of some morning or afternoon suffused with the shade of some isolated and enclosed setting, immovable, arrested, lost, remote from all the rest, and thus the changes gradually wrought not only in the world outside but in our dreams and our evolving character (changes which have imperceptibly carried us through life from one time to another, wholly different) are eliminated, that, if we relive another memory taken from a different year, we find between the two, thanks to lacunae, to vast stretches of oblivion, as it were the gulf of a difference in altitude or the incompatibility of two divergent qualities of breathed atmosphere and surrounding coloration? But between the memories that had now come to me in turn of Combray, of Doncières and of Rivebelle, I was conscious at that moment of much more than a distance in time, of the distance that there would be between two separate universes whose matter and substance were not the same. If I had sought to reproduce in writing the element in which my most insignificant memories of Rivebelle appeared to me to be carved, I should have had to vein it with pink, to render at once translucent, compact, cool and resonant, a substance hitherto analogous to the sombre, rugged sandstone of Combray.

But Robert, having finished giving his instructions to the driver, now joined me in the carriage. The ideas that had appeared before me took flight. They are goddesses who deign at times to make themselves visible to a solitary mortal, at a turning in the road, even in his bedroom while he sleeps, when, standing framed in the doorway, they bring him their annunciation. But as soon as a companion joins him they vanish; in the society of his fellows no man has ever beheld them. And I found myself thrown back upon friendship.

Robert on arriving had indeed warned me that there was a good deal of fog outside, but while we were talking it had grown steadily thicker. It was no longer merely the light mist which I had looked forward to seeing rise from the island and envelop Mme de Stermaria and myself. A few feet away from us the street lamps were blotted out and then it was night, as dark as in open fields, in a forest, or rather on a mild Breton island whither I should have liked to go; I felt lost, as on the stark coast of some northern sea where one risks one's life twenty times over before coming to the solitary inn;

ceasing to be a mirage for which one seeks, the fog had become one of those dangers against which one has to fight, so
that in finding our way and reaching a safe haven, we experienced the difficulties, the anxiety and finally the joy which
safety, so little perceived by him who is not threatened with the
loss of it, gives to the perplexed and benighted traveller. One
thing only came near to destroying my pleasure during our
adventurous ride, owing to the angry astonishment into which
it flung me for a moment. "You know," Saint-Loup suddenly
said to me, "I told Bloch that you didn't like him all that much,
that you found him rather vulgar at times. I'm like that, you see,
I like clear-cut situations," he wound up with a self-satisfied air
and in an unanswerable tone of voice. I was astounded. Not
only had I the most absolute confidence in Saint-Loup, in the
loyalty of his friendship, and he had betrayed it by what he had
said to Bloch, but it seemed to me that he of all men ought to
have been restrained from doing so by his defects as well as
by his good qualities, by that astonishing veneer of breeding
which was capable of carrying politeness to what was positively
a want of frankness. Was his triumphant air the sort that we
assume to cloak a certain embarrassment in admitting a thing
which we know that we ought not to have done? Was it
simply the expression of frivolity, stupidity, making a virtue
out of a defect which I had not associated with him? Or a
passing fit of ill humour towards me, prompting him to make
an end of our friendship, or the registering of a passing fit of
ill humour against Bloch to whom he had wanted to say
something disagreeable even though it would compromise me?
Whatever it was, his face was seared, while he uttered these
vulgar words, by a frightful sinuosity which I saw on it once or
twice only in all the time I knew him, and which, beginning
by running more or less down the middle of his face, when it
came to his lips twisted them, gave them a hideous expression
of baseness, almost of bestiality, quite transitory and no doubt
inherited. There must have been at such moments, which
recurred probably not more than once every other year, a
partial eclipse of his true self by the passage across it of the
personality of some ancestor reflecting itself upon him. Fully
as much as his self-satisfied air, the words "I like clear-cut

situations" encouraged the same doubt and should have
incurred a similar condemnation. I felt inclined to say to him
that if one likes clear-cut situations one ought to confine these
outbursts of frankness to one's own affairs and not to acquire a
too easy merit at the expense of others. But by this time the
carriage had stopped outside the restaurant, the huge front of
which, glazed and streaming with light, alone succeeded in
piercing the darkness. The fog itself, lit up by the comfortable
brightness of the interior, seemed to be waiting outside on
the pavement to show one the way in with the joy of servants
whose faces reflect the hospitable instincts of their master; shot
with the most delicate shades of light, it pointed the way like
the pillar of fire which guided the Hebrews. Many of these, as
it happened, were to be found inside. For this was the place
to which Bloch and his friends, intoxicated by their fast on
coffee and political curiosity, a fast as famishing as the ritual
fast which occurs only once a year, had long been in the habit
of repairing in the evenings. Every mental excitement creating
a value that overrides everything else, a quality superior to the
habits bound up in it, there is no taste at all keenly developed
that does not thus gather round it a society which it unites and
in which the esteem of his fellows is what each of its members
seeks before anything else from life. Here, in their café, be it
in a little provincial town, you will find impassioned music-
lovers; the greater part of their time and all their spare cash
are spent in chamber-concerts, in meetings for musical discussion, in cafés where they find themselves among music-
lovers and rub shoulders with musicians. Others, keen on
flying, seek to stand well with the old waiter in the glazed
bar perched on top of the aerodrome; sheltered from the wind
as in the glass cage of a lighthouse, they can follow in the
company of an airman who is not going up that day the
gyrations of a pilot looping the loop, while another, invisible
a moment ago, comes suddenly swooping down to land with
the great winged roar of an Arabian roc. The little group
which met to try to perpetuate, to explore the fugitive emotions aroused by the Zola trial attached a similar importance to
this particular café. But they were not viewed with favour by the
young nobles who composed the other part of the clientele and

had taken over a second room, separated from the other only by a flimsy parapet topped with a row of plants. These looked upon Dreyfus and his supporters as traitors, although twenty-five years later, ideas having had time to settle down and Dreyfusism to acquire a certain glamour in the light of history, the sons, Bolshevistic and dance-mad, of these same young nobles would declare to the "intellectuals" who questioned them that undoubtedly, had they been alive at the time, they would have been for Dreyfus, without having any clearer idea of what the Affair had been about than Comtesse Edmond de Pourtalès or the Marquise de Galliffet, other luminaries already extinct at the date of their birth. For on the night of the fog the noblemen of the café, who were in due course to become the fathers of these retrospectively Dreyfusard young intellectuals, were still bachelors. Naturally the idea of a rich marriage was present in the minds of all their families, but none of them had yet brought such a marriage off. Still only potential, this rich marriage which was the simultaneous ambition of several of them (there were indeed several "good matches" in view, but after all the number of big dowries was considerably below that of the aspirants to them) merely tended to create among these young men a certain amount of rivalry.

As ill luck would have it, Saint-Loup remaining outside for a few minutes to explain to the driver that he was to call for us again after dinner, I had to go in alone. Now, to begin with, once I had ventured into the revolving door, a contrivance to which I was unaccustomed, I began to fear that I should never succeed in getting out again. (Let me note here for the benefit of lovers of verbal accuracy that the contrivance in question, despite its peaceful appearance, is known as a "revolver," from the English "revolving door.") That evening the proprietor, unwilling either to brave the elements outside or to desert his customers, nevertheless remained standing near the entrance so as to have the pleasure of listening to the joyful complaints of the new arrivals, all aglow with the satisfaction of people who had had trouble getting there and been afraid of getting lost. The smiling cordiality of his welcome was, however, dissipated by the sight of a stranger incapable of disengaging himself from the rotating sheets of glass. This

flagrant sign of ignorance made him frown like an examiner
who has a good mind not to utter the formula: *Dignus est
intrare.* As a crowning error I went and sat down in the room
set apart for the nobility, from which he came at once to extir-
pate me, with a rudeness to which all the waiters immediately
conformed, and showed me to a place in the other room. This
was all the less to my liking because the seat was in the middle
of a crowded bench and I had opposite me the door reserved
for the Hebrews which, since it did not revolve, opened and
closed every other minute and kept me in a horrible draught.
But the proprietor declined to move me, saying: "No, sir, I
cannot disturb everybody just for you." Presently, however,
he forgot this belated and troublesome guest, captivated as
he was by the arrival of each newcomer who, before calling
for his beer, his wing of cold chicken, or his hot grog (it was
by now long past dinner-time), must first, as in the old romances, sing for his supper by relating his adventure as soon
as he entered this asylum of warmth and security where the
contrast with the perils just escaped engendered the sort of
gaiety and sense of comradeship that create a cheerful harmony
round the camp fire.

One reported that his carriage, thinking it had got to the
Pont de la Concorde, had circled the Invalides three times,
another that his, in trying to make its way down the Avenue
des Champs-Elysées, had driven into a clump of trees at the
Rond-Point, from which it had taken three-quarters of an hour
to extricate itself. Then followed lamentations about the fog,
the cold, the deathly silence of the streets, uttered and received
with the same exceptionally jovial air that was attributable
to the pleasant atmosphere of the room which, except where I
sat, was warm, the dazzling light which set blinking eyes
already accustomed to not seeing, and the buzz of talk which
restored their activity to deafened ears.

The new arrivals had the greatest difficulty in keeping silence.
The singularity of the mishaps which each of them thought
unique set their tongues on fire, and their eyes roved in search
of someone to engage in conversation. The proprietor himself
lost all sense of social distinctions: "M. le Prince de Foix lost
his way three times coming from the Porte Saint-Martin," he

was not afraid to say with a laugh, actually pointing out, as though introducing one to the other, the illustrious nobleman to a Jewish barrister who on any evening but this would have been separated from him by a barrier far harder to surmount than the ledge of greenery. "Three times—fancy that!" said the barrister, touching his hat. This note of friendly interest was not at all to the Prince's liking. He belonged to an aristocratic group for whom the practice of rudeness, even at the expense of their fellow-nobles when these were not of the very highest rank, seemed to be the sole occupation. Not to acknowledge a greeting; if the polite stranger repeated the offence, to laugh with sneering contempt or fling back one's head with a look of fury; to pretend not to recognise some elderly man who had done them a service; to reserve their handshakes for dukes and the really intimate friends of dukes whom the latter introduced to them: such was the attitude of these young men, and especially of the Prince de Foix. Such an attitude was encouraged by the thoughtlessness of youth (a period in which, even in the middle class, one appears ungrateful and behaves boorishly because, having forgotten for months to write to a benefactor who has just lost his wife, one then ceases to greet him in the street so as to simplify matters), but it was inspired above all by an acute caste snobbery. It is true that, after the fashion of certain nervous disorders the symptoms of which grow less pronounced in later life, this snobbishness would generally cease to express itself in so offensive a form in these men who had been so intolerable when young. Once youth is outgrown, it is rare for a man to remain confined in insolence. He had supposed it to be the only thing in the world; suddenly he discovers, prince though he is, that there are also such things as music, literature, even standing for parliament. The scale of human values is correspondingly altered and he engages in conversation with people whom at one time he would have dismissed with a withering glance. Good luck to those of the latter who have had the patience to wait, and who are of such a good disposition—if "good" is the right word—that they accept with pleasure in their forties the civility and welcome that had been coldly withheld from them at twenty.

Since we are on the subject of the Prince de Foix, it may be mentioned here that he belonged to a set of a dozen or fifteen young men and to an inner group of four. The dozen or fifteen shared the characteristic (from which the Prince, I fancy, was exempt) that each of them presented a dual aspect to the world. Up to their eyes in debt, they were regarded as bounders by their tradesmen, notwithstanding the pleasure these took in addressing them as "Monsieur le Comte," "Monsieur le Marquis," "Monsieur le Duc." They hoped to retrieve their fortunes by means of the famous rich marriage ("moneybags" as the expression still was) and, as the fat dowries which they coveted numbered at the most four or five, several of them were secretly setting their sights on the same damsel. And the secret would be so well kept that when one of them, on arriving at the café, announced: "My dear fellows, I'm too fond of you all not to tell you of my engagement to Mlle d'Ambresac," there would be a general outburst, more than one of the others imagining that the marriage was as good as settled already between Mlle d'Ambresac and himself, and not having the self-control to stifle a spontaneous cry of stupefaction and rage. "So you like the idea of marriage, do you, Bibi?" the Prince de Châtellerault could not help exclaiming, dropping his fork in surprise and despair, for he had been fully expecting the engagement of this identical Mlle d'Ambresac to be announced, but with himself, Châtellerault, as her bridegroom. And heaven only knew all that his father had cunningly hinted to the Ambresacs about Bibi's mother. "So you think it'll be fun, being married, do you?" he could not help repeating for the second time to Bibi, who, better prepared because he had had plenty of time to decide on the right attitude to adopt since the engagement had reached the semi-official stage, would reply with a smile: "I'm pleased, not to be getting married, which I didn't particularly want to do, but to be marrying Daisy d'Ambresac whom I find charming." In the time taken up by this response M. de Châtellerault would have recovered his composure, but then he would think that he must at the earliest possible moment execute an about-face in the direction of Mlle de la Canourque or Miss Foster, numbers two and three on the list of heiresses, pacify somehow the creditors who were expecting the Ambresac marriage, and, finally, explain to the people to whom he too had declared that Mlle de Ambresac was charming that this marriage was all very well for Bibi, but that he himself would have had all his family down on him like a ton of bricks if he had married her. Mme Soléon (he would say) had actually gone so far as to announce that she would not have them in her house.

But if in the eyes of tradesmen, restaurant proprietors and the like they seemed of little account, conversely, being creatures of dual personality, the moment they appeared in society they ceased to be judged by the dilapidated state of their fortunes and the sordid occupations by which they sought to repair them. They became once more M. le Prince this, M. le Duc that, and were judged only by their quarterings. A duke who was practically a multi-millionaire and seemed to combine in his person every possible distinction would give precedence to them because, being the heads of their various houses, they were by descent sovereign princes of small territories in which they were entitled to mint money and so forth. Often, in this café, one of them would lower his eyes when another came in so as not to oblige the newcomer to greet him. This was because in his imaginative pursuit of riches he had invited a banker to dine. Every time a man about town enters into relations with a banker in such circumstances, the latter leaves him the poorer by a hundred thousand francs, which does not prevent the man about town from at once repeating the process with another. We continue to burn candles in churches and to consult doctors.

But the Prince de Foix, who was himself rich, belonged not only to this fashionable set of fifteen or so young men, but to a more exclusive and inseparable group of four, which included Saint-Loup. These were never asked anywhere separately, they were known as the four gigolos, they were always to be seen riding together, and in country houses their hostesses gave them communicating bedrooms, with the result that, especially as they were all four extremely good-looking, rumours were current as to the extent of their intimacy. I was in a position to give these the lie direct so far as Saint-Loup was concerned. But the curious thing is that if, later on, it was discovered that these rumours were true of all four, each of the quartet had been entirely in the dark as to the other three. And yet each of them had done his utmost to find out about the others, to gratify a desire or (more probably) a grudge, to prevent a marriage or to secure a hold over the friend whose secret he uncovered. A fifth (for in groups of four there are always more than four) had joined this platonic party who was more so than any of the others. But religious scruples restrained him until long after the group had broken up and he himself was a married man, the father of a family, fervently praying at Lourdes that the next baby might be a boy or a girl, and in the meantime flinging himself upon soldiers.

Despite the Prince's arrogant ways, the fact that the barrister's comment, though uttered in his hearing, had not been directly addressed to him made him less angry than he would otherwise have been. Besides, this evening was somehow exceptional. And in any case the barrister had no more chance of getting to know the Prince de Foix than the cabman who had driven that noble lord to the restaurant. The Prince accordingly felt that he might allow himself to reply—in an arrogant tone, however, and as though to the company at large—to this stranger who, thanks to the fog, was in the position of a travelling companion whom one meets at some seaside place at the ends of the earth, scoured by all the winds of heaven or shrouded in mist: "Losing your way isn't so bad; the trouble is finding it again." The wisdom of this aphorism impressed the proprietor, for he had already heard it several times in the course of the evening.

He was, indeed, in the habit of always comparing what he heard or read with an already familiar canon, and felt his admiration quicken if he could detect no difference. This state of mind is by no means to be ignored, for, applied to political conversations, to the reading of newspapers, it forms public opinion and thereby makes possible the greatest events in history. A large number of German landlords, simply by being impressed by a customer or a newspaper when they said that France, England and Russia were "out to crush" Germany, made war possible at the time of Agadir, even if no war occurred. Historians, if they have not been wrong to abandon

the practice of attributing the actions of peoples to the will of
kings, ought to substitute for the latter the psychology of the
individual, the inferior individual at that.

In politics the proprietor of this particular café had for some
time now applied his recitation-teacher's mentality to a certain
number of set-pieces on the Dreyfus case. If he did not find the
terms that were familiar to him in the remarks of a customer
or the columns of a newspaper he would pronounce the article
boring or the speaker insincere. The Prince de Foix, however,
impressed him so forcibly that he barely gave him time to
finish his sentence. "Well said, Prince, well said" (which
meant, more or less, "faultlessly recited"), "that's it, that's
exactly it," he exclaimed, "swelling up," as they say in the
Arabian Nights, "to the extreme limit of satisfaction." But the
Prince had already vanished into the smaller room. Then, as
life resumes its normal course after even the most sensational
happenings, those who had emerged from the sea of fog began
to order whatever they wanted to eat or drink; among them a
party of young men from the Jockey Club who, in view of the
abnormality of the occasion, had no hesitation in taking their
places at a couple of tables in the big room, and were thus
quite close to me. So the cataclysm had established even
between the smaller room and the bigger, among all these
people stimulated by the comfort of the restaurant after their
long wanderings across the ocean of fog, a familiarity from
which I alone was excluded and which was not unlike the
spirit that must have prevailed in Noah's ark.

Suddenly I saw the landlord bent double, bowing and
scraping, and the waiters hurrying to support him in full
force, a scene which drew every eye towards the door. "Quick,
send Cyprien here, a table for M. le Marquis de Saint-Loup,"
cried the proprietor, for whom Robert was not merely a great
nobleman who enjoyed genuine prestige even in the eyes of
the Prince de Foix, but a customer who burned the candle at
both ends and spent a great deal of money in this restaurant.
The customers in the big room looked on with curiosity,
those in the small room vied with one another in hailing
their friend as he finished wiping his shoes. But just as he was
about to make his way into the small room he caught sight of

me in the big one. "Good God," he exclaimed, "what on earth are you doing there? And with the door wide open too?" he added with a furious glance at the proprietor, who ran to shut it, throwing the blame on his staff: "I'm always telling them to keep it shut."

I had been obliged to shift my own table and to disturb others which stood in the way in order to reach him. "Why did you move? Would you sooner dine here than in the little room? Why, my poor fellow, you're freezing. You will oblige me by keeping that door permanently locked," he said to the proprietor. "This very instant, Monsieur le Marquis. The customers who arrive from now on will have to go through the little room, that's all." And the better to prove his zeal, he detailed for this operation a head waiter and several satellites, vociferating the most terrible threats if it were not properly carried out. He proceeded to show me exaggerated marks of respect, to make me forget that these had begun not upon my arrival but only after that of Saint-Loup, while, lest I should think them to have been prompted by the friendliness shown me by this rich and noble client, he gave me now and again a surreptitious little smile which seemed to indicate a regard that was wholly personal.

Something said by one of the diners behind me made me turn my head for a moment. I had caught, instead of the words: "Wing of chicken, excellent; and a glass of champagne, only not too dry," these: "I should prefer glycerine. Yes, hot, excellent." I had wanted to see who the ascetic was who was inflicting upon himself such a diet, but I quickly turned back to Saint-Loup in order not to be recognised by the man of strange appetite. It was simply a doctor whom I happened to know and of whom another customer, taking advantage of the fog to buttonhole him here in the café, was asking his professional advice. Like stockbrokers, doctors employ the first person singular.

Meanwhile I looked at Robert, and my thoughts ran as follows. There were in this café, and I had myself known at other times in my life, plenty of foreigners, intellectuals, budding geniuses of all sorts, resigned to the laughter excited by their pretentious capes, their 1830 ties and still more by the clumsiness of their movements, going so far as to provoke that laughter in order to show that they paid no heed to it, who yet were men of real intellectual and moral worth, of profound sensibility. They repelled—the Jews among them principally, the unassimilated Jews, that is to say, for with the other kind we are not concerned—those who could not endure any oddity or eccentricity of appearance (as Bloch repelled Albertine). Generally speaking, one realised afterwards that, if it could be held against them that their hair was too long, their noses and eyes were too big, their gestures abrupt and theatrical, it was puerile to judge them by this, that they had plenty of wit and good-heartedness, and were men to whom, in the long run, one could become closely attached. Among the Jews especially there were few whose parents and kinsfolk had not a warmth of heart, a breadth of mind, a sincerity, in comparison with which Saint-Loup's mother and the Duc de Guermantes cut the poorest of moral figures by their aridity, their skin-deep religiosity which denounced only the most open scandal, their apology for a Christianity which led invariably (by the unexpected channels of the uniquely prized intellect) to a colossally mercenary marriage. But in Saint-Loup, when all was said, however the faults of his parents had combined to create a new blend of qualities, there reigned the most charming openness of mind and heart. And whenever (it must be allowed to the undying glory of France) these qualities are found in a man who is purely French, whether he belongs to the aristocracy or the people, they flower —flourish would be too strong a word, for moderation persists in this field, as well as restriction—with a grace which the foreigner, however estimable he may be, does not present to us. Of these intellectual and moral qualities others undoubtedly have their share, and, if we have first to overcome what repels us and what makes us smile, they remain no less precious. But it is all the same a pleasant thing, and one which is perhaps exclusively French, that what is fine in all equity of judgment, what is admirable to the mind and the heart, should be first of all attractive to the eyes, pleasingly coloured, consummately chiselled, should express as well in substance as in form an inner perfection. I looked at Saint-Loup, and I said to myself that it is a thing to be glad of when there is no lack of physical grace to serve as vestibule to the graces within, and when the curves of the nostrils are as delicate and as perfectly designed as the wings of the little butterflies that hover over the field-flowers round Combray; and that the true *opus francigenum*, the secret of which was not lost in the thirteenth century, and would not perish with our churches, consists not so much in the stone angels of Saint-André-des-Champs as in the young sons of France, noble, bourgeois or peasant, whose faces are carved with that delicacy and boldness which have remained as traditional as on the famous porch, but are creative still.

After leaving us for a moment in order to supervise personally the barring of the door and the ordering of our dinner (he laid great stress on our choosing "butcher's meat," the fowls being presumably nothing to boast of) the proprietor came back to inform us that M. le Prince de Foix would esteem it a favour if M. le Marquis would allow him to dine at a table next to his. "But they are all taken," objected Robert, casting an eye over the tables which blocked the way to mine. "That doesn't matter in the least. If M. le Marquis is agreeable, I can easily ask these people to move to another table. It is always a pleasure to do anything for M. le Marquis!" "But you must decide," said Saint-Loup to me. "Foix is a good fellow. I don't know whether he'd bore you, but he's not such a fool as most of them." I told Robert that of course I should like to meet his friend but that now that I was dining with him for once in a way and was so happy to be doing so, I should be just as pleased to have him to myself. "He's got a very fine cloak, the Prince has," the proprietor broke in upon our deliberation. "Yes, I know," said Saint-Loup. I wanted to tell Robert that M. de Charlus had concealed from his sister-in-law the fact that he knew me, and ask him what could be the reason for this, but I was prevented from doing so by the arrival of M. de Foix. He had come to see whether his request had been favourably received, and we caught sight of him standing a few feet away. Robert introduced us, but made no secret of the fact that as we had things to talk about he would prefer us to be left alone. The Prince withdrew, adding to the farewell bow which he made me a smile which, pointed at

Saint-Loup, seemed to transfer to him the responsibility for the shortness of a meeting which the Prince himself would have liked to see prolonged. But at that moment Robert, apparently struck by a sudden thought, went off with his friend after saying to me: "Do sit down and start your dinner, I shall be back in a moment," and vanished into the smaller room. I was pained to hear the smart young men whom I did not know telling the most absurd and malicious stories about the adoptive Grand Duke of Luxembourg (formerly Comte de Nassau) whom I had met at Balbec and who had given me such delicate proofs of sympathy during my grand-mother's illness. According to one of these young men, he had said to the Duchesse de Guermantes: "I expect everyone to get up when my wife comes in," to which the Duchess had retorted (with as little truth, had she said any such thing, as wit, the grandmother of the young Princess having always been the very pink of propriety): "Get up when your wife comes in, do they? Well, that's a change from her grand-mother—she expected the gentlemen to lie down." Then someone alleged that, having gone down to see his aunt the Princesse de Luxembourg at Balbec, and put up at the Grand Hotel, he had complained to the manager (my friend) that the royal standard of Luxembourg was not flown in front of the hotel, and that this flag being less familiar and less generally in use than the British or Italian, it had taken him several days to procure one, greatly to the young Grand Duke's annoyance. I did not believe a word of this story, but made up my mind, as soon as I went to Balbec, to question the manager in order to satisfy myself that it was pure invention. While waiting for Saint-Loup to return I asked the restaurant proprietor for some bread. "Certainly, Monsieur le Baron!" "I am not a baron," I told him in a tone of mock sadness. "Oh, beg pardon, Monsieur le Comte!" I had no time to lodge a second protest which would certainly have promoted me to the rank of marquis: faithful to his promise of an immediate return, Saint-Loup reappeared in the doorway carrying over his arm the thick vicuna cloak of the Prince de Foix, from whom I guessed that he had borrowed it in order to keep me warm. He signed to me not to get up, and came towards me, but either my table would have to be moved again, or I must change my seat if he was to get to his. On entering the big room he sprang lightly on to one of the red plush benches which ran round its walls and on which, apart from myself, there were sitting three or four of the young men from the Jockey Club, friends of his, who had not managed to find places in the other room. Between the tables and the wall electric wires were stretched at a certain height; without the slightest hesitation Saint-Loup jumped nimbly over them like a steeplechaser taking a fence; embarrassed that it should be done wholly for my benefit and to save me the trouble of a very minor disturbance, I was at the same time amazed at the precision with which my friend performed this feat of acrobatics; and in this I was not alone; for although they would probably have been only moderately appreciative of a similar display on the part of a more humbly born and less generous client, the proprietor and his staff stood fascinated, like race-goers in the enclosure; one underling, apparently rooted to the ground, stood gaping with a dish in his hand for which a party close beside him were waiting; and when Saint-Loup, having to get past his friends, climbed on to the back of the bench behind them and ran along it, balancing himself like a tight-rope walker, discreet applause broke from the body of the room. On coming to where I was sitting, he checked his momentum with the precision of a tributary chieftain before the throne of a sovereign, and, stooping down, handed to me with an air of courtesy and submission the vicuna cloak which a moment later, having taken his place beside me, without my having to make a single movement, he arranged as a light but warm shawl about my shoulders.

"By the way, while I think of it, my uncle Charlus has something to say to you. I promised I'd send you round to him to-morrow evening."

"I was just going to speak to you about him. But to-morrow evening I'm dining out with your aunt Guermantes."

"Yes, there's a regular beanfeast to-morrow at Oriane's. I'm not asked. But my uncle Palamède doesn't want you to go there. You can't get out of it, I suppose? Well, anyhow, go on to my uncle's afterwards. I think he's very anxious to see

you. Surely you could manage to get there by eleven. Eleven
o'clock, don't forget. I'll let him know. He's very touchy. If
you don't turn up he'll never forgive you. And Oriane's
parties are always over quite early. If you're only going
to dine there you can quite easily be at my uncle's by eleven.
Actually I ought to go and see Oriane, about getting a transfer from Morocco. She's so nice about all that sort of thing,
and she can get anything she likes out of General de
Saint-Joseph, who's the man in charge. But don't say anything
about it to her. I've mentioned it to the Princesse de Parme,
everything will be all right. Interesting place, Morocco. I could
tell you all sorts of things. Very fine lot of men out there. One
feels they're on one's own level, mentally."

"You don't think the Germans are going to go to war
over it?"

"No, they're annoyed with us, as after all they have every
right to be. But the Kaiser is out for peace. They're always
making us think they want war, to force us to give in. Pure
bluff, you know, like poker. The Prince of Monaco, one of
Wilhelm II's agents, comes and tells us in confidence that
Germany will attack us if we don't give in. So then we give in.
But if we didn't give in, there wouldn't be war in any shape or
form. You have only to think what a cosmic thing a war would
be to-day. It'd be a bigger catastrophe than the Flood and the
Götterdämmerung rolled into one. Only it wouldn't last so long."

He spoke to me of friendship, affection, regret, although
like all travellers of his sort he was going off the next morning
for some months which he was to spend in the country and
would only be staying a couple of nights in Paris on his way
back to Morocco (or elsewhere); but the words which he thus
let fall into the warm furnace of my heart this evening kindled
a pleasant glow there. Our infrequent meetings, and this one
in particular, have since assumed epoch-making proportions
in my memory. For him, as for me, this was the evening of
friendship. And yet the friendship that I felt for him at this
moment was scarcely, I feared (and felt therefore some remorse
at the thought), what he would have liked to inspire. Suffused
still with the pleasure that I had had in seeing him canter
towards me and come gracefully to a halt on arriving at his

goal, I felt that this pleasure lay in my recognising that each
of the movements which he had executed on the bench,
along the wall, had its meaning, its cause, in Saint-Loup's
own personal nature perhaps, but even more in that which
by birth and upbringing he had inherited from his race.

A certainty of taste in the domain not of aesthetics but of
behaviour, which when he was faced by a novel combination
of circumstances enabled the man of breeding to grasp at
once—like a musician who has been asked to play a piece he
has never seen—the attitude and the action that were called for
and to apply the appropriate mechanism and technique, which
then allowed this taste to be exercised without the constraint
of any other consideration by which so many young men
of the middle class would have been paralysed from fear both
of making themselves ridiculous in the eyes of strangers by
a breach of propriety and of appearing over-zealous in those
of their friends, and which in Robert's case was replaced by a
lofty disdain which certainly he had never felt in his heart but
which he had received by inheritance in his body, and which
had fashioned the attitudes of his ancestors into a familiarity
which, they imagined, could only flatter and enchant those
to whom it was addressed; together with a noble liberality
which, far from taking undue heed of his boundless material
advantages (lavish expenditure in this restaurant had succeeded
in making him, here as elsewhere, the most fashionable customer and the general favourite, a position which was under-
lined by the deference shown him not only by the waiters but
by all its most exclusive young patrons), led him to trample
them underfoot, just as he had actually and symbolically
trodden upon those crimson benches, suggestive of some
ceremonial way which pleased my friend only because it
enabled him more gracefully and swiftly to arrive at my side:
such were the quintessentially aristocratic qualities that shone
through the husk of this body—not opaque and dim as mine
would have been, but limpid and revealing—as, through a
work of art, the industrious, energetic force which has created
it, and rendered the movements of that light-footed course
which Robert had pursued along the wall as intelligible and
charming as those of horsemen on a marble frieze. "Alas!"

Robert might have thought, "was it worth while to have grown up despising birth, honouring only justice and intellect, choosing, outside the ranks of the friends provided for me, companions who were awkward and ill-dressed but had the gift of eloquence, only to find that the sole personality apparent in me which remains a treasured memory is not the one that my will, with the most praiseworthy effort, has fashioned in my likeness, but one that is not of my making, that is not myself, that I have always despised and striven to overcome; was it worth while to love my chosen friend as I have done, only to find that the greatest pleasure he derives from my company is that of discovering in it something far more general than myself, a pleasure which is not in the least (as he says, though he cannot seriously believe it) the pleasure of friendship, but an intellectual and detached, a sort of artistic pleasure?" This is what I now fear that Saint-Loup may at times have thought. If so, he was mistaken. If he had not (as he steadfastly had) cherished something more lofty than the innate suppleness of his body, if he had not been detached for so long from aristocratic arrogance, there would have been something more studied, more heavy-handed in this very agility, a self-important vulgarity in his manners. Just as a strong vein of seriousness had been necessary for Mme de Villeparisis to convey in her conversation and in her *Memoirs* a sense of the frivolous, which is intellectual, so, in order that Saint-Loup's body should be imbued with so much nobility, the latter had first to desert his mind, which was straining towards higher things, and, reabsorbed into his body, to establish itself there in unconsciously aristocratic lines. In this way his distinction of mind was not inconsistent with a physical distinction which otherwise would not have been complete. An artist has no need to express his thought directly in his work for the latter to reflect its quality; it has even been said that the highest praise of God consists in the denial of him by the atheist who finds creation so perfect that it can dispense with a creator. And I was well aware, too, that it was not merely a work of art that I was admiring in this young man unfolding along the wall the frieze of his flying course; the young prince (a descendant of Catherine de Foix, Queen of

Navarre and grand-daughter of Charles VII) whom he had just left for my sake, the endowments of birth and fortune which he was laying at my feet, the proud and shapely ancestors who survived in the assurance, the agility and the courtesy with which he had arranged about my shivering body the warm woollen cloak—were not all these like friends of longer standing in his life, by whom I might have expected that we should be permanently kept apart, and whom, on the contrary, he was sacrificing to me by a choice that can be made only in the loftiest places of the mind, with that sovereign liberty of which Robert's movements were the image and the symbol and in which perfect friendship is enshrined?

The vulgar arrogance that was to be detected in the familiarity of a Guermantes—as opposed to the distinction that it had in Robert, because hereditary disdain was in him only the outer garment, transmuted into an unconscious grace, of a genuine moral humility—had been brought home to me, not by M. de Charlus, in whom certain characteristic faults for which I had so far been unable to account were superimposed on his aristocratic habits, but by the Duc de Guermantes. And yet he too, in the general impression of commonness which had so repelled my grandmother when she had met him years earlier at Mme de Villeparisis's, showed glimpses of ancient grandeur of which I became conscious when I went to dine at his house the following evening.

They had not been apparent to me either in himself or in the Duchess when I had first met them in their aunt's drawing-room, any more than I had discerned, on first seeing her, the differences that set Berma apart from her colleagues, although in her case the distinctive qualities were infinitely more striking than in any social celebrity, since they become more marked in proportion as the objects are more real, more conceivable by the intellect. And yet, however slight the shades of social distinction may be (and so slight are they that when an accurate portrayer like Sainte-Beuve tries to indicate the shades of difference between the salons of Mme Geoffrin, Mme Récamier and Mme de Boigne, they appear so alike that the cardinal truth which, unknown to the author, emerges from his investigations is the vacuity of that form of life), nevertheless, for the same reason as with Berma, when I had ceased to be dazzled by the Guermantes and their droplet of originality was no longer vaporised by my imagination, I was able to distil and analyse it, imponderable as it was.

The Duchess having made no reference to her husband at her aunt's party, I wondered whether, in view of the rumours of divorce, he would be present at the dinner. But I was soon enlightened on that score, for through the crowd of footmen who stood about in the hall and who (since they must until then have regarded me much as they regarded the children of the evicted cabinet-maker, that is to say with more fellow-feeling perhaps than their master but as a person incapable of being admitted to his house) must have been asking themselves to what this social revolution could be due, I caught sight of M. de Guermantes, who had been watching for my arrival so as to receive me on his threshold and take off my overcoat with his own hands.

"Mme de Guermantes will be as pleased as Punch," he said to me in a glibly persuasive tone. "Let me help you off with your duds." (He felt it to be at once companionable and comic to use popular colloquialisms.) "My wife was just the least bit afraid you might defect, although you had fixed a date. We've been saying to each other all day: 'Depend upon it, he'll never turn up.' I'm bound to say that Mme de Guermantes was a better prophet than I was. You are not an easy man to get hold of, and I was quite sure you were going to let us down." And the Duke was such a bad husband, so brutal even (people said), that one felt grateful to him, as one feels grateful to wicked people for their occasional kindness of heart, for those words "Mme de Guermantes" with which he appeared to be spreading a protective wing over the Duchess, so that she might be one with him. Meanwhile, taking me familiarly by the hand, he set about introducing me into his household. Just as some common expression may delight us coming from the lips of a peasant if it points to the survival of a local tradition or shows the trace of some historic event, unknown, it may be, to the person who thus alludes to it, so this politeness on the part of M. de Guermantes, which he was to continue to show me throughout the evening,

charmed me as a survival of habits many centuries old, habits
of the seventeenth century in particular. The people of bygone
ages seem infinitely remote from us. We do not feel justified in
ascribing to them any underlying intentions beyond those they
formally express; we are amazed when we come upon a sentiment more or less akin to what we feel to-day in a Homeric
hero, or a skilful tactical feint by Hannibal during the battle
of Cannae, where he let his flank be driven back in order to take
the enemy by surprise and encircle him; it is as though we
imagined the epic poet and the Carthaginian general to be as
remote from ourselves as an animal seen in a zoo. Even with
certain personages of the court of Louis XIV, when we find
signs of courtesy in letters written by them to some man of
inferior rank who could be of no service to them whatever,
these letters leave us astonished because they reveal to us
suddenly in these great noblemen a whole world of beliefs
which they never directly express but which govern their
conduct, and in particular the belief that they are bound in
politeness to feign certain sentiments and to exercise with the
most scrupulous care certain obligations of civility.

This imagined remoteness of the past is perhaps one of the
things that may enable us to understand how even great
writers have found an inspired beauty in the works of mediocre
mystifiers such as Ossian. We are so astonished that bards
long dead should have modern ideas that we marvel if in what
we believe to be an ancient Gaelic ode we come across one
which we should have thought at most ingenious in a contemporary. A translator of talent has only to add to an ancient
writer whom he is reconstructing more or less faithfully a
few passages which, signed with a contemporary name and
published separately, would seem agreeable merely; at once he
imparts a moving grandeur to his poet, who is thus made to
play upon the keyboards of several ages at once. The translator was capable only of a mediocre book, if that book had
been published as his original work. Offered as a translation, it
seems a masterpiece. The past is not fugitive, it stays put. It is
not only months after the outbreak of a war that laws passed
without haste can effectively influence its course, it is not only
fifteen years after a crime which has remained obscure that a

magistrate can still find the vital evidence which will throw
light on it; after hundreds and thousands of years the scholar
who has been studying the place-names and the customs of the
inhabitants of some remote region may still extract from them
some legend long anterior to Christianity, already unintelligible, if not actually forgotten, at the time of Herodotus,
which in the name given to a rock, in a religious rite, still
dwells in the midst of the present, like a denser emanation,
immemorial and stable. There was an emanation too, though
far less ancient, of the life of the court, if not in the manners
of M. de Guermantes, which were often vulgar, at least in
the mind that controlled them. I was to experience it again, like
an ancient odour, when I rejoined him a little later in the drawing-room. For I did not go there at once.

As we left the outer hall, I had mentioned to M. de Guermantes that I was extremely anxious to see his Elstirs. "I am
at your service. Is M. Elstir a friend of yours, then? I'm morti-
fied not to have known that you were so interested in him. I
know him slightly, he's an amiable man, what our fathers used
to call an 'honest fellow.' I might have asked him to honour us
with his company at dinner to-night. I'm sure he would have
been highly flattered at being invited to spend the evening in
your company." Very untrue to the old world when he tried
thus to assume its manner, the Duke then relapsed into it
unconsciously. After inquiring whether I wished him to show
me the pictures, he conducted me to them, gracefully standing
aside for me at each door, apologising when, to show me the
way, he was obliged to precede me, a little scene which (since
the time when Saint-Simon relates that an ancestor of the
Guermantes did him the honours of his house with the same
punctilious exactitude in the performance of the frivolous duties
of a gentleman) before reaching our day must have been
enacted by many another Guermantes for many another
visitor. And as I had said to the Duke that I would like very
much to be left alone for a few minutes with the pictures, he
discreetly withdrew, telling me that I should find him in the
drawing-room when I had finished.

However, once I was face to face with the Elstirs, I completely forgot about dinner and the time; here again as at

Balbec I had before me fragments of that world of new and strange colours which was no more than the projection of that great painter's peculiar vision, which his speech in no way expressed. The parts of the walls that were covered by paintings of his, all homogeneous with one another, were like the luminous images of a magic lantern which in this instance was the brain of the artist, and the strangeness of which one could never have suspected so long as one had known only the man, in other words so long as one had only seen the lantern boxing its lamp before any coloured slide had been slid into its groove. Among these pictures, some of those that seemed most absurd to people in fashionable society interested me more than the rest because they recreated those optical illusions which prove to us that we should never succeed in identifying objects if we did not bring some process of reasoning to bear on them. How often, when driving, do we not come upon a bright street beginning a few feet away from us, when what we have actually before our eyes is merely a patch of wall glaringly lit which has given us the mirage of depth. This being the case, it is surely logical, not from any artifice of symbolism but from a sincere desire to return to the very root of the impression, to represent one thing by that other for which, in the flash of a first illusion, we mistook it. Surfaces and volumes are in reality independent of the names of objects which our memory imposes on them after we have recognised them. Elstir sought to wrest from what he had just felt what he already knew; he had often been at pains to break up that medley of impressions which we call vision.

The people who detested these "horrors" were astonished to find that Elstir admired Chardin, Perroneau, any number of painters whom they, the ordinary men and women of society, liked. They did not realise that Elstir for his own part, in striving to reproduce reality (with the particular trademark of his taste for certain experiments), had made the same effort as a Chardin or a Perroneau and that consequently, when he ceased to work for himself, he admired in them attempts of the same kind, anticipatory fragments, so to speak, of works of his own. Nor did these society people add to Elstir's work in their mind's eye that temporal perspective which enabled them to like, or at least to look without discomfort at, Chardin's painting. And yet the older among them might have reminded themselves that in the course of their lives they had gradually seen, as the years bore them away from it, the unbridgeable gulf between what they considered a masterpiece by Ingres and what they had supposed must for ever remain a "horror" (Manet's *Olympia*, for example) shrink until the two canvases seemed like twins. But we never learn, because we lack the wisdom to work backwards from the particular to the general, and imagine ourselves always to be faced with an experience which has no precedents in the past.

I was moved by the discovery in two of the pictures (more realistic, these, and in an earlier manner) of the same person, in one of them in evening dress in his own drawing-room, in the other wearing a frock coat and tall hat at some popular seaside festival where he had evidently no business to be, which proved that for Elstir he was not only a regular sitter but a friend, perhaps a patron, whom he liked to introduce into his paintings, as Carpaccio introduced—and in the most speaking likenesses—prominent Venetian noblemen into his; in the same way as Beethoven, too, found pleasure in inscribing at the top of a favourite work the beloved name of the Archduke Rudolph. There was something enchanting about this waterside carnival. The river, the women's dresses, the sails of the boats, the innumerable reflexions of one thing and another jostled together enchantingly in this little square panel of beauty which Elstir had cut out of a marvellous afternoon. What delighted one in the dress of a woman who had stopped dancing for a moment because she was hot and out of breath shimmered too, and in the same way, in the cloth of a motionless sail, in the water of the little harbour, in the wooden landing-stage, in the leaves of the trees and in the sky. Just as, in one of the pictures that I had seen at Balbec, the hospital, as beautiful beneath its lapis lazuli sky as the cathedral itself, seemed (more daring than Elstir the theorician, than Eltsir the man of taste, the lover of things mediaeval) to be intoning: "There is no such thing as Gothic, there is no such thing as a masterpiece, a hospital with no style is just as good as the glorious porch," so I now heard: "The slightly vulgar lady whom a man of discernment wouldn't bother to look at as he passed her by, whom he would exclude from the poetical composition which nature has set before him—she is beautiful too; her dress is receiving the same light as the sail of that boat, everything is equally precious; the commonplace dress and the sail that is beautiful in itself are two mirrors reflecting the same image; their virtue is all in the painter's eye." This eye had succeeded in arresting for all time the motion of the hours at this luminous instant when the lady had felt hot and had stopped dancing, when the tree was encircled with a perimeter of shadow, when the sails seemed to be gliding over a golden glaze. But precisely because that instant impressed itself on one with such force, this unchanging canvas gave the most fleeting impression: one felt that the lady would presently go home, the boats drift away, the shadow change place, night begin to fall; that pleasure comes to an end, that life passes and that instants, illuminated by the convergence at one and the same time of so many lights, cannot be recaptured. I recognised yet another aspect, quite different it is true, of what the Moment means, in a series of water-colours of mythological subjects, dating from Elstir's first period, which also adorned this room. Society people who held "advanced" views on art went "as far as" this earliest manner, but no further. It was certainly not the best work he had done, but already the sincerity with which the subject had been thought out took away its coldness. Thus the Muses, for instance, were represented as though they were creatures belonging to a species now fossilised, but creatures it would not have been surprising in mythological times to see pass by in the evening, in twos or threes, along some mountain path. Here and there a poet, of a race that would also have been of peculiar interest to a zoologist (characterised by a certain sexlessness), strolled with a Muse, as one sees in nature creatures of different but of kindred species consort together. In one of these water-colours one saw a poet exhausted by a long journey in the mountains, whom a Centaur, meeting him and moved to pity by his weakness, has taken on his back and is carrying home. In others, the vast landscape (in which the mythical scene, the

fabulous heroes occupied a minute place and seemed almost
lost) was rendered, from the mountain tops to the sea, with an
exactitude which told one more than the hour, told one to the
very minute what time of day it was, thanks to the precise
angle of the setting sun and the fleeting fidelity of the shadows.
In this way the artist had managed, by making it instantaneous,
to give a sort of lived historical reality to the fable, painted it
and related it in the past tense.*

While I was examining Elstir's paintings, the bell, rung
by arriving guests, had been pealing uninterruptedly and had
lulled me into a pleasing unawareness. But the silence which
followed its clangour and had already lasted for some time
finally succeeded—less rapidly, it is true—in awakening me from
my reverie as the silence that follows Lindor's music arouses
Bartolo from his sleep. I was afraid that I might have been
forgotten, that they might already have sat down to dinner, and
I hurried to the drawing-room. At the door of the Elstir
gallery I found a servant waiting for me, white-haired, though
whether with age or powder I could not say, and reminiscent
of a Spanish minister, though he treated me with the same
respect that he would have shown to a king. I felt from his
manner that he would have waited for me for another hour,
and I thought with alarm of the delay I had caused in the service of dinner, especially as I had promised to be at M. de
Charlus's by eleven.

It was the Spanish minister (though I also met on the way
the footman persecuted by the porter, who, radiant with
delight when I inquired after his fiancée, told me that to-
morrow was a "day off" for both of them, so that he would be
able to spend the whole day with her, and extolled the kindness
of Madame la Duchesse) who conducted me to the drawing-
room, where I was afraid of finding M. de Guermantes in a
bad humour. He welcomed me, on the contrary, with a joy
that was obviously to some extent factitious and dictated by
politeness, but was in other respects sincere, prompted both
by his stomach which so long a delay had begun to famish,
and his consciousness of a similar impatience in all his other
guests, who completely filled the room. Indeed I learned afterwards that I had kept them waiting for nearly three-quarters

of an hour. The Duc de Guermantes probably thought that to prolong the general torment for two minutes more would make it no worse and that, politeness having driven him to postpone for so long the moment of moving into the dining-room, this politeness would be more complete if, by not having dinner announced immediately, he could succeed in persuading me that I was not late and they had not been waiting for me. And so he asked me, as if we still had an hour before dinner and some of the party had not yet arrived, what I thought of his Elstirs. But at the same time, and without letting the cravings of his stomach become too apparent, in order not to lose another moment he proceeded in concert with the Duchess to the ceremony of introduction. It was only then that I perceived that, having until this evening—save for my novitiate in Mme Swann's salon—been accustomed in my mother's drawing-room, in Combray and in Paris, to the patronising or defensive attitudes of prim bourgeois ladies who treated me as a child, I was now witnessing a change of surroundings comparable to that which introduces Parsifal suddenly into the midst of the flower-maidens. Those who surrounded me now, their necks and shoulders entirely bare (the naked flesh appearing on either side of a sinuous spray of mimosa or the petals of a full-blown rose), accompanied their salutations with long, caressing glances, as though shyness alone restrained them from kissing me. Many of them were nevertheless highly respectable from the moral standpoint; many, not all, for the more virtuous did not feel the same revulsion as my mother would have done for those of easier virtue. The vagaries of conduct, denied by saintlier friends in the face of the evidence, seemed in the Guermantes world to matter far less than the social relations one had been able to maintain. One pretended not to know that the body of a hostess was at the disposal of all comers, provided that her visiting list showed no gaps.

As the Duke showed very little concern for his other guests (from whom he had for long had as little to learn as they from him), but a great deal for me, whose particular kind of superiority, being outside his experience, inspired in him something akin to the respect which the great noblemen of the court of

Louis XIV used to feel for his bourgeois ministers, he evidently considered that the fact of my not knowing his guests mattered not at all—to me at least, though it might to them—and while I was anxious, on his account, as to the impression that I might make on them, he was thinking only of the impression they would make on me.

At the very outset, indeed, there was a little twofold imbroglio. No sooner had I entered the drawing-room than M. de Guermantes, without even allowing me time to shake hands with the Duchess, led me, as though to give a pleasant surprise to the person in question to whom he seemed to be saying: "Here's your friend! You see, I'm bringing him to you by the scruff of the neck," towards a lady of smallish stature. Well before I arrived in her vicinity, the lady had begun to flash at me continuously from her large, soft, dark eyes the sort of knowing smiles which we address to an old friend who perhaps has not recognised us. As this was precisely the case with me and I could not for the life of me remember who she was, I averted my eyes as the Duke propelled me towards her, in order not to have to respond until our introduction should have released me from my predicament. Meanwhile the lady continued to maintain in precarious balance the smile she was aiming at me. She looked as though she was in a hurry to be relieved of it and to hear me say: "Ah, Madame, of course! How delighted Mamma will be to hear that we've met again!" I was as impatient to learn her name as she was to see that I did finally greet her with every indication of recognition, so that her smile, indefinitely prolonged like the note of a tuning-fork, might at length be given a rest. But M. de Guermantes managed things so badly (to my mind, at least) that it seemed to me that only my own name was mentioned and I was given no clue as to the identity of my unknown friend, to whom it never occurred to name herself, so obvious did the grounds of our intimacy, which baffled me completely, seem to her. Indeed, as soon as I had come within reach, she did not offer me her hand, but took mine in a familiar clasp, and spoke to me exactly as though I had been as aware as she was of the pleasant memories to which her mind reverted. She told me how sorry Albert (who I gathered was her son) would be to have missed seeing me. I tried to remember which of my school friends had been called Albert, and could think only of Bloch, but this could not be Bloch's mother since she had been dead for many years. In vain I struggled to identify the past experience common to herself and me to which her thoughts had been carried back. But I could no more distinguish it through the translucent jet of her large, soft pupils which allowed only her smile to pierce their surface than one can distinguish a landscape that lies on the other side of a pane of smoked glass even when the sun is blazing on it. She asked me whether my father was not working too hard, if I would like to come to the theatre some evening with Albert, if my health was better, and as my replies, stumbling through the mental darkness in which I was plunged, became distinct only to explain that I was not feeling well that evening, she pushed forward a chair for me herself, putting herself out in a way to which I had never been accustomed by my parents' other friends. At length the clue to the riddle was furnished me by the Duke: "She thinks you're charming," he murmured in my ear, which felt somehow that it had heard these words before. They were the words Mme de Villeparisis had spoken to my grandmother and myself after we had made the acquaintance of the Princesse de Luxembourg. Everything was now clear; the present lady had nothing in common with Mme de Luxembourg, but from the language of him who was serving her up to me I could discern the nature of the beast. She was a royal personage. She had never before heard of either my family or myself, but, a scion of the noblest race and endowed with the greatest fortune in the world (for, a daughter of the Prince de Parme, she had married an equally princely cousin), she sought always, in gratitude to her Creator, to testify to her neighbour, however poor or lowly he might be, that she did not look down upon him. And indeed I ought to have guessed this from her smile, for I had seen the Princesse de Luxembourg buy little rye-cakes on the beach at Balbec to give to my grandmother, as though to a caged deer in the zoo. But this was only the second princess of the blood royal to whom I had been presented, and I might be excused my failure to discern in her the generic features of the affability of the great. Besides, had not they themselves

gone out of their way to warn me not to count too much on
this affability, since the Duchesse de Guermantes, who had
waved me so effusive a greeting with her gloved hand at the
Opéra, had appeared furious when I bowed to her in the
street, like the people who, having once given somebody a
sovereign, feel that this has released them from any further
obligation towards him. As for M. de Charlus, his ups and
downs were even more sharply contrasted. And I was later to
know, as the reader will learn, highnesses and majesties of
another sort altogether, queens who play the queen and speak
not after the conventions of their kind but like the queens in
Sardou's plays.

If M. de Guermantes had been in such haste to present me,
it was because the presence at a gathering of anyone not
personally known to a royal personage is an intolerable state
of things which must not be prolonged for a single instant.
It was similar to the haste which Saint-Loup had shown to be
introduced to my grandmother. By the same token, in a fragmentary survival of the old life of the court which is called
social etiquette and is by no means superficial, wherein, rather,
by a sort of outside-in reversal, it is the surface that becomes
essential and profound, the Duc and Duchesse de Guermantes
regarded as a duty more essential and more inflexible than those
(all too often neglected by one at least of the pair) of charity,
chastity, pity and justice, that of rarely addressing the Princesse
de Parme save in the third person.

Failing the visit to Parma which I had never yet made (and
which I had wanted to make ever since certain Easter holidays
long ago), meeting its Princess—who, I knew, owned the finest
palace in that unique city where in any case everything must
be in keeping, isolated as it was from the rest of the world
within its polished walls, in the atmosphere, stifling as an
airless summer evening on the piazza of a small Italian town,
of its compact and almost cloying name—ought to have
substituted in a flash, for what I had so often tried to imagine,
all that did really exist at Parma, in a sort of fragmentary
arrival there without having moved; it was, in the algebraical
expression of a journey to the city of Giorgione,[21] a simple
equation, so to speak, of that unknown quantity. But if I had

for many years past—like a perfumer impregnating a solid
block of fat—saturated this name, Princesse de Parme, with
the scent of thousands of violets, in return, when I set eyes on
the Princess, who until then I would have sworn must be the
Sanseverina herself, a second process began which was not,
I may say, completed until several months had passed, and
consisted in expelling, by means of fresh chemical combinations, all the essential oil of violets and all the Stendhalian
fragrance from the name of the Princess, and implanting there
in their place the image of a little dark woman taken up with
good works and so humbly amiable that one felt at once in how
exalted a pride that amiability had its roots. Moreover, while
identical, barring a few points of difference, with any other
great lady, she was as little Stendhalian as is, for example, in
the Europe district of Paris, the Rue de Parme, which bears
far less resemblance to the name of Parma than to any or all of
the neighbouring streets, and reminds one not nearly so much
of the Charterhouse in which Fabrice ends his days as of the
waiting room in the Gare Saint-Lazare.

Her amiability sprang from two causes. The first and more
general was the upbringing which this daughter of kings had
received. Her mother (not merely related to all the royal
families of Europe but furthermore—in contrast to the ducal
house of Parma—richer than any reigning princess) had
instilled into her from her earliest childhood the arrogantly
humble precepts of an evangelical snobbery; and to-day every
line of the daughter's face, the curve of her shoulders, the
movements of her arms, seemed to repeat the lesson: "Remember that if God has caused you to be born on the steps of
a throne you ought not to make that a reason for looking down
upon those to whom Divine Providence has willed (wherefore
His Name be praised) that you should be superior by birth
and fortune. On the contrary, you must be kind to the lowly.
Your ancestors were Princes of Cleves and Juliers from the
year 647; God in His bounty has decreed that you should hold
practically all the shares in the Suez Canal and three times as
many Royal Dutch as Edmond de Rothschild; your pedigree
in a direct line has been established by genealogists from the
year 63 of the Christian era; you have as sisters-in-law two

empresses. Therefore never seem in your speech to be recalling these great privileges, not that they are precarious (for nothing can alter the antiquity of blood, while the world will always need oil), but because it is unnecessary to point out that you are better born than other people or that your investments are all gilt-edged, since everyone knows these facts already. Be helpful to the needy. Give to all those whom the bounty of heaven has been graciously pleased to put beneath you as much as you can give them without forfeiting your rank, that is to say help in the form of money, even your personal service by their sickbeds, but of course never any invitations to your soirées, which would do them no possible good and, by diminishing your prestige, would reduce the efficacy of your benevolent activities."

And so, even at moments when she could not do good, the Princess endeavoured to demonstrate, or rather to let it be thought, by all the external signs of dumb show, that she did not consider herself superior to the people among whom she found herself. She treated each of them with that charming courtesy with which well-bred people treat their inferiors and was continually, to make herself useful, pushing back her chair so as to leave more room, holding my gloves, offering me all those services which would demean the proud spirit of a commoner but are willingly rendered by sovereign ladies or, instinctively and from force of professional habit, by old servants.

The other reason for the amiability shown me by the Princesse de Parme was a more special one, which however was in no way dictated by a mysterious liking for me. But for the moment I did not have time to get to the bottom of it. For already the Duke, who seemed in a hurry to complete the round of introductions, had led me off to another of the flower-maidens. On hearing her name I told her that I had passed by her country house, not far from Balbec. "Oh, I should have been so pleased to show you round it," she said to me almost in a whisper as though to emphasise her modesty, but in a heartfelt tone filled with regret for the loss of an opportunity to enjoy a quite exceptional pleasure; and she added with a meaning look: "I do hope you will come again some day. But I must say that what would interest you even more would be my aunt Brancas's place. It was built by Mansard and it's the jewel of the province." It was not only she herself who would have been glad to show me over her house, but her aunt Brancas would have been no less delighted to do me the honours of hers, or so I was assured by this lady who evidently thought that, especially at a time when the land showed a tendency to pass into the hands of financiers who had no idea how to live, it was important that the great should keep up the lofty traditions of lordly hospitality, by speeches which did not commit them to anything. It was also because she sought, like everyone in her world, to say the things that would give most pleasure to the person she was addressing, to give him the highest idea of himself, to make him think that he flattered people by writing to them, that he honoured those who entertained him, that everyone was longing to know him. The desire to give other people this comforting idea of themselves does, it is true, sometimes exist even among the middle classes. We find there that amiable disposition, in the form of an individual quality compensating for some other defect, not alas in the most trusty male friends but at any rate in the most agreeable female companions. But there it flourishes only in isolation. In an important section of the aristocracy, on the other hand, this characteristic has ceased to be individual; cultivated by upbringing, sustained by the idea of a personal grandeur that need fear no humiliation, that knows no rival, is aware that by being gracious it can make people happy and delights in doing so, it has become the generic feature of a class. And even those whom personal defects of too incompatible a kind prevent from keeping it in their hearts bear the unconscious trace of it in their vocabulary or their gesticulation.

"She's a very kind woman," said the Duc de Guermantes of the Princesse de Parme, "and she knows how to play the *grande dame* better than anyone."

While I was being introduced to the ladies, one of the gentlemen of the party had been showing various signs of agitation: this was Comte Hannibal de Bréauté-Consalvi. Having arrived late, he had not had time to investigate the composition of the party, and when I entered the room, seeing

in me a guest who was not one of the Duchess's regular circle
and must therefore have some quite extraordinary claim to
admission, installed his monocle beneath the groined arch
of his eyebrow, thinking that this would help him, far more
than to see me, to discern what manner of man I was. He
knew that Mme de Guermantes had (the priceless appanage of
truly superior women) what was called a "salon," that is to say
added occasionally to the people of her own set some celebrity
who had recently come into prominence by the discovery
of a new cure for something or the production of a masterpiece. The Faubourg Saint-German had not yet recovered from
the shock of learning that the Duchess had not been afraid
to invite M. Detaille[22] to the reception which she had given
to meet the King and Queen of England. The clever women
of the Faubourg were not easily consolable for not having
been invited, so deliciously thrilling would it have been to
come into contact with that strange genius. Mme de Courvoisier averred that M. Ribot had been there as well, but this
was a pure invention designed to make people believe that
Oriane was aiming at an embassy for her husband. To cap it
all, M. de Guermantes, with a gallantry that would have done
credit to Marshal Saxe, had presented himself at the stage door
of the Comédie-Française and had persuaded Mlle Reichenberg to come and recite before the King, something that
constituted an event without precedent in the annals of routs.
Remembering all these unexpected happenings, which moreover had his entire approval, his own presence being both an
ornament to and, in the same way as that of the Duchesse de
Guermantes but in the masculine gender, an endorsement for
any salon, M. de Bréauté, when he asked himself who I could
be, felt that the field of inquiry was very wide. For a moment
the name of M. Widor flashed before his mind, but he decided
that I was too young to be an organist, and M. Widor not
prominent enough to be "received." It seemed on the whole
more plausible to regard me simply as the new attaché at the
Swedish Legation of whom he had heard, and he was preparing
to ask me for the latest news of King Oscar, by whom he had
several times been very hospitably received; but when the Duke,
in introducing me, had mentioned my name to M. de Bréauté, the

latter, finding the name to be completely unknown to him, had
no longer any doubt that, since I was there, I must be a
celebrity of some sort. It was absolutely typical of Oriane,
who had the knack of attracting to her salon men who were in
the public eye, in a ratio that of course never exceeded one in
a hundred, otherwise she would have lowered its tone.
Accordingly M. de Bréauté began to lick his chops and to sniff
the air greedily, his appetite whetted not only by the good
dinner he could count on, but by the character of the party,
which my presence could not fail to make interesting and which
would furnish him with an intriguing topic of conversation
next day at the Duc de Chartres's luncheon-table. He was not
yet enlightened as to whether I was the man who had just been
making those experiments with a serum against cancer, or the
author of the new "curtain-raiser" then in rehearsal at the
Théâtre-Français; but, a great intellectual, a great collector of
"travellers' tales," he lavished on me an endless series of bows,
signs of mutual understanding, smiles filtered through the
glass of his monocle, either in the misapprehension that a man
of standing would esteem him more highly if he could manage to instil into me the illusion that for him, the Comte de
Bréauté-Consalvi, the privileges of the mind were no less
deserving of respect than those of birth, or simply from the
need to express and the difficulty of expressing his satisfaction,
in his ignorance of the language in which he ought to address
me, precisely as if he had found himself face to face with one of
the "natives" of an undiscovered country on which his raft
had landed, from whom, in the hope of ultimate profit, he
would endeavour, observing with interest the while their
quaint customs and without interrupting his demonstrations
of friendship or forgetting to utter loud cries like them, to
obtain ostrich eggs and spices in exchange for glass beads.
Having responded as best I could to his joy, I shook hands
with the Duc de Châtellerault, whom I had already met at
Mme de Villeparisis's and who observed that she was "a wily
old bird." He was typically Guermantes with his fair hair, his
aquiline profile, the points where the skin of the cheeks was
blemished, all of which may be seen in the portraits of that
family which have come down to us from the sixteenth and

seventeenth centuries. But, as I was no longer in love with the Duchess, her reincarnation in the person of a young man offered me no attraction. I interpreted the hook made by the Duc de Châtellerault's nose as if it had been the signature of a painter whose work I had long studied but who no longer interested me in the least. Next, I said good evening also to the Prince de Foix, and to the detriment of my knuckles, which emerged crushed and mangled, let them be caught in the vice of a German handclasp, accompanied by an ironical or good-natured smile, from the Prince von Faffenheim, M. de Norpois's friend, who, by virtue of the craze for nicknames which prevailed in this circle, was known so universally as Prince Von that he himself used to sign his letters "Prince Von," or, when he wrote to his intimates, "Von." At least this abbreviation was understandable, in view of his triple-barrelled name. It was less easy to grasp the reasons which caused "Elizabeth" to be replaced, now by "Lili," now by "Bebeth," just as another world swarmed with "Kikis." One can understand how people, idle and frivolous though they in general were, should have come to adopt "Quiou" in order not to waste the precious time that it would have taken them to pronounce "Montesquiou." But it is less easy to see what they gained by nicknaming one of their cousins "Dinand" instead of "Ferdinand." It must not be thought, however, that in the invention of nicknames the Guermantes invariably proceeded by curtailing or duplicating syllables. Thus two sisters, the Comtesse de Montpeyroux and the Vicomtesse de Vélude, who were both of them enormously stout, invariably heard themselves addressed, without the least trace of annoyance on their part or of amusement on other people's, so long established was the custom, as "Petite" and "Mignonne." Mme de Guermantes, who adored Mme de Montpeyroux, would, if the latter had fallen seriously ill, have flown to the sister with tears in her eyes and exclaimed: "I hear Petite is dreadfully bad!" Mme de l'Eclin, who wore her hair in bands that entirely hid her ears, was never called anything but "Hungry belly."[23] In some cases people simply added an 'a' to the surname or Christian name of the husband to designate the wife. The most miserly, most sordid, most inhuman man in the

Faubourg having been christened Raphael, his charmer, his flower springing also from the rock, always signed herself "Raphaela." But these are merely a few specimens of countless rules to which we can always return later on if the occasion arises, and explain some of them.

I then asked the Duke to introduce me to the Prince d'Agrigente. "What! do you mean to say you don't know the good Gri-gri!" exclaimed M. de Guermantes, and gave M. d'Agrigente my name. His own, so often quoted by Françoise, had always appeared to me like a transparent sheet of coloured glass through which I beheld, struck by the slanting rays of a golden sun, on the shore of the violet sea, the pink marble cubes of an ancient city of which I had not the least doubt that the Prince—who happened by some brief miracle to be passing through Paris—was himself, as luminously Sicilian and as gloriously weathered, the absolute sovereign. Alas, the vulgar drone to whom I was introduced, and who wheeled round to bid me good evening with a ponderous nonchalance which he considered elegant, was as independent of his name as of a work of art that he owned without betraying in his person any reflexion of it, without, perhaps, ever having looked at it. The Prince d'Agrigente was so entirely devoid of anything princely, anything remotely reminiscent of Agrigento, that one was led to suppose that his name, entirely distinct from himself, bound by no ties to his person, had had the power of attracting to itself every iota of vague poetry that there might have been in this man, as in any other, and enclosing it, after this operation, in the enchanted syllables. If any such operation had been performed, it had certainly been done most efficiently, for there remained not an atom of charm to be drawn from this kinsman of the Guermantes. With the result that he found himself at one and the same time the only man in the world who was Prince d'Agrigente and of all the men in the world the one who was perhaps least so. He was, for all that, very glad to be what he was, but as a banker is glad to hold a number of shares in a mine, without caring whether the said mine answers to the charming name of Ivanhoe or Primrose, or is called merely the Premier. Meanwhile, as these introductions which have taken so long to recount but which, beginning as soon as I entered the room, had lasted only a few moments, were drawing to an end at last, and Mme de Guermantes was saying to me in an almost suppliant tone: "I'm sure Basin is tiring you, dragging you round like that from one person to the next. We want you to know our friends, but we're a great deal more anxious not to tire you, so that you may come again often," the Duke, with a somewhat awkward and timorous wave of the hand, gave the signal (which he would gladly have given at any time during the hour I had spent in contemplation of the Elstirs) that dinner might now be served.

I should add that one of the guests was still missing, M. de Grouchy, whose wife, a Guermantes by birth, had arrived by herself, her husband being due to come straight from the country where he had been shooting all day. This M. de Grouchy, a descendant of his namesake of the First Empire, of whom it has been falsely said that his absence at the start of the Battle of Waterloo was the principal cause of Napoleon's defeat, came of an excellent family which, however, was not good enough in the eyes of certain fanatics for blue blood. Thus the Prince de Guermantes, who was to prove less fastidious in later life as far as he himself was concerned, was in the habit of saying to his nieces: "What a misfortune for that poor Mme de Guermantes" (the Vicomtesse de Guermantes, Mme de Grouchy's mother) "that she has never succeeded in marrying any of her children." "But, uncle, the eldest girl married M. de Grouchy." "I don't call that a husband! However, they say that your uncle François has proposed to the youngest one, so perhaps they won't all die old maids."

No sooner had the order to serve dinner been given than with a vast gyratory whirr, multiple and simultaneous, the double doors of the dining-room swung apart; a butler with the air of a court chamberlain bowed before the Princesse de Parme and announced the tidings "Madame is served," in a tone such as he would have employed to say "Madame is dead," which, however, cast no gloom over the assembly for it was with a sprightly air and as, in summer, at Robinson[24] that the couples advanced one behind the other to the dining-room, separating when they had reached their places, where footmen thrust their chairs in behind them; last of all, Mme de Guermantes advanced towards me to be taken in to dinner, without my feeling the least shadow of the timidity that I might have feared, for, like a huntress whose muscular dexterity has endowed her with natural ease and grace, observing no doubt that I had placed myself on the wrong side of her, she pivoted round me so adroitly that I found her arm resting on mine and was at once naturally attuned to a rhythm of precise and noble movements. I yielded to them all the more readily because the Guermantes attached no more importance to them than does to learning a truly learned man in whose company one is less alarmed than in that of a dunce. Other doors opened through which there entered the steaming soup, as though the dinner were being held in a skilfully contrived puppet-theatre, where, at a signal from the puppet-master, the belated arrival of the young guest set all the machinery in motion.

Timid, rather than majestically sovereign, had been this signal from the Duke, to which that vast, ingenious, subservient and sumptuous clockwork, mechanical and human, had responded. The indecisiveness of the gesture did not spoil for me the effect of the spectacle that was attendant upon it. For I sensed that what had made it hesitant and embarrassed was the fear of letting me see that they had been waiting only for me to begin dinner and that they had been waiting for a long time, in the same way as Mme de Guermantes was afraid that, after looking at so many pictures, I would find it tiring and would be hindered from taking my ease among them if her husband engaged me in a continuous flow of introductions. So that it was the absence of grandeur in this gesture that disclosed the true grandeur which lay in the Duke's indifference to the splendour of his surroundings, in contrast to his deference towards a guest, however insignificant, whom he desired to honour.

Not that M. de Guermantes was not in certain aspects thoroughly commonplace, showing indeed some of the absurd weaknesses of a man with too much money, the arrogance of an upstart which he certainly was not. But just as a public official or a priest sees his own humble talents multiplied to infinity (as a wave is by the whole mass of the sea which presses behind it) by the forces that stand behind him, the

Government of France or the Catholic Church, so M. de
Guermantes was borne up by that other force, aristocratic
courtesy in its truest form. This courtesy excluded a large
number of people. Mme de Guermantes would not have
entertained Mme de Cambremer or M. de Forcheville. But the
moment that anyone (as was the case with me) appeared
eligible for admission into the Guermantes world, this courtesy
disclosed a wealth of hospitable simplicity more splendid still,
if possible, than those historic rooms and the marvellous furniture that remained in them.

When he wished to give pleasure to someone, M. de Guermantes went about making him the most important personage
on that particular day with an art and a skill that made the most
of the circumstances and the place. No doubt at Guermantes
his "distinctions" and "favours" would have assumed another
form. He would have ordered his carriage to take me for a
drive alone with himself before dinner. Such as they were,
one could not help feeling touched by his courteous ways, as
one is, when one reads the memoirs of the period, by those of
Louis XIV when he replies benignly, with a smile and a half-
bow, to someone who has come to solicit his favour. It must
however, in both instances, be borne in mind that this
"politeness" did not go beyond the strict meaning of the word.

Louis XIV (with whom the sticklers for pure nobility of his
day nevertheless find fault for his scant regard for etiquette,
so much so that, according to Saint-Simon, he was only a
very minor king, in terms of rank, by comparison with such
monarchs as Philippe de Valois or Charles V) has the most
meticulous instructions drawn up so that princes of the blood
and ambassadors may know to what sovereigns they ought to
give precedence. In certain cases, in view of the impossibility
of arriving at an agreement, a compromise is arranged by
which the son of Louis XIV, Monseigneur, shall entertain a
certain foreign sovereign only out of doors, in the open air,
so that it may not be said that in entering the palace one has
preceded the other; and the Elector Palatine, entertaining the
Duc de Chevreuse to dinner, in order not to have to make way
for his guest, pretends to be taken ill and dines with him
lying down, thus solving the difficulty. When M. le Duc avoids

occasions when he must wait upon Monsieur, the latter, on the advice of the King, his brother, who is incidentally extremely attached to him, seizes an excuse for making his cousin attend his levee and forcing him to put on the royal shirt. But as soon as deeper feelings are involved, matters of the heart, this rule of duty, so inflexible when politeness only is at stake, changes entirely. A few hours after the death of his brother, one of the people whom he most dearly loved, when Monsieur, in the words of the Duc de Montfort, is "still warm," we find Louis XIV singing snatches from operas, astonished that the Duchesse de Bourgogne, who can scarcely conceal her grief, should be looking so woe begone, and, anxious that the gaiety of the court shall be at once resumed, encouraging his courtiers to sit down to the card-tables by ordering the Duc de Bourgogne to start a game of *brelan*. Now, not only in his social or business activities, but in his most spontaneous utterances, his ordinary preoccupations, his daily routine, one found a similar contrast in M. de Guermantes. The Guermantes were no more susceptible to grief than other mortals; it could indeed be said that they had less real sensibility; on the other hand one saw their names every day in the social columns of the *Gaulois* on account of the prodigious number of funerals at which they would have felt it culpable of them not to have their presence recorded. As the traveller discovers, almost unaltered, the houses roofed with turf, the terraces which may have met the eyes of Xenophon or St Paul, so in the manners of M. de Guermantes, a man who was heart-warming in his graciousness and revolting in his hardness, a slave to the pettiest obligations and derelict as regards the most solemn pacts, I found still intact after more than two centuries that aberration, peculiar to the life of the court under Louis XIV, which transfers the scruples of conscience from the domain of the affections and morality to questions of pure form.

The other reason for the friendliness shown me by the Princesse de Parme was that she was convinced beforehand that everything that she saw at the Duchesse de Guermantes's, people and things alike, was of a superior quality to anything she had at home. It is true that in every other house she also behaved as if this was the case; not merely did she go into raptures over the simplest dish, the most ordinary flowers, but she would ask permission to send round next morning, for the purpose of copying the recipe or examining the variety of blossom, her head cook or head gardener, gentlemen with large emoluments who kept their own carriages and were deeply humiliated at having to come to inquire after a dish they despised or to take a cutting of a variety of carnation that was not half as fine, as variegated, did not produce as large a blossom as those which they had long been growing for her at home. But if, wherever she went, this astonishment on the part of the Princess at the sight of the most commonplace things was factitious, and intended to show that she did not derive from the superiority of her rank and riches a pride forbidden by her early instructors, habitually dissembled by her mother and intolerable in the sight of her Creator, it was, on the other hand, in all sincerity that she regarded the drawing-room of the Duchesse de Guermantes as a privileged place in which she could progress only from surprise to delight. To a certain extent, it is true, though not nearly enough to justify this state of mind, the Guermantes were different from the rest of society; they were rarefied and precious. They had given me at first sight the opposite impression; I had found them vulgar, similar to all other men and women, but this was because before meeting them I had seen them, as I saw Balbec, Florence or Parma, as names. It was evident from this drawing-room, all the women whom I had imagined as being like Dresden figures resembled after all the great majority of women. But, in the same way as Balbec or Florence, the Guermantes, after first disappointing the imagination because they resembled their fellow-men rather more than their name, could subsequently, though to a lesser degree, hold out to one's intelligence certain distinctive characteristics. Their physique, the colour—a peculiar pink that merged at times into purple—of their skins, a certain almost lustrous blondness of the finely spun hair even in the men, massed in soft golden tufts, half wall-growing lichen, half catlike fur (a luminous brilliance to which corresponded a certain intellectual glitter, for if people spoke of the Guermantes complexion, the Guermantes hair, they spoke also of the Guermantes wit, as of the wit of the

Mortemarts), a certain social quality whose superior refinement—pre-Louis XIV—was all the more universally recognised because they promulgated it themselves—all this meant
that in the actual substance, however precious it might be, of
the aristocratic society in which they were to be found embedded here and there, the Guermantes remained recognisable,
easy to detect and to follow, like the veins whose paleness
streaks a block of jasper or onyx, or, better still, like the supple
undulation of those tresses of light whose loosened hairs run
like flexible rays along the sides of a moss-agate.

The Guermantes—those at least who were worthy of the
name—were not only endowed with an exquisite quality of
flesh, of hair, of transparency of gaze, but had a way of holding
themselves, of walking, of bowing, of looking at one before
they shook one's hand, of shaking hands, which made them as
different in all these respects from an ordinary member of
fashionable society as he in turn was from a peasant in a
smock. And despite their affability one asked oneself: "Have
they not indeed the right, though they waive it, when they see
us walk, bow, leave a room, do any of those things which when
performed by them become as graceful as the flight of a swallow
or the droop of a rose on its stem, to think: 'These people are
of a different breed from us, and we are the lords of creation'?"
Later on, I realised that the Guermantes did indeed regard
me as being of a different breed, but one that aroused their
envy because I possessed merits unknown to myself which
they professed to prize above all others. Later still I came to feel
that this profession of faith was only half sincere and that in
them scorn or amazement could co-exist with admiration and
envy. The physical flexibility peculiar to the Guermantes was
twofold: on the one hand always in action, at every moment,
so that if, for example, a male Guermantes were about to
salute a lady, he produced a silhouette of himself formed from
the precarious balance of a series of asymmetrical and nervily
compensated movements, one leg dragging a little, either on
purpose or because, having been broken so often in the hunt-
ing-field, it imparted to his trunk in its effort to keep pace with
the other a curvature to which the upward thrust of one
shoulder gave a counterpoise, while the monocle was inserted

in the eye and raised an eyebrow just as the tuft of hair on the forehead flopped downward in the formal bow; on the other hand, like the shape which wave or wind or wake have permanently imprinted on a shell or a boat, this flexibility was so to speak stylised into a sort of fixed mobility, curving the arched nose which, beneath the blue, protruding eyes, above the thin lips from which, in the women, there emerged a husky voice, recalled the fabulous origin attributed in the sixteenth century by the complaisance of parasitic and Hellenising genealogists to this race, ancient beyond dispute, but not to the extent which they claimed when they gave as its source the mythological impregnation of a nymph by a divine Bird.

The Guermantes were no less idiosyncratic from the intellectual than from the physical point of view. With the exception of Prince Gilbert, the husband of "Marie-Gilbert" with the antiquated ideas, who made his wife sit on his left when they drove out together because her blood, though royal, was inferior to his own (but he was an exception and a perpetual laughing-stock, behind his back, to the rest of his family, for whom he provided an endless source of fresh anecdotes), the Guermantes, while living among the cream of the aristocracy, affected to set no store by nobility. The theories of the Duchesse de Guermantes, who, it must be said, by virtue of being a Guermantes, had become to a certain extent something different and more attractive, put intelligence so much above everything else and were in politics so socialistic that one wondered where in her mansion could be the hiding-place of the genie whose duty it was to ensure the maintenance of the aristocratic way of life and who, always invisible but evidently lurking at one moment in the entrance hall, at another in the drawing-room, at a third in her dressing-room, reminded the servants of this woman who did not believe in titles to address her as "Madame la Duchesse," and reminded this woman herself, who cared only for reading and was no respecter of persons, to go out to dinner with her sister-in-law when eight o'clock struck, and to put on a low-necked dress for the occasion.

The same family genie represented to Mme de Guermantes the social duties of duchesses, at least of the foremost among

them who like herself were also multi-millionaires—the
sacrifice to boring tea-parties, grand dinners, routs of every
kind, of hours in which she might have read interesting books
—as unpleasant necessities like rain, which Mme de Guermantes
accepted while bringing her irreverent humour to bear on
them, though without going so far as to examine the reasons
for her acceptance. The curious coincidence whereby Mme de
Guermantes's butler invariably said "Madame la Duchesse" to
this woman who believed only in the intellect did not appear
to shock her. Never had it entered her head to request him to
address her simply as "Madame." Giving her the utmost
benefit of the doubt one might have supposed that, being
absent-minded, she caught only the word "Madame" and that
the suffix appended to it remained unheard. Only, though she
might feign deafness, she was not dumb. And the fact was that
whenever she had a message to give to her husband she would
say to the butler: "Remind Monsieur le Duc——"

The family genie had other occupations as well, one of
which was to inspire them to talk morality. It is true that there
were Guermantes who went in for intellect and Guermantes
who went in for morals, and that these two groups did not as
a rule coincide. But the former—including a Guermantes who
had forged cheques, who cheated at cards and was the most
delightful of them all, with a mind open to every new and
sensible idea—spoke even more eloquently about morals than
the others, and in the same strain as Mme de Villeparisis, at
the moments when the family genie expressed itself through
the lips of the old lady. At corresponding moments one saw
the Guermantes suddenly adopt a tone almost as antiquated
and as affable as, and (since they themselves had more charm)
more affecting than that of the Marquise, to say of a servant:
"One feels that she has a thoroughly sound nature, she's not
at all a common girl, she must come of decent parents, she's
certainly a girl who has never gone astray." At such moments
the family genie adopted the form of a tone of voice. But at
times it could reveal itself in the bearing also, in the expression
on the face, the same in the Duchess as in her grandfather the
Marshal, a sort of imperceptible convulsion (like that of the
Snake, the genius of the Carthaginian family of Barca) by

which my heart had more than once been made to throb, on my morning walks, when before I had recognised Mme de Guermantes I felt her eyes fastened upon me from the inside of a little dairy. This family genie had intervened in a situation which was far from immaterial not merely to the Guermantes but to the Courvoisiers, the rival faction of the family and, though of as noble stock as the Guermantes (it was, indeed, through his Courvoisier grandmother that the Guermantes explained the obsession which led the Prince de Guermantes always to speak of birth and titles as though they were the only things that mattered), their opposite in every respect. Not only did the Courvoisiers not assign to intelligence the same importance as the Guermantes, they had a different notion of it. For a Guermantes (however stupid), to be intelligent meant to have a sharp tongue, to be capable of saying scathing things, to give short shrift; but it meant also the capacity to hold one's own equally in painting, music, architecture, and to speak English. The Courvoisiers had a less favourable notion of intelligence, and unless one belonged to their world, being intelligent was almost tantamount to "having probably murdered one's father and mother." For them intelligence was the sort of burglar's jemmy by means of which people one did not know from Adam forced the doors of the most reputable drawing-rooms, and it was common knowledge among the Courvoisiers that you always had to pay in the long run for having "those sort" of people in your house. To the most trivial statements made by intelligent people who were not "in society" the Courvoisiers opposed a systematic distrust. Someone having once remarked: "But Swann is younger than Palamède," Mme de Gallardon had retorted: "So he says, at any rate, and if he says it you may be sure it's because he thinks it's in his interest!" Better still, when someone said of two highly distinguished strangers whom the Guermantes had entertained that one of them had been sent in first because she was the elder: "But is she really the elder?" Mme de Gallardon had inquired, not positively as though that sort of person did not have an age, but as if, being very probably devoid of civil or religious status, of definite traditions, they were both more or less of an age, like two kittens of the same litter between which only a veterinary surgeon would be competent to decide. The Courvoisiers however, more than the Guermantes, maintained in a certain sense the integrity of the titled class thanks at once to the narrowness of their minds and the malevolence of their hearts. Just as the Guermantes (for whom, below the royal families and a few others like the Lignes, the La Trémoïlles and so forth, all the rest were a vague jumble of indistinguishable small-fry) were insolent towards various people of ancient stock who lived round Guermantes, precisely because they paid no attention to those secondary distinctions by which the Courvoisiers set enormous store, so the absence of such distinctions affected them little. Certain women who did not enjoy a very exalted rank in their native provinces but had made glittering marriages and were rich, pretty, beloved of duchesses, were for Paris, where people are never very well up in who one's "father and mother" were, desirable and elegant imports. It might happen, though rarely, that such women were, through the medium of the Princesse de Parme, or by virtue of their own attractions, received by certain Guermantes. But towards these the indignation of the Courvoisiers was unrelenting. Having to meet at their cousin's, between five and six in the afternoon, people with whose relatives their own relatives did not care to be seen mixing down in the Perche became for them an ever-increasing source of rage and an inexhaustible fount of rhetoric. Whenever, for instance, the charming Comtesse G—— entered the Guermantes drawing-room, the face of Mme de Villebon assumed exactly the expression that would have befitted it had she been called upon to recite the line:

And should but one stand fast, that one were surely I,

a line which for that matter was unknown to her. This Courvoisier had consumed almost every Monday éclairs stuffed with cream within a few feet of the Comtesse G——, but to no consequence. And Mme de Villebon confessed in secret that she could not conceive how her cousin Guermantes could allow a woman into her house who was not even in the second-best society of Châteaudun. "I really fail to see why my cousin should make such a fuss about whom she knows;

she really has got a nerve!" concluded Mme de Villebon with a
change of facial expression, now smilingly sardonic in its
despair, to which, in a charade, another line of verse would
have been applied, one with which she was no more familiar
than with the first:

> Grâce aux dieux! Mon malheur passe mon espérance.

We may here anticipate events to explain that the *persé-
vérance* (which rhymes, in the following line, with *espérance*)
shown by Mme de Villebon in snubbing Mme G—— was
not entirely wasted. In the eyes of Mme G—— it invested
Mme de Villebon with a distinction so supreme, though
purely imaginary, that when the time came for Mme G——'s
daughter, who was the prettiest girl and the greatest heiress
in the ballrooms of that season, to marry, people were
astonished to see her refuse all the dukes in succession. The
fact was that her mother, remembering the weekly snubs she
had to endure in the Rue de Grenelle in memory of Chateau-
dun, could think of only one possible husband for her
daughter—a Villebon son.

A single point at which Guermantes and Courvoisiers converged was the art (one, moreover, of infinite variety) of keeping
distances. The Guermantes manners were not absolutely uniform throughout the family. And yet, to take an example, all of
them, all those who were genuine Guermantes, when you were
introduced to them proceeded to perform a sort of ceremony
almost as though the fact that they had held out their hands
to you were as significant as if they had been dubbing you a
knight. At the moment when a Guermantes, were he no more
than twenty, but treading already in the footsteps of his
ancestors, heard your name uttered by the person who introduced you, he let fall on you as though he had by no means
made up his mind to say "How d'ye do" to you a gaze generally
blue and always of the coldness of a steel blade which he
seemed ready to plunge into the deepest recesses of your heart.
Which was as a matter of fact what the Guermantes imagined
themselves to be doing, since they all regarded themselves as
psychologists of the first water. They felt moreover that they
enhanced by this inspection the affability of the salute which

was to follow it, and would not be rendered you without full knowledge of your deserts. All this occurred at a distance from yourself which, little enough had it been a question of a passage of arms, seemed immense for a handclasp and had as chilling an effect in the latter case as it would have had in the former, so that when a Guermantes, after a rapid tour round the innermost recesses of your soul to establish your credentials, had deemed you worthy to consort with him thereafter, his hand, directed towards you at the end of an arm stretched out to its fullest extent, appeared to be presenting a rapier to you for a single combat, and that hand was on the whole placed so far in advance of the Guermantes himself at that moment that when he proceeded to bow his head it was difficult to distinguish whether it was yourself or his own hand that he was saluting. Certain Guermantes, lacking any sense of moderation, or being incapable of refraining from repeating themselves incessantly, went further and repeated this ceremony afresh every time they met you. Seeing that they had no longer any need to conduct the preliminary psychological investigation for which the "family genie" had delegated its powers to them and the result of which they had presumably kept in mind, the insistency of the piercing gaze preceding the handclasp could be explained only by the automatism which their gaze had acquired or by some hypnotic power which they believed themselves to possess. The Courvoisiers, whose physique was different, had tried in vain to acquire that searching gaze and had had to fall back upon a haughty stiffness or a hurried negligence. On the other hand, it was from the Courvoisiers that certain very rare Guermantes of the gentler sex seemed to have borrowed the feminine form of greeting. At the moment when you were presented to one of these, she made you a sweeping bow in which she carried towards you, almost at an angle of forty-five degrees, her head and bust, the rest of her body (which was very tall) up to the belt which formed a pivot, remaining stationary. But no sooner had she projected thus towards you the upper part of her person, than she flung it backwards beyond the vertical with a brusque withdrawal of roughly equal length. This subsequent withdrawal neutralised what appeared to have been conceded to you; the ground which you believed yourself to have gained did not even remain in your possession as in a duel; the original positions were retained. This same annulment of affability by the resumption of distance (which was Courvoisier in origin and intended to show that the advances made in the first movement were no more than a momentary feint) displayed itself equally clearly, in the Courvoisier ladies as in the Guermantes, in the letters which you received from them, at any rate in the first period of your acquaintance. The "body" of the letter might contain sentences such as one writes only (you would suppose) to a friend, but in vain might you have thought yourself entitled to boast of being in that relation to the lady, since the letter would begin with "Monsieur" and end with "Croyez, monsieur, à mes sentiments distingués." After which, between this cold opening and frigid conclusion which altered the meaning of all the rest, there might (were it a reply to a letter of condolence) come a succession of the most touching pictures of the grief which the Guermantes lady had felt on losing her sister, of the intimacy that had existed between them, of the beauty of the place in which she was staying, of the consolation that she found in the charm of her grandchildren, in other words it was simply a letter such as one finds in printed collections, the intimate character of which implied, however, no more intimacy between yourself and the writer than if she had been Pliny the Younger or Mme de Simiane.

It is true that certain Guermantes ladies wrote to you from the first as "My dear friend," or "Dear friend." These were not always the most homely among them, but rather those who, living only in the society of kings and being at the same time "of easy virtue," assumed in their pride the certainty that everything that came from them gave pleasure and in their corruption the habit of not grudging you any of the satisfactions they had to offer. However, since to have had a common great-great-grandmother in the reign of Louis XIII was enough to make a young Guermantes invariably refer to the Marquise de Guermantes as "Aunt Adam," the Guermantes were so numerous a clan that, even with these simple rites, that for example of the form of greeting adopted on introduction to a stranger, there existed a wide divergence. Each sub-group of any refinement had its own, which was handed down from parents to children like the prescription for a liniment or a special way of making jam. Thus we have seen Saint-Loup's handshake unleashed as though involuntarily as soon as he heard one's name, without any participation by his eyes, without the addition of a nod or a bow. Any unfortunate commoner who for a particular reason—which in fact very rarely occurred —was presented to a member of the Saint-Loup sub-group would scratch his head over this abrupt minimum of a greeting, which deliberately assumed the appearance of non-recognition, wondering what in the world the Guermantes—male or female —could have against him. And he was highly surprised to learn that the said Guermantes had thought fit to write specially to the introducer to tell him how delighted he or she had been with the stranger, whom he or she looked forward to meeting again. As characteristic as the mechanical gestures of Saint-Loup were the complicated and rapid capers (which M. de Charlus condemned as ridiculous) of the Marquis de Fierbois, or the grave and measured paces of the Prince de Guermantes. But it is impossible to describe here the richness of this Guermantes choreography because of the sheer extent of the corps de ballet.

To return to the antipathy which animated the Courvoisiers against the Duchesse de Guermantes, the former might have had the consolation of feeling sorry for her so long as she was still unmarried, for she was then of comparatively slender means. Unfortunately, at all times and seasons, a sort of fuliginous emanation, quite *sui generis*, enveloped and concealed from view the wealth of the Courvoisiers which, however great it might be, remained obscure. In vain might a young Courvoisier with an enormous dowry find a most eligible bridegroom; it invariably happened that the young couple had no house of their own in Paris, "came up to stay" in the season with the parents-in-law, and for the rest of the year lived down in the country in the midst of a society that was unadulterated but undistinguished. Whereas Saint-Loup, who was up to the eyes in debt, dazzled Doncières with his carriage-horses, a Courvoisier who was extremely rich always went by tram.

Similarly (though of course many years earlier) Mlle de
Guermantes (Oriane), who had scarcely a penny to her name,
created more stir with her clothes than all the Courvoisiers
put together. The very scandalousness of her remarks was a
sort of advertisement for her style of dressing and doing her
hair. She had had the audacity to say to the Russian Grand
Duke: "Well, sir, I hear you would like to have Tolstoy
executed?" at a dinner-party to which none of the Courvoisiers, in any case ill-informed about Tolstoy, had been
asked. They were no better informed about the Greek authors,
if we may judge by the Dowager Duchesse de Gallardon
(mother-in-law of the Princesse de Gallardon who at that time
was still a girl) who, not having been honoured by Oriane
with a single visit in five years, replied to someone who asked
her the reason for this abstention: "It seems she recites
Aristotle" (meaning Aristophanes) "in society. I won't tolerate
that sort of thing in my house!"

One can imagine how greatly this "sally" by Mlle de Guermantes on the subject of Tolstoy, if it enraged the Courvoisiers, delighted the Guermantes, and beyond them everyone
who was not merely closely but even remotely attached to them.
The Dowager Comtesse d'Argencourt (*née* Seineport), who
entertained more or less everyone because she was a bluestocking and in spite of her son's being a terrible snob, retailed
the remark to her literary friends with the comment: "Oriane
de Guermantes, you know, she's as sharp as a needle, as
mischievous as a monkey, gifted at everything, does water-
colours worthy of a great painter, and writes better verses
than most of the great poets, and as for family, you couldn't
imagine anything better, her grandmother was Mlle de
Montpensier, and she's the eighteenth Oriane de Guermantes
in succession, without a single misalliance; it's the purest,
the oldest blood in the whole of France." And so the sham
men of letters, the pseudo-intellectuals whom Mme d'Argencourt entertained, picturing Oriane de Guermantes, whom they
would never have an opportunity of knowing personally,
as something more wonderful and more extraordinary than
Princess Badroul Boudour, not only felt ready to die for her
on learning that so noble a person glorified Tolstoy above all

others, but felt also a quickening in their hearts of their own love of Tolstoy, their longing to resist Tsarism. These liberal ideas might have languished in them, they might have begun to doubt their importance, no longer daring to confess to them, when suddenly from Mlle de Guermantes herself, that is to say from a girl so indisputably cultured and authoritative, who wore her hair flat on her forehead (a thing that no Courvoisier would ever have dreamed of doing), came this vehement support. A certain number of realities, good or bad in themselves, gain enormously in this way by receiving the adhesion of people who are in authority over us. For instance, among the Courvoisiers the rites of civility in a public thoroughfare consisted in a certain form of greeting, very ugly and far from affable in itself, which people nevertheless knew to be the distinguished way of bidding a person good-day, with the result that everyone else, suppressing their instinctive smiles of welcome, endeavoured to imitate these frigid gymnastics. But the Guermantes in general and Oriane in particular, while more conversant than anyone with these rites, did not hesitate, if they caught sight of you from a carriage, to greet you with a friendly wave, and in a drawing-room, leaving the Courvoisiers to give their stiff, self-conscious salutes, offered the most charming bows, held out their hands as though to a comrade with a smile from their blue eyes, so that suddenly, thanks to the Guermantes, there entered into the substance of stylish manners, hitherto rather hollow and dry, everything that one would naturally have liked and had forced oneself to eschew, a genuine welcome, the warmth of true friendliness, spontaneity. It is in a similar fashion (but by a rehabilitation which in this case is less justified) that the people who are most strongly imbued with an instinctive taste for bad music and for melodies, however commonplace, which have something facile and caressing about them, succeed, by dint of education in symphonic culture, in mortifying that appetite. But once they have arrived at this point, when, dazzled—and rightly so— by the brilliant orchestral colouring of Richard Strauss, they see that musician adopt the most vulgar motifs with a self-indulgence worthy of Auber, what those people originally admired finds suddenly in so high an authority a justification which delights them, and they wallow without qualms and with a twofold gratitude, when they listen to *Salomé*, in what it would have been impossible for them to admire in *Les Diamants de la Couronne*.

Authentic or not, Mlle de Guermantes's apostrophe to the Grand Duke, retailed from house to house, provided an opportunity to relate with what excessive elegance Oriane had been turned out at the dinner-party in question. But if such splendour (and this is precisely what rendered it inaccessible to the Courvoisiers) springs not from wealth but from prodigality, the latter nevertheless lasts longer if it enjoys the constant support of the former, which then allows it to pull out all the stops. Now, given the principles openly paraded not only by Oriane but by Mme de Villeparisis, namely that nobility does not count, that it is ridiculous to bother one's head about rank, that money doesn't bring happiness, that intellect, heart, talent are alone of importance, the Courvoisiers were justified in hoping that, as a result of the training she had received from the Marquise, Oriane would marry someone who was not in society, an artist, an ex-convict, a tramp, a free-thinker, that she would enter for good and all into the category of what the Courvoisiers called "ne'er-do-wells." They were all the more justified in this hope because, inasmuch as Mme de Villeparisis was at that time going through an awkward crisis from the social point of view (none of the few bright stars whom I was to meet in her drawing-room had as yet reappeared there), she professed an intense horror of the society which thus excluded her. Even when she spoke of her nephew the Prince de Guermantes, whom she did still see, she never ceased mocking him because he was so infatuated with his pedigree. But the moment it became a question of finding a husband for Oriane, it was no longer the principles publicly paraded by aunt and niece that had guided the operation; it was the mysterious and ubiquitous "family genie." As unerringly as if Mme de Villeparisis and Oriane had never spoken of anything but rent-rolls and pedigrees instead of literary merit and depth of character, and as if the Marquise, for the space of a few days, had been—as she would ultimately be—dead and in her coffin in the church at Combray, where each member of the family became simply a Guermantes, with a forfeiture of individuality and baptismal names attested on the voluminous black drapery of the pall by the single 'G' in purple surmounted by the ducal coronet, it was on the wealthiest and the most nobly born, on the most eligible bachelor of the Faubourg Saint-Germain, on the eldest son of the Duc de Guermantes, the Prince des Laumes, that the family genie had fixed the choice of the intellectual, the rebellious, the evangelical Mme de Villeparisis. And for a couple of hours, on the day of the wedding, Mme de Villeparisis received in her drawing-room all the noble persons whom she had been in the habit of deriding, whom she even derided with the few bourgeois intimates whom she had invited and on whom the Prince des Laumes promptly left cards, preparatory to "cutting the painter" in the following year. And then, making the Courvoisiers' cup of bitterness overflow, the same old maxims according to which intellect and talent were the sole claims to social pre-eminence began once more to be trotted out in the household of the Princesse des Laumes immediately after her marriage. And in this respect, be it said in passing, the point of view which Saint-Loup upheld when he lived with Rachel, frequented the friends of Rachel, would have liked to marry Rachel, entailed—whatever the horror that it inspired in the family—less falsehood than that of the Guermantes young ladies in general, extolling the intellect, barely allowing the possibility that anyone could question the equality of mankind, all of which led, when it came to the point, to the same result as if they had professed the opposite principles, that is to say to marrying an extremely wealthy duke. Saint-Loup, on the contrary, acted in conformity with his theories, which led people to say that he was treading in evil ways. Certainly from the moral standpoint Rachel was not altogether satisfactory. But it is by no means certain that, if she had been no more virtuous but a duchess or the heiress to many millions, Mme de Marsantes would not have been in favour of the match.

However, to return to Mme des Laumes (shortly afterwards Duchesse de Guermantes, on the death of her father-in-law), it was the last agonising straw for the Courvoisiers that the

theories of the young Princess, remaining thus confined to
her speech, should in no way have guided her conduct; with
the result that this philosophy (if one may so call it) did not
impair the aristocratic elegance of the Guermantes drawing-
room. No doubt all the people whom Mme de Guermantes
did not invite imagined that it was because they were not
clever enough, and a rich American lady who had never
possessed any other book except a little old copy, never
opened, of Parny's poems, arranged because it was "of the
period" on one of the tables in her small drawing-room,
showed how much store she set by the things of the mind by
the devouring gaze which she fastened on the Duchesse de
Guermantes when that lady made her appearance at the
Opéra. No doubt, too, Mme de Guermantes was sincere when
she elected a person on account of his or her intelligence.
When she said of a woman: "It appears she's quite charming!"
or of a man that he was the "cleverest person in the world,"
she imagined herself to have no other reason for consenting
to receive them than this charm or cleverness, the family
genie not interposing itself at the last moment; more deeply-
rooted, stationed at the obscure entrance to the region in
which the Guermantes exercised their judgment, this vigilant
spirit precluded them from finding the man clever or the
woman charming if they had no social merit, actual or potential. The man was pronounced learned, but like a dictionary,
or, on the contrary, common, with the mind of a commercial
traveller, the woman pretty, but with a terribly bad style, or
too talkative. As for the people who had no definite position,
they were simply dreadful—such snobs! M. de Bréauté, whose
country house was quite close to Guermantes, mixed with no
one below the rank of Highness. But he was totally indifferent
to them and longed only to spend his days in museums.
Accordingly Mme de Guermantes was indignant when anyone
spoke of M. de Bréauté as a snob. "Babal a snob! But, my
dear man, you must be mad, he's just the opposite. He loathes
smart people; he won't let himself be introduced to anyone.
Even in my house! If I invite him to meet someone he doesn't
know, he never stops grumbling when he comes."

This was not to say that, even in practice, the Guermantes

did not set altogether more store by intelligence than the Courvoisiers. In a positive sense, this difference between the Guermantes and the Courvoisiers had already begun to bear very promising fruit. Thus the Duchesse de Guermantes, enveloped moreover in a mystery which had set so many poets dreaming of her from afar, had given that ball to which I have already referred, at which the King of England had enjoyed himself more thoroughly than anywhere else, for she had had the idea, which would never have occurred to the Courvoisier mind, of inviting, and the audacity, from which the Courvoisier courage would have recoiled, to invite, apart from the personages already mentioned, the musician Gaston Lemaire and the dramatist Grandmougin. But it was chiefly from the negative point of view that intellectuality made itself felt. If the necessary coefficient of cleverness and charm declined steadily as the rank of the person who sought an invitation from the Duchesse de Guermantes became more exalted, vanishing to zero when it came to the principal crowned heads of Europe, conversely the further they fell below this royal level the higher the coefficient rose. For instance, at the Princesse de Parme's receptions there were a number of people whom Her Royal Highness invited because she had known them as children, or because they were related to some duchess, or attached to the person of some sovereign, they themselves being quite possibly ugly, boring or stupid. Now, in the case of a Courvoisier reasons such as "a favourite of the Princesse de Parme," or "a niece on the mother's side of the Duchesse d'Arpajon," or "spends three months every year with the Queen of Spain," would have been sufficient to make her invite such people to her house, but Mme de Guermantes, who had politely acknowledged their greetings for ten years at the Princesse de Parme's, had never once allowed them to cross her threshold, considering that the same rule applied to a drawing-room in a social as in a physical sense, where it only needed a few pieces of furniture which had no particular beauty, but were left there to fill the room and as a sign of the owner's wealth, to render it hideous. Such a drawing-room resembled a book in which the author cannot refrain from the use of language advertising his own learning, brilliance, fluency. Like a book, like a house, the quality of a "salon," Mme de Guermantes rightly thought, is based on the corner-stone of sacrifice.

Many of the friends of the Princesse de Parme, with whom the Duchesse de Guermantes had confined herself for years past to the same conventional greeting, or to returning their cards, without ever inviting them to her house or going to theirs, complained discreetly of these omissions to Her Highness who, on days when M. de Guermantes came by himself to see her, dropped a hint of it to him. But the wily nobleman, a bad husband to the Duchess in so far as he kept mistresses, but her most tried and trusty friend in everything that concerned the proper functioning of her salon (and her own wit, which formed its chief attraction), replied: "But does my wife know her? Indeed! Oh, well, I daresay she ought to have. But the truth is, Ma'am, that Oriane doesn't care for women's conversations. She lives surrounded by a court of superior minds— I'm not her husband, I'm only the first chamberlain. Except for quite a small number, who are all of them very witty indeed, women bore her. Surely, Ma'am, Your Highness with all her fine judgment is not going to tell me that the Marquise de Souvré has any wit. Yes, I quite understand, Your Highness receives her out of kindness. Besides, Your Highness knows her. You tell me that Oriane has met her; it's quite possible, but once or twice at the most, I assure you. And then, I must explain to Your Highness, it's really a little my fault as well. My wife is very easily tired, and she's so anxious to be friendly always that if I allowed her she would never stop going to see people. Only yesterday evening, although she had a temperature, she was afraid of hurting the Duchesse de Bourbon's feelings by not going to see her. I had to show my teeth, I can tell you; I positively forbade them to bring the carriage round. Do you know, Ma'am, I've a very good mind not to mention to Oriane that you've spoken to me about Mme de Souvré. Oriane is so devoted to Your Highness that she'll go round at once to invite Mme de Souvré to the house; that will mean another call to be paid, it will oblige us to make friends with the sister, whose husband I know quite well. I think I shall say nothing at all about it to Oriane, if Your Highness has no objection. We'll save her a great deal of strain and agitation. And I assure you that it will be no loss to Mme de Souvré. She goes everywhere, moves in the most brilliant circles. We scarcely entertain at all, really, just a few little friendly dinners. Mme de Souvré would be bored to death." The Princesse de Parme, innocently convinced that the Duc de Guermantes would not transmit her request to the Duchess, and dismayed by her failure to procure the invitation that Mme de Souvré sought, was all the more flattered to think that she herself was one of the regular frequenters of so exclusive a household. No doubt this satisfaction had its drawbacks also. Thus whenever the Princesse de Parme invited Mme de Guermantes to her own parties she had to rack her brains to be sure that there was no one else on her list whose presence might offend the Duchess and make her refuse to come again.

On her habitual evenings, after dinner, to which she always invited a few people (very early, for she clung to old customs), the Princesse de Parme's drawing-room was thrown open to her regular guests and, generally speaking, to the whole of the higher aristocracy, French and foreign. The order of her receptions was as follows: on issuing from the dining-room the Princess sat down on a settee in front of a large round table and chatted with two of the most important ladies who had dined with her, or else cast her eyes over a magazine, or sometimes played cards (or pretended to play, following a German court custom), either a game of patience or selecting as her real or pretended partner some prominent personage. By nine o'clock the double doors of the big drawing-room were in constant action, opening and shutting and opening again to admit the visitors who had dined quietly at home (or if they had dined "out," skipped coffee, promising to return later, having intended only "to go in at one door and out at the other") in order to conform with the Princess's time-table. She, meanwhile, attentive to her game or conversation, made a show of not seeing the new arrivals, and it was not until they were actually within reach of her that she rose graciously from her seat, with a benevolent smile for the women. The latter thereupon sank before the standing Princess in a curtsey which was tantamount to a genuflexion, in such a way as to bring their lips down to the level of the beautiful hand which hung very low, and to kiss it. But at that moment the Princess, just as if she had been surprised each time by a protocol with which nevertheless she was perfectly familiar, raised the kneeling lady as though by main force, but with incomparable grace and sweetness, and kissed her on both cheeks. A grace and sweetness that were conditional, you may say, upon the meekness with which the arriving guest bent her knee. Very likely; and it would seem that in an egalitarian society social etiquette would vanish, not, as is generally supposed, from want of breeding, but because on the one side would disappear the deference due to a prestige which must be imaginary to be effective, and on the other, more completely still, the affability that is gracefully and generously dispensed when it is felt to be of infinite price to the recipient, a price which, in a world based on equality, would at once fall to nothing like everything that has only a fiduciary value. But this disappearance of social distinctions in a reconstructed society is by no means a foregone conclusion, and we are at times too ready to believe that present circumstances are the only ones in which a state of things can survive. People of first-rate intelligence believed that a republic could not have any diplomacy or foreign alliances, and that the peasant class would not tolerate the separation of Church and State. After all, the survival of etiquette in an egalitarian society would be no more miraculous than the practical success of the railways or the use of the aeroplane in war. Besides, even if politeness were to vanish, there is nothing to show that this would be a misfortune. Finally, would not society become secretly more hierarchical as it became outwardly more democratic? Very possibly. The political power of of the Popes has grown enormously since they ceased to possess either States or an army; our cathedrals meant far less to a devout Catholic of the seventeenth century than they mean to an atheist of the twentieth, and if the Princesse de Parme had been the sovereign ruler of a State, no doubt I should have felt moved to speak of her about as much as of a President of the Republic, that is to say not at all.

As soon as the postulant had been raised up and embraced by the Princess, the latter resumed her seat and returned to her game of patience, unless the newcomer was a lady of some distinction, in which case she sat her down in an armchair and chatted to her for a while.

When the room became too crowded the lady in waiting who had to control the traffic cleared some space by leading the regular guests into an immense hall on to which the drawing-room opened, a hall filled with portraits and minor trophies relating to the House of Bourbon. The intimate friends of the Princess would then volunteer as guides and tell interesting anecdotes, to which the young people had not the patience to listen, more interested in the spectacle of living royalty (with the possibility of getting themselves presented to it by the lady in waiting and the maids of honour) than in examining the relics of dead sovereigns. Too occupied with the acquaintances they might be able to make and the invitations they might be able to pick up, they knew absolutely nothing, even after several years, of what there was in this priceless museum of the archives of the monarchy, and could only recall vaguely that it was decorated with cacti and giant palms which gave this centre of social elegance a look of the palmarium in the Zoological gardens.

Of course the Duchesse de Guermantes, by way of self-mortification, did occasionally appear on these evenings to pay an "after dinner" call on the Princess, who kept her all the time by her side, while exchanging pleasantries with the Duke. But on evenings when the Duchess came to dine, the Princess took care not to invite her regular party, and closed her doors to the world on rising from table, for fear lest a too liberal selection of guests might offend the exacting Duchess. On such evenings, were any of the faithful who had not received warning to present themselves on the royal doorstep, they would be informed by the porter: "Her Royal Highness is not at home this evening," and would turn away. But many of the Princess's friends would have known in advance that on the day in question they would not be asked to her house. These were a special catagory of parties, a category barred to many who must have longed for admission. Those who were excluded could with virtual certainty enumerate the roll of the elect, and would say irritably among themselves: "You know, of course, that Oriane de Guermantes never goes anywhere

without her entire general staff." With the help of this body,
the Princesse de Parme sought to surround the Duchess as
with a protective rampart against those persons the chance of
whose making a good impression on her was at all doubtful.
But there were several of the Duchess's favourites, several
members of this glittering "staff," for whom the Princesse de
Parme resented having to put herself out, seeing that they paid
little or no attention to herself. No doubt the Princess was fully
prepared to admit that people might derive more enjoyment
from the company of the Duchesse de Guermantes than from
her own. She could not deny that there was always a "crush"
at the Duchess's "at homes," or that she herself often met
there three or four royal personages who thought it sufficient
to leave their cards upon her. And in vain might she commit
to memory Oriane's witty sayings, copy her gowns, serve at
her own tea-parties the same strawberry tarts, there were
occasions on which she was left by herself all afternoon with a
lady in waiting and some councillor from a foreign legation.
And so whenever (as had been the case with Swann, for
instance, at an earlier period) there was anyone who never let a
day pass without going to spend an hour or two at the
Duchess's and paid a call once every two years on the Princesse
de Parme, the latter felt no great desire, even for the sake of
amusing Oriane, to make "advances" to this Swann or whoever he was by inviting him to dinner. In a word, having the
Duchess in her house was for the Princess a source of endless
perplexity, so haunted was she by the fear that Oriane would
find fault with everything. But in return, and for the same
reason, when the Princesse de Parme came to dine with Mme
de Guermantes she could be certain in advance that everything
would be perfect, delightful, and she had only one fear, which
was that of being unable to understand, remember, give
satisfaction, being unable to assimilate new ideas and people.
On this score, my presence aroused her attention and excited
her cupidity, just as might a new way of decorating the dinner-
table with garlands of fruit, uncertain as she was which of the
two—the table decorations or my presence—was the more
distinctively one of those charms which were the secret of the
success of Oriane's receptions, and in her uncertainty firmly

resolved to try to have them both at her own next dinner-party. What in fact fully justified the enraptured curiosity which the Princesse de Parme brought to the Duchess's house was that comic, dangerous, exciting element into which the Princess used to plunge with a thrill of anxiety, shock and delight (as at the seaside on one of those days of "big seas" of the danger of which the bathing-attendants warn one for the simple reason that none of them can swim), and from which she would emerge feeling braced, happy, rejuvenated—the element known as the wit of the Guermantes. The wit of the Guermantes—a thing as non-existent as the squared circle, according to the Duchess who regarded herself as the sole Guermantes to possess it—was a family reputation like that of the *rillettes* of Tours or the biscuits of Rheims. However (since an intellectual characteristic does not employ for its propagation the same channels as the colour of hair or complexion) certain intimate friends of the Duchess who were not of her blood were nevertheless endowed with this wit, which on the other hand had failed to inculcate itself into various Guermantes who were all too resistant to wit of any kind. For the most part, the custodians of the Guermantes wit who were not related to the Duchess shared the characteristic feature of having been brilliant men, eminently fitted for a career to which, whether in the arts, diplomacy, parliamentary eloquence or the army, they had preferred the life of society. Possibly this preference could be explained by a certain lack of originality, of initiative, of will power, of health or of luck, or possibly by snobbishness.

With certain of them (though these, it must be admitted, were the exception), if the Guermantes drawing-room had been the stumbling-block in their careers, it had been against their will. Thus a doctor, a painter and a diplomat of great promise had failed to achieve success in the careers for which they were nevertheless more brilliantly endowed than most because their friendship with the Guermantes had resulted in the first two being regarded as men of fashion and the third as a reactionary, and this had prevented all three from winning the recognition of their peers. The mediaeval gown and red cap which are still donned by the electoral colleges of the Faculties are (or were, at least, not so long since) something more than a purely outward survival from a narrow-minded past, from a rigid sectarianism. Under the cap with its golden tassels, like the high priests in the conical mitre of the Jews, the "professors" were still, in the years that preceded the Dreyfus case, fast rooted in rigorously pharisaical ideas. Du Boulbon was at heart an artist, but was safe because he did not care for society. Cottard was always at the Verdurins', but Mme Verdurin was a patient, he was moreover protected by his vulgarity, and at his own house he entertained no one outside the Faculty, at banquets over which there floated an aroma of carbolic acid. But in strongly corporate bodies, where moreover the rigidity of their prejudices is but the price that must be paid for the noblest integrity, the most lofty conceptions of morality, which wither in more tolerant, more liberal, ulti-mately more corrupt atmospheres, a professor in his gown of scarlet satin faced with ermine, like that of a Doge (which is to say a Duke) of Venice shut away in the ducal palace, was as virtuous, as deeply attached to noble principles, but as pitiless towards any alien element as that other admirable but fear-some duke, M. de Saint-Simon. The alien, here, was the worldly doctor, with other manners, other social relations. To make good, the unfortunate of whom we are now speaking, so as not to be accused by his colleagues of looking down on them (who but a man of fashion would think of such an idea!) if he concealed the Duchesse de Guermantes from them, hoped to disarm them by giving mixed dinner-parties in which the medical element was merged in the fashionable. He was unaware that in so doing he signed his own death-warrant, or rather he discovered this when the Council of Ten (a little larger in number) had to fill a vacant chair, and it was in-variably the name of another doctor, more normal if more mediocre, that emerged from the fatal urn, and the "Veto" thundered round the ancient Faculty, as solemn, as absurd and as terrible as the "Juro" that spelt the death of Molière. So too with the painter permanently labelled man of fashion, when fashionable people who dabbled in art had succeeded in getting themselves labelled artists; so with the diplomat who had too many reactionary associations.

But these cases were rare. The prototype of the distinguished men who formed the main substance of the Guermantes salon was someone who had voluntarily (or at least they supposed) renounced all else, everything that was incompatible with the wit of the Guermantes, with the courtesy of the Guermantes, with that indefinable charm odious to any "body" that is at all "corporate."

And the people who were aware that one of the habitués of the Duchess's drawing-room had once been awarded the gold medal of the Salon, that another, Secretary to the Bar Council, had made a brilliant début in the Chamber, that a third had ably served France as chargé d'affaires, might have been led to regard as "failures" people who had now done nothing for twenty years. But there were few who were thus "in the know," and the persons concerned would themselves have been the last to remind one, finding these old distinctions valueless, precisely by virtue of the Guermantes wit: for did not this encourage them to denounce on the one hand as a bore and a pedant, on the other as a counter-jumper, a pair of eminent Ministers, one a trifle solemn, the other addicted to puns, whose praises the newspapers were constantly singing but in whose company Mme de Guermantes would begin to yawn and show signs of impatience if a hostess had rashly placed either of them next to her at the dinner-table. Since being a statesman of the first rank was in no sense a recommendation in the eyes of the Duchess, those of her friends who had abandoned the "Career" or the "Service," who had never stood for parliament, felt, as they came day after day to have lunch and talk with their great friend, or when they met her in the houses of royal personages—incidentally held in low esteem by them (or so they said)—that they had chosen the better part, albeit their melancholy air, even in the midst of the gaiety, seemed somehow to impugn the validity of this judgment.

And it must be acknowledged that the refinement of social life, the sparkle of the conversation at the Guermantes' did have something real about it, however exiguous it may have been. No official title was worth more than the personal charm of certain of Mme de Guermantes's favourites whom

the most powerful ministers would have been unable to attract
to their houses. If in this drawing-room so many intellectual
ambitions and even noble efforts had been for ever buried, still
at least from their dust the rarest flowering of civilised society
had sprung to life. Certainly men of wit, such as Swann for
instance, regarded themselves as superior to men of merit,
whom they despised, but that was because what the Duchess
valued above everything else was not intelligence but—a
superior form of intelligence, according to her, rarer, more
exquisite, raising it up to a verbal variety of talent—wit. And
long ago at the Verdurins', when Swann denounced Brichot
and Elstir, one as a pedant and the other as an oaf, despite all
the learning of the one and the genius of the other, it was the
infiltration of the Guermantes spirit that had led him to
classify them thus. Never would he have dared to introduce
either of them to the Duchess, conscious instinctively of the
air with which she would have listened to Brichot's perorations
and Elstir's "balderdash," the Guermantes spirit consigning
pretentious and prolix speech, whether in a serious or a farcical
vein, to the category of the most intolerable imbecility.

As for the Guermantes of the true flesh and blood, if the
Guermantes spirit had not infected them as completely as we
see occur in, for example, those literary coteries in which
everyone has the same way of pronouncing, enunciating and
consequently thinking, it was certainly not because originality
is stronger in social circles and inhibits imitation therein. But
imitation requires not only the absence of any unconquerable
originality but also a relative fineness of ear which enables
one first of all to discern what one is afterwards to imitate.
And there were several Guermantes in whom this musical
sense was as entirely lacking as in the Courvoisiers.

To take as an instance what is called, in another sense of the
word imitation, "giving imitations" (or among the Guermantes was called "taking off"), for all that Mme de Guermantes could bring these off to perfection, the Courvoisiers
were as incapable of appreciating it as if they had been a tribe
of rabbits instead of men and women, because they had never
managed to observe the particular defect or accent that the
Duchess was endeavouring to mimic. When she "gave an

imitation" of the Duc de Limoges, the Courvoisiers would protest: "Oh, no, he doesn't really speak like that. I met him again only last night at dinner at Bebeth's; he talked to me all evening and he didn't speak like that at all!" whereas any Guermantes who was at all cultivated would exclaim: "Goodness, how droll Oriane is! The amazing thing is that when she's mimicking him she looks exactly like him! I feel I'm listening to him. Oriane, do give us a little more Limoges!" Now these Guermantes (without even including those absolutely remarkable members of the clan who, when the Duchess imitated the Duc de Limoges, would say admiringly: "Oh, you really have got him," or "You do hit him off!") might be devoid of wit according to Mme de Guermantes (in this respect she was right), but by dint of hearing and repeating her sayings they had come to imitate more or less her way of expressing herself, of criticising people, of what Swann, like the Duchess herself, would have called her way of "phrasing" things, so that they presented in their conversation something which to the Courvoisiers appeared appallingly similar to Oriane's wit and was treated by them collectively as the Guermantes wit. As these Guermantes were to her not merely kinsfolk but admirers, Oriane (who kept the rest of the family rigorously at arm's-length and now avenged by her disdain the spitefulness they had shown her in her girlhood) went to call on them now and then, generally in the company of the Duke, when she drove out with him in the summer months. These visits were an event. The Princesse d'Epinay's heart would begin to beat more rapidly, as she entertained in her big drawing-room on the ground floor, when she saw from a distance, like the first glow of an innocuous fire, or the scouting party of an unexpected invasion, making her way slowly across the courtyard in a diagonal course, the Duchess wearing a ravishing hat and holding atilt a sunshade redolent with a summer fragrance. "Why, here comes Oriane," she would say, like an "On guard!" intended to convey a prudent warning to her visitors, so that they should have time to beat an orderly retreat, to evacuate the rooms without panic. Half of those present dared not remain, and rose at once to go. "But no, why? Sit down again, I insist on keeping you a little longer," the Princess would say in an airy, off-hand manner (to show herself the great lady) but in a voice that suddenly rang false. "But you may want to talk to each other." "Really, you're in a hurry? Oh, very well, I shall come and see you," the lady of the house would reply to those whom she would just as soon see leave. The Duke and Duchess would give a very civil greeting to people whom they had seen there regularly for years though without coming to know them any better, while these in return barely said good-day to them, from discretion. Scarcely had they left the room before the Duke would begin asking good-naturedly who they were, so as to appear to be taking an interest in the intrinsic quality of people whom he never saw in his own house owing to the malevolence of fate or the state of Oriane's nerves which the company of women was bad for:

"Tell me, who was that little woman in the pink hat?"

"Why, my dear cousin, you've seen her hundreds of times, she's the Vicomtesse de Tours, who was a Lamarzelle."

"But, do you know, she's very pretty, and she has a witty look. If it weren't for a little flaw in her upper lip she'd be a regular charmer. If there's a Vicomte de Tours, he can't have any too bad a time. Oriane, do you know who her eyebrows and the way her hair grows reminded me of? Your cousin Hedwige de Ligne."

The Duchesse de Guermantes, who languished whenever people spoke of the beauty of any woman other than herself, let the subject drop. She had reckoned without the weakness of her husband for letting it be seen that he knew all about the people who did not come to his house, whereby he believed that he showed himself to be more "serious" than his wife.

"But," he would suddenly resume with emphasis, "you mentioned the name Lamarzelle. I remember, when I was in the Chamber, hearing a really remarkable speech made . . ."

"That was the uncle of the young woman you saw just now."

"Indeed! What talent! No, my dear girl," he assured the Vicomtesse d'Egremont, whom Mme de Guermantes could not endure but who, refusing to stir from the Princesse d'Epinay's drawing-room where she willingly stooped to the role of parlour-maid (though it did not prevent her from slapping her own on returning home), stayed there, tearful and abashed, but nevertheless stayed, when the ducal couple were there, taking their cloaks, trying to make herself useful, discreetly offering to withdraw into the next room, "you're not to make tea for us, let's just sit and talk quietly, we're simple, homely souls. Besides," he went on, turning to the Princesse d'Epinay (leaving the Egremont lady blushing, humble, ambitious and full of zeal), "we can only spare you a quarter of an hour."

This quarter of an hour would be entirely taken up with a sort of exhibition of the witty things which the Duchess had said during the previous week, and to which she herself would certainly have refrained from alluding had not her husband, with great adroitness, by appearing to be rebuking her with reference to the incidents that had provoked them, obliged her as though against her will to repeat them.

The Princesse d'Epinay, who was fond of her cousin and knew that she had a weakness for compliments, would go into ecstasies over her hat, her sunshade, her wit. "Talk to her as much as you like about her clothes," the Duke would say in the surly tone which he had adopted and now tempered with a mocking smile so that his displeasure should not be taken seriously, "but for heaven's sake don't speak of her wit. I could do without having such a witty wife. You're probably alluding to the shocking pun she made about my brother Palamède," he went on, knowing quite well that the Princess and the rest of the family had not yet heard this pun, and delighted to have an opportunity of showing off his wife. "In the first place I consider it unworthy of a person who has occasionally, I must admit, said some quite good things, to make bad puns, but especially about my brother, who is very touchy, and if it's going to lead to bad blood between us, that would really be too much of a good thing."

"But we've no idea! One of Oriane's puns? It's sure to be delicious. Oh, do tell us!"

"No, no," the Duke went on, still surly though with a broader smile, "I'm delighted you haven't heard it. Seriously, I'm very fond of my brother."

"Look here, Basin," the Duchess would break in, the

moment having come for her to take up her husband's cue,
"I can't think why you should say that it might annoy
Palamède, you know quite well it would do nothing of the
sort. He's far too intelligent to be offended by a stupid joke
which has nothing offensive about it. You'll make them think
I said something nasty; I simply made a remark which wasn't
in the least funny, it's you who make it seem important by
getting so indignant. I don't understand you."

"You're being horribly tantalising. What's it all about?"

"Oh, obviously nothing serious!" cried M. de Guermantes.
"You may have heard that my brother offered to give Brézé,
the place he got from his wife, to his sister Marsantes."

"Yes, but we were told she didn't want it, that she didn't
care for that part of the country, that the climate didn't suit
her."

"Precisely. Well, someone was telling my wife all that and
saying that if my brother was giving this place to our sister it
wasn't so much to please her as to tease her. 'He's such a
teaser, Charlus,' was what they actually said. Well, you know
Brézé is really impressive, I should say it's worth millions, it
used to be part of the crown lands, it includes one of the finest
forests in France. There are plenty of people who would be
only too delighted to be teased to that tune. And so when she
heard the words 'teaser' applied to Charlus because he was
giving away such a magnificent property, Oriane couldn't
help exclaiming, quite involuntarily, I must admit, without the
slightest suggestion of malice, for it came out like a flash of
lightning: 'Teaser, teaser? Then he must be Teaser Augustus!'
You understand," he went on, resuming his surly tone, having
first cast a sweeping glance round the room in order to judge
the effect of his wife's witticism—and in some doubt as to
the extent of Mme d'Epinay's acquaintance with ancient
history, "you understand, it's an allusion to Augustus Caesar,
the Roman Emperor. It's too stupid, a bad play on words,
quite unworthy of Oriane. And then, you see, I'm more circumspect than my wife. Even if I haven't her wit, I think of
the consequences. If anyone should be so ill-advised as to
repeat the remark to my brother there'll be the devil to pay.
All the more so," he went on, "because as you know Palamède

is very high and mighty, and very carping also, given to gossip
and all that sort of thing, so that quite apart from the question
of his giving away Brézé you must admit that 'Teaser
Augustus' suits him down to the ground. That's what justifies
my wife's quips; even when she stoops to feeble puns, she's
always witty and does really describe people rather well."

And so, thanks on one occasion to "Teaser Augustus," on
another to something else, the visits paid by the Duke and
Duchess to their kinsfolk replenished the stock of anecdotes,
and the excitement they had caused lasted long after the departure of the sparkling lady and her impresario. The hostess
would begin by going over again with the privileged persons
who had been at the entertainment (those who had remained)
the clever things that Oriane had said. "You hadn't heard
'Teaser Augustus'?" the Princesse d'Epinay would ask.
"Yes," the Marquise de Baveno would reply, blushing as she
spoke, "the Princesse de Sarsina-La Rochefoucauld mentioned
it to me, not quite in the same terms. But of course it was far
more interesting to hear it repeated like that with my cousin
in the room," she went on, as though speaking of a song that
had been accompanied by the composer himself. "We were
speaking of Oriane's latest—she was here just now," her
hostess would greet a visitor who was very disconsolate at not
having arrived an hour earlier.

"What! has Oriane been here?"

"Yes, if you'd come a little sooner . . ." the Princesse
d'Epinay replied, not in reproach but making it clear how
much the blunderer had missed. It was her fault alone if she
had not been present at the creation of the world or at Mme
Carvalho's last performance. "What do you think of Oriane's
latest? I must say I do like 'Teaser Augustus,' " and the "quip"
would be served up again cold next day at lunch before a few
intimate friends invited for the purpose, and would reappear
under various sauces throughout the week. Indeed Mme
d'Epinay happening in the course of that week to pay her
annual visit to the Princesse de Parme, seized the opportunity
to ask whether Her Royal Highness had heard the pun, and
repeated it to her. "Ah! Teaser Augustus," said the Princesse
de Parme, wide-eyed with an instinctive admiration, which

begged however for a complementary elucidation which Mme
d'Epinay was not loth to furnish. "I must say Teaser Augustus
pleases me enormously as a piece of 'phrasing,'" she concluded. As a matter of fact the word "phrasing" was not in the
least applicable to this pun, but the Princesse d'Epinay, who
claimed to have assimilated her share of the Guermantes
wit, had borrowed from Oriane the expressions "phrased"
and "phrasing" and employed them without much discrimina-
tion. Now the Princesse de Parme, who was not at all fond of
Mme d'Epinay, whom she considered plain, knew to be
miserly, and believed, on the authority of the Courvoisiers, to
be malicious, recognised this word "phrasing" which she had
heard on Mme de Guermantes's lips but would not herself
have known how or when to apply. She concluded that it
must indeed be its "phrasing" that formed the charm of
"Teaser Augustus" and, without altogether forgetting her
antipathy towards the plain and miserly lady, could not repress
an impulse of admiration for a person endowed to such a degree
with the Guermantes wit, so much so that she was on the point
of inviting the Princesse d'Epinay to the Opéra. She was held
in check only by the reflexion that it would be wiser perhaps
to consult Mme de Guermantes first. As for Mme d'Epinay,
who, unlike the Courvoisiers, was endlessly obliging towards
Oriane and was genuinely fond of her, but was jealous of her
exalted friends and slightly irritated by the fun which the
Duchess used to make of her in front of everyone on account of
her meanness, she reported on her return home how much
difficulty the Princesse de Parme had had in grasping the point
of "Teaser Augustus," and declared what a snob Oriane must
be to number such a goose among her friends. "I should never
have been able to see much of the Princesse de Parme even if I
had wanted to, because M. d'Epinay would never have allowed
it on account of her immorality," she told the friends who were
dining with her, alluding to certain purely imaginary excesses
on the part of the Princess. "But even if I had had a husband
less strict in his views, I must say I could never have made
friends with her. I don't know how Oriane can bear to see her
every other day, as she does. I go there once a year, and it's all
I can do to sit out my call."

As for those of the Courvoisiers who happened to be at
Victurnienne's on the day of Mme de Guermantes's visit, the
arrival of the Duchess generally put them to flight owing to the
exasperation they felt at the "ridiculous salaams" that were
made to her there. One alone remained on the evening of
"Teaser Augustus." He did not entirely see the point, but he
half-understood it, being an educated man. And the Courvoisiers went about repeating that Oriane had called uncle
Palamède "Caesar Augustus," which was, according to them,
a good enough description of him. But why all this endless
talk about Oriane, they went on. People couldn't make more
fuss about a queen. "After all, what is Oriane? I don't say
the Guermantes aren't an old family, but the Courvoisiers are
every bit as good in rank, antiquity, marriages. We mustn't
forget that on the Field of the Cloth of Gold, when the King
of England asked François I who was the noblest of the lords
there present, 'Sire,' said the King of France, 'Courvoisier.' "
But even if all the Courvoisiers had stayed in the room to hear
them, Oriane's witticisms would have fallen on deaf ears, since
the incidents that usually gave rise to them would have been
regarded by them from a totally different point of view. If, for
instance, a Courvoisier found herself running short of chairs
in the middle of a reception she was giving, or if she used the
wrong name in greeting a guest whose face she did not remember, or if one of her servants said something stupid, the
Courvoisier lady, extremely annoyed, flushed, quivering with
agitation, would deplore so unfortunate an occurrence. And
when she had a visitor in the room, and Oriane was expected,
she would ask in an anxious and imperious tone: "Do you
know her?", fearing that if the visitor did not know her his
presence might make a bad impression on Oriane. But Mme
de Guermantes on the contrary drew from such incidents
opportunities for stories which made the Guermantes laugh
until the tears streamed down their cheeks, so that one was
obliged to envy her for having run short of chairs, for having
herself made or allowed her servant to make a gaffe, for having
had at a party someone whom nobody knew, as one is obliged
to be thankful that great writers have been kept at a distance
by men and betrayed by women when their humiliations and

their sufferings have been if not the direct stimulus of their genius at any rate the subject matter of their works.

The Courvoisiers were equally incapable of rising to the spirit of innovation which the Duchesse de Guermantes introduced into the life of society and which, by adapting it with an unerring instinct to the necessities of the moment, made it into something artistic, where the purely rational application of cut and dried rules would have produced results as unfortunate as would greet a man who, anxious to succeed in love or in politics, reproduced to the letter in his own life the exploits of Bussy d'Amboise. If the Courvoisiers gave a family dinner or a dinner to meet some prince, the addition of a recognised wit, of some friend of their son, seemed to them an anomaly capable of producing the direst consequences. A Courvoisier lady whose father had been a Minister under the Empire, having to give an afternoon party in honour of the Princesse Mathilde, deduced with a geometrical logic that she could invite no one but Bonapartists—of whom she knew practically none. All the smart women of her acquaintance, all the amusing men, were ruthlessly barred because, with their Legitimist views or connexions, they might, according to Courvoisier logic, have given offence to the Imperial Highness. The latter, who in her own house entertained the flower of the Faubourg Saint-Germain, was somewhat surprised when she found at Mme de Courvoisier's only a notorious old sponger whose husband had been a prefect under the Empire, the widow of the Director of Posts, and sundry others known for their loyalty to Napoleon III, for their stupidity and for their dullness. The Princesse Mathilde nevertheless in no way constrained the sweet and generous outpouring of her sovereign grace over these calamitous ugly ducklings, whom the Duchesse de Guermantes, for her part, took good care not to invite when it was her turn to entertain the Princess, but substituted for them, without any *a priori* reasoning about Bonapartism, the most brilliant coruscation of all the beauties, all the talents, all the celebrities whom, by some subtle sixth sense, she felt likely to be acceptable to the niece of the Emperor even when they actually belonged to the Royal House. Not even the Duc d'Aumale was excluded, and when,

on withdrawing, the Princess, raising Mme de Guermantes
from the ground where she had sunk in a curtsey and was
about to kiss the august hand, embraced her on both cheeks, it
was from the bottom of her heart that she was able to assure
the Duchess that never had she spent a happier afternoon nor
attended so successful a party. The Princesse de Parme was
Courvoisier in her incapacity for innovation in social matters
but unlike the Courvoisiers in that the surprise that was
perpetually caused her by the Duchesse de Guermantes engendered in her not, as in them, antipathy, but wonderment.
This feeling was still further enhanced by the infinitely backward state of the Princess's education. Mme de Guermantes
was herself a great deal less advanced than she supposed. But
she had only to be a little ahead of Mme de Parme to astound
that lady, and, as the critics of each generation confine themselves to maintaining the direct opposite of the truths acknowledged by their predecessors, she had only to say that
Flaubert, that arch-enemy of the bourgeoisie, had been bourgeois through and through, or that there was a great deal of
Italian music in Wagner, to open before the Princess, at the
cost of a nervous exhaustion that was constantly renewed,
as before the eyes of a swimmer in a stormy sea, horizons that
seemed to her unimaginable and remained for ever dim. A
stupefaction caused also by the paradoxes uttered not only in
connexion with works of art but with persons of their
acquaintance and with current social events. Doubtless the
incapacity that prevented Mme de Parme from distinguishing
the true wit of the Guermantes from certain rudimentarily
acquired forms of that wit (which made her believe in the
high intellectual worth of certain Guermantes, especially
certain female Guermantes, of whom afterwards she was
bewildered to hear the Duchess confide to her with a smile
that they were mere nitwits) was one of the causes of the
astonishment which the Princess always felt on hearing Mme
de Guermantes criticise other people. But there was another
cause also, one which I, who knew at that time more books
than people and literature better than life, explained to myself
by thinking that the Duchess, living this worldly life the idleness and sterility of which are to a true social activity what,

in art, criticism is to creation, extended to the persons who surrounded her the instability of viewpoint, the unhealthy thirst, of the caviller who, to quench a mind that has grown too dry, goes in search of no matter what paradox that is still fairly fresh, and will not hesitate to uphold the reinvigorating opinion that the really great *Iphigenia* is Piccini's and not Gluck's, and at a pinch that the true *Phèdre* is that of Pradon.

When an intelligent, witty, educated woman had married a shy bumpkin whom one seldom saw and never heard, Mme de Guermantes one fine day would find a rare intellectual pleasure not only in decrying the wife but in "discovering" the husband. In the Cambremer household, for example, if she had lived in that section of society at the time, she would have decreed that Mme de Cambremer was stupid, and that the really interesting person, misunderstood, delightful, condemned to silence by a chattering wife but himself worth a thousand of her, was the Marquis, and the Duchess would have felt on declaring this the same kind of refreshment as the critic who, after people have been admiring *Hernani* for seventy years, confesses to a preference for *Le Lion amoureux*. And from this same morbid need of arbitrary novelties, if from her girlhood everyone had been pitying a model wife, a true saint, for being married to a scoundrel, one fine day Mme de Guermantes would assert that this scoundrel was perhaps a frivolous man but one with a heart of gold, whom the implacable harshness of his wife had driven to commit serious indiscretions. I knew that it was not only between the works of different artists, in the long course of the centuries, but between the different works of the same artist, that criticism enjoyed thrusting back into the shade what for too long had been radiant and bringing to the fore what seemed doomed to permanent obscurity. I had not only seen Bellini, Winterhalter, the Jesuit architects, a Restoration cabinet-maker, come to take the place of men of genius who were called "well-worn" simply because the lazy minds of intellectuals had grown worn and weary of them, as neurasthenics are always worn and weary and fickle; I had seen Sainte-Beuve preferred alternately as critic and as poet, Musset rejected so far as his poetry went save for a few insignificant little plays, and extolled as a story-teller. No doubt certain essayists are mistaken when they set above the most famous scenes in *Le Cid* or *Polyeucte* some speech from *Le Menteur* which, like an old plan, gives us information about the Paris of the day, but their predilection, justified if not by considerations of beauty at least by a documentary interest, is still too rational for our criticism run mad. It will barter the whole of Molière for a line from *L'Etourdi*, and even when it pronounces Wagner's *Tristan* a bore will except a "charming note on the horns" at the point where the hunt goes by. This depravity of taste helped me to understand the similar perversity in Mme de Guermantes that made her decide that a man of their world, who was recognised as a good fellow but a fool, was a monster of egoism, sharper than people thought, that another who was well known for his generosity might be considered the personification of avarice, that a good mother paid no attention to her children, and that a woman generally supposed to be vicious was really actuated by the noblest sentiments. As though corrupted by the nullity of life in society, the intelligence and sensibility of Mme de Guermantes were too vacillating for disgust not to follow pretty swiftly in the wake of infatuation (leaving her still ready to be attracted afresh by the kind of cleverness which she had alternately sought and abandoned) and for the charm which she had found in some warm-hearted man not to change, if he came too often to see her, sought too freely from her a guidance which she was incapable of giving him, into an irritation which she believed to be produced by her admirer but which was in fact due to the utter impossibility of finding pleasure when one spends all one's time seeking it. The Duchess's vagaries of judgment spared no one, except her husband. He alone had never loved her; in him she had always felt an iron character, indifferent to her whims, contemptuous of her beauty, violent, one of those unbreakable wills under whose rule alone highly-strung people can find tranquillity. M. de Guermantes for his part, pursuing a single type of feminine beauty but seeking it in mistresses whom he constantly replaced, had, once he had left them, and to share with him in mocking them, one lasting and identical partner, who irritated him often by her chatter but as to whom he knew

that everyone regarded her as the most beautiful, the most
virtuous, the cleverest, the best-read member of the aristocracy, as a wife whom he, M. de Guermantes, was only too
fortunate to have found, who covered up for all his irregularities, entertained like no one else in the world, and upheld
for their salon its position as the premier in the Faubourg
Saint-Germain. This common opinion he himself shared;
often bad-tempered with his wife, he was proud of her. If,
being as niggardly as he was ostentatious, he refused her the
most trifling sums for her charities or for the servants, yet he
insisted on her having the most sumptuous clothes and the
finest equipages in Paris. And finally, he enjoyed bringing
out his wife's wit. Now, whenever Mme de Guermantes had
just thought up, with reference to the merits and defects,
suddenly transposed, of one of their friends, a new and succulent paradox, she longed to try it out on people capable of
appreciating it, to bring out the full savour of its psychological originality and the brilliance of its epigrammatic
malice. Of course these new opinions contained as a rule no
more truth than the old, often less; but this very element
of arbitrariness and unexpectedness conferred on them an
intellectual quality which made them exciting to communicate.
However, the patient on whom the Duchess was exercising
her psychological skill was generally an intimate friend as to
whom the people to whom she longed to hand on her discovery were entirely unaware that he was not still at the apex
of her favour; thus Mme de Guermantes's reputation for being
an incomparable friend, sentimental, tender and devoted,
made it difficult for her to launch the attack herself; she could
at the most intervene later on, as though under constraint,
by taking up a cue in order to appease, to contradict in appearance but actually to support a partner who had taken it on
himself to provoke her; this was precisely the role in which
M. de Guermantes excelled.

As for social activities, Mme de Guermantes enjoyed yet
another arbitrarily theatrical pleasure in expressing thereon
some of those unexpected judgments which whipped the
Princesse de Parme into a state of perpetual and delicious
surprise. In the case of this particular pleasure of the Duchess's,

it was not so much with the help of literary criticism as from
the example of political life and the reports of parliamentary
debates that I tried to understand in what it might consist. The
successive and contradictory edicts by which Mme de Guermantes continually reversed the scale of values among the
people of her world no longer sufficing to distract her, she
sought also in the manner in which she ordered her own social
behaviour, in which she accounted for her own most trifling
decisions on points of fashion, to savour those artificial emotions, to fulfil those factitious obligations, which stir the feelings of parliaments and impress themselves on the minds of
politicians. We know that when a minister explains to the
Chamber that he believed himself to be acting rightly in
following a line of conduct which does indeed appear quite
straightforward to the commonsense person who reads the
report of the sitting in his newspaper next morning, this
commonsense reader nevertheless feels suddenly stirred and
begins to doubt whether he has been right in approving the
minister's conduct when he sees that the latter's speech was
listened to in an uproar and punctuated with expressions of
condemnation such as: "It's most serious!" ejaculated by a
Deputy whose name and titles are so long, and followed in the
report by reactions so emphatic, that in the whole interruption
the words "It's most serious!" occupy less room than a
hemistich in an alexandrine. For instance in the days when
M. de Guermantes, Prince des Laumes, sat in the Chamber,
one used to read now and then in the Paris newspapers,
although it was intended primarily for the Méséglise division,
to show the electors there that they had not given their votes
to an inactive or voiceless representative:

MONSIEUR DE GUERMANTES-BOUILLON, PRINCE DES LAUMES:
"This is serious!" (*"Hear, hear!" from the centre and some of the benches
on the right, loud exclamations from the extreme left.*)

The commonsense reader still retains a glimmer of loyalty
to the sage minister, but his heart is convulsed with a fresh
palpitation by the first words of the speaker who rises to reply:

"The astonishment, it is not too much to say the stupor" (*keen
sensation on the right side of the House*) "that I have felt at the words of

one who is still, I presume, a member of the Government"
(*thunderous applause ... Several Deputies then crowded round the
ministerial bench. The Under-Secretary of State for Posts and Telegraphs,
without rising from his seat, gives an affirmative nod.*)

This "thunderous applause" carries away the last shred of
resistance in the mind of the commonsense reader: he regards
as an insult to the Chamber, monstrous in fact, a way of proceeding which in itself is of no great significance. It may
be some quite straightforward item such as wanting the rich
to pay more than the poor, bringing to light some piece of
injustice, preferring peace to war, but he will find it scandalous
and will see it as an offence to certain principles to which in
fact he had never given a thought, which are not engraved
in the heart of man, but which move him strongly by reason
of the acclamations which they provoke and the compact
majorities which they assemble.

It must at the same time be recognised that this subtlety
of the politician which served to explain to me the Guermantes
circle, and other groups in society later on, is no more than the
perversion of a certain nicety of interpretation often described
by the expression "reading between the lines." If in representative assemblies there is absurdity owing to the perversion
of this quality, there is equally stupidity, through the lack of it,
in the public who take everything "literally," who do not
suspect a dismissal when a high dignitary is relieved of his
office "at his own request," and say: "He cannot have been
dismissed, since it was he who asked to go," or a defeat when,
in the face of the Japanese advance, the Russians by a strategic
manoeuvre fall back on stronger prepared positions, or a
refusal when, a province having demanded its independence
from the German Emperor, he grants it religious autonomy.
It is possible, moreover (to revert to these sittings of the
Chamber), that when they open the Deputies themselves are
like the commonsense person who will read the published
report. Learning that certain workers on strike have sent their
delegates to confer with a minister, they may ask themselves
naïvely: "There now, I wonder what they can have been saying; let's hope it's all settled," at the moment when the minister
himself rises to address the House in a solemn silence which

has already brought artificial emotions into play. The minister's first words: "There is no necessity for me to inform the Chamber that I have too high a sense of what is the duty of the Government to have received a deputation of which the authority entrusted to me could take no cognisance," produce a dramatic effect, for this was the one hypothesis which the commonsense of the Deputies had failed to foresee. But precisely because of its dramatic effect it is greeted with such applause that it is only after several minutes have passed that the minister can succeed in making himself heard, and on returning to his bench he will receive the congratulations of his colleagues. They are as deeply moved as on the day when the same minister failed to invite to a big official reception the chairman of the municipal council who supported the Opposition, and they declare that on this occasion as on the other he has acted with true statesmanship.

M. de Guermantes at this period of his life had, to the great scandal of the Courvoisiers, frequently been among the crowd of Deputies who came forward to congratulate the minister. I later heard it said that even at a time when he was playing a fairly important role in the Chamber and was being thought of in connexion with ministerial office or an embassy, he was, when a friend came to ask a favour of him, infinitely more simple, behaved politically a great deal less like a person of importance, than anyone else who did not happen to be Duc de Guermantes. For if he said that nobility was of no account, that he regarded his colleagues as equals, he did not believe it for a moment. He sought, and pretended to value, but really despised political position, and as he remained in his own eyes M. de Guermantes it did not envelop his person in that starchiness of high office which makes others unapproachable. And in this way his pride protected against every assault not only his manners, which were of an ostentatious familiarity, but also such true simplicity as he might actually possess.

To return to those artificial and dramatic decisions of hers, so like those of politicians, Mme de Guermantes was no less disconcerting to the Guermantes, the Courvoisiers, the Faubourg in general and, more than anyone, the Princesse de

Parme in her habit of issuing unaccountable decrees behind which one sensed latent principles which impressed one all the more the less one was aware of them. If the new Greek Minister gave a fancy dress ball, everyone chose a costume and wondered what the Duchess would wear. One thought that she would appear as the Duchesse de Bourgogne, another suggested as probable the guise of Princess of Dujabar, a third Psyche. Finally a Courvoisier, having asked her: "What are you going to go as, Oriane?" provoked the one response of which nobody had thought: "Why, nothing at all!" which at once set every tongue wagging, as revealing Oriane's opinion as to the true social position of the new Greek Minister and the proper attitude to adopt towards him, that is to say the opinion which ought to have been foreseen, namely that a duchess "wasn't obliged" to attend the fancy dress ball given by this new Minister. "I don't see that there's any necessity to go to the Greek Minister's. I don't know him; I'm not a Greek; why should I go to his house, I have nothing to do with him?" said the Duchess.

"But everybody will be there, they say it's going to be charming!" cried Mme de Gallardon.

"But it's just as charming sometimes to sit by one's own fireside," replied Mme de Guermantes.

The Courvoisiers could not get over this, but the Guermantes, without copying it, approved of their cousin's attitude: "Naturally, everybody isn't in a position like Oriane to break with all the conventions. But if you look at it in one way you can't say she's wrong to want to show that we do go rather too far in grovelling before these foreigners who appear from heaven knows where."

Naturally, knowing the stream of comment which one or other attitude would not fail to provoke, Mme de Guermantes took as much pleasure in appearing at a party to which her hostess had not dared to count on her coming as in staying at home or spending the evening at the theatre with her husband on the night of a party to which "everybody was going," or, again, when people imagined that she would eclipse the finest diamonds with some historic diadem, by stealing into the room without a single jewel, and in another style of dress than what had been wrongly supposed to be essential to the occasion. Although she was anti-Dreyfusard (while believing Dreyfus to be innocent, just as she spent her life in the social world while believing only in ideas), she had created an enormous sensation at a party at the Princesse de Ligne's, first of all by remaining seated when all the ladies had risen to their feet as General Mercier entered the room, and then by getting up and asking for her carriage in a loud voice when a nationalist orator had begun to address the gathering, thereby showing that she did not consider that society was meant for talking politics in; and all heads had turned towards her at a Good Friday concert at which, although a Voltairean, she had refused to remain because she thought it indecent to bring Christ on the stage. We know how important, even for the great queens of society, is that moment of the year at which the round of entertainment begins: so much so that the Marquise d'Amoncourt, who, from a need to say something, a psychological quirk, and also from a lack of sensitivity, was always making a fool of herself, had actually replied to somebody who had called to condole with her on the death of her father, M. de Montmorency: "What makes it sadder still is that it should come at a time when one's mirror is simply stuffed with cards!" Well, at this point in the social year, when people invited the Duchesse de Guermantes to dinner, hurrying so as to make sure that she was not already engaged, she declined for the one reason of which nobody in society would ever have thought: she was just setting off on a cruise in the Norwegian fjords, which were so interesting. The fashionable world was stunned, and, without any thought of following the Duchess's example, derived nevertheless from her action that sense of relief which one has in reading Kant when, after the most rigorous demonstration of determinism, one finds that above the world of necessity there is the world of freedom. Every invention of which no one has ever thought before excites the interest even of people who can derive no benefit from it. That of steam navigation was a small thing compared with the employment of steam navigation at that sedentary time of year called "the season." The idea that anyone could voluntarily renounce a hundred dinners or luncheons, twice as many afternoon teas,

three times as many receptions, the most brilliant Mondays at
the Opéra and Tuesdays at the Comédie-Française to visit
the Norwegian fjords seemed to the Courvoisiers no more
explicable than the idea of *Twenty Thousand Leagues under the
Sea*, but conveyed to them a similar impression of independence
and charm. So that not a day passed on which somebody might
not be heard to ask, not merely: "You've heard Oriane's latest
joke?" but "You know Oriane's latest?" and on "Oriane's
latest" as on "Oriane's latest joke" would follow the comment: "How typical of Oriane!" "Isn't that pure Oriane?"
Oriane's latest might be, for instance, that, having to write on
behalf of a patriotic society to Cardinal X—, Bishop of Mâcon
(whom M. de Guermantes when he spoke of him invariably
called "Monsieur de Mascon," thinking this to be "old
French"), when everyone was trying to imagine what form
the letter would take, and had no difficulty as to the opening
words, the choice lying between "Eminence" and "Monseigneur," but was puzzled as to the rest, Oriane's letter, to
the general astonishment, began: "Monsieur le Cardinal,"
following an old academic form, or: "My cousin," this term
being in use among the Princes of the Church, the Guermantes
and crowned heads, who prayed to God to take each and all
of them into "His fit and holy keeping." To start people on
the topic of an "Oriane's latest" it was sufficient that at a
performance at which all Paris was present and a most charming
play was being given, when they looked for Mme de Guermantes in the boxes of the Princesse de Parme, the Princesse de
Guermantes, countless other ladies who had invited her, they
discovered her sitting by herself, in black, with a tiny hat on
her head, in a stall in which she had arrived before the curtain
rose. "You hear better, when it's a play that's worth listening
to," she explained, to the scandal of the Courvoisiers and the
admiring bewilderment of the Guermantes and the Princesse
de Parme, who suddenly discovered that the "fashion" of
hearing the beginning of a play was more up to date, was a
proof of greater originality and intelligence (which need not
astonish them, coming from Oriane) than arriving for the last
act after a big dinner-party and having put in an appearance
at a reception. Such were the various kinds of surprise for

which the Princesse de Parme knew that she ought to be prepared if she put a literary or social question to Mme de Guermantes, and because of which, during these dinner-parties at Oriane's, Her Royal Highness never ventured upon the slightest topic save with the uneasy and enraptured prudence of the bather emerging from between two breakers.

Among the elements which, absent from the three or four other more or less equivalent salons that set the fashion for the Faubourg Saint-Germain, differentiated that of the Duchesse de Guermantes from them, just as Leibniz allows that each monad, while reflecting the entire universe, adds to it something of its own, one of the least attractive was habitually furnished by one or two extremely good-looking women who had no other right to be there but their beauty and the use that M. de Guermantes had made of them, and whose presence revealed at once, as does in other drawing-rooms that of certain otherwise unaccountable pictures, that in this household the husband was an ardent appreciator of feminine graces. They were all more or less alike, for the Duke had a taste for tall women, at once statuesque and loose-limbed, of a type half-way between the Venus de Milo and the Winged Victory; often fair, rarely dark, sometimes auburn, like the most recent, who was at this dinner, that Vicomtesse d'Arpajon whom he had loved so well that for a long time he had obliged her to send him as many as ten telegrams daily (which slightly irritated the Duchess), corresponded with her by carrier pigeon when he was at Guermantes, and from whom moreover he had long been so incapable of tearing himself away that, one winter which he had had to spend at Parma, he travelled back regularly every week to Paris, spending two days in the train, in order to see her.

As a rule these handsome "supers" had been his mistresses but were no longer (as was Mme d'Arpajon's case) or were on the point of ceasing to be. It may well have been that the glamour which the Duchess enjoyed in their eyes and the hope of being invited to her house, though they themselves came from thoroughly aristocratic backgrounds, if of the second rank, had prompted them, even more than the good looks and generosity of the Duke, to yield to his desires. Not that the

Duchess would have placed any insuperable obstacle in the way of their crossing her threshold: she was aware that in more than one of them she had found an ally thanks to whom she had obtained countless things which she wanted but which M. de Guermantes pitilessly denied his wife so long as he was not in love with someone else. And so the reason why they were not received by the Duchess until their liaison was already far advanced lay principally in the fact that the Duke, each time he embarked on a love affair, had imagined no more than a brief fling, as a reward for which he considered an invitation from his wife excessive. And yet he found himself offering this as the price for far less, for a first kiss in fact, because he had met with unexpected resistance or, on the contrary, because there had been no resistance. In love it often happens that gratitude, the desire to give pleasure, make us generous beyond the limits of what hope and self-interest had foreseen. But then the realisation of this offer was hindered by conflicting circumstances. In the first place, all the women who had responded to M. de Guermantes's love, and sometimes even when they had not yet given themselves to him, he had one after another kept cut off from the world. He no longer allowed them to see anyone, spent almost all his time in their company, looked after the education of their children, to whom now and again, if one was to judge by certain striking resemblances later on, he had occasion to present a little brother or sister. And then if, at the start of the liaison, the prospect of an introduction to Mme de Guermantes, which had never been envisaged by the Duke, had played a part in the mistress's mind, the liaison in itself had altered the lady's point of view; the Duke was no longer for her merely the husband of the smartest woman in Paris, but a man with whom the new mistress was in love, a man moreover who had given her the means and the inclination for a more luxurious style of living and had transposed the relative importance in her mind of questions of social and of material advantage; while now and then a composite jealousy of Mme de Guermantes, into which all these factors entered, animated the Duke's mistresses. But this case was the rarest of all; besides, when the day appointed for the introduction at length arrived (at a point when as a

rule it had more or less become a matter of indifference to the
Duke, whose actions, like everyone's else, were more often
dictated by previous actions than by the original motive which
had ceased to exist), it frequently happened that it was Mme de
Guermantes who had sought the acquaintance of the mistress
in whom she hoped, and so greatly needed, to find a valuable
ally against her dread husband. This is not to say that, save at
rare moments, in their own house, when, if the Duchess
talked too much, he let fall a few words or, more dreadful still,
preserved a silence which petrified her, M. de Guermantes
failed in his outward relations with his wife to observe what
are called the forms. People who did not know them might
easily be taken in. Sometimes between the races at Deauville,
taking the waters and the return to Guermantes for the
shooting, in the few weeks which people spend in Paris, since
the Duchess had a liking for café-concerts, the Duke would go
with her to spend the evening at one of these. The audience
remarked at once, in one of those little open boxes in which
there is just room for two, this Hercules in his "smoking" (for
in France we give to everything that is more or less British
the one name that it happens not to bear in England), his
monocle screwed in his eye, a fat cigar, from which now and
then he drew a puff of smoke, in his plump but finely shaped
hand, on the ring-finger of which a sapphire glowed, keeping
his eyes for the most part on the stage but, when he did let
them fall upon the audience in which there was absolutely no
one whom he knew, softening them with an air of gentleness,
reserve, courtesy and consideration. When a song struck him
as amusing and not too indecent, the Duke would turn round
with a smile to his wife, would share with her, with a twinkle
of good-natured complicity, the innocent merriment which
the new song had aroused in him. And the spectators might
believe that there was no better husband in the world than he,
nor anyone more enviable than the Duchess—that woman
outside whom every interest in the Duke's life lay, that woman
whom he did not love, to whom he had never ceased to be
unfaithful; and when the Duchess felt tired, they saw M. de
Guermantes rise, put on her cloak with his own hands, arranging her necklaces so that they did not get caught in the lining,

and clear a path for her to the exit with an assiduous and
respectful attention which she received with the coldness of
the woman of the world who sees in such behaviour simply
conventional good manners, at times even with the slightly
ironical bitterness of the disabused spouse who has no illusion
left to shatter. But despite these externals (another element of
that politeness which has transferred duty from the inner
depths to the surface, at a period already remote but which
still continues for its survivors) the life of the Duchess was by
no means easy. M. de Guermantes only became generous
and human again for a new mistress, who would, as it generally
happened, take the Duchess's side; the latter saw the possibility
arising for her once again of generosities towards inferiors,
charities to the poor, and even for herself, later on, a new and
sumptuous motor-car. But from the irritation which was provoked as a rule pretty rapidly in Mme de Guermantes by
people whom she found too submissive, the Duke's mistresses
were not exempt. Presently the Duchess grew tired of them.
As it happened, at that moment too the Duke's liaison with
Mme d'Arpajon was drawing to an end. Another mistress was
in the offing.

No doubt the love which M. de Guermantes had borne each
of them in succession would begin one day to make itself felt
anew: in the first place this love, in dying, bequeathed them to
the household like beautiful marble statues—beautiful to the
Duke, become thus in part an artist, because he had loved them
and was appreciative now of lines which he would not have
appreciated without love—which brought into juxtaposition in
the Duchess's drawing-room their forms that had long been
inimical, devoured by jealousies and quarrels, and finally
reconciled in the peace of friendship; and then this friendship
itself was an effect of the love which had made M. de Guermantes observe in those who had been his mistresses virtues
which exist in every human being but are perceptible only
to the carnal eye, so much so that the ex-mistress who has
become "a good friend" who would do anything in the world
for one has become a cliché, like the doctor or father who is
not a doctor or a father but a friend. But during a period of
transition, the woman whom M. de Guermantes was preparing

to abandon bewailed her lot, made scenes, showed herself exacting, appeared indiscreet, became a nuisance. The Duke would begin to take a dislike to her. Then Mme de Guermantes had a chance to bring to light the real or imagined defects of a person who annoyed her. Known to be kind, she would receive the constant telephone calls, the confidences, the tears of the abandoned mistress and make no complaint. She would laugh at them, first with her husband, then with a few chosen friends. And imagining that the pity which she showed for the unfortunate woman gave her the right to make fun of her, even to her face, whatever the lady might say, provided it could be included among the attributes of the ridiculous character which the Duke and Duchess had recently fabricated for her, Mme de Guermantes had no hesitation in exchanging glances of ironical connivance with her husband.

Meanwhile, as she sat down to table, the Princesse de Parme remembered that she had thought of inviting Mme d'Heudicourt to the Opéra, and, wishing to be assured that this would not in any way offend Mme de Guermantes, was preparing to sound her.

At this moment M. de Grouchy entered, his train having been held up for an hour owing to a derailment. He made what excuses he could. His wife, had she been a Courvoisier, would have died of shame. But Mme de Grouchy was not a Guermantes for nothing. As her husband was apologising for being late, "I see," she broke in, "that even in little things arriving late is a tradition in your family."

"Sit down, Grouchy, and don't let them fluster you," said the Duke.

"Although I move with the times, I must admit that the Battle of Waterloo had its points, since it brought about the Restoration of the Bourbons, and, better still, in a way that made them unpopular. But you seem to be a regular Nimrod!"

"Well, as a matter of fact, I did get quite a good bag. I shall take the liberty of sending the Duchess six brace of pheasant to-morrow."

An idea seemed to flicker in the eyes of Mme de Guermantes. She insisted that M. de Grouchy must not give himself the trouble of sending the pheasants. And making a sign to the betrothed footman with whom I had exchanged a few words on my way from the Elstir room, "Poullein," she told him, "you will go to-morrow and fetch M. le Comte's pheasants and bring them straight back—you won't mind, will you, Grouchy, if I make a few little presents. Basin and I can't eat a dozen pheasants by ourselves."

"But the day after to-morrow will be soon enough," said M. de Grouchy.

"No, to-morrow suits me better," the Duchess insisted.

Poullein had turned pale; he would miss his rendezvous with his sweetheart. This was quite enough for the diversion of the Duchess, who liked to appear to be taking a human interest in everyone.

"I know it's your day off," she went on to Poullein, "all you've got to do is change with Georges; he can take to-morrow off and stay in the day after."

But the day after, Poullein's sweetheart would not be free. He had no interest in going out then. As soon as he had left the room, everyone complimented the Duchess on her kindness towards her servants.

"But I only behave towards them as I'd like people to behave to me."

"That's just it. They can say they've found a good place with you all right."

"Oh, nothing so very wonderful. But I think they all like me. That one is a little irritating because he's in love. He thinks it incumbent on him to go about with a long face."

At this point Poullein reappeared.

"You're quite right," said M. de Grouchy, "he doesn't look very cheerful. With those fellows one has to be kind but not too kind."

"I admit I'm not a very dreadful mistress. He'll have nothing to do all day but call for your pheasants, sit in the house doing nothing and eat his share of them."

"There are plenty of people who would be glad to be in his place," said M. de Grouchy, for envy makes men blind.

"Oriane," began the Princesse de Parme, "I had a visit the other day from your cousin d'Heudicourt; of course she's a highly intelligent woman; she's a Guermantes—need I say more?—but they tell me she has a spiteful tongue."

The Duke fastened on his wife a slow gaze of feigned stupefaction. Mme de Guermantes began to laugh. Gradually the Princess became aware of their pantomime.

"But . . . do you mean to say . . . you don't agree with me?" she stammered with growing uneasiness.

"Really, Ma'am, it's too good of you to pay any attention to Basin's faces. Now, Basin, you're not to hint nasty things about our cousins."

"Does he think she's too malicious?" inquired the Princess briskly.

"Oh, dear me, no!" replied the Duchess. "I don't know who told Your Highness that she was malicious. On the contrary, she's an excellent creature who never spoke ill of anyone, or did any harm to anyone."

"Ah!" sighed Mme de Parme, greatly relieved. "I must say I'd never noticed it either. But I know it's often difficult not to be a bit malicious when one has a great deal of wit . . ."

"Ah! now that is a quality of which she has even less."

"Less wit?" asked the stupefied Princess.

"Come now, Oriane," broke in the Duke in a plaintive tone, casting to right and left of him a glance of amusement, "you heard the Princess tell you that she was a superior woman."

"But isn't she?"

"Superior in chest measurement, at any rate."

"Don't listen to him, Ma'am, he's having you on; she's as stupid as a (h'm) goose," came in a loud and husky voice from Mme de Guermantes, who, a great deal more "old world" even than the Duke when she wasn't trying, often deliberately sought to be, but in a manner entirely different from the deliquescent, lace jabot style of her husband and in reality far more subtle, with a sort of almost peasant pronunciation which had a harsh and delicious flavour of the soil. "But she's the best woman in the world. Besides, I don't really know that one can call it stupidity when it's carried to such a point as that. I don't believe I ever met anyone quite like her; she's a case for a specialist, there's something pathological about her, she's a sort of 'natural' or cretin or 'mental deficient,' like the people you see in melodramas, or in *L'Arlésienne*. I always ask myself, when she comes here, whether the moment may not have arrived at which her intelligence is going to dawn, which makes me a little nervous always."

The Princess marvelled at these expressions, but remained astonished by the verdict. "She repeated to me—and so did Mme d'Epinay—your remark about 'Teaser Augustus.' It's delicious," she put in.

M. de Guermantes explained the joke to me. I wanted to tell him that his brother, who pretended not to know me, was expecting me that very evening at eleven o'clock. But I had not asked Robert whether I might mention this assignation, and as the fact that M. de Charlus had practically fixed it with me himself directly contradicted what he had told the Duchess, I judged it more tactful to say nothing.

" 'Teaser Augustus' isn't bad," said M. de Guermantes, "but Mme d'Heudicourt probably didn't tell you a far wittier remark Oriane made to her the other day in reply to an invitation to luncheon."

"Oh, no! Do tell me!"

"Now Basin, you keep quiet. In the first place, it was a stupid remark, and it will make the Princess think me inferior even to my nitwit of a cousin. Though I don't know why I should call her my cousin. She's one of Basin's cousins. Still, I believe she is related to me in some sort of way."

"Oh!" cried the Princesse de Parme at the idea that she could possibly think Mme de Guermantes stupid, and protesting desperately that nothing could ever make the Duchess fall from the place she held in her estimation.

"Besides, we've already deprived her of the qualities of the mind, and since the remark in question tends to deny certain qualities of the heart, it seems to me inopportune to repeat it."

" 'Deny her!' 'Inopportune!' How well she expresses herself!" said the Duke with a pretence of irony, to win admiration for the Duchess.

"Now, then, Basin, you're not to make fun of your wife."

"I should explain to your Royal Highness," went on the

Duke, "that Oriane's cousin may be superior, good, stout, anything you like to mention, but she is not exactly—what shall I say—lavish."

"Yes, I know, she's terribly close-fisted," broke in the Princess.

"I should not have ventured to use the expression, but you have hit on exactly the right word. It's reflected in her house-keeping, and especially in the cooking, which is excellent, but strictly rationed."

"Which gives rise to some quite amusing scenes," M. de Bréauté interrupted him. "For instance, my dear Basin, I was down at Heudicourt one day when you were expected, Oriane and yourself. They had made the most sumptuous preparations when a footman brought in a telegram during the afternoon to say that you weren't coming."

"That doesn't surprise me!" said the Duchess, who not only was difficult to get, but liked people to know as much.

"Your cousin read the telegram, was duly distressed, then immediately, without missing a trick, telling herself that there was no point in going to unnecessary expense for so unimportant a gentleman as myself, called the footman back: 'Tell the cook not to put on the chicken!' she shouted after him. And that evening I heard her asking the butler: 'Well? What about the beef that was left over yesterday? Aren't you going to let us have that?'"

"All the same, one must admit that the fare you get there is of the very best," said the Duke, who fancied that in using this expression he was showing himself to be very old school. "I don't know any house where one eats better."

"Or less," put in the Duchess.

"It's quite wholesome and quite adequate for what you would call a vulgar yokel like myself," went on the Duke. "One doesn't outrun one's appetite."

"Oh, if it's to be taken as a cure, that's another matter. It's certainly more healthy than sumptuous. Not that it's as good as all that," added Mme de Guermantes, who was not at all pleased that the title of "best table in Paris" should be awarded to any but her own. "With my cousin it's just the same as with those costive authors who turn out a one-act play or a sonnet every fifteen years. The sort of thing people call little master-pieces, trifles that are perfect gems, in fact what I loathe most in the world. The cooking at Zénaïde's is not bad, but you would think it more ordinary if she was less parsimonious. There are some things her cook does quite well, and others he doesn't bring off. I've had some thoroughly bad dinners there, as in most houses, only they've done me less harm there because the stomach is, after all, more sensitive to quantity than to quality."

"Well, to get on with the story," the Duke concluded, "Zénaïde insisted that Oriane should to go luncheon there, and as my wife is not very fond of going out anywhere she resisted, wanted to be sure that under the pretence of a quiet meal she was not being trapped into some great junket, and tried in vain to find out who else would be of the party. 'You must come,' Zénaïde insisted, boasting of all the good things there would be to eat. 'You're going to have a *purée* of chestnuts, I need say no more than that, and there will be seven little *bouchées à la reine.*' 'Seven little *bouchées!*' cried Oriane, 'that means that we shall be at least eight!' "

There was silence for a few seconds, and then the Princess, having seen the point, let her laughter explode like a peal of thunder. "Ah! 'Then we shall be eight'—it's exquisite. How very well phrased!" she said, having by a supreme effort recalled the expression she had heard used by Mme d'Epinay, which this time was more appropriate.

"Oriane, that was very charming of the Princess, she said your remark was well phrased."

"But, my dear, you're telling me nothing new. I know how clever the Princess is," replied Mme de Guermantes, who readily appreciated a remark when it was uttered at once by a royal personage and in praise of her own wit. "I'm very proud that Ma'am should appreciate my humble phrasings. I don't remember, though, that I ever did say such a thing, and if I did, it must have been to flatter my cousin, for if she had ordered seven 'mouthfuls,' the mouths, if I may so express myself, would have been a round dozen if not more."

During this time the Comtesse d'Arpajon, who, before dinner, had told me that her aunt would have been so happy to show me round her house in Normandy, was saying to me over the Prince d'Agrigente's head that where she would most like to entertain me was in the Côte d'Or, because there, at Pont-le-Duc, she would be at home.

"The archives of the château would interest you. There are some absolutely fascinating correspondences between all the most prominent people of the seventeenth, eighteenth and nineteenth centuries. I've spent many wonderful hours there, living in the past," she declared, and I remembered that M. de Guermantes had told me that she was extremely well up in literature.

"She owns all M. de Bornier's manuscripts," went on the Princess, speaking of Mme d'Heudicourt, and anxious to make the most of the good reasons she might have for befriending that lady.

"She must have dreamed it, I don't believe she ever even knew him," said the Duchess.

"What is especially interesting is that these correspondences are with people of different countries," went on the Comtesse d'Arpajon who, allied to the principal ducal and even reigning families of Europe, was always glad to remind people of the fact.

"Surely, Oriane," said M. de Guermantes, meaningly, "you can't have forgotten that dinner-party where you had M. de Bornier sitting next to you!" "But, Basin," the Duchess interrupted him, "if you mean to inform me that I knew M. de Bornier, why of course I did, he even called upon me several times, but I could never bring myself to invite him to the house because I should always have been obliged to have it disinfected afterwards with formol. As for the dinner you mean, I remember it only too well, but it was certainly not at Zénaïde's, who never set eyes on Bornier in her life and would probably think if you spoke to her of *La Fille de Roland* that you meant a Bonaparte princess who is said to be engaged to the son of the King of Greece;[25] no, it was at the Austrian Embassy. Dear Hoyos imagined he was giving me a great treat by planting that pestiferous academician on the chair next to mine. I quite thought I had a squadron of mounted police sitting beside me. I was obliged to stop my nose as best I could all through dinner; I didn't dare breathe until the gruyère came round."

M. de Guermantes, having achieved his secret objective, made a furtive examination of his guests' faces to judge the effect of the Duchess's pleasantry.

"As a matter of fact I find that old correspondences have a peculiar charm," the lady who was well up in literature and had such fascinating letters in her château went on, in spite of the intervening head of the Prince d'Agrigente. "Have you noticed how often a writer's letters are superior to the rest of his work? What's the name of that author who wrote *Salammbô*?"

I should have liked not to have to reply in order not to prolong this conversation, but I felt it would be disobliging to the Prince d'Agrigente, who had pretended to know perfectly well who *Salammbô* was by and out of pure politeness to be leaving it to me to say, but who was now in a painful quandary.

"Flaubert," I ended up by saying, but the vigorous signs of assent that came from the Prince's head smothered the sound of my reply, so that my interlocutress was not exactly sure whether I had said Paul Bert or Fulbert, names which she did not find entirely satisfactory.

"In any case," she went on, "how intriguing his correspondence is, and how superior to his books! It explains him, in fact, because one sees from everything he says about the difficulty he has in writing a book that he wasn't a real writer, a gifted man."

"Talking of correspondence, I must say I find Gambetta's admirable," said the Duchesse de Guermantes, to show that she was not afraid to be found taking an interest in a proletarian and a radical. M. de Bréauté, who fully appreciated the brilliance of this feat of daring, gazed round him with an eye at once tipsy and affectionate, after which he wiped his monocle.

"Gad, it's infernally dull, that *Fille de Roland*," said M. de Guermantes (who was still on the subject of M. de Bornier), with the satisfaction which he derived from the sense of his own superiority over a work which had bored him so much, and perhaps also from the *suave mari magno* feeling one has in the middle of a good dinner, when one recalls such terrible evenings in the past. "Still, there were some quite good lines in it, and a patriotic feeling."

I made a remark that implied that I had no admiration for M. de Bornier.

"Ah! have you got something against him?" the Duke asked with genuine curiosity, for he always imagined when anyone spoke ill of a man that it must be on account of a personal resentment, just as to speak well of a woman marked the beginning of a love affair. "You've obviously got a grudge against him. What did he do to you? You must tell us. Why yes, there must be some skeleton in the cupboard or you wouldn't run him down. It's long winded, *La Fille de Roland*, but it's quite strong in parts."

"Strong is just the word for such an odorous author," Mme de Guermantes broke in sarcastically. "If this poor boy ever found himself in his company I can quite understand that he got up his nostrils!"

"I must confess, though, Ma'am," the Duke went on, addressing the Princesse de Parme, "that quite apart from *La Fille de Roland*, in literature and even in music I'm terribly old-fashioned; no old junk can be too stale for my taste. You won't believe me, perhaps, but in the evenings, if my wife sits down to the piano, I find myself calling for some old tune by Auber or Boieldieu, or even Beethoven! That's the sort of thing I like. As for Wagner, he sends me to sleep at once."

"You're wrong there," said Mme de Guermantes. "In spite of his insufferable long-windedness, Wagner was a genius. *Lohengrin* is a masterpiece. Even in *Tristan* there are some intriguing passages here and there. And the Spinning Chorus in the *Flying Dutchman* is a perfect marvel."

"Aren't I right, Babal," said M. de Guermantes, turning to M. de Bréauté, "what we like is:

> Les rendez-vous de noble compagnie
> Se donnent tous en ce charmant séjour.[26]

It's delightful. And *Fra Diavolo* and the *Magic Flute*, and *Le Chalet*, and the *Marriage of Figaro*, and *Les Diamants de la*

Couronne—there's music for you! It's the same thing in literature. For instance, I adore Balzac, *Le Bal de Sceaux, Les
Mohicans de Paris*."

"Ah! my dear man, if you're off on the subject of Balzac
we'll be here all night. Keep it for some evening when Mémé's
here. He's even better, he knows it all by heart."

Irritated by his wife's interruption, the Duke held her for
some seconds under the fire of a menacing silence. And his
huntsman's eyes looked like a pair of loaded pistols. Meanwhile Mme d'Arpajon had been exchanging with the Princesse
de Parme some remarks about poetry, tragic and otherwise,
which did not reach me distinctly until I caught the following
from Mme d'Arpajon: "Oh, I quite agree with all that, I admit
he makes the world seem ugly because he's unable to distinguish between ugliness and beauty, or rather because his
insufferable vanity makes him believe that everything he says
is beautiful. I agree with your Highness that in the piece in
question there are some ridiculous things, quite unintelligible,
and errors of taste, and that's it's difficult to understand, that
it's as much trouble to read as if it was written in Russian or
Chinese, because obviously it's anything in the world but
French; but still, when one has taken the trouble, how richly
one is rewarded, it's so full of imagination!"

I had missed the opening sentences of this little lecture. I
gathered in the end not only that the poet incapable of distinguishing between beauty and ugliness was Victor Hugo, but
furthermore that the poem which was as difficult to understand
as Chinese or Russian was

Lorsque l'enfant paraît, le cercle de famille
Applaudit à grands cris . . .

a piece dating from the poet's earliest period, and perhaps
even nearer to Mme Deshoulières[27] than to the Victor Hugo
of the *Légende des Siècles*. Far from thinking Mme d'Arpajon
ridiculous, I saw her (the first person at this table, so real and
so ordinary, at which I had sat down with such keen disappointment), I saw her in my mind's eye crowned with that
lace cap, with the long spiral ringlets falling from it on either
side, which was worn by Mme de Rémusat, Mme de Broglie,

Mme de Saint-Aulaire, all those distinguished ladies who in their delightful letters quote with such learning and such aptness Sophocles, Schiller and the *Imitation*, but in whom the earliest poetry of the Romantics induced the alarm and exhaustion inseparable for my grandmother from the later verses of Stéphane Mallarmé.

"Mme d'Arpajon is very fond of poetry," said the Princesse de Parme to her hostess, impressed by the ardent tone in which the speech had been delivered.

"No, she doesn't understand the first thing about it," replied Mme de Guermantes in an undertone, taking advantage of the fact that Mme d'Arpajon, who was dealing with an objection raised by General de Beautreillis, was too intent upon what she herself was saying to hear what was being murmured by the Duchess. "She has become literary since she's been forsaken. I may tell your Highness that it's I who have to bear the brunt of it because it's to me that she comes to complain whenever Basin hasn't been to see her, which is practically every day. But it isn't my fault, after all, if she bores him, and I can't force him to go to her, although I'd rather he were a little more faithful, because then I shouldn't see quite so much of her myself. But she drives him mad and I'm not surprised. She isn't a bad sort, but she's boring to a degree you can't imagine. She gives me such a headache every day that I'm obliged to take a pyramidon tablet whenever she comes. And all this because Basin took it into his head for a year or so to go to bed with her. And on top of that to have a footman who's in love with a little tart and goes about with a long face if I don't ask the young person to leave her profitable pavement for half an hour and come to tea with me! Oh! life is really too tedious!" the Duchess languorously concluded.

Mme d'Arpajon bored M. de Guermantes principally because he had recently fallen in love with another, whom I discovered to be the Marquise de Surgis-le-Duc. As it happened, the footman who had been deprived of his day off was at that moment waiting at table. And it struck me that, still disconsolate, he was doing it with some lack of composure, for I noticed that in handing the dish to M. de Châtellerault he performed his task so awkwardly that the young Duke's elbow

came in contact several times with his. The young Duke
showed no sign of annoyance with the blushing footman, but
on the contrary looked up at him with a smile in his clear blue
eyes. This good humour seemed to me to betoken kindness on
the guest's part. But the insistency of his smile led me to think
that, aware of the servant's discomfiture, what he felt was
perhaps a malicious amusement.

"But, my dear, you know you're not revealing any new
discovery when you tell us about Victor Hugo," went on the
Duchess, this time addressing Mme d'Arpajon whom she had
just seen turn round with a worried look. "You mustn't expect
to launch that young genius. Everybody knows that he has
talent. What is utterly detestable is the Victor Hugo of the last
stage, the *Légende des Siècles*, I forget all their names. But in the
Feuilles d'Automne, the *Chants du Crépuscule*, there's a great deal
that's the work of a poet, a true poet! Even in the *Contempla-
tions*," went on the Duchess, whom none of her listeners dared
to contradict, and with good reason, "there are still some quite
pretty things. But I confess that I prefer not to venture farther
than the *Crépuscule*! And then in the finer poems of Victor
Hugo, and there really are some, one frequently comes across
an idea, even a profound idea."

And with just the right shade of feeling, bringing out the
sorrowful thought with the full force of her intonation,
projecting it somewhere beyond her voice, and fixing straight
in front of her a charming, dreamy gaze, the Duchess slowly
recited:

> "La douleur est un fruit, Dieu ne le fait pas croître
> Sur la branche trop faible encor pour le porter.

Or again:

> Les morts durent bien peu . . .
> Hélas, dans le cercueil ils tombent en poussière,
> Moins vite qu'en nos cœurs!"

And, while a smile of disillusionment puckered her sorrowful lips with a graceful sinuosity, the Duchess fastened on
Mme d'Arpajon the dreamy gaze of her lovely clear blue eyes.

I was beginning to know them, as well as her voice, with its heavy drawl, its harsh savour. In those eyes and in that voice, I recognised much of the life of nature round Combray. Certainly, in the affectation with which that voice betrayed at times a rudeness of the soil, there was more than one element: the wholly provincial origin of one branch of the Guermantes family, which had for long remained more localised, more hardy, wilder, more combative than the rest; and then the ingrained habit of really distinguished people and people of intelligence who know that distinction does not lie in mincing speech, and the habit of nobles who fraternise more readily with their peasants than with the middle classes; peculiarities all of which the regal position of Mme de Guermantes enabled her to display more freely, to bring out in full fig. It appears that the same voice existed also in some of her sisters, whom she detested, and who, less intelligent than herself and almost humbly married, if one may use this adverb to speak of unions with obscure noblemen, holed up on their provincial estates, or, in Paris, in one of the dimmer reaches of Faubourg society, possessed this voice also but had curbed it, corrected it, softened it so far as lay in their power, just as it is very rarely that any of us has the courage of his own originality and does not apply himself diligently to resembling the most approved models. But Oriane was so much more intelligent, so much richer, above all, so much more in vogue than her sisters, she had, when Princesse des Laumes, cut so successful a figure in the company of the Prince of Wales, that she had realised that this discordant voice was an attraction, and had made it, in the social sphere, with the courage of originality rewarded by success, what in the theatrical sphere a Réjane or a Jeanne Granier (which implies no comparison, naturally, between the respective merits and talents of those two actresses) had made of theirs, something admirable and distinctive which possibly certain Réjane and Granier sisters, whom no one has ever known, strove to conceal as a defect.

To all these reasons for displaying her local originality, Mme de Guermantes's favourite writers—Mérimée, Meilhac and Halévy—had brought in addition, together with a respect for "naturalness," a feeling for the prosaic by which she attained to poetry and a purely society spirit which called up distant landscapes before my eyes. Besides, the Duchess was fully capable, adding to these influences an artful refinement of her own, of having chosen for the majority of her words the pronunciation that seemed to her most "Ile-de-France," most "Champenoise," since, if not quite to the same extent as her sister-in-law Marsantes, she rarely strayed beyond the pure vocabulary that might have been used by an old French writer. And when one was tired of the composite patchwork of modern speech, it was very restful to listen to Mme de Guermantes's talk, even though one knew it could express far fewer things—almost as restful, if one was alone with her and she restrained and clarified the flow of her speech still further, as listening to an old song. Then, as I looked at and listened to Mme de Guermantes, I could see, imprisoned in the perpetual afternoon of her eyes, a sky of the Ile-de-France or of Champagne spread itself, grey-blue, oblique, with the same angle of inclination as in the eyes of Saint-Loup.

Thus, through these diverse influences, Mme de Guermantes expressed at once the most ancient aristocratic France, then, much later, the manner in which the Duchesse de Broglie might have enjoyed and found fault with Victor Hugo under the July Monarchy, and, finally, a keen taste for the literature that sprang from Mérimée and Meilhac. The first of these influences attracted me more than the second, did more to console me for the disappointments of my pilgrimage to and arrival in the Faubourg Saint-Germain, so different from what I had imagined it to be; but even the second I preferred to the last. For, while Mme de Guermantes was almost involuntarily Guermantes, her Pailleronism,[28] her taste for the younger Dumas were self-conscious and deliberate. As this taste was the opposite of my own, she furnished my mind with literature when she talked to me of the Faubourg Saint-Germain, and never seemed to me so stupidly Faubourg Saint-Germain as when she talked literature.

Moved by this last quotation, Mme d'Arpajon exclaimed: " 'Ces reliques du cœur ont aussi leur poussière!'—Monsieur, you must write that down for me on my fan," she said to M. de Guermantes.

"Poor woman, I feel sorry for her!" said the Princesse de Parme to Mme de Guermantes.

"No, really, Ma'am, you mustn't be soft-hearted, she has only got what she deserves."

"But—you'll forgive my saying this to you—she does really love him all the same!"

"Oh, not at all; she isn't capable of it; she thinks she loves him just as she thought just now she was quoting Victor Hugo when she was reciting a line from Musset. Look," the Duchess went on in a melancholy tone, "nobody would be more touched than myself by a true feeling. But let me give you an example. Only yesterday she made a terrible scene with Basin. Your Highness thinks perhaps that it was because he's in love with other women, because he no longer loves her; not in the least, it was because he won't put her sons up for the Jockey. Is that the behaviour of a woman in love? No! I will go further," Mme de Guermantes added with precision, "she is a person of rare insensitivity."

Meanwhile it was with an eye sparkling with satisfaction that M. de Guermantes had listened to his wife talking about Victor Hugo "point-blank" and quoting those few lines. The Duchess might frequently irritate him, but at moments such as this he was proud of her. "Oriane is really extraordinary. She can talk about anything, she has read everything. She couldn't possibly have guessed that the conversation this evening would turn on Victor Hugo. Whatever subject you take her on at, she's ready for you, she can hold her own with the most learned scholars. This young man must be quite captivated."

"But do let's change the subject," Mme de Guermantes added, "because she's dreadfully susceptible ... You must think me very old-fashioned," she went on, turning to me, "I know that nowadays it's considered a weakness to care for ideas in poetry, poetry with some thought in it."

"Old-fashioned?" asked the Princesse de Parme, quivering with the slight shock produced by this new wave which she had not expected, although she knew that the Duchess's conversation always held in store for her those continuous and delightful thrills, that breath-catching panic, that wholesome exhaustion after which her thoughts instinctively turned to the necessity of taking a footbath in a dressing cabin and a brisk walk to "restore her circulation."

"For my part, no, Oriane," said Mme de Brissac, "I don't in the least object to Victor Hugo's having ideas, quite the contrary, but I do object to his seeking them in everything that's monstrous. It was he who accustomed us to ugliness in literature. There's quite enough ugliness in life already. Why can't we be allowed at least to forget it while we're reading? A distressing spectacle from which we should turn away in real life, that's what attracts Victor Hugo."

"Victor Hugo is not so realistic as Zola though, surely?" asked the Princesse de Parme.

The name of Zola did not stir a muscle on the face of M. de Beautreillis. The General's anti-Dreyfusism was too deep-rooted for him to seek to give expression to it. And his benign silence when anyone broached these topics touched the layman's heart as a proof of the same delicacy that a priest shows in avoiding any reference to your religious duties, a financier in taking pains not to recommend the companies which he himself controls, a strong man in behaving with lamblike gentleness and not hitting you in the jaw.

"I know you're related to Admiral Jurien de la Gravière," Mme de Varambon, the lady-in-waiting to the Princesse de Parme, said to me with a knowing look. An excellent but limited woman, she had been procured for the Princess long ago by the Duke's mother. She had not previously addressed me, and I could never afterwards, despite the admonitions of the Princess and my own protestations, get out of her mind the idea that I was in some way connected with the admiral-academician, who was a complete stranger to me. The obstinate persistence of the Princesse de Parme's lady-in-waiting in seeing in me a nephew of Admiral Jurien de la Gravière was in itself quite an ordinary form of silliness. But the mistake she made was only an extreme and desiccated sample of the numberless mistakes, more frivolous, more pointed, unwitting or deliberate, which accompany one's name on the label which the world attaches to one. I remember a friend of the Guermantes who expressed a keen desire to meet me, and gave me as his reason that I was a great friend of his cousin, Mme de

Chaussegros. "She's a charming person, and so fond of you."
I scrupulously, though quite vainly, insisted on the fact that
there must be some mistake, as I did not know Mme de
Chaussegros. "Then it's her sister you know; it comes to the
same thing. She met you in Scotland." I had never been to
Scotland, and took the fruitless trouble, in my honesty, to
apprise my interlocutor of the fact. It was Mme de Chaussegros herself who had said that she knew me, and no doubt
sincerely believed it, as a result of some initial confusion, for
from that time onwards she never failed to greet me whenever she saw me. And since, after all, the world in which I
moved was precisely that in which Mme de Chaussegros
moved, my humility had neither rhyme nor reason. To say
that I was an intimate friend of the Chaussegros family was,
literally, a mistake, but from the social point of view it roughly
corresponded to my position, if one can speak of the social
position of so young a man as I then was. It therefore mattered
not in the least that this friend of the Guermantes should tell
me things that were untrue about myself, he neither lowered
nor raised me (from the social point of view) in the idea which
he continued to hold of me. And when all is said, for those of
us who are not professional actors, the tedium of living always
in the same character is dispelled for a moment, as if we were
to go on the boards, when another person forms a false idea of
us, imagines that we are friends with a lady whom we do not
know and are reported to have met in the course of a delightful
journey which we have never made. Errors that multiply
themselves and are harmless when they do not have the
inflexible rigidity of the one which had been committed, and
continued for the rest of her life to be committed, in spite of
my denials, by the imbecile lady-in-waiting to Mme de Parme,
rooted for all time in the belief that I was related to the tiresome Admiral Jurien de la Gravière. "She's not very strong
in the head," the Duke confided to me, "and besides, she ought
not to indulge in too many libations. I fancy she's slightly
under the influence of Bacchus." As a matter of fact Mme de
Varambon had drunk nothing but water, but the Duke liked
to seize opportunities for his favourite phrases.

"But Zola is not a realist, Ma'am, he's a poet!" said Mme de

Guermantes, drawing inspiration from the critical essays she
had read in recent years and adapting them to her own personal genius. Agreeably buffeted hitherto, in the course of
the bath of wit, a bath stirred up specially for her, which she
was taking this evening and which, she considered, must be
particularly good for her health, letting herself be borne up
by the waves of paradox which curled and broke one after
another, at this, even more enormous than the rest, the
Princesse de Parme jumped for fear of being knocked over. And
it was with a catch in her voice, as though she had lost her
breath, that she now gasped: "Zola a poet!"

"Why, yes," answered the Duchess with a laugh, entranced
by this display of suffocation. "Your Highness must have
remarked how he magnifies everything he touches. You will
tell me that he only touches . . . what brings luck! But he makes
it into something colossal. His is the epic dungheap! He is the
Homer of the sewers! He hasn't enough capital letters to write
the *mot de Cambronne.*"[29]

Despite the extreme exhaustion which she was beginning
to feel, the Princess was enchanted; never had she felt better.
She would not have exchanged for an invitation to Schön-
brunn, although that was the one thing that really flattered her,
these divine dinner-parties at Mme de Guermantes's, made
invigorating by so liberal a dose of attic salt.

"He writes it with a big 'C'," exclaimed Mme d'Arpajon.

"Surely with a big 'M', I think, my dear," replied Mme de
Guermantes, exchanging first with her husband a merry glance
which implied: "Did you ever hear such an idiot?"

"Wait a minute, now," Mme de Guermantes turned to me,
fixing on me a tender, smiling gaze, because, as an accomplished
hostess, she was anxious to display her own knowledge of the
artist who interested me particularly and to give me, if need be,
an opportunity to exhibit mine, "wait now," she said, gently
waving her feather fan, so conscious was she at this moment that
she was exercising to the full the duties of hospitality, and, that
she might be found wanting in none of them, making a sign
also to the servants to help me to more of the asparagus with
mousseline sauce, "wait now, I do believe that Zola has actually
written an essay on Elstir, the painter whose paintings you

were looking at just now—the only ones of his I care for, incidentally."

As a matter of fact she hated Elstir's work, but found a unique quality in anything that was in her own house. I asked M. de Guermantes if he knew the name of the gentleman in the tall hat who figured in the picture of the crowd and whom I recognised as the same person whose formal portrait the Guermantes also had and had hung beside the other, both dating more or less from the same early period in which Elstir's personality had not yet completely emerged and he modelled himself a little on Manet.

"Oh, heavens!" he replied, "I know it's a fellow who is quite well-known and no fool either in his own line, but I have no head for names. I have it on the tip of my tongue, Monsieur . . . . Monsieur . . . . oh, well, it doesn't matter, I've forgotten. Swann would be able to tell you. It was he who made Mme de Guermantes buy all that stuff. She's always too good-natured, afraid of hurting people's feelings if she refuses to do things; between ourselves, I believe he's landed us with a lot of daubs. What I *can* tell you is that the gentleman you mean has been a sort of Maecenas to M. Elstir—he launched him and has often helped him out of difficulties by commissioning pictures from him. As a compliment to this man—if you call it a compliment, it's a matter of taste—he painted him standing about among that crowd, where with his Sunday-go-to-meeting look he creates a distinctly odd effect. He may be no end of a pundit but he's evidently not aware of the proper time and place for a top hat. With that thing on his head, among all those bare-headed girls, he looks like a little country lawyer on the spree. But tell me, you seem quite gone on his pictures. If I'd only known, I should have had it all at my fingertips. Not that there's much need to rack one's brains to get to the bottom of M. Elstir's work, as there would be for Ingres's *Source* or the *Princes in the Tower* by Paul Delaroche. What one appreciates in his work is that it's shrewdly observed, amusing, Parisian, and then one passes on to the next thing. One doesn't need to be an expert to look at that sort of thing. I know of course that they're merely sketches, but still, I don't feel myself that he puts enough work into them. Swann had

the nerve to try and make us buy a *Bundle of Asparagus*. In fact
it was in the house for several days. There was nothing else
in the picture, just a bundle of asparagus exactly like the ones
you're eating now. But I must say I refused to swallow M.
Elstir's asparagus. He wanted three hundred francs for them.
Three hundred francs for a bundle of asparagus! A louis, that's
as much as they're worth, even early in the season. I thought
it a bit stiff. When he puts people into his pictures as well,
there's something squalid and depressing about them that I
dislike. I'm surprised to see a man of refinement, a superior
mind like you, admiring that sort of thing."

"I don't know why you should say that, Basin," interrupted
the Duchess, who did not like to hear people run down
anything that her rooms contained. "I'm by no means prepared
to admit that there's no distinction in Elstir's painting. You
have to take it or leave it. But it's not always lacking in talent.
And you must admit that the ones I bought are remarkably
beautiful."

"Well, Oriane, in that style of thing I'd infinitely prefer to
have the little study by M. Vibert we saw at the water-colour
exhibition. There's nothing much in it, if you like, you could
hold it in the palm of your hand, but you can see the man's
got wit to the tips of his fingers: that shabby scarecrow of a
missionary standing in front of the sleek prelate who is making
his little dog do tricks, it's a perfect little poem of subtlety,
and even profundity."

"I believe you know M. Elstir," the Duchess said to me.
"As a man, he's quite pleasant."

"He's intelligent," said the Duke. "You're surprised,
when you talk to him, that his paintings should be so vulgar."

"He's more than intelligent, he's really quite witty," said
the Duchess in the judicious, appraising tone of a person who
knew what she was talking about.

"Didn't he once start a portrait of you, Oriane?" asked the
Princesse de Parme.

"Yes, in shrimp pink," replied Mme de Guermantes, "but
that's not going to make his name live for posterity. It's a
ghastly thing; Basin wanted to have it destroyed."

This last statement was one which Mme de Guermantes

often made. But at other times her appreciation of the picture was different: "I don't care for his painting, but he did once do a good portrait of me." The first of these judgments was addressed as a rule to people who spoke to the Duchess of her portrait, the other to those who did not refer to it and whom therefore she was anxious to inform of its existence. The first was inspired in her by coquetry, the second by vanity.

"Make a portrait of you look ghastly! Why, then it can't be a portrait, it's a lie. I don't know one end of a brush from the other, but I'm sure if I were to paint you, merely putting you down as I see you, I should produce a masterpiece," said the Princesse de Parme ingenuously.

"He probably sees me as I see myself, bereft of allurements," said the Duchesse de Guermantes, with the look, at once melancholy, modest and winning, which seemed to her best calculated to make her appear different from what Elstir had portrayed.

"That portrait ought to appeal to Mme de Gallardon," said the Duke.

"Because she knows nothing about pictures?" asked the Princesse de Parme, who knew that Mme de Guermantes had an infinite contempt for her cousin. "But she's a very kind woman, isn't she?"

The Duke assumed an air of profound astonishment.

"Why, Basin, don't you see the Princess is making fun of you?" (The Princess had never dreamed of doing such a thing.) "She knows as well as you do that Gallardonette is an old *poison*," went on Mme de Guermantes, whose vocabulary, habitually limited to all these old expressions, was as richly flavoured as those dishes which it is possible to come across in the delicious books of Pampille, but which have in real life become so rare, dishes in which the jellies, the butter, the gravy, the quenelles are all genuine and unalloyed, in which even the salt is brought specially from the salt-marshes of Brittany: from her accent, her choice of words, one felt that the basis of the Duchess's conversation came directly from Guermantes. In this way, the Duchess differed profoundly from her nephew Saint-Loup, impregnated by so many new ideas and expressions; it is difficult, when one's mind is troubled by

the ideas of Kant and the yearnings of Baudelaire, to write
the exquisite French of Henri IV, so that the very purity of
the Duchess's language was a sign of limitation and that, in
her, both intelligence and sensibility had remained closed
against innovation. Here again, Mme de Guermantes's mind
attracted me just because of what it excluded (which was
precisely the substance of my own thoughts) and everything
which, by virtue of that exclusion, it had been able to preserve,
that seductive vigour of supple bodies which no exhausting
reflexion, no moral anxiety or nervous disorder has deformed.
Her mind, of a formation so anterior to my own, was for me the
equivalent of what had been offered me by the gait and the
bearing of the girls of the little band along the sea-shore. Mme
de Guermantes offered me, domesticated and subdued by
civility, by respect for intellectual values, all the energy and
charm of a cruel little girl of one of the noble families round
Combray who from her childhood had been brought up in the
saddle, had tortured cats, gouged out the eyes of rabbits, and,
instead of having remained a pillar of virtue, might equally
well have been, a good few years ago now, so much did she
have the same-dashing style, the most brilliant mistress of the
Prince de Sagan. But she was incapable of understanding what I
had looked for in her—the charm of her historic name—and
the tiny quantity of it that I had found in her, a rustic survival
from Guermantes. Our relations were based on a misunderstanding which could not fail to become manifest as soon as
my homage, instead of being addressed to the relatively
superior woman she believed herself to be, was diverted to
some other woman of equal mediocrity and exuding the same
unconscious charm. A misunderstanding that is entirely
natural, and one that will always exist between a young
dreamer and a society woman, but nevertheless profoundly
disturbs him, so long as he has not yet discovered the nature
of his imaginative faculties and has not yet resigned himself
to the inevitable disappointments he is destined to find in
people, as in the theatre, in travel and indeed in love.

M. de Guermantes having declared (following upon Elstir's
asparagus and those that had just been served after the chicken
financière) that green asparagus grown in the open air, which,

as has been so quaintly said by the charming writer who signs herself E. de Clermont-Tonnerre, "have not the impressive rigidity of their sisters," ought to be eaten with eggs. "One man's meat is another man's poison, as they say," replied M. de Bréauté. "In the province of Canton, in China, the greatest delicacy that can be set before one is a dish of completely rotten ortolan's eggs." M. de Bréauté, the author of an essay on the Mormons which had appeared in the *Revue des Deux Mondes*, moved in none but the most aristocratic circles, but among these only such as had a certain reputation for intellect, with the result that from his presence, if it was at all regular, in a woman's house, one could tell that she had a "salon." He claimed to loathe society, and assured each of his duchesses in turn that it was for the sake of her wit and beauty that he came to see her. They all believed him. Whenever he resigned himself, with a heavy heart, to attending a big reception at the Princesse de Parme's, he collected them all around him to keep up his courage, and thus appeared only to be moving in the midst of an intimate circle. So that his reputation as an intellectual might survive his social activity, applying certain maxims of the Guermantes spirit, he would set out with the ladies of fashion on long scientific expeditions at the height of the dancing season, and when a snobbish person, in other words a person not yet socially secure, began to be seen everywhere, he would be ferociously obstinate in his refusal to know that person, to allow himself to be introduced to him or her. His hatred of snobs derived from his snobbishness, but made the simple-minded (in other words, everyone) believe that he was immune from snobbishness.

"Babal always knows everything," exclaimed the Duchesse de Guermantes. "I think it must be charming, a country where you can be quite sure that your dairyman will supply you with really rotten eggs, eggs of the year of the comet. I can just see myself dipping my bread and butter in them. I may say that it sometimes happens at aunt Madeleine's" (Mme de Villeparisis's) "that things are served in a state of putrefaction, eggs included." Then, as Mme d'Arpajon protested, "But my dear Phili, you know it as well as I do. You can see the chicken in the egg. In fact I can't think how they can be so well behaved as to stay in. It's not an omelette you get there, it's a regular chicken-run, but at least it isn't marked on the menu. You were so wise not to come to dinner there the day before yesterday, there was a brill cooked in carbolic! I assure you, it wasn't a dinner-table, it was far more like an isolation ward. Really, Norpois carries loyalty to the pitch of heroism: he had a second helping!"

"I believe I saw you there the time she lashed out at M. Bloch" (M. de Guermantes, perhaps to give a Jewish name a more foreign sound, pronounced the 'ch' in Bloch not like a 'k' but as in the German "*hoch*") "when he said about some poit" (poet) "or other that he was sublime. Châtellerault did his best to break M. Bloch's shins, but the fellow didn't understand and thought my nephew's kicks were aimed at a young woman sitting next to him." (At this point M. de Guermantes coloured slightly.) "He didn't realise that he was irritating our aunt with his 'sublimes' chucked about all over the place like that. Anyhow, aunt Madeleine, who's never at a loss for words, turned on him with: 'Indeed, sir, and what epithet are you going to keep for M. de Bossuet?'" (M. de Guermantes thought that, when one mentioned a famous name, the use of "Monsieur" and a particle was eminently "old school.") "It was absolutely killing."

"And what answer did this M. Bloch make?" came in a careless tone from Mme de Guermantes, who, running short for the moment of original ideas, felt that she must copy her husband's Teutonic pronunciation.

"Ah! I can assure you M. Bloch didn't wait for any more, he fled."

"Yes, I remember very well seeing you there that evening," said Mme de Guermantes with emphasis, as though there must be something highly flattering to myself in this remembrance on her part. "It's always so interesting at my aunt's. At that last party, where I met you, I meant to ask you whether that old gentleman who went past us wasn't François Coppée. You must know who everyone is," she went on, sincerely envious of my relations with poets and poetry, and also out of amiability towards me, the wish to enhance the status, in the eyes of her other guests, of a young man so well versed in literature.

I assured the Duchess that I had not observed any celebrities at Mme de Villeparisis's party. "What!" she exclaimed unguardedly, betraying the fact that her respect for men of letters and her contempt for society were more superficial than she said, perhaps even than she thought, "what, no famous authors there! You astonish me! Why, I saw all sorts of quite impossible-looking people!"

I remembered the evening very well on account of an entirely trivial incident. Mme de Villeparisis had introduced Bloch to Mme Alphonse de Rothschild, but my friend had not caught the name and, thinking he was talking to an old English lady who was a trifle mad, had replied only in monosyllables to the garrulous conversation of the historic beauty, when Mme de Villeparisis, introducing her to someone else, had pronounced, quite distinctly this time: "The Baronne Alphonse de Rothschild." Thereupon so many ideas of millions and of glamour, which it would have been more prudent to subdivide and separate, had suddenly and simultaneously coursed through Bloch's arteries that he had had a sort of heart attack and brainstorm combined, and had cried aloud in the dear old lady's presence: "If I'd only known!"— an exclamation the silliness of which kept him awake at nights for a whole week. This remark of Bloch's was of no great interest, but I remembered it as a proof that sometimes in this life, under the stress of an exceptional emotion, people do say what they think.

"I fancy Mme de Villeparisis is not absolutely . . . moral," said the Princesse de Parme, who knew that the best people did not visit the Duchess's aunt, and, from what the Duchess herself had just been saying, that one might speak freely about her. But, Mme de Guermantes not seeming to approve of this criticism, she hastened to add: "Though, of course, intelligence carried to that degree excuses everything."

"You take the same view of my aunt as everyone else," replied the Duchess, "which is, on the whole, quite mistaken. It's just what Mémé was saying to me only yesterday." (She blushed, her eyes clouding with a memory unknown to me. I conjectured that M. de Charlus had asked her to cancel my invitation, as he had sent Robert to ask me not to go to her

house. I had the impression that the blush—equally incomprehensible to me—which had tinged the Duke's cheeks when he
made some reference to his brother could not be attributed to
to the same cause.) "My poor aunt—she will always have the
reputation of being a lady of the old school, of sparkling wit and
uncontrolled passions. And really there's no more middle-class,
solemn, drab, commonplace mind in Paris. She will go down
as a patron of the arts, which means to say that she was once
the mistress of a great painter, though he was never able to
make her understand what a picture was; and as for her private
life, so far from being a depraved woman, she was so much
made for marriage, so conjugal from her cradle that, not having succeeded in keeping a husband, who incidentally was a
scoundrel, she has never had a love affair which she hasn't
taken just as seriously as if it were holy matrimony, with the
same irritations, the same quarrels, the same fidelity. Mind
you, those relationships are often the most sincere; on the
whole there are more inconsolable lovers than husbands."

"And yet, Oriane, if you take the case of your brother-in-law
Palamède whom you were speaking about just now, no
mistress in the world could ever dream of being mourned as
that poor Mme de Charlus has been."

"Ah!" replied the Duchess, "Your Highness must permit
me to be not altogether of her opinion. People don't all like
to be mourned in the same way, each of us has his prefer-
ences."

"Still, he has made a regular cult of her since her death. It's
true that people sometimes do for the dead what they would
not have done for the living."

"For one thing," retorted Mme de Guermantes in a dreamy
tone which belied her facetious intent, "we go to their funerals,
which we never do for the living!" (M. de Guermantes gave
M. de Bréauté a sly glance as though to provoke him into
laughter at the Duchess's wit.) "At the same time I frankly
admit," went on Mme de Guermantes, "that the manner in
which I should like to be mourned by a man I loved would not
be that adopted by my brother-in-law."

The Duke's face darkened. He did not like to hear his wife
utter random judgments, especially about M. de Charlus.

"You're very particular. His grief set an edifying example to everyone," he reproved her stiffly. But the Duchess had in dealing with her husband that sort of boldness which animal tamers show, or people who live with a madman and are not afraid of provoking him.

"Well, yes, if you like, I suppose it's edifying—he goes every day to the cemetery to tell her how many people he has had to luncheon, he misses her enormously, but as he'd mourn a cousin, a grandmother, a sister. It isn't the grief of a husband. It's true that they were a pair of saints, which makes it all rather exceptional." (M. de Guermantes, infuriated by his wife's chatter, fixed on her with a terrible immobility a pair of eyes already loaded.) "I don't wish to say anything against poor Mémé, who, by the way, couldn't come this evening," went on the Duchess. "I quite admit there's no one like him, he's kind and sweet, he has a delicacy, a warmth of heart that you don't as a rule find in men. He has a woman's heart, Mémé has!"

"What you say is absurd," M. de Guermantes broke in sharply. "There's nothing effeminate about Mémé. Nobody could be more manly than he is."

"But I'm not suggesting for a moment that he's the least bit effeminate. Do at least take the trouble to understand what I say," retorted the Duchess. "He's always like that the moment he thinks one's getting at his brother," she added, turning to the Princesse de Parme.

"It's very charming, it's a pleasure to hear him. There's nothing so nice as two brothers who are fond of each other," replied the Princess, as many a humbler person might have replied, for it is possible to belong to a princely family by blood and a very plebeian family by intellect.

"While we're on the subject of your family, Oriane," said the Princess, "I saw your nephew Saint-Loup yesterday. I believe he wants to ask you a favour."

The Duc de Guermantes knitted his Olympian brow. When he did not care to do someone a favour, he preferred that his wife should not undertake to do so, knowing that it would come to the same thing in the end and that the people to whom she would be obliged to apply would put it down to the common account of the household, just as much as if it had been requested by the husband alone.

"Why didn't he ask me himself?" said the Duchess, "he was here yesterday and stayed a couple of hours, and I can't tell you how boring he was. He would be no stupider than anyone else if he had only had the sense, like many people we know, to remain a fool. It's his veneer of knowledge that's so terrible. He wants to have an open mind—open to all the things he doesn't understand. The way he goes on about Morocco, it's frightful."

"He doesn't want to go back there, because of Rachel," said the Prince de Foix.

"But I thought they'd broken it off," interrupted M. de Bréauté.

"So far from breaking it off, I found her a couple of days ago in Robert's rooms, and they didn't look at all like people who'd quarrelled, I can assure you," replied the Prince de Foix, who liked to spread every rumour that could damage Robert's chances of marrying, and who might, moreover, have been misled by one of the intermittent resumptions of a liaison that was practically at an end.

"That Rachel was speaking to me about you. I run into her occasionally in the morning in the Champs-Elysées. She's a sort of *évaporée* as you say, what you call *dégrafée*, a kind of 'Dame aux Camélias,' figuratively speaking, of course." (This speech was addressed to me by Prince Von, who liked always to appear conversant with French literature and Parisian refinements.)

"Why, that's just what it was—Morocco!" exclaimed the Princess, flinging herself into this opening.

"What on earth can he want in Morocco?" asked M. de Guermantes sternly. "Oriane can do absolutely nothing for him there, as he knows perfectly well."

"He thinks he invented strategy," Mme de Guermantes pursued the theme, "and then he uses impossible words for the simplest thing, which doesn't prevent him from making blots all over his letters. The other day he announced that he'd been given some *sublime* potatoes, and that he'd taken a *sublime* stage box."

"He speaks Latin," the Duke went one better.

"What! Latin?" the Princess gasped.

"On my word of honour! Your Highness can ask Oriane if I'm not telling the truth."

"Why, yes, Ma'am; the other day he said to us straight out, without stopping to think: 'I know of no more touching example of *sic transit gloria mundi*.' I can repeat the phrase now to Your Highness because, after endless inquiries and by appealing to *linguists*, we succeeded in reconstructing it, but Robert flung it out without pausing for breath, one could hardly make out that there was Latin in it, he was just like a character in the *Malade Imaginaire*. And it was simply to do with the death of the Empress of Austria!"

"Poor woman!" cried the Princess, "what a delicious creature she was!"

"Yes," replied the Duchess, "a trifle mad, a trifle headstrong, but she was a thoroughly good woman, a nice, kind-hearted lunatic; the only thing I could never understand was why she never managed to get a set of false teeth that fitted her; they always came loose half-way through a sentence and she was obliged to stop short or she'd have swallowed them."

"That Rachel was telling me that young Saint-Loup worshipped you, that he was fonder of you than he was of her," said Prince Von to me, devouring his food like an ogre as he spoke, his face scarlet, his teeth bared by his perpetual grin.

"But in that case she must be jealous of me and hate me," said I.

"Not at all, she said all sorts of nice things about you. The Prince de Foix's mistress would perhaps be jealous if he preferred you to her. You don't understand? Come home with me, and I'll explain it all to you."

"I'm afraid I can't, I'm going on to M. de Charlus at eleven."

"Why, he sent round to me yesterday to ask me to dine with him this evening, but told me not to come after a quarter to eleven. But if you insist on going to him, at least come with me as far as the Théâtre-Francais, you will be in the periphery," said the Prince, who thought doubtless that this last word meant "proximity" or possibly "centre."

But the bulging eyes in his coarse though handsome red face frightened me and I declined, saying that a friend was coming to call for me. This reply seemed to me in no way offensive. The Prince, however, apparently formed a different impression of it, for he did not say another word to me.

"I really must go and see the Queen of Naples—it must be a great grief to her," said, or at least appeared to me to have said, the Princesse de Parme. For her words had come to me only indistinctly through the intervening screen of those addressed to me, albeit in an undertone, by Prince Von, who had doubtless been afraid of being overheard by the Prince de Foix if he spoke louder.

"Oh, dear, no!" replied the Duchess, "I don't believe she feels any grief at all."

"None at all! You do always fly to extremes, Oriane," said M. de Guermantes, resuming his role as the cliff which, by standing up against the wave, forces it to fling even higher its crest of foam.

"Basin knows even better than I that I'm telling the truth," replied the Duchess, "but he thinks he's obliged to look severe because you are present, Ma'am, and he's afraid of my shocking you."

"Oh, please no, I beg of you," cried the Princesse de Parme, dreading the slightest alteration on her account of these delicious evenings at the Duchesse de Guermantes's, this forbidden fruit which the Queen of Sweden herself had not yet acquired the right to taste.

"Why, it was to Basin himself, when he said to her with a duly sorrowful expression: 'But I see the Queen is in mourning. For whom, pray? Is it a great grief to Your Majesty?' that she replied: 'No, it's not a deep mourning, it's a light mourning, a very light mourning, it's my sister.' The truth is, she's delighted about it, as Basin knows perfectly well. She invited us to a party that very evening, and gave me two pearls. I wish she could lose a sister every day! So far from weeping for her sister's death, she was in fits of laughter over it. She probably says to herself, like Robert, '*sic transit*——' I forget how it goes on," she added modestly, knowing how it went on perfectly well.

In saying all this Mme de Guermantes was only indulging her wit, and in the most disingenuous way, for the Queen of Naples, like the Duchesse d'Alençon, who also died in tragic circumstances, had the warmest heart in the world and sincerely mourned her kinsfolk. Mme de Guermantes knew these noble Bavarian sisters, her cousins, too well not to be aware of this. "He is anxious not to go back to Morocco," said the Princesse de Parme, grasping once more at the name Robert which Mme de Guermantes had held out to her, quite unintentionally, like a lifeline. "I believe you know General de Monserfeuil."

"Very slightly," replied the Duchess, who was an intimate friend of the officer in question. The Princess explained what it was that Saint-Loup wanted.

"Oh dear, well, yes, if I see him . . . It's possible that I may run into him," the Duchess replied, so as not to appear to be refusing, her relations with General de Monserfeuil seeming to have grown rapidly more intermittent since it had become a question of her asking him for something. This uncertainty did not, however, satisfy the Duke, who interrupted his wife.

"You know perfectly well you won't be seeing him, Oriane, and besides you've already asked him for two things which he hasn't done. My wife has a passion for doing people good turns," he went on, getting more and more furious in order to force the Princess to withdraw her request without making her doubt his wife's good nature and so that Mme de Parme should throw the blame on his own essentially crotchety character. "Robert could get anything he wanted out of Monserfeuil. Only, as he happens not to know what he wants, he gets us to ask for it because he knows there's no better way of making the whole thing fall through. A request from her now would be a reason for him to refuse."

"Oh, in that case, it would be better if the Duchess did nothing," said Mme de Parme.

"Obviously!" the Duke closed the discussion.

"That poor General, he's been defeated again at the elections," said the Princess, to change the subject.

"Oh, it's nothing serious, it's only the seventh time," said the Duke, who, having been obliged himself to retire from politics, quite enjoyed hearing of other people's failures at the polls.

"He has consoled himself by giving his wife another baby."

"What! Is that poor Mme de Monserfeuil pregnant again?" cried the Princess.

"Why, of course," replied the Duchess, "it's the one *arrondissement* where the poor General has never failed."

In the period that followed I was continually to be invited, however small the party, to these repasts at which I had at one time imagined the guests as seated like the Apostles in the Sainte-Chapelle. They did assemble there indeed, like the early Christians, not to partake merely of a material nourishment, which was incidentally exquisite, but in a sort of social Eucharist; so that in the course of a few dinner-parties I assimilated the acquaintance of all the friends of my hosts, friends to whom they presented me with a tinge of benevolent patronage so marked (as a person for whom they had always had a sort of parental affection) that there was not one among them who would not have felt himself to be somehow failing the Duke and Duchess if he had given a ball without including my name on his list, and at the same time, while I sipped one of those Yquems which lay concealed in the Guermantes cellars, I tasted ortolans dressed according to a variety of recipes judiciously elaborated and modified by the Duke himself. However, for one who had already sat down more than once at the mystic board, the consumption of these latter was not indispensable. Old friends of M. and Mme de Guermantes came in to see them after dinner, "with the tooth-picks" as Mme Swann would have said, without being expected, and took in winter a cup of *tilleul* in the lighted warmth of the great drawing-room, in summer a glass of orangeade in the darkness of the little rectangular strip of garden outside. No one could remember having ever received from the Guermantes, on these evenings in the garden, anything else but orangeade. It had a sort of ritual meaning. To have added other refreshments would have seemed to be falsifying the tradition, just as a big at-home in the Faubourg Saint-Germain ceases to be an at-home if there is a play also, or music. You must be assumed to have come simply—even if there were five hundred of you—to pay a call on, let us say, the Princesse de Guermantes. People marvelled at my influence because I

managed to procure the addition to this orangeade of a jug
containing the juice of stewed cherries or stewed pears. I took
a dislike on this account to the Prince d'Agrigente, who was
like all those people who, lacking in imagination but not in
covetousness, take a keen interest in what one is drinking and
ask if they may taste a little of it themselves. Which meant that,
every time, M. d'Agrigente, by diminishing my ration,
spoiled my pleasure. For this fruit juice can never be provided
in sufficient quantities to quench one's thirst. Nothing is less
cloying than that transmutation into flavour of the colour of a
fruit, which, when cooked, seems to have travelled backwards
to the season of its blossoming. Blushing like an orchard in
spring, or else colourless and cool like the zephyr beneath the
fruit-trees, the juice can be sniffed and gloated over drop by
drop, and M. d'Agrigente prevented me, regularly, from taking
my fill of it. Despite these distillations, the traditional orangeade persisted like the *tilleul*. In these humble kinds, the social
communion was none the less administered. In this respect,
doubtless, the friends of M. and Mme de Guermantes had
after all, as I had originally imagined them, remained more
different from the rest of humanity than their outward appearance might have misled me into supposing. Numbers of
elderly men came to receive from the Duchess, together with
the invariable drink, a welcome that was often far from warm.
Now this could not have been due to snobbishness, they
themselves being of a rank to which there was none superior;
nor to love of luxury: they did love it perhaps, but, in less
exalted social conditions, might have been enjoying a glittering
example of it, for on those same evenings the charming wife of
a colossally rich financier would have given anything in the
world to have them among the brilliant shooting-party she
was giving for a couple of days for the King of Spain. They had
nevertheless declined her invitation, and had come round
without fail to see whether Mme de Guermantes was at home.
They were not even certain of finding there opinions that conformed entirely with their own, or sentiments of any great cordiality; Mme de Guermantes would throw out from time to time
—on the Dreyfus case, on the Republic, on the anti-religious
laws, or even, in an undertone, on themselves, their weak-

nesses, the dullness of their conversation—comments which they had to appear not to notice. No doubt, if they kept up their habit of coming there, it was owing to their consummate training as epicures in things wordly, to their clear conscious- ness of the prime and perfect quality of the social pabulum, with its familiar, reassuring, sapid flavour, free of admixture or adulteration, with the origin and history of which they were as well acquainted as she who served them with it, remaining more "noble" in this respect than they themselves imagined. Now, on this occasion, among the visitors to whom I was introduced after dinner, it so happened that there was that General de Monserfeuil of whom the Princesse de Parme had spoken and whom Mme de Guermantes, of whose drawing- room he was one of the regular frequenters, had not expected that evening. He bowed before me, on hearing my name, as though I had been the President of the Supreme War Council. I had supposed it to be simply from some deep-rooted un- willingness to oblige, in which the Duke, as in wit if not in love, was his wife's accomplice, that the Duchess had practically refused to recommend her nephew to M. de Monserfeuil. And I saw in this an indifference all the more blameworthy in that I seemed to have gathered from a few words which the Princess had let fall that Robert was in a post of danger from which it would be prudent to have him re- moved. But it was by the genuine malice of Mme de Guer- mantes that I was revolted when, the Princesse de Parme having timidly suggested that she might say something herself and on her own initiative to the general, the Duchess did everything in her power to dissuade her.

"But Ma'am," she cried, "Monserfeuil has no sort of stand- ing or influence whatever with the new Government. You would be wasting your breath."

"I think he can hear us," murmured the Princess, as a hint to the Duchess not to speak so loud.

"Your Highness needn't be afraid, he's as deaf as a post," said the Duchess, without lowering her voice, though the General could hear her perfectly.

"The thing is, I believe M. de Saint-Loup is in a place that is not very safe," said the Princess.

"It can't be helped," replied the Duchess, "he's in the same boat as everybody else, the only difference being that it was he who asked to be sent there. Besides, no, it's not really dangerous; if it was, you can imagine how anxious I should be to help. I'd have spoken to Saint-Joseph about it during dinner. He has far more influence, and he's a real worker. But, as you see, he's gone now. Besides, it would be less awkward than going to this one, who has three of his sons in Morocco just now and has refused to apply for them to be transferred; he might raise that as an objection. Since Your Highness insists, I shall speak to Saint-Joseph—if I see him again, or to Beautreillis. But if I don't see either of them, you mustn't waste your pity on Robert. It was explained to us the other day where he is. I don't think he could be anywhere better."

"What a pretty flower, I've never seen one like it; there's no one like you, Oriane, for having such marvellous things in your house," said the Princesse de Parme, who, fearing that General de Monserfeuil might have overheard the Duchess, sought now to change the subject. I looked and recognised a plant of the sort that I had watched Elstir painting.

"I'm so glad you like them; they are charming, do look at their little purple velvet collars; the only thing against them is—as may happen with people who are very pretty and very nicely dressed—they have a hideous name and a horrid smell. In spite of which I'm very fond of them. But what is rather sad is that they're going to die."

"But they're growing in a pot, they aren't cut flowers," said the Princess.

"No," answered the Duchess with a smile, "but it comes to the same thing, as they're all ladies. It's a kind of plant where the ladies and the gentlemen don't both grow on the same stalk. I'm like the people who keep a lady dog. I have to find a husband for my flowers. Otherwise I shan't have any young ones!"

"How very strange. Do you mean to say that in nature. . .?"

"Yes, there are certain insects whose duty it is to bring about the marriage, as with sovereigns, by proxy, without the bride and bridegroom ever having set eyes on one another. And so, I assure you, I always tell my man to put my plant at the open

window as often as possible, on the courtyard side and the
garden side turn about, in the hope that the necessary insect will
arrive. But the odds are so enormous! Just think, he would have
to have just been to see a person of the same species and the
opposite sex, and he must then have taken it into his head to
come and leave cards at the house. He hasn't appeared so far
—I believe my plant can still qualify for the white flower of
maidenhood, but I must say a little more shamelessness would
please me better. It's just the same with that fine tree we have
in the courtyard—it will die childless because it belongs to a
species that's very rare in these latitudes. In its case, it's the
wind that's responsible for bringing about the union, but the
wall is a trifle high."

"Yes, indeed," said M. de Bréauté, "you ought to have
taken just a couple of inches off the top, that would have been
quite enough. You have to know all the tricks of the trade.
The flavour of vanilla we tasted in the excellent ice you gave us
this evening, Duchess, comes from a plant called the vanilla
tree. This plant produces flowers which are both male and
female, but a sort of partition between them prevents any
communication. And so one could never get any fruit from
them until a young negro, a native of Réunion, by the name
of Albins, which by the way is rather a comic name for a
black man since it means 'white,' had the happy thought of
using the point of a needle to bring the separate organs into
contact."

"Babal, you're divine, you know everything," cried the
Duchess.

"But you yourself, Oriane, have taught me things I had no
idea of," the Princesse de Parme assured her.

"I must explain to Your Highness that it's Swann who has
always talked to me a great deal about botany. Sometimes
when we thought it would be too boring to go to an afternoon
party we would set off for the country, and he would show
me extraordinary marriages between flowers, which was far
more amusing than going to human marriages—no wedding-
breakfast and no crowd in the sacristy. We never had time to
go very far. Now that motor-cars have come in, it would be
delightful. Unfortunately, in the meantime he himself has

made an even more astonishing marriage, which makes everything very difficult. Ah, Ma'am, life is a dreadful business, we spend our whole time doing things that bore us, and when by chance we come across somebody with whom we could go and look at something really interesting, he has to make a marriage like Swann's. Faced with the alternatives of giving up my botanical expeditions and being obliged to call upon a degrading person, I chose the first of these two calamities. Actually, though, there's no need to go quite so far. It seems that even here, in my own little bit of garden, more improper things happen in broad daylight than at midnight . . . in the Bois de Boulogne! Only they attract no attention, because between flowers it's all done quite simply—you see a little orange shower, or else a very dusty fly coming to wipe its feet or take a bath before crawling into a flower. And that does the trick!"

"The cabinet the plant is standing on is splendid, too; it's Empire, I believe," said the Princess, who, not being familiar with the works of Darwin and his followers, was unable to grasp the point of the Duchess's pleasantries.

"It's lovely, isn't it? I'm so glad Your Highness likes it," replied the Duchess, "it's a magnificent piece. I must tell you that I've always adored the Empire style, even when it wasn't in fashion. I remember at Guermantes I got into terrible disgrace with my mother-in-law because I told them to bring down from the attics all the splendid Empire furniture Basin had inherited from the Montesquious, and used it to furnish the wing we lived in."

M. de Guermantes smiled. He must nevertheless have remembered that the course of events had been very different. But, the witticisms of the Princesse des Laumes on the subject of her mother-in-law's bad taste having been a tradition during the short time in which the Prince had been in love with his wife, his love for the latter had been outlasted by a certain contempt for the intellectual inferiority of the former, a contempt which, however, went hand in hand with considerable attachment and respect.

"The Iénas have the same armchair with Wedgwood medallions. It's a fine piece, but I prefer mine," said the Duchess,

with the same air of impartiality as if she had not been the
owner of either of these two pieces of furniture. "I admit,
of course, that they've got some marvellous things which I
haven't."

The Princesse de Parme remained silent.

"But it's quite true; Your Highness hasn't seen their collection. Oh, you ought really to come there one day with me, it's
one of the most magnificent things in Paris. You'd say it was a
museum come to life."

And since this suggestion was one of the most "Guermantes"
of the Duchess's audacities, inasmuch as the Iénas were for the
Princesse de Parme rank usurpers, their son bearing like her
own the title of Duc de Guastalla, Mme de Guermantes in thus
launching it could not refrain (so much did the love that she
bore her own originality prevail over the deference due to the
Princesse de Parme) from glancing round at her other guests
with an amused smile. They too made an effort to smile, at
once alarmed, amazed and above all delighted to think that
they were being witnesses of Oriane's very "latest" and
could serve it up "piping hot." They were only half shocked,
knowing that the Duchess had the knack of throwing all the
Courvoisier prejudices to the wind for the sake of a more
striking and enjoyable triumph. Had she not, within the last
few years, brought together Princesse Mathilde and the Duc
d'Aumale, who had written to the Princess's own brother the
famous letter: "In my family all the men are brave and the
women chaste"? And inasmuch as princes remain princely
even at those moments when they appear anxious to forget
that they are, the Duc d'Aumale and the Princesse Mathilde
had enjoyed themselves so greatly at Mme de Guermantes's
that they had afterwards exchanged visits, with that faculty for
forgetting the past which Louis XVIII showed when he
appointed as a minister Fouché, who had voted the death of
his brother. Mme de Guermantes was now nursing a similar
project of arranging a reconciliation between the Princesse
Murat and the Queen of Naples. In the meantime, the
Princesse de Parme appeared as embarrassed as might have
been the heirs-apparent to the thrones of the Netherlands and
Belgium, styled respectively Prince of Orange and Duke of

Brabant, had one offered to present to them M. de Mailly-
Nesle, Prince d'Orange, and M. de Charlus, Duc de Brabant.
But, before anything further could happen, the Duchess, in
whom Swann and M. de Charlus between them (albeit the
latter was resolute in ignoring the Iénas' existence) had with
great difficulty succeeded in inculcating a taste for the Empire
style, exclaimed:

"Honestly, Ma'am, I can't tell you how beautiful you'll find
it! I must confess that the Empire style has always had a
fascination for me. But at the Iénas' it really is hallucinating.
That sort of—what shall I say—reflux from the Egyptian
expedition, and then, too, the sort of upsurge into our own
times from Antiquity, all those things invading our houses,
the Sphinxes crouching at the feet of the armchairs, the snakes
coiled round candelabra, a huge Muse who holds out a little
torch for you to play cards under, or has quietly climbed on
to the mantelpiece and is leaning against your clock; and then
all the Pompeian lamps, the little boat-shaped beds which
look as if they had been found floating on the Nile so that you
expect to see Moses climb out of them, the classical chariots
galloping along the bedside tables. . . ."

"They're not very comfortable to sit in, those Empire chairs,"
the Princess ventured.

"No," the Duchess agreed, "but I love," she at once added,
stressing the point with a smile, "I love being uncomfortable
on those mahogany seats covered with ruby velvet or green
silk. I love that discomfort of warriors who understand
nothing but the curule chair and weave their fasces and pile
their laurels in the middle of their main living-room. I can
assure you that at the Iénas' one doesn't stop to think for a
moment of how comfortable one is, when one sees in front of
one a great strapping wench of a Victory painted in fresco on
the wall. My husband is going to say that I'm a very bad
royalist, but I'm terribly disloyal, you know, I can assure
you that in those people's house one comes to love all the
big N's and all the bees. Good heavens, after all, since we
hadn't been exactly surfeited with glory for a good many years
under our kings, those warriors who brought home so many
crowns that they stuck them even on the arms of the chairs,

I must say I think it's all rather fetching! Your Highness really must."

"Why, my dear, if you think so," said the Princess, "but it seems to me that it won't be easy."

"But Your Highness will find that it will all go quite smoothly. They are very kind people, and no fools. We took Mme de Chevreuse there," added the Duchess, knowing the force of this example, "and she was enchanted. The son is really very pleasant . . . I'm going to tell you something that's not quite proper," she went on, "but he has a bedroom, and more especially a bed, in which I should love to sleep—without him! What is even less proper is that I went to see him once when he was ill and lying in it. By his side, on the frame of the bed, there was a sculpted Siren, stretched out at full length, absolutely ravishing, with a mother-of-pearl tail and some sort of lotus flowers in her hand. I assure you," went on Mme de Guermantes, reducing the speed of her delivery to bring into even bolder relief the words which she seemed to be modelling with the pout of her fine lips, drawing them out with her long expressive hands, directing on the Princess as she spoke a soft, intent, profound gaze, "that with the palm-leaves and the golden crown on one side, it was most moving, it was precisely the same composition as Gustave Moreau's *Death and the Young Man* (Your Highness must know that masterpiece, of course)."

The Princesse de Parme, who did not know so much as the painter's name, nodded her head vehemently and smiled ardently, in order to manifest her admiration for this picture. But the intensity of her mimicry could not fill the place of that light which is absent from our eyes so long as we do not understand what people are talking to us about.

"A good-looking boy, I believe?" she asked.

"No, he's just like a tapir. The eyes are a little those of a Queen Hortense on a lamp-shade. But he probably came to the conclusion that it would be rather absurd for a man to develop such a resemblance, and so it's lost in the encaustic surface of his cheeks which give him really rather a Mameluke appearance. You feel that the polisher must call round every morning. Swann," she went on, reverting to the young duke's bed, "was struck by the resemblance between that Siren and Gustave Moreau's *Death*. But in fact," she added, in a more rapid but still serious tone of voice, in order to provoke more laughter, "there was nothing really to get worked up about, for it was only a cold in the head, and the young man is now as fit as a fiddle."

"They say he's a snob?" put in M. de Bréauté, with a malicious twinkle, expecting to be answered with the same precision as though he had said: "They tell me that he has only four fingers on his right hand; is that so?"

"G—ood g—racious, n—o," replied Mme de Guermantes with a smile of benign tolerance. "Perhaps just the least little bit of a snob in appearance, because he's extremely young, but I should be surprised to hear that he was in reality, for he's intelligent," she added, as though there were to her mind some absolute incompatibility between snobbishness and intelligence. "He has wit, too, I've known him to be quite amusing," she said again, laughing with the air of an epicure and expert, as though the act of declaring that a person could be amusing demanded a certain expression of merriment from the speaker, or as though the Duc de Guastalla's sallies were recurring to her mind as she spoke. "Anyway, as he is never invited anywhere, he can't have much scope for his snobbishness," she wound up, oblivious of the fact that this was hardly an encouragement to the Princesse de Parme.

"I cannot help wondering what the Prince de Guermantes, who calls her Mme Iéna, will say if he hears that I've been to see her."

"What!" cried the Duchess with extraordinary vivacity. "Don't you know that it was we who gave up to Gilbert" (she bitterly regretted that surrender now) "a complete card-room done in the Empire style which came to us from Quiou-Quiou and is an absolute marvel! There was no room for it here, though I think it would look better here than it does in his house. It's a thing of sheer beauty, half Etruscan, half Egyptian. . . ."

"Egyptian?" queried the Princess, to whom the word Etruscan conveyed little.

"Well, you know, a little of both. Swann told us that, he

explained it all to me, only you know I'm such a dunce. But then, Ma'am, what one has to bear in mind is that the Egypt of the Empire cabinet-makers has nothing to do with the historical Egypt, nor their Romans with the Romans nor their Etruria. . . ."

"Indeed," said the Princess.

"No, it's like what they used to call a Louis XV costume under the Second Empire, when Anna de Mouchy and dear Brigode's mother were girls. Basin was talking to you just now about Beethoven. We heard a thing of his played the other day which was really rather fine, though a little stiff, with a Russian theme in it. It's pathetic to think that he believed it to be Russian. In the same way as the Chinese painters believed they were copying Bellini. Besides, even in the same country, whenever anybody begins to look at things in a slightly new way, nine hundred and ninety-nine people out of a thousand are totally incapable of seeing what he puts before them. It takes at least forty years before they can manage to make it out."

"Forty years!" the Princess cried in alarm.

"Why, yes," went on the Duchess, adding more and more to her words (which were practically my own, for I had just been expressing a similar idea to her), thanks to her way of pronouncing them, the equivalent of what on the printed page are called italics, "it's like a sort of first isolated individual of a species which does not yet exist but is going to multiply in the future, an individual endowed with a kind of *sense* which the human race of his generation does not possess. I can hardly give myself as an instance because I, on the contrary, have always loved any interesting artistic offering from the very start, however novel it might be. But anyway the other day I was with the Grand Duchess in the Louvre and we happened to pass Manet's *Olympia*. Nowadays nobody is in the least surprised by it. It looks just like an Ingres! And yet, heaven knows how I had to take up the cudgels on behalf of that picture, which I don't altogether like but which is unquestionably the work of *somebody*. Perhaps the Louvre isn't quite the place for it."

"And is the Grand Duchess well?" inquired the Princesse de

Parme, to whom the Tsar's aunt was infinitely more familiar than Manet's model.

"Yes; we talked about you. After all," she resumed, clinging to her idea, "the fact of the matter is, as my brother-in-law Palamède always says, that one has between oneself and the rest of the world the barrier of a strange language.* Though I admit that there's no one it's quite so true of as Gilbert. If it amuses you to go to the Iénas', you have far too much sense to let your actions be governed by what that poor fellow may think—he's a dear, innocent creature, but he really lives in another world. I feel nearer, more akin to my coachman, my horses even, than to a man who keeps on harking back to what people would have thought under Philip the Bold or Louis the Fat. Just fancy, when he goes for a walk in the country, he waves the peasants out of his way with his stick, quite affably, saying 'Get along there, churls!' In fact I'm as amazed when he speaks to me as if I heard myself addressed by a recumbent figure on an old Gothic tomb. It's all very well that animated gravestone's being my cousin; he frightens me, and the only idea that comes into my head is to let him stay in his Middle Ages. Apart from that, I quite admit that he's never murdered anyone."

"I've just been seeing him at dinner at Mme de Villeparisis's," said the General, but without either smiling at or endorsing the Duchess's pleasantries.

"Was M. de Norpois there?" asked Prince Von, whose mind still ran on the Academy of Moral Sciences.

"Yes," said the General. "In fact he was talking about your Emperor."

"It seems the Emperor William is highly intelligent, but he doesn't care for Elstir's painting. Not that that's anything against him," said the Duchess, "I quite share his point of view. Although Elstir has done a fine portrait of me. You don't know it? It's not in the least like me, but it's an intriguing piece of work. He's most interesting while one's sitting to him. He has made me like a little old woman. It's modelled on *The Female Regents of the Hospital*, by Hals. I expect you know those sublimities, to borrow one of my nephew's favourite expressions," the Duchess turned to me, gently flapping her black feather fan. More than erect on her chair, she flung her head nobly backwards, for, while always a great lady, she was a trifle inclined to act the part of the great lady too. I said that I had been once to Amsterdam and The Hague, but that to avoid getting everything muddled up, since my time was limited, I had left out Haarlem.

"Ah! The Hague! What a gallery!" cried M. de Guermantes. I said to him that he had doubtless admired Vermeer's *View of Delft*. But the Duke was less erudite than arrogant. Accordingly he contented himself with replying in a self-complacent tone, as was his habit whenever anyone spoke to him of a picture in a gallery, or in the Salon, which he did not remember having seen: "If it's to be seen, I saw it!"

"What? You've been to Holland, and you never visited Haarlem!" cried the Duchess. "Why, even if you had only a quarter of an hour to spend in the place, they're an extraordinary thing to have seen, those Halses. I don't mind saying that a person who only caught a passing glimpse of them from the top of a tram without stopping, supposing they were hung out to view in the street, would open his eyes pretty wide."

This remark shocked me as indicating a misconception of the way in which artistic impressions are formed in our minds, and because it seemed to imply that our eye is in that case simply a recording machine which takes snapshots.

M. de Guermantes, rejoicing that she should be speaking to me with so competent a knowledge of the subjects that interested me, appraised his wife's illustrious presence, listened to what she was saying about Franz Hals, and thought: "She's thoroughly at home in everything. Our young friend can go home and say that he's had before his eyes a great lady of the old school, in the full sense of the word, the like of whom couldn't be found anywhere else to-day." Thus I beheld the pair of them, divorced from that name Guermantes in which long ago I had imagined them leading an unimaginable life, now just like other men and other women, merely lagging a little behind their contemporaries, and that not evenly, as in so many households of the Faubourg Saint-Germain where the wife has had the good taste to stop at the golden, the husband the misfortune to come down to the pinchbeck age of the past, she remaining still Louis XV while her partner is pompously Louis-Philippe. That Mme de Guermantes should be like other women had been for me at first a disappointment; it was now, by a natural reaction, and with the help of so many good wines, almost a miracle. A Don John of Austria, an Isabella d'Este, situated for us in the world of names, have as little communication with the great pages of history as the Méséglise way had with the Guermantes. Isabella d'Este was no doubt in reality a very minor princess, similar to those who under Louis XIV obtained no special place at Court. But because she seems to us to be of a unique and therefore incomparable essence, we cannot conceive of her as being any less great than he, so that a supper-party with Louis XIV would appear to us only to be rather interesting, whereas with Isabella d'Este we should find ourselves miraculously transported into the presence of a heroine of romance. Then, after having studied Isabella d'Este, after having transplanted her patiently from that magic world into the world of history, and discovered that her life, her thought, contained nothing of that mysterious strangeness which had been suggested to us by her name, once we have recovered from our disappointment we feel a boundless gratitude to that princess for having had a knowledge of Mantegna's paintings almost equal to that, hitherto despised by us and put, as Françoise would have said, "lower than the dirt," of M. Lafenestre. After having scaled the inaccessible heights of the name Guermantes, on descending the inner slope of the life of the Duchess, I felt on finding there the names, familiar elsewhere, of Victor Hugo, Franz Hals and, I regret to say, Vibert, the same astonishment that an explorer, after having taken into account, in order to visualise the singularity of the native customs in some wild valley of Central America or Northern Africa, its geographical remoteness, the strangeness of its place-names, of its flora, feels on discovering, once he has made his way through a screen of giant aloes or manchineels, inhabitants who (sometimes indeed among the ruins of a Roman theatre and beneath a column dedicated to Venus) are engaged in reading Voltaire's *Mérope* or *Alzire*. And, so remote, so distinct from, so superior to the educated women of the middle classes whom I had known, the similar culture by which Mme de Guermantes had made herself, with no ulterior motive, to gratify no ambition, descend to the level of people whom she would never know, had the praiseworthy character, almost touching in its uselessness, of a knowledge of Phoenician antiquities in a politician or a doctor.

"I might have been able to show you a very fine one," Mme de Guermantes said to me amiably, still speaking of Hals, "the finest in existence, some people say, which was left to me by a German cousin. Unfortunately, it turned out to be 'enfeoffed' in the castle—you don't know the expression? nor do I," she added, with her fondness for jokes (which made her, she thought, seem modern) at the expense of the old customs to which nevertheless she was unconsciously but fiercely attached. "I'm glad you have seen my Elstirs, but I must admit I should have been a great deal more glad if I could have done you the honours of my Hals, of that 'enfeoffed' picture."

"I know the one," said Prince Von, "it's the Grand Duke of Hesse's Hals."

"Quite so; his brother married my sister," said M. de Guermantes, "and his mother and Oriane's were first cousins as well."

"But so far as M. Elstir is concerned," the Prince went on, "I shall take the liberty of saying, without having any opinion of his work, which I do not know, that the hatred with which the Kaiser pursues him ought not, it seems to me, to be counted against him. The Kaiser is a man of marvellous intelligence."

"Yes, I've met him at dinner twice, once at my aunt Sagan's and once at my aunt Radziwill's, and I must say I found him quite unusual. I didn't find him at all simple! But there's something amusing about him, something 'forced'" (she detached the word) "like a green carnation, that is to say a thing that surprises me and doesn't please me enormously, a thing it's surprising that anyone should have been able to create but which I feel would have been just as well left uncreated. I trust I'm not shocking you?"

"The Kaiser is a man of astounding intelligence," resumed

the Prince, "he is passionately fond of the arts, he has for works of art a taste that is practically infallible, he never makes a mistake: if a thing is good he spots at at once and takes a dislike to it. If he detests anything, there can be no more doubt about it, the thing is excellent."

Everyone smiled.

"You set my mind at rest," said the Duchess.

"I should be inclined to compare the Kaiser," went on the Prince, who, not knowing how to pronounce the word archaeologist (that is to say, as though it were spelt with a "k"), never missed an opportunity of using it, "to an old archaeologist" (but the Prince said "arsheologist") "we have in Berlin. If you put him in front of a genuine Assyrian antique, he weeps. But if it is a modern fake, if it is not really old, he does not weep. And so, when they want to know whether an arsheological piece is really old, they take it to the old arsheologist. If he weeps, they buy the piece for the Museum. If his eyes remain dry, they send it back to the dealer, and prosecute him for fraud. Well, every time I dine at Potsdam, if the Kaiser says to me of a play: 'Prince, you must see it, it's a work of genius,' I make a note not to go to it; and when I hear him fulminating against an exhibition, I rush to see it at the first possible opportunity."

"Norpois is in favour of an Anglo-French understanding, isn't he?" said M. de Guermantes.

"What good would that do you?" asked Prince Von, who could not endure the English, with an air at once irritated and crafty. "The English are so *schtubid*. I know, of course, that it would not be as soldiers that they would help you. But one can judge them, all the same, by the *schtubidity* of their generals. A friend of mine was talking the other day to Botha, you know, the Boer leader. He said to my friend: 'It's terrible, an army like that. I rather like the English, as a matter of fact, but just imagine that I, a mere *peassant*, have beaten them in every battle. And in the last, when I was overpowered by a force twenty times the strength of my own, even while surrendering because I had to, I managed to take two thousand prisoners! That was all right because I was only a leader of an army of *peassants*, but if those poor fools ever have to stand up against

a European army, one trembles to think what may happen to
them!' Besides, you have only to see how their King, whom
you know as well as I do, passes for a great man in England."

I scarcely listened to these stories, of the kind that M. de
Norpois used to tell my father; they supplied no food for my
favourite trains of thought; and besides, even had they possessed the elements which they lacked, they would have had
to be of a very exciting quality for my inner life to awaken
during those hours in which I lived on the surface, my hair
well brushed, my shirt-front starched, in which, that is to say,
I could feel nothing of what constituted for me the pleasure of
life.

"Oh, I don't agree with you at all," said Mme de Guermantes, who felt that the German prince was wanting in tact,
"I find King Edward charming, so simple, and much
cleverer than people think. And the Queen is, even now, the
most beautiful thing I've ever seen in the world."

"But, *Matame* la Duchesse," said the Prince, who was losing
his temper and unable to see that he was giving offence, "you
must admit that if the Prince of Wales had been an ordinary
person there isn't a club that wouldn't have blackballed him,
and nobody would have been willing to shake hands with him.
The Queen is charming, excessively gentle and dim-witted.
But still, there's something shocking about a royal couple who
are literally kept by their subjects, who get the big Jewish
financiers to foot all the bills they ought to pay themselves,
and create them Baronets in return. It's like the Prince of
Bulgaria. . . ."

"He's our cousin," put in the Duchess, "he's a witty
fellow."

"He's mine, too, but we don't think him a good man on
that account. No, it is us you ought to make friends with, it's
the Kaiser's dearest wish, but he insists on its coming from the
heart. He says: 'What I want to see is a hand clasped in mine,
not waving a hat in the air.' With that, you would be in-
vincible. It would be more practical than the Anglo-French
rapprochement M. de Norpois preaches."*

"You know him, of course," said the Duchess, turning to
me, so as not to leave me out of the conversation. Remember-

ing that M. de Norpois had said that I had once looked as though I wanted to kiss his hand, thinking that he had no doubt repeated this story to Mme de Guermantes, and in any event could have spoken of me to her only with malice, since in spite of his friendship with my father he had not hesitated to make me appear so ridiculous, I did not do what a man of the world would have done. He would have said that he detested M. de Norpois, and had let him see it; he would have said this so as to give himself the appearance of being the deliberate cause of the Ambassador's slanders, which would then have been no more than lying and calculated reprisals. I said, on the contrary, that, to my great regret, I was afraid that M. de Norpois did not like me.

"You're quite mistaken," replied the Duchess, "he likes you very much indeed. You can ask Basin, for if people give me the reputation of only saying nice things, he certainly doesn't. He will tell you that we've never heard Norpois speak about anyone so kindly as he spoke about you. And only the other day he was wanting to give you a fine post at the Ministry. As he knew that you were not very strong and couldn't accept it, he had the delicacy not to speak of his kind thought to your father, for whom he has an unbounded admiration."

M. de Norpois was quite the last person whom I should have expected to do me any practical service. The truth was that, his being a mocking and indeed somewhat malicious nature, those who, like me, had let themselves be taken in by his outward appearance of a Saint Louis delivering justice beneath an oak-tree, by the affecting sounds that emerged from his somewhat too tuneful lips, suspected real treachery when they learned of a slander uttered at their expense by a man whose words had always seemed so heartfelt. These slanders were frequent enough with him. But that did not prevent him from taking a liking to people, from praising those he liked and taking pleasure in showing willingness to help them.

"Not that I'm in the least surprised at his appreciating you," said Mme de Guermantes, "he's an intelligent man. And I can quite understand," she added, for the benefit of the rest of the party, alluding to a plan of marriage of which I knew nothing, "that my aunt, who has long ceased to amuse him as an old mistress, may not seem of very much use to him as a new wife. Especially as I understand that even as a mistress she has ceased for years now to serve any practical purpose, and is wrapped up in her devotions. Booz-Norpois can say, in the words of Victor Hugo:

> Voilà longtemps que celle avec qui j'ai dormi,
> O Seigneur, a quitté ma couche pour la vôtre!

Really, my poor aunt is like those avant-garde artists who have railed against the Academy all their lives, and in the end start a little academy of their own, or those unfrocked priests who fabricate a religion of their own. They might as well have stuck to the cloth. But who knows," went on the Duchess with a meditative air, "it may be in anticipation of widowhood— there's nothing sadder than weeds one's not entitled to wear."

"Ah! if Mme de Villeparisis were to become Mme de Norpois, I really believe our cousin Gilbert would have a fit," said General de Monserfeuil. "The Prince de Guermantes is a charming man, but he really is rather taken up with questions of birth and etiquette," said the Princesse de Parme. "I went to spend a few days with them in the country, when the Princess, unfortunately, was ill in bed. I was accompanied by Petite." (This was a nickname that was given to Mme d'Hunolstein because she was enormously stout.) "The Prince came to meet me at the foot of the steps, and pretended not to see Petite. We went up to the first floor, and then at the entrance to the reception rooms, stepping back to make way for me, he said: 'Oh, how d'ye do, Mme d'Hunolstein' (he always calls her that now, since her separation) pretending to have caught sight of Petite for the first time, so as to show her that he didn't have to come down to receive her at the foot of the steps."

"That doesn't surprise me in the least. I don't need to tell you," said the Duke, who regarded himself as extremely modern, more contemptuous than anyone in the world of mere birth, and in fact a Republican, "that I haven't many ideas in common with my cousin. Your Highness can imagine that we are about as much agreed on most subjects as day and night. But I must say that if my aunt were to marry Norpois, for once I should be of Gilbert's opinion. To be the daughter

of Florimond de Guise and then to make a marriage like that
would be enough, as the saying is, to make a cat laugh, when
all's said and done." (These last words, which the Duke uttered
as a rule in the middle of a sentence, were here quite superfluous. But he felt a perpetual need to say them which made
him shift them to the end of a period if he had found no
place for them elsewhere. They were for him, among other
things, almost a question of prosody.) "Mind you," he added,
"the Norpois are excellent people with a good place, of good
stock."

"Listen to me, Basin, it's really not worth your while to
poke fun at Gilbert if you're going to speak the same language
as he does," said Mme de Guermantes, for whom the
"goodness" of a family, no less than that of a wine, consisted
in its age. But, less frank than her cousin and more subtle
than her husband, she made a point of never in her conversation playing false to the Guermantes spirit, and despised rank
in her speech while ready to honour it by her actions.

"But aren't you even some sort of cousins?" asked General
de Monserfeuil. "I seem to remember that Norpois married a
La Rochefoucauld."

"Not in that way at all, she belonged to the branch of the
Ducs de la Rochefoucauld, and my grandmother comes from
the Ducs de Doudeauville. She was own grandmother to
Edouard Coco, the wisest man in the family," replied the Duke,
whose views of wisdom were somewhat superficial, "and the
two branches haven't intermarried since Louis XIV's time; the
connexion would be rather distant."

"Really, how interesting; I never knew that," said the
General.

"However," went on M. de Guermantes, "his mother, I
believe, was the sister of the Duc de Montmorency, and had
originally been married to a La Tour d'Auvergne. But as those
Montmorencys are barely Montmorencys, while those La
Tour d'Auvergnes are not La Tour d'Auvergnes at all, I cannot
see that it gives him any very great position. He says—and
this should be more to the point—that he's descended from
Saintrailles, and as we ourselves are in a direct line of
descent. . . ."

There was at Combray a Rue de Saintrailles to which I had never given another thought. It led from the Rue de la Bretonnerie to the Rue de l'Oiseau. And as Saintrailles, the companion of Joan of Arc, had, by marrying a Guermantes, brought into the family that county of Combray, his arms were quartered with those of Guermantes at the base of one of the windows in Saint-Hilaire. I saw again a vision of dark sandstone steps, while a modulation of sound brought to my ears that name, Guermantes, in the forgotten tone in which I used to hear it long ago, so different from that in which it simply meant the genial hosts with whom I was dining this evening. If the name, Duchesse de Guermantes, was for me a collective name, it was not so merely in history, by the accumulation of all the women who had successively borne it, but also in the course of my own short life, which had already seen, in this single Duchesse de Guermantes, so many different women superimpose themselves, each one vanishing as soon as the next had acquired sufficient consistency. Words do not change their meaning as much in centuries as names do for us in the space of a few years. Our memories and our hearts are not large enough to be able to remain faithful. We have not room enough, in our present mental field, to keep the dead there as well as the living. We are obliged to build on top of what has gone before and is brought to light only by a chance excavation, such as the name Saintrailles had just opened up. I felt that it would be useless to explain all this, and indeed a little while earlier I had lied by implication in not answering when M. de Guermantes said to me: "You don't know our little corner?" Perhaps he was quite well aware that I did know it, and it was only from good breeding that he did not press the question. Mme de Guermantes drew me out of my meditation.

"Really, I find all that sort of thing too deadly. I say, it's not always as boring as this at my house. I hope you'll soon come and dine again as a compensation, with no pedigrees next time," she said to me in a low voice, incapable both of appreciating the kind of charm which I might find in her house and of having sufficient humility to be content to appeal to me simply as a herbarium filled with plants of another day.

What Mme de Guermantes believed to be disappointing my

expectations was on the contrary what in the end—for the
Duke and the General went on to discuss pedigrees now without stopping—saved my evening from being a complete
disappointment. How could I have felt otherwise until now?
Each of my fellow-guests at dinner, decking out the mysterious
name under which I had merely known and dreamed of them
at a distance in a body and a mind similar or inferior to those
of all the people I knew, had given me the impression of a
commonplace dullness which the view on entering the Danish
port of Elsinore would give to any passionate admirer of
Hamlet. No doubt these geographical regions and that ancient
past which put forest glades and Gothic belfries into their
names had in a certain measure formed their faces, their minds
and their prejudices, but survived in them only as does the
cause in the effect, that is to say as a thing possible for the
intelligence to perceive but in no way perceptible to the
imagination.

And these old-time prejudices restored in a flash to the friends
of M. and Mme de Guermantes their lost poetry. Assuredly,
the notions in the possession of the nobility which make them
the scholars, the etymologists of the language not of words
but of names (and even then only in comparison with the
ignorant mass of the middle classes, for if at the same level of
mediocrity a devout Catholic would be better able to stand
questioning on the details of the liturgy than a free-thinker, on
the other hand an anti-clerical archaeologist can often give
points to his parish priest on everything connected even with
the latter's own church), those notions, if we are to keep
to the truth, that is to say to the spirit, did not even have for
these noblemen the charm that they would have had for a
bourgeois. They knew perhaps better than I that the Duchesse
de Guise was Princess of Cleves, of Orléans, of Porcien, and
all the rest, but they had known, long before they knew all
these names, the face of the Duchesse de Guise which thenceforth that name reflected back to them. I had begun with the
fairy, even if she was fated soon to perish; they with the
woman.

In middle-class families one sometimes sees jealousies spring
up if the younger sister marries before the elder. So the

aristocratic world, Courvoisiers especially but Guermantes also, reduced its ennobled greatness to simple domestic superiorities, by virtue of a childishness which I had met originally (and this for me was its sole charm) in books. Is it not just as though Tallemant des Réaux were speaking of the Guermantes, and not of the Rohans, when he relates with evident satisfaction how M. de Guéménée cried to his brother: "You can come in here; this is not the Louvre!" and said of the Chevalier de Rohan (because he was a natural son of the Duc de Clermont): "At any rate he's a prince." The only thing that distressed me in all this talk was to find that the absurd stories which were being circulated about the charming adoptive Grand Duke of Luxembourg found as much credence in this salon as they had among Saint-Loup's friends. Plainly it was an epidemic that would not last longer than perhaps a year or two but had meanwhile infected everyone. People repeated the same old stories, or enriched them with others equally untrue. I gathered that the Princesse de Luxembourg herself, while apparently defending her nephew, supplied weapons for the assault. "You are wrong to stand up for him," M. de Guermantes told me, as Saint-Loup had told me before. "Why, even if you ignore the opinion of our family, which is unanimous, you have only to talk to his servants, and they, after all, are the people who know us best. Mme de Luxembourg gave her little negro page to her nephew. The negro came back in tears: 'Grand Duke beat me; me no bad boy; Grand Duke naughty man,' it's really too much. And I can speak with some knowledge, he's Oriane's cousin."

I cannot, by the way, say how many times in the course of this evening I heard the word "cousin" used. On the one hand, M. de Guermantes, almost at every name that was mentioned, exclaimed: "But he's Oriane's cousin!" with the sudden delight of a man who, lost in a forest, reads at the ends of a pair of arrows pointing in opposite directions on a metal plate, and followed by quite a low number of kilometres, the words: "Belvédère Casimir-Périer" and "Croix du Grand-Veneur," and gathers from them that he is on the right road. On the other hand the word cousin was employed in a wholly different connexion (which was here the exception to the prevailing rule) by the Turkish Ambassadress, who had come in after dinner. Devoured by social ambition and endowed with a real power of assimilating knowledge, she would pick up with equal facility the story of the Retreat of the Ten Thousand or the details of sexual perversion among birds. It would have been impossible to "stump" her on any of the most recent German publications, whether they dealt with political economy, mental aberrations, the various forms of onanism, or the philosophy of Epicurus. She was, incidentally, a dangerous person to listen to, for, perpetually in error, she would point out to you as being of the loosest morals women of irreproachable virtue, would put you on your guard against a man with the most honourable intentions, and would tell you anecdotes of the sort that seem always to have come out of a book, not so much because they are serious as because they are so wildly improbable.

She was at this period little received in society. For some weeks now she had been frequenting the houses of women of real social brilliance, such as the Duchesse de Guermantes, but in general had confined herself, of necessity, as regards the noblest families, to obscure scions whom the Guermantes had ceased to know. She hoped to prove her social credentials by quoting the most historic names of the little-known people who were her friends. At once M. de Guermantes, thinking that she was referring to people who frequently dined at his table, quivered with joy at finding himself once more in sight of a landmark and uttered the rallying-cry: "But he's Oriane's cousin! I know him as well as I know my own name. He lives in the Rue Vaneau. His mother was Mlle d'Uzès." The Ambassadress was obliged to admit that her specimen had been drawn from smaller game. She tried to connect her friends with those of M. de Guermantes by cutting across her track. "I know quite well who you mean. No, it's not those ones, they're cousins." But this cross-current launched by the unfortunate Ambassadress ran but a little way. For M. de Guermantes, losing interest, answered: "Oh, then I don't know who you're talking about." The Ambassadress offered no reply, for if she never knew anyone nearer than the "cousins" of those whom she ought to have known in person, very often these "cousins" were not even related at all. Then, from the lips of M. de Guermantes, would flow a fresh wave of "But she's Oriane's cousin!"—words which seemed to have for the Duke the same practical value in each of his sentences as certain epithets which the Roman poets found convenient because they provided them with dactyls or spondees for their hexameters.

At least the explosion of "But she's Oriane's cousin!" appeared to me quite natural when applied to the Princesse de Guermantes, who was indeed very closely related to the Duchess. The Ambassadress did not seem to care for this Princess. She said to me in an undertone: "She is stupid. No, she's not so beautiful as all that. That reputation is usurped. Anyhow," she went on, with an air at once considered, dismissive and decisive, "I find her extremely antipathetic." But often the cousinship extended a great deal further, Mme de Guermantes making it a point of honour to address as "Aunt" ladies with whom it would have been impossible to find her an ancestress in common without going back at least to Louis XV; just as, whenever the "hardness" of the times brought it about that a multimillionairess married a prince whose great-great-grandfather had married, as had Oriane's also, a daughter of Louvois, one of the chief joys of the fair American was to be able, after a first visit to the Hôtel de Guermantes, where she was, incidentally, somewhat coolly received and critically dissected, to say "Aunt" to Mme de Guermantes, who allowed her to do so with a maternal smile. But little did it matter to me what "birth" meant for M. de Guermantes and M. de Monserfeuil; in the conversations which they held on the subject I sought only a poetic pleasure. Without being conscious of it themselves, they procured me this pleasure as might a couple of farmers or sailors speaking of the soil or the tides, realities too little detached from their own lives for them to be capable of enjoying the beauty which personally I undertook to extract from them.

Sometimes, rather than of a race, it was of a particular fact, of a date, that a name reminded me. Hearing M. de Guermantes recall that M. de Bréauté's mother had been a Choiseul and his grandmother a Lucinge, I fancied I could see beneath the commonplace shirt-front with its plain pearl studs, bleeding

still in two globes of crystal, those august relics, the hearts of
Mme de Praslin and of the Duc de Berri. Others were more
voluptuous: the fine and flowing hair of Mme Tallien or
Mme de Sabran.

Sometimes it was more than a simple relic that I saw. Better
informed than his wife as to what their ancestors had been,
M. de Guermantes had at his command memories which gave
to his conversation a fine air of an ancient mansion, lacking in
real masterpieces but still full of pictures, authentic, indifferent
and majestic, which taken as a whole has an air of grandeur.
The Prince d'Agrigente having asked why the Prince of X . . .
had said, in speaking of the Duc d'Aumale, "my uncle,"
M. de Guermantes replied: "Because his mother's brother, the
Duke of Württemberg, married a daughter of Louis-Philippe."
At once I was lost in contemplation of a reliquary such as
Carpaccio or Memling used to paint, from its first panel in
which the princess, at the wedding festivities of her brother
the Duc d'Orléans, appeared wearing a plain garden dress to
indicate her ill-humour at having seen her ambassadors, who
had been sent to sue on her behalf for the hand of the Prince
of Syracuse, return empty-handed, down to the last, in which
she has just given birth to a son, the Duke of Württemberg
(the uncle of the prince with whom I had just dined), in that
castle called Fantaisie, one of those places which are as aristocratic as certain families, for they too, outlasting a single
generation, see attached to themselves more than one historical
personage: in this one, notably, survive side by side memories
of the Margravine of Bayreuth, of that other somewhat fantastic princess (the Duc d'Orléans's sister), to whom, it was
said, the name of her husband's castle made a distinct appeal,
of the King of Bavaria, and finally of the Prince of X . . .,
whose address it now in fact was, at which he had just asked the
Duc de Guermantes to write to him, for he had succeeded to
it and let it only during the Wagner festivals, to the Prince de
Polignac, another delightful "fantasist." When M. de Guermantes, to explain how he was related to Mme d'Arpajon,
was obliged to go back, so far and so simply, along the chain
formed by the joined hands of three or five ancestresses, to
Marie-Louise or Colbert, it was the same thing again: in each

of these cases, a great historical event appeared only in passing, masked, distorted, reduced, in the name of a property, in the Christian names of a woman, chosen for her because she was the grand-daughter of Louis-Philippe and Marie-Amélie, considered no longer as King and Queen of France but only insofar as, in their capacity as grand-parents, they bequeathed a heritage. (We see for other reasons in a gazetteer of the works of Balzac, where the most illustrious personages figure only to the extent of their connexion with the *Comédie Humaine*, Napoleon occupying a space considerably less than that allotted to Rastignac, and occupying that space solely because he once spoke to Mlle de Cinq-Cygne.) Thus does the aristocracy, in its heavy structure, pierced with rare windows, admitting a scanty daylight, showing the same incapacity to soar but also the same massive and blind force as Romanesque architecture, embody all our history, immure it, beetle over it.

Thus the empty spaces of my memory were covered by degrees with names which in arranging, composing themselves in relation to one another, in linking themselves to one another by increasingly numerous connexions, resembled those finished works of art in which there is not one touch that is isolated, in which every part in turn receives from the rest a justification which it confers on them in turn.

M. de Luxembourg's name having been brought up again, the Turkish Ambassadress told us how, the young bride's grandfather (he who had made that immense fortune out of flour and cereals) having invited M. de Luxembourg to lunch, the latter had written to decline, putting on the envelope: "M. So-and-so, miller," to which the grandfather had replied: "I am all the more disappointed that you were unable to come, my dear friend, in that I should have been able to enjoy your society in privacy, for we were an intimate party and there would have been only the miller, his son, and you."[30] This story was not merely utterly distasteful to me, who knew how inconceivable it was that my dear M. de Nassau could write to his wife's grandfather (whose fortune, moreover, he was expecting to inherit) and address him as "miller"; but furthermore its stupidity was glaring from the start, the

word "miller" having obviously been dragged in only to lead
up to the title of La Fontaine's fable. But there is in the
Faubourg Saint-Germain a silliness so great, when it is aggravated by malice, that everyone agreed that it was "well said"
and that the grandfather, as to whom at once everyone confi-
dently declared that he was a remarkable man, had shown a
prettier wit than his grandson-in-law. The Duc de Châtellerault wanted to take advantage of this story to tell the one
I had heard in the café: "Everyone had to lie down!"—but
scarcely had he begun, or reported M. de Luxembourg's
pretension that in his wife's presence M. de Guermantes
ought to stand up, when the Duchess stopped him with the
protest: "No, he's very absurd, but not as bad as that." I was
privately convinced that all these stories at the expense of
M. de Luxembourg were equally untrue, and that whenever I
found myself face to face with any of the reputed actors or
spectators I should hear the same denial. I wondered, however,
whether the denial just uttered by Mme de Guermantes had
been inspired by regard for truth or by pride. In any event
the latter quality succumbed to malice, for she added with
a laugh: "Not that I haven't had my little snub too, for he
invited me to luncheon, wishing to introduce me to the
Grand Duchess of Luxembourg, which is how he has the good
taste to describe his wife when he's writing to his aunt. I sent
a reply expressing my regret, and adding: As for the 'Grand
Duchess of Luxembourg' (in inverted commas), tell her that
if she wants to come to see me I am at home every Thursday
after five. I even had another snub. Happening to be in
Luxembourg, I telephoned and asked to speak to him. His
Highness was going into luncheon, had just risen from
luncheon, two hours went by and nothing happened; so then
I employed another method: 'Will you tell the Comte de
Nassau to come and speak to me?' Cut to the quick, he was at
the instrument that very minute." Everyone laughed at the
Duchess's story, and at other analogous, that is to say (I am
convinced of it) equally untrue stories, for a man more intelli-
gent, better, more refined, in a word more exquisite than this
Luxembourg-Nassau I have never met. The sequel will show
that it was I who was right. I must admit that, in the midst of

her scurrilous onslaught, Mme de Guermantes nevertheless did have a kind word for him.

"He wasn't always like that," she informed us. "Before he went off his head, like the man in the story-book who thinks he's become king, he was no fool, and indeed in the early days of his engagement he used to speak of it in really quite a nice way, as an undreamed-of happiness: 'It's just like a fairy-tale; I shall have to make my entry into Luxembourg in a fairy coach,' he said to his uncle d'Ornessan, who answered—for you know it's not a very big place, Luxembourg: 'A fairy coach! I'm afraid, my dear fellow, you'd never get it in. I should suggest that you take a goat cart.' Not only did this not annoy Nassau, but he was the first to tell us the story, and to laugh at it."

"Ornessan is a witty fellow, and he has every reason to be; his mother was a Montjeu. He's in a very bad way now, poor Ornessan."

This name had the magic virtue of interrupting the flow of stale witticisms which otherwise would have gone on forever. For M. de Guermantes went on to explain that M. d'Ornessan's great-grandmother had been the sister of Marie de Castille Montjeu, the wife of Timoléon de Lorraine, and consequently Oriane's aunt, with the result that the conversation drifted back to genealogies, while the imbecile Turkish Ambassadress breathed in my ear: "You appear to be very much in the Duke's good books; have a care!" and, on my demanding an explanation: "I mean to say, you understand what I mean, he's a man to whom one could safely entrust one's daughter, but not one's son." Now if ever, on the contrary, there was a man who was passionately and exclusively a lover of women, it was certainly the Duc de Guermantes. But error, untruth fatuously believed, were for the Ambassadress like a vital element out of which she could not move. "His brother Mémé, who is, as it happens, for other reasons altogether" (he ignored her) "profoundly uncongenial to me, is genuinely distressed by the Duke's morals. So is their aunt Villeparisis. Ah, now, her I adore! There is a saint of a woman for you, the true type of the great ladies of the past. She's not only virtue itself but reserve itself. She still says 'Monsieur' to the Ambassador Norpois whom she sees every day, and who, by the way, made an excellent impression in Turkey."

I did not even reply to the Ambassadress, in order to listen to the genealogies. They were not all of them important. It happened indeed that one of the alliances about which I learned from M. de Guermantes in the course of the conversation was a misalliance, but one not without charm, for, uniting under the July Monarchy the Duc de Guermantes and the Duc de Fezensac with the two irresistible daughters of an eminent navigator, it gave to the two duchesses the unexpected piquancy of an exotically bourgeois, "Louisphilippically" Indian grace. Or else, under Louis XIV, a Norpois had married the daughter of the Duc de Mortemart, whose illustrious title struck the name Norpois, which I had found lacklustre and might have supposed to be recent, and engraved it deeply with the beauty of an old medal. And in these cases, moreover, it was not only the less well-known name that benefited by the association; the other, hackneyed by its very lustre, struck me more forcibly in this novel and more obscure aspect, just as among the portraits painted by a brilliant colourist the most striking is sometimes one that is all in black. The sudden mobility with which all these names seemed to me to have been endowed, as they sprang to take their places by the side of others from which I should have supposed them to be remote, was due not to my ignorance alone; the to-ings and fro-ings which they were performing in my mind they had carried out no less readily at these epochs in which a title, being always attached to a piece of land, used to follow it from one family to another, so much so that, for example, in the fine feudal structure that is the title of Duc de Nemours or Duc de Chevreuse, I might discover successively, crouching as in the hospitable abode of a hermit-crab, a Guise, a Prince of Savoy, an Orléans, a Luynes. Sometimes several remained in competition for a single shell: for the Principality of Orange the royal house of the Netherlands and MM. de Mailly-Nesle, for the Duchy of Brabant the Baron de Charlus and the royal house of Belgium, various others for the titles of Prince of Naples, Duke of Parma, Duke of Reggio. Sometimes it was the other way; the shell had been so long uninhabited by proprietors long since dead that it had never occurred to me that this or that name of a castle could have been, at an epoch which after all was comparatively recent, the name of a family. Thus, when M. de Guermantes replied to a question put to him by M. de Monserfeuil: "No, my cousin was a fanatical royalist; she was the daughter of the Marquis de Féterne, who played some part in the Chouan rising," on seeing this name Féterne, which to me, since my stay at Balbec, had been the name of a castle, become, what I had never dreamed that it could possibly be, a family name, I felt the same astonishment as in reading a fairy-tale where turrets and a terrace come to life and turn into men and women. In this sense of the words, we may say that history, even mere family history, restores old stones to life. There have been in Parisian society men who played as considerable a part in it, who were more sought after for their distinction or for their wit, who were equally well born as the Duc de Guermantes or the Duc de La Trémoïlle. They have now fallen into oblivion because, as they left no descendants, their name, which we no longer hear, has an unfamiliar ring; at most, like the name of a thing beneath which we never think to discover the name of any person, it survives in some remote castle or village. The day is not distant when the traveller who, in the heart of Burgundy, stops in the little village of Charlus to look at its church, if he is not studious enough or is in too great a hurry to examine its tombstones, will go away ignorant of that fact that this name, Charlus, was that of a man who ranked with the highest in the land. This thought reminded me that it was time to go, and that while I listened to M. de Guermantes talking pedigrees, the hour was approaching at which I had promised to call on his brother. "Who knows," I continued to muse, "whether one day Guermantes itself may appear nothing more than a place-name, save to the archaeologists who, stopping by chance at Combray and standing beneath the window of Gilbert the Bad, have the patience to listen to the account given them by Théodore's successor or to read the Curé's guide?" But so long as a great name is not extinct it keeps the men and women who bear it in the limelight; and doubtless to some extent the interest which the illustriousness of these families gave them in my eyes lay in the fact that one can, starting from to-day, follow their ascending course, step by step, to a point far beyond the fourteenth century, and find the diaries and correspondence of all the forebears of M. de Charlus, of the Prince d'Agrigente, of the Princesse de Parme, in a past in which an impenetrable darkness would cloak the origins of a middle-class family, and in which we make out, in the luminous backward projection of a name, the origin and persistence of certain nervous characteristics, vices and disorders of one or another Guermantes. Almost pathologically identical with their namesakes of the present day, they excite from century to century the startled interest of their correspondents, whether these be anterior to the Princess Palatine and Mme de Motteville, or subsequent to the Prince de Ligne.

However, my historical curiosity was faint in comparison with my aesthetic pleasure. The names cited had the effect of disembodying the Duchess's guests, whose masks of flesh and unintelligence or vulgar intelligence had transformed them into ordinary mortals, so much so that I had made my landing on the ducal door-mat not as upon the threshold (as I had supposed) but as at the terminus of the enchanted world of names. The Prince d'Agrigente himself, as soon as I heard that his mother had been a Damas, a grand-daughter of the Duke of Modena, was delivered, as from an unstable chemical alloy, from the face and speech that prevented one from recognising him, and went to form with Damas and Modena, which themselves were only titles, an infinitely more seductive combination. Each name displaced by the attraction of another with which I had never suspected it of having any affinity left the unalterable position which it had occupied in my brain, where familiarity had dulled it, and, speeding to join the Mortemarts, the Stuarts or the Bourbons, traced with them branches of the most graceful design and ever-changing colour. The name Guermantes itself received from all the beautiful names—extinct, and so all the more glowingly rekindled— with which I learned only now that it was connected, a new and purely poetic sense and purpose. At the most, at the extremity of each spray that burgeoned from the exalted stem, I could see it flower in some face of a wise king or illustrious princess, like the sire of Henri IV or the Duchesse de Longue-ville. But as these faces, different in this respect from those of the party around me, were not overlaid for me by any residue of physical experience or social mediocrity, they remained, in their handsome outlines and rainbow iridescence, homo-geneous with those names which at regular intervals, each of a different hue, detached themselves from the genealogical tree of Guermantes, and disturbed with no foreign or opaque matter the translucent, alternating, multicoloured buds which like the ancestors of Jesus in the old Jesse windows, blos-somed on either side of the tree of glass.

Already I had made several attempts to slip away, on account, more than for any other reason, of the insignificance which my presence in it imparted to the gathering, although it was one of those which I had long imagined as being so beautiful—as it would doubtless have been had there been no inconvenient witness present. At least my departure would allow the guests, once the interloper had gone, to form them-selves into a closed group. They would be free to celebrate the mysteries for which they had assembled there, since it could obviously not have been to talk of Franz Hals or of avarice, and to talk of them in the same way as people talk in bourgeois society. They spoke nothing but trivialities, doubt-less because I was in the room, and I felt with some compunc-tion, on seeing all these pretty women kept apart, that I was preventing them by my presence from carrying on, in the most precious of its drawing-rooms, the mysterious life of the Faubourg Saint-Germain. But M. and Mme de Guermantes carried the spirit of self-sacrifice so far as to keep postponing, by detaining me, this departure which I was constantly trying to effect. A more curious thing still, several of the ladies who had come hurrying, ecstatic, decked out in their finery, bespangled with jewels, only to attend a party which, through my fault, differed in essence from those that are given elsewhere than in the Faubourg Saint-Germain no more than one feels oneself at Balbec to be in a town that differs from what one's eyes are accustomed to see—several of these ladies left, not at all disappointed, as they had every reason to be, but thanking Mme de Guermantes most effusively for the delightful evening which they had spent, as though on other days, those on which I was not present, nothing more occurred.

Was it really for the sake of dinners such as this that all these people dressed themselves up and refused to allow middle-class women to penetrate into their so exclusive drawing-rooms—for dinners such as this, identical had I been absent? The suspicion flashed across my mind for a moment, but it was too absurd. Plain commonsense enabled me to brush it aside. And then, if I had adopted it, what would have been left of the name Guermantes, already so debased since Combray?

It struck me that these flower-maidens were, to a strange extent, easily pleased with another person or anxious to please that person, for more than one of them, to whom I had not uttered during the whole course of the evening more than two or three casual remarks the stupidity of which had left me blushing, made a point, before leaving the drawing-room, of coming to tell me, fastening on me her fine caressing eyes, straightening as she spoke the garland of orchids that followed the curve of her bosom, what an intense pleasure it had been to her to make my acquaintance, and to speak to me—a veiled allusion to an invitation to dinner—of her desire to "arrange something" after she had "fixed a day" with Mme de Guermantes.

None of these flower ladies left the room before the Princesse de Parme. The presence of the latter—one must never depart before royalty—was one of the two reasons, neither of which I had guessed, for which the Duchess had insisted so strongly on my remaining. As soon as Mme de Parme had risen, it was like a deliverance. Each of the ladies, having made a genuflexion before the Princess, who then raised her up from the ground, received from her in a kiss, and as it were a benediction which they had craved on their knees, the permission to ask for their cloaks and carriages. With the result that there followed, at the front door, a sort of stentorian recital of great names from the History of France. The Princesse de Parme had forbidden Mme de Guermantes to accompany her downstairs to the hall for fear of her catching cold, and the Duke had added: "There, Oriane, since Ma'am gives you leave, remember what the doctor told you."

"I think the Princesse de Parme was *very pleased* to dine with you." I knew the formula. The Duke had come the whole way across the drawing-room in order to utter it for my benefit with an obliging, earnest air, as though he were handing me a diploma or offering me a plateful of biscuits. And I guessed from the pleasure which he appeared to be feeling as he spoke, and which brought so gentle an expression momentarily into his face, that the duties and concerns which it represented for him were of the kind which he would continue to discharge to the very end of his life, like one of those honorific and easy posts which one is still allowed to retain even when senile.

Just as I was about to leave, the Princess's lady-in-waiting reappeared in the drawing-room, having forgotten to take away some wonderful carnations, sent up from Guermantes, which the Duchess had presented to Mme de Parme. The lady-in-waiting was somewhat flushed, and one felt that she had just been receiving a scolding, for the Princess, so kind to everyone else, could not contain her impatience at the stupidity of her attendant. And so the latter picked up the flowers quickly and ran, but to preserve an air of nonchalance and independence, flung at me as she passed: "The Princess says I'm keeping her waiting; she wants to be gone, and to have the carnations as well. After all, I'm not a little bird, I can't be in several places at once."

Alas! the rule of not leaving before royalty was not the only one. I could not depart at once, for there was another: this was that the famous prodigality, unknown to the Courvoisiers, with which the Guermantes, whether opulent or practically ruined, excelled in entertaining their friends, was not only a material prodigality, of the kind that I had often experienced with Robert de Saint-Loup, but also a prodigality of charming words, of courteous gestures, a whole system of verbal elegance fed by a positive cornucopia within. But as this last, in the idleness of fashionable existence, remains unemployed, it overflowed at times, sought an outlet in a sort of fleeting effusion which was all the more intense, and which might, on

the part of Mme de Guermantes, have led one to suppose a
genuine affection. She did in fact feel it at the moment when
she let it overflow, for she found then, in the society of the
friend, man or woman, with whom she happened to be, a
sort of intoxication, in no way sensual, similar to that which
music produces in certain people; she would suddenly pluck
a flower from her bodice, or a medallion, and present it to
someone with whom she would have liked to prolong the
evening, with a melancholy feeling the while that such a
prolongation could have led to nothing but idle talk, into which
nothing could have passed of the nervous pleasure, the fleeting
emotion, reminiscent of the first warm days of spring in the
impression they leave behind them of lassitude and regret.
As for the friend, it did not do for him to put too implicit a
faith in the promises, more exhilarating than anything he had
ever heard, tendered by these women who, because they feel
with so much more force the sweetness of a moment, make of
it, with a delicacy, a nobility of which normally constituted
creatures are incapable, a compelling masterpiece of grace and
kindness, and no longer have anything of themselves left to
give when the next moment has arrived. Their affection does
not outlive the exaltation that has dictated it; and the subtlety
of mind which had then led them to divine all the things that
you wished to hear, and to say them to you, will enable them
just as easily, a few days later, to seize hold of your absurdities
and use them to entertain another of their visitors with whom
they will then be in the act of enjoying one of those "musical
moments" which are so brief.

In the hall where I asked the footmen for my snowboots,
which I had brought, not realising how unfashionable they
were, as a precaution against the snow, a few flakes of which
had already fallen, to be converted rapidly into slush, I felt,
at the contemptuous smiles on all sides, a shame which rose
to its highest pitch when I saw that Mme de Parme had not yet
gone and was watching me put on my American "rubbers."
The Princess came towards me. "Oh! what a good idea," she
exclaimed, "it's so practical! There's a sensible man for you.
Madame, we shall have to get a pair of those," she said to her
lady-in-waiting, while the mockery of the footmen turned to

respect and the other guests crowded round me to inquire where I had managed to find these marvels. "With those on, you will have nothing to fear even if it starts snowing again and you have a long way to go. You're independent of the weather," the Princess said to me.

"Oh! if it comes to that, Your Royal Highness can rest assured," broke in the lady-in-waiting with a knowing air, "it won't snow again."

"What do you know about it, Madame?" came witheringly from the excellent Princesse de Parme, whose temper only the stupidity of her lady-in-waiting could succeed in ruffling.

"I can assure Your Royal Highness that it can't snow again. It's a physical impossibility."

"But why?"

"It can't snow any more, because they've taken the necessary steps to prevent it: they've sprinkled salt in the streets!"

The simple-minded lady did not notice either the anger of the Princess or the mirth of the rest of her audience, for instead of remaining silent she said to me with a genial smile, paying no heed to my repeated denials of any connexion with Admiral Jurien de la Gravière: "Not that it matters, after all. Monsieur must have stout sea-legs. What's bred in the bone!"

Having escorted the Princesse de Parme to her carriage, M. de Guermantes said to me, taking hold of my great-coat: "Let me help you into your skin." He had ceased even to smile when he employed this expression, for those that were most vulgar had for that very reason, because of the Guermantes affectation of simplicity, become aristocratic.

An exhilaration relapsing only into melancholy, because it was artificial, was what I also, although quite differently from Mme de Guermantes, felt once I had finally left her house, in the carriage that was to take me to that of M. de Charlus. We can as we choose abandon ourselves to one or other of two forces, of which one rises in ourselves, emanates from our deepest impressions, while the other comes to us from without. The first brings with it naturally a joy, the joy that springs from the life of those who create. The other current, that which endeavours to introduce into us the impulses by which persons external to ourselves are stirred, is not accompanied by pleasure; but we can add a pleasure to it, by a sort of recoil, in an intoxication so artificial that it turns swiftly into boredom, into melancholy—whence the gloomy faces of so many men of the world, and all those nervous conditions which may even lead to suicide. Now, in the carriage which was taking me to M. de Charlus, I was a prey to this second sort of exaltation, very different from that which is given us by a personal impression, such as I had received in other carriages, once at Combray, in Dr Percepied's gig, from which I had seen the spires of Martinville against the setting sun, another day at Balbec, in Mme de Villeparisis's barouche, when I strove to identify the reminiscence that was suggested to me by an avenue of trees. But in this third carriage, what I had before my mind's eye were those conversations that had seemed to me so tedious at Mme de Guermantes's dinner-table, for example Prince Von's stories about the German Emperor, General Botha and the British Army. I had just slid them into the internal stereoscope through the lenses of which, as soon as we are no longer ourselves, as soon as, endowed with a worldly spirit, we wish to receive our life only from other people, we give depth and relief to what they have said and done. Like a tipsy man filled with tender feeling for the waiter who has been serving him, I marvelled at my good fortune, a good fortune not recognised by me, it is true, at the actual moment, in having dined with a person who knew Wilhelm II so well and had told stories about him that were—upon my word— extremely witty. And, as I repeated to myself, with the Prince's German accent, the story of General Botha, I laughed out loud, as though this laugh, like certain kinds of applause which increase one's inward admiration, were necessary to the story as a corroboration of its hilariousness. Through the magnifying lenses, even those of Mme de Guermantes's pronouncements which had struck me as being stupid (as for example the one about the Hals pictures which one ought to see from the top of a tram-car) took on an extraordinary life and depth. And I must say that, even if this exaltation was quick to subside, it was not altogether unreasonable. Just as there may always come a day when we are glad to know the person whom we despise more than anyone in the world because he happens to be connected with a girl with whom we are in love, to whom he can introduce us, and thus offers us both utility and agreeableness, attributes in which we should have supposed him to be permanently lacking, so there is no conversation, any more than there are personal relations, from which we can be certain that we shall not one day derive some benefit. What Mme de Guermantes had said to me about the pictures which it would be interesting to see, even from a tram-car, was untrue, but it contained a germ of truth which was of value to me later on.

Similarly the lines of Victor Hugo which I had heard her quote were, it must be admitted, of a period earlier than that in which he became something more than a new man, in which he brought to light, in the order of evolution, a literary species hitherto unknown, endowed with more complex organs. In these early poems, Victor Hugo is still a thinker, instead of contenting himself, like Nature, with providing food for thought. His "thoughts" he at that time expressed in the most direct form, almost in the sense in which the Duke understood the word when, feeling it to be "old hat" and otiose for the guests at his big parties at Guermantes to append to their signatures in the visitors' book a philosophico-poetical reflexion, he used to warn newcomers in a beseeching tone: "Your name, my dear fellow, but no 'thoughts,' please!" Now, it was these "thoughts" of Victor Hugo's (almost as absent from the *Légende des Siècles* as "tunes," as "melodies" are from Wagner's later manner) that Mme de Guermantes admired in the early Hugo. Nor was she altogether wrong. They were touching, and already round about them, before their form had yet achieved the depth which it was to acquire only in later years, the rolling tide of words and of richly articulated rhymes rendered them unassimilable to the lines that one can discover in a Corneille, for example, lines in which a romanticism that is intermittent, restrained, and thus all the more moving, has nevertheless in no way penetrated to the physical sources of life, modified the unconscious and generalisable organism in which the idea is latent. And so I had been wrong in confining myself, hitherto, to the later volumes of Hugo. Of the earlier ones, of course, it was only with a fractional part that Mme de Guermantes embellished her conversation. But it is precisely by thus quoting an isolated line that one multiplies its power of attraction tenfold. The lines that had entered or returned to my mind during this dinner magnetised in turn, summoned to themselves with such force, the poems within which they were normally embedded, that my electrified hands could not hold out for longer than forty-eight hours against the force that drew them towards the volume in which were bound up the *Orientales* and the *Chants du Crépuscule*. I cursed Françoise's footman for having made a present to his native village of my copy of the *Feuilles d'Automne*, and sent him off without a moment's delay to buy me another. I read these volumes from cover to cover and found peace of mind only when I suddenly came across, awaiting me in the light in which she had bathed them, the lines which Mme de Guermantes had quoted to me. For all these reasons, conversations with the Duchess resembled the discoveries that we make in the library of a country house, out of date, incomplete, incapable of forming a mind, lacking in almost everything that we value, but offering us now and then some curious scrap of information, or even a quotation from a fine passage which we did not know and as to which we are glad to remember in after years that we owe our knowledge of it to a stately baronial mansion. We are then, as a result of having found Balzac's preface to the *Chartreuse*, or some unpublished letters of Joubert, tempted to exaggerate the value of the life we led there, the barren frivolity of which we forget for this windfall of a single evening.

From this point of view, if this world had been unable at the outset to respond to what my imagination expected, and was consequently to strike me first of all by what it had in common with every other world rather than by the ways in which it differed from them, it yet revealed itself to me by degrees as something quite distinct. Noblemen are almost the only people from whom one learns as much as one does from peasants; their conversation is adorned with everything that concerns the land, dwellings as people used to live in them long ago, old customs, everything of which the world of money is profoundly ignorant. Even supposing that the aristocrat

most moderate in his aspirations has finally caught up with
the period in which he lives, his mother, his uncles, his great-
aunts keep him in touch, when he recalls his childhood, with
the conditions of a life almost unknown to-day. In the death-
chamber of a contemporary corpse Mme de Guermantes
would not have pointed out, but would immediately have
noticed, all the lapses from traditional customs. She was
shocked to see women mingling with the men at a funeral,
when there was a particular ceremony which ought to be
celebrated for the women. As for the pall, the use of which
Bloch would doubtless have believed to be confined to coffins,
on account of the pall bearers of whom one reads in the
reports of funerals, M. de Guermantes could remember the
time when, as a child, he had seen it borne at the wedding of
M. de Mailly-Nesle. While Saint-Loup had sold his priceless
"genealogical tree," old portraits of the Bouillons, letters of
Louis XIII, in order to buy Carrières and furniture in the
modern style, M. and Mme de Guermantes, moved by a
sentiment in which a fervent love of art may have played
very little part and which left them themselves more commonplace, had kept their marvellous Boulle furniture, which
presented an ensemble altogether more seductive to an artist.
A literary man would similarly have been enchanted by their
conversation, which would have been for him—for a hungry
man has no need of another to keep him company—a living
dictionary of all those expressions which every day are becoming more and more forgotten: St Joseph ties, children
pledged to wear blue for Our Lady, and so forth, which one
finds to-day only among those who have constituted themselves the amiable and benevolent custodians of the past. The
pleasure that a writer experiences among them, far more than
among other writers, is not without danger, for there is a
risk of his coming to believe that the things of the past have a
charm in themselves, of his transferring them bodily into his
work, still-born in that case, exhaling a tedium for which he
consoles himself with the reflexion: "It's attractive because it's
true; that's how people do talk." These aristocratic conversations had moreover the charm, in Mme de Guermantes's case,
of being couched in excellent French. For this reason they made

permissible on the Duchess's part her hilarity at the words "vatic," "cosmic," "pythian," "supereminent," which Saint-Loup used to employ—as well as his Bing furniture.

When all was said, the stories I had heard at Mme de Guermantes's, very different in this respect from what I had felt in the case of the hawthorns, or when I tasted a *madeleine,* remained alien to me. Entering me for a moment and possessing me only physically, it was as though being of a social, not an individual nature, they were impatient to escape. I writhed in my seat in the carriage like the priestess of an oracle. I looked forward to another dinner-party at which I might myself become a sort of Prince of X . . ., of Mme de Guermantes, and repeat them. In the meantime they made my lips quiver as I stammered them to myself, and I tried in vain to bring back and concentrate a mind that was carried away by a centrifugal force. And so it was with a feverish impatience not to have to bear the whole weight of them any longer by myself in a carriage where indeed I made up for the lack of conversation by soliloquising aloud, that I rang the bell at M. de Charlus's door, and it was in long monologues with myself, in which I rehearsed everything that I was going to tell him and gave scarcely a thought to what he might have to say to me, that I spent the whole of the time during which I was kept waiting in a drawing-room into which a footman showed me and which I was incidentally too excited to inspect. I felt so urgent a need for M. de Charlus to listen to the stories I was burning to tell him that I was bitterly disappointed to think that the master of the house was perhaps in bed, and that I might have to go home to work off by myself my verbal intoxication. I had just noticed, in fact, that I had been twenty-five minutes—that they had perhaps forgotten about me—in this room of which, despite this long wait, I could at the most have said that it was immense, greenish in colour, and contained a large number of portraits. The need to speak prevents one not merely from listening but from seeing, and in this case the absence of any description of external surroundings is tantamount to a description of an internal state. I was about to leave the room to try to get hold of someone, and, if I found no one, to make my way back to the hall and have myself let out, when, just as I had risen from my chair and taken a few steps across the mosaic parquet of the floor, a manservant came in with a troubled expression and said to me: "Monsieur le Baron has been engaged all evening, sir. There are still several people waiting to see him. I shall do everything I possibly can to get him to receive you; I have already telephoned up twice to the secretary."

"No; please don't bother. I had an appointment with M. le Baron, but it's now very late, and if he's busy this evening I can come back another day."

"Oh no, sir, you mustn't go away," cried the servant. "M. le Baron might be vexed. I will try again."

I was reminded of the things I had heard about M. de Charlus's servants and their devotion to their master. One could not quite say of him as of the Prince de Conti that he sought to give pleasure as much to the valet as to the minister, but he had shown such skill in making of the least thing that he asked of them a sort of personal favour that at night, when his body-servants were assembled round him at a respectful distance, and after running his eye over them he said: "Coignet, the candlestick!" or "Ducret, the nightshirt!" it was with an envious murmur that the rest used to withdraw, jealous of him who had been singled out by his master's favour. Two of them, indeed, who could not abide one another, used each to try to snatch the favour from his rival by going on the most flimsy pretext with a message to the Baron, if he had gone upstairs earlier than usual, in the hope of being invested for the evening with the charge of candlestick or nightshirt. If he addressed a few words directly to one of them on some subject outside the scope of his duty, still more if in winter, in the garden, knowing that one of his coachmen had caught cold, he said to him after ten minutes: "Put your cap on!" the others would not speak to the fellow again for a fortnight, in their jealousy of the great distinction that had been conferred on him.

I waited ten minutes more, and then, after requesting me not to stay too long as M. le Baron was tired and had had to send away several most important people who had made appointments with him many days before, they admitted me to his presence. These histrionic trappings with which M. de Charlus surrounded himself seemed to me a great deal less impressive than the simplicity of his brother Guermantes, but already the door stood open, and I could see the Baron, in a Chinese dressing-gown, with his throat bare, lying on a settee. My eye was caught at the same moment by a tall hat, its nap flashing like a mirror, which had been left on a chair with a cape, as though the Baron had but recently come in. The valet withdrew. I supposed that M. de Charlus would rise to greet me. Without moving a muscle he fastened on me a pair of implacable eyes. I went towards him and said good evening; he did not hold out his hand, made no reply, did not ask me to take a chair. After a moment's silence I asked him, as one would ask an ill-mannered doctor, whether it was necessary for me to remain standing. I said this with no ill intent, but my words seemed only to intensify the cold fury on M. de Charlus's face. I was not aware, moreover, that at home, in the country, at the Château de Charlus, he was in the habit after dinner (so much did he love to play the king) of sprawling in an armchair in the smoking-room, letting his guests remain standing round him. He would ask for a light from one, offer a cigar to another and then, after a few minutes' interval, would say: "But Argencourt, why don't you sit down? Take a chair, my dear fellow," and so forth, having made a point of keeping them standing simply to remind them that it was from him that they must receive permission to be seated. "Put yourself in the Louis XIV seat," he answered me with an imperious air, as though rather to force me to move further away from him than to invite me to be seated. I took an armchair which was comparatively near. "Ah! so that is what you call a Louis XIV seat! I can see you are a well-educated young man," he exclaimed in derision. I was so taken aback that I did not move, either to leave the house, as I ought to have done, or to change my seat, as he wished. "Sir," he next said to me, weighing each of his words, to the more insulting of which he prefixed a double yoke of consonants, "the interview which I have condescended to grant you, at the request of a person who desires to remain nameless, will mark the final point in our relations. I make no secret of the fact that I had hoped for better things! I should perhaps be straining the meaning of the words a little—which one ought not to do, even with people who are ignorant of their value, simply out of the respect due to oneself—were I to tell you that I had felt a certain *liking* for you. I think, however, that *benevolence*, in its most effectively patronising sense, would exceed neither what I felt nor what I was proposing to display. I had, immediately on my return to Paris, given you to understand, while you were still at Balbec, that you could count upon me." I who remembered with what a torrent of abuse M. de Charlus had parted from me at Balbec made an instinctive gesture of denial. "What!" he shouted angrily, and indeed his face, convulsed and white, differed as much from his ordinary face as does the sea when, on a stormy morning, one sees instead of its customary smiling surface a myriad writhing snakes of spray and foam, "do you mean to pretend that you did not receive my message—almost a declaration—that you were to remember me? What was there in the way of decoration round the cover of the book that I sent you?"

"Some very pretty twined garlands with tooled ornaments," I told him.

"Ah!" he replied contemptuously, "the young in France know little of the treasures of our land. What would be said of a young Berliner who had never heard of the *Walküre*? Besides, you must have eyes to see and see not, since you yourself told me that you had spent two hours contemplating that particular treasure. I can see that you know no more about flowers than you do about styles. Don't protest that you know about styles," he cried in a shrill scream of rage, "you don't even know what you are sitting on. You offer your hindquarters a Directory *chauffeuse* as a Louis XIV *bergère*. One of these days you'll be mistaking Mme de Villeparisis's lap for the lavatory, and goodness knows what you'll do in it. Similarly, you did not even recognise on the binding of Bergotte's book the lintel of myosotis over the door of Balbec church. Could there have been a clearer way of saying to you: 'Forget me not!'?"

I looked at M. de Charlus. Undoubtedly his magnificent head, though repellent, yet far surpassed that of any of his relatives; he was like an ageing Apollo; but an olive-hued, bilious juice seemed ready to start from the corners of his malevolent mouth; as for intellect, one could not deny that his, over a vast compass, had a grasp of many things which would always remain unknown to his brother Guermantes. But whatever the fine words with which he embellished all his hatreds, one felt that, whether he was moved by offended pride or disappointed love, whether his motivating force was rancour, sadism, teasing or obsession, this man was capable of committing murder, and of proving by dint of logic that he had been right in doing it and was still head and shoulders above his brother, his sister-in-law, or any of the rest.

"As, in Velazquez's *Surrender of Breda*," he went on, "the victor advances towards him who is the humbler in rank, and as is the duty of every noble nature, since I was everything and you were nothing, it was I who took the first steps towards you. You have made an imbecilic reply to what it is not for me to describe as an act of grandeur. But I did not allow myself to be discouraged. Our religion enjoins patience. The patience I have shown towards you will be counted, I hope, to my credit, and also my having only smiled at what might be denounced as impertinence, were it within your power to be impertinent to one who is so infinitely your superior. However, all this is now neither here nor there. I have subjected you to the test which the one eminent man of our world has ingeniously named the test of untoward kindness, and which he rightly declares to be the most terrible of all, the only one that can separate the wheat from the chaff. I can scarcely reproach you for having undergone it without success, for those who emerge from it triumphant are very few. But at least, and this is the conclusion which I am entitled to draw from the last words that we shall exchange on this earth, at least I intend to protect myself against your calumnious fabrications."

So far, I had never dreamed that M. de Charlus's rage could have been caused by an unflattering remark which had been repeated to him; I searched my memory; I had not spoken about him to anyone. Some ill-wisher had invented the whole thing. I protested to M. de Charlus that I had said absolutely nothing about him. "I don't think I can have annoyed you by saying to Mme de Guermantes that I was a friend of yours." He gave a disdainful smile, raised his voice to the supreme pitch of its highest register, and there, softly attacking the shrillest and most contumelious note, "Oh! Sir," he said, returning by the most gradual stages to a natural intonation, and seeming to revel as he went in the oddities of this descending scale, "I think you do yourself an injustice when you accuse yourself of having said that we were *friends*. I do not look for any great verbal accuracy in one who could all too easily mistake a piece of Chippendale for a rococo *chaire*, but really I do not believe," he went on, with vocal caresses that grew more and more sardonically winning until a charming smile actually began to play about his lips, "I do not believe that you can ever have said, or thought, that we were *friends*! As for your having boasted that you had been *presented* to me, had *talked* to me, *knew* me slightly, had obtained, almost without solicitation, the prospect of becoming my *protégé*, I find it on the contrary very natural and intelligent of you to have done so. The extreme difference in age that there is between us enables me to recognise without absurdity that that *presentation*, those *talks*, that vague prospect of future *relations* were for you, it is not for me to say an honour, but still, when all is said and done, an advantage as to which I consider that your folly lay not in divulging it but in not having had the sense to keep it. I will even go so far as to say," he went on, switching suddenly and momentarily from haughty anger to a gentleness so tinged with melancholy that I thought he was going to burst into tears, "that when you left unanswered the proposal I made to you here in Paris, it seemed to me so unbelievable on your part, you who had struck me as well brought up and of a good *bourgeois* family" (on this adjective alone his voice gave a little hiss of impertinence), "that I was ingenuous enough to imagine all the excuses that never really happen, letters miscarrying, addresses misread. I recognise that it was extremely naïve of me, but St Bonaventure preferred to believe that an ox could fly rather than that his brother was capable of lying. However, all that is over: the idea did not appeal to you, there is no more to be said. It seems to me only that you might have brought yourself" (and there were genuine tears in his voice), "were it only out of consideration for my age, to write to me. I had conceived and planned for you infinitely seductive things, which I had taken good care not to divulge to you. You preferred to refuse without knowing what they were; that is your affair. But, as I say, one can always *write*. In your position, and indeed in my own, I should have done so. For that reason I prefer mine to yours—I say 'for that reason,' because I believe that all our positions are equal, and I have more fellow-feeling for an intelligent labourer than for many a duke. But I can say that I prefer my position, because in the whole course of my life, which is beginning now to be a pretty long one, I am conscious that I have never done what you did." (His head was turned away from the light, and I could not see if tears were falling from his eyes, as his voice led one to suppose.) "I said that I had advanced a long way towards you; the effect that had was to make you withdraw twice as far. Now it is for me to withdraw, and we shall know one another no longer. I shall retain not your name but your case, so that at moments when I might be tempted to believe that men have good manners, or simply the intelligence not to let slip an unparalleled opportunity, I may remember that that is ranking them too highly. No, that you should have said that you knew me when it was true—for henceforward it will cease to be true—I regard that as only natural, and I take it as an act of homage, that is to say something agreeable. Unfortunately, elsewhere and in other circumstances, you have uttered remarks of a very different nature."

"Monsieur, I swear to you that I have said nothing that could offend you."

"And who says that I am offended?" he furiously screamed, raising himself into an erect posture on the sofa on which hitherto he had been reclining motionless, while, as the pallid, frothing snakes twisted and stiffened in his face, his voice became alternately shrill and solemn like the deafening onrush of a storm. (The force with which he habitually spoke, which made strangers turn round in the street, was multiplied a hundredfold, as is a musical *forte* if, instead of being played on the piano, it is played by an orchestra, and changed into a

fortissimo as well. M. de Charlus roared.) "Do you suppose
that it is within your power to offend me? You are evidently
not aware to whom you are speaking? Do you imagine that
the envenomed spittle of five hundred little gentlemen of your
type, heaped one upon another, would succeed in slobbering
so much as the tips of my august toes?"

While he was speaking, my desire to persuade M. de Charlus
that I had never spoken or heard anyone else speak ill of him
had given place to a wild rage, provoked by the words which,
to my mind, were dictated to him solely by his colossal pride.
Perhaps they were indeed the effect, in part at any rate, of this
pride. Almost all the rest sprang from a feeling of which I
was then still ignorant, and for which I could not therefore be
blamed for not making due allowance. Failing this unknown
element, I might, had I remembered the words of Mme de
Guermantes, have been tempted to assume a trace of madness
in his pride. But at that moment the idea of madness never
even entered my head. There was in him, in my view, only
pride, while in me there was only fury. This fury (at the moment when M. de Charlus ceased to shout, in order to refer
to his august toes, with a majesty that was accompanied by a
grimace, a vomit of disgust at his obscure blasphemers), this
fury could contain itself no longer. I felt a compulsive desire
to strike something, and, a lingering trace of discernment
making me respect the person of a man so much older than
myself, and even, in view of their dignity as works of art, the
pieces of German porcelain that were grouped around him,
I seized the Baron's new silk hat, flung it to the ground,
trampled it, picked it up again, began blindly pulling it to
pieces, wrenched off the brim, tore the crown in two, heedless
of the continuing vociferations of M. de Charlus, and, crossing
the room in order to leave, opened the door. To my intense
astonishment, two footmen were standing one on either side
of it, who moved slowly away, so as to appear only to have
been casually passing in the course of their duty. (I afterwards
learned their names; one was called Burnier, the other
Charmel.) I was not taken in for a moment by the explanation which their leisurely gait seemed to offer me. It was highly
improbable; three others appeared to me to be less so: one was

that the Baron sometimes entertained guests against whom, in case he happened to need assistance (but why?), he deemed it necessary to keep reinforcements posted close at hand; the second was that, drawn by curiosity, they had stopped to listen at the keyhole, not thinking that I should come out so quickly; the third, that, the whole of the scene which M. de Charlus had made having been a piece of play-acting rehearsed in advance, he had himself told them to listen, from a love of spectacle combined, perhaps, with a "*nunc erudimini*" by which everyone would profit.

My anger had not calmed that of M. de Charlus, and my departure from the room seemed to cause him acute distress; he called me back, shouted to his servants to stop me, and finally, forgetting that a moment earlier, when he spoke of his "august toes," he had thought to make me a witness of his own deification, came running after me at full speed, overtook me in the hall, and stood barring the door. "Come, now," he said, "don't be childish; come back for a minute; he that loveth well chasteneth well, and if I have chastened you well it is because I love you well." My anger had subsided; I let the word "chasten" pass and followed the Baron who, summoning a footman, ordered him without a trace of self-consciousness to clear away the remains of the shattered hat, which was replaced by another.

"If you will tell me, Monsieur, who it is that has treacherously maligned me," I said to M. de Charlus, "I will stay here to learn his name and to confute the impostor."

"Who? Do you not know? Do you retain no memory of the things you say? Do you think that the people who are so good as to inform me of such things do not begin by demanding secrecy? And do you imagine that I'm going to betray a person to whom I have given my promise?"

"So it's impossible for you to tell me?" I asked, racking my brains in a last fruitless effort to discover to whom I could have spoken about M. de Charlus.

"Did you not hear me say that I had given a promise of secrecy to my informant?" he said in a snarling voice. "I see that with your fondness for abject utterances you combine one for futile persistence. You ought at least to have the intelligence to profit from a final interview with me, and not go on talking for the sake of talking drivel."

"Monsieur," I replied, moving away from him, "you insult me. I am disarmed, because you are several times my age, we are not equally matched. Moreover, I cannot convince you. I have already sworn to you that I have said nothing."

"So I'm lying!" he screamed in a terrifying tone, and with a bound forward that brought him within a yard of me.

"Someone has misinformed you."

Then in a gentle, affectionate, melancholy voice, as in those symphonies which are played without a break between the different movements, in which a graceful *scherzo*, amiable and idyllic, follows the thunder-peals of the opening pages, "It is quite possible," he said. "Generally speaking, a remark repeated at second hand is rarely true. It is your fault if, not having profited by the opportunities of seeing me which I had held out to you, you have not furnished me, by those frank and open words of daily intercourse which create confidence, with the unique and sovereign remedy against a remark which made you out a traitor. Either way, true or false, the allegation has done its work. I can never rid myself of the impression it made on me. I cannot even say that he who chasteneth well loveth well, for I have chastened you well enough but I no longer love you."

While saying this he had forced me to sit down and had rung the bell. A different footman appeared. "Bring something to drink and order the brougham." I said that I was not thirsty, that it was very late, and that in any case I had a carriage waiting. "They have probably paid him and sent him away," he told me, "you needn't worry about that. I'm ordering a carriage to take you home. . . . If you're anxious about the time . . . I could have given you a room here. . . ." I said that my mother would be worried. "Ah! of course, yes. Well, true or false, the remark has done its work. My affection, a trifle premature, had flowered too soon, and, like those apple trees of which you spoke so poetically at Balbec, it has been unable to withstand the first frost."

If M. de Charlus's affection for me had not been destroyed, he could hardly have acted differently, since, while assuring me that we had quarrelled irrevocably, he made me sit down and drink, asked me to stay the night, and was now going to send me home. He had indeed an air of dreading the moment at which he must part from me and find himself alone, that sort of slightly anxious fear which his sister-in-law and cousin Guermantes had appeared to me to be feeling when she had tried to force me to stay a little longer, with something of the same momentary fondness for me, of the same effort to prolong the passing minute.

"Unfortunately," he went on, "I have not the power to cause what has once been destroyed to blossom again. My affection for you is quite dead. Nothing can revive it. I believe that it is not unworthy of me to confess that I regret it. I always feel myself to be a little like Victor Hugo's Booz: 'I am widowed and alone, and the darkness gathers o'er me.'"

I walked back through the big green drawing-room with him. I told him, speaking quite at random, how beautiful I thought it. "Isn't it?" he replied. "It's a good thing to be fond of something. The panelling is by Bagard. What is rather charming, d'you see, is that it was made to match the Beauvais chairs and the consoles. You observe, it repeats the same decorative design. There used to be only two places where you could see this, the Louvre and M. d'Hinnisdal's house. But naturally, as soon as I had decided to come and live in this street, there cropped up an old family house of the Chimays which nobody had ever seen before because it came here expressly for *me*. On the whole it's quite good. It might perhaps be better, but after all it's not bad. Some pretty things, are there not? These are portraits of my uncles, the King of Poland and the King of England, by Mignard. But why am I telling you all this? You must know it as well as I do, since you were waiting in this room. No? Ah, then they must have put you in the blue drawing-room," he said with an air that might have been either rudeness, on the score of my lack of curiosity, or personal superiority, in not having taken the trouble to ask where I had been kept waiting. "Look, in this cabinet I have all the hats worn by Madame Elisabeth, by the Princesse de Lamballe, and by the Queen. They don't interest you; it's as though you couldn't see. Perhaps you are suffering from an affection of the optic nerve. If you like this kind of beauty better, here is a rainbow by Turner beginning to shine out between these two Rembrandts, as a sign of our reconciliation. You hear: Beethoven has come to join him." And indeed one could hear the first chords of the last movement of the Pastoral Symphony, "Joy after the Storm," performed somewhere not far away, on the first floor no doubt, by a band of musicians. I innocently inquired how they happened to be playing that, and who the musicians were. "Ah, well, one doesn't know. One never does know. It's invisible music. Pretty, isn't it?" he said to me in a slightly insolent tone, which nevertheless suggested somehow the influence and accent of Swann. "But you don't care two hoots about it. You want to go home, even if it means showing disrespect for Beethoven and for me. You are pronouncing judgment on yourself," he added, with an affectionate and mournful air, when the moment had come for me to go. "You will excuse my not accompanying you home, as good manners ordain that I should. Since I have decided not to see you again, spending five minutes more in your company would make very little difference to me. But I am tired, and I have a great deal to do." However, seeing that it was a fine night: "Ah, well, perhaps I will come in the carriage after all," he said. "There's a superb moon which I shall go on to admire from the Bois after I have taken you home. What, you don't know how to shave!—even on a night when you've been dining out, you have still a few hairs here," he said, taking my chin between two fingers which seemed as it were magnetised, and after a moment's resistance ran up to my ears like the fingers of a barber. "Ah! how pleasant it would be to look at the 'blue light of the moon' in the Bois with someone like yourself," he said to me with a sudden and almost involuntary gentleness, and then, sadly: "For you're nice, really; you could be nicer than anyone," he went on, laying his hand in a fatherly way on my shoulder. "Originally, I must confess that I found you quite insignificant." I ought to have reflected that he must find me so still. I had only to recall the rage with which he had spoken to me, barely half an hour before. In spite of this I had the impression that he was, for the moment, sincere, that his kindness of heart was prevailing over what I regarded as an almost frenzied condition of susceptibility and pride. The carriage was waiting beside us, and still he prolonged the conversation. "Come along," he said abruptly, "jump in, in five minutes we shall be at your door. And I shall bid you a good-night which will cut short our relations, for all time. It is better, since we must part for ever, that we should do so, as in music, on a perfect chord." Despite these solemn affirmations that we should never see one another again, I could have sworn that M. de Charlus, annoyed at having forgotten himself earlier in the evening and afraid of having hurt my feelings, would not have been displeased to see me once again. Nor was I mistaken, for, a moment later: "There, now," he said, "if I hadn't forgotten the most important thing of all. In memory of your grandmother, I have had a rare edition of Mme de Sévigné bound for you. I fear that that will prevent this from being our last meeting. One must console oneself with the reflexion that complicated affairs are rarely settled in a day. Just look how long they took over the Congress of Vienna."

"But I could send round for it without disturbing you," I said obligingly.

"Will you hold your tongue, you little fool," he replied angrily, "and not assume the grotesque air of regarding as a small matter the honour of being probably (I do not say certainly, for it will perhaps be one of my servants who hands you the volumes) received by me."

Then, regaining possession of himself: "I do not wish to part from you on these words. No dissonance; before the eternal silence, the dominant chord!" It was for his own nerves that he seemed to dread an immediate return home after harsh words of dissension. "You would not care to come to the Bois," he said to me in a tone that was not so much interrogative as affirmative, not, it seemed to me, because he did not wish to make me the offer, but because he was afraid that his self-esteem might meet with a refusal. "Ah, well," he went on, still postponing our separation, "it is the moment when, as Whistler says, the *bourgeois* go to bed" (perhaps he wished now to appeal to my self-esteem) "and it is meet to begin to look at things. But you don't even know who Whistler is!" I changed the subject and asked him whether the Princesse d'Iéna was an intelligent person. M. de Charlus stopped me, and, adopting the most contemptuous tone that I had yet heard him use, "Ah! there, sir," he said, "you are alluding to an order of nomenclature with which I do not hold. There is perhaps an aristocracy among the Tahitians, but I must confess that I know nothing about it. The name which you have just pronounced did sound in my ears, strangely enough, only a few days ago. Someone asked me whether I would condescend to allow the young Duc de Guastalla to be presented to me. The request astonished me, for the Duc de Guastalla has no need of an introduction to me, for the simple reason that he is my cousin, and has known me all his life; he is the son of the Princesse de Parme, and, as a well brought-up young kinsman, he never fails to come and pay his respects to me on New Year's Day. But, on making inquiries, I discovered that the young man in question was not my kinsman but the son of the person in whom you are interested. As there exists no princess of that title, I supposed that my friend was referring to some poor wanton sleeping under the Pont d'Iéna, who had picturesquely assumed the title of Princesse d'Iéna, as one talks about the Panther of the Batignolles, or the Steel King. But no, the reference was to a rich person who possesses some remarkable furniture which I had seen and admired at an exhibition, and which enjoys the superiority over the name of its owner of being genuine. As for this self-styled Duc de Guastalla, I supposed him to be my secretary's stockbroker; one can procure so many things with money. But no; it was the Emperor, it appears, who amused himself by conferring on these people a title which simply was not his to give. It was perhaps a sign of power, or of ignorance, or of malice, but in any case, I consider that it was an exceedingly scurvy trick to play on these unwitting usurpers. However, I cannot enlighten you on the subject; my knowledge begins and ends with the Faubourg Saint-Germain, where, among all the Courvoisiers and Gallardons, you will find, if you can manage to secure an introduction, plenty of old harridans taken straight out of Balzac who will amuse you. Naturally, all that has nothing to do with the prestige of the Princesse de Guer-

mantes, but without me and my 'Open Sesame' her portals are
inaccessible."

"The Princesse de Guermantes's house is really very
beautiful."

"Oh, it's not very beautiful. It's the most beautiful thing in
the world. Next to the Princess herself, of course."

"Is the Princesse de Guermantes superior to the Duchesse de
Guermantes?"

"Oh! there's no comparison." (It is to be observed that,
whenever people in society have the least touch of imagination,
they will crown or dethrone, at the whim of their affections or
their quarrels, those whose position appeared most solid and
unalterably fixed.) "The Duchesse de Guermantes" (perhaps
in not calling her "Oriane" he wished to set a greater distance
between her and myself) "is delightful, far superior to anything you can have guessed. But really she is incommensurable
with her cousin. The Princess is exactly what the people in the
market-place might imagine Princess Metternich to have been,
but *la* Metternich believed she had launched Wagner, because
she knew Victor Maurel.[31] The Princesse de Guermantes,
or rather her mother, knew the man himself. Which is a distinction, not to mention the incredible beauty of the lady.
And the Esther gardens alone!"

"Can one not visit them?"

"No, you would have to be invited, but they never invite
anyone unless I intercede."

But at once withdrawing the bait of this offer after having
dangled it in front of me, he held out his hand, for we had
reached my door.

"My role is at an end, sir. I will simply add these few words.
Another person will perhaps offer you his affection some day
as I have done. Let the present example serve for your instruction. Do not neglect it. Affection is always precious. What one
cannot do alone in this life, because there are things which one
cannot ask, or do, or wish, or learn by oneself, one can do in
company, and without needing to be thirteen, as in Balzac's
story, or four, as in *The Three Musketeers*. Good-bye."

He must have been feeling tired and have abandoned the idea
of going to look at the moonlight, for he asked me to tell his

coachman to drive home. At once he made a sharp movement as though he had changed his mind. But I had already given the order, and, so as not to lose any more time, I went and rang my door-bell. It had not recurred to me for a moment that I had been meaning to tell M. de Charlus, on the subject of the German Emperor and General Botha, stories which had been such an obsession an hour ago but which his unexpected and crushing reception had sent flying far from my mind.

On entering my room I saw on my desk a letter which Françoise's young footman had written to one of his friends and had left lying there. Now that my mother was away, there was no liberty that he hesitated to take. I was even more at fault for taking the liberty of reading the letter which lay spread out before me with no envelope and (this was my sole excuse) seemed to be offering itself to my eyes.

"Dear Friend and Cousin,

"I hope this finds you in good health, and the same with all the young folk, particularily my young godson Joseph who I have not yet had the pleasure of meeting but who I preffer to you all as being my godson, these relics of the heart they also have their dust, upon their blest remains let us not lay our hands. Besides dear friend and cousin who can say that to-morrow you and your dear wife my cousin Marie, will not both be cast hedlong down into the bottom of the sea, like the sailor clinging to the mast on high, for this life is but a dark valley. Dear friend I must tell you that my principal ocupation, which will astonish you I'm sure, is now poetry which I love passionately, for we must wile away the time. And so dear friend do not be too surprised if I have not ansered your last letter before now, in place of pardon let oblivion come. As you know, Madame's mother has past away amid unspeakable sufferings which fairly exausted her as she saw as many as three doctors. The day of her internment was a great day for all Monsieur's relations came in crowds as well as several Ministers. It took them more than two hours to get to the cemetry, which will make you all open your eyes pretty wide in your village for they certainly wont do as much for mother Michu. So all my life to come can be but one long sob. I am enjoying myself imensely with the motorcycle which Ive recently learned. What would you say my dear friends if I arived suddenly like that at full speed at Les Ecorres. But on that head I shall no more keep silence for I feel that the frenzy of greif sweeps its reason away. I am associating with the Duchesse de Guermantes, poeple whose names you have never even heard in our ignorant villages. Therefore it is with pleasure that Im going to send the works of Racine, of Victor Hugo, of Pages Choisies de Chenédollé, of Alfred de Musset, for I would cure the land which give me birth of ignorance which leads innevitably to crime. I cant think of anything more to say to you and send you like the pelican wearied by a long flite my best regards as well as to your wife my godson and your sister Rose. May it never be said of her: And Rose she lived only as live the roses, as has been said by Victor Hugo, the sonnet of Arvers, Alfred de Musset all those great geniuses who because of that were sent to die at the steak like Joan of Arc. Hoping for your next missive soon, your loving cousin Périgot Joseph."

We are attracted by any life which represents for us something unknown and strange, by a last illusion still unshattered. Many of the things that M. de Charlus had told me had given a vigorous spur to my imagination and, making it forget how much the reality had disappointed it at Mme de Guermantes's (people's names are in this respect like the names of places), had swung it towards Oriane's cousin. Moreover, M. de Charlus misled me for some time as to the imaginary worth and variety of society people only because he was himself misled. And this, perhaps, because he did nothing, did not write, did not paint, did not even read anything in a serious and thorough manner. But, superior as he was by several degrees to society people, if it was from them and the spectacle they afforded that he drew the material for his conversation, he was still not understood by them. Speaking as an artist, he could at the most bring out the deceptive charm of society people—but for artists only, in relation to whom he might be said to play the part played by the reindeer among the Eskimos: this precious animal plucks for them from the barren rocks lichens and mosses which they themselves could neither discover nor utilise, but which, once they have been digested by the reindeer, become for the inhabitants of the far North an assimilable form of food.

To which I may add that the pictures which M. de Charlus drew of society were animated with plenty of life by the blend of his ferocious hatreds and his passionate affections—hatreds directed mainly against young men, adoration aroused principally by certain women.

If among these the Princesse de Guermantes was placed by M. de Charlus upon the most exalted throne, his mysterious words about the "inaccessible Aladdin's palace" in which his cousin dwelt were not sufficient to account for my amazement, speedily followed by the fear that I might be the victim of some bad joke concocted by someone who wanted to get me thrown out of a house to which I had gone without being invited, when, about two months after my dinner with the Duchess and while she was at Cannes, having opened an envelope the appearance of which had not led me to suppose that it contained anything out of the ordinary, I read the following words engraved on a card: "The Princesse de Guermantes, *née* Duchesse en Bavière, At Home, the ——th." No doubt to be invited to the Princesse de Guermantes's was perhaps not, from the social point of view, any more difficult than to dine with the Duchess, and my slight knowledge of heraldry had taught me that the title of Prince is not superior to that of Duke. Besides, I told myself that the intelligence of a society woman could not be essentially so dissimilar from that of the rest of her kind as M. de Charlus made out. But my imagination, like Elstir engaged upon rendering some effect of perspective without reference to the notions of physics which he might quite well possess, depicted for me not what I knew but what it saw; what it saw, that is to say what the name showed it. Now, even before I had met the Duchess, the name Guermantes preceded by the title of Princess, like a note or a colour or a quantity profoundly modified by surrounding values, by the mathematical or aesthetic "sign" that governs it, had always evoked for me something entirely different. With that title, it is to be found chiefly in the memoirs of the days of Louis XIII and Louis XIV; and I imagined the town house of the Princesse de Guermantes as being regularly frequented by the Duchesse de Longueville and the great Condé, whose presence there rendered it highly improbable that I should ever penetrate it.

In spite of whatever may stem from various subjective points of view, of which I shall have something to say later,

in these artificial magnifications, the fact remains that there is
a certain objective reality in all these people, and consequently
a difference between them.

How, in any case, could it be otherwise? The humanity with
which we consort and which bears so little resemblance to our
dreams is none the less the same that, in the memoirs and in
the letters of eminent persons, we have seen described and have
felt a desire to know. The utterly insignificant old man we
meet at dinner is the same who wrote that proud letter to Prince
Friedrich-Karl which we read with such emotion in a book
about the war of 1870. We are bored at the dinner-table
because our imagination is absent, and, because it is keeping us company, we are interested in a book. But the
people in question are the same. We should like to have
known Mme de Pompadour, who was so valuable a patron
of the arts, and we should have been as bored in her company as among the modern Egerias at whose houses we
cannot bring ourselves to pay a second call, so uninteresting
do we find them. The fact remains that these differences do
exist. People are never completely alike; their behaviour with
regard to ourselves, at, one might say, the same level of
friendship, reveals differences which, in the end, counterbalance one another. When I knew Mme de Montmorency,
she enjoyed saying disagreeable things to me, but if I asked her
a favour she would use all her influence as unstintingly and
as effectively as possible in order to obtain what I needed.
Whereas another woman, Mme de Guermantes for example,
would never have wished to hurt my feelings, never said
anything about me except what might give me pleasure,
showered on me all those tokens of friendship which formed
the rich texture of the Guermantes's moral life, but, if I asked
her for the smallest thing above and beyond that, would not
have moved an inch to procure it for me, as in those country
houses where one has at one's disposal a motor-car and a
valet but where it is impossible to obtain a glass of cider for
which no provision has been made in the arrangements for a
party. Which was for me the true friend, Mme de Montmorency, so happy to ruffle my feelings and always so ready
to oblige, or Mme de Guermantes, distressed by the slightest

offence that might have been given me and incapable of the slightest effort to be of use to me? Similarly, it was said that the Duchesse de Guermantes spoke only about frivolities, and her cousin, intellectually so mediocre, invariably about interesting things. Types of mind are so varied, so conflicting, not only in literature but in society, that Baudelaire and Mérimée are not the only people who have the right to despise one another mutually. These distinctive characteristics form in each person a system of looks, words and actions so coherent, so despotic, that when we are in his or her presence it seems to us superior to the rest. With Mme de Guermantes, her words, deduced like a theorem from her type of mind, seemed to me the only ones that could possibly be said. And at heart I was of her opinion when she told me that Mme de Montmorency was stupid and kept an open mind towards all the things she did not understand, or when, having heard of some malicious remark made by that lady, she said: "So that's what you call a kind woman. I call her a monster." But this tyranny of the reality which confronts us, this self-evidence of the lamplight which turns the already distant dawn as pale as the faintest memory, disappeared when I was away from Mme de Guermantes and a different lady said to me, putting herself on my level and considering the Duchess as being far below either of us: "Oriane takes no interest, really, in anything or anybody," or even (something that in the presence of Mme de Guermantes it would have seemed impossible to believe, so loudly did she herself proclaim the opposite): "Oriane is a snob." Since no mathematical process would have enabled one to convert Mme d'Arpajon and Mme de Montpensier into commensurable quantities, it would have been impossible for me to answer had anyone asked me which of the two seemed to me superior to the other.

Now, among the characteristics peculiar to the Princesse de Guermantes's salon, the one most generally cited was an exclusiveness due in part to the Princess's royal birth but more especially to the almost fossilised rigidity of the Prince's aristocratic prejudices—which, incidentally, the Duke and Duchess had had no hesitation in deriding in front of me. This exclusiveness made me regard it as even more improbable that I should have been invited by this man who reckoned only in royal personages and dukes and at every dinner-party made a scene because he had not been put in the place to which he would have been entitled under Louis XIV, a place which, thanks to his immense erudition in matters of history and genealogy, he was the only person who knew. For this reason, many society people came down on the side of the Duke and Duchess when discussing the differences that distinguished them from their cousins. "The Duke and Duchess are far more modern, far more intelligent, they aren't simply interested, like the other couple, in how many quarterings one has, their house is three hundred years in advance of their cousins'," were customary remarks, the memory of which made me tremble as I looked at the invitation card, since they made it all the more probable that it had been sent to me by some practical joker.

If the Duke and Duchess had not been still at Cannes, I might have tried to find out from them whether the invitation I had received was genuine. This state of doubt in which I was plunged is not in fact, as I deluded myself for a time by supposing, a sentiment which a man of fashion would not have felt and which consequently a writer, even if he otherwise belonged to the world of society, ought to reproduce in order to be thoroughly "objective" and to depict each class differently. I happened indeed, only the other day, in a charming volume of memoirs, to come upon the record of uncertainties analogous to those which the Princesse de Guermantes's card engendered in me. "Georges and I" (or "Hély and I"—I haven't the book at hand to verify the reference) "were so longing to be asked to Mme Delessert's that, having received an invitation from her, we thought it prudent, each of us independently, to make certain that we were not the victims of an April fool hoax." And the writer is none other than the Comte d'Haussonville (he who married the Duc de Broglie's daughter), while the other young man who "independently" tries to ascertain whether he is the victim of a hoax is, according to whether he is called Georges or Hély, one or other of the two inseparable friends of M. d'Haussonville, either M. d'Harcourt or the Prince de Chalais.

The day on which the reception at the Princesse de Guermantes's was to be held, I learned that the Duke and Duchess had returned to Paris the night before, and I made up my mind to go and see them that morning. But, having gone out early, they had not yet returned; I watched first of all from a little room, which had seemed to me to be a good look-out post, for the arrival of their carriage. As a matter of fact I had made a singularly bad choice of observatory, for I could scarcely see into our courtyard, but I caught a glimpse of several others, and this, though of no practical use to me, diverted me for a time. It is not only in Venice that one has these views on to several houses at once which have proved so tempting to painters; it is just the same in Paris. Nor do I cite Venice at random. It is of its poorer quarters that certain poor quarters of Paris remind one, in the morning, with their tall, splayed chimneys to which the sun imparts the most vivid pinks, the brightest reds—like a garden flowering above the houses, and flowering in such a variety of tints as to suggest the garden of a tulip-fancier of Delft or Haarlem planted above the town. And then the extreme proximity of the houses, with their windows looking across at one another over a common courtyard, makes of each casement the frame in which a cook sits dreamily gazing down at the ground below, or, further off, a girl is having her hair combed by an old woman with a witchlike face, barely distinguishable in the shadow: thus each courtyard provides the neighbours in the adjoining house, suppressing sound by its width and framing silent gestures in a series of rectangles placed under glass by the closing of the windows, with an exhibition of a hundred Dutch paintings hung in rows. True, from the Hôtel de Guermantes one did not have the same kind of views, but one had curious ones none the less, especially from the strange trigonometrical point at which I had placed myself and from which there was nothing to arrest one's gaze, across the relatively featureless and steeply sloping intervening area, until the distant heights formed by the mansion of the Marquise de Plassac and Mme de Tresmes, extremely noble cousins of M. de Guermantes whom I did not know. Between me and this house (which was that of their father, M. de Bréquigny) nothing but blocks of buildings of low elevation, facing in every conceivable direction, which, without blocking the view, prolonged the distance with their oblique planes. The red-tiled turret of the coach-house in which the Marquis de Fré-court kept his carriages did indeed end in a spire that rose rather higher, but was so slender that it concealed nothing, and reminded one of those picturesque old buildings in Switzerland which spring up in isolation at the foot of a mountain. All these vague and divergent points on which my eyes came to rest made Mme de Plassac's house, actually quite near but misleadingly distant as in an Alpine landscape, appear as though it were separated from us by several streets or by a series of foothills. When its large rectangular windows, glittering in the sunlight like flakes of rock crystal, were thrown open to air the rooms, one felt, in following from one floor to the next the footmen whom it was impossible to see clearly but who were visibly shaking carpets, the same pleasure as when one sees in a landscape by Turner or Elstir a traveller in a stage-coach, or a guide, at different degrees of altitude on the Saint-Gothard. But from the vantage-point where I had placed myself I should have been in danger of not seeing M. or Mme de Guermantes come in, so that when in the afternoon I was free to resume my watch I simply stood on the staircase, from which the opening of the carriage-gate could not escape my notice, and it was on this staircase that I posted myself, although the Alpine beauties of the Hôtel de Bréquigny, so entrancing with their footmen rendered minute by distance and busily cleaning, were not visible from there. Now this wait on the staircase was to have for me consequences so considerable, and to reveal to me so important a landscape, no longer Turneresque but moral, that it is preferable to postpone the account of it for a little while by interposing first that of my visit to the Guermantes when I knew that they had come home.

It was the Duke alone who received me in his library. As I was approaching the door there emerged a little man with snow-white hair, a rather shabby appearance, a little black tie such as was worn by the Combray notary and by several of my grandfather's friends, but of a more timid aspect than

they, who, making me a series of deep bows, refused absolutely
to go downstairs until I had passed him. The Duke shouted
after him from the library something which I did not understand, and the other responded with further bows, addressed
to the wall, for the Duke could not see him, but endlessly
repeated nevertheless, like the purposeless smiles on the faces
of people who are talking to one on the telephone; he had a
falsetto voice, and saluted me afresh with the humility of a
steward. And he might indeed have been a steward from Combray, so much was he in the style, provincial, antiquated and
mild, of the small folk, the modest elders of those parts.

"You'll see Oriane presently," the Duke said to me when I
entered the room. "As Swann is coming round soon with
the proofs of his essay on the coinage of the Order of Malta,
and, what is worse, an immense photograph he has had taken
showing both sides of each of the coins, Oriane decided to
get dressed first in order to be able to stay with him until it's
time to go out to dinner. We're already so cluttered with things
that we don't know where to put them all, and I wonder where
on earth we're going to stick this photograph. But my wife's
too good-natured—she can't resist obliging people. She
thought it would be nice to ask Swann to let her see side by
side on one sheet the heads of all those Grand Masters of the
Order whose medals he found at Rhodes. I said Malta, didn't
I—it's Rhodes, but it's the same Order of St John of Jerusalem. The truth is that she's interested in all that only because
Swann makes a hobby of it. Our family is very much mixed up
in the whole story; even to-day, my brother, whom you know,
is one of the highest dignitaries in the Order of Malta. But if
I'd talked to Oriane about it all she simply wouldn't have
listened to me. On the other hand, Swann's researches into the
Templars (it's astonishing the passion people of one religion
have for studying others) only had to lead him on to the history
of the Knights of Rhodes, who succeeded the Templars, for
Oriane at once to insist on seeing the heads of these knights.
They were very small fry indeed compared with the Lusignans,
Kings of Cyprus, from whom we descend in a direct line. But
so far Swann hasn't taken them up, so Oriane doesn't care to
hear anything about the Lusignans."

I could not at once explain to the Duke why I had come. The fact was that several relatives or friends, including Mme de Silistrie and the Duchesse de Montrose, came to call on the Duchess, who was often at home before dinner, and not finding her, stayed for a short while with the Duke. The first of these ladies (the Princesse de Silistrie), simply attired, with a curt but friendly manner, was carrying a stick. I was afraid at first that she had injured herself, or was a cripple. She was on the contrary most alert. She spoke sadly to the Duke, of a first cousin of his—not on the Guermantes side, but more illustrious still, were that possible—whose health, which had been in a grave condition for some time past, had grown suddenly worse. But it was evident that the Duke, while sympathising with his cousin and repeating "Poor Mama! He's such a good fellow," had formed a favourable prognosis. The fact was that the Duke was looking forward to the dinner-party he was to attend, and far from bored at the prospect of the big reception at the Princesse de Guermantes's, but above all he was to go on at one o'clock in the morning with his wife to a great supper and fancy dress ball, with a view to which a costume as Louis XI for himself, and one as Isabella of Bavaria for the Duchess, were waiting in readiness. And the Duke was determined not to be disturbed amid all these gaieties by the sufferings of the worthy Amanien d'Osmond. Two other ladies carrying sticks, Mme de Plassac and Mme de Tresmes, both daughters of the Comte de Bréquigny, came in next to pay Basin a visit, and declared that cousin Mama's state was now beyond hope. The Duke shrugged his shoulders, and to change the subject asked whether they were going that evening to Marie-Gilbert's. They replied that they were not, in view of the state of Amanien who was *in extremis*, and indeed they had excused themselves from the dinner to which the Duke was going, the other guests at which they proceeded to enumerate to him: the brother of King Theodosius, the Infanta Maria Concepción, and so forth. As the Marquis d'Osmond was less closely related to them than he was to Basin, their "defection" appeared to the Duke to be a sort of indirect reproach for his own conduct, and he was rather curt with them. And so, although they had come down from the heights of the Hôtel de Bréquigny to see the Duchess (or rather to announce to her the alarming character, incompatible for his relatives with attendance at social gatherings, of their cousin's illness), they did not stay long: each armed with her alpenstock, Walpurge and Dorothée (such were the names of the two sisters) retraced the craggy path to their citadel. I never thought to ask the Guermantes what was the meaning of these sticks, so common in a certain part of the Faubourg Saint-Germain. Possibly, looking upon the whole parish as their domain, and not caring to hire cabs, they were in the habit of taking long walks, for which some old fracture, due to immoderate indulgence in the chase and to the falls from horseback which are often the fruit of that indulgence, or simply rheumatism caused by the damp-ness of the left bank and of old country houses, made a stick necessary. Perhaps they had not set out upon any such long expedition through the neighbourhood, but, having merely come down into their garden (which lay at no great distance from that of the Duchess) to pick the fruit required for their compotes, had looked in on their way home to bid good evening to Mme de Guermantes, though without going so far as to bring a pair of secateurs or a watering-can into her house.

The Duke appeared touched that I should have come to see them on the very day of their return to Paris. But his face clouded over when I told him I had come to ask his wife to find out whether her cousin really had invited me. I had touched upon one of those services which M. and Mme de Guermantes were not fond of rendering. The Duke explained to me that it was too late, that if the Princess had not sent me an invitation it would make him appear to be asking her for one, that his cousins had refused him one once before, and he had no wish to appear either directly or indirectly to be interfering with their visiting list, to be "meddling," that anyhow he could not even be sure that he and his wife, who were dining out that evening, would not come straight home afterwards, that in that case their best excuse for not having gone to the Princess's party would be to conceal from her the fact of their return to Paris, instead of hastening to inform her of it, as they must do if they sent her a note or spoke to her over the telephone about

me, and certainly too late to be of any use, since, in all
probability, the Princess's list of guests would be closed by
now. "You've not fallen foul of her in any way?" he asked in
a suspicious tone, the Guermantes living in constant fear of not
being informed of the latest society quarrels, and of people's
trying to climb back into favour on their shoulders. Finally,
as the Duke was in the habit of taking upon himself all
decisions that might seem ungracious, "Listen, my boy," he
said to me suddenly, as though the idea had just come into his
head, "I'd really rather not mention at all to Oriane that
you've spoken to me about this. You know how kind-hearted
she is, and besides, she's enormously fond of you—she'd insist
on sending to ask her cousin, in spite of anything I might say
to the contrary, and if she's tired after dinner, there'll be no
getting out of it, she'll be forced to go to the party. No,
decidedly, I shall say nothing to her about it. Anyhow, you'll
see her yourself in a minute. But not a word about this matter, I
beg of you. If you decide to go to the party, I've no need to
tell you what a pleasure it will be for us to spend the evening
there with you."

Humane motives are too sacred for the person before whom
they are invoked not to bow to them, whether he believes them
to be sincere or not; I did not wish to appear to be weighing
in the balance for a moment the relative importance of my
invitation and the possible tiredness of Mme de Guermantes,
and I promised not to speak to her of the object of my visit,
exactly as though I had been taken in by the little farce which
M. de Guermantes had performed for my benefit. I asked him
if he thought there was any chance of my seeing Mme de
Stermaria at the Princess's.

"Why, no," he replied with the air of a connoisseur. "I
know the name you mention, from having seen it in club direc-
tories—it isn't at all the type of person who goes to Gilbert's.
You'll see nobody there who is not excessively well-bred and
intensely boring, duchesses bearing titles which one thought
were extinct years ago and which have been trotted out for the
occasion, all the ambassadors, heaps of Coburgs, foreign royalties, but you mustn't expect even the ghost of a Stermaria.
Gilbert would be taken ill at the mere thought of such a thing.

Wait now, you're fond of painting, I must show you a superb picture I bought from my cousin, partly in exchange for the Elstirs, which frankly didn't appeal to us. It was sold to me as a Philippe de Champaigne, but I believe myself that it's by someone even greater. Would you like to know what I think? I think it's a Velazquez, and of the best period," said the Duke, looking me boldly in the eyes, either to ascertain my impression or in the hope of enhancing it. A footman came in.

"Mme la Duchesse wishes to know if M. le Duc will be so good as to see M. Swann, as Mme la Duchesse is not quite ready."

"Show M. Swann in," said the Duke, after looking at his watch and seeing that he himself still had a few minutes before he need go to dress. "Naturally my wife, who told him to come, isn't ready. No point in saying anything in front of Swann about Marie-Gilbert's party," said the Duke. "I don't know whether he's been invited. Gilbert likes him immensely, because he believes him to be the natural grandson of the Duc de Berri, but that's a long story. (Otherwise you can imagine! —my cousin, who has a fit if he sees a Jew a mile off.) But now of course the Dreyfus case has made things more serious. Swann ought to have realised that he more than anyone must drop all connexion with those fellows, instead of which he says the most regrettable things."

The Duke called back the footman to know whether the man who had been sent to inquire at cousin Osmond's had returned. His plan was as follows: since he rightly believed that his cousin was dying, he was anxious to obtain news of him before his death, that is to say before he was obliged to go into mourning. Once covered by the official certainty that Amanien was still alive, he would sneak off to his dinner, to the Prince's reception, to the midnight revel where he was to appear as Louis XI and where he had a most tantalising assignation with a new mistress, and would make no more inquiries until the following day, when his pleasures would be over. Then he would put on mourning if the cousin had passed away in the night. "No, M. le Duc, he is not back yet." "Hell and damnation! Nothing is ever done in this house till the last minute," cried the Duke, at the thought that Amanien might still be in time to "croak" for an evening paper, and to make him miss his revel. He sent for *Le Temps*, in which there was nothing.

I had not seen Swann for a long time, and found myself wondering momentarily whether in the old days he used to clip his moustache, or whether his hair had not been *en brosse*, for I found him somehow changed. It was simply that he was indeed greatly "changed" because he was very ill, and illness produces in the face modifications as profound as are created by growing a beard or by changing one's parting. (Swann's illness was the same that had killed his mother, who had been struck down by it at precisely the age which he had now reached. Our lives are in truth, owing to heredity, as full of cabalistic ciphers, of horoscopic castings as if sorcerers really existed. And just as there is a certain duration of life for humanity in general, so there is one for families in particular, that is to say, in any one family, for the members of it who resemble one another.) Swann was dressed with an elegance which, like that of his wife, associated with what he now was what he once had been. Buttoned up in a pearl-grey frock coat which emphasised his tall, slim figure, his white gloves stitched in black, he had a grey topper of a flared shape which Delion no longer made except for him, the Prince de Sagan, M. de Charlus, the Marquis de Modène, M. Charles Haas and Comte Louis de Turenne. I was surprised at the charming smile and affectionate handclasp with which he replied to my greeting for I had imagined that after so long an interval he would not recognise me at once; I told him of my astonishment; he received it with a shout of laughter, a trace of indignation and a further squeeze of my hand, as if it were to throw doubt on the soundness of his brain or the sincerity of his affection to suppose that he did not recognise me. And yet that was in fact the case; he did not identify me, as I learned long afterwards, until several minutes later when he heard my name mentioned. But no change in his face, in his speech, in the things he said to me betrayed the discovery which a chance word from M. de Guermantes had enabled him to make, with such mastery, with such absolute sureness did he play the social game. He brought to it, moreover, that spontaneity in manners and that personal enterprise, even in matters of dress, which characterised the Guermantes style. Thus it was that the greeting which the old clubman had given me without recognising me was not the cold, stiff greeting of the purely formalist man of the world, but a greeting full of real friendliness, genuine charm, such as the Duchesse de Guermantes, for instance, possessed (carrying it so far as to smile at you first, before you had bowed to her, if she met you in the street), in contrast to the more mechanical greeting customary among the ladies of the Faubourg Saint-Germain. In the same way, the hat which, in conformity with a custom that was beginning to disappear, he laid on the floor by his feet, was lined with green leather, a thing not usually done, because (he said) it showed the dirt far less, in reality because (but this he did not say) it was highly becoming.

"Now, Charles, you're a great expert, come and see what I've got to show you, after which, my boys, I'm going to ask your permission to leave you together for a moment while I go and change my clothes. Besides, I expect Oriane won't be long now." And he showed his "Velazquez" to Swann. "But it seems to me that I know this," said Swann with the grimace of a sick man for whom the mere act of speaking requires an effort.

"Yes," said the Duke, perturbed by the time which the expert was taking to express his admiration. "You've probably seen it at Gilbert's."

"Oh, yes, of course, I remember."

"What do you suppose it is?"

"Oh, well, if it comes from Gilbert's house it's probably one of your *ancestors*," said Swann with a blend of irony and deference towards a grandeur which he would have felt it impolite and absurd to belittle, but to which for reasons of good taste he preferred to make only a playful reference.

"Of course it is," said the Duke bluntly. "It's Boson, the I forget how manyeth de Guermantes. Not that I care a damn about that. You know I'm not as feudal as my cousin. I've heard the names of Rigaud, Mignard, even Velazquez mentioned," he went on, fastening on Swann the look of both an inquisitor and a torturer in an attempt at once to read into his mind and to influence his response. "Well," he concluded (for when he was led to provoke artificially an opinion which he desired to hear, he had the faculty, after a few moments, of believing that it had been spontaneously uttered), "come, now, none of your flattery. Do you think it's by one of those big guns I've mentioned?"

"Nnnnno," said Swann.

"Well anyway, I know nothing about these things, it's not for me to decide who daubed the canvas. But you're a dilettante, a master of the subject, what would you say it was?"

Swann hesitated for a moment in front of the picture, which obviously he thought atrocious.

"A bad joke!" he replied with a smile at the Duke who could not restrain an impulse of rage. When this had subsided: "Be good fellows, both of you, wait a moment for Oriane, I must go and put on my swallow-tails and then I'll be back. I shall send word to the missus that you're both waiting for her."

I chatted for a minute or two with Swann about the Dreyfus case and asked him how it was that all the Guermantes were anti-Dreyfusards. "In the first place because at heart all these people are anti-semites," replied Swann, who nevertheless knew very well from experience that certain of them were not, but, like everyone who holds a strong opinion, preferred to explain the fact that other people did not share it by imputing to them preconceptions and prejudices against which there was nothing to be done, rather than reasons which might permit of discussion. Besides, having come to the premature term of his life, like a weary animal that is being tormented, he cried out against these persecutions and was returning to the spiritual fold of his fathers.

"Yes, it's true I've been told that the Prince de Guermantes is anti-semitic."

"Oh, that fellow! I don't even bother to consider him. He carries it to such a point that when he was in the army and had a frightful toothache he preferred to grin and bear it rather than go to the only dentist in the district, who happened to be a Jew, and later on he allowed a wing of his castle to be burned to the ground because he would have had to send for extinguishers to the place next door, which belongs to the Rothschilds."

"Are you going to be there this evening, by any chance?"

"Yes," Swann replied, "although I don't really feel up to it. But he sent me a wire to tell me that he has something to say to me. I feel that I shall soon be too unwell to go there or to receive him at my house, it will be too agitating, so I prefer to get it over at once."

"But the Duc de Guermantes is not anti-semitic?"

"You can see quite well that he is, since he's an anti-Dreyfusard," replied Swann, without noticing the logical fallacy. "All the same I'm sorry to have disappointed the fellow—His Grace I should say!—by not admiring his Mignard or whatever he calls it."

"But at any rate," I went on, reverting to the Dreyfus case, "the Duchess, now, is intelligent."

"Yes, she is charming. To my mind, however, she was even more charming when she was still known as the Princesse des Laumes. Her mind has become somehow more angular—it was all much softer in the juvenile great lady. But after all, young or old, men or women, when all's said and done these people belong to a different race, one can't have a thousand years of feudalism in one's blood with impunity. Naturally they imagine that it counts for nothing in their opinions."

"All the same, Robert de Saint-Loup is a Dreyfusard."

"Ah! So much the better, especially as his mother is extremely 'anti.' I had heard that he was, but I wasn't certain of it. That gives me a great deal of pleasure. It doesn't surprise me, he's highly intelligent. It's a great thing, that is."

Swann's Dreyfusism had brought out in him an extraordinary naïvety and imparted to his way of looking at things an impulsiveness, an inconsistency more noticeable even than had been the similar effects of his marriage to Odette; this new "declassing" would have been better described as a "reclassing" and was entirely to his credit, since it made him return to the paths which his forebears had trodden and from which he had been deflected by his aristocratic associations. But precisely at the moment when, with all his clear-sightedness, and thanks to the principles he had inherited from his

ancestors, he was in a position to perceive a truth that was still
hidden from people of fashion, Swann showed himself
nevertheless quite comically blind. He subjected all his admira-
tions and all his contempts to the test of a new criterion,
Dreyfusism. That the anti-Dreyfusism of Mme Bontemps
should make him think her a fool was no more astonishing
than that, when he had got married, he should have thought her
intelligent. It was not very serious, either, that the new wave
should also affect his political judgments and make him lose
all memory of having denounced Clemenceau—whom, he
now declared, he had always regarded as a voice of conscience,
a man of steel, like Cornély—as a man with a price, a British
spy (this latter was an absurdity of the Guermantes set).
"No, no, I never told you anything of the sort. You're thinking
of someone else." But, sweeping past his political judgments,
the wave overturned Swann's literary judgments too, down to
his way of expressing them. Barrès was now devoid of talent,
and even his early books were feeble, could scarcely bear
re-reading. "You try, you'll find you can't struggle to the end.
What a difference from Clemenceau! Personally I'm not anti-
clerical, but when you compare them together you must see
that Barrès is invertebrate. He's a very great man, is old
Clemenceau. How he knows the language!" However, the
anti-Dreyfusards were in no position to criticise these follies.
They explained that one was only a Dreyfusard because one
was of Jewish origin. If a practising Catholic like Saniette
was also in favour of revision, that was because he was cornered
by Mme Verdurin, who behaved like a wild radical. She was
first and foremost against the "frocks." Saniette was more
fool than knave, and had no idea of the harm that the Mistress
was doing him. If you pointed out that Brichot was equally a
friend of Mme Verdurin and was a member of the "Patrie
Française," that was because he was more intelligent.

"You see him occasionally?" I asked Swann, referring to
Saint-Loup.

"No, never. He wrote to me the other day asking me to
persuade the Duc de Mouchy and various other people to vote
for him at the Jockey, where for that matter he got through
like a letter through the post."

"In spite of the Affair!"

"The question was never raised. However I must tell you that since all this business began I never set foot in the place."

M. de Guermantes returned and was presently joined by his wife, all ready now for the evening, tall and proud in a gown of red satin the skirt of which was bordered with sequins. She had in her hair a long ostrich feather dyed purple, and over her shoulders a tulle scarf of the same red as her dress. "How nice it is to have one's hat lined in green," said the Duchess, who missed nothing. "However, with you Charles, everything is always charming, whether it's what you wear or what you say, what you read or what you do." Swann meanwhile, without apparently listening, was considering the Duchess as he would have studied the canvas of a master, and then sought her eyes, making a face which implied the exclamation "Gosh!" Mme de Guermantes rippled with laughter. "So my clothes please you? I'm delighted. But I must say they don't please me much," she went on with a sulky air. "God, what a bore it is to have to dress up and go out when one would ever so much rather stay at home!"

"What magnificent rubies!"

"Ah! my dear Charles, at least one can see that you know what you're talking about, you're not like that brute Monserfeuil who asked me if they were real. I must say I've never seen anything quite like them. They were a present from the Grand Duchess. They're a little too big for my liking, a little too like claret glasses filled to the brim, but I've put them on because we shall be seeing the Grand Duchess this evening at Marie-Gilbert's," added Mme de Guermantes, never suspecting that this assertion destroyed the force of those previously made by the Duke.

"What's on at the Princess's?" inquired Swann.

"Practically nothing," the Duke hastened to reply, the question having made him think that Swann was not invited.

"What do you mean, Basin? The whole world has been invited. It will be a deathly crush. What will be pretty, though," she went on, looking soulfully at Swann, "if the storm I can feel in the air now doesn't break, will be those marvellous gardens. You know them, of course. I was there a month ago, when the lilacs were in flower. You can't imagine how lovely they were. And then the fountain—really, it's Versailles in Paris."

"What sort of person is the Princess?" I asked.

"Why, you know quite well, since you've seen her here, that she's as beautiful as the day, and also a bit of a fool, but very nice, in spite of all her Germanic high-and-mightiness, full of good nature and gaffes."

Swann was too shrewd not to perceive that the Duchess was trying to show off the "Guermantes wit," and at no great cost to herself, for she was only serving up in a less perfect form a few of her old quips. Nevertheless, to prove to the Duchess that he appreciated her intention to be funny, and as though she had really succeeded in being funny, he gave a somewhat forced smile, causing me by this particular form of insincerity the same embarrassment as I used to feel long ago when I heard my parents discussing with M. Vinteuil the corruption of certain sections of society (when they knew very well that a corruption far greater reigned at Montjouvain), or simply on hearing Legrandin embellishing his utterances for the benefit of fools, choosing delicate epithets which he knew perfectly well would not be understood by a rich or smart but illiterate audience.

"Come now, Oriane, what on earth are you saying?" broke in M. de Guermantes. "Marie a fool? Why, she's read everything, and she's as musical as a fiddle."

"But, my poor little Basin, you're as innocent as a new-born babe. As if one couldn't be all that, and rather an idiot as well. Idiot is too strong a word; no, she's in the clouds, she's Hesse-Darmstadt, Holy Roman Empire, and wa-wa-wa. Even her pronunciation gets on my nerves. But I quite admit that she's a charming loony. In the first place, the very idea of stepping down from her German throne to go and marry, in the most bourgeois way, a private individual. It's true that she chose him! Ah, but of course," she went on, turning to me, "you don't know Gilbert. Let me give you an idea of him: he took to his bed once because I had left a card on Mme Carnot. . . . But, my dear Charles" (the Duchess changed the subject when she saw that the story of the card left on the Carnots appeared to irritate M. de Guermantes), "you know, you've never sent me that photograph of our Knights of Rhodes, whom I've learned to love through you and with whom I'm so anxious to become acquainted." The Duke meanwhile had not taken his eyes from his wife's face: "Oriane, you might at least tell the story properly and not cut out half. I ought to explain," he corrected, addressing Swann, "that the British Ambassadress at that time, who was a very worthy woman but lived rather in the moon and was in the habit of making up these odd combinations, conceived the distinctly quaint idea of inviting us with the President and his wife. Even Oriane was rather surprised, especially as the Ambassadress knew quite enough of the same sort of people as us not to invite us to such an ill-assorted gathering. There was a Minister there who's a swindler . . . however I'll draw a veil over all that— the fact was that we hadn't been warned, we were trapped, and to be honest I'm bound to admit that all these people behaved most civilly. Still, that was quite enough of a good thing. But Mme de Guermantes, who does not often do me the honour of consulting me, felt it incumbent upon her to leave a card in the course of the following week at the Elysée. Gilbert may perhaps have gone rather far in regarding it as a stain upon our name. But it must not be forgotten that, politics apart, M. Carnot, who incidentally filled his post quite respectably, was the grandson of a member of the revolutionary tribunal which slaughtered eleven of our people in a single day."

"In that case, Basin, why used you to go every week to dine at Chantilly? The Duc d'Aumale was just as much the grandson of a member of the revolutionary tribunal, with this difference, that Carnot was a decent man and Philippe-Egalité a frightful scoundrel."

"Excuse my interrupting you to explain that I did send the photograph," said Swann. "I can't understand how it hasn't reached you."

"It doesn't altogether surprise me," said the Duchess, "my servants tell me only what they think fit. They probably don't approve of the Order of St John." And she rang the bell.

"You know, Oriane, that when I used to go to Chantilly it was without much enthusiasm."

"Without much enthusiasm, but with a nightshirt in case

the Prince asked you to stay the night, which in fact he very rarely did, being a perfect boor like all the Orléans lot ... Do you know who else we're dining with at Mme de Saint-Euverte's?" Mme de Guermantes asked her husband.

"Besides the people you know already, she's asked King Theodosius's brother at the last moment."

At these tidings the Duchess's features exuded contentment and her speech boredom: "Oh, God, more princes!"

"But that one is amiable and intelligent," Swann remarked.

"Not altogether, though," replied the Duchess, apparently seeking for words that would give more novelty to her thought. "Have you ever noticed with princes that the nicest of them are never entirely nice? They must always have an opinion about everything. And as they have no opinions of their own, they spend the first half of their lives asking us ours and the second half serving them up to us again. They positively must be able to say that this has been well played and that not so well. When there's no difference. Do you know, this little Theodosius junior (I forget his name) asked me once what an orchestral motif was called. I answered" (the Duchess's eyes sparkled and a laugh exploded from her beautiful red lips) " 'It's called an orchestral motif.' I don't think he was any too well pleased, really. Oh, my dear Charles," she went on with a languishing air, "what a bore it can be, dining out. There are evenings when one would sooner die! It's true that dying may be perhaps just as great a bore, because we don't know what it's like."

A servant appeared. It was the young lover who had had a quarrel with the concierge, until the Duchess, out of the kindness of her heart, had brought about an apparent peace between them.

"Am I to go round this evening to inquire after M. le Marquis d'Osmond?" he asked.

"Most certainly not, nothing before to-morrow morning. In fact I don't want you to remain in the house to-night. His footman, whom you know, might very well come and bring you the latest report and send you out after us. Be off with you, go anywhere you like, have a spree, sleep out, but I don't want to see you here before to-morrow morning."

The footman's face glowed with happiness. At last he would be able to spend long hours with his betrothed, whom he had practically ceased to see ever since, after a final scene with the concierge, the Duchess had considerately explained to him that it would be better, to avoid further conflicts, if he did not go out at all. He floated, at the thought of having an evening free at last, on a tide of happiness which the Duchess saw and the reason for which she guessed. She felt a sort of pang and as it were an itching in all her limbs at the thought of this happiness being snatched behind her back, unbeknownst to her, and it made her irritated and jealous.

"No, Basin, he must stay here; he's not to stir out of the house."

"But Oriane, that's absurd, the house is crammed with servants, and you have the costumier's people coming as well at twelve to dress us for our ball. There's absolutely nothing for him to do, and he's the only one who's a friend of Mama's footman; I'd much sooner get him right away from the house."

"Listen, Basin, let me do what I want. I shall have a message for him during the evening, as it happens—I'm not yet sure at what time. In any case you're not to budge from here for a single instant, do you hear?" she said to the despairing footman.

If there were continual quarrels, and if servants did not stay long with the Duchess, the person to whose charge this guerrilla warfare was to be laid was indeed irremovable, but it was not the concierge. No doubt for the rougher tasks, for the tortures it was particularly tiring to inflict, for the quarrels which ended in blows, the Duchess entrusted the heavier instruments to him; but even then he played his role without the least suspicion that he had been cast for it. Like the household servants, he was impressed by the Duchess's kindness, and the imperceptive footmen who came back, after leaving her service, to visit Françoise used to say that the Duke's house would have been the finest "place" in Paris if it had not been for the porter's lodge. The Duchess made use of the lodge in the same way as at different times clericalism, freemasonry, the Jewish peril and so on have been made use of. Another footman came into the room.

"Why haven't they brought up the package M. Swann sent

here? And, by the way (you've heard, Charles, that Mama is seriously ill?), Jules went round to inquire for news of M. le Marquis d'Osmond: has he come back yet?"

"He's just arrived this instant, M. le Duc. They're expecting M. le Marquis to pass away at any moment."

"Ah, he's alive!" exclaimed the Duke with a sigh of relief. "They're expecting, are they? Well, they can go on expecting. While there's life there's hope," he added cheerfully for our benefit. "They've been talking to me about him as though he were dead and buried. In a week from now he'll be fitter than I am."

"It's the doctors who said that he wouldn't last out the evening. One of them wanted to call again during the night. The head one said it was no use. M. le Marquis would be dead by then; they've only kept him alive by injecting him with camphorated oil."

"Hold your tongue, you damned fool," cried the Duke in a paroxysm of rage. "Who the devil asked you for your opinion? You haven't understood a word of what they told you."

"It wasn't me they told, it was Jules."

"Will you hold your tongue!" roared the Duke, and, turning to Swann: "What a blessing he's still alive! He'll regain his strength gradually, don't you know. Still alive, after being in such a critical state—that in itself is an excellent sign. One mustn't expect everything at once. It can't be at all unpleasant, a little injection of camphorated oil." He rubbed his hands. "He's alive; what more could anyone want? After all that he's gone through, it's a great step forward. Upon my word, I envy him having such a constitution. Ah! these invalids, you know, people do all sorts of little things for them that they don't do for us. For instance, to-day some beggar of a chef sent me up a leg of mutton with *béarnaise* sauce—it was done to a turn, I must admit, but just for that very reason I took so much of it that it's still lying on my stomach. However, that doesn't make people come to inquire after me as they do after dear Amanien. We do too much inquiring. It only tires him. We must leave him room to breathe. They're killing the poor fellow by sending round to him all the time."

"Well," said the Duchess to the footman as he was leaving

the room, "I gave orders for the envelope containing a photograph which M. Swann sent me to be brought up here."

"Madame la Duchesse, it's so large that I didn't know if I could get it through the door. We've left it in the hall. Does Madame la Duchesse wish me to bring it up?"

"Oh, in that case, no; they ought to have told me, but if it's so big I shall see it in a moment when I come downstairs."

"I forgot to tell Mme la Duchesse that Mme la Comtesse Molé left a card this morning for Mme la Duchesse."

"What, this morning?" said the Duchess with an air of disapproval, feeling that so young a woman ought not to take the liberty of leaving cards in the morning.

"About ten o'clock, Madame la Duchesse."

"Show me the cards."

"In any case, Oriane, when you say that it was a funny idea on Marie's part to marry Gilbert," went on the Duke, reverting to the original topic of conversation, "it's you who have an odd way of writing history. If either of them was a fool, it was Gilbert, for having married of all people a woman so closely related to the King of the Belgians, who has usurped the name of Brabant which belongs to us. To put it briefly, we are of the same blood as the Hesses, and of the elder branch. It's always stupid to talk about oneself," he apologised to me, "but after all, whenever we've been not only to Darmstadt, but even to Cassel and all over electoral Hesse, all the landgraves have always been most courteous in giving us precedence as being of the elder branch."

"But really, Basin, you don't mean to tell me that a person who was matron of every regiment in her country, who had been engaged to the King of Sweden . . ."

"Oh, Oriane, that's too much; anyone would think you didn't know that the King of Sweden's grandfather was tilling the soil at Pau when we had been ruling the roost for nine hundred years throughout the whole of Europe."

"That doesn't alter the fact that if somebody were to say in the street: 'Hallo, there's the King of Sweden,' everyone would at once rush to see him as far as the Place de la Concorde, and if he said: 'There's M. de Guermantes,' nobody would know who it was."

"What an argument!"

"Besides, I can't understand how, once the title of Duke of Brabant has passed to the Belgian royal family, you can continue to claim it."

The footman returned with the Comtesse Molé's card, or rather what she had left in place of a card. On the pretext that she did not have one with her, she had taken from her pocket a letter addressed to herself, and keeping the contents had handed in the envelope which bore the inscription: "La Comtesse Molé." As the envelope was rather large, following the fashion in note-paper which prevailed that year, this manuscript "card" was almost twice the size of an ordinary visiting card.

"That's what people call Mme Molé's 'simplicity,' " said the Duchess sarcastically. "She wants to make us think that she had no cards on her to show her originality. But we know all about that, don't we, my little Charles, we're quite old enough and quite original enough ourselves to see through the tricks of a little lady who has only been going about for four years. She is charming, but she doesn't seem to me, all the same, to have the weight to imagine that she can stun the world with so little effort as merely by leaving an envelope instead of a card and leaving it at ten o'clock in the morning. Her old mother mouse will show her that she knows a thing or two about that."

Swann could not help smiling at the thought that the Duchess, who was, as it happened, a trifle jealous of Mme Molé's success, would find it quite in accordance with the "Guermantes wit" to make some insolent retort to her visitor.

"So far as the title of Duc de Brabant is concerned, I've told you a hundred times, Oriane . . ." the Duke continued, but the Duchess, without listening, cut him short.

"But, my dear Charles, I'm longing to see your photograph."

"Ah! *Extinctor draconis latrator Anubis*," said Swann.

"Yes, it was so charming what you said about that apropos of San Giorgio at Venice. But I don't understand why Anubis?"

"What's the one like who was an ancestor of Babal?" asked M. de Guermantes.

"You want to see his bauble," said his wife drily, to show that she herself despised the pun. "I want to see them all," she added.

"I'll tell you what, Charles, let's go downstairs till the carriage comes," said the Duke. "You can pay your call on us in the hall, because my wife won't let us have any peace until she's seen your photograph. I'm less impatient, I must say," he added complacently. "I'm not easily stirred myself, but she would see us all dead rather than miss it."

"I entirely agree with you, Basin," said the Duchess, "let's go into the hall; we shall at least know why we have come down from your study, whereas we shall never know how we have come down from the Counts of Brabant."

"I've told you a hundred times how the title came into the House of Hesse," said the Duke (while we were going downstairs to look at the photograph, and I thought of those that Swann used to bring me at Combray), "through the marriage of a Brabant in 1241 with the daughter of the last Landgrave of Thuringia and Hesse, so that really it's the title of Prince of Hesse that came to the House of Brabant rather than that of Duke of Brabant to the House of Hesse. You will remember that our battle-cry was that of the Dukes of Brabant: 'Limbourg to her conqueror!' until we exchanged the arms of Brabant for those of Guermantes, in which I think myself that we were wrong, and the example of the Gramonts will not make me change my opinion."

"But," replied Mme de Guermantes, "as it's the King of the Belgians who is the conqueror . . . Besides, the Belgian Crown Prince calls himself Duc de Brabant."

"But, my dear child, your argument will not hold water for a moment. You know as well as I do that there are titles of pretension which can perfectly well survive even if the territory is occupied by usurpers. For instance, the King of Spain describes himself equally as Duke of Brabant, claiming in virtue of a possession less ancient than ours, but more ancient than that of the King of the Belgians. He also calls himself Duke of Burgundy, King of the West and East Indies, and Duke of Milan. Well, he's no more in possession of Burgundy, the Indies or Brabant than I possess Brabant myself, or the

Prince of Hesse either, for that matter. The King of Spain likewise proclaims himself King of Jerusalem, as does the Austrian Emperor, and Jerusalem belongs to neither one nor the other."

He stopped for a moment, perturbed by the thought that the mention of Jerusalem might have embarrassed Swann, in view of "current events," but only went on more rapidly: "What you said just now might be said of anyone. We were at one time Dukes of Aumale, a duchy that has passed as regularly to the House of France as Joinville and Chevreuse have to the House of Albert. We make no more claim to those titles than to that of Marquis de Noirmoutiers, which was at one time ours, and became perfectly regularly the appanage of the House of La Trémoïlle, but because certain cessions are valid, it does not follow that they all are. For instance," he went on, turning to me, "my sister-in-law's son bears the title of Prince d'Agrigente, which comes to us from Joan the Mad, as that of Prince de Tarente comes to the La Trémoïlles. Well, Napoleon went and gave this title of Tarente to a soldier, who may have been an excellent campaigner, but in doing so the Emperor was disposing of what belonged to him even less than Napoleon III when he created a Duc de Montmorency, since Périgord had at least a mother who was a Montmorency, while the Tarente of Napoleon I had no more Tarente about him than Napoleon's wish that he should become so. That didn't prevent Chaix d'Est-Ange, alluding to our uncle Condé, from asking the Imperial Attorney if he had picked up the title of Duc de Montmorency in the moat at Vincennes."

"Look, Basin, I ask for nothing better than to follow you to the moat of Vincennes, or even to Taranto. And that reminds me, Charles, of what I was going to say to you when you were telling me about your San Giorgio of Venice. We have a plan, Basin and I, to spend next spring in Italy and Sicily. If you were to come with us, just think what a difference it would make! I'm not thinking only of the pleasure of seeing you, but imagine, after all you've told me about the remains of the Norman Conquest and of antiquity, imagine what a trip like that would become if you were with us! I mean to say that even Basin—what am I saying, Gilbert!—would benefit by it, because I feel that even his claims to the throne of Naples and all that sort of thing would interest me if they were explained by you in old Romanesque churches in little villages perched on hills as in primitive paintings. But now we're going to look at your photograph. Open the envelope," she said to a footman.

"Please, Oriane, not this evening; you can look at it to-morrow," implored the Duke, who had already been making signs of alarm to me on seeing the enormous size of the photograph.

"But I want to look at it with Charles," said the Duchess, with a smile at once spuriously concupiscent and subtly psychological, for in her desire to be amiable to Swann she spoke of the pleasure which she would derive from looking at the photograph as of the kind an invalid feels he would derive from eating an orange, or as though she had simultaneously contrived an escapade with some friends and informed a biographer of tastes flattering to herself.

"Well, he'll come and see you specially," declared the Duke, to whom his wife was obliged to yield. "You can spend three hours in front of it, if that amuses you," he added sarcastically. "But where are you going to stick a toy that size?"

"In my room, of course. I want to have it before my eyes."

"Oh, just as you please; if it's in your room, there's a chance I shall never see it," said the Duke, oblivious of the revelation he was thus blindly making of the negative character of his conjugal relations.

"Make sure you undo it with the greatest care," Mme de Guermantes told the servant, underlining her instructions out of deference to Swann. "And don't crumple the envelope, either."

"Even the envelope has to be respected!" the Duke murmured to me, raising his eyes to the ceiling. "But, Swann," he added, "what amazes me, a poor prosaic husband, is how you managed to find an envelope that size. Where on earth did you dig it up?"

"Oh, at the photographer's; they're always sending out things like that. But the man is an oaf, for I see he's written on it 'La Duchesse de Guermantes,' without putting 'Madame.'"

"I forgive him," said the Duchess carelessly; then, seeming to be struck by a sudden idea which amused her, repressed a faint smile; but at once returning to Swann: "Well, you don't say whether you're coming to Italy with us?"

"Madame, I'm very much afraid that it won't be possible."

"Indeed! Mme de Montmorency is more fortunate. You went with her to Venice and Vicenza. She told me that with you one saw things one would never see otherwise, things no one had ever thought of mentioning before, that you showed her things she'd never dreamed of, and that even in the well-known things she was able to appreciate details which without you she might have passed by a dozen times without ever noticing. She's certainly been more highly favoured than we are to be. . . . You will take the big envelope which contained M. Swann's photograph," she said to the servant, "and you will hand it in, from me, this evening at half past ten at Mme la Comtesse Molé's."

Swann burst out laughing.

"I should like to know, all the same," Mme de Guermantes asked him, "how you can tell ten months in advance that a thing will be impossible."

"My dear Duchess, I'll tell you if you insist, but, first of all, you can see that I'm very ill."

"Yes, my little Charles, I don't think you look at all well. I'm not pleased with your colour. But I'm not asking you to come with us next week, I'm asking you to come in ten months' time. In ten months one has time to get oneself cured, you know."

At this point a footman came in to say that the carriage was at the door. "Come, Oriane, to horse," said the Duke, already pawing the ground with impatience as though he were himself one of the horses that stood waiting outside.

"Very well, give me in one word the reason why you can't come to Italy," the Duchess put it to Swann as she rose to say good-bye to us.

"But, my dear lady, it's because I shall then have been dead for several months. According to the doctors I've consulted, by the end of the year the thing I've got—which may, for that matter, carry me off at any moment—won't in any case leave me more than three or four months to live, and even that is a

generous estimate," replied Swann with a smile, while the
footman opened the glazed door of the hall to let the Duchess
out.

"What's that you say?" cried the Duchess, stopping for a
moment on her way to the carriage and raising her beautiful,
melancholy blue eyes, now clouded by uncertainty. Placed for
the first time in her life between two duties as incompatible as
getting into her carriage to go out to dinner and showing
compassion for a man who was about to die, she could find
nothing in the code of conventions that indicated the right line
to follow; not knowing which to choose, she felt obliged to
pretend not to believe that the latter alternative need be
seriously considered, in order to comply with the first, which
at the moment demanded less effort, and thought that the best
way of settling the conflict would be to deny that any existed.
"You're joking," she said to Swann.

"It would be a joke in charming taste," he replied ironically.
"I don't know why I'm telling you this. I've never said a word
to you about my illness before. But since you asked me, and
since now I may die at any moment . . . But whatever I do I
mustn't make you late; you're dining out, remember," he
added, because he knew that for other people their own
social obligations took precedence over the death of a friend,
and he put himself in their place thanks to his instinctive
politeness. But that of the Duchess enabled her also to perceive
in a vague way that the dinner-party to which she was going
must count for less to Swann than his own death. And so,
while continuing on her way towards the carriage, she let her
shoulders droop, saying: "Don't worry about our dinner. It's
not of any importance!" But this put the Duke in a bad humour
and he exclaimed: "Come, Oriane, don't stop there chattering
like that and exchanging your jeremiads with Swann; you
know very well that Mme de Saint-Euverte insists on sitting down to table at eight o'clock sharp. We must know
what you propose to do; the horses have been waiting for a
good five minutes. Forgive me, Charles," he went on, turning
to Swann, "but it's ten minutes to eight already. Oriane is
always late, and it will take us more than five minutes to get to
old Saint-Euverte's."

Mme de Guermantes advanced resolutely towards the carriage and uttered a last farewell to Swann. "You know, we'll talk about that another time; I don't believe a word you've been saying, but we must discuss it quietly. I expect they've frightened you quite unnecessarily. Come to luncheon, any day you like" (with Mme de Guermantes things always resolved themselves into luncheons), "just let me know the day and the time," and, lifting her red skirt, she set her foot on the step. She was just getting into the carriage when, seeing this foot exposed, the Duke cried out in a terrifying voice: "Oriane, what have you been thinking of, you wretch? You've kept on your black shoes! With a red dress! Go upstairs quick and put on red shoes, or rather," he said to the footman, "tell Mme la Duchesse's lady's maid at once to bring down a pair of red shoes."

"But, my dear," replied the Duchess gently, embarrassed to see that Swann, who was leaving the house with me but had stood back to allow the carriage to pass out in front of us, had heard, "seeing that we're late . . ."

"No, no, we have plenty of time. It's only ten to; it won't take us ten minutes to get to the Parc Monceau. And after all, what does it matter? Even if we turn up at half past eight they'll wait for us, but you can't possibly go there in a red dress and black shoes. Besides, we shan't be the last, I can tell you; the Sassenages are coming, and you know they never arrive before twenty to nine."

The Duchess went up to her room.

"Well," said M. de Guermantes to Swann and myself, "people laugh at us poor downtrodden husbands, but we have our uses. But for me, Oriane would have gone out to dinner in black shoes."

"It's not unbecoming," said Swann, "I noticed the black shoes and they didn't offend me in the least."

"I don't say you're wrong," replied the Duke, "but it looks better to have them to match the dress. Besides, you needn't worry, no sooner had she got there than she'd have noticed them, and I should have been obliged to come home and fetch the others. I should have had my dinner at nine o'clock. Goodbye, my boys," he said, thrusting us gently from the door, "off you go before Oriane comes down again. It's not that she doesn't like seeing you both. On the contrary, she's too fond of your company. If she finds you still here she'll start talking again. She's already very tired, and she'll reach the dinner-table quite dead. Besides, I tell you frankly, I'm dying of hunger. I had a wretched luncheon this morning when I came from the train. There was the devil of a *béarnaise* sauce, I admit, but in spite of that I shan't be sorry, not at all sorry to sit down to dinner. Five minutes to eight! Ah, women! She'll give us both indigestion before to-morrow. She's not nearly as strong as people think."

The Duke felt no compunction in speaking thus of his wife's ailments and his own to a dying man, for the former interested him more and therefore appeared to him more important. And so it was simply from good breeding and good fellowship that, after politely showing us out, he shouted in a stentorian voice from the porch to Swann, who was already in the courtyard: "You, now, don't let yourself be alarmed by the nonsense of those damned doctors. They're fools. You're as sound as a bell. You'll bury us all!"

CITIES OF THE
PLAIN

PART ONE

THE reader will remember that, well before going that day
(the day on which the Princesse de Guermantes's reception was to be held) to pay the Duke and Duchess the visit
I have just described, I had kept watch for their return and
in the course of my vigil had made a discovery which concerned M. de Charlus in particular but was in itself so important that I have until now, until the moment when I could give
it the prominence and treat it with the fullness that it demanded, postponed giving an account of it. I had, as I have
said, left the marvellous point of vantage, so snugly contrived
at the top of the house, commanding the hilly slopes which led
up to the Hôtel de Bréquigny, and which were gaily decorated
in the Italian manner by the rose-pink campanile of the Marquis
de Frécourt's coach-house. I had thought it more practical,
when I suspected that the Duke and Duchess were on the point
of returning, to post myself on the staircase. I rather missed
my Alpine eyrie. But at that time of day, namely the hour immediately after lunch, I had less cause for regret, for I should
not then have seen, as in the morning, the footmen of the
Bréquigny household, converted by distance into minute
figures in a picture, make their leisurely ascent of the steep
hillside, feather-brush in hand, behind the large, transparent
flakes of mica which stood out so pleasingly upon its ruddy
bastions. Failing the geologist's field of contemplation, I had
at least that of the botanist, and was peering through the
shutters of the staircase window at the Duchess's little tree
and at the precious plant, exposed in the courtyard with that
assertiveness with which mothers "bring out" their marriage-
able offspring, and asking myself whether the unlikely insect
would come, by a providential hazard, to visit the offered and
neglected pistil. My curiosity emboldening me by degrees, I
went down to the ground-floor window, which also stood
open with its shutters ajar. I could distinctly hear Jupien getting

ready to go out, but he could not detect me behind my blind, where I stood perfectly still until the moment when I drew quickly aside in order not to be seen by M. de Charlus, who, on his way to call upon Mme de Villeparisis, was slowly crossing the courtyard, corpulent, greying, aged by the strong light. Nothing short of an indisposition from which Mme de Villeparisis might be suffering (consequent on the illness of the Marquis de Fierbois, with whom he personally was at daggers drawn) could have made M. de Charlus pay a call, perhaps for the first time in his life, at that hour of the day. For with that eccentricity of the Guermantes, who, instead of conforming to the ways of society, tended to modify them to suit their own personal habits (habits not, they thought, social, and deserving in consequence the abasement before them of that worthless thing, society life—thus it was that Mme de Marsantes had no regular "day," but was at home to her friends every morning between ten o'clock and noon), the Baron, reserving those hours for reading, hunting for old curios and so forth, paid calls only between four and six in the evening. At six o'clock he went to the Jockey Club, or took a stroll in the Bois. A moment later, I again recoiled, in order not to be seen by Jupien. It was nearly time for him to set out for the office, from which he would return only for dinner, and not always even then during the last week since his niece and her apprentices had gone to the country to finish a dress for a customer. Then, realising that no one could see me, I decided not to let myself be disturbed again for fear of missing, should the miracle be fated to occur, the arrival, almost beyond the possibility of hope (across so many obstacles of distance, of adverse risks, of dangers), of the insect sent from so far away as ambassador to the virgin who had been waiting for so long. I knew that this expectancy was no more passive than in the male flower, whose stamens had spontaneously curved so that the insect might more easily receive their offering; similarly the female flower that stood here would coquettishly arch her "styles" if the insect came, and, to be more effectively penetrated by him, would imperceptibly advance, like a hypocritical but ardent damsel, to meet him half-way. The laws of the vegetable kingdom are themselves governed by increasingly higher laws. If the visit of an insect, that is to say the transportation of the seed from another flower, is generally necessary for the fertilisation of a flower, that is because self-fertilisation, the insemination of a flower by itself, would lead, like a succession of intermarriages in the same family, to degeneracy and sterility, whereas the crossing effected by insects gives to the subsequent generations of the same species a vigour unknown to their forebears. This invigoration may, however, prove excessive, and the species develop out of all proportion; then, as an anti-toxin protects us against disease, as the thyroid gland regulates our adiposity, as defeat comes to punish pride, as fatigue follows indulgence, and as sleep in turn brings rest from fatigue, so an exceptional act of self-fertilisation comes at the crucial moment to apply its turn of the screw, its pull on the curb, brings back within the norm the flower that has exaggeratedly overstepped it. My reflexions had followed a trend which I shall describe in due course, and I had already drawn from the visible stratagems of flowers a conclusion that bore upon a whole unconscious element of literary production, when I saw M. de Charlus coming away from the Marquise's door. Only a few minutes had passed since his entry. Perhaps he had learned from his elderly relative herself, or merely from a servant, of a great improvement in her condition, or rather her complete recovery from what had been nothing more than a slight indisposition. At this moment, when he did not suspect that anyone was watching him, his eyelids lowered as a screen against the sun, M. de Charlus had relaxed that artificial tension, softened that artificial vigour in his face which were ordinarily sustained by the animation of his talk and the force of his will. Pale as a marble statue, his fine features with the prominent nose no longer received from an expression de-liberately assumed a different meaning which altered the beauty of their contours; no more now than a Guermantes, he seemed already carved in stone, he, Palamède XV, in the chapel at Combray. These general features of a whole family took on, however, in the face of M. de Charlus a more spiritual-ised, above all a softer refinement. I regretted for his sake that he should habitually adulterate with so many violent out-bursts, offensive eccentricities, calumnies, with such harshness, touchiness and arrogance, that he should conceal beneath a spurious brutality the amenity, the kindness which, as he emerged from Mme de Villeparisis's, I saw so innocently displayed upon his face. Blinking his eyes in the sunlight, he seemed almost to be smiling, and I found in his face seen thus in repose and as it were in its natural state something so affectionate, so defenceless, that I could not help thinking how angry M. de Charlus would have been could he have known that he was being watched; for what was suggested to me by the sight of this man who was so enamoured of, who so prided himself upon, his virility, to whom all other men seemed odiously effeminate, what he suddenly suggested to me, to such an extent had he momentarily assumed the features, the expression, the smile thereof, was a woman.

I was about to change my position again, so that he should not catch sight of me; I had neither the time nor the need to do so. For what did I see! Face to face, in that courtyard where they had certainly never met before (M. de Charlus coming to the Hôtel de Guermantes only in the afternoon, during the time when Jupien was at his office), the Baron, having suddenly opened wide his half-shut eyes, was gazing with extraordinary attentiveness at the ex-tailor poised on the threshold of his shop, while the latter, rooted suddenly to the spot in front of M. de Charlus, implanted there like a tree, contemplated with a look of wonderment the plump form of the ageing Baron. But, more astounding still, M. de Charlus's pose having altered, Jupien's, as though in obedience to the laws of an occult art, at once brought itself into harmony with it. The Baron, who now sought to disguise the impression that had been made on him, and yet, in spite of his affectation of indifference, seemed unable to move away without regret, came and went, looked vaguely into the distance in the way which he felt would most enhance the beauty of his eyes, assumed a smug, nonchalant, fatuous air. Meanwhile Jupien, shedding at once the humble, kindly expression which I had always associated with him, had —in perfect symmetry with the Baron—thrown back his head, given a becoming tilt to his body, placed his hand with grotesque effrontery on his hip, stuck out his behind, struck poses with the coquetry that the orchid might have adopted on the providential arrival of the bee. I had not supposed that he could appear so repellent. But I was equally unaware that he was capable of improvising his part in this sort of dumb show which (although he found himself for the first time in the presence of M. de Charlus) seemed to have been long and carefully rehearsed; one does not arrive spontaneously at that pitch of perfection except when one meets in a foreign country a compatriot with whom an understanding then develops of itself, the means of communication being the same and, even though one has never seen each other before, the scene already set.

This scene was not, however, positively comic; it was stamped with a strangeness, or if you like a naturalness, the beauty of which steadily increased. Try as M. de Charlus might to assume a detached air, to let his eyelids nonchalantly droop, every now and then he raised them, and at such moments turned on Jupien an attentive gaze. But (doubtless because he felt that such a scene could not be prolonged indefinitely in this place, whether for reasons which we shall understand later on, or possibly from that feeling of the brevity of all things which makes us determine that every blow must strike home, and renders so moving the spectacle of every kind of love), each time that M. de Charlus looked at Jupien, he took care that his glance should be accompanied by a word, which made it infinitely unlike the glances we usually direct at a person whom we scarcely know or do not know at all; he stared at Jupien with the peculiar fixity of the person who is about to say to you: "Excuse my taking the liberty, but you have a long white thread hanging down your back," or else: "Surely I can't be mistaken, you come from Zürich too; I'm certain I must have seen you there often at the antique dealer's." Thus, every other minute, the same question seemed to be put to Jupien intently in M. de Charlus's ogling, like those questioning phrases of Beethoven's, indefinitely repeated at regular intervals and intended—with an exaggerated lavishness of preparation—to introduce a new theme, a change of key, a "re-entry." On the other hand, the beauty of the reciprocal glances of M. de Charlus and Jupien arose precisely from the fact that they did not, for the moment at least, seem

to be intended to lead to anything further. It was the first time
I had seen the manifestation of this beauty in the Baron and
Jupien. In the eyes of both of them, it was the sky not of
Zurich but of some Oriental city, the name of which I had not
yet divined, that I saw reflected. Whatever the point might be
that held M. de Charlus and the ex-tailor thus arrested, their
pact seemed concluded and these superfluous glances to be
but ritual preliminaries, like the parties people give before a
marriage which has been definitely "arranged." Nearer still to
nature—and the multiplicity of these analogies is itself all the
more natural in that the same man, if we examine him for a few
minutes, appears in turn a man, a man-bird, a man-fish, a man-
insect—one might have thought of them as a pair of birds,
the male and the female, the male seeking to make advances,
the female—Jupien—no longer giving any sign of response to
these overtures, but regarding her new friend without surprise,
with an inattentive fixity of gaze, doubtless considered more
disturbing and all that was called for now that the male had
taken the first steps, and contenting herself with preening
her feathers. At length Jupien's indifference seemed to suffice
him no longer; from the certainty of having conquered to
getting himself pursued and desired was but a step, and
Jupien, deciding to go off to his work, went out through the
carriage gate. It was only, however, after turning his head
two or three times that he disappeared into the street, towards
which the Baron, trembling lest he should lose the trail
(boldly humming a tune, and not forgetting to fling a "Good-
day" to the porter, who, half-tipsy and engaged in treating a
few friends in his back kitchen, did not even hear him),
hurried briskly to catch up with him. At the same instant as
M. de Charlus disappeared through the gate humming like a
great bumble-bee, another, a real one this time, flew into the
courtyard. For all I knew this might be the one so long awaited
by the orchid, coming to bring it that rare pollen without
which it must die a virgin. But I was distracted from following
the gyrations of the insect, for, a few minutes later, engaging
my attention afresh, Jupien (perhaps to pick up a parcel which
he did take away with him ultimately and which, in the
emotion aroused in him by the appearance of M. de Charlus,

he had forgotten, perhaps simply for a more natural reason)
returned, followed by the Baron. The latter, deciding to precipitate matters, asked the tailor for a light, but at once observed: "I ask you for a light, but I see I've left my cigars at
home." The laws of hospitality prevailed over the rules of
coquetry. "Come inside, you shall have everything you wish,"
said the tailor, on whose features disdain now gave place to
joy. The door of the shop closed behind them and I could
hear no more. I had lost sight of the bumble-bee. I did not
know whether he was the insect that the orchid required,
but I had no longer any doubt, in the case of a very rare
insect and a captive flower, of the miraculous possibility
of their conjunction when I considered that M. de Charlus
(this is simply a comparison of providential chances, whatever
they may be, without the slightest scientific claim to establish
a relation between certain botanical laws and what is sometimes, most ineptly, termed homosexuality), who for years
past had never come to the house except at hours when Jupien
was not there, had, by the mere accident of Mme de Villeparisis's indisposition, encountered the tailor and with him the
good fortune reserved for men of the Baron's kind by one of
those fellow-creatures who may even be, as we shall see,
infinitely younger than Jupien and better-looking, the man
predestined to exist in order that they may have their share of
sensual pleasure on this earth: the man who cares only for
elderly gentlemen.

All that I have just said, however, I was not to understand
until several minutes had elapsed, to such an extent is reality
encumbered by those properties of invisibility until a chance
occurrence has divested it of them. At all events, for the
moment I was greatly annoyed at not being able to hear any
more of the conversation between the ex-tailor and the Baron.
I then bethought myself of the vacant shop, separated from
Jupien's only by an extremely thin partition. In order to get to
it, I had merely to go up to our flat, pass through the kitchen,
go down by the service stairs to the cellars, make my way
through them across the breadth of the courtyard above, and
on arriving at the place in the basement where a few months
ago the joiner had still been storing his timber and where

Jupien intended to keep his coal, climb the flight of steps which led to the interior of the shop. Thus the whole of my journey would be made under cover, and I should not be seen by anyone. This was the most prudent method. It was not the one that I adopted; instead, keeping close to the walls, I edged my way round the courtyard in the open, trying not to let myself be seen. If I was not, I owe it more, I am sure, to chance than to my own sagacity. And for the fact that I took so imprudent a course, when the way through the cellar was so safe, I can see three possible reasons, assuming that I had any reason at all. First of all, my impatience. Secondly, perhaps, a dim memory of the scene at Montjouvain, when I crouched concealed outside Mlle Vinteuil's window. Certainly, the affairs of this sort of which I have been a spectator have always been, as far as their setting is concerned, of the most imprudent and least probable character, as if such revelations were to be the reward of an action full of risk, though in part clandestine. I hardly dare confess to the third and final reason, so childish does it seem, but I suspect that it was unconsciously decisive. Ever since, in order to follow—and see controverted—the military principles enunciated by Saint-Loup, I had been following in close detail the course of the Boer War, I had been led on from that to re-read old accounts of travel and exploration. These narratives had thrilled me, and I applied them to the events of my daily life to give myself courage. When attacks of illness had compelled me to remain for several days and nights on end not only without sleep but without lying down, without tasting food or drink, at the moment when my pain and exhaustion became so intense that I felt that I should never escape from them, I would think of some traveller cast up on a shore, poisoned by noxious herbs, shivering with fever in clothes drenched by the salt water, who nevertheless in a day or two felt stronger, rose and went blindly on his way, in search of possible inhabitants who might turn out to be cannibals. His example acted on me as a tonic, restored my hope, and I felt ashamed of my momentary discouragement. Thinking of the Boers who, with British armies facing them, were not afraid to expose themselves at the moment when they had to cross a tract of open country in order to reach cover,

"It would be a fine thing," I thought to myself, "if I were to show less courage when the theatre of operations is simply our own courtyard, and when the only steel that I, who fought more than one duel fearlessly at the time of the Dreyfus case, have to fear is that of the eyes of the neighbours who have other things to do besides looking into the courtyard."

But when I was inside the shop, taking care not to let the wooden floor make the slightest creak, as I realised that the least sound in Jupien's shop could be heard from mine, I thought to myself how rash Jupien and M. de Charlus had been, and how luck had favoured them.

I did not dare move. The Guermantes groom, taking advantage no doubt of his master's absence, had, as it happened, transferred to the shop in which I now stood a ladder which hitherto had been kept in the coach-house, and if I had climbed this I could have opened the fanlight above and heard as well as if I had been in Jupien's shop itself. But I was afraid of making a noise. Besides, it was unnecessary. I had not even cause to regret my not having arrived in the shop until several minutes had elapsed. For from what I heard at first in Jupien's quarters, which was only a series of inarticulate sounds, I imagine that few words had been exchanged. It is true that these sounds were so violent that, if they had not always been taken up an octave higher by a parallel plaint, I might have thought that one person was slitting another's throat within a few feet of me, and that subsequently the murderer and his resuscitated victim were taking a bath to wash away the traces of the crime. I concluded from this later on that there is another thing as vociferous as pain, namely pleasure, especially when there is added to it—in the absence of the fear of an eventual parturition, which could not be the case here, despite the hardly convincing example in the *Golden Legend*—an immediate concern about cleanliness. Finally, after about half an hour (during which time I had stealthily hoisted myself up my ladder so as to peep through the fanlight which I did not open), the Baron emerged and a conversation began. Jupien refused with insistence the money that M. de Charlus was trying to press upon him.

"Why do you have your chin shaved like that," he inquired

of the Baron in a winsome tone. "It's so becoming, a nice beard." "Ugh! It's disgusting," the Baron replied.

Meanwhile he still lingered on the threshold and plied Jupien with questions about the neighbourhood. "You don't know anything about the man who sells chestnuts round the corner, not the one on the left, he's a horror, but on the other side, a big dark fellow? And the chemist opposite, he has a charming cyclist who delivers his parcels." These questions must have ruffled Jupien, for, drawing himself up with the indignation of a courtesan who has been betrayed, he replied: "I can see you are thoroughly fickle." Uttered in a pained, frigid, affected tone, this reproach must have had its effect on M. de Charlus, who, to counteract the bad impression his curiosity had produced, addressed to Jupien, in too low a tone for me to be able to make out his words, a request the granting of which would doubtless necessitate their prolonging their sojourn in the shop, and which moved the tailor sufficiently to make him forget his annoyance, for he studied the Baron's face, plump and flushed beneath his grey hair, with the supremely blissful air of a person whose self-esteem has just been profoundly flattered, and, deciding to grant M. de Charlus the favour that he had just asked of him, after various remarks lacking in refinement such as "What a big bum you have!" said to the Baron with an air at once smiling, impassioned, superior and grateful: "All right, you big baby, come along!"

"If I hark back to the question of the tram conductor," M. de Charlus tenaciously pursued, "it is because, apart from anything else, it might provide some interest for my homeward journey. For it occurs to me now and then, like the Caliph who used to roam the streets of Bagdad in the guise of a common merchant, to condescend to follow some curious little person whose profile may have taken my fancy." At this point I was struck by the same observation as had occurred to me in the case of Bergotte. If he should ever have to answer for himself before a court, he would employ not the sentences calculated to convince the judges, but such Bergottesque sentences as his peculiar literary temperament suggested to him and made him find pleasure in using. Similarly M. de Charlus, in conversing with the tailor, made use of the same language as he would have used in speaking to fashionable people of his own set, even exaggerating its eccentricities, whether because the shyness which he was striving to overcome drove him to an excess of pride or, by preventing him from mastering himself (for we are always less at our ease in the company of someone who is not of our milieu), forced him to unveil, to lay bare his true nature, which was indeed arrogant and a trifle mad, as Mme de Guermantes had remarked. "In order not to lose the trail," he went on, "I spring like a little usher, like a young and good-looking doctor, into the same tram-car as the little person herself, of whom we speak in the feminine gender only so as to conform with the rules of grammar (as one says in speaking of a prince, 'Is *Her* Highness enjoying *her* usual health').[32] If she changes trams, I take, with possibly the germs of the plague, that incredible thing called a 'transfer'—a number, and one which, although it is presented to *me*, is not always number one! I change 'carriages' in this way as many as three or four times, I end up sometimes at eleven o'clock at night at the Gare d'Orléans, and then have to come home. Still, if only it was just the Gare d'Orléans! Once, I must tell you, not having managed to engage in conversation sooner, I went all the way to Orleans itself, in one of those frightful compartments where all one has to rest one's eyes upon, between those triangular objects made of netting, are photographs of the principal architectural features of the line. There was only one vacant seat; I had in front of me, by way of historic monument, a 'view' of the Cathedral of Orleans, quite the ugliest in France, and as tiring a thing to have to stare at in that way against my will as if somebody had forced me to focus its towers in the lens of one of those optical penholders which give one ophthalmia. I got out of the train at Les Aubrais together with my young person, for whom alas his family (when I had imagined him to possess every defect except that of having a family) were waiting on the platform! My sole consolation, as I waited for a train to take me back to Paris, was the house of Diane de Poitiers. For all that she charmed one of my royal ancestors, I should have preferred a more living beauty. That is why, as an antidote to the boredom of returning home alone, I should rather like to make friends with a sleeping-car attendant or a bus conductor. Now, don't be shocked," the Baron wound up, "it is all a question of type. With what you might call 'young gentlemen,' for instance, I feel no desire for physical possession, but I am never satisfied until I have touched them, I don't mean physically, but touched a responsive chord. As soon as, instead of leaving my letters unanswered, a young man starts writing to me incessantly, when he is morally, as it were, at my disposal, I am assuaged, or at least I would be were I not immediately seized with an obsession for another. Rather curious, is it not?—Speaking of 'young gentlemen,' those that come to the house here, do you know any of them?" "No, my pet. Oh, yes, I do, a dark one, very tall, with an eyeglass, who keeps smiling and turning round." "I don't know who you mean." Jupien filled in the portrait, but M. de Charlus was unable to identify its subject, not knowing that the ex-tailor was one of those persons, more common than is generally supposed, who never remember the colour of the hair of people they do not know well. But to me, who was aware of this infirmity in Jupien and substituted "fair" for "dark," the portrait appeared to be an exact description of the Duc de Châtellerault. "To return to young men not of the lower orders," the Baron went on, "at the present moment my head has been turned by a strange little fellow, an intelligent little cit who shows with regard to myself a prodigious want of civility. He has absolutely no idea of the prodigious personage that I am, and of the microscopic animalcule that he is in comparison. But what does it matter, the little donkey may bray his head off before my august bishop's mantle." "Bishop!" cried Jupien, who had understood nothing of M. de Charlus's last remarks, but was completely taken aback by the word bishop. "But that sort of thing doesn't go with religion," he said. "I have three Popes in my family," replied M. de Charlus, "and enjoy the right to mantle in gules by virtue of a cardinalate title, the niece of the Cardinal, my great-uncle, having brought to my grandfather the title of Duke which was substituted for it. I see, though, that you are deaf to metaphor and indifferent to French history. Besides," he added, less perhaps by way of conclusion than as a warning, "this attraction that I feel towards young people who avoid me, from fear of course, for only their natural respect stops their mouths from crying out to me that they love me, requires in them a superior social position. Even then their feigned indifference may produce nevertheless a directly opposite effect. Fatuously prolonged, it sickens me. To take an example from a class with which you are more familiar, when they were doing up my house, so as not to create jealousies among all the duchesses who were vying with one another for the honour of being able to say that they had given me lodging, I went for a few days to an 'hotel,' as they say nowadays. One of the room waiters was known to me, and I pointed out to him an interesting little page who opened carriage doors and who remained recalcitrant to my proposals. Finally, in my exasperation, in order to prove to him that my intentions were pure, I made him an offer of a ridiculously high sum simply to come upstairs and talk to me for five minutes in my room. I waited for him in vain. I then took such a dislike to him that I used to go out by the service door so as not to see his villainous little mug at the other. I learned afterwards that he had never had any of my notes, which had been intercepted, the first by the room waiter who was jealous, the next by the day porter who was virtuous, the third by the night porter who was in love with the little page, and used to couch with him at the hour when Dian rose. But my disgust persisted none the less, and were they to bring me the page like a dish of venison on a silver platter, I should thrust him away with a retching stomach. There now, what a pity—we have spoken of serious matters and now it's all over between us as regards what I was hoping for. But you could be of great service to me, act as my agent ... Why no, the mere thought of such a thing arouses my lubricity again, and I feel that all is by no means over."

From the beginning of this scene my eyes had been opened by a transformation in M. de Charlus as complete and as immediate as if he had been touched by a magician's wand. Until then, because I had not understood, I had not seen. Each man's vice (we use the term for the sake of linguistic convenience) accompanies him through life after the manner of the familiar genius who was invisible to men so long as they were unaware of his presence. Our kindness, our treachery, our name, our social relations do not disclose themselves to the eye, we carry them hidden within us. Ulysses himself did not recognise Athena at first. But the gods are immediately perceptible to one another, like as quickly to like, and so too had M. de Charlus been to Jupien. Until that moment, in the presence of M. de Charlus I had been in the position of an unobservant man who, standing before a pregnant woman whose distended outline he has failed to remark, persists, while she smilingly reiterates "Yes, I'm a little tired just now," in asking her tactlessly: "Why, what's the matter with you?" But let someone say to him: "She is expecting a child," and suddenly he catches sight of her stomach and ceases to see anything else. It is the explanation that opens our eyes; the dispelling of an error gives us an additional sense.

People who do not care to refer, for examples of this law, to the Messieurs de Charlus of their acquaintance whom for long years they had never suspected until the day when, upon the smooth surface of an individual indistinguishable from everyone else, there suddenly appears, traced in an ink hitherto invisible, the characters that compose the word dear to the ancient Greeks, have only to remind themselves, in order to be persuaded that the world which surrounds them appears to them naked at first, stripped of a thousand ornaments which it offers to the eyes of others better informed, of the number of times in the course of their lives they have found themselves on the point of committing a social blunder. Nothing upon the blank, undocumented face of this man or that could have led them to suppose that he was precisely the brother, or the fiancé, or the lover of a woman of whom they were about to remark: "What a cow!" But then, fortunately, a word whispered to them by someone standing near arrests the fatal expression on their lips. At once there appear, like a *Mene, Tekel, Upharsin*, the words: "he is engaged to," or "he is the brother of," or "he is the lover of" the woman whom it is inadvisable to describe in his hearing as a cow. And this single new notion will bring about an entire regrouping, thrusting some back, others forward, of the fractional notions, henceforward a complete whole, which we possessed of the rest of the family. Although in the person of M. de Charlus another creature was coupled, as the horse in the centaur, which made him different from other men, although this creature was one with the Baron, I had never perceived it. Now the abstraction had become materialised, the creature at last discerned had lost its power of remaining invisible, and the transformation of M. de Charlus into a new person was so complete that not only the contrasts of his face and of his voice, but, in retrospect, the very ups and downs of his relations with myself, everything that hitherto had seemed to my mind incoherent, became intelligible, appeared self-evident, just as a sentence which presents no meaning so long as it remains broken up in letters arranged at random expresses, if these letters be rearranged in the proper order, a thought which one can never afterwards forget.

I now understood, moreover, why earlier, when I had seen him coming away from Mme de Villeparisis's, I had managed to arrive at the conclusion that M. de Charlus looked like a woman: he was one! He belonged to that race of beings, less paradoxical than they appear, whose ideal is manly precisely because their temperament is feminine, and who in ordinary life resemble other men in appearance only; there where each of us carries, inscribed in those eyes through which he beholds everything in the universe, a human form engraved on the surface of the pupil, for them it is not that of a nymph but that of an ephebe. A race upon which a curse is laid and which must live in falsehood and perjury because it knows that its desire, that which constitutes life's dearest pleasure, is held to be punishable, shameful, an inadmissible thing; which must deny its God, since its members, even when Christians, when at the bar of justice they appear and are arraigned, must before Christ and in his name refute as a calumny what is their very life; sons without a mother, to whom they are obliged to lie all her life long and even in the hour when they close her dying eyes; friends without friendships, despite all those which their frequently acknowledged charm inspires and their often generous hearts would gladly feel—but can we describe as friendships those relationships which flourish only by virtue of a lie and from which the first impulse of trust and sincerity to which they might be tempted to yield would cause them to be rejected with disgust, unless they are dealing with an impartial or perhaps even sympathetic spirit, who however in that case, misled with regard to them by a conventional psychology, will attribute to the vice confessed the very affection that is most alien to it, just as certain judges assume and are more inclined to pardon murder in inverts and treason in Jews for reasons derived from original sin and racial predestination? And lastly—according at least to the first theory which I sketched in outline at the time, which we shall see subjected to some modification in the sequel, and in which this would have angered them above all else had not the paradox been hidden from their eyes by the very illusion that made them see and live—lovers who are almost precluded from the possibility of that love the hope of which gives them the strength to endure so many risks and so much loneliness, since they are enamoured of precisely the type of man who has nothing feminine about him, who is not an invert and consequently cannot love them in return; with the result that their desire would be for ever unappeased did not their money procure for them real men, and their imagination end by making them take for real men the inverts to whom they have prostituted themselves. Their honour precarious, their liberty provisional, lasting only until the discovery of their crime; their position unstable, like that of the poet one day fêted in every drawing-room and applauded in every theatre in London, and the next driven from every lodging, unable to find a pillow upon which to lay his head, turning the mill like Samson and saying like him: "The two sexes shall die, each in a place apart!";[33] excluded even, save on the days of general misfortune when the majority rally round the victim as the Jews rallied round Dreyfus, from the sympathy—at times from the society—of their fellows, in whom they inspire only disgust at seeing themselves as they are, portrayed in a mirror which, ceasing to flatter them, accentuates every blemish that they have refused to observe in themselves, and makes them understand that what they have been calling their love (and to which, playing upon the word, they have by association annexed all that poetry,

painting, music, chivalry, asceticism have contrived to add to
love) springs not from an ideal of beauty which they have
chosen but from an incurable disease; like the Jews again
(save some who will associate only with those of their race
and have always on their lips the ritual words and the accepted
pleasantries), shunning one another, seeking out those who
are most directly their opposite, who do not want their company, forgiving their rebuffs, enraptured by their condescen-
sions; but also brought into the company of their own kind
by the ostracism to which they are subjected, the opprobrium
into which they have fallen, having finally been invested, by
a persecution similar to that of Israel, with the physical and
moral characteristics of a race, sometimes beautiful, often
hideous, finding (in spite of all the mockery with which one
who, more closely integrated with, better assimilated to the
opposing race, is in appearance relatively less inverted, heaps
upon one who has remained more so) a relief in frequenting
the society of their kind, and even some support in their
existence, so much so that, while steadfastly denying that they
are a race (the name of which is the vilest of insults), they
readily unmask those who succeed in concealing the fact that
they belong to it, with a view less to injuring them, though
they have no scruple about that, than to excusing themselves,
and seeking out (as a doctor seeks out cases of appendicitis)
cases of inversion in history, taking pleasure in recalling that
Socrates was one of themselves, as the Jews claim that Jesus
was one of them, without reflecting that there were no
abnormal people when homosexuality was the norm, no anti-
Christians before Christ, that the opprobrium alone makes the
crime because it has allowed to survive only those who remained obdurate to every warning, to every example, to every
punishment, by virtue of an innate disposition so peculiar that
it is more repugnant to other men (even though it may be
accompanied by high moral qualities) than certain other vices
which exclude those qualities, such as theft, cruelty, breach of
faith, vices better understood and so more readily excused by
the generality of men; forming a freemasonry far more extensive, more effective and less suspected than that of the
Lodges, for it rests upon an identity of tastes, needs, habits,

dangers, apprenticeship, knowledge, traffic, vocabulary, and one in which even members who do not wish to know one another recognise one another immediately by natural or conventional, involuntary or deliberate signs which indicate one of his kind to the beggar in the person of the nobleman whose carriage door he is shutting, to the father in the person of his daughter's suitor, to the man who has sought healing, absolution or legal defence in the doctor, the priest or the barrister to whom he has had recourse; all of them obliged to protect their own secret but sharing with the others a secret which the rest of humanity does not suspect and which means that to them the most wildly improbable tales of adventure seem true, for in this life of anachronistic fiction the ambassador is a bosom friend of the felon, the prince, with a certain insolent aplomb born of his aristocratic breeding which the timorous bourgeois lacks, on leaving the duchess's party goes off to confer in private with the ruffian; a reprobate section of the human collectivity, but an important one, suspected where it does not exist, flaunting itself, insolent and immune, where its existence is never guessed; numbering its adherents everywhere, among the people, in the army, in the church, in prison, on the throne; living, in short, at least to a great extent, in an affectionate and perilous intimacy with the men of the other race, provoking them, playing with them by speaking of its vice as of something alien to it—a game that is rendered easy by the blindness or duplicity of the others, a game that may be kept up for years until the day of the scandal when these lion-tamers are devoured; obliged until then to make a secret of their lives, to avert their eyes from the direction in which they would wish to stray, to fasten them on what they would naturally turn away from, to change the gender of many of the adjectives in their vocabulary, a social constraint that is slight in comparison with the inward constraint imposed upon them by their vice, or what is improperly so called, not so much in relation to others as to themselves, and in such a way that to themselves it does not appear a vice. But certain among them, more practical, busier men who have not the time to go and drive their bargains, or to dispense with the simplification of life and the saving of time which may result from co-operation,

have formed two societies of which the second is composed
exclusively of persons similar to themselves.

This is noticeable in those who are poor and have come up
from the country, without friends, with nothing but their
ambition to be some day a celebrated doctor or barrister, with
a mind still barren of opinions, a person devoid of social
graces which they intend as soon as possible to adorn, just
as they might buy furniture for their little attic in the Latin
Quarter, modelling themselves on what they observe among
those who have already "arrived" in the useful and serious
profession in which they also intend to establish themselves
and to become famous; in these their special predisposition,
unconsciously inherited like a proclivity for drawing, for
music, a tendency towards blindness, is perhaps the only
inveterate and overriding peculiarity—which on certain evenings compels them to miss some meeting, advantageous to
their career, with people whose ways of speaking, thinking,
dressing, parting their hair, they otherwise adopt. In their
neighbourhood, where for the rest they mix only with brother
students, teachers or some fellow-provincial who has graduated
and can help them on, they have speedily discovered other
young men who are drawn to them by the same special inclination, as in a small town the assistant schoolmaster and the solicitor are brought together by a common interest in chamber
music or mediaeval ivories; applying to the object of their
distraction the same utilitarian instinct, the same professional spirit which guides them in their career, they meet these
young men at gatherings to which no outsider is admitted
any more than to those that bring together collectors of old
snuff-boxes, Japanese prints or rare flowers, and at which,
what with the pleasure of gaining information, the practical
value of making exchanges and the fear of competition, there
prevail simultaneously, as in a stamp market, the close co-
operation of specialists and the fierce rivalries of collectors.
No one moreover in the café where they have their table
knows what the gathering is, whether it is that of an angling
club, of an editorial staff, or of the "Sons of the Indre," so
correct is their attire, so cold and reserved their manner, so
modestly do they refrain from any but the most covert glance

at the young men of fashion, the young "lions" who, a few
feet away, are boasting about their mistresses, and among
whom those who now admire them without venturing to raise
their eyes will learn only twenty years later, when some are on
the eve of admission to the Academy, and others middle-aged
clubmen, that the most attractive among them, now a stout
and grizzled Charlus, was in reality one of themselves, but
elsewhere, in another circle of society, beneath other external
symbols, with different signs whose unfamiliarity misled them.
But these groups are at varying stages of evolution; and, just
as the "Union of the Left" differs from the "Socialist Federa-
tion" or some Mendelssohnian musical club from the Schola
Cantorum, on certain evenings, at another table, there are
extremists who allow a bracelet to slip down from beneath a
cuff, or sometimes a necklace to gleam in the gap of a collar,
who by their persistent stares, their cooings, their laughter,
their mutual caresses, oblige a band of students to depart in
hot haste, and are served with a civility beneath which indignation smoulders by a waiter who, as on the evenings when he
has to serve Dreyfusards, would have the greatest pleasure in
summoning the police did he not find profit in pocketing their
gratuities.

It is with these professional organisations that the mind
contrasts the taste of the solitaries, and in one sense without
too much contrivance, since it is doing no more than imitate the
solitaries themselves who imagine that nothing differs more
widely from organised vice than what appears to them to be
a misunderstood love, but with some contrivance nevertheless,
for these different classes correspond, no less than to diverse
physiological types, to successive stages in a pathological or
merely social evolution. And it is, in fact, very rarely that the
solitaries do not eventually merge themselves in some such
organisation, sometimes from simple lassitude, or for convenience (just as the people who have been most strongly
opposed to such innovations end by having the telephone
installed, inviting the Iénas to their parties, or shopping at
Potin's). They meet with none too friendly a reception as a
rule, for, in their relatively pure lives, their want of experience,
the saturation in day-dreams to which they have been reduced,

have branded more strongly upon them those special marks of effeminacy which the professionals have sought to efface. And it must be admitted that, among certain of these newcomers, the woman is not only inwardly united to the man but hideously visible, convulsed as they are by a hysterical spasm, by a shrill laugh which sets their knees and hands trembling, looking no more like the common run of men than those apes with melancholy ringed eyes and prehensile feet who dress up in dinner-jackets and black ties; so that these new recruits are judged by others, themselves less chaste, to be compromising associates, and their admission is hedged with difficulties; they are accepted nevertheless, and they benefit then from those facilities by which commerce and big business have transformed the lives of individuals by bringing within their reach commodities hitherto too costly to acquire and indeed hard to find, which now submerge them beneath a plethora of what by themselves they had never succeeded in discovering amid the densest crowds.

But, even with these innumerable outlets, the burden of social constraint is still too heavy for some, recruited principally among those who have not practised mental constraint and who still take to be rarer than it actually is their way of love. Let us ignore for the moment those who, the exceptional character of their inclinations making them regard themselves as superior to the other sex, look down on women, regard homosexuality as the appurtenance of genius and the great periods of history, and, when they wish to share their taste with others, seek out not so much those who seem to them to be predisposed towards it, like drug-addicts with their morphine, as those who seem to them to be worthy of it, from apostolic zeal, just as others preach Zionism, conscientious objection, Saint-Simonianism, vegetarianism or anarchy. There are some who, should we intrude upon them in the morning, still in bed, will present to our gaze an admirable female head, so generalised and typical of the entire sex is the expression of the face; the hair itself affirms it, so feminine is its ripple; unbrushed, it falls so naturally in long curls over the cheek that one marvels how the young woman, the girl, the Galatea barely awakened to life in the unconscious mass of this male body in which she is imprisoned has contrived so ingeniously, by herself, without instruction from anyone else, to take advantage of the narrowest apertures in her prison wall to find what was necessary to her existence. No doubt the young man who sports this delicious head does not say: "I am a woman." Even if—for any of the countless possible reasons—he lives with a woman, he can deny to her that he is himself one, can swear to her that he has never had intercourse with men. But let her look at him as we have just revealed him, lying back in bed, in pyjamas, his arms bare, his throat and neck bare too beneath the dark tresses: the pyjama jacket becomes a woman's shift, the head that of a pretty Spanish girl. The mistress is appalled by these confidences offered to her gaze, truer than any spoken confidence could be, or indeed any action, which his actions indeed, if they have not already done so, cannot fail later on to confirm, for every individual follows the line of his own pleasure, and if he is not too depraved, seeks it in a sex complementary to his own. And for the invert vice begins, not when he enters into relations (for there are all sorts of reasons that may enjoin these), but when he takes his pleasure with women. The young man whom we have been attempting to portray was so evidently a woman that the women who looked upon him with desire were doomed (failing a special taste on their part) to the same disappointment as those who in Shakespeare's comedies are taken in by a girl disguised as a youth. The deception is mutual, the invert is himself aware of it, he guesses the disillusionment which the woman will experience once the mask is removed, and feels to what an extent this mistake as to sex is a source of poetical imaginings. Moreover it is in vain that he keeps back the admission "I am a woman" even from his demanding mistress (if she is not a denizen of Gomorrah) when all the time, with the cunning, the agility, the obstinacy of a climbing plant, the unconscious but visible woman in him seeks the masculine organ. We have only to look at that curly hair on the white pillow to understand that if, in the evening, this young man slips through his guardians' fingers in spite of them, in spite of himself, it will not be to go in pursuit of women. His mistress may castigate him, may lock him up, but next day the man-woman will have

found some way of attaching himself to a man, as the convolvu-
lus throws out its tendrils wherever it finds a pick or a rake
up which to climb. Why, when we admire in the face of this
man a delicacy that touches our hearts, a grace, a natural
gentleness such as men do not possess, should we be dismayed
to learn that this young man runs after boxers? They are
different aspects of the same reality. And indeed, what repels
us is the most touching thing of all, more touching than any
refinement of delicacy, for it represents an admirable though
unconscious effort on the part of nature: the recognition of
sex by itself, in spite of the deceptions of sex, appears as an
unavowed attempt to escape from itself towards what an
initial error on the part of society has segregated it from. Some
—those no doubt who have been most timid in childhood—
are not greatly concerned with the kind of physical pleasure
they receive, provided that they can associate it with a masculine face. Whereas others, whose sensuality is doubtless more
violent, feel an imperious need to localise their physical
pleasure. These latter, perhaps, would shock the average
person with their avowals. They live perhaps less exclusively
beneath the sway of Saturn's outrider, since for them women
are not entirely excluded as they are for the former sort, in
relation to whom women have no existence apart from conversation, flirtation, loves not of the heart but of the head. But
the second sort seek out those women who love other women,
who can procure for them a young man, enhance the pleasure
they experience in his company; better still, they can, in the
same fashion, enjoy with such women the same pleasure as
with a man. Whence it arises that jealousy is kindled in those
who love the first sort only by the pleasure which they may
enjoy with a man, which alone seems to their lovers a betrayal,
since they do not participate in the love of women, have
practised it only out of habit and to preserve for themselves the
possibility of eventual marriage, visualising so little the pleasure
that it is capable of giving that they cannot be distressed by
the thought that he whom they love is enjoying that pleasure;
whereas the other sort often inspire jealousy by their love-
affairs with women. For, in their relations with women, they
play, for the woman who loves her own sex, the part of another

woman, and she offers them at the same time more or less what they find in other men, so that the jealous friend suffers from the feeling that the man he loves is riveted to the woman who is to him almost a man, and at the same time feels his beloved almost escape him because, to these women, he is something which the lover himself cannot conceive, a sort of woman. Nor need we pause here to consider those young fools who out of childish exhibitionism, to tease their friends or to shock their families, go out of their way to choose clothes that resemble women's dresses, to redden their lips and blacken their eyelashes; let us leave them aside, for it is they whom we shall find later on, when they have suffered the all too cruel penalty of their affectation, spending what remains of their lifetime in vain attempts to repair by a sternly protestant demeanour the wrong that they did to themselves when they were carried away by the same demon that urges young women of the Faubourg Saint-Germain to live scandalous lives, to defy all the conventions, to scoff at the entreaties of their families, until the day when they set themselves with perseverance but without success to reascend the slope down which they had found it so amusing to slide or rather had not been able to stop themselves from sliding. Let us, finally, leave until later the men who have sealed a pact with Gomorrah. We shall speak of them when M. de Charlus comes to know them. Let us leave all those, of one sort or another, who will appear each in his turn, and, to conclude this first sketch of the subject, let us simply say a word about those whom we began to speak of just now, the solitaries. Supposing their vice to be more exceptional than it is, they have retired into solitude from the day on which they discovered it, after having carried it within themselves for a long time without knowing it, longer, that is, than certain others. For no one can tell at first that he is an invert, or a poet, or a snob, or a scoundrel. The boy who has been reading erotic poetry or looking at obscene pictures, if he then presses his body against a schoolfellow's, imagines himself only to be communing with him in an identical desire for a woman. How should he suppose that he is not like everybody else when he recognises the substance of what he feels in reading Mme de La Fayette, Racine, Baudelaire, Walter Scott, at a time when he is still too little capable of observing himself to take into account what he has added from his own store to the picture, and to realise that if the sentiment be the same the object differs, that what he desires is Rob Roy and not Diana Vernon? With many, by a defensive prudence on the part of the instinct that precedes the clearer vision of the intellect, the mirror and walls of their bedroom vanish beneath a cloud of coloured prints of actresses, and they compose verses such as:

> I love but Chloe in the world,
>   For Chloe is divine;
> Her golden hair is sweetly curled,
>   For her my heart doth pine.

Must we on that account attribute to the opening phase of such lives a taste which we shall not find in them later on, like those flaxen ringlets on the heads of children which are destined to change to the darkest brown? Who can tell whether the photographs of women are not a first sign of hypocrisy, a first sign also of horror at other inverts? But the solitaries are precisely those to whom hypocrisy is painful. Possibly even the example of the Jews, of a different type of colony, is not strong enough to account for the frail hold that their upbringing has upon them, and for the skill and cunning with which they find their way back, not, perhaps, to anything so sheerly terrible as suicide (to which madmen return, whatever precautions one may take with them, and, having been pulled out of the river into which they have flung themselves, take poison, procure revolvers, and so forth), but to a life whose compulsive pleasures the men of the other race not only cannot understand, cannot imagine, abominate, but whose frequent danger and constant shame would horrify them. Perhaps, to form a picture of these, we ought to think, if not of the wild animals that never become domesticated, of the lion-cubs, allegedly tamed, which are still lions at heart, then at least of the negroes whom the comfortable existence of the white man renders desperately unhappy and who prefer the risks of life in the wild and its incomprehensible joys. When the day has dawned on which they have discovered themselves to be incapable at once of lying to others and of lying to themselves, they go away to live in the country, shunning the society of their own kind (whom they believe to be few in number) from horror of the monstrosity or fear of the temptation, and that of the rest of humanity from shame. Never having arrived at true maturity, plunged in a constant melancholy, from time to time, on a moonless Sunday evening, they go for a solitary walk as far as a crossroads where, although not a word has been said, there has come to meet them one of their boyhood friends who is living in a house in the neighbourhood. And they begin again the pastimes of long ago, on the grass, in the night, without exchanging a word. During the week, they meet in their respective houses, talk of this and that, without any allusion to what has occurred between them—exactly as though they had done nothing and would not do anything again—save, in their relations, a trace of coldness, of irony, of irritability and rancour, sometimes of hatred. Then the neighbour sets out on a strenuous expedition on horseback, scales mountain peaks, sleeps in the snow; his friend, who identifies his own vice with a weakness of constitution, a timid, stay-at-home life, assumes that vice can no longer exist in his emancipated friend, so many thousands of feet above sea-level. And, sure enough, the other takes a wife. Yet the forsaken one is not cured (although there are cases where, as we shall see, inversion is curable). He insists upon going down himself every morning to the kitchen to receive the milk from the hands of the dairyman's boy, and on the evening when desire is too strong for him will go out of his way to set a drunkard on the right road or to "adjust the dress" of a blind man. No doubt the life of certain inverts appears at times to change, their vice (as it is called) is no longer apparent in their habits; but nothing is ever lost: a missing jewel turns up again; when the quantity of a sick man's urine decreases, it is because he is perspiring more freely, but the excretion must invariably occur. One day this homosexual hears of the death of a young cousin, and from his inconsolable grief we learn that it was to this love, chaste possibly and aimed rather at retaining esteem than at obtaining possession, that his desires have turned by a sort of transfer as, in a budget, without any

alteration in the total, certain expenditure is carried under
another head. As is the case with invalids in whom a sudden
attack of urticaria makes their chronic ailments temporarily
disappear, this pure love for a young relative seems, in the
invert, to have momentarily replaced, by metastasis, habits
that will one day or another return to fill the place of the
vicarious cured malady.

Meanwhile the married neighbour of our recluse has returned; and on the day when he is obliged to invite them to
dinner, seeing the beauty of the young bride and the demon-
strative affection of the husband, he feels ashamed of the past.
Already in an interesting condition, she must return home early,
leaving her husband behind; the latter, when the time has come
for him to go home also, asks his host to accompany him for
part of the way; at first, no suspicion enters his mind, but at
the crossroads he finds himself thrown down on to the grass
without a word by the mountaineer who is shortly to become
a father. And their meetings begin again, and continue until
the day when there comes to live not far off a male cousin
of the young wife's, with whom her husband is now constantly
to be seen. And the latter, if the twice-abandoned friend calls
round and endeavours to approach him, indignantly repulses
him, furious that he has not had the tact to sense the disgust
which he must henceforward inspire. Once, however, there appears a stranger, sent to him by his faithless friend; but being
busy at the time, the abandoned one cannot see him, and only
afterwards learns with what object his visitor had come.

Then the solitary languishes alone. He has no other diversion than to go to the neighbouring watering-place to ask for
some information or other from a certain railwayman there.
But the latter has obtained promotion, has been transferred to
the other end of the country; the solitary will no longer be
able to go and ask him the times of the trains or the price of a
first-class ticket, and, before retiring to dream, Griselda-like,
in his tower, loiters upon the beach, a strange Andromeda
whom no Argonaut will come to free, a sterile jellyfish that
must perish upon the sand, or else he stands idly on the platform until his train leaves, casting over the crowd of passengers a look that will seem indifferent, disdainful or abstracted

to those of another race, but, like the luminous glow with which certain insects bedeck themselves in order to attract others of their species, or like the nectar which certain flowers offer to attract the insects that will fertilise them, would not escape the almost undiscoverable connoisseur of a pleasure too singular, too hard to place, which is offered him, the confrère with whom our specialist could converse in the strange tongue—in which at best some seedy loafer on the platform will put up a show of interest, but for pecuniary gain alone, like those people who, at the Collège de France, in the room in which the Professor of Sanskrit lectures without an audience, attend his course only for the sake of keeping warm. Jellyfish! Orchid! When I followed my instinct only, the jellyfish used to revolt me at Balbec; but if I had the eyes to regard them, like Michelet, from the standpoint of natural history and aesthetics, I saw an exquisite blue girandole. Are they not, with the transparent velvet of their petals, as it were the mauve orchids of the sea? Like so many creatures of the animal and vegetable kingdoms, like the plant which would produce vanilla but, because in its structure the male organ is separated by a partition from the female, remains sterile unless the hummingbirds or certain tiny bees convey the pollen from one to the other, or man fertilises them by artificial means, M. de Charlus (and here the word fertilise must be understood in a moral sense, since in the physical sense the union of male with male is and must be sterile, but it is no small matter for a person to be able to encounter the sole pleasure which he is capable of enjoying, and that "every creature here below" can impart to some other "his music or his fragrance or his flame"), M. de Charlus was one of those men who may be called exceptional because, however many they may be, the satisfaction, so easy for others, of their sexual needs depends upon the coincidence of too many conditions, and of conditions too difficult to meet. For men like M. de Charlus (subject to the compromises which will appear in the course of this story and which the reader may already have sensed, enforced by the need of pleasure which resigns itself to partial acceptations), mutual love, apart from the difficulties, so great as to be almost insurmountable, which

it encounters in the ordinary run of mortals, entails others so
exceptional that what is always extremely rare for everyone
becomes in their case well-nigh impossible, and, if they should
chance to have an encounter which is really fortunate, or which
nature makes appear so to them, their happiness is somehow
far more extraordinary, selective, profoundly necessary than
that of the normal lover. The feud of the Capulets and Mon-
tagues was as nothing compared with the obstacles of every
sort which have been surmounted, the special eliminations
to which nature has had to subject the chances, already far
from common, which bring about love, before a retired tailor,
who was intending to set off soberly for his office, can stand
quivering in ecstasy before a stoutish man of fifty; this Romeo
and this Juliet may believe with good reason that their love is
not a momentary whim but a true predestination, determined
by the harmonies of their temperaments, and not only by
their own personal temperaments but by those of their
ancestors, by their most distant strains of heredity, so much so
that the fellow-creature who is conjoined with them has belonged to them from before their birth, has attracted them by a
force comparable to that which governs the worlds on which
we spent our former lives. M. de Charlus had distracted me
from looking to see whether the bumble-bee was bringing
to the orchid the pollen it had so long been waiting to receive, and had no chance of receiving save by an accident so
unlikely that one might call it a sort of miracle. But it was a
miracle also that I had just witnessed, almost of the same order
and no less marvellous. As soon as I considered the encounter
from this point of view, everything about it seemed to me
instinct with beauty. The most extraordinary stratagems that
nature has devised to compel insects to ensure the fertilisation
of flowers which without their intervention could not be
fertilised because the male flower is too far away from the
female—or the one which, if it is the wind that must provide
for the transportation of the pollen, makes it so much more
easily detachable from the male, so much more easily snatched
from the air by the female flower, by eliminating the secretion
of the nectar, which is no longer of any use since there are no
insects to be attracted, and even the brilliance of the corollas

which attract them—and the device which, in order that the flower may be kept free for the right pollen, which can fructify only in that particular flower, makes it secrete a liquid which renders it immune to all other pollens—seemed to me no more marvellous than the existence of the subvariety of inverts destined to guarantee the pleasures of love to the invert who is growing old: men who are attracted not by all other men, but—by a phenomenon of correspondence and harmony similar to those that govern the fertilisation of heterostyle trimorphous flowers like the *lythrum salicaria*—only by men considerably older than themselves. Of this subvariety Jupien had just furnished me with an example, one less striking however than certain others which every human herbalist, every moral botanist, will be able to observe in spite of their rarity, and which will show them a frail young man awaiting the advances of a robust and paunchy quinquagenarian, and remaining as indifferent to those of other young men as the hermaphrodite flowers of the short-styled *primula veris* remain sterile so long as they are fertilised only by other *primulae veris* of short style also, whereas they welcome with joy the pollen of the *primula veris* with the long style. As for M. de Charlus's part in the transaction, I noticed later on that there were for him various kinds of conjunction, some of which, by their multiplicity, their scarcely visible instantaneousness, and above all the absence of contact between the two actors, recalled still more forcibly those flowers that in a garden are fertilised by the pollen of a neighbouring flower which they may never touch. There were in fact certain persons whom it was sufficient for him to invite to his house, and to hold for an hour or two under the domination of his talk, for his desire, inflamed by some earlier encounter, to be assuaged. By a simple use of words the conjunction was effected, as simply as it can be among the infusoria. Sometimes, as had doubtless been the case with me on the evening on which I had been summoned by him after the Guermantes dinner-party, the relief was effected by a violent diatribe which the Baron flung in his visitor's face, just as certain flowers, by means of a hidden spring, spray from a distance the disconcerted but unconsciously collaborating insect. M. de Charlus, the dominated

one turned dominator, feeling purged of his agitation and
calmed, would send away the visitor who had at once ceased to
appear to him desirable. Finally, inasmuch as inversion itself
springs from the fact that the invert is too closely akin to
woman to be capable of having any effective relations with
her, it relates to a higher law which ordains that so many
hermaphrodite flowers shall remain infertile, that is to say
to the sterility of self-fertilisation. It is true that inverts, in
their search for a male, often content themselves with other
inverts as effeminate as themselves. But it is enough that they
do not belong to the female sex, of which they have in them an
embryo which they can put to no useful purpose, as happens
with so many hermaphrodite flowers, and even with certain
hermaphrodite animals, such as the snail, which cannot be
fertilised by themselves, but can by other hermaphrodites.
In this respect the race of inverts, who readily link themselves
with the ancient East or the golden age of Greece, might be
traced back further still, to those experimental epochs in which
there existed neither dioecious plants nor monosexual animals,
to that initial hermaphroditism of which certain rudiments of
male organs in the anatomy of women and of female organs in
that of men seem still to preserve the trace. I found the pantomime, incomprehensible to me at first, of Jupien and M. de
Charlus as curious as those seductive gestures addressed,
Darwin tells us, to insects by the flowers called composite
which erect the florets of their capitula so as to be seen from
a greater distance, like certain heterostyled flowers which
turn back their stamens and bend them to open the way for
the insect, or which offer him an ablution, and indeed quite
simply comparable to the nectar-fragrance and vivid hue of
the corollas that were at that moment attracting insects into
the courtyard. From this day onwards M. de Charlus was to
alter the time of his visits to Mme de Villeparisis, not that he
could not see Jupien elsewhere and with greater convenience,
but because to him just as much as to me the afternoon sunshine and the blossoming plant were no doubt linked with his
memories. Moreover, not only did he recommend the Jupiens
to Mme de Villeparisis, to the Duchesse de Guermantes, to a
whole brilliant clientele who were all the more assiduous in

their patronage of the young seamstress when they saw that the few ladies who had resisted, or had merely delayed their submission, were subjected to the direst reprisals by the Baron, whether in order that they might serve as examples or because they had aroused his wrath and had stood out against his attempted domination, but he made Jupien's position more and more lucrative, until he finally engaged him as his secretary and established him in the state in which we shall see him later on. "Ah, now! There's a happy man, if you like, that Jupien," said Françoise, who had a tendency to minimise or exaggerate people's generosity according as it was bestowed on herself or on others. Not that, in this instance, she had any need to exaggerate, nor for that matter did she feel any jealousy, being genuinely fond of Jupien. "Oh, he's such a good man, the Baron," she went on, "such a nice, religious, proper sort of man. If I had a daughter to marry and was one of the rich myself, I'd give her to the Baron with my eyes shut." "But, Françoise," my mother observed gently, "she'd be well supplied with husbands, that daughter of yours. Don't forget you've already promised her to Jupien." "Ah! Lordy, now," replied Françoise, "there's another of them that would make a woman happy. It doesn't matter whether you're rich or poor, it makes no difference to your nature. The Baron and Jupien, they're just the same sort of person."

However, I greatly exaggerated at the time, on the strength of this first revelation, the elective character of so carefully selected a combination. Admittedly, every man of M. de Charlus's kind is an extraordinary creature since, if he does not make concessions to the possibilities of life, he seeks out essentially the love of a man of the other race, that is to say a man who is a lover of women (and incapable consequently of loving him); contrary to what I had imagined in the courtyard, where I had seen Jupien hovering round M. de Charlus like the orchid making overtures to the bumble-bee, these exceptional creatures with whom we commiserate are a vast crowd, as we shall see in the course of this book, for a reason which will be disclosed only at the end of it, and commiserate with themselves for being too many rather than too few. For the two angels who were posted at the gates of Sodom to learn whether its inhabitants (according to Genesis) had indeed done all the things the report of which had ascended to the Eternal Throne must have been, and of this one can only be glad, exceedingly ill chosen by the Lord, who ought to have entrusted the task to a Sodomite. Such a one would never have been persuaded by such excuses as "I'm the father of six and I've two mistresses," to lower his flaming sword benevolently and mitigate the punishment. He would have answered: "Yes, and your wife lives in a torment of jealousy. But even when these women have not been chosen by you from Gomorrah, you spend your nights with a watcher of flocks upon Hebron." And he would at once have made him retrace his steps to the city which the rain of fire and brimstone was to destroy. On the contrary, they allowed all the shameless Sodomites to escape, even if these, on catching sight of a boy, turned their heads like Lot's wife, though without being on that account changed like her into pillars of salt. With the result that they engendered a numerous progeny with whom this gesture has remained habitual, like that of the dissolute women who, while apparently studying a row of shoes displayed in a shop window, turn their heads to keep track of a passing student. These descendants of the Sodomites, so numerous that we may apply to them that other verse of Genesis: "If a man can number the dust of the earth, then shall thy seed also be numbered," have established themselves throughout the entire world; they have had access to every profession and are so readily admitted into the most exclusive clubs that, whenever a Sodomite fails to secure election, the black balls are for the most part cast by other Sodomites, who make a point of condemning sodomy, having inherited the mendacity that enabled their ancestors to escape from the accursed city. It is possible that they may return there one day. Certainly they form in every land an oriental colony, cultured, musical, malicious, which has charming qualities and intolerable defects. We shall study them with greater thoroughness in the course of the following pages; but I have thought it as well to utter here a provisional warning against the lamentable error of proposing (just as people have encouraged a Zionist movement) to create a Sodomist movement and to rebuild

Sodom. For, no sooner had they arrived there than the Sodomites would leave the town so as not to have the appearance of belonging to it, would take wives, keep mistresses in other cities where they would find, incidentally, every diversion that appealed to them. They would repair to Sodom only on days of supreme necessity, when their own town was empty, at those seasons when hunger drives the wolf from the woods. In other words, everything would go on very much as it does to-day in London, Berlin, Rome, Petrograd or Paris.

At all events, on the day in question, before paying my call on the Duchess, I did not look so far ahead, and I was distressed to find that, by my engrossment in the Jupien-Charlus conjunction, I had missed perhaps an opportunity of witnessing the fertilisation of the blossom by the bumble-bee.

PART TWO

CHAPTER ONE

As I was in no hurry to arrive at the Guermantes reception to which I was not certain that I had been invited, I remained sauntering out of doors; but the summer day seemed to be in no greater haste to stir. Although it was after nine o'clock, it was still the daylight that was giving the Luxor obelisk on the Place de la Concorde the appearance of pink nougat. Then it diluted the tint and changed the surface to a metallic substance, so that the obelisk not only became more precious but seemed more slender and almost flexible. One felt that one might have been able to twist this jewel, that one had perhaps already slightly bent it. The moon was now in the sky like a section of an orange delicately peeled although slightly bruised. But a few hours later it was to be fashioned of the most enduring gold. Nestling alone behind it, a poor little star was to serve as sole companion to the lonely moon, while the latter, keeping its friend protected but striding ahead more boldly, would brandish like an irresistible weapon, like an oriental symbol, its broad, magnificent golden crescent.

Outside the mansion of the Princesse de Guermantes I ran into the Duc de Châtellerault. I no longer remembered that half an hour earlier I had still been tormented by the fear—which in fact was soon to grip me again—that I might be entering the house uninvited. We get anxious, and it is sometimes long after the hour of danger, which a subsequent distraction has made us forget, that we remember our anxiety. I greeted the young Duke and made my way into the house. But here I must first of all record a trifling incident, which will enable us to understand something that was presently to occur.

There was one person who, on that evening as on the previous evenings, had been thinking a great deal about the Duc de Châtellerault, without however suspecting who he was: this was the Princesse de Guermantes's usher (styled at that time the "barker"). M. de Châtellerault, so far from being

657

one of the Princess's intimate friends, although he was one of
her cousins, had been invited to her house for the first time.
His parents, who had not been on speaking terms with her for
ten years, had made it up with her within the last fortnight,
and, obliged to be out of Paris that evening, had requested
their son to represent them. Now, a few days earlier, the
Princess's usher had met in the Champs-Elysées a young man
whom he had found charming but whose identity he had been
unable to establish. Not that the young man had not shown
himself as obliging as he had been generous. All the favours
that the usher had supposed that he would have to bestow
upon so young a gentleman, he had on the contrary received.
But M. de Châtellerault was as cowardly as he was rash; he
was all the more determined not to unveil his incognito since
he did not know with whom he was dealing; his fear would
have been far greater, although ill-founded, if he had known. He
had confined himself to posing as an Englishman, and to all
the passionate questions with which he was plied by the usher,
desirous to meet again a person to whom he was indebted for
so much pleasure and largesse, the Duke had merely replied,
from one end of the Avenue Gabriel to the other: "I do not
speak French."

Although, in spite of everything—remembering his cousin
Gilbert's maternal ancestry—the Duc de Guermantes affected
to find a touch of Courvoisier in the drawing-room of the
Princesse de Guermantes-Bavière, the general estimate of that
lady's initiative and intellectual superiority was based upon
an innovation that was to be found nowhere else in these
circles. After dinner, however important the party that was
to follow, the chairs at the Princesse de Guermantes's were
arranged in such a way as to form little groups whose backs
were necessarily sometimes turned on one another. The Princess then displayed her social sense by going to sit down, as
though by preference, in one of these. She did not however
hesitate to pick out and draw into it a member of another
group. If, for instance, she had remarked to M. Detaille, who
had naturally agreed with her, on the beauty of Mme de
Villemur's neck, of which that lady's position in another
group made her present a back view, the Princess had no

hesitation in raising her voice: "Madame de Villemur, M. Detaille, with his wonderful painter's eye, has just been admiring your neck." Mme de Villemur interpreted this as a direct invitation to join in the conversation; with the agility of a practised horsewoman, she would swivel round slowly in her chair through three quadrants of a circle, and, without in any way disturbing her neighbours, come to rest almost facing the Princess. "You don't know M. Detaille?" exclaimed their hostess, for whom her guest's skilful and discreet about-face was not enough. "I don't know him, but I know his work," Mme de Villemur would reply with a respectful and winning air and an aptness which many of the onlookers envied her, addressing the while an imperceptible bow to the celebrated painter whom this invocation had not been sufficient to introduce to her in a formal manner. "Come, Monsieur Detaille," said the Princess, "let me introduce you to Mme de Villemur." That lady thereupon showed as much ingenuity in making room for the creator of the *Dream* as she had shown a moment earlier in wheeling round to face him. And the Princess would draw forward a chair for herself, having in fact addressed Mme de Villemur only in order to have an excuse for leaving the first group, in which she had spent the statutory ten minutes, and bestow a similar allowance of her time upon the second. In three quarters of an hour, all the groups would have received a visit from her, which seemed to have been determined in each instance by impulse and predilection, but had the paramount object of making it apparent how naturally "a great lady knows how to entertain." But now the guests for the reception were beginning to arrive and the lady of the house was seated not far from the door— erect and proud in her quasi-regal majesty, her eyes ablaze with their own incandescence—between two unattractive royalties and the Spanish Ambassadress.

I stood waiting behind a number of guests who had arrived before me. Facing me was the Princess, whose beauty is probably not the only thing, among so many other beauties, that reminds me of this party. But the face of my hostess was so perfect, stamped like so beautiful a medal, that it has retained a commemorative virtue in my mind. The Princess was in the habit of saying to her guests when she met them a day or two before one of her parties: "You will come, won't you?" as though she felt a great desire to talk to them. But since, on the contrary, she had nothing to talk to them about, when they entered her presence she contented herself, without rising, with breaking off for an instant her vapid conversation with the two royalties and the Ambassadress and thanking them with: "How good of you to have come," not because she thought that the guest had shown goodness by coming, but to enhance her own; then, at once dropping him back into the stream, she would add: "You will find M. de Guermantes by the garden door," so that the guest proceeded on his way and ceased to bother her. To some indeed she said nothing, contenting herself with showing them her admirable onyx eyes, as though they had come merely to visit an exhibition of precious stones.

The person immediately in front of me was the Duc de Châtellerault.

Having to respond to all the smiles, all the greetings waved to him from inside the drawing-room, he had not noticed the usher. But from the first moment the usher had recognised him. In another instant he would know the identity of this stranger, which he had so ardently desired to learn. When he asked his "Englishman" of the other evening what name he was to announce, the usher was not merely stirred, he considered that he was being indiscreet, indelicate. He felt that he was about to reveal to the whole world (which would, however, suspect nothing) a secret which it was criminal of him to ferret out like this and to proclaim in public. Upon hearing the guest's reply: "Le Duc de Châtellerault," he was overcome with such pride that he remained for a moment speechless. The Duke looked at him, recognised him, saw himself ruined, while the servant, who had recovered his composure and was sufficiently versed in heraldry to complete for himself an appellation that was too modest, roared with a professional vehemence softened with intimate tenderness: "Son Altesse Monseigneur le Duc de Châtellerault!" But now it was my turn to be announced. Absorbed in contemplation of my hostess, who had not yet seen me, I had not thought of the function—terrible to me, although not in the same sense as to M. de Châtellerault—of this usher garbed in black like an executioner, surrounded by a group of lackeys in the most cheerful livery, strapping fellows ready to seize hold of an intruder and fling him out. The usher asked me my name, and I gave it to him as mechanically as the condemned man allows himself to be strapped to the block. At once he lifted his head majestically and, before I could beg him to announce me in a lowered tone so as to spare my own feelings if I were not invited and those of the Princesse de Guermantes if I were, roared the disquieting syllables with a force capable of bringing down the roof.

The famous Huxley (whose grandson occupies a leading position in the English literary world of to-day) relates that one of his patients no longer dared go out socially because often, on the very chair that was offered to her with a courteous gesture, she saw an old gentleman already seated. She was quite certain that either the gesture of invitation or the old gentleman's presence was a hallucination, for her hostess would not have offered her a chair that was already occupied. And when Huxley, to cure her, forced her to reappear in society, she had a moment of painful hesitation wondering whether the friendly sign that was being made to her was the real thing, or whether, in obedience to a non-existent vision, she was about to sit down in public upon the knees of a gentleman of flesh and blood. Her brief uncertainty was agonising. Less so perhaps than mine. From the moment I had taken in the sound of my name, like the rumble that warns us of a possible cataclysm, I was obliged, in order at least to plead my good faith, and as though I were not tormented by any doubts, to advance towards the Princess with a resolute air.

She caught sight of me when I was still a few feet away and (leaving me in no further doubt that I had been the victim of a plot), instead of remaining seated, as she had done for her other guests, rose and came towards me. A moment later, I was able to heave the sigh of relief of Huxley's patient when, having made up her mind to sit down in the chair, she found it vacant and realised that it was the old gentleman who was the hallucination. The Princess had just held out her hand to me with a smile. She remained standing for some moments with the kind of charm enshrined in the verse of Malherbe which ends:

To do them honour all the angels rise.

She apologised because the Duchess had not yet arrived, as though I must be bored there without her. In offering me this greeting, she executed around me, holding me by the hand, a graceful pirouette, by the whirl of which I felt myself swept away. I almost expected her to offer me next, like the leader of a cotillon, an ivory-headed cane or a wrist-watch. She did not, however, give me anything of the sort, and as though, instead of dancing the Boston, she had been listening to a sacrosanct Beethoven quartet the sublime strains of which she was afraid of interrupting, she cut short the conversation there and then, or rather did not begin it, and, still radiant at having seen me come in, merely informed me where the Prince was to be found.

I moved away from her and did not venture to approach her again, feeling that she had absolutely nothing to say to me and that, in her immense good will, this marvellously handsome and stately woman, noble as were so many great ladies who stepped so proudly on to the scaffold, could only, short of offering me a draught of honeydew, repeat what she had already said to me twice: "You will find the Prince in the garden." Now, to go in search of the Prince was to feel my doubts revive in a different form.

In any case I should have to find somebody to introduce me. Above all the din of conversation was to be heard the inexhaustible chattering of M. de Charlus, talking to H.E. the Duke of Sidonia, whose acquaintance he had just made. Members of the same profession recognise each other instinctively; so do those with the same vice. M. de Charlus and M. de Sidonia had each of them immediately detected the other's, which was in both cases that of being monologuists in society, to the extent of not being able to stand any interruption. Having decided at once that, in the words of a famous sonnet, there was "no help," they had made up their minds, not to remain silent, but each to go on talking without any regard to what the other might say. This had resulted in the sort of confused babble produced in Molière's comedies by a number of people saying different things simultaneously. The Baron, with his deafening voice, was moreover certain of keeping the upper hand, of drowning the feeble voice of M. de Sidonia—without however discouraging him, for, whenever M. de Charlus paused for a moment to draw breath, the gap was filled by the murmuring of the Spanish grandee who had imperturbably continued his discourse. I might well have asked M. de Charlus to introduce me to the Prince de Guermantes, but I feared (and with good reason) that he might be displeased with me. I had treated him in the most ungrateful fashion by letting his offers pass unheeded for the second time and by giving him no sign of life since the evening when he had so affectionately escorted me home. And yet I could not plead the excuse of having anticipated the scene which I had witnessed that very afternoon enacted by himself and Jupien. I suspected nothing of the sort. It is true that shortly before this, when my parents reproached me for my laziness and for not having taken the trouble to write a line to M. de Charlus, I had accused them of wanting me to accept a degrading proposal. But anger alone, and the desire to hit upon the expression that would be most offensive to them, had dictated this mendacious retort. In reality, I had imagined nothing sensual, nothing sentimental even, underlying the Baron's offers. I had said this to my parents out of pure fantasy. But sometimes the future is latent in us without our knowing it, and our supposedly lying words foreshadow an imminent reality.

M. de Charlus would doubtless have forgiven me my want of gratitude. But what made him furious was that my presence this evening at the Princesse de Guermantes's, as for some time past at her cousin's, seemed to flout his solemn declaration: "There is no admission to those houses save through me." I had not followed the hierarchical path—a grave fault, a perhaps inexpiable crime. M. de Charlus knew all too well that the thunderbolts which he hurled at those who did not comply with his orders, or to whom he had taken a dislike, were beginning to be regarded by many people, however furiously he might brandish them, as mere pasteboard, and had no longer the force to banish anybody from anywhere. But he believed perhaps that his diminished power, still considerable, remained intact in the eyes of novices like myself. And so I did not consider it very advisable to ask a favour of him at a party where the mere fact of my presence seemed an ironical refutation of his pretensions.

I was buttonholed at that moment by a rather vulgar man, Professor E——. He had been surprised to see me at the Guermantes's. I was no less surprised to see him there, for nobody of his sort had ever been seen before or was ever to be seen again in the Princess's drawing-room. He had just cured the Prince, after the last sacraments had been administered, of infectious pneumonia, and the special gratitude that Mme de Guermantes felt towards him was the reason for her thus departing from custom and inviting him to her house. As he knew absolutely nobody there, and could not wander about indefinitely by himself like a minister of death, having recognised me he had discovered for the first time in his life that he had an infinite number of things to say to me, which enabled him to keep some sort of countenance. This was one of the reasons for his approaching me. There was also another. He attached great importance to never being mistaken in his diagnoses. Now his correspondence was so voluminous that he could not always remember, when he had seen a patient once only, whether the disease had really followed the course that he had traced for it. The reader may perhaps remember that, immediately after my grandmother's stroke, I had taken her to see him, on the afternoon when he was having all his decorations stitched to his coat. After so long an interval, he had forgotten the formal announcement which had been sent to him at the time. "Your grandmother *is* dead, isn't she?" he said to me in a voice in which a semi-certainty calmed a slight apprehension. "Ah! indeed! Well, from the moment I saw her my prognosis was extremely grave, I remember it quite well."

It was thus that Professor E—— learned or recalled the death of my grandmother, and (I must say this to his credit, and to the credit of the medical profession as a whole) without displaying, without perhaps feeling any satisfaction. The mistakes made by doctors are innumerable. They err habitually on the side of optimism as to treatment, of pessimism as to the outcome. "Wine? In moderation, it can do you no harm, it's always a tonic. . . . Sexual enjoyment? After all it's a natural function. But you mustn't overdo it, you understand. Excess in anything is wrong." At once, what a temptation to the patient to renounce those two life-givers, water and chastity! If, on the other hand, he has trouble with his heart, an excess of albumin, or something of the sort, he has very little hope. Disorders that are grave but purely functional are at once ascribed to an imaginary cancer. Useless to continue visits which are powerless to check an ineluctable disease. Let the patient, left to his own devices, thereupon subject himself to an implacable regimen and in time recover, or at any rate survive, and the doctor, to whom he touches his hat in the Avenue de l'Opéra when he supposed him to have long been lying in Père-Lachaise, will interpret the gesture as an act of sardonic insolence. An innocent stroll taken beneath his nose and venerable beard would arouse no greater wrath in the Assize Judge who two years earlier had sentenced the stroller, now passing him with apparent impunity, to death. Doctors (we do not here include them all, of course, and make a mental reservation of certain admirable exceptions) are in general more displeased, more irritated by the invalidation of their verdicts than pleased by their execution. This explains why Professor E——, despite the intellectual satisfaction that he doubtless felt at finding that he had not been mistaken, was able to speak to me with due regret of the blow that had fallen upon us. He was in no hurry to cut short the conversation, which kept him in countenance and gave him a reason for remaining. He spoke to me of the heat-wave through which we were passing, but although he was a well-read man and capable of expressing himself in good French, he asked me: "You are none the worse for this hyperthermia?" The fact is that medicine has made some slight advance in knowledge since Molière's days, but none in its vocabulary. My interlocutor went on: "The great thing is to avoid the sudations that are caused by weather like this, especially in overheated rooms. You can remedy them, when you go home and feel thirsty, by the application of heat" (by which he apparently meant hot drinks).

Owing to the circumstances of my grandmother's death, the subject interested me, and I had recently read in a book by a great specialist that perspiration was injurious to the kidneys by discharging through the skin something whose proper outlet was elsewhere. I thought with regret of those dog-days at the time of my grandmother's death, and was inclined to blame them for it. I did not mention this to Dr E——, but of his own accord he said to me: "The advantage of this very hot weather in which perspiration is abundant is that the kidney is correspondingly relieved." Medicine is not an exact science.

Clinging on to me, Professor E—— asked only not to be forced to leave me. But I had just seen the Marquis de Vaugoubert, bowing and scraping this way and that to the Princesse de Guermantes after first taking a step backwards. M. de Norpois had recently introduced me to him and I hoped that I might find in him a person capable of presenting me to our host. The proportions of this work do not permit me to explain here in consequence of what incidents in his youth M. de Vaugoubert was one of the few men (possibly the only man) in society who happened to be in what is called in Sodom the "confidence" of M. de Charlus. But, if our Minister to the court of King Theodosius had some of the same defects as the Baron, they were only very pale reflexions of them. It was only in an infinitely diluted, sentimental and inane form that he displayed those alternations of affection and hatred through which the desire to charm, and then the fear—equally imaginary—of being, if not scorned, at any rate unmasked, made the Baron pass. These alternations—made ridiculous by a chastity, a "platonicism," to which as a man of keen ambition he had, from the moment of passing his examination, sacrificed all pleasure, above all by his intellectual nullity—M. de Vaugoubert did nevertheless display. But whereas M. de Charlus's immoderate eulogies were proclaimed with a positively dazzling eloquence, and seasoned with the subtlest, the most mordant banter which marked a man for ever, M. de

Vaugoubert's predilections were by contrast expressed with the banality of a man of the lowest intelligence, a man of fashionable society, and a functionary, and his grievances (made up on the spur of the moment like the Baron's) with a malevolence that was as witless as it was remorseless, and was all the more startling in that it was invariably a direct contradiction of what the Minister had said six months earlier and might soon perhaps be saying again: a regularity of change which gave an almost astronomic poetry to the various phases of M. de Vaugoubert's life, albeit apart from this nobody was ever less suggestive of a star.

His response to my greeting had nothing in common with that which I should have received from M. de Charlus. He imparted to it, in addition to countless mannerisms which he supposed to be typical of the social and diplomatic worlds, a brisk, cavalier, smiling air calculated to make him seem on the one hand delighted with his existence—at a time when he was inwardly brooding over the mortifications of a career with no prospect of advancement and threatened with enforced retirement—and on the other hand young, virile and charming, when he could see and no longer dared to go and examine in the glass the wrinkles gathering on a face which he would have wished to remain infinitely seductive. Not that he hoped for real conquests, the mere thought of which filled him with terror on account of gossip, scandal, blackmail. Having gone from an almost infantile corruption to an absolute continence dating from the day on which his thoughts had turned to the Quai d'Orsay and he had begun to plan a great career for himself, he had the air of a caged animal, casting in every direction glances expressive of fear, craving and stupidity. This last was so dense that it did not occur to him that the street-arabs of his adolescence were boys no longer, and when a newsvendor bawled in his face: "*La Presse!*" he shuddered with terror even more than with longing, imagining himself recognised and denounced.

But in default of the pleasures sacrificed to the ingratitude of the Quai d'Orsay, M. de Vaugoubert—and it was for this that he was still anxious to please—was liable to sudden stirrings of the heart. He would pester the Ministry with endless letters, would employ every personal ruse, would draw shamelessly on the considerable credit of Mme de Vaugoubert (who, on account of her corpulence, her high birth, her masculine air, and above all the mediocrity of her husband, was reputed to be endowed with eminent capacities and to be herself for all practical purposes the Minister), to introduce for no valid reason a young man destitute of all merit on to the staff of the legation. It is true that a few months or a few years later, the insignificant attaché had only to appear, without the least trace of any hostile intention, to have shown signs of coldness towards his chief for the latter, supposing himself scorned or betrayed, to devote the same hysterical ardour to punishing as formerly to gratifying him. He would move heaven and earth to have him recalled and the head of the political section would receive a letter daily, saying: "Why don't you hurry up and rid me of the brute? Give him a dressing down in his own interest. What he needs is a slice of humble pie." The post of attaché at the court of King Theodosius was for that reason far from enjoyable. But in all other respects, thanks to his perfect common sense as a man of the world, M. de Vaugoubert was one of the best representatives of the French Government abroad. When a man who was reckoned a superior person, a Jacobin with an expert knowledge of all subjects, replaced him later on, it was not long before war broke out between France and the country over which that monarch reigned.

M. de Vaugoubert, like M. de Charlus, did not care to be the first to greet one. Both of them preferred to "respond," being constantly afraid of the gossip which the person to whom otherwise they would have offered their hand might have heard about them since their last meeting. In my case, M. de Vaugoubert had no need to ask himself this question, for I had gone up of my own accord to greet him, if only because of the difference in our ages. He replied with an air of wonder and delight, his eyes continuing to stray as though there had been a patch of forbidden clover to be grazed on either side of me. I felt that it would be more seemly to ask him to introduce me to Mme de Vaugoubert before effecting the introduction to the Prince, which I decided not to mention to him until afterwards. The idea of making me acquainted with his wife seemed to fill him with joy, for his own sake as well as for hers, and he led me with a resolute step towards the Marquise. Arriving in front of her, and indicating me with his hand and eyes, with every conceivable mark of consideration, he nevertheless remained silent and withdrew after a few moments, with a wriggling, sidelong motion, leaving me alone with his wife. She had at once given me her hand, but without knowing to whom this gesture of affability was addressed, for I realised that M. de Vaugoubert had forgotten my name, perhaps even had failed to recognise me, and being reluctant, out of politeness, to confess his ignorance, had made the introduction consist in a mere dumb show. And so I was no further advanced; how was I to get myself introduced to my host by a woman who did not know my name? Worse still, I found myself obliged to remain for some moments chatting to Mme de Vaugoubert. And this irked me for two reasons. I had no wish to remain all night at this party, having arranged with Albertine (I had given her a box for *Phèdre*) that she was to pay me a visit shortly before midnight. I was not in the least in love with her; in asking her to come this evening, I was yielding to a purely sensual desire, although we were at that torrid period of the year when sensuality, evaporating, is more readily inclined to visit the organs of taste, seeks above all things coolness. More than for the kiss of a girl, it thirsts for orangeade, for a bath, or even to gaze at that peeled and juicy moon that was quenching the thirst of heaven. I counted however upon ridding myself, in Albertine's company—which moreover reminded me of the coolness of the sea—of the regrets I was bound to feel for many a charming face (for it was a party quite as much for young girls as for married women that the Princess was giving). On the other hand, the face of the imposing Mme de Vaugoubert, Bourbonesque and morose, was in no way attractive.

It was said at the Ministry, without any suggestion of malice, that in their household it was the husband who wore the petticoats and the wife the trousers. Now there was more truth in this than was supposed. Mme de Vaugoubert really was a man. Whether she had always been one, or had grown to be as I now saw her, matters little, for in either case we are faced with one of the most touching miracles of nature which, in the latter alternative especially, makes the human kingdom resemble the kingdom of flowers. On the former hypothesis— if the future Mme de Vaugoubert had always been so heavily mannish—nature, by a fiendish and beneficent ruse, bestows on the girl the deceptive aspect of a man. And the youth who has no love for women and is seeking to be cured greets with joy this subterfuge of discovering a bride who reminds him of a market porter. In the alternative case, if the woman has not at first these masculine characteristics, she adopts them by degrees, to please her husband, and even unconsciously, by that sort of mimicry which makes certain flowers assume the appearance of the insects which they seek to attract. Her regret at not being loved, at not being a man, makes her mannish. Indeed, quite apart from the case that we are now considering, who has not remarked how often the most normal couples end by resembling each other, at times even by exchanging qualities? A former German Chancellor, Prince von Bülow, married an Italian. In the course of time it was remarked on the Pincio how much Italian delicacy the Teutonic husband had absorbed, and how much German coarseness the Italian princess. To go outside the confines of the laws which we are now tracing, everyone knows an eminent French diplomat whose origins were suggested only by his name, one of the most illustrious in the East. As he matured, as he aged, the Oriental whom no one had even suspected in him emerged, and now when we see him we regret the absence of the fez that would complete the picture.[34]

To revert to habits completely unknown to the ambassador whose ancestrally thickened profile we have just recalled, Mme de Vaugoubert personified the acquired or predestined type, the immortal example of which is the Princess Palatine, never out of a riding habit, who, having borrowed from her husband more than his virility, embracing the defects of the men who do not care for women, reports in her gossipy letters the mutual relations of all the great noblemen of the court of Louis XIV. One of the reasons which enhance still further the masculine air of women like Mme de Vaugoubert is that the neglect which they receive from their husbands, and the shame that they feel at such neglect, gradually dry up everything that is womanly in them. They end by acquiring both the good and the bad qualities which their husbands lack. The more frivolous, effeminate, indiscreet their husbands are, the more they grow into the charmless effigies of the virtues which their husbands ought to practise.

Traces of opprobrium, boredom, indignation, tarnished the regular features of Mme de Vaugoubert. Alas, I felt that she was considering me with interest and curiosity as one of those young men who appealed to M. de Vaugoubert and whom she herself would so much have liked to be now that her ageing husband showed a preference for youth. She was gazing at me with the close attention shown by provincial ladies who from an illustrated catalogue copy the tailor-made dress so becoming to the charming person in the picture (actually the same person on every page, but deceptively multiplied into different creatures, thanks to the differences of pose and the variety of attire). The instinctive attraction which urged Mme de Vaugoubert towards me was so strong that she went as far as to seize me by the arm so that I might take her to get a glass of orangeade. But I extricated myself on the pretext that I must presently be going, and had not yet been introduced to our host.

The distance between me and the garden door where he stood talking to a group of people was not very great. But it alarmed me more than if, in order to cross it, I had had to expose myself to a continuous hail of fire.

A number of women from whom I felt that I might be able to secure an introduction were in the garden, where, while feigning an ecstatic admiration, they were at a loss for something to do. Parties of this sort are as a rule premature. They have little reality until the following day, when they occupy the attention of the people who were not invited. A real writer, devoid of the foolish self-esteem of so many literary people, when he reads an article by a critic who has always expressed the greatest admiration for his works and sees the names of various inferior writers mentioned but not his own, has no time to stop and consider what might be to him a matter for astonishment; his books are calling him. But a society woman has nothing to do and, on seeing in the *Figaro*: "Last night the Prince and Princesse de Guermantes gave a large party," etc., exclaims: "What! Only three days ago I talked to Marie-Gilbert for an hour, and she never said a word about it!" and racks her brain to discover how she can have offended the Guermantes. It must be said that, so far as the Princess's parties were concerned, the astonishment was sometimes as great among those who were invited as among those who were not. For they would burst forth at the moment when one least expected them, and mobilised people whose existence Mme de Guermantes had forgotten for years. And almost all society people are so insignificant that others of their sort adopt, in judging them, only the measure of their social success, cherish them if they are invited, detest them if they are omitted. As to the latter, if it was the fact that the Princess did not invite them even though they were her friends, that was often due to her fear of annoying "Palamède," who had excommunicated them. And so I might be certain that she had not spoken of me to M. de Charlus, for otherwise I should not have found myself there. He meanwhile was posted between the house and the garden, beside the German Ambassador, leaning upon the balustrade of the great staircase which led from the garden to the house, so that the other guests, in spite of the three or four female admirers who were grouped round the Baron and almost concealed him, were obliged to greet him as they passed. He responded by naming each of them in turn. And one heard successively: "Good evening, Monsieur du Hazay, good evening, Madame de la Tour du Pin-Verclause, good evening, Madame de la Tour du Pin-Gouvernet, good evening, Philibert, good evening, my dear Ambassadress," and so on. This created a continuous yapping interspersed with benevolent suggestions or inquiries (the answers to which he ignored), which M. de Charlus addressed to them in an artificially soft and benign tone of voice that betrayed his indifference: "Take care the child doesn't catch cold, it's always rather damp in the gardens. Good evening, Madame de Brantes. Good evening, Madame de Mecklem-bourg. Have you brought your daughter? Is she wearing that delicious pink frock? Good evening, Saint-Géran." True, there was an element of pride in this attitude. M. de Charlus was aware that he was a Guermantes, and that he occupied a predominant place at this festivity. But there was more in it than pride, and the very word festivity suggested, to the man with aesthetic gifts, the luxurious, rarefied sense that it might bear if it were being given not by people in contemporary society but in a painting by Carpaccio or Veronese. It is even more probable that the German prince M. de Charlus was must rather have been picturing to himself the reception that occurs in *Tannhäuser*, and himself as the Margrave, standing at the entrance to the Warburg with a kind word of condescension for each of the guests, while their procession into the castle or the park is greeted by the long phrase, a hundred times repeated, of the famous March.

Meanwhile I had to make up my mind. I recognised beneath the trees various women with whom I was on more or less friendly terms, but they seemed transformed because they were at the Princess's and not at her cousin's, and because I saw them seated not in front of Dresden china plates but beneath the boughs of a chestnut-tree. The elegance of the setting mattered nothing. Had it been infinitely less elegant than at "Oriane's," I should have felt the same uneasiness. If the electric light in our drawing-room fails, and we are obliged to replace it with oil lamps, everything seems altered. I was rescued from my uncertainty by Mme de Souvré. "Good evening," she said, coming towards me. "Have you seen the Duchesse de Guermantes lately?" She excelled in giving to remarks of this sort an intonation which proved that she was not uttering them from sheer silliness, like people who, not knowing what to talk about, come up to you again and again to mention some mutual acquaintance, often extremely vague. She had on the contrary a subtle way of intimating with her eyes: "Don't imagine for a moment that I haven't recognised you. You are the young man I met at the Duchesse de Guermantes's. I remember very well." Unfortunately, the patronage extended to me by this remark, stupid in appearance but delicate in intention, was extremely fragile, and vanished as soon as I tried to make use of it. Mme de Souvré had the art, if called upon to convey a request to some influential person, of appearing at once in the petitioner's eyes to be recommending him, and in those of the influential person not to be recommending the petitioner, so that this ambiguous gesture gave her a credit balance of gratitude with the latter without putting her in debit with the former. Encouraged by this lady's civilities to ask her to introduce me to M. de Guermantes, I found that she took advantage of a moment when our host was not looking in our direction, laid a motherly hand on my shoulder, and, smiling at the averted face of the Prince who could not see her, thrust me towards him with a would-be protective but deliberately ineffectual gesture which left me stranded almost where I had started. Such is the cowardice of society people.

That of a lady who came to greet me, addressing me by my name, was greater still. I tried to recall hers as I talked to her; I remembered quite well having met her at dinner, and could remember things that she had said. But my attention, concentrated upon the inward region in which these memories of her lingered, was unable to discover her name there. It was there none the less. My thoughts began playing a sort of game with it to grasp its outlines, its initial letter, and finally to bring the whole name to light. It was labour in vain; I could more or less sense its mass, its weight, but as for its forms, confronting them with the shadowy captive lurking in the interior darkness, I said to myself: "That's not it." Certainly my mind would have been capable of creating the most difficult names. Unfortunately, it was not called upon to create but to reproduce. Any mental activity is easy if it need not be subjected to reality. Here I was forced to subject myself to it. Finally, in a flash, the name came back to me in its entirety: "Madame d'Arpajon." I am wrong in saying that it came, for it did not, I think, appear to me by a spontaneous propulsion. Nor do I think that the many faint memories associated with the lady, to which I did not cease to appeal for help (by such exhortations as: "Come now, it's the lady who is a friend of Mme de Souvré, who feels for Victor Hugo so artless an admiration mingled with so much alarm and horror")—nor do I think that all these memories, hovering between me and her name, served in any way to bring it to light. That great game of hide and seek which is played in our memory when we seek to recapture a name does not entail a series of gradual approximations. We see nothing, then suddenly the correct name appears and is very different from what we were trying to guess. It is not the name that has come to us. No, I believe rather that, as we go on living, we move further and further away from the zone in which a name is distinct, and it was by an exercise of my will and attention, which heightened the acuteness of my inward vision, that all of a sudden I had pierced the semi-darkness and seen daylight. In any case, if there are transitions between oblivion and memory, then these transitions are unconscious. For the intermediate names through which we pass before finding the real name are themselves false, and bring us nowhere nearer to it. They are not even, strictly speaking, names at all, but often mere consonants which are not to be found in the recaptured name. And yet this labour of the mind struggling from blankness to reality is so mysterious that it is possible after all that these false consonants are really lifelines clumsily thrown out to enable us to seize hold of the correct name. "All this," the reader will remark, "tells us nothing as to the lady's failure to oblige; but since you have made so long a digression, allow me, dear author, to waste another moment of your time by telling you that it is a pity that, young as you were (or as your hero was, if he be not yourself), you had already so feeble a memory that you could not remember the name of a lady whom you knew quite well." It is indeed a pity, dear reader. And sadder than you think when one feels that it heralds the time when names and words will vanish from the bright zone of consciousness and one must forever cease to name to oneself the people whom one has known most intimately. It is indeed regrettable that one should require this effort, when one is still young, to remember names which one knows well. But if this infirmity occurred only in the case of names barely known and quite naturally forgotten, names which one would not take the trouble to remember, the infirmity would not be without its advantages. "And what are they, may I ask?" Well, sir, infirmity alone makes us take notice and learn, and enables us to analyse mechanisms of which otherwise we should know nothing. A man who falls straight into bed night after night, and ceases to live until the moment when he wakes and rises, will surely never dream of making, I don't say great discoveries, but even minor observations about sleep. He scarcely knows that he is asleep. A little insomnia is not without its value in making us appreciate sleep, in throwing a ray of light upon that darkness. An unfailing memory is not a very powerful incentive to the study of the phenomena of memory. "Well, did Mme d'Arpajon introduce you to the Prince?" No, but be quiet and let me go on with my story.

Mme d'Arpajon was even more cowardly than Mme de Souvré, but there was more excuse for her cowardice. She knew that she had always had very little influence in society. This influence, such as it was, had been reduced still further by her liaison with the Duc de Guermantes; his desertion of her dealt it the final blow. The ill-humour aroused in her by my request that she should introduce me to the Prince produced a silence which she was ingenuous enough to imagine a convincing pretence of not having heard what I said. She was not even aware that her anger made her frown. Perhaps, on the other hand, she was aware of it, did not bother about the inconsistency, and made use of it for the lesson in tact which she was thus able to teach me without undue rudeness; I mean a silent lesson, but none the less eloquent for that.

Apart from this, Mme d'Arpajon was extremely nettled, for many eyes were raised in the direction of a Renaissance balcony at the corner of which, instead of one of those monumental statues which were so often used as ornaments at that period, there leaned, no less sculptural than they, the magnificent Duchesse de Surgis-le-Duc, who had recently succeeded Mme d'Arpajon in the affections of Basin de Guermantes. Beneath the flimsy white tulle which protected her from the cool night air, one saw the supple form of a winged victory.

I had no one else to turn to save M. de Charlus, who had withdrawn to a room downstairs which opened on to the garden. I had plenty of time (as he was pretending to be absorbed in a fictitious game of whist which enabled him to appear not to notice people) to admire the deliberate, artful simplicity of his evening coat which, by the merest trifles which only a tailor's eye could have picked out, had the air of a "Harmony in Black and White" by Whistler; black, white and red, rather, for M. de Charlus was wearing, suspended from a broad ribbon over his shirt-front, the cross, in white, black and red enamel, of a Knight of the religious Order of Malta. At that moment the Baron's game was interrupted by Mme de Gallardon, escorting her nephew, the Vicomte de Courvoisier, a young man with a pretty face and an impertinent air. "Cousin," said Mme de Gallardon, "allow me to introduce my nephew Adalbert. Adalbert, you remember the famous Uncle Pala-mède of whom you have heard so much." "Good evening, Madame de Gallardon," M. de Charlus replied. And he added, without so much as a glance at the young man: "Good evening, sir," with a truculent air and in a tone so violently discourteous that everyone in the room was stunned. Perhaps M. de Charlus, knowing that Mme de Gallardon had her doubts as to his morals and had once been unable to resist the temptation to hint at them, was determined to nip in the bud any scandal that she might embroider upon a friendly reception of her nephew, and at the same time make a resounding profession of indifference with regard to young men in general; perhaps he did not consider that the said Adalbert had responded to his aunt's words with a sufficiently respectful air; perhaps, desirous of making his mark later with so attractive a cousin, he wished to give himself the advantage of a pre-emptive attack, like those sovereigns who, before engaging upon diplomatic action, reinforce it with an act of war.

It was not so difficult as I supposed to secure M. de Charlus's consent to my request that he should introduce me to the Prince de Guermantes. For one thing, in the course of the last twenty years this Don Quixote had tilted against so many windmills (often relatives who he claimed had behaved badly to him), he had so frequently banned people as being "impossible to have in the house" from being invited by various male or female Guermantes, that these were beginning to be afraid of quarrelling with all the people they knew and liked, of condemning themselves to a lifelong deprivation of the society of certain newcomers whom they were curious to meet, by espousing the thunderous but unexplained grudges of a brother-in-law or cousin who expected them to abandon wife, brother, children for his sake. More intelligent than the other Guermantes, M. de Charlus realised that people were ceasing to pay attention to more than one in every two of his vetoes, and, with an eye to the future, fearing lest it might be he himself whose society they dispensed with, had begun to cut his losses, to lower, as the saying is, his sights. Furthermore, if he had the faculty of keeping up a feud with a detested person for months, for years on end—to such a one he would not have tolerated their sending an invitation, and would have fought like a trooper even against a queen, the status of the person who stood in his way ceasing to count for anything in his eyes—on the other hand, his explosions of rage were too frequent not to be somewhat fragmentary. "The imbecile, the scoundrel! We shall have to put him in his place, sweep him into the gutter, where unfortunately he will not be innocuous to the health of the town," he would scream, even when he was alone in his own room, on reading a letter that he considered irreverent, or on recalling some remark that had been repeated to him. But a fresh outburst against a second imbecile cancelled the first, and the former victim had only to show due deference for the fit of rage that he had occasioned to be forgotten, it not having lasted long enough to establish a foundation of hatred upon which to build. And so, perhaps—despite his ill-humour towards me—I might have been successful when I asked him to introduce me to the Prince, had I not been so ill-inspired as to add, from a scruple of conscience, and so that he might not suppose me guilty of the indelicacy of entering the house on the off chance, counting upon him to enable me to remain there: "You are aware that I know them quite well, the Princess was very nice to me." "Very well, if you know them, why do you need me to introduce you?" he replied in a waspish tone, and, turning his back, resumed his make-believe game with the Nuncio, the German Ambassador and another personage whom I did not know by sight.

Then, from the depths of those gardens where in days past the Duc d'Aiguillon used to breed rare animals, there came to my ears, through the great open doors, the sound of a sniffing nose that was savouring all those refinements and determined to miss none of them. The sound approached, I moved at a venture in its direction, with the result that the words "Good evening" were murmured in my ear by M. de Bréauté, not like the rusty metallic sound of a knife being sharpened on a grindstone, even less like the cry of the wild boar, devastator of tilled fields, but like the voice of a possible saviour.

Less influential than Mme de Souvré, but less deeply ingrained than she with unwillingness to oblige, far more at his ease with the Prince than was Mme d'Arpajon, entertaining some illusions, perhaps, as to my position in the Guermantes set, or perhaps knowing more about it than myself, he was, however, for the first few moments difficult to pin down, for he was turning in every direction, with quivering and distended nostrils, staring inquisitively through his monocle as though he were confronted with five hundred matchless works of art. But, having heard my request, he received it with satisfaction, led me towards the Prince and presented me to him with a lip-smacking, ceremonious, vulgar air, as though he had been handing him a plate of cakes with a word of commendation. Whereas the Duc de Guermantes's greeting was, when he chose, friendly, instinct with good fellowship, cordial and familiar, I found that of the Prince stiff, solemn and haughty. He barely smiled at me, addressed me gravely as "Sir." I had often heard the Duke make fun of his cousin's hauteur. But from the first words that he addressed to me, which by their cold and serious tone formed the most complete contrast with Basin's comradely language, I realised at once that the fundamentally disdainful man was the Duke, who spoke to you at your first meeting with him as "man to man," and that, of the two cousins, the one who was genuinely simple and natural was the Prince. I found in his reserve a stronger feeling if not of equality, for that would have been inconceivable to him, at least of the consideration which one may show for an inferior, such as may be found in all strongly hierarchical societies, in the Law Courts, for instance, or in a Faculty, where a public prosecutor or a dean, conscious of their high charge, conceal perhaps more genuine simplicity, and, when you come to know them better, more kindness and cordiality, beneath their traditional aloofness than the more modern brethren beneath their jocular affectation of comradeship. "Do you intend to follow the career of your distinguished father?" he inquired with a distant but interested air. I answered the question briefly, realising that he had asked it only out of politeness, and moved away to allow him to greet new arrivals.

I caught sight of Swann, and wanted to speak to him, but at that moment I saw that the Prince de Guermantes, instead of waiting where he was to receive the greeting of Odette's husband, had immediately carried him off, with the force of a suction pump, to the further end of the garden, in order, some people said, "to show him the door."

So bewildered in the midst of the glittering company that I did not learn until two days later, from the newspapers, that a Czech orchestra had been playing throughout the evening, and that fireworks had been going off in constant succession, I recovered some power of attention with the thought of going to look at the famous Hubert Robert fountain.

It could be seen from a distance, slender, motionless, rigid, set apart in a clearing surrounded by fine trees, several of which were as old as itself, only the lighter fall of its pale and quivering plume stirring in the breeze. The eighteenth century had refined the elegance of its lines, but, by fixing the style of the jet, seemed to have arrested its life; at this distance one had the impression of art rather than the sensation of water. Even the moist cloud that was perpetually gathering at its summit preserved the character of the period like those that assemble in the sky round the palaces of Versailles. But from a closer view one realised that, while it respected, like the stones of an ancient palace, the design traced for it beforehand, it was a constantly changing stream of water that, springing upwards and seeking to obey the architect's original orders, performed them to the letter only by seeming to infringe them, its thousand separate bursts succeeding only from afar in giving the impression of a single thrust. This was in reality as often interrupted as the scattering of the fall, whereas from a distance it had appeared to me dense, inflexible, unbroken in its continuity. From a little nearer, one saw that this continuity, apparently complete, was assured, at every point in the ascent of the jet where it must otherwise have been broken, by the entering into line, by the lateral incorporation of a parallel jet which mounted higher than the first and was itself, at a greater altitude which was however already a strain upon its endurance, relieved by a third. From close to, exhausted drops could be seen falling back from the column of water, passing their sisters on the way up, and at times, torn and scattered, caught in an eddy of the night air, disturbed by this unremitting surge, floating awhile before being drowned in the basin. They teased with their hesitations, with their journey in the opposite direction, and blurred with their soft vapour the vertical tension of the shaft that bore aloft an oblong cloud composed of countless tiny drops but seemingly painted in an unchanging golden brown which rose, unbreakable, fixed, slender, swift, to mingle with the clouds in the sky. Unfortunately, a gust of wind was enough to scatter it obliquely on the ground; at times indeed a single disobedient jet swerved and, had they not kept a respectful distance, would have drenched to their skins the incautious crowd of gazers.

One of these little accidents, which occurred only when the breeze freshened for a moment, was somewhat unpleasant. Mme d'Arpajon had been led to believe that the Duc de Guermantes, who in fact had not yet arrived, was with Mme de Surgis in one of the galleries of pink marble to which one ascended by the double colonnade, hollowed out of the wall, which rose from the brink of the fountain. Now, just as Mme d'Arpajon was making for one of these colonnades, a strong gust of warm air deflected the jet of water and inundated the fair lady so completely that, the water streaming down from her low neckline inside her dress, she was as thoroughly soaked as if she had been plunged into a bath. Whereupon, a few feet away, a rhythmical roar resounded, loud enough to be heard by a whole army, and at the same time periodically prolonged as though it were being addressed not to the army as a whole but to each unit in turn; it was the Grand Duke Vladimir, laughing whole-heartedly on seeing the immersion of Mme d'Arpajon, one of the funniest sights, as he was never tired of repeating afterwards, that he had ever seen in his life. Some charitable persons having suggested to the Muscovite that a word of sympathy from himself was perhaps called for and would give pleasure to the lady who, notwithstanding her forty years and more, mopping herself up with her scarf without appealing to anyone for help, was bravely extricating herself in spite of the water that was mischievously spilling over the edge of the basin, the Grand Duke, who had a kind heart, felt that he ought to comply, and before the last military tattoo of his laughter had altogether subsided, one heard a fresh roar, even more vociferous than the last. "Bravo, old girl!" he cried, clapping his hands as though at the theatre. Mme d'Arpajon was not at all pleased that her dexterity should be commended at the expense of her youth. And when someone remarked to her, in a voice drowned by the roar of the water, over which the princely thunder could nevertheless be heard: "I think His Imperial Highness said something to you," "No! It was to Mme de Souvré," was her reply.

I passed through the gardens and returned by the stair, upon which the absence of the Prince, who had vanished with Swann, swelled the crowd of guests round M. de Charlus, just as, when Louis XIV was not at Versailles, there was a more numerous attendance upon Monsieur, his brother. I was stopped on my way by the Baron, while behind me two ladies and a young man came up to greet him.

"It's nice to see you here," he said to me, holding out his hand. "Good evening, Madame de la Trémoïlle, good evening, my dear Herminie." But doubtless the memory of what he had said to me as to his own supreme position in the Hôtel Guermantes made him wish to appear to be drawing, from a circumstance which displeased him but which he had been unable to prevent, a satisfaction which his lordly insolence and hysterical glee immediately invested in a cloak of exaggerated sarcasm: "It's nice," he went on, "but above all it's extremely funny." And he broke into peals of laughter which appeared to be indicative at once of his amusement and of the inadequacy of human speech to express it. Certain of the guests, meanwhile, who knew both how difficult he was of access and how prone to offensive outbursts, had been drawn towards us by curiosity and now, with an almost indecent haste, took to their heels. "Come, now, don't be cross," he said to me, patting me gently on the shoulder, "you know I'm fond of you. Good evening, Antioche, good evening, Louis-René. Have you been to look at the fountain?" he asked me in a tone that was more affirmative than questioning. "Very pretty, is it not? Marvellous though it is, it could be better still, naturally, if certain things were removed, and then there would be nothing like it in France. But even as it stands, it's quite one of the best things. Bréauté will tell you that it was a mistake to put lamps round it, to try and make people forget that it was he who was responsible for that absurd idea. But on the whole he didn't manage to spoil it too much. It's far more difficult to disfigure a great work of art than to create one. Not that we hadn't a shrewd suspicion all the time that Bréauté was not quite a match for Hubert Robert."

I drifted back into the stream of guests who were going into the house. "Have you seen my delicious cousin Oriane lately?" I was asked by the Princess who had now deserted her post by the door and with whom I found myself making my way back to the rooms. "She's coming to-night. I saw her this afternoon," my hostess added, "and she promised she would. Incidentally, I gather that you will be dining with us both to meet the Queen of Italy at the embassy on Thursday. There'll be every imaginable royalty—it will be most alarming." They could not in any way alarm the Princesse de Guermantes, whose rooms swarmed with them and who would say "my little Coburgs" as she might have said "my little dogs." And so she said "It will be most alarming," out of sheer silliness, a characteristic which, in society people, overrides even their vanity. With regard to her own genealogy, she knew less than a history graduate. As regards the people of her circle, she liked to show that she knew the nicknames with which they had been labelled. Having asked me whether I was dining the following week with the Marquise de la Pommelière, who was often called "la Pomme," the Princess, having elicited a negative reply, remained silent for some moments. Then, without any other motive than a deliberate display of involuntary erudition, banality, and conformity to the prevailing spirit, she added: "She's quite an agreeable woman, la Pomme!"

While the Princess was talking to me, it so happened that the Duc and Duchesse de Guermantes made their entrance. But I was unable to go at once to meet them, for I was waylaid by the Turkish Ambassadress, who, pointing to our hostess whom I had just left, exclaimed as she seized me by the arm: "Ah! What a delightful woman the Princess is! What a superior person! I feel sure that, if I were a man," she went on, with a trace of Oriental servility and sensuality, "I would give my life for that heavenly creature." I replied that I did indeed find her charming, but that I knew her cousin the Duchess better. "But there is no comparison," said the Ambassadress. "Oriane is a charming society woman who gets her wit from Mémé and Babal, whereas Marie-Gilbert is *somebody*."

I never much like to be told like this, without a chance to reply, what I ought to think about people whom I know. And there was no reason why the Turkish Ambassadress should be in any way better qualified than myself to judge the merits of the Duchesse de Guermantes. On the other hand (and this also explained my irritation with the Ambassadress), the defects of a mere acquaintance, and even of a friend, are to us real poisons, against which we are fortunately immunised. But, without applying any standard of scientific comparison and talking of anaphylaxis, we may say that, at the heart of our friendly or purely social relations, there lurks a hostility momentarily cured but sporadically recurrent. As a rule, we suffer little from these poisons so long as people are "natural." By saying "Babal" and "Mémé" to indicate people with whom she was not acquainted, the Turkish Ambassadress suspended the effects of the immunisation which normally made me find her tolerable. She irritated me, and this was all the more unfair inasmuch as she did not speak like this to make me think that she was an intimate friend of "Mémé," but owing to a too rapid education which made her name these noble lords in accordance with what she believed to be the custom of the country. She had crowded her course into a few months instead of working her way up gradually.

But on thinking it over, I found another reason for my

disinclination to remain in the Ambassadress's company. It was not so very long since, at "Oriane's," this same diplomatic personage had said to me, with a purposeful and serious air, that she found the Princesse de Guermantes frankly antipathetic. I felt that I need not stop to consider this change of front: the invitation to the party this evening had brought it about. The Ambassadress was perfectly sincere in saying that the Princesse de Guermantes was a sublime creature. She had always thought so. But, having never before been invited to the Princess's house, she had felt herself bound to give this non-invitation the appearance of a deliberate abstention on principle. Now that she had been asked, and would presumably continue to be asked in the future, she could give free expression to her feelings. There is no need, in accounting for nine out of ten of the opinions that we hold about other people, to go so far as crossed love or exclusion from public office. Our judgment remains uncertain: the withholding or bestowal of an invitation determines it. At all events, the Turkish Ambassadress, as the Duchesse de Guermantes remarked while making a tour of inspection through the rooms with me, "looked well." She was, above all, extremely useful. The real stars of society are tired of appearing there. He who is curious to gaze at them must often migrate to another hemisphere, where they are more or less alone. But women like the Ottoman Ambassadress, a newcomer to society, are never weary of shining there, and, so to speak, everywhere at once. They are of value at entertainments of the sort known as receptions or routs, to which they would let themselves be dragged from their deathbeds rather than miss one. They are the supers upon whom a hostess can always count, determined never to miss a party. Hence foolish young men, unaware that they are false stars, take them for the queens of fashion, whereas it would require a formal lecture to explain to them by virtue of what reasons Mme Standish, who remains unknown to them, painting cushions far away from society, is at least as great a lady as the Duchesse de Doudeauville.

In the ordinary course of life, the eyes of the Duchesse de Guermantes were abstracted and slightly melancholy; she made them sparkle with a flame of wit only when she had

to say how-d'ye-do to a friend, precisely as though the said
friend had been some witty remark, some charming touch,
some titbit for delicate palates, the sampling of which has
brought an expression of refined delight to the face of the
connoisseur. But at big receptions, as she had too many
greetings to bestow, she decided that it would be tiring to
have to switch off the light after each. Just as a literary en-
thusiast, when he goes to the theatre to see a new play by one
of the masters of the stage, testifies to his certainty that he is
not going to spend a dull evening by having, while he hands
his hat and coat to the attendant, his lip adjusted in readiness
for a sapient smile, his eye kindled for knowing approval;
similarly it was from the very moment of her arrival that the
Duchess lit up for the whole evening. And while she was
handing over her evening cloak, of a magnificent Tiepolo red,
exposing a huge collar of rubies round her neck, having cast
over her dress that final rapid, meticulous and exhaustive
dressmaker's glance which is also that of a woman of the world,
Oriane made sure that her eyes were sparkling no less brightly
than her other jewels. In vain did sundry "kind friends" such
as M. de Jouville fling themselves upon the Duke to keep him
from entering: "But don't you know that poor Mama is at his
last gasp? He has just been given the last sacraments." "I know,
I know," answered M. de Guermantes, thrusting the tiresome
fellow aside in order to enter the room. "The viaticum has
had an excellent effect," he added with a smile of pleasure at the
thought of the ball which he was determined not to miss after
the Prince's party. "We didn't want people to know that we
had come back," the Duchess said to me, unaware of the fact
that the Princess had already disproved this statement by telling
me that she had seen her cousin for a moment and that she
had promised to come. The Duke, after a protracted stare with
which he proceeded to crush his wife for the space of five
minutes, observed: "I told Oriane about your misgivings."
Now that she saw that they were unfounded, and that she need
take no action to dispel them, she pronounced them absurd,
and continued to chaff me about them. "The idea of supposing
that you weren't invited! One's always invited! Besides, there
was me. Do you think I couldn't have got you an invitation to

my cousin's house?" I must admit that subsequently she often did things for me that were far more difficult; nevertheless, I took care not to interpret her words in the sense that I had been too modest. I was beginning to learn the exact value of the language, spoken or mute, of aristocratic affability, an affability that is happy to shed balm upon the sense of inferiority of those towards whom it is directed, though not to the point of dispelling that inferiority, for in that case it would no longer have any *raison d'être*. "But you are our equal, if not our superior," the Guermantes seemed, in all their actions, to be saying; and they said it in the nicest way imaginable, in order to be loved and admired, but not to be believed; that one should discern the fictitious character of this affability was what they called being well-bred; to suppose it to be genuine, a sign of ill-breeding. Shortly after this, as it happened, I was to receive a lesson which finally enlightened me, with the most perfect accuracy, as to the extent and limits of certain forms of aristocratic affability. It was at an afternoon party given by the Duchesse de Montmorency for the Queen of England. There was a sort of royal procession to the buffet, at the head of which walked Her Majesty on the arm of the Duc de Guermantes. I happened to arrive at that moment. With his free hand the Duke conveyed to me, from a distance of nearly fifty yards, countless signs of friendly welcome, which appeared to mean that I need not be afraid to approach, that I should not be devoured alive instead of the Cheshire cheese sandwiches. But I, who was becoming word-perfect in the language of the court, instead of going even one step nearer, made a deep bow from where I was, without smiling, the sort of bow that I should have made to someone I scarcely knew, then proceeded in the opposite direction. Had I written a masterpiece, the Guermantes would have given me less credit for it than I earned by that bow. Not only did it not pass unperceived by the Duke, although he had that day to acknowledge the greetings of more than five hundred people; it also caught the eye of the Duchess, who, happening to meet my mother, told her of it, and, so far from suggesting that I had done wrong, that I ought to have gone up to him, said that her husband had been lost in admiration of my bow, that it would have been impossible for anyone to put more into it. They never ceased to find in that bow every possible merit, without however mentioning the one which had seemed the most precious of all, to wit that it had been tactful; nor did they cease to pay me compliments which I understood to be even less a reward for the past than a hint for the future, after the fashion of a hint delicately conveyed to his pupils by the head of an educational establishment: "Do not forget, my boys, that these prizes are intended not so much for you as for your parents, so that they may send you back next term." So it was that Mme de Marsantes, when someone from a different world entered her circle, would praise in his hearing those unobtrusive people "who are there when you want them and the rest of the time let you forget their existence," as one indirectly reminds a servant who smells that the practice of taking a bath is beneficial to the health.

While, before she had even left the entrance hall, I was talking to Mme de Guermantes, I could hear a voice of a sort which henceforth I was able to identify without the least possibility of error. It was, in this particular instance, the voice of M. de Vaugoubert talking to M. de Charlus. A skilled physician need not even make his patient unbutton his shirt, nor listen to his breathing—the sound of his voice is enough. How often, in time to come, was my ear to be caught in a drawing-room by the intonation or laughter of some man whose artificial voice, for all that he was reproducing exactly the language of his profession or the manners of his class, affecting a stern aloofness or a coarse familiarity, was enough to indicate "He is a Charlus" to my trained ear, like the note of a tuning-fork! At that moment the entire staff of one of the embassies went past, pausing to greet M. de Charlus. For all that my discovery of the sort of malady in question dated only from that afternoon (when I had surprised M. de Charlus with Jupien) I should have had no need to ask questions or to sound the chest before giving a diagnosis. But M. de Vaugoubert, when talking to M. de Charlus, appeared uncertain. And yet he should have known where he stood after the doubts of his adolescence. The invert believes himself to be the only one of his kind in the universe; it is only in later years that

he imagines—another exaggeration—that the unique exception is the normal man. But, ambitious and timorous, M. de
Vaugoubert had not for many years past surrendered himself
to what would to him have meant pleasure. The career of
diplomacy had had the same effect upon his life as taking orders.
Combined with his assiduous frequentation of the School of
Political Sciences, it had doomed him from his twentieth year
to the chastity of a Desert Father. And so, as each of our senses
loses some of its strength and keenness, becomes atrophied
when it is no longer exercised, M. de Vaugoubert, just as
the civilised man is no longer capable of the feats of strength,
of the acuteness of hearing of the cave-dweller, had lost that
special perspicacity which was rarely lacking in M. de Charlus;
and at official banquets, whether in Paris or abroad, the
Minister Plenipotentiary was no longer capable of identifying
those who, beneath the disguise of their uniform, were at
heart his congeners. Certain names mentioned by M. de
Charlus, indignant if he himself was cited for his inclinations,
but always delighted to give away those of other people, caused
M. de Vaugoubert an exquisite surprise. Not that, after all
these years, he dreamed of taking advantage of any windfall.
But these rapid revelations, similar to those which in Racine's
tragedies inform Athalie and Abner that Joas is of the House of
David, that Esther, "enthroned in the purple," has "Yid"
parents, changing the aspect of the X—— Legation, or of one
or another department of the Ministry of Foreign Affairs,
rendered those palaces as mysterious, in retrospect, as the
Temple at Jerusalem or the throne-room at Susa. At the sight
of the youthful staff of his embassy advancing in a body to
shake hands with M. de Charlus, M. de Vaugoubert assumed
the astonished air of Elise exclaiming, in *Esther*: "Great
heavens! What a swarm of innocent beauties issuing from all
sides presents itself to my gaze! How charming a modesty is
depicted on their faces!" Then, athirst for more definite
information, he glanced smilingly at M. de Charlus with a
fatuously interrogative and concupiscent expression: "Why,
of course they are," said M. de Charlus with the learned air of
a scholar speaking to an ignoramus. From that instant M. de
Vaugoubert (greatly to the annoyance of M. de Charlus) could

not tear his eyes away from these young secretaries whom the
X—— Ambassador to France, an old stager, had not chosen
blindfold. M. de Vaugoubert remained silent; I could only see
his eyes. But, being accustomed from my childhood to apply,
even to what is voiceless, the language of the classics, I read
into M. de Vaugoubert's eyes the lines in which Esther explains to Elise that Mardochée, in his zeal for his religion,
has made it a rule that only those maidens who profess it shall
be employed about the Queen's person. "And now his love
for our nation has peopled this palace with daughters of Zion,
young and tender flowers wafted by fate, transplanted like
myself beneath a foreign sky. In a place set apart from profane
eyes, he" (the worthy Ambassador) "devotes his skill and
labour to shaping them."

At length M. de Vaugoubert spoke, otherwise than with his
eyes. "Who knows," he said sadly, "whether in the country
where I live the same thing does not exist also?" "It is
probable," replied M. de Charlus, "starting with King
Theodosius, though I don't know anything definite about
him." "Oh, dear, no! not in the least!" "Then he has no right
to look it so completely. Besides, he has all the little tricks.
He has that 'my dear' manner, which I detest more than anything in the world. I should never dare to be seen walking in
the street with him. Anyhow, you must know him for what he
is, he's quite notorious." "You're entirely mistaken about him.
In any case he's quite charming. On the day the agreement with
France was signed, the King embraced me. I've never been
so moved." "That was the moment to tell him what you
wanted." "Oh, good heavens! What an idea! If he were even
to suspect such a thing! But I have no fear in that direction."
Words which I heard, for I was standing close by, and which
made me recite to myself: "The King unto this day knows not
who I am, and this secret keeps my tongue still enchained."

This dialogue, half mute, half spoken, had lasted only a few
moments, and I had barely entered the first of the drawing-
rooms with the Duchesse de Guermantes, when a little dark
lady, extremely pretty, stopped her:

"I've been looking for you everywhere. D'Annunzio saw
you from a box in the theatre, and he wrote the Princesse de

T—— a letter in which he says that he never saw anything so
lovely. He would give his life for ten minutes' conversation
with you. In any case, even if you can't or won't, the letter is
in my possession. You must fix a day to come and see me.
There are some secrets which I cannot tell you here. I see you
don't remember me," she added, turning to me; "I met you
at the Princesse de Parme's" (where I had never been). "The
Emperor of Russia is anxious for your father to be sent to
Petersburg. If you could come in on Tuesday, Isvolski himself
will be there, and he'll talk to you about it. I have a present
for you, my dear," she went on, turning back to the Duchess,
"which I should not dream of giving to anyone but you. The
manuscripts of three of Ibsen's plays, which he sent to me by
his old attendant. I shall keep one and give you the other two."

The Duc de Guermantes was not overpleased by these
offers. Uncertain whether Ibsen or D'Annunzio were dead or
alive, he could see in his mind's eye a tribe of authors and
playwrights coming to call upon his wife and putting her in
their works. People in society are too apt to think of a book
as a sort of cube one side of which has been removed, so that
the author can at once "put in" the people he meets. This is
obviously rather underhand, and writers are a pretty low class.
True, it's not a bad thing to meet them once in a way, for
thanks to them, when one reads a book or an article, one
"gets to know the inside story," one "sees people in their true
colours." On the whole, though, the wisest thing is to stick
to dead authors. M. de Guermantes considered "perfectly
decent" only the gentleman who did the funeral notices in the
Gaulois. He, at any rate, was content to include M. de Guermantes at the head of the list of people present "among others"
at funerals at which the Duke had given his name. When he
preferred that his name should not appear, instead of giving it,
he sent a letter of condolence to the relatives of the deceased,
assuring them of his deep and heartfelt sympathy. If, then, the
family inserted an announcement in the paper: "Among the
letters received, we may mention one from the Duc de Guermantes," etc., this was the fault not of the ink-slinger but of
the son, brother, father of the deceased whom the Duke
thereupon denounced as upstarts, and with whom he decided

for the future to have no further dealings (what he called, not being very well up in the meaning of such expressions, "having a crow to pick"). At all events, the names of Ibsen and D'Annunzio, and his uncertainty as to their continued survival, brought a frown to the brow of the Duke, who was not yet far enough away from us to avoid hearing the various blandishments of Mme Timoléon d'Amoncourt. She was a charming woman, her wit, like her beauty, so entrancing that either of them by itself would have made her shine. But, born outside the world in which she now lived, having aspired at first merely to a literary salon, the friend successively—and nothing more than a friend, for her morals were above reproach—and exclusively of all the great writers, who gave her their manuscripts, wrote books for her, chance having once introduced her into the Faubourg Saint-Germain, these literary privileges served her well there. She had now an established position, and no longer needed to dispense other graces than those that were shed by her presence. But, accustomed in the past to social manoeuvring, to worldly stratagems, she persevered in these things even when they were no longer necessary. She had always a state secret to reveal to you, a potentate whom you must meet, a water-colour by a master to present to you. There was indeed in all these superfluous attractions a trace of falsehood, but they made her life a comedy that scintillated with complications, and it was no exaggeration to say that she was responsible for the appointment of prefects and generals.

As she strolled by my side, the Duchesse de Guermantes allowed the azure light of her eyes to float in front of her, but vaguely, so as to avoid the people with whom she did not wish to enter into relations, whose presence she discerned from time to time like a menacing reef in the distance. We advanced between a double hedge of guests, who, conscious that they would never come to know "Oriane," were anxious at least to point her out, as a curiosity, to their wives: "Quick, Ursule, come and look at Madame de Guermantes talking to that young man." And one felt that in another moment they would be clambering upon the chairs for a better view, as at the military review on the 14th July or the Grand Prix. Not that the Duchesse de Guermantes had a more aristocratic salon than her cousin. The former's was frequented by people whom the latter would never have been willing to invite, chiefly because of her husband. She would never have been at home to Mme Alphonse de Rothschild, who, an intimate friend of Mme de la Trémoïlle and of Mme de Sagan, as was Oriane herself, was constantly to be seen in the house of the last-named. It was the same with Baron Hirsch, whom the Prince of Wales had brought to her house but not to that of the Princess, who would not have approved of him, and also with certain outstanding Bonapartist or even Republican celebrities whom the Duchess found interesting but whom the Prince, a convinced Royalist, would on principle not have allowed inside his house. His antisemitism, being also founded on principle, did not yield before any social distinction, however strongly accredited, and if he was at home to Swann, whose friend he had been from time immemorial—being, however, the only Guermantes who addressed him as Swann and not as Charles—this was because, knowing that Swann's grandmother, a Protestant married to a Jew, had been the Duc de Berry's mistress, he endeavoured, from time to time, to believe in the legend which made out Swann's father to be that prince's natural son. On this hypothesis, which incidentally was false, Swann, the son of a Catholic father himself the son of a Bourbon by a Catholic mother, was a gentile to his finger-tips.

"What, you don't know these splendours?" said the Duchess, referring to the rooms through which we were moving. But, having given its due meed of praise to her cousin's "palace," she hastened to add that she infinitely preferred her own "humble den." "This is an admirable house to *visit*. But I should die of misery if I had to stay and sleep in rooms that have witnessed so many historic events. It would give me the feeling of having been left behind after closing-time, forgotten, in the Château of Blois, or Fontainebleau, or even the Louvre, with no antidote to my depression except to tell myself that I was in the room in which Monaldeschi was murdered. As a sedative, that is not good enough. Why, here comes Mme de Saint-Euverte. We've just been dining with her. As she is giving her great annual beanfeast to-morrow,

I supposed she would be going straight to bed. But she can never miss a party. If this one had been in the country, she would have jumped on a delivery-van rather than not go to it."

As a matter of fact, Mme de Saint-Euverte had come this evening less for the pleasure of not missing another person's party than in order to ensure the success of her own, recruit the latest additions to her list, and, so to speak, hold an eleventh-hour review of the troops who were on the morrow to perform such brilliant manoeuvres at her garden-party. For in the course of the years the guests at the Saint-Euverte parties had almost entirely changed. The female celebrities of the Guermantes world, formerly so sparsely scattered, had—loaded with attentions by their hostess—begun gradually to bring their friends. At the same time, by a similarly gradual process, but in the opposite direction, Mme de Saint-Euverte had year by year reduced the number of persons unknown to the world of fashion. One after another had ceased to be seen. For some time the "batch" system was in operation, which enabled her, thanks to parties over which a veil of silence was drawn, to summon the ineligibles separately to entertain one another, which dispensed her from having to invite them with the best people. What cause had they for complaint? Were they not given (*panem et circenses*) light refreshments and a select musical programme? And so, in a kind of symmetry with the two exiled duchesses whom formerly, when the Saint-Euverte salon was only starting, one used to see holding up its shaky pediment like a pair of caryatids, in these later years one could distinguish, mingling with the fashionable throng, only two heterogeneous persons: old Mme de Cambremer and the architect's wife with a fine voice who often had to be asked to sing. But, no longer knowing anybody at Mme de Saint-Euverte's, bewailing their lost comrades, feeling out of place, they looked as though they might at any moment die of cold, like two swallows that have not migrated in time. And so, the following year, they were not invited. Mme de Franquetot made an appeal on behalf of her cousin, who was so fond of music. But as she could obtain for her no more explicit reply than the words: "Why, people can always come in and listen to music, if they like; there's nothing criminal about that!" Mme de Cambremer did not find the invitation sufficiently pressing, and abstained.

Such a transformation having been effected by Mme de Saint-Euverte, from a leper colony to a gathering of great ladies (the latest form, apparently ultra-smart, that it had assumed), it might seem odd that the person who on the following day was to give the most brilliant party of the season should need to appear overnight to address a final appeal to her troops. But the fact was that the pre-eminence of Mme de Saint-Euverte's salon existed only for those whose social life consists exclusively in reading the accounts of afternoon and evening parties in the *Gaulois* or the *Figaro*, without ever having been present at any of them. To these worldlings who see the world only through the newspapers, the enumeration of the British, Austrian, etc., ambassadresses, of the Duchesses d'Uzès, de la Trémoïlle, etc., etc., was sufficient to make them automatically imagine the Saint-Euverte salon to be the first in Paris, whereas it was among the last. Not that the reports were mendacious. The majority of the persons mentioned had indeed been present. But each of them had come in response to entreaties, civilities, favours, and with the sense of doing infinite honour to Mme de Saint-Euverte. Such salons, shunned rather than sought after, which are attended as a sort of official duty, deceive no one but the fair readers of the "Society" columns. They pass over a really fashionable party, the sort at which the hostess, who could have had all the duchesses in existence, every one of them athirst to be "numbered among the elect," has invited only two or three. And so these hostesses, who do not send a list of their guests to the papers, ignorant or contemptuous of the power that publicity has acquired to-day, are considered fashionable by the Queen of Spain but are overlooked by the crowd, because the former knows and the latter does not know who they are.

Mme de Saint-Euverte was not one of these women, and, like the busy bee she was, had come to gather up for the morrow everyone who had been invited. M. de Charlus was not among these, having always refused to go to her house. But he had quarrelled with so many people that Mme de Saint-Euverte might put this down to his peculiar nature.

Of course, if it had been only Oriane, Mme de Saint-Euverte need not have put herself to the trouble, for the invitation had been given by word of mouth, and moreover accepted with that charming and deceptive grace which is practised to perfection by those Academicians from whose doors the candidate emerges with a warm glow, never doubting that he can count upon their support. But there were others as well. The Prince d'Agrigente—would he come? And Mme de Durfort? And so, keeping a weather eye open, Mme de Saint-Euverte had thought it expedient to appear on the scene in person; insinuating with some, imperative with others, to all alike she hinted in veiled words at unimaginable attractions which could never be seen anywhere again, and promised each of them that they would find at her house the person they most desired or the personage they most needed to meet. And this sort of function with which she was invested on one day in the year—like certain public offices in the ancient world—as the person who is to give on the morrow the biggest garden-party of the season, conferred upon her a momentary authority. Her lists were made up and closed, so that while she wandered slowly through the Princess's rooms dropping into one ear after another: "You won't forget to-morrow," she had the ephemeral glory of averting her eyes, while continuing to smile, if she caught sight of some ugly duckling who was to be avoided or some country squire for whom the bond of a schoolboy friendship had secured admission to "Gilbert's," and whose presence at her garden-party would be no gain. She preferred not to speak to him so as to be able to say later on: "I issued my invitations verbally, and unfortunately I didn't meet you anywhere." And so she, a mere Saint-Euverte, set to work with her gimlet eyes to pick and choose among the guests at the Princess's party. And she imagined herself, in so doing, to be every inch a Duchesse de Guermantes.

It must be said that the latter too did not enjoy to the extent that one might suppose the unrestricted use of her greetings and smiles. Sometimes, no doubt, when she withheld them, it was deliberately: "But the woman bores me to tears," she would say. "Am I expected to talk to her about the party for the next hour?" (A duchess of swarthy complexion went past, whose ugliness and stupidity, and certain irregularities of conduct, had exiled her not from society as a whole but from certain intimate friendships. "Ah!" murmured Mme de Guermantes, with the sharp, unerring glance of the connoisseur who is shown a false jewel, "so they invite *that* here!" From the mere sight of this semi-tarnished lady, whose face was burdened with a surfeit of moles from which black hairs sprouted, Mme de Guermantes gauged the mediocrity of this party. They had been brought up together, but she had severed all relations with the lady; and responded to her greeting only with the curtest little nod. "I cannot understand," she said to me as if to excuse herself, "how Marie-Gilbert can invite us with all these dregs. It looks as though there are people from every parish. Mélanie Pourtalès arranged things far better. She could have the Orthodox Synod and the Oratoire Protestants in her house if she liked, but at least she didn't invite us on those days.") But in many cases, it was from timidity, fear of a scene with her husband, who did not like her to entertain artists and such-like (Marie-Gilbert took a kindly interest in dozens of them: you had to take care not to be accosted by some illustrious German diva), from some misgivings, too, with regard to nationalist feeling, which, inasmuch as she was endowed like M. de Charlus with the wit of the Guermantes, she despised from the social point of view (people were now, for the greater glory of the General Staff, sending a plebeian general in to dinner before certain dukes), but to which nevertheless, as she knew that she was considered unsound in her views, she made large concessions, even dreading the prospect of having to shake hands with Swann in these anti-semitic surroundings. With regard to this, her mind was soon set at rest, for she learned that the Prince had refused to have Swann in the house and had had "a sort of an altercation" with him. There was no risk of her having to converse in public with "poor Charles," whom she preferred to cherish in private.

"And who in the world is that?" Mme de Guermantes exclaimed, on seeing a little lady with a slightly lost air, in a black dress so simple that you would have taken her for a pauper, make her a deep bow, as did also her husband. She did not recognise the lady and, in her insolent way, drew herself up as though offended and stared at her without responding: "Who is that person, Basin?" she asked with an air of astonishment, while M. de Guermantes, to atone for Oriane's impoliteness, bowed to the lady and shook hands with her husband. "Why, it's Mme de Chaussepierre, you were most impolite." "I've never heard of Chaussepierre." "Old mother Chanlivault's nephew." "I haven't the faintest idea what you're talking about. Who is the woman, and why does she bow to me?" "But you know perfectly well; she's Mme de Charleval's daughter, Henriette Montmorency." "Oh, but I knew her mother quite well. She was charming, extremely intelligent. What made her go and marry all these people I've never heard of? You say she calls herself Mme de Chaussepierre?" she asked, spelling out the name with a questioning look, as though she were afraid of getting it wrong. The Duke looked at her sternly. "It's not so ridiculous as you appear to think, to be called Chaussepierre! Old Chaussepierre was the brother of the aforesaid Chanlivault, of Mme de Sennecour and of the Vicomtesse du Merlerault. They're excellent people." "Oh, do stop," cried the Duchess, who, like a lion-tamer, never cared to give the impression of being intimidated by the devouring glare of the animal. "Basin, you are the joy of my life. I can't imagine where you unearthed those names, but I congratulate you on them. If I did not know Chaussepierre, I have at least read Balzac—you're not the only one—and I've even read Labiche. I can appreciate Chanlivault, I do not object to Charleval, but I must confess that du Merlerault is a masterpiece. However, I must admit that Chaussepierre is not bad either. You must have gone about collecting them, it's not possible. You mean to write a book," she added, turning to me, "you ought to make a note of Charleval and du Merlerault. You won't find anything better." "He'll find himself in the dock, and will go to prison; you're giving him very bad advice, Oriane." "I hope, for his own sake, that he has younger people than me at his disposal if he wishes to ask for bad advice, especially if he means to follow it. But if he means to do nothing worse than write a book!"

At some distance from us, a wonderful, proud young woman

stood out delicately from the throng in a white dress, all diamonds and tulle. Mme de Guermantes watched her talking to a whole group of people fascinated by her grace.

"Your sister is the belle of the ball, as usual; she is charming to-night," she said, as she took a chair, to the Prince de Chimay who was passing.

Colonel de Froberville (the General of that name was his uncle) came and sat down beside us, as did M. de Bréauté, while M. de Vaugoubert, after hovering about us (by an excess of politeness which he maintained even when playing tennis, thus, by dint of asking leave of the eminent personages present before hitting the ball, invariably losing the game for his partner), returned to M. de Charlus (until that moment almost concealed by the huge skirt of the Comtesse Molé, whom he professed to admire above all other women), just as several members of the latest diplomatic mission to Paris chanced to be greeting the Baron. At the sight of a young secretary with a particularly intelligent look, M. de Vaugoubert fastened on M. de Charlus a smile in which a single question visibly shone. M. de Charlus would perhaps readily have compromised someone else, but he was exasperated to feel himself compromised by a smile on another person's lips which could have but one meaning. "I know absolutely nothing about the matter. I beg you to keep your curiosity to yourself. It leaves me more than cold. Besides, in this instance, you are making a mistake of the first order. I believe this young man to be absolutely the opposite." Here M. de Charlus, irritated at being thus given away by a fool, was not speaking the truth. Had the Baron been correct, the secretary would have been the exception to the rule in that embassy. It was in fact composed of widely different personalities, many of them extremely second-rate, so that, if one sought to discover what could have been the motive of the selection that had brought them together, the only one possible seemed to be inversion. By setting at the head of this little diplomatic Sodom an ambassador on the contrary enamoured of women with the comic exaggeration of a revue compère, who drilled his battalion of transvestites like clockwork, the authorities seemed to have been obeying the law of contrasts. In spite of what he had beneath his nose, he did not believe in inversion. He gave an immediate proof of this by marrying his sister to a chargé d'affaires whom he believed, quite mistakenly, to be a womaniser. After this he became rather a nuisance and was soon replaced by a new Excellency, who ensured the homogeneity of the party. Other embassies sought to rival this one, but could never dispute the prize (as in the *concours général*, where a certain *lycée* always heads the list), and more than ten years had to pass before, heterogeneous attachés having been introduced into this too perfect unit, another could at last wrest the disreputable palm from it and march out in front.

Reassured as regards her fear of having to talk to Swann, Mme de Guermantes now felt merely curious as to the subject of the conversation he had had with their host. "Do you know what it was about?" the Duke asked M. de Bréauté. "I did hear," the other replied, "that it was about a little play which the writer Bergotte produced at their house. It was a delightful show, I gather. But it seems the actor made himself up to look like Gilbert, whom, as it happens, Master Bergotte had intended to take off." "Oh, I should have loved to see Gilbert taken off," said the Duchess with a dreamy smile. "It was about this little performance," M. de Bréauté went on, thrusting forward his rodent jaw, "that Gilbert demanded an explanation from Swann, who merely replied what everyone thought very witty: 'Why, not at all, it wasn't the least bit like you, you are far funnier!' It appears, though," M. de Bréauté continued, "that the little play was quite delightful. Mme Molé was there, and she was immensely amused." "What, does Mme Molé go there?" said the Duchess in astonishment. "Ah! that must be Mémé's doing. That's what always happens in the end to that sort of house. One fine day everybody begins to flock to it, and I, who have deliberately remained aloof on principle, find myself left to mope alone in my corner." Already, since M. de Bréauté's speech, the Duchesse de Guermantes (with regard, if not to Swann's house, at least to the hypothesis of encountering him at any moment) had, as we see, adopted a fresh point of view. "The explanation that you have given us," said Colonel de Froberville to M. de

Bréauté, "is entirely unfounded. I have good reason to know. The Prince purely and simply gave Swann a dressing down and intimated to him in no uncertain terms that he was not to show his face in the house again, in view of the opinions he flaunts. And, to my mind, my uncle Gilbert was right a thousand times over, not only in giving Swann a piece of his mind—he ought to have broken off relations with a professed Dreyfusard six months ago."

Poor M. de Vaugoubert, from being a too dawdling tennis-player having now become a mere inert tennis-ball which is driven to and fro without compunction, found himself projected towards the Duchesse de Guermantes, to whom he made obeisance. He was none too well received, Oriane living in the belief that all the diplomats—or politicians—of her world were nincompoops.

M. de Froberville had inevitably benefited from the preferential position that had of late been accorded to military men in the social world. Unfortunately, if the wife of his bosom was a quite authentic relative of the Guermantes, she was also an extremely poor one, and, as he himself had lost his fortune, they went scarcely anywhere, and were the sort of people who were apt to be overlooked except on big occasions, when they had the good fortune to bury or marry a relation. Then, they did really enter into communion with high society, like those nominal Catholics who approach the altar rails only once a year. Their material situation would indeed have been deplorable had not Mme de Saint-Euverte, faithful to her affection for the late General de Froberville, done everything to help the household, providing frocks and entertainments for the two girls. But the Colonel, though generally considered a good fellow, was lacking in the spirit of gratitude. He was envious of the splendours of a benefactress who celebrated them herself without pause or restraint. The annual garden-party was for him, his wife and children a marvellous pleasure which they would not have missed for all the gold in the world, but a pleasure poisoned by the thought of the joy of self-satisfied pride that Mme de Saint-Euverte derived from it. The accounts of this garden-party in the newspapers, which, after giving a detailed report, would add with Machiavellian guile: "We shall come back to this brilliant gathering," the complementary details about the women's clothes, appearing for several days in succession—all this was so painful to the Frobervilles that although they were cut off from most pleasures and knew that they could count upon the pleasure of this one afternoon, they were moved every year to hope that bad weather would spoil the success of the party, to consult the barometer and to anticipate with delight the threatenings of a storm that might ruin everything.

"I shall not discuss politics with you, Froberville," said M. de Guermantes, "but, so far as Swann is concerned, I can tell you frankly that his conduct towards ourselves has been beyond words. Although he was originally introduced into society by ourselves and the Duc de Chartres, they tell me now that he is openly Dreyfusard. I should never have believed it of him, an epicure, a man of practical judgment, a collector, a connoisseur of old books, a member of the Jockey, a man who enjoys the respect of all, who knows all the good addresses and used to send us the best port you could wish to drink, a dilettante, a family man. Ah! I feel badly let down. I don't mind about myself, it's generally agreed that I'm only an old fool whose opinion counts for nothing, mere ragtag and bobtail, but if only for Oriane's sake, he ought not to have done that, he should have openly disavowed the Jews and the partisans of the accused.

"Yes, after the friendship my wife has always shown him," went on the Duke, who evidently considered that to denounce Dreyfus as guilty of high treason, whatever opinion one might hold in one's heart of hearts as to his guilt, constituted a sort of thank-offering for the manner in which one had been received in the Faubourg Saint-Germain, "he ought to have dissociated himself. For, you can ask Oriane, she had a real friendship for him."

The Duchess, thinking that a quiet, ingenuous tone would give a more dramatic and sincere value to her words, said in a schoolgirl voice, as though simply letting the truth fall from her lips, and merely allowing a slightly melancholy expression to becloud her eyes: "Yes, it's true, I have no reason to conceal the fact that I did feel a sincere affection for Charles!"

"There, you see, I don't have to make her say it. And after that, he carries his ingratitude to the point of being a Dreyfusard!"

"Talking of Dreyfusards," I said, "it appears that Prince Von is one."

"Ah, I'm glad you reminded me of him," exclaimed M. de Guermantes, "I was forgetting that he had asked me to dine with him on Monday. But whether he's a Dreyfusard or not is entirely immaterial to me, since he's a foreigner. I don't give two straws for his opinion. With a Frenchman it's another matter. It's true that Swann is a Jew. But, until to-day—forgive me, Froberville—I have always been foolish enough to believe that a Jew can be a Frenchman, I mean an honourable Jew, a man of the world. Now, Swann was that in every sense of the word. Well, now he forces me to admit that I was mistaken, since he has taken the side of this Dreyfus (who, guilty or not, never moved in his world, whom he wouldn't ever have met) against a society that had adopted him, had treated him as one of its own. There's no question about it, we were all of us prepared to vouch for Swann, I would have answered for his patriotism as for my own. And this is how he repays us! I must confess that I should never have expected such a thing from him. I thought better of him. He was a man of intelligence (in his own line, of course). I know that he had already been guilty of the aberration of that shameful marriage. And by the way, do you know someone who was really hurt by Swann's marriage? My wife. Oriane often has what I might call an affectation of insensibility. But at heart she feels things with extraordinary keenness." (Mme de Guermantes, delighted by this analysis of her character, listened to it with a modest air but did not utter a word, from a scrupulous reluctance to acquiesce in it but principally from fear of cutting it short. M. de Guermantes might have gone on talking for an hour on this subject and she would have sat as still, or even stiller than if she had been listening to music.) "Well, I remember when she heard of Swann's marriage she was genuinely hurt. She felt that it was very bad on the part of someone to whom we had shown so much friendship. She was very fond of Swann; she was deeply grieved. Am I not right, Oriane?"

Mme de Guermantes felt that she ought to reply to so direct a challenge on a point of fact which would enable her unobtrusively to confirm the tribute which she felt had come to an end. In a shy and simple tone, and with an air all the more studied in that it sought to appear "heartfelt," she said with a meek reserve: "It's true, Basin is quite right."

"But still, that wasn't quite the same thing as this. After all, love is love, although, in my opinion, it ought to confine itself within certain limits. I could excuse a young fellow, a snotty-nosed youth, for letting himself be carried away by utopian ideas. But Swann, a man of intelligence, of proved refinement, a fine judge of pictures, an intimate friend of the Duc de Chartres, of Gilbert himself!"

The tone in which M. de Guermantes said this was, incidentally, quite inoffensive, without a trace of the vulgarity which he too often showed. He spoke with a slightly indignant melancholy, but his whole manner exuded that gentle gravity which constitutes the broad and unctuous charm of certain portraits by Rembrandt, that of the Burgomaster Six, for example. One felt that for the Duke there was no question of the immorality of Swann's conduct with regard to the "Affair," so self-evident was it; it caused him the grief of a father who sees one of his sons, for whose education he has made the greatest sacrifices, deliberately ruin the magnificent position he has created for him and dishonour a respected name by escapades which the principles or prejudices of his family cannot allow. It is true that M. de Guermantes had not displayed so profound and pained an astonishment when he learned that Saint-Loup was a Dreyfusard. But, for one thing, he regarded his nephew as a young man gone astray, from whom nothing would be surprising until he began to mend his ways, whereas Swann was what M. de Guermantes called "a level-headed man, a man occupying a position in the front rank." Moreover, and above all, a considerable period of time had elapsed during which, if, from the historical point of view, events had to some extent seemed to justify the Dreyfusard thesis, the anti-Dreyfusard opposition had greatly increased in violence, and from being purely political had become social. It was now a question of militarism, of patriotism, and the waves of anger that had been stirred up in society had had time to gather the force which they never have at the beginning of a storm. "Don't you see," M. de Guermantes went on, "even from the point of view of his beloved Jews, since he is absolutely determined to stand by them, Swann has made a bloomer of incalculable significance. He has proved that they're all secretly united and are somehow forced to give their support to anyone of their own race, even if they don't know him personally. It's a public menace. We've obviously been too easy-going, and the mistake Swann is making will create all the more stir since he was respected, not to say received, and was almost the only Jew that anyone knew. People will say: *Ab uno disce omnes.*" (Satisfaction at having hit at the right moment upon so apt a quotation alone brightened with a proud smile the melancholy countenance of the betrayed nobleman.)

I was longing to know exactly what had happened between the Prince and Swann, and to catch the latter, if he had not already gone home. "I don't mind telling you," the Duchess answered me when I spoke to her of this desire, "that I for my part am not over-anxious to see him, because it appears, from what I was told just now at Mme de Saint-Euverte's, that he wants me to make the acquaintance of his wife and daughter before he dies. God knows I'm terribly distressed that he should be ill, but in the first place I hope it isn't as serious as all that. And besides, it isn't a valid reason, because otherwise it would be really too easy. A writer with no talent would only have to say: 'Vote for me at the Academy because my wife is dying and I wish to give her this last happiness.' There would be no more entertaining if one was obliged to make friends with all the dying. My coachman might come to me with: 'My daughter is seriously ill, get me an invitation to the Princesse de Parme's.' I adore Charles, and I should hate having to refuse him, and so I prefer to avoid the risk of his asking me. I hope with all my heart that he isn't dying, as he says, but really, if it has to happen, it wouldn't be the moment for me to make the acquaintance of those two creatures who have deprived me of the most agreeable of my friends for the last fifteen years, and whom he would leave on my hands

without my even being able to make use of their society to
see him, since he would be dead!"

Meanwhile M. de Bréauté had not ceased to brood upon the
refutation of his story by Colonel de Froberville.

"I don't question the accuracy of your version, my dear
fellow," he said, "but I had mine from a good source. It was
the Prince de la Tour d'Auvergne who told me."

"I'm surprised that a learned man like yourself should still
say 'Prince de la Tour d'Auvergne,' " the Duc de Guermantes
broke in. "You know that he's nothing of the kind. There is
only one member of that family left: Oriane's uncle, the Duc
de Bouillon."

"Mme de Villeparisis's brother?" I asked, remembering that
she had been Mlle de Bouillon.

"Precisely. Oriane, Mme de Lambresac is saying how-d'ye-
do to you."

And indeed, one saw from time to time, forming and fading
like a shooting star, a faint smile directed by the Duchesse de
Lambresac at somebody whom she had recognised. But this
smile, instead of taking definite shape in an active affirmation,
in a language mute but clear, was drowned almost immediately
in a sort of ideal ecstasy which expressed nothing, while her
head drooped in a gesture of blissful benediction, recalling
that which a slightly senile prelate bestows upon a crowd of
communicants. There was not the least trace of senility about
Mme de Lambresac. But I was already acquainted with this
particular type of old-fashioned distinction. At Combray and
in Paris, all my grandmother's friends were in the habit of
greeting one another at a social gathering with as seraphic an
air as if they had caught sight of someone of their acquaintance
in church, at the moment of the Elevation or during a funeral,
and were offering him a languid greeting which ended in
prayer. At this point a remark made by M. de Guermantes was
to complete the comparison that I was making. "But you
have seen the Duc de Bouillon," he said to me. "He was just
leaving my library this afternoon as you came in, a short
gentleman with white hair." It was the man I had taken for a
man of business from Combray, and yet, now that I came to
think it over, I could see the resemblance to Mme de Ville-

parisis. The similarity between the evanescent greetings of the Duchesse de Lambresac and those of my grandmother's friends had began to arouse my interest by showing me how in all narrow and closed societies, be they those of the minor gentry or of the great nobility, the old manners persist, enabling us to recapture, like an archaeologist, something of the up-bringing, and the ethos it reflects, that prevailed in the days of the Vicomte d'Arlincourt and Loisa Puget. Better still now, the perfect conformity in appearance between a petty bour-geois from Combray of his generation and the Duc de Bouillon reminded me of what had already struck me so forcibly when I had seen Saint-Loup's maternal grandfather, the Duc de La Rochefoucauld, in a daguerreotype in which he was exactly similar, in dress, appearance and manner, to my great-uncle—that social, and even individual, differences are merged when seen from a distance in the uniformity of an epoch. The truth is that similarity of dress and also the reflexion of the spirit of the age in facial composition occupy so much more important a place in a person's make-up than his caste, which bulks large only in his own self-esteem and the imagin-ation of other people, that in order to realise that a nobleman of the time of Louis-Philippe differs less from an ordinary citizen of the time of Louis-Philippe than from a nobleman of the time of Louis XV, it is not necessary to visit the galleries of the Louvre.

At that moment, a Bavarian musician with long hair, whom the Princesse de Guermantes had taken under her wing, bowed to Oriane. She responded with a nod, but the Duke, furious at seeing his wife greet a person whom he did not know, who looked rather weird, and, so far as M. de Guermantes under-stood, had an extremely bad reputation, turned upon his wife with a terrible and inquisitorial air, as much as to say: "Who in the world is that vulgar fellow?" Poor Mme de Guermantes's position was already distinctly complicated, and if the musician had felt a little pity for this martyred wife, he would have made off as quickly as possible. But, whether from a desire not to submit to the humiliation that had just been inflicted on him in public, before the eyes of the Duke's oldest and most intimate friends, whose presence there had perhaps been responsible to some extent for his silent bow, and to show that it was on the best of grounds and not without knowing her already that he had greeted the Duchesse de Guermantes, or whether in obedience to an obscure but irresistible impulse to commit a social blunder which drove him—at a moment when he ought to have trusted to the spirit—to apply the whole letter of the law of etiquette, the musician came closer to Mme de Guermantes and said to her: "Madame la Duchesse, I should like to have the honour of being presented to the Duke." Mme de Guermantes was miserable in the extreme. But after all, even if she was a forsaken wife, she was still Duchesse de Guermantes and could not allow herself to appear to have forfeited the right to introduce to her husband the people whom she knew. "Basin," she said, "allow me to present to you M. d'Herweck."

"I need not ask whether you are going to Mme de Saint-Euverte's to-morrow," Colonel de Froberville said to Mme de Guermantes, to dispel the painful impression produced by M. d'Herweck's ill-timed request. "The whole of Paris will be there."

Meanwhile, turning towards the indiscreet musician with a single movement and as though he were carved out of a solid block, the Duc de Guermantes, drawing himself up, monumental, mute, wrathful, like Jupiter Tonans, remained thus motionless for some seconds, his eyes ablaze with anger and astonishment, his crinkly hair seeming to emerge from a crater. Then, as though carried away by an impulse which alone enabled him to perform the act of politeness that was demanded of him, and after appearing by his aggressive demeanour to be calling the entire company to witness that he did not know the Bavarian musician, clasping his white-gloved hands behind his back, he jerked his body forward and bestowed upon the musician a bow so profound, instinct with such stupefaction and rage, so abrupt, so violent, that the trembling artist recoiled, bowing as he went, in order not to receive a formidable butt in the stomach.

"Well, the fact is I shan't be in Paris," the Duchess answered Colonel de Froberville. "I must tell you (though I ought to be ashamed to confess such a thing) that I have lived all these years without seeing the stained-glass windows at Montfort-l'Amaury. It's shocking, but there it is. And so, to make amends for my shameful ignorance, I decided that I would go and see them to-morrow."

M. de Bréauté smiled a subtle smile. For he was well aware that, if the Duchess had been able to live all these years without seeing the windows at Montfort-l'Amaury, this artistic excursion had not all of a sudden taken on the urgent character of an "emergency" operation and might without danger, after having been put off for more than twenty-five years, be retarded for twenty-four hours. The plan that the Duchess had formed was simply the Guermantes way of decreeing that the Saint-Euverte establishment was definitely not a socially respectable house, but a house to which you were invited so that your name might afterwards be flaunted in the account in the *Gaulois*, a house that would award the seal of supreme elegance to those, or at any rate to her (should there be but one), who would not be seen there. The delicate amusement of M. de Bréauté, coupled with the poetical pleasure which society people felt when they saw Mme de Guermantes do things which their own inferior position did not allow them to imitate but the mere sight of which brought to their lips the smile of the peasant tied to his glebe when he sees freer and more fortunate men pass by above his head—this delicate pleasure could in no way be compared with the concealed but frantic delight which M. de Froberville instantaneously experienced.

The efforts that this gentleman was making so that people should not hear his laughter had made him turn as red as a turkey-cock, in spite of which it was with a running interruption of hiccoughs of joy that he exclaimed in a pitying tone: "Oh! poor Aunt Saint-Euverte, she'll be so upset. No, the unhappy woman isn't to have her duchess! What a blow! It'll be enough to kill her!" He doubled up with laughter, and in his exhilaration could not help stamping his feet and rubbing his hands. Smiling out of one eye and one small corner of her lips at M. de Froberville, whose amiable intention she appreciated, though she found less tolerable the deadly boredom of his company, Mme de Guermantes finally decided to leave him.

"I say, I'm afraid I'm going to *have* to bid you good-night," she said to him as she rose with an air of melancholy resignation, and as though it were a bitter grief to her. Beneath the magic spell of her blue eyes her gently musical voice made one think of the poetical lament of a fairy. "Basin wants me to go and talk to Marie for a while."

In reality, she was fed up with listening to Froberville, who went on envying her her visit to Montfort-l'Amaury, when she knew quite well that he had never heard of the windows before in his life, and besides would not for anything in the world have missed going to the Saint-Euverte party. "Good-bye, I've barely said a word to you, but it's always like that at parties—we never really see each other, we never say the things we should like to; in fact it's the same everywhere in this life. Let's hope that when we are dead things will be better arranged. At any rate we shan't always be having to put on low-cut dresses. And yet one never knows. We may perhaps have to display our bones and worms on great occasions. Why not? Just look at old mother Rampillon—do you see any great difference between her and a skeleton in an open dress? It's true that she has every right to look like that, for she must be at least a hundred. She was already one of those sacred monsters before whom I refused to bow the knee when I made my first appearance in society. I thought she had been dead for years; which for that matter would be the only possible explanation for the spectacle she presents. It's most impressive and liturgical; quite *Campo Santo*!"

The Duchess had moved away from Froberville. He followed her: "Just one word in your ear." Slightly irritated, "Well, what is it now?" she said to him stiffly. And he, having been afraid lest at the last moment she might change her mind about Montfort-l'Amaury: "I didn't like to mention it for Mme de Saint-Euverte's sake, so as not to upset her, but since you don't intend to be there, I may tell you that I'm glad for your sake, because she has measles in the house!" "Oh, good gracious!" said Oriane, who had a horror of diseases. "But that wouldn't matter to me, I've had them already. You can't get them twice." "So the doctors say. I know people who've had them four times. Anyhow, you are warned." As for himself, these fictitious measles would have needed to attack him in reality and to chain him to his bed before he would have resigned himself to missing the Saint-Euverte party to which he had looked forward for so many months. He would have the pleasure of seeing so many smart people there, the still greater pleasure of remarking that certain things had gone wrong, and the supreme pleasure of being able for long afterwards to boast that he had mingled with the former and, exaggerating or inventing them, of deploring the latter.

I took advantage of the Duchess's moving to rise also in order to make my way to the smoking-room and find out the truth about Swann. "Don't believe a word of what Babal told us," she said to me. "Little Molé would never poke her nose into a place like that. They tell us that to entice us. Nobody ever goes to them and they are never asked anywhere either. He admits it himself: 'We spend the evenings alone by our own fireside.' As he always says *we*, not like royalty, but to include his wife, I don't press him. But I know all about it." We passed two young men whose great and dissimilar beauty derived from the same woman. They were the two sons of Mme de Surgis, the latest mistress of the Duc de Guermantes. Both were resplendent with their mother's perfections, but each in a different way. To one had passed, rippling through a virile body, the regal bearing of Mme de Surgis, and the same glowing, rufous, pearly paleness flooded the marmoreal cheeks of mother and son; but his brother had received the Grecian brow, the perfect nose, the statuesque neck, the eyes of infinite depth; composed thus of separate gifts, which the goddess had shared between them, their twofold beauty offered one the abstract pleasure of thinking that the cause of that beauty was something outside themselves; it was as though the principal attributes of their mother had been incarnated in two different bodies; this one was her stature and her complexion, the other her gaze, as Mars and Venus were simply the strength and the beauty of Jupiter or Minerva. Full of respect though they were for M. de Guermantes, of whom they said: "He is a great friend of our parents," the elder nevertheless thought that it would be wiser not to come up and greet the Duchess, of whose hostility towards his mother he was aware though without perhaps understanding the reason, and at the sight of us he slightly averted his head. The younger, who imitated his brother in everything, because, being stupid and moreover short-sighted, he did not dare to have his own opinion, inclined his head at the same angle, and the pair slipped past us towards the card-room, one behind the other, like a pair of allegorical figures.

Just as I reached this room, I was stopped by the Marquise de Citri, still beautiful but almost foaming at the mouth. Of decently noble birth, she had sought and made a brilliant match in marrying M. de Citri, whose great-grandmother had been an Aumale-Lorraine. But no sooner had she tasted this satisfaction than her natural cantankerousness had given her a horror of high society which did not absolutely preclude social life. Not only, at a party, did she deride everyone present, but her derision was so violent that mere laughter was not sufficiently acrid and developed into a guttural hiss. "Ah!" she said to me, pointing to the Duchesse de Guermantes who had now left my side and was already some way off, "what defeats me is that she can lead this sort of existence." Was this the remark of a righteously indignant saint, astonished that the Gentiles did not come of their own accord to perceive the Truth, or that of an anarchist athirst for carnage? In any case there could be no possible justification for this criticism. In the first place, the "existence led" by Mme de Guermantes differed very little (except in indignation) from that led by Mme de Citri. Mme de Citri was amazed to find the Duchess capable of that mortal sacrifice: attendance at one of Marie-Gilbert's parties. It must be said in this particular instance that Mme de Citri was genuinely fond of the Princess, who was indeed the kindest of women, and knew that by attending her reception she was giving her great pleasure. Hence, in order to come to the party, she had put off a dancer whom she regarded as a genius and who was to have initiated her into the mysteries of Russian choreography. Another reason which to some extent stultified the concentrated rage which Mme de Citri felt on seeing Oriane greet one or other of the guests was that the Duchess, although at a far less advanced stage, showed the symptoms of the malady that was devouring Mme de Citri.

We have seen, moreover, that she had carried the germs of it from her birth. In fact, being more intelligent than Mme de Citri, Mme de Guermantes would have had more justification than she for this nihilism (which was more than merely social), but it is true that certain qualities help us to endure the defects of our neighbour more than they make us suffer from them; and a man of great talent will normally pay less attention to other people's foolishness than would a fool. We have already described at sufficient length the nature of the Duchess's wit to convince the reader that, if it had nothing in common with high intelligence, it was at least wit, a wit adroit in making use (like a translator) of different grammatical forms. Now nothing of this sort seemed to entitle Mme de Citri to look down upon qualities so closely akin to her own. She found everyone idiotic, but in her conversation, in her letters, showed herself distinctly inferior to the people whom she treated with such disdain. She had moreover such a thirst for destruction that, when she had more or less given up society, the pleasures that she then sought were subjected, each in turn, to her terrible undermining power. After she had given up parties for musical evenings, she used to say: "You like listening to that sort of thing, to music? Goodness me, it depends on the mood. But how deadly it can be! Ah, Beethoven!—what a bore! (*la barbe*)." With Wagner, then with Franck, with Debussy, she did not even take the trouble to say the word *barbe*, but merely drew her hand over her face with a tonsorial gesture. Presently, everything became boring. "Beautiful things are such a bore. Ah, pictures!—they're enough to drive you mad. How right you are, it is such a bore having to write letters!" Finally it was life itself that she declared to be boring (*rasante*), leaving you to wonder where she took her term of comparison.

I do not know whether it was the effect of what the Duchesse de Guermantes, on the evening when I first dined at her house, had said of this interior, but the card-room or smoking-room, with its pictorial floor, its tripods, its figures of gods and animals that gazed at you, the sphinxes stretched out along the arms of the chairs, and most of all the huge table of marble or enamelled mosaic, covered with symbolical signs more or less imitated from Etruscan and Egyptian art, gave me the impression of a magician's cell. And, indeed, on a chair drawn up to the glittering augural table, M. de Charlus in person, never touching a card, oblivious of what was going on around him, incapable of observing that I had entered the room, seemed precisely a magician applying all the force of his will and reason to drawing a horoscope. Not only were his eyes starting from his head like the eyes of a Pythian priestess on her tripod, but, so that nothing might distract him from labours which required the cessation of the most simple movements, he had (like a mathematician who will do nothing else until he has solved his problem) laid down beside him the cigar which he had previously been holding between his lips but had no longer the necessary equanimity of mind to think of smoking. Seeing the two crouching deities on the arms of the chair that stood facing him, one might have thought that the Baron was endeavouring to solve the riddle of the Sphinx, had it not been rather that of a young and living Oedipus seated in that very armchair where he had settled down to play. Now, the figure to which M. de Charlus was applying all his mental powers with such concentration, and which was not in fact one of the sort that are commonly studied *more geometrico*, was that which was proposed to him by the lineaments of the young Comte de Surgis; it appeared, so profound was M. de Charlus's absorption in front of it, to be some rebus, some riddle, some algebraical problem, of which he must try to penetrate the mystery or to work out the formula. In front of him the sibylline signs and the figures inscribed upon that Table of the Law seemed the gramarye which would enable the old sorcerer to tell in what direction the young man's destiny was shaping. Suddenly he became aware that I was watching him, raised his head as though he were waking from a dream, smiled at me and blushed. At that moment Mme de Surgis's other son came up behind the one who was playing, to look at his cards. When M. de Charlus had learned from me that they were brothers, his face could not conceal the admiration that he felt for a family which could create masterpieces so splendid and so diverse. And what would have added to the Baron's enthusiasm would have been the discovery that the two sons of Mme de Surgis-le-Duc were sons not only of the same mother but of the same father. The children of Jupiter are dissimilar, but that is because he married first Metis, whose destiny it was to bring into the world wise children, then Themis, and after her Eurynome, and Mnemosyne, and Leto, and only as a last resort Juno. But to a single father Mme de Surgis had borne these two sons who had each received beauty from her, but a different beauty.

At last I had the pleasure of seeing Swann come into this room, which was extremely large, so large that he did not at first catch sight of me. A pleasure mingled with sadness, a sadness which the other guests did not, perhaps, feel, their feeling consisting rather in that sort of fascination which is exercised by the strange and unexpected signs of an approaching death, a death that a man already has, in the popular saying, written on his face. And it was with an almost offensive amazement, in which there were elements of tactless curiosity, of cruelty, of relieved and at the same time anxious self-scrutiny (a blend of *suave mari magno* and *memento quia pulvis*, Robert would have said), that all eyes were fastened on that face the cheeks of which had been so eaten away, so whittled down, by illness, like a waning moon, that except at a certain angle, the angle doubtless from which Swann looked at himself, they stopped short like a flimsy piece of scenery to which only an optical illusion can add the appearance of depth. Whether because of the absence of those cheeks, no longer there to modify it, or because arteriosclerosis, which is also a form of intoxication, had reddened it as would drunkenness, or deformed it as would morphine, Swann's punchinello nose, absorbed for long years into an agreeable face, seemed now enormous, tumid, crimson, the nose of an old Hebrew rather than of a dilettante Valois. Perhaps, too, in these last days, the physical type that characterises his race was becoming more pronounced in him, at the same time as a sense of moral solidarity with the rest of the Jews, a solidarity which Swann seemed to have forgotten throughout his life, and which, one after another, his mortal illness, the Dreyfus case and the anti-semitic propaganda had reawakened. There are certain Jews, men of great refinement and social delicacy, in whom neverthe-less there remain in reserve and in the wings, ready to enter their lives at a given moment, as in a play, a boor and a prophet. Swann had arrived at the age of the prophet. Certainly, with that face of his from which, under the influence of his disease, whole segments had vanished, as when a block of ice melts and whole slabs of it fall off, he had of course "changed." But I could not help being struck by the much greater extent to which he had changed in relation to myself. Admirable and cultivated though he was, a man I was anything but bored to meet, I could not for the life of me understand how I had been able to invest him long ago with such mystery that his appearance in the Champs-Elysées in his silk-lined cape would make my heart beat to the point where I was ashamed to approach him, and that at the door of the flat where such a being dwelt I could not ring the bell without being overcome with boundless agitation and alarm. All this had vanished not only from his house but from his person, and the idea of talking to him might or might not be agreeable to me, but had no effect whatever upon my nervous system.

And furthermore, how he had changed since that very afternoon, when I had met him—after all, only a few hours earlier—in the Duc de Guermantes's study! Had he really had a scene with the Prince, which had deeply upset him? The supposition was not necessary. The slightest efforts that are demanded of a person who is very ill quickly become for him an excessive strain. He has only to be exposed, when already tired, to the heat of a crowded drawing-room, for his features to change dramatically and turn blue, as happens in a few hours with an overripe pear or milk that is about to turn. Besides this, Swann's hair was worn thin in patches, and, as Mme de Guermantes remarked, needed attention from the furrier, looked as if it had been camphorated, and camphorated badly. I was just crossing the room to speak to Swann when unfortunately a hand fell upon my shoulder:

"Hallo, old boy, I'm in Paris for forty-eight hours. I called at your house and they told me you were here, so that it's to you that my aunt is indebted for the honour of my company at her party." It was Saint-Loup. I told him how greatly I admired the house. "Yes, it's very much the historic monument. Personally I find it deadly. We mustn't go near my uncle

Palamède, or we shall be caught. Now that Mme Molé has gone (she's the one who rules the roost just now) he's rather at a loose end. I gather it was quite a spectacle, he never let her out of his sight for a moment, and didn't leave her until he'd seen her safely into her carriage. I bear my uncle no ill will, only I do think it odd that my family council, which has always been so hard on me, should be composed of the very ones who have led the most debauched lives themselves, beginning with the biggest roisterer of the lot, my uncle Charlus, who is my surrogate guardian, has had more women than Don Juan, and is still carrying on in spite of his age. There was talk at one time of having me made a ward of court. I bet when all those gay old dogs met to consider the question and had me up to preach to me and tell me I was breaking my mother's heart, they dared not look one another in the face for fear of laughing. If you examined the composition of the council, you'd think they had deliberately chosen the biggest womanisers."

Leaving aside M. de Charlus, with regard to whom my friend's astonishment seemed to me to be no more justified—though for different reasons, and reasons which, moreover, were afterwards to undergo some modification in my mind—Robert was quite wrong to think it extraordinary that lessons in worldly wisdom should be given to a young man by people who have played the fool or are still doing so. Even if it is simply a question of atavism and family likeness, it is inevitable that the uncle who delivers the lecture should have more or less the same failings as the nephew whom he has been deputed to scold. Nor is the uncle in the least hypocritical in so doing, deluded as he is by the faculty people have of believing, in every new set of circumstances, that "this is quite different," a faculty which enables them to adopt artistic, political and other errors without perceiving that they are the same errors which they exposed, ten years ago, in another school of painting which they condemned, another political affair which they felt to deserve a loathing that they no longer feel, and espouse those errors without recognising them in a fresh disguise. Besides, even if the faults of the uncle are different from those of the nephew, heredity may none the less to a certain extent be responsible, for the effect does not always resemble the cause, as a copy resembles its original, and even if the uncle's faults are worse, he may easily believe them to be less serious.

When M. de Charlus had made indignant remonstrances to Robert, who in any case was unaware of his uncle's true inclinations at the time—and even if it had still been the time when the Baron used to denounce his own inclinations—he might perfectly well have been sincere in considering, from the point of view of a man of the world, that Robert was infinitely more culpable than himself. Had not Robert, at the time when his uncle had been deputed to make him listen to reason, come within an inch of getting himself ostracised by society? Had he not very nearly been blackballed at the Jockey? Had he not made himself a public laughing-stock by the vast sums that he threw away upon a woman of the lowest type, by his friendships with people—authors, actors, Jews—not one of whom moved in society, by his opinions, which were indistinguishable from those held by traitors, by the grief he was causing to all his family? How could this scandalous existence be compared with that of M. de Charlus who had managed, so far, not only to retain but to enhance still further his position as a Guermantes, being in society an absolutely privileged person, sought after, adulated in the most exclusive circles, and a man who, married to a Bourbon princess, a woman of eminence, had succeeded in making her happy, had shown a devotion to her memory more fervent, more scrupulous than is customary in society, and had thus been as good a husband as a son!

"But are you sure that M. de Charlus has had all those mistresses?" I asked, not, of course, with the diabolical intention of revealing to Robert the secret that I had discovered, but irritated, nevertheless, at hearing him maintain an erroneous theory with such smug assurance. He merely shrugged his shoulders in response to what he took for ingenuousness on my part. "Not that I blame him in the least, I consider that he's perfectly right." And he proceeded to outline to me a theory of conduct that would have horrified him at Balbec (where he was not content with denouncing seducers, death seeming to him the only punishment adequate to their crime). Then, however, he had still been in love and jealous. Now he even went so far as to sing the praises of houses of assignation. "They're the only places where you can find a shoe to fit you, sheathe your weapon, as we say in the Army." He no longer felt for places of that sort the disgust that had inflamed him at Balbec when I made an allusion to them, and hearing what he now said, I told him that Bloch had introduced me to one, but Robert replied that the one which Bloch frequented must be "pretty vile, a poor man's paradise!—It all depends, though: where was it?" I remained vague, for I had just remembered that it was there that Rachel whom Robert had so passionately loved used to give herself for a louis. "Anyhow, I can take you to some far better ones, full of stunning women." Hearing me express the desire that he should take me as soon as possible to the ones he knew, which must indeed be far superior to the house to which Bloch had introduced me, he expressed sincere regret that he would be unable to do so on this occasion as he was leaving Paris next day. "It will have to be my next leave," he said. "You'll see, there are young girls there, even," he added with an air of mystery. "There's a little Mademoiselle de . . . I think it's d'Orgeville—I can let you have the exact name —who is the daughter of quite tip-top people; her mother was by way of being a La Croix-l'Evêque, and they're really out of the top drawer—in fact they're more or less related, if I'm not mistaken, to my aunt Oriane. Anyhow, you have only to see the child to realise at once that she must be somebody's daughter" (I could detect, hovering for a moment over Robert's voice, the shadow of the Guermantes family genie, which passed like a cloud, but at a great height and without stopping). "She looks to me a marvellous proposition. The parents are always ill and can't look after her. Gad, the child must have some amusement, and I count upon you to provide it!" "Oh, when are you coming back?" "I don't know. If you don't absolutely insist upon duchesses" (duchess being for the aristocracy the only title that denotes a particularly brilliant rank, as the lower orders talk of "princesses"), "in a different class of goods there's Mme Putbus's chambermaid."

At this moment, Mme de Surgis entered the room in search of her sons. As soon as he saw her M. de Charlus went up to her with a friendliness by which the Marquise was all the more agreeably surprised in that an icy coldness was what she had expected from the Baron, who had always posed as Oriane's protector and alone of the family—the rest being too often inclined to indulgence towards the Duke's irregularities because of his wealth and from jealousy of the Duchess—kept his brother's mistresses ruthlessly at a distance. And so Mme de Surgis would have fully understood the motives for the attitude that she dreaded to find in the Baron, but never for a moment suspected those for the wholly different welcome that she did receive from him. He spoke to her with admiration of the portrait that Jacquet had painted of her years before. This admiration waxed indeed to an enthusiasm which, if it was partly calculating, with the object of preventing the Marquise from going away, of "engaging" her, as Robert used to say of enemy armies whose forces one wants to keep tied down at a particular point, was also perhaps sincere. For, if everyone was pleased to admire in her sons the regal bearing and the beautiful eyes of Mme de Surgis, the Baron could taste an inverse but no less keen pleasure in finding those charms combined in the mother, as in a portrait which does not in itself provoke desire, but feeds, with the aesthetic admiration that it does provoke, the desires that it awakens. These now gave in retrospect a voluptuous charm to Jacquet's portrait itself, and at that moment the Baron would gladly have purchased it to study therein the physiological pedigree of the two Surgis boys.

"You see, I wasn't exaggerating," Robert said in my ear. "Just look at my uncle's attentiveness to Mme de Surgis. Though I must say it does surprise me. If Oriane knew, she would be furious. Really, there are enough women in the world without his having to go and pounce on her," he went on. Like everybody who is not in love, he imagined that one chooses the person one loves after endless deliberation and on the strength of diverse qualities and advantages. Besides, while completely mistaken about his uncle, whom he supposed to be devoted to women, Robert, in his rancour, spoke too lightly of M. de Charlus. One is not always somebody's nephew with impunity. It is often through him that a hereditary habit is transmitted sooner or later. We might indeed arrange a whole gallery of portraits, named like the German comedy *Uncle and Nephew*, in which we should see the uncle watching jealously, albeit unconsciously, for his nephew to end by becoming like himself. I might even add that this gallery would be incomplete were we not to include in it uncles who are not blood relations, being the uncles only of their nephews' wives. For the Messieurs de Charlus of this world are so convinced that they themselves are the only good husbands, and what is more the only husbands of whom their wives are not jealous, that generally, out of affection for their niece, they make her marry another Charlus. Which tangles the skein of family likenesses. And, to affection for the niece, is added at times affection for her betrothed as well. Such marriages are not uncommon, and are often what is called happy.

"What were we talking about? Oh yes, that big, fair girl, Mme Putbus's maid. She goes with women too, but I don't suppose you mind that. I tell you frankly, I've never seen such a gorgeous creature." "I imagine her as being rather Giorgionesque?" "Wildly Giorgionesque! Oh, if I only had a little time in Paris, what wonderful things there are to be done! And then one goes on to the next. Because love is all rot, you know, I've finished with all that."

I soon discovered, to my surprise, that he had equally finished with literature, whereas it was merely with regard to literary men that he had struck me as being disillusioned at our last meeting. ("They're practically all a pack of scoundrels," he had said to me, a remark that was to be explained by his justified resentment towards certain of Rachel's friends. For they had persuaded her that she would never have any talent if she allowed "Robert, scion of an alien race" to acquire an influence over her, and with her used to make fun of him, to his face, at the dinners he gave for them.) But in reality Robert's love of Letters was in no sense profound, did not spring from his true nature, was only a by-product of his love of Rachel, and had faded with the latter at the same time as his loathing for voluptuaries and his religious respect for the virtue of women.

"There's something rather strange about those two young

men. Look at that curious passion for gambling, Marquise,"
said M. de Charlus, drawing Mme de Surgis's attention to her
two sons, as though he were completely unaware of their
identity. "They must be a pair of Orientals, they have certain
characteristic features, they're perhaps Turks," he went on,
so as to give further support to his feigned innocence and
at the same time to exhibit a vague antipathy, which, when in
due course it gave place to affability, would prove that the
latter was addressed to the young men solely in their capacity
as sons of Mme de Surgis, having begun only when the Baron
discovered who they were. Perhaps, too, M. de Charlus,
whose insolence was a natural gift which he delighted in
exercising, was taking advantage of the few moments in which
he was supposed not to know the name of these two young
men to have a little fun at Mme de Surgis's expense and to
indulge in his habitual mockery, as Scapin takes advantage of
his master's disguise to give him a sound drubbing.

"They are my sons," said Mme de Surgis, with a blush
that would not have coloured her cheeks had she been shrewder
without necessarily being more virtuous. She would then
have understood that the air of absolute indifference or of
sarcasm which M. de Charlus displayed towards a young man
was no more sincere than the wholly superficial admiration
which he showed for a woman expressed his true nature. The
woman to whom he could go on indefinitely paying the
prettiest compliments might well be jealous of the look which,
while talking to her, he shot at a man whom he would pretend
afterwards not to have noticed. For that look was different
from the looks which M. de Charlus kept for women; a special
look, springing from the depths, which even at a party could
not help straying naïvely in the direction of young men, like
the look in a tailor's eye which betrays his profession by
immediately fastening upon your attire.

"Oh, how very odd!" replied M. de Charlus with some
insolence, as though his mind had to make a long journey to
arrive at a reality so different from what he had pretended to
suppose. "But I don't know them," he added, fearing lest he
might have gone a little too far in the expression of his antipathy and have thus paralysed the Marquise's intention of

effecting an introduction. "Would you allow me to introduce them to you?" Mme de Surgis inquired timidly. "Why, good gracious, just as you please, I don't mind, but I'm perhaps not very entertaining company for such young people," M. de Charlus intoned with the air of chilly reluctance of someone allowing himself to be forced into an act of politeness.

"Arnulphe, Victurnien, come here at once," said Mme de Surgis. Victurnien rose purposefully. Arnulphe, though he could not see further than his brother, followed him meekly.

"It's the sons' turn, now," muttered Saint-Loup. "It's enough to make one die laughing. He tries to curry favour with everyone, down to the dog in the yard. It's all the funnier as my uncle detests pretty boys. And just look how seriously he's listening to them. If it was me who tried to introduce them to him, he'd send me away with a flea in my ear. Listen, I shall have to go and say how-d'ye-do to Oriane. I have so little time in Paris that I want to try and see all the people here that otherwise I ought to leave cards on."

"How well brought-up they seem, what charming manners," M. de Charlus was saying.

"Do you think so?" Mme de Surgis replied, highly delighted.

Swann, having caught sight of me, came over to Saint-Loup and myself. His Jewish gaiety was less subtle than his socialite witticisms: "Good evening," he said to us. "Heavens! all three of us together—people will think it's a meeting of the Syndicate. In another minute they'll be looking for the money-box!" He had not observed that M. de Beauserfeuil was just behind him and could hear what he said. The General could not help wincing. We heard the voice of M. de Charlus close beside us: "What, so you're called Victurnien, after the *Cabinet des Antiques*," the Baron was saying, to prolong his conversation with the two young men. "By Balzac, yes," replied the elder Surgis, who had never read a line of that novelist's work, but to whom his tutor had remarked, a few days earlier, upon the similarity of his Christian name and d'Esgrignon's. Mme de Surgis was delighted to see her son shine, and M. de Charlus in ecstasy at such a display of learning.

"It appears that Loubet[35] is entirely on our side, I have it

from an absolutely trustworthy source," Swann informed
Saint-Loup, but this time in a lower tone so as not to be overheard by the General. He had begun to find his wife's Republican connexions more interesting now that the Dreyfus case
had become his chief preoccupation. "I tell you this because
I know that you are with us up to the hilt."

"Not quite to that extent; you're completely mistaken,"
Robert replied. "It's a bad business, and I'm sorry I ever got
involved in it. It was no affair of mine. If it were to begin
over again, I should keep well clear of it. I'm a soldier, and
my first loyalty is to the Army. If you stay with M. Swann for a
moment, I shall be back presently. I must go and talk to my
aunt."

But I saw that it was with Mlle d'Ambresac that he went to
talk, and was distressed by the thought that he had lied to me
about the possibility of their engagement. My mind was set
at rest when I learned that he had been introduced to her half
an hour earlier by Mme de Marsantes, who was anxious for
the marriage, the Ambresacs being extremely rich.

"At last," said M. de Charlus to Mme de Surgis. "I find a
young man with some education, who has read a bit, who
knows who Balzac is. And it gives me all the more pleasure
to meet him where that sort of thing has become most rare,
in the house of one of my peers, one of ourselves," he added,
laying stress upon the words. It was all very well for the Guermantes to profess to regard all men as equal; on the great
occasions when they found themselves among "well-born"
people, especially if they were not quite so "well-born" as
themselves, whom they were anxious and able to flatter, they
did not hesitate to trot out old family memories. "At one time,"
the Baron went on, "the word aristocrat meant the best people,
in intellect and in heart. Now, here is the first person I've
come across in our world who has ever heard of Victurnien
d'Esgrignon. No, I'm wrong in saying the first. There are
also a Polignac and a Montesquiou," added M. de Charlus,
who knew that this twofold association must inevitably thrill
the Marquise. "However, in your sons' case it runs in the
family: their maternal grandfather had a famous eighteenth-
century collection. I will show you mine if you will give me

the pleasure of coming to luncheon with me one day," he said to the young Victurnien. "I can show you an interesting edition of the *Cabinet des Antiques* with corrections in Balzac's own hand. I shall be charmed to bring the two Victurniens face to face."

I could not bring myself to leave Swann. He had arrived at that stage of exhaustion in which a sick man's body becomes a mere retort in which to study chemical reactions. His face was mottled with tiny spots of Prussian blue, which seemed not to belong to the world of living things, and emitted the sort of odour which, at school, after "experiments," makes it so unpleasant to have to remain in a "science" classroom. I asked him if it was true that he had had a long conversation with the Prince de Guermantes and if he would tell me what it had been about.

"Yes," he said, "but go for a moment first with M. de Charlus and Mme de Surgis. I'll wait for you here."

And indeed M. de Charlus, having suggested to Mme de Surgis that they should leave this room, which was too hot, and go and sit for a while in another, had invited not the two sons to accompany their mother, but myself. In this way he had made himself appear, after having successfully hooked them, to have lost all interest in the two young men. He was moreover paying me an inexpensive compliment, Mme de Surgis-le-Duc being socially in rather bad odour.

Unfortunately, no sooner had we sat down in an alcove from which there was no way of escape than Mme de Saint-Euverte, a favourite butt for the Baron's jibes, came past. She, perhaps to mask or else openly to disregard the ill will which she inspired in M. de Charlus, and above all to show that she was on intimate terms with a woman who was talking so familiarly to him, gave a disdainfully friendly greeting to the famous beauty, who acknowledged it while peeping out of the corner of her eye at M. de Charlus with a mocking smile. But the alcove was so narrow that Mme de Saint-Euverte, when she went behind us to continue her canvass of her guests for the morrow, found herself cornered and could not easily escape—a heaven-sent opportunity which M. de Charlus, anxious to display his insolent wit before the mother of the two young men, took good care not to let slip. A silly question which I put to him without any malicious intent gave him the cue for a triumphal tirade of which the wretched Saint-Euverte, more or less immobilised behind us, could not have missed a single word.

"Would you believe it, this impertinent young man," he said, indicating me to Mme de Surgis, "has just asked me, without the slightest concern for the proper reticence in regard to such needs, whether I was going to Mme de Saint-Euverte's, in other words, I suppose, whether I was suffering from diarrhoea. I should endeavour in any case to relieve myself in some more comfortable place than the house of a person who, if my memory serves me, was celebrating her centenary when I first began to move in society, that is to say, not in her house. And yet who could be more interesting to listen to? What a host of historic memories, seen and lived through in the days of the First Empire and the Restoration, and intimate revelations, too, which certainly had nothing of the 'Saint' about them but must have been extremely 'vertes'[36] if one may judge by the friskiness still left in those venerable hams. What would prevent me from questioning her about those thrilling times is the sensitiveness of my olfactory organ. The proximity of the lady is enough. I suddenly say to myself: oh, good lord, someone has broken the lid of my cesspool, when it's simply the Marquise opening her mouth to emit some invitation. And you can imagine that if I had the misfortune to go to her house, the cesspool would expand into a formidable sewage-cart. She bears a mystic name, though, which has always made me think with jubilation, although she has long since passed the date of her jubilee, of that stupid line of so-called 'deliquescent' poetry: 'Ah, green, how green my soul was on that day. . . .' But I require a cleaner sort of verdure. They tell me that the indefatigable old street-walker gives 'garden-parties.' Myself, I should describe them as 'invitations to explore the sewers.' Are you going to wallow there?" he asked Mme de Surgis, who now found herself in a quandary. Wishing to pretend for the Baron's benefit that she was not going, and knowing that she would give days of her life rather than miss the Saint-Euverte party, she got out of it by a compromise, that is to say by expressing uncertainty. This uncertainty took so clumsily amateurish, so sordidly material a form, that M. de Charlus, not afraid of offending Mme de Surgis, whom nevertheless he was anxious to please, began to laugh to show her that "it didn't wash."

"I always admire people who make plans," she said. "I often change mine at the last moment. There's a question of a summer frock which may alter everything. I shall act upon the inspiration of the moment."

For my part, I was incensed at the abominable little speech that M. de Charlus had just made. I would have liked to shower blessings upon the giver of garden-parties. Unfortunately, in the social as in the political world, the victims are such cowards that one cannot for long remain indignant with their executioners. Mme de Saint-Euverte, who had succeeded in escaping from the alcove to which we were barring the entry, brushed against the Baron inadvertently as she passed him, and, by a reflex of snobbishness which wiped out all her anger, perhaps even in the hope of securing an opening of a kind at which this could not be the first attempt, exclaimed: "Oh! I beg your pardon, Monsieur de Charlus, I hope I did not hurt you," as though she were kneeling before her lord and master. The latter did not deign to reply otherwise than by a broad ironical smile, and conceded only a "Good evening," which, uttered as though he had noticed the Marquise's presence only after she had greeted him, was an additional insult. Finally, with an extreme obsequiousness which pained me for her sake, Mme de Saint-Euverte came up to me and, drawing me aside, murmured in my ear: "Tell me, what have I done to offend M. de Charlus? They say that he doesn't consider me smart enough for him," she added, laughing heartily. I remained serious. For one thing, I thought it stupid of her to appear to believe or to wish other people to believe that nobody, really, was as smart as herself. For another thing, people who laugh so heartily at what they themselves have said, when it is not funny, dispense us accordingly, by taking upon themselves the responsibility for the mirth, from joining in it.

"Other people assure me that he is cross because I don't

invite him. But he doesn't give me much encouragement. He seems to avoid me." (This expression struck me as inadequate.) "Try to find out, and come and tell me to-morrow. And if he feels remorseful and wishes to come too, bring him. I shall forgive and forget. Indeed, I shall be quite glad to see him, because it will annoy Mme de Surgis. I give you a free hand. You have the most perfect judgment in these matters and I do not wish to appear to be begging my guests to come. In any case, I count upon you absolutely."

It occurred to me that Swann must be getting tired of waiting for me. Moreover I did not wish to be too late in returning home because of Albertine, and, taking leave of Mme de Surgis and M. de Charlus, I went in search of my invalid in the card-room. I asked him whether what he had said to the Prince in their conversation in the garden was really what M. de Bréauté (whom I did not name) had reported to us, about a little play by Bergotte. He burst out laughing: "There's not a word of truth in it, not one, it's a complete fabrication and would have been an utterly stupid thing to say. It's really incredible, this spontaneous generation of falsehood. I won't ask who it was that told you, but it would be really interesting, in a field as limited as this, to work back from one person to another and find out how the story arose. Anyhow, what concern can it be of other people, what the Prince said to me? People are very inquisitive. I've never been inquisitive, except when I was in love, and when I was jealous. And a lot I ever learned! Are you jealous?" I told Swann that I had never experienced jealousy, that I did not even know what it was. "Well, you can count yourself lucky. A little jealousy is not too unpleasant, for two reasons. In the first place, it enables people who are not inquisitive to take an interest in the lives of others, or of one other at any rate. And then it makes one feel the pleasure of possession, of getting into a carriage with a woman, of not allowing her to go about by herself. But that's only in the very first stages of the disease, or when the cure is almost complete. In between, it's the most agonising torment. However, I must confess that I haven't had much experience even of the two pleasures I've mentioned—the first because of my own nature, which is incapable of sustained reflexion; the second because of circumstances, because of the woman, I should say the women, of whom I've been jealous. But that makes no difference. Even when one is no longer attached to things, it's still something to have been attached to them; because it was always for reasons which other people didn't grasp. The memory of those feelings is something that's to be found only in ourselves; we must go back into ourselves to look at it. You mustn't laugh at this idealistic jargon, but what I mean to say is that I've been very fond of life and very fond of art. Well, now that I'm a little too weary to live with other people, those old feelings, so personal and individual, that I had in the past, seem to me—it's the mania of all collectors—very precious. I open my heart to myself like a sort of showcase, and examine one by one all those love affairs of which the rest of the world can have known nothing. And of this collection, to which I'm now even more attached than to my others, I say to myself, rather as Mazarin said of his books, but in fact without the least distress, that it will be very tiresome to have to leave it all. But, to come back to my conversation with the Prince, I shall tell one person only, and that person is going to be you."

My attention was distracted by the conversation that M. de Charlus, who had returned to the card-room, was carrying on endlessly nearby. "And are you a reader too? What do you do?" he asked Comte Arnulphe, who had never heard even the name of Balzac. But his short-sightedness, since it caused him to see everything very small, gave him the appearance of seeing great distances, so that—rare poetry in a statuesque Greek god—remote, mysterious stars seemed to be engraved upon his pupils.

"Suppose we took a turn in the garden," I said to Swann, while Comte Arnulphe, in a lisping voice which seemed to indicate that mentally at least his development was incomplete, replied to M. de Charlus with an artlessly obliging precision: "Oh, you know, mainly golf, tennis, football, running, and especially polo." Thus had Minerva, having subdivided herself, ceased in certain cities to be the goddess of wisdom, and had become partly incarnated in a purely sporting, horse-loving deity, Athene Hippia. And he went to St Moritz also to ski, for

Pallas Tritogeneia frequents the high peaks and outruns swift
horsemen. "Ah!" replied M. de Charlus with the transcendental
smile of the intellectual who does not even take the trouble to
conceal his derision, but, on the other hand, feels himself so
superior to other people and so far despises the intelligence
of those who are least stupid that he barely differentiates between them and the most stupid, as long as the latter are attractive to him in some other way. While talking to Arnulphe, M.
de Charlus felt that by the mere act of addressing him he was
conferring upon him a superiority which everyone else must
recognise and envy. "No," Swann replied, "I'm too tired to
walk about. Let's sit down somewhere in a corner, I cannot remain on my feet any longer." This was true, and yet the act of
beginning to talk had already restored to him a certain vivacity.
For it is a fact that in the most genuine exhaustion there is, especially in highly-strung people, an element that depends on
attention and is preserved only by an act of memory. We feel
suddenly weary as soon as we are afraid of feeling weary, and, to
throw off our fatigue, it suffices us to forget about it. To be sure,
Swann was far from being one of those indefatigable invalids
who, entering a room worn out and ready to drop, revive in
conversation like a flower in water and are able for hours on
end to draw from their own words a reserve of strength which
they do not, alas, communicate to their hearers, who appear
more and more exhausted the more the talker comes back to
life. But Swann belonged to that stout Jewish race, in whose
vital energy, its resistance to death, its individual members
seem to share. Stricken severally by their own diseases, as it is
stricken itself by persecution, they continue indefinitely to
struggle against terrible agonies which may be prolonged
beyond every apparently possible limit, when already one can
see only a prophet's beard surmounted by a huge nose which
dilates to inhale its last breath, before the hour strikes for the
ritual prayers and the punctual procession of distant relatives
begins, advancing with mechanical movements as upon an
Assyrian frieze.

We went to sit down, but, before moving away from the
group formed by M. de Charlus with the two young Surgis and
their mother, Swann could not resist fastening upon the lady's

bosom the lingering, dilated, concupiscent gaze of a connoisseur. He even put up his monocle for a better view, and,
while he talked to me, kept glancing in her direction.

"Here, word for word," he said to me when we were seated,
"is my conversation with the Prince, and if you remember what
I said to you just now, you will see why I choose you as my
confidant. There is another reason as well, which you will
learn one day. 'My dear Swann,' the Prince de Guermantes
said to me, 'you must forgive me if I have appeared to be
avoiding you for some time past.' (I had never even noticed it,
having been ill and avoiding society myself.) 'In the first place,
I had heard it said, and I fully expected, that in the unhappy
affair which is splitting the country in two your views were
diametrically opposed to mine. Now, it would have been
extremely painful to me to hear you express these views in my
presence. I was so sensitive on the matter that when the
Princess, two years ago, heard her brother-in-law, the Grand
Duke of Hesse, say that Dreyfus was innocent, she was not
content with promptly denying the assertion but refrained from
repeating it to me in order not to upset me. At about the same
time, the Crown Prince of Sweden came to Paris and, having
probably heard someone say that the Empress Eugénie was a
Dreyfusist, confused her with the Princess (a strange confusion,
you will admit, between a woman of the rank of my wife and
a Spaniard who is a great deal less well-born than people make
out and who was married to a mere Bonaparte) and said to
her: Princess, I am doubly glad to meet you, for I know that
you hold the same view as myself of the Dreyfus case, which
does not surprise me since Your Highness is Bavarian. Which
drew down upon the Prince the answer: Sir, I am now a
French princess, and I share the views of all my fellow-
countrymen. Well, my dear Swann, about eighteen months
ago, a conversation I had with General de Beauserfeuil made
me suspect that, not an error, but grave illegalities, had been
committed in the conduct of the trial.'"

We were interrupted (Swann did not want his story to be
overheard) by the voice of M. de Charlus who (without, as it
happened, paying us the slightest attention) came past escorting Mme de Surgis and stopped in the hope of detaining her

for a moment longer, either on account of her sons or from that reluctance common to all the Guermantes to bring anything to an end, which kept them plunged in a sort of anxious inertia. Swann informed me in this connexion, a little later, of something that, for me, stripped the name Surgis-le-Duc of all the poetry that I had found in it. The Marquise de Surgis-le-Duc boasted a far higher social position, far grander connexions by marriage, than her cousin the Comte de Surgis, who had no money and lived on his estate in the country. But the suffix to her title, "le Duc," had not at all the origin which I attributed to it, and which had made me associate it in my imagination with Bourg-l'Abbé, Bois-le-Roi, etc. All that had happened was that a Comte de Surgis had married, under the Restoration, the daughter of an immensely rich industrial magnate, M. Leduc, or Le Duc, himself the son of a chemical manufacturer, the richest man of his day and a peer of France. King Charles X had created for the son born of this marriage the marquisate of Surgis-le-Duc, a marquisate of Surgis existing already in the family. The addition of the bourgeois surname had not prevented this branch from allying itself, on the strength of its enormous fortune, with the first families of the realm. And the present Marquise de Surgis-le-Duc, being extremely well-born, could have enjoyed a very high position in society. A demon of perversity had driven her, scorning the position ready-made for her, to flee from the conjugal roof and live a life of open scandal. Whereupon the society she had scorned at twenty, when it was at her feet, had cruelly spurned her at thirty, when, after ten years, nobody except a few faithful friends greeted her any longer, and she had had to set to work to reconquer laboriously, inch by inch, what she had possessed as a birthright (a return journey that is not uncommon).

As for the great nobles, her kinsmen, whom she had disowned in the past, and who in their turn had disowned her, she found an excuse for the joy that she would feel in gathering them again to her bosom in the memories of childhood that she would be able to recall with them. And in saying this, with the object of disguising her snobbery, she was perhaps being less untruthful than she supposed. "Basin is all my girlhood!" she said on the day on which he came back to her.

And indeed it was partly true. But she had miscalculated when she chose him for her lover. For all the women friends of the Duchesse de Guermantes were to rally round her, and so Mme de Surgis must descend for the second time that slope up which she had so laboriously toiled. "Well!" M. de Charlus was saying to her in an effort to prolong the conversation, "you must lay my tribute at the feet of the beautiful portrait. How is it? What has become of it?" "Why," replied Mme de Surgis, "you know I haven't got it now; my husband wasn't pleased with it." "Not pleased! With one of the greatest works of art of our time, equal to Nattier's Duchesse de Châteauroux, and, moreover, perpetuating no less majestic and heart-shattering a goddess. Oh, that little blue collar! I swear, Vermeer himself never painted a fabric more consummately—but we must not say it too loud or Swann will fall upon us to avenge his favourite painter, the Master of Delft." The Marquise, turning round, addressed a smile and held out her hand to Swann, who had risen to greet her. But almost without concealment, because his advanced years had deprived him either of the will, from indifference to the opinion of others, or the physical power, from the intensity of his desire and the weakening of the controls that help to disguise it, as soon as Swann, on taking the Marquise's hand, had seen her bosom at close range and from above, he plunged an attentive, serious, absorbed, almost anxious gaze into the depths of her corsage, and his nostrils, drugged by her perfume, quivered like the wings of a butterfly about to alight upon a half-glimpsed flower. Abruptly he shook off the intoxication that had seized him, and Mme de Surgis herself, although embarrassed, stifled a deep sigh, so contagious can desire prove at times. "The painter was offended," she said to M. de Charlus, "and took it back. I have heard that it is now at Diane de Saint-Euverte's." "I decline to believe," said the Baron, "that a great picture can have such bad taste."*

"He is talking to her about her portrait. I could talk to her about that portrait just as well as Charlus," said Swann, affecting a drawling, raffish tone as he followed the retreating couple with his eyes. "And I should certainly enjoy talking about it more than Charlus," he added.

I asked him whether the things that were said about M. de
Charlus were true, in doing which I was lying twice over, for
if I had no proof that anybody ever had said anything, I had
on the other hand been perfectly aware since that afternoon
that what I was hinting at was true. Swann shrugged his
shoulders, as though I had suggested something quite absurd.

"It's quite true that he's a charming friend. But I need hardly
add that his friendship is purely platonic. He is more sentimental than other men, that's all; on the other hand, as he
never goes very far with women, that has given a sort of
plausibility to the idiotic rumours to which you refer. Charlus is
perhaps greatly attached to his men friends, but you may be
quite certain that the attachment is only in his head and in his
heart. However, now we may perhaps be left in peace for a
moment. Well, the Prince de Guermantes went on to say: 'I
don't mind telling you that this idea of a possible illegality in
the conduct of the trial was extremely painful to me, because I
have always, as you know, worshipped the Army. I discussed
the matter again with the General, and, alas, there could be no
room for doubt. I need hardly tell you that, all this time, the
idea that an innocent man might be undergoing the most
infamous punishment had never even crossed my mind. But
tormented by this idea of illegality, I began to study what I
had always declined to read, and then the possibility, this
time not only of illegality but of the prisoner's innocence, began
to haunt me. I did not feel that I could talk about it to the
Princess. Heaven knows that she has become just as French
as myself. From the day of our marriage, I took such pride
in showing her our country in all its beauty, and what to me
is its greatest splendour, its Army, that it would have been too
painful for me to tell her of my suspicions, which involved,
it is true, a few officers only. But I come of a family of soldiers,
and I was reluctant to believe that officers could be mistaken.
I discussed the case again with Beauserfeuil, and he admitted
that there had been culpable intrigues, that the *bordereau* was
possibly not in Dreyfus's writing, but that an overwhelming
proof of his guilt did exist. This was the Henry document.
And a few days later we learned that it was a forgery. After
that, unbeknownst to the Princess, I began to read the *Siècle*

and the *Aurore* every day. Soon I had no more doubts, and I couldn't sleep. I confided my distress to our friend, the abbé Poiré, who, I was astonished to find, held the same conviction, and I got him to say masses for the intention of Dreyfus, his unfortunate wife and their children. Meanwhile, one morning as I went into the Princess's room, I saw her maid trying to hide something from me that she had in her hand. I asked her, chaffingly, what it was, and she blushed and refused to tell me. I had the greatest confidence in my wife, but this incident disturbed me considerably (and the Princess too, no doubt, who must have heard about it from her maid), for my dear Marie barely uttered a word to me that day at luncheon. I asked the abbé Poiré that day whether he could say my mass for Dreyfus the following morning. . . .' And so much for that!" exclaimed Swann, breaking off his narrative.

I looked up, and saw the Duc de Guermantes bearing down upon us. "Forgive me for interrupting you, my boys. Young man," he went on, addressing me, "I am instructed to give you a message from Oriane. Marie and Gilbert have asked us to stay and have supper at their table with only five or six other people: the Princess of Hesse, Mme de Ligne, Mme de Tarente, Mme de Chevreuse, the Duchesse d'Arenberg. Unfortunately, we can't stay—we're going on to a little ball of sorts." I was listening, but whenever we have something definite to do at a given moment, we depute a certain person inside us who is accustomed to that sort of duty to keep an eye on the clock and warn us in time. This inner servant reminded me, as I had asked him to remind me a few hours before, that Albertine, who at the moment was far from my thoughts, was to come and see me immediately after the theatre. And so I declined the invitation to supper. This does not mean that I was not enjoying myself at the Princesse de Guermantes's. The truth is that men can have several sorts of pleasure. The true pleasure is the one for which they abandon the other. But the latter, if it is apparent, or rather if it alone is apparent, may put people off the scent of the other, reassure or mislead the jealous, create a false impression. And yet, all that is needed to make us sacrifice it to the other is a little happiness or a little suffering. Sometimes a third category of pleasures,

more serious, but more essential, does not yet exist for us, its
potential existence betraying itself only by arousing regrets and
discouragement. And yet it is to these pleasures that we shall
devote ourselves in time to come. To give a very minor
example, a soldier in time of peace will sacrifice social life to
love, but, once war is declared (and without there being
any need to introduce the idea of patriotic duty), will sacrifice
love to the passion, stronger than love, for fighting. For all
that Swann assured me that he was happy to tell me his story,
I could feel that his conversation with me, because of the lateness of the hour, and because he was so ill, was one of those
exertions for which those who know that they are killing
themselves by sitting up late, by overdoing things, feel an
angry regret when they return home, a regret similar to that
felt at the wild extravagance of which they have again been
guilty by the spendthrifts who will nevertheless be unable to
restrain themselves from throwing money out of the window
again to-morrow. Once we have reached a certain degree of
enfeeblement, whether it be caused by age or by ill health, all
pleasure taken at the expense of sleep outside our normal
habits, every disturbance of routine, becomes a nuisance. The
talker continues to talk, from politeness, from excitement, but
he knows that the hour at which he might still have been able
to go to sleep has already passed, and he knows also the
reproaches that he will heap upon himself during the insomnia
and fatigue that must ensue. Already, moreover, even the
momentary pleasure has come to an end, body and brain are
too far drained of their strength to welcome with any readiness
what seems entertaining to one's interlocutor. They are like a
house on the morning before a journey or removal, where
visitors become a perfect plague, to be received sitting upon
locked trunks, with our eyes on the clock.

"At last we're alone," he said. "I quite forget where I was.
Oh yes, I had just told you, hadn't I, that the Prince asked the
abbé Poiré if he could say his mass next day for Dreyfus.
'No, the abbé informed me' (I say *me*," Swann explained to me,
"because it's the Prince who is speaking, you understand?),
'for I have another mass that I've been asked to say for him
to-morrow as well.—What, I said to him, is there another

Catholic as well as myself who is convinced of his innocence?—
It appears so.—But this other supporter's conviction must be
more recent than mine.—Maybe, but this other was asking me
to say masses when you still believed Dreyfus guilty.—Ah, I
can see that it's no one in our world.—On the contrary!—
Really, there are Dreyfusists among us, are there? You intrigue me; I should like to unbosom myself to this rare bird,
if it is someone I know.—It is.—What is his name?—The
Princesse de Guermantes. While I was afraid of offending my
dear wife's nationalistic opinions, her faith in France, she had
been afraid of alarming my religious opinions, my patriotic
sentiments. But privately she had been thinking as I did, though
for longer than I had. And what her maid had been hiding as
she went into her room, what she went out to buy for her every
morning, was the *Aurore*. My dear Swann, from that moment
I thought of the pleasure that I should give you if I told you
how closely akin my views upon this matter were to yours;
forgive me for not having done so sooner. If you bear in mind
that I had never said a word to the Princess, it will not surprise
you to be told that thinking the same as yourself must at that
time have kept me further apart from you than thinking differently. For it was an extremely painful topic for me to broach.
The more I believe that an error, that crimes even, have been
committed, the more my heart bleeds for the Army. It had
never occurred to me that opinions like mine could possibly
cause you similar pain, until I was told the other day that you
emphatically condemned the insults to the Army and the fact
that the Dreyfusists agreed to ally themselves with those who
insulted it. That settled it. I admit that it has been most painful
for me to confess to you what I think of certain officers, few
in number fortunately, but it is a relief to me not to have to
keep away from you any longer, and above all a relief to make
it clear to you that if I had other feelings it was because I
hadn't a shadow of doubt as to the soundness of the verdict.
As soon as my doubts began, I could wish for only one thing,
that the mistake should be rectified.' I confess that I was deeply
moved by the Prince de Guermantes's words. If you knew him
as I do, if you could realise the distance he has had to travel
in order to reach his present position, you would admire him

as he deserves. Not that his opinion surprises me, his is such an upright nature!"

Swann was forgetting that during the afternoon he had on the contrary told me that people's opinions as to the Dreyfus case were dictated by atavism. At the most he had made an exception on behalf of intelligence, because in Saint-Loup it had managed to overcome atavism and had made a Dreyfusard of him. Now he had just seen that this victory had been of short duration and that Saint-Loup had passed into the opposite camp. And so it was to moral uprightness that he now assigned the role which had previously devolved upon intelligence. In reality we always discover afterwards that our adversaries had a reason for being on the side they espoused, which has nothing to do with any element of right that there may be on that side, and that those who think as we do do so because their intelligence, if their moral nature is too base to be invoked, or their uprightness, if their perception is weak, has compelled them to.

Swann now found equally intelligent anybody who was of his opinion, his old friend the Prince de Guermantes as well as my schoolfellow Bloch, whom previously he had avoided and whom he now invited to lunch. Swann interested Bloch greatly by telling him that the Prince de Guermantes was a Dreyfusard. "We must ask him to sign our appeal on behalf of Picquart; a name like his would have a tremendous effect." But Swann, blending with his ardent conviction as a Jew the diplomatic moderation of a man of the world, whose habits he had too thoroughly acquired to be able to shed them at this late hour, refused to allow Bloch to send the Prince a petition to sign, even on his own initiative. "He cannot do such a thing, we mustn't expect the impossible," Swann repeated. "There you have a charming man who has travelled thousands of miles to come over to our side. He can be very useful to us. If he were to sign your petition, he would simply be compromising himself with his own people, would be made to suffer on our account, might even repent of his confidences and do nothing more." Nor was this all: Swann even refused his own signature. He felt that his name was too Hebraic not to create a bad effect. Besides, even if he approved of everything that concerned revision, he did not wish to be mixed up in any way in the anti-militarist campaign. He wore, a thing he had never done previously, the decoration he had won as a young militiaman in '70, and added a codicil to his will asking that, contrary to its previous provisions, he might be buried with the military honours due to his rank as Chevalier of the Legion of Honour. A request which assembled round the church of Combray a whole squadron of those troopers over whose fate Françoise used to weep in days gone by, when she envisaged the prospect of war. In short, Swann refused to sign Bloch's petition, with the result that, if he passed in the eyes of many people as a fanatical Dreyfusard, my friend found him lukewarm, infected with nationalism, deeply jingoistic.

Swann left me without shaking hands so as not to be forced into a general leave-taking in this room which swarmed with his friends, but said to me: "You ought to come and see your friend Gilberte. She has really grown up now and altered, you wouldn't know her. She would be so pleased!" I no longer loved Gilberte. She was for me like a dead person for whom one has long mourned, and then forgetfulness has come, and if she were to be resuscitated would no longer fit into a life which has ceased to be fashioned for her. I no longer had any desire to see her, not even that desire to show her that I did not wish to see her which, every day, when I was in love with her, I vowed to myself that I would flaunt before her when I loved her no longer.

Hence, seeking now only to give myself in Gilberte's eyes the air of having longed with all my heart to meet her again and of having been prevented by circumstances of the kind called "beyond our control," which indeed only occur, with any consistency at least, when we do nothing to thwart them, so far from accepting Swann's invitation with reserve, I did not leave him until he had promised to explain in detail to his daughter the mischances that had prevented and would continue to prevent me from going to see her. "In any case I shall write to her as soon as I get home," I added. "But be sure to tell her it will be a threatening letter, for in a month or two I shall be quite free, and then let her tremble, for I shall be coming to your house as regularly as in the old days."

Before parting from Swann, I had a word with him about

his health. "No, it's not as bad as all that," he told me. "Still, as I was saying, I'm pretty worn out, and I accept with resignation whatever may be in store for me. Only, I must say that it would be very irritating to die before the end of the Dreyfus case. Those scoundrels have more than one card up their sleeves. I have no doubt of their being defeated in the end, but still they're very powerful, they have supporters everywhere. Just as everything is going on splendidly, it all collapses. I should like to live long enough to see Dreyfus rehabilitated and Picquart a colonel."

When Swann had left, I returned to the big drawing-room to find the Princesse de Guermantes, with whom I did not then know that I was one day to be so intimate. Her passion for M. de Charlus did not reveal itself to me at first. I noticed only that the Baron, after a certain date, and without having taken to the Princesse de Guermantes one of those sudden dislikes so familiar with him, while continuing to feel for her just as strong if not a stronger affection perhaps than ever, appeared irritated and displeased whenever one mentioned her name to him. He never included it now in his list of people with whom he wished to dine.

It is true that before this time I had heard an extremely malicious man about town say that the Princess had completely changed, that she was in love with M. de Charlus, but this slander had appeared to me absurd and had made me angry. I had indeed remarked with astonishment that, when I was telling her something that concerned myself, if M. de Charlus's name cropped up in the middle, the Princess's attention at once became screwed up to a higher pitch, like that of a sick man who, hearing us talk about ourselves and listening, in consequence, in a listless and absent-minded fashion, suddenly realises that a name we have mentioned is that of the disease from which he is suffering, which at once interests and delights him. Thus, if I said to her: "Actually, M. de Charlus was telling me . . ." the Princess at once gathered up the slackened reins of her attention. And having on one occasion said in her hearing that M. de Charlus had at that time a warm regard for a certain person, I was astonished to see in the Princess's eyes that momentary glint, like the trace of a fissure in the pupils, which is due to a thought that our words have unwittingly aroused in the mind of the person to whom we are talking, a secret thought that will not find expression in words but will rise from the depths which we have stirred to the momentarily altered surface of his gaze. But if my remark had moved the Princess, I did not then suspect in what way.

At all events, shortly after this she began to talk to me about M. de Charlus, and almost without circumlocution. If she made any allusion to the rumours which a few people here and there were spreading about the Baron, it was merely to reject them as absurd and infamous inventions. But on the other hand she said: "I feel that any woman who fell in love with a man of such immense worth as Palamède ought to be magnanimous enough and devoted enough to accept him and understand him as a whole, for what he is, to respect his freedom, humour his whims, seek only to smooth out his difficulties and console him in his griefs." Now, by such words, vague as they were, the Princesse de Guermantes gave away what she was seeking to idealise, just as M. de Charlus himself did at times. Have I not heard him, again and again, say to people who until then had been uncertain whether or not he was being slandered: "I, who have had so many ups and downs in my life, who have known all manner of people, thieves as well as kings, and indeed, I must confess, with a slight preference for the thieves, I who have pursued beauty in all its forms," and so forth; and by these words which he thought adroit, and by contradicting rumours the currency of which no one suspected (or, from inclination, restraint or concern for verisimilitude, to make a concession to the truth that he was alone in regarding as minimal), he removed the last doubts from the minds of some of his hearers, and inspired others, who had not yet begun to doubt him, with their first. For the most dangerous of all forms of concealment is that of the crime itself in the mind of the guilty party. His constant awareness of it prevents him from imagining how generally unknown it is, how readily a complete lie would be accepted, and on the other hand from realising at what degree of truth other people will begin to detect an admission in words which he believes to be innocent.

In any case he would not have been entirely wrong in seeking to hush it up, for there is no vice that does not find ready tolerance in the best society, and one has seen a country house turned upside down in order that two sisters might sleep in adjoining rooms as soon as their hostess learned that theirs was a more than sisterly affection. But what revealed to me all of a sudden the Princess's love was a particular incident on which I shall not dwell here, for it forms part of quite another story, in which M. de Charlus allowed a queen to die rather than miss an appointment with the hairdresser who was to singe his hair for the benefit of a bus conductor whom he found prodigiously intimidating.* However, to finish with the Princess's love, I shall say briefly what the trifle was that opened my eyes. I was, on the day in question, alone with her in her carriage. As we were passing a post-box she stopped the coachman. She had come out without a footman. She half drew a letter from her muff and was preparing to step down from the carriage to put it into the box. I tried to stop her, she made a show of resistance, and we both realised that our instinctive movements had been, hers compromising, in appearing to be protecting a secret, mine indiscreet, in thwarting that protection. She was the first to recover. Suddenly turning very red, she gave me the letter. I no longer dared not to take it, but, as I slipped it into the box, I could not help seeing that it was addressed to M. de Charlus.

To return to this first evening at the Princesse de Guermantes's, I went to bid her good-night, for her cousins, who had promised to take me home, were in a hurry to be gone. M. de Guermantes wished, however, to say good-bye to his brother, Mme de Surgis having found time to mention to the Duke as she left that M. de Charlus had been charming to her and to her sons. This great kindness on his brother's part, the first moreover that he had ever shown in that line, touched Basin deeply and aroused in him old family feelings which were never entirely dormant. As we were saying good-bye to the Princess he insisted, without actually thanking M. de Charlus, on expressing his fondness for him, either because he genuinely had difficulty in containing it or in order that the Baron might remember that actions of the sort he had performed that evening did not escape the eyes of a brother, just as, with the object of creating salutary associations of memory for the future, we give a lump of sugar to a dog that has done its trick. "Well, little brother!" said the Duke, stopping M. de Charlus and taking him tenderly by the arm, "so we walk past our elders without so much as a word. I never see you now, Mémé, and you can't think how I miss you. I was turning over some old letters the other day and came upon some from poor Mamma, which are all so full of tenderness for you."

"Thank you, Basin," M. de Charlus replied in a broken voice, for he could never speak of their mother without emotion.

"You must let me fix up a cottage for you at Guermantes," the Duke went on.

"It's nice to see the two brothers being so affectionate towards each other," the Princess said to Oriane.

"Yes, indeed! I don't suppose you could find many brothers like them. I shall invite you with him," the Duchess promised me. "You've not quarrelled with him? . . . But what can they be talking about?" she added in an anxious tone, for she could catch only an occasional word of what they were saying. She had always felt a certain jealousy of the pleasure that M. de Guermantes found in talking to his brother of a past from which he was inclined to keep his wife shut out. She felt that, when they were happily together like this and she, unable to restrain her impatient curiosity, came and joined them, her arrival was not well received. But this evening, this habitual jealousy was reinforced by another. For if Mme de Surgis had told M. de Guermantes how kind his brother had been to her so that the Duke might thank his brother, at the same time certain devoted female friends had felt it their duty to warn the Duchess that her husband's mistress had been seen in close conversation with his brother. And Mme de Guermantes was tormented by this.

"Think of the fun we used to have at Guermantes long ago," the Duke went on. "If you came down sometimes in summer we could take up our old life again. Do you remember old Father Courveau: 'Why is Pascal disturbing? Because he is dis . . . dis . . .'" "Turbed," put in M. de Charlus as though he were still answering his tutor's question. "'And why is

Pascal disturbed?; because he is dis . . . because he is dis . . .' "
"Turbing." " 'Very good, you'll pass, you're certain to get a
distinction, and Madame la Duchesse will give you a Chinese
dictionary.' How it all comes back to me, Mémé, and the old
Chinese vase Hervey de Saint-Denys[37] brought back for you,
I can see it now. You used to threaten us that you would go
and spend your life in China, you were so enamoured of the
country; even then you used to love going for long rambles.
Ah, you were always an odd one, for I can honestly say that you
never had the same tastes as other people in anything . . ." But
no sooner had he uttered these words than the Duke blushed
scarlet, for he was aware of his brother's reputation, if not of
his actual habits. As he never spoke to him about it, he was all
the more embarrassed at having said something which might
be taken to refer to it, and still more at having shown his
embarrassment. After a moment's silence: "Who knows," he
said, to cancel the effect of his previous words, "you were perhaps in love with a Chinese girl before loving so many white
ones, and finding favour with them, if I am to judge by a
certain lady to whom you have given great pleasure this
evening by talking to her. She was delighted with you." The
Duke had vowed to himself that he would not mention Mme
de Surgis, but, in the confusion that the gaffe he had just made
had wrought in his ideas, he had pounced on the one that
was uppermost in his mind, which happened to be precisely
the one that ought not to have appeared in the conversation,
although it had started it. But M. de Charlus had observed his
brother's blush. And, like guilty persons who do not wish to
appear embarrassed that you should talk in their presence of the
crime which they are supposed not to have committed, and feel
obliged to prolong a dangerous conversation: "I am charmed
to hear it," he replied, "but I should like to go back to what you
were saying before, which struck me as being profoundly true.
You were saying that I never had the same ideas as other
people—how right you are!—and you said that I had unorthodox tastes." "No I didn't," protested M. de Guermantes, who,
as a matter of fact, had not used those words, and may not
have believed that their meaning was applicable to his brother.
Besides, what right had he to bully him about idiosyncrasies

which in any case were vague enough or secret enough to have in no way impaired the Baron's tremendous position in society? What was more, feeling that the resources of his brother's position were about to be placed at the service of his mistresses, the Duke told himself that this was well worth a little tolerance in exchange; had he at that moment known of some "unorthodox" relationship of his brother's M. de Guermantes would, in the hope of the support that the other might give him, have passed it over, shutting his eyes to it, and if need be lending a hand. "Come along, Basin; good-night, Palamède," said the Duchess, who, devoured by rage and curiosity, could endure no more, "if you have made up your minds to spend the night here, we might just as well stay to supper. You've been keeping Marie and me standing for the last half-hour." The Duke parted from his brother after a meaningful embrace, and the three of us began to descend the immense staircase of the Princess's house.

On either side of us, on the topmost steps, were scattered couples who were waiting for their carriages to come to the door. Erect, isolated, flanked by her husband and myself, the Duchess kept to the left of the staircase, already wrapped in her Tiepolo cloak, her throat clasped in its band of rubies, devoured by the eyes of women and men alike, who sought to divine the secret of her beauty and elegance. Waiting for her carriage on the same step of the staircase as Mme de Guermantes, but at the opposite side of it, Mme de Gallardon, who had long abandoned all hope of ever receiving a visit from her cousin, turned her back so as not to appear to have seen her, and, what was more important, so as not to offer proof of the fact that the other did not greet her. Mme de Gallardon was in an extremely bad temper because some gentlemen in her company had taken it upon themselves to speak to her of Oriane: "I haven't the slightest desire to see her," she had replied to them, "I did see her, as a matter of fact, just now, and she's beginning to show her age. It seems she can't get over it, Basin says so himself. And I can well understand it, because, since she hasn't any brains, is as nasty as can be, and has shocking manners, she must know very well that, once her looks go, she'll have nothing left to fall back on."

I had put on my overcoat, for which M. de Guermantes, who dreaded chills, reproached me as we went down together, because of the heated atmosphere indoors. And the generation of noblemen who more or less passed through the hands of Mgr Dupanloup speak such bad French (except the Castellane brothers) that the Duke expressed what was in his mind thus: "It is better not to put on your coat before going out of doors, at least *as a general thesis*." I can see all that departing crowd now; I can see, if I am not mistaken in placing him upon that staircase, a portrait detached from its frame, the Prince de Sagan, whose last appearance in society this must have been, paying his respects to the Duchess with so ample a sweep of his top hat in his white-gloved hand, harmonising with the gardenia in his buttonhole, that one was surprised that it was not a plumed felt hat of the *ancien régime*, several ancestral faces from which were exactly reproduced in the face of this noble lord. He stopped for only a short time in front of her, but his attitudes in that brief moment were sufficient to compose a complete tableau vivant and, as it were, an historical scene. Moreover, as he has since died, and as I never had more than a glimpse of him in his lifetime, he has become for me so much a character in history, social history at least, that I am sometimes astonished when I think that a woman and a man whom I know are his sister and nephew.

While we were going down the staircase, a woman who appeared to be about forty but was in fact older was climbing it with an air of lassitude that became her. This was the Princesse d'Orvillers, a natural daughter, it was said, of the Duke of Parma, whose pleasant voice rang with a vaguely Austrian accent. She advanced, tall and stooping, in a gown of white flowered silk, her exquisite bosom throbbing and heaving with exhaustion beneath a harness of diamonds and sapphires. Tossing her head like a royal palfrey embarrassed by its halter of pearls, of an incalculable value but an inconvenient weight, she let fall here and there a soft and charming gaze, of an azure which, as it gradually began to fade, became more caressing still, and greeted most of the departing guests with a friendly nod. "You choose a nice time to arrive, Paulette!" said the Duchess. "Yes, I am so sorry! But really it was a physical impossibility," replied the Princesse d'Orvillers, who had acquired this sort of expression from the Duchesse de Guermantes, but added to it her own natural sweetness and the air of sincerity conveyed by the force of a distantly Teutonic accent in so tender a voice. She appeared to be alluding to complications of life too elaborate to be related, and not merely to parties, although she had just come on from a succession of these. But it was not they that forced her to come so late. As the Prince de Guermantes had for many years forbidden his wife to receive Mme d'Orvillers, the latter, when the ban was lifted, contented herself with replying to the other's invitations, so as not to appear to be thirsting after them, by simply leaving cards. After two or three years of this method, she came in person, but very late, as though after the theatre. In this way she gave herself the appearance of attaching no importance to the party, nor to being seen at it, but simply of having come to pay the Prince and Princess a visit, for their own sakes, because she liked them, at an hour when, the great majority of their guests having already gone, she would "have them more to herself."

"Oriane has really sunk very low," muttered Mme de Gallardon. "I cannot understand Basin's allowing her to speak to Mme d'Orvillers I'm sure M. de Gallardon would never have allowed me." For my part, I had recognised in Mme d'Orvillers the woman who, outside the Hôtel Guermantes, used to cast languishing glances at me, turn round, stop and gaze into shop windows. Mme de Guermantes introduced me. Mme d'Orvillers was charming, neither too friendly nor piqued. She gazed at me as at everyone else with her soft eyes. . . . But I was never again, when I met her, to receive from her one of those overtures with which she had seemed to be offering herself. There is a special kind of look, apparently of recognition, which a young man receives from certain women—and from certain men—only until the day on which they have made his acquaintance and have learned that he is the friend of people with whom they too are intimate.

We were told that the carriage was at the door. Mme de Guermantes gathered up her red skirt as though to go down-stairs and get into the carriage, but, seized perhaps by remorse, or by the desire to give pleasure and above all to profit by the brevity which the material obstacle to prolonging it imposed upon so boring an action, looked at Mme de Gallardon; then, as though she had only just caught sight of her, acting upon a sudden inspiration, before going down she tripped across the whole width of the step and, upon reaching her delighted cousin, held out her hand. "Such a long time," said the Duchess, who then, so as not to have to enlarge upon all the regrets and legitimate excuses that this formula might be supposed to contain, turned with a look of alarm towards the Duke, who indeed, having gone down with me to the carriage, was storming with rage on seeing that his wife had gone over to Mme de Gallardon and was holding up the stream of carriages. "Oriane is really very beautiful still!" said Mme de Gallardon. "People amuse me when they say that we've quarrelled; we may (for reasons which we have no need to tell other people) go for years without seeing one another, but we have too many memories in common ever to be separated, and deep down she must know that she cares far more for me than for all sorts of people whom she sees every day and who are not of her blood." Mme de Gallardon was in fact like those scorned lovers who try desperately to make people believe that they are better loved than those whom their fair one cherishes. And (by the praises which, heedless of the contradiction with what she had been saying shortly before, she now lavished on the Duchesse de Guermantes) she proved indirectly that the other was thoroughly conversant with the maxims that ought to guide in her career a great lady of fashion who, at the selfsame moment when her most marvellous gown is exciting an admiration not unmixed with envy, must be able to cross the whole width of a staircase to disarm it. "Do at least take care not to wet your shoes" (a brief but heavy shower of rain had fallen), said the Duke, who was still furious at having been kept waiting.

On our homeward drive, in the confined space of the coupé, those red shoes were of necessity very close to mine, and Mme de Guermantes, fearing that she might actually have touched me, said to the Duke: "This young man is going to be obliged to say to me, like the person in some cartoon or other:

'Madame, tell me at once that you love me, but don't tread on my feet like that.' " My thoughts, however, were far from Mme de Guermantes. Ever since Saint-Loup had spoken to me of a young girl of good family who frequented a house of ill-fame, and of the Baroness Putbus's chambermaid, it was in these two persons that had now become coalesced and embodied the desires inspired in me day by day by countless beauties of two classes, on the one hand the vulgar and magnificent, the majestic lady's maids of great houses, swollen with pride and saying "we" in speaking of duchesses, and on the other hand those girls of whom it was enough for me sometimes, without even having seen them go past in carriages or on foot, to have read the names in the account of a ball for for me to fall in love with them and, having conscientiously searched the social directory for the country houses in which they spent the summer (as often as not letting myself be led astray by a similarity of names), to dream alternately of going to live amid the plains of the West, the dunes of the North, the pine-woods of the South. But in vain did I fuse together all the most exquisite fleshly matter to compose, after the ideal outline traced for me by Saint-Loup, the young girl of easy virtue and Mme Putbus's maid, my two possessible beauties still lacked what I should never know until I had seen them: individual character. I was to wear myself out in vain trying to picture, during the months when my desires were focused on young girls, what the one Saint-Loup had spoken of looked like, and who she was, and during the months in which I would have preferred a lady's maid, the lineaments of Mme Putbus's. But what peace of mind, after having been perpetually troubled by my restless desires for so many fugitive creatures whose very names I often did not know and who were in any case so hard to find, harder still to get to know, impossible perhaps to conquer, to have drawn from all that scattered, fugitive, anonymous beauty two choice specimens duly labelled, whom I was at least certain of being able to procure when I wished! I kept putting off the hour for getting down to this twofold pleasure, as I put off the hour for getting down to work, but the certainty of having it whenever I chose dispensed me almost from the necessity of taking it, like those sleeping tablets which one has only to have within hand's reach to be able to do without them and to fall asleep. In the whole universe I now desired only two women, of whose faces I could not, it is true, form any picture, but whose names Saint-Loup had given me and whose compliance he had guaranteed. So that if, by what he had said this evening, he had set my imagination a heavy task, he had at the same time procured an appreciable relaxation, a prolonged rest for my will.

"Well!" said the Duchess, "apart from your parties, can I be of any use to you? Have you found a salon to which you would like me to introduce you?" I replied that I was afraid the only one that tempted me was hardly elegant enough for her. "Whose is that?" she asked in a husky monotone, scarcely opening her lips. "Baroness Putbus." This time she pretended to be really angry. "Ah, no, really! I believe you're trying to make a fool of me. I don't even know how I come to have heard the creature's name. But she is the dregs of society. It's as though you were to ask me for an introduction to my dressmaker. In fact worse, for my dressmaker is charming. You must be a little bit cracked, my poor boy. In any case, I beseech you to be polite to the people I've introduced you to, to leave cards on them, and go and see them, and not talk to them about Baroness Putbus of whom they have never heard." I asked whether Mme d'Orvillers was not inclined to be flighty. "Oh, not in the least, you're mixing her up with someone else. She's rather a prude, if anything. Isn't she, Basin?" "Yes, in any case I don't think there has ever been any talk about her," said the Duke.

"You won't come with us to the ball?" he asked me. "I can lend you a Venetian cloak and I know someone who will be deucedly glad to see you there—Oriane for one, that goes without saying—but the Princesse de Parme. She never tires of singing your praises, and swears by you. It's lucky for you—since she's a trifle mature—that she is a model of virtue. Otherwise she would certainly have taken you on as a cicisbeo, as they used to say in my young days, a sort of cavaliere servente."

I was interested not in the ball but in my rendezvous with

Albertine. And so I refused. The carriage had stopped, the footman was shouting for the gate to be opened, the horses pawed the ground until it was flung apart and the carriage passed into the courtyard. "So long," said the Duke. "I've sometimes regretted living so close to Marie," the Duchess said to me, "because although I'm very fond of her, I'm not quite so fond of her company. But I've never regretted it so much as to-night, since it has allowed me so little of yours." "Come, Oriane, no speechmaking."

The Duchess would have liked me to come inside for a minute. She laughed heartily, as did the Duke, when I said that I could not because I was expecting a girl to call at any moment. "You choose a funny time to receive visitors," she said to me.

"Come along, my sweet, there's no time to lose," said M. de Guermantes to his wife. "It's a quarter to twelve, and time we were dressed. . . ." He came into collision, outside his front door which they were grimly guarding, with the two ladies with the walking-sticks, who had not been afraid to descend at dead of night from their mountain-top to prevent a scandal. "Basin, we felt we must warn you, in case you were seen at that ball: poor Amanien has just died, an hour ago." The Duke was momentarily dismayed. He saw the famous ball collapsing in ruins for him now that these accursed mountaineers had informed him of the death of M. d'Osmond. But he quickly recovered himself and flung at his cousins a retort which reflected, together with his determination not to forgo a pleasure, his incapacity to assimilate exactly the niceties of the French language: "He's dead! No, no, they're exaggerating, they're exaggerating!" And without giving a further thought to his two relatives who, armed with their alpenstocks, prepared to make their nocturnal ascent, he fired off a string of questions at his valet:

"Are you sure my helmet has come?" "Yes, Monsieur le Duc." "You're sure there's a hole in it I can breathe through? I don't want to be suffocated, damn it!" "Yes, Monsieur le Duc." "Oh, hell and damnation, everything's going wrong this evening. Oriane, I forgot to ask Babal whether the shoes with pointed toes were for you!" "But, my dear, the dresser

from the Opéra-Comique is here, he will tell us. I don't see
how they could go with your spurs." "Let's go and find the
dresser," said the Duke. "Good-bye, my boy, I'd ask you to
come in while we are trying on our costumes—it would
amuse you. But we should only waste time talking, it's nearly
midnight and we mustn't be late in getting there or we shall
spoil the show."

I too was in a hurry to get away from M. and Mme de
Guermantes as quickly as possible. *Phèdre* finished at about
half past eleven. Albertine must have arrived by now. I went
straight to Françoise: "Is Mlle Albertine here?" "No one has
called."

Good God, did that mean that no one would call! I was in
torment, Albertine's visit seeming to me now all the more
desirable the less certain it had become.

Françoise was upset too, but for quite a different reason.
She had just installed her daughter at the table for a succulent
repast. But, on hearing me come in, and seeing that there was
no time to whip away the dishes and put out needles and
thread as though it were a work party and not a supper party:
"She's just had a spoonful of soup, and I forced her to gnaw
a bit of bone," Françoise explained to me, to reduce thus to
nothing her daughter's supper, as though its copiousness were
a crime. Even at lunch or dinner, if I committed the sin of
going into the kitchen, Françoise would pretend that they had
finished, and would even excuse herself by saying: "I just felt
like a *scrap*," or "a *mouthful*." But I was speedily reassured on
seeing the multitude of dishes that covered the table, which
Françoise, surprised by my sudden entry, like a thief in the
night which she was not, had not had time to whisk out of
sight. Then she added: "Go along to your bed now, you've
done enough work to-day" (for she wished to make it appear
that her daughter not only cost us nothing and lived frugally,
but was actually working herself to death in our service).
"You're only cluttering up the kitchen and disturbing Monsieur, who is expecting a visitor. Go on, upstairs," she repeated,
as though she were obliged to use her authority to send her
daughter to bed when in fact she was only there for appearances's sake now that supper had been ruined, and if I had

stayed five minutes longer would have withdrawn of her own accord. And turning to me, in that charming, popular and yet highly individual French that was hers, Françoise added: "Monsieur can see that her face is just cut in two with want of sleep." I remained, delighted not to have to talk to Françoise's daughter.

I have said that she came from a small village which was quite close to her mother's, and yet differed from it in the nature of the soil and its cultivation, in dialect, and above all in certain characteristics of the inhabitants. Thus the "butcheress" and Françoise's niece did not get on at all well together, but had this point in common, that when they went out on an errand, they would linger for hours at "the sister's" or "the cousin's," being themselves incapable of finishing a conversation, in the course of which the purpose with which they had set out faded so completely from their minds that, if we said to them on their return: "Well! will M. le Marquis de Norpois be at home at a quarter past six?" they did not even slap their foreheads and say: "Oh, I forgot all about it," but "Oh! I didn't understand that Monsieur wanted to know that, I thought I had just to go and bid him good-day." If they "lost their heads" in this way about something that had been said to them an hour earlier, it was on the other hand impossible to get out of their heads what they had once heard said by "the" sister or "the" cousin. Thus, if the butcheress had heard it said that the English made war on us in '70 at the same time as the Prussians (and I explained to her until I was tired that this was not the case), every three weeks the butcheress would repeat to me in the course of conversation: "It's all because of that war the English made on us in '70 with the Prussians." "But I've told you a hundred times that you're wrong," I would say, and she would then answer, implying that her conviction was in no way shaken: "In any case, that's no reason for wishing them any harm. Plenty of water has flowed under the bridges since '70," and so forth. On another occasion, advocating a war with England which I opposed, she said: "To be sure, it's always better not to go to war; but when you must, it's best to do it at once. As the sister was explaining just now, ever since that war the English made on us in '70, the commercial treaties have ruined us. After we've beaten them, we won't allow one Englishman into France unless he pays three hundred francs admission, as we have to pay now to land in England."

Such was, in addition to great decency and civility and, when they were talking, an obstinate refusal to allow any interruption, going back time and time again to the point they had reached if one did interrupt them, thus giving their talk the unshakeable solidity of a Bach fugue, the character of the inhabitants of this tiny village which did not boast five hundred, set among its chestnuts, its willows, and its fields of potatoes and beetroot.

Françoise's daughter, on the other hand (regarding herself as an up-to-date woman who had got out of the old ruts), spoke Parisian slang and was well versed in all the jokes of the day. Françoise having told her that I had come from the house of a princess: "Oh, indeed! The Princess of Brazil, I suppose, where the nuts come from." Seeing that I was expecting a visitor, she pretended to believe that my name was Charles. I replied innocently that it was not, which enabled her to get in: "Oh, I thought it was! And I was just saying to myself, *Charles attend* (charlatan)." This was not in the best of taste. But I was less unmoved when, to console me for Albertine's delay, she said to me: "I expect you'll go on waiting till doomsday. She's never coming. Ah, these modern flappers!"

And so her speech differed from her mother's; but, what is more curious, her mother's speech was not the same as that of her grandmother, a native of Bailleau-le-Pin, which was so close to Françoise's village. And yet the dialects differed slightly, like the two landscapes, Françoise's mother's village, on a slope descending into a ravine, being overgrown with willows. And, miles away from either of them, there was a small area of France where the people spoke almost precisely the same dialect as in Méséglise. I made this discovery at the same time as I experienced its tediousness, for I once came upon Françoise deep in conversation with a neighbour's housemaid, who came from this village and spoke its dialect. They could more or less understand one another, I could not understand a word, and they knew this but nevertheless continued (excused, they felt, by the joy of being fellow-countrywomen although born so far apart) to converse in this strange tongue in front of me, like people who do not wish to be understood. These picturesque studies in linguistic geography and below-stairs comradeship were renewed weekly in the kitchen, without my deriving any pleasure from them.

Since, whenever the outer gate opened, the concierge pressed an electric button which lighted the stairs, and since all the occupants of the building had already come in, I left the kitchen immediately and went to sit down in the hall, keeping my eyes fastened on the point where the slightly too narrow curtain did not completely cover the glass panel of our front door, leaving visible a vertical strip of semi-darkness from the stairs. If, suddenly, this strip turned to a golden yellow, that would mean that Albertine had just entered the building and would be with me in a minute; nobody else could be coming at that time of night. And I sat there, unable to take my eyes from the strip which persisted in remaining dark; I bent my whole body forward to make certain of noticing any change; but, gaze as I might, the vertical black band, despite my impassioned longing, did not give me the intoxicating delight that I should have felt had I seen it changed by a stroke of sudden and significant magic to a luminous bar of gold. This was indeed a great fuss to make about Albertine, to whom I had not given three minutes' thought during the Guermantes reception! But, reviving the feelings of anxious expectancy I had had in the past over other girls, Gilberte especially when she was late in coming, the prospect of having to forgo a simple physical pleasure caused me an intense mental suffering.

I was obliged to go back to my room. Françoise followed me. She felt that, as I had come away from my party, there was no point in my keeping the rose that I had in my buttonhole, and approached to take it from me. Her action, by reminding me that Albertine might perhaps not come, and by obliging me also to confess that I wished to look smart for her benefit, caused me an irritation that was intensified by the fact that, in tugging myself free, I crushed the flower and Françoise said to me: "It would have been better to let me take it than to go and spoil it like that." Indeed, her slightest word exasperated me. When we are waiting, we suffer so keenly from the absence of the person for whom we are longing that we cannot endure the presence of anyone else.

Françoise having left the room, it occurred to me that if I was now so concerned about my appearance for Albertine's sake, it was a great pity that I had so often let her see me unshaved, with several days' growth of beard, on the evenings when I let her come round to renew our caresses. I felt that she was indifferent to me and was giving me the cold shoulder. To make my room look a little more attractive, in case Albertine should still come, and because it was one of the prettiest things that I possessed, for the first time in years I placed on the bedside table the turquoise-studded cover which Gilberte had had made for me to hold Bergotte's booklet and which for so long I had insisted on keeping by me while I slept, together with the agate marble. As much perhaps as Albertine herself, who still did not come, her presence at that moment in an "elsewhere" which she had evidently found more agreeable, and of which I knew nothing, gave me a painful feeling which, in spite of what I had said to Swann scarcely an hour before as to my incapacity for being jealous, might, if I had seen her at less protracted intervals, have changed into an anxious need to know where, and with whom, she was spending her time. I dared not send round to Albertine's house, as it was too late, but in the hope that, having supper perhaps with some other girls in a café, she might take it into her head to tele-phone me, I turned the switch and, restoring the connexion to my own room, cut it off between the post office and the porter's lodge to which it was generally switched at that hour. A receiver in the little passage on to which Françoise's room opened would have been simpler, less inconvenient, but use-less. The advance of civilisation enables people to display unsuspected qualities or fresh defects which make them dearer or more insupportable to their friends. Thus Dr Bell's inven-tion had enabled Françoise to acquire an additional defect, which was that of refusing, however important, however urgent the occasion might be, to make use of the telephone. She would manage to disappear whenever anybody tried to teach her how to use it, as people disappear when it is time for them to be vaccinated. And so the telephone was installed in my bedroom, and, so that it might not disturb my parents, a whirring noise had been substituted for the bell. I did not move, for fear of not hearing it. So motionless did I remain that, for the first time for months, I noticed the tick of the clock. Françoise came in to tidy up the room. She chatted to me, but I hated her conversation, beneath the uniformly trivial continuity of which my feelings were changing from one minute to the next, passing from fear to anxiety, from anxiety to complete despair. Belying the vaguely cheerful words which I felt obliged to address to her, I could sense that my face was so wretched that I pretended to be suffering from rheumatism, to account for the discrepancy between my feigned indifference and that woe-begone expression; then I was afraid that her talk, although carried on in a low voice (not on account of Albertine, for Françoise considered that all possibility of her coming was long past), might prevent me from hearing the saving call which now would never come. At length Françoise went off to bed; I dismissed her firmly but gently, so that the noise she made in leaving the room should not drown that of the telephone. And I settled down again to listen, to suffer; when we are waiting, from the ear which takes in sounds to the mind which dissects and analyses them, and from the mind to the heart to which it transmits its results, the double journey is so rapid that we cannot even perceive its duration, and imagine that we have been listening directly with our heart.

I was tortured by the incessant recurrence of my longing, ever more anxious and never gratified, for the sound of a call; having arrived at the culminating point of a tortuous ascent through the coils of my lonely anguish, from the depths of a populous, nocturnal Paris brought miraculously close to me, there beside my bookcase, I suddenly heard, mechanical and sublime, like the fluttering scarf or the shepherd's pipe in *Tristan*, the top-like whirr of the telephone. I sprang to the intrument; it was Albertine. "I'm not disturbing you, ringing you up at this hour?" "Not at all . . ." I said, restraining my joy, for her remark about the lateness of the hour was doubtless meant as an apology for coming round in a moment, so late, and did not mean that she was not coming. "Are you coming round?" I asked in a tone of indifference. "Well . . . no, unless you absolutely must see me."

Part of me, which the other part sought to join, was in Albertine. It was essential that she should come, but I did not tell her so at first; now that we were in communication, I said to myself that I could always oblige her at the last moment either to come to me or to let me rush round to her. "Yes, I'm near home," she said, "and miles away from you. I hadn't read your note properly. I've just found it again and was afraid you might be waiting up for me." I felt sure she was lying, and now, in my fury, it was from a desire not so much to see her as to inconvenience her that I was determined to make her come. But I felt it better to refuse at first what in a few moments I should try to procure. But where was she? With the sound of her voice were blended other sounds: the braying of a bicyclist's horn, a woman's voice singing, a brass band in the distance, rang out as distinctly as the beloved voice, as though to show me that it was indeed Albertine in her actual surroundings who was beside me at that moment, like a clod of earth together with which we have carried away all the grass that was growing from it. The same sounds that I heard were striking her ear also, and were distracting her attention: true-to-life details, extraneous to the subject, valueless in themselves, all the more necessary to our perception of the miracle for what it was; simple, charming features descriptive of some Parisian street, bitter, cruel features, too, of some unknown festivity which, after she had come away from *Phèdre*, had prevented Albertine from coming to me. "I must warn you first of all that it's not that I wanted you to come, because, at this time of night, it would be a frightful nuisance . . ." I said to her. "I'm dropping with sleep. And besides, well, there are endless complications. I'm bound to say that there was no possibility of your misunderstanding my letter. You answered that it was all right. Well then, if you hadn't understood, what did you mean by that?" "I said it was all right, only I couldn't quite remember what we had arranged. But I see you're cross with me, I'm sorry. I wish now I'd never gone to *Phèdre*. If I'd known there was going to be all this fuss about it . . ." she went on, as people invariably do when, being in the wrong over one thing, they pretend to believe that they are being blamed for another. "I'm not in the least annoyed about *Phèdre*, seeing it was I who asked you to go to it." "Then you *are* angry with me; it's a nuisance it's so late now, otherwise I should have come round, but I shall call to-morrow or the day after and make it up." "Oh, please don't, Albertine, I beg of you; after making me waste an entire evening, the least you can do is to leave me in peace for the next few days. I shan't be free for a fortnight or three weeks. Listen, if it worries you to think that we seem to be parting in anger—and perhaps you're right, after all—then I'd much prefer, all things considered, since I've been waiting for you all this time and you're still out, that you should come at once. I'll have a cup of coffee to keep myself awake." "Couldn't you possibly put it off till to-morrow? Because the trouble is. ..." As I listened to these words of excuse, uttered as though she did not intend to come, I felt that, with the longing to see again the velvet-soft face which in the past, at Balbec, used to direct all my days towards the moment when, by the mauve September sea, I should be beside that roseate flower, a very different element was painfully endeavouring to combine. This terrible need of a person was something I had learned to know at Combray in the case of my mother, to the point of wanting to die if she sent word to me by Françoise that she could not come upstairs. This effort on the part of the old feeling to combine and form a single element with the other, more recent, which had for its voluptuous object only the coloured surface, the flesh-pink bloom of a flower of the sea-shore, was one that often results simply in creating (in the chemical sense) a new body, which may last only a few moments. That evening, at any rate, and for long afterwards, the two elements remained apart. But already, from the last words that had reached me over the telephone, I was beginning to understand that Albertine's life was situated (not in a physical sense, of course) at so great a distance from mine that I should always have to make exhausting explorations in order to seize hold of it, and moreover was organised like a system of earthworks which, for greater security, were of the kind that at a later period we learned to call "camouflaged." Albertine, in fact, belonged, although at a slightly higher social level, to that type of person to whom the concierge promises your messenger that she will deliver your letter when she comes in—until the day when you realise that it is precisely she, the person you have met in a public place and to whom you have ventured to write, who is the concierge. So that she does indeed live—though in the lodge only—at the address she has given you (which moreover is a private brothel of which the concierge is the madame). Lives entrenched behind five or six lines of defence, so that when you try to see this woman, or to find out about her, you invariably aim too far to the right, or to the left, or too far in front, or too far behind, and can remain in total ignorance for months, even years. In the case of Albertine, I felt that I should never discover anything, that, out of that tangled mass of details of fact and falsehood, I should never unravel the truth: and that it would always be so, unless I were to shut her up in prison (but prisoners escape) until the end. That evening, this conviction gave me only a vague anxiety, in which however I could detect a shuddering anticipation of prolonged suffering to come.

"No," I replied, "I told you a moment ago that I wouldn't be free for the next three weeks—to-morrow no more than any other day." "Very well, in that case . . . I shall come this very instant . . . It's a nuisance, because I'm at a friend's house, and she. . . ." I sensed that she had not believed that I would accept her offer to come, which therefore was not sincere, and I decided to force her hand. "What do you suppose I care about your friend? Either come or don't, it's for you to decide. I'm not asking you to come, it was you who suggested it." "Don't be angry. I'll jump into a cab now and I'll be with you in ten minutes."

Thus, from that nocturnal Paris out of whose depths the invisible message had already wafted into my very room, delimiting the field of action of a faraway person, what was now about to materialise, after this preliminary annunciation, was the Albertine whom I had known long ago beneath the sky of Balbec, when the waiters of the Grand Hotel, as they laid the tables, were blinded by the glow of the setting sun, when, the glass panels having been drawn wide open, the faintest evening breeze passed freely from the beach, where the last strolling couples still lingered, into the vast dining-room in which the first diners had not yet taken their places, and, across the mirror placed behind the cashier's desk, there passed the red reflexion of the hull and lingered long after it the grey reflexion of the smoke of the last steamer for Rivebelle. I had ceased to ask myself what could have made Albertine late, and when Françoise came into my room to inform me: "Mademoiselle Albertine is here," if I answered without even turning my head: "What in the world makes Mademoiselle Albertine come at this time of night?" it was only out of dissimulation. But then, raising my eyes to look at Françoise, as though curious to hear her answer which must corroborate the apparent sincerity of my question, I perceived, with admiration and fury, that, capable of rivalling Berma herself in the art of endowing with speech inanimate garments and the lines of her face, Françoise had taught their parts to her bodice, her hair— the whitest threads of which had been brought to the surface, were displayed there like a birth-certificate—and her neck, bent with fatigue and obedience. They commiserated with her for having been dragged from her sleep and from her warm bed, in the middle of the night, at her age, obliged to bundle into her clothes in haste, at the risk of catching pneumonia. And so, afraid that I might have seemed to be apologising for Albertine's late arrival, I added: "Anyhow, I'm very glad she has come, it's just what I wanted," and I gave free vent to my profound joy. It did not long remain unclouded, when I had heard Françoise's reply. Without uttering a word of complaint, seeming indeed to be doing her best to stifle an irrepressible cough, and simply folding her shawl over her bosom as though she felt cold, she began by telling me everything that she had said to Albertine, having not forgotten to ask after her aunt's health. "I was just saying, Monsieur must have been afraid that Mademoiselle wasn't coming, because this is no time to pay visits, it's nearly morning. But she must have been in some place that she was having a good time because she never so much as said she was sorry she had kept Monsieur waiting, she answered me as saucy as you please: 'Better late

than never!' " And Françoise added these words that pierced
my heart: "When she spoke like that she gave herself away. She
would have liked to hide what she was thinking, perhaps,
but. . . ."

I had little cause for astonishment. I have said that Françoise
rarely brought back word, when she was sent on an errand,
if not of what she herself had said, on which she readily enlarged, at any rate of the answer that was expected. But if,
exceptionally, she repeated to us the words that our friends
had said, however brief, she generally contrived, thanks if
need be to the expression, the tone that, she assured us, had
accompanied them, to make them somehow wounding. At a
pinch, she would admit to having received a snub (probably
quite imaginary) from a tradesman to whom we had sent her,
provided that, being addressed to her as our representative,
who had spoken in our name, it might rebound on us. The
only thing then would be to tell her that she had misunderstood
the man, that she was suffering from persecution mania and
that the shopkeepers were not in league against her. However,
their sentiments affected me little. Those of Albertine were a
different matter. And in repeating the sarcastic words: "Better
late than never!" Françoise at once evoked for me the friends
with whom Albertine had finished the evening, thus preferring
their company to mine. "She's a comical sight, she has a little
flat hat on, and with those big eyes of hers it does make her
look funny, especially with her cloak which she did ought to
have sent to the amender's, for it's all in holes. She amuses me,"
Françoise added, as though mocking Albertine. Though she
rarely shared my impressions, she felt the need to communicate
her own. I refused even to appear to understand that this laugh
was indicative of scorn and derision, but, to give tit for tat,
replied, although I had never seen the little hat to which she
referred: "What you call a 'little flat hat' is simply ravishing. . . ." "That is to say, it's just a bit of rubbish," said
Françoise, giving expression, frankly this time, to her genuine
contempt. Then (in a mild and leisurely tone so that my mendacious answer might appear to be the expression not of my
anger but of the truth, though without wasting any time in
order not to keep Albertine waiting) I addressed these cruel

words to Françoise: "You are excellent," I said to her in a
honeyed voice, "you are kind, you have endless qualities, but
you have never learned a single thing since the day you first
came to Paris, either about ladies' clothes or about how to
pronounce words without making silly howlers." And this
reproach was particularly stupid, for those French words
which we are so proud of pronouncing accurately are themselves only blunders made by Gaulish lips which mispro-
nounced Latin or Saxon, our language being merely a defective
pronunciation of several others. The genius of language in its
living state, the future and past of French, that is what ought
to have interested me in Françoise's mistakes. Her "amender"
for "mender" was no less curious than those animals that
survive from remote ages, such as the whale or the giraffe,
and show us the states through which animal life has passed.

"And," I went on, "since you haven't managed to learn
in all these years, you never will. But don't let that distress
you: it doesn't prevent you from being a very good soul, and
making spiced beef with jelly to perfection, and lots of other
things as well. The hat that you think so simple is copied from
a hat belonging to the Princesse de Guermantes which cost
five hundred francs. In fact I mean to give Mlle Albertine an
even finer one very soon."

I knew that what would annoy Françoise more than anything
was the thought of my spending money on people she disliked.
She answered me in a few words which were made almost
unintelligible by a sudden attack of breathlessness. When I
discovered afterwards that she had a weak heart, how remorseful I felt that I had never denied myself the fierce and sterile
pleasure of thus answering her back! Françoise detested Albertine, moreover, because, being poor, Albertine could not
enhance what Françoise regarded as my superior position. She
smiled benevolently whenever I was invited by Mme de Villeparisis. On the other hand, she was indignant that Albertine
did not practise reciprocity. I found myself being obliged to
invent fictitious presents from the latter, in the existence of
which Françoise never for an instant believed. This want of
reciprocity shocked her most of all in the matter of food. That
Albertine should accept dinners from Mamma, when we were

not invited to Mme Bontemps's (who in any case spent half her time out of Paris, her husband accepting "posts" as in the old days when he had had enough of the Ministry), seemed to her an indelicacy on the part of my friend which she rebuked indirectly by repeating a saying current at Combray:

> "Let's eat my bread."
> "Ay, that's the stuff."
> "Let's eat thy bread."
> "I've had enough."

I pretended that I was obliged to write a letter.

"Who were you writing to?" Albertine asked me as she entered the room.

"To a pretty little friend of mine, Gilberte Swann. Don't you know her?"

"No."

I decided not to question Albertine as to how she had spent the evening, feeling that I should only reproach her and that we should have no time left, seeing how late it was already, to be reconciled sufficiently to proceed to kisses and caresses. And so it was with these that I chose to begin from the first moment. Besides, if I was a little calmer, I was not feeling happy. The loss of all equanimity, of all sense of direction, that we feel when we are kept waiting, persists after the arrival of the person awaited, and, taking the place inside us of the calm spirit in which we had been picturing her coming as so great a pleasure, prevents us from deriving any from it. Albertine was in the room: my disordered nerves, continuing to flutter, were still awaiting her.

"I want a nice kiss, Albertine."

"As many as you like," she said to me in her good-natured way. I had never seen her looking so pretty.

"Another?" she asked.

"Why, you know it's a great, great pleasure to me."

"And a thousand times greater to me," she replied. "Oh, what a pretty book-cover you have there!"

"Take it, I give it to you as a keep-sake."

"You really are nice. . . ."

One would be cured for ever of romanticism if one could

make up one's mind, in thinking of the woman one loves, to try to be the man one will be when one no longer loves her. Gilberte's book-cover, her agate marble, must have derived their importance in the past from some purely inward state, since now they were to me a book-cover, a marble like any others.

I asked Albertine if she would like something to drink. "I seem to see oranges over there and water," she said. "That will be perfect." I was thus able to taste, together with her kisses, that refreshing coolness which had seemed to me to be superior to them at the Princesse de Guermantes's. And the orange squeezed into the water seemed to yield to me, as I drank, the secret life of its ripening growth, its beneficent action upon certain states of that human body which belongs to so different a kingdom, its powerlessness to make that body live but on the other hand the process of irrigation by which it was able to benefit it—countless mysteries unveiled by the fruit to my sensory perception, but not at all to my intelligence.

When Albertine had gone, I remembered that I had promised Swann that I would write to Gilberte, and courtesy, I felt, demanded that I should do so at once. It was without emotion, and as though finishing off a boring school essay, that I traced upon the envelope the name *Gilberte Swann* with which at one time I used to cover my exercise-books to give myself the illusion that I was corresponding with her. For if, in the past, it had been I who wrote that name, now the task had been deputed by Habit to one of the many secretaries whom she employs. He could write down Gilberte's name all the more calmly in that, placed with me only recently by Habit, having but recently entered my service, he had never known Gilberte, and knew only, without attaching any reality to the words, because he had heard me speak of her, that she was a girl with whom I had once been in love.

I could not accuse her of coldness. The person I now was in relation to her was the clearest possible proof of what she herself had been: the book-cover, the agate marble had simply become for me in relation to Albertine what they had been for Gilberte, what they would have been to anybody who had not suffused them with the glow of an internal flame. But now there was in me a new turmoil which in its turn distorted the real force of things and words. And when Albertine said to me, in a further outburst of gratitude: "I do love turquoises!" I answered her: "Don't let these die," entrusting to them as to some precious jewel the future of our friendship, which in fact was no more capable of inspiring a sentiment in Albertine than it had been of preserving the sentiment that had once bound me to Gilberte.

There occurred at about this time a phenomenon which deserves mention only because it recurs in every important period of history. At the very moment I was writing to Gilberte, M. de Guermantes, just home from his ball, still wearing his helmet, was thinking that next day he would be compelled to go into formal mourning, and decided to bring forward by a week the cure he was due to take at a spa. When he returned from it three weeks later (to anticipate for a moment, since I have only just finished my letter to Gilberte), those friends of his who had seen him, so indifferent at the start, turn into a fanatical anti-Dreyfusard, were left speechless with amazement when they heard him (as though the action of the cure had not been confined to his bladder) declare: "Oh, well, there'll be a fresh trial and he'll be acquitted. You can't sentence a fellow without any evidence against him. Did you ever see anyone so gaga as Froberville? An officer leading the French people to the slaughter (meaning war)! Strange times we live in." The fact was that, in the meantime, the Duke had met at the spa three charming ladies (an Italian princess and her two sisters-in-law). After hearing them make a few remarks about the books they were reading or a play that was being given at the Casino, the Duke had at once realised that he was dealing with women of superior intellect whom, as he expressed it, he "wasn't up to." He had been all the more delighted to be asked to play bridge by the princess. But, the moment he entered her sitting-room, as he began to say to her, in the fervour of his double-dyed anti-Dreyfusism: "Well, we don't hear very much about the famous Dreyfus re-trial," his stupefaction had been great when he heard the princess and her sisters-in-law say: "It's becoming more certain every day. They can't keep a man in prison who has done nothing."

"Eh? Eh?" the Duke had gasped at first, as at the discovery of a fantastic nickname employed in his household to turn to ridicule a person whom he had always regarded as intelligent. But, after a few days, just as, from cowardice and the spirit of imitation, we shout "Hallo, Jojotte" without knowing why at a great artist whom we hear so addressed by the rest of the household, the Duke, still greatly embarrassed by the novelty of this attitude, began nevertheless to say: "After all, if there's no evidence against him." The three charming ladies considered that he was not progressing rapidly enough and bullied him a bit: "But really, nobody with a grain of intelligence can ever have believed for a moment that there was anything." Whenever any revelation came out that was "damning" to Dreyfus, and the Duke, supposing that now he was going to convert the three charming ladies, came to inform them of it, they burst out laughing and had no difficulty in proving to him, with great dialectic subtlety, that his argument was worthless and quite absurd. The Duke had returned to Paris a fanatical Dreyfusard. And of course we do not suggest that the three charming ladies were not, in this instance, messengers of truth. But it is to be observed that, every ten years or so, when we have left a man imbued with a genuine conviction, it so happens that an intelligent couple, or simply a charming lady, comes into his life and after a few months he is won over to the opposite camp. And in this respect there are many countries that behave like the sincere man, many countries which we have left full of hatred for another race and which, six months later, have changed their minds and reversed their alliances.

I ceased for some time to see Albertine, but continued, failing Mme de Guermantes who no longer spoke to my imagination, to visit other fairies and their dwellings, as inseparable from themselves as is from the mollusc that fashioned it and takes shelter within it the pearly or enamelled valve or crenellated turret of its shell. I should not have been able to classify these ladies, the problem being insignificant and impossible not only to resolve but to pose. Before coming to the lady, one had first to approach the faery mansion. Now as one of them was always at home after lunch in the summer months, before I reached her house I would be obliged to lower the hood of my cab, so scorching were the sun's rays, the memory of which, without my realising it, was to enter into my general impression. I supposed that I was merely being driven to the Cours-la-Reine; in reality, before arriving at the gathering which a man of wider experience might well have derided, I would receive, as though on a journey through Italy, a delicious, dazzled sensation from which the house was never afterwards to be separated in my memory. What was more, in view of the heat of the season and the hour, the lady would have hermetically closed the shutters of the vast rectangular saloons on the ground floor in which she entertained. I would have difficulty at first in recognising my hostess and her guests, even the Duchesse de Guermantes, who in her husky voice bade me come and sit down next to her, in a Beauvais armchair illustrating the Rape of Europa. Then I would begin to make out on the walls the huge eighteenth-century tapestries representing vessels whose masts were holly-hocks in blossom, beneath which I sat as though in the palace not of the Seine but of Neptune, by the brink of the river Oceanus, where the Duchesse de Guermantes became a sort of goddess of the waters. I should never get to the end of it if I began to describe all the different types of drawing-room. This example will suffice to show that I introduced into my social judgments poetical impressions which I never took into account when I came to add up the sum, so that, when I was calculating the merits of a drawing-room, my total was never correct.

Certainly, these were by no means the only sources of error, but I have no time left, before my departure for Balbec (where to my sorrow I am going to make a second stay which will also be my last), to start upon a series of pictures of society which will find their place in due course. Here I need only say that to this first erroneous reason (my relatively frivolous existence which made people suppose that I was fond of society) for my letter to Gilberte, and for that reconciliation with the Swann family to which it seemed to point, Odette might very well, and with equal inaccuracy, have added a second. I have suggested hitherto the different aspects that the social world assumes in the eyes of a single person only by supposing that it does not change: if the selfsame woman who the other day knew nobody now goes everywhere, and another who occupied a commanding position is ostracised, one is inclined to see in these changes merely those purely personal ups and downs which from time to time bring about, in the same section of society, in consequence of speculations on the stock exchange, a resounding collapse or enrichment beyond the dreams of avarice. But there is more to it than that. To a certain extent social manifestations (vastly less important than artistic movements, political crises, the trend that leads public taste towards the theatre of ideas, then towards Impressionist painting, then towards music that is German and complicated, then music that is Russian and simple, or towards ideas of social service, ideas of justice, religious reaction, outbursts of patriotism) are nevertheless an echo of them, distant, disjointed, uncertain, changeable, blurred. So that even salons cannot be portrayed in a static immobility which has been conventionally employed up to this point for the study of characters, though these too must be carried along as it were in a quasi-historical momentum. The thirst for novelty that leads men of the fashionable world who are more or less sincere in their eagerness to keep abreast of intellectual developments to frequent the circles in which they can follow them makes them prefer as a rule some hostess as yet undiscovered, who represents still in their first freshness the hopes of a superior culture so faded and tarnished in the women who for long years have wielded the social sceptre and who, having no secrets from these men, no longer appeal to their imagination. And every period finds itself personified thus in new women, in a new group of women, who, closely identified with whatever may be the latest object of curiosity, seem, in their new attire, to be at that moment making their first appearance, like an unknown species born of the last deluge, irresistible beauties of each new Consulate, each new Directory. But very often the new hostesses are simply, like certain statesmen who may be in office for the first time but have for the last forty years been knocking at every door without seeing any open, women who were not known in society but who nevertheless had been entertaining for years past, for want of anyone better, a few "chosen friends." To be sure, this is not always the case, and when, with the prodigious flowering of the Russian Ballet, revealing one after another Bakst, Nijinsky, Benoist and the genius of Stravinsky, Princess Yourbeletieff, the youthful sponsor of all these new great men, appeared wearing on her head an immense, quivering aigrette that was new to the women of Paris and that they all sought to copy, it was widely supposed that this marvellous creature had been imported in their copious luggage, and as their most priceless treasure, by the Russian dancers; but when presently, by her side in her stage box at every performance of the "Russians," seated like a true fairy godmother, unknown until that moment to the aristocracy, we see Mme Verdurin, we shall be able to tell the society people who may well suppose her to have recently entered the country with Diaghileff's troupe, that this lady, too, had already existed in different periods and had passed through various avatars from which this one differed only in being the first to bring about at last, henceforth assured, and more and more swiftly on the march, the success so long awaited by the Mistress. In Mme Swann's case, it is true, the novelty she represented had not the same collective character. Her salon had crystallised round one man, a dying man, who had progressed almost overnight, at the moment when his talent was exhausted, from obscurity to a blaze of glory. The passion for Bergotte's works was unbounded. He spent the whole day, on show, at Mme Swann's, who would whisper to some influential man: "I shall say a word to him: he'll write an article for you." He was, in fact, in a condition to do so, and even to write a little play for Mme Swann. A stage nearer to death, he was not quite so ill as at the time when he used to come and inquire after my grandmother. This was because intense physical pain had enforced a regime on him. Illness is the most heeded of doctors: to kindness and wisdom we make promises only; pain we obey.

It is true that the Verdurins and their little clan were at this time of far more lively interest than the faintly nationalist, more markedly literary, and pre-eminently Bergottesque salon of Mme Swann. The little clan was in fact the active centre of a long political crisis which had reached its maximum of intensity: Dreyfusism. But society people were for the most part so violently anti-revisionist that a Dreyfusian salon seemed to them as inconceivable a phenomenon as, at an earlier period, a Communard salon. True, the Principessa di Caprarola, who had made Mme Verdurin's acquaintance over a big exhibition which she had organised, had been to pay her a long visit in the hope of seducing a few interesting specimens of the little clan and incorporating them in her own salon, a visit in the course of which the Princess (playing a poor man's Duchesse de Guermantes) had taken the opposing view to accepted opinion and declared that the people in her world were idiots, all of which Mme Verdurin had thought most courageous. But this courage did not subsequently take her to the point of daring, under the gimlet eyes of nationalist ladies, to bow to Mme Verdurin at the Balbec races. As for Mme Swann, on the other hand, the anti-Dreyfusards gave her credit for being "sound," which, in a woman married to a Jew, was doubly meritorious. Nevertheless, people who had never been to her house imagined her as visited only by a few obscure Jews and disciples of Bergotte. In this way women far better qualified than Mme Swann are placed on the lowest rung of the social ladder, whether on account of their origins, or because they do not care about dinner-parties and receptions, at which they are never seen (an absence erroneously assumed to be due to their not having been invited), or because they never speak of their social connexions but only of literature and art, or because people conceal the fact that they go to their houses, or they, to avoid impoliteness to yet other people, conceal the fact that they entertain them—in short for countless reasons which, added together, make of this or that woman, in certain people's eyes, the sort of woman whom one does not know. So it was with Odette. Mme d'Epinoy, when busy collecting some subscriptions for the "Patrie française," having been obliged to go and see her, as she would have gone to her dress-maker, convinced moreover that she would find only a lot of faces that were not even despised but completely unknown, stood rooted to the ground when the door opened not upon the drawing-room she imagined but upon a magic hall in which, as in the transformation scene of a pantomime, she recognised in the dazzling chorus, reclining upon divans, seated in armchairs, addressing their hostess by her Christian name, the royalties, the duchesses whom she, the Princesse d'Epinoy, had the greatest difficulty in enticing into her own drawing-room, and to whom at that moment, beneath the benevolent gaze of Odette, the Marquis du Lau, Comte Louis de Turenne, Prince Borghese, the Duc d'Estrées, carrying orangeade and cakes, were acting as cupbearers and pantlers. The Princesse d'Epinoy, as she instinctively took people's social status to be inherent in themselves, was obliged to disincarnate Mme Swann and reincarnate her in a fashionable woman. Ignorance of the real existence led by women who do not advertise it in the newspapers draws a veil of mystery over certain situations, thereby contributing to the diversification of salons. In Odette's case, at the start, a few men of the highest society, anxious to meet Bergotte, had gone to dine in privacy at her house. She had had the tact, recently acquired, not to advertise their presence; they found when they went there— a memory perhaps of the little nucleus, whose traditions Odette had preserved in spite of the schism—a place laid for them at table, and so forth. Odette took them with Bergotte (whom these excursions, incidentally, finished off) to interesting first nights. They spoke of her to various women of their own world who were capable of taking an interest in such novelty. These women were convinced that Odette, an intimate friend of Bergotte, had more or less collaborated in his works, and believed her to be a thousand times more intelligent than the most outstanding women of the Faubourg, for the same reason that made them pin all their political faith to certain staunch Republicans such as M. Doumer and M. Deschanel, whereas they visualised France on the brink of ruin were her destinies entrusted to the monarchists who were in the habit of dining with them, men like Charette or Doudeauville. This change in Odette's status had been achieved with a discretion on her part that made it more secure and more rapid but allowed no suspicion to filter through to the public, which is prone to refer to the social columns of the *Gaulois* for evidence as to the advance or decline of a salon, with the result that one day, at

the dress rehearsal of a play by Bergotte given in one of the
most fashionable theatres in aid of a charity, the really dramatic
moment was when people saw coming in and sitting down
beside Mme Swann in the centre box, which was that reserved
for the author, Mme de Marsantes and the lady who, by
the gradual self-effacement of the Duchesse de Guermantes
(glutted with honours, and taking the easy way out), was on
the way to becoming the lioness, the queen of the age: the
Comtesse Molé. "We never even imagined that she had begun
to climb," people said of Odette as they saw the Comtesse
Molé enter the box, "and look, she has reached the top of the
ladder."

So that Mme Swann might suppose that it was from snobbery that I was taking up again with her daughter.

Odette, notwithstanding her brilliant friends, listened with
close attention to the play, as though she had come there solely
to see it performed, just as in the past she used to walk across
the Bois for her health, as a form of exercise. Men who in the
past had been less assiduously attentive to her came to the
edge of the box, disturbing the whole audience, to reach up to
her hand and so approach the imposing circle that surrounded
her. She, with a smile that was still one of friendliness rather
than of irony, replied patiently to their questions, affecting
greater calm than might have been expected, a calm that was
perhaps sincere, this exhibition being only the belated revela-
lation of a habitual and discreetly hidden intimacy. Behind
these three ladies to whom every eye was drawn was Bergotte
flanked by the Prince d'Agrigente, Comte Louis de Turenne,
and the Marquis de Bréauté. And it is easy to understand that,
to men who were received everywhere and could not expect
any further distinction save one for original research, this
demonstration of their merit which they considered they were
making in succumbing to the allurements of a hostess with a
reputation for profound intellectuality, in whose house they
expected to meet all the fashionable dramatists and novelists of
the day, was more exciting, more lively than those evenings
at the Princesse de Guermantes's, which, without any change
of programme or fresh attraction, had been going on year after
year, all more or less like the one we have described at such

length. In that exalted world, the world of the Guermantes, in which people were beginning to lose interest, the latest intellectual fashions were not embodied in entertainments fashioned in their image, as in those sketches that Bergotte used to write for Mme Swann, or those veritable Committees of Public Safety (had society been capable of taking an interest in the Dreyfus case) at which, in Mme Verdurin's house, Picquart, Clemenceau, Zola, Reinach and Labori used to assemble.

Gilberte, too, helped to strengthen her mother's position, for an uncle of Swann's had just left her nearly eighty million francs, which meant that the Faubourg Saint-Germain was beginning to take notice of her. The reverse of the medal was that Swann (who, however, was dying) held Dreyfusard opinions, though even this did not injure his wife and was actually of service to her. It did not injure her because people said: "He is dotty, his mind has quite gone, nobody pays any attention to him, his wife is the only person who counts and she is charming." But Swann's Dreyfusism was positively useful to Odette. Left to herself, she might have been unable to resist making advances to fashionable women which would have been her undoing. Whereas on the evenings when she dragged her husband out to dine in the Faubourg Saint-Germain, Swann, sitting sullenly in his corner, would not hesitate, if he saw Odette seeking an introduction to some nationalist lady, to exclaim aloud: "Really, Odette, you must be mad. Why can't you keep yourself to yourself. It's very sycophantic of you to ask to be introduced to anti-semites. I forbid you." People in society whom everyone else runs after are not accustomed either to such pride or to such ill-breeding. For the first time they were seeing someone who thought himself "superior" to them. Swann's growlings were much talked about, and cards with turned-down corners rained upon Odette. When she came to call upon Mme d'Arpajon there was a lively stir of friendly curiosity. "You didn't mind my introducing her to you," said Mme d'Arpajon. "She's very nice. It was Marie de Marsantes who told me about her." "No, not at all, I hear she's so wonderfully clever, and she is charming. I'd been longing to meet her; do tell me where she lives." Mme d'Arpajon told Mme Swann that she had enjoyed herself hugely at the latter's house the other evening, and had joyfully forsaken Mme de Saint-Euverte for her. And it was true, for to prefer Mme Swann was to show that one was intelligent, like going to concerts instead of to tea-parties. But when Mme de Saint-Euverte called on Mme d'Arpajon at the same time as Odette, as Mme de Saint-Euverte was a great snob and Mme d'Arpajon, albeit she treated her without ceremony, valued her invitations, she did not introduce Odette, so that Mme de Saint-Euverte should not know who she was. The Marquise imagined that it must be some princess who seldom went out since she had never seen her before, prolonged her call, replied indirectly to what Odette was saying, but Mme d'Arpajon remained adamant. And when Mme de Saint-Euverte admitted defeat and took her leave, "I didn't introduce you," her hostess told Odette, "because people don't much care about going to her house and she's always inviting one; you'd never have heard the last of her." "Oh, that's all right," said Odette with a pang of regret. But she retained the idea that people did not care to go to Mme de Saint-Euverte's, which was to a certain extent true, and concluded that she herself held a position in society vastly superior to Mme de Saint-Euverte's, although that lady had a very high position, and Odette, so far, none at all.

She was not aware of this, and although all Mme de Guermantes's friends were friends also of Mme d'Arpajon, whenever the latter invited Mme Swann, she would say with an air of compunction: "I'm going to Mme d'Arpajon's, but—you'll think me dreadfully old-fashioned, I know—it shocks me because of Mme de Guermantes" (whom, as it happened, she had never met). Elegant men thought that the fact that Mme Swann knew hardly anyone in high society meant that she must be a superior woman, probably a great musician, and that it would be a sort of extra-social distinction, as for a duke to be a Doctor of Science, to go to her house. Utterly insignificant society women were attracted towards Odette for a diametrically opposite reason; hearing that she attended the Colonne concerts and professed herself a Wagnerian, they concluded from this that she must be "rather a lark," and were greatly excited by the idea of getting to know her. But, being themselves none too firmly established, they were afraid of compromising themselves in public if they appeared to be on friendly terms with Odette, and if they caught sight of her at a charity concert, would turn away their heads, deeming it impossible to greet, under the very nose of Mme de Roche-chouart, a woman who was perfectly capable of having been to Bayreuth, which was as good as saying that she would stick at nothing.

Since everybody becomes different when a guest in another's house—quite apart from the marvellous metamorphoses that were accomplished thus in the faery palaces—in Mme Swann's drawing-room M. de Bréauté, suddenly transfigured by the absence of the people with whom he was normally surrounded, by his air of self-satisfaction at finding himself there, just as if instead of going out to a party he had slipped on his spectacles to shut himself up in his study and read the *Revue des Deux Mondes*, by the mystic rite that he appeared to be performing in coming to see Odette, M. de Bréauté himself seemed a new man. I would have given a great deal to see what transformations the Duchesse de Montmorency-Luxembourg would have undergone in this new environment. But she was one of the people who could never be induced to meet Odette. Mme de Montmorency, a great deal kinder about Oriane than Oriane was about her, surprised me greatly by saying of Mme de Guermantes: "She knows some quite clever people, and everybody likes her. I believe that if she had had a little more consistency and application she would have succeeded in forming a salon. The fact is, she never bothered about it, and she's quite right, she's very well off as she is, sought after by everyone." If Mme de Guermantes did not have a "salon," what in the world could a "salon" be? The stupefaction which these words induced in me was no greater than that which I caused Mme de Guermantes when I told her that I enjoyed going to Mme de Montmorency's. Oriane thought her an old cretin. "I go there," she said, "because I'm forced to, she's my aunt; but you! She doesn't even know how to get agreeable people to come to her house." Mme de Guermantes did not realise that agreeable people left me cold, that when she spoke to me of "the Arpajon salon" I saw a yellow butterfly, and of "the Swann salon" (Mme Swann was at home in the winter months between 6 and 7) a black butterfly with its wings powdered with snow. At a pinch this last salon, which was not one at all, she considered, although out of bounds for herself, permissible for me on account of the "clever people" to be found there. But Mme de Luxembourg! Had I already "produced" something that had attracted attention, she would have concluded that an element of snobbishness may be combined with talent. But I put the finishing touch to her disillusionment; I confessed to her that I did not go to Mme de Montmorency's (as she supposed) to "take notes "and "make a study." Mme de Guermantes was in this respect no more in error than the social novelists who analyse mercilessly from the outside the actions of a snob or supposed snob, but never place themselves inside his skin, at the moment when a whole social springtime is bursting into blossom in one's imagination. I myself, when I sought to analyse the great pleasure that I found in going to Mme de Montmorency's, was somewhat taken aback. She occupied, in the Faubourg Saint-Germain, an old mansion ramifying into pavilions which were separated by small gardens. In the outer hall a statuette, said to be by Falconet, represented a spring which did indeed exude a perpetual moisture. A little further on the concierge, her eyes always red, either from grief or neurasthenia, a headache or a cold in the head, never answered your inquiry, waved her arm vaguely to indicate that the Duchess was at home, and let a drop or two trickle from her eyelids into a bowl filled with forget-me-nots. The pleasure that I felt on seeing the statuette, because it reminded me of a "little gardener" in plaster that stood in one of the Combray gardens, was nothing to that which was given me by the great staircase, damp and resonant, full of echoes, like the stairs in certain old-fashioned bathing establishments, the vases filled with cinerarias—blue against blue—in the ante-room, and most of all the tinkle of the bell, which was exactly that of the bell in Eulalie's room. This tinkle brought my enthusiasm to its peak, but seemed to me too humble a matter for me to be able to explain it to Mme

de Montmorency, with the result that she invariably saw me
in a state of rapture of which she never guessed the cause.

THE INTERMITTENCIES OF THE HEART

My second arrival at Balbec was very different from the
first. The manager had come in person to meet me at Pont-à-
Couleuvre, reiterating how greatly he valued his titled patrons,
which made me afraid that he had ennobled me until I realised
that, in the obscurity of his grammatical memory, *titré* meant
simply *attitré*, or accredited. In fact, the more new languages
he learned the worse he spoke the others. He informed me
that he had placed me at the very top of the hotel. "I hope,"
he said, "that you will not interpolate this as a want of discourtesy. I was worried about giving you a room of which
you are unworthy, but I did it in connexion with the noise,
because in that room you will not have anyone above your
head to disturb your trepanum" (tympanum). "And do not
worry, I shall have the windows closed, so that they don't
bang. Upon that point, I am intolerable" (this last word
expressing not his own thought, which was that he would
always be found inexorable in that respect, but, quite possibly,
the thoughts of his underlings). The rooms were, as it proved,
those we had had before. They were no humbler, but I had
risen in the manager's esteem. I could light a fire if I liked (for,
on the doctors' orders, I had left Paris at Easter), but he was
afraid there might be "fixtures" in the ceiling. "See that you
always wait before alighting a fire until the preceding one is
extenuated" (extinguished). "The important thing is to take
care not to avoid setting fire to the chimney, especially as, to
cheer things up a bit, I have put an old china pottage on the
mantelpiece which might become damaged."
He informed me with great sorrow of the death of the leader
of the Cherbourg bar: "He was an old retainer," he said
(meaning probably "campaigner") and gave me to understand
that his end had been hastened by the quickness, otherwise
the fastness, of his life. "For some time past I noticed that after

dinner he would doss off in the reading-room" (doze off, presumably). "The last times, he was so changed that if you hadn't known who it was, to look at him, he was barely recognisant" (presumably recognisable).

A happy compensation: the senior judge from Caen had just received his "rope" (ribbon) as Commander of the Legion of Honour. "Surely enough, he has capacities, but seems they gave him it principally because of his general 'impotence.'" There was a mention of this decoration, as it happened, in the previous day's *Echo de Paris*, of which the manager had as yet read only "the first paraph," in which M. Caillaux's foreign policy was severely trounced. "I consider they're quite right," he said. "He is putting us too much under the thimble of Germany" (under the thumb). As the discussion of a subject of this sort with a hotel-keeper seemed to me boring, I ceased to listen. I thought of the visual images that had made me decide to return to Balbec. They were very different from those of the earlier time, for the vision in quest of which I had come was as dazzlingly clear as the former had been hazy; they were to prove no less disappointing. The images selected by memory are as arbitrary, as narrow, as elusive as those which the imagination had formed and reality has destroyed. There is no reason why, existing outside ourselves, a real place should conform to the pictures in our memory rather than to those in our dreams. And besides, a fresh reality will perhaps make us forget, detest even, the desires on account of which we set out on our journey.

Those that had made me set out for Balbec sprang to some extent from my discovery that the Verdurins (whose invitations I had never taken up, and who would certainly be delighted to see me, if I went to call upon them in the country with apologies for never having been able to call upon them in Paris), knowing that several of the faithful would be spending the holidays on that part of the coast, and having, for that reason, taken for the whole season one of M. de Cambremer's houses (la Raspelière), had invited Mme Putbus to stay with them. The evening on which I learned this (in Paris) I lost my head completely and sent our young footman to find out whether that lady would be taking her chambermaid to

Balbec with her. It was eleven o'clock. The porter was a long
time opening the front door, and for a wonder did not send my
messenger packing, did not call the police, merely gave him a
dressing down, but with it the information that I desired. He
said that the head lady's maid would indeed be accompanying
her mistress, first of all to the waters in Germany, then to
Biarritz, and at the end of the season to Mme Verdurin's.
From that moment my mind had been set at rest, content to
have this iron in the fire. I had been able to dispense with those
pursuits in the streets, wherein I lacked that letter of introduction to the beauties I encountered which I should have to the
"Giorgione" in the fact of my having dined that very evening
with her mistress at the Verdurins'. Besides, she might perhaps
form a still better opinion of me when she learned that I knew
not merely the middle-class tenants of la Raspelière but its
owners, and above all Saint-Loup who, unable to commend
me to the chambermaid from a distance (since she did not
know him by name), had written an enthusiastic letter about
me to the Cambremers. He believed that, quite apart from any
service that they might be able to render me, Mme de Cambremer, the Legrandin daughter-in-law, would interest me by
her conversation. "She is an intelligent woman," he had
assured me. "She won't say anything definitive" (*definitive*
having taken the place of *sublime* with Robert, who, every five
or six years, would modify a few of his favourite expressions
while preserving the more important intact), "but she's a real
personality, she has character and intuition, and throws out
quite pertinent remarks. From time to time she's maddening,
she talks pretentious rubbish to put on 'dog,' which is all the
more ridiculous as nobody could be less grand than the
Cambremers, she's not always 'in the swim,' but, taking her
all round, she is one of the people it's more or less possible to
talk to."

No sooner had Robert's letter of introduction reached them
than the Cambremers, whether from a snobbishness that made
them anxious to oblige Saint-Loup, even indirectly, or from
gratitude for what he had done for one of their nephews at
Doncières, or (most probably) from kindness of heart and
traditions of hospitality, had written long letters insisting that

I should stay with them, or, if I preferred to be more independent, offering to find me lodgings. When Saint-Loup had pointed out that I should be staying at the Grand Hotel at Balbec, they replied that at least they would expect a call from me as soon as I arrived and, if I did not appear, would come without fail to hunt me out and invite me to their garden-parties.

No doubt there was no essential connexion between Mme Putbus's maid and the country round Balbec; she would not be for me like the peasant girl whom, as I strayed alone along the Méséglise way, I had so often summoned up in vain with all the force of my desire. But I had long since given up trying to extract from a woman as it were the square root of her unknown quantity, the mystery of which a mere introduction was generally enough to dispel. At least at Balbec, where I had not been for so long, I should have the advantage, failing the necessary connexion between the place and this woman, that my sense of reality would not be destroyed by habit as in Paris, where, whether in my own home or in a bedroom that I already knew, pleasure indulged in with a woman could not give me for one instant, amid everyday surroundings, the illusion that it was opening the door for me to a new life. (For if habit is a second nature, it prevents us from knowing our first, whose cruelties it lacks as well as its enchantments.) But I might perhaps experience this illusion in a strange place, where one's sensibility is revived by a ray of sunshine, and where my ardour would be finally consummated by the woman I desired. However, we shall see that circumstances conspired in such a way that not only did this woman fail to come to Balbec, but I dreaded nothing so much as the possibility of her coming, so that the principal object of my expedition was neither attained nor indeed pursued.

It was true that Mme Putbus was not to be at the Verdurins' so early in the season; but pleasures which we have chosen beforehand may be remote if their coming is assured and if, in the interval of waiting, we can devote ourselves to the pastime of seeking to attract while powerless to love. Moreover, I was not going to Balbec in the same poetical frame of mind as on the first occasion; there is always less egoism in pure imagination than in recollection; and I knew that I was going to find myself in one of those very places where fair strangers must abound; a beach offers them in no less profusion than a ball-room, and I looked forward to strolling up and down outside the hotel, on the front, with the same sort of pleasure that Mme de Guermantes would have procured me if, instead of getting me invited to brilliant dinner-parties, she had given my name more often for their lists of partners to hostesses who gave dances. To make female acquaintances at Balbec would be as easy for me now as it had been difficult before, for I was now as well supplied with friends and resources there as I had been destitute of them on my first visit.

I was roused from my meditations by the voice of the manager, to whose political dissertations I had not been listening. Changing the subject, he told me of the judge's delight on hearing of my arrival, and said that he was coming to pay me a visit in my room that very evening. The thought of this visit so alarmed me (for I was beginning to feel tired) that I begged him to prevent it (which he promised to do) and, as a further precaution, to post members of his staff on guard, for the first night, on my landing. He did not seem overfond of his staff. "I am obliged to keep running after them all the time because they are lacking in inertia. If I was not there they would never stir. I shall post the lift-boy on sentry outside your door." I asked him if the boy had yet become "head page." "He is not old enough yet in the house," was the answer. "He has comrades more aged than he is. It would cause an outcry. We must act with granulation in everything. I quite admit that he strikes a good aptitude at the door of his lift. But he is still a trifle young for such positions. With others in the place of longer standing, it would make a contrast. He is a little wanting in seriousness, which is the primitive quality" (doubtless, the primordial, the most important quality). "He needs his leg screwed on a bit tighter" (my interlocutor meant to say his head). "Anyhow, he can leave it all to me. I know what I'm about. Before I won my stripes as manager of the Grand Hotel, I smelt powder under M. Paillard." I was impressed by this simile, and thanked the manager for having come in person as far as Pont-à-Couleuvre. "Oh, that's nothing! The

loss of time has been quite infinite" (for infinitesimal). Meanwhile, we had arrived.

Disruption of my entire being. On the first night, as I was
suffering from cardiac fatigue, I bent down slowly and cau-
tiously to take off my boots, trying to master my pain. But
scarcely had I touched the topmost button than my chest
swelled, filled with an unknown, a divine presence, I was
shaken with sobs, tears streamed from my eyes. The being
who had come to my rescue, saving me from barrenness of
spirit, was the same who, years before, in a moment of identical
distress and loneliness, in a moment when I had nothing left
of myself, had come in and had restored me to myself, for
that being was myself and something more than me (the container that is greater than the contained and was bringing
it to me). I had just perceived, in my memory, stooping over
my fatigue, the tender, preoccupied, disappointed face of my
grandmother, as she had been on that first evening of our
arrival, the face not of that grandmother whom I had been
astonished and remorseful at having so little missed, and who
had nothing in common with her save her name, but of my
real grandmother, of whom, for the first time since the afternoon of her stroke in the Champs-Elysées, I now recaptured
the living reality in a complete and involuntary recollection.
This reality does not exist for us so long as it has not been
recreated by our thought (otherwise men who have been
engaged in a titanic struggle would all of them be great epic
poets); and thus, in my wild desire to fling myself into her
arms, it was only at that moment—more than a year after her
burial, because of the anachronism which so often prevents the
calendar of facts from corresponding to the calendar of feelings—that I became conscious that she was dead. I had often
spoken about her since then, and thought of her also, but
behind my words and thoughts, those of an ungrateful,
selfish, cruel young man, there had never been anything that
resembled my grandmother, because, in my frivolity, my love
of pleasure, my familiarity with the spectacle of her ill health,
I retained within me only in a potential state the memory of
what she had been. At any given moment, our total soul has
only a more or less fictitious value, in spite of the rich inventory

of its assets, for now some, now others are unrealisable, whether they are real riches or those of the imagination—in my own case, for example, not only of the ancient name of Guermantes but those, immeasurably graver, of the true memory of my grandmother. For with the perturbations of memory are linked the intermittencies of the heart. It is, no doubt, the existence of our body, which we may compare to a vase enclosing our spiritual nature, that induces us to suppose that all our inner wealth, our past joys, all our sorrows, are perpetually in our possession. Perhaps it is equally inexact to suppose that they escape or return. In any case if they remain within us, for most of the time it is in an unknown region where they are of no use to us, and where even the most ordinary are crowded out by memories of a different kind, which preclude any simultaneous occurrence of them in our consciousness. But if the context of sensations in which they are preserved is recaptured, they acquire in turn the same power of expelling everything that is incompatible with them, of installing alone in us the self that originally lived them. Now, inasmuch as the self that I had just suddenly become once again had not existed since that evening long ago when my grandmother had undressed me after my arrival at Balbec, it was quite naturally, not at the end of the day that had just passed, of which that self knew nothing, but—as though Time were to consist of a series of different and parallel lines—without any solution of continuity, immediately after the first evening at Balbec long ago, that I clung to the minute in which my grandmother had stooped over me. The self that I then was, that had disappeared for so long, was once again so close to me that I seemed still to hear the words that had just been spoken, although they were now no more than a phantasm, as a man who is half awake thinks he can still make out close by the sound of his receding dream. I was now solely the person who had sought a refuge in his grandmother's arms, had sought to obliterate the traces of his sorrow by smothering her with kisses, that person whom I should have had as much difficulty in imagining when I was one or other of those that for some time past I had successively been as now I should have had in making the sterile effort to experience the desires and joys of one of those that for a time at least I no longer was. I remembered how, an hour before the moment when my grandmother had stooped in her dressing-gown to unfasten my boots, as I wandered along the stiflingly hot street, past the pastry-cook's, I had felt that I could never, in my need to feel her arms round me, live through the hour that I had still to spend without her. And now that this same need had reawakened, I knew that I might wait hour after hour, that she would never again be by my side. I had only just discovered this because I had only just, on feeling her for the first time alive, real, making my heart swell to breaking-point, on finding her at last, learned that I had lost her for ever. Lost for ever; I could not understand, and I struggled to endure the anguish of this contradiction: on the one hand an existence, a tenderness, surviving in me as I had known them, that is to say created for me, a love which found in me so totally its complement, its goal, its constant lodestar, that the genius of great men, all the genius that might have existed from the beginning of the world, would have been less precious to my grandmother than a single one of my defects; and on the other hand, as soon as I had relived that bliss, as though it were present, feeling it shot through by the certainty, throbbing like a recurrent pain, of an annihilation that had effaced my image of that tenderness, had destroyed that existence, retrospectively abolished our mutual predestination, made of my grandmother, at the moment when I had found her again as in a mirror, a mere stranger whom chance had allowed to spend a few years with me, as she might have done with anyone else, but to whom, before and after those years, I was and would be nothing.

Instead of the pleasures that I had been experiencing of late, the only pleasure that it would have been possible for me to enjoy at that moment would have been, by touching up the past, to diminish the sorrows and sufferings of my grandmother's life. But I did not remember her only in that dressing-gown, a garment so appropriate as to have become almost symbolic of the pains, unhealthy no doubt but comforting too, which she took for me; gradually I began to remember all the opportunities that I had seized, by letting her see my sufferings and exaggerating them if necessary, to cause her a grief which I imagined as being obliterated immediately by my kisses, as though my tenderness had been as capable as my happiness of creating hers; and, worse than that, I who could conceive of no other happiness now but that of finding happiness shed in my memory over the contours of that face, moulded and bowed by love, had striven with such insensate frenzy to expunge from it even the smallest pleasures, as on the day when Saint-Loup had taken my grandmother's photograph and I, unable to conceal from her what I thought of the ridiculous childishness of the coquetry with which she posed for him, with her wide-brimmed hat, in a flattering half light, had allowed myself to mutter a few impatient, wounding words, which, I had sensed from a contraction of her features, had struck home; it was I whose heart they were rending, now that the consolation of countless kisses was forever impossible.

But never should I be able to eradicate from my memory that contraction of her face, that anguish of her heart, or rather of mine; for as the dead exist only in us, it is ourselves that we strike without respite when we persist in recalling the blows that we have dealt them. I clung to this pain, cruel as it was, with all my strength, for I realised that it was the effect of the memory I had of my grandmother, the proof that this memory was indeed present within me. I felt that I did not really remember her except through pain, and I longed for the nails that riveted her to my consciousness to be driven yet deeper. I did not try to mitigate my suffering, to embellish it, to pretend that my grandmother was only somewhere else and momentarily invisible, by addressing to her photograph (the one taken by Saint-Loup, which I had with me) words and entreaties as to a person who is separated from us but, retaining his personality, knows us and remains bound to us by an indissoluble harmony. Never did I do this, for I was determined not merely to suffer, but to respect the original form of my suffering as it had suddenly come upon me unawares, and I wanted to continue to feel it, following its own laws, whenever that contradiction of survival and annihilation, so strangely intertwined within me, returned. I did not know whether I should one day distil a grain of truth from this painful and for the moment incomprehensible impression, but I knew that if I ever did extract some truth from life, it could only be from such an impression and from none other, an impression at once so particular and so spontaneous, which had neither been traced by my intelligence nor attenuated by my pusillanimity, but which death itself, the sudden revelation of death, striking like a thunderbolt, had carved within me, along a supernatural and inhuman graph, in a double and mysterious furrow. (As for the state of forgetfulness of my grandmother in which I had been living until that moment, I could not even think of clinging to it to find some truth; since in itself it was nothing but a negation, a weakening of the faculty of thought incapable of recreating a real moment of life and obliged to substitute for it conventional and neutral images.) Perhaps, however, the instinct of self-preservation, the ingenuity of the mind in safeguarding us from pain, already beginning to lay the foundations of its necessary but baneful edifice on the still smoking ruins, I relished too keenly the sweet joy of recalling this or that opinion held by the beloved being, recalling them as though she had been able to hold them still, as though she existed, as though I continued to exist for her. But as soon as I had succeeded in falling asleep, at that more truthful hour when my eyes closed to the things of the outer world, the world of sleep (on whose frontier my intelligence and my will, momentarily paralysed, could no longer strive to rescue me from the cruelty of my real impressions) reflected, refracted the agonising synthesis of survival and annihilation, once more reformed, in the organic and translucent depths of the mysteriously lighted viscera. The world of sleep, in which our inner consciousness, subordinated to the disturbances of our organs, accelerates the rhythm of the heart or the respiration, because the same dose of terror, sorrow or remorse acts with a strength magnified a hundredfold if it is thus injected into our veins: as soon as, to traverse the arteries of the subterranean city, we have embarked upon the dark current of our own blood as upon an inward Lethe meandering sixfold, tall solemn forms appear to us, approach and glide away, leaving us in tears. I sought in vain for my grandmother's form when I had entered beneath the sombre portals; yet I knew that she did exist still, if with a diminished vitality, as pale as that of memory; the darkness was increasing, and the wind; my father, who was to take me to her, had not yet arrived. Suddenly my breath failed me, I felt my heart turn to stone; I had just remembered that for weeks on end I had forgotten to write to my grandmother. What must she be thinking of me? "Oh God," I said to myself, "how wretched she must be in that little room which they have taken for her, no bigger than what one would give to an old servant, where she's all alone with the nurse they have put there to look after her, from which she cannot stir, for she's still slightly paralysed and has always refused to get up! She must think that I've forgotten her now that she's dead; how lonely she must be feeling, how deserted! Oh, I must hurry to see her, I mustn't lose a minute, I can't wait for my father to come—but where is it? How can I have forgotten the address? Will she know me again, I wonder? How can I have forgotten her all these months? It's so dark, I shan't be able to find her; the wind is holding me back; but look! there's my father walking ahead of me . . ." I call out to him: "Where is grandmother? Tell me her address. Is she all right? Are you quite sure she has everything she needs?" "Yes, yes," says my father, "you needn't worry. Her nurse is well trained. We send her a little money from time to time, so that she can get your grandmother anything she may need. She sometimes asks what's become of you. She was told you were going to write a book. She seemed pleased. She wiped away a tear." And then I seemed to remember that shortly after her death, my grandmother had said to me, sobbing, with a humble look, like an old servant who has been given notice, like a stranger: "You will let me see something of you occasionally, won't you; don't let too many years go by without visiting me. Remember that you were my grandson, once, and that grandmothers never forget." And seeing again that face of hers, so submissive, so sad, so tender, I wanted to run to her at once and say to her, as I ought to have said to her then: "Why, grandmother, you can see me as often as you like, I have only you in the world, I shall never leave you any more." What tears my silence must have made her shed through all those months in which I have never been to the place where she is lying! What can she have been saying to herself? And it is in a voice choked with tears that I too shout to my father: "Quick, quick, her address, take me to her." But he says: "Well . . . I don't know whether you will be able to see her. Besides, you know, she's very frail now, very frail, she's not at all herself, I'm afraid you would find it rather painful. And I can't remember the exact number of the avenue." "But tell me, you who know, it's not true that the dead have ceased to exist. It can't possibly be true, in spite of what they say, because grandmother still exists." My father smiles a mournful smile: "Oh, hardly at all, you know, hardly at all. I think it would be better if you didn't go. She has everything that she wants. They come and keep the place tidy for her." "But is she often alone?" "Yes, but that's better for her. It's better for her not to think, it could only make her unhappy. Thinking often makes people unhappy. Besides, you know, she is quite lifeless now. I shall leave a note of the exact address, so that you can go there; but I don't see what good you can do, and I don't suppose the nurse will allow you to see her." "But you know quite well I shall always live by her side, dear, deer, deer, Francis Jammes, fork." But already I had retraced the dark meanderings of the stream, had ascended to the surface where the world of the living opens, so that if I still repeated: "Francis Jammes, deer, deer," the sequence of these words no longer offered me the limpid meaning and logic which they had expressed so naturally for me only a moment before, and which I could not now recall. I could not even understand why the word "Aias" which my father had said to me just now had immediately signified: "Take care you don't catch cold," without any possibility of doubt. I had forgotten to close the shutters, and so probably the daylight had awakened me. But I could not bear to have before my eyes those sea vistas on which my grandmother used to gaze for hours on end; the fresh image of their heedless beauty was at once supplemented by the thought that she could not see them; I should have liked to stop my ears against their sound, for now the luminous plenitude of the beach carved out an emptiness in my heart; everything seemed to be saying to me, like those paths and lawns of a public garden in which I had once lost her, long ago, when I was still a little child: "We haven't seen her," and beneath the roundness of the pale vault of heaven I felt crushed as though beneath a huge bell of bluish glass forming an horizon from which my grandmother was excluded. To escape from the sight of it, I turned towards the wall, but alas, what was now facing me was that partition which used to serve us as a morning messenger, that partition which, as responsive as a violin in rendering every nuance of a feeling, reported so exactly to my grandmother my fear at once of waking her and, if she were already awake, of not being heard by her and so of her not coming, then immediately, like a second instrument taking up the melody, informing me of her coming and bidding me be calm. I dared not put out my hand to that wall, any more than to a piano on which my grandmother had been playing and which still vibrated from her touch. I knew that I might knock now, even louder, and that I should hear no response, that my grandmother would never come again. And I asked nothing more of God, if a paradise exists, than to be able, there, to knock on that wall with the three little raps which my grandmother would recognise among a thousand, and to which she would give those answering knocks which meant: "Don't fuss, little mouse, I know you're impatient, but I'm just coming," and that he would let me stay with her throughout eternity, which would not be too long for the two of us.

The manager came in to ask whether I should like to come down. He had most carefully supervised, just in case, my "placement" in the dining-room. As he had seen no sign of me, he had been afraid that I might have had a recurrence of my spasms. He hoped that it might be only a little "sore throats" and assured me that he had heard it said that they could be soothed with what he called "calyptus."

He brought me a message from Albertine. She had not been due to come to Balbec that year but, having changed her plans, had been for the last three days not in Balbec itself but ten minutes away by train at a neighbouring watering-place. Fearing that I might be tired after the journey, she had stayed away the first evening, but sent word now to ask when I could see her. I inquired whether she had called in person, not because I wished to see her, but so that I might arrange not to see her. "Yes," replied the manager. "But she would like it to be as soon as possible, unless you have not some quite necessitous reasons. You see," he concluded, "that everybody here desires you eventually." But for my part, I wished to see nobody.

And yet the day before, on my arrival, I had been seized once again by the indolent charm of seaside existence. The same taciturn lift-boy, silent this time from respect and not from disdain, and glowing with pleasure, had set the lift in motion. As I rose upon the ascending column, I had travelled once again through what had formerly been for me the mystery of a strange hotel, in which when you arrive, a tourist without protection or prestige, each resident returning to his room, each young girl going down to dinner, each chambermaid passing along the eerie perspective of a corridor, not to mention the young lady from America with her chaperon, gives you a look in which you can read nothing that you would have liked to read there. This time, on the contrary, I had felt the almost too soothing pleasure of passing up through an hotel that I knew, where I felt at home, where I had performed once again that operation which we must always start afresh, longer, more difficult than the turning inside out of an eyelid, and which consists in the imposition of our own familiar soul on the terrifying soul of our surroundings. Must I now, I had asked myself, little suspecting the sudden change of mood that was in store for me, go always to new hotels where I shall be dining for the first time, where Habit will not yet have killed upon each landing, outside each door, the terrible dragon that seemed to be watching over a magical existence, where I shall have to approach those unknown women whom grand hotels, casinos, watering-places seem to bring together to live a communal existence as though in vast polyparies?

I had found pleasure even in the thought that the tedious judge was so eager to see me; I could see, on the first evening, the waves, the azure mountain ranges of the sea, its glaciers and its cataracts, its elevation and its careless majesty, merely upon smelling for the first time after so long an interval, as I washed my hands, that peculiar odour of the over-scented

soap of the Grand Hotel—which, seeming to belong at once
to the present moment and to my past visit, floated between
them like the real charm of a particular form of existence in
which one comes home only to change one's tie. The sheets
on my bed, too fine, too light, too large, impossible to tuck
in, to keep in position, which billowed out from beneath the
blankets in shifting whorls, would have distressed me before.
Now they merely cradled upon the awkward, swelling fullness
of their sails the glorious sunrise, big with hopes, of my first
morning. But that sun did not have time to appear. That very
night the terrible, divine presence had returned to life. I asked
the manager to leave me, and to give orders that no one was
to enter my room. I told him that I should remain in bed and
rejected his offer to send to the chemist's for the excellent drug.
He was delighted by my refusal for he was afraid that other
visitors might be bothered by the smell of the "calyptus."
It earned me the compliment: "You are in the movement"
(he meant: "in the right"), and the warning: "Take care you
don't defile yourself at the door, I've had the lock 'elucidated'
with oil; if any of the servants dares to knock at your door,
he'll be beaten 'black and white.' And they can mark my
words, for I'm not a repeater" (this evidently meant that he
did not say a thing twice). "But wouldn't you care for a drop
of old wine, just to set you up; I have a pig's head of it downstairs" (presumably hogshead). "I shan't bring it to you on a
silver dish like the head of Jonathan, and I warn you that it is
not Château-Lafite, but it is virtually equivocal" (equivalent).
"And as it's quite light, they might fry you a little sole." I
declined everything, but was surprised to hear the name of the
fish pronounced like that of the first king of Israel, Saul, by a
man who must have ordered so many in his life.

Despite the manager's promises, a little later I was brought
a calling-card from the Marquise de Cambremer. Having come
over to see me, the old lady had inquired whether I was there
and when she heard that I had arrived only the day before and
was unwell, had not insisted but (not without stopping,
doubtless, at the chemist's or the haberdasher's, while the footman jumped down from the box and went in to pay a bill or
to give an order) had driven back to Féterne in her old ba-

rouche upon eight springs drawn by a pair of horses. Not
infrequently indeed was the rumble of the latter to be heard
and its trappings admired in the streets of Balbec and of various
other little places along the coast, between Balbec and Féterne.
Not that these halts outside shops were the object of these
excursions. It was on the contrary some tea-party or garden-
party at the house of some squire or burgess, socially quite
unworthy of the Marquise. But she, though completely over-
shadowing, by her birth and her wealth, the petty nobility of
the district, was in her perfect goodness and simplicity of
heart so afraid of disappointing anyone who had invited her
that she would attend all the most insignificant social gatherings in the neighbourhood. Certainly, rather than travel
such a distance to listen, in the stifling heat of a tiny drawing-
room, to a singer who generally had no voice and whom in
her capacity as the lady bountiful of the countryside and as a
renowned musician she would afterwards be compelled to
congratulate with exaggerated warmth, Mme de Cambremer
would have preferred to go for a drive or to remain in her
marvellous gardens at Féterne, at the foot of which the drowsy
waters of a little bay float in to die amid the flowers. But she
knew that the probability of her coming had been announced
by the host, whether he was a noble or a freeman of Maineville-la-Teinturière or of Chattoncourt-l'Orgueilleux. And if
Mme de Cambremer had driven out that afternoon without
making a formal appearance at the party, one or other of the
guests who had come from one of the little places that lined
the coast might have seen or heard the Marquise's barouche,
thus depriving her of the excuse that she had not been able to
get away from Féterne. Moreover, for all that these hosts had
often seen Mme de Cambremer appear at concerts given in
houses which they considered were no place for her, the slight
depreciation which in their eyes the position of the too obliging
Marquise suffered thereby vanished as soon as it was they who
were entertaining her, and it was with feverish anxiety that
they would ask themselves whether or not they were going to
see her at their little party. What an assuagement of the doubts
and fears of days if, after the first song had been sung by the
daughter of the house or by some amateur on holiday in the

neighbourhood, one of the guests announced (an infallible sign that the Marquise was coming to the party) that he had seen the famous barouche and pair drawn up outside the watchmaker's or the chemist's! Thereupon Mme de Cambremer (who indeed would arrive before long, followed by her daughter-in-law and the guests who were staying with her at the moment and whom she had asked permission, joyfully granted, to bring) shone once more with undiminished lustre in the eyes of the host and hostess, for whom the hoped-for reward of her coming had perhaps been the determining if unavowed cause of the decision they had made a month earlier to burden themselves with the trouble and expense of an afternoon party. Seeing the Marquise present at their gathering, they remembered no longer her readiness to attend those given by their less qualified neighbours, but the antiquity of her family, the splendour of her house, the rudeness of her daughter-in-law, *née* Legrandin, who by her arrogance emphasised the slightly insipid good-nature of the dowager. Already they could see in their mind's eye, in the social column of the *Gaulois*, the paragraph which they would concoct themselves in the family circle, with all the doors shut and barred, about "the little corner of Brittany which is at present a whirl of gaiety, the ultra-select party from which the guests could hardly tear themselves away, promising their charming host and hostess that they would soon pay them another visit." Day after day they would watch for the newspaper to arrive, worried that they had not yet seen any notice in it of their party, and afraid lest they should have had Mme de Cambremer for their other guests alone and not for the whole reading public. At length the blessed day would arrive: "The season is exceptionally brilliant this year at Balbec. Small afternoon concerts are the fashion. ..." Heaven be praised, Mme de Cambremer's name had been spelt correctly, and included "among others we may mention" but at the head of the list. All that remained would be to appear annoyed at this journalistic indiscretion which might get them into difficulties with people whom they had not been able to invite, and to ask hypocritically in Mme de Cambremer's hearing who could have been so treacherous as to send the notice, upon which the

Marquise, every inch the lady bountiful, would say: "I can understand your being annoyed, but I must say I'm only too delighted that people should know I was at your party."

On the card that was brought me, Mme de Cambremer had scribbled the message that she was giving an afternoon party "the day after to-morrow." And indeed only two days earlier, tired as I was of social life, it would have been a real pleasure to me to taste it, transplanted amid those gardens in which, thanks to the exposure of Féterne, fig trees, palms, rose bushes grew out in the open and stretched down to a sea often as blue and calm as the Mediterranean, upon which the hosts' little yacht would sail across, before the party began, to fetch the most important guests from the places on the other side of the bay, would serve, with its awnings spread to shut out the sun, as an open-air refreshment room after the party had assembled, and would set sail again in the evening to take back those whom it had brought. A charming luxury, but so costly that it was partly to meet the expenditure that it entailed that Mme de Cambremer had sought to increase her income in various ways, notably by letting for the first time one of her properties, very different from Féterne: la Raspelière. Yes, two days earlier, how welcome such a party, peopled with minor nobles all unknown to me, in a new setting, would have been to me as a change from the "high life" of Paris! But now pleasures had no longer any meaning for me. And so I wrote to Mme de Cambremer to decline, just as, an hour ago, I had sent Albertine away: grief had destroyed in me the possibility of desire as completely as a high fever takes away one's appetite. . . . My mother was to arrive the following day. I felt that I was less unworthy to live in her company, that I should understand her better, now that a whole alien and degrading existence had given way to the resurgence of the heartrending memories that encircled and ennobled my soul, like hers, with their crown of thorns. So I thought; but in reality there is a world of difference between real grief, like my mother's—which literally crushes the life out of one for years if not for ever, when one has lost the person one loves—and that other kind of grief, transitory when all is said, as mine was to be, which passes as quickly as it has been slow in coming, which we do not experience until long after the event because in order to feel it we need first to "understand" the event; grief such as so many people feel, from which the grief that was torturing me at this moment differed only in assuming the form of involuntary memory.

That I was one day to experience a grief as profound as that of my mother will be seen in the course of this narrative, but it was neither then nor thus that I imagined it. Nevertheless, like an actor who ought to have learned his part and to have been in his place long beforehand but, having arrived only at the last moment and having read over once only what he has to say, manages to improvise so skilfully when his cue comes that nobody notices his unpunctuality, my new-found grief enabled me, when my mother came, to talk to her as though it had existed always. She supposed merely that the sight of these places which I had visited with my grandmother (which was not at all the case) had revived it. For the first time then, and because I felt a sorrow which was as nothing compared with hers but which opened my eyes, I realised with horror what she must be suffering. For the first time I understood that the blank, tearless gaze (because of which Françoise had little pity for her) that she had worn since my grandmother's death was fixed on that incomprehensible contradiction between memory and non-existence. Moreover, since, though still in deep mourning, she was more "dressed up" in this new place, I was more struck by the transformation that had occurred in her. It is not enough to say that she had lost all her gaiety; fused, congealed into a sort of imploring image, she seemed to be afraid of affronting by too sudden a movement, by too loud a tone of voice, the sorrowful presence that never left her. But above all, as soon as I saw her enter in her crape overcoat, I realised—something that had escaped me in Paris—that it was no longer my mother that I had before my eyes, but my grandmother. As, in royal and ducal families, on the death of the head of the house his son takes his title and, from being Duc d'Orléans, Prince de Tarente or Prince des Laumes, becomes King of France, Duc de la Trémoïlle, Duc de Guermantes, so by an accession of a different order and more profound origin, the dead annex the living who become their replicas and successors, the continuators of their interrupted life. Perhaps the great sorrow that, in a daughter such as Mamma, follows the death of her mother simply breaks the chrysalis a little sooner, hastens the metamorphosis and the appearance of a being whom we carry within us and who, but for this crisis which annihilates time and space, would have emerged more gradually. Perhaps, in our regret for her who is no more, there is a sort of auto-suggestion which ends by bringing out in our features resemblances which potentially we already bore, and above all a cessation of our most characteristically individual activity (in my mother, her common sense and the mocking gaiety that she inherited from her father), which, so long as the beloved person was alive, we did not shrink from exercising, even at her expense, and which counterbalanced the traits that we derived exclusively from her. Once she is dead, we hesitate to be different, we begin to admire only what she was, what we ourselves already were, only blended with something else, and what in future we shall be exclusively. It is in this sense (and not in that other sense, so vague, so false, in which the phrase is generally understood) that we may say that death is not in vain, that the dead continue to act upon us. They act upon us even more than the living because, true reality being discoverable only by the mind, being the object of a mental process, we acquire a true knowledge only of things that we are obliged to recreate by thought, things that are hidden from us in everyday life. . . . Lastly, in this cult of grief for our dead, we pay an idolatrous worship to the things that they loved. My mother could not bear to be parted, not only from my grandmother's bag, which had become more precious than if it had been studded with sapphires and diamonds, from her muff, from all those garments which served to accentuate the physical resemblance between them, but even from the volumes of Mme de Sévigné which my grandmother took with her everywhere, copies which my mother would not have exchanged even for the original manuscript of the *Letters*. She had often teased my grandmother, who could never write to her without quoting some phrase of Mme de Sévigné or Mme de Beausergent. In each of the three letters that I received from Mamma before her arrival at Balbec, she quoted Mme de Sévigné to me as though those three letters had been written not by her to me but by my grandmother to her. She must at once go out on to the front to see that beach of which my grandmother had spoken to her every day in her letters. I saw her from my window, dressed in black, and carrying her mother's sunshade, advancing with timid, pious steps over the sands which beloved feet had trodden before her, and she looked as though she were going in search of a corpse which the waves would cast up at her feet. So that she should not have to dine alone, I had to join her downstairs. The judge and the barrister's widow asked to be introduced to her. And everything that was in any way connected with my grandmother was so precious to her that she was deeply touched, and remembered ever afterwards with gratitude what the judge said to her, just as she was hurt and indignant that on the contrary the barrister's wife had not a word to say in memory of the dead woman. In reality, the judge cared no more about my grandmother than the barrister's wife. The affecting words of the one and the other's silence, for all that my mother put so vast a distance between them, were but alternative ways of expressing that indifference which we feel towards the dead. But I think that my mother found most comfort in the words in which I unintentionally betrayed a little of my own anguish. It could not but make Mamma happy (notwithstanding all her affection for myself), like everything else that guaranteed my grandmother survival in people's hearts. Daily after this my mother went down and sat on the beach, in order to do exactly what her mother had done, and read her two favourite books, the *Memoirs* of Mme de Beausergent and the *Letters* of Mme de Sévigné. She, like all the rest of us, could not bear to hear the latter called the "witty Marquise" any more than to hear La Fontaine called "le Bonhomme." But when, in reading the *Letters*, she came upon the words "my daughter," she seemed to be listening to her mother's voice.

    She had the misfortune, on one of these pilgrimages during which she did not like to be disturbed, to meet on the beach a lady from Combray, accompanied by her daughters. Her name was, I think, Mme Poussin. But among ourselves we always referred to her as "Just You Wait," for it was by the perpetual repetition of this phrase that she warned her daughters of the evils that they were laying up for themselves, saying for instance if one of them was rubbing her eyes: "Just you wait until you go and get ophthalmia." She greeted my mother from afar with long, lachrymose bows, a sign not of condolence but of the nature of her social training. Living in comparative retirement at Combray within the walls of her large garden, she could never find anything soft enough for her liking, and subjected words and even proper names to a softening process. She felt "spoon" to be too hard a word to apply to the piece of silverware which measured out her syrups, and said, in consequence, "spune"; she would have been afraid of offending the gentle bard of Télémaque by calling him bluntly Fénelon— as I myself did with every reason to know, having as my dearest friend the best, bravest, most intelligent of men, whom no one who knew him could forget: Bertrand de Fénelon—and invariably said "Fénélon," feeling that the acute accent added a certain softness. The far from soft son-in-law of this Mme Poussin, whose name I have forgotten, having been notary public at Combray, ran off with the contents of the safe, and relieved my uncle, in particular, of a considerable sum of money. But most of the inhabitants of Combray were on such friendly terms with the rest of the family that no coolness ensued and people were merely sorry for Mme Poussin. She never entertained, but whenever people passed by her railings they would stop to admire the shade of her trees, without being able to make out anything else. She gave us no trouble at Balbec, where I encountered her only once, at a moment when she was saying to a daughter who was biting her nails: "Just you wait till you get a good whitlow."

While Mamma sat reading on the beach I remained in my room by myself. I recalled the last weeks of my grandmother's life, and everything connected with them, the outer door of the flat which had been propped open when I went out with her for the last time. In contrast with all this the rest of the world seemed scarcely real and my anguish poisoned everything in it. Finally my mother insisted on my going out. But at every step, some forgotten view of the casino, of the street along which, while waiting for her that first evening, I had walked as far as the Duguay-Trouin monument, prevented me, like a wind against which it is hopeless to struggle, from going further; I lowered my eyes in order not to see. And after I had recovered my strength a little I turned back towards the hotel, the hotel in which I knew that it was henceforth impossible that, however long I might wait, I should find my grand-mother as I had found her there before, on the evening of our arrival. As it was the first time that I had gone out of doors, a number of servants whom I had not yet seen gazed at me curiously. On the very threshold of the hotel a young page took off his cap to greet me and at once put it on again. I supposed that Aimé had, to borrow his own expression, "tipped him the wink" to treat me with respect. But I saw a moment later that, as someone else entered the hotel, he doffed it again. The fact of the matter was that this young man had no other occupation in life than to take off and put on his cap, and did it to perfection. Having realised that he was incapable of doing anything else but excelled in that, he practised it as many times a day as possible, thus winning a discreet but widespread regard from the hotel guests, coupled with great regard from the hall porter upon whom devolved the duty of engaging the boys and who, until this rare bird alighted, had never succeeded in finding one who did not receive notice within a week, greatly to the astonishment of Aimé who used to say: "After all, in that job they've only got to be polite, which can't be so very difficult." The manager required in addition that they should have what he called a good "presence," meaning thereby that they should not be absent from their posts, or perhaps having heard the word "presence" used of personal appearance. The appearance of the lawn behind the hotel had been altered by the creation of several flower-beds and by the removal not only of an exotic shrub but of the page who, at the time of my former visit, used to provide an external decoration with the supple stem of his figure and the curious colouring of his hair. He had gone off with a Polish countess who had taken him as her secretary, following the example of his two elder brothers and their typist sister, snatched from the hotel by persons of different

nationality and sex who had been attracted by their charm.
The only one remaining was the youngest, whom nobody
wanted because he squinted. He was highly delighted when the
Polish countess or the protectors of the other two brothers
came on a visit to the hotel at Balbec. For, although he envied
his brothers, he was fond of them and could in this way cultivate his family feelings for a few weeks in the year. Was not
the Abbess of Fontevrault, deserting her nuns for the occasion,
in the habit of going to partake of the hospitality which Louis
XIV offered to that other Mortemart, his mistress, Madame
de Montespan? The boy was still in his first year at Balbec; he
did not as yet know me, but having heard his comrades of
longer standing supplement the word "Monsieur" with my
surname when they addressed me, he copied them from the
first with an air of self-satisfaction, either at showing his
familiarity with a person whom he supposed to be well-known,
or at conforming with a usage of which five minutes earlier he
had been unaware but which he felt it to be indispensable that
he should not fail to observe. I could well appreciate the charm
that this great hotel might have for certain persons. It was
arranged like a theatre, and was filled to the flies with a
numerous and animated cast. For all that the visitor was only
a sort of spectator, he was perpetually involved in the performance, not simply as in one of those theatres where the
actors play a scene in the auditorium, but as though the life of
the spectator was going on amid the sumptuous fittings of the
stage. The tennis-player might come in wearing a white flannel
blazer, but the porter would have put on a blue frock coat with
silver braid in order to hand him his letters. If this tennis-
player did not choose to walk upstairs, he was equally involved
with the actors in having by his side, to propel the lift, its
attendant no less richly attired. The corridors on each floor
engulfed a flock of chambermaids and female couriers, fair
visions against the sea, like the frieze of the Panathenaea, to
whose modest rooms devotees of ancillary feminine beauty
would penetrate by cunning detours. Downstairs, it was the
masculine element that predominated and that made this
hotel, in view of the extreme and idle youth of the servants,
a sort of Judaeo-Christian tragedy given bodily form and

perpetually in performance. And so I could not help reciting
to myself, when I saw them, not indeed the lines of Racine
that had come into my head at the Princesse de Guermantes's
while M. de Vaugoubert stood watching young embassy secretaries greet M. de Charlus, but other lines of Racine, taken this
time not from *Esther* but from *Athalie*: for in the doorway of
the hall, what in the seventeenth century was called the portico,
"a flourishing race" of young pages clustered, especially at tea-
time, like the young Israelites of Racine's choruses. But I do
not believe that a single one of them could have given even
the vague answer that Joas finds to satisfy Athalie when she
inquires of the infant Prince: "What is your office, then?" for
they had none. At the most, if one had asked of any of them,
like the old Queen: "But all this race, what do they then,
within the confines of this place?" he might have said: "I
watch the solemn pomp and bear my part." Now and then one
of the young supers would approach some more important
personage, then this young beauty would rejoin the chorus,
and, unless it was the moment for a spell of contemplative
relaxation, they would proceed with their useless, respectful,
decorative, daily evolutions. For, except on their "day off,"
"reared in seclusion from the world" and never crossing
the threshold, they led the same ecclesiastical existence as
the Levites in *Athalie*, and as I gazed at that "young and
faithful troop" playing at the foot of the steps draped with
sumptuous carpets, I felt inclined to ask myself whether I
was entering the Grand Hotel at Balbec or the Temple of
Solomon.

I went straight up to my room. My thoughts kept constantly
turning to the last days of my grandmother's illness, to her
sufferings which I relived, intensifying them even more: when
we think we are merely recreating the grief and pain of a
beloved person, our pity exaggerates them; but perhaps it is
our pity that speaks true, more than the sufferers' own consciousness of their pain, they being blind to that tragedy of
their existence which pity sees and deplores. But my pity would
have transcended my grandmother's sufferings in a renewed
outpouring had I known then what I did not know until long
afterwards, that on the eve of her death, in a moment of

consciousness and after making sure that I was not in the
room, she had taken Mamma's hand, and, after pressing her
fevered lips to it, had said: "Good-bye, my child, good-bye for
ever." And this may also perhaps have been the memory upon
which my mother never ceased to gaze so fixedly. Then
sweeter memories returned to me. She was my grandmother
and I was her grandson. Her facial expressions seemed written
in a language intended for me alone; she was everything in my
life, other people existed merely in relation to her, to the
opinion she would express to me about them. But no, our
relations were too fleeting to have been anything but accidental.
She no longer knew me, I should never see her again. We had
not been created solely for one another; she was a stranger to
me. This stranger was before my eyes at the moment in the
photograph taken of her by Saint-Loup. Mamma, who had met
Albertine, had insisted upon my seeing her because of the nice
things she had said about my grandmother and myself. I had
accordingly made an appointment with her. I told the manager
that she was coming, and asked him to put her in the drawing-
room to wait for me. He told me that he had known her for
years, herself and her friends, long before they had attained
"the age of purity," but that he was annoyed with them because
of certain things they had said about the hotel. "They can't be
very 'illegitimate' if they talk like that. Unless people have been
slandering them." I had no difficulty in guessing that "purity"
here meant "puberty." "Illegitimate" puzzled me more. Was
it perhaps a confusion with "illiterate," which in that case
was a further confusion with "literate"? As I waited until it
was time to go down and meet Albertine, I kept my eyes fixed,
as on a drawing which one ceases to see by dint of staring at it,
upon the photograph that Saint-Loup had taken, and all of a
sudden I thought once again: "It's grandmother, I am her
grandson," as a man who has lost his memory remembers his
name, as a sick man changes his personality. Françoise came
in to tell me that Albertine was there, and, catching sight of
the photograph: "Poor Madame, it's the very image of her,
down to the beauty spot on her cheek; that day the Marquis
took her picture, she was very poorly, she had been taken bad
twice. 'Whatever happens, Françoise,' she says to me, 'you

must never let my grandson know.' And she hid it well, she was always cheerful in company. When she was by herself, though, I used to find that she seemed to be in rather monotonous spirits now and then. But she soon got over it. And then she says to me, she says: 'If anything happened to me, he ought to have a picture of me to keep. And I've never had one taken in my life.' So then she sent me along with a message to the Marquis, and he was never to let you know that it was she had asked him, but could he take her photograph. But when I came back and told her he would, she changed her mind again, because she was looking so poorly. 'It would be even worse,' she says to me, 'than no photograph at all.' But she was a clever one, she was, and in the end she got herself up so well in that big shady hat that it didn't show at all when she was out of the sun. She was very pleased with her photograph, because at that time, so she said, she didn't think she would ever leave Balbec alive. It was no use me saying to her: 'Madame, it's wrong to talk like that, I don't like to hear Madame talk like that,' she'd got it into her head. And, lord, there were plenty of days when she couldn't eat a thing. That was why she used to make Monsieur go and dine away out in the country with M. le Marquis. Then instead of going in to dinner she'd pretend to be reading a book, and as soon as the Marquis's carriage had started, up she'd go to bed. Some days she wanted to send word to Madame to come down so's she could see her once more. And then she was afraid of alarming her, as she hadn't said anything to her about it. 'It will be better for her to stay with her husband, don't you see, Françoise.' " Looking me in the face, Françoise asked me all of a sudden if I was "feeling queer." I said that I was not; and she went on: "Here you are keeping me chatting to you. And your visitor has been here all this time. I must go down and tell her. She's not the sort of person to have here. Why, a fast one like that, she may be gone again by now. She doesn't like to be kept waiting. Oh, nowadays, Mademoiselle Albertine, she's somebody!" "You are quite wrong, she's a very respectable person, too good for this place. But go and tell her that I shan't be able to see her to-day."

What compassionate declamations I should have provoked

from Françoise if she had seen me cry. I carefully hid myself
from her. Otherwise I should have had her sympathy. But I
gave her mine. We do not put ourselves sufficiently in the
place of these poor maidservants who cannot bear to see us
cry, as though crying hurt us; or hurt them, perhaps, for
Françoise used to say to me when I was a child: "Don't cry
like that, I don't like to see you crying like that." We dislike
high-sounding phrases, asseverations, but we are wrong, for
we close our hearts to the pathos of country folk, to the legend
which the poor serving woman, dismissed, unjustly perhaps,
for theft, pale as death, grown suddenly more humble, as if it
were a crime merely to be accused, unfolds, invoking her
father's honesty, her mother's principles, her grandmother's
admonitions. It is true that those same servants who cannot
bear our tears will have no hesitation in letting us catch
pneumonia because the maid downstairs likes draughts and it
would not be polite to her to shut the windows. For it is
necessary that even those who are right, like Françoise, should
be wrong also, so that Justice may be made an impossible thing.
Even the humble pleasures of servants provoke either the
refusal or the ridicule of their masters. For it is always a mere
nothing, but foolishly sentimental, unhygienic. And so
they are in a position to say: "I only ask for this one thing in
the whole year, and I'm not allowed it." And yet their masters
would allow them far more, provided it was not stupid and
dangerous for them—or for the masters themselves. To be sure,
the humility of the wretched maid, trembling, ready to confess
the crime that she has not committed, saying "I shall leave
to-night if you wish," is a thing that nobody can resist. But we
must learn also not to remain unmoved, despite the solemn
and threatening banality of the things that she says, her maternal heritage and the dignity of the family "kailyard," at the
sight of an old cook draped in the honour of her life and of
her ancestry, wielding her broom like a sceptre, putting on a
tragic act, her voice broken with sobs, drawing herself up
majestically. That afternoon, I remembered or imagined scenes
of this sort which I associated with our old servant, and from
then onwards, in spite of all the harm that she might do to
Albertine, I loved Françoise with an affection, intermittent

it is true, but of the strongest kind, the kind that is founded upon pity.

True, I suffered all day long as I sat gazing at my grandmother's photograph. It tortured me. Not so acutely, though, as the visit I received that evening from the manager. When I had spoken to him about my grandmother, and he had reiterated his condolences, I heard him say (for he enjoyed using the words that he pronounced wrongly): "Like the day when Madame your grandmother had that sincup, I wanted to tell you about it, because you see, on account of the other guests it might have given the place a bad name. She ought really to have left that evening. But she begged me to say nothing about it and promised me that she wouldn't have another sincup, or the first time she had one, she would go. However, the floor waiter reported to me that she had had another. But, lord, you were old clients we wanted to please, and since nobody made any complaint. . ." And so my grandmother had had syncopes which she never mentioned to me. Perhaps at the very moment when I was being least kind to her, when she was obliged, in the midst of her pain, to make an effort to be good-humoured so as not to irritate me, and to appear well so as not to be turned out of the hotel. "Sincup" was a word which, so pronounced, I should never have imagined, which might perhaps, applied to other people, have struck me as ridiculous, but which in its strange tonal novelty, like that of an original discord, long retained the faculty of arousing in me the most painful sensations.

Next day I went, at Mamma's request, to lie down for a while on the beach, or rather among the dunes, where one is hidden by their folds, and where I knew that Albertine and her friends would not be able to find me. My drooping eyelids allowed but one kind of light to pass, entirely pink, the light of the inner walls of the eyes. Then they shut altogether. Whereupon my grandmother appeared to me, seated in an armchair. So feeble was she that she seemed to be less alive than other people. And yet I could hear her breathe; now and again she made a sign to show that she had understood what we were saying, my father and I. But in vain did I take her in my arms, I could not kindle a spark of affection in her eyes, a flush of

colour in her cheeks. Absent from herself, she appeared somehow not to love me, not to know me, perhaps not to see me.
I could not interpret the secret of her indifference, of her dejection, of her silent displeasure. I drew my father aside. "You
can see, all the same," I said to him, "there's no doubt about
it, she understands everything perfectly. It's a perfect imitation
of life. If only we could fetch your cousin, who maintains that
the dead don't live. Why, she's been dead for more than a year
and yet she's still alive. But why won't she give me a kiss?"
"Look, her poor head is drooping again." "But she wants to
go to the Champs-Elysées this afternoon." "It's madness!"
"You really think it can do her any harm, that she can die any
further? It isn't possible that she no longer loves me. I keep on
hugging her, won't she ever smile at me again?" "What can
you expect, when people are dead they're dead."

A few days later I was able to look with pleasure at the
photograph that Saint-Loup had taken of her; it did not
revive the memory of what Françoise had told me, because that
memory had never left me and I was growing used to it. But
by contrast with what I imagined to have been her grave and
pain-racked state that day, the photograph, still profiting by the
ruses which my grandmother had adopted, which succeeded in
taking me in even after they had been disclosed to me, showed
her looking so elegant, so carefree, beneath the hat which
partly hid her face, that I saw her as less unhappy and in better
health than I had supposed. And yet, her cheeks having without
her knowing it an expression of their own, leaden, haggard,
like the expression of an animal that feels that it has been
marked down for slaughter, my grandmother had an air of
being under sentence of death, an air involuntarily sombre,
unconsciously tragic, which escaped me but prevented Mamma
from ever looking at that photograph, that photograph which
seemed to her a photograph not so much of her mother as of
her mother's disease, of an insult inflicted by that disease on
my grandmother's brutally buffeted face.

Then one day I decided to send word to Albertine that I
would see her presently. This was because, on a morning of
intense and premature heat, the myriad cries of children at
play, of bathers disporting themselves, of newsvendors, had

traced for me in lines of fire, in wheeling, interlacing flashes, the scorching beach which the little waves came up one by one to sprinkle with their coolness; then the symphony concert had begun, mingled with the lapping of the surf, through which the violins hummed like a swarm of bees that had strayed out over the sea. At once I had longed to hear Albertine's laughter and to see her friends again, those girls silhouetted against the waves who had remained in my memory the inseparable charm, the characteristic flora of Balbec; and I had decided to send a line via Françoise to Albertine, making an appointment for the following week, while the sea, gently rising, with the unfurling of each wave completely buried in layers of crystal the melody whose phrases appeared to be separated from one another like those angel lutanists which on the roof of an Italian cathedral rise between the pinnacles of blue porphyry and foaming jasper. But on the day on which Albertine came, the weather had turned dull and cold again, and moreover I had no opportunity of hearing her laugh; she was in a very bad mood. "Balbec is deadly dull this year," she said to me. "I don't mean to stay any longer than I can help. You know I've been here since Easter, that's more than a month. There's not a soul here. You can imagine what fun it is." Notwithstanding the recent rain and a sky that changed every moment, after escorting Albertine as far as Epreville, for she was, to borrow her expression, "shuttling" between that little watering-place, where Mme Bontemps had her villa, and Incarville, where she had been taken "en pension" by Rosemonde's family, I went off by myself in the direction of the highroad that Mme de Villeparisis's carriage used to take when we went for drives with my grandmother; pools of water, which the sun, now bright again, had not yet dried, made a regular quagmire of the ground, and I thought of my grandmother who could never walk a yard without covering herself in mud. But on reaching the road I found a dazzling spectacle. Where I had seen with my grandmother in the month of August only the green leaves and, so to speak, the disposition of the apple-trees, as far as the eye could reach they were in full bloom, unbelievably luxuriant, their feet in the mire beneath their ball-dresses, heedless of spoiling the most marvellous pink satin that was ever seen, which glittered in the sunlight; the distant horizon of the sea gave the trees the background of a Japanese print; if I raised my head to gaze at the sky through the flowers, which made its serene blue appear almost violent, they seemed to draw apart to reveal the immensity of their paradise. Beneath that azure a faint but cold breeze set the blushing bouquets gently trembling. Blue-tits came and perched upon the branches and fluttered among the indulgent flowers, as though it had been an amateur of exotic art and colours who had artificially created this living beauty. But it moved one to tears because, to whatever lengths it went in its effects of refined artifice, one felt that it was natural, that these apple-trees were there in the heart of the country, like peasants on one of the highroads of France. Then the rays of the sun gave place suddenly to those of the rain; they streaked the whole horizon, enclosing the line of apple-trees in their grey net. But these continued to hold aloft their pink and blossoming beauty, in the wind that had turned icy beneath the drenching rain: it was a day in spring.

CHAPTER TWO

IN my fear lest the pleasure I found in this solitary excursion might weaken my memory of my grandmother, I sought to revive it by thinking of some great sorrow that she had experienced; in response to my appeal that sorrow tried to reconstruct itself in my heart, threw up vast pillars there; but my heart was doubtless too small for it, I had not the strength to bear so great a pain, my attention was distracted at the moment when it was approaching completion, and its arches collapsed before they had joined, as the waves crumble before reaching their pinnacle.

And yet, if only from my dreams when I was asleep, I might have learned that my grief for my grandmother's death was diminishing, for she appeared in them less crushed by the idea that I had formed of her non-existence. I saw her an invalid still, but on the road to recovery; I found her in better health. And if she made any allusion to what she had suffered, I stopped her mouth with my kisses and assured her that she was now permanently cured. I should have liked to call the sceptics to witness that death is indeed a malady from which one recovers. Only, I no longer found in my grandmother the rich spontaneity of old. Her words were no more than a feeble, docile response, almost a mere echo of mine; she was now no more than the reflexion of my own thoughts.

Although I was still incapable of feeling a renewal of physical desire, Albertine was beginning nevertheless to inspire in me a desire for happiness. Certain dreams of shared affection, always hovering within us, readily combine, by a sort of affinity, with the memory (provided that this has already become slightly vague) of a woman with whom we have taken our pleasure. This sentiment recalled to me aspects of Albertine's face more gentle, less gay, quite different from those that would have been evoked by physical desire; and as it was also less pressing than that desire, I would gladly have postponed its realisation until the following winter, without seeking to see Albertine again at Balbec before her departure. But, even in the midst of a grief that is still acute, physical desire will revive. From my bed, where I was made to spend hours every day resting, I longed for Albertine to come and resume our former amusements. Do we not see, in the very room in which they have lost a child, its parents soon come together again to give the little angel a baby brother? I tried to distract my mind from this desire by going to the window to look at that day's sea. As in the former year, the seas, from one day to another, were rarely the same. Nor indeed did they at all resemble those of that first year, whether because it was now spring with its storms, or because, even if I had come down at the same time of year as before, the different, more change-able weather might have discouraged from visiting this coast certain indolent, vaporous, fragile seas which on blazing summer days I had seen slumbering upon the beach, their bluish breasts faintly stirring with a soft palpitation or above all because my eyes, taught by Elstir to retain precisely those elements that once I had deliberately rejected, would now gaze for hours at what in the former year they had been incapable of seeing. The contrast that used then to strike me so forcibly, between the country drives that I took with Mme de Ville-parisis and the fluid, inaccessible, mythological proximity of the eternal Ocean, no longer existed for me. And there were days now when, on the contrary, the sea itself seemed almost rural. On the days, few and far between, of really fine weather, the heat had traced upon the waters, as though across fields, a dusty white track at the end of which the pointed mast of a fishing-boat stood up like a village steeple. A tug, of which only the funnel was visible, smoked in the distance like a factory set apart, while alone against the horizon a convex patch of white, sketched there doubtless by a sail but seemingly solid and as it were calcareous, was reminiscent of the sunlit corner of some isolated building, a hospital or a school. And the clouds and the wind, on the days when these were added to the sun, completed, if not the error of judgment, at any rate the illusion of the first glance, the suggestion that it aroused in the imagination. For the alternation of sharply defined patches of colour like those produced in the country by the proximity of different crops, the rough, yellow, almost muddy irregularities of the marine surface, the banks, the slopes that hid from sight a vessel upon which a crew of nimble sailors seemed to be harvesting, all this on stormy days made the sea a thing as varied, as solid, as undulating, as populous, as civilised as the earth with its carriage roads over which I used to travel and was soon to be travelling again. And once, unable any longer to hold out against my desire, instead of going back to bed I put on my clothes and set off for Incarville to find Albertine. I would ask her to come with me to Douville, where I would pay calls on Mme de Cambremer at Féterne and on Mme Verdurin at la Raspelière. Albertine would wait for me meanwhile upon the beach and we would return together after dark. I went to take the train on the little local railway, of which I had picked up from Albertine and her friends all the nicknames current in the district, where it was known as the *Twister* because of its numberless windings, the *Crawler* because the train never seemed to move, the *Transatlantic* because of a horrible siren which it sounded to clear people off the line, the *Decauville* and the *Funi*, albeit there was nothing funicular about it but because it climbed the cliff, and, though not strictly speaking a Decauville, had a 60 centimetre gauge, the *B. A. G.* because it ran between Balbec and Grattevast *via* Angerville, the *Tram* and the *T. S. N.* because it was a branch of the Tramways of Southern Normandy. I took my seat in a compartment in which I was alone; it was a day of glorious sunshine, and stiflingly hot; I drew down the blue blind which shut off all but a single ray of sunlight. But immediately I saw my grandmother, as she had appeared sitting in the train on our departure from Paris for Balbec, when, in her distress at seeing me drink beer, she had preferred not to look, to shut her eyes and pretend to be asleep. I, who in my childhood had been unable to endure her anguish when my grandfather took a drop of brandy, had not only inflicted upon her the anguish of seeing me accept, at the invitation of another, a drink which she regarded as harmful to me, but had forced her to leave me free to swill it down to my heart's content; worse still, by my bursts of anger, my fits of breathlessness, I had forced her to help, to advise me to do so, with a supreme resignation of which I saw now in my memory the mute, despairing image, her eyes closed to shut out the sight. So vivid a memory had, like the stroke of a magic wand, restored the mood that I had been gradually outgrowing for some time past; what could I have done with Rosemonde when my lips were wholly possessed by the desperate longing to kiss a dead woman? What could I have said to the Cambremers and the Verdurins when my heart was beating so violently because the pain that my grandmother had suffered was being constantly renewed in it? I could not remain in the compartment. As soon as the train stopped at Maineville-la-Teinturière, abandoning all my plans, I alighted. Maineville had of late acquired considerable importance and a reputation all its own, because a director of various casinos, a purveyor of pleasure, had set up just outside it, with a luxurious display of bad taste that could vie with that of any grand hotel, an establishment to which we shall return anon and which was, to put it bluntly, the first brothel for smart people that it had occurred to anyone to build upon the coast of France. It was the only one. True, every port has its own, but intended for sailors only, and for lovers of the picturesque who are amused to see, next door to the age-old parish church, the hardly less ancient, venerable and moss-grown bawd standing in front of her ill-famed door waiting for the return of the fishing fleet.

Hurrying past the glittering house of "pleasure," insolently erected there despite the protests which the heads of families had addressed in vain to the mayor, I reached the cliff and followed its winding paths in the direction of Balbec. I heard, without responding to it, the appeal of the hawthorns. Less opulent neighbours of the blossoming apple trees, they found them rather heavy, without denying the fresh complexion of the rosy-petalled daughters of those wealthy brewers of cider. They knew that, though less well endowed, they were more sought after, and were more than attractive enough simply in their crumpled whiteness.*

On my return, the hotel porter handed me a black-bordered letter in which the Marquis and the Marquise de Gonneville,

the Vicomte and the Vicomtesse d'Amfreville, the Comte and
the Comtesse de Berneville, the Marquis and the Marquise de
Graincourt, the Comte d'Amenoncourt, the Comtesse de
Maineville, the Comte and the Comtesse de Franquetot, the
Comtesse de Chaverny *née* d'Aigleville, begged to announce,
and from which I understood at length why it had been sent
to me when I caught sight of the names of the Marquise de
Cambremer *née* du Mesnil la Guichard, the Marquis and the
Marquise de Cambremer, and saw that the deceased, a cousin
of the Cambremers, was named Eléonore-Euphrasie-Humber-
tine de Cambremer, Comtesse de Criquetot. In the whole
expanse of this provincial family, the enumeration of which
filled several closely printed lines, not a single commoner, and
on the other hand not a single known title, but the entire
muster-roll of the nobles of the region who made their names
—those of all the interesting places in the neighbourhood—
ring out with their joyous endings in *ville*, in *court*, or sometimes
on a duller note (in *tot*). Garbed in the roof-tiles of their castle
or in the roughcast of their parish church, their nodding
heads barely reaching above the vault of the nave or hall, and
then only to cap themselves with the Norman lantern or the
timbers of the pepperpot turret, they gave the impression of
having sounded the rallying call to all the charming villages
straggling or scattered over a radius of fifty leagues, and to
have paraded them in massed formation, without a single
absentee or a single intruder, on the compact, rectangular
chess-board of the aristocratic letter edged with black.

My mother had gone upstairs to her room, meditating this
sentence from Mme de Sévigné: "I see none of the people who
seek to distract me; in veiled words they seek to prevent me
from thinking of you, and that offends me"—because the
judge had told her that she ought to find some distraction.
To me he whispered: "That's the Princesse de Parme!" My
fears were dispelled when I saw that the woman whom the
judge pointed out to me bore not the slightest resemblance
to Her Royal Highness. But as she had engaged a room
in which to spend the night after paying a visit to Mme de
Luxembourg, the report of her coming had the effect upon
many people of making them take each newcomer for the

Princesse de Parme—and upon me of making me go and shut myself up in my attic.

I had no wish to remain there by myself. It was barely four o'clock. I asked Françoise to go and find Albertine, so that she might spend the evening with me.

It would be untrue, I think, to say that there were already symptoms of that painful and perpetual mistrust which Albertine was to inspire in me, not to mention the special character, emphatically Gomorrhan, which that mistrust was to assume. Certainly, even that afternoon—but not for the first time— I waited a little anxiously. Françoise, once she had started, stayed away so long that I began to despair. I had not lighted the lamp. The daylight had almost gone. The flag over the Casino flapped in the wind. And, feebler still in the silence of the beach over which the tide was rising, and like a voice expressing and intensifying the jarring emptiness of this restless, unnatural hour, a little barrel-organ that had stopped outside the hotel was playing Viennese waltzes. At length Françoise arrived, but unaccompanied. "I have been as quick as I could but she wouldn't come because she didn't think she was looking smart enough. If she was five minutes painting herself and powdering herself, she was a good hour. It'll be a regular scentshop in here. She's coming, she stayed behind to tidy herself at the mirror. I thought I should find her here." There was still a long time to wait before Albertine appeared. But the gaiety and the charm that she showed on this occasion dispelled my gloom. She informed me (contrary to what she had said the other day) that she would be staying for the whole season and asked me whether we could not arrange, as in the former year, to meet daily. I told her that at the moment I was too sad and that I would rather send for her from time to time at the last moment, as I did in Paris. "If ever you're feeling gloomy or if you're in the mood, don't hesitate," she told me, "just send for me and I shall come at once, and if you're not afraid of its creating a scandal in the hotel, I shall stay as long as you like." Françoise, in bringing her to me, had assumed the joyous air she wore whenever she had gone to some trouble on my behalf and had succeeded in giving me pleasure. But her joy had nothing to do with Albertine herself, and the very next day she was to greet me with these penetrating words: "Monsieur ought not to see that young lady. I know quite well the sort she is, she'll make you unhappy." As I escorted Albertine to the door I saw in the lighted dining-room the Princesse de Parme. I merely gave her a glance, taking care not to be seen. But I must confess that I found a certain grandeur in the royal politeness which had made me smile at the Guermantes's. It is a fundamental rule that sovereign princes are at home wherever they are, and this rule is conventionally expressed in obsolete and useless customs such as that which requires the host to carry his hat in his hand in his own house to show that he is not in his own home but in the Prince's. Now the Princesse de Parme may not have formulated this idea to herself, but she was so imbued with it that all her actions, spontaneously invented to suit the circumstances, expressed it. When she rose from table she handed a lavish tip to Aimé, as though he had been there solely for her and she were rewarding, before leaving a country house, a butler who had been detailed to wait upon her. Nor did she stop at the tip, but with a gracious smile bestowed on him a few friendly, flattering words, with a store of which her mother had provided her. She all but told him that, just as the hotel was perfectly managed, so Normandy was a garden of roses and that she preferred France to any other country in the world. Another coin slipped from the Princess's fingers for the wine waiter whom she had sent for and to whom she insisted on expressing her satisfaction like a general after an inspection. The lift-boy had come up at that moment with a message for her; he too received a word, a smile and a tip, all this interspersed with simple, encouraging remarks intended to prove to them that she was only one of themselves. As Aimé, the wine waiter, the lift-boy and the rest felt that it would be impolite not to grin from ear to ear at a person who smiled at them, she was presently surrounded by a cluster of servants with whom she chatted benevolently; such ways being unfamiliar in smart hotels, the people who passed by, not knowing who she was, thought they were seeing a regular visitor to Balbec who because of her mean extraction or for professional reasons (she was perhaps the wife of an agent for champagne) was less different from the domestics than the really smart visitors. As for me, I thought of the palace at Parma, of the advice, partly religious, partly political, given to this Princess, who behaved towards the lower orders as though she had been obliged to conciliate them in order to reign over them one day; or indeed, as though she were already reigning.

I went upstairs to my room, but I was not alone there. I could hear someone mellifluously playing Schumann. No doubt it happens at times that people, even those whom we love best, become permeated with the gloom or irritation that emanates from us. There is however an inanimate object which is capable of a power of exasperation to which no human being will ever attain: to wit, a piano.

Albertine had made me take a note of the dates on which she would be going away for a few days to visit various friends, and had made me write down their addresses as well, in case I should want her on one of those evenings, for none of them lived very far away. This meant that in seeking her out, from one girl friend to another, I found her more and more entwined in ropes of flowers. I must confess that many of her friends— I was not yet in love with her—gave me, at one watering-place or another, moments of pleasure. These obliging young playmates did not seem to me to be very many. But recently I thought of them again, and their names came back to me. I counted that, in that one season, a dozen conferred on me their ephemeral favours. Another name came back to me later, which made thirteen. I then had a sort of childishly cruel impulse to settle for that number. Alas, I realised that I had forgotten the first, Albertine who was no more and who made the fourteenth.

To resume the thread of my narrative, I had written down the names and addresses of the girls with whom I should find her on the days when she was not to be at Incarville, but privately had decided that on those days I would instead take the opportunity to call on Mme Verdurin. In any case, our desires for different women vary in intensity. One evening we cannot bear to be deprived of one who, after that, for the next month or two, will trouble us scarcely at all. And then there are the laws of alternation—which it is not the place to study here—whereby, after an over-exertion of the flesh, the woman whose image haunts our momentary senility is one to whom we would barely give more than a kiss on the forehead. As for Albertine, I saw her seldom, and only on the very infrequent evenings when I felt that I could not do without her. If such a desire seized me when she was too far from Balbec for Françoise to be able to go and fetch her, I used to send the lift-boy to Egreville, to La Sogne, to Saint-Frichoux, asking him to finish his work a little earlier than usual. He would come into my room, but would leave the door open, for although he was conscientious at his "job" which was pretty hard, consisting in endless cleanings from five o'clock in the morning, he could never bring himself to make the effort to shut a door, and, if one pointed out to him that it was open, would turn back and, summoning up all his strength, give it a gentle push. With the democratic pride that marked him, a pride to which, in the liberal avocations, the members of a profession that is at all numerous never attain, barristers, doctors and men of letters speaking simply of a "brother" barrister, doctor or man of letters, he, rightly employing a term that is confined to close corporations like the Academy, would say to me in speaking of a page who was in charge of the lift on alternate days: "I'll see if I can get my *colleague* to take my place." This pride did not prevent him from accepting remuneration for his errands, with a view to increasing what he called his "salary," a fact which had made Françoise take a dislike to him: "Yes, the first time you see him you'd think butter wouldn't melt in his mouth, but there's days when he's as friendly as a prison gate. It's your money he's after." This was the category in which she had so often included Eulalie, and in which, alas (when I think of all the trouble that it was eventually to bring), she already placed Albertine, because she saw me often asking Mamma for trinkets and other little presents on behalf of my impecunious friend, something which Françoise considered inexcusable because Mme Bontemps had only a general help.

A moment later the lift-boy, having removed what I should have called his livery and he called his tunic, would appear wearing a straw hat, carrying a cane and holding himself

stiffly erect, for his mother had warned him never to adopt
a "working-class" or "messenger boy" manner. Just as, thanks
to books, all knowledge is open to a working man, who ceases
to be such when he has finished his work, so, thanks to a
"boater" and a pair of gloves, elegance became accessible to
the lift-boy who, having ceased for the evening to take the
guests upstairs, imagined himself, like a young surgeon who
has taken off his smock, or Sergeant Saint-Loup out of uniform,
a typical young man about town. He was not for that matter
lacking in ambition, or in talent either in manipulating his
machine and not bringing you to a standstill between two
floors. But his vocabulary was defective. I credited him with
ambition because he said in speaking of the porter, who was
his immediate superior, "my porter," in the same tone in
which a man who owned what the lift-boy would have called
a "private mansion" in Paris would have referred to his footman. As for the lift-boy's vocabulary, it is curious that someone
who heard people, fifty times a day, calling for the "lift,"
should never himself call it anything but a "liff." There were
certain things about this lift-boy that were extremely irritating:
whatever I might say to him he would interrupt with the
phrase: "I should think so!" or "Of course!" which seemed
either to imply that my remark was so obvious that anybody
would have thought of it, or else to take all the credit for it to
himself, as though it were he that was drawing my attention
to the subject. "I should think so!" or "Of course!", exclaimed
with the utmost emphasis, issued from his lips every other
minute, in connexion with things he would never have
dreamed of, a trick which irritated me so much that I immediately began to say the opposite to show him that he had
no idea what he was talking about. But to my second assertion,
although it was incompatible with the first, he would reply no
less stoutly: "I should think so!" "Of course!" as though these
words were inevitable. I found it difficult, also, to forgive him
the trick of employing certain terms that were proper to his
calling, and would therefore have sounded perfectly correct in
their literal sense, in a figurative sense only, which gave them
an air of feeble witticism—for instance the verb "to pedal."
He never used it when he had gone anywhere on his

bicycle. But if, on foot, he had hurried to arrive somewhere in time, then, to indicate that he had walked fast, he would exclaim: "I should say I didn't half pedal!" The lift-boy was on the small side, ill-made and rather ugly. This did not prevent him, whenever one spoke to him of some tall, slim, lithe young man, from saying: "Oh, yes, I know, a fellow who is just my height." And one day when I was expecting him to bring me a message, hearing somebody come upstairs, I had in my impatience opened the door of my room and caught sight of a page as handsome as Endymion, with incredibly perfect features, who was bringing a message to a lady whom I did not know. When the lift-boy returned, in telling him how impatiently I had waited for the message, I mentioned to him that I had thought I heard him come upstairs but that it had turned out to be a page from the Hôtel de Normandie. "Oh, yes, I know," he said, "they have only the one, a fellow about my build. He's so like me in face, too, that we could easily be mistaken for one another; anybody would think he was my brother." Lastly, he always wanted to appear to have understood you perfectly from the first second, which meant that as soon as you asked him to do anything he would say: "Yes, yes, yes, yes, I understand all that," with a precision and a tone of intelligence which for some time deceived me; but other people, as we get to know them, are like a metal dipped in an acid bath, and we see them gradually lose their qualities (and their defects too, at times). Before giving him my instructions, I saw that he had left the door open; I pointed this out to him, for I was afraid that people might hear us; he acceded to my request and returned, having reduced the gap. "Anything to oblige. But there's nobody on this floor except us two." Immediately I heard one, then a second, then a third person go by. This annoyed me partly because of the risk of my being overheard, but mainly because I could see that it did not in the least surprise him and was a perfectly normal coming and going. "Yes, that'll be the maid next door going for her things. Oh, that's of no importance, it's the wine waiter putting away his keys. No, no, it's nothing, you can say what you want, it's my colleague just going on duty." Then, as the reasons that all these people had for passing did not diminish my dislike of the thought that they might overhear me, at a formal order from me he went, not to shut the door, which was beyond the strength of this cyclist who longed for a "motor-bike," but to push it a little closer to. "Now we'll be nice and peaceful." So peaceful were we that an American lady burst in and withdrew with apologies for having mistaken the number of her room. "You are to bring this young lady back with you," I told him, after banging the door shut with all my might (which brought in another page to see whether a window had been left open). "You remember the name: Mlle Albertine Simonet. Anyhow it's on the envelope. You need only say to her that it's from me. She will be delighted to come," I added, to encourage him and preserve my own self-esteem. "I should think so!" "On the contrary, it isn't at all natural to suppose that she should be glad to come. It's very inconvenient getting here from Berneville." "Don't I know it!" "You will tell her to come with you." "Yes, yes, yes, yes, I understand perfectly," he replied, in that shrewd and precise tone which had long ceased to make a "good impression" upon me because I knew that it was almost mechanical and covered with its apparent clearness a great deal of vagueness and stupidity. "When will you be back?" "Shan't take too long," said the lift-boy, who, carrying to extremes the grammatical rule that forbids the repetition of personal pronouns before co-ordinate verbs, omitted the pronoun altogether. "Should be able to go all right. Actually, leave was stopped this afternoon, because there was a dinner for twenty at lunch-time. And it was my turn off duty to-day. Should be all right if I go out a bit this evening, though. Take my bike with me. Get there in no time." And an hour later he reappeared and said: "Monsieur's had to wait, but the young lady's come with me. She's down below." "Oh, thanks very much; the porter won't be cross with me?" "Monsieur Paul? Doesn't even know where I've been. Even the head doorman didn't say a word." But once, after I had told him: "You absolutely must bring her back with you," he reported to me with a smile: "You know I couldn't find her. She's not there. Couldn't wait any longer because I was afraid of copping it like my colleague who was 'missed from the hotel" (for the lift-boy, who used the word "rejoin" of a profession which one joined for the first time—"I should like to rejoin the post office"—to make up for this, or to mitigate the calamity if his own career was at stake, or to insinuate it more suavely and treacherously if the victim was someone else, elided the prefix and said: "I know he's been 'missed"). It was not out of malice that he smiled, but out of sheer timidity. He thought that he was diminishing the magnitude of his offence by making a joke of it. In the same way, when he said to me: "*You know* I couldn't find her," this did not mean that he really thought that I knew it already. On the contrary, he was all too certain that I did not know it, and, what was more, was scared of the fact. And so he said "you know" to spare himself the torments he would have to go through in uttering the words that would bring me the knowledge. We ought never to lose our tempers with people who, when we find them at fault, begin to snigger. They do so not because they are laughing at us, but because they are afraid of our displeasure. Let us show all pity and tenderness to those who laugh. For all the world as though he were having a stroke, the lift-boy's anxiety had wrought in him not merely an apoplectic flush but an alteration in his speech, which had suddenly become familiar. He wound up by telling me that Albertine was not at Egreville, that she would not be coming back there before nine o'clock, and that if betimes (which meant, by chance) she came back earlier, my message would be given her and in any case she would be with me before one o'clock in the morning.

It was not on that evening, however, that my cruel mistrust began to take solid form. No, to reveal it here and now, although the incident did not occur until some weeks later, it arose out of a remark made by Cottard. On the day in question Albertine and her friends had wanted to drag me to the casino at Incarville where, to my ultimate good fortune, I would not have joined them (having decided to pay a visit to Mme Verdurin who had invited me several times), had I not been held up at Incarville itself by a train breakdown which required a considerable time to repair. As I strolled up and down waiting for the men to finish working at it, I found myself all of a sudden

face to face with Dr Cottard, who had come to Incarville
to see a patient. I almost hesitated to greet him as he had not
answered any of my letters. But friendliness does not express
itself in everyone in the same way. Not having been brought
up to observe the same fixed rules of behaviour as society
people, Cottard was full of good intentions of which one
knew nothing and even denied the existence, until the day
when he had an opportunity of displaying them. He apologised,
had indeed received my letters, had reported my whereabouts
to the Verdurins who were most anxious to see me and whom
he urged me to go and see. He even proposed to take me there
that very evening, for he was waiting for the little local train
to take him back there for dinner. As I was uncertain and as
he had still some time before his train (for the breakdown
threatened to be a fairly long one), I made him come with me
to the little casino, one of those that had struck me as being so
gloomy on the evening of my first arrival, now filled with the
tumult of the girls, who, in the absence of male partners, were
dancing together. Andrée came sliding along the floor towards
me; I was meaning to go off with Cottard in a moment to the
Verdurins', when I finally declined his offer, seized by an irresistible desire to stay with Albertine. The fact was that I had
just heard her laugh. And this laugh at once evoked the
flesh-pink, fragrant surfaces with which it seemed to have just
been in contact and of which it seemed to carry with it,
pungent, sensual and revealing as the scent of geraniums, a
few almost tangible and mysteriously revealing particles.

One of the girls, a stranger to me, sat down at the piano,
and Andrée invited Albertine to waltz with her. Happy in the
thought that I was going to remain in this little casino with
these girls, I remarked to Cottard how well they danced together. But he, taking the professional point of view of a
doctor and with an ill-breeding which overlooked the fact
that they were my friends, although he must have seen me
greet them, replied: "Yes, but parents are very rash to allow
their daughters to form such habits. I should certainly never
let mine come here. Are they pretty, though? I can't make out
their features. There now, look," he went on, pointing to
Albertine and Andrée who were waltzing slowly, tightly

clasped together, "I've left my glasses behind and I can't see very well, but they are certainly keenly roused. It's not sufficiently known that women derive most excitement through their breasts. And theirs, as you see, are touching completely." And indeed the contact between the breasts of Andrée and of Albertine had been constant. I do not know whether they heard or guessed Cottard's observation, but they drew slightly apart while continuing to waltz. At that moment Andrée said something to Albertine, who laughed with the same deep and penetrating laugh that I had heard before. But the turmoil it roused in me this time was a painful one; Albertine appeared to be conveying by it, to be making Andrée share, some secret and voluptuous thrill. It rang out like the first or the last strains of a ball to which one has not been invited. I left the place with Cottard, absorbed in conversation with him, thinking only at odd moments of the scene I had just witnessed. Not that Cottard's conversation was interesting. It had indeed, at that moment, become rather sour, for we had just seen Dr du Boulbon go past without noticing us. He had come down to spend some time on the other side of the bay from Balbec, where he was greatly in demand. Now, albeit Cottard was in the habit of declaring that he did no professional work during the holidays, he had hoped to build up a select practice along the coast, an ambition which du Boulbon's presence there was likely to hinder. Certainly, the Balbec doctor could not stand in Cottard's way. He was merely a thoroughly conscientious doctor who knew everything, and to whom you could not mention the slightest itch without his immediately prescribing, in a complicated formula, the ointment, lotion or liniment that would put you right. As Marie Gineste used to say in her charming speech, he knew how to "charm" cuts and sores. But he was in no way eminent. True, he had caused Cottard some slight annoyance. The latter, now that he was anxious to exchange his chair for that of Therapeutics, had begun to specialise in toxic actions. These, a perilous innovation in medicine, give an excuse for changing the labels in the chemists' shops, where every preparation is declared to be in no way toxic, unlike its substitutes, and indeed to be disintoxicant. It is the fashionable cry; at the most there may survive below in illegible lettering, like the faint trace of an older fashion, the assurance that the preparation has been carefully antisepticised. Toxic actions serve also to reassure the patient, who learns with joy that his paralysis is merely a toxic disturbance. Now, a grand duke who had come for a few days to Balbec and whose eye was extremely swollen had sent for Cottard who, in return for a wad of hundred-franc notes (the Professor refused to see anyone for less), had put down the inflammation to a toxic condition and prescribed a disintoxicant treatment. As the swelling did not go down, the grand duke fell back upon the general practitioner of Balbec, who in five minutes had removed a speck of dust. The following day, the swelling had gone. A celebrated specialist in nervous diseases was, however, a more dangerous rival. He was a rubicund, jovial man, at once because the constant society of nervous wrecks did not prevent him from enjoying excellent health, and also in order to reassure his patients by the hearty merriment of his "Good morning" and "Good-bye," while quite ready to lend the strength of his muscular arms to fastening them in strait-waistcoats later on. Nevertheless, whenever you spoke to him at a gathering, whether political or literary, he would listen to you with benevolent attention, as though he were saying: "What can I do for you?" without at once giving an opinion, as though it were a medical consultation. But anyhow he, whatever his talent might be, was a specialist. And so the whole of Cottard's rage was concentrated upon du Boulbon. But I soon took my leave of the Verdurins' professional friend, and returned to Balbec, after promising him that I would pay them a visit before long.

The mischief that his remarks about Albertine and Andrée had done me was extreme, but its worst effects were not immediately felt by me, as happens with those forms of poisoning which begin to act only after a certain time.

Albertine, on the night the lift-boy had failed to find her, did not appear, in spite of his assurances. There is no doubt that a person's charms are a less frequent cause of love than a remark such as: "No, this evening I shan't be free." We barely notice this remark if we are with friends; we remain gay all the evening, a certain image never enters our mind; during those hours it remains dipped in the necessary solution; when we return home we find the plate developed and perfectly clear. We become aware that life is no longer the life which we would have surrendered for a trifle the day before, because, even if we continue not to fear death, we no longer dare think of a parting.

From, however, not one o'clock in the morning (the limit fixed by the lift-boy), but three o'clock, I no longer felt as in former times the anguish of seeing the chance of her coming diminish. The certainty that she would not now come brought me a complete and refreshing calm; this night was simply a night like so many others during which I did not see her—such was the notion on which I based myself. And thenceforth the thought that I should see her next day or some other day, outlining itself upon the blank which I submissively accepted, became comforting. Sometimes, during these nights of waiting, our anguish is due to a drug which we have taken. The sufferer, misinterpreting his own symptoms, thinks that he is anxious about the woman who fails to appear. Love is engendered in these cases, as are certain nervous ailments, by the inaccurate interpretation of a painful discomfort. An interpretation which it is useless to correct, at any rate so far as love is concerned, it being a sentiment which (whatever its cause) is invariably erroneous.

Next day, when Albertine wrote to me that she had only just got back to Egreville, and so had not received my note in time, and would come, if she might, to see me that evening, behind the words of her letter, as behind those that she had said to me once over the telephone, I thought I could detect the presence of pleasures, of people, whom she had preferred to me. Once again, my whole body was stirred by the painful longing to know what she could have been doing, by the latent love which we always carry within us; I almost thought for a moment that it was going to bind me to Albertine, but it confined itself to a stationary throbbing, the last echo of which died away without the machine's having been set in motion.

I had failed, during my first visit to Balbec—and perhaps, for that matter, Andrée had failed equally—to understand Albertine's character. I had put it down as frivolous, but had not known whether our combined supplications might not succeed in keeping her with us and making her forgo a garden-party, a donkey-ride, a picnic. During my second visit to Balbec, I began to suspect that this frivolity was merely a semblance, the garden-party a mere screen, if not an invention. There occurred in a variety of forms a phenomenon of which the following is an example (a phenomenon as seen by me, of course, from my side of the glass, which was by no means transparent, and without my having any means of determining what reality there was on the other side). Albertine was making me the most passionate protestations of affection. She looked at the time because she had to go and call upon a lady who was at home, it appeared, every afternoon at five o'clock, at Infreville. Tormented by suspicion, and feeling at the same time far from well, I asked Albertine, I implored her to stay with me. It was impossible (and indeed she could stay only five minutes longer) because it would anger the lady who was far from hospitable, extremely susceptible and, said Albertine, very boring. "But one can easily cut a social call." "No, my aunt has always told me that one must above all be polite." "But I've often seen you being impolite." "It's not the same thing, this lady would be angry with me and would get me into trouble with my aunt. I'm pretty well in her bad books already. She insists that I should go and see her at least once." "But if she's at home every day?" Here Albertine, feeling that she was caught, changed her line of argument. "I know she's at home every day. But to-day I've made arrangements to meet some other girls there. It will be less boring that way." "So then, Albertine, you prefer this lady and your friends to me, since, rather than miss paying an admittedly boring call, you prefer to leave me here alone, sick and wretched?" "I wouldn't care two hoots if it was boring. I'm going for their sake. I shall bring them home in my trap. Otherwise they won't have any way of getting back." I pointed out to Albertine that there were trains from Infreville up to ten o'clock at night. "Quite true, but don't you see, it's possible that we may be asked to stay to dinner. She's very hospitable." "Very well then, you'll refuse." "I should only make my aunt angry." "Besides, you can dine with her and catch the ten o'clock train." "It's cutting it rather fine." "Then I can never go and dine in town and come back by train. But listen, Albertine, I'll tell you what we'll do. I feel that the fresh air will do me good; since you can't give up your lady, I'll come with you to Infreville. Don't be alarmed, I shan't go as far as the Tour Elisabeth" (the lady's villa), "I shall see neither the lady nor your friends." Albertine looked as though she had received a violent blow. For a moment, she was unable to speak. She explained that the sea bathing was not doing her any good. "If you don't want me to come with you?" "How can you say such a thing, you know that there's nothing I enjoy more than going out with you." A sudden change of tactics had occurred. "Since we're going out together," she said to me, "why not go in the other direction. We might dine together. It would be so nice. After all, that side of Balbec is much the prettier. I'm getting sick and tired of Infreville and all those little cabbage-green places." "But your aunt's friend will be annoyed if you don't go and see her." "Very well, let her be." "No, it's wrong to annoy people." "But she won't even notice that I'm not there, she has people every day; I can go to-morrow, the next day, next week, the week after, it's exactly the same." "And what about your friends?" "Oh, they've ditched me often enough. It's my turn now." "But from the direction you suggest there's no train back after nine." "Well, what's the matter with that? Nine will do perfectly. Besides, one should never worry about how to get back. We can always find a cart, a bike or, if the worst comes to the worst, we have legs." " 'We can always find.' Albertine, how you go on! Out Infreville way, where the villages run into one another, well and good. But the other way, it's a very different matter." "That way too. I promise to bring you back safe and sound." I sensed that Albertine was giving up for my sake some plan arranged beforehand of which she refused to tell me, and that there was someone else who would be as unhappy as I was. Seeing that what she had intended to do was out of the question, since I insisted upon accompanying her, she was giving it up altogether. She knew that the loss was not irremediable. For, like all women who have a number of irons in the fire, she could rely on something that never fails: suspicion and jealousy. Of course she did not

seek to arouse them, quite the contrary. But lovers are so
suspicious that they instantly scent out falsehood. With the
result that Albertine, being no better than anyone else, knew
from experience (without for a moment imagining that she
owed it to jealousy) that she could always be sure of not losing
the people she had jilted for an evening. The unknown person
whom she was deserting for me would be hurt, would love her
all the more for that (though Albertine did not know that this
was the reason), and, so as not to prolong the agony, would
return to her of his own accord, as I should have done. But I
had no desire either to give pain to another, or to tire myself,
or to enter upon the terrible path of investigation, of multiform, unending vigilance. "No, Albertine, I don't want to
spoil your pleasure. You can go to your lady at Infreville,
or rather the person for whom she is a pseudonym, it's all the
same to me. The real reason why I'm not coming with you is
that you don't want me to, because the outing with me is not
the one you wanted—the proof of it is that you've contradicted
yourself at least five times without noticing it." Poor Albertine
was afraid that her contradictions, which she had not noticed,
had been more serious than they were. Not knowing exactly
what fibs she had told me, "It's quite on the cards that I did
contradict myself," she said. "The sea air makes me lose my
head altogether. I'm always calling things by the wrong
names." And (what proved to me that she would not, now,
require many tender affirmations to make me believe her) I
felt a stab in my heart as I listened to this admission of what
I had but faintly imagined. "Very well, that's settled, I'm off,"
she said in a tragic tone, not without looking at the time to see
whether she was making herself late for the other person, now
that I had provided her with an excuse for not spending the
evening with myself. "It's too bad of you. I alter all my plans
to spend a nice evening with you, and it's you that won't have
it, and you accuse me of telling lies. I've never known you be
so cruel. The sea shall be my tomb. I shall never see you any
more." At these words my heart missed a beat, although I was
certain that she would come again next day, as she did. "I shall
drown myself, I shall throw myself into the sea." "Like
Sappho." "There you go, insulting me again. You suspect not

only what I say but what I do." "But, my lamb, I didn't mean anything, I swear to you. You know Sappho flung herself into the sea." "Yes, yes, you have no faith in me." She saw from the clock that it was twenty minutes to the hour; she was afraid of missing her appointment, and choosing the shortest form of farewell (for which as it happened she apologised on coming to see me again next day, the other person presumably not being free then), she dashed from the room, crying: "Good-bye for ever," in a heartbroken tone. And perhaps she was heartbroken. For, knowing what she was about at that moment better than I, at once more severe and more indulgent towards herself than I was towards her, she may after all have had a fear that I might refuse to see her again after the way in which she had left me. And I believe that she was attached to me, so much so that the other person was more jealous than I was.

Some days later, at Balbec, while we were in the ballroom of the casino, there entered Bloch's sister and cousin, who had both turned out extremely pretty, but whom I refrained from greeting on account of my girl friends, because the younger one, the cousin, was notoriously living with the actress whose acquaintance she had made during my first visit. Andrée, at a whispered allusion to this scandal, said to me: "Oh! about that sort of thing I'm like Albertine; there's nothing we both loathe so much as that sort of thing." As for Albertine, sitting down to talk to me on the sofa, she had turned her back on the disreputable pair. I had noticed, however, that, before she changed her position, at the moment when Mlle Bloch and her cousin appeared, a look of deep attentiveness had momentarily flitted across her eyes, a look that was wont to impart to the face of this mischievous girl a serious, indeed a solemn air, and left her pensive afterwards. But Albertine had at once turned back towards me a gaze which nevertheless remained strangely still and dreamy. Mlle Bloch and her cousin having finally left the room after laughing very loud and uttering the most unseemly cries, I asked Albertine whether the little fair one (the one who was the friend of the actress) was not the girl who had won the prize the day before in the procession of flowers. "I don't know," said Albertine, "is one of them fair? I must confess they don't interest me particularly, I never looked at them. Is one of them fair?" she asked her friends with a detached air of inquiry. When applied to people whom Albertine passed every day on the front, this ignorance seemed to me too extreme to be entirely genuine. "They didn't appear to be looking at us much either," I said to Albertine, perhaps (on the assumption, which I did not however consciously envisage, that Albertine loved her own sex) to free her from any regret by pointing out to her that she had not attracted the attention of these girls and that, generally speaking, it is not customary even for the most depraved of women to take an interest in girls whom they do not know. "They weren't looking at us?" Albertine replied without thinking. "Why, they did nothing else the whole time." "But you can't possibly tell," I said to her, "you had your back to them." "Well then, what about that?" she replied, pointing out to me, set in the wall in front of us, a large mirror which I had not noticed and upon which I now realised that my friend, while talking to me, had never ceased to fix her beautiful preoccupied eyes.

From the day when Cottard accompanied me into the little casino at Incarville, although I did not share the opinion that he had expressed, Albertine seemed to me to be different; the sight of her made me angry. I myself had changed, quite as much as she had changed in my eyes. I had ceased to wish her well; to her face, behind her back when there was a chance of my words being repeated to her, I spoke of her in the most wounding terms. There were, however, moments of respite. One day I learned that Albertine and Andrée had both accepted an invitation to Elstir's. Feeling certain that this was in order that they might, on the return journey, amuse themselves like schoolgirls on holiday by imitating the manners of fast young women, and in so doing find an unmaidenly pleasure the thought of which tormented me, without announcing my intention, to embarrass them and to deprive Albertine of the pleasure on which she was counting, I paid an unexpected call at Elstir's studio. But I found only Andrée there. Albertine had chosen another day when her aunt was to go there with her. Then I told myself that Cottard must have been mistaken; the favourable impression that I received from

Andrée's presence there without her friend remained with me and made me feel more kindly disposed towards Albertine. But this feeling lasted no longer than the healthy moments of those delicate people who are subject to intermittent recoveries, and are prostrated again by the merest trifle. Albertine incited Andrée to actions which, without going very far, were perhaps not altogether innocent; pained by this suspicion, I would finally succeed in banishing it. No sooner was I cured of it than it revived under another form. I had just seen Andrée, with one of those graceful gestures that came naturally to her, lay her head lovingly on Albertine's shoulder and kiss her on the neck, half shutting her eyes; or else they had exchanged a glance; or a remark had been made by somebody who had seen them going down together to bathe: little trifles such as habitually float in the surrounding atmosphere where the majority of people absorb them all day long without injury to their health or alteration of their mood, but which have a morbid effect and breed fresh suffering in a nature predisposed to receive them. Sometimes even without my having seen Albertine, without anyone having spoken to me about her, I would suddenly call to mind some memory of her with Gisèle in a posture which had seemed to me innocent at the time but was enough now to destroy the peace of mind that I had managed to recover; I had no longer any need to go and breathe dangerous germs outside—I had, as Cottard would have said, supplied my own toxin. I thought then of all that I had been told about Swann's love for Odette, of the way in which Swann had been tricked all his life. Indeed, when I come to think of it, the hypothesis that made me gradually build up the whole of Albertine's character and give a painful interpretation to every moment of a life that I could not control in its entirety, was the memory, the rooted idea of Mme Swann's character, as it had been described to me. These accounts contributed towards the fact that, in the future, my imagination played with the idea that Albertine might, instead of being the good girl that she was, have had the same immorality, the same capacity for deceit as a former prostitute, and I thought of all the sufferings that would in that case have been in store for me if I had happened to love her.

One day, outside the Grand Hotel, where we were gathered on the front, I had just been addressing Albertine in the harshest, most humiliating language, and Rosemonde was saying: "Ah, how you've changed towards her; she used to be the only one who counted, it was she who ruled the roost, and now she isn't even fit to be thrown to the dogs." I was proceeding, in order to make my attitude towards Albertine still more marked, to say all the nicest possible things to Andrée, who, if she was tainted with the same vice, seemed to me more excusable since she was sickly and neurasthenic, when we saw Mme de Cambremer's barouche, drawn by its two horses at a jog-trot, coming into the side street at the corner of which we were standing. The judge, who at that moment was advancing towards us, sprang back upon recognising the carriage, in order not to be seen in our company; then, when he thought that the Marquise's eye might catch his, bowed to her with a immense sweep of his hat. But the carriage, instead of continuing along the Rue de la Mer as might have been expected, disappeared through the gate of the hotel. It was quite ten minutes later when the lift-boy, out of breath, came to announce to me: "It's the Marquise de Camembert who's come to see Monsieur. I've been up to the room, I looked in the reading-room, I couldn't find Monsieur anywhere. Luckily I thought of looking on the beach." He had barely ended his speech when, followed by her daughter-in-law and by an extremely ceremonious gentleman, the Marquise advanced towards me, having probably come on from some tea-party in the neighbourhood, bowed down not so much by age as by the mass of costly trinkets with which she felt it more sociable and more befitting her rank to cover herself, in order to appear as "dressed up" as possible to the people whom she went to visit. It was in fact that "descent" of the Cambremers on the hotel which my grandmother had so greatly dreaded when she wanted us not to let Legrandin know that we might perhaps be going to Balbec. Then Mamma used to laugh at these fears inspired by an event which she considered impossible. And here it was actually happening, but by different channels and without Legrandin's having had any part of it. "Do you mind my staying here, if

I shan't be in your way?" asked Albertine (in whose eyes there lingered, brought there by the cruel things I had just been saying to her, a few tears which I observed without seeming to see them, but not without rejoicing inwardly at the sight), "there's something I want to say to you." A hat with feathers, itself surmounted by a sapphire pin, was perched haphazardly on Mme de Cambremer's wig, like a badge the display of which was necessary but sufficient, its position immaterial, its elegance conventional and its stability superfluous. Notwithstanding the heat, the good lady had put on a jet-black cloak, like a dalmatic, over which hung an ermine stole the wearing of which seemed to depend not upon the temperature and season, but upon the nature of the ceremony. And on Mme de Cambremer's bosom a baronial torse, fastened to a chain, dangled like a pectoral cross. The gentleman was an eminent lawyer from Paris, of noble family, who had come down to spend a few days with the Cambremers. He was one of those men whose consummate professional experience inclines them to look down upon their profession, and who say, for instance: "I know I'm a good advocate, so it no longer amuses me to go through the motions," or: "I'm no longer interested in operating, because I know I'm a good surgeon." Intelligent, "artistic," they see themselves in their maturity, richly endowed by success, shining with that "intelligence," that "artistic" nature which their professional brethren acknowledge in them and which confer upon them an approximation of taste and discernment. They develop a passion for the paintings not of a great artist, but of an artist who nevertheless is highly distinguished, and spend upon the purchase of his work the fat incomes that their career procures for them. Le Sidaner was the artist chosen by the Cambremers' friend, who incidentally was extremely agreeable. He talked well about books, but not about the books of the true masters, those who have mastered themselves. The only irritating defect that this amateur displayed was his constant use of certain ready-made expressions, such as "for the most part," which gave an air of importance and incompleteness to the matter of which he was speaking. Mme de Cambremer had taken advantage, she told me, of a party which some friends of hers had been giving

that afternoon in the Balbec direction to come and call upon
me, as she had promised Robert de Saint-Loup. "You know
he's coming down to these parts quite soon for a few days.
His uncle Charlus is staying near here with his sister-in-law,
the Duchesse de Luxembourg, and M. de Saint-Loup means
to take the opportunity of paying his aunt a visit and going to
see his old regiment, where he is very popular, highly respected.
We often have visits from officers who are never tired of singing
his praises. How nice it would be if you and he would give
us the pleasure of coming together to Féterne."

I presented Albertine and her friends. Mme de Cambremer
introduced us all to her daughter-in-law. The latter, so frigid
towards the petty nobility with whom her seclusion at Féterne
forced her to associate, so reserved, so afraid of committing
herself, held out her hand to me with a radiant smile, feeling
secure and delighted at seeing a friend of Robert de Saint-
Loup, whom he, possessing a sharper social intuition than he
allowed himself to betray, had mentioned to her as being a
great friend of the Guermantes. So, unlike her mother-in-law,
the young Mme de Cambremer employed two vastly different
forms of politeness. It was at the most the former kind, curt
and insufferable, that she would have conceded me had I met
her through her brother Legrandin. But for a friend of the
Guermantes she had not smiles enough. The most convenient
room in the hotel for entertaining visitors was the reading-
room, that place once so terrible into which I now went a
dozen times every day, emerging freely, my own master, like
those mildly afflicted lunatics who have so long been inmates
of an asylum that the superintendent trusts them with a latch-
key. And so I offered to take Mme de Cambremer there.
And as this room no longer filled me with shyness and no
longer held any charm for me, since the faces of things change
for us like the faces of people, it was without any trepidation
that I made this suggestion. But she declined it, preferring
to remain out of doors, and we sat down in the open air,
on the terrace of the hotel. I found there and rescued a
volume of Mme de Sévigné which Mamma had not had time
to carry off in her precipitate flight, when she heard that visitors
had called for me. No less than my grandmother, she dreaded

these invasions of strangers, and, in her fear of being too late
to escape if she let herself be cornered, would flee with a
rapidity which always made my father and me laugh at her.
Mme de Cambremer carried in her hand, together with the
handle of a sunshade, a number of embroidered bags, a hold-
all, a gold purse from which there dangled strings of garnets,
and a lace handkerchief. I could not help thinking that it would
be more convenient for her to deposit them on a chair; but I
felt that it would be improper and useless to ask her to lay
aside the ornaments of her pastoral round and her social
ministry. We gazed at the calm sea upon which, here and there,
a few gulls floated like white petals. Because of the level of
mere "medium" to which social conversation reduces us, and
also of our desire to please not by means of those qualities of
which we are ourselves unaware but of those which we think
likely to be appreciated by the people who are with us, I began
instinctively to talk to Mme de Cambremer *née* Legrandin in
the strain in which her brother might have talked. "They
have," I said, referring to the gulls, "the immobility and
whiteness of water-lilies." And indeed they did appear to be
offering a lifeless object to the little waves which tossed them
about, so much so that the waves, by contrast, seemed in their
pursuit of them to be animated by a deliberate intention, to
have become imbued with life. The dowager Marquise could
not find words enough to do justice to the superb view of the
sea that we had from Balbec, and envied me, since from la
Raspelière (where in fact she was not living that year), she
had only such a distant glimpse of the waves. She had two
remarkable habits, due at once to her exalted passion for the
arts (especially for music) and to her want of teeth. Whenever
she talked of aesthetic subjects her salivary glands—like those
of certain animals when in rut—became so overcharged that
the old lady's edentate mouth allowed to trickle from the
corners of her faintly mustachioed lips a few drops of misplaced moisture. Immediately she drew it in again with a deep
sigh, like a person recovering his breath. Secondly, if some
overwhelming musical beauty was at issue, in her enthusiasm
she would raise her arms and utter a few summary opinions,
vigorously masticated and if necessary issuing from her nose.

Now it had never occurred to me that the vulgar beach at Balbec could indeed offer a "seascape," and Mme de Cambremer's simple words changed my ideas in that respect. On the other hand, as I told her, I had always heard people praise the matchless view from la Raspelière, perched on the summit of the hill, where, in a great drawing-room with two fireplaces, one whole row of windows swept the gardens and, through the branches of the trees, the sea as far as Balbec and beyond, and another row the valley. "How nice of you to say so, and how well you put it: the sea through the branches. It's exquisite—reminiscent of . . . a painted fan." And I gathered, from a deep breath intended to catch the falling spittle and dry the moustaches, that the compliment was sincere. But the Marquise *née* Legrandin remained cold, to show her contempt not for my words but for those of her mother-in-law. Indeed she not only despised the latter's intellect but deplored her affability, being always afraid that people might not form a sufficiently high idea of the Cambremers.

"And how charming the name is," said I. "One would like to know the origin of all those names."

"That one I can tell you," the old lady answered modestly. "It is a family place, it came from my grandmother Arrachepel, not an illustrious family, but good and very old country stock."

"What! not illustrious!" her daughter-in-law tartly interrupted her. "A whole window in Bayeux cathedral is filled with their arms, and the principal church at Avranches has all their tombs. If these old names interest you," she added, "you've come a year too late. We managed to appoint to the living at Criquetot, in spite of all the difficulties about changing from one diocese to another, the parish priest of a place where I myself have some land, a long way from here, Combray, where the worthy cleric felt that he was becoming neurasthenic. Unfortunately, the sea air didn't agree with him at his age; his neurasthenia grew worse and he has returned to Combray. But he amused himself while he was our neighbour in going about looking up all the old charters, and he compiled quite an interesting little pamphlet on the place-names of the district. It has given him a fresh interest, too, for it seems he is spending his last years in writing a magnum opus about Combray and

its surroundings. I shall send you his pamphlet on the surroundings of Féterne. It's a most painstaking piece of scholarship. You'll find the most interesting things in it about our
old Raspelière, of which my mother-in-law speaks far too
modestly."

"In any case, this year," replied the dowager Mme de
Cambremer, "la Raspelière is no longer ours and does not
belong to me. But I can see that you have a painter's instincts;
I am sure you sketch, and I should so like to show you
Féterne, which is far finer than la Raspelière."

For ever since the Cambremers had let this latter residence
to the Verdurins, its commanding situation had at once
ceased to appear to them as it had appeared for so many years
past, that is to say to offer the advantage, without parallel in the
neighbourhood, of looking out over both sea and valley, and
had on the other hand, suddenly and retrospectively, presented
the drawback that one had always to go up or down hill to
get to or from it. In short, one might have supposed that if
Mme de Cambremer had let it, it was not so much to add to
her income as to spare her horses. And she proclaimed herself
delighted at being able at last to have the sea always so close
at hand, at Féterne, she who for so many years (forgetting the
two months that she spent there) had seen it only from up
above and as though at the end of a vista. "I'm discovering it
at my age," she said, "and how I enjoy it! It does me a world
of good. I would let la Raspelière for nothing so as to be
obliged to live at Féterne."

"To return to more interesting topics," went on Legrandin's
sister, who addressed the old Marquise as "Mother" but with
the passing of the years had come to treat her with insolence,
"you mentioned water-lilies: I suppose you know Claude
Monet's pictures of them. What a genius! They interest me
particularly because near Combray, that place where I told
you I had some land. . . ." But she preferred not to talk too
much about Combray.

"Why, that must be the series that Elstir told us about, the
greatest living painter," exclaimed Albertine, who had said
nothing so far.

"Ah! I can see that this young lady loves the arts," cried

old Mme de Cambremer; and drawing a deep breath, she recaptured a trail of spittle.

"You will allow me to put Le Sidaner before him, Mademoiselle," said the lawyer, smiling with the air of a connoisseur. And as he had appreciated, or seen others appreciating, years ago, certain "daring" innovations of Elstir's, he added: "Elstir was gifted, indeed he almost belonged to the avant-garde, but for some reason or other he never kept up, he has wasted his life."

Mme de Cambremer-Legrandin agreed with the lawyer so far as Elstir was concerned, but, greatly to the chagrin of her guest, bracketed Monet with Le Sidaner. It would be untrue to say that she was a fool; she overflowed with a kind of intelligence that meant nothing to me. As the sun was beginning to set, the seagulls were now yellow, like the water-lilies on another canvas of that series by Monet. I said that I knew it, and (continuing to imitate the language of her brother, whom I had not yet ventured to name) added that it was a pity that she had not thought of coming a day earlier, for, at the same hour, there would have been a Poussin light for her to admire. Had some Norman squireen, unknown to the Guermantes, told her that she ought to have come a day earlier, Mme de Cambremer-Legrandin would doubtless have drawn herself up with an offended air. But I might have been far more familiar still, and she would have been all smiles and sweetness; I might in the warmth of that fine afternoon devour my fill of that rich honey cake which the young Mme de Cambremer so rarely was and which took the place of the dish of pastries that it had not occurred to me to offer my guests. But the name of Poussin, without altering the amenity of the society lady, aroused the protests of the connoisseur. On hearing that name, she produced six times in almost continuous succession that little smack of the tongue against the lips which serves to convey to a child who is misbehaving at once a reproach for having begun and a warning not to continue. "In heaven's name, after a painter like Monet, who is quite simply a genius, don't go and mention an old hack without a vestige of talent, like Poussin. I don't mind telling you frankly that I find him the deadliest bore. I mean to say, you can't really call that sort of thing painting. Monet, Degas, Manet, yes, there are painters if you like! It's a curious thing," she went on, fixing a searching and ecstatic gaze upon a vague point in space where she could see what was in her mind, "it's a curious thing, I used at one time to prefer Manet. Nowadays I still admire Manet, of course, but I believe I like Monet even more. Ah, the cathedrals!" She was as scrupulous as she was condescending in informing me of the development of her taste. And one felt that the phases through which that taste had evolved were not, in her eyes, any less important than the different manners of Monet himself. Not that I had any reason to feel flattered by her confiding her enthusiasms to me, for even in the presence of the most dim-witted provincial lady, she could not remain for five minutes without feeling the need to confess them. When a noble lady of Avranches, who would have been incapable of distinguishing between Mozart and Wagner, said in the young Mme de Cambremer's hearing: "We saw nothing of any interest while we were in Paris. We went once to the Opéra-Comique, they were doing *Pelléas et Mélisande*, it's dreadful stuff," Mme de Cambremer not only boiled with rage but felt obliged to exclaim: "Not at all, it's a little gem," and to "argue the point." It was perhaps a Combray habit which she had picked up from my grandmother's sisters, who called it "fighting the good fight," and loved the dinner-parties at which they knew all through the week that they would have to defend their idols against the Philistines. Similarly, Mme de Cambremer-Legrandin enjoyed "getting worked up" and having "a good set-to" about art, as other people do about politics. She stood up for Debussy as she would have stood up for a woman friend whose conduct had been criticised. She must however have known very well that when she said: "Not at all, it's a little gem," she could not improvise, for the person whom she was putting in her place, the whole progression of artistic culture at the end of which they would have reached agreement without any need of discussion. "I must ask Le Sidaner what he thinks of Poussin," the lawyer remarked to me. "He's a regular recluse, never opens his mouth, but I know how to get things out of him."

"Anyhow," Mme de Cambremer-Legrandin went on, "I

have a horror of sunsets, they're so romantic, so operatic. That is why I can't abide my mother-in-law's house, with its tropical plants. You'll see, it's just like a public garden at Monte-Carlo. That's why I prefer your coast here. It's more sombre, more sincere. There's a little lane from which one doesn't see the sea. On rainy days, there's nothing but mud, it's a little world apart. It's just the same at Venice, I detest the Grand Canal and I don't know anything so touching as the little rios. But it's all a question of atmosphere."

"But," I remarked to her, feeling that the only way to rehabilitate Poussin in her eyes was to inform her that he was once more in fashion. "M. Degas affirms that he knows nothing more beautiful than the Poussins at Chantilly."

"Really? I don't know the ones at Chantilly," said Mme de Cambremer, who had no wish to differ from Degas, "but I can speak about the ones in the Louvre, which are hideous."

"He admires them immensely too."

"I must look at them again. My memory of them is a bit hazy," she replied after a moment's silence, and as though the favourable opinion which she was certain to form of Poussin before very long would depend, not upon the information that I had just communicated to her, but upon the supplementary and this time definitive examination that she intended to make of the Poussins in the Louvre in order to be in a position to change her mind.

Contenting myself with what was a first step towards retraction, since, if she did not yet admire the Poussins, she was adjourning the matter for further consideration, in order not to keep her on the rack any longer I told her mother-in-law how much I had heard of the wonderful flowers at Féterne. In modest terms she spoke of the little presbytery garden that she had behind the house, into which in the mornings, by simply pushing open a door, she went in her dressing-gown to feed her peacocks, hunt for newlaid eggs, and gather the zinnias or roses which, on the sideboard, framing the creamed eggs or fried fish in a border of flowers, reminded her of her garden paths. "It's true, we have a great many roses," she told me, "our rose garden is almost too near the house, there are days when it makes my head ache. It's nicer on the terrace at la Raspelière where the breeze wafts the scent of the roses, but not so headily."

I turned to her daughter-in-law: "It's just like *Pelléas*," I said to her, to gratify her taste for the modern, "that scent of roses wafted up to the terraces. It's so strong in the score that, as I suffer from hay-fever and rose-fever, it sets me sneezing every time I listen to that scene."

"What a marvellous thing *Pelléas* is," cried the young Mme de Cambremer, "I'm mad about it"; and, drawing closer to me with the gestures of a wild woman seeking to captivate me, picking out imaginary notes with her fingers, she began to hum something which I took to represent for her Pelléas's farewell, and continued with a vehement insistency as though it were important that she should at that moment remind me of that scene, or rather should prove to me that she remembered it. "I think it's even finer than *Parsifal*," she added, "because in *Parsifal* the most beautiful things are surrounded with a sort of halo of melodic phrases, outworn by the very fact of being melodic."

"I know you are a great musician, Madame," I said to the dowager. "I should so much like to hear you play."

Mme de Cambremer-Legrandin gazed at the sea so as not to be drawn into the conversation. Being of the opinion that what her mother-in-law liked was not music at all, she regarded the talent, bogus according to her, but in reality of the very highest order, that the other was acknowledged to possess as a technical accomplishment devoid of interest. It was true that Chopin's only surviving pupil declared, and with justice, that the Master's style of playing, his "feeling," had been transmitted, through herself, to Mme de Cambremer alone, but to play like Chopin was far from being a recommendation in the eyes of Legrandin's sister, who despised nobody so much as the Polish composer.

"Oh! they're flying away," exclaimed Albertine, pointing to the gulls which, casting aside for a moment their flowery incognito, were rising in a body towards the sun.

"Their giant wings from walking hinder them," quoted Mme de Cambremer-Legrandin, confusing the seagull with the albatross.

"I do love them; I saw some in Amsterdam," said Albertine. "They smell of the sea, they come and sniff the salt air even through the paving stones."

"Ah! so you've been in Holland. Do you know the Vermeers?" Mme de Cambremer-Legrandin asked imperiously, in the tone in which she would have said: "You know the Guermantes?"—for snobbishness in changing its object does not change its accent. Albertine replied in the negative, thinking that they were living people. But her mistake was not apparent.

"I should be delighted to play to you," the dowager Mme de Cambremer said to me. "But you know I only play things that no longer appeal to your generation. I was brought up in the worship of Chopin," she said in a lowered tone, for she was afraid of her daughter-in-law, and knew that to the latter, who considered that Chopin was not music, to talk of playing him well or badly was meaningless. She admitted that her mother-in-law had technique, played the notes to perfection. "Nothing will ever make me say that she is a musician," was Mme de Cambremer-Legrandin's conclusion. Because she considered herself "advanced," because (in matters of art only) "one could never be far enough to the Left," she maintained not merely that music progressed, but that it progressed along a single straight line, and that Debussy was in a sense a super-Wagner, slightly more advanced again than Wagner. She did not realise that if Debussy was not as independent of Wagner as she herself was to suppose in a few years' time, because an artist will after all make use of the weapons he has captured to free himself finally from one whom he has momentarily defeated, he nevertheless sought, when people were beginning to feel surfeited with works that were too complete, in which everything was expressed, to satisfy an opposite need. There were theories, of course, to bolster this reaction temporarily, like those theories which, in politics, come to the support of the laws against the religious orders, or of wars in the East (unnatural teaching, the Yellow Peril, etc., etc.). People said that an age of speed required rapidity in art, precisely as they might have said that the next war could not last longer than a fortnight, or that the coming of railways would kill the little places beloved of the coaches, which the motor-car was none the less to restore to favour. Composers were warned not to strain the attention of their audience, as though we had not at our disposal different degrees of attention, among which it rests precisely with the artist himself to arouse the highest. For those who yawn with boredom after ten lines of a mediocre article have journeyed year after year to Bayreuth to listen to the *Ring*. In any case, the day was to come when, for a time, Debussy would be pronounced as trivial as Massenet, and the throbbings of Mélisande degraded to the level of Manon's. For theories and schools, like microbes and corpuscles, devour one another and by their warfare ensure the continuity of life. But that time was still to come.

As on the Stock Exchange, when a rise occurs, a whole group of securities profit by it, so a certain number of despised artists benefited from the reaction, either because they did not deserve such scorn, or simply—which enabled one to be original when one sang their praises—because they had incurred it. And people even went so far as to seek out, in an isolated past, men of independent talent upon whose reputation the present movement would not have seemed likely to have any influence, but of whom one of the new masters was understood to have spoken favourably. Often it was because a master, whoever he may be, however exclusive his school, judges in the light of his own untutored instincts, gives credit to talent wherever it is to be found, or rather not so much to talent as to some agreeable inspiration which he has enjoyed in the past, which reminds him of a precious moment in his adolescence. At other times it was because certain artists of an earlier generation have in some fragment of their work achieved something that resembles what the master has gradually become aware that he himself wanted to do. Then he sees the old master as a sort of precursor; he values in him, under a wholly different form, an effort that is momentarily, partially fraternal. There are bits of Turner in the work of Poussin, phrases of Flaubert in Montesquieu. Sometimes, again, this rumoured predilection of a master was due to an error, starting heaven knows where and circulated among his followers. But in that case the name mentioned profited by the auspices under which it was introduced in the nick of time, for if there is some independence, some genuine taste expressed in the master's choice, artistic schools go only by theory. Thus it was that the spirit of the times, following its habitual course which advances by digression, inclining first in one direction, then in the other, had brought back into the limelight a number of works to which the need for justice or for renewal, or the taste of Debussy, or a whim of his, or some remark that he had perhaps never made, had added the works of Chopin. Commended by the most trusted judges, profiting by the admiration that was aroused by *Pelléas*, they had acquired a fresh lustre, and even those who had not heard them again were so anxious to admire them that they did so in spite of themselves, albeit preserving the illusion of free will. But Mme de Cambremer-Legrandin spent part of the year in the country. Even in Paris, being an invalid, she was often confined to her room. It is true that the drawbacks of this mode of existence were noticeable chiefly in her choice of expressions, which she supposed to be fashionable but which would have been more appropriate to the written language, a distinction that she did not perceive, for she derived them more from reading than from conversation. The latter is not so necessary for an exact knowledge of current opinion as of the latest expressions. However, this rehabilitation of the *Nocturnes* had not yet been announced by the critics. The news of it had been transmitted only by word of mouth among the "young." Mme de Cambremer-Legrandin remained unaware of it. I gave myself the pleasure of informing her, but by addressing my remark to her mother-in-law, as when, at billiards, in order to hit a ball one plays off the cushion, that Chopin, so far from being out of date, was Debussy's favourite composer. "Really, how amusing," said the daughter-in-law with a knowing smile as though it had been merely a deliberate paradox on the part of the composer of *Pelléas*. Nevertheless it was now quite certain that in future she would always listen to Chopin with respect and even pleasure. Hence my words, which had sounded the hour of deliverance for the dowager, produced on her face an expression of gratitude to myself and above all of joy. Her eyes shone like the eyes of Latude in the play entitled *Latude, or Thirty-five Years in Captivity*, and her bosom inhaled the sea air with that dilatation which Beethoven has depicted so well in *Fidelio*, at the point where his prisoners at last breathe again "this life-giving air." I thought that she was going to press her hirsute lips to my cheek. "What, you like Chopin? He likes Chopin, he likes Chopin," she cried in an impassioned nasal twang, as she might have said: "What, you know Mme de Franquetot too?" with this difference, that my relations with Mme de Franquetot would have been a matter of profound indifference to her, whereas my knowledge of Chopin plunged her into a sort of artistic delirium. Her salivary hyper-secretion no longer sufficed. Not having even attempted to understand the part played by Debussy in the rediscovery of Chopin, she felt only that my judgment of him was favourable. Her musical enthusiasm overpowered her. "Elodie! Elodie! He likes Chopin!" Her bosom rose and she beat the air with her arms. "Ah! I knew at once that you were a musician," she cried, " I can quite understand your liking his work, *artistic* as you are. It's so beautiful!" And her voice was as pebbly as if, to express her ardour for Chopin, she had imitated Demosthenes and filled her mouth with all the shingle on the beach. Then came the ebb-tide, reaching as far as her veil which she had not time to lift out of harm's way and which was drenched, and finally the Marquise wiped away with her embroidered handkerchief the tidemark of foam in which the memory of Chopin had steeped her moustaches.

"Good heavens," Mme de Cambremer-Legrandin exclaimed to me, "I'm afraid my mother-in-law's cutting it rather fine: she's forgotten that we've got my uncle de Ch'nouville dining. And besides, Cancan doesn't like to be kept waiting." The name "Cancan" meant nothing to me, and I supposed that she might perhaps be referring to a dog. But as for the Ch'nouville relatives, the explanation was as follows. With the passage of time the young Marquise had outgrown the pleasure that she had once found in pronouncing their name in this manner. And yet it was the prospect of enjoying that pleasure that had decided her choice of a husband. In other social circles, when one referred to the Chenouville family, the custom was (whenever, that is to say, the particle was preceded by a word ending in a vowel, for in the opposite case you were obliged to lay stress upon the *de*, the tongue refusing to utter Madam' d'Ch'nonceaux) that it was the mute *e* of the particle that was sacrificed. One said: "Monsieur d'Chenouville." The Cambremer tradition was different, but no less imperious. It was the mute *e* of Chenouville that was suppressed. Whether the name was preceded by *mon cousin* or by *ma cousine*, it was always *de Ch'nouville* and never *de Chenouville*. (Of the father of these Chenouvilles they said "our uncle," for they were not sufficiently "upper crust" at Féterne to pronounce the word "unk" like the Guermantes, whose studied jargon, suppressing consonants and naturalising foreign words, was as difficult to understand as old French or a modern dialect.) Every new-comer into the family circle at once received, in the matter of the Ch'nouvilles, a lesson which Mlle Legrandin had not required. When, paying a call one day, she had heard a girl say: "my aunt d'Uzai," "my unk de Rouan," she had not at first recognised the illustrious names which she was in the habit of pronouncing Uzès and Rohan; she had felt the astonishment, embarrassment and shame of a person who sees before him on the table a recently invented implement of which he does not know the proper use and with which he dare not begin to eat. But during that night and the next day she had rapturously repeated: "my aunt d'Uzai," with that suppression of the final *s* that had stupefied her the day before but which it now seemed to her so vulgar not to know that, one of her friends having spoken to her of a bust of the Duchesse d'Uzès, Mlle Legrandin had answered her crossly and in a haughty tone: "You might at least pronounce her name properly: Mame d'Uzai." From that moment she had realised that, by virtue of the transmutation of solid bodies into more and more subtle elements, the considerable and so honourably acquired fortune that she had inherited from her father, the finished education that she had received, her assiduous attendance at the Sorbonne, whether at Caro's lectures or at Brunetière's, and at the Lamoureux concerts, all this was to vanish into thin air, to find its ultimate sublimation in the pleasure of being able one day to say: "my aunt d'Uzai." This did not exclude the thought that she would continue to associate, at least in the early days of her married life, not indeed with certain friends whom she liked and had resigned herself to sacrificing, but with certain others whom she did not like and to whom she looked forward to being able to say (since that, after all, was why she was marrying): "I must introduce you to my aunt d'Uzai," and, when she saw that such an alliance was beyond her reach, "I must introduce you to my aunt de Ch'nouville," and "I shall ask you to dinner with the Uzai." Her marriage to M. de Cambremer had procured for Mlle Legrandin the opportunity to use the former of these sentences but not the latter, the circle in which her parents-in-law moved not being that which she had supposed and of which she continued to dream. Thus, after saying to me of Saint-Loup (adopting for the purpose one of his expressions, for if in talking to her I employed Legrandin's expressions, she by a reverse suggestion answered me in Robert's dialect which she did not know had been borrowed from Rachel), bringing her thumb and forefinger together and half-shutting her eyes as though she were gazing at something infinitely delicate which she had succeeded in capturing: "He has a charming quality of mind," she began to extol him with such warmth that one might have supposed that she was in love with him (it had indeed been alleged that, some time back, when he was at Doncières, Robert had been her lover), in reality simply in order that I might repeat her words to him, and ended up with: "You're a great friend of the Duchesse de Guermantes. I'm an invalid, I seldom go out, and I know that she sticks to a close circle of chosen friends, which I do think so wise of her, and so I know her very slightly, but I know she is a really remarkable woman." Aware that Mme de Cambremer barely knew her, and anxious to put myself on a level with her, I glossed over the subject and answered the Marquise that the person whom I did know well was her brother, M. Legrandin. At the sound of his name she assumed the same evasive air as I had on the subject of Mme de Guermantes, but combined with it an expression of displeasure, for she imagined that I had said this with the object of humiliating not myself but her. Was she gnawed by despair at having been

born a Legrandin? So at least her husband's sisters and sisters-
in-law asserted, noble provincial ladies who knew nobody and
nothing, and were jealous of Mme de Cambremer's intelligence, her education, her fortune, and the physical attractions
that she had possessed before her illness. "She can think of
nothing else, that is what is killing her," these spiteful provincial ladies would say whenever they spoke of Mme de Cambremer to no matter whom, but preferably to a commoner,
either—if he was conceited and stupid—to enhance, by this
affirmation of the shamefulness of the commoner's condition,
the value of the affability that they were showing him, or—if
he was shy and clever and applied the remark to himself—to
give themselves the pleasure, while receiving him hospitably,
of insulting him indirectly. But if these ladies thought that they
were speaking the truth about their sister-in-law, they were
mistaken. She suffered not at all from having been born
Legrandin, for she had forgotten the fact altogether. She was
offended by my reminding her of it, and remained silent as
though she had failed to understand, not thinking it necessary
to enlarge upon or even to confirm my statement.

"Our cousins are not the chief reason for our cutting short
our visit," said the dowager Mme de Cambremer, who was
probably more satiated than her daughter-in-law with the
pleasure to be derived from saying "Ch'nouville." "But, so
as not to bother you with too many people, Monsieur," she
went on, indicating the lawyer, "was reluctant to bring his
wife and son to the hotel. They are waiting for us on the
beach, and must be getting impatient." I asked for an exact
description of them and hastened in search of them. The wife
had a round face like certain flowers of the ranunculus family,
and a large vegetable growth at the corner of her eye. And,
the generations of mankind preserving their characteristics like
a family of plants, just as on the blemished face of his mother,
an identical growth, which might have helped towards the
classification of a variety of the species, protruded below the
eye of the son. The lawyer was touched by my civility to his
wife and son. He expressed an interest in the subject of my
stay at Balbec. "You must find yourself a bit homesick, for the
people here are for the most part foreigners." And he kept his

eye on me as he spoke, for, not caring for foreigners, albeit he had many foreign clients, he wished to make sure that I was not hostile to his xenophobia, in which case he would have beaten a retreat, saying: "Of course, Mme X—— may be a charming woman. It's a question of principle." As at that time I had no definite opinion about foreigners, I showed no sign of disapproval, and he felt himself to be on safe ground. He went so far as to invite me to come one day to his house in Paris to see his collection of Le Sidaners, and to bring with me the Cambremers, with whom he evidently supposed me to be on intimate terms. "I shall invite you to meet Le Sidaner," he said to me, confident that from that moment I would live only in expectation of that happy day. "You shall see what a delightful man he is. And his pictures will enchant you. Of course, I can't compete with the great collectors, but I do believe that I own the largest number of his favourite canvases. They will interest you all the more, coming from Balbec, since they're marine subjects, for the most part at least." The wife and son, blessed with a vegetable nature, listened composedly. One felt that their house in Paris was a sort of temple to Le Sidaner. Temples of this sort are not without their uses. When the god has doubts as to his own merits, he can easily stop the cracks in his opinion of himself with the irrefutable testimony of people who have dedicated their lives to his work.

At a signal from her daughter-in-law, the dowager Mme de Cambremer prepared to depart, and said to me: "Since you won't come and stay at Féterne, won't you at least come to luncheon, one day this week, to-morrow for instance?" And in her benevolence, to make the invitation irresistible, she added: "You will *find* the Comte de Crisenoy," whom I had never lost, for the simple reason that I did not know him. She was beginning to dazzle me with yet further temptations, but stopped short; for the judge, who, on returning to the hotel, had been told that she was on the premises, had crept about searching for her everywhere, then waited his opportunity, and pretending to have caught sight of her by chance, came up now to pay her his respects. I gathered that Mme de Cambremer did not mean to extend to him the invitation to lunch that she had just addressed to me. And yet he had known her far longer than I, having for years past been one of the regular guests at the afternoon parties at Féterne whom I used so to envy during my former visit to Balbec. But old acquaintance is not the only thing that counts in society. And hostesses are more inclined to reserve their luncheons for new acquaintances who still whet their curiosity, especially when they arrive preceded by a warm and glowing recommendation from a Saint-Loup. The dowager Mme de Cambremer calculated that the judge could not have heard what she was saying to me, but, to salve her conscience, spoke to him in the most friendly terms. In the sunlight on the horizon that flooded the golden coastline of Rivebelle, invisible as a rule, we could just make out, barely distinguishable from the luminous azure, rising from the water, rose-pink, silvery, faint, the little bells that were sounding the Angelus round about Féterne. "That is rather *Pelléas*, too," I suggested to Mme de Cambremer-Legrandin. "You know the scene I mean." "Of course I do" was what she said; but "I haven't the faintest idea" was the message proclaimed by her voice and features, which did not mould themselves to the shape of any recollection, and by her smile, which floated in the air, without support. The dowager could not get over her astonishment that the sound of bells should carry so far, and rose, reminded of the time: "But, as a rule," I said, "we never see that part of the coast from Balbec, nor hear it either. The weather must have changed and enlarged the horizon in more ways than one. Unless the bells have come to look for you, since I see that they are making you leave; to you they are a dinner bell." The judge, little interested in the bells, glanced furtively along the esplanade, on which he was sorry to see so few people that evening. "You are a true poet," the dowager Mme de Cambremer said to me. "One feels you are so responsive, so artistic. Do come, I shall play you some Chopin," she went on, raising her arms with an air of ecstasy and pronouncing the words in a raucous voice that seemed to be shifting pebbles. Then came the deglutition of saliva, and the old lady instinctively wiped the stubble of her toothbrush moustache with her handkerchief. The judge unwittingly did me a great favour by offering the old Marquise his arm to escort her to her carriage, a certain blend of vulgarity, boldness and love of ostentation prompting him to a mode of conduct which other people would hesitate to adopt but which is by no means unwelcome in society. He was in any case, and had been for years past, far more in the habit of such conduct than myself. While blessing him I did not venture to emulate him, and walked by the side of Mme de Cambremer-Legrandin who insisted upon seeing the book that I had in my hand. The name of Mme de Sévigné drew a grimace from her; and using a word which she had read in certain "advanced" journals, but which, used in speech, given a feminine form and applied to a seventeenth-century writer, had an odd effect, she asked me: "Do you really think she's 'talentuous'?" The dowager gave her footman the address of a pastry-cook where she had to call before taking the road, which was pink in the evening haze, with the humped cliffs stretching away into the bluish distance. She asked her old coachman whether one of the horses which was apt to catch cold had been kept warm enough, and whether the other's shoe were not hurting him. "I shall write to you and make a definite arrangement," she murmured to me. "I heard you talking about literature to my daughter-in-law. She's adorable," she added, not that she really thought so, but she had acquired the habit—and kept it up out of the kindness of her heart—of saying so, in order that her son might not appear to have married for money. "Besides," she added with a final enthusiastic mumble, "she's so harttissttick!" With this she stepped into her carriage, nodding her head, holding the crook of her sunshade aloft like a crozier, and set off through the streets of Balbec, overloaded with the ornaments of her ministry, like an old bishop on a confirmation tour.

"She has asked you to lunch," the judge said to me sternly when the carriage had passed out of sight and I came indoors with the girls. "We're not on the best of terms just now. She feels that I neglect her. Gad, I'm easy enough to get on with. If anybody needs me, I'm always there to say: Adsum! But they tried to get their hooks on me. And that," he went on with a shrewd look, waving his finger like a man arguing some subtle distinction, "that is a thing I will not allow. It is a threat to the liberty of my holidays. I was obliged to say: Stop! You seem to be in her good books. When you reach my age you will see that society is a very trumpery thing, and you will be sorry you attached so much importance to these trifles. Well, I'm going to take a turn before dinner. Good-bye, children," he shouted back at us, as though he were already fifty yards away.

When I had said good-bye to Rosemonde and Gisèle, they saw with astonishment that Albertine was staying behind instead of accompanying them. "Why, Albertine, what are you doing, don't you know what time it is?" "Go home," she replied in a tone of authority. "I want to talk to him," she added, pointing to me with a submissive air. Rosemonde and Gisèle stared at me, filled with a new and strange respect. I enjoyed the feeling that, for a moment at least, in the eyes even of Rosemonde and Gisèle, I was to Albertine something more important than the time, or her friends, and might indeed share solemn secrets with her into which it was impossible for them to be admitted. "Shan't we see you again this evening?" "I don't know, it will depend on this person. Anyhow, to-morrow." "Let's go up to my room," I said to her when her friends had gone. We took the lift; she remained silent in the lift-boy's presence. The habit of being obliged to resort to personal observation and deduction in order to find out the business of their masters, those strange beings who converse among themselves and do not speak to them, develops in "employees" (as the lift-boy styled servants) a greater power of divination than "employers" possess. Our organs become atrophied or grow stronger or more subtle according as our need of them increases or diminishes. Since railways came into existence, the necessity of not missing trains has taught us to take account of minutes, whereas among the ancient Romans, who not only had a more cursory acquaintance with astronomy but led less hurried lives, the notion not only of minutes but even of fixed hours barely existed. Hence the lift-boy had gathered, and meant to inform his "colleagues," that Albertine and I were preoccupied. But he talked to us without ceasing because he had no tact. And yet I discerned upon his face, in place of the customary expression of friendliness and joy at taking me up in his lift, an air of extraordinary dejection and anxiety. Since I knew nothing of the cause of this, in an attempt to distract his thoughts—although I was more preoccupied with Albertine—I told him that the lady who had just left was called the Marquise de Cambremer and not de Camembert. On the floor which we were passing at that moment, I caught sight of a hideous chambermaid carrying a bolster, who greeted me with respect, hoping for a tip when I left. I should have liked to know if she was the one whom I had so ardently desired on the evening of my first arrival at Balbec, but I could never arrive at any certainty. The lift-boy swore to me with the sincerity of most false witnesses, but without shedding his woe-begone expression, that it was indeed by the name of Camembert that the Marquise had told him to announce her. And as a matter of fact it was quite natural that he should have heard her say a name which he already knew. Besides, having only those very vague notions of nobility, and of the names with which titles are composed, which are shared by many people who are not lift-boys, the name Camembert had seemed to him all the more probable inasmuch as, that cheese being universally known, it was not in the least surprising that a marquisate should have been extracted from so glorious a renown, unless it were the marquisate that had bestowed its celebrity upon the cheese. Nevertheless, as he saw that I refused to admit that I might be mistaken, and as he knew that masters like to see their most futile whims obeyed and their most obvious lies accepted, he promised me like a good servant that in future he would say Cambremer. It is true that none of the shopkeepers in the town, none of the peasants in the district, where the name and persons of the Cambremers were perfectly familiar, could ever have made the lift-boy's mistake. But the staff of the "Grand Hotel of Balbec" were none of them natives. They came direct, together with all the equipment and stock, from Biarritz, Nice and Monte-Carlo, one division having been transferred to Deauville, another to Dinard and the third reserved for Balbec.

But the lift-boy's anxious gloom continued to grow. For him thus to forget to show his devotion to me by the customary smiles, some misfortune must have befallen him.

Perhaps he had been " 'missed." I made up my mind in that
case to try to secure his reinstatement, the manager having
promised to ratify all my wishes with regard to his staff.
"You can always do just what you like, I rectify everything in
advance." Suddenly, as I stepped out of the lift, I guessed the
meaning of the lift-boy's air of stricken misery. Because of
Albertine's presence I had not given him the five francs which
I was in the habit of slipping into his hand when I went up.
And the idiot, instead of realising that I did not wish to make
a display of largesse in front of a third person, had begun to
tremble, supposing that it was all finished once and for all,
that I would never give him anything again. He imagined
that I was "on the rocks" (as the Duc de Guermantes would
have said), and the supposition inspired him with no pity
for myself but with a terrible selfish disappointment. I told
myself that I was less unreasonable than my mother thought
when I had not dared, one day, not to give the extravagant
but feverishly awaited sum that I had given the day before.
But at the same time the meaning that I had until then, and
without a shadow of doubt, ascribed to his habitual expression
of joy, in which I had no hesitation in seeing a sign of devotion, seemed to me to have become less certain. Seeing him
ready, in his despair, to fling himself down from the fifth
floor of the hotel, I asked myself whether, if our respective
social stations were to be altered, in consequence let us say of
a revolution, instead of politely working his lift for me the
lift-boy, having become a bourgeois, would not have flung me
down the well, and whether there was not, in certain of the
lower orders, more duplicity than in society, where, no doubt,
people reserve their offensive remarks until we are out of
earshot, but their attitude towards us would not be insulting
if we were reduced to poverty.

One cannot however say that the lift-boy was the most
commercially minded person in the Balbec hotel. From this
point of view the staff might be divided into two categories:
on the one hand, those who drew distinctions between the
guests, and were more grateful for the modest tip of an old
nobleman (who, moreover, was in a position to relieve them
from 28 days of military service by saying a word for them to

General de Beautreillis) than for the thoughtless liberalities
of a flashy vulgarian who by his very extravagance revealed
a lack of breeding which only to his face did they call generosity; on the other hand, those to whom nobility, intellect,
fame, position, manners were non-existent, concealed under
a cash valuation. For these there was but a single hierarchy,
that of the money one has, or rather the money one gives.
Perhaps even Aimé himself, although pretending, in view of
the great number of hotels in which he had served, to a great
knowledge of the world, belonged to this latter category. At
the most he would give a social turn, showing that he knew
who was who, to this sort of appreciation, as when he said of
the Princesse de Luxembourg: "There's a pile of money
among that lot?" (the question mark at the end being to
ascertain the facts, or to check such information as he had
already ascertained, before supplying a client with a "chef"
for Paris, or promising him a table on the left, by the door,
with a view of the sea, at Balbec). In spite of this, without
being free from mercenary tendencies, he would not have displayed them with the fatuous despair of the lift-boy. And yet
the latter's artlessness helped perhaps to simplify things. It is
a convenient feature of a big hotel, or of a house such as
Rachel used at one time to frequent, that, without any intermediary, at the sight of a hundred-franc note, still more a
thousand-franc one, even though it is being given on that particular occasion to someone else, the hitherto stony face of a
servant or a woman will light up with smiles and offers of
service. Whereas in politics, or in the relations between lover
and mistress, there are too many things interposed between
money and docility—so many things indeed that the very
people upon whose faces money finally evokes a smile are
often incapable of following the internal process that links
them together, and believe themselves to be, indeed are, more
refined. Besides, it rids polite conversation of such speeches
as: "There's only one thing left for me to do—you'll find me
to-morrow in the mortuary." Hence one meets in polite
society few novelists, or poets, few of all those sublime
creatures who speak of the things that are not to be mentioned.
    As soon as we were alone and had moved along the corridor,

Albertine began: "What have you got against me?" Had my
harsh treatment of her been painful to myself? Had it been
merely an unconscious ruse on my part, with the object of
bringing her round to that attitude of fear and supplication
which would enable me to interrogate her, and perhaps to find
out which of the alternative hypotheses that I had long since
formed about her was the correct one? However that may be,
when I heard her question I suddenly felt the joy of one who
attains to a long-desired goal. Before answering her, I escorted
her to the door of my room. Opening it, I scattered the roseate
light that was flooding the room and turning the white muslin
of the curtains drawn for the night to golden damask. I went
across to the window; the gulls had settled again upon the
waves; but this time they were pink. I drew Albertine's attention
to them. "Don't change the subject," she said, "be frank with
me." I lied. I told her that she must first listen to a confession,
that of a violent passion I had had for Andrée for some time
past, and I made her this confession with a simplicity and
frankness worthy of the stage, but seldom expressed in real
life except in declaring a love which one does not feel. Reverting to the fiction I had employed with Gilberte before my first
visit to Balbec, but varying it, I went so far (in order to make
her more ready to believe me when I told her now that I did
not love her) as to let fall the admission that at one time I had
been on the point of falling in love with her, but that too long
an interval had elapsed, that she was no more to me now than
a good friend, and that, even if I wished, it would no longer be
possible for me to feel a more ardent sentiment for her. As it
happened, in thus underlining to Albertine these protestations
of coldness towards her, I was merely—because of a particular
circumstance and with a particular object in view—making
more perceptible, accentuating more markedly, that binary
rhythm which love adopts in all those who have too little
confidence in themselves to believe that a woman can ever
fall in love with them, and also that they themselves can
genuinely fall in love with her. They know themselves well
enough to have observed that in the presence of the most
divergent types of woman they felt the same hopes, the same
agonies, invented the same romances, uttered the same words,

to have deduced therefore that their feelings, their actions, bear no close and necessary relation to the woman they love, but pass to one side of her, splash her, encircle her, like the incoming tide breaking against the rocks, and their sense of their own instability increases still further their misgivings that this woman, by whom they so long to be loved, does not love them. Why should chance have brought it about, when she is simply an accident placed in the path of our surging desires, that we should ourselves be the object of the desires that she feels? And so, while feeling the need to pour out to her all those sentiments, so different from the merely human sentiments that our neighbour inspires in us, those highly specialised sentiments which are those of lovers, after having taken a step forward, in avowing to the one we love our passion for her, our hopes, we are overcome at once by the fear of offending her, and ashamed too that the language we have used to her was not fashioned expressly for her, that it has served us already, will serve us again for others, that if she does not love us she cannot understand us, and that we have spoken in that case with the lack of taste and discretion of a pedant who addresses an ignorant audience in subtle phrases which are not for them; and this fear and shame provoke the counter-rhythm, the reflux, the need, if only by first drawing back, hotly denying the affection previously confessed, to resume the offensive and regain respect and domination; the double rhythm is perceptible in the various periods of a single love affair, in all the corresponding periods of similar love affairs, in all those people whose self-analysis outweighs their self-esteem. If it was however somewhat more forcefully accentuated than usual in this speech which I was now making to Albertine, this was simply to allow me to pass more rapidly and more vigorously to the opposite rhythm which would be measured by my tenderness.

As though it must be painful to Albertine to believe what I was saying to her as to the impossibility of my loving her again after so long an interval, I justified what I called an eccentricity in my nature by examples taken from people with whom I had, by their fault or my own, allowed the time for loving them to pass, and been unable, however keenly I might have desired it, to recapture it. I thus appeared at one and the same time to be apologising to her, as for a want of courtesy, for this inability to begin loving her again, and to be seeking to make her understand the psychological reasons for that incapacity as though they had been peculiar to myself. But by explaining myself in this fashion, by dwelling upon the case of Gilberte, in regard to whom the argument had indeed been strictly true which was becoming so far from true when applied to Albertine, I was merely rendering my assertions as plausible as I pretended to believe that they were not. Sensing that Albertine appreciated what she believed to be my "plain speaking" and recognised my deductions as clearly self-evident, I apologised for the former by telling her that I knew that the truth was always unpleasant and in this intance must seem to her incomprehensible. She thanked me, on the contrary, for my sincerity and added that so far from being puzzled she understood perfectly a state of mind so frequent and so natural.

This avowal to Albertine of an imaginary sentiment for Andrée, and, towards herself, of an indifference which, so that it might appear altogether sincere and without exaggeration, I assured her incidentally, as though out of scrupulous politeness, must not be taken too literally, enabled me at length, without any danger that Albertine might interpret it as love, to speak to her with a tenderness which I had so long denied myself and which seemed to me exquisite. I almost caressed my confidante; as I spoke to her of her friend whom I loved, tears came to my eyes. But, coming at last to the point, I said to her that she knew what love was, its susceptibilities, its sufferings, and that perhaps, as the old friend that she now was, she might feel it in her heart to put an end to the distress she was causing me, not directly, since it was not herself that I loved, if I might venture to repeat that without offending her, but indirectly by wounding me in my love for Andrée. I broke off to admire and point out to Albertine a great, solitary, speeding bird which, far out in front of us, lashing the air with the regular beat of its wings, flew at full speed over the beach, which was stained here and there with gleaming reflexions like little torn scraps of red paper, and crossed it from end to end without slackening its pace, without diverting its attention, without deviating from its path, like an envoy carrying far afield an urgent and vital message. "It at least goes straight to the point!" said Albertine reproachfully. "You say that because you don't know what I was going to tell you. But it's so difficult that I prefer to leave it; I'm certain to make you angry; and then all that will have happened will be this: I shall in no way be better off with the girl I really love and I shall have lost a good friend." "But I swear to you that I won't be angry." She looked so sweet, so wistfully docile, as though her whole happiness depended on me, that I could barely restrain myself from kissing—with almost the same kind of pleasure that I should have had in kissing my mother— this new face which no longer presented the lively, flushed mien of a cheeky and perverse kitten with its little pink tip-tilted nose, but seemed, in the plenitude of its crestfallen sadness, moulded in broad, flattened, drooping slabs of pure goodness. Leaving aside my love as though it were a chronic mania that had no connexion with her, putting myself in her place, I let my heart melt at the sight of this sweet girl, accustomed to being treated in a friendly and loyal fashion, whom the good friend that she might have supposed me to be had been pursuing for weeks past with persecutions which had at last arrived at their culminating point. It was because I placed myself at a standpoint that was purely human, external to both of us, from which my jealous love had evaporated, that I felt for Albertine that profound pity, which would have been less profound if I had not loved her. However, in that rhythmical oscillation which leads from a declaration to a quarrel (the surest, the most effectively perilous way of forming by opposite and successive movements a knot which will not be loosened and which attaches us firmly to a person), in the midst of the movement of withdrawal which constitutes one of the two elements of the rhythm, of what use is it to analyse further the refluences of human pity, which, the opposite of love, though springing perhaps unconsciously from the same cause, in any case produce the same effects? When we count up afterwards the sum of all that we have done for a woman, we often dis-cover that the actions prompted by the desire to show that

we love her, to make her love us, to win her favours, bulk
scarcely larger than those due to the human need to repair the
wrongs that we do to the loved one, from a mere sense of
moral duty, as though we did not love her. "But tell me,
what on earth have I done?" Albertine asked me. There was
a knock at the door; it was the lift-boy; Albertine's aunt, who
was passing the hotel in a carriage, had stopped on the chance
of finding her there and taking her home. Albertine sent word
that she could not come down, that they were to begin dinner .
without her, that she could not say at what time she would
return. "But won't your aunt be angry?" "Not at all! She'll
understand perfectly well." In other words—at this moment
at least, which perhaps would never recur—a conversation
with me was in Albertine's eyes, because of the circumstances,
a thing of such self-evident importance that it must be given
precedence over everything, a thing to which, referring no
doubt instinctively to a family code, enumerating certain
crises in which, when the career of M. Bontemps was at stake,
a journey had been made without a thought, my friend never
doubted that her aunt would think it quite natural to see her
sacrifice the dinner-hour. Having relinquished for my benefit
that remote hour which she spent without me, among her own
people, Albertine was giving it to me; I might make what use
of it I chose. I finally made bold to tell her what had been
reported to me about her way of life, and said that notwithstanding the profound disgust I felt for women tainted with
that vice, I had not given it a thought until I had been told
the name of her accomplice, and that she could readily understand, loving Andrée as I did, the pain that this had caused me.
It would have been more astute perhaps to say that other
women had also been mentioned but that they were of no
interest to me. But the sudden and terrible revelation that
Cottard had made to me had struck home, had lacerated me,
just as it was, complete in itself without any accretions. And
just as, before that moment, it would never have occurred
to me that Albertine was enamoured of Andrée, or at any rate
could find pleasure in caressing her, if Cottard had not drawn
my attention to their posture as they waltzed together, so I
had been incapable of passing from that idea to the idea, so

different for me, that Albertine might have, with women other
than Andrée, relations which could not even be excused by
affection. Albertine, even before swearing to me that it was not
true, expressed, like everyone upon learning that such things
are being said about them, anger, concern, and, with regard
to the unknown slanderer, a fierce curiosity to know who he
was and a desire to be confronted with him so as to be able to
confound him. But she assured me that she bore me, at least,
no resentment. "If it had been true, I would have told you.
But Andrée and I both loathe that sort of thing. We haven't
reached our age without seeing women with cropped hair
who behave like men and do the things you mean, and
nothing revolts us more." Albertine merely gave me her word,
a categorical word unsupported by proof. But this was precisely what was best calculated to calm me, jealousy belonging
to that family of morbid doubts which are eliminated by the
vigour of an affirmation far more surely than by its probability.
It is moreover the property of love to make us at once more
distrustful and more credulous, to make us suspect the loved
one, more readily than we should suspect anyone else, and
be convinced more easily by her denials. We must be in love
before we can care that all women are not virtuous, which
is to say before we can be aware of the fact, and we must be
in love too before we can hope, that is to say assure ourselves,
that some are. It is human to seek out what hurts us and then
at once to seek to get rid of it. Statements that are capable of
so relieving us seem all too readily true: we are not inclined
to cavil at a sedative that works. Besides, however multiform
the person we love may be, she can in any case present to us
two essential personalities according to whether she appears to
us as ours, or as turning her desires elsewhere. The first of
these personalities possesses the peculiar power which prevents us from believing in the reality of the second, the secret
remedy to heal the sufferings that this latter has caused us.
The beloved object is successively the malady and the remedy
that suspends and aggravates it. Doubtless I had long been
conditioned, by the powerful impression made on my imagination and my faculty for emotion by the example of Swann, to
believe in the truth of what I feared rather than of what I

should have wished. Hence the comfort brought me by Albertine's affirmations came near to being jeopardised for a moment because I remembered the story of Odette. But I told myself that, if it was right to allow for the worst, not only when, in order to understand Swann's sufferings, I had tried to put myself in his place, but now that it concerned myself, in seeking the truth as though it concerned someone else I must nevertheless not, out of cruelty to myself, like a soldier who chooses the post not where he can be of most use but where he is most exposed, end up with the mistake of regarding one supposition as more true than the rest simply because it was the most painful. Was there not a vast gulf between Albertine, a girl of good middle-class parentage, and Odette, a whore sold by her mother in her childhood? There could be no comparison of their respective credibility. Besides, Albertine had in no sense the same interest in lying to me that Odette had had in lying to Swann. And in any case to him Odette had admitted what Albertine had just denied. I should therefore be guilty of an error of reasoning as serious—though in the opposite sense—as that which would have inclined me towards a certain assumption because it caused me less pain than any other, in not taking into account these material differences in their situations, and in reconstructing the real life of my beloved solely from what I had been told about Odette's. I had before me a new Albertine, of whom I had already, it was true, caught more than one glimpse towards the end of my previous visit to Balbec, a frank, kind Albertine who, out of affection for myself, had just forgiven me my suspicions and tried to dispel them. She made me sit down by her side on my bed. I thanked her for what she had said to me, assuring her that our reconciliation was complete, and that I would never be harsh to her again. I told her that she ought neverthelesss to go home to dinner. She asked me whether I was not glad to have her with me. And drawing my head towards her for a caress which she had never given me before and which I owed perhaps to the healing of our quarrel, she drew her tongue lightly over my lips, which she attempted to force apart. At first I kept them tight shut. "What an old spoilsport you are!" she said to me.

I ought to have gone away that evening and never seen her again. I sensed there and then that in a love that is not shared—one might almost say in love, for there are people for whom there is no such thing as shared love—we can enjoy only that simulacrum of happiness which had been given to me at one of those unique moments in which a woman's good nature, or her caprice, or mere chance, respond to our desires, in perfect coincidence, with the same words, the same actions, as if we were really loved. The wiser course would have been to consider with curiosity, to appropriate with delight, that little particle of happiness failing which I should have died without ever suspecting what it could mean to hearts less difficult to please or more highly privileged; to pretend that it formed part of a vast and enduring happiness of which this fragment only was visible to me; and—lest the next day should give the lie to this fiction—not to attempt to ask for any fresh favour after this one, which had been due only to the artifice of an exceptional moment. I ought to have left Balbec, to have shut myself up in solitude, to have remained there in harmony with the last vibrations of the voice which I had contrived to render loving for an instant, and of which I should have asked nothing more than that it might never address another word to me; for fear lest, by an additional word which henceforth could not but be different, it might shatter with a discord the sensory silence in which, as though by the pressure of a pedal, there might long have survived in me the throbbing chord of happiness.

Calmed by my confrontation with Albertine, I began once again to live in closer intimacy with my mother. She loved to talk to me gently about the days when my grandmother had been younger. Fearing that I might reproach myself with the sorrows with which I had perhaps darkened the close of my grandmother's life, she preferred to turn back to the years when my first studies had given my grandmother a satisfaction which until now had always been kept from me. We talked of the old days at Combray. My mother reminded me that there at least I used to read, and that at Balbec I might well do the same, if I was not going to work. I replied that, to surround myself with memories of Combray and of the charming coloured plates, I should like to re-read the *Thousand and One Nights*. As, long ago at Combray, when she gave me books for my birthday, so it was in secret, as a surprise for me, that my mother now sent for both the *Thousand and One Nights* of Galland and the *Thousand Nights and One Night* of Mardrus.[38] But, after casting her eye over the two translations, my mother would have preferred that I should stick to Galland's, albeit hesitating to influence me because of her respect for intellectual liberty, her dread of interfering with my intellectual life and the feeling that, being a woman, on the one hand she lacked, or so she thought, the necessary literary equipment, and on the other hand ought not to judge a young man's reading by what she herself found shocking. Happening upon certain of the tales, she had been revolted by the immorality of the subject and the coarseness of the expression. But above all, preserving like precious relics not only her mother's brooch, her sunshade, her cloak, her volume of Mme. de Sévigné, but also her habits of thought and speech, invoking on every occasion the opinion that she would have expressed, my mother could have no doubt of the unfavourable judgment which my grandmother would have passed on Mardrus's version. She remembered that at Combray, while I sat reading Augustin Thierry before setting out for a walk along the Méséglise way, my grandmother, pleased with my reading and my walks, was indignant nevertheless at seeing the person whose name remained enshrined in the hemistich "Then reignèd Mérovée" called Merowig, and refused to say "Carolingians" for the "Carlovingians" to which she remained loyal. And then I told her what my grandmother had thought of the Greek names which Bloch, following Lecomte de Lisle, used to give to Homer's gods, going so far, in the simplest matters, as to make it a religious duty, in which he supposed literary talent to consist, to adopt a Greek system of spelling. Having occasion, for instance, to mention in a letter that the wine which they drank at his home was real nectar, he would write "nektar," with a *k*, which enabled him to titter at the mention of Lamartine. Now if an *Odyssey* from which the names of Ulysses and Minerva were missing was no longer the *Odyssey* to her, what would she have said upon seeing corrupted, even on the cover, the title of her *Thousand*

and One Nights, upon no longer finding, exactly transcribed
as she had all her life been in the habit of pronouncing them,
the immortally familiar names of Scheherazade or Dinarzade,
while, themselves debaptised (if one may use the expression of
Moslem tales), even the charming Caliph and the powerful
Genies were barely recognisable, being renamed, he the
"Khalifa" and they the "Gennis." However, my mother
handed over both books to me, and I told her that I would read
them on the days when I felt too tired to go out.

These days were not very frequent, however. We used to go
out picnicking as before in a band, Albertine, her friends and
myself, on the cliff or to the farm called Marie-Antoinette.
But there were times when Albertine bestowed on me a great
pleasure. She would say to me: "To-day I want to be alone with
you for a while; it will be nicer if we are just by ourselves."
Then she would give out that she had things to do—not that
she had to account for her movements—and so that the others,
if they went out for a picnic all the same without us, should
not be able to find us, we would steal away like a pair of lovers,
all by ourselves to Bagatelle or the Cross of Heulan, while the
band, who would never think of looking for us there and never
went there, waited indefinitely at Marie-Antoinette in the hope
of seeing us appear. I remember the hot weather that we had
then, when from the foreheads of the farm labourers toiling
in the sun drops of sweat would fall, vertical, regular, intermittent, like drops of water from a cistern, alternating with
the fall of the ripe fruit dropping from the tree in the adjoining
orchard; they have remained to this day, together with that
mystery of a woman's secret, the most enduring element in
every love that offers itself to me. For a woman who is mentioned to me and to whom ordinarily I would not give a
moment's thought, I will upset all my week's engagements to
make her acquaintance, if it is a week of similar weather, and
if I am to meet her in some isolated farmhouse. Even if I am
aware that this kind of weather, this kind of assignation,
have nothing to do with her, they are still the bait which,
however familiar, I allow myself to be tempted by, and which
is sufficient to hook me. I know that in cold weather, in a town,
I might perhaps have desired this woman, but without the

accompaniment of romantic feelings, without falling in love;
my love is none the less strong as soon as, by force of circumstances, it has enchained me—it is simply more melancholy,
as over the years our feelings for other people become, in
proportion as we become more aware of the ever smaller part
they play in our lives and realise that the new love which we
would like to be so enduring, cut short in the same moment as
life itself, will be the last.

There were still few people at Balbec, few girls. Sometimes
I would see one standing on the beach, one devoid of charm
and yet whom various coincidences seemed to identify as a
girl whom I had been in despair at not being able to approach
when she emerged with her friends from the riding school
or gymnasium. If it was the same one (and I took care not to
mention the matter to Albertine), then the girl that I had
thought so intoxicating did not exist. But I could not arrive
at any certainty, for the faces of these girls did not fill a constant
space, did not present a constant form upon the beach, contracted, dilated, transmogrified as they were by my own
expectancy, the anxiousness of my desire, or by a sense of self-
sufficient well-being, the different clothes they wore, the
rapidity of their walk or their stillness. From close to, however,
two or three of them seemed to me adorable. Whenever I saw
one of these, I longed to take her to the Avenue des Tamaris,
or among the sandhills, or better still on to the cliff. But
although in desire, as opposed to indifference, there is already
that element of audacity which a first step, if only unilateral,
towards realisation entails, all the same, between my desire and
the action that my request to be allowed to kiss her would
have been, there was all the indefinite hiatus of hesitation and
shyness. Then I went into the café-bar, and proceeded to drink,
one after another, seven or eight glasses of port wine. At
once, instead of the impassable gulf between my desire and
action, the effect of the alcohol traced a line that joined them
together. No longer was there any room for hesitation or fear.
It seemed to me that the girl was about to fly into my arms.
I went up to her, and there sprang to my lips of their own
accord the words: "I should like to go for a walk with you.
You wouldn't care to go along the cliff? We shan't be

disturbed behind the little wood that keeps the wind off the wooden bungalow that is empty just now." All the difficulties of life were smoothed away, there were no longer any obstacles to the conjunction of our two bodies. No longer any obstacles for me, at least. For they had not been dissipated for her, who had not been drinking port wine. Had she done so, had the outer world lost some of its reality in her eyes, the long-cherished dream that would then have appeared to her to be suddenly realisable might perhaps have been not at all that of falling into my arms.

Not only were the girls few in number but, at this season which was not yet "the season," they stayed only a short time. There is one I remember with a russet skin, green eyes and a pair of ruddy cheeks, whose slight symmetrical face resembled the winged seeds of certain trees. I cannot say what breeze wafted her to Balbec or what other bore her away. So sudden was her removal that for some days afterwards I was haunted by a chagrin which I made bold to confess to Albertine when I realised that the girl had gone forever.

I should add that several of them were girls whom I either did not know at all or had not seen for years. Often I wrote to them before meeting them. If their answers allowed me to believe in the possibility of love, what joy! One cannot, at the outset of a friendship with a woman, even if that friendship is destined to come to nothing, bear to be parted from these first letters that we receive. We like to have them with us all the time, like a present of rare flowers, still fresh, at which one ceases to gaze only to breathe their scent. The sentence that one knows by heart is pleasant to read again, and in those that one has committed less accurately to memory one wants to verify the degree of affection in some expression. Did she write: "Your dear letter"? A slight marring of one's bliss, which must be ascribed either to one's having read too quickly, or to the illegible handwriting of one's correspondent; she did not say: "Your dear letter" but "From your letter." But the rest is so tender. Oh, that more such flowers may come to-morrow! Then that is no longer enough, one must with the written words compare the writer's eyes, her voice. One makes a rendezvous, and—without her having altered, perhaps—

whereas one expected, from the description received or one's personal memory, to meet a Fairy Queen, one finds Puss-in-Boots. One makes another rendezvous, nevertheless, for the following day, for it is, after all, *she*, and it was she that one desired. For these desires for a woman of whom one has dreamed do not make the beauty of this or that particular feature absolutely essential. These desires are only the desire for this or that person; vague as perfumes, as styrax was the desire of Prothyraia, saffron the ethereal desire, spices the desire of Hera, myrrh the perfume of the clouds, manna the desire of Nike, incense the perfume of the sea. But these perfumes that are sung in the Orphic hymns are far fewer in number than the deities they cherish. Myrrh is the perfume of the clouds, but also of Protogonos, Neptune, Nereus, Leto; incense is the perfume of the sea, but also of the fair Dike, of Themis, of Circe, of the Nine Muses, of Eos, of Mnemosyne, of the Day, of Dikaiosyne. As for styrax, manna and spices, it would be impossible to name all the deities that inspire them, so many are they. Amphietes has all the perfumes except incense, and Gaia rejects only beans and spices. So it was with these desires that I felt for different girls. Less numerous than the girls themselves, they changed into disappointments and regrets closely similar one to another. I never wished for myrrh. I reserved it for Jupien and for the Princesse de Guermantes, for it is the desire of Protogonos "of twofold sex, with the roar of a bull, of countless orgies, memorable, indescribable, descending joyously to the sacrifices of the Orgiophants."

But presently the season was in full swing; every day there was some new arrival, and for the sudden increase in the frequency of my outings, which took the place of the charmed perusal of the *Thousand and One Nights*, there was an unpleasurable reason which poisoned them all. The beach was now peopled with girls, and, since the idea suggested to me by Cottard, while not imbuing me with fresh suspicions, had rendered me sensitive and vulnerable in that quarter and careful not to let any suspicion take shape in my mind, as soon as a young woman arrived at Balbec I began to feel ill at ease and proposed to Albertine the most distant excursions so that she might not make the newcomer's acquaintance and if possible might not even set eyes on her. I dreaded naturally even more those women whose dubious ways were remarked or their bad reputation already known; I tried to persuade my beloved that this bad reputation had no foundation, was a slander, perhaps, without admitting it to myself, from a fear, as yet unconscious, that she might seek to make friends with the depraved woman or regret her inability to do so because of me, or might conclude from the number of examples that a vice so widespread could not be blameworthy. In denying it of every guilty woman, I was not far from contending that sapphism did not exist. Albertine adopted my incredulity as to the viciousness of this one or that: "No, I think it's just a pose, she wants to put on airs." But then I regretted almost that I had pleaded their innocence, for it offended me that Albertine, formerly so severe, could believe that this "pose" was a thing so flattering, so advantageous, that a woman innocent of such tastes should seek to adopt it. I began to wish that no more women would come to Balbec; I trembled at the thought that, as it was about the time when Mme Putbus was due to arrive at the Verdurins', her maid, whose tastes Saint-Loup had not concealed from me, might take it into her head to come down to the beach, and, if it were a day on which I was not with Albertine, might seek to corrupt her. I went as far as to ask myself whether, as Cottard had made no secret of the fact that the Verdurins thought highly of me and, while not wishing to appear, as he put it, to be running after me, would give a great deal to have me come to their house, I might not, on the strength of promises to bring all the Guermantes in existence to call on them in Paris, induce Mme Verdurin on some pretext or other to inform Mme Putbus that it was impossible to keep her there any longer and make her leave the place at once.

Notwithstanding these thoughts, and as it was chiefly the presence of Andrée that disturbed me, the soothing effect that Albertine's words had had upon me to some extent persisted— I knew moreover that presently I should have less need of it, since Andrée would be leaving with Rosemonde and Gisèle just about the time when the crowd began to arrive and would be spending only a few weeks more with Albertine. During these weeks, moreover, Albertine seemed to plan everything that she did, everything that was said, with a view to destroying my suspicions if any remained, or to preventing their recurrence. She contrived never to be left alone with Andrée, and insisted, when we came back from an excursion, on my accompanying her to her door, and on my coming to fetch her when we were going anywhere. Andrée meanwhile took just as much trouble on her side, seemed to avoid meeting Albertine. And this apparent understanding between them was not the only indication that Albertine must have informed her friend of our conversation and have asked her to be so kind as to calm my absurd suspicions.

About this time there occurred at the Grand Hotel a scandal which was not calculated to alter the trend of my anxieties. Bloch's sister had for some time past been indulging, with a retired actress, in secret relations which presently ceased to suffice them. They felt that to be seen would add perversity to their pleasure, and chose to flaunt their dangerous embraces before the eyes of all the world. They began with caresses, which might, after all, be attributed to a friendly intimacy, in the card-room, round the baccarat-table. Then they grew bolder. And finally, one evening, in a corner of the big ballroom that was not even dark, on a sofa, they made no more attempt to conceal what they were doing than if they had been in bed. Two officers, who happened to be nearby with their wives, complained to the manager. It was thought for a moment that their protest would be effective. But they suffered from the disadvantage that, having come over for the evening from Netteholme, where they lived, they could not be of any use to the manager. Whereas, without her even knowing it, and whatever remarks the manager might make to her, there hovered over Mlle Bloch the protection of M. Nissim Bernard. I must explain why. M. Nissim Bernard practised the family virtues in the highest degree. Every year he rented a magnificent villa at Balbec for his nephew, and no invitation would have dissuaded him from going home to dine at his own table, which was really theirs. But he never lunched at home. Every day at noon he was at the Grand Hotel. The fact of the matter was that he was keeping, as other men keep a dancer from the *corps de ballet*, a fledgling waiter of much the same type as the pages of whom we have spoken, and who made us think of the young Israelites in *Esther* and *Athalie*. It is true that the forty years' difference in age between M. Nissim Bernard and the young waiter ought to have preserved the latter from a contact that could scarcely have been agreeable. But, as Racine so wisely observes in those same choruses:

> Great God, with what uncertain tread
> A budding virtue 'mid such perils goes!
> What stumbling-blocks do lie before a soul
> That seeks Thee and would fain be innocent.

For all that the young waiter had been brought up "remote from the world" in the Temple-Caravanserai of Balbec, he had not followed the advice of Joad:

> In riches and in gold put not thy trust.

He had perhaps justified himself by saying: "The wicked cover the earth." However that might be, and albeit M. Nissim Bernard had not expected so rapid a conquest, on the very first day,

> Were't in alarm, or anxious to caress,
> He felt those childish arms about him thrown.

And by the second day, M. Nissim Bernard having taken the young waiter out,

> The dire assault his innocence destroyed.

From that moment the boy's life was altered. He might only carry bread and salt, as his superior bade him, but his whole face sang:

> From flowers to flowers, from joys to keener joys
> Let our desires now range.
> Uncertain is our tale of fleeting years,
> Let us then hasten to enjoy this life!
> Honours and fame are the reward
> Of blind and meek obedience.
> For moping innocence
> Who now would raise his voice?

Since that day, M. Nissim Bernard had never failed to come and occupy his seat at the lunch-table (as a man might occupy his seat in the stalls who was keeping a dancer, a dancer in this case of a distinct and special type which still awaits its Degas). It was M. Nissim Bernard's delight to follow round the restaurant, as far as the remote vistas where beneath her palm the cashier sat enthroned, the gyrations of the adolescent in zealous attendance—attendance on everyone, and less on M. Nissim Bernard now that the latter was keeping him, whether because the young altar-boy did not think it necessary to display the same civility to a person by whom he supposed himself to be sufficiently well loved, or because that love annoyed him or he feared lest, if discovered, it might make him lose other opportunities. But this very coldness pleased M. Nissim Bernard, because of all that it concealed; whether from Hebraic atavism or in profanation of its Christian feeling, he took a singular pleasure in the Racinian ceremony, were it Jewish or Catholic. Had it been a real performance of *Esther* or *Athalie*, M. Bernard would have regretted that the gulf of centuries must prevent him from making the acquaintance of the author, Jean Racine, so that he might obtain for his protégé a more substantial part. But as the luncheon ceremony came from no author's pen, he contented himself with being on good terms with the manager and with Aimé, so that the "young Israelite" might be promoted to the coveted post of under-waiter, or even put in charge of a row of tables. A post in the cellars had been offered him. But M. Bernard made him decline it, for he would no longer have been able to come every day to watch him race about the green dining-room and to be waited upon by him like a stranger. Now this pleasure was so keen that every year M. Bernard returned to Balbec and had his lunch away from home, habits in which M. Bloch saw, in the former a poetical fancy for the beautiful light and the sunsets of this coast favoured above all others, in the latter the inveterate eccentricity of an old bachelor.

As a matter of fact, this misapprehension on the part of M. Nissim Bernard's relatives, who never suspected the true reason for his annual return to Balbec, and for what the pedantic Mme Bloch called his gastronomic absenteeism, was a deeper truth, at one remove. For M. Nissim Bernard himself was unaware of the extent to which a love for the beach at Balbec and for the

view over the sea which one enjoyed from the restaurant, together with eccentricity of habit, contributed to the fancy that
he had for keeping, like a little dancing girl of another kind
which still lacks a Degas, one of his equally nubile servers. And
so M. Nissim Bernard maintained excellent relations with the
director of this theatre which was the hotel at Balbec, and with
the stage-manager and producer Aimé—whose roles in this
whole affair were far from clear. One day they would all contrive to procure an important part for his protégé, perhaps a
post as head waiter. In the meantime M. Nissim Bernard's
pleasure, poetical and calmly contemplative as it might be, was
somewhat reminiscent of those women-loving men who always
know—Swann, for example, in the past—that if they go out in
society they will meet their mistress. No sooner had M. Nissim
Bernard taken his seat than he would see the object of his
affections appear on the scene, bearing in his hands fruit or cigars
upon a tray. And so every morning, after kissing his niece,
inquiring about my friend Bloch's work, and feeding his horses
with lumps of sugar from the palm of his outstretched hand,
he would betray a feverish haste to arrive in time for lunch at
the Grand Hotel. Had the house been on fire, had his niece had
a stroke, he would doubtless have started off just the same. So
that he dreaded like the plague a cold that would confine him
to his bed—for he was a hypochondriac—and would oblige
him to ask Aimé to send his young friend across to visit him
at home, between lunch and tea-time.

He loved moreover all the labyrinth of corridors, private
offices, reception-rooms, cloakrooms, larders, galleries which
composed the hotel at Balbec. With a strain of oriental atavism
he loved a seraglio, and when he went out at night might be
seen furtively exploring its purlieus.

While, venturing down to the basement and endeavouring
at the same time to escape notice and to avoid a scandal, M.
Nissim Bernard, in his quest of the young Levites, put one in
mind of those lines in *La Juive*:

> O God of our Fathers, come down to us again,
> Our mysteries veil from the eyes of wicked men!

I on the contrary would go up to the room of two sisters who had come to Balbec with an old foreign lady as her maids. They were what the language of hotels called two *courrières*, and that of Françoise, who imagined that a courier was a person who was there to run errands (*faire des courses*) two *coursières*. The hotels have remained, more nobly, in the period when people sang: "*C'est un courrier de cabinet.*"[39]

Difficult as it was for a guest to penetrate to the servants' quarters, and vice versa, I had very soon formed a mutual bond of friendship, as strong as it was pure, with these two young persons, Mlle Marie Gineste and Mme Céleste Albaret. Born at the foot of the high mountains in the centre of France, on the banks of rivulets and torrents (the water flowed actually under the family home, turning a millwheel, and the house had often been damaged by floods), they seemed to embody the spirit of those waters. Marie Gineste was more regularly rapid and abrupt, Céleste Albaret softer and more languishing, spread out like a lake, but with terrible boiling rages in which her fury suggested the peril of spates and gales that sweep everything before them. They often came in the morning to see me when I was still in bed. I have never known people so deliberately ignorant, who had learned absolutely nothing at school, and yet whose language was somehow so literary that, but for the almost wild naturalness of their tone, one would have thought their speech affected. With a familiarity which I reproduce verbatim, notwithstanding the eulogies (which I set down here in praise not of myself but of the strange genius of Céleste) and the criticisms, equally unfounded but absolutely sincere, which her remarks seem to imply towards me, while I dipped croissants in my milk, Céleste would say to me: "Oh! little black devil with raven hair, oh deep-dyed mischief! I don't know what your mother was thinking of when she made you, you're just like a bird. Look, Marie, wouldn't you say he was preening his feathers, and the supple way he turns his head right round, he looks so light, you'd think he was just learning to fly. Ah! it's lucky for you that you were born into the ranks of the rich, otherwise what would ever have become of you, spendthrift that you are. Look at him throwing away his croissant because it touched the bed. There he goes, now, look, he's spilling his milk. Wait till I tie a napkin round you, because you'll never do it for yourself, I've never seen anyone so helpless and clumsy as you." I would then hear the more regular sound of the torrent of Marie Gineste furiously reprimanding her sister: "Will you hold your tongue, now, Céleste. Are you mad, talking to Monsieur like that?" Céleste merely smiled; and as I detested having a napkin tied round my neck: "No, Marie, look at him, bang, he's shot straight up on end like a snake. A proper snake, I tell you." She was full of zoological similes, for, according to her, it was impossible to tell when I slept, I fluttered about all night like a moth, and in the day-time I was as swift as the squirrels, "you know, Marie, which we used to see at home, so nimble that even with your eyes you can't follow them." "But, Céleste, you know he doesn't like having a napkin when he's eating." "It isn't that he doesn't like it, it's so that he can say nobody can make him do anything against his will. He's a grand gentleman and he wants to show that he is. You change the sheets ten times over if need be, but he still won't be satisfied. Yesterday's had served their time, but to-day they've only just been put on the bed and they have to be changed already. Oh, I was right when I said that he was never meant to be born among the poor. Look, his hair's standing on end, puffing out with rage like a bird's feathers. Poor *ploumissou!*" Here it was not only Marie who protested, but myself, for I did not feel in the least like a grand gentleman. But Céleste would never believe in the sincerity of my modesty and would cut me short: "Oh, what a bag of tricks! Oh, the soft talk, the deceitfulness! Ah, the cunning rogue! Ah, Molière!" (This was the only writer's name that she knew, but she applied it to me, meaning thereby a person who was capable both of writing plays and of acting them.) "Céleste!" came the imperious cry from Marie, who, not knowing the name of Molière, was afraid that it might be some fresh insult. Céleste continued to smile: "Then you haven't seen the photograph of him in his drawer, when he was little? He tried to make us believe that he was always dressed quite simply. And there, with his little cane, he's all furs and lace, such as not even a prince ever wore. But that's nothing compared with his tremendous majesty and his even more profound kindness." "So you go rummaging in his drawers

now, do you?" growled the torrent Marie. To calm Marie's
fears I asked her what she thought of M. Nissim Bernard's
behaviour. . . . "Ah! Monsieur, there are things I wouldn't
have believed could exist until I came here." And for once
going one better than Céleste with an even more profound
observation, she added: "Ah! You see, Monsieur, one can
never tell what there may be in a person's life." To change the
subject, I spoke to her of the life led by my father, who worked
night and day. "Ah! Monsieur, there are people who keep
nothing of their life for themselves, not one minute, not one
pleasure, the whole thing is a sacrifice for others, they are
lives that are *offered up* . . . Look, Céleste, simply the way he puts
his hand on the counterpane and picks up his croissant, what
distinction! He can do the most insignificant things, and you'd
think that the whole nobility of France, from here to the
Pyrenees, was stirring in each of his movements."

Overwhelmed by this portrait that was so far from lifelike,
I remained silent; Céleste interpreted my silence as a further
instance of guile: "Ah! forehead that looks so pure and hides
so many things, nice, cool cheeks like the inside of an almond,
little hands all soft and satiny, nails like claws," and so forth.
"There, Marie, look at him sipping his milk with a reverence
that makes me want to say my prayers. What a serious air!
Someone really ought to take a picture of him as he is just
now. He's just like a child. Is it by drinking milk, like them,
that you've kept that clear complexion? Ah, what youth!
Ah, what lovely skin! You'll never grow old. You're lucky,
you'll never need to raise your hand against anyone, for you
have eyes that know how to impose their will. Look at him
now, he's angry. He shoots up, straight as a sign-post."

Françoise did not at all approve of those she called the two
"wheedlers" coming to talk to me like this. The manager, who
made his staff keep watch over everything that went on, even
pointed out to me gravely that it was not proper for a customer
to talk to servants. I, who found the "wheedlers" better
company than any visitor in the hotel, merely laughed in his
face, convinced that he would not understand my explanations.
And the sisters returned. "Look, Marie, at his delicate features.
Oh, perfect miniature, finer than the most precious you could

see in a glass case, because he has movement, and words you could listen to for days and nights."

It was a miracle that a foreign lady could have brought them there, for, without knowing anything of history or geography, they heartily detested the English, the Germans, the Russians, the Italians, all foreign "vermin," and cared, with certain exceptions, for French people alone. Their faces had so far preserved the moisture of the malleable clay of their native river beds, that, as soon as one mentioned a foreigner who was staying in the hotel, in order to repeat what he had said Céleste and Marie at once took on his facial expression, their mouths became his mouth, their eyes his eyes—one would have liked to preserve these admirable comic masks. Céleste indeed, while pretending merely to be repeating what the manager or one of my friends had said, would insert in her little narrative, apparently quite unwittingly, fictitious remarks in which were maliciously portrayed all the defects of Bloch, the judge, and others. Under the form of a report on a simple errand which she had obligingly undertaken, she would provide an inimitable portrait. They never read anything, not even a newspaper. One day, however, they found a book lying on my bed. It was a volume of the admirable but obscure poems of Saint-Léger Léger.[40] Céleste read a few pages and said to me: "But are you quite sure that it's poetry? Mightn't it just be riddles?" Obviously, to a person who had learned in her childhood a single poem: "Here below the lilacs die," there was a lack of transition. I fancy that their obstinate refusal to learn anything was due in part to the unhealthy climate of their early home. They had nevertheless all the gifts of a poet with more modesty than poets generally show. For if Céleste had said something noteworthy and, unable to remember it correctly, I asked her to repeat it, she would assure me that she had forgotten. They will never read any books, but neither will they ever write any.

Françoise was considerably impressed when she learned that the two brothers of these humble women had married, one the niece of the Archbishop of Tours, the other a relative of the Bishop of Rodez. To the manager, this would have conveyed nothing. Céleste would sometimes reproach her husband with his failure to understand her, and I myself was astonished that he could put up with her. For at certain moments, raging, furious, destroying everything, she was detestable. It is said that the salt liquid which is our blood is only an internal survival of the primitive marine element. Similarly, I believe that Céleste, not only in her bursts of fury, but also in her hours of depression, preserved the rhythm of her native streams. When she was exhausted, it was after their fashion; she had literally run dry. Nothing could then have revitalised her. Then all of a sudden the circulation was restored in her tall, slender, magnificent body. The water flowed in the opaline transparence of her bluish skin. She smiled in the sun and became bluer still. At such moments she was truly celestial.

In spite of the fact that Bloch's family had never suspected the reason why their uncle never lunched at home, and had accepted it from the first as the idiosyncrasy of an elderly bachelor, attributable perhaps to the demands of a liaison with some actress, everything that concerned M. Nissim Bernard was taboo to the manager of the Balbec hotel. And it was for this reason that, without even referring to the uncle, he had finally not ventured to find fault with the niece, albeit recommending her to be a little more circumspect. Mlle Bloch and her friend, who for some days had imagined themselves to have been excluded from the Casino and the Grand Hotel, seeing that all was well, were delighted to show those respectable family men who held aloof from them that they might with impunity take the utmost liberties. No doubt they did not go so far as to repeat the public exhibition which had revolted everybody. But gradually they returned to their old ways. And one evening as I came out of the Casino, which was half in darkness, with Albertine and Bloch whom we had met there, they came by, linked together, kissing each other incessantly, and, as they passed us, crowed and chortled and uttered indecent cries. Bloch lowered his eyes so as to seem not to have recognised his sister, and I was tortured by the thought that this private and horrifying language was addressed perhaps to Albertine.

Another incident focused my preoccupations even more in the direction of Gomorrah. I had noticed on the beach a handsome young woman, slender and pale, whose eyes, round their centre, scattered rays so geometrically luminous that one was reminded, on meeting her gaze, of some constellation. I thought how much more beautiful she was than Albertine, and how much wiser it would be to give up the other. But the face of this beautiful young woman had been scoured by the invisible plane of a thoroughly depraved life, of the constant acceptance of vulgar expedients, so much so that her eyes, though nobler than the rest of her face, could radiate nothing but appetites and desires. On the following day, this young woman being seated a long way away from us in the Casino, I saw that she never ceased to fasten upon Albertine the alternating and revolving beam of her gaze. It was as though she were making signals to her with a lamp. It pained me that Albertine should see that she was being so closely observed, and I was afraid that these incessantly rekindled glances might be the agreed signal for an amorous assignation next day. For all I knew, this assignation might not be the first. The young woman with the flashing eyes might have come another year to Balbec. It was perhaps because Albertine had already yielded to her desires, or to those of a friend, that this woman allowed herself to address to her those flashing signals. If so, they were doing more than demand something for the present; they invoked a justification for it in pleasant hours in the past.

This assignation, in that case, must be not the first, but the sequel to adventures shared in past years. And indeed her glance did not say: "Will you?" As soon as the young woman had caught sight of Albertine, she had turned her head and beamed upon her glances charged with recollection, as though she were afraid and amazed that my beloved did not remember. Albertine, who could see her plainly, remained phlegmatically motionless, with the result that the other, with the same sort of discretion as a man who sees his old mistress with a new lover, ceased to look at her and paid no more attention to her than if she had not existed.

But a day or two later, I received proof of this young woman's tendencies, and also of the probability of her having known Albertine in the past. Often, in the hall of the Casino, when two girls were smitten with mutual desire, a sort of luminous phenomenon occurred, as it were a phosphorescent trail flashing from one to the other. It may be noted, incidentally, that it is by the aid of such materialisations, impalpable though they be, by these astral signs that set a whole section of the atmosphere ablaze, that dispersed Gomorrah strives, in every town, in every village, to reunite its separated members, to reconstruct the biblical city while everywhere the same efforts are being made, be it in view of but a momentary reconstruction, by the nostalgic, the hypocritical, sometimes the courageous exiles of Sodom.

One day I saw the unknown woman whom Albertine had appeared not to recognise at a moment when Bloch's cousin was passing by. The young woman's eyes flashed, but it was quite evident that she did not know the Jewish girl. She beheld her for the first time, felt a desire, scarcely any doubt, but by no means the same certainty as in the case of Albertine, Albertine upon whose friendship she must so far have counted that, in the face of her coldness, she had felt the surprise of a foreigner familiar with Paris but not resident there, who, having returned to spend a few weeks there, finds the site of the little theatre where he was in the habit of spending pleasant evenings occupied now by a bank.

Bloch's cousin went and sat down at a table where she turned the pages of a magazine. Presently the young woman came and sat down beside her with an abstracted air. But under the table one could presently see their feet wriggling, then their legs and hands intertwined. Words followed, a conversation began, and the young woman's guileless husband, who had been looking everywhere for her, was astonished to find her making plans for that very evening with a girl whom he did not know. His wife introduced Bloch's cousin to him as a childhood friend, under an inaudible name, for she had forgotten to ask her what her name was. But the husband's presence made their intimacy advance a stage further, for they addressed each other as *tu*, having known each other at their convent, an incident at which they laughed heartily later on, as well as at the hoodwinked husband, with a gaiety which afforded them an excuse for further caresses.

As for Albertine, I cannot say that anywhere, whether at the

Casino or on the beach, her behaviour with any girl was unduly free. I found in it indeed an excess of coldness and indifference which seemed to be more than good breeding, to be a ruse planned to avert suspicion. When questioned by some girl, she had a quick, icy, prim way of replying in a very loud voice: "Yes, I shall be at the tennis-court about five. I shall go for a bathe to-morrow morning about eight," and of at once turning away from the person to whom she had said this —all of which had a horrible appearance of being meant to put one off the scent, and either to make an assignation, or rather, the assignation having already been made in a whisper, to utter these perfectly harmless words aloud so as not to attract undue attention. And when later on I saw her mount her bicycle and scorch away into the distance, I could not help thinking that she was on her way to join the girl to whom she had barely spoken.

However, when some handsome young woman stepped out of a motor-car at the end of the beach, Albertine could not help turning round. And she would at once explain: "I was looking at the new flag they've put up over the bathing place. They might have spent a bit more on it! The old one was pretty moth-eaten, but I really think this one is mouldier still."

On one occasion Albertine was not content with cold indifference, and this made me all the more wretched. She knew that I was concerned about the possibility of her meeting a friend of her aunt, who had a "bad name" and came now and again to spend a few days with Mme Bontemps. Albertine had pleased me by telling me that she would not speak to her again. And when this woman came to Incarville Albertine would say: "By the way, you know she's here. Have they told you?" as though to show me that she was not seeing her in secret. One day, when she told me this, she added: "Yes, I ran into her on the beach, and knocked against her as I passed, on purpose, to be rude to her." When Albertine told me this, there came back to my mind a remark made by Mme Bontemps, to which I had never given a second thought, when she had said to Mme Swann in my presence how brazen her niece Albertine was, as though that were a merit, and how Albertine reminded the wife of some official or other that her father had been a kitchen-boy. But a thing said by the woman we love does not long retain its purity; it cankers, it putrefies. An evening or two later, I thought again of Albertine's remark, and it was no longer the ill-breeding of which she boasted—and which could only make me smile—that it seemed to me to signify; it was something else, to wit that Albertine, perhaps even without any precise object, to tease this woman's senses, or wantonly to remind her of former propositions, accepted perhaps in the past, had swiftly brushed against her, had thought that I had perhaps heard of this as it had been done in public, and had wished to forestall an unfavourable interpretation.

However, the jealousy that was caused me by the women whom Albertine perhaps loved was abruptly to cease.

Albertine and I were waiting at the Balbec station of the little local railway. We had driven there in the hotel omnibus, because it was raining. Not far away from us was M. Nissim Bernard, who had a black eye. He had recently forsaken the chorister from *Athalie* for the waiter at a much frequented farmhouse in the neighbourhood, known as the "Cherry Orchard." This rubicund youth, with his blunt features, appeared for all the world to have a tomato instead of a head. A tomato exactly similar served as head to his twin brother. To the detached observer, the charm of these perfect resemblances between twins is that nature, as if momentarily industrialised, seems to be turning out identical products. Unfortunately M. Nissim Bernard looked at it from another point of view, and this resemblance was only external. Tomato No. 2 showed a frenzied zeal in catering exclusively to the pleasures of ladies; Tomato No. 1 was not averse to complying with the tastes of certain gentlemen. Now on every occasion when, stirred, as though by a reflex, by the memory of pleasant hours spent with Tomato No. 1, M. Bernard presented himself at the Cherry Orchard, being short-sighted (not that one had to be short-sighted to mistake them), the old Jewish gentleman, unwittingly playing Amphitryon, would accost the twin brother with: "Will you meet me somewhere this evening?" He at once received a thorough "hiding." It might even be repeated in the course of a single meal, when he continued with the second

brother a conversation he had begun with the first. In the end
this treatment, by association of ideas, so put him off tomatoes,
even of the edible variety, that whenever he heard a newcomer
order that vegetable at a neighbouring table in the Grand
Hotel, he would murmur to him: "You must excuse me,
Monsieur, for addressing you without an introduction. But I
heard you order tomatoes. They are bad to-day. I tell you in
your own interest, for it makes no difference to me, I never
touch them myself." The stranger would thank this philan-
thropic and disinterested neighbour effusively, call back the
waiter, and pretend to have changed his mind: "No, on second
thoughts, definitely no tomatoes." Aimé, who had seen it all
before, would laugh to himself, and think: "He's an old rascal,
that Monsieur Bernard, he's gone and made another of them
change his order." M. Bernard, as he waited for the already
overdue train, showed no eagerness to speak to Albertine and
myself, because of his black eye. We were even less eager to
speak to him. It would however have been almost inevitable if,
at that moment, a bicycle had not come swooping towards us;
the lift-boy sprang from its saddle, out of breath. Mme
Verdurin had telephoned shortly after we left the hotel, to
know whether I would dine with her two days later; we shall
presently see why. Then, having given me the message in detail,
the lift-boy left us, explaining, as one of those democratic
"employees" who affect independence with regard to the
gentry and restore the principle of authority among themselves, "I must be off, because of my chiefs."

Albertine's friends had gone away for some time. I was
anxious to provide her with distractions. Even supposing that
she might have found some happiness in spending the afternoons with no company but my own, at Balbec, I knew that
such happiness is never complete and that Albertine, being still
at the age (which some people never outgrow) when one has
not yet discovered that this imperfection resides in the person
who experiences the happiness and not in the person who gives
it, might have been tempted to trace the cause of her disappointment back to me. I preferred that she should impute it to
circumstances which, arranged by myself, would not give us an
opportunity of being alone together, while at the same time

preventing her from remaining in the Casino and on the beach without me. And so I had asked her that day to come with me to Doncières, where I was going to meet Saint-Loup. With the same object of keeping her occupied, I advised her to take up painting, in which she had had lessons in the past. While working she would not ask herself whether she was happy or unhappy. I would gladly have taken her also to dine now and again with the Verdurins and the Cambremers, who certainly would have been delighted to see any friend introduced by myself, but I must first make certain that Mme Putbus was not yet at la Raspelière. It was only by going there in person that I could make sure of this, and, as I knew beforehand that on the next day but one Albertine would be going on a visit with her aunt, I had seized this opportunity to send Mme Verdurin a telegram asking her whether I could visit her on Wednesday. If Mme Putbus was there, I would contrive to see her maid, ascertain whether there was any danger of her coming to Balbec, and if so find out when, so as to take Albertine out of reach on that day. The little local railway, making a loop which did not exist at the time when I had taken it with my grandmother, now extended to Doncières-la-Goupil, a big station at which important trains stopped, among them the express by which I had come down to visit Saint-Loup from Paris and thence returned. And, because of the bad weather, the omnibus from the Grand Hotel took Albertine and myself to the station of Balbec-Plage.

The little train had not yet arrived, but one could see the lazy, sluggish plume of smoke which it had left in its wake and which now, reduced to its own power of locomotion as a not very mobile cloud, was slowly mounting the green slope of the cliff of Criquetot. Finally the little train, which it had preceded by taking a vertical course, arrived in its turn, at a leisurely crawl. The passengers who were waiting to board it stepped back to make way for it, but without hurrying, knowing that they were dealing with a good-natured, almost human traveller, who, guided like the bicycle of a beginner by the obliging signals of the station-master, under the capable supervision of the engine-driver, was in no danger of running over anybody, and would come to a halt at the proper place.

My telegram explained the Verdurins' telephone message and had been all the more opportune since Wednesday (the next day but one happened to be a Wednesday) was the day set apart for big dinner-parties by Mme Verdurin, at la Raspelière as in Paris, a fact of which I was unaware. Mme Verdurin did not give "dinners," but she had "Wednesdays." These Wednesdays were works of art. While fully conscious that they had not their match anywhere, Mme Verdurin introduced shades of distinction between them. "Last Wednesday wasn't as good as the one before," she would say. "But I believe the next will be one of the most successful I've ever given." Sometimes she went so far as to admit: "This Wednesday wasn't worthy of the others. But I have a big surprise for you next week." In the closing weeks of the Paris season, before leaving for the country, the Mistress would announce the approaching end of the Wednesdays. It gave her an opportunity to spur on the faithful. "There are only three more Wednesdays left," or "Only two more," she would say, in the same tone as though the world were coming to an end. "You aren't going to let us down next Wednesday, for the finale." But this finale was a sham, for she would announce: "Officially, there will be no more Wednesdays. To-day was the last for this year. But I shall be at home all the same on Wednesday. We'll celebrate Wednesday by ourselves; I dare say these little private Wednesdays will be the nicest of all." At la Raspelière, the Wednesdays were of necessity restricted, and since, if they met a friend who was passing that way, they would invite him for any evening he chose, almost every day of the week became a Wednesday. "I don't remember all the guests, but I know there's Madame la Marquise de Camembert," the lift-boy had told me; his memory of our discussion of the name Cambremer had not succeeded in conclusively supplanting that of the old word, whose syllables, familiar and full of meaning, came to the young employee's rescue when he was flummoxed by this difficult name, and were immediately preferred and readopted by him, not from laziness or as an old and ineradicable usage, but because of the need for logic and clarity which they satisfied.

We hastened in search of an empty carriage in which I could hold Albertine in my arms throughout the journey. Having failed to find one, we got into a compartment in which there was already installed a lady with a massive face, old and ugly, and a masculine expression, very much in her Sunday best, who was reading the *Revue des Deux Mondes*. Notwithstanding her vulgarity, she was ladylike in her gestures, and I amused myself wondering to what social category she could belong; I at once concluded that she must be the manageress of some large brothel, a procuress on holiday. Her face and her manner proclaimed the fact aloud. Only, I had hitherto been unaware that such ladies read the *Revue des Deux Mondes*. Albertine drew my attention to her with a wink and a smile. The lady wore an air of extreme dignity; and as I, for my part, was inwardly aware that I was invited, two days hence, to the house of the celebrated Mme Verdurin at the terminal point of the little railway line, that at an intermediate station I was awaited by Robert de Saint-Loup, and that a little further on I would have given great pleasure to Mme de Cambremer by going to stay at Féterne, my eyes sparkled with irony as I gazed at this self-important lady who seemed to think that, because of her elaborate attire, the feathers in her hat, her *Revue des Deux Mondes*, she was a more considerable personage than myself. I hoped that the lady would not remain in the train much longer than M. Nissim Bernard, and that she would alight at least at Toutainville, but no. The train stopped at Egreville, and she remained seated. Similarly at Montmartin-sur-Mer, at Parville-la-Bingard, at Incarville, so that in desperation, when the train had left Saint-Frichoux, which was the last station before Doncières, I began to embrace Albertine without bothering about the lady.

At Doncières, Saint-Loup had come to meet me at the station, with the greatest difficulty, he told me, for, as he was staying with his aunt, my telegram had only just reached him and he could not, having been unable to make any arrangements beforehand, spare me more than an hour of his time. This hour seemed to me, alas, far too long, for as soon as we had left the train Albertine devoted her attention exclusively to Saint-Loup. She did not say a word to me, barely answered me if I addressed her, repulsed me when I approached her. With Robert, on the other hand, she laughed her provoking laugh, she talked to him volubly, played with the dog he had brought with him, and, while teasing the animal, deliberately rubbed against its master. I remembered that, on the day when Albertine had allowed me to kiss her for the first time, I had smiled with inward gratitude towards the unknown seducer who had wrought so profound a change in her and had so simplified my task. I thought of him now with horror. Robert must have realized that I was not indifferent to Albertine, for he did not respond to her advances, which put her in a bad humour with myself; then he spoke to me as though I was alone, and this, when she noticed it, raised me again in her esteem. Robert asked me if I would like to try and find, among the friends with whom he used to take me to dine every evening at Doncières when I was staying there, those who were still in the garrison. And as he himself indulged in that sort of teasing affectation which he reproved in others, "What's the good of your having worked so hard to *charm* them if you don't want to see them again?" he asked. I declined his offer, for I did not wish to run the risk of being parted from Albertine, but also because now I was detached from them. From them, which is to say from myself. We passionately long for there to be another life in which we shall be similar to what we are here below. But we do not pause to reflect that, even without waiting for that other life, in this life, after a few years, we are unfaithful to what we once were, to what we wished to remain immortally. Even without supposing that death is to alter us more completely than the changes that occur in the course of our lives, if in that other life we were to encounter the self that we have been, we should turn away from ourselves as from those people with whom we were once on friendly terms but whom we have not seen for years—such as Saint-Loup's friends whom I used so much to enjoy meeting every evening at the Faisan Doré, and whose conversation would now have seemed to me merely a boring importunity. In this respect, and because I preferred not to go there in search of what had given me pleasure in the past, a stroll through Doncières might have seemed to me a prefiguration of an arrival in paradise. We dream much of paradise, or rather of a number of successive paradises, but each of them is, long before we die, a paradise lost, in which we should feel ourself lost too.

He left us at the station. "But you may have nearly an hour to wait," he told me. "If you spend it here, you'll probably see my uncle Charlus, who is catching the train to Paris, ten minutes before yours. I've already said good-bye to him, because I have to be back before his train leaves. I didn't tell him about you, because I hadn't got your telegram."

To the reproaches which I heaped upon her when Saint-Loup had left us, Albertine replied that she had intended, by her coldness towards me, to dispel any idea that he might have formed if, at the moment when the train stopped, he had seen me leaning against her with my arm round her waist. He had indeed noticed this attitude (I had not caught sight of him, otherwise I should have sat up decorously beside Albertine), and had had time to murmur in my ear: "So *that's* one of those priggish little girls you told me about, who wouldn't go near Mlle de Stermaria because they thought her fast?" I had indeed mentioned to Robert, and in all sincerity, when I went down from Paris to visit him at Doncières, and when we were talking about our time at Balbec, that there was nothing to be done with Albertine, that she was virtue itself. And now that I had long since discovered for myself that this was false, I was even more anxious that Robert should believe it to be true. It would have been sufficient for me to tell Robert that I was in love with Albertine. He was one of those people who are capable of denying themselves a pleasure to spare a friend sufferings which they would feel as though they were their own. "Yes, she's still rather childish. But you don't know anything against her?" I added anxiously. "Nothing, except that I saw you clinging together like a pair of lovers."

"Your attitude dispelled absolutely nothing," I told Albertine when Saint-Loup had left us. "Quite true," she said to me, "it was stupid of me, I hurt your feelings, I'm far more unhappy about it than you are. You'll see, I shall never be like that again; forgive me," she pleaded, holding out her hand with a sorrowful air. At that moment, from the waiting-room in which we were sitting, I saw M. de Charlus pass slowly by, followed at a respectful distance by a porter loaded with his baggage.

In Paris, where I encountered him only at evening receptions, immobile, strapped up in dress-clothes, maintained in a vertical posture by his proud erectness, his eagerness to be admired, his conversational verve, I had not realised how much he had aged. Now, in a light travelling suit which made him appear stouter, as he waddled along with his swaying paunch and almost symbolic behind, the cruel light of day decomposed, into paint on his lips, into face-powder fixed by cold cream on the tip of his nose, into mascara on his dyed moustache whose ebony hue contrasted with his grizzled hair, everything that in artificial light would have seemed the healthy complexion of a man who was still young.

While I stood talking to him, though briefly, because of his train, I kept my eye on Albertine's carriage to show her that I was coming. When I turned my head towards M. de Charlus, he asked me to be so kind as to summon a soldier, a relative of his, who was standing on the opposite platform, as though he were waiting to take our train, but in the opposite direction, away from Balbec. "He is in the regimental band," said M. de Charlus. "As you are so fortunate as to be still young enough, and I unfortunately am old enough for you to save me the trouble of going across to him . . ." I felt obliged to go across to the soldier in question, and saw from the lyres embroidered on his collar that he was a bandsman. But, just as I was preparing to execute my commission, what was my surprise, and, I may say, my pleasure, on recognising Morel, the son of my uncle's valet, who recalled to me so many memories. They made me forget to convey M. de Charlus's message. "What, are you at Doncières?" "Yes, and they've put me in the band attached to the artillery." But he made this answer in a dry and haughty tone. He had become an intense "poseur," and evidently the sight of myself, reminding him of his father's profession, was displeasing to him. Suddenly I saw M. de Charlus descending upon us. My dilatoriness had evidently taxed his patience. "I should like to listen to a little music this evening," he said to Morel without any preliminaries. "I pay five hundred francs for the evening, which may perhaps be of interest to one of your friends, if you have any in the band." Knowing as I did the insolence of M. de Charlus, I was none the less astonished at his not even saying how-d'ye-do to his young friend. He did not however give me time for reflexion. Holding out his hand to me affectionately, "Good-bye, my dear fellow," he said, implying that I might now leave them. I had in any case left my dear Albertine too long alone. "D'you know," I said to her as I climbed into the carriage, "the seaside life and the life of travel make me realise that the theatre of the world is stocked with fewer settings than actors, and with fewer actors than situations." "What makes you say that?" "Because M. de Charlus asked me just now to fetch one of his friends, whom this instant, on the platform of this station, I have just discovered to be one of my own." But as I uttered these words, I began to wonder how the Baron could have bridged the social gulf to which I had not given a thought. It occurred to me first of all that it might be through Jupien, whose niece, as the reader may remember, had seemed to become enamoured of the violinist. However, what baffled me completely was that, when due to leave for Paris in five minutes, the Baron should have asked for a musical evening. But, visualising Jupien's niece again in my memory, I was beginning to think that "recognitions" might indeed express an important part of life, if one knew how to penetrate to the romantic core of things, when all of a sudden the truth flashed across my mind and I realised that I had been absurdly ingenuous. M. de Charlus had never in his life set eyes upon Morel, nor Morel upon M. de Charlus, who, dazzled but also intimidated by a soldier even though he carried no weapon but a lyre, in his agitation had called upon me to bring him the person whom he never suspected that I already knew. In any case, for Morel, the offer of five hundred francs must have made up for the absence of any previous relations, for I saw that they were going on talking, oblivious of the fact that they were standing close beside our train. And remembering the manner in which M. de Charlus had come up to Morel and myself, I saw at once the resemblance to certain of his relatives when they picked up a woman in the street. The desired object had merely changed sex. After a certain age, and even if we develop in quite different ways, the more we become ourselves, the more our family traits are accentuated. For Nature, even while harmoniously fashioning the design of its tapestry, breaks the monotony of the composition thanks to the variety of the faces it catches. Besides, the haughtiness with

which M. de Charlus had eyed the violinist is relative, and
depends upon the point of view one adopts. It would have been
recognised by three out of four society people, who bowed to
him, not by the prefect of police who, a few years later, was to
keep him under surveillance.

"The Paris train has been signalled, sir," said the porter who
was carrying his suitcases. "But I'm not taking the train; put
them in the cloakroom, damn you!" said M. de Charlus, giving
twenty francs to the porter, who was astonished by the change
of plan and charmed by the tip. This generosity at once
attracted a flower-seller. "Take these carnations, look, this
lovely rose, kind gentleman, it will bring you luck." M. de
Charlus, exasperated, handed her a couple of francs, in exchange
for which the woman gave him her blessing, and her flowers as
well. "Good God, why can't she leave us alone," said M. de
Charlus, addressing himself to Morel in an ironically querulous
tone, as though he were at the end of his tether and found a
certain comfort in appealing to him for support; "what we have
to say to each other is quite complicated enough as it is."
Perhaps, the porter not yet being out of earshot, M. de Charlus
did not care to have too numerous an audience; perhaps these
incidental remarks enabled his lofty timidity not to broach too
directly the request for an assignation. The musician, turning
with a frank, imperious and determined air to the flower-seller,
raised a hand which repulsed her and indicated to her that her
flowers were not wanted and that she was to clear off at once.
M. de Charlus observed with ecstasy this authoritative, virile
gesture, wielded by the graceful hand for which it ought still to
have been too weighty, too massively brutal, with a precocious
firmness and suppleness which gave to this still beardless
adolescent the air of a young David capable of challenging
Goliath. The Baron's admiration was unconsciously blended
with the sort of smile with which we observe in a child an expression of gravity beyond his years. *"There's* somebody I
should like to have to accompany me on my travels and help me
in my business. How he would simplify my life," M. de Charlus
said to himself.

The train for Paris started, without M. de Charlus. Then
Albertine and I took our seats in our own train, without my

discovering what had become of M. de Charlus and Morel. "We must never quarrel any more, I beg your pardon again," Albertine said to me, alluding to the Saint-Loup incident. "We must always be nice to each other," she added tenderly. "As for your friend Saint-Loup, if you think that I'm the least bit interested in him, you're quite mistaken. All that I like about him is that he seems so very fond of you." "He's a very good fellow," I said, taking care not to attribute to Robert those imaginary excellences which I should not have failed to invent, out of friendship for him, had I been with anybody but Albertine. "He's an excellent creature, frank, devoted, loyal, someone you can rely on in any circumstances." In saying this I confined myself, restrained by my jealousy, to speaking the truth about Saint-Loup, but what I said was indeed the truth. But it expressed itself in precisely the same terms as Mme de Villeparisis had used in speaking to me of him, when I did not yet know him, imagined him to be so different, so proud, and said to myself: "People think him kind because he's a blue-blooded nobleman." In the same way, when she had said to me: "He would be so pleased," I thought to myself, after seeing him outside the hotel preparing to take the reins, that his aunt's words had been mere social banality, intended to flatter me. And I had realised afterwards that she had spoken sincerely, thinking of the things that interested me, of my reading, and because she knew that that was what Saint-Loup liked, as it was later to happen to me to say sincerely to somebody who was writing a history of his ancestor La Rochefoucauld, the author of the *Maximes*, and wished to consult Robert about him: "He will be so pleased." It was simply that I had learned to know him. But, when I set eyes on him for the first time, I had not supposed that an intelligence akin to my own could be enveloped in so much outward elegance of dress and attitude. By his feathers I had judged him to be a bird of another species. It was Albertine now who, perhaps a little because Saint-Loup, out of kindness to myself, had been so cold to her, said to me what I had once thought: "Ah, he's as devoted as all that! I notice that people are invariably credited with all the virtues when they belong to the Faubourg Saint-Germain." And yet, the fact that Saint-Loup belonged to the Faubourg Saint-

German was something I had never once thought of again in the course of all these years in which, stripping himself of his prestige, he had demonstrated his virtues to me. Such a change of perspective in looking at other people, more striking already in friendship than in merely social relations, is all the more striking still in love, where desire so enlarges the scale, so magnifies the proportions of the slightest signs of coldness, that it had required far less than Saint-Loup had shown at first sight for me to believe myself disdained at first by Albertine, to imagine her friends as fabulously inhuman creatures, and to ascribe Elstir's judgment, when he said to me of the little band with exactly the same sentiment as Mme de Villeparisis speaking of Saint-Loup: "They're good girls," simply to the indulgence people have for beauty and a certain elegance. Yet was this not the verdict I would automatically have expressed when I heard Albertine say: "In any case, whether he's devoted or not, I sincerely hope I shall never see him again, since he's made us quarrel. We must never quarrel again. It isn't nice." Since she had seemed to desire Saint-Loup, I felt more or less cured for the time being of the idea that she cared for women, assuming that the two things were irreconcilable. And, looking at Albertine's mackintosh, in which she seemed to have become another person, the tireless vagrant of rainy days, and which, close-fitting, malleable and grey, seemed at that moment not so much intended to protect her clothes from the rain as to have been soaked by it and to be clinging to her body as though to take the imprint of her form for a sculptor, I tore off that tunic which jealously enwrapped a longed-for breast and, drawing Albertine towards me:

"But won't you, indolent traveller, rest your head
And dream your dreams upon my shoulder?"

I said, taking her head in my hands, and showing her the wide meadows, flooded and silent, which extended in the gathering dusk to an horizon closed by the parallel chains of distant blue hills.

Two days later, on the famous Wednesday, in that same little train which I had again taken at Balbec to go and dine at la

Raspelière, I was extremely anxious not to miss Cottard at
Graincourt-Saint-Vast, where a second telephone message from
Mme Verdurin had told me that I should find him. He was to
join my train and would tell me where we had to get out to
pick up the carriages that would be sent from la Raspelière to
the station. And so, as the little train stopped for only a moment
at Graincourt, the first station after Doncières, I had posted
myself in readiness at the open window for fear of not seeing
Cottard or of his not seeing me. Vain fears! I had not realised to
what an extent the little clan had moulded all its regular members after the same type, so that, as they stood waiting on the
platform, being moreover in full evening dress, they were
immediately recognisable by a certain air of assurance, elegance
and familiarity, by a look in their eyes which seemed to sweep
across the serried ranks of the common herd as across an empty
space in which there was nothing to arrest their attention,
watching for the arrival of some fellow-member who had taken
the train at an earlier station, and sparkling in anticipation of
the talk that was to come. This sign of election, with which the
habit of dining together had marked the members of the little
group, was not all that distinguished them when they were
massed together in full strength, forming a more brilliant patch
in the midst of the troop of passengers—what Brichot called
the *pecus*—upon whose drab faces could be discerned no notion
relating to the name Verdurin, no hope of ever dining at la
Raspelière. To be sure, these common travellers would have
been less interested than myself—notwithstanding the fame that
several of the faithful had achieved—had anyone quoted in
their hearing the names of these men whom I was astonished
to see continuing to dine out when many of them had already
been doing so, according to the stories that I had heard, before
my birth, at a period at once so distant and so vague that I was
inclined to exaggerate its remoteness. The contrast between the
continuance not only of their existence, but of the fullness of
their powers, and the obliteration of so many friends whom I
had already seen vanish here or there, gave me the same feeling
that we experience when in the stop-press column of the newspapers we read the very announcement that we least expected,
for instance that of an untimely death, which seems to us

fortuitous because the causes that have led up to it have remained outside our knowledge. This is the feeling that death does not descend uniformly upon all men, but that a more advanced wave of its tragic tide carries off a life situated at the same level as others which the waves that follow will long continue to spare. We shall see later on that the diversity of the forms of death that circulate invisibly is the cause of the peculiar unexpectedness of obituary notices in the newspapers. Then I saw that, with the passage of time, not only do real talents that may coexist with the most commonplace conversation reveal and impose themselves, but furthermore that mediocre persons arrive at those exalted positions, attached in the imagination of our childhood to certain famous elders, when it never occurred to us that a certain number of years later, their disciples, now become masters, would be famous too, and would inspire the respect and awe that they themselves once felt. But if the names of the faithful were unknown to the *pecus*, their aspect still singled them out in its eyes. Even in the train, when the coincidence of what they had been doing during the day assembled them all together, and they had to collect at a subsequent station only one isolated companion, the carriage in which they were gathered, designated by the sculptor Ski's elbow, flagged by Cottard's *Temps*, stood out from a distance like a special saloon, and rallied at the appointed station the tardy comrade. The only one who, because of his semi-blindness, might have missed these welcoming signals was Brichot. But one of the party would always volunteer to keep a look-out for him, and, as soon as his straw hat, his green umbrella and blue spectacles had been spotted, he would be gently but hastily guided towards the chosen compartment. So that it was inconceivable that one of the faithful, without exciting the gravest suspicions of his being "on the loose," or even of his not having come "by the train," should not pick up the others in the course of the journey. Sometimes the opposite process occurred: one of the faithful might have had to go some distance down the line during the afternoon and would be obliged in consequence to make part of the journey alone before being joined by the group; but even when thus isolated, alone of his kind, he did not fail as a rule to produce a certain effect.

The Future towards which he was travelling marked him out
to the person on the seat opposite, who would say to himself
"He must be somebody," would discern a vague halo round
the trilby of Cottard or of the sculptor Ski, and would be only
half-astonished when at the next station an elegant crowd, if it
were their terminal point, greeted the faithful one at the carriage
door and escorted him to one of the waiting vehicles, all of
them receiving a deep bow from the factotum of Doville
station, or, if it were an intermediate station, invaded the
compartment. This was what now occurred, with some preci-
pitation, for several had arrived late, just as the train which was
already in the station was about to start, with the troupe which
Cottard led at the double towards the carriage at the window of
which he had seen me signalling. Brichot, who was among this
group of the faithful, had become more faithful than ever in
the course of these years which had diminished the assiduity of
others. As his sight became steadily weaker, he had been
obliged, even in Paris, to reduce more and more his work after
dark. Besides, he was out of sympathy with the modern Sorbonne, where ideas of scientific exactitude, after the German
model, were beginning to prevail over humanism. He now
confined himself exclusively to his lectures and to his duties as
an examiner; hence he had a great deal more time to devote to
social pursuits, that is to say to evenings at the Verdurins', or
to those that now and again were given for the Verdurins by
one or other of the faithful, tremulous with emotion. It is true
that on two occasions love had almost succeeded in achieving
what his work could no longer do: in detaching Brichot from
the little clan. But Mme Verdurin, who "kept a weather eye
open," and moreover, having acquired the habit in the interests
of her salon, had come to take a disinterested pleasure in this
sort of drama and execution, had brought about an irremediable
breach between him and the dangerous person, being skilled
(as she put it) at "putting things in order" and "stopping the
rot." This she had found all the easier in the case of one of
the dangerous persons in that the latter was simply Brichot's
laundress, and Mme Verdurin, having free access to the fifth-
floor rooms of the Professor, who was crimson with pride
whenever she deigned to climb his stairs, had only had to

throw the wretched woman out. "What!" the Mistress had said to Brichot, "a woman like myself does you the honour of calling upon you, and you entertain a creature like that?" Brichot had never forgotten the service that Mme Verdurin had rendered him by preventing his old age from foundering in the mire, and became more and more attached to her, whereas, in contrast to this renewal of affection and possibly because of it, the Mistress was beginning to be tired of this too docile follower of whose obedience she could be certain in advance. But Brichot acquired from his intimacy with the Verdurins a glamour which set him apart from all his colleagues at the Sorbonne. They were dazzled by the accounts that he gave them of dinner-parties to which they would never be invited, by the mention made of him in the reviews, or the portrait of him exhibited in the Salon, by some writer or painter of repute whose talent the occupants of the other chairs in the Faculty of Letters esteemed but whose attention they had no prospect of attracting, and in particular by the elegance of the mundane philosopher's attire, an elegance which they had mistaken at first for slovenliness until their colleague had benevolently explained to them that a top hat could quite acceptably be placed on the floor when one was paying a call and was not the right thing for dinners in the country, however smart, where it should be replaced by a trilby, which was perfectly all right with a dinner-jacket.

For the first few moments after the little group had swept into the carriage, I could not even speak to Cottard, for he was completely breathless, not so much from having run in order not to miss the train as from astonishment at having caught it at the last second. He felt more than the joy of success, almost the hilarity of a merry prank. "Ah! that was a good one!" he said when he had recovered himself. "A minute later! 'Pon my soul, that's what they call arriving in the nick of time!" he added with a wink, intended not so much to inquire whether the expression were apt, for he now overflowed with confidence, but to express his self-satisfaction. At length he was able to introduce me to the other members of the little clan. I was dismayed to see that they were almost all in the dress which in Paris is called a "smoking." I had forgotten that the Verdurins

were beginning to make tentative moves in the direction of
fashionable ways, moves which, slowed down by the Dreyfus
case, accelerated by the "new" music, they in fact denied, and
would continue to deny until they were complete, like those
military objectives which a general does not announce until
he has reached them, so as not to appear defeated if he fails.
Society for its part was quite prepared to go half-way to meet
them. At the moment it had reached the point of regarding
them as people to whose house nobody in Society went but
who were not in the least perturbed by the fact. The Verdurin
salon was understood to be a Temple of Music. It was there,
people affirmed, that Vinteuil had found inspiration and
encouragement. And although Vinteuil's sonata remained
wholly unappreciated and almost unknown, his name, referred
to as that of the greatest of modern composers, enjoyed an
extraordinary prestige. Finally, certain young men of the
Faubourg having decided that they ought to be as well educated
as the middle classes, three of them had studied music and
among these Vinteuil's sonata enjoyed an enormous vogue.
They would speak of it, on returning to their homes, to the
intelligent mothers who had encouraged them to improve
their minds. And, taking an interest in their sons' studies, these
mothers would gaze with a certain respect at Mme Verdurin
in her front box at concerts, following the music from the
score. So far, this latent social success of the Verdurins had
expressed itself in two facts only. In the first place, Mme
Verdurin would say of the Principessa di Caprarola: "Ah! she's
intelligent, that one, she's a charming woman. What I cannot
endure are the imbeciles, the people who bore me—they drive
me mad." Which would have made anybody at all perspicacious
realise that the Principessa di Caprarola, a woman who moved
in the highest society, had called upon Mme Verdurin. She had
even mentioned the Verdurins' name in the course of a visit of
condolence which she had paid to Mme Swann after the death
of her husband, and had asked whether she knew them. "What
name did you say?" Odette had asked with sudden wistfulness.
"Verdurin? Oh, yes, of course," she had continued glumly,
"I don't know them, or rather, I know them without really
knowing them, they're people I used to meet with friends

years ago, they're quite nice." When the Principessa di Caprarola had gone, Odette regretted not having told the bare truth.
But the immediate falsehood was not the fruit of her calcula-
tions, but the revelation of her fears and her desires. She denied
not what it would have been adroit to deny, but what she would
have liked not to be the case, even if her interlocutor was
bound to hear an hour later that it was indeed the case. A little
later she had recovered her self-assurance, and would even
anticipate questions by saying, so as not to appear to be afraid
of them: "Mme Verdurin, why, I used to know her terribly
well," with an affectation of humility, like a great lady who tells
you that she has taken the tram. "There has been a great deal of
talk about the Verdurins lately," Mme de Souvré would
remark. Odette, with the smiling disdain of a duchess, would
reply: "Yes, I do seem to have heard a lot about them lately.
Every now and then there are new people like that who arrive
in society," without reflecting that she herself was among the
newest. "The Principessa di Caprarola has dined there,"
Mme de Souvré would continue. "Ah!" Odette would reply,
accentuating her smile, "that doesn't surprise me. That sort of
thing always begins with the Principessa di Caprarola, and then
someone else follows suit, like Comtesse Molé." Odette, in
saying this, appeared to be filled with a profound contempt for
the two great ladies who made a habit of "house-warming"
in recently established salons. One felt from her tone that
the implication was that she, Odette, like Mme de Souvré,
was not the sort of person to let herself in for that sort of
thing.

After the admission that Mme Verdurin had made of the
Principessa di Caprarola's intelligence, the second indication
that the Verdurins were conscious of their future destiny was
that (without, of course, their having formally requested it)
they were most anxious that people should now come to dine
with them in evening dress. M. Verdurin could now have been
greeted without shame by his nephew, the one who was "a wash-
out."

Among those who entered my carriage at Graincourt was
Saniette, who long ago had been driven from the Verdurins'
by his cousin Forcheville, but had since returned. His faults,

from the social point of view, had originally been—notwithstanding his superior qualities—somewhat similar to Cottard's: shyness, anxiety to please, fruitless attempts to succeed in doing so. But if the course of life, by making Cottard assume (if not at the Verdurins', where, because of the influence that past associations exert over us when we find ourselves in familiar surroundings, he had remained more or less the same, at least in his practice, in his hospital work, and at the Academy of Medicine) an outer shell of coldness, disdain, gravity, that became more and more pronounced as he trotted out his puns to his indulgent students, had created a veritable gulf between the old Cottard and the new, the same defects had on the contrary become more extreme in Saniette the more he sought to correct them. Conscious that he was frequently boring, that people did not listen to him, instead of then slackening his pace as Cottard would have done, and forcing their attention by an air of authority, not only did he try to win forgiveness for the unduly serious turn of his conversation by adopting a playful tone, but he speeded up his delivery, rushed his remarks, used abbreviations in order to appear less long-winded, more familiar with the matters of which he spoke, and succeeded only, by making them unintelligible, in appearing interminable. His self-assurance was not like that of Cottard, who so petrified his patients that when other people lauded his social affability they would reply: "He's a different man when he receives you in his consulting room, you with your face to the light, and he with his back to it, and those piercing eyes." It failed to make any effect, one felt that it cloaked an excessive shyness, that the merest trifle would be enough to dispel it. Saniette, whose friends had always told him that he was wanting in self-confidence, and who had indeed seen men whom he rightly considered greatly inferior to himself obtain with ease the successes that were denied to him, now never began a story without smiling at its drollery, fearing lest a serious air might make his hearers underestimate the value of his wares. Sometimes, taking on trust the humour which he himself appeared to see in what he was about to say, his audience would oblige him with a general silence. But the story would fall flat. A kind-hearted fellow-guest would sometimes give Saniette the private, almost secret encouragement of a smile of approbation, conveying it to him furtively, without attracting attention, as one slips a note into someone's hand. But nobody went so far as to assume the responsibility, to risk the glaring publicity of an honest laugh. Long after the story was ended and had fallen flat, Saniette, crestfallen, would remain smiling to himself, as though relishing in it and for himself the delectation which he pretended to find adequate and which the others had not felt.

As for the sculptor Ski—so styled on account of the difficulty they found in pronouncing his Polish surname, and because he himself, since he had begun to move in a certain social sphere, affected not to wish to be associated with his perfectly respectable but slightly boring and very numerous relations—he had, at forty-four and with no pretension to good looks, a sort of boyishness, a dreamy wistfulness which was the result of his having been, until the age of ten, the most ravishing child prodigy imaginable, the darling of all the ladies. Mme Verdurin maintained that he was more of an artist than Elstir. Any resemblance that there may have been between them was, however, purely external. It was sufficient to make Elstir, who had met Ski once, feel for him the profound repulsion that is inspired in us not so much by the people who are completely different from us as by those who are less satisfactory versions of ourselves, in whom are displayed our less attractive qualities, the faults of which we have cured ourselves, unpleasantly reminding us of how we must have appeared to certain other people before we became what we now are. But Mme Verdurin thought that Ski had more temperament than Elstir because there was no art in which he did not have some aptitude, and she was convinced that he would have developed that aptitude into talent if he had been less indolent. This indolence seemed to the Mistress to be actually an additional gift, being the opposite of hard work which she regarded as the lot of people devoid of genius. Ski would paint anything you asked, on cuff-links or on overdoors. He sang very musically and played from memory, giving the piano the effect of an orchestra, less by his virtuosity than by his vamped basses which suggested the inability of the fingers to indicate that at a certain point the cornet entered, which in any case he would imitate with his lips. Searching for words when he spoke so as to convey an interesting impression, just as he would pause before banging out a chord with the exclamation "Ping!" to bring out the brass, he was regarded as being marvellously intelligent, but as a matter of fact his ideas boiled down to two or three, extremely limited. Bored with his reputation for whimsicality, he had taken it into his head to show that he was a practical, down-to-earth person, whence a triumphant affectation of fake precision, of fake common sense, aggravated by his having no memory and a fund of information that was always inaccurate. The movements of his head, his neck and his limbs would have been graceful if he had still been nine years old, with golden curls, a wide lace collar and red leather bootees. Having arrived at Graincourt station in the company of Cottard and Brichot with time to spare, he and Cottard had left Brichot in the waiting-room and had gone for a stroll. When Cottard proposed to turn back, Ski had replied: "But there's no hurry. It isn't the local train to-day, it's the departmental train." Delighted by the effect that this refinement of accuracy produced upon Cottard, he added, with reference to himself: "Yes, because Ski loves the arts, because he models in clay, people think he's not practical. Nobody knows this line better than I do." Nevertheless, when they had turned back towards the station, Cottard, all of a sudden catching sight of the smoke of the approaching train, had let out a bellow and exclaimed: "We shall have to run like the wind." And they had in fact arrived with not a moment to spare, the distinction between local and departmental trains having never existed save in the mind of Ski.

"But isn't the Princess on the train?" came in ringing tones from Brichot, whose huge spectacles, glittering like the reflectors that throat specialists attach to their foreheads to see into their patients' larynxes, seemed to have taken their life from the Professor's eyes, and, possibly because of the effort he made to adjust his sight to them, seemed themselves to be looking, even at the most trivial moments, with sustained attention and extraordinary fixity. Brichot's malady, as it gradually deprived him of his sight, had revealed to him the beauties of that sense, just as, frequently, we have to make up our minds to part with some object, to make a present of it for instance, in order to study it, regret it, admire it.

"No, no, the Princess went over to Maineville with some of Mme Verdurin's guests who were taking the Paris train. It isn't beyond the bounds of possibility that Mme Verdurin, who had some business at Saint-Mars, may be with her! In that case, she'll be coming with us, and we shall all travel together, which will be delightful. We shall have to keep our eyes skinned at Maineville and see what we shall see! Ah, well, never mind— we certainly came very near to missing the bus. When I saw the train I was flabbergasted. That's what you call arriving at the psychological moment. What if we'd missed the train and Mme Verdurin had seen the carriages come back without us? You can just picture it," added the doctor, who had not yet recovered from his excitement. "I must say we really are having quite a jaunt. Eh, Brichot, what have you to say about our little escapade?" inquired the doctor with a note of pride.

"Upon my soul," replied Brichot, "why, yes, if you'd found the train gone, that would have been a heck of a to-do, as Villemain, our late professor of eloquence, would have said."

But I, engrossed from the very first by these people whom I did not know, was suddenly reminded of what Cottard had said to me in the ballroom of the little casino, and, as though it were possible for an invisible link to join an organ to the images of one's memory, the image of Albertine pressing her breasts against Andrée's brought a terrible pain to my heart. This pain did not last: the idea of Albertine's having relations with women seemed no longer possible since the occasion, forty-eight hours earlier, when the advances she had made to Saint-Loup had excited in me a new jealousy which had made me forget the old. I was innocent enough to believe that one taste necessarily excludes another.

At Harambouville, as the train was full, a farm labourer in a blue smock who had only a third-class ticket got into our compartment. The doctor, feeling that the Princess could not be allowed to travel with such a person, called a porter, showed a card which described him as medical officer to one of the big railway companies, and obliged the station-master to eject the intruder. This incident so pained and alarmed Saniette's timid spirit that, as soon as he saw it beginning, fearing already lest, in view of the crowd of peasants on the platform, it should assume the proportions of a jacquerie, he pretended to be suffering from a stomach-ache, and to avoid being accused of any share in the responsibility for the doctor's violence, rushed down the corridor pretending to be looking for what Cottard called the "waters." Failing to find it, he stood and gazed at the scenery from the other end of the "twister."

"If this is your first appearance at Mme Verdurin's, Monsieur," Brichot said to me, anxious to show off his talents before a newcomer, "you will find that there is no place where one feels more the '*douceur de vivre*,' to quote one of the inventors of dilettantism, of pococurantism, of all sorts of 'isms' that are in fashion among our little snobbesses—I refer to M. le Prince de Talleyrand." For, when he spoke of these great noblemen of the past, he felt that it was witty and added "period colour" to prefix their titles with "Monsieur," and said "M. le Duc de La Rochefoucauld," "M. le Cardinal de Retz," referring to these also as "That *struggle for lifer* de Gondi," "that *Boulangist* de Marcillac." And he never failed, when referring to Montesquieu, to call him, with a smile, "Monsieur le Président Secondat de Montesquieu." An intelligent man of society would have been irritated by this pedantry, which reeked of the lecture-room. But in the perfect manners of the man of society there is a pedantry too, when speaking of a prince, which betrays a different caste, that in which one prefixes the name "William" with "the Emperor" and addresses a Royal Highness in the third person. "Ah, now, that is a man," Brichot continued, still referring to "Monsieur le Prince de Talleyrand," "to whom we take off our hats. He is an ancestor."

"It's a delightful circle," Cottard told me, "you'll find a little of everything, for Mme Verdurin is not exclusive—distinguished scholars like Brichot, the nobility, for example Princess Sherbatoff, an aristocratic Russian lady, a friend of the Grand Duchess Eudoxie, who even sees her alone at hours when no one else is admitted."

As a matter of fact the Grand Duchess Eudoxie, not wishing Princess Sherbatoff, who for years past had been ostracised by

everyone, to come to her house when there might be other
people, allowed her to come only in the early morning, when
Her Imperial Highness was not at home to any of those friends
to whom it would have been as disagreeable to meet the Princess
as it would have been awkward for the Princess to meet them.
Since, for the last three years, as soon as she came away from
the Grand Duchess, like a manicurist, Mme Sherbatoff would
go to Mme Verdurin, who had just woken up, and stick to her
for the rest of the day, one might say that the Princess's loyalty
surpassed even that of Brichot, constant as he was at those
Wednesdays, both in Paris, where he had the pleasure of
fancying himself a sort of Chateaubriand at l'Abbaye-aux-Bois,[41]
and in the country, where he saw himself becoming the equivalent of what the man whom he always referred to (with the
knowing sarcasm of the man of letters) as "M. de Voltaire"
must have been in the salon of Mme du Châtelet.

 Her want of friends had enabled Princess Sherbatoff for some
years past to display towards the Verdurins a fidelity which
made her more than an ordinary member of the "faithful,"
the classic example of the breed, the ideal which Mme Verdurin
had long thought unattainable and which now, in her later
years, she at length found incarnate in this new feminine recruit.
However keenly the Mistress might feel the pangs of jealousy, it
was without precedent for the most assiduous of her faithful
not to have "defected" at least once. The most stay-at-home
yielded to the temptation to travel; the most continent fell from
virtue; the most robust might catch influenza, the idlest be
caught for his month's soldiering, the most indifferent go to
close the eyes of a dying mother. And it was in vain that Mme
Verdurin told them then, like the Roman Empress, that she
was the sole general whom her legion must obey, or like Christ
or the Kaiser, that he who loved his father or mother more than
her and was not prepared to leave them and follow her was not
worthy of her, that instead of wilting in bed or letting themselves be made fools of by whores they would do better to
stay with her, their sole remedy and sole delight. But destiny,
which is sometimes pleased to brighten the closing years of a
life that stretches beyond the normal span, had brought Mme
Verdurin in contact with the Princess Sherbatoff. Estranged

from her family, an exile from her native land, knowing nobody
but the Baroness Putbus and the Grand Duchess Eudoxie, to
whose houses, because she herself had no desire to meet the
friends of the former, and the latter no desire that her friends
should meet the Princess, she went only in the early morning
hours when Mme Verdurin was still asleep, never once, so far
as she could remember, having been confined to her bed since
she was twelve years old, when she had had the measles, having
on the 31st of December replied to Mme Verdurin who, afraid
of being left alone, had asked her whether she would not
"shake down" there for the night, in spite of its being New
Year's Eve: "Why, what is there to prevent me, any day of the
year? Besides, to-morrow is a day when one stays at home with
one's family, and you are my family," living in a boarding-
house and moving from it whenever the Verdurins moved,
accompanying them on their holidays, the Princess had so
completely exemplified to Mme Verdurin the line of Vigny:

> Thou only didst appear that which one seeks always,

that the Lady President of the little circle, anxious to make sure
of one of her "faithful" even after death, had made her promise
that whichever of them survived the other should be buried by
her side. In front of strangers—among whom we must always
reckon the one to whom we lie the most because he is the one
whose contempt would be most painful to us: ourselves—
Princess Sherbatoff took care to represent her only three friendships—with the Grand Duchess, the Verdurins, and the Baroness Putbus—as the only ones, not which cataclysms beyond
her control had allowed to emerge from the destruction of
all the rest, but which a free choice had made her elect in
preference to any other, and to which a taste for solitude and
simplicity had made her confine herself. "I see *nobody* else,"
she would say, underlining the inflexible character of what
appeared to be rather a rule that one imposes upon oneself than
a necessity to which one submits. She would add: "I visit only
three houses," as a dramatist who fears that it may not run to
a fourth announces that there will be only three performances of
his play. Whether or not M. and Mme Verdurin gave credence
to this fiction, they had helped the Princess to instil it into the

minds of the faithful. And they in turn were persuaded both
that the Princess, among the thousands of invitations that were
available to her, had chosen the Verdurins' alone, and that the
Verdurins, deaf to the overtures with which they were bombarded by the entire aristocracy, had consented to make but a
single exception, in favour of a great lady of more intelligence
than the rest of her kind, the Princess Sherbatoff.

The Princess was very rich; she engaged for every first night
a large box, to which, with Mme Verdurin's assent, she invited
the faithful and nobody else. People would point out to one
another this pale and enigmatic person who had grown old
without turning white, turning red, rather, like certain tough
and shrivelled hedgerow fruits. They admired both her
influence and her humility, for, having always with her an
Academician, Brichot, a famous doctor, Cottard, the leading
pianist of the day, and at a later date M. de Charlus, she
remained in the background, made a point of securing the least
prominent box in the theatre, paid no attention to the rest of
the house, lived exclusively for the little group, who, shortly
before the end of the performance, would withdraw in the wake
of this strange sovereign, who was not without a certain shy,
bewitching, faded beauty. But if Mme Sherbatoff did not look
at the audience, if she effaced herself, it was to try to forget that
there existed a living world which she passionately desired and
was unable to enjoy; the coterie in a box was to her what is to
certain animals their almost corpselike immobility in the
presence of danger. Nevertheless the thirst for novelty and for
the curious which possesses society people made them pay even
more attention perhaps to this mysterious stranger than to the
celebrities in the front boxes to whom everybody paid a visit.
They imagined that she must be different from the people they
knew, that a marvellous intellect combined with a discerning
bounty retained round about her that little circle of eminent
men. The Princess was compelled, if you spoke to her about
anyone, or introduced her to anyone, to feign an intense coldness, in order to keep up the fiction of her loathing of society.
Nevertheless, with the support of Cottard or of Mme Verdurin,
several new recruits succeeded in getting to know her and such
was her excitement at making a fresh acquaintance that she

forgot the fable of her deliberate isolation, and went to the wildest extremes to please the newcomer. If he was something of a nonentity, the rest would be astonished. "How strange that the Princess, who refuses to know anyone, should make an exception of such an uninteresting person." But these fertilising acquaintances were rare, and the Princess lived narrowly confined in the midst of the faithful.

Cottard said far more often: "I shall see him on Wednesday at the Verdurins'," than: "I shall see him on Tuesday at the Academy." He also spoke of the Wednesdays as of an equally important and inescapable occupation. But Cottard was one of those people, little sought-after, who make it as imperious a duty to obey an invitation as if such invitations were orders, like a military or judicial summons. It required a very important call to make him "fail" the Verdurins on a Wednesday, the importance depending moreover rather upon the rank of the patient than upon the gravity of his complaint. For Cottard, excellent fellow as he was, would forgo the delights of a Wednesday not for a workman who had had a stroke, but for a minister's cold. Even then he would say to his wife: "Make my apologies to Mme Verdurin. Tell her that I shall be coming later on. His Excellency really might have chosen some other day to catch a cold." One Wednesday, their old cook having cut open a vein in her arm, Cottard, already in his dinner-jacket to go to the Verdurins', had shrugged his shoulders when his wife had timidly inquired whether he could not bandage the wound: "Of course I can't, Léontine," he had groaned; "can't you see I've got my white waistcoat on?" So as not to annoy her husband, Mme Cottard had sent posthaste for the house surgeon. The latter, to save time, had taken a cab, with the result that, his carriage entering the courtyard just as Cottard's was emerging to take him to the Verdurins, five minutes had been wasted in manoeuvring backwards and forwards to let one another pass. Mme Cottard was worried that the house surgeon should see his chief in evening dress. Cottard sat cursing the delay, from remorse perhaps, and started off in a villainous temper which it took all the Wednesday's pleasures to dispel.

If one of Cottard's patients were to ask him: "Do you ever see the Guermantes?" it was with the utmost sincerity that the

Professor would reply: "Perhaps not actually the Guermantes, I can't be certain. But I meet all those people at the house of some friends of mine. You must, of course, have heard of the Verdurins. They know everybody. Besides, they at least aren't grand people who've come down in the world. They've got the goods, all right. It's generally estimated that Mme Verdurin is worth thirty-five million. Gad, thirty-five million, that's quite a figure. And so she doesn't go in for half-measures. You mentioned the Duchesse de Guermantes. I'll tell you the difference. Mme Verdurin is a great lady, the Duchesse de Guermantes is probably a nobody. You see the distinction, of course? In any case, whether the Guermantes go to Mme Verdurin's or not, she entertains all the very best people, the d'Sherbatoffs, the d'Forchevilles, *e tutti quanti*, people of the top flight, all the nobility of France and Navarre, with whom you would see me conversing as man to man. Of course, those sort of people are only too glad to meet the princes of science," he would add, with a smile of fatuous conceit, brought to his lips by his proud satisfaction not so much that the expression formerly reserved for men like Potain and Charcot should now be applicable to himself, as that he knew at last how to employ all these expressions that were sanctioned by usage, and, after a long course of study, had learned them by heart. And so, after mentioning to me Princess Sherbatoff as one of the people who went to Mme Verdurin's, Cottard added with a wink: "That gives you an idea of the style of the house, if you see what I mean?" He meant that it was the very height of fashion. Now, to entertain a Russian lady who knew nobody but the Grand Duchess Eudoxie meant very little. But Princess Sherbatoff might not have known even her, and it would in no way have diminished Cottard's estimate of the supreme elegance of the Verdurin salon or his joy at being invited there. The splendour with which the people whose houses we visit seem to us to be endowed is no more intrinsic than that of stage characters in dressing whom it is useless for a producer to spend hundreds and thousands of francs in purchasing authentic costumes and real jewels which will make no impression, when a great designer will procure a far more sumptuous impression by focusing a ray of light on a doublet of coarse cloth studded with glass spangles and on a paper cloak. A man may have spent his life among the great ones of the earth, who to him have been merely boring relatives or tedious acquaintances because a familiarity engendered in the cradle had stripped them of all glamour in his eyes. Yet on the other hand, such glamour need only, by some accident, have come to be attached to the most obscure people, for innumerable Cottards to be permanently dazzled by titled ladies whose drawing-rooms they imagined as the centres of aristocratic elegance, ladies who were not even what Mme de Villeparisis and her friends were (noble ladies fallen from grace, whom the aristocracy that had been brought up with them no longer visited); no, if the ladies whose friendship has been the pride of so many people were to be named in the memoirs of these people together with those whom they entertained, no one, Mme de Cambremer no more than Mme de Guermantes, would be able to identify them. But what of that! A Cottard has thus his baroness or his marquise, who is for him "the Baroness" or "the Marquise," as, in Marivaux, the baroness whose name is never mentioned and who for all one knows may never even have had one. A Cottard is all the more convinced that she epitomises the aristocracy—which has never heard of the lady—in that, the more dubious titles are, the more prominently coronets are displayed upon wine glasses, silver, note-paper and luggage. Many Cottards who have supposed that they were living in the heart of the Faubourg Saint-Germain have perhaps had their imaginations more beguiled by feudal dreams than the men who really have lived among princes, just as, for the small shopkeeper who sometimes goes on a Sunday to look at buildings of the "olden days," it is often those of which every stone is of our own, the vaults of which have been painted blue and sprinkled with golden stars by pupils of Viollet-le-Duc, that provide the most potent sensation of the Middle Ages.

"The Princess will be at Maineville," Cottard went on. "She will be coming with us. But I shan't introduce you to her at once. It will be better to leave that to Mme Verdurin. Unless I find a loophole. Then you can rely on me to take the bull by the horns."

"What were you saying?" asked Saniette, as he rejoined us, pretending to have been taking the air.

"I was quoting to this gentleman," said Brichot, "a saying, which you will remember, of the man who, to my mind, is the first of the *fins-de-siècle* (of the eighteenth century, that is), by name Charles-Maurice, Abbé de Périgord. He began by promising to be an excellent journalist. But he took a wrong turning, by which I mean that he became a minister! Such misfortunes happen in life. A far from scrupulous politician to boot, who, with all the lofty contempt of a thoroughbred nobleman, did not hesitate to play both ends against the middle—there are no two ways about it—and remained an incorrigible trimmer until his dying day."

At Saint-Pierre-des-Ifs we were joined by a glorious girl who, unfortunately, was not a member of the little group. I could not take my eyes off her magnolia skin, her dark eyes, the bold and admirable composition of her forms. After a moment she wanted to open a window, for it was hot in the compartment, and not wishing to ask leave of everybody, as I alone was without an overcoat she said to me in a quick, cool, cheerful voice: "Do you mind a little fresh air, Monsieur?" I would have liked to say to her: "Come with us to the Verdurins" or "Give me your name and address." I answered: "No, fresh air doesn't bother me, Mademoiselle." Whereupon, without stirring from her seat: "Your friends don't object to smoke?" and she lit a cigarette. At the third station she sprang from the train. Next day, I inquired of Albertine who she could be. For, stupidly thinking that people could have but one sort of love, in my jealousy of Albertine's attitude towards Robert, I was reassured so far as women were concerned. Albertine told me, I believe quite sincerely, that she did not know. "I should so like to see her again," I exclaimed. "Don't worry, one always sees people again," replied Albertine. In this particular instance she was wrong; I never saw again, and never identified, the handsome girl with the cigarette. We shall see, moreover, why for a long time I ceased to look for her. But I never forgot her. I find myself at times, when I think of her, seized by a wild longing. But these recurrences of desire oblige us to reflect that if we wish to rediscover these girls with the same pleasure we must also return to the year which has since been followed by ten others in the course of which her bloom has faded. We can sometimes find a person again, but we cannot abolish time. And so on until the unforeseen day, gloomy as a winter night, when one no longer seeks that girl, or any other, when to find her would actually scare one. For one no longer feels that one has attractions enough to please, or strength enough to love. Not, of course, that one is in the strict sense of the word impotent. And as for loving, one would love more than ever. But one feels that it is too big an undertaking for the little strength one has left. Eternal rest has already interposed intervals during which one can neither go out nor even speak. Setting one's foot on the right step is an achievement, like bringing off a somersault. To be seen in such a state by a girl one loves, even if one has kept the features and all the golden locks of one's youth! One can no longer face the strain of keeping up with the young. Too bad if carnal desire increases instead of languishing! One procures for it a woman whom one need make no effort to attract, who will share one's couch for one night only and whom one will never see again.

"Still no news, I suppose, of the violinist," said Cottard. For the event of the day in the little clan was the defection of Mme Verdurin's favourite violinist. The latter, who was doing his military service near Doncières, came three times a week to dine at la Raspelière, having a midnight pass. But two days ago, for the first time, the faithful had been unable to discover him on the train. It was assumed that he had missed it. But in vain had Mme Verdurin sent to meet the next train, and the next, and so on until the last, the carriage had returned empty.

"He's certain to have been put in quod," Cottard went on, "there's no other explanation of his desertion. Gad, in the Army, you know, with those fellows, it only needs a bad-tempered sergeant."

"It will be all the more mortifying for Mme Verdurin," said Brichot, "if he defects again this evening, because our kind hostess has invited to dinner for the first time the neighbours from whom she rented la Raspelière, the Marquis and Marquise de Cambremer."

"This evening, the Marquis and Marquise de Cambremer!" exclaimed Cottard. "But I knew absolutely nothing about it.

Naturally, I knew like everybody else that they would be coming one day, but I had no idea it was to be so soon. By Jove!" he went on, turning to me, "what did I tell you? The Princess Sherbatoff, the Marquis and Marquise de Cambremer." And, after repeating these names, lulling himself with their melody: "You see that we move in good company," he said to me. "No doubt about it, for your first appearance you've really struck lucky. It's going to be an exceptionally brilliant roomful." And, turning to Brichot, he went on: "The Mistress will be furious. It's time we got there to lend her a hand."

Ever since Mme Verdurin had been at la Raspelière she had pretended for the benefit of the faithful to be under the disagreeable obligation of inviting her landlords for one evening. By so doing she would obtain better terms next year, she explained, and was inviting them merely out of self-interest. But she affected to regard with such terror, to make such a bugbear of the idea of dining with people who did not belong to the little group, that she kept putting off the evil day. The prospect did indeed alarm her slightly for the reasons which she professed, albeit exaggerating them, if at the same time it enchanted her for reasons of snobbery which she preferred to keep to herself. She was therefore partly sincere, for she believed the little clan to be something so unique, one of those perfect entities which it takes centuries to produce, that she trembled at the thought of seeing these provincials, ignorant of the *Ring* and the *Meistersinger*, introduced into its midst, people who would be unable to play their part in the concert of general conversation and were capable of ruining one of those famous Wednesdays, masterpieces as incomparably fragile as those Venetian glasses which one false note is enough to shatter. "Besides, they're bound to be absolutely *anti*, and jingoistic," M. Verdurin had said. "Oh, as to that I don't really mind, we've heard quite enough about that business," Mme Verdurin had replied, for, though a sincere Dreyfusard, she would nevertheless have been glad to discover a social counterpoise to the preponderant Dreyfusism of her salon. For Dreyfusism was triumphant politically but not socially. Labori, Reinach, Picquart, Zola were still, to people in society, more or less traitors, who could only keep them estranged from the little nucleus. And so, after this incursion into politics, Mme Verdurin was anxious to return to the world of art. Besides, were not d'Indy and Debussy on the "wrong" side in the Affair! "As far as the Affair goes, we have only to put them beside Brichot," she said (the Professor being the only one of the faithful who had sided with the General Staff, thus forfeiting a great deal of esteem in the eyes of Mme Verdurin). "There's no need to be eternally discussing the Dreyfus case. No, the fact of the matter is that the Cambremers bore me." As for the faithful, no less excited by their unavowed desire to meet the Cambremers than they were taken in by Mme Verdurin's affected reluctance to invite them, they returned, day after day, in conversation with her, to the base arguments which she herself produced in favour of the invitation, and tried to make them irresistible. "Make up your mind to it once and for all," Cottard repeated, "and you'll get a reduction of the rent, they'll pay the gardener, you'll have the use of the meadow. That will be well worth a boring evening. I'm thinking only of you," he added, although his heart had leapt on one occasion when, in Mme Verdurin's carriage, he had passed old Mme de Cambremer's on the road, and he felt humiliated in the eyes of the railway employees when he found himself standing beside the Marquis. For their part, the Cambremers, living much too far outside the social "swim" ever to suspect that certain ladies of fashion now spoke of Mme Verdurin with a certain respect, imagined that she was a person who could know none but Bohemians, was perhaps not even legally married, and so far as people of "birth" were concerned would never meet any but themselves. They had resigned themselves to the thought of dining with her only in order to be on good terms with a tenant who, they hoped, would return again for many seasons, especially since they had learned, during the previous month, that she had recently inherited all those millions. It was in silence and without any vulgar pleasantries that they prepared themselves for the fatal day. The faithful had given up hope of its ever coming, so often had Mme Verdurin already fixed in their hearing a date that was invariably postponed. These false alarms were intended not merely to make a show of the boredom that she felt at the thought of this dinner-party, but to keep in suspense those members of the little group who were staying in the neighbourhood and were sometimes inclined to defect. Not that the Mistress guessed that the "great day" was as delightful a prospect to them as to herself, but in order that, having persuaded them that this dinner-party was for her the most terrible of social duties, she might appeal to their devotion and loyalty. "You're not going to leave me all alone with those freaks! We must assemble in full force to support the boredom. Naturally we shan't be able to talk about any of the things that interest us. It will be a Wednesday spoiled, but what is one to do!"

"Actually," Brichot observed for my benefit, "I fancy that Mme Verdurin, who is highly intelligent and takes infinite pains in the elaboration of her Wednesdays, was by no means anxious to entertain these squireens of ancient lineage but small wit. She could not bring herself to invite the dowager Marquise, but has resigned herself to having the son and daughter-in-law."

"Ah! we are to see the young Marquise de Cambremer?" said Cottard with a smile into which he felt called upon to introduce a tinge of lecherous gallantry, although he had no idea whether Mme de Cambremer was good-looking or not. But the title of Marquise conjured up in his mind images of glamour and dalliance.

"Ah! I know her," said Ski, who had met her once when he was out for a drive with Mme Verdurin.

"Not in the biblical sense of the word, I trust," said the doctor, darting a sly glance through his eyeglass; this was one of his favourite pleasantries.

"She is intelligent," Ski informed me. "Naturally," he went on, seeing that I said nothing, and dwelling with a smile upon each word, "she is intelligent and at the same time she is not, she lacks education, she is frivolous, but she has an instinct for pretty things. She may say nothing, but she will never say anything silly. And besides, her colouring is charming. She would be fun to paint," he addded, half shutting his eyes as though he saw her posing in front of him.

As my opinion of her was quite the opposite of what Ski was expressing with so many qualifications, I observed merely that she was the sister of a very distinguished engineer, M. Legrandin.

"There, you see, you are going to be introduced to a pretty woman," Brichot said to me, "and one never knows what may come of that. Cleopatra was not even a great lady, she was the little woman, the thoughtless, dreadful little woman of our Meilhac, and just think of the consequences, not only to that idiot Antony, but to the whole of the ancient world."

"I've already been introduced to Mme de Cambremer," I replied.

"Ah! In that case, you will find yourself on familiar ground."

"I shall be all the more delighted to meet her," I answered him, "because she has promised me a book by the former curé of Combray about the place-names of this region, and I shall be able to remind her of her promise. I'm interested in that priest, and also in etymologies."

"Don't put too much faith in the ones he gives," replied Brichot, "there's a copy of the book at la Raspelière, which I've glanced through casually without finding anything of any value; it's a tissue of errors. Let me give you an example. The word *bricq* is found in a number of place-names in this neighbourhood. The worthy cleric had the distinctly eccentric idea that it comes from *briga*, a height, a fortified place. He finds it already in the Celtic tribes, Latobriges, Nemetobriges, and so forth, and traces it down to such names as Briand, Brion, and so forth. To confine ourselves to the region through which we have the pleasure of travelling with you at this moment, Bricquebosc, according to him, would mean the wood on the height, Bricqueville the habitation on the height, Bricquebec, where we shall be stopping presently before coming to Maineville, the height by the stream. Now there is not a word of truth in all this, for the simple reason that *bricq* is the old Norse word which means simply a bridge. Just as *fleur*, which Mme de Cambremer's protégé takes infinite pains to connect, in one place with the Scandinavian words *floi*, *flo*, in another with the Irish words *ae* and *aer*, is, beyond any doubt, the *fjord* of the Danes, and means harbour. Similarly, the excellent priest thinks that the station of Saint-Martin-le-Vêtu, which adjoins la Raspelière, means Saint-Martin-le-Vieux (*vetus*). It is unquestionable that the word *vieux* has played an important part in the toponymy of this region. *Vieux* comes as a rule from *vadum*, and means a ford, as at the place called les Vieux. It is what the English call *ford* (Oxford, Hereford). But, in this particular instance, Vêtu is derived not from *vetus*, but from *vastatus*, a place that is devastated and bare. You have, round about here, Sottevast, the *vast* of Setold, Brillevast, the *vast* of Berold. I am all the more certain of the curé's mistake in that Saint-Martin-le-Vêtu was formerly called Saint-Martin-du-Gast and even Saint-Martin-de-Terregate. Now the *v* and the *g* in these words are the same letter. We say *dévaster*, but also *gâcher*. *Jachères* and *gâtines*[42] (from the High German *wastinna*) have the same meaning: Terregate is therefore *terra vastata*. As for Saint-Mars, formerly (save the mark) Saint-Merd, it is Saint-Medardus, which appears variously as Saint-Médard, Saint-Mard, Saint-Marc, Cinq-Mars, and even Dammas. Nor must we forget that, quite close to here, places bearing the name Mars simply attest to a pagan origin (the god Mars) which has remained alive in this country but which the holy man refuses to recognise. The high places dedicated to the gods are especially frequent, such as the mount of Jupiter (Jeumont). Your curé declines to admit this, and yet, on the other hand, wherever Christianity has left traces, they escape his notice. He has gone as far afield as Loctudy, a barbarian name, according to him, whereas it is simply *Locus sancti Tudeni*; nor, in the name Sammercoles, has he divined *Sanctus Martialis*. Your curé," Brichot continued, seeing that I was interested, "derives the terminations *hon*, *home*, *holm*, from the word *holl* (*hullus*), a hill, whereas it comes from the Norse *holm*, an island, with which you are familiar in Stockholm, and which is so widespread throughout this region: la Houlme, Engohomme, Tahoume, Robehomme, Néhomme, Quetteholme, and so forth."

These names reminded me of the day when Albertine had wished to go to Amfreville-la-Bigot (from the name of two successive lords of the manor, Brichot told me), and had then suggested that we should dine together at Robehomme. "Isn't Néhomme," I asked, "somewhere near Carquethuit and Clitourps?"

"Precisely; Néhomme is the *holm*, the island or peninsula of the famous Viscount Nigel, whose name has survived also in Néville. The Carquethuit and Clitourps that you mention provide Mme de Cambremer's protégé with an occasion for further errors. Of course he realises that *carque* is a church, the *Kirche* of the Germans. You will remember Querqueville, not to mention Dunkerque. For there we should do better to stop and consider the famous word *dun*, which to the Celts meant high ground. And that you will find over the whole of France. Your abbé was hypnotised by Duneville, which recurs in the Eure-et-Loir; he would have found Châteaudun, Dun-le-Roi in the Cher, Duneau in the Sarthe, Dun in the Ariège, Dune-les-Places in the Nièvre, and many others. This word *dun* leads him into a curious error with regard to Douville, where we shall be alighting, where we shall find Mme Verdurin's comfortable carriages awaiting us. Douville, in Latin *donvilla*, says he. And Douville does indeed lie at the foot of high hills. Your curé, who knows everything, feels all the same that he has made a blunder. And indeed he has found, in an old cartulary, the name *Domvilla*. Whereupon he retracts; Douville, according to him, is a fief belonging to the abbot, *domino abbati*, of Mont-Saint-Michel. He is delighted with the discovery, which is distinctly odd when one thinks of the scandalous life that, according to the capitulary of Saint-Clair-sur-Epte, was led at Mont-Saint-Michel, though no more extraordinary than to picture the King of Denmark as suzerain of all this coast, where he encouraged the worship of Odin far more than that of Christ. On the other hand, the supposition that the *n* has been changed to *m* doesn't shock me, and requires less alteration than the perfectly correct Lyon, which also is derived from *Dun* (*Lugdunum*). But the fact is, the abbé is mistaken. Douville was never Donville, but Doville, *Eudonis villa*, the village of Eudes. Douville was formerly called Escalecliff, the steps up the cliff. About the year 1233, Eudes le Bouteiller, Lord of Escalecliff, set out for the Holy Land; on the eve of his departure he made over the church to the Abbey of Blanchelande. By an exchange of courtesies, the village took his name, whence we have Douville to-day. But I must add that toponymy, of which moreover I know little or nothing, is not an exact science; had we not this historical evidence, Douville might quite well come from Ouville, that is to say the Waters. The forms in *ai* (Aigues-Mortes) of *aqua* are constantly changed to *eu* or *ou*. Now there were, quite close to Douville, certain famous springs, Carquebut. You can imagine that the curé was only too glad to find Christian traces there, especially as this area seems to have been pretty hard to evangelise, since successive attempts were made by St Ursal, St Gofroi, St Barsanore, St Laurent of Brèvedent, who finally handed over the task to the monks of Beaubec. But as regards *thuit* the writer is mistaken; he sees it as a form of *toft*, a building, as in Cricquetot, Ectot, Yvetot, whereas it is the *thveit*, the assart or reclaimed land, as in Braquetuit, le Thuit, Regnetuit, and so forth. Similarly, if he recognises in Clitourps the Norman *thorp* which means village, he maintains that the first syllable of the word must come from *clivus*, a slope, whereas it comes from *cliff*, a precipice. But his biggest blunders are due not so much to his ignorance as to his prejudices. However good a Frenchman one is, there is no need to fly in the face of the evidence and take Saint-Laurent-en-Bray to be the Roman priest who was so famous at one time, when he is actually Saint Lawrence O'Toole, Archbishop of Dublin. But even more than his patriotic sentiments, your friend's religious bigotry leads him into outrageous errors. Thus you have not far from our hosts at la Raspelière two places called Montmartin, Mont-martin-sur-Mer and Montmartin-en-Graignes. In the case of Graignes, the good curé is quite right, he has recognised that Graignes, in Latin *Grania*, in Greek *Krene*, means ponds, marshes; how many instances of Gresmays, Croen, Grenneville, Lengronne, could one not cite? But when he comes to Mont-martin, your self-styled linguist positively insists that these must be parishes dedicated to St Martin. He bases his assertion on the fact that that saint is the patron of the two villages, but does not realise that he was only recognized as such subsequently; or rather he is blinded by his hatred of paganism; he refuses to see that we should say Mont-Saint-Martin as we say Mont-Saint-Michel if it were a question of St Martin, whereas the name Montmartin refers in a far more pagan fashion to temples dedicated to the god Mars, temples of which, it is true, no other vestige remains, but which the undisputed existence in the neighbourhood of vast Roman camps would render highly probable even without the name Montmartin, which removes all doubt. You see that the little book which you will find at la Raspelière is far from perfect."

I protested that at Combray the curé had often given us interesting etymological dissertations.

"He was probably better on his own ground. The move to Normandy must have made him lose his bearings."

"Nor did it do him any good," I added, "for he came here with neurasthenia and went away again with rheumatism."

"Ah, his neurasthenia is to blame. He has lapsed from neurasthenia into philology, as my worthy master Poquelin would have said. Tell us, Cottard, do you suppose that neurasthenia can have a pernicious effect on philology, philology a soothing effect on neurasthenia, and the relief from neurasthenia lead to rheumatism?"

"Absolutely: rheumatism and neurasthenia are vicarious forms of neuro-arthritism. You may pass from one to the other by metastasis."

"The eminent professor," said Brichot, "expresses himself in a French as highly infused with Latin and Greek as M. Purgon himself, of Moliéresque memory! Our sainted uncle Sarcey. . .[43]

But he was prevented from finishing his sentence for Cottard had leapt from his seat with a wild shout: "The devil!" he exclaimed on regaining his power of articulate speech, "we've passed Maineville (d'you hear?) and Renneville too." He had just noticed that the train was stopping at Saint-Mars-le-Vieux, where most of the passengers alighted. "They can't have run through without stopping. We must have failed to notice while we were talking about the Cambremers. Listen to me, Ski, wait a moment, I'm going to tell you something" (Cottard had taken a fancy to this expression, in common use in certain medical circles). "The Princess must be on the train, she can't have seen us, and will have got into another compartment. Come along and find her. Let's hope this won't land us in trouble!"

And he led us all off in search of Princess Sherbatoff. He found her in the corner of an empty compartment, reading the *Revue des Deux Mondes*. She had long ago, from fear of rebuffs, acquired the habit of keeping her place, or remaining in her corner, in life as in trains, and of not offering her hand until the other person had greeted her. She went on reading as the faithful trooped into her carriage. I recognised her immediately;

this woman who might have forfeited her social position but was nevertheless of exalted birth, who in any event was the pearl of a salon such as the Verdurins', was the lady whom, on the same train, I had put down two days earlier as possibly the keeper of a brothel. Her social personality, which had been so doubtful, became clear to me as soon as I learned her name, just as when, after racking our brains over a puzzle, we at length hit upon the word which clears up all the obscurity, and which, in the case of a person, is his name. To discover two days later who the person is with whom one has travelled in a train is a far more amusing surprise than to read in the next number of a magazine the clue to the problem set in the previous number. Big restaurants, casinos, local trains, are the family portrait galleries of these social enigmas.

"Princess, we must have missed you at Maineville! May we come and sit in your compartment?"

"Why, of course," said the Princess who, upon hearing Cottard address her, but only then, raised from her magazine a pair of eyes which, like the eyes of M. de Charlus, although gentler, saw perfectly well the people of whose presence she pretended to be unaware. Cottard, reflecting that the fact of my having been invited to meet the Cambremers was a sufficient recommendation, decided, after a momentary hesitation, to introduce me to the Princess, who bowed with great courtesy but appeared to be hearing my name for the first time.

"Confound it!" cried the Doctor, "my wife has forgotten to have the buttons on my white waistcoat changed. Ah, women! They never remember anything. Don't you ever marry, my boy," he said to me. And as this was one of the pleasantries which he considered appropriate when he had nothing else to say, he peeped out of the corner of his eye at the Princess and the rest of the faithful, who, because he was a professor and an Academician, smiled back at him, admiring his good humour and lack of arrogance.

The Princess informed us that the young violinist had been found. He had been confined to bed the day before by a sick headache, but was coming that evening and bringing with him a friend of his father whom he had met at Doncières. She had learned this from Mme Verdurin with whom she had lunched that morning, she told us in a rapid voice, rolling her *r*s, with her Russian accent, softly at the back of her throat, as though they were not *r*s but *l*s. "Ah! you lunched with her this morning," Cottard said to the Princess, but his eyes were on me, for the object of this remark was to show me on what intimate terms the Princess was with the Mistress. "You really are one of the faithful!"

"Yes, I love this little gloup, so intelligent, so agleeable, so simple, not snobbish or spiteful, and clevel to their fingle-tips."

"Devil take it! I must have lost my ticket, I can't find it anywhere," cried Cottard, without being unduly alarmed. He knew that at Douville, where a couple of landaus would be awaiting us, the collector would let him pass without a ticket, and would only touch his cap the more deferentially in order to provide an explanation for his leniency, which was that he had of course recognised Cottard as one of the Verdurins' regular guests. "They won't shove me in the lock-up for that," the Doctor concluded.

"You were saying Monsieur," I inquired of Brichot, "that there used to be some famous waters near here. How do we know that?"

"The name of the next station is one of a multitude of proofs. It is called Fervaches."

"I don't undlestand what he's talking about," mumbled the Princess, as though she were saying to me out of kindness: "He's rather a bore, isn't he?"

"Why, Princess, Fervaches means hot springs. *Fervidae aquae.* But to return to the young violinist," Brichot went on, "I was quite forgetting, Cottard, to tell you the great news. Had you heard that our poor friend Dechambre, who used to be Mme Verdurin's favourite pianist, has just died? It's dreadful."

"He was still quite young," replied Cottard, "but he must have had some trouble with his liver, there must have been something sadly wrong in that quarter, he'd been looking very queer indeed for a long time past."

"But he wasn't as young as all that," said Brichot. "In the days when Elstir and Swann used to come to Mme Verdurin's, Dechambre had already made himself a reputation in Paris, and, what is remarkable, without having first received the baptism of success abroad. Ah! he was no follower of the Gospel according to St Barnum, that fellow."

"You must be mistaken, he couldn't have been going to Mme Verdurin's at that time, he was still in the nursery."

"But, unless my old memory plays me false, I was under the impression that Dechambre used to play Vinteuil's sonata for Swann when that clubman, being at odds with the aristocracy, had still no idea that he was one day to become the embourgeoised prince consort of our sainted Odette."

"That's impossible. Vinteuil's sonata wasn't played at Mme Verdurin's until long after Swann ceased to come there," said the Doctor, for he was one of those people who work very hard and think they remember a great many things which they imagine to be useful, but forget many others, a condition which enables them to go into ecstasies over the memories of people who have nothing else to do. "You are not doing justice to your reputation for learning, and yet you don't seem to be suffering from softening of the brain," he added with a smile. Brichot admitted that he was mistaken.

The train stopped. We were at la Sogne. The name stirred my curiosity. "How I should like to know what all these names mean," I said to Cottard.

"Ask M. Brichot, he may know, perhaps."

"Why, la Sogne is la Cicogne, *Siconia*," replied Brichot, whom I was longing to interrogate about many other names.

Forgetting her attachment to her "corner," Mme Sherbatoff kindly offered to change places with me so that I might talk more easily with Brichot, whom I wanted to ask about other etymologies that interested me, and assured me that she did not mind in the least whether she travelled with her face or her back to the engine, standing, or seated, or anyhow. She remained on the defensive until she had discovered a newcomer's intentions, but as soon as she had realised that these were friendly, she would do everything in her power to oblige. At length the train stopped at the station of Douville-Féterne, which being more or less equidistant from the villages of Féterne and Douville, bore for this reason their hyphenated names. "Gadzooks!" exclaimed Dr Cottard when we came to the barrier where the tickets were collected, pretending to have only just discovered his loss, "I can't find my ticket, I must have lost it." But the collector, taking off his cap, assured him that it did not matter and smiled respectfully. The Princess (giving instructions to the coachman, as though she were a sort of lady-in-waiting to Mme Verdurin, who, because of the Cambremers, had not been able to come to the station, as, for that matter, she rarely did) took me, and also Brichot, with herself in one of the carriages. The Doctor, Saniette and Ski got into the other.

The driver, although quite young, was the Verdurins' head coachman, the only one who was strictly qualified for the post. He took them, in the day-time, on all their excursions, for he knew all the roads, and in the evening went down to meet the faithful and brought them back to the station later on. He was accompanied by extra helpers (whom he chose himself) if the necessity arose. He was an excellent fellow, sober and skilled, but with one of those melancholy faces on which a fixed stare indicates a person who will worry himself sick over the merest trifle and even harbour black thoughts. But at the moment he was quite happy, for he had managed to secure a place for his brother, another excellent young man, with the Verdurins. We began by driving through Douville. Grassy knolls ran down from the village to the sea, spreading out into broad pastures which were extraordinarily thick, lush and vivid in hue from saturation in moisture and salt. The islands and indentations of Rivebelle, much closer here than at Balbec, gave this part of the coast the appearance, novel to me, of a relief map. We passed several little bungalows, almost all of which were let to painters, turned into a track upon which some loose cattle, as frightened as were our horses, barred our way for ten minutes, and emerged upon the cliff road.

"But, by the immortal gods," Brichot suddenly asked, "to return to that poor Dechambre, do you suppose Mme Verdurin *knows*? Has anyone *told* her?"

Mme Verdurin, like most people who move in society, simply because she needed the society of other people, never thought of them again for a single day as soon as, being dead, they could no longer come to her Wednesdays, or her Saturdays, or drop in for dinner. And it could not be said of the little clan, akin in this respect to every other salon, that it was composed of more dead than living members, seeing that, as soon as you were dead, it was as though you had never existed. But, to avoid the tedium of having to talk about the deceased, and even suspend the dinners—an inconceivable thing for the Mistress—as a token of mourning, M. Verdurin used to pretend that the death of the faithful had such an effect on his wife that, in the interest of her health, the subject must never be mentioned to her. Moreover, and perhaps just because the death of other people seemed to him so conclusive and so vulgar an accident, the thought of his own death filled him with horror and he shunned any reflexion that might have any bearing on it. As for Brichot, since he was a good-natured man and completely taken in by what M. Verdurin said about his wife, he dreaded for her sake the distress that such a bereavement must cause her.

"Yes, she *knew the worst* this morning," said the Princess, "it was impossible to *keep it from her*."

"Ye gods!" cried Brichot, "ah! it must have been a terrible blow, a friend of twenty-five years standing. There was a man who was one of us."

"Of course, of course, but it can't be helped," said Cottard. "Such events are bound to be painful; but Mme Verdurin is a brave woman, she is even more cerebral than emotive."

"I don't altogether agree with the Doctor," said the Princess, whose rapid speech and garbled diction made her somehow appear at once sulky and mischievous. "Beneath a cold exterior, Mme Verdurin conceals treasures of sensibility. M. Verdurin told me that he had had great difficulty in preventing her from going to Paris for the funeral; he was obliged to let her think that it was all to be held in the country."

"The devil! She wanted to go to Paris, did she? Of course, I know that she has a heart, too much heart perhaps. Poor Dechambre! As Madame Verdurin remarked not two months ago: 'Compared with him, Planté, Paderewski, even Risler himself are nowhere!' Ah, he could say with better reason than that show-off Nero, who has managed to hoodwink even German scholarship: *Qualis artifex pereo!* But he at least, Dechambre, must have died in the fulfilment of his vocation, in the odour of Beethovenian devotion; and bravely, I have no doubt; he had every right, that interpreter of German music, to pass away while celebrating the *Missa Solemnis*. But at any rate he was the man to greet the Reaper with a trill, for that inspired performer would produce at times, from the Parisianised Champagne ancestry of which he came, the gallantry and swagger of a guardsman."

From the height we had now reached, the sea no longer appeared, as it did from Balbec, like an undulating range of hills, but on the contrary like the view, from a mountain-peak or from a road winding round its flank, of a blue-green glacier or a glittering plain situated at a lower level. The ripples of eddies and currents seemed to be fixed upon its surface, and to have traced there forever their concentric circles; the enamelled face of the sea, imperceptibly changing colour, assumed towards the head of the bay, where an estuary opened, the blue whiteness of milk in which little black boats that did not move seemed entangled like flies. I felt that from nowhere could one discover a vaster prospect. But at each turn in the road a fresh expanse was added to it and when we arrived at the Douville toll-house, the spur of the cliff which until then had concealed from us half the bay receded, and all of a sudden I saw upon my left a gulf as profound as that which I had already had in front of me, but one that changed the proportions of the other and doubled its beauty. The air at this lofty point had a keenness and purity that intoxicated me. I adored the Verdurins; that they should have sent a carriage for us seemed to me a touching act of kindness. I should have liked to kiss the Princess. I told her that I had never seen anything so beautiful. She professed that she too loved this spot more than any other. But I could see that to her as to the Verdurins the thing that really mattered was not to gaze at the view like tourists, but to partake of good meals there, to entertain people whom they liked, to write letters, to read books, in short to live in these surroundings, passively allowing the beauty of the scene to soak into them rather than making it the object of their conscious attention.

After the toll-house, where the carriage had stopped for a moment at such a height above the sea that, as from a mountain-top, the sight of the blue gulf beneath almost made one dizzy,

I opened the window; the sound, distinctly caught, of each wave breaking in turn had something sublime in its softness and clarity. Was it not like an index of measurement which, upsetting all our ordinary impressions, shows us that vertical distances may be compared with horizontal ones, contrary to the idea that our mind generally forms of them; and that, though they bring the sky nearer to us in this way, they are not great; that they are indeed less great for a sound which traverses them, as did the sound of those little waves, because the medium through which it has to pass is purer? And in fact if one drew back only a couple of yards behind the toll-house, one could no longer distinguish that sound of waves which six hundred feet of cliff had not robbed of its delicate, minute and soft precision. I thought to myself that my grandmother would have listened to it with the delight that she felt in all manifestations of nature or art that combine simplicity with grandeur. My exaltation was now at its height and raised everything round about me accordingly. It melted my heart that the Verdurins should have sent to meet us at the station. I said as much to the Princess, who seemed to think that I was greatly exaggerating so simple an act of courtesy. I know that she admitted subsequently to Cottard that she found me remarkably enthusiastic; he replied that I was too emotional, that I needed sedatives and ought to take to knitting. I pointed out to the Princess every tree, every little house smothered in its mantle of roses, I made her admire everything, I would have liked to take her in my arms and press her to my heart. She told me that she could see that I had a gift for painting, that I ought to take up sketching, that she was surprised that nobody had told me before. And she confessed that the country was indeed picturesque. We drove through the little village of Englesqueville perched on its hill—*Engleberti villa*, Brichot informed us. "But are you quite sure that this evening's dinner party will take place in spite of Dechambre's death, Princess?" he went on, without stopping to think that the arrival at the station of the carriage in which we were sitting was in itself an answer to his question.

"Yes," said the Princess, "M. Veldulin insisted that it should not be put off, precisely in order to keep his wife from *thinking*.

And besides, after never failing for all these years to entertain on Wednesdays, such a change in her habits would have been bound to upset her. Her nerves are velly bad just now. M. Verdurin was particularly pleased that you were coming to dine this evening, because he knew that it would be a great distraction for Mme Verdurin," the Princess said to me, forgetting her pretence of having never heard my name before. "I think that it will be as well not to say *anything* in front of Mme Verdurin," she added.

"Ah! I'm glad you warned me," Brichot artlessly replied. "I shall pass on your advice to Cottard."

The carriage stopped for a moment. It moved on again, but the sound that the wheels had been making in the village street had ceased. We had turned into the drive of la Raspelière, where M. Verdurin stood waiting for us on the steps. "I did well to put on a dinner-jacket," he said, observing with pleasure that the faithful had put on theirs, "since I have such smart gentlemen in my party." And as I apologised for not having changed: "Why, that's quite all right. We're all friends here. I should be delighted to offer you one of my own dinner-jackets, but it wouldn't fit you."

The handclasp throbbing with emotion which, by way of condolence at the death of the pianist, Brichot gave our host as he entered the hall of la Raspelière elicited no response from the latter. I told him how greatly I admired the scenery. "Ah! I'm delighted, and you've seen nothing yet; we must take you round. Why not come and spend a week or two here, the air is excellent."

Brichot was afraid that his handclasp had not been understood. "Ah! poor Dechambre!" he said, but in an undertone, in case Mme Verdurin was within earshot.

"It's dreadful," replied M. Verdurin cheerfully.

"So young," Brichot pursued the point.

Annoyed at being detained over these futilities, M. Verdurin replied hurriedly and with a high-pitched moan, not of grief but of irritated impatience: "Ah well, there we are, it's no use crying over spilt milk, talking about him won't bring him back to life, will it?" And, his civility returning with his joviality: "Come along, my dear Brichot, get your things off quickly. We have a bouillbaisse which mustn't be kept waiting. But, in heaven's name, don't start talking about Dechambre to Mme Verdurin. You know that she always hides her feelings, but she's quite morbidly sensitive. No, but I swear to you, when she heard that Dechambre was dead, she almost wept," said M. Verdurin in a tone of profound irony. Hearing him, one might have concluded that it implied a form of insanity to regret the death of a friend of thirty years' standing, and at the same time one gathered that the perpetual union of M. Verdurin and his wife did not preclude constant censure and frequent irritation on his part. "If you mention it to her, she'll go and make herself ill again. It's deplorable, three weeks after her bronchitis. When that happens, it's I who have to be sicknurse. You can understand that I've had more than enough of it. Grieve for Dechambre's fate in your heart as much as you like. Think of him, but don't speak about him. I was very fond of Dechambre, but you cannot blame me for being fonder still of my wife. Here's Cottard, now, you can ask him." And indeed he knew that a family doctor can do many little services, such as prescribing that one must not give way to grief.

The docile Cottard had said to the Mistress: "Upset yourself like that, and to-morrow you'll give *me* a temperature of 102," as he might have said to the cook: "Tomorrow you'll give me a *ris de veau*." Medicine, when it fails to cure, busies itself with changing the sense of verbs and pronouns.

M. Verdurin was glad to find that Saniette, notwithstanding the snubs that he had had to endure two days earlier, had not deserted the little nucleus. And indeed Mme Verdurin and her husband had acquired, in their idleness, cruel instincts for which the great occasions, occurring too rarely, no longer sufficed. They had succeeded in effecting a breach between Odette and Swann, and between Brichot and his mistress. They would try it again with others, that was understood. But the opportunity did not present itself every day. Whereas, thanks to his quivering sensibility, his timorous and easily alarmed shyness, Saniette provided them with a whipping-boy for every day in the year. And so, for fear of his defecting, they took care always to invite him with friendly and persuasive words, such as the bigger boys at school or the old soldiers in a regiment

address to a greenhorn whom they are anxious to cajole so that
they may get him into their clutches with the sole object of
ragging and bullying him when he can no longer escape.

"Whatever you do," Cottard reminded Brichot, not having
heard what M. Verdurin had been saying, "mum's the word in
front of Mme Verdurin."

"Have no fear, O Cottard, you are dealing with a sage, as
Theocritus says. Besides, M. Verdurin is right, what is the use
of lamentations?" Brichot added, for, though capable of assimilating verbal forms and the ideas which they suggested
to him, but lacking subtlety, he had discerned and admired
in M. Verdurin's remarks the most courageous stoicism.
"All the same, it's a great talent that has gone from the
world."

"What, are you still talking about Dechambre?" said M.
Verdurin, who had gone on ahead of us, and, seeing that we
were not following him, turned back. "Listen," he said to
Brichot, "don't let's exaggerate. The fact of his being dead is
no excuse for making him out a genius, which he was not. He
played well, I admit, but the main thing was that he was in the
right surroundings here; transplanted, he ceased to exist. My
wife was infatuated with him and made his reputation. You
know what she's like. I will go further: in the interest of his
own reputation he died at the right moment, *à point*, as the
lobsters, grilled according to Pampille's incomparable recipe,
are going to be, I hope (unless you keep us standing here all
night with your jeremiads in this kasbah exposed to all the
winds of heaven). You don't seriously expect us all to die of
hunger because Dechambre is dead, when for the last year he
was obliged to practise scales before giving a concert, in order
to recover for the moment, and for the moment only, the
suppleness of his wrists. Besides, you're going to hear this
evening, or at any rate to meet, for the rascal is too fond of
deserting his art for the card-table after dinner, somebody who
is a far greater artist than Dechambre, a youngster whom my
wife has discovered" (as she had discovered Dechambre, and
Paderewski, and the rest), "called Morel. The beggar hasn't
arrived yet. I shall have to send a carriage down to meet the
last train. He's coming with an old friend of his family whom he

ran into, and who bores him to tears, but otherwise, so as not to get into trouble with his father, he would have been obliged to stay down at Doncières and keep him company: the Baron de Charlus."

The faithful entered the drawing-room. M. Verdurin, who had remained behind with me while I took off my things, took my arm by way of a joke, as one's host does at a dinner-party when there is no lady for one to take in. "Did you have a pleasant journey?" "Yes, M. Brichot told me things which interested me greatly," said I, thinking of the etymological dissertation, and because I had heard that the Verdurins greatly admired Brichot. "I'm surprised to hear that he told you anything," said M. Verdurin, "he's such a retiring man, and talks so little about the things he knows." This compliment did not strike me as being very apt. "He seems charming," I remarked. "Exquisite, delightful, not an ounce of pedantry, such a light, fantastic touch, my wife adores him, and so do I!" replied M. Verdurin in an exaggerated tone, as though reciting a lesson. Only then did I grasp that what he had said to me about Brichot was ironical. And I wondered whether M. Verdurin, since those far-off days of which I had heard reports, had not shaken off the yoke of his wife's tutelage.

The sculptor was greatly astonished to learn that the Verdurins were willing to have M. de Charlus in their house. Whereas in the Faubourg Saint-Germain, where M. de Charlus was so well known, nobody ever referred to his morals (of which the majority had no suspicion and others remained doubtful, crediting him rather with intense but platonic friendships, with indiscretions, while the enlightened few carefully concealed them, shrugging their shoulders at any insinuation upon which some malicious Gallardon might venture), these morals, the nature of which was known to only a handful of intimates, were on the contrary denounced daily far from the circle in which he moved, just as, at times, the sound of artillery fire is audible only beyond an intervening zone of silence. Moreover, in those professional and artistic circles where he was regarded as the personification of inversion, his high social position and his noble origin were completely unknown, by a process analogous to that which, among the people of Rumania,

has brought it about that the name of Ronsard is known as that
of a great nobleman, while his poetical work is unknown there.
Furthermore, the Rumanian estimate of Ronsard's nobility is
founded upon an error. Similarly, if in the world of painters
and actors M. de Charlus had such a bad reputation, this was
due to their confusing him with a certain Comte Leblois de
Charlus who was not even related to him (or, if so, the connexion was extremely remote), and who had been arrested,
possibly by mistake, in the course of a notorious police raid.
In short, all the stories related of our M. de Charlus referred to
the other. Many professionals swore that they had had relations
with M. de Charlus, and did so in good faith, believing that the
false M. de Charlus was the true one, the false one possibly
encouraging, partly from an affectation of nobility, partly to
conceal his vice, a confusion which was for a long time
prejudicial to the real one (the Baron we know), and afterwards,
when he had begun to go down the hill, became a convenience,
for it enabled him likewise to say: "It isn't me." And in the
present instance it was not him to whom the rumours referred.
Finally, what added even more to the falseness of the comments
on a true fact (the Baron's sexual proclivities) was the fact that
he had had an intimate but perfectly pure friendship with an
author who, in the theatrical world, had for some reason acquired a similar reputation which he in no way deserved.
When they were seen together at a first night, people would
say: "You see," just as it was supposed that the Duchesse de
Guermantes had immoral relations with the Princesse de
Parme—an indestructible legend, for it would have been dispelled only by a proximity to those two noble ladies to which
the people who spread it would presumably never attain other
than by staring at them through their glasses in the theatre and
slandering them to the occupant of the next stall. From M. de
Charlus's morals, the sculptor concluded all the more readily
that the Baron's social position must be equally low, since he
had no information whatsoever about the family to which
M. de Charlus belonged, his title or his name. Just as Cottard
imagined that everybody knew that the title of doctor of
medicine meant nothing and the title of hospital consultant
meant something, so people in society are mistaken when they

suppose that everybody has the same idea of the social importance of their name as they themselves and the other people of their circle.

The Prince d'Agrigente was regarded as a flashy foreigner by a club servant to whom he owed twenty-five louis, and regained his importance only in the Faubourg Saint-Germain where he had three sisters who were duchesses, for it is not among humble people, in whose eyes he is of small account, but among smart people, who know who is who, that a nobleman can hope to make an impression. M. de Charlus, indeed, was to learn in the course of the evening that his host had only the most superficial notions about the most illustrious ducal families.

Convinced that the Verdurins were making a grave mistake in allowing an individual of tarnished reputation to be admitted to so "select" a household as theirs, the sculptor felt it his duty to take the Mistress aside. "You are entirely mistaken; besides, I never pay any attention to such tales, and even if it were true, I may be allowed to point out that it could hardly compromise *me*!" replied Mme Verdurin angrily, for, Morel being the principal feature of the Wednesdays, she was particularly anxious not to give him any offence. As for Cottard, he could not express an opinion, for he had asked leave to go upstairs for a moment to "do a little job" in the *buen retiro* and afterwards, in M. Verdurin's bedroom, to write an extremely urgent letter for a patient.

An eminent publisher from Paris who had come to call, expecting to be invited to stay to dinner, withdrew with savage abruptness, realising that he was not smart enough for the little clan. He was a tall, stout man, very dark, with a studious and somewhat trenchant look about him. He reminded one of an ebony paper-knife.

Mme Verdurin, who, to welcome us in her immense drawing-room, in which displays of grasses, poppies, field-flowers, picked only that morning, alternated with a similar theme painted in monochrome two centuries earlier by an artist of exquisite taste, had risen for a moment from a game of cards which she was playing with an old friend, begged us to excuse her for a minute or two until she finished her game while

continuing to talk to us. What I told her about my impressions
was not entirely pleasing to her. For one thing I was shocked to
observe that she and her husband came indoors every day long
before the hour of those sunsets which were considered so fine
when seen from that cliff, and finer still from the terrace of la
Raspelière, and which I would have travelled miles to see.
"Yes, it's incomparable," said Mme Verdurin carelessly, with a
glance at the huge windows which gave the room a wall of
glass. "Even though we have it in front of us all the time, we
never grow tired of it," and she turned her attention back to her
cards. But my very enthusiasm made me exacting. I complained
of not being able to see from the drawing-room the rocks of
Darnetal which Elstir had told me were quite lovely at that
hour, when they reflected so many colours. "Ah! you can't see
them from here, you'd have to go to the end of the gardens, to
the 'view of the bay.' From the seat there, you can take in the
whole panorama. But you can't go there by yourself, you'll
lose your way. I can take you there, if you like," she added
half-heartedly. "Come now, no," said her husband, "haven't
you had enough of those rheumatic pains you had the other
day? Do you want to get them again? He can come back and
see the view of the bay another time." I did not insist, and
realised that it was enough for the Verdurins to know that this
sunset made its way into their drawing-room or dining-room,
like a magnificent painting, like a priceless Japanese enamel,
justifying the high rent they were paying for la Raspelière,
furnished, without their having constantly to raise their eyes
towards it; the important thing here for them was to live
comfortably, to go for drives, to eat well, to talk, to entertain
agreeable friends whom they provided with amusing games of
billiards, good meals, merry tea-parties. I noticed, however,
later on, how intelligently they had got to know the district,
taking their guests for excursions as "novel" as the music to
which they made them listen. The part which the flowers of la
Raspelière, the paths along the edge of the sea, the old houses,
the undiscovered churches, played in M. Verdurin's life was so
great that those who saw him only in Paris and who themselves
substituted urban luxuries for seaside and country life could
barely understand the exalted idea that he himself had of his

own life, or the importance that his pleasures gave him in his own eyes. This importance was further enhanced by the fact that the Verdurins were convinced that la Raspelière, which they hoped to purchase, was a property without its match in the world. This superiority which their self-esteem made them attribute to la Raspelière justified in their eyes my enthusiasm which, but for that, would have annoyed them slightly, because of the disappointments which it involved (like those which my first experience of Berma had once caused me) and which I frankly admitted to them.

"I hear the carriage coming back," the Mistress suddenly murmured. Let us here briefly remark that Mme Verdurin, quite apart from the inevitable changes due to increasing years, no longer resembled what she had been at the time when Swann and Odette used to listen to the little phrase in her house. Even when she heard it played, she was no longer obliged to assume the air of exhausted admiration which she used to assume then, for that had become her normal expression. Under the influence of the countless headaches which the music of Bach, Wagner, Vinteuil, Debussy had given her, Mme Verdurin's forehead had assumed enormous proportions, like limbs that become permanently deformed by rheumatism. Her temples, suggestive of a pair of throbbing, pain-stricken, milk-white spheres, in which Harmony endlessly revolved, flung back silvery locks on either side, and proclaimed, on the Mistress's behalf, without any need for her to say a word: "I know what is in store for me to-night." Her features no longer took the trouble to formulate, one after another, aesthetic impressions of undue violence, for they had themselves become as it were their permanent expression on a superbly ravaged face. This attitude of resignation to the ever-impending sufferings inflicted by the Beautiful, and the courage required to make her dress for dinner when she had barely recovered from the effects of the last sonata, caused Mme Verdurin, even when listening to the most heartrending music, to preserve a disdainfully impassive countenance, and even to withdraw into privacy to swallow her two spoonfuls of aspirin.

"Why, yes, here they are!" M. Verdurin exclaimed with relief on seeing the door open to admit Morel followed by

M. de Charlus. The latter, to whom dining with the Verdurins meant not so much going into society as going into a place of ill repute, was as apprehensive as a schoolboy entering a brothel for the first time and showing the utmost deference towards its mistress. Hence the Baron's habitual desire to appear virile and cold was overshadowed (when he appeared in the open doorway) by those traditional ideas of politeness which are awakened as soon as shyness destroys an artificial pose and falls back on the resources of the subconscious. When it is a Charlus, whether he be noble or plebeian, who is stirred by such a sentiment of instinctive and atavistic politeness to strangers, it is always the spirit of a relative of the female sex, attendant like a goddess, or incarnate as a double, that undertakes to introduce him into a strange drawing-room and to mould his attitude until he comes face to face with his hostess. Thus a young painter, brought up by a godly, Protestant, female cousin, will enter a room, his trembling head to one side, his eyes raised to the ceiling, his hands clutching an invisible muff, the remembered shape of which and its real and tutelary presence will help the frightened artist to cross without agoraphobia the yawning abyss between the hall and the inner drawing-room. Thus it was that the pious relative whose memory is guiding him to-day used to enter a room years ago, and with so plaintive an air that one wondered what calamity she had come to announce until from her first words one realised, as now in the case of the painter, that she had come to pay an after-dinner call. By virtue of the same law, which ordains that life, in the interests of the still unfulfilled act, shall bring into play, utilise, adulterate, in a perpetual prostitution, the most respectable, sometimes the most sacred, occasionally only the most innocent legacies of the past, and albeit in this instance it engendered a different aspect, a nephew of Mme Cottard, who distressed his family by his effeminate ways and the company he kept, would always make a joyous entry as though he had a surprise in store for you or were going to inform you that he had been left a fortune, radiant with a happiness which it would have been futile to ask him to explain, it being due to his unconscious heredity and his misplaced sex. He walked on tiptoe, was no doubt himself astonished that he

was not holding a cardcase, offered you his hand with a simper
as he had seen his aunt do, and his only anxious look was
directed at the mirror in which he seemed to wish to verify,
although he was bare-headed, whether, as Mme Cottard had
once inquired of Swann, his hat was askew. As for M. de
Charlus, whom the society in which he had lived furnished at
this critical moment with different examples, with other
arabesques of amiability, and especially with the maxim that one
must in certain cases, for the benefit of people of humble rank,
bring into play and make use of one's rarest graces, normally
held in reserve, it was with a fluttering, mincing gait and the
same sweep with which a skirt would have enlarged and
impeded his waddling motion that he advanced upon Mme
Verdurin with so flattered and honoured an air that one would
have said that to be presented to her was for him a supreme
favour. His face, bent slightly forward, on which satisfaction
vied with decorum, was creased with tiny wrinkles of affability.
One might have thought that it was Mme de Marsantes who
was entering the room, so salient at that moment was the
woman whom a mistake on the part of Nature had enshrined
in the body of M. de Charlus. Of course the Baron had made
every effort to conceal this mistake and to assume a masculine
appearance. But no sooner had he succeeded than, having
meanwhile retained the same tastes, he acquired from this habit
of feeling like a woman a new feminine appearance, due not to
heredity but to his own way of living. And as he had gradually
come to regard even social questions from the feminine point
of view, and that quite unconsciously, for it is not only by dint
of lying to other people but also by lying to oneself that one
ceases to be aware that one is lying, although he had called upon
his body to manifest (at the moment of his entering the Verdurins' house) all the courtesy of a great nobleman, that body,
which had so well grasped what M. de Charlus had ceased
to understand, displayed, to such an extent that the Baron
would have deserved the epithet *ladylike*, all the seductions of a
great lady. Besides, can one entirely separate M. de Charlus's
appearance from the fact that sons, who do not always take
after their fathers, even without being inverts and even though
seekers after women, may consummate upon their faces the

profanation of their mothers? But let us not consider here a subject that deserves a chapter to itself: the Profanation of the Mother.

Although other reasons may have dictated this transformation of M. de Charlus, and purely physical ferments may have set his chemistry "working" and made his body gradually change into the category of women's bodies, nevertheless the change that we record here was of spiritual origin. By dint of imagining oneself to be ill one becomes ill, one grows thin, one is too weak to rise from one's bed, one suffers from nervous enteritis. By dint of thinking tenderly of men one becomes a woman, and an imaginary skirt hampers one's movements. The obsession, as in the other instance it can affect one's health, may in this instance alter one's sex.

Morel, who accompanied him, came up to greet me. From that first moment, owing to a twofold change that occurred in him, he made (and alas, I was not quick enough to take account of it!) a bad impression on me. I have said that Morel, having risen above his father's menial status, was generally pleased to indulge in a contemptuous familiarity. He had spoken to me, on the day when he brought me the photographs, without once addressing me as Monsieur, treating me superciliously. What was my surprise at Mme Verdurin's to see him bow very low before me, and before me alone, and to hear, before he had even uttered a syllable to anyone else, words of infinite respect —words such as I thought could not possibly flow from his pen or fall from his lips—addressed to myself. I at once suspected that he had some favour to ask of me. Taking me aside a minute later: "Monsieur would be doing me a very great service," he said to me, going so far this time as to address me in the third person, "by keeping from Mme Verdurin and her guests the nature of the profession that my father practised in his uncle's household. It would be best to say that he was the intendant of family estates so considerable as to put him almost on a level with your parents." Morel's request annoyed me intensely not because it obliged me to magnify his father's position, which was a matter of complete indifference to me, but by requiring me to exaggerate the apparent wealth of my own, which I felt to be absurd. But he appeared so wretched so pressing, that I could not refuse him. "No, before dinner," he said in an imploring tone, "Monsieur can easily find some excuse for taking Mme Verdurin aside." This was what I in fact did, trying to enhance to the best of my ability the glamour of Morel's father without unduly exaggerating the "style," the "worldly goods" of my own family. It went off very smoothly, despite the astonishment of Mme Verdurin, who had had a nodding acquaintance with my grandfather. And as she had no tact and hated family life (that dissolvent of the little nucleus), after telling me that she remembered seeing my great-grand-father long ago, and speaking to me of him as of somebody who was more or less an idiot who would have been incapable of understanding the little group and who, to use her expression, "was not one of us," she said to me: "Families are such a bore, one longs to get away from them"; and at once proceeded to tell me of a trait in my great-grandfather's character of which I was unaware, although I had suspected it at home (I had never known him, but he was much spoken of), his remarkable stingi-ness (in contrast to the somewhat excessive generosity of my great-uncle, the friend of the lady in pink and Morel's father's employer): "The fact that your grandparents had such a smart intendant only goes to show that there are all sorts of people in a family. Your grandfather's father was so stingy that at the end of his life when he was almost gaga—between you and me, he was never anything very special, you make up for the lot of them—he could not bring himself to pay a penny for his ride on the omnibus. So that they were obliged to have him followed by somebody who paid his fare for him, and to let the old miser think that his friend M. de Persigny, the Cabinet Minister, had given him a permit to travel free on the omnibuses. But I'm delighted to hear that *our* Morel's father was so distinguished. I was under the impression that he had been a schoolmaster, but it doesn't matter, I must have misunderstood. In any case, it makes not the slightest difference, for I must tell you that here we appreciate only true worth, the personal contribution, what I call participation. Provided that a person is artistic, provided in a word that he is one of the confraternity, nothing else matters." The way in which Morel was one of the con-fraternity was—so far as I was able to discover—that he was

sufficiently fond of both women and men to satisfy either sex
with the fruits of his experience of the other—as we shall see
later on. But what it is essential to note here is that as soon as I
had given him my word that I would speak on his behalf to
Mme Verdurin, as soon, especially, as I had actually done so
without any possibility of subsequent retractation, Morel's
"respect" for myself vanished as though by magic, the formal
language of respect melted away, and indeed for some time he
avoided me, contriving to appear to despise me, so that if Mme
Verdurin wanted me to give him a message, to ask him to play
something, he would continue to talk to one of the faithful,
then move on to another, changing his seat if I approached him.
The others were obliged to tell him three or four times that I
had spoken to him, after which he would reply, with an air of
constraint, briefly—unless we were by ourselves. Then he was
expansive and friendly, for there was a charming side to him.
I concluded all the same from this first evening that his must be
a vile nature, that he would not shrink from any act of servility
if the need arose, and was incapable of gratitude. In which he
resembled the majority of mankind. But inasmuch as I had
inherited a strain of my grandmother's nature, and enjoyed
the diversity of other people without expecting anything of
them or resenting anything that they did, I overlooked his
baseness, rejoiced in his gaiety when it was in evidence, and
indeed in what I believe to have been a genuine affection on his
part when, having run through the whole gamut of his false
ideas of human nature, he realised (in fits and starts, for he had
strange reversions to blind and primitive savagery) that my
gentleness with him was disinterested, that my indulgence arose
not from a want of perception but from what he called kindness; and above all I was enraptured by his art, through which,
although it was little more than an admirable virtuosity, and
although he was not, in the intellectual sense of the word, a real
musician, I heard again or for the first time so much beautiful
music. Moreover a manager (M. de Charlus, in whom I had
not suspected these talents, although Mme de Guermantes,
who had known him as a very different person in their younger
days, asserted that he had composed a sonata for her, painted a
fan, and so forth), a manager modest in regard to his true

merits, extremely gifted, contrived to place this virtuosity at the service of a versatile artistic sense which increased it tenfold. Imagine a purely skilful performer in the Russian ballet, trained, taught, developed in all directions by M. Diaghilev.

I had just given Mme Verdurin the message with which Morel had entrusted me and was talking to M. de Charlus about Saint-Loup, when Cottard burst into the room announcing, as though the house were on fire, that the Cambremers had arrived. Mme Verdurin, not wishing to appear, in front of "newcomers" such as M. de Charlus (whom Cottard had not seen) and myself, to attach any great importance to the arrival of the Cambremers, did not move, made no response to the announcement of these tidings, and merely said to the Doctor, fanning herself gracefully and adopting the tone of a marquise in the Théâtre-Français: "The Baron has just been telling us. . . ." This was too much for Cottard. Less abruptly than he would have done in the old days, for learning and high positions had added weight to his utterance, but nevertheless with the excitement which he recaptured at the Verdurins', he exclaimed: "A Baron! What Baron? Where's the Baron?" staring round the room with an astonishment that bordered on incredulity. With the affected indifference of a hostess when a servant has broken a valuable glass in front of her guests, and with the artificial, high-pitched tone of a Conservatoire prize-winner acting in a play by the younger Dumas, Mme Verdurin replied, pointing with her fan to Morel's patron: "Why, the Baron de Charlus, to whom let me introduce you . . . M. le Professeur Cottard." Mme Verdurin was for that matter by no means sorry to have an opportunity of playing the leading lady. M. de Charlus proffered two fingers which the Professor clasped with the kindly smile of a "prince of science." But he stopped short upon seeing the Cambremers enter the room, while M. de Charlus led me into a corner to have a word with me, not without fingering my muscles, which is a German habit.

M. de Cambremer bore little resemblance to the old Marquise. As she was wont to remark tenderly, he took entirely "after his papa." To anyone who had only heard of him, or of letters written by him, brisk and suitably expressed, his personal appearance was startling. No doubt one grew accustomed to it. But his nose had chosen, in placing itself askew above his mouth, perhaps the only oblique line, among so many possible ones, that one would never have thought of tracing upon this face, and one that indicated a vulgar stupidity, aggravated still further by the proximity of a Norman complexion on cheeks that were like two red apples. It is possible that M. de Cambremer's eyes retained between their eyelids a trace of the sky of the Cotentin, so soft upon sunny days when the wayfarer amuses himself counting in their hundreds the shadows of the poplars drawn up by the roadside, but those eyelids, heavy, bleared and drooping, would have prevented the least flash of intelligence from escaping. And so, discouraged by the meagreness of that azure gaze, one returned to the big crooked nose. By a transposition of the senses, M. de Cambremer looked at you with his nose. This nose of his was not ugly; it was if anything too handsome, too bold, too proud of its own importance. Arched, polished, gleaming, brand-new, it was amply prepared to make up for the spiritual inadequacy of the eyes. Unfortunately, if the eyes are sometimes the organ through which our intelligence is revealed, the nose (whatever the intimate solidarity and the unsuspected repercussion of one feature on another), the nose is generally the organ in which stupidity is most readily displayed.

Although the propriety of the dark clothes which M. de Cambremer invariably wore, even in the morning, might well reassure those who were dazzled and exasperated by the insolent brightness of the seaside attire of people whom they did not know, it was none the less impossible to understand why the wife of the judge should have declared with an air of discernment and authority, as a person who knows far more than you about the high society of Alençon, that on seeing M. de Cambremer one immediately felt oneself, even before one knew who he was, in the presence of a man of supreme distinction, of a man of perfect breeding, a change from the sort of person one saw at Balbec, a man in short in whose company one could breathe freely. He was to her, asphyxiated by all those Balbec tourists who did not know her world, like a bottle of smelling salts. It seemed to me on the contrary that he was one

of those people whom my grandmother would at once have
set down as "very common," and since she had no conception
of snobbishness, she would no doubt have been stupefied that
he could have succeeded in winning the hand of Mlle Legrandin, who must surely be difficult to please, having a brother
who was "so well-bred." At best one might have said of M. de
Cambremer's plebeian ugliness that it was to some extent
redolent of the soil and had a hint of something very anciently
local; one was reminded, on examining his faulty features,
which one would have liked to correct, of those names of little
Norman towns as to the etymology of which my friend the curé
was mistaken because the peasants, mispronouncing or having
misunderstood the Latin or Norman words that underlay
them, have finally perpetuated in a barbarism to be found already in the cartularies, as Brichot would have said, a misinterpretation and a faulty pronunciation. Life in these little old
towns may, for all that, be pleasant enough, and M. de Cambremer must have had his good points, for if it was in a mother's
nature that the old Marquise should prefer her son to her
daughter-in-law, on the other hand she who had other children,
of whom two at least were not devoid of merit, was often
heard to declare that the Marquis was, in her opinion, the best
of the family. During the short time he had spent in the Army,
his messmates, finding Cambremer too long a name to pronounce, had given him the nickname Cancan, implying a flow
of gossip, which he had done nothing to deserve. He knew how
to brighten a dinner-party to which he was invited by saying
when the fish (even if it were putrescent) or the entrée came in:
"I say, that looks a fine beast." And his wife, who had adopted
on entering the family everything that she supposed to form
part of their ethos, put herself on the level of her husband's
friends and perhaps sought to please him like a mistress and as
though she had been involved in his bachelor existence, by
saying in a casual tone when she spoke of him to officers:
"You shall see Cancan presently. Cancan has gone to Balbec,
but he will be back this evening." She was furious at having
compromised herself this evening by coming to the Verdurins'
and had done so only in response to the entreaties of her
mother-in-law and her husband, in the interests of a renewal of

the lease. But, being less well-brought-up than they, she made
no secret of the ulterior motive and for the last fortnight had
been making fun of this dinner-party to her women friends.
"You know we're going to dine with our tenants. That will be
well worth an increased rent. As a matter of fact, I'm rather
curious to see what they've done to our poor old Raspelière"
(as though she had been born in the house, and would find there
all her old family associations). "Our old keeper told me only
yesterday that you wouldn't know the place. I can't bear to
think of all that must be going on there. I'm sure we shall have
to have the whole place disinfected before we move in again."
She arrived haughty and morose, with the air of a great lady
whose castle, owing to a state of war, is occupied by the enemy,
but who nevertheless feels herself at home and makes a point of
showing the conquerors that they are intruding. Mme de Cambremer could not see me at first for I was in a bay at the side of
the room with M. de Charlus, who was telling me that he had
heard from Morel that his father had been an "intendant" in my
family, and that he, Charlus, credited me with sufficient intelligence and magnanimity (a term common to himself and Swann)
to forgo the mean and ignoble pleasure which vulgar little
idiots (I was warned) would not have failed, in my place, to
give themselves by revealing to our hosts details which they
might regard as demeaning. "The mere fact that I take an
interest in him and extend my protection over him, gives him a
pre-eminence and wipes out the past," the Baron concluded.
As I listened to him and promised the silence which I would
have kept even without the hope of being considered in return
intelligent and magnanimous, I looked at Mme de Cambremer.
And I had difficulty in recognising the melting, savoury morsel
I had had beside me the other day at tea-time on the terrace
at Balbec in the piece of Norman shortbread I now saw, hard
as rock, in which the faithful would in vain have tried to insert
their teeth. Irritated in advance by the good-nature which her
husband had inherited from his mother, and which would
make him assume a flattered expression when the faithful were
presented to him, but nevertheless anxious to perform her duty
as a society woman, when Brichot was introduced to her she
wanted to introduce him to her husband, as she had seen her

more fashionable friends do, but, rage or pride prevailing over the desire to show her knowledge of the world, instead of saying, as she ought to have done, "Allow me to present my husband," she said "I present you to my husband," holding aloft thus the banner of the Cambremers, but to no avail, for her husband bowed as low before Brichot as she had expected. But all Mme de Cambremer's ill humour vanished in an instant when her eye fell on M. de Charlus, whom she knew by sight. Never had she succeeded in obtaining an introduction, even at the time of her liaison with Swann. For as M. de Charlus always sided with the woman—with his sister-in-law against M. de Guermantes's mistresses, with Odette, at that time still unmarried, but an old flame of Swann's, against the new—he had, as a stern defender of morals and faithful protector of homes, given Odette—and kept—the promise that he would never allow himself to be introduced to Mme de Cambremer. She had certainly never imagined that it was at the Verdurins' that she was at length to meet this unapproachable person. M. de Cambremer knew that this was a great joy to her, so great that he himself was moved by it and gave his wife a look that implied: "You're glad you decided to come, aren't you?" He spoke in fact very little, knowing that he had married a superior woman. "Unworthy as I am," he would say at every moment, and readily quoted a fable of La Fontaine and one of Florian which seemed to him to apply to his ignorance and at the same time to enable him, beneath the outward form of a disdainful flattery, to show the men of science who were not members of the Jockey that one might be a sportsman and yet have read fables. The unfortunate thing was that he knew only two. And so they kept cropping up. Mme de Cambremer was no fool, but she had a number of extremely irritating habits. With her, the corruption of names had absolutely nothing to do with aristocratic disdain. She was not the person to say, like the Duchesse de Guermantes (whom the mere fact of her birth ought to have preserved even more than Mme de Cambremer from such an absurdity), with a pretence of not remembering the unfashionable name (although it is now that of one of the women whom it is most difficult to approach) of Julien de Monchâteau: "a little Madame . . . Pico della Mirandola." No, when Mme de Cambremer said a name wrong it was out of kindness of heart, so as not to appear to know some damaging fact, and when, out of truthfulness, she admitted it, she tried to conceal it by distorting it. If, for instance, she was defending a woman, she would try to conceal, while determined not to lie to the person who had asked her to tell the truth, the fact that Madame So-and-so was at the moment the mistress of M. Sylvain Lévy, and would say: "No ... I know absolutely nothing about her, I believe that people used to accuse her of having inspired a passion in a gentleman whose name I don't know, something like Cahn, Kohn, Kuhn; anyhow, I believe the gentleman has been dead for years and that there was never anything between them." This is an analogous—but inverse— process to that adopted by liars who, in falsifying what they have done when giving an account of it to a mistress or merely to a friend, imagine that their listener will not immediately see that the crucial phrase (as with Cahn, Kohn, Kuhn) is interpolated, is of a different texture from the rest of the conversation, is false-bottomed.

Mme Verdurin whispered in her husband's ear: "Shall I offer my arm to the Baron de Charlus? As you'll have Mme de Cambremer on your right, we might divide the honours." "No," said M. Verdurin, "since the other is higher in rank" (meaning that M. de Cambremer was a marquis), "M. de Charlus is, after all, his inferior." "Very well, I shall put him beside the Princess." And Mme Verdurin introduced Mme Sherbatoff to M. de Charlus; each of them bowed in silence, with an air of knowing all about the other and of promising a mutual secrecy. M. Verdurin introduced me to M. de Cambremer. Before he had even begun to speak to me in his loud and slightly stammering voice, his tall figure and high complexion displayed in their oscillation the martial hesitation of a commanding officer who tries to put you at your ease and says: "I have heard about you, I shall see what can be done; your punishment shall be remitted; we don't thirst for blood here; everything will be all right." Then, as he shook my hand: "I believe you know my mother," he said to me. The verb "believe" seemed to him appropriate to the discretion of a first meeting but not to imply any uncertainty, for he went on:

"I have a note for you from her." M. de Cambremer was
childishly happy to revisit a place where he had lived for so
long. "I'm at home again," he said to Mme Verdurin, while his
eyes marvelled at recognising the flowers painted on panels
over the doors, and the marble busts on their high pedestals.
He might, all the same, have felt somewhat at sea, for Mme
Verdurin had brought with her a quantity of fine old things of
her own. In this respect Mme Verdurin, while regarded by the
Cambremers as having turned everything upside down, was
not revolutionary but intelligently conservative, in a sense
which they did not understand. They thus wrongly accused her
of hating the old house and of degrading it by hanging plain
cloth curtains instead of their rich plush, like an ignorant
parish priest reproaching a diocesan architect for putting back
in its place the old carved wood which the cleric had discarded
and seen fit to replace with ornaments purchased in the Place
Saint-Sulpice. Furthermore, a herb garden was beginning to
take the place, in front of the house, of the flower-beds that
were the pride not merely of the Cambremers but of their
gardener. The latter, who regarded the Cambremers as his sole
masters and groaned beneath the Verdurins' yoke, as though
the place were momentarily occupied by an invading army of
roughneck soldiery, went in secret to unburden his grievances
to its dispossessed mistress, complained bitterly of the contempt with which his araucarias, begonias, sempervivum and
double dahlias were treated, and that they should dare in so
grand a place to grow such common plants as camomile and
maidenhair fern. Mme Verdurin sensed this silent opposition
and had made up her mind, if she took a long lease of la
Raspelière or even bought the place, to make one of her conditions the dismissal of the gardener, by whom his old mistress,
on the contrary, set great store. He had worked for her for
nothing when times were bad, and he adored her; but by that
odd multiformity of opinion which we find among the people,
whereby the most profound moral scorn is embedded in the
most passionate admiration, which in turn overlaps old and
undying grudges, he used often to say of Mme de Cambremer,
who, caught by the invasion of '70 in a house that she owned in
the East of France, had been obliged to endure for a month the

contact of the Germans: "What many people can't forgive
Madame la Marquise is that during the war she took the side
of the Prussians and even had them to stay in her house. At
any other time, I could understand it; but in wartime she
shouldn't have done it. It's not right." So that at one and the
same time he was faithful to her unto death, venerated her for
her kindness, and firmly believed that she had been guilty of
treason. Mme Verdurin was annoyed that M. de Cambremer
should claim to recognise la Raspelière so well. "You must
notice a good many changes, all the same," she replied. "For
one thing there were those big bronze Barbedienne devils
and some horrid little plush chairs which I packed off at once
to the attic, though even that's too good a place for them."
After this acerbic riposte to M. de Cambremer, she offered him
her arm to go in to dinner. He hesitated for a moment, saying
to himself: "I can't really go in before M. de Charlus." But
assuming the other to be an old friend of the house, since he
did not have the place of honour, he decided to take the arm
that was offered him and told Mme Verdurin how proud he
felt to be admitted into the cenacle (it was thus that he styled
the little nucleus, not without a smile of self-congratulation at
knowing the term). Cottard, who was seated next to M. de
Charlus, beamed at him through his pince-nez, to make his
acquaintance and to break the ice, with a series of winks far
more insistent than they would have been in the old days, and
not interrupted by fits of shyness. And these winning glances,
enhanced by the smile that accompanied them, were no longer
contained by the glass of his pince-nez but overflowed on all
sides. The Baron, who was only too inclined to see people of
his sort everywhere, had no doubt that Cottard was one of
them and was making eyes at him. At once he turned on the
Professor the cold shoulder of the invert, as contemptuous of
those who are attracted by him as he is ardent in pursuit of
those he finds attractive. Although everyone speaks men-
daciously of the pleasure of being loved, which fate constantly
withholds, it is undoubtedly a general law, the application of
which is by no means confined to the Charluses of this world,
that the person whom we do not love and who loves us seems
to us insufferable. To such a person, to a woman of whom we

say not that she loves us but that she clings to us, we prefer the society of any other, no matter who, with neither her charm, nor her looks, nor her brains. She will recover these, in our estimation, only when she has ceased to love us. In this sense, we might regard the invitation aroused in an invert by a man he finds repellent who pursues him as simply the transposition, in a comical form, of this universal rule. But in his case it is much stronger. Hence, whereas the normal man seeks to conceal the irritation he feels, the invert is implacable in making it clear to the man who provokes it, as he would certainly not bring it home to a woman, M. de Charlus for instance to the Princesse de Guermantes, whose passion for him he found irksome but flattering. But when they see another man display a particular predilection towards them, then, whether because they fail to recognise that it is the same as their own, or because it is a painful reminder that this predilection, exalted by them as long as it is they themselves who feel it, is regarded as a vice, or from a desire to rehabilitate themselves by making a scene in circumstances in which it costs them nothing, or from a fear of being unmasked which suddenly overtakes them when desire no longer leads them blindfold from one imprudence to another, or from rage at being subjected, by the equivocal attitude of another person, to the injury which by their own attitude, if that other person attracted them, they would not hesitate to inflict on him, men who do not in the least mind following a young man for miles, never taking their eyes off him in the theatre even if he is with friends, thereby threatening to compromise him with them, may be heard to say, if a man who does not attract them merely looks at them, "Monsieur, what do you take me for?" (simply because he takes them for what they are) "I don't understand you, no, don't attempt to explain, you are quite mistaken," may proceed at a pinch from words to blows, and, to a person who knows the imprudent stranger, wax indignant: "What, you know this loathsome creature. The way he looks at one! . . . A fine way to behave!" M. de Charlus did not go quite so far as this, but assumed the offended, glacial air adopted, when one appears to suspect them of being of easy virtue, by women who are not, and even more by women who are. Furthermore, the invert brought face to

face with an invert sees not merely an unpleasing image of
himself which, being purely inanimate, could at the worst
only injure his self-esteem, but a second self, living, active in
the same field, capable therefore of injuring him in his loves.
And so it is from an instinct of self-preservation that he will
speak ill of the possible rival, whether to people who are able
to do the latter some injury (nor does Invert No. 1 mind being
thought a liar when he thus denounces Invert No. 2 in front of
people who may know all about his own case), or to the young
man whom he has "picked up," who is perhaps about to be
snatched away from him and whom it is important to persuade
that the very things which it is to his advantage to do with the
speaker would be the bane of his life if he allowed himself to do
them with the other person. To M. de Charlus, who was thinking perhaps of the wholly imaginary dangers in which the
presence of this Cottard whose smile he misinterpreted might
involve Morel, an invert who did not attract him was not
merely a caricature of himself but also an obvious rival. A
tradesman practising an uncommon trade who on his arrival
in the provincial town where he intends to settle for life discovers that in the same square, directly opposite, the same trade
is being carried on by a competitor, is no more discomfited
than a Charlus who goes down to a quiet country spot to make
love unobserved and, on the day of his arrival, catches sight
of the local squire or the barber, whose aspect and manner
leave no room for doubt. The tradesman often develops a
hatred for his competitor; this hatred degenerates at times into
melancholy, and, if there is the slightest suggestion of tainted
heredity, one has seen in small towns the tradesman begin to
show signs of insanity which is cured only by his being persuaded to "sell up" and move elsewhere. The invert's rage is
even more obsessive. He has realised that from the very first
instant the squire and the barber have coveted his young
companion. Even though he repeats to him a hundred times a
day that the barber and the squire are scoundrels whose
company would bring disgrace on him, he is obliged, like
Harpagon, to watch over his treasure, and gets up in the night
to make sure that it is not being stolen. And it is this, no
doubt, even more than desire, or the convenience of habits

shared in common, and almost as much as that experience of oneself which is the only true experience, that makes one invert detect another with a rapidity and certainty that are almost infallible. He may be mistaken for a moment, but a rapid divination brings him back to the truth. Hence M. de Charlus's error was brief. His divine discernment showed him after the first minute that Cottard was not of his kind, and that he need fear his advances neither for himself, which would merely have annoyed him, nor for Morel, which would have seemed to him a more serious matter. He recovered his calm, and as he was still beneath the influence of the transit of Venus Androgyne, from time to time he smiled a faint smile at the Verdurins without taking the trouble to open his mouth, merely uncreasing a corner of his lips, and for an instant kindled a coquettish light in his eyes, he so obsessed with virility, exactly as his sister-in-law the Duchesse de Guermantes might have done.

"Do you shoot much, Monsieur?" said Mme Verdurin contemptuously to M. de Cambremer.

"Has Ski told you of the near shave we had to-day?" Cottard inquired of the Mistress.

"I shoot mostly in the forest of Chantepie," replied M. de Cambremer.

"No, I've told her nothing," said Ski.

"Does it deserve its name?" Brichot asked M. de Cambremer, after a glance at me from the corner of his eye, for he had promised me that he would introduce the topic of etymology, begging me at the same time to conceal from the Cambremers the scorn that he felt for the researches of the Combray priest.

"I'm afraid I must be very stupid, but I don't grasp your question," said M. de Cambremer.

"I mean: do many magpies sing in it?" replied Brichot.

Cottard meanwhile could not bear Mme Verdurin's not knowing that they had nearly missed the train.

"Out with it," Mme Cottard said to her husband encouragingly, "tell us about your odyssey."

"Well, it really is rather out of the ordinary," said the doctor, and repeated his narrative from the beginning. "When I saw that the train was in the station, I was dumbfounded. It was all Ski's fault. You're pretty eccentric with your information, my dear fellow! And there was Brichot waiting for us at the station!"

"I assumed," said the scholar, casting around him what he could still muster of a glance and smiling with his thin lips, "that if you had been detained at Graincourt, it would mean that you had encountered some peripatetic siren."

"Will you hold your tongue! What if my wife were to hear you?" said the Doctor. "This wife of mine, it is jealous."

"Ah! that Brichot," cried Ski, moved to traditional merriment by Brichot's spicy witticism, "he's always the same," although he had no reason to suppose that the worthy academic had ever been specially lecherous. And, to embellish these time-honoured words with the ritual gesture, he made as though he could not resist the desire to pinch Brichot's leg. "He never changes, the rascal," Ski went on, without stopping to think of the effect, at once sad and comic, that Brichot's semi-blindness gave to his words: "Always an eye for the ladies."

"You see," said M. de Cambremer, "what it is to meet a scholar. Here have I been shooting for fifteen years in the forest of Chantepie, and I've never even thought of what the name meant."

Mme de Cambremer cast a stern glance at her husband; she did not like him to humiliate himself thus before Brichot. She was even more displeased when, at every "ready-made" expression that Cancan employed, Cottard, who knew the ins and outs of them all, having himself laboriously acquired them, pointed out to the Marquis, who admitted his stupidity, that they meant nothing: "Why 'stupid as an owl'? Do you suppose owls are stupider than any other creature? We say: 'Mind your p's and q's.' Why p's and q's specially? Why do we say: 'sleep like a top'? Why 'Thundering snakes!'? Why 'at sixes and sevens'?"

But at this, the defence of M. de Cambremer was taken up by Brichot who explained the origin of each of these expressions. But Mme de Cambremer was chiefly occupied in examining the changes that the Verdurins had introduced at la Raspelière, in order that she might be able to criticise some and import others, or possibly the same ones, to Féterne. "I keep wondering what that chandelier is that's hanging all skew-whiff. I hardly recognise my old Raspelière," she went on, with a familiarly aristocratic air, as she might have spoken of an old servant meaning not so much to indicate his age as to say that he had seen her in her cradle. And as she was a trifle bookish in her speech: "All the same," she added in an undertone, "I can't help feeling that if I were living in another person's house I should feel some compunction about altering everything like this."

"It's a pity you didn't come with them," said Mme Verdurin to M. de Charlus and Morel, hoping that M. de Charlus was now "enrolled" and would submit to the rule that they must all arrive by the same train. "You're sure that Chantepie means the singing magpie, Chochotte?" she went on, to show that, like the great hostess that she was, she could join in every conversation at once.

"Tell me something about this violinist," Mme de Cambremer said to me, "he interests me. I adore music, and it seems to me that I have heard of him before. Complete my education." She had heard that Morel had come with M. de Charlus and hoped, by getting the former to come to her house, to make friends with the latter. She added, however, so that I might not guess her reason for asking, "M. Brichot interests me too." For, although she was highly cultivated, just as certain persons who are prone to obesity eat hardly anything and take exercise all day long without ceasing to grow visibly fatter, so Mme de Cambremer might spend her time, especially at Féterne, delving into ever more recondite philosophy, ever more esoteric music, and yet she emerged from these studies only to hatch intrigues that would enable her to break with the middle-class friends of her girlhood and to form the connexions which she had originally supposed to be part of the social life of her "in-laws" and had since discovered to be far more exalted and remote. A philosopher who was not modern enough for her, Leibnitz, has said that the way is long from the intellect to the heart. It was a journey that Mme de Cambremer had been no more capable of making than her brother. Abandoning the study of John Stuart Mill only for that of Lachelier, the less she believed in the reality of the external world, the more desperately she sought to establish herself in a good position in it before she died. In her passion for realism in art, no object seemed to her humble enough to serve as a model to painter or writer. A fashionable picture or novel would have made her sick; Tolstoy's mujiks, or Millet's peasants, were the extreme social boundary beyond which she did not allow the artist to pass. But to cross the boundary that limited her own social relations, to raise herself to an intimate acquaintance with duchesses, this was the goal of all her efforts, so ineffective had the spiritual treatment to which she subjected herself by the study of great masterpieces proved in overcoming the congenital and morbid snobbery that had developed in her. This snobbery had even succeeded in curing certain tendencies to avarice and adultery to which in her younger days she had been inclined, just as certain peculiar and permanent pathological conditions seem to render those who are subject to them immune to other maladies. I could not however refrain, as I listened to her, from admiring, though without deriving any pleasure therefrom, the refinement of her expressions. They were those that are employed in a given period by all the people of the same intellectual range, so that the refined expression provides at once, like the arc of a circle, the means to describe and limit the entire circumference. And so the effect of these expressions is that the people who employ them bore me immediately, because I feel that I already know them, but are generally regarded as superior persons, and have often been offered me as delightful and unappreciated dinner neighbours.

"You cannot fail to be aware, Madame, that many forest regions take their name from the animals that inhabit them. Next to the forest of Chantepie, you have the wood Chantereine."

"I don't know who the queen may be, but you're not very courteous to her," said M. de Cambremer.

"Take that, Chochotte," said Mme de Verdurin. "And otherwise, did you have a pleasant journey?"

"We encountered only vague specimens of humanity who thronged the train. But I must answer M. de Cambremer's question; *reine*, in this instance, is not the wife of a king, but a frog. It is the name that the frog has long retained in this district, as is shown by the station Renneville, which ought to be spelt Reineville."

"I say, that looks a fine beast," said M. de Cambremer to Mme Verdurin, pointing to a fish. (It was one of the compliments by means of which he considered that he paid his whack at a dinner-party, and gave an immediate return of hospitality. "There's no need to invite them back," he would often say, in speaking to his wife of one or other couple of their acquaintance: "They were delighted to have us. It was they who thanked me for coming.") "I may tell you, though, that I've been going to Renneville every day for years, and I've never seen any more frogs there than anywhere else. Madame de Cambremer brought over to these parts the curé of a parish where she owns a considerable property, who has very much the same turn of mind as yourself, it seems to me. He has written a book."

"I know, I've read it with immense interest," Brichot replied hypocritically.

The satisfaction that his pride received indirectly from this answer made M. de Cambremer laugh long and loud. "Ah, well, the author of, what shall I call it, this geography, this glossary, dwells at great length upon the name of a little place of which we were formerly, if I may say so, the lords, and which is called Pont-à-Couleuvre. Of course I am only an ignorant rustic compared with such a fountain of learning, but I have been to Pont-à-Couleuvre a thousand times if he's been there once, and devil take me if I ever saw one of those beastly snakes there—I say beastly in spite of the tribute the worthy La Fontaine pays them." (*The Man and the Snake* was one of his two fables.)

"You haven't seen any, and you've been quite right," replied Brichot. "Undoubtedly, the writer you mention knows his subject through and through, he has written a remarkable book."

"He has indeed!" exclaimed Mme de Cambremer. "That book, there's no doubt about it, is a real work of scholarship."

"No doubt he consulted various terriers (by which we mean the lists of benefices and cures of each diocese), which may have furnished him with the names of lay patrons and ecclesiastical collators. But there are other sources. One of the most learned of my friends has delved into them. He found that the place in question was named Pont-à-Quileuvre. This odd name encouraged him to carry his researches further, to a Latin text in which the bridge that your friend supposes to be infested with snakes is styled *Pons cui aperit:* a closed bridge that was opened only upon due payment."

"You were speaking of frogs. I, when I find myself among such learned folk, feel like the frog before the Areopagus" (this being his other fable), said Cancan who often indulged, with a hearty laugh, in this pleasantry thanks to which he imagined himself to be making at one and the same time, with a mixture of humility and aptness, a profession of ignorance and a display of learning.

Meanwhile Cottard, blocked on one side by M. de Charlus's silence, and driven to seek an outlet elsewhere, turned to me with one of those questions which impressed his patients when it hit the mark and showed them that he could put himself so to speak inside their bodies, and if on the other hand it missed the mark, enabled him to check certain theories, to widen his previous standpoints. "When you come to a relatively high altitude, such as this where we now are, do you find that the change increases your tendency to breathlessness?" he asked me with the certainty of either arousing admiration or enlarging his own knowledge.

M. de Cambremer heard the question and smiled. "I can't tell you how delighted I am to hear that you have fits of breathlessness," he flung at me across the table. He did not mean that it cheered him up, though in fact it did. For this worthy man could not hear any reference to another person's sufferings without a feeling of well-being and a spasm of hilarity which speedily gave place to the instinctive pity of a kind heart. But his words had another meaning which was indicated more precisely by the sentence that followed: "I'm delighted," he explained, "because my sister has them too." In short, he was delighted in the same way as if he had heard me mention as one of my friends a person who was constantly coming to their house. "What a small world!" was the reflexion which he formed mentally and which I saw written upon his smiling face when Cottard spoke to me of my attacks. And these began to establish themselves, from the evening of this dinner-party, as a sort of common acquaintance, after whom M. de

Cambremer never failed to inquire, if only to hand on a report to his sister.

As I answered the questions with which his wife kept plying me about Morel, my thoughts returned to a conversation I had had with my mother that afternoon. Without attempting to dissuade me from going to the Verdurins' if there was a chance of my enjoying myself there, she had pointed out that it was a circle of which my grandfather would not have approved, which would have made him exclaim: "On guard!" Then she had gone on to say: "By the way, Judge Toureuil and his wife told me they had been to lunch with Mme Bontemps. They asked me no questions. But I seemed to gather from what was said that a marriage between you and Albertine would be the joy of her aunt's life. I think the real reason is that they are all extremely fond of you. At the same time the style in which they imagine that you would be able to keep her, the sort of connexions they more or less know that we have—all that is not, I fancy, entirely irrelevant, although it may be a minor consideration. I wouldn't have mentioned it to you myself, because I'm not keen on it, but as I imagine they'll mention it to you, I thought I'd get a word in first." "But you yourself, what do you think of her?" I asked my mother. "Well, I'm not the one who's going to marry her. You could certainly do a great deal better in terms of marriage. But I feel that your grandmother would not have liked me to influence you. As a matter of fact, I can't say what I think of Albertine; I don't think of her. All I can say to you is, like Madame de Sévigné: 'She has good qualities, or so I believe. But at this first stage I can praise her only by negatives. She is not this: she has not the Rennes accent. In time, I shall perhaps say: she is that.' And I shall always think well of her if she can make you happy." But by these very words which left it to me to decide my own happiness, my mother had plunged me into that state of doubt in which I had been plunged long ago when, my father having allowed me to go to *Phèdre* and, what was more, to take up writing as a career, I had suddenly felt myself burdened with too great a responsibility, the fear of distressing him, and that melancholy which we feel when we cease to obey orders which, from one day to another, keep the future hidden, and realise that we have at last begun to live in real earnest, as a grown-up person, the life, the only life that any of us has at his disposal.

Perhaps the best thing would be to wait a little longer, to begin by seeing Albertine as I had seen her in the past, so as to find out whether I really loved her. I might take her, as a diversion, to see the Verdurins, and this thought reminded me that I had come there myself that evening only to learn whether Mme Putbus was staying there or was expected. In any case, she was not dining with them.

"Speaking of your friend Saint-Loup," said Mme de Cambremer, using an expression which betrayed more consistency in her train of thought than her remarks might have led one to suppose, for if she spoke to me about music she was thinking about the Guermantes, "you know that everybody is talking about his marriage to the niece of the Princesse de Guermantes. Though I may say that, for my part, all that society gossip concerns me not one whit." I was seized by a fear that I might have spoken unfeelingly to Robert about the girl in question, a girl full of sham originality, whose mind was as mediocre as her temper was violent. Hardly ever do we hear anything that does not make us regret something we have said. I replied to Mme de Cambremer, truthfully as it happened, that I knew nothing about it, and that anyhow I thought that the girl seemed rather young to be engaged.

"That is perhaps why it's not yet official. Anyhow there's a lot of talk about it."

"I ought to warn you," Mme Verdurin observed drily to Mme de Cambremer, having heard her talking to me about Morel and supposing, when she had lowered her voice to speak of Saint-Loup's engagement, that Morel was still under discussion. "You needn't expect any light music here. In matters of art, you know, the faithful who come to my Wednesdays, my children as I call them, are all fearfully advanced," she added with an air of terrified pride. "I say to them sometimes: My dear people, you move too fast for your Mistress, and she's not exactly notorious for being afraid of daring innovations. Every year it goes a little further; I can see the day coming when they will have no more use for Wagner or d'Indy."

"But it's splendid to be advanced, one can never be advanced enough," said Mme de Cambremer, scrutinising every corner of the dining-room as she spoke, trying to identify the things that her mother-in-law had left there and those that Mme Verdurin had brought with her, and to catch the latter red-handed in an error of taste. At the same time she tried to get me to talk of the subject that interested her most, M. de Charlus. She thought it touching that he should offer his patronage to a violinist: "He seems intelligent."

"Yes, his mind is extremely active for a man of his age," I replied.

"Age? But he doesn't seem at all old, look, the hair is still young." (For, during the last three or four years, the word hair had been used with the article by one of those unknown persons who launch the literary fashions, and everybody at the same radius from the centre as Mme de Cambremer would say "the hair," not without an affected smile. At the present day, people still say "the hair," but from an excessive use of the article the pronoun will be born again.)[44] "What interests me most about M. de Charlus," she went on, "is that one can feel that he is naturally gifted. I may tell you that I attach little importance to knowledge. I'm not interested in what's learnt."

These words were not incompatible with Mme de Cambremer's own particular quality, which was precisely imitated and acquired. But it so happened that one of the things one was required to know at that moment was that knowledge is nothing, and is not worth a straw when compared with originality. Mme de Cambremer had learned, with everything else, that one ought not to learn anything. "That is why," she explained to me, "Brichot, who has an interesting side to him, for I'm not one to despise a certain lively erudition, interests me far less."

But Brichot, at that moment, was occupied with one thing only: hearing people talk about music, he trembled lest the subject should remind Mme Verdurin of the death of Dechambre. He wanted to say something that would avert that harrowing memory. M. de Cambremer provided him with an opportunity with the question: "You mean to say that wooded places always take their names from animals?"

"Not so," replied Brichot, happy to display his learning

before so many strangers, among whom, I had told him, he would be certain to interest one at least. "We have only to consider how often, even in the names of people, a tree is preserved, like a fern in a seam of coal. One of our eminent Senators is called M. de Saulces de Freycinet, which means, if I be not mistaken, a spot planted with willow and ash, *salix et fraxinetum*; his nephew M. de Selves combines more trees still, since he is named de Selves, *de sylvis*."

Saniette was delighted to see the conversation take so animated a turn. Since Brichot was talking all the time, he himself could preserve a silence which would save him from being the butt of M. and Mme Verdurin's wit. And growing even more sensitive in his joy and relief, he had been touched when he heard M. Verdurin, notwithstanding the formality of so grand a dinner-party, tell the butler to put a jug of water in front of him since he never drank anything else. (The generals responsible for the death of most soldiers insist upon their being well fed.) Moreover, Mme Verdurin had actually smiled at him once. Decidedly, they were kind people. He was not going to be tortured any more

At this moment the meal was interrupted by one of the party whom I have forgotten to mention, an eminent Norwegian philosopher who spoke French very well but very slowly, for the twofold reason that, in the first place, having learned the language only recently and not wishing to make mistakes (though he did make a few), he referred each word to a sort of mental dictionary, and secondly, being a metaphysician, he always thought of what he intended to say while he was saying it, which, even in a Frenchman, is a cause of slowness. For the rest, he was a delightful person, although similar in appearance to many other people, save in one respect. This man who was so slow in his diction (there was an interval of silence after every word) developed a startling rapidity in escaping from the room as soon as he had said good-bye. His haste made one suppose, the first time one saw it, that he was suffering from colic or some even more urgent need.

"My dear—colleague," he said to Brichot, after deliberating in his mind whether colleague was the correct term, "I have a sort of—desire to know whether there are other trees in the—

nomenclature of your beautiful French—Latin—Norman tongue. Madame" (he meant Mme Verdurin, although he dared not look at her) "has told me that you know everything. Is not this precisely the moment?"

"No, it's the moment for eating," interrupted Mme Verdurin, who saw the dinner becoming interminable.

"Very well," the Scandinavian replied, bowing his head over his plate with a resigned and sorrowful smile. "But I must point out to Madame that if I have permitted myself this questionnaire—pardon me, this questation—it is because I have to return to-morrow to Paris to dine at the Tour d'Argent or at the Hôtel Meurice. My French—confrère—M. Boutroux is to address us there about certain séances of spiritualism—pardon me, certain spirituous evocations—which he has verified."

"The Tour d'Argent is not nearly as good as they make out," said Mme Verdurin sourly. "In fact, I've had some disgusting dinners there."

"But am I mistaken, is not the food that one consumes at Madame's table an example of the finest French cookery?"

"Well, it's not positively bad," replied Mme Verdurin, mollified. "And if you come next Wednesday, it will be better."

"But I am leaving on Monday for Algiers, and from there I am going to the Cape. And when I am at the Cape of Good Hope, I shall no longer be able to meet my illustrious colleague —pardon me, I shall no longer be able to meet my confrère."

And he set to work obediently, after offering these retrospective apologies, to devour his food at a headlong pace. But Brichot was only too delighted to be able to furnish other vegetable etymologies, and replied, so greatly interesting the Norwegian that he again stopped eating, but with a sign to the servants that they might remove his full plate and go on to the next course.

"One of the Immortals," said Brichot, "is named Houssaye, or a place planted with holly-trees; in the name of a brilliant diplomat, d'Ormesson, you will find the elm, the *ulmus* beloved of Virgil, which gave its name to the town of Ulm; in the names of his colleagues, M. de la Boulaye, the birch (*bouleau*), M. d'Aunay, the alder (*aune*), M. de Bussière, the box-tree (*buis*), M. Albaret, the sapwood (*aubier*)" (I made a mental note that I must tell this to Céleste), "M. de Cholet, the cabbage (*chou*), and the apple-tree (*pommier*) in the name of M. de la Pommeraye, whose lectures we used to attend, do you remember, Saniette, in the days when the worthy Porel had been sent to the furthest ends of the earth, as Proconsul in Odéonia?"

On hearing the name Saniette on Brichot's lips, M. Verdurin glanced at his wife and at Cottard with an ironical smile which disconcerted their timid guest.

"You said that Cholet was derived from *chou*," I remarked to Brichot. "Does the name of a station I passed before reaching Doncières, Saint-Frichoux, also come from *chou*?"

"No, Saint-Frichoux is *Sanctus Fructuosus*, as *Sanctus Ferreolus* gave rise to Saint-Fargeau, but that's not Norman in the least."

"He knows too much, he's boring us," the Princess gurgled softly.

"There are so many other names that interest me, but I can't ask you everything at once." And turning to Cottard, "Is Madame Putbus here?" I asked him.

"No, thank heaven," replied Mme Verdurin, who had overheard my question, "I've managed to divert her holiday plans towards Venice, so we are rid of her for this year."

"I shall myself be entitled presently to two trees," said M. de Charlus, "for I have more or less taken a little house between Saint-Martin-du-Chêne and Saint-Pierre-des-Ifs."

"But that's quite close to here. I hope you'll come over often with Charlie Morel. You have only to come to an arrangement with our little group about the trains, you're just a stone's throw from Doncières," said Mme Verdurin, who hated people not coming by the same train and at the hours when she sent carriages to meet them. She knew how stiff the climb was to la Raspelière, even by the zigzag path behind Féterne which was half an hour longer; she was afraid that those of her guests who came on their own might not find carriages to take them, or even, having in reality stayed away, might plead the excuse that they had not found a carriage at Douville-Féterne, and had not felt strong enough to make so stiff a climb on foot. To this invitation M. de Charlus responded with a silent nod.

"I bet he's an awkward customer, he's got a very starchy look," the Doctor whispered to Ski, for, having remained very unassuming in spite of a surface-dressing of arrogance, he made no attempt to conceal the fact that Charlus was snubbing him. "He's obviously unaware that at all the fashionable spas, and even in Paris, in all the clinics, the physicians, who naturally regard me as the 'big boss,' make it a point of honour to introduce me to all the noblemen present, not that they need to be asked twice. It makes my stay at the spas quite enjoyable," he added lightly. "Indeed at Doncières the medical officer of the regiment, who is the doctor who attends the Colonel, invited me to lunch to meet him, saying that I was fully entitled to dine with the General. And that general is a Monsieur *de* something. I don't know whether his title-deeds are more or less ancient than those of this Baron."

"Don't you worry about him, his is a very humble coronet," replied Ski in an undertone, and he added something indistinct including a word of which I caught only the last syllable, *-ast*, being engaged in listening to what Brichot was saying to M. de Charlus.

"No, as to that, I'm sorry to have to tell you, you have probably one tree only, for if Saint-Martin-du-Chêne is obviously *Sanctus Martinus juxta quercum*, on the other hand the word *if* [yew] may be simply the root *ave*, *eve*, which means moist, as in Aveyron, Lodève, Yvette, and which you see survive in our kitchen-sinks (*éviers*). It is the word *eau* which in Breton is represented by *ster*, Stermaria, Sterlaer, Sterbouest, Ster-en-Dreuchen."

I did not hear the rest, for whatever the pleasure I might feel on hearing again the name Stermaria, I could not help listening to Cottard, near whom I was seated, as he murmured to Ski: "Really! I didn't know that. So he's a gentleman who has the *mens conscia recti*! He's one of the happy band, is he? And yet he hasn't got rings of fat round his eyes. I shall have to watch out for my feet under the table or he might take a fancy to me. But I'm not at all surprised. I'm used to seeing noblemen in the shower-room, in their birthday suits, they're all more or less degenerates. I don't talk to them, because after all I'm in an official position and it might do me harm. But they know quite well who I am."

Saniette, who had been scared by Brichot's interpellation,

was beginning to breathe again, like a man who is afraid of
storms when he finds that the lightning has not been followed
by any sound of thunder, when he heard M. Verdurin interrogate him, fastening upon him a stare which did not let go of the
poor man until he had finished speaking, so as to disconcert
him from the start and prevent him from recovering his composure. "But you never told us that you went to those *matinées*
at the Odéon, Saniette?"

Trembling like a recruit before a bullying sergeant, Saniette
replied, making his reply as exiguous as possible, so that it
might have a better chance of escaping the blow: "Only once,
to the *Chercheuse*."

"What's that he says?" shouted M. Verdurin, with an air of
disgust and fury combined, knitting his brows as though he
needed all his concentration to grasp something unintelligible.
"It's impossible to understand what you say. What have you got
in your mouth?" inquired M. Verdurin, growing more and
more furious, and alluding to Saniette's speech defect.

"Poor Saniette, I won't have him made unhappy," said Mme
Verdurin in a tone of false pity, so as to leave no one in doubt
as to her husband's rudeness.

"I was at the Ch . . . Che . . ."

"Che, che, try to speak distinctly," said M. Verdurin, "I can't
understand a word you say."

Almost without exception, the faithful burst out laughing,
looking like a group of cannibals in whom the sight of a
wounded white man has aroused the thirst for blood. For the
instinct of imitation and absence of courage govern society and
the mob alike. And we all of us laugh at a person whom we see
being made fun of, though it does not prevent us from
venerating him ten years later in a circle where he is admired. It is
in like manner that the populace banishes or acclaims its kings.

"Come, now, it's not his fault," said Mme Verdurin.

"It's not mine either, people ought not to dine out if they
can't speak properly."

"I was at the *Chercheuse d'Esprit* by Favart."

"What! It's the *Chercheuse d'Esprit* that you call the *Chercheuse*? Why, that's marvellous! I might have gone on trying for
a hundred years without guessing it," cried M. Verdurin, who

nevertheless would have decided immediately that you were not literary, were not artistic, were not "one of us," if he had heard you quote the full title of certain works. For instance, one was expected to say the *Malade*, the *Bourgeois*), and anyone who added *imaginaire* or *gentilhomme* would have shown that he did not "belong," just as in a drawing-room a person proves that he is not in society by saying "M. de Montesquiou-Fezensac" instead of "M. de Montesquiou."

"But it isn't so extraordinary," said Saniette, breathless with emotion but smiling, although he was in no smiling mood.

Mme Verdurin could not contain herself: "Oh yes it is!" she exclaimed with a snigger. "You may be quite sure that nobody would ever have guessed that you meant the *Chercheuse d'Esprit*."

M. Verdurin went on in a gentler tone, addressing both Saniette and Brichot: "It's not a bad play, actually, the *Chercheuse d'Esprit*."

Uttered in a serious tone, this simple remark, in which no trace of malice was to be detected, did Saniette as much good and aroused in him as much gratitude as a deliberate compliment. He was unable to utter a single word and preserved a happy silence. Brichot was more loquacious. "It's true," he replied to M. Verdurin, "and if it could be passed off as the work of some Sarmatian or Scandinavian author, we might put it forward as a candidate for the vacant post of masterpiece. But, be it said without any disrespect to the shade of the gentle Favart, he had not the Ibsenian temperament." (Immediately he blushed to the roots of his hair, remembering the Norwegian philosopher, who looked unhappy because he was trying in vain to discover what vegetable the *buis* might be that Brichot had cited a little earlier in connexion with the name Bussière.) "However, now that Porel's satrapy is filled by a functionary who is a Tolstoyan of rigorous observance, it may come to pass that we shall witness *Anna Karenina* or *Resurrection* beneath the Odéonian architrave."

"I know the portrait of Favart to which you allude," said M. de Charlus. "I have seen a very fine print of it at the Comtesse Molé's."

This name made a great impression upon Mme Verdurin. "Oh! so you go to Mme de Molé's!" she exclaimed. She

supposed that people said "the Comtesse Molé," "Madame
Molé," simply as an abbreviation, as she heard people say
"the Rohans" or in contempt, as she herself said, "Madame la
Trémoïlle." She had no doubt that the Comtesse Molé, who
knew the Queen of Greece and the Principessa di Caprarola,
must have as much right as anybody to the particle, and for
once in a way had decided to bestow it upon so brilliant a
personage, and one who had been extremely civil to herself.
And so, to make it clear that she had spoken thus on purpose
and did not grudge the Comtesse her "de," she went on:
"But I had no idea that you knew Madame de Molé!" as though
it was doubly extraordinary, both that M. de Charlus should
know the lady and that Mme Verdurin should not know that
he knew her. Now society, or at least the people to whom M. de
Charlus gave that name, forms a relatively homogeneous and
compact entity. And whereas it is understandable that in the
disparate vastness of the middle classes a barrister should say
to somebody who knows one of his schoolfriends: "But how
in the world do you come to know him?" to be surprised at a
Frenchman's knowing the meaning of the word *temple* or *forest*
would be hardly more extraordinary than to wonder at the
accidents that might have brought together M. de Charlus and
the Comtesse Molé. Moreover, even if such an acquaintance
had not followed quite naturally from the laws that govern
society, even if it had been fortuitous, how could there be
anything strange in the fact that Mme Verdurin did not know
of it, since she was meeting M. de Charlus for the first time, and
his relations with Mme Molé were far from being the only
thing she did not know about him, for in fact she knew
nothing. "Who was in this *Chercheuse d'Esprit*, my good
Saniette?" asked M. Verdurin.

Although he felt that the storm had passed, the old archivist
hesitated before answering.

"There you go," said Mme Verdurin, "you frighten him,
you make fun of everything he says, and then you expect him
to answer. Come along, tell us who was in it, and you shall
have some galantine to take home," said Mme Verdurin,
making a cruel allusion to the penury into which Saniette had
plunged himself by trying to rescue the family of a friend.

"I can remember only that it was Mme Samary who played the Zerbina," said Saniette.

"The Zerbina? What in the world is that?" M. Verdurin shouted, as though the house were on fire.

"It's one of the stock types in the old repertory, see *Le Capitaine Fracasse*, as who should say the Braggart, the Pedant."

"Ah, the pedant, that's you. The Zerbina! No, really the man's mad," exclaimed M. Verdurin. (Mme Verdurin looked at her guests and laughed as though to apologise for Saniette.) "The Zerbina, he imagines that everybody will know at once what it means. You're like M. de Longepierre, the stupidest man I know, who said to us quite familiarly the other day 'the Banat.' Nobody had any idea what he meant. Finally we were informed that it was a province of Serbia."

To put an end to Saniette's torture, which hurt me more than it hurt him, I asked Brichot if he knew what the word Balbec meant. "Balbec is probably a corruption of Dalbec," he told me. "One would have to consult the charters of the Kings of England, suzerains of Normandy, for Balbec was a dependency of the barony of Dover, for which reason it was often styled Balbec d'Outre-Mer, Balbec-en-Terre. But the barony of Dover itself came under the bishopric of Bayeux, and, notwithstanding the rights that were temporarily enjoyed in the abbey by the Templars, from the time of Louis d'Harcourt, Patriarch of Jerusalem and Bishop of Bayeux, it was the bishops of that diocese who collated to the benefice of Balbec. So it was explained to me by the incumbent of Douville, a bald, eloquent, fanciful man and a devotee of the table, who lives by the rule of Brillat-Savarin, and who expounded to me in somewhat sibylline terms a loose pedagogy, while he fed me upon some admirable fried potatoes."

While Brichot smiled to show how witty it was to juxtapose such disparate matters and to employ an ironically lofty diction in treating of commonplace things, Saniette was trying to find a loophole for some witticism which would raise him from the abyss into which he had fallen. The witticism was what was known as an "approximation," but it had changed its form, for there is an evolution in puns as in literary styles, an epidemic that disappears is replaced by another, and so forth. . . . At one

time the typical "approximation" was the "height of. ..."
But this was out of date, no one used it any more, except for
Cottard who might still say, on occasion, in the middle of a
game of piquet: "Do you know what is the height of absent-
mindedness? It's to think that the Edict of [*l'édit de*] Nantes
was an Englishwoman." These "heights" had been replaced by
nicknames. In reality it was still the old "approximation," but,
as the nickname was in fashion, people did not notice. Unfortunately for Saniette, when these "approximations" were not
his own, and as a rule were unknown to the little nucleus, he
produced them so timidly that, in spite of the laugh with which
he followed them up to indicate their humorous nature, nobody
saw the point. And if on the other hand the joke was his own,
as he had generally hit upon it in conversation with one of the
faithful, and the latter had repeated it, appropriating the
authorship, the joke was in that case known, but not as being
Saniette's. And so when he slipped in one of these it was
recognised, but, because he was its author, he was accused of
plagiarism.

"Thus," Brichot continued, "*bec*, in Norman, is a stream;
there is the Abbey of Bec, Mobec, the stream from the marsh
(*mor* or *mer* meant a marsh, as in Morville, or in Bricquemar,
Alvimare, Cambremer), Bricquebec, the stream from the high
ground, coming from *briga*, a fortified place, as in Bricqueville,
Bricquebosc, le Bric, Briand, or from *brice*, bridge, which is
the same as *bruck* in German (Innsbruck), and as the English
bridge which ends so many place-names (Cambridge, for
instance). You have moreover in Normandy many other
instances of *bec*: Caudebec, Bolbec, le Robec, le Bec-Hellouin,
Becquerel. It's the Norman form of the German *bach*, Offenbach, Anspach; Varaguebec, from the old word *varaigne*,
equivalent to *warren*, means protected woods or ponds. As for
dal," Brichot went on, "it is a form of *thal*, a valley: Darnetal,
Rosendal, and indeed, close to Louviers, Becdal. The river
that has given its name to Balbec is, by the way, charming.
Seen from a *falaise* (*fels* in German, in fact not far from here,
standing on a height, you have the picturesque town of Falaise),
it runs close under the spires of the church, which is actually a
long way from it, and seems to be reflecting them."

"I can well believe it," said I, "it's an effect that Elstir is very fond of. I've seen several sketches of it in his studio."

"Elstir! You know Tiche?" cried Mme Verdurin. "But do you know that we used to be the closest friends. Thank heaven, I never see him now. No, but ask Cottard or Brichot, he used to have his place laid at my table, he came every day. Now, there's a man of whom you can say that it did him no good to leave our little nucleus. I shall show you presently some flowers he painted for me; you'll see the difference from the things he's doing now, which I don't care for at all, not at all! Why, I got him to do a portrait of Cottard, not to mention all the sketches he did of me."

"And he gave the Professor purple hair," said Mme Cottard, forgetting that at the time her husband had not been even a Fellow of the College. "Would you say that my husband had purple hair, Monsieur?"

"Never mind!" said Mme Verdurin, raising her chin with an air of contempt for Mme Cottard and of admiration for the man of whom she was speaking, "it was the work of a bold colourist, a fine painter. Whereas," she added, turning again to me, "I don't know whether you call it painting, all those outlandish great compositions, those hideous contraptions he exhibits now that he has given up coming to me. I call it daubing, it's all so hackneyed, and besides, it lacks relief and personality. There are bits of everybody in it."

"He has revived the grace of the eighteenth century, but in a modern form," Saniette burst out, fortified and emboldened by my friendliness, "but I prefer Helleu."

"There's not the slightest connexion with Helleu," said Mme Verdurin.

"Yes, yes, it's hotted-up eighteenth century. He's a steam Watteau," and he began to laugh.[45]

"Old, old as the hills. I've had that served up to me for years," said M. Verdurin, to whom indeed Ski had once repeated the remark, but as his own invention. "It's unfortunate that when once in a way you say something quite amusing and make it intelligible, it isn't your own."

"I'm sorry about it," Mme Verdurin went on, "because he was really gifted, he has wasted a very remarkable painterly talent. Ah, if only he'd stayed with us! Why, he would have become the greatest landscape painter of our day. And it was a woman who dragged him down so low! Not that that surprises me, for he was an attractive enough man, but common. At bottom, he was a mediocrity. I may tell you that I felt it at once. Really, he never interested me. I was quite fond of him, that was all. For one thing, he was so dirty! Tell me now, do *you* like people who never wash?"

"What is this prettily coloured thing that we're eating?" asked Ski.

"It's called strawberry mousse," said Mme Verdurin.

"But it's ex-qui-site. You ought to open bottles of Château-Margaux, Château-Lafite, port wine."

"I can't tell you how he amuses me, he never drinks anything but water," said Mme Verdurin, seeking to cloak with her delight at this flight of fancy her alarm at the thought of such extravagance.

"But not to drink," Ski went on. "You shall fill all our glasses, and they will bring in marvellous peaches, huge nectarines; there, against the sunset, it will be as luscious as a beautiful Veronese."

"It would cost almost as much," M. Verdurin murmured.

"But take away those cheeses with their hideous colour," said Ski, trying to snatch the plate from in front of his host, who defended his gruyère with all his might.

"You can see why I don't miss Elstir," Mme Verdurin said to me, "this one is far more gifted. Elstir is simply hard work, the man who can't tear himself away from his painting when he feels like it. He's the good pupil, the exam fiend. Ski, now, only follows his own fancy. You'll see him light a cigarette in the middle of dinner."

"By the way, I can't think why you wouldn't invite his wife," said Cottard, "he would be with us still."

"Will you mind what you're saying, please. I don't open my doors to trollops, Monsieur le Professeur," said Mme Verdurin, who had, on the contrary, done everything in her power to make Elstir return, even with his wife. But before they were married she had tried to separate them, had told Elstir that the woman he loved was stupid, dirty, immoral, a thief. For once in a way she had failed to effect a breach. It was with the Verdurin salon that Elstir had broken; and he was glad of it, as converts bless the illness or misfortune that has caused them to withdraw from the world and has shown them the way of salvation.

"He really is magnificent, the Professor," she said. "Why not declare outright that I keep a disorderly house. Anyone would think you didn't know what Madame Elstir was. I'd sooner have the lowest streetwalker at my table! Oh no, I'm not stooping to that! But in any case it would have been stupid of me to overlook the wife when the husband no longer interests me—he's out of date, he can't even draw."

"It's extraordinary in a man of his intelligence," said Cottard.

"Oh, no!" replied Mme Verdurin, "even at the time when he had talent—for he did have talent, the wretch, and to spare—what was tiresome about him was that he hadn't a spark of intelligence."

In order to form this opinion, Mme Verdurin had not waited for their quarrel, or until she had ceased to care for his painting. The fact was that, even at the time when he formed part of the little group, it sometimes happened that Elstir would spend whole days in the company of some woman whom, rightly or wrongly, Mme Verdurin considered a goose, and this, in her opinion, was not the conduct of an intelligent man. "No," she observed judiciously, "I consider that his wife and he are made for one another. Heaven knows, there isn't a more boring creature on the face of the earth, and I should go mad if I had to spend a couple of hours with her. But people say that he finds her very intelligent. There's no use denying it, our Tiche was *extremely stupid*. I've seen him bowled over by women you can't conceive, amiable idiots we'd never have allowed into our little clan. Well, he used to write to them, and argue with them, he, Elstir! That doesn't prevent his having charming qualities, oh, charming, and deliciously absurd, naturally." For Mme Verdurin was convinced that men who are truly remarkable are capable of all sorts of follies. A false idea in which there is nevertheless a grain of truth. Certainly, people's "follies" are insupportable. But a want of balance which we discover only in course of time is the consequence of the entering into a human

brain of refinements for which it is not normally adapted. So
that the oddities of charming people exasperate us, but there
are few if any charming people who are not, at the same time,
odd. "There, I shall be able to show you his flowers now," she
said to me, seeing that her husband was making signals to her
to rise. And she took M. de Cambremer's arm again. M.
Verdurin wanted to apologise for this to M. de Charlus, as
soon as he had got rid of Mme de Cambremer, and to give him
his reasons, chiefly for the pleasure of discussing these social
distinctions with a man of title, momentarily the inferior of
those who assigned to him the place to which they considered
him entitled. But first of all he was anxious to make it clear
to M. de Charlus that intellectually he esteemed him too highly
to suppose that he could pay any attention to these trivialities.

"Forgive my mentioning these trifles," he began, "for I can
well imagine how little importance you attach to them. Middle-
class minds take them seriously, but the others, the artists, the
people who are really *of our sort*, don't give a rap for them.
Now, from the first words we exchanged, I realised that you
were *one of us!*" M. de Charlus, who attached a very different
meaning to this expression, gave a start. After the Doctor's
oglings, his host's insulting frankness took his breath away.
"Don't protest, my dear sir, you are *one of us*, it's as clear as
daylight," M. Verdurin went on. "Mind you, I don't know
whether you practise any of the arts, but that's not necessary.
Nor is it always sufficient. Dechambre, who has just died,
played exquisitely, with the most vigorous execution, but he
wasn't *one of us*, you felt at once that he wasn't. Brichot isn't
one of us. Morel is, my wife is, I can feel that you are. . . ."

"What were you going to say to me?" interrupted M. de
Charlus, who was beginning to feel reassured as to M. Verdurin's meaning, but preferred that he should not utter these
equivocal remarks quite so loud.

"Only that we put you on the left," replied M. Verdurin.

M. de Charlus, with a tolerant, genial, insolent smile, replied:
"Why, that's not of the slightest importance, *here*!" And he
gave a little laugh that was all his own—a laugh that came
down to him probably from some Bavarian or Lorraine grandmother, who herself had inherited it, in identical form, from an

ancestress, so that it had tinkled now, unchanged, for a good many centuries in little old-fashioned European courts, and one could appreciate its precious quality, like that of certain old musical instruments that have become very rare. There are times when, to paint a complete portrait of someone, we should have to add a phonetic imitation to our verbal description, and our portrait of the figure that M. de Charlus presented is liable to remain incomplete in the absence of that little laugh, so delicate, so light, just as certain works of Bach are never accurately rendered because our orchestras lack those small, high trumpets, with a sound so entirely their own, for which the composer wrote this or that part.

"But," explained M. Verdurin, hurt, "we did it on purpose. I attach no importance whatever to titles of nobility," he went on, with that contemptuous smile which I have seen so many people I have known, unlike my grandmother and my mother, assume when they speak of something they do not possess to those who will thereby, they imagine, be prevented from using it to show their superiority over them. "But you see, since we happened to have M. de Cambremer here, and he's a marquis, while you're only a baron. . . ."

"Pardon me," M. de Charlus haughtily replied to the astonished Verdurin, "I am also Duke of Brabant, Squire of Montargis, Prince of Oléron, of Carency, of Viareggio and of the Dunes. However, it's not of the slightest importance. Please don't distress yourself," he concluded, resuming his delicate smile which blossomed at these final words: "I could see at a glance that you were out of your depth."

Mme Verdurin came across to me to show me Elstir's flowers. If the act of going out to dinner, to which I had grown so indifferent, by taking the form, which entirely revivified it, of a journey along the coast followed by an ascent in a carriage to a point six hundred feet above the sea, had produced in me a sort of intoxication, this feeling had not been dispelled at la Raspelière. "Just look at this, now," said the Mistress, showing me some huge and splendid roses by Elstir, whose unctuous scarlet and rich whiteness stood out, however, with almost too creamy a relief from the flower-stand on which they were arranged. "Do you suppose he would still have the touch to achieve that? Don't you call that striking? And what marvellous texture! One longs to feel it. I can't tell you what fun it was to watch him painting them. One could feel that he was interested in trying to get just that effect." And the Mistress's gaze rested musingly on this present from the artist which epitomised not merely his great talent but their long friendship which survived only in these mementoes of it that he had bequeathed to her; behind the flowers that long ago he had picked for her, she seemed to see the shapely hand that had painted them, in the course of a morning, in their freshness, so that, they on the table, it leaning against the back of a chair in the dining-room, had been able to meet face to face at the Mistress's lunch-party, the still-living roses and their almost lifelike portrait. "Almost" only, for Elstir was unable to look at a flower without first transplanting it to that inner garden in which we are obliged always to remain. He had shown in this water-colour the appearance of the roses which he had seen, and which, but for him, no one would ever have known; so that one might say that they were a new variety with which this painter, like a skilful horticulturist, had enriched the rose family. "From the day he left the little nucleus, he was finished. It seems my dinners made him waste his time, that I hindered the development of his *genius*," she said in a tone of irony. "As if the society of a woman like myself could fail to be beneficial to an artist!" she exclaimed with a burst of pride.

Close beside us, M. de Cambremer, who was already seated, seeing that M. de Charlus was standing, made as though to rise and offer him his chair. This offer may have arisen, in the Marquis's mind, from nothing more than a vague wish to be polite. M. de Charlus preferred to attach to it the sense of a duty which the simple squire knew that he owed to a prince, and felt that he could not establish his right to this precedence better than by declining it. And so he exclaimed: "Good gracious me! Please! The idea!" The astutely vehement tone of this protest had in itself something typically "Guermantes" which became even more evident in the imperious, supererogatory and familiar gesture with which he brought both his hands down, as though to force him to remain seated, upon the shoulders of M. de Cambremer who had not risen: "Come, come, my dear fellow," the Baron insisted, "that would be the last straw! There's really no need! In these days we keep that for Princes of the Blood."

I made no more impression on the Cambremers than on Mme Verdurin by my enthusiasm for their house. For the beauties they pointed out to me left me cold, whilst I was carried away by confused reminiscences; at times I even confessed to them my disappointment at not finding something correspond to what its name had made me imagine. I enraged Mme de Cambremer by telling her that I had supposed the place to be more rustic. On the other hand I broke off in an ecstasy to sniff the fragrance of a breeze that crept in through the chink of the door. "I see you like draughts," they said to me. My praise of a piece of green lustre plugging a broken pane met with no greater success: "How frightful!" exclaimed the Marquise. The climax came when I said: "My greatest joy was when I arrived. When I heard my footsteps echoing in the gallery, I felt I had walked into some village *mairie*, with a map of the district on the wall." This time, Mme de Cambremer resolutely turned her back on me.

"You didn't find the arrangement too bad?" her husband asked her with the same compassionate anxiety with which he would have inquired how his wife had stood some painful ceremony. "They have some fine things."

But since malice, when the hard and fast rules of a sure taste do not confine it within reasonable limits, finds fault with everything in the persons or in the houses of the people who have supplanted you, "Yes, but they are not in the right places," replied Mme de Cambremer. "Besides, are they really as fine as all that?"

"You noticed," said M. de Cambremer, with a melancholy that was tempered with a note of firmness, "there are some Jouy hangings that are worn away, some quite threadbare things in this drawing-room!"

"And that piece of stuff with its huge roses, like a peasant woman's quilt," said Mme de Cambremer, whose entirely spurious culture was confined exclusively to idealist philosophy, Impressionist painting and Debussy's music. And, so as not to criticise merely in the name of luxury but in that of taste: "And they've put up draught-curtains! Such bad form!

But what do you expect? These people simply don't know, where could they possibly have learned? They must be retired tradespeople. It's really not bad for them."

"I thought the chandeliers good," said the Marquis, though it was not evident why he should make an exception of the chandeliers, in the same way as, inevitably, whenever anyone spoke of a church, whether it was the Cathedral of Chartres, or of Rheims, or of Amiens, or the church at Balbec, what he would always make a point of mentioning as admirable would be: "the organ-case, the pulpit and the misericords."

"As for the garden, don't speak about it," said Mme de Cambremer. "It's sheer butchery. Those paths running all lopsided."

I took the opportunity while Mme Verdurin was serving coffee to go and glance over the letter which M. de Cambremer had brought me and in which his mother invited me to dinner. With that faint trace of ink, the handwriting revealed an individuality which in the future I should be able to recognise among a thousand, without any more need to have recourse to the hypothesis of special pens than to suppose that rare and mysteriously blended colours are necessary to enable a painter to express his original vision. Indeed a paralytic, stricken with agraphia after a stroke and reduced to looking at the script as at a drawing without being able to read it, would have gathered that the dowager Mme de Cambremer belonged to an old family in which the zealous cultivation of literature and the arts had brought a breath of fresh air to its aristocratic traditions. He would have guessed also the period in which the Marquise had learned simultaneously to write and to play Chopin's music. It was the time when well-bred people observed the rule of affability and what was called the rule of the three adjectives. Mme de Cambremer combined both rules. One laudatory adjective was not enough for her, she followed it (after a little dash) with a second, then (after another dash) with a third. But, what was peculiar to her was that, in defiance of the literary and social aim which she set herself, the sequence of the three epithets assumed in Mme de Cambremer's letters the aspect not of a progression but of a diminuendo. Mme de Cambremer told me, in this first letter, that she had seen Saint-Loup and had appreciated more than ever his "unique—rare—

real" qualities, that he was coming to them again with one of his friends (the one who was in love with her daughter-in-law), and that if I cared to come, with or without them, to dine at Féterne she would be "delighted—happy—pleased." Perhaps it was because her desire to be amiable outran the fertility of her imagination and the riches of her vocabulary that the lady, while determined to utter three exclamations, was incapable of making the second and third anything more than feeble echoes of the first. Had there only been a fourth adjective, nothing would have remained of the initial amiability. Finally, with a certain refined simplicity which cannot have failed to produce a considerable impression upon her family and indeed her circle of acquaintance, Mme de Cambremer had acquired the habit of substituting for the word "sincere" (which might in time begin to ring false) the word "true." And to show that it was indeed by sincerity that she was impelled, she broke the conventional rule that would have placed the adjective "true" before its noun, and planted it boldly after. Her letters ended with: *"Croyez à mon amitié vraie"*; *"Croyez à ma sympathie vraie."* Unfortunately, this had become so stereotyped a formula that the affectation of frankness was more suggestive of a polite fiction than the time-honoured formulas to whose meaning one no longer gives a thought.

I was, however, hindered from reading her letter by the confused hubbub of conversation over which rang out the louder accents of M. de Charlus, who, still on the same topic, was saying to M. de Cambremer: "You reminded me, when you offered me your chair, of a gentleman from whom I received a letter this morning addressed 'To His Highness the Baron de Charlus,' and beginning: 'Monseigneur.' "[46]

"To be sure, your correspondent was exaggerating a bit," replied M. de Cambremer, giving way to a discreet show of mirth.

M. de Charlus had provoked this, but he did not partake in it. "Well, if it comes to that, my dear fellow," he said, "I may tell you that, heraldically speaking, he was entirely in the right. I'm not making a personal issue of it, you understand. I'm speaking of it as though it were someone else. But one has to face the facts, history is history, there's nothing we can do

about it and it's not for us to rewrite it. I need not cite the case
of the Emperor William, who at Kiel invariably addressed me
as 'Monseigneur.' I have heard it said that he gave the same title
to all the dukes of France, which is improper, but is perhaps
simply a delicate attention aimed over our heads at France
herself."

"More delicate, perhaps, than sincere," said M. de Cambremer.

"Ah! there I must differ from you. Mind you, speaking
personally, a gentleman of the lowest rank such as that Hohenzollern, a Protestant to boot, and one who has usurped the
throne of my cousin the King of Hanover, can be no favourite
of mine," added M. de Charlus, with whom the annexation of
Hanover seemed to rankle more than that of Alsace-Lorraine.
"But I believe the penchant that the Emperor feels for us to
be profoundly sincere. Fools will tell you that he is a stage
emperor. He is on the contrary marvellously intelligent; it's
true that he knows nothing about painting, and has forced
Herr Tschudi to withdraw the Elstirs from the public galleries.
But Louis XIV did not appreciate the Dutch masters, he had
the same fondness for pomp and ceremony, and yet he was,
when all is said, a great monarch. Besides, William II has
armed his country from the military and naval point of view in
a way that Louis XIV failed to do, and I hope that his reign
will never know the reverses that darkened the closing days of
him who is fatuously styled the Sun King. The Republic
committed a grave error, to my mind, in rejecting the overtures
of the Hohenzollern, or responding to them only in driblets.
He is very well aware of it himself and says, with that gift of
expression that is his: 'What I want is a handclasp, not a
raised hat.' As a man, he is vile; he abandoned, betrayed,
repudiated his best friends, in circumstances in which his silence
was as deplorable as theirs was noble," continued M. de Charlus, who was irresistibly drawn by his own tendencies to the
Eulenburg affair,[47] and remembered what one of the most highly
placed of the accused had said to him: "How the Emperor
must have relied upon our delicacy to have dared to allow such
a trial! But he was not mistaken in trusting to our discretion.
We would have gone to the scaffold with our lips sealed." "All

that, however, has nothing to do with what I was trying to explain, which is that, in Germany, mediatised princes like ourselves are *Durchlaucht*, and in France our rank of Highness was publicly recognised. Saint-Simon claims that we acquired it improperly, in which he is entirely mistaken. The reason that he gives, namely that Louis XIV forbade us to style him the Most Christian King and ordered us to call him simply the King, proves merely that we held our title from him, and not that we did not have the rank of prince. Otherwise, it would have had to be withheld from the Duc de Lorraine and God knows how many others. Besides, several of our titles come from the House of Lorraine through Thérèse d'Espinoy, my great-grandmother, who was the daughter of the Damoiseau de Commercy."

Observing that Morel was listening, M. de Charlus proceeded to develop the reasons for his claim. "I have pointed out to my brother that it is not in the third part of the Gotha, but in the second, not to say the first, that the account of our family ought to be included," he said, without stopping to think that Morel did not know what the "Gotha" was. "But that is his affair, he is the head of our house, and so long as he raises no objection and allows the matter to pass, I can only shut my eyes."

"I found M. Brichot most interesting," I said to Mme Verdurin as she joined me, and I slipped Mme de Cambremer's letter into my pocket.

"He has a cultured mind and is an excellent man," she replied coldly. "Of course what he lacks is originality and taste, and he has a fearsome memory. They used to say of the 'forebears' of the people we have here this evening, the *émigrés*, that they had forgotten nothing. But they had at least the excuse," she said, borrowing one of Swann's epigrams, "that they had learned nothing. Whereas Brichot knows everything, and hurls chunks of dictionary at our heads during dinner. I'm sure there's nothing you don't know now about the names of all the towns and villages."

While Mme Verdurin was speaking, it occurred to me that I had intended to ask her something, but I could not remember what it was. I could not now say what Mme Verdurin was wearing that evening. Perhaps even then I was no more able to, for I have not an observant mind. But feeling that her dress was not unambitious, I said to her something polite and even admiring. She was like almost all women, who imagine that a compliment that is paid to them is a literal statement of the truth, a judgment impartially, irresistibly pronounced as though it referred to a work of art that has no connexion with a person. And so it was with an earnestness which made me blush for my own hypocrisy that she replied with the proud and artless question that is habitual in such circumstances: "Do you like it?"

"I'm sure you're talking about Brichot," said M. Verdurin as he came towards us. "Eh, Chantepie, Freycinet, he spared you nothing. I had my eye on you, my little Mistress!"

"Yes, I saw you, and it was all I could do not to burst out laughing."

I had been alone, as I thought of my strip of green cloth and of a scent of wood, in failing to notice that, while he enumerated these etymological derivations, Brichot had been provoking derision. And since the impressions that for me gave things their value were of the sort which other people either do not feel or unthinkingly reject as insignificant, they were entirely useless to me and had the additional drawback of making me appear stupid in the eyes of Mme Verdurin who saw that I had "swallowed" Brichot, as I had already appeared stupid to Mme de Guermantes because I had enjoyed myself at Mme d'Arpajon's. With Brichot, however, there was another reason. I was not one of the little clan. And in every clan, whether it be social, political, or literary, one contracts a perverse facility for discovering in a conversation, in an official speech, in a story, in a sonnet, everything that the plain reader would never have dreamed of finding there. How often have I found myself, after reading with a certain excitement a tale skilfully told by a fluent and slightly old-fashioned Academician, on the point of saying to Bloch or to Mme de Guermantes: "How charming this is!" when before I had opened my mouth they exclaimed, each in a different language: "If you want to be really amused, read a story by So-and-so. Human stupidity has never sunk to greater depths." Bloch's scorn derived mainly from the fact that certain effects of style, pleasing enough in themselves, were slightly faded; that of Mme de Guermantes from the notion that the story seemed to prove the direct opposite of what the author meant, for reasons of fact which she had the ingenuity to deduce but which would never have occurred to me. I was no less surprised to discover the irony that underlay the Verdurins' apparent friendliness for Brichot than to hear some days later, at Féterne, the Cambremers say to me, on hearing my enthusiastic praise of la Raspelière: "You can't be sincere, after what they've done to it." It is true that they admitted that the china was good. Like the shocking draught-curtains, it had escaped my notice. "Anyhow, when you go back to Balbec, you'll now know what Balbec means," said M. Verdurin sarcastically. It was precisely the things Brichot had taught me that interested me. As for what was called his wit, it was exactly the same as had at one time been so highly appreciated by the little clan. He talked with the same irritating fluency, but his words no longer struck a chord, having to overcome a hostile silence or disagreeable echoes; what had changed was not what he said but the acoustics of the room and the attitude of his audience. "Take care," Mme Verdurin murmured, pointing to Brichot. The latter, whose hearing remained keener than his vision, darted at the Mistress a short-sighted and philosophical glance which he hastily withdrew. If his outward eyes had deteriorated, those of his mind had on the contrary begun to take a larger view of things. He saw how little was to be expected of human affection, and had resigned himself to the fact. Undoubtedly the discovery pained him. It may happen that even the man who on one evening only, in a circle where he is usually greeted with pleasure, realises that the others have found him too frivolous or too pedantic or too clumsy or too cavalier, or whatever it may be, returns home miserable. Often it is a difference of opinion, or of approach, that has made him appear to other people absurd or old-fashioned. Often he is perfectly well aware that those others are inferior to himself. He could easily dissect the sophistries with which he has been tacitly condemned, and is tempted to pay a call, to write a letter: on second thoughts, he does nothing, and awaits the invitation for the following week. Sometimes, too, these falls from grace, instead of ending with the evening, last for months. Arising from the instability of social judgments, they increase that instability further. For the man who knows that Mme X despises him, feeling that he is respected at Mme Y's, pronounces her far superior to the other and migrates to her salon. This, however, is not the proper place to describe those men, superior to the life of society but lacking the capacity to realise themselves outside it, glad to be invited, embittered at being underrated, discovering annually the defects of the hostess to whom they have been offering incense and the genius of the other whom they have never properly appreciated, ready to return to the old love when they have experienced the drawbacks to be found equally in the new, and when they have begun to forget those of the old. We may judge by such temporary falls from grace of the chagrin that Brichot felt at this one, which he knew to be final. He was not unaware that Mme Verdurin sometimes laughed at him publicly, even at his infirmities, and knowing how little was to be expected of human affection, he continued nevertheless to regard the Mistress as his best friend. But, from the blush that crept over the scholar's face, Mme Verdurin realised that he had heard her, and made up her mind to be kind to him for the rest of the evening. I could not help remarking to her that she had not been very kind to Saniette. "What! Not kind to him! Why, he adores us, you've no idea what we are to him. My husband is sometimes a little irritated by his stupidity, and you must admit with some reason, but when that happens why doesn't he hit back instead of cringing like a whipped dog? It's so unmanly. I can't bear it. That doesn't mean that I don't always try to calm my husband, because if he went too far, all that would happen would be that Saniette would stay away; and I don't want that because I may tell you that he hasn't a penny in the world, he needs his dinners. But after all, if he takes offence, he can stay away, it's nothing to do with me. When you rely on other people you should try not to be such an idiot."

"The Duchy of Aumale was in our family for years before passing to the House of France," M. de Charlus was explaining to M. de Cambremer in front of a flabbergasted Morel, for whose benefit the whole dissertation was intended, if it was not actually addressed to him. "We took precedence over all foreign

princes; I could give you a hundred examples. The Princesse de
Croy having attempted, at the burial of Monsieur, to fall on her
knees after my great-great-grandmother, the latter reminded
her sharply that she had no right to the hassock, made the
officer on duty remove it, and reported the matter to the King,
who ordered Mme de Croy to call upon Mme de Guermantes
and offer her apologies. The Duc de Bourgogne having come
to us with ushers with raised batons, we obtained the King's
authority to have them lowered. I know it is not good form to
speak of the merits of one's own family. But it is well known
that our people were always to the fore in the hour of danger.
Our battle-cry, after we abandoned that of the Dukes of
Brabant, was *Passavant!* So that it is not unjust on the whole
that this right to be everywhere the first, which we had
established for so many centuries in war, should afterwards
have been granted to us at Court. And, egad, it was always
acknowledged there. I may give you a further instance, that of
the Princess of Baden. As she had so far forgotten herself as to
attempt to challenge the precedence of that same Duchesse de
Guermantes of whom I was speaking just now, and had
attempted to go in first to the King's presence by taking advantage of a momentary hesitation which my ancestress may perhaps have shown (although there was no reason for it), the
King called out: 'Come in, cousin, come in; Mme de Baden
knows very well what her duty is to you.' And it was as
Duchesse de Guermantes that she held this rank, albeit she was
of no mean family herself, since she was through her mother
niece to the Queen of Poland, the Queen of Hungary, the
Elector Palatine, the Prince of Savoy-Carignano and the Elector
of Hanover, afterwards King of England."

"*Maecenas atavis edite regibus!*" said Brichot, addressing M. de
Charlus, who acknowledged the compliment with a slight nod.

"What did you say?" Mme Verdurin asked Brichot, anxious
to make amends to him for her earlier words.

"I was referring, Heaven forgive me, to a dandy who was the
flower of the nobility" (Mme Verdurin winced) "about the
time of Augustus" (Mme Verdurin, reassured by the remoteness
in time of this nobility, assumed a more serene expression), "to
a friend of Virgil and Horace who carried their sycophancy to

the extent of proclaiming to his face his more than aristocratic, his royal descent. In a word, I was referring to Maecenas, a bookworm who was the friend of Horace, Virgil, Augustus. I am sure that M. de Charlus knows all about Maecenas."

With a gracious sidelong glance at Mme Verdurin, because he had heard her make a rendezvous with Morel for the day after next and was afraid that she might not invite him also, "I should say," said M. de Charlus, "that Maecenas was more or less the Verdurin of antiquity."

Mme Verdurin could not altogether suppress a smile of self-satisfaction. She went over to Morel. "He's nice, your father's friend," she said to him. "One can see that he's an educated man, and well bred. He will get on well in our little nucleus. Where does he live in Paris?"

Morel preserved a haughty silence and merely proposed a game of cards. Mme Verdurin demanded a little violin music first. To the general astonishment, M. de Charlus, who never spoke of his own considerable gifts, accompanied, in the purest style, the closing passage (uneasy, tormented, Schumannesque, but, for all that, earlier than Franck's sonata) of the sonata for piano and violin by Fauré. I felt that he would provide Morel, marvellously endowed as to tone and virtuosity, with just those qualities that he lacked, culture and style. But I thought with curiosity of this combination in a single person of a physical blemish and a spiritual gift. M. de Charlus was not very different from his brother, the Duc de Guermantes. Indeed, a moment ago (though this was rare), he had spoken as bad a French as his brother. He having reproached me (doubtless in order that I might speak in glowing terms of Morel to Mme Verdurin) with never coming to see him, and I having pleaded discretion, he had replied: "But, since it is I who ask, there's no one but me who could possibly take huff." This might have been said by the Duc de Guermantes. M. de Charlus was only a Guermantes when all was said. But it had sufficed that nature should have upset the balance of his nervous system enough to make him prefer, to the woman that his brother the Duke would have chosen, one of Virgil's shepherds or Plato's disciples, and at once qualities unknown to the Duc de Guermantes and often combined with this lack of equilibrium had made M. de

Charlus an exquisite pianist, an amateur painter who was not devoid of taste, and an eloquent talker. Who would ever have detected that the rapid, nervous, charming style with which M. de Charlus played the Schumannesque passage of Fauré's sonata had its equivalent—one dare not say its cause—in elements entirely physical, in the Baron's nervous weaknesses? We shall explain later on what we mean by nervous weaknesses, and why it is that a Greek of the time of Socrates, a Roman of the time of Augustus, might be what we know them to have been and yet remain absolutely normal, not men-women such as we see around us to-day. Just as he had real artistic aptitudes which had never come to fruition, so M. de Charlus, far more than the Duke, had loved their mother and loved his own wife, and indeed, years afterwards, if anyone spoke of them to him, would shed tears, but superficial tears, like the perspiration of an over-stout man, whose forehead will glisten with sweat at the slightest exertion. With this difference, that to the latter one says: "How hot you are," whereas one pretends not to notice other people's tears. One, that is to say, society; for simple people are as distressed by the sight of tears as if a sob were more serious than a haemorrhage. Thanks to the habit of lying, his sorrow after the death of his wife did not debar M. de Charlus from a life which was not in conformity with it. Indeed later on, he was ignominious enough to let it be known that, during the funeral ceremony, he had found an opportunity of asking the acolyte for his name and address. And it may have been true.

When the piece came to an end, I ventured to ask for some Franck, which appeared to cause Mme de Cambremer such acute pain that I did not insist. "You can't admire that sort of thing," she said to me. Instead she asked for Debussy's *Fêtes*, which made her exclaim: "Ah! how sublime!" from the first note. But Morel discovered that he could remember only the opening bars, and in a spirit of mischief, without any intention to deceive, began a March by Meyerbeer. Unfortunately, as he left little interval and made no announcement, everybody supposed that he was still playing Debussy, and continued to exclaim "Sublime!" Morel, by revealing that the composer was that not of *Pelléas* but of *Robert le Diable*, created

a certain chill. Mme de Cambremer had scarcely time to feel it
for herself, for she had just discovered a volume of Scarlatti
and had flung herself upon it with an hysterical shriek. "Oh!
play this, look, this piece, it's divine," she cried. And yet, of
this composer long despised but recently promoted to the
highest honours, what she had selected in her feverish impatience was one of those infernal pieces which have so often
kept us from sleeping, while a merciless pupil repeats them
ad infinitum on the next floor. But Morel had had enough
music, and as he insisted upon cards, M. de Charlus, to be able
to join in, proposed a game of whist.

"He was telling the Boss just now that he's a prince," said
Ski to Mme Verdurin, "but it's not true, they're quite a humble
family of architects."

"I want to know what it was you were saying about
Maecenas. It interests me, don't you know!" Mme Verdurin
repeated to Brichot, with an affability that carried him off his
feet. And so, in order to shine in the Mistress's eyes, and
possibly in mine: "Why, to tell you the truth, Madame,
Maecenas interests me chiefly because he is the earliest apostle
of note of that oriental god who numbers more followers in
France today than Brahma, than Christ himself, the all-powerful
God Ubedamd." Mme Verdurin was no longer content, on
these occasions, with burying her head in her hands. She
would descend with the suddenness of the insects called
ephemerids upon Princess Sherbatoff; were the latter within
reach the Mistress would cling to her shoulder, dig her nails
into it, and hide her face against it for a few moments like a
child playing hide and seek. Concealed by this protecting
screen, she was understood to be laughing until she cried, but
could as well have been thinking of nothing at all as the people
who, while saying a longish prayer, take the wise precaution of
burying their faces in their hands. Mme Verdurin imitated
them when she listened to Beethoven quartets, in order at the
same time to show that she regarded them as a prayer and not
to let it be seen that she was asleep. "I speak quite seriously,
Madame," said Brichot. "Too numerous, I consider, to-day
are the persons who spend their time gazing at their navels as
though they were the hub of the universe. As a matter of

doctrine, I have no objection to offer to any Nirvana which
will dissolve us in the great Whole (which, like Munich and
Oxford, is considerably nearer to Paris than Asnières or
Bois-Colombes), but it is unworthy either of a true Frenchman,
or of a true European even, when the Japanese are possibly at
the gates of our Byzantium, that socialised anti-militarists
should be gravely discussing the cardinal virtues of free verse."
Mme Verdurin felt that she might dispense with the Princess's
mangled shoulder, and allowed her face to become once more
visible, not without pretending to wipe her eyes and gasping
two or three times for breath. But Brichot was determined that
I should have my share in the entertainment, and having
learned, from those oral examinations which he conducted like
nobody else, that the best way to flatter the young is to lecture
them, to make them feel important, to make them regard you
as a reactionary: "I have no wish to blaspheme against the Gods
of Youth," he said, with that furtive glance at myself which an
orator turns upon a member of his audience when he mentions
him by name, "I have no wish to be damned as a heretic and
renegade in the Mallarméan chapel in which our new friend,
like all the young men of his age, must have served the esoteric
mass, at least as an acolyte, and have shown himself deliquescent or Rosicrucian. But really, we have seen more than
enough of these intellectuals worshipping art with a capital A,
who, when they can no longer intoxicate themselves upon
Zola, inject themselves with Verlaine. Having become
etheromaniacs out of Baudelairean devotion, they would no
longer be capable of the virile effort which the country may
one day or another demand of them, anaesthetised as they are
by the great literary neurosis in the heated, enervating atmosphere, heavy with unwholesome vapours, of a symbolism of
the opium-den."

Incapable of feigning the slightest admiration for Brichot's
inept and motley tirade, I turned to Ski and assured him that he
was entirely mistaken as to the family to which M. de Charlus
belonged; he replied that he was certain of his facts, and added
that I myself had said that his real name was Gandin, Le
Gandin. "I told you," was my answer, "that Mme de Cambremer was the sister of an engineer called M. Legrandin. I

never said a word to you about M. de Charlus. There is about
as much connexion between him and Mme de Cambremer
as between the Great Condé and Racine."

"Ah! I thought there was," said Ski lightly, with no more
apology for his mistake than he had made a few hours earlier
for the mistake that had nearly made his party miss the
train.

"Do you intend to remain long on this coast?" Mme
Verdurin asked M. de Charlus, in whom she foresaw an
addition to the faithful and trembled lest he should be returning
too soon to Paris.

"Goodness me, one never knows," replied M. de Charlus in
a nasal drawl. "I should like to stay until the end of September."

"You are quite right," said Mme Verdurin; "that's when we
get splendid storms at sea."

"To tell you the truth, that is not what would influence me.
I have for some time past unduly neglected the Archangel
Michael, my patron saint, and I should like to make amends to
him by staying for his feast, on the 29th of September, at the
Abbey on the Mount."

"You take an interest in all that sort of thing?" asked Mme
Verdurin, who might perhaps have succeeded in hushing the
voice of her outraged anti-clericalism had she not been afraid
that so long an expedition might make the violinist and the
Baron "defect" for forty-eight hours.

"You are perhaps afflicted with intermittent deafness," M.
de Charlus replied insolently. "I have told you that Saint
Michael is one of my glorious patrons." Then, smiling with a
benevolent ecstasy, his eyes gazing into the distance, his voice
reinforced by an exaltation which seemed now to be not
merely aesthetic but religious: "It is so beautiful at the Offertory
when Michael stands erect by the altar, in a white robe,
swinging a golden censer heaped so high with perfumes that
the fragrance of them mounts up to God."

"We might go there in a party," suggested Mme Verdurin,
notwithstanding her horror of the clergy.

"At that moment, when the Offertory begins," went on M.
de Charlus who, for other reasons but in the same manner as
good speakers in Parliament, never replied to an interruption

and would pretend not to have heard it, "it would be wonderful to see our young friend Palestrinising and even performing an aria by Bach. The worthy Abbot, too, would be
wild with joy, and it is the greatest homage, at least the greatest
public homage, that I can pay to my patron saint. What an
edification for the faithful! We must mention it presently to
the young Angelico of music, himself a warrior like Saint
Michael."

Saniette, summoned to make a fourth, declared that he did
not know how to play whist. And Cottard, seeing that there
was not much time left before the train, embarked at once on a
game of écarté with Morel. M. Verdurin was furious, and bore
down with a terrible expression upon Saniette: "Is there
nothing you know how to play?" he shouted, furious at being
deprived of the opportunity for a game of whist, and delighted
to have found one for insulting the ex-archivist. The latter,
terror-stricken, did his best to look clever: "Yes, I can play the
piano," he said. Cottard and Morel were seated face to face.
"Your deal," said Cottard. "Suppose we go nearer to the card-
table," M. de Charlus, worried by the sight of Morel in
Cottard's company, suggested to M. de Cambremer. "It's quite
as interesting as those questions of etiquette which in these days
have ceased to count for very much. The only kings that we have
left, in France at least, are the kings in packs of cards, who seem
to me to be positively swarming in the hand of our young
virtuoso," he added a moment later, from an admiration for
Morel which extended to his way of playing cards, to flatter
him also, and finally to account for his suddenly leaning over
the young violinist's shoulder. "I-ee trrump," said Cottard,
putting on a vile foreign accent; his children would burst out
laughing, like his students and the house surgeon, whenever
the Master, even by the bedside of a serious case, uttered one
of his hackneyed witticisms with the impassive expression
of an epileptic. "I don't know what to play," said Morel,
seeking advice from M. de Cambremer. "Just as you please,
you're bound to lose, whatever you play, it's all the same (*c'est
égal*)." "Galli-Marié?" said the Doctor with a benign and knowing glance at M. de Cambremer. "She was what we call a
true diva, she was a dream, a Carmen such as we shall never see

again. She was wedded to the part. I used to enjoy too listening to Engalli." "Marié?"

The Marquis rose, and with that contemptuous vulgarity of well-born people who do not realise that they are insulting their host by appearing uncertain whether they ought to associate with his guests, and plead English habits as an excuse for a disdainful expression, asked: "Who is that gentleman playing cards? What does he do for a living? What does he *sell*? I rather like to know who I'm with, so as not to make friends with any Tom, Dick or Harry. But I didn't catch his name when you did me the honour of introducing me to him." If M. Verdurin, on the strength of these last words, had indeed introduced M. de Cambremer *to* his fellow-guests, the other would have been greatly annoyed. But, knowing that it was the opposite procedure that had been observed, he thought it gracious to assume a genial and modest air, without risk to himself. The pride that M. Verdurin took in his intimacy with Cottard had gone on increasing ever since the Doctor had become an eminent professor. But it no longer found expression in the same ingenuous form as of old. Then, when Cottard was scarcely known to the public, if you spoke to M. Verdurin of his wife's facial neuralgia, "There is nothing to be done," he would say, with the naïve complacency of people who assume that anyone whom they know must be famous, and that everybody knows the name of their daughter's singing-teacher. "If she had an ordinary doctor, one might look for a second opinion, but when that doctor is called Cottard" (a name which he pronounced as though it were Bouchard or Charcot) "one simply has to bow to the inevitable." Adopting a reverse procedure, knowing that M. de Cambremer must certainly have heard of the famous Professor Cottard, M. Verdurin assumed an artless air. "He's our family doctor, a worthy soul whom we adore and who would bend over backwards for our sakes; he's not a doctor, he's a friend. I don't suppose you have ever heard of him or that his name would convey anything to you, but in any case to us it's the name of a very good man, of a very dear friend, Cottard." This name, murmured in a modest tone, surprised M. de Cambremer who supposed that his host was referring to someone else. "Cottard? You don't mean Professor

Cottard?" At that moment one heard the voice of the said Professor who, at an awkward point in the game, was saying as he looked at his cards: "This is where Greek meets Greek." "Why, yes, to be sure, he is a professor," said M. Verdurin. "What! Professor Cottard! You're sure you're not mistaken! You're certain it's the same man! The one who lives in the Rue du Bac!" "Yes, his address is 43, Rue du Bac. You know him?" "But everybody knows Professor Cottard. He's a leading light. It's as though you asked me if I knew Bouffe de Saint-Blaise or Courtois-Suffit. I could see when I heard him speak that he was not an ordinary person. That's why I took the liberty of asking you." "Well then, what shall I play, trumps?" asked Cottard. Then abruptly, with a vulgarity which would have been irritating even in heroic circumstances, as when a soldier uses a coarse expression to convey his contempt for death, but became doubly stupid in the safe pastime of a game of cards, Cottard, deciding to play a trump, assumed a sombre, death-defying air and flung down his card as though it were his life, with the exclamation: "There it is, and be damned to it!" It was not the right card to play, but he had a consolation. In a deep armchair in the middle of the room, Mme Cottard, yielding to the effect, which she always found irresistible, of a good dinner, had succumbed after vain efforts to the vast if gentle slumbers that were overpowering her. In vain did she sit up now and then, and smile, either in self-mockery or from fear of leaving unanswered some polite remark that might have been addressed to her, she sank back, in spite of herself, into the clutches of the implacable and delicious malady. More than the noise, what awakened her thus, for an instant only, was the glance (which, in her wifely affection, she could see even when her eyes were shut, and anticipated, for the same scene occurred every evening and haunted her dreams like the thought of the hour at which one will have to rise), the glance with which the Professor drew the attention of those present to his wife's slumbers. To begin with, he merely looked at her and smiled, for if as a doctor he disapproved of this habit of falling asleep after dinner (or at least gave this scientific reason for getting angry later on, though it is not certain whether it was a determining reason, so many and diverse were the views that he held on the subject), as an all-powerful and teasing husband he was delighted to be able to make fun of his wife, to half-waken her only at first, so that she might fall asleep again and he have the pleasure of waking her anew.

By this time, Mme Cottard was sound asleep. "Now then, Léontine, you're snoring," the Professor called to her. "I'm listening to Mme Swann, my dear," Mme Cottard replied faintly, and dropped back into her lethargy. "It's absolute madness," exclaimed Cottard, "she'll be telling us presently that she wasn't asleep. She's like the patients who come to a consultation and insist that they never sleep at all." "They imagine it, perhaps," said M. de Cambremer with a laugh. But the doctor enjoyed contradicting no less than teasing, and would on no account allow a layman to talk medicine to him. "One doesn't imagine that one can't sleep," he promulgated in a dogmatic tone. "Ah!" replied the Marquis with a respectful bow, such as Cottard at one time would have made. "It's easy to see," Cottard went on, "that you've never administered, as I have, as much as two grains of trional without succeeding in provoking somnolence." "Quite so, quite so," replied the Marquis, laughing with a superior air, "I've never taken trional, or any of those drugs which soon cease to have any effect but ruin your stomach. When a man has been out shooting all night, like me, in the forest of Chantepie, I can assure you he doesn't need any trional to make him sleep." "It's only fools who say that," replied the Professor. "Trional frequently has a remarkable effect on the tonicity of the nerves. You mention trional, have you any idea what it is?" "Well . . . I've heard people say that it's a drug to make one sleep." "You're not answering my question," replied the Professor, who, thrice weekly, at the Faculty, sat on the board of examiners. "I'm not asking you whether it makes you sleep or not, but what it is. Can you tell me what percentage it contains of amyl and ethyl?" "No," replied M. de Cambremer, abashed. "I prefer a good glass of old brandy or even 345 Port." "Which are ten times as toxic," the Professor interrupted. "As for trional," M. de Cambremer ventured, "my wife goes in for all that sort of thing, you'd better talk to her about it." "She probably knows as much about it as you do. In any case, if your wife takes trional to make her sleep, you can see that mine has no need of it. Come along, Léontine, wake up, you'll get stiff. Did you ever see me fall asleep after dinner? What will you be like when you're sixty, if you fall asleep now like an old woman? You'll get fat, you're arresting your circulation. She doesn't even hear what I'm saying." "They're bad for one's health, these little naps after dinner, aren't they, Doctor?" said M. de Cambremer, seeking to rehabilitate himself with Cottard. "After a heavy meal one ought to take exercise." "Stuff and nonsense!" replied the Doctor. "Identical quantities of food have been taken from the stomach of a dog that has lain quiet and from the stomach of a dog that has been running about, and it's in the former that digestion has been found to be more advanced." "Then it's sleep that interrupts the digestion." "That depends whether you mean oesophagic digestion, stomachic digestion or intestinal digestion. It's pointless giving you explanations which you wouldn't understand since you've never studied medicine. Now then, Léontine, quick march, it's time we were going." This was not true, for the Doctor was merely going to continue his game, but he hoped thus to cut short in a more drastic fashion the slumbers of the deaf mute to whom he had been addressing without a word of response the most learned exhortations. Either because a determination to remain awake survived in Mme Cottard, even in her sleep, or because the armchair offered no support to her head, it was jerked mechanically from left to right and up and down in the empty air, like a lifeless object, and Mme Cottard, with her nodding poll, appeared now to be listening to music, now to be in her death-throes. Where her husband's increasingly vehement admonitions failed of their effect, her sense of her own stupidity proved successful: "My bath is nice and hot," she murmured. "But the feathers on the dictionary . . ." she exclaimed, sitting up. "Oh, good gracious, what a fool I am! Whatever have I been saying? I was thinking about my hat, and I'm sure I said something silly. In another minute I would have dozed off. It's that wretched fire." Everybody laughed, for there was no fire in the room.

"You're making fun of me," said Mme Cottard, herself laughing, and raising her hand to her forehead with the light touch of a hypnotist and the deftness of a woman putting her hair straight, to erase the last traces of sleep, "I must offer my humble apologies to dear Mme Verdurin and get the truth from her." But her smile at once grew mournful, for the Professor, who knew that his wife sought to please him and trembled lest she fail to do so, had shouted at her: "Look at yourself in the mirror. You're as red as if you had an eruption of acne. You look just like an old peasant."

"You know, he's charming," said Mme Verdurin, "he has such a delightfully sardonic good-nature. And then, he snatched my husband from the jaws of death when the whole medical profession had given him up. He spent three nights by his bedside, without ever lying down. And so for me, you know," she went on in a grave and almost menacing tone, raising her hand to the twin spheres, shrouded in white tresses, of her musical temples, and as though we had threatened to assault the Doctor, "Cottard is sacred! He could ask me for anything in the world! As it is, I don't call him Doctor Cottard, I call him Doctor God! And even in saying that I'm slandering him, for this God does everything in his power to remedy some of the disasters for which the other is responsible."

"Play a trump," M. de Charlus said to Morel with a delighted air.

"A trump, here goes," said the violinist.

"You ought to have declared your king first," said M. de Charlus, "you're not paying attention to the game, but how well you play!"

"I have the king," said Morel.

"He's a fine man," replied the Professor.

"What's that thing up there with the sticks?" asked Mme Verdurin, drawing M. de Cambremer's attention to a superb escutcheon carved over the mantelpiece. "Are they your *arms*?" she added with sarcastic scorn.

"No, they're not ours," replied M. de Cambremer. "We bear *barry of five, embattled counterembattled or and gules, as many trefoils countercharged*. No, those are the arms of the Arrachepels, who were not of our stock, but from whom we inherited the house, and nobody of our line has ever made any changes here." ("That's one in the eye for her," muttered Mme de

Cambremer.) "The Arrachepels (formerly Pelvilains, we are told) bore *or five piles couped in base gules*. When they allied themselves with the Féterne family, their blazon changed, but remained *cantoned within twenty cross crosslets fitchee in base or, a dexter canton ermine*. My great-grandmother was a d'Arrachepel or de Rachepel, whichever you like, for both forms are found in the old charters," continued M. de Cambremer, blushing deeply, for only then did the idea for which his wife had given him credit occur to him, and he was afraid that Mme Verdurin might have applied to herself words which had in no way been aimed at her. "History relates that in the eleventh century the first Arrachepel, Macé, known as Pelvilain, showed a special aptitude, in siege warfare, in tearing up piles. Whence the nickname Arrachepel under which he was ennobled, and the piles which you see persisting through the centuries in their arms. These are the piles which, to render fortifications more impregnable, used to be driven, plugged, if you will pardon the expression, into the ground in front of them, and fastened together laterally. They are what you quite rightly called sticks, though they had nothing to do with the floating sticks of our good La Fontaine. For they were supposed to render a stronghold impregnable. Of course, with our modern artillery, they make one smile. But you must bear in mind that I'm speaking of the eleventh century."

"Yes, it's not exactly up-to-date," said Mme Verdurin, "but the little campanile has character."

"You have," said Cottard, "the luck of a fiddlededee," a word which he regularly repeated to avoid using Molière's.[48] "Do you know why the king of diamonds was invalided out of the army?"

"I shouldn't mind being in his shoes," said Morel, who was bored with military service.

"Oh! how unpatriotic!" exclaimed M. de Charlus, who could not refrain from pinching the violinist's ear.

"You don't know why the king of diamonds was invalided out of the army?" Cottard pursued, determined to make his joke, "it's because he has only one eye."

"You're up against it, Doctor," said M. de Cambremer, to show Cottard that he knew who he was.

"This young man is astonishing," M. de Charlus interrupted naïvely, pointing to Morel. "He plays like a god."

This observation did not find favour with the Doctor, who replied: "Wait and see. He who laughs last laughs longest."

"Queen, ace," Morel announced triumphantly, for fortune was favouring him.

The Doctor bowed his head as though powerless to deny this good fortune, and admitted, spellbound: "That's beautiful."

"We're so pleased to have met M. de Charlus," said Mme de Cambremer to Mme Verdurin.

"Had you never met him before? He's rather nice, most unusual, very much *of a period*" (she would have found it difficult to say which), replied Mme Verdurin with the complacent smile of a connoisseur, a judge and a hostess.

Mme de Cambremer asked me if I was coming to Féterne with Saint-Loup. I could not suppress a cry of admiration when I saw the moon hanging like an orange lantern beneath the vault of oaks that led away from the house. "That's nothing," said Mme Verdurin. "Presently, when the moon has risen higher and the valley is lit up, it will be a thousand times more beautiful. That's something you haven't got at Féterne!" she added scornfully to Mme de Cambremer, who did not know how to answer, not wishing to disparage her property, especially in front of the tenants.

"Are you staying much longer in the neighbourhood, Madame?" M. de Cambremer asked Mme Cottard, a speech that might be interpreted as a vague intention to invite her, but which dispensed him for the moment from making any more precise commitment. "Oh, certainly, Monsieur, I regard this annual exodus as most important for the children. Say what you like, they need air. The doctors wanted to send me to Vichy; but it's too stuffy there, and I can look after my stomach when those big boys of mine have grown a little bigger. Besides, the Professor, with all the examining he has to do, has always got his shoulder to the wheel, and the heat tires him dreadfully. I feel that a man needs a thorough rest after he has been on the go all the year like that. Whatever happens we shall stay another month at least."

"Ah! in that case we shall meet again."

"In any case I shall be obliged to stay here as my husband has to go on a visit to Savoy, and won't be finally settled here for another fortnight."

"I like the view of the valley even more than the sea view," Mme Verdurin went on. "You're going to have a splendid night for your journey."

"We ought really to find out whether the carriages are ready, if you are absolutely determined to go back to Balbec to-night," M. Verdurin said to me, "for I see no necessity for it myself. We could drive you over to-morrow morning. It's certain to be fine. The roads are excellent."

I said that it was impossible. "But in any case it isn't time to go yet," the Mistress protested. "Leave them alone, they have heaps of time. A lot of good it will do them to arrive at the station with an hour to wait. They're far better off here. And you, my young Mozart," she said to Morel, not venturing to address M. de Charlus directly, "won't you stay the night? We have some nice rooms overlooking the sea."

"No, he can't," M. de Charlus replied on behalf of the absorbed card-player who had not heard. "He has a pass until midnight only. He must go back to bed like a good little boy, obedient and well-behaved," he added in a smug, affected, insistent voice, as though he found a sadistic pleasure in employing this chaste comparison and also in letting his voice dwell, in passing, upon something that concerned Morel, in touching him, if not with his hand, with words that seemed to be tactile.

From the sermon that Brichot had addressed to me, M. de Cambremer had concluded that I was a Dreyfusard. As he himself was as anti-Dreyfusard as possible, out of courtesy to a foe he began to sing me the praises of a Jewish colonel who had always been very decent to a cousin of the Chevregnys and had secured for him the promotion he deserved. "And my cousin's opinions were the exact opposite," said M. de Cambremer. He omitted to mention what those opinions were, but I sensed that they were as antiquated and misshapen as his own face, opinions which a few families in certain small towns must long have entertained. "Well, you know, I call that really fine!" was M. de Cambremer's conclusion. It is true that he was hardly employing the word "fine" in the aesthetic sense in which his wife or his mother would have applied it to different works of art. M. de Cambremer often made use of this term, when for instance he was congratulating a delicate person who had put on a little weight. "What, you've gained half a stone in two months? I say, that's really fine!"

Refreshments were set out on a table. Mme Verdurin invited the gentlemen to go and choose whatever drink they preferred. M. de Charlus went and drank his glass and at once returned to a seat by the card-table from which he did not stir. Mme Verdurin asked him: "Did you have some of my orangeade?" Whereupon M. de Charlus, with a gracious smile, in a crystalline tone which he rarely adopted, and with endless simperings and wrigglings of the hips, replied: "No, I preferred its neighbour, which is strawberry-juice, I think. It's delicious." It is curious that a certain category of secret impulses has as an external consequence a way of speaking or gesticulating which reveals them. If a man believes or disbelieves in the Immaculate Conception, or in the innocence of Dreyfus, or in a plurality of worlds, and wishes to keep his opinion to himself, you will find nothing in his voice or in his gait that will betray his thoughts. But on hearing M. de Charlus say, in that shrill voice and with that smile and those gestures, "No, I preferred its neighbour, the strawberry-juice," one could say: "Ah, he likes the stronger sex," with the same certainty as enables a judge to sentence a criminal who has not confessed, or a doctor a patient suffering from general paralysis who himself is perhaps unaware of his malady but has made some mistake in pronunciation from which it can be deduced that he will be dead in three years. Perhaps the people who deduce, from a man's way of saying: "No, I preferred its neighbour, the strawberry-juice," a love of the kind called unnatural, have no need of any such scientific knowledge. But that is because here there is a more direct relation between the revealing sign and the secret. Without saying so to oneself in so many words, one feels that it is a gentle, smiling lady who is answering and who appears affected because she is pretending to be a man and one is not accustomed to seeing men put on such airs. And it is perhaps more gracious to think that a certain number of angelic women have long been included by mistake in the masculine sex where, feeling exiled, ineffectually flapping their wings towards men in whom they inspire a physical repulsion, they know how to arrange a drawing-room, to compose "interiors." M. de Charlus was not in the least perturbed that Mme Verdurin should be standing, and remained ensconced in his armchair so as to be nearer to Morel. "Don't you think it criminal," said Mme Verdurin to the Baron, "that that creature who might be enchanting us with his violin should be sitting there at a card-table. When one can play the violin like that!" "He plays cards well, he does everything well, he's so intelligent," said M. de Charlus, keeping his eye on the game, so as to be able to advise Morel. This was not his only reason, however, for not rising from his chair for Mme Verdurin. With the singular amalgam that he had made of his social conceptions at once as a great nobleman and as an art-lover, instead of being courteous in the same way as a man of his world would have been, he invented as it were tableaux-vivants for himself after Saint-Simon; and at that moment he was amusing himself by impersonating the Maréchal d'Huxelles, who interested him from other aspects also, and of whom it is said that he was so arrogant as to remain seated, with an air of indolence, before all the most distinguished persons at Court. "By the way, Charlus," said Mme Verdurin, who was beginning to grow familiar, "you don't know of any penniless old nobleman in your Faubourg who would come to me as porter?" "Why, yes . . . why, yes," replied M. de Charlus with a genial smile, "but I don't advise it." "Why not?" "I should be afraid for your sake that the more elegant visitors would go no further than the lodge." This was the first skirmish between them. Mme Verdurin barely noticed it. There were to be others, alas, in Paris. M. de Charlus remained glued to his chair. He could not, moreover, restrain a faint smile on seeing how his favourite maxims as to aristocratic prestige and bourgeois cowardice were confirmed by the so easily won submission of Mme Verdurin. The Mistress appeared not at all surprised by the Baron's posture, and if she left him it was only because she had been perturbed by seeing me taken up by M. de Cambremer. But first of all, she wished to clear up the mystery of M. de Charlus's relations with Com-

tesse Molé. "You told me that you knew Mme de Molé. Does
that mean you go there?" she asked, giving to the words "go
there" the sense of being received there, of having received
permission from the lady to go and call on her. M. de Charlus
replied with an inflexion of disdain, an affectation of precision
and in a sing-song tone: "Yes, sometimes." This "sometimes"
inspired doubts in Mme Verdurin, who asked: "Have you ever
met the Duc de Guermantes there?" "Ah! that I don't remember." "Oh!" said Mme Verdurin, "you don't know the Duc de
Guermantes?" "And how could I not know him?" replied
M. de Charlus, his lips curving in a smile. This smile was
ironical; but as the Baron was afraid of letting a gold tooth be
seen, he checked it with a reverse movement of his lips, so that
the resulting sinuosity was that of a smile of benevolence.
"Why do you say: 'How could I not know him?' " "Because
he is my brother," said M. de Charlus carelessly, leaving Mme
Verdurin plunged in stupefaction and uncertain whether her
guest was making fun of her, was a natural son, or a son by
another marriage. The idea that the brother of the Duc de
Guermantes might be called Baron de Charlus never entered
her head. She bore down upon me. "I heard M. de Cambremer
invite you to dinner just now. It has nothing to do with me, you
understand. But for your own sake, I very much hope you
won't go. For one thing, the place is infested with bores. Oh, if
you like dining with provincial counts and marquises whom
nobody knows, you'll have all you could wish." "I think I shall
be obliged to go there once or twice. I'm not altogether free,
however, for I have a young cousin whom I can't leave by
herself" (I felt that this fictitious kinship made it easier for me
to take Albertine about), "but in the case of the Cambremers, as
I've already introduced her to them. . . ." "You shall do just as
you please. One thing I can tell you: it's extremely unhealthy;
when you've caught pneumonia, or a nice little chronic rheumatism, what good will that do you?" "But isn't the place itself
very pretty?" "Mmmmyesss. . . . If you like. Frankly, I must
confess that I'd far sooner have the view from here over this
valley. In any case, I wouldn't have taken the other house if
they'd paid us because the sea air is fatal to M. Verdurin. If
your cousin is at all delicate. . . . But you yourself are delicate, I

believe . . . you have fits of breathlessness. Very well! You shall see. Go there once, and you won't sleep for a week after it; but it's not my business." And regardless of the inconsistency with what had gone before, she went on: "If it would amuse you to see the house, which is not bad, pretty is too strong a word, still it's amusing with its old moat and its old drawbridge, as I shall have to sacrifice myself and dine there once, very well, come that day, I shall try to bring all my little circle, then it will be quite nice. The day after to-morrow we're going to Harambouville in the carriage. It's a magnificent drive, and the cider is delicious. Come with us. You, Brichot, you shall come too. And you too, Ski. It will make a party which, as a matter of fact, my husband must have arranged already. I don't know whom all he has invited. Monsieur de Charlus, are you one of them?" The Baron, who had not heard the whole speech and did not know that she was talking of an excursion to Harambouville, gave a start. "A strange question," he murmured in a sardonic tone that nettled Mme Verdurin. "Anyhow," she said to me, "before you dine with the Cambremers, why not bring your cousin here? Does she like conversation, and intelligent people? Is she agreeable? Yes, very well then. Bring her with you. The Cambremers aren't the only people in the world. I can understand their being glad to invite her, they must find it difficult to get anyone. Here she will have plenty of fresh air, and lots of clever men. In any case, I'm counting on you not to fail me next Wednesday. I heard you were having a tea-party at Rivebelle with your cousin, and M. de Charlus, and I forget who else. You should arrange to bring the whole lot on here, it would be nice if you all came in a body. It's the easiest thing in the world to get here, and the roads are charming; if you like I can send down for you. I can't imagine what you find attractive in Rivebelle, it's infested with foreign riffraff. Perhaps you're thinking of the reputation of the local pancakes. My cook makes them far better. I'll give you some Norman pancakes, the real article, and shortbread; just let me show you. Ah! if you want the sort of filth they give you at Rivebelle, you won't get it from me, I don't poison my guests, Monsieur, and even if I wished to, my cook would refuse to make such unspeakable muck and would give in his notice. Those pancakes you get down there, you can't tell what they're made of. I knew a poor girl who got peritonitis from them, which carried her off in three days. She was only seventeen. It was sad for her poor mother," added Mme Verdurin with a mournful air beneath the spheres of her temples charged with experience and suffering. "However, go and have tea at Rivebelle if you enjoy being fleeced and flinging money out of the window. But one thing I beg of you—it's a confidential mission I'm entrusting you with—on the stroke of six bring all your party here, don't allow them to go straggling away by themselves. You can bring whom you please. I wouldn't say that to everybody. But I'm sure your friends are nice, I can see at once that we understand one another. Apart from the little nucleus, there are some very agreeable people coming next Wednesday, as it happens. You don't know little Mme de Longpont? She's charming, and so witty, not in the least snobbish, you'll find you'll like her immensely. And she's going to bring a whole troupe of friends too," Mme Verdurin added to show me that this was the right thing to do and encourage me by the other's example. "We shall see which of you has most influence and brings most people, Barbe de Longpont or you. And then I believe somebody's going to bring Bergotte," she added vaguely, this attendance of a celebrity being rendered far from likely by a paragraph which had appeared in the papers that morning to the effect that the great writer's health was causing grave anxiety. "Anyhow, you'll see that it will be one of my most successful Wednesdays. I don't want to have any boring women. You mustn't judge by this evening, which has been a complete failure. Don't try to be polite, you can't have been more bored that I was, I myself thought it was deadly. It won't always be like to-night, you know! I'm not thinking of the Cambremers, who are impossible, but I've known society people who were supposed to be agreeable, and compared with my little nucleus they didn't exist. I heard you say that you thought Swann clever. I must say, to my mind it's greatly exaggerated, but without even speaking of the character of the man, which I've always found fundamentally antipathetic, sly, underhand, I often had him to dinner on Wednesdays. Well, you can ask the others, even compared with Brichot, who is far from being a genius, who's a good secondary schoolmaster whom I got into the Institute all the same, Swann was simply nowhere. He was so dull!" And as I expressed a contrary opinion: "It's the truth. I don't want to say a word against him since he was your friend, indeed he was very fond of you, he spoke to me about you in the most charming way, but ask the others here if he ever said anything interesting, at our dinners. That, after all, is the test. Well, I don't know why it was, but Swann, in my house, never seemed to come off, one got nothing out of him. And yet the little he had he picked up here." I assured her that he was highly intelligent. "No, you only thought that because you didn't know him as long as I did. Really, one got to the end of him very soon. I was always bored to death by him." (Translation: "He went to the la Trémoïlles and the Guermantes and knew that I didn't.") "And I can put up with anything except being bored. That I cannot stand!" Her horror of boredom was now the reason upon which Mme Verdurin relied to explain the composition of the little group. She did not yet entertain duchesses because she was incapable of enduring boredom, just as she was incapable of going for a cruise because of sea-sickness. I thought to myself that what Mme Verdurin said was not entirely false, and, whereas the Guermantes would have declared Brichot to be the stupidest man they had ever met, I remained uncertain whether he was not in reality superior, if not to Swann himself, at least to the people endowed with the wit of the Guermantes who would have had the good taste to avoid and the delicacy to blush at his pedantic pleasantries; I asked myself the question as though the nature of intelligence might be to some extent clarified by the answer that I might give, and with the earnestness of a Christian influenced by Port-Royal when he considers the problem of Grace. "You'll see," Mme Verdurin continued, "when one has society people together with people of real intelligence, people of our set, that's where one has to see them—the wittiest society man in the kingdom of the blind is only one-eyed here. Besides, he paralyses the others, who don't feel at home any longer. So much so that I'm inclined to wonder whether, instead of attempting mixtures that spoil everything, I shan't start special evenings confined to the bores so as to have the full benefit of my little nucleus. However: you're coming again with your cousin. That's settled. Good. At any rate you'll get something to eat here, the pair of you. Féterne is starvation corner. Oh, by the way, if you like rats, go there at once, you'll get as many as you want. And they'll keep you there as long as you're prepared to stay. Why, you'll die of hunger. When I go there, I shall dine before I start. To make it a bit gayer, you must come here first. We shall have a good high tea, and supper when we get back. Do you like apple-tarts? Yes, very well then, our chef makes the best in the world. You see I was quite right when I said you were made to live here. So come and stay. There's far more room here than you'd think. I don't mention it, so as not to let myself in for bores. You might bring your cousin to stay. She would get a change of air from Balbec. With the air here, I maintain that I can cure incurables. My word, I've cured some, and not only this time. For I've stayed near here before—a place I discovered and got for a mere song, and which had a lot more character than their Raspelière. I can show it to you if we go for a drive together. But I admit that even here the air is really invigorating. Still, I don't want to say too much about it, or the whole of Paris would begin to take a fancy to my little corner. That's always been my luck. Anyhow, give your cousin my message. We'll put you in two nice rooms looking over the valley. You ought to see it in the morning, with the sun shining through the mist! By the way, who is this Robert de Saint-Loup you were speaking of?" she said anxiously, for she had heard that I was to pay him a visit at Doncières, and was afraid that he might make me defect. "Why not bring him here instead, if he's not a bore. I've heard of him from Morel; I fancy he's one of his greatest friends," she added, lying in her teeth, for Saint-Loup and Morel were not even aware of one another's existence. But having heard that Saint-Loup knew M. de Charlus, she supposed that it was through the violinist, and wished to appear in the know. "He's not taking up medicine, by any chance, or literature? You know, if you want any help about examinations, Cottard can do anything, and I make what use of him I please. As for the Academy later on—for I suppose he's not old enough yet—I have several votes in my pocket. Your friend would find himself on friendly soil here, and it might amuse him perhaps to see over the house. Doncières isn't much fun. Anyhow, do just as you please, whatever suits you best," she concluded, without insisting, so as not to appear to be trying to know people of noble birth, and because she always maintained that the system by which she governed the faithful, to wit despotism, was named liberty. "Why, what's the matter with you," she said, at the sight of M. Verdurin who, gesticulating impatiently, was making for the wooden terrace that ran along the side of the drawing-room above the valley, like a man who is bursting with rage and needs fresh air. "Has Saniette been irritating you again? But since you know what an idiot he is, you must resign yourself and not work yourself up into such a state . . . I hate it when he gets like this," she said to me, "because it's bad for him, it sends the blood to his head. But I must say that one would need the patience of an angel at times to put up with Saniette, and one must always remember that it's an act of charity to have him in the house. For my part I must admit that he's so gloriously silly that I can't help enjoying him. I dare say you heard what he said after dinner: 'I can't play whist, but I can play the piano.' Isn't it superb? It's positively colossal, and incidentally quite untrue, for he's incapable of doing either. But my husband, beneath his rough exterior, is very sensitive, very kind-hearted, and Saniette's self-centred way of always thinking about the effect he's going to make drives him crazy . . . Come, dear, calm down, you know Cottard told you that it was bad for your liver. And I'm the one who'll have to bear the brunt of it all. To-morrow Saniette will come back and have his little fit of hysterics. Poor man, he's very ill. But still, that's no reason why he should kill other people. And then, even at moments when he's really suffering, when one would like to comfort him, his silliness hardens one's heart. He's really too stupid. You ought to tell him quite politely that these scenes make you both ill, and he'd better not come back, and since that's what he's most afraid of, it will have a calming effect on his nerves," Mme Verdurin concluded.

The sea was only just discernible from the windows on the right. But those on the other side revealed the valley, now shrouded in a snowy cloak of moonlight. From time to time one heard the voices of Morel and Cottard. "Have you any trumps?" "*Yes.*" "You must be joking," said M. de Cambremer to Morel, in answer to his question, for he had seen that the Doctor's hand was full of trumps. "Here comes the lady of diamonds," said the Doctor. "Zat iss trump, you know? My trick. But there isn't a Sorbonne any longer," said the Doctor to M. de Cambremer, "there's only the University of Paris." M. de Cambremer confessed that he did not see the point of this remark. "I thought you were talking about the Sorbonne," continued the Doctor. "I understood you to say: *tu nous la sors bonne,*" he added, with a wink, to show that this was a pun. "Just wait a moment," he said, pointing to his opponent, "I have a Trafalgar in store for him." And the prospect must have been excellent for the Doctor, for in his joy his shoulders began to shake rapturously with laughter, a motion which in his family, in the "genus" Cottard, was an almost zoological sign of satisfaction. In the previous generation the movement used to be accompanied by that of rubbing the hands together as though one were soaping them. Cottard himself had originally employed both forms of mimicry simultaneously, but one fine day, nobody ever knew by whose intervention, wifely or perhaps professional, the rubbing of the hands had disappeared. The Doctor, even at dominoes, when he forced his opponent into a corner and made him take the double six, which was to him the keenest of pleasures, contented himself with the shoulder-shake. And when—which was as seldom as possible—he went down to his native village for a few days and met his first cousin who was still at the hand-rubbing stage, he would say to Mme Cottard on his return: "I thought poor René very common." "Have you any little dears?" he said, turning to Morel. "No? Then I play this old David." "Then you have five, you've won!" "*Si signor.*" "A splendid victory, Doctor," said the Marquis. "A Pyrrhic victory," said Cottard, turning to face the Marquis and looking at him over his glasses to judge the effect of his remark. "If there's still time," he said to Morel, "I give you your revenge. It's my deal. Ah! no, here come the carriages, it will have to be Friday, and I shall show you a trick you don't see every day."

M. and Mme Verdurin accompanied us to the door. The Mistress was particularly affectionate to Saniette so as to make certain of his returning next time. "But you don't look to me as if you were properly wrapped up, my boy," said M. Verdurin, whose age allowed him to address me in this paternal tone. "It looks as though the weather has changed." These words filled me with joy, as though the dormant life, the resurgence of different combinations which they implied in nature, heralded other changes, occurring in my own life, and created fresh possibilities in it. Merely by opening the door on to the garden, before leaving, one felt that a different weather had, at that moment, taken possession of the scene; cooling breezes, one of the joys of summer, were rising in the fir plantation (where long ago Mme de Cambremer had dreamed of Chopin) and almost imperceptibly, in caressing coils, in fitful eddies, were beginning their gentle nocturnes. I declined the rug which, on subsequent evenings, I was to accept when Albertine was with me, more to preserve the secrecy of pleasure than to avoid the risk of cold. A vain search was made for the Norwegian philosopher. Had he been seized by a colic? Had he been afraid of missing the train? Had an aeroplane come to fetch him? Had he been carried aloft in an Assumption? In any case he had vanished without anyone's noticing his departure, like a god. "You are unwise," M. de Cambremer said to me, "it's as cold as charity." "Why charity?" the Doctor inquired. "Beware of your spasms," the Marquis went on. "My sister never goes out at night. However, she is in a pretty bad state at present. In any case you oughtn't to stand about bare-headed, put your tile on at once." "They are not *a frigore* spasms," said Cottard sententiously. "Ah, well," M. de Cambremer bowed, "of course, if that's your view. . . ." "View halloo," said the Doctor, his eyes twinkling behind his glasses. M. de Cambremer laughed, but, convinced that he was in the right, insisted: "All the same," he said, "whenever my sister goes out after dark, she has an attack." "It's no use quibbling," replied the Doctor, oblivious of his own discourtesy. "However, I don't practise medicine by the seaside, unless I'm called in for a consultation. I'm here on holiday." He was perhaps even more on holiday than he would have liked. M. de Cambremer having said to him as they got into the carriage together: "We're fortunate in having quite close to us (not on your side of the bay, on the opposite side, but it's quite narrow at that point) another medical celebrity, Dr du Boulbon," Cottard, who as a rule, from "deontology," abstained from criticising his colleagues, could not help exclaiming, as he had exclaimed to me on the fatal day when we had visited the little casino: "But he isn't a doctor. He practises a sort of literary medicine, whimsical therapy, pure charlatanism. All the same, we're on quite good terms. I'd take the boat and go over and pay him a visit if I didn't have to go away." But, from the air which Cottard assumed in speaking of du Boulbon to M. de Cambremer, I felt that the boat which he would gladly have taken to call upon him would have greatly resembled that vessel which, in order to go and spoil the waters discovered by another literary doctor, Virgil (who took all their patients from them as well), the doctors of Salerno had chartered, but which sank with them during the crossing. "Good-bye, my dear Saniette. Don't forget to come to-morrow, you know how fond of you my husband is. He enjoys your wit and intelligence; yes indeed, you know quite well he does. He likes putting on a show of brusqueness, but he can't do without you. It's always the first thing he asks me: 'Is Saniette coming? I do so enjoy seeing him.'" "I never said anything of the sort," said M. Verdurin to Saniette with a feigned frankness which seemed perfectly to reconcile what the Mistress had just said with the manner in which he treated Saniette. Then, looking at his watch, doubtless so as not to prolong the leave-taking in the damp night air, he warned the coachmen not to lose any time, but to be careful when going down the hill, and assured us that we should be in plenty of time for our train. The latter was to set down the faithful, one at one station, another at a second, and so on, ending with myself, for no one else was going as far as Balbec, and beginning with the Cambremers, who, in order not to bring their horses all the way up to la Raspelière at night, took the train with us at Douville-Féterne. For the station nearest to them was not this one, which, being already at some distance from the village, was further still from the château, but la Sogne. On arriving at the station of Douville-Féterne, M. de Cambremer made a point of "crossing the palm," as Françoise used to say, of the Verdurins' coachman (the nice, sensitive

coachman, with the melancholy thoughts), for M. de Cambremer was generous, in that respect "taking after his mamma."
But, possibly because his "papa's side" intervened at this point,
in the process of giving he had qualms about the possibility of
an error—either on his part, if, for instance, in the dark, he
were to give a sou instead of a franc, or on the part of the
recipient who might not notice the size of the present that was
being given him. And so he drew attention to it: "It is a franc
I'm giving you, isn't it?" he said to the coachman, turning the
coin until it gleamed in the lamplight, and so that the faithful
might report his action to Mme Verdurin. "Isn't it? Twenty
sous is right, as it's only a short drive." He and Mme de Cambremer left us at la Sogne. "I shall tell my sister," he repeated to
me once more, "about your spasms. I'm sure she'll be interested." I understood that he meant: "will be pleased." As for
his wife, she employed, in saying good-bye to me, two abbreviations which even in writing, used to shock me at that time in
a letter, although one has grown accustomed to them since, but
which, when spoken, seem to me still, even today, insufferably
pedantic in their deliberate carelessness, in their studied
familiarity: "Delighted to have met you," she said; "greetings to Saint-Loup, if you see him." In making this speech,
Mme de Cambremer pronounced the name "Saint-Loupe." I
never discovered who had pronounced it thus in her hearing,
or what had led her to suppose that it ought to be so pronounced. However that may be, for some weeks afterwards she
continued to say "Saint-Loupe," and a man who had a great
admiration for her and echoed her in every way did the same.
If other people said "Saint-Lou," they would insist, would say
emphatically "Saint-Loupe," either to teach the others a lesson
indirectly, or to distinguish themselves from them. But no
doubt women of greater social prestige than Mme de Cambremer
told her, or gave her indirectly to understand, that this was not
the correct pronunciation, and that what she regarded as a
sign of originality was a solecism which would make people
think her little conversant with the usages of society, for
shortly afterwards Mme de Cambremer was again saying
"Saint-Lou," and her admirer similarly ceased to hold out,
either because she had admonished him, or because he had

noticed that she no longer sounded the final consonant and had said to himself that if a woman of such distinction, energy and ambition had yielded, it must have been on good grounds. The worst of her admirers was her husband. Mme de Cambremer loved to tease other people in a way that was often highly impertinent. As soon as she began to attack me, or anyone else, in this fashion, M. de Cambremer would start watching her victim with a laugh. As the Marquis had a squint—a blemish which gives an impression of intended wit to the mirth even of imbeciles—the effect of this laughter was to bring a segment of pupil into the otherwise complete whiteness of his eye. Thus does a sudden rift bring a patch of blue into an otherwise clouded sky. His monocle moreover protected, like the glass over a valuable picture, this delicate operation. As for the actual intention of his laughter, it was hard to say whether it was friendly: "Ah! you rascal, you're a lucky man and no mistake! You've won the favour of a woman with a very pretty wit." Or vicious: "Well then, I hope you'll learn your lesson when you've swallowed all those insults." Or obliging: "I'm here, you know. I take it with a laugh because it's all pure fun, but I shan't let you be ill-treated." Or cruelly conniving: "I don't need to add my little pinch of salt, but you can see I'm enjoying all the snubs she's handing out to you. I'm laughing myself silly, because I approve, and I'm her husband. So if you should take it into your head to answer back, you'd have me to deal with, young fellow. First of all I'd fetch you a couple of monumental clouts, and then we should go and cross swords in the forest of Chantepie."

Whatever the correct interpretation of the husband's merriment, the wife's whimsical banter soon came to an end. Whereupon M. de Cambremer ceased to laugh, the temporary pupil vanished, and as one had forgotten for a minute or two to expect an entirely white eyeball, it gave this ruddy Norman an air at once anaemic and ecstatic, as though the Marquis had just undergone an operation, or were imploring heaven, through his monocle, for a martyr's crown.

CHAPTER THREE

I was dropping with sleep. I was taken up to my floor not
by the lift-boy but by the squinting page, who to make
conversation informed me that his sister was still with the
gentleman who was so rich, and that once, when she had taken
it into her head to return home instead of sticking to her
business, her gentleman friend had paid a visit to the mother of
the squinting page and of the other more fortunate children,
who had very soon made the silly creature return to her protector. "You know, sir, she's a fine lady, my sister is. She plays the
piano, she talks Spanish. And, you'd never believe it of the
sister of the humble employee who's taking you up in the lift,
but she denies herself nothing; Madame has a maid to herself,
and she'll have her own carriage one day, I shouldn't wonder.
She's very pretty, if you could see her, a bit too high and
mighty, but well, you can understand that. She's full of fun.
She never leaves a hotel without relieving herself first in a
wardrobe or a drawer, just to leave a little keepsake with the
chambermaid who'll have to clean up. Sometimes she does it in
a cab, and after she's paid her fare, she'll hide behind a tree, and
she doesn't half laugh when the cabby finds he's got to clean his
cab after her. My father had another stroke of luck when he
found my young brother this Indian prince he used to know
long ago. It's not the same style of thing, of course. But it's a
superb position. If it wasn't for the travelling, it would be a
dream. I'm the only one still on the shelf. But you never know.
We're a lucky family; perhaps one day I shall be President of
the Republic. But I'm keeping you babbling" (I had not
uttered a single word and was beginning to fall asleep as I
listened to the flow of his). "Good-night, sir. Oh! thank you,
sir. If everybody had as kind a heart as you, there wouldn't be
any poor people left. But, as my sister says, 'there must always
be poor people so that now that I'm rich I can shit on them.'
You'll pardon the expression. Good-night, sir."

Perhaps every night we accept the risk of experiencing, while we are asleep, sufferings which we regard as null and void because they will be felt in the course of a sleep which we suppose to be unconscious. And indeed on these evenings when I came back late from la Raspelière I was very sleepy. But after the weather turned cold I could not get to sleep at once, for the fire lighted up the room as though there were a lamp burning in it. Only it was nothing more than a brief blaze, and —like a lamp too, or like the daylight when night falls—its too bright light was not long in fading; and I entered the realm of sleep, which is like a second dwelling into which we move for that one purpose. It has noises of its own and we are sometimes violently awakened by the sound of bells, perfectly heard by our ears, although nobody has rung. It has its servants, its special visitors who call to take us out, so that we are ready to get up when we are compelled to realise, by our almost immediate transmigration into the other dwelling, our waking one, that the room is empty, that nobody has called. The race that inhabits it, like that of our first human ancestors, is androgynous. A man in it appears a moment later in the form of a woman. Things in it show a tendency to turn into men, men into friends and enemies. The time that elapses for the sleeper, during these spells of slumber, is absolutely different from the time in which the life of the waking man is passed. Sometimes its course is far more rapid—a quarter of an hour seems a day— at other times far longer—we think we have taken only a short nap, when we have slept through the day. Then, in the chariot of sleep, we descend into depths in which memory can no longer keep up with it, and on the brink of which the mind has been obliged to retrace its steps.

The horses of sleep, like those of the sun, move at so steady a pace, in an atmosphere in which there is no longer any resistance, that it requires some little aerolith extraneous to ourselves (hurled from the azure by what Unknown?) to strike our regular sleep (which otherwise would have no reason to stop, and would continue with a similar motion world without end) and to make it swing sharply round, return towards reality, travel without pause, traverse the regions bordering on life— whose sounds the sleeper will presently hear, still vague but already perceptible even if distorted—and come to earth suddenly at the point of awakening. Then from those profound slumbers we awake in a dawn, not knowing who we are, being nobody, newly born, ready for anything, the brain emptied of that past which was life until then. And perhaps it is more wonderful still when our landing at the waking-point is abrupt and the thoughts of our sleep, hidden by a cloak of oblivion, have no time to return to us gradually, before sleep ceases. Then, from the black storm through which we seem to have passed (but we do not even say *we*), we emerge prostrate, without a thought, a *we* that is void of content. What hammer-blow has the person or thing that is lying there received to make it unconscious of everything, stupefied until the moment when memory, flooding back, restores to it consciousness or personality? However, for both these kinds of awakening, we must avoid falling asleep, even into a deep sleep, under the law of habit. For everything that habit ensnares in her nets, she watches closely; we must escape her, take our sleep at a moment when we thought we were doing something quite other than sleeping, take, in a word, a sleep that does not dwell under the tutelage of foresight, in the company, albeit latent, of reflexion.

At all events, in these awakenings which I have just described, and which I experienced as a rule when I had been dining overnight at la Raspelière, everything occurred as though by this process, and I can testify to it, I, the strange human who, while he waits for death to release him, lives behind closed shutters, knows nothing of the world, sits motionless as an owl, and like that bird can only see things at all clearly in the darkness. Everything occurs as though by this process, but perhaps only a wad of cotton-wool has prevented the sleeper from taking in the internal dialogue of memories and the incessant verbiage of sleep. For (and this may be equally manifest in the other, vaster, more mysterious, more astral system) at the moment of his entering the waking state, the sleeper hears a voice inside him saying: "Will you come to this dinner to-night, my dear friend, it would be so nice?" and thinks: "Yes, how nice it would be, I shall go"; then, growing wider awake, he suddenly remembers: "My grandmother has only a few weeks to live, so the doctor assures us." He rings, he weeps at the thought that it will not be, as in the past, his grandmother, his dying grandmother, but an indifferent valet that will come in answer to his summons. Moreover, when sleep bore him so far away from the world inhabited by memory and thought, through an ether in which he was alone, more than alone, without even the companionship of self-perception, he was outside the range of time and its measurements. But now the waiter is in the room, and he dares not ask him the time, for he does not know whether he has slept, for how many hours he has slept (he wonders whether it should not be how many days, with such a weary body, such a rested mind, such a homesick heart has he returned, as from a journey too distant not to have taken a long time).

One can of course maintain that there is but one time, for the futile reason that it is by looking at the clock that one established as being merely a quarter of an hour what one had supposed a day. But at the moment of establishing this, one is precisely a man awake, immersed in the time of waking men, having deserted the other time. Perhaps indeed more than another time: another life. We do not include the pleasures we enjoy in sleep in the inventory of the pleasures we have experienced in the course of our existence. To take only the most grossly sensual of them all, which of us, on waking, has not felt a certain irritation at having experienced in his sleep a pleasure which, if he is anxious not to tire himself, he is not, once he is awake, at liberty to repeat indefinitely during that day. It seems a positive waste. We have had pleasure in another life which is not ours. If we enter up in a budget the pains and pleasures of dreams (which generally vanish soon enough after our waking), it is not in the current account of our everyday life.

Two times, I have said; perhaps there is only one after all, not that the time of the waking man has any validity for the sleeper, but perhaps because the other life, the life in which he sleeps, is not—in its profounder aspect—included in the category of time. I came to this conclusion when, after those dinner-parties at la Raspelière, I used to sleep so thoroughly. For this reason: I was beginning to despair, on waking, when I found that, after I had rung the bell ten times, the valet did not appear. At the eleventh ring he came. It was only the first after all. The other ten had been mere adumbrations, in my sleep which still hung about me, of the ring that I had been meaning to give. My numbed hands had never even moved. Now, on those mornings (and it is this that makes me think that sleep is perhaps independent of the law of time) my effort to wake up consisted chiefly in an effort to bring the obscure, undefined mass of the sleep in which I had just been living into the framework of time. It is no easy task; sleep, which does not know whether we have slept for two hours or two days, cannot provide us with any point of reference. And if we do not find one outside, not being able to re-enter time, we fall asleep again, for five minutes which seem to us three hours.

I have always said—and have proved by experience—that the most powerful soporific is sleep itself. After having slept profoundly for two hours, having fought with so many giants, and formed so many lifelong friendships, it is far more difficult to awake than after taking several grammes of veronal. And so, reasoning from one thing to the other, I was surprised to hear from the Norwegian philosopher, who had it from M. Boutroux, "my eminent colleague—pardon me, confrère," what M. Bergson thought of the peculiar effects upon the memory of soporific drugs. "Naturally," M. Bergson had said to M. Boutroux, according to the Norwegian philosopher, "soporifics taken from time to time in moderate doses have no effect upon that solid memory of our everyday life which is so firmly established within us. But there are other forms of memory, loftier but also more unstable. One of my colleagues lectures on ancient history. He tells me that if, overnight, he has taken a sleeping pill, he has great difficulty, during his lecture, in recalling the Greek quotations that he requires. The doctor who recommended these tablets assured him that they had no effect on the memory. 'That is perhaps because you do not have to quote Greek,' the historian answered, not without a note of sarcastic pride."

I cannot say whether this conversation between M. Bergson and M. Boutroux is accurately reported. The Norwegian philosopher, albeit so profound and so lucid, so passionately attentive, may have misunderstood. Personally, my own experience has produced the opposite results. The moments of forgetfulness that come to us in the morning after we have taken certain narcotics have a resemblance that is only partial, though disturbing, to the oblivion that reigns during a night of natural and deep sleep. Now what I find myself forgetting in either case is not some line of Baudelaire, which on the contrary keeps sounding in my ear "like a dulcimer," not some concept of one of the philosophers above-named, it is—if I am asleep—the actual reality of the ordinary things that surround me, my non-perception of which makes me an idiot; it is—if I am awakened and go out after an artificial slumber—not the system of Porphyry or Plotinus, which I can discuss as fluently as on any other day, but the answer that I have promised to give to an invitation, the memory of which has been replaced by a pure blank. The lofty thought remains in its place; what the soporific has put out of action is the power to act in little things, in everything that demands exertion in order to recapture at the right moment, to grasp some memory of everyday life. In spite of all that may be said about survival after the destruction of the brain, I observe that each alteration of the brain is a partial death. We possess all our memories, but not the faculty of recalling them, said, echoing M. Bergson, the eminent Norwegian philosopher whose speech I have made no attempt to imitate in order not to slow things down even more. But not the faculty of recalling them. What, then, is a memory which we do not recall? Or, indeed, let us go further. We do not recall our memories of the last thirty years; but we are wholly steeped in them; why then stop short at thirty years, why not extend this previous life back to before our birth? If I do not know a whole section of the memories that are behind me, if they are invisible to me, if I do not have the faculty of calling them to me, how do I know whether in that mass that is unknown to me there may not be some that extend back much further than my human existence? If I can have in me and round me so many memories which I do not remember, this oblivion (a *de facto* oblivion, at least, since I have not the faculty of seeing anything) may extend over a life which I have lived in the body of another man, even on another planet. A common oblivion obliterates everything. But what, in that case, is the meaning of that immortality of the soul the reality of which the Norwegian philosopher affirmed? The being that I shall be after death has no more reason to remember the man I have been since my birth than the latter to remember what I was before it.

The valet came in. I did not mention to him that I had rung several times, for I was beginning to realise that hitherto I had only dreamed that I was ringing. I was alarmed nevertheless by the thought that this dream had had the clarity of consciousness. By the same token, might consciousness have the unreality of a dream?

Instead I asked him who it was that had been ringing so often during the night. He told me: "Nobody," and could prove his statement, for the bell-board would have registered any ring. And yet I could hear the repeated, almost furious peals which were still echoing in my ears and were to remain perceptible for several days. It is, however, unusual for sleep thus to project into our waking life memories that do not perish with it. We can count these aeroliths. If it is an idea that sleep has forged, it soon breaks up into tenuous, irrecoverable fragments. But, in this instance, sleep had fashioned sounds. More material and simpler, they lasted longer.

I was astonished to hear from the valet how relatively early it was. I felt none the less rested. It is light sleeps that have a long duration, because, being an intermediate state between waking and sleeping, preserving a somewhat faded but constant impression of the former, they require infinitely more time to make us feel rested than a deep sleep, which may be short. I felt entirely relaxed for another reason. If remembering that we have tired ourselves is enough to make us feel our tiredness, saying to oneself "I've rested" is enough to create rest. Now I had been dreaming that M. de Charlus was a hundred and ten years old, and had just boxed the ears of his own mother, Mme Verdurin, because she had paid five billion francs for a bunch of violets; I was thus assured of having slept profoundly, had dreamed back to front what had been in my thoughts overnight and all the possibilities of life at the moment; this was enough to make me feel entirely rested.

I should greatly have astonished my mother, who could not understand M. de Charlus's assiduity in visiting the Verdurins, had I told her whom (on the very day on which Albertine's toque had been ordered, without a word about it to her, in order that it might come as a surprise) M. de Charlus had brought to dine in a private room at the Grand Hotel, Balbec. His guest was none other than the footman of a lady who was a cousin of the Cambremers. This footman was very smartly dressed, and, as he crossed the hall with the Baron, "looked the man of fashion," as Saint-Loup would have said, in the eyes of the visitors. Indeed, the young page-boys, the Levites who were swarming down the temple steps at that moment because it was the time when they came on duty, paid no attention to the two newcomers, one of whom, M. de Charlus, kept his eyes lowered to show that he was paying little if any to them. He appeared to be trying to carve his way through their midst. "Thrive then, dear hope of a sacred nation," he said, recalling a passage from Racine, and applying to it a wholly different meaning. "Pardon?" asked the footman, who was not well up in the classics. M. de Charlus made no reply, for he took a certain pride in never answering questions and in walking straight ahead as though there were no other visitors in the hotel and no one else existed in the world except himself, Baron de Charlus. But, having continued to quote the speech of Josabeth: "Come, then, my daughters," he felt a revulsion and did not, like her, add: "Bid them approach," for these young people had not yet reached the age at which sex is completely developed and which appealed to M. de Charlus.

Moreover, if he had written to Mme de Chevregny's footman, because he had had no doubt of his docility, he had expected someone more virile. On seeing him, he found him more effeminate than he would have liked. He told him that he had been expecting someone else, for he knew by sight another of Mme de Chevregny's footmen, whom he had noticed upon the box of her carriage. This was an extremely rustic type of peasant, the very opposite of the present footman, who, regarding his mincing ways as a mark of his superiority and never doubting that it was these man-of-fashion airs that had captivated M. de Charlus, could not even guess whom the

Baron meant. "But there's nobody else except one you can't have had your eye on—he's hideous, just like a great peasant." And at the thought that it was perhaps this lout whom the Baron had seen, he felt wounded in his self-esteem. The Baron guessed this, and, widening his quest, "But I haven't made a vow to know only Mme de Chevregny's people," he said. "Surely there are plenty of fellows in one house or another here, or in Paris, since you're going back there soon, that you could introduce to me?" "Oh, no!" replied the footman, "I never associate with anyone of my own class. I only speak to them on duty. But there's one very nice person I could introduce you to." "Who?" asked the Baron. "The Prince de Guermantes." M. de Charlus was vexed at being offered only a man so advanced in years, one moreover to whom he had no need to apply to a footman for an introduction. And so he declined the offer curtly, and, refusing to be put off by the menial's social pretensions, began to explain to him again what he wanted, the style, the type, a jockey, for instance, and so on. Fearing lest the notary, who went past at that moment, might have heard him, he thought it cunning to show that he was speaking of anything in the world rather than what his hearer might suspect, and said with emphasis and in ringing tones, but as though he were simply continuing his conversation: "Yes, in spite of my age, I still retain a passion for collecting, a passion for pretty things. I will do anything to secure an old bronze, an early chandelier. I adore the Beautiful."

But to make clear to the footman the change of subject he had so rapidly executed, M. de Charlus laid such stress upon each word, and furthermore, in order to be heard by the notary, he shouted his words so loud, that this charade would have been enough to betray what it concealed to ears more alert than those of the legal gentleman. The latter suspected nothing, any more than did any of the other residents in the hotel, all of whom saw a fashionable foreigner in the footman so smartly attired. On the other hand, if the men of the world were deceived and took him for a distinguished American, no sooner did he appear before the servants than he was spotted by them, as one convict recognises another, indeed scented afar off, as certain animals scent one another. The waiters raised their eyebrows. Aimé cast a suspicious glance. The wine waiter, shrugging his shoulders, uttered behind his hand (because he thought it polite) a disobliging remark which everybody heard.

And even our old Françoise, whose sight was failing and who arrived at the foot of the staircase at that moment on her way to dine in the guests' servants' hall, raised her head, recognised a servant where the hotel guests never suspected one—as the old nurse Euryclea recognises Ulysses long before the suitors seated at the banquet—and seeing M. de Charlus arm in arm with him, assumed an appalled expression, as though all of a sudden slanders which she had heard repeated and had not believed had acquired a distressing verisimilitude in her eyes. She never spoke to me, or to anyone else, of this incident, but it must have caused a considerable commotion in her brain, for afterwards, whenever in Paris she happened to see "Julien," to whom until then she had been so greatly attached, she still treated him with politeness, but with a politeness that had cooled and was always tempered with a strong dose of reserve. This same incident, however, led someone else to confide in me: this was Aimé. When I passed M. de Charlus, the latter, not having expected to meet me, raised his hand and called out "Good evening" with the indifference—outwardly, at least— of a great nobleman who thinks he can do anything he likes and considers it shrewder not to appear to be hiding anything. Aimé, who at that moment was watching him with a suspicious eye and saw that I greeted the companion of the person in whom he was certain that he detected a servant, asked me that same evening who he was.

For, for some time past, Aimé had shown a fondness for chatting, or rather, as he himself put it, doubtless in order to emphasise the (to him) philosophical character of these chats, "discussing" with me. And as I often said to him that it distressed me that he should have to stand beside the table while I ate instead of being able to sit down and share my meal, he declared that he had never seen a guest show such "sound reasoning." He was chatting at that moment to two waiters. They had greeted me, I did not know why; their faces were unfamiliar, although their conversation reverberated with echoes that were not entirely new to me. Aimé was scolding them both because of their matrimonial engagements, of which he disapproved. He appealed to me, and I said that I could not have any opinion on the matter since I did not know them. They reminded me of their names, and said that they had often waited upon me at Rivebelle. But one had let his moustache grow, the other had shaved his off and had had his head cropped; and for this reason, although it was the same head as before that rested upon the shoulders of each of them (and not a different head as in the faulty restorations of Notre-Dame), it had remained almost as invisible to me as those objects which escape the most minute search and are actually staring everybody in the face where nobody notices them, on the mantelpiece. As soon as I knew their names, I recognised exactly the uncertain music of their voices because I saw once more the old faces which determined it. "They want to get married and they haven't even learned English!" Aimé said to me, overlooking the fact that I was little versed in the ways of the hotel trade, and could not be aware that if one does not know foreign languages one cannot be certain of getting a job.

Assuming that Aimé would have no difficulty in finding out that the newcomer was M. de Charlus, and indeed convinced that he must remember him, having waited on him in the dining-room when the Baron had come to see Mme de Villeparisis during my former visit to Balbec, I told him his name. Not only did Aimé not remember the Baron de Charlus, but the name appeared to make a profound impression on him. He told me that he would look next day in his room for a letter which I might perhaps be able to explain to him. I was all the more astonished because M. de Charlus, when he had wished to give me one of Bergotte's books at Balbec the first year, had specially asked for Aimé, whom he must have recognised later on in that Paris restaurant where I had had lunch with Saint-Loup and his mistress and where M. de Charlus had come to spy on us. It is true that Aimé had not been able to execute these commissions in person, being on the former occasion in bed, and on the latter engaged in serving. I had nevertheless grave doubts as to his sincerity when he claimed not to know M. de Charlus. For one thing, he must have been to the Baron's liking. Like all the floor waiters of the Balbec hotel, like several of the Prince de Guermantes's footmen, Aimé belonged to a race more ancient than that of the Prince, and therefore more noble. When one asked for a private room, one thought at first that one was alone. But presently, in the pantry, one caught sight of a sculptural waiter, of that ruddy Etruscan kind of which Aimé was the epitome, slightly aged by excessive consumption of champagne and seeing the inevitable hour for mineral water approach. Not all the guests asked them merely to wait upon them. The underlings, who were young, scrupulous, and in a hurry, having mistresses waiting for them outside, made off. Hence Aimé reproached them with not being serious. He had every right to do so. He himself was certainly serious. He had a wife and children, and was ambitious on their behalf. And so he never repulsed the advances made to him by a strange lady or gentleman, even if it meant his staying all night. For business must come first. He was so much of the type that might attract M. de Charlus that I suspected him of falsehood when he told me that he did not know him. I was wrong. The page had been perfectly truthful when he told the Baron that Aimé (who had given him a dressing-down for it next day) had gone to bed (or gone out), and on the other occasion was busy serving. But imagination outreaches reality. And the page-boy's embarrassment had probably aroused in M. de Charlus doubts as to the sincerity of his excuses, doubts that had wounded feelings on his part of which Aimé had no suspicion. We have seen moreover that Saint-Loup had prevented Aimé from going out to the carriage and that M. de Charlus, who had managed somehow or other to discover the head waiter's new address, had suffered a further disappointment. Aimé, who had not noticed him, felt an astonishment that may be imagined when, on the evening of that very day on which I had had lunch with Saint-Loup and his mistress, he received a letter sealed with the Guermantes arms from which I shall quote a few pasages here as an example of unilateral insanity in an intelligent man addressing a sensible idiot.

"Monsieur, I have been unsuccessful, notwithstanding efforts that would astonish many who have sought in vain to be received and greeted by me, in persuading you to listen to certain explanations which you have not asked of me but which

I have felt it to be incumbent upon my dignity and your own to offer you. I propose therefore to write down here what it would have been simpler to say to you in person. I make no secret of the fact that, the first time I set eyes upon you at Balbec, I found your face frankly antipathetic." Here followed reflexions on the resemblance—remarked only on the following day—to a deceased friend to whom M. de Charlus had been deeply attached. "The thought then suddenly occurred to me that you might, without in any way encroaching upon the demands of your profession, come to see me and, by joining me in the card games with which his gaiety used to dispel my gloom, give me the illusion that he was not dead. Whatever the nature of the more or less fatuous suppositions which you probably formed, suppositions more within the mental range of a servant (who does not even deserve the name of servant since he has declined to serve) than the comprehension of so lofty a sentiment, you no doubt thought to give yourself an air of importance, ignoring who I was and what I was, by sending word to me, when I asked you to fetch me a book, that you were in bed; but it is a mistake to imagine that impolite behaviour ever adds to charm, a quality in which in any case you are entirely lacking. I should have ended matters there had I not by chance had occasion to speak to you the following day. Your resemblance to my poor friend was so pronounced, banishing even the intolerable protuberance of your too prominent chin, that I realised that it was the deceased who at that moment was lending you his own kindly expression so as to permit you to regain your hold over me and to prevent you from missing the unique opportunity that was being offered you. Indeed, although I have no wish, since there is no longer any object and it is unlikely that I shall meet you again in this life, to introduce coarse questions of material interest, I should have been only too glad to obey the prayer of my dead friend (for I believe in the Communion of Saints and in their desire to intervene in the destiny of the living), that I should treat you as I used to treat him, who had his carriage and his servants, and to whom it was quite natural that I should consecrate the greater part of my fortune since I loved him as a father loves his son. You have decided otherwise. To my request that you should fetch me a book you sent the reply that you were obliged to go out. And this morning when I sent to ask you to come to my carriage, you then, if I may so speak without blasphemy, denied me for the third time. You will forgive me for not enclosing in this envelope the lavish gratuity which I intended to give you at Balbec and to which it would be too painful for me to restrict myself in dealing with a person with whom I had thought for a moment of sharing all that I possess. At the very most you could spare me the trouble of coming to your restaurant to make a fourth futile overture to which my patience will not extend." (Here M. de Charlus gave his address, stated the hours at which he would be at home, etc.) "Farewell, Monsieur. Since I assume that, resembling so strongly the friend whom I have lost, you cannot be entirely stupid, otherwise physiognomy would be a false science, I am convinced that if, one day, you think of this incident again, it will not be without a feeling of some regret and remorse. For my part, believe me, I am quite sincere in saying that I retain no bitterness. I should have preferred that we should part with a less unpleasant memory than this third futile approach. It will soon be forgotten. We are like those vessels which you must often have seen at Balbec, which have crossed one another's paths for a moment; it might have been to the advantage of each of them to stop; but one of them has decided otherwise; presently they will no longer even see one another on the horizon, and their meeting is a thing out of mind; but before this final parting, each of them salutes the other, and so at this point, Monsieur, wishing you all good fortune, does the Baron de Charlus."

Aimé had not even read this letter to the end, being able to make nothing of it and suspecting a hoax. When I had explained to him who the Baron was, he appeared to be lost in thought and to be feeling the regret that M. de Charlus had anticipated. I would not be prepared to swear that he might not at that moment have written a letter of apology to a man who gave carriages to his friends. But in the interval M. de Charlus had made Morel's acquaintance. At most, his relations with Morel being possibly platonic, M. de Charlus occasionally sought to spend an evening in company such as that in which I had just met him in the hall. But he was no longer able to divert from Morel the violent feelings which, unfettered a few years earlier, had been only too ready to fasten themselves upon Aimé and had dictated the letter which had embarrassed me for its writer's sake when the head waiter showed me it. It was, because of the anti-social nature of M. de Charlus's love, a more striking example of the insensible, sweeping force of those currents of passion by which the lover, like a swimmer, is very soon carried out of sight of land. No doubt the love of a normal man may also, when the lover, through the successive fabrications of his desires, regrets, disappointments, plans, constructs a whole novel about a woman whom he does not know, cause the two legs of the compass to gape at a fairly considerable angle. All the same, such an angle was singularly widened by the character of a passion which is not generally shared and by the difference in social position between M. de Charlus and Aimé.

Every day I went out with Albertine. She had decided to take up painting again and had chosen as the subject of her first attempts the church of Saint-Jean-de-la-Haise which nobody ever visited and very few had even heard of, which was difficult to get directions to, impossible to find without being guided, and laborious to reach in its isolation, more than half an hour from Epreville station, after one had long left behind one the last houses of the village of Quetteholme. As to the name Epreville, I found that the curé's book and Brichot's information were at variance. According to one, Epreville was the ancient Sprevilla; the other derived the name from Aprivilla. On our first visit we took a little train in the opposite direction from Féterne, that is to say towards Grattevast. But we were in the dog days and it had been a terrible strain to leave immediately after lunch. I should have preferred not to set out so early; the luminous and burning air provoked thoughts of indolence and cool retreats. It filled my mother's room and mine, according to their exposure, at varying temperatures, like rooms in a Turkish bath. Mamma's bathroom, festooned by the sun with a dazzling, Moorish whiteness, appeared to be sunk at the bottom of a well, because of the four plastered walls on which it looked out, while far above, in the square gap, the sky, whose fleecy white waves could be seen gliding past, one above the other, seemed (because of the longing that one felt) like a tank filled with blue water and reserved for ablutions, either built on a terrace or seen upside down in a mirror fixed to the window. Notwithstanding this scorching temperature, we had taken the one o'clock train. But Albertine had been very hot in the carriage, hotter still in the long walk across country, and I was afraid of her catching cold when afterwards she had to sit still in that damp hollow where the sun's rays did not penetrate. However, having realised as long ago as our first visits to Elstir that she would appreciate not merely luxury but even a certain degree of comfort of which her want of money deprived her, I had made arrangements with a Balbec jobmaster for a carriage to be sent to fetch us every day. To escape from the heat we took the road through the forest of Chantepie. The invisibility of the innumerable birds, some of them sea-birds, that conversed with one another from the trees on either side of us, gave the same impression of repose as one has when one shuts one's eyes. By Albertine's side, clasped in her arms in the depths of the carriage, I listened to these Oceanides. And when by chance I caught sight of one of these musicians as he flitted from one leaf to the shelter of another, there was so little apparent connexion between him and his songs that I could not believe that I was seeing their cause in that tiny body, fluttering, humble, startled and unseeing. The carriage could not take us all the way to the church. I stopped it when we had passed through Quetteholme and bade Albertine good-bye. For she had alarmed me by saying to me of this church as of other monuments and of certain pictures: "What a pleasure it would be to see it with you!" This pleasure was one that I did not feel myself capable of giving her. I felt it myself in front of beautiful things only if I was alone or pretended to be alone and did not speak. But since she had hoped to be able, thanks to me, to experience artistic sensations that cannot be communicated thus, I thought it more prudent to say that I must leave her, that I would come back to fetch her at the end of the day, but that in the meantime I must go back with the carriage to pay a call on Mme Verdurin or on the Cambremers, or even spend an hour with Mamma at Balbec, but never further afield.

To begin with, that is to say. For, Albertine having once said to me petulantly: "It's a bore that nature has arranged things so badly and put Saint-Jean-de-la-Haise in one direction, la Raspelière in another, so that you're imprisoned for the whole day in the spot you've chosen," as soon as the toque and veil had come I ordered, to my eventual undoing, a motor-car from Saint-Fargeau (*Sanctus Ferreolus*, according to the curé's book). Albertine, whom I had kept in ignorance and who had come to call for me, was surprised when she heard in front of the hotel the purr of the engine, delighted when she learned that this motor was for ourselves. I took her upstairs to my room for a moment. She jumped for joy. "Are we going to pay a call on the Verdurins?" "Yes, but you'd better not go dressed like that since you'll have your motor-car. Here, you'll look better in these." And I brought out the toque and veil which I had hidden. "They're for me? Oh! you are an angel," she cried, throwing her arms round my neck. Aimé, who met us on the stairs, proud of Albertine's smart attire and of our means of transport, for these vehicles were still comparatively rare at Balbec, could not resist the pleasure of coming downstairs behind us. Albertine, anxious to display herself in her new garments, asked me to have the hood raised; we could lower it later on when we wished to be more private. "Now then," said Aimé to the driver, with whom he was not acquainted and who had not stirred, "don't you (*tu*) hear, you're to raise the hood?" For Aimé, sophisticated as a result of hotel life, in which moreover he had won his way to exalted rank, was not as shy as the cab driver to whom Françoise was a "lady"; despite the absence of any formal introduction, plebeians whom he had never seen before he addressed as *tu*, though it was hard to say whether this was aristocratic disdain on his part or democratic fraternity. "I'm engaged," replied the chauffeur, who did not know me by sight. "I'm ordered for Mlle Simonet. I can't take this gentleman." Aimé burst out laughing: "Why, you great bumpkin," he said to the driver, whom he at once convinced, "this is Mademoiselle Simonet, and Monsieur, who wants you to open the roof of your car, is the person who has engaged you." And since, although personally he had no great liking for Albertine, Aimé was for my sake proud of her get-up, he whispered to the chauffeur: "Don't get the chance of driving a princess like that every day, do you?" On this first occasion I was unable to go to la Raspelière alone as I did on other days, while Albertine painted; she wanted to come there with me. Although she realised that it would be possible to stop here and there on our way, she could not believe that we could start by going to Saint-Jean-de-la-Haise, that is to say in another direction, and then make an excursion which seemed to be reserved for a different day. She learned on the contrary from the driver that nothing could be easier than to go to Saint-Jean, which he could do in twenty minutes, and that we might stay there if we chose for hours, or go on much further, for from Quetteholme to la Raspelière would not take more than thirty-five minutes. We realised this as soon as the vehicle, starting off, covered in one bound twenty paces of an excellent horse. Distances are only the relation of space to time and vary with it. We express the difficulty that we have in getting to a place in a system of miles or kilometres which becomes false as soon as that difficulty decreases. Art is modified by it also, since a village which seemed to be in a different world from some other village becomes its neighbour in a landscape whose dimensions are altered. In any case, to learn that there may perhaps exist a universe in which two and two make five and a straight line is not the shortest distance between two points would have astonished Albertine far less than to hear the driver say that it was easy to go in a single afternoon to Saint-Jean and la Raspelière. Douville and Quetteholme, Saint-Mars-le-Vieux and Saint-Mars-le-Vêtu, Gourville and Balbec-le-Vieux, Tourville and Féterne, prisoners hitherto as hermetically confined in the cells of distinct days as long ago were Méséglise and Guermantes, upon which the same eyes could not gaze in the course of a single afternoon, delivered now by the giant with the seven-league boots, clustered around our tea-time with their towers and steeples and their old gardens which the neighbouring wood sprang back to reveal.

Coming to the foot of the cliff road, the car climbed effortlessly, with a continuous sound like that of a knife being ground, while the sea, falling away, widened beneath us. The old rustic houses of Montsurvent came rushing towards us,

clasping to their bosoms vine or rose-bush; the firs of la Raspelière, more agitated than when the evening breeze was rising,
ran in every direction to escape from us, and a new servant
whom I had never seen before came to open the door for us on
the terrace while the gardener's son, betraying a precocious
bent, gazed intently at the engine. As it was not a Monday we
did not know whether we should find Mme Verdurin, for except on that day, when she had guests, it was unsafe to call upon
her without warning. No doubt she was "in principle" at home,
but this expression, which Mme Swann employed at the time
when she too was seeking to form her little clan and attract customers without herself moving (even though she often did not
get her money's worth) and which she mistranslated into "on
principle," meant no more than "as a general rule," that is to
say with frequent exceptions. For not only did Mme Verdurin
like going out, but she carried her duties as a hostess to extreme
lengths, and when she had had people to lunch, immediately
after the coffee, liqueurs and cigarettes (notwithstanding the
first somnolent effects of heat and digestion in which they
would have preferred to watch through the leafy boughs of
the terrace the Jersey packet sailing across the enamelled sea),
the programme included a series of excursions in the course of
which her guests, forced into carriages, were conveyed willy-
nilly to look at one or other of the beauty spots that abound in
the neighbourhood of Douville. This second part of the entertainment was, as it happened (once the effort to get up and climb
into a carriage had been made), no less satisfying than the
other to the guests, already conditioned by the succulent dishes,
the vintage wines or sparkling cider to be easily intoxicated by
the purity of the breeze and the magnificence of the sights. Mme
Verdurin used to show these to visitors rather as though they
were annexes (more or less detached) of her property, which
you could not help going to see if you came to lunch with her
and which conversely you would never have known had you
not been entertained by the Mistress. This claim to arrogate to
herself the exclusive right over the local sights, as over Morel's
and formerly Dechambre's playing, and to compel the landscapes to form part of the little clan, was not in fact as absurd
as it appears at first sight. Mme Verdurin deplored not only the

lack of taste which in her opinion the Cambremers showed in the furnishing of la Raspelière and the arrangement of the garden, but still more their want of initiative in the excursions they made, with or without their guests, in the surrounding countryside. Just as, according to her, la Raspelière was only beginning to become what it should always have been now that it was the asylum of the little clan, so she insisted that the Cambremers, perpetually exploring in their barouche, along the railway line, by the shore, the one ugly road in the district, had been living in the place all their lives but did not know it. There was a grain of truth in this assertion. From force of habit, lack of imagination, want of interest in a country which seemed hackneyed because it was so near, the Cambremers when they left their home went always to the same places and by the same roads. To be sure, they laughed heartily at the Verdurins' pretensions to teach them about their own countryside. But if they were driven into a corner they and even their coachman would have been incapable of taking us to the splendid, more or less secret places to which M. Verdurin brought us, now breaking through the fence of a private but deserted property into which other people would not have thought it possible to venture, now leaving the carriage to follow a path which was not wide enough for wheeled traffic, but in either case with the certain recompense of a marvellous view. It must also be said that the garden at la Raspelière was in a sense a compendium of all the excursions to be made in a radius of many miles—in the first place because of its commanding position, overlooking on one side the valley, on the other the sea, and also because, on one and the same side, the seaward side for instance, clearings had been made through the trees in such a way that from one point you embraced one horizon, from another a different one. There was at each of these vantage points a bench; you went and sat down in turn upon the bench from which there was the view of Balbec, or Parville, or Douville. Even to command a single direction, one bench would have been placed more or less on the edge of the cliff, another set back. From the latter you had a foreground of verdure and a horizon which seemed already the vastest imaginable, but which became infinitely larger if, continuing along a little path, you went to the next bench from which you embraced the whole amphitheatre of the sea. There you could catch distinctly the sound of the waves, which did not penetrate to the more secluded parts of the garden, where the sea was still visible but no longer audible. These resting-places were known by the occupants of la Raspelière by the name of "views." And indeed they assembled round the château the finest views of the neighbouring villages, beaches or forests, seen greatly diminished by distance, as Hadrian collected in his villa reduced models of the most famous monuments of different regions. The name that followed the word "view" was not necessarily that of a place on the coast, but often that of the opposite shore of the bay which you could make out, standing out in a certain relief notwithstanding the extent of the panorama. Just as you took a book from M. Verdurin's library to go and read for an hour at the "view of Balbec," so if the sky was clear the liqueurs would be served at the "view of Rivebelle," on condition however that the wind was not too strong, for, in spite of the trees planted on either side, the air up there was keen.

To revert to the afternoon drives which Mme Verdurin used to organise, if on her return she found the cards of some social butterfly "on a visit to the coast," the Mistress would pretend to be overjoyed but was actually broken-hearted at having missed his visit and (albeit people at this date came only to "see the house" or to make the acquaintance for a day of a woman whose artistic salon was famous but outside the pale in Paris) would at once get M. Verdurin to invite him to dine on the following Wednesday. As the tourist was often obliged to leave before that day, or was afraid to be out late, Mme Verdurin had arranged that on Mondays she was always to be found at tea-time. These tea-parties were not at all large, and I had known more brilliant gatherings of the sort in Paris, at the Princesse de Guermantes's, at Mme de Galliffet's or Mme d'Arpajon's. But this was not Paris, and the charm of the setting enhanced, in my eyes, not merely the pleasantness of the occasion but the merits of the visitors. A meeting with some society person, which in Paris would have given me no pleasure but which at la Raspelière, whither he or she had come from a distance via Féterne or the forest of Chantepie, changed in character and importance, became an agreeable incident. Sometimes it was a person whom I knew quite well and would not have gone a yard to meet at the Swanns'. But his name had a different reverberation on this cliff, like the name of an actor one has constantly seen in the theatre printed in a different colour on a poster for some special gala performance, where his fame is suddenly heightened by the unexpectedness of the context. As in the country people behave without ceremony, the social celebrity often took it upon himself to bring the friends with whom he was staying, murmuring to Mme Verdurin by way of excuse that he could not leave them behind as he was living in their house; to his hosts on the other hand he pretended to be offering as a sort of courtesy this diversion, in a monotonous seaside life, of being taken to a centre of wit and intellect, of visiting a magnificent mansion and of having an excellent tea. This composed at once an assembly of several persons of semi-distinction; and if a little slice of garden with a few trees, which would seem paltry in the country, acquires an extraordinary charm in the Avenue Gabriel or the Rue de Monceau, where only multi-millionaires can afford such a luxury, conversely noblemen who would be background figures at a Parisian reception were shown to full advantage on a Monday afternoon at la Raspelière. No sooner did they sit down at the table covered with a cloth embroidered in red, beneath the painted panels, to partake of pancakes, Norman puff pastry, trifles, boat-shaped tartlets filled with cherries like coral beads, than these guests were subjected, by the proximity of the great bowl of azure upon which the window opened and which you could not help seeing at the same time as them, to a profound alteration, a transmutation which changed them into something more precious than before. What was more, even before you set eyes on them, when you came on a Monday to Mme Verdurin's, people who in Paris would scarcely turn their jaded heads to look at the string of elegant carriages stationed outside a great house, felt their hearts throb at the sight of the two or three shabby dog-carts drawn up in front of la Raspelière, beneath the tall firs. No doubt this was because the rustic setting was different, and social impressions thanks to this transposition regained a certain freshness. It was also because the broken-down carriage that one hired to pay a call upon Mme Verdurin conjured up a pleasant drive and a costly bargain struck with a coachman who had demanded "so much" for the whole day. But the slight stir of curiosity with regard to fresh arrivals whom it was still impossible to distinguish arose also from the fact that everyone wondered, "Who can this be?" —a question which it was difficult to answer, when one did not know who might have come down to spend a week with the Cambremers or elsewhere, but which people always enjoy putting to themselves in rustic, solitary environments where a meeting with a human being whom one has not seen for a long time, or an introduction to somebody one does not know, ceases to be the tedious affair that it is in the life of Paris, and forms a delicious break in the empty monotony of lives that are too isolated, in which even the arrival of the mail becomes a pleasure. And on the day on which we arrived by motor-car at la Raspelière, as it was not Monday, M. and Mme Verdurin must have been devoured by that craving to see people which attacks both men and women and inspires a longing to throw himself out of the window in the patient who has been shut up away from his family and friends in an isolation clinic. For the new and more swift-footed servant, who had already made himself familiar with these expressions, having replied that "if Madame hasn't gone out she must be at the view of Douville," and that he would go and look for her, came back immediately to tell us that she was coming to welcome us. We found her slightly dishevelled, for she had come from the flower-beds, the poultry-yard and the kitchen garden, where she had gone to feed her peacocks and hens, to look for eggs, to gather fruit and flowers to "make her table-runner," which would recall her garden path in miniature, but would confer on the table the distinction of making it support the burden of only such things as were useful and good to eat; for round those other presents from the garden—the pears, the whipped eggs—rose the tall stems of bugloss, carnations, roses and coreopsis, between which one saw, as between blossoming boundary posts, the ships out at sea moving slowly across the glazed windows. From the astonishment which M. and Mme Verdurin, interrupted while arranging their flowers to receive the visitors who had been announced, showed upon finding that these visitors were merely Albertine and myself, it was easy to see that the new servant, full of zeal but not yet familiar with my name, had repeated it wrongly and that Mme Verdurin, hearing the names of guests whom she did not know, had nevertheless bidden him let them in, in her need of seeing somebody, no matter whom. And the new servant stood contemplating this spectacle from the door in order to learn what part we played in the household. Then he made off at a loping run, for he had entered upon his duties only the day before. When Albertine had quite finished displaying her toque and veil to the Verdurins, she gave me a warning look to remind me that we had not too much time left for what we meant to do. Mme Verdurin begged us to stay to tea, but we refused, when all of a sudden a suggestion was mooted which would have made an end of all the pleasures that I had promised myself from my drive with Albertine: the Mistress, unable to face the thought of leaving us, or perhaps of letting slip a new diversion, decided to accompany us. Accustomed for years past to the experience that similar offers on her part were not well received, and being probably uncertain whether this offer would find favour with us, she concealed beneath an excessive assurance the timidity that she felt in making it to us and, without even appearing to suppose that there could be any doubt as to our answer, asked us no question but said to her husband, referring to Albertine and myself, as though she were conferring a favour on us: "I shall see them home myself." At the same time there hovered over her lips a smile that did not strictly belong to them, a smile which I had already seen on the faces of certain people when they said to Bergotte with a knowing air: "I've bought your book, it's not bad," one of those collective, universal smiles which, when they feel the need of them—as one makes use of railways and removal vans—individuals borrow, except a few who are extremely refined, like Swann or M. de Charlus, on whose lips I never saw that smile appear. From that moment my visit was ruined. I pretended not to have understood. A moment later it became evident that M. Verdurin was to be of the party. "But it will be too far for M. Verdurin," I objected. "Not at all," replied Mme Verdurin with a condescending, cheerful air, "he says it will amuse him immensely to go with you young people over a road he has travelled so many times; if necessary, he will sit beside the driver, that doesn't frighten him, and we shall come back quietly by the train like good spouses. Look at him, he's quite delighted." She seemed to be speaking of an aged and famous painter full of good nature, who, younger than the youngest, takes a delight in daubing pictures to amuse his grandchildren. What added to my gloom was that Albertine seemed not to share it and to find some amusement in the thought of dashing all over the country-side with the Verdurins. As for myself, the pleasure that I had been looking forward to enjoying with her was so imperious that I refused to allow the Mistress to spoil it; I made up lies which were justified by Mme Verdurin's irritating threats but which Albertine unfortunately contradicted. "But we have a call to make," I said. "What call?" asked Albertine. "I'll explain to you later, there's no getting out of it." "Very well, we can wait outside," said Mme Verdurin, resigned to anything. At the last minute my anguish at being deprived of a happiness for which I had so longed gave me the courage to be impolite. I refused point-blank, whispering in Mme Verdurin's ear that because of some trouble which had befallen Albertine and about which she wished to consult me, it was absolutely essential that I should be alone with her. The Mistress looked furious: "All right, we shan't come," she said to me in a voice trembling with rage. I felt her to be so angry that, so as to appear to be giving way a little: "But we might perhaps . . ." I began. "No," she replied, more furious than ever, "when I say no, I mean no." I supposed that I had irrevocably offended her, but she called us back at the door to urge us not to "let her down" on the following Wednesday, and not to come with that contraption, which was dangerous at night, but by the train with the little group, and she stopped the car, which was already moving downhill through the park, because the footman had forgotten to put in the back the slice of tart and the shortbread which she had had wrapped up for us. We set off again, escorted for a moment by the little houses that came running to meet us with their flowers. The face of the countryside seemed to us entirely changed, for in the topographical image that we form in our minds of separate places the notion of space is far from being the most important factor. We have said that the notion of time segregates them even further. It is not the only factor either. Certain places which we see always in isolation seem to us to have no common measure with the rest, to be almost outside the world, like those people whom we have known in exceptional periods of our life, in the army or during our childhood, and whom we do not connect with anything. During my first stay at Balbec there was a hill which Mme de Villeparisis liked to take us up because from it you saw only the sea and the woods, and which was called Beaumont. As the road that she took to approach it, and preferred to other routes because of its old trees, went uphill all the way, her carriage was obliged to go at a crawling pace and took a very long time. When we reached the top we used to get down, walk for a while, get back into the carriage, and return by the same road, without seeing a single village, a single country house. I knew that Beaumont was something very special, very remote, very high, but I had no idea of the direction in which it was to be found, having never taken the Beaumont road to go anywhere else; besides, it took a very long time to get there in a carriage. It was obviously in the same department (or in the same province) as Balbec, but was situated for me on another plane, enjoyed a special privilege of extra-territoriality. But the motor-car respects no mystery, and, having passed through Incarville, whose houses still danced before my eyes, as we were going down the by-road that leads to Parville (*Paterni villa*), catching sight of the sea from a natural terrace over which we were passing, I asked the name of the place, and before the chauffeur had time to reply recognised Beaumont, close by which I passed thus without knowing it whenever I took the little train, for it was within two minutes of Parville. Like an officer in my regiment who might have struck me as someone special, too kindly and unassuming to be a nobleman, or altogether too remote and mysterious to be merely a nobleman, and whom I then might have discovered to be the brother-in-law or the cousin of people with whom I often dined, so Beaumont, suddenly linked with places from which I supposed it to be so distinct, lost its mystery and took its place in the district, making me think with terror that Madame Bovary and the Sanseverina might perhaps have seemed to me to be like ordinary people, had I met them elsewhere than in the closed atmosphere of a novel. It may be thought that my love of enchanted journeys by train ought to have kept me from sharing Albertine's wonder at the motor-car which takes even an invalid wherever he wishes to go and prevents one from thinking—as I had done hitherto—of the actual site as the individual mark, the irreplaceable essence of irremovable beauties. And doubtless this site was not, for the motor-car, as it had formerly been for the railway train when I came from Paris to Balbec, a goal exempt from the contingencies of ordinary life, almost ideal at the moment of departure and remaining so at the moment of arrival in that great dwelling where nobody lives and which bears only the name of the town, the station, with its promise at last of accessibility to the place of which it is, as it were, the materialisation. No, the motor-car did not convey us thus by magic into a town which we saw at first as the collectivity summed up in its name, and with the illusions of a spectator in a theatre. It took us backstage into the streets, stopped to ask an inhabitant the way. But, as compensation for so homely a mode of progress, there are the gropings of the chauffeur himself, uncertain of his way and going back over his tracks; the "general post" of the perspective which sets a castle dancing about with a hill, a church and the sea, while one draws nearer to it however much it tries to huddle beneath its age-old foliage; those ever-narrowing circles described by the motor-car round a spellbound town which darts off in every direction to escape, and which finally it swoops straight down upon in the depths of the valley where it lies prone on the ground; so that this site, this unique point, which on the one hand the motor-car seems to have stripped of the mystery of express trains, on the other hand it gives us the impression of discovering, of pinpointing for ourselves as with a compass, and helps us to feel with a more lovingly exploring hand, with a more delicate precision, the true geometry, the beautiful proportions of the earth.

What unfortunately I did not know at that moment and did not learn until more than two years later was that one of the chauffeur's customers was M. de Charlus, and that Morel, instructed to pay him and keeping part of the money for himself (making the chauffeur triple and quintuple the mileage), had become very friendly with him (while pretending not to know him in front of other people) and made use of his car for long journeys. If I had known this at the time, and that the confidence which the Verdurins were presently to feel in this chauffeur came, unknown to them perhaps, from that source, many of the sorrows of my life in Paris in the following year, much of my trouble over Albertine, would have been avoided; but I had not the slightest suspicion of it. In themselves, M. de Charlus's excursions by motor-car with Morel were of no direct interest to me. They were confined as a rule to a lunch or dinner in some restaurant along the coast where M. de Charlus was taken for an old and penniless servant and Morel, whose duty it was to pay the bill, for a too kind-hearted gentleman. I report the conversation at one of these meals, which may give an idea of the others. It was in a restaurant of elongated shape at Saint-Mars-le-Vêtu.

"Can't you get them to remove this thing?" M. de Charlus asked Morel, as though appealing to an intermediary without having to address the staff directly. "This thing" was a vase containing three withered roses with which a well-meaning head waiter had seen fit to decorate the table.

"Yes . . ." said Morel, embarrassed. "Don't you like roses?"

"My request ought on the contrary to prove that I do like them, since there are no roses here" (Morel appeared surprised) "but as a matter of fact I do not care much for them. I am rather susceptible to names; and whenever a rose is at all beautiful, one learns that it is called Baronne de Rothschild or Maréchale Niel, which casts a chill. Do you like names? Have you found pretty titles for your little concert numbers?"

"There is one that's called *Poème triste*."

"That's hideous," replied M. de Charlus in a shrill voice that rang out like a slap in the face. "But I ordered champagne," he said to the head waiter, who had supposed he was obeying the order by placing by the diners two glasses of sparkling liquid.

"Yes, sir."

"Take away that filth, which has no connexion with the worst champagne in the world. It is the emetic known as *cup*, which consists, as a rule, of three rotten strawberries swimming in a mixture of vinegar and soda-water. ... Yes," he went on, turning again to Morel, "you don't seem to know what a title is. And even in the interpretation of the things you play best, you seem not to be aware of the mediumistic side."

"What's that you say?" asked Morel, who, not having understood one word of what the Baron had said, was afraid that he might be missing something of importance, such as an invitation to lunch. M. de Charlus not having deigned to consider "What's that you say?" as a question, Morel in consequence received no answer, and thought it best to change the subject and give the conversation a sensual turn.

"I say, look at the little blonde selling the flowers you don't like; I bet she's got a little girlfriend. And the old woman dining at the table at the end, too."

"But how do you know all that?" asked M. de Charlus, amazed at Morel's intuition.

"Oh! I can spot them in an instant. If we walked together through a crowd, you'd see that I never make a mistake." And anyone looking at Morel at that moment, with his girlish air enshrined in his masculine beauty, would have understood the obscure divination which marked him out to certain women no less than them to him. He was anxious to supplant Jupien, vaguely desirous of adding to his regular salary the income which, he supposed, the tailor derived from the Baron. "And with gigolos I'm surer still. I could save you from making mistakes. They'll be having the fair at Balbec soon. We'll find lots of things there. And in Paris too, you'll see, you'll have a fine time." But the inherited caution of a servant made him give a different turn to the sentence on which he had already embarked. So that M. de Charlus supposed that he was still referring to girls. "Do you know," said Morel, anxious to excite the Baron's senses in a fashion which he considered less compromising for himself (although it was actually more immoral), "what I'd like would be to find a girl who was absolutely pure, make her fall in love with me, and take her virginity."

M. de Charlus could not refrain from pinching Morel's ear affectionately, but added ingenuously: "What good would that do you? If you took her maidenhead, you would be obliged to marry her."

"Marry her?" cried Morel, feeling that the Baron must be tipsy, or else giving no thought to the sort of man, more scrupulous in reality than he supposed, to whom he was speaking. "Marry her? No fear! I'd promise, but once the little operation was performed, I'd ditch her that very evening."

M. de Charlus was in the habit, when a fiction was capable of causing him a momentary sensual pleasure, of giving it his support and then withdrawing it a few minutes later, when his pleasure was at an end. "Would you really do that?" he said to Morel with a laugh, squeezing him more tightly still.

"Wouldn't I half!" said Morel, seeing that he was not displeasing the Baron by continuing to expound to him what was indeed one of his desires.

"It's dangerous," said M. de Charlus.

"I should have my kit packed and ready, and buzz off without leaving an address."

"And what about me?" asked M. de Charlus.

"I should take you with me, of course," Morel made haste to add, never having thought of what would become of the Baron, who was the least of his worries. "I say, there's a kid I should love to try that game on, she's a little seamstress who keeps a shop in M. le Duc's house."

"Jupien's girl," the Baron exclaimed as the wine-waiter entered the room. "Oh! never," he added, whether because the presence of a third person had cooled him down, or because even in this sort of black mass in which he took pleasure in defiling the most sacred things, he could not bring himself to allow the mention of people to whom he was bound by ties of friendship. "Jupien is a good man, and the child is charming. It would be terrible to cause them distress."

Morel felt that he had gone too far and was silent, but his eyes continued to gaze into space at the girl for whose benefit he had once begged me to address him as "*cher maître*" and from whom he had ordered a waistcoat. An industrious worker, the child had not taken any holiday, but I learned afterwards that while the violinist was in the neighbourhood of Balbec she never ceased to think of his handsome face, ennobled by the fact that having seen Morel in my company she had taken him for a "gentleman."

"I never heard Chopin play," said the Baron, "and yet I might have done so. I took lessons from Stamati, but he forbade me to go and hear the Master of the Nocturnes at my aunt Chimay's."

"That was damned silly of him," exclaimed Morel.

"On the contrary," M. de Charlus retorted warmly, in a shrill voice. "It was a proof of his intelligence. He had realised that I was a 'natural' and that I would succumb to Chopin's influence. It's of no importance, since I gave up music when I was quite young, and everything else, for that matter. Besides, one can more or less imagine him," he added in a slow, nasal, drawling voice, "there are still people who did hear him, who can give you an idea. However, Chopin was only an excuse to come back to the mediumistic aspect which you are neglecting."

The reader will observe that, after an interpolation of common parlance, M. de Charlus had suddenly become once more as precious and haughty in his speech as he normally was. The idea of Morel's "ditching" without compunction a girl whom he had outraged had enabled him to enjoy an abrupt and consummate pleasure. From that moment his sensual appetites were satisfied for a time and the sadist (a true medium, he) who had for a few moments taken the place of M. de Charlus had fled, handing over to the real M. de Charlus, full of artistic refinement, sensibility and kindness. "You were playing the other day the piano transcription of the Fifteenth Quartet, which in itself is absurd because nothing could be less pianistic. It is meant for people whose ears are offended by the over-taut strings of the glorious Deaf One. Whereas it is precisely that almost sour mysticism that is divine. In any case you played it very badly and altered all the *tempi*. You ought to play it as though you were composing it: the young Morel, afflicted with a momentary deafness and with a non-existent genius, stands motionless for an instant; then, seized by the divine frenzy, he plays, he composes the opening bars; after which, exhausted by this trance-like effort, he collapses, letting his pretty forelock drop to please Mme Verdurin, and, moreover, giving himself time to restore the prodigious quantity of grey matter which he has drawn upon for the Pythian objectivation; then, having regained his strength, seized by a fresh and overmastering inspiration, he flings himself upon the sublime, imperishable phrase which the virtuoso of Berlin" (we suppose M. de Charlus to have meant Mendelssohn) "was to imitate unceasingly. It is in this, the only truly dynamic and transcendent fashion, that I shall make you play in Paris."

When M. de Charlus gave him advice of this sort, Morel was far more alarmed than when he saw the head waiter remove his spurned roses and "cup," for he wondered anxiously what effect it would create at his classes. But he was unable to dwell upon these reflexions, for M. de Charlus said to him imperiously: "Ask the head waiter if he has a Bon Chrétien."

"A good Christian, I don't understand."

"Can't you see we've reached the dessert. It's a pear. You may be sure Mme de Cambremer has them in her garden, for the Comtesse d'Escarbagnas, whose double she is, had them. M. Thibaudier sends them to her and she says: 'Here is a Bon Chrétien which is worth tasting.' "

"No, I didn't know."

"I can see that you know nothing. If you have never even read Molière. . . . Oh, well, since you are no more capable of ordering food than of anything else, just ask for a pear which happens to be grown in this neighbourhood, the Louise-Bonne d'Avranches."

"The what?"

"Wait a minute, since you're so stupid, I shall ask him myself for others, which I prefer. Waiter, have you any Doyennée des Comices? Charlie, you must read the exquisite passage written about that pear by the Duchesse Emilie de Clermont-Tonnerre."

"No, sir, I haven't."

"Have you any Triomphe de Jodoigne?"

"No, sir."

"Any Virginie-Baltet? Or Passe-Colmar? No? Very well, since you've nothing, we may as well go. The Duchesse d'Angoulême is not in season yet. Come along, Charlie."

Unfortunately for M. de Charlus, his lack of common sense, and perhaps, too, the probable chastity of his relations with

Morel, made him go out of his way at this period to shower upon the violinist strange bounties which the other was incapable of understanding, and to which his nature, impulsive in its own way, but mean and ungrateful, could respond only by an ever-increasing coldness or violence which plunged M. de Charlus—formerly so proud, now quite timid—into fits of genuine despair. We shall see how, in the smallest matters, Morel, who now fancied himself an infinitely more important M. de Charlus, completely misunderstood, by taking them literally, the Baron's arrogant teachings with regard to the aristocracy. Let us for the moment simply say, while Albertine waits for me at Saint-Jean-de-la-Haise, that if there was one thing which Morel set above the nobility (and this was in itself fairly noble, especially in a person whose pleasure was to pursue little girls—on the sly—with the chauffeur), it was his artistic reputation and what the others might think of him in the violin class. No doubt it was an ugly trait in his character that, because he felt M. de Charlus to be entirely devoted to him, he appeared to disown him, to make fun of him, in the same way as, once I had promised not to reveal the secret of his father's position with my great-uncle, he treated me with contempt. But on the other hand his name as that of a qualified artist, Morel, appeared to him superior to a "name." And when M. de Charlus, in his dreams of platonic affection, wanted to make him adopt one of his family titles, Morel stoutly refused.

When Albertine thought it more sensible to remain at Saint-Jean-de-la-Haise and paint, I would take the car, and it was not merely to Gourville and Féterne, but to Saint-Mars-le-Vieux and as far as Criquetot that I was able to penetrate before returning to fetch her. While pretending to be occupied with something else besides her, and to be obliged to forsake her for other pleasures, I thought only of her. As often as not I went no further than the great plain which overlooks Gourville, and as it resembles slightly the plain that begins above Combray, in the direction of Méséglise, even at a considerable distance from Albertine I had the joy of thinking that, even if my eyes could not reach her, the powerful, soft sea breeze that was flowing past me, carrying further than they, must sweep down, with nothing to arrest it, as far as Quetteholme, until it stirred the

branches of the trees that bury Saint-Jean-de-la-Haise in their
foliage, caressing my beloved's face, and thus create a double
link between us in this retreat indefinitely enlarged but free of
dangers, as in those games in which two children find themselves momentarily out of sight and earshot of one another, and
yet while far apart remain together. I returned by those roads
from which there is a view of the sea, and where in the past,
before it appeared among the branches, I used to shut my eyes
to reflect that what I was about to see was indeed the plaintive
ancestress of the earth, pursuing, as in the days when no living
creature yet existed, her insane and immemorial agitation. Now,
these roads were simply the means of rejoining Albertine;
when I recognised them, completely unchanged, knowing how
far they would run in a straight line, where they would turn, I
remembered that I had followed them while thinking of Mlle
de Stermaria, and also that this impatience to be back with
Albertine was the same feeling as I had had when I walked the
streets along which Mme de Guermantes might pass; they
assumed for me the profound monotony, the moral significance
of a sort of ruled line that my character must follow. It was
natural, and yet it was not without importance; they reminded
me that it was my fate to pursue only phantoms, creatures
whose reality existed to a great extent in my imagination; for
there are people—and this had been my case since youth—
for whom all the things that have a fixed value, assessable by
others, fortune, success, high positions, do not count; what
they must have is phantoms. They sacrifice all the rest, devote
all their efforts, make everything else subservient to the pursuit
of some phantom. But this soon fades away; then they run after
another only to return later on to the first. It was not the first
time that I had gone in quest of Albertine, the girl I had seen
that first year silhouetted against the sea. Other women, it is
true, had been interposed between the Albertine whom I had
first loved and the one whom I rarely left now; other women,
notably the Duchesse de Guermantes. But, the reader will say,
why torment yourself so much with regard to Gilberte, why
take such trouble over Mme de Guermantes, if, having become
the friend of the latter, it is with the sole result of thinking no
more of her, but only of Albertine? Swann, before his death,

might have answered the question, he who had been a lover of phantoms. Of phantoms pursued, forgotten, sought anew, sometimes for a single meeting, in order to establish contact with an unreal life which at once faded away, these Balbec roads were full. When I reflected that their trees—pear trees, apple trees, tamarisks—would outlive me, I seemed to be receiving from them a silent counsel to set myself to work at last, before the hour of eternal rest had yet struck.

I got out of the car at Quetteholme, ran down the sunken lane, crossed the brook by a plank and found Albertine painting in front of the church, all spires and crockets, thorny and red, blossoming like a rose bush. The tympanum alone showed an unbroken front; and the smiling surface of the stone was abloom with angels who continued, before the twentieth-century couple that we were, to celebrate, taper in hand, the ceremonies of the thirteenth. It was they that Albertine was endeavouring to portray on her prepared canvas, and, imitating Elstir, she painted in sweeping brush-strokes, trying to obey the noble rhythm which, the master had told her, made those angels so different from all others that he knew. Then she collected her things. Leaning upon one another we walked back up the sunken path, leaving the little church, as quiet as though it had never seen us, to listen to the perpetual murmur of the brook. Presently the car set off, taking us home by a different way. We passed Marcouville-l'Orgueilleuse. Over its church, half new, half restored, the setting sun spread its patina, as fine as that of the centuries. Through it the great bas-reliefs seemed to be visible only beneath a fluid layer, half liquid, half luminous; the Blessed Virgin, St Elizabeth, St Joachim still swam in the impalpable tide, almost detached, at the surface of the water or the sunlight. Rising up in a warm haze, the innumerable modern statues towered on their pillars half-way up the golden webs of sunset. In front of the church a tall cypress seemed to be standing in a sort of consecrated enclosure. We got out of the car to look, and strolled around for a while. No less than of her limbs, Albertine was directly conscious of her toque of Leghorn straw and of the silken veil (which were for her no less a source of sensations of well-being), and derived from them, as we walked round the church, a different sort of impetus, expressed by a lethargic contentment in which I found a certain charm. This veil and toque were but a recent, adventitious part of her, but a part that was already dear to me, as I followed its trail with my eyes, past the cypress, in the evening air. She herself could not see it, but guessed that the effect was pleasing, for she smiled at me, harmonising the poise of her head with the headgear that rounded it off. "I don't like it, it's restored," she said to me, pointing to the church and remembering what Elstir had said to her about the priceless, inimitable beauty of old stone. Albertine could tell a restoration at a glance. One could not help but marvel at the sureness of the taste she had already acquired in architecture, as contrasted with the deplorable taste she still retained in music. I cared no more than Elstir for this church; it was with no pleasure to myself that its sunlit front had come and posed before my eyes, and I had got out of the car to examine it only to oblige Albertine. And yet I felt that the great impressionist had contradicted himself; why exalt this fetish of objective architectural value, and not take into account the transfiguration of the church by the sunset? "No, definitely not," said Albertine, "I don't like it. But I like its name *orgueilleuse*. But what I must remember to ask Brichot is why Saint-Mars is called *le Vêtu*. We shall be going there the next time, shan't we?" she said, gazing at me out of her black eyes over which her toque was pulled down like the little "polo" of old. Her veil floated behind her. I got back into the car with her, happy in the thought that we should be going next day to Saint-Mars, where, in this blazing weather when one could think only of the delights of bathing, the two ancient steeples, salmon-pink, with their diamond-shaped tiles, slightly inflected and as it were palpitating, looked like a pair of old, sharp-snouted fish, moss-grown and coated with scales, which without seeming to move were rising in a blue, transparent water. On leaving Marcouville, we took a short cut by turning off at a crossroads where there was a farm. Sometimes Albertine made the car stop there and asked me to go alone and get some Calvados or cider for her to drink in the car. Although I was assured that it was not effervescent it proceeded to drench us from head to foot. We sat pressed close together. The people of the farm could scarcely see Albertine in the closed car as I handed them back their bottles; and we would drive off again as though to continue that lovers' existence which they might suppose us to lead, and in which this halt for refreshment had been only an insignificant moment —a supposition that would have appeared only too plausible if they had seen us after Albertine had drunk her bottle of cider; for she seemed then positively unable to endure the existence of a gap between herself and me which as a rule did not trouble her; beneath her linen skirt her legs were pressed against mine, and she brought her face closer too, the cheeks pallid now and warm, with a touch of red on the cheekbones, and something ardent and faded about them such as one sees in girls from the slums. At such moments, her voice changed almost as quickly as her personality; she forsook her own to adopt another that was hoarse, brazen, almost dissolute. Night began to fall. What a delight to feel her leaning against me, with her toque and her veil, reminding me that it is always thus, seated side by side, that we find couples who are in love! I was perhaps in love with Albertine, but I did not dare to let her see my love, so that, if it existed in me, it could only be like an abstract truth, of no value until it had been tested by experience; as it was, it seemed to me unrealisable and outside the plane of life. As for my jealousy, it urged me to leave Albertine as little as possible, although I knew that it would not be completely cured until I had parted from her forever. I could even feel it in her presence, but would then take care that the circumstances which had aroused it should not be repeated. Once, for example, on a fine morning, we went to lunch at Rivebelle. The great glazed doors of the dining-room and of the hall shaped like a corridor in which tea was served stood open on the same level as the sun-gilt lawns of which the vast restaurant seemed to form a part. The waiter with the pink face and black hair that writhed like flames was flying from end to end of that vast expanse less swiftly than in the past, for he was no longer an assistant but was now in charge of a row of tables; nevertheless, because of his natural briskness, he was to be glimpsed, now here now there—sometimes at a distance, in the dining-room, sometimes nearby, but out of doors serving customers who preferred to eat in the garden—like successive statues of a young god running, some in the interior, incidentally well-lighted, of a dwelling that extended on to green lawns, others beneath the trees, in the bright radiance of open-air life. For a moment he was close by us. Albertine replied absent-mindedly to what I had just said to her. She was gazing at him with rounded eyes. For a minute or two I felt that one may be close to the person one loves and yet not have her with one. They had the appearance of being engaged in a mysterious private conversation, rendered mute by my presence, which might have been the sequel to meetings in the past of which I knew nothing, or merely to a glance that he had given her—at which I was the *terzo incomodo* from whom their secret must be kept. Even when, peremptorily called away by his boss, he had finally left us, Albertine while continuing her meal seemed to be regarding the restaurant and its gardens merely as a lighted running-track, on which the swift-foot god with the black hair appeared here and there amid the varied scenery. For a moment I wondered whether she was not about to rise up and follow him, leaving me alone at my table. But in the days that followed I began to forget for ever this painful impression, for I had decided never to return to Rivebelle, and had extracted a promise from Albertine, who assured me that she had never been there before, that she would never go there again. And I denied that the nimble-footed waiter had had eyes only for her, so that she should not believe that my company had deprived her of a pleasure. It did happen now and again that I would revisit Rivebelle, but alone, and there to drink too much, as I had done in the past. As I drained a final glass I gazed at a rosette painted on the white wall, and focused on it the pleasure that I felt. It alone in the world had any existence for me; I pursued it, touched it and lost it by turns with my wavering glance, and felt indifferent to the future, contenting myself with my rosette like a butterfly circling about another, stationary butterfly with which it is about to end its life in an act of supreme consummation.

It would perhaps have been a peculiarly opportune moment for giving up a woman whom no very recent or very keen suffering obliged me to ask for the balm against a malady which those who have caused it possess. I was calmed by these very outings, which, even if I considered them at the time merely as a foretaste of a morrow which itself, notwithstanding the longing with which it filled me, would not be different from to-day, had the charm of having been pre-empted from the places which Albertine had frequented hitherto and where I had not been with her, at her aunt's or with her girlfriends—the charm not of a positive joy but simply of the assuagement of an anxiety, and yet extremely potent. For at an interval of a few days, when my thoughts turned to the farm outside which we had sat drinking cider, or simply to the stroll we had taken round Saint-Mars-le-Vêtu, remembering that Albertine had been walking by my side in her toque, the sense of her presence added of a sudden so strong a healing virtue to the indifferent image of the modern church that at the moment when the sunlit façade came thus of its own accord to pose before me in memory, it was like a great soothing compress laid upon my heart. I would drop Albertine at Parville, but only to join her again in the evening and lie stretched out by her side, in the darkness, upon the beach. True, I did not see her every day, yet I could say to myself: "If she were to give an account of how she spent her time, her life, it would still be me who played the largest part in it"; and we spent together long hours on end which brought into my days so sweet an intoxication that even when, at Parville, she jumped from the car which I was to send to fetch her an hour later, I felt no more alone in it than if before leaving me she had strewn it with flowers. I could have dispensed with seeing her every day; I was happy when I left her, and I knew that the calming effect of that happiness might last for several days. But at that moment I would hear Albertine as she left me say to her aunt or to a girl-friend: "To-morrow at eight-thirty, then. We mustn't be late, the others will be ready at a quarter past." The conversation of a woman one loves is like the ground above a dangerous sub-terranean stretch of water; one senses constantly beneath the words the presence, the penetrating chill of an invisible pool; one perceives here and there its treacherous percolation, but the water itself remains hidden. The moment I heard these words of Albertine's my calm was destroyed. I wanted to ask her to let me see her the following morning, so as to prevent her from going to this mysterious rendezvous at half past eight which had been mentioned in my presence only in veiled terms. She would no doubt have begun by obeying me, while regretting that she had to give up her plans; in time she would have discovered my permanent need to upset them; I should have become the person from whom one hides things. And yet it is probable that these gatherings from which I was excluded amounted to very little, and that it was perhaps from the fear that I might find one or other of the participants vulgar or boring that I was not invited to them. Unfortunately this life so closely involved with Albertine's had an effect not only upon myself; to me it brought calm; to my mother it caused anxieties, her confession of which destroyed my calm. Once, as I entered the hotel happy in my own mind, resolved to terminate some day or other an existence the end of which I imagined to depend upon my own volition, my mother said to me, hearing me send a message to the chauffeur to go and fetch Albertine: "How you do waste your money." (Françoise in her simple and expressive language used to say with greater force: "That's the way the money goes.") "Try," Mamma went on, "not to become like Charles de Sévigné, of whom his mother said: 'His hand is a crucible in which gold melts.' Besides, I do really think you've gone about with Albertine quite enough. I assure you you're overdoing it, even to her it may seem ridiculous. I was delighted that you'd found some sort of distraction, and I'm not asking you never to see her again, but simply that it should be possible to meet one of you without the other." My life with Albertine, a life devoid of keen pleasures—that is to say of keen pleasures that I could feel—that life which I intended to change at any moment, choosing a moment of calm, became suddenly necessary to me once more when, by these words of Mamma's, it seemed to be threatened. I told my mother that her words would delay for perhaps two months the decision for which they asked, which otherwise I would have reached before the end of that week. In order not to sadden me, Mamma laughed at this instantaneous effect of her advice, and promised not to raise the subject again so as not to prevent the rebirth of my good intention. But, since my grandmother's death, whenever Mamma gave way to mirth, the incipient laugh would be cut short and would end in an almost heartbroken expression of sorrow, whether from remorse at having been able for an instant to forget, or else from the recrudescence which this brief moment of forgetfulness had brought to her painful obsession. But to the thoughts aroused in her by the memory of my grandmother, a memory that was rooted in my mother's mind, I felt that on this occasion there were added others relating to myself, to what my mother dreaded as the sequel of my intimacy with Albertine; an intimacy which she dared not, however, hinder in view of what I had just told her. But she did not appear convinced that I was not mistaken. She remembered all the years in which my grandmother and she had refrained from speaking to me about my work and the need for a healthier way of life which, I used to say, the agitation into which their exhortations threw me alone prevented me from beginning, and which, notwithstanding their obedient silence, I had failed to pursue.

After dinner the car would bring Albertine back; there was still a glimmer of daylight; the air was less warm, but after a scorching day we both dreamed of delicious coolness; then to our fevered eyes the narrow slip of moon would appear at first (as on the evening when I had gone to the Princesse de Guermantes's and Albertine had telephoned me) like the delicate rind, then like the cool section of a fruit which an invisible knife was beginning to peel in the sky. Sometimes it was I who would go to fetch my beloved, a little later in that case; she would be waiting for me under the arcade of the market at Maineville. At first I could not make her out; I would begin to fear that she might not be coming, that she had misunderstood me. Then I would see her, in her white blouse with blue spots, spring into the car by my side with the light bound of a young animal rather than a girl. And it was like a dog too that she would begin to caress me interminably. When night had completely fallen and, as the manager of the hotel remarked to me, the sky was all "studied" with stars, if we did not go for a drive in the forest with a bottle of champagne, then, heedless of the late strollers on the faintly lighted esplanade, who in any case could not have seen anything a yard away on the dark sand, we would stretch out in the shelter of the dunes; that same body whose suppleness contained all the feminine, marine and sportive grace of the girls whom I had seen that first time against the horizon of the waves, I held pressed against my own, beneath the same rug, by the edge of the motionless sea divided by a tremulous path of light; and we listened to it with the same untiring pleasure, whether it held back its breath, suspended for so long that one thought the reflux would never come, or whether at last it gasped out at our feet the long-awaited murmur. Finally I would take Albertine back to Parville. When we reached her house, we were obliged to break off our kisses for fear that someone might see us; not wishing to go to bed, she would return with me to Balbec, from whence I would take her back for the last time to Parville; the chauffeurs of those early days of the motor-car were people who went to bed at all hours. And indeed I would return to Balbec only with the first dews of morning, alone this time, but still surrounded with the presence of my beloved, gorged with an inexhaustible provision of kisses. On my table I would find a telegram or a postcard. Albertine again! She had written them at Quetteholme when I had gone off by myself in the car, to tell me that she was thinking of me. I would re-read them as I got into bed. Then, above the curtains, I would glimpse the bright streak of the daylight and would say to myself that we must be in love with one another after all, since we had spent the night in one another's arms. When, next morning, I caught sight of Albertine on the front, I was so afraid of her telling me that she was not free that day, and could not accede to my request that we should go out together, that I would delay it for as long as possible. I would be all the more uneasy since she had a cold, preoccupied air; people were passing whom she knew; doubtless she had made plans for the afternoon from which I was excluded. I would gaze at her, I would gaze at that rosy face of Albertine's, tantalising me with the enigma of her intentions, the unknown decision which was to create the happiness or misery of my afternoon. It was a whole state of soul, a whole future existence that had assumed before my eyes the allegorical and fateful form of a girl. And when at last I made up my mind, when, with the most indifferent air that I could muster, I asked: "Are we going

out together now, and again this evening?" and she replied:
"With the greatest pleasure," then the sudden replacement, in
the rosy face, of my long uneasiness by a delicious sense of
ease would make even more precious to me those forms to
which I was perpetually indebted for the sense of well-being
and relief that we feel after a storm has broken. I repeated to
myself: "How sweet she is, what an adorable creature!" in an
excitement less fertile than that caused by intoxication, scarcely
more profound than that of friendship, but far superior to that
of social life. We would cancel our order for the car only on the
days when there was a dinner-party at the Verdurins' and on
those when, Albertine not being free to go out with me, I took
the opportunity to inform anybody who wished to see me that
I should be remaining at Balbec. I gave Saint-Loup permission
to come on these days, but on these days only. For on one
occasion when he had arrived unexpectedly, I had preferred to
forgo the pleasure of seeing Albertine rather than run the risk
of his meeting her, than endanger the state of happy calm in
which I had dwelt for some time and see my jealousy revive.
And my mind had not been set at rest until after Saint-Loup
had gone. Therefore he made it a rule, regretfully but scrupulously observed, never to come to Balbec unless summoned
there by me. In the past, when I thought with longing of the
hours that Mme de Guermantes spent in his company, how I
had valued the privilege of seeing him! People never cease to
change place in relation to ourselves. In the imperceptible but
eternal march of the world, we regard them as motionless, in a
moment of vision too brief for us to perceive the motion that is
sweeping them on. But we have only to select in our memory
two pictures taken of them at different moments, close enough
together however for them not to have altered in themselves—
perceptibly, that is to say—and the difference between the two
pictures is a measure of the displacement that they have undergone in relation to us. Robert alarmed me dreadfully by speaking to me of the Verdurins, for I was afraid that he might ask
me to take him there, which would have been enough, because
of the jealousy I should constantly feel, to spoil all the pleasure
that I found in going there with Albertine. But fortunately
he assured me that, on the contrary, the one thing he desired

above all others was not to know them. "No," he said to me,
"I find that sort of clerical atmosphere maddening." I did not at
first understand the application of the adjective "clerical" to the
Verdurins, but the sequel to his remark clarified his meaning,
betraying his concessions to those fashions in words which one
is often astonished to see adopted by intelligent men. "I mean
the sort of circles," he said, "where people form a tribe, a
religious order, a chapel. You aren't going to tell me that
they're not a little sect; they're all butter and honey to the
people who belong, no words bad enough for those who don't.
The question is not, as for Hamlet, to be or not to be, but to
belong or not to belong. You belong, my uncle Charlus
belongs. But I can't help it, I've never gone in for that sort of
thing, it isn't my fault."

I need hardly say that the rule I had imposed upon Saint-
Loup, never to come and see me unless I had expressly invited
him, I promulgated no less strictly in the case of the various
persons with whom I had gradually made friends at la Raspelière, Féterne, Montsurvent, and elsewhere; and when I saw
from the hotel the smoke of the three o'clock train which, in
the anfractuosity of the cliffs of Parville, left a stationary plume
which long remained clinging to the flank of the green slopes,
I had no doubts as to the identity of the visitor who was
coming to tea with me and was still, like a classical deity, concealed from me beneath that little cloud. I am obliged to confess that this person whose visit I had authorised in advance
was hardly ever Saniette, and I have often reproached myself
for this omission. But Saniette's own consciousness of being a
bore (even more so, naturally, when he came to pay a call than
when he told a story) had the effect that, although he was more
learned, more intelligent and better than most people, it seemed
impossible to feel in his company, not only any pleasure, but
anything save an almost intolerable irritation which spoiled
one's whole afternoon. Probably, if Saniette had frankly
admitted this boredom which he was afraid of causing, one
would not have dreaded his visits. Boredom is one of the least
of the evils that we have to endure, and his boringness existed
perhaps only in the imagination of other people, or had been
inoculated into him by some process of suggestion which had

taken hold on his agreeable modesty. But he was so anxious
not to let it be seen that he was not sought after that he dared
not propose himself. Certainly he was right not to behave like
the people who are so glad to be able to raise their hats in a
public place that, not having seen you for years and catching
sight of you in a box at the theatre with smart people whom
they do not know, they give you a furtive but resounding good-
evening on the pretext of the pleasure and delight they have
felt on seeing you, on realising that you are going about again,
that you are looking well, etc. But Saniette went to the other
extreme. He might, at Mme Verdurin's or in the little train,
have told me that he would have great pleasure in coming to
see me at Balbec were he not afraid of disturbing me. Such a
suggestion would not have alarmed me. On the contrary, he
offered nothing, but, with a tortured expression on his face and
a stare as indestructible as a fired enamel, into the composition
of which, however, there entered, together with a passionate
desire to see one—unless he found someone else who was more
entertaining—the determination not to let this desire be
manifest, would say to me with a casual air: "You don't happen
to know what you will be doing in the next few days, because
I shall probably be somewhere in the neighbourhood of Balbec?
Not that it makes the slightest difference, I just thought I'd
ask." This casual air deceived nobody, and the reverse signs
whereby we express our feelings by their opposites are so
clearly legible that one asks oneself how there can still be
people who say, for instance: "I have so many invitations that
I don't know which way to turn" to conceal the fact that they
have been invited nowhere. But what was more, this casual
air, probably on account of the dubious elements that had gone
to form it, gave you, what the fear of boredom or a frank
admission of the desire to see you would never have done, the
sort of discomfort, of repulsion, which in the category of
relations of simple social courtesy is the equivalent of what, in
amatory relations, is provoked by the lover's disguised offer,
to a lady who does not return his love, to see her next day,
while protesting that he does not greatly care—or not even that
offer but an attitude of sham coldness. There emanated at once
from Saniette's person an indefinable aura which made you

answer him in the tenderest of tones: "No, unfortunately, this week, I must explain to you. . . ." And I allowed to call upon me instead people who were a long way his inferiors but whose eyes were not filled with melancholy or their mouths twisted with bitter regret as his were at the thought of all the visits which he longed, while saying nothing about them, to pay to various people. Unfortunately, Saniette rarely failed to meet in the "crawler" the guest who was coming to see me, if indeed the latter had not said to me at the Verdurins': "Don't forget I'm coming to see you on Thursday," the very day on which I had just told Saniette that I should not be at home. So that he came in the end to imagine life as filled with entertainments arranged behind his back, if not actually at his expense. On the other hand, as none of us is ever all of a piece, this most discreet of men was morbidly tactless and indiscreet. On the one occasion on which he happened to come and see me uninvited, a letter, I forget from whom, had been left lying on my table. After the first few minutes, I saw that he was paying only the vaguest attention to what I was saying. The letter, of whose provenance he knew absolutely nothing, fascinated him and at any moment I expected his glittering eyeballs to detach themselves from their sockets and fly to the letter, insignificant in itself, which his curiosity had magnetised. He was like a bird irresistibly drawn towards a snake. Finally he could restrain himself no longer. He began by altering its position, as though he were tidying up my room; then, this not sufficing him, he picked it up, turned it over, turned it back again, as though mechanically. Another form of his tactlessness was that once he had fastened himself on to you he could not tear himself away. As I was feeling unwell that day, I asked him to go back by the next train, in half an hour's time. He did not doubt that I was feeling unwell, but replied: "I shall stay for an hour and a quarter, and then I shall go." Since then I have regretted that I did not tell him to come and see me whenever I was free. Who knows? Possibly I might have exorcised his ill fate, and other people would have invited him for whom he would immediately have deserted me, so that my invitations would have had the twofold advantage of restoring him to happiness and ridding me of his company.

On the days following those on which I had been "at home," I naturally did not expect any visitors and the motor-car would come again to fetch Albertine and me. And when we returned, Aimé, on the lowest step of the hotel, could not help looking, with passionate, curious, greedy eyes, to see what tip I was giving the chauffeur. However tightly I enclosed my coin or note in my clenched fist, Aimé's gaze tore my fingers apart. He would turn his head away a moment later, for he was discreet and well-mannered, and indeed was himself content with relatively modest remuneration. But the money that another person received aroused in him an irrepressible curiosity and made his mouth water. During these brief moments, he had the attentive, feverish air of a boy reading a Jules Verne novel, or of a diner seated at a neighbouring table in a restaurant who, seeing the waiter carving you a pheasant to which he himself either cannot or will not treat himself, abandons for an instant his serious thoughts to fasten upon the bird eyes lit with a smile of love and longing.

Thus, day after day, these excursions in the motor-car followed one another. But once, as I was going up to my room, the lift-boy said to me: "That gentleman has been, he gave me a message for you." The lift-boy uttered these words in a hoarse croak, coughing and expectorating in my face. "I haven't half got a cold!" he went on, as though I were incapable of perceiving this for myself. "The doctor says it's whooping-cough," and he began once more to cough and expectorate over me. "Don't tire yourself trying to talk," I said to him with an air of kindly concern, which was feigned. I was afraid of catching the whooping-cough which, with my tendency to choking spasms, would have been a serious matter for me. But he made it a point of honour, like a virtuoso who refuses to go sick, to go on talking and spitting all the time. "No, it doesn't matter," he said ("Perhaps not to you," I thought, "but to me it does"). "Besides, I shall be returning to Paris soon" ("So much the better, provided he doesn't give it to me first"). "They say Paris is very superb," he went on. "It must be even more superb than here or Monte-Carlo, although some of the pages and some of the guests, in fact even head waiters who've been to Monte-Carlo for the season have often told me that Paris was not so superb as Monte-Carlo. Perhaps they were being stupid, you've got to have your wits about you to be a head waiter—taking all the orders, reserving tables, you need quite a brain. I've heard it said that it's even tougher than writing plays and books."

We had almost reached my landing when the lift-boy carried me down again to the ground floor because he found that the button was not working properly, and in a moment he had put it right. I told him that I would prefer to walk upstairs, by which I meant, without putting it in so many words, that I preferred not to catch whooping-cough. But with a cordial and contagious burst of coughing the boy thrust me back into the lift. "There's no danger now, I've fixed the button." Seeing that he was still talking incessantly, and preferring to learn the name of my visitor and the message that he had left rather than the comparative beauties of Balbec, Paris, and Monte-Carlo, I said to him (as one might say to a tenor who is wearying one with Benjamin Godard, "Won't you sing me some Debussy?") "But who is the person who called to see me?" "It's the gentleman you went out with yesterday. I'll go and fetch his card, it's with my porter." As, the day before, I had dropped Robert de Saint-Loup at Doncières station before going to meet Albertine, I supposed that the lift-boy was referring to him, but it was the chauffeur. And by describing him in the words: "The gentleman you went out with," he taught me at the same time that a working man is just as much a gentleman as a man about town. A lesson in the use of words only. For in point of fact I had never made any distinction between the classes. And if, on hearing a chauffeur called a gentleman, I had felt the same astonishment as Count X who had only held that rank for a week and who, when I said "the Countess looks tired," turned his head round to see who I was talking about, it was simply because I was unaccustomed to that particular usage; I had never made any distinction between working people, the middle classes and the nobility, and I should have been equally ready to make any of them my friends. With a certain preference for working people, and after them for the nobility, not because I liked them better but because I knew that one could expect greater courtesy from them towards working people than one finds among the middle classes, either because the nobility are less disdainful or else because they are naturally polite to anybody, as beautiful women are glad to bestow a smile which they know will be joyfully welcomed. I cannot however pretend that this habit that I had of putting people of humble station on a level with people in society, even if it was quite understood by the latter, was always entirely pleasing to my mother. Not that, humanly speaking, she made the slightest distinction between one person and another, and if Françoise was ever in sorrow or in pain she was comforted and tended by Mamma with the same devotion as her best friend. But my mother was too much my grandfather's daughter not to accept, in social matters, the rule of caste. People at Combray might have kind hearts and sensitive natures, might have adopted the noblest theories of human equality, yet my mother, when a footman showed signs of forgetting his place, began to say "you" and gradually slipped out of the habit of addressing me in the third person, was moved by these presumptions to the same wrath that breaks out in Saint-Simon's *Memoirs* whenever a nobleman who is not entitled to it seizes a pretext for assuming officially the style of "Highness," or for not paying dukes the deference he owes to them and is gradually beginning to lay aside. There was a "Combray spirit" so deep-rooted that it would take centuries of natural kindness (my mother's was boundless) and egalitarian conviction to succeed in dissolving it. I cannot swear that in my mother certain particles of this spirit had not remained insoluble. She would have been as reluctant to shake hands with a footman as she was ready to give him ten francs (which for that matter gave him far more pleasure). To her, whether she admitted it or not, masters were masters and servants were the people who fed in the kitchen. When she saw the driver of a motor-car dining with me in the restaurant, she was not altogether pleased, and said to me: "It seems to me you might have a more suitable friend than a mechanic," as she might have said, had it been a question of my marriage: "You might have found somebody better than that." This particular chauffeur (fortunately I never dreamed of inviting him to dinner) had come to tell me that the motor-car company which had sent him to Balbec for the season had ordered him to return to Paris on the following day. This excuse, especially as the chauffeur was charming and expressed himself so simply that one would always have taken anything he said for Gospel, seemed to us to be most probably true. It was only half so. There was as a matter of fact no more work for him at Balbec. And in any case, the company being only half convinced of the veracity of the young evangelist, bowed over his wheel of consecration, was anxious that he should return to Paris as soon as possible. And indeed if the young apostle wrought a miracle in multiplying his mileage when he was calculating it for M. de Charlus, when, on the other hand, it was a matter of rendering his account to the company, he divided what he had earned by six. In consequence of which the company, coming to the conclusion either that nobody wanted a car now at Balbec, which, so late in the season, was not improbable, or that it was being robbed, decided that, upon either hypothesis, the best thing was to recall him to Paris, not that there was very much work for him there. What the chauffeur wished was to avoid, if possible, the dead season. I have said—though I was unaware of this at the time, and the knowledge of it would have saved me much unhappiness—that he was on very friendly terms with Morel, although they showed no sign even of knowing each other in front of other people. From the day on which he was recalled, without knowing as yet that he had a means of avoiding departure, we were obliged to content ourselves for our excursions with hiring a carriage, or sometimes, as an amusement for Albertine and because she was fond of riding, a pair of saddle-horses. The carriages were unsatisfactory. "What a rattle-trap," Albertine would say. I would, in any case, often have preferred to be alone in it. Without being ready to fix a date, I longed to put an end to this existence which I blamed for making me renounce not so much work as pleasure. It sometimes happened too, however, that the habits which bound me were suddenly abolished, generally when some former self, full of the desire to live an exhilarating life, momentarily took the place of my present self. I felt this longing to escape especially strongly one day when, having left Albertine at her aunt's, I had gone on horseback to call on the Verdurins and had taken an unfrequented path through the woods the beauty of which they had extolled to me. Hugging the contours of the cliff, it alternately climbed and then, hemmed in by dense woods on either side, dived into wild gorges. For a moment the barren rocks by which I was surrounded, and the sea that was visible through their jagged gaps, swam before my eyes like fragments of another universe: I had recognised the mountainous and marine landscape which Elstir had made the scene of those two admirable watercolours, "Poet meeting a Muse" and "Young Man meeting a Centaur," which I had seen at the Duchesse de Guermantes's. The memory of them transported the place in which I now found myself so far outside the world of to-day that I should not have been surprised if, like the young man of the prehistoric age that Elstir had painted, I had come upon a mythological personage in the course of my ride. Suddenly, my horse reared; he had heard a strange sound; it was all I could do to hold him and remain in the saddle; then I raised my tear-filled eyes in the direction from which the sound seemed to come and saw, not two hundred feet above my head, against the sun, between two great wings of flashing metal which were bearing him aloft, a creature whose indistinct face appeared to me to resemble that of a man. I was as deeply moved as an ancient Greek on seeing for the first time a demi-god. I wept—for I had been ready to weep the moment I realised that the sound came from above my head (aeroplanes were still rare in those days), at the thought that what I was going to see for the first time was an aeroplane. Then, just as when in a newspaper one senses that one is coming to a moving passage, the mere sight of the machine was enough to make me burst into tears. Meanwhile the airman seemed to be uncertain of his course; I felt that there lay open before him—before me, had not habit made me a prisoner—all the routes in space, in life itself; he flew on, let himself glide for a few moments over the sea, then quickly making up his mind, seeming to yield to some attraction that was the reverse of gravity, as though returning to his native element, with a slight adjustment of his golden wings he headed straight up into the sky.

To return to the subject of the chauffeur, he demanded of Morel that the Verdurins should not merely replace their break by a motor-car (which, given their generosity towards the faithful, was comparatively easy), but, what was more difficult, replace their head coachman, the sensitive young man with the tendency to black thoughts, by himself, the chauffeur. This change was carried out in a few days by the following device. Morel had begun by seeing that the coachman was robbed of everything that he needed for harnessing up. One day it was the bit that was missing, another day the curb. At other times it was the cushion of his box-seat that had vanished, or his whip, his rug, the martingale, the sponge, the chamois-leather. He always managed to borrow what he required from a neighbour, but he was late in bringing round the carriage, which put him in M. Verdurin's bad books and plunged him into a state of melancholy and gloom. The chauffeur, who was in a hurry to take his place, told Morel that he would have to return to Paris. It was time to do something drastic. Morel persuaded M. Verdurin's servants that the young coachman had declared that he would lay an ambush for the lot of them, boasting that he could take on all six of them at once, and told them that they could not let this pass. He himself did not want to get involved, but he was warning them so that they might forestall the coachman. It was agreed that while M. and Mme Verdurin and their guests were out walking the servants should set about the young man in the stables. Although it merely provided the opportunity for what was to happen, I may mention the fact—because the people concerned interested me later on—that the Verdurins had a friend staying with them that day whom they had promised to take for a walk before his departure, which was fixed for that same evening.

What surprised me greatly when we started off for our walk was that Morel, who was coming with us and was to play his violin under the trees, said to me: "Listen, I have a sore arm, and I don't want to say anything about it to Mme Verdurin, but you might ask her to send for one of her footmen, Howsler for instance, to carry my things."

"I think someone else would be more suitable," I replied. "He will be wanted here for dinner."

A look of anger flitted across Morel's face. "No, I'm not going to entrust my violin to any Tom, Dick or Harry."

I realised later on his reason for this choice. Howsler was the beloved brother of the young coachman, and, if he had been left at home, might have gone to his rescue. During our walk, dropping his voice so that the elder Howsler should not overhear: "What a good fellow he is," said Morel. "So is his brother, for that matter. If he hadn't that fatal habit of drinking. . . ."

"Did you say drinking?" said Mme Verdurin, turning pale at the idea of having a coachman who drank.

"You've never noticed it? I always say to myself it's a miracle that he's never had an accident while he's been driving you."

"Does he drive anyone else, then?"

"You can easily see how many spills he's had, his face to-day is a mass of bruises. I don't know how he's escaped being killed, he's broken his shafts."

"I haven't seen him to-day," said Mme Verdurin, trembling at the thought of what might have happened to her, "you appal me."

She tried to cut short the walk so as to return at once, but Morel chose an air by Bach with endless variations to keep her away from the house. As soon as we got back she went to the stable, saw the new shafts and Howsler streaming with blood. She was on the point of telling him without more ado that she did not require a coachman any longer, and of paying him his wages, but of his own accord, not wishing to accuse his fellow-servants, to whose animosity he attributed retrospectively the theft of all his saddlery, and seeing that further patience would only end in his being left for dead on the ground, he asked leave to go at once, which settled matters. The chauffeur began his duties next day and, later on, Mme Verdurin (who had been obliged to engage another) was so well satisfied with him that she recommended him to me warmly as a man of the utmost reliability. I, knowing nothing of all this, engaged him by the day in Paris. But I am anticipating events; I shall come to all this when I reach the story of Albertine. At the present moment we are at la Raspelière, where I have just come to dine for the first time with my beloved, and M. de Charlus with Morel, the alleged son of an "intendant" who drew a fixed salary of thirty thousand francs annually, kept his own carriage, and had any number of major-domos, subordinates, gardeners, stewards and farmers at his beck and call. But, since I have so far anticipated, I do not wish to leave the reader under the impression that Morel was entirely wicked. He was, rather, a mass of contradictions, capable on certain days of being genuinely kind.

I was naturally greatly surprised to hear that the coachman had been dismissed, and even more surprised when I recognised his successor as the chauffeur who had been driving Albertine and myself in his car. But he poured out to me a complicated story, according to which he was supposed to have been summoned back to Paris, where an order had come for him to go to the Verdurins, and I did not doubt his word for an instant. The coachman's dismissal was the cause of Morel's talking to me for a few minutes, to express his regret at the departure of that worthy fellow. In fact, even apart from the moments when I was alone and he literally bounded towards me beaming with joy, Morel, seeing that everybody made much of me at la Raspelière and feeling that he was deliberately cutting himself off from the society of a person who was no danger to him, since he had made me burn my boats and had destroyed all possibility of my treating him patronisingly (something which in any case I had never dreamed of doing), ceased to hold aloof from me. I attributed his change of attitude to the influence of M. de Charlus, which as a matter of fact did make him in certain respects less blinkered, more artistic, but in others, when he applied literally the grandiloquent, insincere, and moreover transient formulas of his master, made him stupider than ever. That M. de Charlus might have said something to him was as a matter of fact the only thing that occurred to me. How could I have guessed then what I was told afterwards (and was never certain of its truth, Andrée's assertions about anything that concerned Albertine, especially later on, having always seemed to me to be highly dubious, for, as we have already seen, she did not genuinely like her and was jealous of her), something which in any event, even if it was true, was remarkably well concealed from me by both of them: that Albertine was on the best of terms with Morel? The new attitude which, about the time of the coachman's dismissal,

Morel adopted with regard to myself, enabled me to revise my opinion of him. I retained the ugly impression of his character which had been suggested by the servility which this young man had shown me when he needed me, followed, as soon as the favour had been done, by a scornful aloofness which he took to the point of seeming not to notice me. To this one had to add the evidence of his venal relations with M. de Charlus, and also of his gratuitously brutish impulses, the non-gratification of which (when it occurred) or the complications that they involved, were the cause of his sorrows; but his character was not so uniformly vile and was full of contradictions. He resembled an old book of the Middle Ages, full of mistakes, of absurd traditions, of obscenities; he was extraordinarily composite. I had supposed at first that his art, in which he was really a past master, had endowed him with qualities that went beyond the virtuosity of the mere performer. Once, when I spoke of my wish to start work, "Work, and you will achieve fame," he said to me. "Who said that?" I inquired. "Fontanes, to Chateaubriand." He also knew certain love letters of Napoleon. Good, I thought to myself, he's well-read. But this remark, which he had read God knows where, was evidently the only one that he knew in the whole of ancient or modern literature, for he repeated it to me every evening. Another, which he quoted even more frequently to prevent me from breathing a word about him to anybody, was the following, which he considered equally literary, whereas it is more or less meaningless, or at any rate makes no kind of sense except perhaps to a mystery-loving servant: "Beware of the wary." In fact, if one went from this stupid maxim to Fontanes's remark to Chateaubriand, one would have covered a whole stretch, varied but less contradictory than it might seem, of Morel's character. This youth who, provided there was money to be made by it, would have done anything in the world, and without remorse —perhaps not without an odd sort of vexation, amounting to nervous agitation, to which however the name remorse could not for a moment be applied—who would, had it been to his advantage, have plunged whole families into misery or even into mourning, this youth who put money above everything else, not merely above kindness, but above the most natural feelings of common humanity, this same youth nevertheless put above money his diploma as first prize-winner at the Conservatoire and the risk of anything being said to his discredit in the flute or counterpoint class. Hence his most violent rages, his most sombre and unjustifiable fits of ill-temper arose from what he himself (generalising doubtless from certain particular cases in which he had met with malevolent people) called universal treachery. He flattered himself on eluding it by never speaking about anyone, by keeping his cards close to his chest, by distrusting everybody. (Alas for me, in view of what was to happen after my return to Paris, his distrust had not "held" in the case of the Balbec chauffeur, in whom he had doubtless recognised a peer, that is to say, contrary to his maxim, a wary person in the proper sense of the word, a wary person who remains obstinately silent in front of decent people and at once comes to an understanding with a blackguard.) It seemed to him—and he was not absolutely wrong—that his distrust would enable him always to save his bacon, to come through the most dangerous adventures unscathed, without anyone in the Rue Bergère being able to suggest anything against him, let alone to prove it. He would work, become famous, would perhaps one day, with his respectability still intact, be examiner in the violin on the board of that great and glorious Conservatoire.

But it is perhaps crediting Morel's brain with too much logic to attempt to disentangle all these contradictions. His nature was really like a sheet of paper that has been folded so often in every direction that it is impossible to straighten it out. He seemed to have quite lofty principles, and in a magnificent hand, marred by the most elementary mistakes in spelling, spent hours writing to his brother to point out that he had behaved badly to his sisters, that he was their elder, their natural support, etc., and to his sisters that they had shown a want of respect for himself.

Presently, as summer came to an end, when one got out of the train at Douville, the sun, blurred by the prevailing mist, had ceased to be more than a red blotch in a sky that was uniformly mauve. To the great peace which descends at dusk over these lush, saline meadows, and which had tempted a large number of Parisians, painters mostly, to spend their holidays at Douville, was added a humidity which made them seek shelter early in their little bungalows. In several of these the lamp was already lit. Only a few cows remained out of doors gazing at the sea and lowing, while others, more interested in humanity, turned their attention towards our carriages. A single painter who had set up his easel on a slight eminence was striving to render that great calm, that hushed luminosity. Perhaps the cattle would serve him unconsciously and benevolently as models, for their contemplative air and their solitary presence, when the human beings had withdrawn, contributed in their own way to the powerful impression of repose that evening diffuses. And, a few weeks later, the transposition was no less agreeable when, as autumn advanced, the days became really short, and we were obliged to make our journey in the dark. If I had been out in the afternoon, I had to go back to change at the latest by five o'clock, when at this season the round, red sun had already sunk half-way down the slanting mirror which formerly I had detested, and, like a Greek fire, was setting the sea alight in the glass fronts of all my bookcases. Some incantatory gesture having resuscitated, as I put on my dinner-jacket, the alert and frivolous self that was mine when I used to go with Saint-Loup to dine at Rivebelle and on the evening when I had thought to take Mme de Stermaria to dine on the island in the Bois, I began unconsciously to hum the same tune as I had hummed then; and it was only when I realised this as by the song I recognised the sporadic singer, who indeed knew no other tune. The first time I had sung it, I was beginning to fall in love with Albertine, but I imagined that I would never get to know her. Later, in Paris, it was when I had ceased to love her and some days after I had enjoyed her for the first time. Now it was when I loved her again and was on the point of going out to dinner with her, to the great regret of the manager who believed that I would end up living at la Raspelière altogether and deserting his hotel, and assured me that he had heard that fever was prevalent in that neighbourhood, due to the marshes of the Bec and their "stagning" water. I was delighted by the multiplicity in which I saw my

life thus spread over three planes; and besides, when one becomes for an instant one's former self, that is to say different
from what one has been for some time past, one's sensibility,
being no longer dulled by habit, receives from the slightest
stimulus vivid impressions which make everything that has
preceded them fade into insignificance, impressions to which,
because of their intensity, we attach ourselves with the momentary enthusiasm of a drunkard. It was already dark when we
got into the omnibus or carriage which was to take us to the
station to catch the little train. And in the hall the judge
would say to us: "Ah! so you're off to la Raspelière! Good
God, she has a nerve, your Mme Verdurin, making you travel
an hour by train in the dark, simply to dine with her. And then
having to set out again at ten o'clock at night with a wind
blowing like the very devil. It's easy to see that you have
nothing better to do," he added, rubbing his hands together.
No doubt he spoke thus from annoyance at not having been
invited, and also from the self-satisfaction felt by "busy" men—
however idiotic their business— at "not having time" to do
what you are doing.

It is of course justifiable for the man who draws up reports,
adds up figures, answers business letters, follows the movements of the stock exchange, to feel an agreeable sense of
superiority when he says to you with a sneer: "It's all very well
for you; you having nothing better to do." But he would
be no less contemptuous, would be even more so (for dining
out is a thing that the busy man does also), were your recreation
writing *Hamlet* or merely reading it. Wherein busy men show a
lack of forethought. For the disinterested culture which seems
to them a comic pastime of idle people when they find them
engaged in it is, they ought to reflect, the same as that which,
in their own profession, brings to the fore men who may not be
better judges or administrators than themselves but before
whose rapid advancement they bow their heads, saying: "It
appears he's extremely well-read, a most distinguished individual." But above all the judge was oblivious of the fact
that what pleased me about these dinners at la Raspelière was
that, as he himself said quite rightly, though as a criticism,
they "represented a real journey," a journey whose charm

appeared to me all the more intense in that it was not an end in itself and one did not look to find pleasure in it—this being reserved for the gathering for which we were bound and which could not fail to be greatly modified by all the atmosphere that surrounded it. Night would already have fallen now when I exchanged the warmth of the hotel—the hotel that had become my home—for the railway carriage into which I climbed with Albertine, in which a glimmer of lamp-light on the window showed, at certain halts of the wheezy little train, that we had arrived at a station. So that there should be no risk of Cottard's missing us, and not having heard the name of the station being called, I would open the door, but what burst into the carriage was not any of the faithful, but the wind, the rain and the cold. In the darkness I could make out fields and hear the sea; we were in the open country. Before we joined the little nucleus, Albertine would examine herself in a little mirror, extracted from a gold vanity case which she carried about with her. The fact was that on our first visit, Mme Verdurin having taken her upstairs to her dressing-room so that she might tidy up before dinner, I had felt, amid the profound calm in which I had been living for some time, a slight stir of uneasiness and jealousy at being obliged to part from Albertine at the foot of the stairs, and had become so anxious while I was alone in the drawing-room among the little clan, wondering what she could be doing, that I had telegraphed the next day, after finding out from M. de Charlus what the correct thing was at the moment, to order from Cartier's a vanity case which was the joy of Albertine's life and also of mine. It was for me a guarantee of peace of mind, and also of my mistress's solicitude. For she had evidently seen that I did not like her to be parted from me at Mme Verdurin's and arranged to do all the titivation necessary before dinner in the train.

Among Mme Verdurin's regular guests, and reckoned the most faithful of them all, M. de Charlus had now figured for some months. Regularly, thrice weekly, the passengers sitting in the waiting-rooms or standing on the platform at Doncières-Ouest used to see this stout gentleman go by, with his grey hair, his black moustaches, his lips reddened with a salve less noticeable at the end of the season than in summer when the daylight made it look more garish and the heat liquefied it. As he made his way towards the little train, he could not refrain (simply from force of habit, as a connoisseur, since he now had a sentiment which kept him chaste or at least, for most of the time, faithful) from casting a furtive glance, at once inquisitorial and timorous, at the labourers, the soldiers, the young men in tennis clothes, after which he immediately let his eye-lids droop over his half-shut eyes with the unctuousness of an ecclesiastic engaged in telling his beads, and with the modesty of a bride vowed to the one love of her life or of a well-brought-up young girl. The faithful were all the more convinced that he had not seen them, since he got into a different compartment from theirs (as Princess Sherbatoff often did too), like a man who does not know whether one will be pleased or not to be seen with him and who leaves you the option of coming and joining him if you choose. This option had not been taken, at first, by the Doctor, who had advised us to leave him by himself in his compartment. Making a virtue of his natural hesitancy now that he occupied a great position in the medical world, it was with a smile, a toss of the head, and a glance over his pince-nez at Ski, that he said in a whisper, either from malice or in the hope of eliciting the views of his companions in a roundabout way: "You see, if I was on my own, a bachelor . . . but because of my wife I wonder whether I ought to allow him to travel with us after what you told me." "What's that you're saying?" asked Mme Cottard. "Nothing, it doesn't concern you, it's not meant for women to hear," the Doctor replied with a wink, and with a majestic self-satisfaction which steered a middle course between the impassive expression he maintained in front of his pupils and patients and the uneasiness that used in the past to accompany his shafts of wit at the Verdurins', and went on talking *sotto voce*. Mme Cottard picked up only the words "a member of the confraternity" and "*tapette*,"[49] and as in the Doctor's vocabulary the former expression denoted the Jewish race and the latter a wagging tongue, Mme Cottard concluded that M. de Charlus must be a garrulous Jew. She could not understand why they should cold-shoulder the Baron for that reason, and felt it her duty as the senior lady of the clan to insist that he should not be left alone; and so we proceeded in a body to M. de Charlus's compartment, led by Cottard who was still perplexed. From the corner in which he was reading a volume of Balzac, M. de Charlus observed this indecision; and yet he had not raised his eyes. But just as deaf-mutes detect, from a movement of air imperceptible to other people, that someone has approached behind them, so the Baron, to apprise him of people's coldness towards him, had a veritable sensory hyper-acuity. This, as it habitually does in every sphere, had engendered in M. de Charlus imaginary sufferings. Like those neuropaths who, feeling a slight lowering of the temperature, and deducing therefrom that there must be a window open on the floor above, fly into a rage and start sneezing, M. de Charlus, if a person appeared preoccupied in his presence, concluded that somebody had repeated to that person a remark that he had made about him. But there was no need even for the other person to have an absent-minded, or a sombre, or a smiling air; he would invent them. On the other hand, cordiality easily concealed from him the slanders of which he had not heard. Having detected Cottard's initial hesitation, while he held out his hand to the rest of the faithful when they were at a convenient distance (greatly to their surprise, for they did not think that they had yet been observed by the reader's lowered eyes), for Cottard he contented himself with a forward inclination of his whole person which he at once sharply retracted, without taking in his own gloved hand the hand which the Doctor had held out to him.

"We felt we simply must come and keep you company, Monsieur," Mme Cottard said kindly to the Baron, "and not leave you alone like this in your little corner. It is a great pleasure to us."

"I am greatly honoured," the Baron intoned, bowing coldly.

"I was so pleased to hear that you have definitely chosen this neighbourhood to set up your taber. . . ."

She was going to say "tabernacle" but it occurred to her that the word was Hebraic and discourteous to a Jew who might see some innuendo in it. And so she pulled herself up in order to choose another of the expressions that were familiar to her, that is to say a ceremonious expression: "to set up, I should say, your *penates*." (It is true that these deities do not appertain to the Christian religion either, but to one which has been dead for so long that it no longer claims any devotees whose feelings one need be afraid of hurting.) "We, unfortunately, what with term beginning, and the Doctor's hospital duties, can never take up residence for very long in one place." And glancing down at a cardboard box: "You see too how we poor women are less fortunate than the sterner sex; even to go such a short distance as to our friends the Verdurins', we are obliged to take a whole heap of impedimenta."

I meanwhile was examining the Baron's volume of Balzac. It was not a paper-covered copy, picked up on a bookstall, like the volume of Bergotte which he had lent me at our first meeting. It was a book from his own library, and as such bore the device: "I belong to the Baron de Charlus," for which was substituted at times, to show the studious tastes of the Guermantes: "*In proeliis non semper*," or yet another motto: "*Non sine labore.*" But we shall see these presently replaced by others, in an attempt to please Morel.

Mme Cottard, after a moment or two, hit upon a subject which she felt to be of more personal interest to the Baron. "I don't know whether you agree with me, Monsieur," she said to him presently, "but I am very broad-minded, and in my opinion there is a great deal of good in all religions as long as people practise them sincerely. I am not one of the people who get hydrophobia at the sight of a . . . Protestant."

"I was taught that mine is the true religion," replied M. de Charlus.

"He's a fanatic," thought Mme Cottard. "Swann, until towards the end, was more tolerant; it's true that he was a convert."

Now the Baron, on the contrary, was not only a Christian, as we know, but endued with a mediaeval piety. For him, as for the sculptors of the thirteenth century, the Christian church was, in the living sense of the word, peopled with a swarm of beings whom he believed to be entirely real: prophets, apostles, angels, holy personages of every sort, surrounding the incarnate Word, his mother and her spouse, the Eternal Father, all the martyrs and doctors of the Church, as they may be seen in high relief thronging the porches or lining the naves of cathedrals.

Out of all these M. de Charlus had chosen as his patrons and intercessors the Archangels Michael, Gabriel and Raphael, with whom he discoursed regularly so that they might convey his prayers to the Eternal Father before whose throne they stand. And so Mme Cottard's mistake amused me greatly.

To leave the religious sphere, let us note that the Doctor, who had come to Paris with the meagre equipment of a peasant mother's advice, and had then been absorbed in the almost purely material studies to which those who seek to advance in a medical career are obliged to devote themselves for a great many years, had never cultivated his mind; he had acquired increasing authority but no experience; he took the word "honoured" in its literal sense and was at once flattered by it because he was vain, and distressed because he had a kind heart. "That poor de Charlus," he said to his wife that evening, "he made me feel sorry for him when he said he was honoured to travel with us. One feels, poor devil, that he knows nobody, that he has to humble himself."

But soon, without any need to be guided by the charitable Mme Cottard, the faithful had succeeded in overcoming the qualms which they had all more or less felt at first on finding themselves in the company of M. de Charlus. No doubt in his presence they were incessantly reminded of Ski's revelations, and conscious of the sexual abnormality embodied in their travelling companion. But this abnormality itself had a sort of attraction for them. It gave to the Baron's conversation, remarkable in itself but in ways which they could scarcely appreciate, a savour which, they felt, made the most interesting conversation, even Brichot's, appear slightly insipid in comparison. From the very outset, moreover, they had been pleased to admit that he was intelligent. "Genius is sometimes akin to madness," the Doctor declared, and when the Princess, athirst for knowledge, questioned him further, said not another word, this axiom being all that he knew about genius and in any case seeming to him less demonstrable than everything relating to typhoid and arthritis. And as he had become proud and remained ill-bred: " No questions, Princess, do not interrogate me, I'm at the seaside for a rest. Besides, you wouldn't understand, you know nothing about medicine." And the Princess apologised and held her peace, deciding that Cottard was a charming man and realising that celebrities were not always approachable. In this initial period, then, they had ended by finding M. de Charlus intelligent in spite of his vice (or what is generally so named). Now it was, quite unconsciously, because of that vice that they found him more intelligent than others. The simplest maxims to which, adroitly provoked by the sculptor or the scholar, M. de Charlus gave utterance concerning love, jealousy, beauty, because of the strange, secret, refined and monstrous experience on which they were based, assumed for the faithful that charm of unfamiliarity with which a psychology analogous to that which our own dramatic literature has offered us from time immemorial is clothed in a Russian or Japanese play performed by native actors. They might still venture, when he was not listening, upon a malicious witticism at his expense. "Oh!" the sculptor would whisper, seeing a young railwayman with the sweeping eyelashes of a dancing girl at whom M. de Charlus could not help staring, "if the Baron begins making eyes at the conductor, we shall never get there, the train will start going backwards. Just look at the way he's staring at him: this isn't a puffer-train but a pooftertrain." But when all was said, if M. de Charlus did not appear, they were almost disappointed to be travelling only with people who were just like everybody else, and not to have with them this painted, paunchy, tightly-buttoned personage, reminiscent of a box of exotic and dubious origin exhaling a curious odour of fruits the mere thought of tasting which would turn the stomach. From this point of view, the faithful of the masculine sex enjoyed a keener satisfaction in the short stage of the journey between Saint-Martin-du-Chêne, where M. de Charlus got in, and Doncières, the station at which Morel joined the party. For so long as the violinist was not there (and provided that the ladies and Albertine, keeping to themselves so as not to inhibit the conversation, were out of hearing), M. de Charlus made no attempt to appear to be avoiding certain subjects and did not hesitate to speak of "what it is customary to call immoral practices." Albertine could not hamper him, for she was always with the ladies, like a well-brought-up girl who does not wish her presence to restrict the freedom of grown-up conversation. And I was quite resigned to not having her by my side, on condition however that she remained in the same compartment. For though I no longer felt any jealousy and scarcely any love for her, and never thought about what she might be doing on the days when I did not see her, on the other hand, when I was there, a mere partition which might at a pinch be concealing a betrayal was intolerable to me, and if she withdrew with the ladies to the next compartment, a moment later, unable to remain in my seat any longer, at the risk of offending whoever might be talking, Brichot, Cottard or Charlus, to whom I could not explain the reason for my flight, I would get up, leave them without ceremony, and, to make certain that nothing abnormal was going on, go next door. And until we came to Doncières M. de Charlus, without any fear of shocking his audience, would speak sometimes in the plainest terms of practices which, he declared, for his own part he did not consider either good or bad. He did this from cunning, to show his broad-mindedness, convinced as he was that his own morals aroused no suspicion in the minds of the faithful. He was well aware that there did exist in the world several persons who were, to use an expression which became habitual with him later on, "in the know" about himself. But he imagined that these persons were not more than three or four, and that none of them was at that moment on the Normandy coast. This illusion may appear surprising in so shrewd and so suspicious a man. Even in the case of those whom he believed to be more or less informed, he deluded himself that it was in the vaguest way, and hoped, by telling them this or that fact about someone, to clear the person in question from all suspicion on the part of a listener who out of politeness pretended to accept his statements. Even in my case, while he was aware of what I knew or guessed about him, he imagined that my conviction, which he believed to be of far longer standing than it actually was, was quite general, and that it was sufficient for him to deny this or that detail to be believed, whereas on the contrary, if a knowledge of the whole always precedes a knowledge of the details, it makes investigation of the latter infinitely easier and, having destroyed his cloak of invisibility, no longer allows the dissembler to hide

whatever he chooses. Certainly when M. de Charlus, invited to
a dinner-party by one of the faithful or a friend of one of the
faithful, adopted the most devious means to introduce Morel's
name among ten others which he mentioned, he never
imagined that for the reasons, always different, which he gave
for the pleasure or convenience he would find that evening in
being invited with him, his hosts, while appearing to believe
him implicitly, would substitute a single and invariable
reason, of which he supposed them to be ignorant, namely that
he was in love with him. Similarly, Mme Verdurin, seeming
always entirely to acknowledge the motives, half-artistic, half-
humanitarian, which M. de Charlus gave her for the interest
that he took in Morel, never ceased to thank the Baron warmly
for his kindness—his touching kindness, she called it—to the
violinist. Yet how astonished M. de Charlus would have been
if, one day when Morel and he were delayed and had not come
by the train, he had heard the Mistress say: "We're all here now
except the young ladies." The Baron would have been all the
more amazed in that, scarcely stirring from la Raspelière, he
played the part there of a family chaplain, a stage priest, and
would sometimes (when Morel had 48 hours' leave) sleep there
for two nights in succession. Mme Verdurin would then give
them adjoining rooms, and, to put them at their ease, would
say: "If you want to have a little music, don't worry about us.
The walls are as thick as a fortress, you have nobody else on
your floor, and my husband sleeps like a log." On such days
M. de Charlus would relieve the Princess of the duty of going
to meet newcomers at the station, apologising for Mme
Verdurin's absence on the grounds of a state of health which
he described so vividly that the guests entered the drawing-
room with solemn faces and uttered cries of astonishment on
finding the Mistress up and doing and dressed for the evening.

For M. de Charlus had for the moment become for Mme
Verdurin the faithfullest of the faithful, a second Princess
Sherbatoff. Of his position in society she was not nearly so
certain as of that of the Princess, imagining that if the latter
cared to see no one outside the little nucleus it was out of
contempt for other people and preference for it. As this
pretence was precisely the Verdurins' own, they treating as

bores everyone to whose society they were not admitted, it is incredible that the Mistress can have believed the Princess to have an iron-willed loathing for everything fashionable. But she stuck to her guns and was convinced that in the case of the Princess too it was in all sincerity and from a love of things intellectual that she avoided the company of bores. The latter were, as it happened, diminishing in numbers from the Verdurins' point of view. Life by the seaside exempted an introduction from the consequences for the future which might have been feared in Paris. Brilliant men who had come down to Balbec without their wives (which made everything much easier) made overtures to la Raspelière and, from being bores, became delightful. This was the case with the Prince de Guermantes, whom the absence of his Princess would not, however, have decided to go as a "grass widower" to the Verdurins' had not the magnet of Dreyfusism been so powerful as to carry him at one stroke up the steep ascent to la Raspelière, unfortunately on a day when the Mistress was not at home. Mme Verdurin as it happened was not certain that he and M. de Charlus moved in the same world. The Baron had indeed said that the Duc de Guermantes was his brother, but this was perhaps the untruthful boast of an adventurer. However elegant he had shown himself to be, however amiable, however "faithful" to the Verdurins, the Mistress still almost hesitated to invite him to meet the Prince de Guermantes. She consulted Ski and Brichot: "The Baron and the Prince de Guermantes, will they be all right together?"

"Good gracious, Madame, as to one of the two I think I can safely say. . . ."

"One of the two—what good is that to me?" Mme Verdurin had retorted crossly. "I asked you whether they would get on all right together."

"Ah! Madame, that sort of thing is very difficult to know."

Mme Verdurin had been impelled by no malice. She was certain of the Baron's proclivities, but when she expressed herself in these terms she had not for a moment been thinking about them, but had merely wished to know whether she could invite the Prince and M. de Charlus on the same evening without their clashing. She had no malevolent intention when she employed these ready-made expressions which are popular in artistic "little clans." To make the most of M. de Guermantes, she proposed to take him in the afternoon, after her lunch-party, to a charity entertainment at which sailors from the neighbourhood would give a representation of a ship setting sail. But, not having time to attend to everything, she delegated her duties to the faithfullest of the faithful, the Baron. "You understand, I don't want them to hang about like mussels on a rock, they must keep coming and going, and we must see them weighing anchor or whatever it's called. Since you're always going down to the harbour at Balbec-Plage, you can easily arrange a dress rehearsal without tiring yourself. You must know far better than I do, M. de Charlus, how to get round young sailors. . . . But we really are giving ourselves a lot of trouble for M. de Guermantes. Perhaps he's only one of those idiots from the Jockey Club. Oh! heavens, I'm running down the Jockey Club, and I seem to remember that you're one of them. Eh, Baron, you don't answer me, are you one of them? You don't want to come out with us? Look, here's a book that has just come which I think you'll find interesting. It's by Roujon. The title is attractive: *Among Men*."

For my part, I was all the more pleased that M. de Charlus often took the place of Princess Sherbatoff inasmuch as I was thoroughly in her bad books, for a reason that was at once trivial and profound. One day when I was in the little train being as attentive as ever to Princess Sherbatoff, I saw Mme de Villeparisis get in. She had, I knew, come down to spend some weeks with the Princesse de Luxembourg, but, chained to the daily necessity of seeing Albertine, I had never replied to the repeated invitations of the Marquise and her royal hostess. I felt remorse at the sight of my grandmother's friend, and, purely from a sense of duty (without deserting Princess Sherbatoff), sat talking to her for some time. I was, as it happened, entirely unaware that Mme de Villeparisis knew perfectly well who my companion was but did not wish to acknowledge her. At the next station, Mme de Villeparisis left the train, and indeed I reproached myself for not having helped her on to the platform. I resumed my seat by the side of the Princess. But it was as though (a cataclysm frequent among people who are socially insecure and afraid that one may have heard something to their discredit and hence may despise them) the curtain had risen upon a new scene. Buried in her *Revue des Deux Mondes*, Mme Sherbatoff could scarcely bring herself to reply to my questions and finally told me that I was giving her a headache. I had not the faintest idea of the nature of my crime. When I bade the Princess good-bye, the customary smile did not light up her face, her chin drooped in a curt acknowledgement, she did not even offer me her hand, and she never spoke to me again. But she must have spoken— though I have no idea what she said—to the Verdurins; for as soon as I asked them whether I ought not to make some polite gesture to Princess Sherbatoff, they replied in chorus: "No! No! No! Absolutely not! She doesn't care for polite speeches." They did not say this in order to cause bad blood between us, but she had succeeded in persuading them that she was unmoved by civilities, impervious to the vanities of this world. One needs to have seen the politician who is reckoned the most unbending, the most intransigent, the most unapproachable, now that he is in office; one needs to have seen him at the time of his eclipse, humbly soliciting, with a bright, ingratiating smile, the haughty greeting of some second-rate journalist; one needs to have seen the transformation of Cottard (whom his new patients regarded as a ramrod), and to know what disappointments in love, what rebuffs to snobbery were the basis of the apparent pride, the universally acknowledged anti-snobbery of Princess Sherbatoff, in order to grasp that the rule among the human race—a rule that naturally admits of exceptions—is that the reputedly hard are the weak whom nobody wanted, and that the strong, caring little whether they are wanted or not, have alone that gentleness which the vulgar herd mistakes for weakness.

Besides, I ought not to judge Princess Sherbatoff severely. Her case is so common! One day, at the funeral of a Guermantes, a distinguished man who was standing next to me drew my attention to a tall, slender individual with handsome features. "Of all the Guermantes," my neighbour informed me, "that one is the most strange and remarkable. He is the Duke's brother." I replied imprudently that he was mistaken, that the

gentleman in question, who was in no way related to the Guermantes, was named Fournier-Sarlovèze. The distinguished man
turned his back on me and has never even looked at me since.

An eminent musician, a member of the *Institut*, occupying a
high official position, who was acquainted with Ski, came to
Harambouville, where he had a niece, and appeared at one of
the Verdurins' Wednesdays. M. de Charlus was especially polite
to him (at Morel's request), principally in order that on his
return to Paris the Academician would allow him to attend
various private concerts, rehearsals and so forth at which the
violinist would be playing. The Academician, who was
flattered, and was moreover a charming man, promised to do so
and kept his promise. The Baron was deeply touched by all the
kindness and courtesy which this important personage (who,
for his own part, was exclusively and passionately a lover of
women) showed him, all the facilities that he procured for him
to see Morel in those official premises from which outsiders
are excluded, all the opportunities which the celebrated artist
secured for the young virtuoso to perform, to get himself
known, by naming him in preference to others of equal talent
for auditions which were likely to make a special stir. But
M. de Charlus never suspected that he owed the maestro all the
more gratitude in that the latter, doubly deserving, or alternatively guilty twice over, was fully aware of the relations
between the young violinist and his noble patron. He abetted
them, certainly not out of any sympathy for them since he was
incapable of understanding any other love than the love of
women, which had inspired the whole of his music, but from
moral indifference, a kindness and readiness to oblige characteristic of his profession, social affability, and snobbery. He had
so little doubt as to the character of those relations that, at his
first dinner at la Raspelière, he had inquired of Ski, speaking of
M. de Charlus and Morel as he might have spoken of a man
and his mistress: "Have they been long together?" But, too
much the man of the world to let the parties concerned see
that he knew, prepared, should any gossip arise among
Morel's fellow-students, to rebuke them and to reassure Morel
by saying to him in a fatherly tone: "One hears that sort of
thing about everybody nowadays," he continued to overwhelm

the Baron with civilities which the latter thought charming, but quite natural, being incapable of suspecting the eminent maestro of so much vice or of so much virtue. For nobody was ever base enough to repeat to M. de Charlus the things that were said behind his back, and the jokes about Morel. And yet this simple situation is enough to show that even that thing which is universally decried, which no one would dream of defending—gossip—has itself, whether it is aimed at ourselves and thus becomes especially disagreeable to us, or whether it tells us something about a third person of which we were unaware, a certain psychological value. It prevents the mind from falling asleep over the factitious view which it has of what it imagines things to be and which is actually no more than their outward appearance. It turns this appearance inside out with the magic dexterity of an idealist philosopher and rapidly presents to our gaze an unsuspected corner of the reverse side of the fabric. Could M. de Charlus ever have imagined these words spoken by a certain tender relative: "How on earth can you suppose that Mémé is in love with me? You forget that I'm a woman!" And yet she was genuinely, deeply attached to M. de Charlus. Why then need we be surprised that in the case of the Verdurins, on whose affection and good-will he had no reason to rely, the remarks which they made behind his back (and they did not, as we shall see, confine themselves to remarks) should have been so different from what he imagined them to be, that is to say no more than a reflexion of the remarks that he heard when he was present? These latter alone decorated with affectionate inscriptions the little ideal bower to which M. de Charlus retired at times to dream, when he introduced his imagination for a moment into the idea that the Verdurins had of him. Its atmosphere was so congenial, so cordial, the repose it offered so comforting, that when M. de Charlus, before going to sleep, had withdrawn to it for a momentary relaxation from his worries, he never emerged from it without a smile. But, for each one of us, a bower of this sort is double: opposite the one which we imagine to be unique, there is the other which is normally invisible to us, the real one, symmetrical with the one we know, but very different, whose decoration, in which we should recognise nothing of what we expected to see, would horrify us as though it were composed of the odious symbols of an unsuspected hostility. What a shock it would have been for M. de Charlus if he had found his way into one of these hostile bowers, thanks to some piece of scandal, as though by one of those service staircases where obscene graffiti are scribbled outside the back doors of flats by unpaid tradesmen or dismissed servants! But, just as we do not possess that sense of direction with which certain birds are endowed, so we lack the sense of our own visibility as we lack that of distances, imagining as quite close to us the interested attention of people who on the contrary never give us a thought, and not suspecting that we are at that same moment the sole preoccupation of others. Thus M. de Charlus lived in a fool's paradise like the fish that thinks that the water in which it is swimming extends beyond the glass wall of its aquarium which mirrors it, while it does not see close beside it in the shadow the amused stroller who is watching its gyrations, or the all-powerful keeper who, at the unforeseen and fatal moment, postponed for the present in the case of the Baron (for whom the keeper, in Paris, will be Mme Verdurin), will extract it without compunction from the environment in which it was happily living to fling it into another. Moreover, the races of mankind, insofar as they are no more than collections of individuals, may furnish us with examples more extensive, but identical in each of their parts, of this profound, obstinate and disconcerting blindness. Up to the present, if it was responsible for the fact that M. de Charlus addressed to the little clan remarks of a futile subtlety or of an audacity which made his listeners smile to themselves, it had not yet caused him, nor was it to cause him, at Balbec, any serious inconvenience. A trace of albumen, of sugar, of cardiac arythmia, does not prevent life from continuing normally for the man who is not even aware of it, while the physician alone sees in it a prophecy of catastrophes in store. At present the Baron's predilection for Morel—whether platonic or not—merely led him to say spontaneously in Morel's absence that he thought him very good-looking, assuming that this would be interpreted quite innocently, and thereby acting like a clever man who, when summoned to testify before a court of law, will not be afraid to enter into details which are apparently to his disadvantage but for that very reason are more natural and less vulgar than the conventional protestations of a stage culprit. With the same freedom, always between Saint-Martin-du-Chêne and Doncières-Ouest—or conversely on the return journey—M. de Charlus would readily speak of people who had, it appeared, very peculiar ways, and would even add: "But after all, although I say peculiar, I don't really know why, for there's nothing so very peculiar about it," to prove to himself how thoroughly at his ease he was with his audience. And so indeed he was, provided that it was he who retained the initiative and knew that the gallery was mute and smiling, disarmed by credulity or good manners.

When M. de Charlus was not speaking of his admiration for Morel's beauty as though it had no connexion with a proclivity known as a vice, he would discuss that vice, but as though he himself were in no way addicted to it. Sometimes indeed he did not hesitate to call it by its name. When after examining the fine binding of his volume of Balzac, I asked him which was his favourite novel in the *Comédie humaine,* he replied, his thoughts irresistibly attracted towards an obsession: "Impossible to choose between tiny miniatures like the *Curé de Tours* and the *Femme abandonnée,* or the great frescoes like the series of the *Illusions perdues.* What! you've never read *Les Illusions perdues*? It's so beautiful—the scene where Carlos Herrera asks the name of the château he is driving past, and it turns out to be Rastignac, the home of the young man he used to love; and then the abbé falling into a reverie which Swann once called, and very aptly, the *Tristesse d'Olympio* of pederasty. And the death of Lucien! I forget who the man of taste was who, when he was asked what event in his life had grieved him most, replied: 'The death of Lucien de Rubempré in *Splendeurs et Misères.*' "

"I know that Balzac is all the rage this year, as pessimism was last," Brichot interrupted. "But, at the risk of giving pain to hearts that are smitten with the Balzacian fever, without laying any claim, God forbid, to the role of policeman of letters, and drawing up a list of offences against the laws of grammar, I must confess that the copious improviser whose alarming lucubrations you appear to me singularly to overrate has always struck me as being an insufficiently meticulous scribe. I have read these *Illusions perdues* of which you speak, Baron, flagellating myself to attain to the fervour of an initiate, and I confess in all simplicity of heart that those serial instalments of sentimental balderdash, composed in double or triple Dutch—*Esther heureuse*, *Où mènent les mauvais chemins*, *A combien l'amour revient aux vieillards*—have always had the effect on me of the mysteries of *Rocambole*, exalted by an inexplicable preference to the precarious position of a masterpiece."

"You say that because you know nothing of life," said the Baron, doubly irritated, for he felt that Brichot would not understand either his aesthetic reasons or the other kind.

"I quite realise," replied Brichot, "that, to speak like Master François Rabelais, you mean that I am *moult sorbonagre, sorbonicole et sorboniforme*. And yet, just as much as any of our friends here, I like a book to give an impression of sincerity and real life, I am not one of those clerks . . ."

"The *quart d'heure de Rabelais*,"[50] the Doctor broke in, with an air no longer of uncertainty but of confidence in his own wit.

". . . who take a vow of literature following the rule of the Abbaye-aux-Bois under the obedience of M. le Vicomte de Chateaubriand, Grand Master of humbug, according to the strict rule of the humanists. M. le Vicomte de Chateaubriand . . ."

"Chateaubriand *aux pommes*?" put in Dr Cottard.

"He is the patron saint of the brotherhood," continued Brichot, ignoring the Doctor's joke, while the latter, alarmed by the scholar's phrase, glanced anxiously at M. de Charlus. Brichot had seemed wanting in tact to Cottard, whose pun meanwhile had brought a subtle smile to the lips of Princess Sherbatoff: "With the Professor, the mordant irony of the complete sceptic never forfeits its rights," she said kindly, to show that Cottard's "quip" had not passed unperceived by herself.

"The sage is of necessity sceptical," replied the Doctor. "What do I know? *Gnōthi seauton*, said Socrates. He was quite right, excess in anything is a mistake. But I am dumbfounded when I think that those words have sufficed to keep Socrates's name alive all this time. What does his philosophy amount to?

Very little when all is said. When one thinks that Charcot and others have done work that is a thousand times more remarkable and is at least based on something, on the suppression of the pupillary reflex as a syndrome of general paralysis, and that they are almost forgotten. After all, Socrates was nothing out of the common. Those people had nothing better to do than spend all their time strolling about and splitting hairs. Like Jesus Christ: 'Love one another!' it's all very pretty."

"My dear," Mme Cottard implored.

"Naturally my wife protests, women are all neurotic."

"But, my dear Doctor, I'm not neurotic," murmured Mme Cottard.

"What, she's not neurotic! When her son is ill, she develops all the symptoms of insomnia. Still, I quite admit that Socrates, and all the rest of them, are necessary for a superior culture, to acquire the talent of exposition. I always quote his *gnōthi seauton* to my students at the beginning of the course. Old Bouchard, when he heard of it, congratulated me."

"I am not an upholder of form for form's sake, any more than I am inclined to treasure millionaire rhymes in poetry," Brichot went on. "But all the same, the not very human *Comédie humaine* is all too egregiously the antithesis of those works in which the art exceeds the matter, as that worthy hack Ovid says. And it is permissible to prefer a middle way, which leads to the presbytery of Meudon or the hermitage of Ferney, equidistant from the Valley of Wolves, in which René arrogantly performed the duties of a merciless pontificate, and from les Jardies, where Honoré de Balzac, harried by the bailiffs, never ceased voiding upon paper, like a zealous apostle of gibberish, to please a Polish lady."

"Chateaubriand is far more alive now than you say, and Balzac is, after all, a great writer," replied M. de Charlus, still too much impregnated with Swann's tastes not to be irritated by Brichot, "and Balzac was acquainted even with those passions which the rest of the world ignores, or studies only to castigate them. Without referring again to the immortal *Illusions perdues*, stories like *Sarrazine*, *La Fille aux yeux d'or*, *Une passion dans le désert*, even the distinctly enigmatic *Fausse Maîtresse*, can be adduced in support of my argument. When I spoke of this 'extra-natural' aspect of Balzac to Swann, he said to me: 'You are of the same opinion as Taine.' I never had the honour of knowing Monsieur Taine," M. de Charlus continued (with that irritating habit of inserting an otiose "Monsieur" to which people in society are addicted, as though they imagine that by styling a great writer "Monsieur" they are doing him an honour, perhaps keeping him at his proper distance, and making it quite clear that they do not know him personally), "I never knew Monsieur Taine, but I felt myself greatly honoured by being of the same opinion as he."

Nevertheless, in spite of these ridiculous social affectations, M. de Charlus was extremely intelligent, and it is probable that if some remote marriage had established a connexion between his family and that of Balzac, he would have felt (no less than Balzac himself, for that matter) a satisfaction on which he would yet have been unable to resist preening himself as on a praiseworthy sign of condescension.

Occasionally, at the station after Saint-Martin-du-Chêne, some young men would get into the train. M. de Charlus could not refrain from looking at them, but as he cut short and concealed the attention that he paid them, he gave the impression of hiding a secret that was even more personal than the real one; it was as though he knew them, and betrayed the knowledge in spite of himself, after having accepted the sacrifice, before turning again to us, like children who, in consequence of a quarrel between parents, have been forbidden to speak to certain of their schoolfellows, but who when they meet them cannot forbear to raise their heads before lowering them again beneath the menacing gaze of their tutor.

At the word borrowed from the Greek with which M. de Charlus, in speaking of Balzac, had followed his allusion to *Tristesse d'Olympio* in connexion with *Splendeurs et Misères*, Ski, Brichot and Cottard had glanced at one another with a smile perhaps not so much ironical as tinged with that satisfaction which people at a dinner-party would show who had succeeded in making Dreyfus talk about his own case, or the Empress Eugénie about her reign. They were hoping to press him a little further upon this subject, but we were already at Doncières, where Morel joined us. In his presence, M. de

Charlus kept a careful guard over his conversation and, when Ski tried to bring it back to the love of Carlos Herrera for Lucien de Rubempré, the Baron assumed the vexed, mysterious, and finally (seeing that nobody was listening to him) severe and judicial air of a father who hears a man saying something indecent in front of his daughter. Ski having shown some determination to pursue the subject, M. de Charlus, his eyes starting out of his head, raised his voice and with a meaningful glance at Albertine—who in fact could not hear what we were saying, being engaged in conversation with Mme Cottard and Princess Sherbatoff—and the hint of a double meaning of someone who wishes to teach ill-bred people a lesson, said: "I think it's high time we began to talk of subjects that might interest this young lady." But I realised that, for him, the young lady was not Albertine but Morel, and he confirmed, later on, the accuracy of my interpretation by the expressions he employed when he begged that there might be no more such conversations in front of Morel. "You know," he said to me, speaking of the violinist, "he's not at all what you might suppose, he's a very decent boy who has always been very serious and well-behaved." One sensed from these words that M. de Charlus regarded sexual inversion as a danger as menacing to young men as prostitution is to women, and that if he employed the epithet "serious" of Morel it was in the sense that it has when applied to a young shop-girl.

Then Brichot, to change the subject, asked me whether I intended to remain much longer at Incarville. Although I had pointed out to him more than once that I was staying not at Incarville but at Balbec, he always repeated the mistake, for it was by the name of Incarville or Balbec-Incarville that he referred to this section of the coast. One often finds people speaking thus about the same things as oneself by a slightly different name. A certain lady of the Faubourg Saint-Germain used invariably to ask me, when she meant to refer to the Duchesse de Guermantes, whether I had seen Zénaïde lately, or Oriane-Zénaïde, so that at first I did not understand her. Probably there had been a time when, some relative of Mme de Guermantes being named Oriane, she herself, to avoid confusion, had been known as Oriane-Zénaïde. Perhaps, too, there had originally been a station only at Incarville, from which one went on by carriage to Balbec.

"Why, what have you been talking about?" said Albertine, astonished at the solemn, paternal tone which M. de Charlus had suddenly adopted.

"About Balzac," the Baron hastily replied, "and you are wearing this evening the very same costume as the Princesse de Cadignan, not the first, which she wears at the dinner-party, but the second."

This coincidence was due to the fact that, in choosing Albertine's clothes, I drew my inspiration from the taste that she had acquired thanks to Elstir, who had a liking for the sort of sobriety that might have been called British had it not been tempered with a softness that was purely French. As a rule the clothes he preferred offered to the eye a harmonious combination of grey tones, like the dress of Diane de Cadignan. M. de Charlus was almost the only person capable of appreciating Albertine's clothes at their true value; his eye detected at a glance what constituted their rarity, their worth; he would never have mistaken one material for another, and could always recognise the maker. But he preferred—in women—a little more brightness and colour than Elstir would allow. And so, that evening, Albertine glanced at me with a half-smiling, half-apprehensive expression, wrinkling her little pink cat's nose. Meeting over her skirt of grey crêpe de chine, her jacket of grey cheviot did indeed give the impression that she was dressed entirely in grey. But, signing to me to help her, because her puffed sleeves needed to be smoothed down or pulled up for her to get into or out of her jacket, she took it off, and as these sleeves were of a Scottish plaid in soft colours, pink, pale blue, dull green, pigeon's breast, the effect was as though in a grey sky a rainbow had suddenly appeared. And she wondered whether this would find favour with M. de Charlus.

"Ah!" he exclaimed in delight, "now we have a ray, a prism of colour. I offer you my sincerest compliments."

"But it's this gentleman who has earned them," Albertine replied politely, pointing to myself, for she liked to show off what she had received from me.

"It's only the women who don't know how to dress that are

afraid of colours," went on M. de Charlus. "One can be brilliant without vulgarity and soft without being dull. Besides, you have not the same reasons as Mme de Cadignan for wishing to appear detached from life, for that was the idea which she wished to instil into d'Arthez with her grey gown."

Albertine, who was interested in this mute language of clothes, questioned M. de Charlus about the Princesse de Cadignan. "Oh! it's such a delightful story," said the Baron in a dreamy tone. "I know the little garden in which Diane de Cadignan used to stroll with Mme d'Espard. It belongs to one of my cousins."

"All this talk about his cousin's garden," Brichot murmured to Cottard, "may, like his pedigree, be of some importance to this worthy Baron. But what interest can it have for us who are not privileged to walk in it, do not know the lady, and possess no titles of nobility?" For Brichot had no idea that one might be interested in a dress and in a garden as works of art, and that it was as though in the pages of Balzac that M. de Charlus saw Mme de Cadignan's garden paths in his mind's eye. The Baron went on: "But you know her," he said to me, speaking of this cousin, and flatteringly addressing himself to me as to a person who, exiled amid the little clan, was to him, if not a citizen of his world, at any rate a frequenter of it. "Anyhow you must have seen her at Mme de Villeparisis's."

"Is that the Marquise de Villeparisis who owns the château at Baucreux?" asked Brichot, captivated.

"Yes, do you know her?" inquired M. de Charlus dryly.

"No, not at all," replied Brichot, "but our colleague Norpois spends part of his holidays every year at Baucreux. I have had occasion to write to him there."

I told Morel, thinking to interest him, that M. de Norpois was a friend of my father. But not by the slightest flicker of his features did he show that he had heard me, so little did he think of my parents, so far short did they fall in his estimation of what my great-uncle had been, who had employed Morel's father as his valet, and who moreover, being fond of "cutting a dash," unlike the rest of the family, had left a golden memory among his servants.

"It appears that Mme de Villeparisis is a superior woman,"

Brichot went on, "but I have never been allowed to judge of
that for myself, nor for that matter has any of my colleagues.
For Norpois, who is the soul of courtesy and affability at the
Institut, has never introduced any of us to the Marquise. I
know of no one who has been received by her except our friend
Thureau-Dangin, who had an old family connexion with her,
and also Gaston Boissier, whom she was anxious to meet
because of a study of his that particularly interested her. He
dined with her once and came back quite enthralled by her
charm. Mme Boissier, however, was not invited."

At the sound of these names, Morel melted into a smile.
"Ah! Thureau-Dangin," he said to me with an air of interest as
great as had been his indifference when he heard me speak of
the Marquis de Norpois and my father. "Thureau-Dangin; why
he and your uncle were as thick as thieves. Whenever a lady
wanted a front seat for a reception at the Academy, your uncle
would say: 'I shall write to Thureau-Dangin.' And of course he
got it at once, because you can imagine that M. Thureau-
Dangin would never have dared refuse your uncle anything,
because he'd soon have got his own back. I'm amused to hear
the name Boissier, too, because that was where your uncle
ordered all the presents he used to give the ladies at New Year.
I know all about it, because I knew the person he used to send
for them." He did indeed know him, for it was his father. Some
of these affectionate allusions by Morel to my uncle's memory
were prompted by the fact that we did not intend to remain
permanently in the Hôtel Guermantes, where we had taken an
apartment only on account of my grandmother. From time to
time there would be talk of a possible move. Now, to understand
the advice that Charles Morel gave me in this connexion, the
reader must know that my great-uncle had lived, in his day, at
40*bis* Boulevard Malesherbes. The consequence was that, in
the family, as we often went to visit my uncle Adolphe until
the fatal day when I caused a breach between my parents and
him by telling them the story of the lady in pink, instead of
saying "at your uncle's" we used to say "at 40*bis*." Some
cousins of Mamma's used to say to her in the most natural
tone: "Ah! so we can't expect you on Sunday since you're
dining at 40*bis*." If I were going to call on some relations, I

would be warned to go first of all "to 40*bis*," in order that my uncle might not be offended by my not having begun my round with him. He was the owner of the house and was very particular as to the choice of his tenants, all of whom either were or became his personal friends. Colonel the Baron de Vatry used to look in every day and smoke a cigar with him in the hope of making him consent to repairs. The carriage entrance was always kept shut. If my uncle caught sight of some washing or a rug hanging from one of the window-sills he would storm in and have it removed in less time than the police would take to do so nowadays. All the same, he did let part of the house, reserving for himself only two floors and the stables. In spite of this, knowing that he was pleased when people praised the excellent upkeep of the house, we used always to extol the comfort of the "little mansion" as though my uncle had been its sole occupant, and he encouraged the pretence, without issuing the formal contradiction that might have been expected. The "little mansion" was certainly comfortable (my uncle having installed in it all the most recent inventions). But it was in no way out of the ordinary. Only my uncle, while referring with false modesty to "my little hovel," was convinced, or at any rate had instilled into his valet, the valet's wife, the coachman, the cook, the idea that there was no place in Paris to compare, for comfort, luxury, and general attractiveness, with the little mansion. Charles Morel had grown up in this belief. He had not outgrown it. And so, even on days when he was not talking to me, if in the train I mentioned the possibility of our moving, at once he would smile at me and say with a knowing wink: "Ah! What you want is something in the style of 40*bis*! That's a place that would suit you down to the ground! Your uncle knew what he was about. I'm quite sure that in the whole of Paris there's nothing to compare with 40*bis*."

The melancholy air which M. de Charlus had assumed in speaking of the Princesse de Cadignan left me in no doubt that the tale in question had not reminded him only of the little garden of a cousin to whom he was not particularly attached. He became lost in thought, and as though he were talking to himself: "*The Secrets of the Princesse de Cadignan!*" he exclaimed,

"what a masterpiece! How profound, how heartrending
the evil reputation of Diane, who is afraid that the man
she loves may hear of it. What an eternal truth, and more
universal than it might appear! How far-reaching it is!" He
uttered these words with a sadness in which one nevertheless
felt that he found a certain charm. Certainly M. de Charlus,
unaware to what extent precisely his proclivities were or were
not known, had been trembling for some time past at the
thought that when he returned to Paris and was seen there in
Morel's company, the latter's family might intervene and so his
future happiness be jeopardised. This eventuality had probably
not appeared to him hitherto save as something profoundly
disagreeable and painful. But the Baron was an artist to his
finger-tips. And now that he had suddenly begun to identify his
own situation with that described by Balzac, he took refuge,
as it were, in the story, and for the calamity which was perhaps
in store for him and which he certainly feared, he had the
consolation of finding in his own anxiety what Swann and also
Saint-Loup would have called something "very Balzacian."
This identification of himself with the Princesse de Cadignan
had been made easier for M. de Charlus by virtue of the mental
transposition which was becoming habitual with him and of
which he had already given several examples. It sufficed, moreover, to make the mere conversion of a woman, as the beloved
object, into a young man immediately set in motion around him
the whole sequence of social complications which develop
round a normal love affair. When, for some reason or other, a
change in the calendar or in time-tables is introduced once and
for all, if we make the year begin a few weeks later, or if we
make midnight strike a quarter of an hour earlier, since the days
will still consist of twenty-four hours and the months of thirty
days, everything that depends upon the measure of time will
remain unaltered. Everything can have been changed without
causing any disturbance, since the ratio between the figures is
still the same. So it is with lives which adopt "Central European
time" or the Eastern calendar. It would even seem that the
gratification a man derives from keeping an actress played a
part in this liaison. When, after their first meeting, M. de
Charlus had made inquiries as to Morel's background, he had

of course learned that he was of humble extraction, but a demi-mondaine with whom we are in love does not forfeit our esteem because she is the child of poor parents. On the other hand, the well-known musicians to whom he had addressed his inquiries had answered him—not even from any personal motive, like the friends who, when introducing Swann to Odette, had described her to him as more difficult and more sought after than she actually was, but simply in the stereotyped manner of men in a prominent position overpraising a beginner: "Ah, yes, a great talent, a considerable reputation considering that he's still young, highly esteemed by the experts, will go far." And, with the habit which people who are innocent of inversion have of speaking of masculine beauty: "Besides, he's charming to watch when he plays; he looks better than anyone at a concert, with his pretty hair and distinguished poses; he has an exquisite head, in fact he's the very picture of the romantic violinist." And so M. de Charlus, in any case overexcited by Morel, who did not fail to let him know how many offers had been addressed to him, was flattered to take him home with him, to make a little dovecot for him to which he would often return. For during the rest of the time he wished him to be free, since this was essential to his career, which M. de Charlus wanted him to continue, however much money he had to give him, either because of the thoroughly "Guermantes" idea that a man must do something, that talent is the sole criterion of merit, and that nobility or money are simply the nought that multiplies a value, or because he was afraid lest, having nothing to do and remaining perpetually in his company, the violinist might grow bored. Moreover he did not wish to deprive himself of the pleasure which he felt, at certain grand concerts, in saying to himself: "The person they are applauding at this moment is coming home with me to-night." Elegant people, when they are in love, and whatever the nature of their love, exercise their vanity in ways that can destroy the previous advantages in which their vanity would have found satisfaction.

Morel, feeling that I bore him no malice, that I was sincerely attached to M. de Charlus and that I was at the same time absolutely indifferent physically to both of them, ended by displaying the same warm feelings towards me as a courtesan who knows that you do not desire her and that her lover has in you a sincere friend who will not try to turn him against her. Not only did he speak to me exactly as Rachel, Saint-Loup's mistress, had spoken to me long ago, but what was more, to judge by what M. de Charlus reported to me, he said to him about me in my absence the same things that Rachel used to say about me to Robert. Indeed M. de Charlus said to me: "He likes you very much," as Robert had said: "She likes you very much." And like the nephew on behalf of his mistress, so it was on Morel's behalf that the uncle often invited me to come and dine with them. There were, moreover, just as many storms between them as there had been between Robert and Rachel. To be sure, after Charlie (Morel) had left us, M. de Charlus never stopped singing his praises, repeating—something by which he felt flattered—that the violinist was so kind to him. But it was evident nevertheless that often Charlie, even in front of all the faithful, looked irritated instead of always appearing happy and submissive as the Baron would have wished. This irritation became so extreme in course of time, in consequence of the weakness which led M. de Charlus to forgive Morel his want of politeness, that the violinist made no attempt to conceal it, or even deliberately affected it. I have seen M. de Charlus, on entering a railway carriage in which Morel was sitting with some of his fellow-soldiers, greeted by the musician with a shrug of the shoulders, accompanied by a wink in the direction of his comrades. Or else he would pretend to be asleep, as though this intrusion bored him beyond words. Or he would begin to cough, and the others would laugh, derisively mimicking the affected speech of men like M. de Charlus, and draw Charlie into a corner from which he would eventually return, as though forced to do so, to sit by M. de Charlus, whose heart was pierced by all these cruelties. It is inconceivable how he can have put up with them; and these ever-varied forms of suffering posed the problem of happiness in fresh terms for M. de Charlus, compelled him not only to demand more, but to desire something else, the previous combination being vitiated by a hideous memory. And yet, painful as these scenes came to be, it must be acknowledged that in the early days the genius of the Frenchman of the people instinctively invested Morel with charming forms of simplicity, of apparent candour, even of an independent pride which seemed to be inspired by disinterestedness. This was not the case, but the advantage of this attitude was all the more on Morel's side in that, whereas the person who is in love is continually forced to return to the charge, to go one better, it is on the other hand easy for the person who is not in love to proceed along a straight line, inflexible and dignified. It existed by virtue of the privilege of heredity in the face—so open—of this Morel whose heart was so tightly shut, that face endued with the neo-Hellenic grace which blooms in the basilicas of Champagne. Notwithstanding his affectation of pride, often when he caught sight of M. de Charlus at a moment when he was not expecting to see him, he would be embarrassed by the presence of the little clan, would blush and lower his eyes, to the delight of the Baron, who read a whole novel into it. It was simply a sign of irritation and shame. The former sometimes expressed itself openly; for, calm and severely proper as Morel's attitude generally was, it was not infrequently belied. At times, indeed, at something which the Baron said to him, Morel would burst out in the harshest tones with an insolent retort which shocked everybody. M. de Charlus would lower his head with a sorrowful air, would make no reply, and with that faculty which doting fathers possess of believing that the coldness and rudeness of their children has passed unnoticed, would continue undeterred to sing the violinist's praises. M. de Charlus was not always so submissive, but as a rule his attempts at rebellion proved abortive, principally because, having lived among society people, in calculating the reactions that he might provoke he made allowance for the baser instincts, whether congenital or acquired; whereas, instead of these, he encountered in Morel a plebeian tendency to momentary indifference. Unfortunately for M. de Charlus, he did not understand that, for Morel, everything else gave precedence when the Conservatoire and his good reputation at the Conservatoire (but this, which was to be a more serious matter, did not arise for the moment) were in question. Thus, for instance, people of the middle class will readily change their surnames out of vanity, and noblemen for personal advantage. To the young violinist, on the contrary, the name Morel was inseparably linked with his first prize for the violin, and so impossible to alter. M. de Charlus would have liked Morel to owe everything to him, including his name. Reflecting that Morel's Christian name was Charles, which resembled Charlus, and that the house where they usually met was called les Charmes, he sought to persuade Morel that, a pretty name that is agreeable to pronounce being half the battle in establishing an artistic reputation, the virtuoso ought without hesitation to take the name Charmel, a discreet allusion to the scene of their assignations. Morel shrugged his shoulders. As a conclusive argument, M. de Charlus was unfortunately inspired to add that he had a valet of that name. He succeeded only in arousing the furious indignation of the young man. "There was a time when my ancestors were proud of the title of chamberlain or butler to the King," said the Baron. "There was also a time," replied Morel haughtily, 'when my ancestors cut off your ancestors' heads." M. de Charlus would have been greatly surprised had he been capable of realising that, having resigned himself, failing "Charmel," to adopting Morel and conferring on him one of the titles of the Guermantes family which were at his disposal—but which circumstances, as we shall see, did not permit him to offer the violinist—he would have met with a refusal on the latter's part on the grounds of the artistic reputation attached to the name Morel, and of the things that would be said about him at his classes. So far above the Faubourg Saint-Germain did he place the Rue Bergère! M. de Charlus was obliged to content himself with having symbolical rings made for Morel, bearing the antique device: PLVS VLTRA CAR'LVS. Certainly, in the face of an adversary of a sort with which he was unfamiliar, M. de Charlus ought to have changed his tactics. But which of us is capable of that? Moreover, if M. de Charlus made blunders, Morel was not guiltless of them either. Far more than the actual circumstance which brought about the rupture between them, what was destined, temporarily at least (but the temporary turned out to be permanent), to be his downfall with M. de Charlus was that his nature included not only the baseness which made him obsequious in the face of harshness and respond with insolence to kindness. Running parallel with this innate baseness, there was in him a complicated neurasthenia of ill breeding, which, springing up on every occasion when he was in the wrong or was becoming a nuisance, meant that at the very moment when he needed all his niceness, all his gentleness, all his gaiety to disarm the Baron, he became sombre and aggressive, tried to provoke discussions on matters where he knew that the other did not agree with him, and maintained his own hostile attitude with a weakness of argument and a peremptory violence which enhanced that weakness. For, very soon running short of arguments, he invented fresh ones as he went along, in which he displayed the full extent of his ignorance and stupidity. These were barely noticeable when he was in a friendly mood and sought only to please. On the other hand, nothing else was visible in his black moods, when, from being inoffensive, they became odious. Whereupon M. de Charlus felt that he could endure no more and that his only hope lay in a brighter morrow, while Morel, forgetting that the Baron was keeping him in the lap of luxury, would give an ironical smile of condescending pity, and say: "I've never taken anything from anybody. Which means that there's nobody to whom I owe a single word of thanks."

In the meantime, as though he were dealing with a man of the world, M. de Charlus continued to give vent to his rage, whether genuine or feigned, but in either case ineffective. It was not always so, however. Thus one day (which in fact came after this initial period) when the Baron was returning with Charlie and myself from a lunch-party at the Verdurins' expecting to spend the rest of the afternoon and evening with the violinist at Doncières, the latter's dismissal of him, as soon as we left the train, with: "No, I've an engagement," caused M. de Charlus so keen a disappointment that, although he tried to put a brave face on it, I saw the tears trickling down and melting the make-up on his eyelashes as he stood dazed beside the carriage door. Such was his grief that, as Albertine and I intended to spend the rest of the day at Doncières, I whispered to her that I would prefer not to leave M. de Charlus by himself, as he seemed for some reason or other upset. The dear girl

readily assented. I then asked M. de Charlus if he would like
me to accompany him for a little. He also assented, but did not
want to put my "cousin" to any trouble. I took a certain fond
pleasure (doubtless for the last time, since I had made up my
mind to break with her) in saying to her gently, as though she
were my wife: "Go back home by yourself, I shall see you this
evening," and in hearing her, as a wife might, give me permission to do as I thought fit and authorise me, if M. de Charlus,
of whom she was fond, needed my company, to place myself at
his disposal. We proceeded, the Baron and I, he waddling
obesely, his jesuitical eyes downcast, and I following him, to a
café where we ordered some beer. I felt M. de Charlus's eyes
anxiously absorbed in some plan. Suddenly he called for paper
and ink, and began to write at an astonishing speed. While he
covered sheet after sheet, his eyes glittered with furious
fancies.

When he had written eight pages: "May I ask you to do me a
great service?" he said to me. "You will excuse my sealing this
note. But I must. You will take a carriage, a motor-car if you
can find one, to get there as quickly as possible. You are
certain to find Morel in his quarters, where he has gone to
change. Poor boy, he tried to bluster a little when we parted,
but you may be sure that his heart is heavier than mine. You
will give him this note, and, if he asks you where you saw me,
you will tell him that you stopped at Doncières (which, for that
matter, is the truth) to see Robert, which is not quite the truth
perhaps, but that you met me with a person whom you do not
know, that I seemed to be extremely angry, that you thought
you heard something about sending seconds (I am in fact
fighting a duel to-morrow). Whatever you do, don't say that
I'm asking for him, don't make any effort to bring him here,
but if he wishes to come with you, don't prevent him from
doing so. Go, my boy, it is for his own good, you may be the
means of averting a great tragedy. While you are away, I shall
write to my seconds. I have prevented you from spending the
afternoon with your cousin. I hope that she will bear me no ill
will for that, indeed I am sure of it. For hers is a noble soul, and
I know that she is one of those rare persons who are capable of
rising to the grandeur of an occasion. You must thank her on

my behalf. I am personally indebted to her, and I am glad that it should be so."

I was extremely sorry for M. de Charlus; it seemed to me that Charlie might have prevented this duel, of which he was perhaps the cause, and I was revolted, if that were the case, that he should have gone off with such indifference, instead of staying to help his protector. My indignation was even greater when, on reaching the house in which Morel lodged, I recognised the voice of the violinist, who, feeling the need to give vent to his cheerfulness, was singing boisterously: "Some Sunday morning, when the wedding-bells rrring!" If only poor M. de Charlus, who wished me to believe, and doubtless himself believed, that Morel's heart was heavy, had heard him at that moment!

Charlie began to dance with joy when he caught sight of me. "Hallo, old boy! (excuse me addressing you like that; in this blasted military life one picks up bad habits), what a stroke of luck seeing you! I have nothing to do all evening. Do let's spend it together. We can stay here if you like, or take a boat if you prefer that, or we can have some music, it's all the same to me."

I told him that I was obliged to dine at Balbec, and he seemed anxious that I should invite him to dine there also, but I had no desire to do so.

"But if you're in such a hurry, why have you come here?"

"I've brought you a note from M. de Charlus."

At this name all his gaiety vanished; his face tensed.

"What! he can't leave me alone even here. I'm nothing but a slave. Old boy, be a sport. I'm not going to open his letter. Tell him you couldn't find me."

"Wouldn't it be better to open it? I suspect it's something serious."

"Not on your life. You've no idea what lies, what infernal tricks that old scoundrel gets up to. It's a dodge to make me go and see him. Well, I'm not going. I want to spend the evening in peace."

"But isn't there going to be a duel to-morrow?" I asked him, having assumed that he was in the know.

"A duel?" he repeated with an air of stupefaction, "I never

heard a word about it. Anyhow, I don't give a damn—the dirty old beast can go and get plugged in the guts if he likes. But wait a minute, this is interesting, I'd better look at his letter after all. You can tell him you left it here for me, in case I should come in."

While Morel was speaking, I looked with amazement at the beautiful books which M. de Charlus had given him and which littered his room. The violinist having refused to accept those labelled: "I belong to the Baron" etc., a device which he felt to be insulting to himself, as a mark of vassalage, the Baron, with the sentimental ingenuity in which his ill-starred love abounded, had substituted others, borrowed from his ancestors, but ordered from the binder according to the circumstances of a melancholy friendship. Sometimes they were terse and confident, as *Spes mea* or *Exspectata non eludet*; sometimes merely resigned, as *J'attendrai*. Others were gallant: *Mesmes plaisir du mestre*, or counselled chastity, such as that borrowed from the family of Simiane, sprinkled with azure towers and fleurs-de-lis, and given a fresh meaning: *Sustentant lilia turres*. Others, finally, were despairing, and made an appointment in heaven with him who had spurned the donor upon earth: *Manet ultima coelo*; and (finding the grapes which he had failed to reach too sour, pretending not to have sought what he had not secured) M. de Charlus said in yet another: *Non mortale quod opto*. But I had no time to examine them all.

If M. de Charlus, in dashing this letter down upon paper, had seemed to be carried away by the daemon that was inspiring his flying pen, as soon as Morel had broken the seal (a leopard between two roses gules, with the motto: *Atavis et armis*) he began to read the letter as feverishly as M. de Charlus had written it, and over those pages covered at breakneck speed his eye ran no less swiftly than the Baron's pen. "Good God!" he exclaimed, "this is the last straw! But where am I to find him? Heaven only knows where he is now." I suggested that if he made haste he might still find him perhaps at a tavern where he had ordered beer as a restorative. "I don't know whether I shall be coming back," he said to his landlady, and added to himself, "it will depend on how things turn out." A few minutes later we reached the café. I noticed M. de Charlus's expression at the

moment when he caught sight of me. It was as though, seeing
that I had not returned unaccompanied, he could breathe again,
had been restored to life. Being in a mood not to be deprived
of Morel's company that evening, he had pretended to have
been informed that two officers of the regiment had spoken ill
of him in connexion with the violinist and that he was going to
send his seconds to call upon them. Morel had foreseen the
scandal—his life in the regiment made impossible—and had
come at once. In doing which he had not been altogether
wrong. For to make his lie more plausible, M. de Charlus had
already written to two friends (one was Cottard) asking them to
be his seconds. And if the violinist had not appeared, we may be
certain that, mad as he was (and in order to change his sorrow
into rage), M. de Charlus would have sent them with a challenge to some officer or other with whom it would have been a
relief to him to fight. In the meantime M. de Charlus, remembering that he came of a race that was of purer blood than the
House of France, told himself that it was really very good of
him to make such a fuss about the son of a butler whose
employer he would not have condescended to know. Furthermore, if he now enjoyed almost exclusively the society of riffraff, the latter's profoundly ingrained habit of not replying to
letters, of failing to keep appointments without warning you
beforehand or apologising afterwards, caused him such agitation and distress when, as was often the case, his heart was
involved, and the rest of the time such irritation, inconvenience
and anger, that he would sometimes begin to miss the endless
letters over the most trifling matters and the scrupulous
punctuality of ambassadors and princes who, even if he was,
alas, indifferent to their charms, gave him at any rate some sort
of peace of mind. Accustomed to Morel's ways, and knowing
how little hold he had over him, how incapable he was of
insinuating himself into a life in which vulgar friendships
consecrated by habit occupied too much space and time to leave
a spare hour for a forsaken, touchy, and vainly imploring
nobleman, M. de Charlus was so convinced that the musician
would not come, was so afraid of having lost him forever by
going too far, that he could barely repress a cry of joy when he
saw him appear. But, feeling himself the victor, he was deter-

mined to dictate the terms of peace and to extract from them such advantages as he might.

"What are you doing here?" he said to him. "And you?" he added, looking at me, "I told you, whatever you did, not to bring him back with you."

"He didn't want to bring me," said Morel, turning upon M. de Charlus, in the artlessness of his coquetry, a conventionally mournful and languorously old-fashioned gaze which he doubtless thought irresistible, and looking as though he wanted to kiss the Baron and to burst into tears. "It was I who insisted on coming in spite of him. I come, in the name of our friendship, to implore you on my bended knees not to commit this rash act."

M. de Charlus was wild with joy. The reaction was almost too much for his nerves; he managed, however, to control them.

"The friendship which you somewhat inopportunely invoke," he replied curtly, "ought, on the contrary, to make you give me your approval when I decide that I cannot allow the impertinences of a fool to pass unheeded. Besides, even if I chose to yield to the entreaties of an affection which I have known better inspired, I should no longer be in a position to do so, since my letters to my seconds have been dispatched and I have no doubt of their acceptance. You have always behaved towards me like a young idiot and, instead of priding yourself, as you had every right to do, upon the predilection which I had shown for you, instead of making known to the rabble of sergeants or servants among whom the law of military service compels you to live, what a source of incomparable pride a friendship such as mine was to you, you have sought to apologise for it, almost to make an idiotic merit of not being grateful enough. I know that in so doing," he went on, in order not to let it appear how deeply certain scenes had humiliated him, "you are guilty merely of having let yourself be carried away by the jealousy of others. But how is it that at your age you are childish enough (and ill-bred enough) not to have seen at once that your election by myself and all the advantages that must accrue from it were bound to excite jealousies, that all your comrades, while inciting you to quarrel with me, were plotting to take your place? I did not think it advisable to warn you of the letters I have received in that connexion from all those in whom you place most trust. I scorn the overtures of those flunkeys as I scorn their ineffectual mockery. The only person for whom I care is yourself, since I am fond of you, but affection has its limits and you ought to have guessed as much."

Harsh as the word flunkey might sound in the ears of Morel, whose father had been one, but precisely because his father had been one, the explanation of all social misadventures by "jealousy," an explanation simplistic and absurd but indestructible, which in a certain social class never fails to "work" as infallibly as the old tricks of the stage with a theatre audience or the threat of the clerical peril in a parliamentary assembly, found credence with him almost as strongly as with Françoise or with Mme de Guermantes's servants, for whom jealousy was the sole cause of the misfortunes that beset humanity. He had no doubt that his comrades had tried to oust him from his position and was all the more wretched at the thought of this disastrous albeit imaginary duel.

"Oh, how dreadful," exclaimed Charlie. "I shall never be able to hold up my head again. But oughtn't they to see you before they go and call upon this officer?"

"I don't know. I imagine so. I've sent word to one of them that I shall be here all evening, and I shall give him his instructions."

"I hope that before he comes I can make you listen to reason. Allow me at least to stay with you," Morel pleaded tenderly.

It was all that M. de Charlus wanted. He did not however yield at once.

"You would do wrong to apply in this case the proverbial 'spare the rod and spoil the child,' for you were the child in question, and I do not intend to spare the rod, even after our quarrel, for those who have basely sought to do you injury. Until now, in response to their inquisitive insinuations, when they dared to ask me how a man like myself could associate with a gigolo of your sort, sprung from the gutter, I have answered only in the words of the motto of my La Rochefoucauld cousins: 'It is my pleasure.' I have indeed pointed out to you more than once that this pleasure was capable of becoming my chiefest pleasure, without there resulting from your arbitrary elevation any debasement of myself." And in an impulse of almost insane pride he exclaimed, raising his arms in the air: "*Tantus ab uno splendor!* To condescend is not to descend," he added in a calmer tone, after this delirious outburst of pride and joy. "I hope at least that my two adversaries, notwithstanding their inferior rank, are of a blood that I can shed without reproach. I have made certain discreet inquiries in that direction which have reassured me. If you retained a shred of gratitude towards me, you ought on the contrary to be proud to see that for your sake I am reviving the bellicose humour of my ancestors, saying like them, in the event of a fatal outcome, now that I have learned what a little rascal you are: 'Death to me is life.'"

And M. de Charlus said this sincerely, not only because of his love for Morel, but because a pugnacious instinct which he quaintly supposed to have come down to him from his ancestors filled him with such joy at the thought of fighting that he would now have regretted having to abandon this duel which he had originally concocted with the sole object of bringing Morel to heel. He had never engaged in any affair of the sort without at once preening himself on his valour and identifying himself with the illustrious Constable de Guermantes, whereas in the case of anyone else this same action of taking the field would appear to him to be of the utmost triviality.

"I am sure it will be a splendid sight," he said to us in all sincerity, dwelling upon each word. "To see Sarah Bernhardt in *L'Aiglon*, what is that but trash? Mounet-Sully in *Oedipus*, trash! At the most it assumes a certain pallid transfiguration when it is performed in the Arena of Nîmes. But what is it compared to that unimaginable spectacle, the lineal descendant of the Constable engaged in battle?" And at the mere thought of it M. de Charlus, unable to contain himself for joy, began to make passes in the air reminiscent of Molière, causing us to move our glasses prudently out of the way, and to fear that, when the swords crossed, not only the combatants but the doctor and seconds would at once be wounded. "What a tempting spectacle it would be for a painter. You who know Monsieur Elstir," he said to me, "you ought to bring him." I replied that he was not in the neighbourhood. M. de Charlus suggested that he might be summoned by telegraph. "Oh, I'm only saying it for his sake," he added in response to my silence. "It is always interesting for a master—and in my opinion he is one—to record such instances of ethnic reviviscence. And they occur perhaps once in a century."

But if M. de Charlus was enchanted at the thought of a duel which he had meant at first to be entirely fictitious, Morel was thinking with terror of the stories which, thanks to the stir that this duel would cause, might be peddled around from the regimental band all the way to the holy of holies in the Rue Bergère. Seeing in his mind's eye the "class" fully informed, he became more and more insistent with M. de Charlus, who continued to gesticulate before the intoxicating idea of a duel. He begged the Baron to allow him not to leave him until two days later, the supposed day of the duel, so that he might keep him within sight and try to make him listen to the voice of reason. So tender a proposal overcame M. de Charlus's final hesitations. He promised to try to find a way out, and to postpone his decision until the day. In this way, by not settling the matter at once, M. de Charlus knew that he could keep Charlie with him for at least two days, and take the opportunity of obtaining from him undertakings for the future in exchange for abandoning the duel, an exercise, he said, which in itself delighted him and which he would not forgo without regret. And in saying this he was quite sincere, for he had always enjoyed taking the field when it was a question of crossing swords or exchanging shots with an opponent.

Cottard arrived at length, although extremely late, for, delighted to act as second but even more terrified at the prospect, he had been obliged to halt at all the cafés or farms on the way, asking the occupants to be so kind as to show him the way to "No. 100" or "a certain place." As soon as he arrived, the Baron took him into another room, for he thought it more in keeping with the rules for Charlie and I not to be present at the interview, and he excelled in making the most ordinary room serve as a temporary throne-room or council chamber. When

he was alone with Cottard he thanked him warmly, but informed him that it seemed probable that the remark which had
been repeated to him had never really been made, and requested
that in view of this the Doctor would be so good as to let the
other second know that, barring possible complications, the
incident might be regarded as closed. Now that the prospect of
danger had receded, Cottard was disappointed. He was indeed
tempted for a moment to give vent to anger, but he remembered that one of his masters, who had enjoyed the most
successful medical career of his generation, having failed to
enter the Academy at his first election by two votes only, had
put a brave face on it and had gone and shaken hands with his
successful rival. And so the Doctor refrained from an expression of indignation which could have made no difference,
and, after murmuring, he the most timorous of men, that there
were certain things which one could not overlook, added that
in this case it was better so, that this solution delighted him.
M. de Charlus, desirous of showing his gratitude to the Doctor,
just as the Duke his brother might have straightened the collar
of my father's great-coat or rather as a duchess might put her
arm round the waist of a plebeian lady, brought his chair close
to the Doctor's, notwithstanding the distaste which the latter
inspired in him. And, not only without any physical pleasure,
but having first to overcome a physical repulsion—as a Guermantes, not as an invert—in taking leave of the Doctor he
clasped his hand and caressed it for a moment with the kindly
affection of a master stroking his horse's nose and giving it a
lump of sugar. But Cottard, who had never allowed the Baron
to see that he had so much as heard the vaguest rumours as to
his morals, but nevertheless regarded him in his heart of hearts
as belonging to the category of "abnormals" (indeed, with his
habitual inaccuracy in the choice of terms, and in the most
serious tone, he had said of one of M. Verdurin's footmen:
"Isn't he the Baron's mistress?"), persons of whom he had little
personal experience, imagined that this stroking of his hand
was the immediate prelude to an act of rape for the accomplishment of which, the duel being a mere pretext, he had been
enticed into a trap and led by the Baron into this remote
apartment where he was about to be forcibly outraged. Not

daring to leave his chair, to which fear kept him glued, he rolled his eyes in terror, as though he had fallen into the hands of a savage who, for all he knew, fed upon human flesh. At length M. de Charlus, releasing his hand and anxious to be hospitable to the end, said: "Won't you come and have one with us, as they say—what in the old days used to be called a *mazagran* or a *gloria*, drinks that are no longer to be found except, as archaeological curiosities, in the plays of Labiche and the cafés of Doncières. A *gloria* would be distinctly appropriate to the place, eh? And also to the occasion, what?"

"I am President of the Anti-Alcohol League," replied Cottard. "Some country sawbones has only got to pass, and it will be said that I do not practise what I preach. *Os homini sublime dedit coelumque tueri*," he added, not that this had any bearing on the matter, but because his stock of Latin quotations was extremely limited, albeit sufficient to astound his pupils.

M. de Charlus shrugged his shoulders and led Cottard back to where we were, after exacting a promise of secrecy which was all the more important to him since, the motive for the abortive duel being purely imaginary, it must on no account reach the ears of the officer whom he had arbitrarily selected as his adversary. While the four of us sat drinking, Mme Cottard, who had been waiting for her husband outside, where M. de Charlus had seen her perfectly well but had made no effort to summon her, came in and greeted the Baron, who held out his hand to her as though to a housemaid, without rising from his chair, partly in the manner of a king receiving homage, partly as a snob who does not wish a distinctly inelegant woman to sit down at his table, partly as an egoist who enjoys being alone with his friends and does not wish to be bothered. So Mme Cottard remained standing while she talked to M. de Charlus and her husband. But, possibly because politeness, the knowledge of the "done" thing, is not the exclusive prerogative of the Guermantes, and may all of a sudden illuminate and guide the dimmest brains, or else because, being constantly unfaithful to his wife, Cottard felt at odd moments, by way of compensation, the need to protect her against anyone who showed disrespect to her, the Doctor suddenly frowned, a thing I had never seen him do before, and, without consulting M. de

Charlus, said in a tone of authority: "Come, Léontine, don't stand about like that, sit down." "But are you sure I'm not disturbing you?" Mme Cottard inquired timidly of M. de Charlus, who, surprised by the Doctor's tone, had made no observation. Whereupon, without giving him a second chance, Cottard repeated with authority: "I told you to sit down."

Presently the party broke up, and then M. de Charlus said to Morel: "I conclude from this whole affair, which has ended more happily than you deserved, that you do not know how to behave and that, at the expiry of your military service, I must take you back myself to your father, like the Archangel Raphael sent by God to the young Tobias." And the Baron smiled with an air of magnanimity, and a joy which Morel, to whom the prospect of being thus led home afforded no pleasure, did not appear to share. In the exhilaration of comparing himself to the Archangel, and Morel to the son of Tobit, M. de Charlus no longer thought of the purpose of his remark, which had been to explore the ground to see whether, as he hoped, Morel would consent to come with him to Paris. Intoxicated by his love, or by his self-love, the Baron did not see or pretended not to see the violinist's wry grimace, for, leaving him by himself in the café, he said to me with a proud smile: "Did you notice how, when I compared him to the son of Tobit, he became wild with joy? That was because, being extremely intelligent, he at once understood that the Father with whom he was henceforth to live was not his father after the flesh, who must be some horrible mustachioed valet, but his spiritual father, that is to say Myself. What a triumph for him! How proudly he reared his head! What joy he felt at having understood me! I am sure that he will now repeat day after day: 'O God who didst give the blessed Archangel Raphael as *guide* to thy servant Tobias upon a long journey, grant to us, thy servants, that we may ever be protected by him and armed with his succour.' I did not even need," added the Baron, firmly convinced that he would one day sit before the throne of God, "to tell him that I was the heavenly messenger. He realised it for himself, and was struck dumb with joy!" And M. de Charlus (whom joy, on the contrary, did not deprive of speech), heedless of the passers-by who turned to stare at him, assuming that he must be a lunatic, cried out alone and at the top of his voice, raising his hands in the air: "Alleluia!"

This reconciliation gave but a temporary respite to M. de Charlus's torments. Often, when Morel had gone on man-oeuvres too far away for M. de Charlus to be able to go and visit him or to send me to talk to him, he would write the Baron desperate and affectionate letters, in which he assured him that he would have to put an end to his life because, owing to a ghastly affair, he needed twenty-five thousand francs. He did not mention what this ghastly affair was, and had he done so, it would doubtless have been an invention. As far as the money was concerned, M. de Charlus would willingly have sent it had he not felt that it would make Charlie independent of him and free to receive the favours of someone else. And so he refused, and his telegrams had the dry, cutting tone of his voice. When he was certain of their effect, he longed for Morel to fall out with him forever, for, knowing very well that it was the contrary that would happen, he could not help dwelling upon all the drawbacks that would be revived with this inevitable liaison. But if no answer came from Morel, he lay awake all night, had not a moment's peace, so great is the number of the things of which we live in ignorance, and of the deep, inner realities that remain hidden from us. Then he would think up every conceivable supposition as to the enormity which had put Morel in need of twenty-five thousand francs, would give it every possible form, attach to it, one after another, a variety of proper names. I believe that at such moments M. de Charlus (in spite of the fact that his snobbishness, which was now diminishing, had already been overtaken if not outstripped by his increasing curiosity as to the ways of the people) must have recalled with a certain nostalgia the graceful, many-coloured whirl of the fashionable gatherings at which the most charming men and women sought his company only for the disinterested pleasure that it afforded them, where nobody would have dreamed of "doing him down," of inventing a "ghastly affair" because of which one is prepared to take one's life if one does not at once receive twenty-five thousand francs. I believe that then, and perhaps because he had after all remained more "Combray" at heart than myself, and had grafted a feudal dignity on to his Germanic arrogance, he must have felt that one cannot with impunity lose one's heart to a servant, that the people are by no means the same thing as society: in short he did not "trust the people" as I have always done.

The next station on the little railway, Maineville, reminds me of an incident in which Morel and M. de Charlus were concerned. Before I speak of it, I ought to mention that the halt of the train at Maineville (when one was escorting to Balbec an elegant new arrival who, to avoid giving trouble, preferred not to stay at la Raspelière) was the occasion of scenes less painful than that which I shall describe in a moment. The new arrival, having his light luggage with him in the train, generally found that the Grand Hotel was rather too far away, but, as there was nothing before Balbec except small beach-resorts with uncomfortable villas, had yielded to a preference for luxury and well-being and resigned himself to the long journey when, as the train came to a standstill at Maineville, he suddenly saw looming up in front of him the Palace, which he could never have suspected of being a house of ill fame. "Well, don't let us go any further," he would invariably say to Mme Cottard, a woman well-known for her practical judgment and sound advice. "There's the very thing I want. What's the point of going on to Balbec, where I certainly shan't find anything better. I can tell at a glance that it has every modern comfort, and I can perfectly well invite Mme Verdurin there, for I intend, in return for her hospitality, to give a few little parties in her honour. She won't have so far to come as if I stay at Balbec. It seems to me the very place for her, and for your wife, my dear Professor. There are bound to be reception rooms, and we shall bring the ladies there. Between you and me, I can't imagine why Mme Verdurin didn't come and settle here instead of taking la Raspelière. It's far healthier than an old house like la Raspelière, which is bound to be damp, and isn't clean either; they have no hot water laid on, one can never get a wash. Maineville strikes me as being far more agreeable. Mme Verdurin could have played her role as hostess here to perfection. However, tastes differ; anyhow I intend to remain here. Mme Cottard, won't you come along with me? We shall have to be quick, of course, for the train will be starting again in a minute. You can pilot me through this establishment, which you doubtless know inside out, since you must often have visited it. It's an ideal setting for you." The others would have the greatest difficulty in making the unfortunate new arrival hold his tongue, and still more in preventing him from leaving the train, while he, with the obstinacy which often arises from a gaffe, would insist, would gather his luggage together and refuse to listen to a word until they had assured him that neither Mme Verdurin nor Mme Cottard would ever come to call upon him there. "Anyhow, I'm going to take up residence there. Mme Verdurin can write to me if she wishes to see me."

The incident that concerns Morel was of a more highly specialised order. There were others, but I confine myself at present, as the little train halts and the porter calls out "Doncières," "Grattevast," "Maineville" etc., to noting down the particular memory that the watering-place or garrison town recalls to me. I have already mentioned Maineville (*media villa*) and the importance that it had acquired from that luxurious house of prostitution which had recently been built there, not without arousing futile protests from the local mothers. But before I proceed to say why Maineville is associated in my memory with Morel and M. de Charlus, I must mention the disproportion (which I shall have occasion to examine more thoroughly later on) between the importance that Morel attached to keeping certain hours free, and the triviality of the occupations to which he pretended to devote them, this same disproportion recurring amid the explanations of another sort which he gave to M. de Charlus. He who played the disinterested artist for the Baron's benefit (and might do so with impunity in view of the generosity of his patron), when he wished to have the evening to himself in order to give a lesson, etc., never failed to add to his excuse the following words, uttered with a smile of cupidity: "Besides, there may be forty francs to be got out of it. That's not to be sneezed at. You must let me go, because as you see it's in my interest. Damn it all, I haven't got a regular income like you, I have my way to make in the world, it's a chance of earning a little money." In professing his anxiety to give his lesson, Morel was not altogether insincere. For one thing, it is false to say that money has no colour. A new way of earning it gives a fresh lustre to coins that are tarnished with use. Had he really gone out to give a lesson, it is probable that a couple of louis handed to him as he left the house by a girl pupil would have produced a different effect on him from a couple of louis coming from the hand of M. de Charlus. Besides, for a couple of louis the richest of men would travel miles, which become leagues when one is the son of a valet. But frequently M. de Charlus had his doubts as to the reality of the violin lesson, doubts which were increased by the fact that often the musician would offer pretexts of another sort, entirely disinterested from the material point of view, and at the same time absurd. Thus Morel could not help presenting a picture of his life, but one that was intentionally, and unintentionally too, so obscured that only certain parts of it were distinguishable. For a whole month he placed himself at M. de Charlus's disposal on condition that he might keep his evenings free, for he was anxious to put in a regular attendance at a course of algebra. Come and see M. de Charlus after his classes? Oh, that was impossible; the classes sometimes went on very late. "Even after two o'clock in the morning?" the Baron asked. "Sometimes." "But you can learn algebra just as easily from a book." "More easily, for I don't get very much out of the lessons." "Well then! Besides, algebra can't be of any use to you." "I like it. It soothes my nerves." "It cannot be algebra that makes him ask for night leave," M. de Charlus said to himself. "Can he be working for the police?" In any case Morel, whatever objection might be made, reserved certain evening hours, whether for algebra or for the violin. On one occasion it was for neither, but for the Prince de Guermantes who, having come down for a few days to that part of the coast to pay the Princesse de Luxembourg a visit, met the musician without knowing who he was or being known to him either, and offered him fifty francs to spend the night with him in the brothel at Maineville; a twofold pleasure for Morel, in the remuneration received from M. de Guermantes and in the delight of being surrounded by women who would flaunt their tawny breasts uncovered. In some way or other M. de Charlus got wind of what had occurred and of the place appointed, but did not discover the name of the seducer. Mad with jealousy, and in the hope of identifying the latter, he telegraphed to Jupien, who arrived two days later, and when, early the following week, Morel announced that he would again be absent, the Baron asked Jupien if he would undertake to bribe the woman who kept the establishment to hide them in some place where they could witness what occurred. "That's all right. I'll see to it, dearie," Jupien assured the Baron. It is hard to imagine the extent to which this anxiety agitated the Baron's mind, and by the very fact of doing so had momentarily enriched it. Love can thus be responsible for veritable geological upheavals of the mind. In that of M. de Charlus, which a few days earlier had resembled a plain so uniform that as far as the eye could reach it would have been impossible to make out an idea rising above the level surface, there had suddenly sprung into being, hard as stone, a range of mountains, but mountains as elaborately carved as if some sculptor, instead of quarrying and carting away the marble, had chiselled it on the spot, in which there writhed in vast titanic groups Fury, Jealousy, Curiosity, Envy, Hatred, Suffering, Pride, Terror and Love.

Meanwhile the evening on which Morel was to be absent had come. Jupien's mission had proved successful. He and the Baron were to be there about eleven o'clock, and would be put in a place of concealment. When they were still three streets away from this luxurious house of prostitution (to which people came from all the fashionable resorts in the neighbourhood), M. de Charlus had begun to walk on tiptoe, to disguise his voice, to beg Jupien not to speak so loud, lest Morel should hear them from inside. But, on creeping stealthily into the entrance hall, the Baron, who was not accustomed to places of the sort, found himself, to his terror and amazement, in a gathering more clamorous than the Stock Exchange or a sale-room. It was in vain that he begged the maids who gathered round him to moderate their voices; in any case their voices were drowned by the stream of auctioneering cries from an old "madame" in a very brown wig with the grave, wrinkled face of a notary or a Spanish priest, who kept shouting in a thunderous voice, ordering the doors to be alternately opened and shut, like a policeman regulating the flow of traffic: "Take this gentleman to number 28, the Spanish room." "Let no more

in." "Open the door again, these gentlemen want Mademoiselle
Noémie. She's expecting them in the Persian parlour." M. de
Charlus was as terrified as a countryman who has to cross the
boulevards; while, to take a simile infinitely less sacrilegious
than the subject represented on the capitals of the porch of the
old church of Couliville, the voices of the young maids repeated
in a lower tone, unceasingly, the madame's orders, like the
catechisms that one hears schoolchildren chanting beneath the
echoing vaults of a country church. Alarmed though he was,
M. de Charlus, who in the street had trembled lest he should be
heard, convinced in his own mind that Morel was at the window, was perhaps not so frightened after all in the din of those
huge staircases on which one realised that from the rooms
nothing could be seen. Coming at last to the end of his calvary,
he found Mlle Noémie, who was to conceal him with Jupien
but began by shutting him up in a sumptuously furnished
Persian sitting-room from which he could see nothing at all.
She told him that Morel had asked for some orangeade, and
that as soon as he was served the two visitors would be taken to
a room with a transparent panel. In the meantime, as she was
wanted, she promised them, like a fairy godmother, that to
help them to pass the time she was going to send them a "clever
little lady." For she herself had to go. The clever little lady
wore a Persian wrapper, which she wanted to remove. M. de
Charlus begged her to do nothing of the sort, and she rang for
champagne which cost 40 francs a bottle. Morel, during this
time, was in fact with the Prince de Guermantes; he had, for
form's sake, pretended to go into the wrong room by mistake,
and had entered one in which there were two women, who had
made haste to leave the two gentlemen undisturbed. M. de
Charlus knew nothing of this, but stormed with rage, tried to
open the doors, and sent for Mlle Noémie, who, hearing the
clever little lady give M. de Charlus certain information about
Morel which was not in accordance with what she herself had
told Jupien, banished her promptly and presently sent, as a
substitute for the clever little lady, a "dear little lady" who also
showed them nothing but told them how respectable the house
was and called, like her predecessor, for champagne. The Baron,
foaming with rage, sent again for Mlle Noémie, who said to

them: "Yes, it is taking rather long, the ladies are doing poses, he doesn't look as if he wanted to do anything." Finally, yielding to the promises and threats of the Baron, Mlle Noémie went away with an air of irritation, assuring them that they would not be kept waiting more than five minutes. The five minutes stretched to an hour, after which Noémie came and escorted an enraged Charlus and a disconsolate Jupien on tiptoe to a door which stood ajar, telling them: "You'll see splendidly from here. However, it's not very interesting just at present. He's with three ladies, and he's telling them about his army life." At length the Baron was able to see through the cleft of the door and also the reflexion in the mirrors beyond. But a mortal terror forced him to lean back against the wall. It was indeed Morel that he saw before him, but, as though the pagan mysteries and magic spells still existed, it was rather the shade of Morel, Morel embalmed, not even Morel restored to life like Lazarus, an apparition of Morel, a phantom of Morel, Morel "walking" or "called up" in this room (in which the walls and couches everywhere repeated the emblems of sorcery), that was visible a few feet away from him, in profile. Morel had, as happens to the dead, lost all his colour; among these women, with whom one might have expected him to be making merry, he remained livid, fixed in an artificial immobility; to drink the glass of champagne that stood before him, his listless arm tried in vain to reach out, and dropped back again. One had the impression of that ambiguous state implied by a religion which speaks of immortality but means thereby something that does not exclude extinction. The women were plying him with questions: "You see," Mlle Noémie whispered to the Baron, "they're talking to him about his army life. It's amusing, isn't it?"—here she laughed— "You're glad you came? He's calm, isn't he," she added, as though she were speaking of a dying man. The women's questions came thick and fast, but Morel, inanimate, had not the strength to answer them. Even the miracle of a whispered word did not occur. M. de Charlus hesitated for barely a moment before he grasped what had really happened, namely that— whether from clumsiness on Jupien's part when he had called to make the arrangements, or from the expansive power of

secrets once confided which ensures that they are never kept,
or from the natural indiscretion of these women, or from their
fear of the police—Morel had been told that two gentlemen had
paid a large sum to be allowed to spy on him, unseen hands had
spirited away the Prince de Guermantes, metamorphosed into
three women, and the unhappy Morel had been placed,
trembling, paralysed with fear, in such a position that if M. de
Charlus could scarcely see him, he, terrified, speechless, not
daring to lift his glass for fear of letting it fall, had a perfect
view of the Baron.

The story, as it happened, ended no more happily for the
Prince de Guermantes. When he had been sent away so that
M. de Charlus should not see him, furious at his disappointment without suspecting who was responsible for it, he had
implored Morel, still without letting him know who he was, to
meet him the following night in the tiny villa which he had
taken and which, despite the shortness of his projected stay in
it, he had, obeying the same quirkish habit which we have
already observed in Mme de Villeparisis, decorated with a
number of family keepsakes so that he might feel more at home.
And so, next day, Morel, constantly looking over his shoulder
for fear of being followed and spied upon by M. de Charlus,
had finally entered the villa, having failed to observe any suspicious passer-by. He was shown into the sitting-room by a
valet, who told him that he would inform "Monsieur" (his
master had warned him not to utter the word "Prince" for fear
of arousing suspicions). But when Morel found himself alone,
and went to the mirror to see that his forelock was not dis-
arranged, he felt as though he was the victim of a hallucination.
The photographs on the mantelpiece (which the violinist
recognised, for he had seen them in M. de Charlus's room) of
the Princesse de Guermantes, the Duchesse de Luxembourg
and Mme de Villeparisis, left him at first petrified with fright.
At the same moment he caught sight of the photograph of
M. de Charlus, which was placed a little behind the rest. The
Baron seemed to be transfixing him with a strange, unblinking
stare. Mad with terror, Morel, recovering from his preliminary
stupor and no longer doubting that this was a trap into which
M. de Charlus had led him in order to put his fidelity to the test,

leapt down the steps of the villa four at a time and set off along the road as fast as his legs would carry him, and when the Prince (thinking he had put a casual acquaintance through the required period of waiting, not without wondering whether the whole thing was entirely prudent and whether the individual in question might not be dangerous) came into the sitting-room, he found nobody there. In vain did he and his valet, fearful of burglary, and armed with revolvers, search the whole house, which was not large, the basement, and every corner of the garden, the companion of whose presence he had been certain had completely vanished. He met him several times in the course of the week that followed. But on each occasion it was Morel, the dangerous customer, who turned tail and fled, as though the Prince were more dangerous still. Stubborn in his suspicions, Morel never outgrew them, and even in Paris the sight of the Prince de Guermantes was enough to make him take to his heels. Thus was M. de Charlus protected from an infidelity which filled him with despair, and avenged without ever realising that he had been, still less how.

But already my memories of what I was told about all this are giving place to others, for the T. S. N., resuming its slow crawl, continues to set down or take up passengers at the succeeding stations.

At Grattevast, where his sister lived and where he had been spending the afternoon, M. Pierre de Verjus, Comte de Crécy (who was called simply the Comte de Crécy), would occasionally appear—a gentleman without means but of extreme distinction, whom I had come to know through the Cambremers, although he was by no means intimate with them. As he was reduced to an extremely modest, almost a penurious existence, I felt that a cigar and a drink were things that gave him so much pleasure that I formed the habit, on the days when I could not see Albertine, of inviting him to Balbec. A man of great refinement who expressed himself beautifully, with snow-white hair and a pair of charming blue eyes, he generally spoke, unassumingly and very delicately, of the comforts of life in a country house, which he had evidently known from experience, and also of pedigrees. On my inquiring what was engraved on his ring, he told me with a modest smile: "It is a sprig of verjuice grapes." And he added with degustatory relish: "Our arms are a sprig of verjuice grapes—symbolic, since my name is Verjus—slipped and leaved vert." But I fancy that he would have been disappointed if at Balbec I had offered him nothing better to drink than verjuice. He liked the most expensive wines, doubtless because he was deprived of them, because of his profound knowledge of what he was deprived of, because he had a taste for them, perhaps also because he had an exorbitant thirst. And so when I invited him to dine at Balbec, he would order the meal with a refined skill but eat a little too much, and drink copiously, making the waiters warm the wines that needed warming and place those that needed cooling upon ice. Before dinner and after, he would give the right date or number for a port or an old brandy, as he would have given the date of the creation of a marquisate which was not generally known but with which he was no less familiar.

As I was in Aimé's eyes a favoured customer, he was delighted that I should give these special dinners and would shout to the waiters: "Quick, lay number 25 for me," as though the table were for his own use. And, as the language of head waiters is not quite the same as that of sub-heads, assistants, boys, and so forth, when the time came for me to ask for the bill he would say to the waiter who had served us, making a continuous, soothing gesture with the back of his hand, as though he were trying to calm a horse that was ready to take the bit in its teeth: "Don't overdo it" (in adding up the bill), "gently does it." Then, as the waiter withdrew with this guidance, Aimé, fearing lest his recommendations might not be carried out to the letter, would call him back: "Here, let me make it out." And as I told him not to bother: "It's one of my principles that we ought never, as the saying is, to sting a customer." As for the manager, since my guest was attired simply, always in the same clothes, which were rather thread-bare (albeit nobody would so well have practised the art of dressing expensively, like one of Balzac's dandies, had he possessed the means), he confined himself, out of respect for me, to watching from a distance to see that everything was all right, and beckoning to someone to place a wedge under one leg of the table which was not steady. This is not to say that he was not qualified, though he concealed his beginnings as a scullion, to lend a hand like anyone else. It required some exceptional circumstance nevertheless to induce him one day to carve the turkeys himself. I was out, but I heard afterwards that he carved them with a sacerdotal majesty, surrounded, at a respectful distance from the service-table, by a ring of waiters who, endeavouring thereby not so much to learn the art as to curry favour with him, stood gaping in open-mouthed admiration. The manager, however, as he plunged his knife with solemn deliberation into the flanks of his victims, from which he no more deflected his eyes, filled with a sense of his high function, than if he were expecting to read some augury therein, was totally oblivious of their presence. The hierophant was not even conscious of my absence. When he heard of it, he was distressed: "What, you didn't see me carving the turkeys myself?" I replied that having failed, so far, to see Rome, Venice, Siena, the Prado, the Dresden gallery, the Indies, Sarah in *Phèdre*, I had learned to resign myself, and that I would add his carving of turkeys to my list. The comparison with the dramatic art (Sarah in *Phèdre*) was the only one that he seemed to understand, for he had learned through me that on days of gala performances the elder Coquelin had accepted beginners' roles, even those of characters who had only a single line or none at all. "All the same, I'm sorry for your sake. When shall I be carving again? It will need some great event, it will need a war." (It needed the armistice, in fact.) From that day onwards, the calendar was changed, and time was reckoned thus: "That was the day after the day I carved the turkeys myself." "It was exactly a week after the manager carved the turkeys himself." And so this prosectomy furnished, like the Nativity of Christ or the Hegira, the starting point for a calendar different from the rest, but neither so extensively adopted nor so long observed.

The sadness of M. de Crécy's life was due, just as much as to his no longer keeping horses and a succulent table, to his mixing exclusively with people who were capable of supposing that Cambremers and Guermantes were one and the same thing. When he saw that I knew that Legrandin, who had now taken to calling himself Legrand de Méséglise, had no sort of right to that name, being moreover lit up by the wine that he was drinking, he burst into a sort of transport of joy. His sister would say to me with a knowing look: "My brother is never so happy as when he has a chance to talk to you." He felt indeed that he was alive now that he had discovered somebody who knew the unimportance of the Cambremers and the grandeur of the Guermantes, somebody for whom the social universe existed. So, after the burning of all the libraries on the face of the globe and the emergence of a race entirely unlettered, might an old Latin scholar recover his confidence in life if he heard somebody quoting a line of Horace. Hence, if he never left the train without saying to me: "When is our next little reunion?", it was not only with the avidity of a parasite but with the relish of a scholar, and because he regarded our Balbec agapes as an opportunity for talking about subjects which were precious to him and of which he was never able to talk to anyone else, and in that sense analogous to those dinners at which the Society of Bibliophiles assembles on certain specified dates round the particularly succulent board of the Union Club. He was extremely modest so far as his own family was concerned, and it was not from M. de Crécy himself that I learned that it was a very noble family and an authentic branch transplanted to France of the English family which bears the title of Crecy. When I learned that he was a real Crécy, I told him that one of Mme de Guermantes's nieces had married an American named Charles Crecy, and said that I did not suppose there was any connexion between them. "None," he said. "Any more than—not, of course, that my family is so distinguished—heaps of Americans who are called Montgomery, Berry, Chandos or Capel have with the families of Pembroke, Buckingham or Essex, or with the Duc de Berry." I thought more than once of telling him, as a joke, that I knew Mme Swann, who as a courtesan had been known at one time by the name Odette de Crécy; but although the Duc d'Alençon could not have been offended if one spoke to him of Emilienne d'Alençon, I did not feel that I was on sufficiently intimate terms with M. de Crécy to carry the joke so far. "He comes of a very great family," M. de Montsurvent said to me one day. "His patronymic is Saylor." And he went on to say that on the wall of his old castle above Incarville, which was now almost uninhabitable and which he, although born very rich, was now too impoverished to put in repair, was still to be read the old motto of the family. I thought this motto very fine, whether applied to the impatience of a predatory race niched in that eyrie from which its members must have swooped down in the past, or, at the present day, to its contemplation of its own decline, awaiting the approach of death in that towering, grim retreat. It is in this double sense indeed that this motto plays upon the name Saylor, in the words: *"Ne sçais l'heure."*

At Hermenonville M. de Chevregny would sometimes get in, a gentleman whose name, Brichot told us, signified like that of Mgr de Cabrières "a place where goats assemble." He was related to the Cambremers, for which reason, and from a false appreciation of elegance, the latter often invited him to Féterne, but only when they had no other guests to dazzle. Living all the year round at Beausoleil, M. de Chevregny had remained more provincial than they. And so when he went for a few weeks to Paris, there was not a moment to waste if he was to "see everything" in the time; so much so that sometimes, a little dazed by the number of spectacles too rapidly digested, when he was asked if he had seen a particular play he would find that he was no longer absolutely sure. But this uncertainty was rare, for he had that detailed knowledge of Paris only to be found in people who seldom go there. He advised me which of the "novelties" I ought to see ("It's well worth your while"), regarding them however solely from the point of view of the pleasant evening that they might help to spend, and so completely ignoring the aesthetic point of view as never to suspect that they might indeed occasionally constitute a "novelty" in the history of art. So it was that, speaking of everything in the same tone, he told us: "We went once to the Opéra-Comique, but the show there isn't up to much. It's called *Pelléas et Mélisande*. It's trivial. Périer always acts well, but it's better to see him in something else. At the Gymnase, on the other hand, they're doing *La Châtelaine*. We went back to it twice; don't miss it, whatever you do, it's well worth seeing; besides, it's played to perfection; there's Frévalles, Marie Magnier, Baron fils"; and he went on to cite the names of actors of whom I had never heard, and without prefixing Monsieur, Madame or Mademoiselle like the Duc de Guermantes, who used to speak in the same ceremoniously contemptuous tone of the "songs of Mademoiselle Yvette Guilbert" and the "experiments of Monsieur Charcot." This was not M. de Chevregny's way: he said "Cornaglia and Dehelly" as he might have said "Voltaire and Montesquieu." For in him, with regard to actors as to everything that was Parisian, the aristocrat's desire to show his disdain was overcome by the provincial's desire to appear on familiar terms with everyone.

Immediately after the first dinner-party that I had attended at la Raspelière with what was still called at Féterne "the young couple," although M. and Mme de Cambremer were no longer, by any means, in their first youth, the old Marquise had written me one of those letters which one can pick out by their handwriting from among a thousand. She said to me: "Bring your delicious—charming—nice cousin. It will be a delight, a pleasure," failing always to observe the sequence that the recipient of her letter would naturally have expected, and with such unerring dexterity that I finally changed my mind as to the nature of these diminuendos, decided that they were deliberate, and found in them the same depravity of taste—transposed into the social key—that drove Sainte-Beuve to upset all the normal relations between words, to alter any expression that was at all habitual. Two methods, taught probably by different masters, were juxtaposed in this epistolary style, the second making Mme de Cambremer redeem the monotony of her multiple adjectives by employing them in a descending scale, and avoiding an ending on the common chord. On the other hand, I was inclined to see in these inverse gradations, no longer a stylistic refinement, as when they were the handiwork of the dowager Marquise, but a stylistic awkwardness whenever they were employed by the Marquis her son or by his lady cousins. For throughout the family, to quite a remote degree of kinship and in admiring imitation of Aunt Zélia, the rule of the three adjectives was held in great favour, as was a certain enthusiastic way of catching your breath when talking. An imitation that had passed into the blood, moreover; and whenever, in the family, a little girl from her earliest childhood took to stopping short while she was talking to swallow her saliva, her parents would say: "She takes after Aunt Zélia," would sense that as she grew older her upper lip would soon tend to be shadowed by a faint moustache, and would make up their minds to cultivate her inevitable talent for music.

It was not long before the relations of the Cambremers with Mme Verdurin were less satisfactory than with myself, for different reasons. They felt they must invite her to dine. The "young" Marquise said to me contemptuously: "I don't see why we shouldn't invite that woman. In the country one meets anybody, it's of no great consequence." But being at heart considerably awed, they frequently consulted me as to how they should put into effect their desire to make a polite gesture. Since they had invited Albertine and myself to dine with some friends of Saint-Loup, smart people of the neighbourhood who owned the château of Gourville and represented a little more than the cream of Norman society, to which Mme Verdurin, while pretending to despise it, was partial, I advised the Cambremers to invite the Mistress to meet them. But the lord and lady of Féterne, in their fear (so timorous were they) of offending their noble friends, or else (so ingenuous were they) of the possibility that M. and Mme Verdurin might be bored by people who were not intellectual, or yet again (since they were impregnated with a spirit of routine which experience had not fertilised) of mixing different kinds of people and committing a solecism, declared that it would not "work," that they "wouldn't hit it off together," and that it would be much better to keep Mme Verdurin (whom they would invite with all her little group) for another evening. For this coming evening—the smart one, to meet Saint-Loup's friends—they invited nobody from the little nucleus but Morel, in order that M. de Charlus might indirectly be informed of the brilliant people whom they had to their house, and also that the musician might help to entertain their guests, for he was to be asked to bring his violin. They threw in Cottard as well, because M. de Cambremer declared that he had some "go" about him and would "go down well" at a dinner-party; besides, it might turn out useful to be on friendly terms with a doctor if they should ever have anybody ill in the house. But they invited him by himself, so as not to "start anything with the wife." Mme Verdurin was outraged when she heard that two members of the little group had been invited without herself to dine "informally" at Féterne. She dictated to the Doctor, whose first impulse had been to accept, a stiff reply in which he said: "*We* are dining that evening with Mme Verdurin," a plural intended to teach the Cambremers a lesson and to show them that he was not detachable from Mme Cottard. As for Morel, Mme Verdurin had no need to draw up for him an impolite course of behaviour, for he adopted one of his own accord, for the following reason. If he preserved with regard to M. de Charlus, insofar as his pleasures were concerned, an independence which distressed the Baron, we have seen that the latter's influence had made itself felt more strongly in other areas, and that he had for instance enlarged the young virtuoso's knowledge of music and purified his style. But it was still, at this point in our story at least, only an influence. At the same time there was one domain where anything that M. de Charlus might say was blindly accepted and acted upon by Morel. Blindly and foolishly, for not only were M. de Charlus's instructions false, but, even had they been valid in the case of a nobleman, when applied literally by Morel they became grotesque. The domain in which Morel was becoming so credulous and obeyed his master with such docility was the social domain. The violinist, who before meeting M. de Charlus had had no notion of society, had taken literally the brief and arrogant sketch of it that the Baron had outlined for him: "There are a certain number of outstanding families," M. de Charlus had told him, "first and foremost the Guermantes, who claim fourteen alliances with the House of France, which is flattering to the House of France if anything, for it was to Aldonce de Guermantes and not to Louis the Fat, his younger half-brother, that the throne of France should have passed. Under Louis XIV, we 'draped' at the death of Monsieur, as having the same grandmother as the king. A long way below the Guermantes, one may however mention the La Trémoïlles, descended from the Kings of Naples and the Counts of Poitiers; the d'Uzès, not very old as a family but the oldest peers; the

Luynes, of very recent origin but with the lustre of distinguished marriages; the Choiseuls, the Harcourts, the La Rochefoucaulds. Add to these the Noailles (notwithstanding the Comte de Toulouse), the Montesquious and the Castellanes, and, I think I am right in saying, those are all. As for all the little people who call themselves Marquis de Cambremerde or de Vatefairefiche, there is no difference between them and the humblest private in your regiment. Whether you go and do wee-wee at the Countess Caca's or caca at the Baroness Wee-wee's, it's exactly the same, you will have compromised your reputation and have used a fetid rag instead of toilet paper. Which is unsavoury."

Morel had piously taken in this history lesson, which was perhaps a trifle cursory; he looked upon these matters as though he were himself a Guermantes and hoped that he might some day have an opportunity of meeting the false La Tour d'Auvergnes in order to let them see, by the contemptuous way he shook hands with them, that he did not take them very seriously. As for the Cambremers, here was his very chance to prove to them that they were no better than "the humblest private in his regiment." He did not answer their invitation, and on the evening of the dinner declined at the last moment by telegram, as pleased with himself as if he had behaved like a Prince of the Blood. It must be added here that it is impossible to imagine the degree to which, in a more general sense, M. de Charlus could be intolerable, meddlesome and even—he who was so clever—stupid, in all the circumstances where the flaws in his character came into play. We may say indeed that these flaws are like an intermittent disease of the mind. Who has not observed the phenomenon in women, and even in men, endowed with remarkable intelligence but afflicted with nervous irritability? When they are happy, calm, satisfied with their surroundings, we marvel at their precious gifts; it is the truth, literally, that speaks through their lips. A touch of headache, the slightest prick to their self-esteem, is enough to alter everything. The luminous intelligence, become brusque, convulsive and shrunken, no longer reflects anything but an irritable, suspicious, teasing self, doing everything possible to displease.

The anger of the Cambremers was extreme; and in the meantime other incidents brought about a certain tension in their relations with the little clan. As we were returning, the Cottards, Charlus, Brichot, Morel and I, from a dinner at la Raspelière one evening after the Cambremers, who had been to lunch with friends at Harambouville, had accompanied us for part of our outward journey, "Since you're so fond of Balzac, and can find examples of him in the society of to-day," I had remarked to M. de Charlus, "you must feel that those Cambremers come straight out of the *Scènes de la vie de Province*." But M. de Charlus, for all the world as though he had been their friend and I had offended him by my remark, at once cut me short: "You say that because the wife is superior to the husband," he remarked drily. "Oh, I wasn't suggesting that she was the *Muse du département*, or Mme de Bargeton, although . . ." M. de Charlus again interrupted me: "Say rather, Mme de Mortsauf." The train stopped and Brichot got out. "Didn't you see us making signs to you? You're incorrigible." "What do you mean?" "Why, haven't you noticed that Brichot is madly in love with Mme de Cambremer?" I could see from the attitude of the Cottards and Charlie that there was not a shadow of doubt about this in the little nucleus. I thought that it must be malice on their part. "What, you didn't notice how distressed he became when you mentioned her," went on M. de Charlus, who liked to show that he had experience of women, and spoke of the sentiment they inspire as naturally as if it was what he himself habitually felt. But a certain equivocally paternal tone in addressing all young men—in spite of his exclusive affection for Morel—gave the lie to the womanising views which he expressed. "Oh! these children," he said in a shrill, mincing, sing-song voice, "one has to teach them everything, they're as innocent as newborn babes, they can't even tell when a man is in love with a woman. I was more fly than that at your age," he added, for he liked to use the expressions of the underworld, perhaps because they appealed to him, perhaps so as not to appear, by avoiding them, to admit that he consorted with people whose current vocabulary they were. A few days later, I was obliged to bow to the facts and acknowledge that Brichot was enamoured of the

Marquise. Unfortunately he accepted several invitations to lunch with her. Mme Verdurin decided that it was time to put a stop to these proceedings. Quite apart from what she saw as the importance of such an intervention for the politics of the little nucleus, she had developed an ever-keener taste for remonstrations of this sort and the dramas to which they gave rise, a taste which idleness breeds just as much in the bourgeoisie as in the aristocracy. It was a day of great excitement at la Raspelière when Mme Verdurin was seen to disappear for a whole hour with Brichot, whom (it transpired) she proceeded to inform that Mme de Cambremer cared nothing for him, that he was the laughing-stock of her drawing-room, that he would be dishonouring his old age and compromising his situation in the academic world. She went so far as to refer in touching terms to the laundress with whom he lived in Paris, and to their little girl. She won the day; Brichot ceased to go to Féterne, but his grief was such that for two days it was thought that he would lose his sight altogether, and in any case his disease had taken a leap forward from which it never retreated. In the meantime, the Cambremers, who were furious with Morel, deliberately invited M. de Charlus on one occasion without him. Receiving no reply from the Baron, they began to fear that they had committed a gaffe, and, deciding that rancour was a bad counsellor, wrote somewhat belatedly to Morel, an ineptitude which made M. de Charlus smile by proving to him the extent of his power. "You shall answer for us both that I accept," he said to Morel. When the evening of the dinner came, the party assembled in the great drawing-room of Féterne. In reality, the Cambremers were giving this dinner for those fine flowers of fashion M. and Mme Féré. But they were so afraid of displeasing M. de Charlus that although she had got to know the Férés through M. de Chevregny, Mme de Cambremer went into a frenzy of alarm when, on the day of the dinner-party, she saw him arrive to pay a call on them at Féterne. She thought up every imaginable excuse for sending him back to Beausoleil as quickly as possible, not quickly enough, however, for him not to run into the Férés in the courtyard, who were as shocked to see him dismissed like this as he himself was ashamed. But, whatever happened, the Cambremers wished to spare M. de Charlus the sight of M. de Chevregny, whom they judged to be provincial because of certain little points which can be overlooked within the family but have to be taken into account in front of strangers, who are in fact the last people in the world to notice them. But we do not like to display to them relatives who have remained at the stage which we ourselves have struggled to outgrow. As for M. and Mme Féré, they were in the highest degree what is described as "out of the top drawer." In the eyes of those who so defined them, no doubt the Guermantes, the Rohans and many others were also out of the top drawer, but their name made it unnecessary to say so. Since not everyone was aware of the exalted birth of Mme Féré's mother and the extraordinarily exclusive circle in which she and her husband moved, when you mentioned their name you invariably added by way of explanation that they were "out of the very top drawer." Did their obscure name prompt them to a sort of haughty reserve? The fact remains that the Férés refused to know people on whom a La Trémoïlle would not have forborne to call. It had needed the position of queen of her particular stretch of coast, which the old Marquise de Cambremer held in the Manche, to make the Férés consent to come to one of her afternoons every year. The Cambremers had invited them to dinner and were counting largely on the effect that M. de Charlus was going to make on them. It was discreetly announced that he was to be one of the party. It chanced that Mme Féré did not know him. Mme de Cambremer, on learning this, felt a keen satisfaction, and the smile of a chemist who is about to bring into contact for the first time two particularly important bodies hovered over her lips. The door opened, and Mme de Cambremer almost fainted when she saw Morel enter the room alone. Like a private secretary conveying his minister's apologies, like a morganatic wife expressing the Prince's regret that he is unwell (as Mme de Clinchamp used to do on behalf of the Duc d'Aumale), Morel said in the airiest of tones: "The Baron can't come. He's not feeling very well, at least I think that's the reason ... I haven't seen him this week," he added, these last words completing the despair of Mme de Cambremer, who had told M. and Mme Féré that Morel saw M. de Charlus at every hour

of the day. The Cambremers pretended that the Baron's absence
was a blessing in disguise, and, without letting Morel hear
them, said to their other guests: "We can do very well without
him, can't we, it will be all the more agreeable." But they were
furious, suspected a plot hatched by Mme Verdurin, and, tit
for tat, when she invited them again to la Raspelière, M. de
Cambremer, unable to resist the pleasure of seeing his house
again and of mingling with the little group, came, but came
alone, saying that the Marquise was so sorry, but her doctor
had ordered her to stay at home. The Cambremers hoped by
this partial attendance at the same time to teach M. de Charlus a
lesson and to show the Verdurins that they were not obliged to
treat them with more than a limited politeness, as Princesses of
the Blood used in the old days to show duchesses out, but only
as far as the middle of the second chamber. After a few weeks,
they were scarcely on speaking terms.

M. de Cambremer explained it to me as follows: "I must tell
you that with M. de Charlus it was rather difficult. He is an
extreme Dreyfusard. . . ."

"Oh, no!"

"Yes he is. . . . Anyhow his cousin the Prince de Guermantes
is, and they've come in for a lot of abuse because of it. I have
some relatives who are very particular about that sort of thing.
I can't afford to mix with those people, I should alienate the
whole of my family."

"Since the Prince de Guermantes is a Dreyfusard, that will
make things all the easier," said Mme de Cambremer, "because
Saint-Loup, who is said to be going to marry his niece, is one
too. In fact it may well be the reason for the marriage."

"Come now, my dear," her husband replied, "you mustn't
say that Saint-Loup, who's a great friend of ours, is a Dreyfusard. One oughtn't to make such allegations lightly. You'll
make him highly popular in the Army!"

"He was once, but he isn't any longer," I explained to M. de
Cambremer. "As for his marrying Mlle de Guermantes-
Brassac, is there any truth in that?"

"People are talking of nothing else, but you should be in a
position to know."

"But I tell you, he himself told me he was a Dreyfusard,"

said Mme de Cambremer, "—not that there isn't every excuse for him, the Guermantes are half German."

"As regards the Guermantes of the Rue de Varenne, you can say entirely," said Cancan, "but Saint-Loup is another kettle of fish; he may have any number of German relations, but his father insisted on maintaining his title as a French nobleman; he joined the colours in 1871 and was killed in the war in the most gallant fashion. Although I'm a stickler in these matters, it doesn't do to exaggerate either one way or the other. *In medio . . . virtus*, ah, I forget the exact words. It's a remark I've heard Dr Cottard make. Now, there's a man who always has a word for it. You ought to have a *Petit Larousse* here."

To avoid having to give a verdict on the Latin quotation, and to get away from the subject of Saint-Loup, as to whom her husband seemed to think that she was wanting in tact, Mme de Cambremer fell back upon the Mistress, whose quarrel with them was even more in need of an explanation. "We were delighted to let la Raspelière to Mme Verdurin," said the Marquise. "The only trouble is that she appears to imagine that together with the house and everything else that she has managed to lay her hands on, the use of the meadow, the old hangings, all sorts of things which weren't in the lease at all, she should also be entitled to make friends with us. The two things are entirely distinct. Our mistake lay in not getting everything done quite simply through a lawyer or an agency. At Féterne it doesn't much matter, but I can just imagine the face my aunt de Ch'nouville would make if she saw old mother Verdurin come marching in on one of my days with her hair all over the place. As for M. de Charlus, of course he knows some very nice people, but he knows some very nasty people too." I asked who. Driven into a corner, Mme de Cambremer finally said: "People say that it was he who was keeping a certain Monsieur Moreau, Morille, Morue, I can't remember exactly. Nothing to do, of course, with Morel the violinist," she added, blushing. "When I realised that Mme Verdurin imagined that because she was our tenant in the Manche she would have the right to come and call upon me in Paris, I saw that it was time to cut the painter."

Notwithstanding this quarrel with the Mistress, the Cambremers were on quite good terms with the faithful, and would readily get into our compartment when they were travelling by the train. Just before we reached Douville, Albertine, taking out her mirror for the last time, would sometimes deem it necessary to change her gloves or to take off her hat for a moment, and, with the tortoiseshell comb which I had given her and which she wore in her hair, to smooth out the knots, to fluff up the curls, and if necessary, over the waves which descended in regular valleys to the nape of her neck, to push up her chignon. Once we were in the carriages which had come to meet us, we no longer had any idea where we were; the roads were not lighted; we could tell by the louder noise of the wheels that we were passing through a village, we thought we had arrived, we found ourselves once more in the open country, we heard bells in the distance, we forgot that we were in evening dress, and we had almost fallen asleep when, at the end of this long stretch of darkness which, what with the distance we had travelled and the hitches and delays inseparable from railway journeys, seemed to have carried us on to a late hour of the night and almost half-way back to Paris, suddenly, after the crunching of the carriage wheels over a finer gravel had revealed to us that we had turned into the drive, there burst forth, reintroducing us into a social existence, the dazzling lights of the drawing-room, then of the dining-room where we were suddenly taken aback by hearing eight o'clock strike when we imagined we were long since past it, while the endless dishes and vintage wines would circulate among the men in black and the women with bare arms, at a dinner glittering with light like a real metropolitan dinner-party but surrounded, and thereby changed in character, by the strange and sombre double veil which, diverted from their primal solemnity, the nocturnal, rural, maritime hours of the journey there and back had woven for it. Soon indeed the return journey obliged us to leave the radiant and quickly forgotten splendour of the lighted drawing-room for the carriages, in which I arranged to be with Albertine so that she should not be alone with other people, and often for another reason as well, which was that we could both do many things in a dark carriage, in which the jolts of the downward drive would moreover give us an excuse, should a sudden ray of light fall upon us, for clinging to one another. When M. de Cambremer was still on visiting terms with the Verdurins, he would ask me: "You don't think this fog will bring on your spasms? My sister's were terribly bad this morning. Ah! you've been having them too," he said with satisfaction. "I shall tell her to-night. I know that as soon as I get home the first thing she'll ask will be whether you've had any lately." He spoke to me of my sufferings only to lead up to his sister's, and made me describe mine in detail simply that he might point out the difference between them and hers. But notwithstanding these differences, as he felt that his sister's spasms entitled him to speak with authority, he could not believe that what "succeeded" with hers was not indicated as a cure for mine, and it irritated him that I would not try these remedies, for if there is one thing more difficult than submitting oneself to a regime it is refraining from imposing it on other people. "Not that I need speak, a mere layman, when you are here before the Areopagus, at the fountainhead of wisdom. What does Professor Cottard think about them?"

I saw his wife once again, as a matter of fact, because she had said that my "cousin" behaved rather weirdly, and I wished to know what she meant by this. She denied having said it, but at length admitted that she had been speaking of a person whom she thought she had seen with my cousin. She did not know the person's name and said finally that, if she was not mistaken, it was the wife of a banker, who was called Lina, Linette, Lisette, Lia, anyhow something like that. I felt that "wife of a banker" was inserted merely to put me off the scent. I wanted to ask Albertine whether it was true. But I preferred to give the impression of knowing rather than inquiring. Besides, Albertine would not have answered me at all, or would have answered me only with a "no" of which the "n" would have been too hesitant and the "o" too emphatic. Albertine never related facts that were damaging to her, but always other facts which could be explained only by the former, the truth being rather a current which flows from what people say to us, and which we pick up, invisible though it is, than the actual thing they have said. Thus, when I assured her that a woman whom she had known at Vichy was disreputable, she swore to me that this woman was not at all what I supposed and had never attempted to make her do anything improper. But she added, another day, when I was speaking of my curiosity as to people of that sort, that the Vichy lady had a friend too, whom she, Albertine, did not know, but whom the lady had "*promised* to introduce to her." That she should have promised her this could only mean that Albertine wished it, or that the lady had known that by offering the introduction she would be giving her pleasure. But if I had pointed this out to Albertine, I should have given the impression that my revelations came exclusively from her; I should have put a stop to them at once, never have learned anything more, and ceased to make myself feared. Besides, we were at Balbec, and the Vichy lady and her friend lived at Menton; the remoteness, the impossibility of the danger made short work of my suspicions.

Often, when M. de Cambremer hailed me from the station, I had just been taking advantage of the darkness with Albertine, not without some difficulty as she had struggled a little, fearing that it was not dark enough. "You know, I'm sure Cottard saw us; anyhow, if he didn't, he must have noticed your breathless voice, just when they were talking about your other kind of breathlessness," Albertine said to me when we arrived at Douville station where we took the little train home. But if this return journey, like the outward one, by giving me a certain impression of poetry, awakened in me the desire to travel, to lead a new life, and so made me want to abandon any intention of marrying Albertine, and even to break off our relations for good, it also, by the very fact of their contradictory nature, made this breach easier. For, on the homeward journey just as much as on the other, at every station we were joined in the train or greeted from the platform by people whom we knew; the furtive pleasures of the imagination were overshadowed by those other, continual pleasures of sociability which are so soothing, so soporific. Already, before the stations themselves, their names (which had so fired my imagination ever since the day I had first heard them, that first evening when I had travelled down to Balbec with my grandmother) had become humanised, had lost their strangeness since the evening when

Brichot, at Albertine's request, had given us a more complete account of their etymology. I had been charmed by the "flower" that ended certain names, such as Fiquefleur, Honfleur, Flers, Barfleur, Harfleur, etc., and amused by the "beef" that comes at the end of Bricquebœuf. But the flower vanished, and also the beef, when Brichot (and this he had told me on the first day in the train) informed us that *fleur* means a harbour (like *fiord*), and that *bœuf*, in Norman *budh*, means a hut. As he cited a number of examples, what had appeared to me a particular instance became general: Bricquebœuf took its place by the side of Elbeuf, and even in a name that was at first sight as individual as the place itself, like the name Pennedepie, in which peculiarities too impenetrable for reason to elucidate seemed to me to have been blended from time immemorial in a word as coarse, flavoursome and hard as a certain Norman cheese, I was disappointed to find the Gallic *pen* which means mountain and is as recognisable in Penmarch as in the Apennines. Since, at each halt of the train, I felt that we should have friendly hands to shake if not visitors to receive in our carriage, I said to Albertine: "Hurry up and ask Brichot about the names you want to know. You mentioned to me Marcouville-l'Orgueilleuse."

"Yes, I love that *orgueil*, it's a proud village," said Albertine.

"You would find it prouder still," Brichot replied, "if, instead of its French or even its low Latin form, as we find it in the cartulary of the Bishop of Bayeux, *Marcouvilla superba*, you were to take the older form, more akin to the Norman, *Marculphivilla superba*, the village, the domain of Merculph. In almost all these names which end in *ville*, you might see still marshalled upon this coast the ghosts of the rude Norman invaders. At Hermenonville, you had, standing at the carriage door, only our excellent Doctor, who, obviously, has nothing of the Norse chieftain about him. But, by shutting your eyes, you might have seen the illustrious Herimund (*Herimundivilla*). Although, I can never understand why, people choose these roads, between Loigny and Balbec-Plage, rather than the very picturesque roads that lead from Loigny to old Balbec, Mme Verdurin has perhaps taken you out that way in her carriage. If so, you have seen Incarville, or the village of Wiscar; and Tourville, before you come to Mme Verdurin's, is the village of Turold. Moreover, there were not only the Normans. It seems that the Germans (*Alemanni*) came as far as here: Aumenancourt, *Alemanicurtis*—don't let us speak of it to that young officer I see there; he would be capable of refusing to visit his cousins there any more. There were also Saxons, as is proved by the springs of Sissonne (the goal of one of Mme Verdurin's favourite excursions, and rightly so), just as in England you have Middlesex, Wessex, etc. And what is inexplicable, it seems that the Goths, *gueux* as they were called, came as far as this, and even the Moors, for Mortagne comes from *Mauretania*. Their traces still remain at Gourville—*Gothorumvilla*. Some vestige of the Latins subsists also, for instance Lagny (*Latiniacum*)."

"I should like to know the explanation of Thorpehomme," said M. de Charlus. "I understand *homme*," he added, at which the sculptor and Cottard exchanged meaning glances. "But *Thorpe*?"

"*Homme* does not in the least mean what you are naturally led to suppose, Baron," replied Brichot, glancing mischievously at Cottard and the sculptor. "*Homme* has nothing to do, in this instance, with the sex to which I am not indebted for my mother. *Homme* is *holm*, which means a small island, etc. . . . As for *Thorpe*, or village, we find that in any number of words with which I have already bored our young friend. Thus in Thorpehomme there is not the name of a Norman chief, but words of the Norman language. You see how the whole of this country has been Germanised."

"I think that is an exaggeration," said M. de Charlus. "Yesterday I was at Orgeville."

"This time I give you back the man I took from you in Thorpehomme, Baron. Without wishing to be pedantic, a charter of Robert I gives us, for Orgeville, *Otgervilla*, the domain of Otger. All these names are those of ancient lords. Octeville-la-Venelle is a corruption of l'Avenel. The Avenels were a family of repute in the Middle Ages. Bourguenolles, where Mme Verdurin took us the other day, used to be written Bourg de Môles, for that village belonged in the eleventh century to Baudoin de Môles, as also did la Chaise-Baudoin; but here we are at Doncières."

"Heavens, look at all these subalterns trying to get in," said

M. de Charlus with feigned alarm. "I'm thinking of you, for it doesn't affect me, I'm getting out here."

"You hear, Doctor?" said Brichot. "The Baron is afraid of officers passing over his body. And yet it's quite appropriate for them to be here in strength, for Doncières is precisely the same as Saint-Cyr, *Dominus Cyriacus*. There are plenty of names of towns in which *Sanctus* and *Sancta* are replaced by *Dominus* and *Domina*. Besides, this peaceful military town sometimes has a spurious look of Saint-Cyr, of Versailles, and even of Fontainebleau."

During these homeward journeys (as on the outward ones) I used to tell Albertine to put on her things, for I knew very well that at Aumenancourt, Doncières, Epreville, Saint-Vast we should be receiving brief visits from friends. Nor did I find these disagreeable, whether it might be, at Hermenonville (the domain of Herimund) a visit from M. de Chevregny, seizing the opportunity, when he had come down to meet other guests, of asking me to come over to lunch next day at Beausoleil, or (at Doncières) the sudden irruption of one of Saint-Loup's charming friends, sent by him (if he himself was not free) to convey to me an invitation from Captain de Borodino, from the officers' mess at the Coq-Hardi, or from the sergeants' at the Faisan Doré. Saint-Loup often came in person, and during the whole of the time he was with us I contrived, without letting anyone notice, to keep Albertine a prisoner under my unnecessarily vigilant eye. On one occasion however my watch was interrupted. During a protracted stop, Bloch, after greeting us, was making off at once to join his father—who, having just succeeded to his uncle's fortune, and having leased a country house by the name of la Commanderie, thought it befitting a country gentleman always to go about in a post-chaise, with postilions in livery—and asked me to accompany him to the carriage. "But make haste, for these quadrupeds are impatient. Come, O beloved of the gods, thou wilt give pleasure to my father." But I could not bear to leave Albertine in the train with Saint-Loup; they might, while my back was turned, get into conversation, go into another compartment, smile at one another, touch one another; my eyes, glued to Albertine, could not detach themselves from her so long as Saint-Loup was there. Now I could see quite well that Bloch, who had asked me as a favour to go and pay my respects to his father, in the first place thought it very ungracious of me to refuse when there was nothing to prevent me from doing so, the porters having told us that the train would remain for at least a quarter of an hour in the station, and almost all the passengers, without whom it would not leave, having alighted; and, what was more, had not the least doubt that it was because quite clearly—my conduct on this occasion furnished him with a decisive proof of it—I was a snob. For he was not unaware of the names of the people in whose company I was. In fact M. de Charlus had said to me some time before this, without remembering or caring that the introduction had been made long ago: "But you must introduce your friend to me; your behaviour shows a lack of respect for myself," and had talked to Bloch, who had seemed to please him immensely, so much so that he had gratified him with an: "I hope to meet you again." "Then it's final—you won't walk a hundred yards to say how-d'ye-do to my father, who would be so pleased?" Bloch said to me. I was sorry to appear to be lacking in comradeship, and even more so for the reason for which Bloch supposed that I was lacking in it, and to feel that he imagined that I was not the same towards my middle-class friends when I was with people of "birth." From that day he ceased to show the same friendliness towards me, and, what pained me more, had no longer the same regard for my character. But, in order to disabuse him as to the motive which made me remain in the carriage, I should have had to tell him something—to wit, that I was jealous of Albertine—which would have distressed me even more than letting him suppose that I was stupidly worldly. So it is that in theory we find that we ought always to explain ourselves frankly, to avoid misunderstandings. But very often life arranges these in such a way that, in order to dispel them, in the rare circumstances in which it might be possible to do so, we must reveal either—which was not the case here—something that would annoy our friend even more than the imaginary wrong that he imputes to us, or a secret the disclosure of which —and this was my predicament—appears to us even worse than the misunderstanding. And moreover, even without my explaining to Bloch, since I could not, my reason for not accompanying him, if I had begged him not to be offended, I should only have increased his umbrage by showing him that I had observed it. There was nothing to be done but to bow before the decree of fate which had willed that Albertine's presence should prevent me from accompanying him, and that he should suppose that it was on the contrary the presence of important people—the only effect of which, had they been a hundred times more important, would have been to make me devote my attention exclusively to Bloch and reserve all my civility for him. In this way, accidentally and absurdly, a minor incident (in this case the juxtaposition of Albertine and Saint-Loup) has only to be interposed between two destinies whose lines have been converging towards one another, for them to deviate, stretch further and further apart, and never converge again. And there are friendships more precious than Bloch's for myself which have been destroyed without the involuntary author of the offence having any opportunity to explain to the offended party what would no doubt have healed the injury to his self-esteem and called back his fugitive affection.

Friendships more precious than Bloch's would not, for that matter, be saying very much. He had all the faults that I most disliked, and it happened by chance that my affection for Albertine made them altogether intolerable. Thus in that brief moment in which I was talking to him while keeping my eye on Robert, Bloch told me that he had been to lunch at Mme Bontemps's and that everybody had spoken about me in the most glowing terms until the "decline of Helios." "Good," thought I, "since Mme Bontemps regards Bloch as a genius, the enthusiastic approval that he will have expressed for me will do more than anything that the others can have said, it will get back to Albertine. Any day now she is bound to learn—I'm surprised that her aunt has not repeated it to her already—that I'm a 'superior person.'" "Yes," Bloch went on, "everybody sang your praises. I alone preserved a silence as profound as though, in place of the repast (poor, as it happened) that was set before us, I had absorbed poppies, dear to the blessed brother of Thanatos and Lethe, the divine Hypnos, who enwraps in pleasant bonds the body and the tongue. It is not that I admire you less than the band of ravening dogs with whom I had been bidden to feed. But I admire you because I understand you, and they admire you without understanding you. To tell the truth, I admire you too much to speak of you thus in public. It would have seemed to me a profanation to praise aloud what I carry in the profoundest depths of my heart. In vain did they question me about you, a sacred Pudor, daughter of Kronion, kept me mute."

I did not have the bad taste to appear annoyed, but this Pudor seemed to me akin—far more than to Kronion—to the reticence that prevents a critic who admires you from speaking of you because the secret temple in which you sit enthroned would be invaded by the mob of ignorant readers and journalists; to the reticence of the statesman who does not recommend you for a decoration because you would be lost in a crowd of people who are not your equals; to the reticence of the Academician who refrains from voting for you in order to spare you the shame of being the colleague of X—— who is devoid of talent; to the reticence, finally, more respectworthy and at the same time more criminal, of the sons who implore us not to write about their dead father who abounded in merit, in order to ensure silence and repose, to prevent us from maintaining the stir of life and the sound of glory round the deceased, who himself would prefer the echo of his name upon the lips of men to all the wreaths upon his tomb, however piously borne.

If Bloch, while grieving me by his inability to understand the reason that prevented me from going to greet his father, had exasperated me by confessing that he had depreciated me at Mme Bontemps's (I now understood why Albertine had never made any allusion to this lunch-party and remained silent when I spoke to her of Bloch's affection for myself), my young Jewish friend had produced upon M. de Charlus an impression that was quite the opposite of annoyance.

Of course, Bloch now believed not only that I was incapable of depriving myself for a second of the company of smart people, but that, jealous of the advances that they might make to him (M. de Charlus, for instance), I was trying to put a spoke in his wheel and to prevent him from making friends with them; but for his part the Baron regretted that he had not seen more of my friend. As was his habit, he took care not to betray this feeling. He began by asking me various questions about Bloch, but in so casual a tone, with an interest that seemed so feigned, that it was as though he was not listening to the answers. With an air of detachment, in a monotonous singsong voice that expressed not merely indifference but a total lack of attention, and as though simply out of politeness to myself: "He looks intelligent, he said he wrote, has he any talent?" M. de Charlus asked. I told him that it had been very kind of him to say that he hoped to see Bloch again. The Baron gave not the slightest sign of having heard my remark, and as I repeated it four times without eliciting a reply, I began to wonder whether I had been the victim of an acoustic mirage when I thought I heard M. de Charlus utter those words. "He lives at Balbec?" crooned the Baron in a tone so far from interrogatory that it is regrettable that the written language does not possess a sign other than the question mark to end such apparently unquestioning remarks. It is true that such a sign would be of little use except to M. de Charlus. "No, they've taken a place near here, la Commanderie." Having learned what he wished to know, M. de Charlus pretended to despise Bloch. "How appalling," he exclaimed, his voice resuming all its clarion vigour. "All the places or properties called la Commanderie were built or owned by the Knights of the Order of Malta (of whom I am one), as the places called Temple or Cavalerie were by the Templars. That I should live at la Commanderie would be the most natural thing in the world. But a Jew! However, I am not surprised; it comes from a curious instinct for sacrilege, peculiar to that race. As soon as a Jew has enough money to buy a place in the country he always chooses one that is called Priory, Abbey, Minster, Chantry. I had some business once with a Jewish official, and guess where he lived: at Pont-l'Evêque. When he fell into disfavour, he had himself transferred to Brittany, to Pont-l'Abbé. When they perform in Holy Week those indecent spectacles that are called 'the Passion,' half the audience are Jews, exulting in the thought that they are about to hang Christ a second time on the Cross, at least in effigy. At one of the Lamoureux concerts, I had a wealthy Jewish banker sitting next to me. They played the *Childhood of Christ* by

Berlioz, and he was thoroughly dismayed. But he soon recovered his habitually blissful expression when he heard the
Good Friday music. So your friend lives at the Commanderie,
the wretch! What sadism! You must show me the way to it," he
added, resuming his air of indifference, "so that I may go there
one day and see how our former domains endure such a
profanation. It is unfortunate, for he has good manners, and he
seems cultivated. The next thing I shall hear will be that his
address in Paris is Rue du Temple!"

M. de Charlus gave the impression, by these words, that he
was seeking merely to find a fresh example in support of his
theory; but in reality he was asking me a question with a dual
purpose, the principal one being to find out Bloch's address.

"Yes indeed," put in Brichot, "the Rue du Temple used to be
called Rue de la Chevalerie-du-Temple. And in that connexion
will you allow me to make a remark, Baron?"

"What? What is it?" said M. de Charlus tartly, the proffered
remark preventing him from obtaining his information.

"No, it's nothing," replied Brichot in alarm. "It was in
connexion with the etymology of Balbec, about which they were
asking me. The Rue du Temple was formerly known as the
Rue Barre-du-Bec, because the Abbey of Bec in Normandy
had its Bar of Justice there in Paris."

M. de Charlus made no reply and looked as if he had not
heard, which was one of his favourite forms of rudeness.

"Where does your friend live in Paris? As three streets out of
four take their name from a church or an abbey, there seems
every chance of further sacrilege there. One can't prevent Jews
from living in the Boulevard de la Madeleine, the Faubourg
Saint-Honoré or the Place Saint-Augustin. So long as they do
not carry their perfidy a stage further, and pitch their tents in
the Place du Parvis-Notre-Dame, Quai de l'Archevêché, Rue
Chanoinesse or Rue de l'Ave-Maria, we must make allowance
for their difficulties."

We could not enlighten M. de Charlus, not being aware of
Bloch's address at the time. But I knew that his father's office
was in the Rue des Blancs-Manteaux.

"Oh, isn't that the last word in perversity!" exclaimed M. de
Charlus, appearing to find a profound satisfaction in his own

cry of ironical indignation. "Rue des Blancs-Manteaux!" he
repeated, dwelling with emphasis upon each syllable and laughing as he spoke. "What sacrilege! To think that these White
Mantles polluted by M. Bloch were those of the mendicant
friars, styled Serfs of the Blessed Virgin, whom Saint Louis
established there. And the street has always housed religious
orders. The profanation is all the more diabolical since within a
stone's throw of the Rue des Blancs-Manteaux there is a street
whose name escapes me, which is entirely conceded to the
Jews, with Hebrew characters over the shops, bakeries for
unleavened bread, kosher butcheries—it's positively the
Judengasse of Paris. That is where M. Bloch ought to reside.
Of course," he went on in a lofty, grandiloquent tone suited to
the discussion of aesthetic matters, and giving, by an unconscious atavistic reflex, the air of an old Louis XIII musketeer to
his uptilted face, "I take an interest in all that sort of thing only
from the point of view of art. Politics are not in my line, and I
cannot condemn wholesale, because Bloch belongs to it, a
nation that numbers Spinoza among its illustrious sons. And I
admire Rembrandt too much not to realise the beauty that can
be derived from frequenting the synagogue. But after all a
ghetto is all the finer the more homogeneous and complete it is.
You may be sure, moreover, so far are business instincts and
avarice mingled in that race with sadism, that the proximity of
the Hebraic street in question, the convenience of having close
at hand the fleshpots of Israel, will have made your friend
choose the Rue des Blancs-Manteaux. How curious it all is! It
was there, by the way, that there lived a strange Jew who boiled
the Host, after which I think they boiled him, which is stranger
still since it seems to suggest that the body of a Jew can be
equivalent to the Body of Our Lord. Perhaps it might be possible to arrange for your friend to take us to see the church of
the White Mantles. Just think that it was there that they laid the
body of Louis d'Orléans after his assassination by Jean sans
Peur, which unfortunately did not rid us of the Orléans family.
Personally, I have always been on the best of terms with my
cousin the Duc de Chartres, but they are nevertheless a race of
usurpers who caused the assassination of Louis XVI and the
dethronement of Charles X and Henri V. Of course it runs in

the family, since their ancestors include Monsieur, who was so styled doubtless because he was the most astounding old woman, and the Regent and the rest of them. What a family!"

This speech, anti-Jewish or pro-Hebrew—according to whether one pays attention to the overt meaning of its sentences or the intentions that they concealed—had been comically interrupted for me by a remark which Morel whispered to me, to the chagrin of M. de Charlus. Morel, who had not failed to notice the impression that Bloch had made, murmured his thanks in my ear for having "given him the push," adding cynically: "He wanted to stay, it's all jealousy, he'd like to take my place. Just like a yid!"

"We might have taken advantage of this prolonged halt," M. de Charlus went on, "to ask your friend for some interpretations of ritual. Couldn't you fetch him back?" he pleaded desperately.

"No, it's impossible, he has gone away in a carriage, and besides, he's vexed with me."

"Thank you, thank you," Morel murmured.

"Your excuse is preposterous, one can always overtake a carriage, there is nothing to prevent your taking a motor-car," replied M. de Charlus, in the tone of a man accustomed to carry everything before him. But observing my silence: "What is this more or less imaginary carriage?" he said to me insolently, and with a last ray of hope.

"It is an open post-chaise which must by this time have reached la Commanderie."

M. de Charlus bowed before the impossible and made a show of jocularity. "I can understand their recoiling from the idea of a new brougham. It might have swept them clean."

At last we were warned that the train was about to start, and Saint-Loup left us. But this was the only day on which by getting into our carriage he unwittingly caused me pain, when I momentarily thought of leaving him with Albertine in order to go with Bloch. On every other occasion his presence did not torment me. For of her own accord Albertine, to spare me any uneasiness, would on some pretext or other place herself in such a position that she could not even unintentionally brush against Robert, almost too far away even to shake hands with him; turning her eyes away from him, she would plunge, as soon as he appeared, into ostentatious and almost affected conversation with one of the other passengers, continuing this make-believe until Saint-Loup had gone. So that the visits which he paid us at Doncières, causing me no pain, no worry even, were in no way discordant from the rest, all of which I found pleasing because they brought me so to speak the homage and the hospitality of this land. Already, as the summer drew to a close, on our journeys from Balbec to Douville, when I saw in the distance the little resort of Saint-Pierre-des-Ifs where, for a moment in the evening, the crest of the cliffs glittered pink like the snow on a mountain at sunset, it no longer recalled to my mind—let alone the melancholy which its strange, sudden emergence had aroused in me on the first evening, when it filled me with such a longing to take the train back to Paris instead of going on to Balbec—the spectacle that in the morning, Elstir had told me, might be enjoyed from there, at the hour before sunrise, when all the colours of the rainbow are refracted from the rocks, and when he had so often wakened the little boy who had served him as model one year, to paint him, nude, upon the sands. The name Saint-Pierre-des-Ifs announced to me merely that there would presently appear a strange, witty, painted fifty-year-old with whom I should be able to talk about Chateaubriand and Balzac. And now, in the mists of evening, behind that cliff of Incarville which had filled my mind with so many dreams in the past, what I saw, as though its old sandstone wall had become transparent, was the comfortable house of an uncle of M. de Cambremer in which I knew that I should always find a warm welcome if I did not wish to dine at la Raspelière or return to Balbec. So that it was not merely the place-names of this district that had lost their initial mystery, but the places themselves. The names, already half-stripped of a mystery which etymology had replaced by reasoning, had now come down a stage further still. On our homeward journeys, at Hermenonville, at Incarville, at Harambouville, as the train came to a standstill, we could make out shadowy forms which we did not at first identify and which Brichot, who could see nothing at all, might perhaps have mistaken in the darkness for the ghosts of Herimund, Wiscar and Herimbald. But they came up to our carriage. It was merely M. de Cambremer, now completely estranged from the Verdurins, who had come to see off his own guests and who, on behalf of his wife and his mother, came to ask me whether I would not let him "snatch me away" to spend a few days at Féterne where I should be entertained successively by a lady of great musical talent who would sing me the whole of Gluck, and a famous chess-player with whom I could have some splendid games, which would not interfere with the fishing expeditions and yachting trips in the bay, or even with the Verdurin dinner-parties, for which the Marquis gave me his word of honour that he would "lend" me, sending me there and fetching me back again, for my greater convenience and also to make sure of my returning. "But I cannot believe that it's good for you to go so high up. I know my sister could never stand it. She would come back in a fine state! She's not at all well just now. . . . Really, you had such a bad attack as that! To-morrow you'll hardly be able to stand!" And he shook with laughter, not from malevolence but for the same reason which made him laugh whenever he saw a lame man hobbling along the street, or had to talk to a deaf person. "And before that? What, you hadn't had an attack for a fortnight? Do you know, that's simply marvellous. Really, you ought to come and stay at Féterne, you could talk to my sister about your attacks."

At Incarville it was the Marquis de Montpeyroux who, not having been able to go to Féterne, for he had been away shooting, had come "to meet the train" in top boots and with a pheasant's plume in his hat, to shake hands with the departing guests and at the same time with myself, bidding me expect, on the day of the week that would be most convenient to me, a visit from his son, whom he thanked me for inviting, adding that he would be very glad if I would make the boy read a little; or else M. de Crécy, come out to digest his dinner, he explained, smoking his pipe, accepting a cigar or indeed more than one, and saying to me: "Well, you haven't named a day for our next Lucullan evening. We have nothing to say to each other? Allow me to remind you that we left unsettled the question of the two Montgomery families. We really must settle it. I'm relying on you." Others had come simply to buy newspapers.

And many others came and chatted with us who, I have often
suspected, were to be found upon the platform of the station
nearest to their little manor simply because they had nothing
better to do than to converse for a moment with people of their
acquaintance. They were a setting for social intercourse like
any other, in fact, these halts of the little train, which itself
appeared conscious of the role that had been allotted to it, had
contracted a sort of human kindliness: patient, of a docile
nature, it waited as long as one wished for the stragglers, and
even after it had started, would stop to pick up those who
signalled to it; they would then run after it panting, in which
they resembled it, though they differed from it in that they were
running to overtake it at full speed whereas it was merely
exercising a wise deliberation. And so Hermenonville, Harambouville, Incarville no longer suggested to me even the rugged
grandeurs of the Norman Conquest, not content with having
entirely rid themselves of the unaccountable melancholy in
which I had seen them steeped long ago in the moist evening
air. Doncières! To me, even after I had come to know it and
had awakened from my dream, how long there had survived in
that name those pleasantly glacial streets, lighted windows,
succulent fowls! Doncières! Now it was merely the station at
which Morel joined the train, Egleville (*Aquilae villa*) the one
at which Princess Sherbatoff generally awaited us, Maineville
the station at which Albertine left the train on fine evenings,
when, if she was not too tired, she felt inclined to enjoy a
moment more of my company, having, if she took a footpath,
little if any further to walk than if she had alighted at Parville
(*Paterni villa*). Not only did I no longer feel the anxious dread of
loneliness which had gripped my heart the first evening; I had
no longer any need to fear its reawakening, nor to feel myself a
homesick stranger in this land productive not only of chestnut
trees and tamarisks, but of friendships which from beginning to
end of the route formed a long chain, interrupted like that of
the blue hills, hidden here and there in the anfractuosity of the
rock or behind the lime trees of the avenue, but delegating at
each stopping-place an amiable gentleman who came to
punctuate my journey with a cordial handclasp, to prevent me
from feeling its length, to offer if need be to continue it with me.

Another would be at the next station, so that the whistle of the little train parted us from one friend only to enable us to meet others. Between the most isolated properties and the railway which skirted them almost at the pace of a person walking fairly fast, the distance was so slight that at the moment when, from the platform, outside the waiting-room, their owners hailed us, we might almost have imagined that they were doing so from their own doorstep, from their bedroom window, as though the little departmental line had been merely a provincial street and the isolated country house an urban mansion; and even at the few stations where no "good evening" sounded, the silence had a nourishing and calming plenitude, because I knew that it was formed from the slumber of friends who had gone to bed early in the neighbouring manor, where my arrival would have been greeted with joy if I had been obliged to arouse them to ask for some hospitable service. Apart from the fact that habit so fills up our time that we have not, after a few months, a free moment in a town where on our first arrival the day offered us the absolute disposal of all its twelve hours, if one of these had by any chance fallen vacant it would no longer have occurred to me to devote it to visiting some church for the sake of which I had first come to Balbec, or even to compare a scene painted by Elstir with the sketch that I had seen of it in his studio, but rather to go and play one more game of chess with M. Féré. It was indeed the corrupting effect, as it was also the charm, of this country round Balbec, to have become for me a land of familiar acquaintances; if its territorial distribution, its extensive cultivation, along the entire length of the coast, with different forms of agriculture, gave of necessity to the visits which I paid to these different friends the aspect of a journey, they also reduced that journey to the agreeable proportions of a series of visits. The same place-names, so disturbing to me in the past that the mere Country House Directory, when I leafed through the section devoted to the Department of the Manche, caused me as much dismay as the railway time-table, had become so familiar to me that even in that time-table itself I could have consulted the page headed *Balbec to Douville via Doncières* with the same happy tranquillity as an address-book. In this too social valley, along the flanks of which I felt that there clung, whether visible or not, a numerous company of friends, the poetical cry of the evening was no longer that of the owl or the frog, but the "How goes it?" of M. de Criquetot or the "Khaire" of Brichot. Its atmosphere no longer aroused anguish, and, charged with purely human exhalations, was easily breathable, indeed almost too soothing. The benefit that I did at least derive from it was that of looking at things only from a practical point of view. The idea of marrying Albertine appeared to me to be madness.

CHAPTER FOUR

I WAS only waiting for an opportunity for a final rupture. And, one evening, as Mamma was setting out next day for Combray, where she was to attend the deathbed of one of her mother's sisters, leaving me behind so that I might continue to benefit, as my grandmother would have wished, from the sea air, I had announced to her that I had irrevocably decided not to marry Albertine and would very soon stop seeing her. I was glad to have been able, by these words, to gratify my mother's wishes on the eve of her departure. She had made no secret of the fact that she was indeed extremely gratified. I also had to have things out with Albertine. As I was on my way back with her from la Raspelière, the faithful having alighted, some at Saint-Mars-le-Vêtu, others at Saint-Pierre-des-Ifs, others again at Doncières, feeling particularly happy and detached from her, I had decided, now that there were only our two selves in the carriage, to broach the subject at last. The truth of the matter was that the member of the band of Balbec girls whom I really loved, although she was absent at that moment, as were the rest of her friends, but was coming back there (I enjoyed being with them all, because each of them had for me, as on the day when I first saw them, something of the essence of all the rest, as though they belonged to a race apart), was Andrée. Since she was coming back again to Balbec in a few days' time, it was certain that she would at once pay me a visit, and then, in order to remain free, not to have to marry her if I did not wish to do so, to be able to go to Venice, but at the same time to have her entirely to myself in the meantime, the plan that I would adopt would be that of not seeming at all eager to come to her, and as soon as she arrived, when we were talking together, I would say to her: "What a pity I didn't see you a few weeks earlier. I should have fallen in love with you; now my heart is bespoken. But that makes no difference, we shall see one another frequently, for I am unhappy about my other love, and you will help to console me." I smiled inwardly as I thought of this conversation, for in this way I should give Andrée the impression that I was not really in love with her; hence she would not grow tired of me and I should take a joyful and pleasant advantage of her affection. But all this only made it all the more necessary that I should at last speak seriously to Albertine, in order not to behave dishonourably, and, since I had decided to devote myself to her friend, she herself must be given clearly to understand that I was not in love with her. I must tell her so at once, as Andrée might arrive any day. But as we were approaching Parville, I felt that we might not have time that evening and that it was better to put off until next day what was now irrevocably settled. I confined myself, therefore, to discussing with her our dinner that evening at the Verdurins'. As she was putting on her coat, the train having just left Incarville, the last station before Parville, she said to me: "To-morrow then, more Verdurin. You won't forget that you're coming to call for me." I could not help answering rather tersely: "Yes, that is if I don't 'defect,' because I'm beginning to find that sort of life really stupid. In any case, if we do go, in order that my time at la Raspelière may not be totally wasted, I must remember to ask Mme Verdurin about something that could interest me a great deal, provide me with a subject for study, and give me pleasure as well, because I've really had very little this year at Balbec."

"That's not very polite to me, but I forgive you, because I can see that you're overwrought. What is this pleasure?"

"That Mme Verdurin should let me hear some things by a musician whose work she knows very well. I know one of his things myself, but it seems there are others and I should like to know if the rest of his work is published, if it's different from what I know."

"What musician?"

"My dear child, when I've told you that his name is Vinteuil, will you be any the wiser?"

We may have revolved every possible idea in our minds, and yet the truth has never occurred to us, and it is from without, when we are least expecting it, that it gives us its cruel stab and wounds us forever.

"You can't think how you amuse me," replied Albertine,

getting up, for the train was about to stop. "Not only does it mean a great deal more to me than you suppose, but even without Mme Verdurin I can get you all the information that you require. You remember my telling you about a friend, older than me, who had been a mother, a sister to me, with whom I spent the happiest years of my life, at Trieste, and whom in fact I'm expecting to join in a few weeks at Cherbourg, where we shall set out on a cruise together (it sounds a bit weird, but you know how I love the sea)? Well, this friend (oh! not at all the type of woman you might suppose!), isn't this extraordinary, is the best friend of your Vinteuil's daughter, and I know Vinteuil's daughter almost as well as I know her. I always call them my two big sisters. I'm not sorry to show you that your little Albertine can be of use to you in this question of music, about which you say, and quite rightly, that I know nothing at all."

At the sound of these words, uttered as we were entering the station of Parville, so far from Combray and Montjouvain, so long after the death of Vinteuil, an image stirred in my heart, an image which I had kept in reserve for so many years that even if I had been able to guess, when I stored it up long ago, that it had a noxious power, I should have supposed that in the course of time it had entirely lost it; preserved alive in the depths of my being—like Orestes whose death the gods had prevented in order that, on the appointed day, he might return to his native land to avenge the murder of Agamemnon—as a punishment, as a retribution (who knows?) for my having allowed my grandmother to die; perhaps rising up suddenly from the dark depths in which it seemed forever buried, and striking like an Avenger, in order to inaugurate for me a new and terrible and only too well-merited existence, perhaps also to make dazzlingly clear to my eyes the fatal consequences which evil actions eternally engender, not only for those who have committed them but for those who have done no more, or thought that they were doing no more, than look on at a curious and entertaining spectacle, as I, alas, had done on that afternoon long ago at Montjouvain, concealed behind a bush where (as when I had complacently listened to the account of Swann's love affairs) I had perilously allowed to open up within me the fatal and inevitably painful road of Knowledge. And at the same time, from my bitterest grief I derived a feeling almost of pride, almost of joy, that of a man whom the shock he has just received has carried at a bound to a point to which no voluntary effort could have brought him. The notion of Albertine as the friend of Mlle Vinteuil and of Mlle Vinteuil's friend, a practising and professional Sapphist, was as momentous, compared to what I had imagined when I doubted her most, as are the telephones that soar over streets, cities, fields, seas, linking one country to another, compared to the little acousticon of the 1889 Exhibition which was barely expected to transmit sound from one end of a house to the other. It was a terrible *terra incognita* on which I had just landed, a new phase of undreamed-of sufferings that was opening before me. And yet this deluge of reality that engulfs us, however enormous it may be compared with our timid and microscopic suppositions, has always been foreshadowed by them. It was doubtless something akin to what I had just learned, something akin to Albertine's friendship with Mlle Vinteuil, something which my mind would never have been capable of inventing, that I had obscurely apprehended when I became so uneasy at the sight of Albertine and Andrée together. It is often simply from lack of creative imagination that we do not go far enough in suffering. And the most terrible reality brings us, at the same time as suffering, the joy of a great discovery, because it merely gives a new and clear form to what we have long been ruminating without suspecting it.

The train had stopped at Parville, and, as we were the only passengers in it, it was in a voice weakened by a sense of the futility of his task, by the force of habit which nevertheless made him perform it and inspired in him simultaneously exactitude and indolence, and even more by a longing for sleep, that the porter shouted: "Parville!" Albertine, who stood facing me, seeing that she had arrived at her destination, stepped across the compartment and opened the door. But this movement which she thus made to get off the train tore my heart unendurably, just as if, contrary to the position independent of my body which Albertine's seemed to be occupying a yard away from it, this separation in space, which an accurate draughtsman would have been obliged to indicate between us, was only apparent, and anyone who wished to make a fresh drawing of things as they really were would now have had to place Albertine, not at a certain distance from me, but inside me. She gave me such pain by her withdrawal that, reaching after her, I caught her desperately by the arm.

"Would it be physically possible," I asked her, "for you to come and spend the night at Balbec?"

"Physically, yes. But I'm dropping with sleep."

"You'd be doing me an enormous favour . . ."

"Very well, then, though I don't in the least understand. Why didn't you tell me sooner? I'll stay, though."

My mother was asleep when, after engaging a room for Albertine on a different floor, I entered my own. I sat down by the window, suppressing my sobs so that my mother, who was separated from me only by a thin partition, might not hear me. I had not even remembered to close the shutters, for at one moment, raising my eyes, I saw facing me in the sky that same faint glow as of a dying fire which one saw in the restaurant at Rivebelle in a study that Elstir had made of a sunset effect. I remembered the exaltation I had felt when, on the day of my first arrival at Balbec, I had seen from the railway this same image of an evening which preceded not the night but a new day. But no day now would be new to me any more, would arouse in me the desire for an unknown happiness; it would only prolong my sufferings, until the point when I should no longer have the strength to endure them. The truth of what Cottard had said to me in the casino at Incarville was now confirmed beyond a shadow of doubt. What I had long dreaded, had vaguely suspected of Albertine, what my instinct deduced from her whole personality and my reason controlled by my desire had gradually made me repudiate, was true! Behind Albertine I no longer saw the blue mountains of the sea, but the room at Montjouvain where she was falling into the arms of Mlle Vinteuil with that laugh in which she gave utterance as it were to the strange sound of her pleasure. For, with a girl as pretty as Albertine, was it possible that Mlle Vinteuil, having the desires she had, had not asked her to gratify them? And the proof that Albertine had not been shocked by the request, but had consented, was that they had not quarrelled, that indeed their intimacy had steadily increased. And that graceful movement with which Albertine had laid her chin upon Rosemonde's shoulder, gazed at her smilingly, and deposited a kiss upon her neck, that movement which had reminded me of Mlle Vinteuil but in interpreting which I had nevertheless hesitated to admit that an identical line traced by a gesture must of necessity be the result of an identical inclination, who knew whether Albertine might not quite simply have learned it from Mlle Vinteuil? Gradually, the lifeless sky took fire. I who until then had never awakened without a smile at the humblest things, the bowl of coffee, the sound of the rain, the roar of the wind, felt that the day which in a moment was about to dawn, and all the days to come, would no longer bring me the hope of an unknown happiness, but only the prolongation of my agony. I still clung to life; but I knew that I had nothing now but bitterness to expect from it. I ran to the lift, heedless of the hour, to ring for the lift-boy who acted as night watchman, and asked him to go to Albertine's room and to tell her that I had something of importance to say to her, if she could see me there. "Mademoiselle says she would rather come to you," was the answer he brought me. "She will be here in a moment." And presently, sure enough, in came Albertine in her dressing-gown.

"Albertine," I said to her in a low voice, warning her not to raise hers so as not to wake my mother, from whom we were separated only by that partition whose thinness, to-day a nuisance, because it confined us to whispers, resembled in the past, when it so clearly echoed my grandmother's intentions, a sort of musical diaphanousness, "I'm ashamed to have disturbed you. Listen to me. To make you understand, I must tell you something which you do not know. When I came here, I left a woman whom I was to have married, who was ready to sacrifice everything for me. She was to start on a journey this morning, and every day for the last week I have been wondering whether I should have the courage not to telegraph to her that I was coming back. I did have the courage, but it made me so wretched that I thought I would kill myself. That is why I asked you last night if you would come and sleep at Balbec. If I had to die, I should have liked to bid you farewell."

And I let the tears which my fiction rendered natural flow freely.

"My poor boy, if I had only known, I should have spent the night beside you," cried Albertine, the idea that I might perhaps marry this woman, and that her own chance of making a "good marriage" was thus vanishing, never even crossing her mind, so sincerely was she moved by a grief the cause of which I was able to conceal from her, but not its reality and strength. "As a matter of fact," she said to me, "last night, throughout the entire journey from la Raspelière, I could see that you were nervous and unhappy, and I was afraid there must be something wrong." In reality my grief had begun only at Parville, and my nervous irritability, which was very different but which fortunately Albertine identified with it, arose from the tedium of having to spend a few more days in her company. She added: "I shan't leave you any more, I'm going to spend all my time here." She was offering me, in fact—and she alone could offer me—the sole remedy for the poison that was consuming me, a remedy homogeneous with it indeed, for although one was sweet and the other bitter, both were alike derived from Albertine. At that moment Albertine—my sickness—ceasing to cause me to suffer, left me—she, Albertine the remedy—as weak as a convalescent. But I reflected that she would presently be leaving Balbec for Cherbourg, and from there going to Trieste. Her old habits would be reviving. What I wished above everything else was to prevent Albertine from taking the boat, to make an attempt to carry her off to Paris. It was true that from Paris, more easily even than from Balbec, she might, if she wished, go to Trieste, but in Paris we should see; perhaps I might ask Mme de Guermantes to exert her influence indirectly upon Mlle Vinteuil's friend so that she should not remain at Trieste, to make her accept a situation elsewhere, perhaps with the Prince de ——, whom I had met at Mme de Villeparisis's and, indeed, at Mme de Guermantes's. And he, even if Albertine wished to go to his house to see her friend, might, warned by Mme de Guermantes, prevent them from meeting. Of course I might have reminded myself that in Paris, if Albertine had those tastes, she would find many other people with whom to gratify them. But every impulse of jealousy is unique and bears the imprint of the creature—in this instance Mlle Vinteuil's friend—who has aroused it. It was Mlle Vinteuil's friend who remained my chief preoccupation. The mysterious passion with which I had once thought of Austria because it was the country from which Albertine came (her uncle had been a counsellor at the Embassy there), because I could study its geographical peculiarities, the race that inhabited it, its historic buildings, its scenery, in Albertine's smile and in her ways, as in an atlas or an album of photographs —this mysterious passion I still felt but, by an inversion of symbols, in the domain of horror. Yes, it was from there that Albertine came. It was there that, in every house, she could be sure of finding, if not Mlle Vinteuil's friend, others of her kind. The habits of her childhood would revive, they would be meeting in three months' time for Christmas, then for the New Year, dates which were already painful to me in themselves, owing to an unconscious memory of the misery that I had felt on those days when, long ago, they separated me, for the whole of the Christmas holidays, from Gilberte. After the long dinner-parties, after the midnight revels, when everybody was gay and animated, Albertine would adopt the same poses with her friends there that I had seen her adopt with Andrée—albeit her friendship for Andrée might for all I knew be innocent—the same, perhaps, that Mlle Vinteuil, pursued by her friend, had revealed before my eyes at Montjouvain. To Mlle Vinteuil, while her friend titillated her desires before flinging herself upon her, I now gave the inflamed face of Albertine, of an Albertine whom I heard utter as she fled, then as she surrendered herself, her strange, deep laugh. What, in comparison with the anguish that I was now feeling, was the jealousy I had felt on the day when Saint-Loup had met Albertine with me at Doncières and she had flirted with him, or that I had felt when I thought of the unknown initiator to whom I was indebted for the first kisses that she had given me in Paris, on the day when I was waiting for a letter from Mlle de Stermaria? That other kind of jealousy, provoked by Saint-Loup or by any young man, was nothing. I should have had at the most in that case to fear a rival over whom I should have tried to gain the upper hand. But here the rival was not of the same kind as myself, had different weapons; I could not compete on the same ground, give Albertine the same pleasures, nor indeed conceive what those pleasures might be. In many moments of our life, we would barter the whole of our future for a power that in itself is insignificant. I would at one time have forsworn all the good things in life to get to know Mme Blatin, because she was a friend of Mme Swann. To-day, in order that Albertine might not go to Trieste, I would have endured every possible torment, and if that proved insufficient, would have inflicted torments on her, would have isolated her, kept her under lock and key, would have taken from her the little money that she had so that it should be physically impossible for her to make the journey. Just as, long ago, when I was anxious to go to Balbec, what had urged me to set off was the longing for a Persian church, for a stormy sea at daybreak, so what was now rending my heart as I thought that Albertine might perhaps be going to Trieste, was that she would be spending Christmas night there with Mlle Vinteuil's friend: for the imagination, when it changes its nature and turns into sensibility, does not thereby acquire control of a larger number of simultaneous images. Had anyone told me that she was not at that moment either at Cherbourg or at Trieste, that there was no possibility of her seeing Albertine, how I should have wept for joy! How my whole life and its future would have been changed! And yet I knew quite well that this localisation of my jealousy was arbitrary, that if Albertine had these tastes, she could gratify them with others. And perhaps even these same girls, if they could have seen her elsewhere, would not have tortured my heart so acutely. It was Trieste, it was that unknown world in which I could feel that Albertine took a delight, in which were her memories, her friendships, her childhood loves, that exhaled that hostile, inexplicable atmosphere, like the atmosphere that used to float up to my bedroom at Combray, from the dining-room in which I could hear, talking and laughing with strangers amid the clatter of knives and forks, Mamma who would not be coming upstairs to say good-night to me; like the atmosphere that, for Swann, had filled the houses to which Odette went at night in search of inconceivable joys. It was no longer as of a delightful place where the people were pensive, the sunsets golden, the church bells melancholy, that I thought now of Trieste, but as of an accursed city which I should have liked to see instantaneously burned down and eliminated from the real world. That city was embedded in my heart as a fixed and permanent point. The thought of letting Albertine leave presently for Cherbourg and Trieste filled me with horror; as did even that of remaining at Balbec. For now that the revelation of her intimacy with Mlle Vinteuil had become almost a certainty, it seemed to me that at every moment when Albertine was not with me (and there were whole days on which, because of her aunt, I was unable to see her), she was giving herself to Bloch's sister and cousin, possibly to other girls as well. The thought that that very evening she might see the Bloch girls drove me mad. And so, when she told me that for the next few days she would stay with me all the time, I replied: "But the fact is, I want to go back to Paris. Won't you come with me? And wouldn't you like to come and live with us for a while in Paris?"

At all costs I must prevent her from being alone, for some days at any rate, must keep her with me so as to be certain that she could not meet Mlle Vinteuil's friend. In reality it would mean her living alone with me, for my mother, seizing the opportunity of a tour of inspection which my father had to make, had taken it upon herself as a duty, in obedience to my grandmother's wishes, to go down to Combray and spend a few days there with one of my grandmother's sisters. Mamma had no love for her aunt because she had not been to my grandmother, so loving to her, what a sister should be. Thus, when they grow up, do children remember with resentment the people who have been unkind to them. But having become my grandmother, Mamma was incapable of resentment; her mother's life was to her like a pure and innocent childhood from which she would draw those memories whose sweetness or bitterness regulated her actions with other people. Her aunt might have been able to provide Mamma with certain priceless details, but now she would have difficulty in obtaining them, the aunt being seriously ill (they spoke of cancer). Reproaching herself for not having gone sooner, because she wanted to keep my father company, she saw this as an additional reason for doing what her mother would have done, and, just as she went on the anniversary of the death of my grandmother's father, who had been such a bad parent, to lay upon his grave the flowers which my grandmother had been in the habit of taking there, so, to the side of the grave which was about to open, my mother wished to convey the soft words which her aunt had not come to offer to my grandmother. While she was at Combray, my mother would busy herself with certain alterations which my grandmother had always wished to have made, but only under her daughter's supervision. So that they had not yet been begun, Mamma not wishing, by leaving Paris before my father, to make him feel too keenly the burden of a grief in which he shared but which could not afflict him as it afflicted her.

"Ah! that wouldn't be possible just at present," Albertine replied. "Besides, why should you need to go back to Paris so soon, if the lady has gone?"

"Because I shall feel calmer in a place where I knew her than at Balbec, which she has never seen and which I've begun to loathe."

Did Albertine realise later on that this other woman had never existed, and that if, that night, I had really longed for death, it was because she had thoughtlessly revealed to me that she had been on intimate terms with Mlle Vinteuil's friend? It is possible. There are moments when it appears to me probable. At any rate, that morning, she believed in the existence of this other woman.

"But you ought to marry this lady," she said to me, "it would make you happy, my sweet, and I'm sure it would make her happy as well."

I replied that the thought that I might make this woman happy had almost made me decide to marry her; when, not long since, I had inherited a fortune which would enable me to provide my wife with ample luxury and pleasures, I had been on the point of accepting the sacrifice of the woman I loved. Intoxicated by the gratitude that I felt for Albertine's kindness, coming so soon after the terrible blow she had dealt me, just as one would think nothing of promising a fortune to the waiter who pours one out a sixth glass of brandy, I told her that my wife would have a motor-car and a yacht, that from that point of view, since Albertine was so fond of motoring and yachting, it was unfortunate that she was not the woman I loved, that I should have been the perfect husband for her, but that we should see, we should no doubt be able to meet on friendly terms. Nevertheless, since even when we are drunk we refrain from hailing passers-by for fear of blows, I was not guilty of the imprudence (if such it was) that I should have committed in Gilberte's time, of telling her that it was she, Albertine, whom I loved.

"You see, I came very near to marrying her. But I didn't dare do it, after all, for I wouldn't have wanted to make a young woman live with anyone so sickly and troublesome as myself."

"But you must be mad. Anybody would be delighted to live with you, just look how people run after you. They're always talking about you at Mme Verdurin's, and in high society too, I'm told. She can't have been at all nice to you, that lady, to make you lose confidence in yourself like that. I can see what she is, she's a wicked woman, I detest her. Ah, if I were in her shoes!"

"Not at all, she is very kind, far too kind. As for the Verdurins and all the rest, I don't care a hang. Apart from the woman I love, whom in any case I've given up, I care only for my little Albertine; she is the only person in the world who, by letting me see a great deal of her—that is, during the first few days," I added, in order not to alarm her and to be able to ask anything of her during those days, "—can bring me a little consolation."

I made only a vague allusion to the possibility of marriage, adding that it was quite impracticable since our characters were too different. Being, in spite of myself, still pursued in my jealousy by the memory of Saint-Loup's relations with "Rachel when from the Lord" and of Swann's with Odette, I was too inclined to believe that, once I was in love, I could not be loved in return, and that pecuniary interest alone could attach a woman to me. No doubt it was foolish to judge Albertine by Odette and Rachel. But it was not her that I was afraid of, it was myself; it was the feelings that I was capable of inspiring that my jealousy made me underestimate. And from this judgment, possibly erroneous, sprang no doubt many of the calamities that were to befall us.

"Then you decline my invitation to come to Paris?"

"My aunt wouldn't like me to leave just at present. Besides, even if I can come later on, wouldn't it look rather odd, my descending on you like that? In Paris everybody will know that I'm not your cousin."

"Very well, then. We can say that we're more or less engaged. It can't make any difference, since you know that it isn't true."

Albertine's neck, which emerged in its entirety from her nightdress, was strongly built, bronzed, grainy in texture. I kissed it as purely as if I had been kissing my mother to calm a childish grief which I did not believe that I would ever be able to eradicate from my heart. Albertine left me in order to go and dress. Already her devotion was beginning to falter; earlier she had told me that she would not leave me for a second (and I felt sure that her resolution would not last long, since I was afraid, if we remained at Balbec, that that very evening, in my absence, she might see the Bloch girls), whereas now she had just told me that she wished to call at Maineville and that she would come back and see me in the afternoon. She had not gone home the evening before; there might be letters there for her, and besides, her aunt might be anxious about her. I had replied: "If that's all, we can send the lift-boy to tell your aunt that you're here and to pick up your letters." And, anxious to appear amenable but annoyed at being tied down, she had frowned for a moment and then, at once, very sweetly, had said: "All right" and had sent the lift-boy. Albertine had not been out of the room a moment before the boy came and tapped gently on my door. I could not believe that, while I was talking to Albertine, he had had time to go to Maineville and back. He came now to tell me that Albertine had written a note to her aunt and that she could, if I wished, come to Paris that very day. It was unfortunate that she had given him this message orally, for already, despite the early hour, the manager was about, and came to me in a great state to ask me whether there was anything wrong, whether I was really leaving, whether I could not stay just a few days longer, the wind that day being rather "frightened" (frightful). I did not wish to explain to him that at all costs I wanted Albertine to be out of Balbec before the hour at which the Bloch girls took the air, especially since Andrée, who alone might have protected her, was not there, and that Balbec was like one of those places in which an invalid who can no longer bear it is determined, even if he should die on the journey, not to spend another night. Moreover I should have to struggle against similar entreaties, in the hotel first of all, where the eyes of Marie Gineste and Céleste Albaret were red. (Marie indeed was giving vent to the swift-flowing tears of a mountain stream; Céleste, who was gentler, urged her to be calm; but, Marie having murmured the only line of poetry that she knew: "Here below the lilacs die," Céleste could contain herself no longer, and a flood of tears spilled over her lilac-hued face; I dare say they had forgotten my existence by that evening.) Later, on the the little local railway, despite all my precautions against being seen, I met M. de Cambremer who turned pale at the sight of my boxes, for he was counting upon me for the day after to-morrow; he infuriated me by trying to persuade me that my breathless fits were caused by the change in the weather, and that October would do them all the good in the world, and asked me whether I could not "postpone my departure by a sennight," an expression the fatuity of which enraged me perhaps only because what he was suggesting to me made me feel ill. And while he talked to me in the railway carriage, at each station I was afraid of seeing, more terrible than Herimbald or Guiscard, M. de Crécy imploring me to invite him, or, more dreadful still, Mme Verdurin bent upon inviting me. But this was not to happen for some hours. I had not got there yet. I had to face only the despairing entreaties of the manager. I ushered him out of the room, for I was afraid that, although he kept his voice low, he would end by disturbing Mamma. I remained alone in my room, that room with the too lofty ceiling in which I had been so wretched on my first arrival, in which I had thought with such longing of Mlle de Stermaria, had watched for the appearance of Albertine and her friends, like migratory birds alighting upon the beach, in which I had possessed her with such indifference after I had sent the lift-boy to fetch her, in which I had experienced my grandmother's kindness, then realised that she was dead; those shutters, beneath which shone the early morning light, I had opened the first time to look out upon the first ramparts of the sea (those shutters which Albertine made me close in case anybody should see us kissing). I became aware of my own transformations by contrasting them with the unchangingness of my surroundings. One grows accustomed to these as to people, and when, all of a sudden, one recalls the different meaning that they used to convey to one and then, after they had lost all meaning, the events, very different from those of to-day, which they en-shrined, the diversity of the acts performed beneath the same ceiling, between the same glazed bookshelves, the change in one's heart and in one's life which that diversity implies, seem to be increased still further by the unalterable permanence of the setting, reinforced by the unity of the scene.

Two or three times it occurred to me, for a moment, that the world in which this room and these bookshelves were situated, and in which Albertine counted for so little, was perhaps an intellectual world, which was the sole reality, and my grief something like what we feel when we read a novel, a thing of which only a madman would make a lasting and permanent grief that prolonged itself through his life; that a tiny flicker of my will would suffice, perhaps, to attain to this real world, to re-enter it by breaking through my grief as one breaks through a paper hoop, and to think no more about what Albertine had done than we think about the actions of the imaginary heroine of a novel after we have finished reading it. For that matter, the mistresses whom I have loved most passionately have never coincided with my love for them. That love was genuine, since I subordinated everything else to seeing them, keeping them for myself alone, and would weep aloud if, one evening, I had waited for them in vain. But it was more because they had the faculty of arousing that love, of raising it to a paroxysm, than because they were its image. When I saw them, when I heard their voices, I could find nothing in them which resembled my love and could account for it. And yet my sole joy lay in seeing them, my sole anxiety in waiting for them to come. It was as though a virtue that had no connexion with them had been artificially attached to them by nature, and that this virtue, this quasi-electric power, had the effect upon me of exciting my love, that is to say of controlling all my actions and causing all my sufferings. But from this, the beauty, or the intelligence, or the kindness of these women was entirely distinct. As by an electric current that gives us a shock, I have been shaken by my loves, I have lived them, I have felt them: never have I succeeded in seeing or thinking them. Indeed I am inclined to believe that in these relationships (I leave out of account the physical pleasure which is their habitual accompaniment but is not enough in itself to constitute them), beneath the outward appearance of the woman, it is to those invisible forces with which she is incidentally accompanied that we address ourselves as to obscure deities. It is they whose good will is necessary to us, with whom we seek to establish contact without finding any positive pleasure in it. The woman herself, during our assignation with her, does little more than put us in touch with these goddesses. We have, by way of oblation, promised jewels and travels, uttered incantations which mean that we adore and, at the same time, contrary incantations which mean that we are indifferent. We have used all our power to obtain a fresh assignation, but one that is accorded to us without constraint. Would we in fact go to so much trouble for the woman herself, if she were not complemented by these occult forces, considering that, once she has left us, we are unable to say how she was dressed and realise that we never even looked at her?

What a deceptive sense sight is! A human body, even a beloved one, as Albertine's was, seems to us, from a few yards, from a few inches away, remote from us. And similarly with the soul that inhabits it. But if something brings about a violent change in the position of that soul in relation to us, shows us that it is in love with others and not with us, then by the beating of our shattered heart we feel that it is not a few feet away from us but within us that the beloved creature was. Within us, in regions more or less superficial. But the words: "That friend is Mlle Vinteuil" had been the *Open sesame*, which I should have been incapable of discovering by myself, that had made Albertine penetrate to the depths of my lacerated heart. And I might search for a hundred years without discovering how to open the door that had closed behind her.

I had ceased for a moment to hear these words ringing in my ears while Albertine had been with me just now. While kissing her, as I used to kiss my mother at Combray, to calm my anguish, I believed almost in Albertine's innocence, or at least did not think continuously of the discovery that I had made of her vice. But now that I was alone the words rang out afresh like those noises inside the ear which one hears as soon as someone stops talking to one. Her vice now seemed to me to be beyond any doubt. The light of approaching sunrise, by modifying the appearance of the things around me, made me once again, as if for a moment I were shifting my position in relation to it, even more bitterly aware of my suffering. I had never seen the dawn of so beautiful or so sorrowful a morning. And thinking of all the indifferent landscapes which were about to be lit up and which, only yesterday, would have filled me simply with the desire to visit them, I could not repress a sob when, with a gesture of oblation mechanically performed and symbolising, in my eyes, the bloody sacrifice which I was about to have to make of all joy, every morning, until the end of my life, a solemn renewal, celebrated as each day dawned, of my daily grief and of the blood from my wound, the golden egg of the sun, as though propelled by the rupture of equilibrium brought about at the moment of coagulation by a change of density, barbed with tongues of flame as in a painting, burst through the curtain behind which one had sensed it quivering for a moment, ready to appear on the scene and to spring forward, and whose mysterious frozen purple it annihilated in a flood of light. I heard myself weeping. But at that moment, to my astonishment, the door opened and, with a throbbing heart, I seemed to see my grandmother standing before me, as in one of those apparitions that had already visited me, but only in my sleep. Was it all only a dream, then? Alas, I was wide awake. "You see a likeness to your poor grandmother," said Mamma, for it was she, speaking gently as though to calm my fear, acknowledging however the resemblance, with a beautiful smile of modest pride which had always been innocent of coquetry. Her dishevelled hair, whose grey tresses were not hidden and strayed about her troubled eyes, her ageing cheeks, my grandmother's own dressing-gown which she was wearing, all these had for a moment prevented me from recognising her and had made me uncertain whether I was still asleep or my grandmother had come back to life. For a long time past my mother had resembled my grandmother far more than the young and smiling Mamma of my childhood. But I had ceased to think of this resemblance. So it is, when one has been sitting reading for a long time, one's mind absorbed, not noticing how the time was passing, that suddenly one sees round about one the sun that shone yesterday at the same hour call up the same harmonies, the same effects of colour that precede a sunset. It was with a smile that my mother drew my attention to my error, for it was pleasing to her that she should bear so strong a resemblance to her mother.

"I came," she said, "because while I was asleep I thought I heard someone crying. It wakened me. But how is it that you aren't in bed? And your eyes are filled with tears. What's the matter?"

I took her head in my arms: "Mamma, listen, I'm afraid you'll think me very changeable. But first of all, yesterday I spoke to you not at all nicely about Albertine; what I said was unfair."

"But what difference can that make?" said my mother, and, catching sight of the rising sun, she smiled sadly as she thought of her own mother, and, so that I might not lose the benefit of a spectacle which my grandmother used to regret that I never watched, she pointed to the window. But beyond the beach of Balbec, the sea, the sunrise, which Mamma was pointing out to me, I saw, with a gesture of despair which did not escape her notice, the room at Montjouvain where Albertine, curled up like a great cat, with her mischievous pink nose, had taken the place of Mlle Vinteuil's friend and was saying amid peals of her voluptuous laughter: "Well, all the better if they do see us! What, I wouldn't dare to spit on that old monkey?" It was this scene that I saw, beyond the scene which was framed in the open window and which was no more than a dim veil drawn over the other, superimposed upon it like a reflexion. It seemed, indeed, itself almost unreal, like a painted view. Facing us, where the cliff of Parville jutted out, the little wood in which we had played "ferret" dipped the picture of its foliage down into the sea, beneath the still-golden varnish of the water, as at the hour when often, at the close of day, after I had gone there to rest in the shade with Albertine, we had risen as we saw the sun sink in the sky. In the confusion of the night mists which still hung in pink and blue tatters over the water littered with the pearly debris of the dawn, boats sailed by, smiling at the slanting light which gilded their sails and the points of their bowsprits as when they are homeward bound at evening: an imaginary scene, chilling and deserted, a pure evocation of the sunset which did not rest, as at evening, upon the sequence of the hours of the day which I was accustomed to see precede it, detached, interpolated, more insubstantial even than the horrible image of Montjouvain which it did not succeed in cancelling, covering, concealing—a poetical, vain image of memory and dreams.

"But come," my mother was saying, "you said nothing unpleasant about her, you told me that she bored you a little, that you were glad you had given up the idea of marrying her. That's no reason for you to cry like that. Remember that your Mamma is going away to-day and couldn't bear to leave her big pet in such a state. Especially, my poor child, as I haven't time to comfort you. Even if my things are packed, one never has any time on the morning of a journey."

"It's not that."

And then, calculating the future, weighing up my desires, realising that such an affection on Albertine's part for Mlle Vinteuil's friend, and one of such long standing, could not have been innocent, that Albertine had been initiated, and, as every one of her instinctive actions made plain to me, had moreover been born with a predisposition towards that vice which my anxiety had all too often sensed in her, in which she must never have ceased to indulge (in which she was indulging perhaps at that moment, taking advantage of an instant in which I was not present), I said to my mother, knowing the pain that I was causing her, which she did not reveal and which betrayed itself only by that air of serious preoccupation which she wore when she was comparing the gravity of making me unhappy or making me ill, that air which she had worn at Combray for the first time when she had resigned herself to spending the night in my room, that air which at this moment was extraordinarily like my grandmother's when she had allowed me to drink brandy, I said to my mother: "I know how unhappy I'm going to make you. First of all, instead of remaining here as you wished, I want to leave at the same time as you. But that too is nothing. I don't feel well here, I'd rather go home. But listen to me, don't be too distressed. This is what I want to say. I was deceiving myself, I deceived you in good faith yesterday, I've been thinking it over all night. I absolutely must—and let's settle the matter at once, because I'm quite clear about it now, because I won't change my mind again, because I couldn't live without it—I absolutely must marry Albertine."

NOTES, ADDENDA
SYNOPSIS

NOTES

1 (p. 14) The French is *s'ennuyer de*, which can mean to miss, to suffer from the absence of.

2 (p. 16) Françoise says *avoir d'argent* instead of *avoir de l'argent*.

3 (p. 16) *Ce n'est pas mon père*: celebrated remark by the *môme* Crevette in Feydeau's *La Dame de chez Maxim*. It became a popular all-purpose catch-phrase. John Mortimer translated it as "How's your father?" in his adaptation of the Feydeau play for the National Theatre.

4 (p. 21) The French is *plaindre*, to pity, which used also to mean to deplore or regret. The sense here is that Mme Octave did not regret her expenditure on rich fare.

5 (p. 101) A somewhat inaccurate quotation from Pascal's famous "memorial."

6 (p. 105) The allusion is to the Rumanian-born Comtesse Anna de Noailles (*née* Brancovan), friend and correspondent of Proust, who was an extravagant admirer of her verse.

7 (p. 149) Popular abbreviation of the newspaper *l'Intransigeant*.

8 (p. 153) The Academy in question is *l'Académie des Sciences morales et politiques*, one of the five (including the *Académie Française*) which comprise the *Institut de France*.

9 (p. 154) Jules Méline, Prime Minister for two years during the Dreyfus Case.

10 (p. 171) Bernard de Jussieu (1699-1777), the best-known member of an illustrious family of botanists.

11 (p. 183) *La barbe* has the colloquial meaning "tedious" or "boring."

12 (p. 196) Duc Decazes: minister and favourite of Louis XVIII.

13 (p. 207) Carmen Sylva was the pen-name of Elizabeth, Queen of Rumania (1843-1916).

14 (p. 235) *"Qu'importe le flacon pourvu qu'on ait l'ivresse!"*—the line is in fact by Alfred de Musset.

15 (p. 244) *Le Syndicat* was the term used by anti-semites to describe the secret power of the Jews.

16 (p. 249) Prince Henri d'Orléans, son of the Duc de Chartres, publicly embraced the notorious Esterhazy after he had given evidence at the Zola trial.

17 (p. 262) "Quand on parle du Saint-Loup!" is what the Duchess says. The French for "Talk of the devil" is "Quand on parle du loup." The pun doesn't work in English.

18 (p. 322) Paraphrase of a famous line from Molière's *Le Misanthrope*: "*Ah, qu'en termes galants ces choses-là sont mises!*"

19 (p. 370) A word introduced by Pierre Loti from the Japanese *musume*, meaning girl or young woman.

20 (p. 374) There is a complicated pun here, impossible to convey in English. Françoise says: "Faut-il que j'éteinde?" instead of "éteigne." Albertine's "Teigne?" is not only a tentative correction of Françoise's faulty subjunctive; it also suggests that she is an old shrew (a secondary meaning of *teigne* = tinea, moth).

21 (p. 442) An aberration on Proust's part: Giorgione was of course Venetian, and had no connection with Parma.

22 (p. 446) A Proustian joke here: Edouard Detaille was a mediocre academic painter known especially for his paintings of military life. Alexandre Ribot was a familiar middle-of-the-road political figure, twice Prime Minister under the Third Republic. Suzanne Reichenberg was for thirty years the principal *ingénue* at the Comédie-Française.

23 (p. 448) *Ventre affamé*—from the expression "Ventre affamé n'a pas d'oreilles," meaning "Words are wasted on a starving man."

24 (p. 450) A riverside restaurant/cabaret with "tree-houses" where, the notion was, patrons could imagine themselves the *Swiss Family Robinson*. It gave its name to the spot where it was situated, now incorporated in the Paris suburb of Le Plessis-Robinson.

25 (p. 507) *La Fille de Roland* was a popular verse drama by Henri de Bornier. The Duchess's joke refers to Princess Marie, daughter of Prince Roland Bonaparte, who married Prince George, second son of King George I of Greece.

26 (p. 509) An aria from Hérold's *Le Pré-aux-clercs*.

27 (p. 510) A seventeenth-century poetess noted for rather mawkish verses.

28 (p. 514) A reference to the playwright Edouard Pailleron, noted for his quick, sharp-witted, rather shallow comedies.

29 (p. 518) Euphemism for *merde* (shit), hence the joke about capital C or M.

30 (p. 558) A reference to La Fontaine's fable *The Miller and his Son*, in which the third party is an ass.

31 (p. 587) A well-known French opera singer, who had no connection with Wagner.

32 (p. 633) *Altesse*, like *majesté*, being feminine, takes the feminine pronoun.

33 (p. 638) *Les deux sexes mourront chacun de son côté*: from Alfred de Vigny's *La Colère de Samson*.

34 (p. 670) The reference is to Maurice Paléologue, French Ambassador in St Petersburg during the Great War.

35 (p. 723) Emile Loubet, President of the Republic from 1899 to 1906.

36 (p. 726) *Vert* = spicy, risqué.

37 (p. 744) Marquis d'Hervey de Saint-Denys: a distinguished French sinologist.

38 (p. 865) Of the two French versions of the *Arabian Nights*, Galland's *Les Mille et une Nuits* (1704) is elegant, scholarly but heavily bowdlerised, and Mardrus's *Les Mille Nuits et une Nuit* (1898-1904) coarser and unexpurgated.

39 (p. 875) A popular tune from Offenbach's *Les Brigands*. A *courrier de cabinet* is the equivalent of a King's or Queen's Messenger.

40 (p. 878) Better known under his pen-name Saint-John Perse.

41 (p. 906) Mme Récamier's property on the outskirts of Paris, where she held her salon.

42 (p. 918) *Jachères* = fallow land; *gâtines* = sterile marshland.

43 (p. 921) Francisque Sarcey: middlebrow drama critic noted for his avuncular style.

44 (p. 960) The French has *le cheveu* instead of the normal *les cheveux*.

45 (p. 970) Untranslatable pun. The French of course is *Watteau à vapeur*, echoing *bateau à vapeur* = steamer.

46 (p. 978) *Monseigneur* is the formula for addressing royalty.

47 (p. 979) Philipp, Prince Eulenburg, a close friend and adviser of William II, was involved in a homosexual scandal in 1906.

48 (p. 996) The French say *une veine de cocu* for "the luck of the devil."

49 (p. 1071) *Tapette* can mean both "chatterbox" and "pansy" or "queer."

50 (p. 1085) Idiomatic expression meaning "the moment of reckoning."

ADDENDA

Page 438. *This passage continues as follows in Proust's manuscript:*—

And the legendary scenes depicted in this landscape gave it the curious grandeur of having become contemporaneous with them. The myth dated the landscape; it swept the sky, the sun, the mountains which were its witnesses back with it to a past in the depths of which they already appeared to me to be identical to what they are to-day. It pushed back through endless time the unfurling of the waves which I had seen at Balbec. I said to myself: that sunset, that ocean which I can contemplate once again, whenever I wish, from the hotel or from the cliff, those identical waves, constitute a setting analogous, especially in the summer when the light orientalises it, to that in which Hercules killed the Hydra of Lerna, in which Orpheus was torn to pieces by the Bacchantes. Already, in those immemorial days of kings whose palaces are unearthed by archaeologists and of whom mythology has made its demi-gods, the sea at evening washed against the shore with that plaint which so often aroused in me a similar vague disquiet. And when I walked along the esplanade at the close of day, the sea which formed such a large part of the picture before my eyes, made up of so many contemporary images such as the band-stand and the casino, was the sea that the Argonauts saw, the sea of pre-history, and it was only by the alien elements I introduced into it that it was of to-day, it was only because I adjusted it to the hour of my quotidian vision that I found a familiar echo in the melancholy murmur which Theseus heard.

Page 543. *The following development appears in the original manuscript:*—

"That is why life is so horrible, since nobody can understand anybody else," Mme de Guermantes concluded with a self-consciously pessimistic air, but also with the animation induced by the pleasure of shining before the Princesse de Parme. And when I saw this woman who was so difficult to please, who had claimed to be bored to death by M. and Mme Ribot [*changed to*: with an extremely impressive minister-academician], going to so much trouble for this uninspiring princess, I understood how a man of such refinement as Swann could have enjoyed the company of M. Bontemps [*changed to*: Mme Bontemps]. Indeed if she had had reasons for adopting the latter, the Duchess might have preferred him to the celebrated statesman, for, outside the ranks of the princely families, only charm and distinction, either proved or imaginary but in the latter case its existence having been decreed in the same way as a monarch ennobles people, counted in the Guermantes circle. Political or professional hierarchies meant nothing. And if Cottard, a professor and an academician, who was not received there, had been called in as a consultant, he might have found there a complete unknown, Dr Percepied, whom for purely self-interested motives it was convenient for the Duchess to have to lunch now and then and whom she declared to be rather distinguished because she received him.

"Really?" replied the Princess, astonished by the assertion that life is horrible. "At least," she added, "one can do a great deal of good."

"Not even that, when you come down to it," said the Duchess, fearful lest the conversation should turn to philanthropy, which she found boring. "How can one do good to people one doesn't understand? And besides, one doesn't know which people to do good to—one tries to do good to the wrong people. That's what is so frightful. But to get back to Gilbert and his being shocked at your visiting the Iénas, Your Highness has far too much sense to let her actions be governed . . ."

Page 548.   *Additional passage of dialogue in the manuscript:*—

"I think he's mainly preoccupied by a Villeparisis-Norpois rapprochement," said the Duchess, in order to change the subject.

"But is there any room for a closer rapprochement in that direction?" asked the Prince. "I thought they were already very close."

"Good heavens!" said the Duchess with a gesture of alarm at the image of coupling which the Prince conjured up for her, "I believe at any rate that they have been. But I'm told, ridiculous though it may seem, that my aunt would like to marry him. No, seriously, it seems incredible, but I gather she's the one who wants it, and he doesn't because she already bores him enough as it is. Really, she can't have any sense of the ridiculous. Why, I wonder, when one has so seldom 'resisted' in the course of one's life, should one suddenly feel the need to sanction a liaison with matrimony, after dispensing with it on so many other occasions? There really isn't much point in having caused every door to be closed to one if one cannot bear the idea of a union remaining illicit, especially when it's as respectable as this one, and, we all hope, as platonic."

Page 733.   *The manuscript has a longer version of M. de Charlus's reply:*—

"Good heavens, what a fate for that unfortunate canvas to be a prisoner in the house of such a person! To go there once by chance is in itself an error of taste; but to spend one's life there, especially if one is a thing of beauty, is so painful as to be quite unpardonable. There are certain forms of disgrace which it's a crime to resign oneself to . . . [As a good Catholic, I honour St Euverte: *crossed out*] and I can remember very well from the Lives of the Saints what this confessor's qualifications for canonisation were; and indeed, if you like, as a no less good pagan, I respect Diana and admire her crescent, especially when it is placed in your hair by Elstir. But as for the contradictory monster, or even the monster pure and simple, whom you call Diane de Saint-Euverte, I confess I do not take the desire for a union of the churches as far as that. The name recalls the time when altars used to be raised to St Apollo. It is a very distant time—a time from which the person you speak of must incidentally date, judging by her face, which has strangely survived exhumation. And yet, in spite of everything, she is a person with whom one has certain things in common; she has always manifested a singular love of beauty." This observation would have appeared incomprehensible to the Marquise if for some minutes past, having ceased to understand, she had not given up listening. The love of beauty which caused M. de Charlus to cherish, together with a great deal of social contempt, a more deep-rooted respect for Mme de Saint-Euverte, was deduced from the fact that she always had as footmen a numerous and carefully selected pack of irreproachably vigorous young men. "Yes, what a destiny for a beautiful work of art which was spoiled from the start by living face to face with you! There is something tragic about the fate of these captive paintings. Just think, if ever you pay a brief visit to that lady from the *Golden Legend*, with what despair the poor portrait, imprisoned in its blue and rose-pink tones, must be saying to you:

> How different are our fates! I must remain,
> But you are free to go. . .

And yet both of you are flowers. Flowers, themselves too in bondage, have contrived in their captivity sublime stratagems for passing on their messages. I confess that I should not be surprised if, with similar intelligence, some day when the windows of the Burgundian saint's wife were left open, your portrait unfolded its canvas wings and flew off, thus solving the problem of aerial navigation before mankind, and making Elstir, in a second and more unexpected form, the successor of Leonardo da Vinci."

Page 742. *In place of this sentence the manuscript has a long passage which was not included in the original edition and which Proust here declares his explicit intention to return to later in the novel, though he did not have time to do so:*—

People in society noticed the Princess's febrility, and her fear, though she was still very far from ageing, lest the state of nervous agitation in which she now lived might prevent her from keeping her young appearance. Indeed one evening, at a dinner party to which M. de Charlus was also invited and at which, for that reason, she arrived looking radiant but somehow strange, I realised that this strangeness arose from the fact that, thinking to improve her complexion and to look younger—and probably for the first time in her life—she was heavily made up. She exaggerated even further the eccentricity of dress which had always been a slight weakness of hers. She had only to hear M. de Charlus speak of a portrait to have its sitter's elaborate finery copied and to wear it herself. One day when, thus bedecked with an immense hat copied from a Gainsborough portrait (*it would be better to think of a painter whose hats were really extraordinary*), she was harping on the theme, which had now become a familiar one with her, of how sad it must be to grow old, and quoted in this connexion Mme Récamier's remark to the effect that she would know she was no longer beautiful when the little chimney-sweeps no longer turned to look at her in the street. "Don't worry, my dear little Marie," replied the Duchesse de Guermantes in a caressing voice, so that the affectionate gentleness of her tone should prevent her cousin from taking offence at the irony of the words, "you've only to go on wearing hats like the one you have on and you can be sure that they'll always turn round."

This love of hers for M. de Charlus which was beginning to be bruited abroad, combined with what was gradually becoming known about the latter's way of life, was almost as much of a help to the anti-Dreyfusards as the Princess's Germanic origin. When some wavering spirit pointed out in favour of Dreyfus's innocence the fact that a nationalist and anti-semitic Christian like the Prince de Guermantes had been converted to a belief in it, people would reply:

"But didn't he marry a German?" "Yes, but . . ." "And isn't that
German woman rather highly strung? Isn't she infatuated with a
man who has bizarre tastes?" And in spite of the fact that the Prince's
Dreyfusism had not been prompted by his wife and had no connexion with the Baron's sexual proclivities, the philosophical
anti-Dreyfusard would conclude: "There, you see! The Prince de
Guermantes may be Dreyfusist in the best of good faith; but foreign
influence may have been brought to bear on him by occult means.
That's the most dangerous way. But let me give you a piece of
advice. Whenever you come across a Dreyfusard, just scratch a bit.
Not far underneath you'll find the ghetto, foreign blood, inversion
or Wagneromania." And cravenly the subject would be dropped, for
it had to be admitted that the Princess was a passionate Wagnerian.

Whenever the Princess was expecting a visit from me, since she
knew that I often saw M. de Charlus, she would evidently prepare in
advance a certain number of questions which she then put to me
adroitly enough for me not to detect what lay behind them and
which must have been aimed at verifying whether such and such
an assertion, such and such an excuse by M. de Charlus in connexion
with a certain address or a certain evening, were true or not. Sometimes, throughout my entire visit, she would not ask me a single
question, however insignificant it might have appeared, and would
try to draw my attention to this. Then, having said good-bye to me,
she would suddenly, on the doorstep, ask me five or six as though
without premeditation. So it went on, until one evening she sent for
me. I found her in a state of extraordinary agitation, scarcely able
to hold back her tears. She asked if she could entrust me with a
letter for M. de Charlus and begged me to deliver it to him at all
costs. I hurried round to his house, where I found him in front of
the mirror wiping a few specks of powder from his face. He perused
the letter—the most desperate appeal, I later learned—and asked
me to reply that it was physically impossible that evening, that he
was ill. While he was talking to me, he plucked from a vase one
after another a number of roses each of a different hue, tried them in
his buttonhole, and looked in the mirror to see how they matched
his complexion, without being able to decide on any of them. His
valet came in to announce that the barber had arrived, and the
Baron held out his hand to say good-bye to me. "But he's forgotten
his curling tongs," said the valet. The Baron flew into a terrible
rage; only the unsightly flush which threatened to ruin his complexion persuaded him to calm down a little, though he remained
plunged in an even more bitter despair than before because not only
would his hair be less wavy than it might have been but his face

would be redder and his nose shiny with sweat. "He can go and get them," suggested the valet. "But I haven't the time," wailed the Baron in an ululation calculated to produce as terrifying an effect as the most violent rage while generating less heat in him who emitted it. "I haven't the time," he moaned. "I must leave in half an hour or I shall miss everything." "Would Monsieur le Baron like him to come in, then?" "I don't know, I can't do without a touch of the curling tongs. Tell him he's a brute, a scoundrel. Tell him . . ."

At this point I left and hurried back to the Princess. Her breast heaving with emotion, she scribbled another message and asked me to go round to him again: "I'm taking advantage of your friendship, but if you only knew why . . ." I returned to M. de Charlus. Just before reaching his house, I saw him join Jupien beside a parked cab. The headlights of a passing car lit up for a moment the peaked cap and the face of a bus conductor. Then I could see him no longer, for the cab had been halted in a dark corner near the entrance to a completely unlit cul-de-sac. I turned into this cul-de-sac so that M. de Charlus should not see me.

"Give me a second before I get in," M. de Charlus said to Jupien. "My moustache isn't ruffled?"

"No, you look superb."

"You're kidding me."

"Don't use such expressions, they don't suit you. They're all right for the fellow you're going to see."

"Ah, so he's a bit loutish! I'm not averse to that. But tell me, what sort of man is he, not too skinny?"

I realised from all this that if M. de Charlus was failing to go to the help of a glorious princess who was wild with grief, it was not for the sake of a rendezvous with someone he loved, or even desired, but of an arranged introduction to someone he had never met before.

"No, he isn't skinny; in fact he's rather plump and fleshy. Don't worry, he's just your type, you'll see, you'll be very pleased with him, my little lambkin," Jupien added, employing a form of address which seemed as personally inappropriate, as ritual, as when the Russians call a passer-by "little father."

He got into the cab with M. de Charlus, and I might have heard no more had not the Baron, in his agitation, omitted to shut the window and moreover begun, without realising, in order to appear at his ease, to speak in the shrill, reverberating tone of voice which he assumed when he was putting on a social performance.

"I'm delighted to make your acquaintance, and I really must apologise for keeping you waiting in this nasty cab," he said, in order to fill the vacuum in his anxious mind with words, and oblivious of the fact that the nasty cab must on the contrary seem perfectly nice to a bus conductor. "I hope you will give me the pleasure of spending an evening, a comfortable evening with me. Are you never free except in the evenings?"

"Only on Sundays."

"Ah! you're free on Sunday afternoons? Excellent. That makes everything much simpler. Do you like music? Do you ever go to concerts?"

"Yes, I often goes."

"Ah! very good indeed. You see how nicely we're getting on already? I really am delighted to know you. We might go to a Colonne concert—I often have the use of my cousin de Guermantes's box, or my cousin Philippe de Coburg's" (he did not dare say the King of Bulgaria for fear of seeming to be "showing off," but although the bus conductor had no idea what the Baron was talking about and had never heard of the Coburgs, this princely name seemed already too showy to M. de Charlus, who in order not to give the impression of over-rating what he was offering, modestly proceeded to disparage it). "Yes, my cousin Philippe de Coburg—you don't know him?" and at once, as a rich man might say to a third-class traveller: "One's so much more comfortable than in first-class," he went on: "All the more reason for envying you, really, because he's a bit of a fool, poor fellow. Or rather, it's not so much that he's a fool, but he's irritating—all the Coburgs are. But in any case I envy you: that open-air life must be so agreeable, seeing so many different people, and in a charming spot, surrounded by trees —for I believe my friend Jupien told me that the terminus of your line was at La Muette. I've often wanted to live out there. There's nowhere more beautiful in the whole of Paris. So it's agreed, then: we'll go to a Colonne concert. We can have the box closed. Not that I shouldn't be extremely flattered to be seen with you, but we'd be more peaceful . . . Society is so boring, isn't it? Of course I don't mean my cousin Guermantes who is charming and so beautiful."

Just as shy scholars who are afraid of being accused of pedantry abbreviate an erudite allusion and only succeed in appearing more long-winded by becoming totally obscure, so the Baron, in seeking to belittle the splendour of the names he cited, made his discourse completely unintelligible to the bus conductor. The latter, failing to understand its terms, tried to interpret it according to its tone, and as the tone was that of someone who is apologising, he was beginning to fear that he might not receive the sum that Jupien had led him to expect.

"When you go to concerts on Sunday, do *you* go to the Colonne ones too?"

"Pardon?"

"What concert-hall do you go to on Sundays?" the Baron repeated, slightly irritated.

"Sometimes to Concordia, sometimes to the Apéritif Concert, or to the Concert Mayol. But I prefer to stretch me legs a bit. It ain't much fun having to stay sitting down all day long."

"I don't like Mayol. He has an effeminate manner that I find horribly unpleasant. On the whole I detest all men of that type."

Since Mayol was popular, the conductor understood what the Baron said, but was even more puzzled as to why he had wanted to see him, since it could not be for something he hated.

"We might go to a museum together," the Baron went on. "Have you ever been to a museum?"

"I only know the Louvre and the Musée Grévin."*

I returned to the Princess, bringing back her letter. In her disappointment, she burst out at me angrily, but apologised at once.

"You're going to hate me," she said. "I hardly dare ask you to go back a third time."

I stopped the cab a little before the cul-de-sac, and turned into it. The carriage was still there. M. de Charlus was saying to Jupien: "Well, the most sensible thing is for you to get out first with him, and see him on his way, and then rejoin me here . . . All right, then, I hope to see you again. How shall we arrange it?"

"Well, you could send me a message when you go out for a meal at noon," said the conductor.

If he used this expression, which applied less accurately to the life of M. de Charlus, who did not "go out for a meal at noon," than to that of omnibus employees and others, this was doubtless not from lack of intelligence but from contempt for local colour. In the tradition of the old masters, he treated the character of M. de Charlus as a Veronese or a Racine treats the husband at the marriage feast of Cana or of Orestes, whom they depict as though this legendary Jew and this legendary Greek had belonged, the one to the luxury-loving patriciate of Venice, the other to the court of Louis XIV. M. de Charlus was content to overlook the inaccuracy, and replied: "No, it would be simpler if you would arrange it with Jupien. I'll speak to him about it. Good-night, it's been delightful," he added, unable to relinquish either his worldly courtesy or his aristocratic hauteur. Perhaps he was even more formally polite at such moments than he was in society; for when one steps outside one's habitual sphere,

* The waxwork museum.

shyness renders one incapable of invention, and it is the memory of
one's habits that one calls upon for practically everything; hence it is
upon the actions whereby one hoped to emancipate oneself from
one's habits that the latter are most forcibly brought to bear, almost
in the manner of those toxic states which intensify when the toxin is
withdrawn.

Jupien got out with the conductor.

"Well then, what did I tell you?"

"Ah, I wouldn't mind a few evenings like that! I quite like
hearing someone chatting away like that, steady like, a chap who
doesn't get worked up. He isn't a priest?"

"No, not at all."

"He looks like a photographer I went to one time to get my
picture taken. It's not him?"

"No, not him either."

"Come off it," said the conductor, who thought that Jupien was
trying to deceive him and feared, since M. de Charlus had remained
rather vague about future assignations, that he might "stand him
up," "come off it, you can't tell me it isn't the photographer. I
recognised him all right. He lives at 3, Rue de l'Echelle, and he's got
a little black dog called Love, I think—so you see I know."

"You're talking rubbish," said Jupien. "I don't say there isn't a
photographer who has a little black dog, but I do say he's not the
man I introduced you to."

"All right, all right, you can say what you like, but I'm sticking
to my own opinion."

"You can stick to it as long as you like for all I care. I'll call round
to-morrow about the rendezvous."

Jupien returned to the cab, but the Baron, restive, had already got
out of it.

"He's nice, most agreeable and well-mannered. But what's his
hair like? He isn't bald, I hope? I didn't dare ask him to take his
cap off. I was as nervous as a kitten."

"What a big baby you are!"

"Anyway we can discuss it, but the next time I should prefer to
see him performing his professional functions. For instance I could
take the corner seat beside him in his tram. And if it was possible by
doubling the price, I should even like to see him do some rather
cruel things—for example, pretend not to see the old ladies signalling to the tram and then having to go home on foot."

"You vicious thing! But that, dearie, would not be very easy,
because there's also the driver, you see. He wants to be well thought
of at work."

As I emerged from the cul-de-sac, I remembered the evening at the Princesse de Guermantes's (the evening which I interrupted in the middle of describing it with this anticipatory digression, but to which I shall return) when M. de Charlus denied being in love with the Comtesse Molé, and I thought to myself that if we could read the thoughts of the people we know we would often be astonished to find that the biggest space in them was occupied by something quite other than what we suspected. I walked round to M. de Charlus's house. He had not yet returned. I left the letter. It was learned next day that the Princesse de Guermantes had poisoned herself by mistaking one medicine for another, an accident after which she was for several months at death's door and withdrew from society for several years. It sometimes happened to me also after that evening, on taking a bus, to pay my fare to the conductor whom Jupien had "introduced" to M. de Charlus in the cab. He was a big man, with an ugly, pimpled face and a short-sightedness that made him now wear what Françoise called "specicles." I could never look at him without thinking of the perturbation followed by amazement which the Princesse de Guermantes would have shown if I had had her with me and had said to her: "Wait a minute, I'm going to show you the person for whose sake M. de Charlus resisted your three appeals on the evening you poisoned yourself, the person responsible for all your misfortunes. You'll see him in a moment, he isn't far from here." Doubtless the Princess's heart would have beaten wildly in anticipation. And her curiosity would perhaps have been mixed with a secret admiration for a person who had been so attractive as to make M. de Charlus, as a rule so kind to her, deaf to her entreaties. How often, in her grief mingled with hatred and, in spite of everything, a certain fellow-feeling, must she not have attributed the most noble features to that person, whether she believed it to be a man or a woman! And then, on seeing this creature, ugly, pimpled, vulgar, with red-rimmed, myopic eyes, what a shock! Doubtless the cause of our sorrows, embodied in a human form beloved of another, is sometimes comprehensible to us; the Trojan elders, seeing Helen pass by, said to one another:

> One glance from her eclipses all our griefs.

But the opposite is perhaps more common, because (just as, conversely, admirable and beautiful wives are always being abandoned by their husbands) it often happens that people who are ugly in the eyes of almost everyone excite inexplicable passions; for what Leonardo said of painting can equally well be said of love, that it is *cosa mentale*, something in the mind. Moreover one cannot even say

that the reaction of the Trojan elders is more or less common than
the other (stupefaction on seeing the person who has caused our
sorrows): for one has only to let a little time go by and the case of the
Trojan elders almost always merges with the other; in other words
there is only one case. Had the Trojan elders never seen Helen, and
had she been fated to grow old and ugly, if one had said to them
one day: "You're about to see the famous Helen," it is probable
that, confronted with a dumpy, red-faced, misshapen old woman,
they would have been no less stupefied than the Princesse de
Guermantes would have been at the sight of the bus conductor.

Page 813.   *In place of this paragraph, the manuscript gives the following
long development*:—

Moving away from the dazzling "house of pleasure" insolently
erected there despite the protests fruitlessly addressed to the mayor
by the local families, I made for the cliffs and followed the sinuous
paths leading towards Balbec. And I remembered certain walks
along these paths with my grandmother. I had had a brief meeting
earlier with a local doctor whom I was never to see again and who
had told me that my grandmother would die soon; he was one of
those people, perhaps malevolent, perhaps mad, perhaps afflicted
with a fear of death which they want to induce in others as well, who
later remind one of those witch-like vagrants encountered on a
roadside who hurl some baneful and plausible prophecy at you. It
was the first time I had thought of the possibility of her death. I
could neither confide my anguish to her nor bear it myself when she
left me. And whenever we took some particularly beautiful path
together, I told myself that one day she would no longer be there
when I took that path, and the mere idea that she would die one
day turned my happiness in being with her to such torment that
what I longed to do more than anything else was to forestall her and
to die myself then and there. Now it was these same paths or similar
ones that I was taking, and already the anguish I had felt in the train
was fading, and if I had met Rosemonde I would have asked her to
come with me. Suddenly I was attracted by the scent of the hawthorns which, as at Combray in the month of May, array themselves
alongside a hedge in their large white veils and decorate this green
French countryside with the Catholic whiteness of their demure
procession. I went nearer, but my eyes did not know at what
adjustment to set their optical apparatus in order to see the flowers
at the same time along the hedge and in myself. Belonging at one
and the same time to many springtimes, the petals stood out

against a sort of magical deep background which, in spite of the strong sunlight, was plunged in semi-darkness either because of the twilight of my indistinct memories or because of the nocturnal hour of the Month of Mary. And then, in the flower which opened up before me in the hedge and which seemed to be animated by the clumsy flickering of my blurred and double vision, the flower that rose from my memory revolved without being able to fit itself exactly on to the elusive living blossoms in the tremulous hesitancy of their petals.

The hawthorns brought out the heaviness of the blossom of an apple tree sumptuously established opposite them, like those dowryless girls of good family who, while being friends of the daughters of a big cider-maker and acknowledging their fresh complexions and good appearance, know that they themselves have more *chic* in their crumpled white dresses. I did not have the heart to remain beside them, and yet I had been unable to resist stopping. But Bloch's sisters, whom I caught sight of without their seeing me, did not even turn their heads towards the hawthorns. The latter had made no sign to them, had said nothing to them; they were like those devout young girls who never miss a Month of Mary, during which they are not afraid to steal a glance at a young man with whom they will make an assignation in the countryside, and by whom they will even allow themselves to be kissed in the chapel when there is no one about, but would never dream—because it has been strictly forbidden—of speaking to or playing with children of another religion.

SYNOPSIS

THE GUERMANTES WAY

Chapter One

Move into a new apartment in a wing of the Hôtel de Guermantes (3). Poetic dreams conjured up by the name Guermantes dispelled one by one (5).

Françoise holds court at lunch-time below stairs (11). Jupien (13); his niece (14).

The name Guermantes, having shed its feudal connotations, now offers my imagination a new mystery, that of the Faubourg Saint-Germain (23). The Guermantes's doormat: threshold of the Faubourg (25).

A gala evening at the Opéra (32). Berma in *Phèdre* once more (32, 40). The Prince of Saxony? (32). The Faubourg Saint-Germain in their boxes (35). The Princesse de Guermantes's *baignoire:* the water-goddesses and the bearded tritons (36). Berma in a modern piece (47). Berma and Elstir (47). The Princesse and the Duchesse de Guermantes (49). Mme de Cambremer (51).

My stratagems for seeing the Duchesse de Guermantes out walking (55); her different faces (60). Françoise's impenetrable feelings (64). I decide to visit Saint-Loup in his garrison, hoping to approach the Duchess through him (67).

Doncières. The cavalry barracks (68). The Captain, the Prince de Borodino (71). Saint-Loup's room (71). Noises and silence (72). My Doncières hotel (79). The world of sleep (82). Field manoeuvres (89). Saint-Loup's popularity (91). The streets of Doncières in the evening (93). Dinner at Saint-Loup's *pension* (97). I ask him to speak to his aunt about me (98). He wants me to shine in front of his friends (102). He denies the rumour of his engagement to Mlle d'Ambresac (103). Major Duroc (105). The Army and the Dreyfus Case (107). Aesthetics of the military art (108). Saint-Loup and his mistress (121). Captain de Borodino and his barber (127). My grandmother's voice on the telephone (133). Saint-Loup's strange salute (139; cf. 179).

Return to Paris. I discover how much my grandmother has changed as a result of her illness (141). End of winter (144). Mme de Guermantes in lighter dresses (145). Work-plans, constantly postponed (151). Mme Sazerat a Dreyfusard (153). Legrandin's professed hatred of society (156). Visit to the suburbs to meet Saint-Loup's mistress (157). I recognise her as "Rachel when from the Lord" (160). Pear trees in blossom (163). Jealous scenes in the restaurant (167). In the theatre after lunch (175). Rachel's cruelty (176). Her transformation on stage (177). Rachel and the dancer (180). Saint-Loup and the journalist (184). Saint-Loup and the passionate stranger (186).

An afternoon party at Mme de Villeparisis's (187). Her social decline (188; cf. Vol. Three p. 296); her literary qualities (189). The social kaleidoscope and the Dreyfus Case (194). Mme de Villeparisis's *Memoirs* (198). The three Parcae (201). The portrait of the Duchesse de Montmorency (203). Legrandin in society (205). Mme de Guermantes's face and her conversation lack the mysterious glamour of her name (209, 214). Mme de Guermantes's luncheons (211); the Mérimée and Meilhac and Halévy type of mind (213). Bloch's bad manners (224). Entry of M. de Norpois (227). Entry of the Duc de Guermantes (229). Norpois and my father's candidature for the Academy (231). Generality of psychological laws (233). Various opinions on Rachel (233; cf. 223, 230, 235), on Odette (235), on Mme de Cambremer (238). Norpois and the Dreyfus Case (239, 247). The laws of the imagination and of language (242). Mme de Villeparisis's by-play with Bloch (256). The Vicomtesse de Marsantes (257). Entry of Robert de Saint-Loup (262). Mme de Guermantes's amiability towards me (262, 272). Norpois and Prince von Faffenheim (265). Oriane refuses to meet Mme Swann (272). Entry of Charlus and Morel (272). Mme Swann and "the Lady in pink" (275). Charlus and Odette (276). Charlus's strange behaviour to his aunt (276). Mme de Marsantes and her son (279, 289). I learn that Charlus is the Duc de Guermantes's brother (287). The affair of the necklace (288, 291). Mme de Villeparisis tries to prevent me from going home with M. de Charlus (293). Charlus offers to guide my life (295). "Terrible, almost insane" remarks about the Bloch family (298). M. d'Argencourt's coldness towards me (302). Strange choice of a cab (306).

The Dreyfus Case below-stairs (306). My grandmother's illness (308). The thermometer (309). Dr de Boulbon's diagnosis (310). Expedition to the Champs-Elysées with my grandmother (319). The "marquise" (319). My grandmother has a slight stroke (323).

sadress (555). The poetry of genealogy (557). Exaltation in the cab on the way to M. de Charlus (568).

Waiting in M. de Charlus's drawing-room (574). His strange welcome (575). Gentleness succeeding rage (582). He accompanies me home in his carriage (584).

Letter from the young footman to his cousin (588). Invitation from the Princesse de Guermantes (590). Diversity of society people in spite of their apparently monotonous insignificance (591). Visit to the Duke and Duchess: view of the neighbouring houses (594). Remarkable discovery which will be described later (595; cf. 623). The Duc de Bouillon (595). The coins of the Order of Malta (596). The Duc de Guermantes's "Philippe de Champaigne" (600). Swann greatly "changed" (601). His Dreyfusism (603). The Duke's ball and Amanien's illness (611). Swann's illness (617). The Duchess's red shoes (619).

CITIES OF THE PLAIN

Part I

Discovery concerning M. de Charlus (623). Reflections on the laws of the vegetable kingdom (624). Meeting between M. de Charlus and Jupien (626); amatory display (627). Eavesdropping (630). M. de Charlus's revelations on the peculiarities of his amatory behaviour (632).

The race of men-women. The curse that weighs upon it (637); its freemasonry (639); varieties of invert (643); the solitaries (646). The Charlus-Jupien conjunction a miracle of nature (651). M. de Charlus becomes Jupien's patron, to Françoise's sentimental delight (653). Numerous progeny of the original Sodomites (655).

Part II

Chapter One

Reception at the Princesse de Guermantes's. My fear of not having been invited (657; cf. 590). The Duc de Châtellerault and the usher (658). The Princess's social technique (658). Her welcome (661). I look for someone to introduce me to the Prince (662). M. de Charlus's chattering (662). Professor E— (664). M. de Vaugoubert (666); his amatory tastes (667); Mme de Vaugoubert (669). M. de Charlus "on show" (672). Mme de Souvré and the cowardice of society people (673). Mme d'Arpajon, whose name escapes me for a moment (674), pretends not to hear my request to be introduced to the Prince (676). Failure of my clumsy request to M. de Charlus

(677). M. de Bréauté effects the introduction (679). The Prince's reserved but unaffected welcome (679). He takes Swann into the garden (680). The Hubert Robert fountain (680). Mme d'Arpajon gets a soaking, much to the hilarity of the Grand Duke Vladimir (681). A chat with the Princess (683). The Turkish Ambassadress (684; cf. 555). The Duchesse de Guermantes's eyes (685). My progress in worldly diplomacy (687). Diplomatic Sodoms; references to *Esther* (689). Mme d'Amoncourt and her offers to Mme de Guermantes (690). Mme de Saint-Euverte recruiting for her garden-party (694). A slightly tarnished duchess (697). Mme de Guermantes's rudeness to Mme de Chaussepierre (697). Different conjectures about Swann's conversation with the Prince de Guermantes (700). The Duc de Guermantes's strictures on Swann's Dreyfusism (702). Mme de Guermantes refuses to meet his wife and daughter (705). Mme de Lambresac's smile (706). Mme de Guermantes intends to forgo the Saint-Euverte garden-party (708), much to the delight of M. de Froberville (709). Beauty of Mme de Surgis-le-Duc's two sons (711). Mme de Citri and her nihilism (711). M. de Charlus absorbed in contemplation of the Surgis boys (714). Swann: signs of his approaching death (715). Arrival of Saint-Loup (716), who expresses approval of his uncle Charlus's womanising (718), sings the praises of bawdy-houses (719), and tells me of a house of assignation frequented by Mlle d'Orgeville and Mme Putbus's chambermaid (719, 721; cf. Vol. Three p. 574). M. de Charlus is presented to the Surgis boys by their mother (719, 722). Saint-Loup's changed attitude towards the Dreyfus Case (724).

Curious conversation between Swann and the Prince de Guermantes (725). M. de Charlus exercises his insolent wit at the expense of Mme de Saint-Euverte (726). Swann's concupiscent stares at Mme de Surgis's bosom (730, 733). His account of the Prince de Guermantes's conversion to Dreyfusism (731, 734), and also his wife's (736). Swann invites me to visit Gilberte (739). The Princesse de Guermantes's secret passion for M. de Charlus (740; cf. 1179).

Departure and return home. M. de Guermantes takes leave of his brother: affectionate reminiscences and a gaffe (742). I leave with the Duke and Duchess: scene on the staircase (745). Mme d'Orvillers (746; cf. 387). Mme de Gallardon (747). Return home in the Guermantes's coupé (748). The Duchess's refusal to introduce me to Baroness Putbus (750). The Guermantes prepare for their fancy-dress ball in spite of the death of their cousin d'Osmond (751; cf. 611).

Visit from Albertine. Françoise and her daughter (752). Linguistic geography (754). I await Albertine's arrival with growing anxiety (755). A telephone call from Albertine (757). "This terrible need of a person": my mother and Albertine (759). How Françoise announces Albertine (761); the latter's visit (764). Afterwards I write to Gilberte Swann, with none of the emotion of old (765). The Duc de Guermantes's conversion to Dreyfusism (766).

Social visiting before my second trip to Balbec. I continue to see other fairies and their dwellings (767). Changes in the social picture (768); the Verdurin salon (770) and the rise of Odette's salon, centred round Bergotte (771). Mme de Montmorency (776).

The intermittencies of the heart (778).

My second stay in Balbec. The hotel manager's malapropisms (778). Principal motive for coming to Balbec: the hope of meeting at the Verdurins' Mme de Putbus's maid (779) and other unknown beauties (781). Disruption of my entire being (783): the living presence of my grandmother is restored to me (783; cf. Vol. One p. 719); at the same time I discover that I have lost her forever (785). My dream, my awakening and my heart-rending memories (787-790). A message from Albertine: I have no desire to see her, or anyone (790). An invitation from Mme de Cambremer (792), which I decline (795). My grief, however, is less profound than my mother's (796). Her resemblance to my grandmother (797). Meeting with Mme Poussin (798). The new young page at the hotel (800) and the domestic staff from the chorus of *Athalie* (802). Françoise's revelations about the circumstances in which Saint-Loup's photograph of my grandmother had been taken (803; cf. Vol. One p. 843). Further revelations, from the manager: my grandmother's fainting fits (806). Another dream about her (806). I suddenly decide to see Albertine (807). Apple trees in blossom (808).

Chapter Two

Resumption of intimacy with Albertine, and first suspicions. My grief at the death of my grandmother wanes and Albertine begins to inspire me with a desire for happiness (810). Sudden return of my grief in the little train (812). Albertine's first visit to Balbec (815). The Princesse de Parme (816). My links with Albertine's friends (817). The lift-boy goes to fetch her (818): his manners and his speech (819). Beginnings of my mistrust of Albertine (822): Cottard's remark while she is dancing with Andrée (823). Albertine fails to turn up one evening (825). Painful curiosity about her secret life (826). Her lies about her proposed visit to a lady in Infreville (827-830). In the casino at Balbec: the girls she sees in the mirror (830). The memory of Odette's character applied to Albertine (832).

Visit from Mme de Cambremer while I am on the esplanade with Albertine and her friends (833). Her paraphernalia (834). Her daughter-in-law's two forms of politeness (835). Etymological curiosities (837). Aesthetic prejudices and snobbery of the young Mme de Cambremer (838); evolution of artistic theories (843); her pronunciation of Chenouville (846). She has forgotten her Legrandin origins (849). The Cambremers' friend, a worshipper at the shrine of Le Sidaner (850).

Albertine comes up to my room (853). The lift-boy's anxious and despondent air (854); its cause: the absence of the customary tip (855). The hotel staff and money (855). My calculated protestations of coldness towards Albertine and love for Andrée (857). Albertine denies having had relations with Andrée (861-863). Reconciliation and caresses (863). Excursions with Albertine (866). Brief desires for other girls (867). Jealousy (870).

Scandal in the Grand Hotel provoked by Bloch's sister and an actress (871), hushed up through the good offices of M. Nissim Bernard (871). Why the latter likes the hotel (872). My friendship with two young "couriers" (875); their language (876-878). Renewed suspicions about Albertine's Gomorrhan proclivities (880): the unknown woman in the casino (881); suspect rudeness to a friend of her aunt's (882). M. Nissim Bernard and the tomatoes (883). I go to Doncières with Albertine (885). A fat, vulgar, pretentious lady on the train (887). Albertine and Saint-Loup (887-889). M. de Charlus appears on the platform at Doncières (890). His first meeting with Morel (890-892).

An evening with the Verdurins at la Raspelière. The little train (895) and its "habitués": Cottard, Ski, Brichot (895). Social development of the Verdurin salon (899). Saniette (900); Ski (902). Princess Sherbatoff (905). Cottard and the Verdurin "Wednesdays" (909). The unknown girl from Saint-Pierre-des-Ifs (912). Mme Verdurin has invited the Cambremers, whose tenant she is (914). Remarks of the "faithful" about the Cambremers (916). Brichot's etymologies (917-921). I recognise Princess Sherbatoff as the fat lady in the train to Doncières (921; cf. 887). News of the death of Dechambre, formerly Mme Verdurin's favourite pianist (923). Mme Verdurin and the death of the faithful (925). Beauty of the countryside (927). Dechambre disowned (930) in the interests of Morel, who is coming with Charlus (931). The latter's sexual proclivities better known among the "faithful" than in the Faubourg Saint-Germain (932). The Verdurins' indifference to the beauties of nature (935).

Arrival of Morel and M. de Charlus (937); evidence of the latter's femininity (937). Morel's request to me (939); his rudeness once he has obtained satisfaction (941). Arrival of the Cambremers (942), he vulgarly ugly (943), she haughty and morose (945); introductions (946). Mme Verdurin and social etiquette (947). The Cambremers' garden (948). M. de Charlus's momentary mistake about Cottard (949). The name Chantepie (952). Combination of culture and snobbery in Mme de Cambremer (954). M. de Cambremer takes an interest in my fits of breathlessness (957). My mother and Albertine (958).

More etymology from Brichot (960). The Norwegian philosopher (961). M. Verdurin bullies Saniette (965). Conversation about Elstir (970). A letter from the dowager Marquise de Cambremer: the rule of the three adjectives (977). M. de Charlus's claim to the rank of Highness (978). The Verdurins' attitude to Brichot (981). M. de Charlus's historical anecdotes (983). Mme de Cambremer's musical snobbery (986). Brichot holds forth (987). M. de Charlus and the Archangel Michael (990). M. de Cambremer discovers the identity of Professor Cottard (991). Mme Cottard dozes off (992). Sleeping draughts (993). A game of cards (995). The arms of the Arrachepels (996). M. de Charlus expresses a preference for strawberry-juice (999). His first skirmish with Mme Verdurin (1000). She invites me to her next "Wednesday" with my "cousin" (1002) and even suggests that I should bring her to stay (1005). Renewed outburst by M. Verdurin against Saniette (1006). Cottard and du Boulbon (1009). M. de Cambremer's tip (1009). Mme de Cambremer's good-bye (1010).

Chapter Three

The squinting page (1012). Sleep after a visit to la Raspelière (1013); reflections on sleep (1013). M. de Charlus dines at the Grand Hotel with a footman (1019). His strange letter to Aimé (1023).

Drives in a motor-car with Albertine (1026). Through the forest of Chantepie (1027). Presents for Albertine (1028). Virtues of the motor-car (1029, 1037). Visit to the Verdurins (1030). The views from la Raspelière (1031). Charm of social life in the country (1032). Other customers of our chauffeur: Charlus and Morel (1039). One of their luncheons on the coast (1039). Morel's cynical projects and the Baron's sensual excitement (1040). My obsession with Albertine (1045). Norman churches (1046). A loving couple (1048). My increasing jealousy: the Rivebelle waiter (1049). Remonstrances from my mother and their negative effect (1051). Evening assignations with Albertine (1052) followed by morning anxiety about her day-time activities (1053). A lesson in the use of words from the lift-boy (1058). Weariness of life with Albertine (1061). The aeroplane (1062).

Morel, the chauffeur, and Mme Verdurin's coachman (1063). Morel's change of attitude towards me (1065); his composite character (1066). Charm of setting out for la Raspelière on late summer evenings (1063). M. de Charlus in the little train (1070). He becomes temporarily the most faithful of the faithful (1077). Princess Sherbatoff gives me the cold shoulder after a meeting on the train with Mme de Villeparisis (1079). M. de Charlus's blindness (1082). Discussion between Brichot and Charlus about Chateaubriand and Balzac (1084). M. de Charlus's discretion about his favourite subject in Morel's presence (1088). Albertine's clothes, inspired by Elstir's taste, admired by M. de Charlus (1089). Morel's admiration for my great-uncle and his house (1091). M. de Charlus's "Balzacian" melancholy (1092). Morel reminds me of Rachel (1095).

M. de Charlus's fictitious duel (1099). Morel dissuades him (1104). Cottard, an alarmed but disappointed second (1106). Morel's demands for money (1110).

The stations on the "Transatlantic." The *de luxe* brothel at Maineville (1111). Morel's assignation there with the Prince de Guermantes, of which M. de Charlus gets wind (1112). Discomfiture of the Prince de Guermantes (1117). Grattevast: the Comte de Crécy (1118). The turkeys carved by the hotel manager (1120). Origins of the Crécy family: Odette's first husband (1121). Hermenonville: M. de Chevregny: a provincial with a passion for Paris (1122). Mme de Cambremer's three adjectives again (1123; cf. 977). Unsatisfactory relations between the Verdurins and the Cambremers (1124, 1131). Brichot's secret passion for the Mme de Cambremer junior (1127). M. and Mme Féré (1129). The long drive between the station and la Raspelière (1132). More Brichot etymologies (1135). Brief visits from friends at various stations (1137). A misunderstanding with Bloch (1138). M. de Charlus's interest in Bloch (1140). Familiarity and social relations rob these places of their poetry and mystery (1145). I feel it would be madness to marry Albertine (1149).

Chapter Four

Albertine's revelation about Mlle Vinteuil and her friend (1151). Recollection of Montjouvain (1152; cf. Vol. One p. 173). I take her

back to the Grand Hotel (1154). Solitary misery until dawn (1154).
Albertine consoles me (1156). I ask her to accompany me to Paris
(1159). Her objections (1160), then her sudden decision to come with
me that very day (1162; cf. Vol. Three p. 397). Reflections on love
(1164). I tell my mother that I must marry Albertine (1168).